D1279263

TOWARDS AN INDEFINITE SHORE

TOWARDS AN INDEFINITE SHORE

The Final Months of the Civil War December 1864 - May 1865

Don Lowry

HIPPOCRENE BOOKS
New York

For information, address:
HIPPOCRENE BOOKS, INC.
171 Madison Avenue
New York, NY 10016

Library of Congress Cataloging-in-Publication Data

Lowry, Don.
Towards an indefinite shore : the final months of the Civil War, December 1864 – May 1865 / Don Lowry.
p. cm.
Includes bibliographical references (p.) and index.
ISBN 0-7818-0422-1
1. United States—History—Civil War, 1861-1865—Campaigns. 2. United States—History—Civil War, 1861-1865—Chronology. 3. Grant, Ulysses S. (Ulysses Simpson), 1822-1885. 4. Generals-United States—Biography. 5. United States. Army—Biography. I. Title.
E470.L88 1995
973.7'3—dc20 95-23240
CIP

Printed in the United States of America.

"...for he had last night the usual dream which he had preceding nearly every great and important event of the War... and the dream itself was always the same... He... seemed to be in some singular, indescribable vessel, and ...he was moving with great rapidity towards an indefinite shore."

Gideon Welles, Secretary of the Navy
on President Lincoln's final dream

CONTENTS

PART THREE—RICHMOND

PART FIVE—ASSASSINATION AND FLIGHT

MAPS

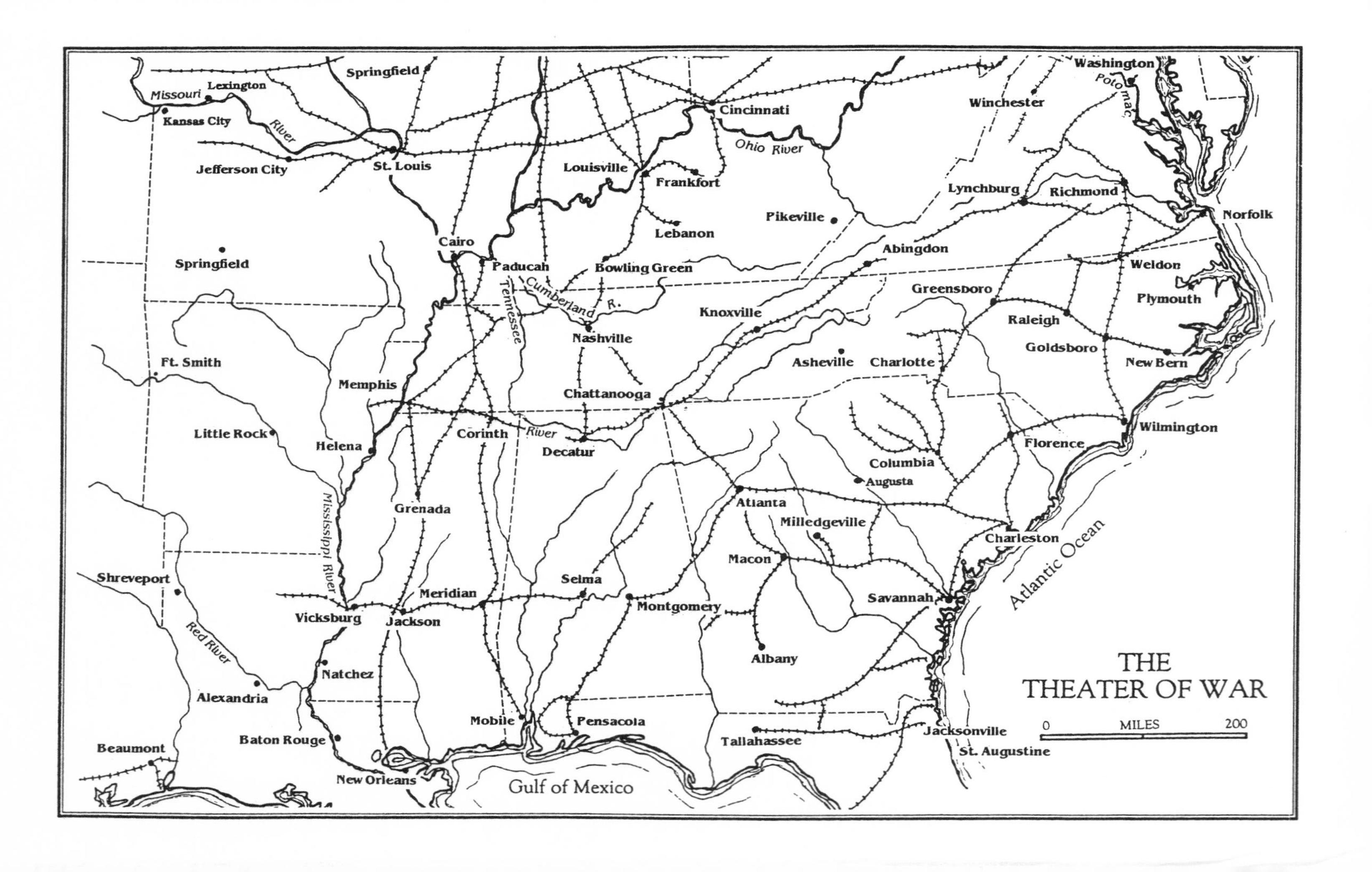
THE
THEATER OF WAR
0
MILES
200
Springfield
Missouri
Lexington
Kansas City
River
Jefferson City
St. Louis
Cincinnati
Ohio River
Louisville
Frankfort
Lebanon
Pikeville
Winchester
Washington
Potomac
Lynchburg
Richmond
Norfolk
Springfield
Cairo
Paducah
Bowling Green
Abingdon
Weldon
Plymouth
Greensboro
Raleigh
Goldsboro
New Bern
Tennessee
Cumberland R.
Nashville
Knoxville
Asheville
Charlotte
Ft. Smith
Memphis
Chattanooga
Little Rock
Helena
Corinth
River
Decatur
Wilmington
Florence
Columbia
Augusta
Mississippi River
Grenada
Atlanta
Milledgeville
Charleston
Atlantic Ocean
Macon
Shreveport
Meridian
Selma
Savannah
Vicksburg
Jackson
Montgomery
Red River
Albany
Natchez
Alexandria
Mobile
Pensacola
Baton Rouge
Tallahassee
Jacksonville
St. Augustine
Beaumont
New Orleans
Gulf of Mexico

PROLOGUE

This is the final book in a four-volume history of the final year of the Civil War, from the time Lieutenant General Ulysses S. Grant took overall command of the Union war effort. However, it can easily stand alone as a history of the final months of the war. For those who insist on coming in at the beginning: The first volume, *No Turning Back*, ends with Grant's crossing of the James River to get at Richmond's supply lines running through Petersburg; the second volume, *Fate of the Country*, begins with the first attacks on Petersburg and ends with Sherman's capture of Atlanta; and the third volume, *Dark and Cruel War*, begins with Sheridan's victories in the Shenandoah Valley and ends with the completion of Sherman's march to the sea.

The final months of the Civil War, covered here, have received rather mixed coverage by historians. The pursuit of Lee to Appomattox and his surrender there have been well covered in popular histories, but the battles that caused Lee to retreat and the weeks that followed Lee's surrender, during which the rest of the Confederacy collapsed, have not. And the two-pronged Union offensive into Alabama from the Gulf coast and from the Tennessee River has received very little attention. While much has been written about the assassination of Abraham Lincoln, only recently has much attention been paid to the evidence of Confederate involvement in that plot.

As in the previous volumes of this series, it has been my purpose to weave these and other related events into a chronological narrative. It is my belief that such an approach can be highly instructive by better showing how these thing were all interrelated.

Notes are provided only to indicate the source of quotations. Quotes in the text are presented with the same spelling and punctuation as found in the sources noted. For instance, Sayler's Creek was often called Sailor's Creek by those who fought there, and I have kept whichever spelling was found in the source.

As with the previous volumes, I would like to thank my wife, Julie, and my son, James, for their continued assistance, encouragement, faith and forebearance through what must have seemed at times a never-ending project.

PART ONE

FORT FISHER

Between Bragg and Lee, Sherman and Grant, old North Carolina is in a pretty fix.

—Brigadier General W.H.C. Whiting, C.S.A.

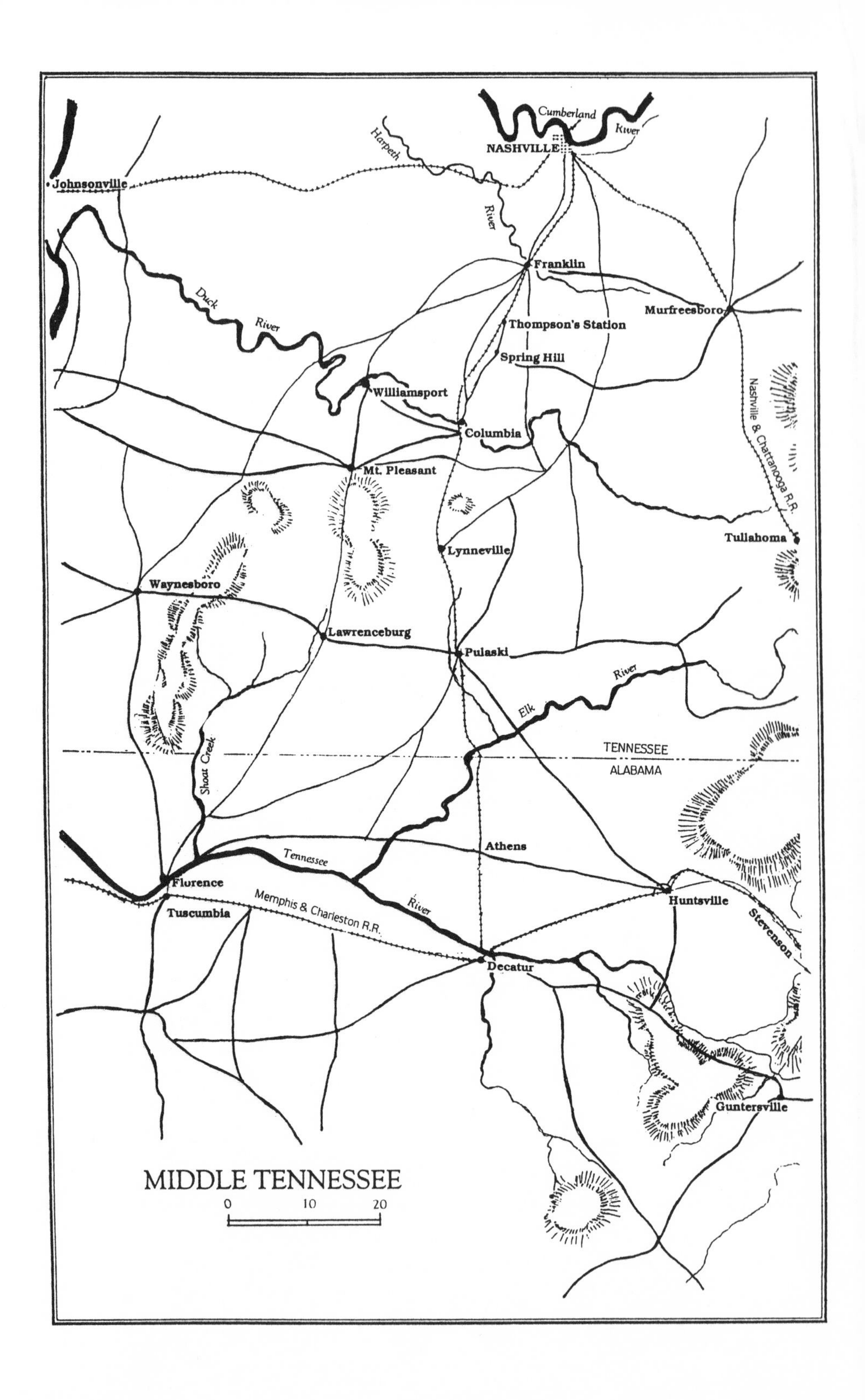
Cumberland
River
NASHVILLE
Harpeth
River
Johnsonville
Duck
River
Franklin
Murfreesboro
Thompson's Station
Spring Hill
Williamsport
Columbia
Nashville & Chattanooga R.R.
Mt. Pleasant
Tullahoma
Lynneville
Waynesboro
Lawrenceburg
Pulaski
River
Elk
TENNESSEE
ALABAMA
Shoal Creek
Athens
Tennessee
Florence
Huntsville
Tuscumbia
Memphis & Charleston R.R.
River
Stevenson
Decatur
Guntersville
MIDDLE TENNESSEE
0
10
20

CHAPTER ONE

The Once Proud Army of Tennessee

22 - 23 December 1864

The winter of 1864-65 was the coldest the state of Tennessee had known for many years. And through the alternating snows, rains, thaws, and freezes the Confederate Army of Tennessee streamed southward in a weary retreat reminiscent of Napoleon's escape from Russia. "The ground was frozen and rough," Private Sam Watkins remembered, "and our soldiers were poorly clad, while many, yes, very many, were entirely barefoot. Our wagon trains had either gone on, we knew not whither, or had been left behind. Everything and nature, too, seemed to be working against us. Even the keen, cutting air that whistled through our tattered clothes and over our poorly covered heads, seemed to lash us in its fury. The floods of waters that had overflowed their banks, seemed to laugh at our calamity, and to mock us in our misfortunes."[1]

General John Bell Hood, that army's commander, after evacuating Atlanta in early September 1864 to avoid being cut off and starved out by Union Major General William Tecumseh Sherman, had seized the initiative by swinging around to the west of the city to attack the Federal army's vulnerable railroad supply line running back to Chattanooga. Sherman had left part of his forces to hold Atlanta and had chased after Hood with the rest. The Confederate had then moved westward into Alabama, and Sherman had dispaired of ever catching him. Instead, he cut loose from his supply line, destroyed everything in Atlanta of possible use to the Confederacy, and marched for the Atlantic coast, cutting a swath of destruction across Georgia fifty or sixty miles wide. Hood, meanwhile, moved westward, crossed the Tennessee River at Florence, Alabama, and marched north into Tennessee with the hope of reclaiming that state from almost three years of Federal occupation.

Sherman had left his principal subordinate, Major General George H. Thomas, in charge in Tennessee with a hodge-podge of forces, but Hood had advanced before Thomas had assembled them. The 4th Corps of Thomas's own Army of the Cumberland and the 23rd Corps of Major General John M. Schofield's Army of the Ohio, both under Schofield, had retreated toward Nashville before Hood's advance and had only narrowly escaped being cut off near the village of Spring Hill due to an effective Union holding action and miscommunication among the Confederate generals. The following day, 30 November 1864, the frustrated Hood had launched an all-out frontal assault on Schofield's entrenchments at Franklin, Tennessee, on the south bank of the Harpeth River. In the bloody hand-to-hand struggle that had followed, the Confederate army had suffered crippling losses in men and officers, including a large number of generals.

Union losses had been light. Nevertheless, Schofield, running low on ammunition and considering himself badly outnumbered, had continued his retreat to Nashville, followed by Hood. At Nashville the two Union corps from Franklin had been joined by a corps-sized detachment of the Army of the Tennessee, commanded by Major General A. J. Smith, which had just arrived from a brief stint in Missouri chasing Confederate raiders, and by a provisional force, under Major General James B. Steedman, brought up from the Union garrisons in northern Georgia and around Chattanooga. Hood had entrenched his army on the hills south of the city, cutting off a sizable Union garrison to the southeast at Murfreesboro. But the latter had been well supplied and it had easily defeated a Confederate attempt to attack it. Hood nevertheless had hoped that Thomas would be forced to come to its assistance and attack his entrenchments south of Nashville.

The Union high command—consisting of President Abraham Lincoln, Secretary of War Edwin M. Stanton, and Chief of Staff Major General Henry W. Halleck, all in Washington, and the general-in-chief,

Lieutenant General Ulysses S. Grant, personally supervising the siege of the Confederate capital, Richmond, Virginia, and the town of Petersburg through which most of its railroads ran—had been worried that Hood would somehow slip past Thomas, cross the Cumberland River, and invade Kentucky. Thomas had been bombarded with suggestions, pleas, and orders to attack Hood before he got away. Thomas, however, had continually pleaded the necessity of organizing his ad hoc army and especially the need for remounting and reorganizing the cavalry corps commanded by Brevet Major General James H. Wilson. Then a sudden drop of temperature and a freezing rain had turned the hills and fields around Nashville into sheets of ice, making any attack impossible. Grant had finally grown so impatient with Thomas's delays that he had started for Nashville to take personal command there, but he had gone only as far as Washington on 15 December before word reached him that, after a break in the weather, Thomas had attacked the Confederates and driven them from their position that day.

Hood had fallen back only far enough to establish a new line of defenses on another series of hills, but Thomas had attacked again on the sixteenth and had driven the Rebels from their defenses in great confusion. Hood's army had fallen apart as it retreated by every road back through Franklin, where it destroyed the bridges over the Harpeth River. However, Wilson's cavalry had been able to ford that river before renewed rains had caused it to rise too far, and the horsemen had pushed on after the routed Confederates while the Union infantry rebuilt the bridges over the Harpeth. But other rising streams and a small but stubborn Rebel rear guard had managed to protect the rest of Hood's army from the Union pursuit.

At 5 a.m. on 22 December 1864 work began on a Federal pontoon bridge across the Duck River at Columbia, Tennessee. However, two hours later Major General Nathan Bedford Forrest's Confederate cavalry began to fire on the working party from the southern bank. A regiment of Union infantry had to be sent across the swollen, icy stream in canvas pontoon boats to chase the Rebel horsemen away and establish a bridgehead. A young courier sent by Forrest to bring up reinforcements was so nearly frozen by his six-mile ride that he was unable to dismount by himself and could only manage to whisper "Boots and saddles," the name of the bugle call that told the cavalry to mount up.[2]

Even without the distraction of Confederate fire, the bridge progressed slowly. There were only three pontoniers with the boats, and the infantrymen who were pressed into service knew next to nothing about how to string them together to make a floating bridge. The

15-degree weather did not make the job any easier. Two or three times the bridge broke apart, and it was 6:30 p.m., well after dark, before the job was completed. Wilson's cavalry had already gone into bivouac for the night, so Brigadier General Thomas J. Wood's 4th Corps was the first to cross.

By then the head of Hood's column had already started down the frozen unpaved road running south from Pulaski, Tennessee, toward the Tennessee River, pursued only by a piercing northwest wind. The men did not march by brigades, regiments, or even companies. Almost all formation had been lost in the headlong retreat. Instead, they moved along in clumps of from six to twenty men, each group stopping to rest whenever it pleased. Many of these Confederates had long since thrown away their rifles in order to lighten their load and hasten their march. The side of the road was strewn with discarded weapons, equipment, ammunition and abandoned wagons. The weary, freezing men made only six miles that day before staggering to the side of the road to build campfires and bivouac on the snow and frozen mud. Most of them had nothing to eat other than a bit of parched corn. That night, General Hood dined on oyster stew at the warm and comfortable Jones residence in Pulaski.

Hood's foray into central Tennessee had been supplied, with considerable difficulty, up the Nashville & Decatur Railroad, which, along with the roads, gave his army a tenuous connection with northwestern Alabama. This area, in turn, was connected, or had been, via the east-west Memphis & Charleston Railroad, with Corinth, in the northeastern part of Mississippi. Over the course of two and a half years of war, both sides had alternately attacked that line and rebuilt it, depending on whether they were trying to use it at the time or trying to keep the other side from using it. And it had long lain unused by either side. It was not in good condition now, but the Confederates had been trying to fix it up as well as they could because another line, the Mobile & Ohio, ran south from Corinth to Mobile. This line had also been attacked occasionally, but not so well or so often, and it connected the Army of Tennessee with the supply depots of the deep South.

As Sherman had marched away from Atlanta toward the Atlantic coast, the Union garrisons of western Tennessee and Mississippi, which had belonged to the Department of Tennessee, had been renamed the Department of the Mississippi and transferred from Sherman's Military Division of the Mississippi to Major General E.R.S. Canby's Military Division of West Mississippi, which also included the Department of the Gulf, and the Department of Arkansas. This new department included a cavalry division commanded by Brigadier General Benjamin

H. Grierson, and Major General N.J.T. Dana, commander of the Department of the Mississippi, had sent Grierson and his 3,500 troopers eastward out of Memphis on the 21st to raid these important Confederate supply lines. Grierson is best known today for a famous and very successful raid he had made back in the summer of 1863 during Grant's Vicksburg campaign. On that occasion he had ridden the length of Mississippi from La Grange, Tennessee, to Baton Rouge, Louisiana, tearing up railroads and scattering Rebels along the way. Since then he had commanded the cavalry portion of three other forays into Mississippi from West Tennessee. The first of these, under the overall command of Brigadier General Sam Sturgis, had been decisively defeated by Forrest six months back. The other two had been commanded by A. J. Smith and had included his veteran infantry before both he and they had been sent off to Missouri to chase Rebel raiders. Smith's first expedition had defeated Forrest in a defensive battle near Tupelo, Mississippi, and the other had ended inconclusively when unseasonal rains had bogged it down while Forrest rode off to raid Memphis.

Now, at last, Grierson was again unimpeded with superior officers or accompanying infantry. In fact, he was not even taking any artillery or wagons along, and all his supplies were being carried by pack mules. What was even better, from his point of view, Forrest was off playing rear guard for Hood's retreating army. So, on the 22nd of December, Grierson turned south from the line of the Memphis & Charleston Railroad and crossed from Tennessee into Mississippi once again while sending the 10th Missouri Cavalry on to the east to destroy the railroad stations and telegraph lines at La Grange and Grand Junction, Tennessee.

In Virginia, General Robert E. Lee's Army of Northern Virginia had been virtually besieged in Richmond and Petersburg since Grant had slipped the Army of the Potomac away from Lee and across the James River back in June. Initial attempts to capture the town of Petersburg, through which ran most of the railroads supplying Richmond, had failed, but the Federals had been gradually extending their lines to the southwest ever since, to cut those rail lines one by one. As the year 1864 drew to a close, only four lines of supply remained open to the Confederate capital: the Southside Railroad, which ran west from Petersburg, south of the Appomattox River, to Lynchburg, where there was an important Confederate supply depot; the James River canal, which also connected with Lynchburg; the Richmond & Danville Railroad, which ran southwest from Richmond, crossed the

Apppomattox well to the northwest of Petersburg, and continued on to Danville, where it connected with a line running into North Carolina; and the Virginia Central Railroad, which ran north from Richmond about twenty miles to Hanover Junction, where it turned to the northwest to Gordonsville. From there it dipped to the southwest to Charlottesville and then turned to the west, crossing the Blue Ridge near Waynesborough into the fertile Shenandoah Valley.

Lieutenant General Ulysses S. Grant, in addition to being the general-in-chief of the army and thus in overall charge of all land combat operations of the United States, was in direct command of what were known semi-officially as the Armies Operating Against Richmond. These were Major General George G. Meade's Army of the Potomac, manning the lines south of the Appomattox River facing Petersburg, and Major General Benjamin F. Butler's Army of the James, manning Union lines across the Bermuda Hundred Peninsula between the Appomattox and James rivers and north of the James southeast of Richmond.

Butler's army was the main field force drawn from his Department of Virginia and North Carolina. However, he and a sizable portion of his command were floating on transport ships down on the coast of North Carolina just then. With the help of a large fleet of warships and gunboats, he planned to capture Fort Fisher, a very formidable Confederate earthwork that controlled the mouth of the Cape Fear River, allowing blockade-runners to get in and out of Wilmington, the South's last lifeline to the outside world. However, rough seas had delayed the operation, and word of it had eventually reached the ears of Robert E. Lee. Reluctantly the Confederate commander had stripped his own defenses in order to send a division under Major General Robert F. Hoke to reinforce the Wilmington defenses. The last of Hoke's brigades left the Richmond area on that same day, 22 December.

Back in June, at the same time that Grant had slipped away from Lee to cross the James, Lee had sent off one corps of his army, under Lieutenant General Jubal A. Early, to chase away a Union raid on Lynchburg and then to march down the Shenandoah Valley to threaten Washington and Baltimore. This had led Grant to send reinforcements to protect those areas and one of his favorite subordinates to command them. Several small military departments in the area had been united to form the Middle Military Division under Major General Philip H. Sheridan, who had previously been the commander of the Cavalry Corps of the Army of the Potomac. Sheridan had eventually defeated Early in three pitched battles and devastated much of the Shenandoah Valley so that it could no longer supply Early's army or send supplies to Richmond. Then, as winter weather had seemingly put an end to active campaigning, Lee had recalled most of Early's forces to help defend Richmond and Petersburg, and Sheridan had sent off much of his infantry to Grant.

Ever since Sheridan had first defeated Early, Grant had been trying to talk him into crossing the Blue Ridge for an attack upon the Virginia Central Railroad. He would not order such a move against the judgment of the commander on the spot, but he continually returned to the subject in his telegrams to Sheridan, urging the importance of cutting this vital Confederate supply line. Sheridan had been extremely reluctant to comply, complaining that he could not carry enough supplies for his entire army that far, nor spare the troops it would take to defend a railroad supply line of his own. However, with most of Early's forces sent to Richmond and the remainder withdrawing up the Valley to go into winter quarters near Staunton, Sheridan finally decided to send his cavalry to make the attack. Despite the cold weather, two divisions of cavalry under Brevet Major General A.T.A. Torbert, commander of the Cavalry Corps, were sent across the Blue Ridge to raid the railroad while the 3rd Division of cavalry, commanded by Brevet Major General George A. Custer, was sent up the Valley to divert Early's attention.

On the 22nd, Torbert drove one brigade of Confederate cavalry from Madison Court House to Liberty Mill, where it was joined by a second Rebel brigade. The Confederates blew up the bridge over the Rapidan River there and planted two guns to cover the crossing, but Torbert sent one division upstream and the other down, got them both across the river, and captured both guns along with several of their gunners. However, Early had been informed of Sheridan's moves by observers who watched the Union camps from high atop a mountain. He sent one of his cavalry divisions, under Major General Tom Rosser, and his sole remaining infantry division, under Brigadier General Gabriel C. Wharton, to deal with Custer, and his other cavalry division, under Major General Lunsford Lomax, to protect the railroad. Rosser had surprised Custer with a pre-dawn attack on the 21st that had caused the Federal horsemen to retreat back down the Valley. Then Wharton's infantry had been loaded onto railroad cars for transfer to Gordonsville. Lee also responded quickly to this threat to one of his few remaining supply lines. He ordered Lieutenant General James Longstreet, commander of his 1st Corps, to send troops to defend Gordonsville. Longstreet ordered one brigade from Major General Charles Field's division, north of the James, and one from Major General George Pickett's division, on the Bermuda Hundred Peninsula, to be pulled out of the defenses and marched to the railroad station in Richmond that night. Colonel Robert M. Mayo's small brigade of Major General Henry Heth's division of Lieutenant General A.P. Hill's 3rd Corps was also pulled out of the lines around Petersburg as a potential reinforcement but was held in reserve for the time being.

The well-known actor John Wilkes Booth had spent the night of 21-22 December at the home of Dr. Samuel Mudd near Bryantown, Maryland, southeast of Washington, D.C. He had gone to Bryantown the day before so that Mudd could introduce him to Thomas H. Harbin, alias Thomas A. Wilson, an agent of the Confederate Secret Service. Booth was involved in a Confederate plot to capture President Lincoln, and Harbin's job would be to help smuggle the captors and their victim across the lower Potomac to Virginia. On the morning of the 22nd, Booth and Mudd walked across a field for a look at some horses owned by Mudd's neighbor. Booth bought a one-eyed animal for $80, acquired a saddle and bridle in Bryantown, and rode back to Washington, where he checked into the National Hotel.

The next day, Dr. Mudd went to Washington and checked into the Pennsylvania House. He met with Booth that evening and the two proceeded toward Mary Surratt's boardinghouse. They found the landlady's son, John H. Surratt, Jr., who was a courier on the Confederate Secret Service's clandestine line of communication through Maryland, standing out in front of the house with an old college chum who was one of the boarders, and Louis J. Weichmann, a clerk at the War Department. Introductions were made all around, but either Weichmann was confused or Dr. Mudd intentionally deceived him into believing that the other man's name was Boone. "I noticed that he was a young man of medium figure, apparently about twenty-eight years of age," Weichmann later wrote. "A heavy black mustache rendered the pallor of his contenance very noticeable. He possessed an abundance of black curly hair and a voice that was musical and rich in its tones. His bearing was that of a man of the world and a gentleman. In dress, he was faultless. His companion, Dr. Mudd, was the very opposite, slender, about six feet in height, with fair and finely cut features. He was not blessed with as much hair as his friend and such as he did have was quite florid in color and straight."[3]

The four men went back to Booth's rooms at the National Hotel, where they had some milk punch. Then Booth and Mudd, and later Surratt as well, engaged in private conversations which they later explained to Weichmann related to the purchase of Mudd's farm by Booth—or Boone, as Weichmann still knew him. After about twenty minutes of this they went down to the Pennsylvania House, where Dr. Mudd was staying. Mudd and Weichmann, who was dressed in the uniform of the War Department Rifles, a regiment composed of government clerks used to defend the capital in emergencies, had a long talk on a settee in the hotel's public room while Surratt and Booth sat apart, engaged in animated conversation in front of the fire. "Probably by this time," Weichmann wrote, "Surratt was duly impressed with the greatness of his new-found friend. Certain it is he acted as if he had known him all his life. What pictures Boone drew before this country boy's vision, what glittering baubles he held out to him, no one knows. Boone, at any rate, found him an easy victim, for from that hour Surratt was his, as completely as Doctor Faust belonged to Mephistopheles."[4]

Some seventy miles southwest of Washington, Torbert's Union cavalry approached Gordonsville, on the Virginia Central Railroad, on the twenty-third. But they found that the cavalry from Early's Army of the Valley had been reinforced by infantry sent by rail from Lee's army. The Union troopers were cold and wet and many of them suffered from frostbite. They had been pelted by snow, sleet, and hail almost continuously since leaving the Shenandoah, and the frozen, rutted, muddy roads made every step dangerous for man and horse. Finding his objective too well defended, Torbert turned back without attacking.

Down in northern Mississippi on the twenty-third, Grierson's Union raiders passed through Lamar and Salem, having ridden some thirty miles that day.

In Tennessee, Wilson's cavalry began crossing the newly constructed pontoon bridge over the Duck River at Columbia, but the bridge was in such poor condition and its approaches so slippery with ice and mud that the entire day was consumed in the crossing. Wood's 4th Corps tired of waiting for the horsemen and began to march south again at 2:30 p.m. Five miles south of Columbia they came upon a few of Forrest's Confederate cavalry deployed across a gorge between two high hills. A few shells from a battery of artillery soon chased the Rebels off, but by then it was after 4 p.m. and darkness was approaching, so the Federals went into camp. Three hours later Wilson's cavalry began to trot past their bivouac, taking over the lead again.

Much of Hood's escaping army reached Lexington, Tennessee, that day, having covered about two-thirds of the distance from Pulaski to the Tennessee River. "The once proud Army of Tennessee had degenerated to a mob," wrote Private Sam Watkins. "We were pinched by hunger and cold. The rains, and sleet, and snow never ceased falling from the winter sky, while the winds pierced the old, ragged, gray-back Rebel soldier to his very marrow. The clothing of many were hanging around them in shreds of rags and tatters, while an old slouched hat covered their frozen ears."[5]

The ordnance and quartermaster's wagons of the leading Confederate corps found it so difficult to get up one icy hill that the corps commander, Major General Frank Cheatham, told his adjutant to pick out a hundred well-shod men to help push the wagons. The adjutant was only able to find 25 men in the entire corps with shoes adequate for the job.

---

1. Sam R. Watkins, *Co. Aytch: A Side Show of the Big Show* (Nashville, 1882), Collier Books paperback edition, 241.
2. Wiley Sword, *Embrace an Angry Wind: The Confederacy's Last Hurrah:* Spring Hill, Franklin, and Nashville (New York, 1992), 414.
3. Louis J. Weichmann, *A True History of the Assassination of Abraham Lincoln and of the Conspiracy of 1865* (New York, 1975), 32.
4. Ibid., 34.
5. Watkins, *Co. Aytch*, 242.

CHAPTER TWO

There's a Fizzle

23 - 24 December 1864

Like Private Sam Watkins in Tennessee, Major General Benjamin Franklin Butler may well have felt that "everything and nature, too" was working against him. Everything seemed to be going wrong with the combined army-navy operation to capture Fort Fisher and close the port of Wilmington, North Carolina.

That town was now the Confederacy's last remaining port where fast, sleek ships from Bermuda and the Bahamas could slip past the Union blockade with desperately needed supplies for the Rebel armies and otherwise-unobtainable luxuries that sold at grossly inflated prices. "The staid old town of Wilmington was turned topsy turvy during the war," the commander of the Confederate blockade-runner *Robert E. Lee* wrote. "Here resorted the speculators from all parts of the South, to attend the weekly auctions of imported cargoes; and the town was infested with rogues and desperadoes, who made a livelihood by robbery and murder. It was unsafe to venture into the suburbs at night, and even in daylight there were frequent conflicts in the public streets, between the crews of the steamers in port and the soldiers stationed in the town, in which knives and pistols would be freely used; and not unfrequently a dead body would rise to the surface of the water in one of the docks with marks of violence upon it. The civil authorities were powerless to prevent crime.... The agents and employees of different blockade-running companies lived in magnificent style, paying a king's ransom (in Confederate money) for their household expenses, and nearly monopolized the supplies in the country market. Towards the end of the war, indeed, fresh provisions were almost beyond the reach of every one."[1]

The Federal navy had been wanting to launch an expedition to capture Wilmington for a long time, for it was not only the entrepot for supplies and equipment bound for the Confederate army but the home port of naval raiders such as the CSS *Tallahassee*, which had taken over thirty Northern vessels along the Atlantic coast back in August. And, because of its location, it was a very difficult port to blockade. It was situated about 20 miles up the Cape Fear River from the coast, but the river had two mouths. A peninsula that separated the southward-flowing river from the southwestward-tending coast ended in what had been known before the war as Federal Point. Southerners now called it Confederate Point. Between the point and Smith's Island, to the south, was the mouth of the river known as New Inlet. The southeastern tip of Smith's Island was the Cape Fear that gave the river its name, and between the mainland and the western side of the island was the other mouth of the river, the Old Inlet. The Confederates had numerous forts along these shores to keep the Union navy out of the river and to make the Federals keep their distance. And, so far as Union ships off the coast were concerned, these two inlets were not only separated by Smith's Island but by miles of shallow water, known as Frying Pan Shoals, that extended eastward from Cape Fear. So the navy had to maintain a semicircle of some 33 ships to cover the approaches to the two inlets.

"The pleasures of blockade service had to be experienced to be fully appreciated," one Union sailor wrote with more than a touch of sarcasm. "There may have been an occasional spot of monotony here and there, but upon the average station the experience was as varied as it was exciting. An occasional skirmish on shore with an outlying picket of observation; a midnight alarm, which sometimes resulted in a beat to quarters merely to receive on board a boat-load of contrabands seeking refuge under cover of darkness on the 'Lincum' gunboat; frequent dashes after blockade runners that somehow or other so often managed to elude our grasp; a cutting-out expedition that often resulted in the gallant capture of a very hostile fishing-smack; the destruction of salt works that increased in number the more they were destroyed; and... 'laying low' for the monthly visit of the beef boat, that brought our supplies of fresh meat, ice, blockade sherry, and our mail, made up a round of duty that could not be fairly termed monotonous. Then it afforded a splendid opportunity for the development and study of character as well as for the exercise of qualities that under other circumstances would not have been so prominently called into requisition. If you want to find out what a man really is, go and spend a year with him on the blockade and you will discover what kind of stuff he is made of as well as what kind of a fellow you are yourself."[2]

The key to the Cape Fear system was Fort Fisher, just north of Federal/Confederate Point. It was thought to be the strongest earthwork ever built and was called the Gibraltar of the South. It was shaped roughly like the letter L. The short leg, known as the land face, stretched almost a half-mile across the peninsula north of the point, running southeast from the river to the ocean. The longer leg, the sea face, ran southwest from the east end of the land face for more than a mile. Both faces were studded with heavy artillery pieces separated by huge earthen mounds, called traverses, designed to protect them from flanking fire.

Each traverse on the land face was some 30 feet high and 25 feet thick and hollowed out to provide shelters known as bombproofs. North of the land face the peninsula had been cleared of trees and brush for a half-mile to provide its defenders a clear field of fire, and a nine-foot-high fence of sharpened pine logs, known as a palisade, ran parallel with the land face and just north of it to block the approach of any enemy force. The sandy road running down the western side of the peninsula penetrated the palisade through a gate, crossed some marshy ground on a narrow wooden bridge, and entered the fort at the western end of the land face. Halfway across the land face the earthwork was penetrated by a tunnel known as the sally port. This led to an elevated artillery position between the land face and the wooden palisade. From there field pieces could be run out to fire into the flanks of any enemy attempting to scale the palisade or the sloping earthen walls of the land face. Beyond the palisade, Confederate ordnance experts had planted 24 explosive devices in the ground. Some were artillery shells and others, known in the parlance of the day as torpedoes, were iron cylinders filled with 100 pounds of gunpowder. All were connected by a network of underground wires to an electric battery inside the fort, by means of which they could be detonated at will.

At the angle where the land face met the sea face there was a massive earthwork known as the Northeast Bastion. Its sodded walls rose 43 feet above the nearby beach. Next to it was the Pulpit Battery, from which enemy ships and approaching blockade-runners could be seen miles away. The huge bombproof below the Pulpit Battery would serve as a field hospital should the fort be attacked. Behind the Northeast Bastion was a 60-foot-wide bombproof that held the fort's main magazine of 13,000 pounds of gunpowder. And just behind the magazine were some smaller earthworks protecting the rear of the Northeast Bastion and the eastern half of the land face.

From the Northeast Bastion the sea face ran down the peninsula in a continuous line of alternating gun chambers and traverses. Halfway down the sea face was located the fort's most potent weapon, a huge 150-pounder Armstrong rifle that was said to be a gift from the gun's British manufacturer to Confederate president Jefferson Davis. This powerful, accurate, long-range gun kept the Union blockaders at a respectful distance, but in a serious battle it would be severly hampered by a shortage of ammunition to fit it. At the southern end of the sea face the Mound Battery rose sixty feet above the beach. It had taken a year and a half and tons of sand to construct, and was visible from miles out to sea. It held two large guns, a 10-inch smoothbore and a 6.4-inch rifle, and these could blast any ship attempting to enter New Inlet. Beyond the Mound Battery the peninsula turned to the west and a detached work with four guns, known as Battery Buchanan, would have the final shots at any ship that made it past the fort. It also served to cover a wharf on the river side of the point, where supplies for the fort could be brought by riverboats. Other than that, the rear of the fort was open to the river, except for a line of rifle pits running diagonally across the L. Altogether, Fort Fisher contained 44 heavy guns, three mortars, and several field pieces. But its weakness was its lack of manpower. "The garrison," one Rebel officer observed, "consisted of one raw, inexperienced regiment that had never smelled powder."[3]

It had taken months for the Union navy to convince the army to provide the troops necessary to capture Fort Fisher. General Grant had finally agreed to send a couple of divisions from Ben Butler's Army of the James under the command of Brigadier General Godfrey Weitzel, one of Butler's corps commanders, but the move had been postponed back in September when Grant had instead made a one-two punch at the defenses of Richmond and Petersburg to keep Lee from sending reinforcements to the Shenandoah Valley following Sheridan's first two victories there. However, when Sherman had marched from Atlanta for the coast two months later the Confederates had sent General Braxton Bragg with over half the troops in the Wilmington area to Augusta to defend that city from Sherman. And when Grant had learned of this by reading the Southern newspapers he had urged Butler to get Weitzel's expedition on the way before Bragg returned. A number of factors had served to further delay the launching of the expedition, however, including bad weather.

The Federals—some said the navy, others said Butler—had come up with the idea of destroying or at least damaging Fort Fisher by exploding a ship filled with hundreds of tons of gunpowder within a few hundred yards of it. But the preparation of the ship and the procurement of the powder had proven troublesome. Finally, on 12 December, it had been ready, and the next day it and the transports carrying the army's 5,000 soldiers had steamed out of the James River into Chesapeake Bay. After a brief feint up the Potomac River to fool any Confederate spies who might be watching, the transports had turned to the south under the cover of night and headed for the point of rendezvous with the navy off the North Carolina coast. Butler had gone along in person, telling Grant that Weitzel was a good general, but too young for such an important expedition, and besides, Butler wanted to make sure the exploding of the powder boat was handled correctly. Also he probably hoped to garner the credit and the glory for the capture of the Confederacy's strongest fort, which would be of considerable aid to his presidential ambitions. Grant had no faith in the powder boat experiment and very little in Butler either, but the latter was within his rights to accompany an expedition of his own soldiers within his own department.

Benjamin Franklin Butler was a highly effective, if not scrupulously honest, administrator of conquered territory, and a capable military planner, but he was out of his depth as an army commander. "A vivacious, prying man, this Butler," a British correspondent observed, "full of life, self-esteem, revelling in the exercise of power."[4] He owed his position as one of the most senior generals in the Union army mostly to his political influence, for he was an important Democratic politician in Massachusetts, and his support for the Lincoln administration and the war effort had made him too valuable for Grant or even Lincoln to remove him. What the scheming and ambitious Butler may not have considered, however, was that, with Lincoln's reelection the month before, Butler's political support was no longer as important as it had been.

The transport ships carrying Butler's soldiers had been anchored about twenty miles offshore and eighteen miles north of Fort Fisher for two days and three nights of beautiful weather and calm seas before Rear Admiral David Dixon Porter's fleet had finally arrived at the rendezvous point on the night of 18 December. Although the naval ships had preceded the army transports down the coast, they had run into Union-held Beaufort, North Carolina, where the outfitting of the powder boat, the *Louisiana*, was to be completed. This had taken longer than expected, and then the fleet had had to wait for a high tide in order to leave Beaufort.

Porter was a career naval officer, son of a hero of the old sailing navy and foster brother of Admiral David Farragut, but for ambition and scheming he was second only to Butler. He had developed a disliking for Butler ever since the capture of New Orleans in early 1862, when that general, then in command of the army's garrison of that city, had publicly criticized Porter's role in that expedition, in which he had commanded a squadron of mortar ships. Porter had served with Grant on the Mississippi River in 1863 and did not care much for him either, although there was no personal animosity and Grant liked him well enough. Evidently Porter felt that he had received less than his fair share of the credit and glory for the Vicksburg campaign and that Grant had received more. The admiral had told the general-in-chief that he could not get along with Butler, and he thought he had extracted a promise that the latter would not be coming on this expedition. But here he was after all. "Butler is too cunning for Grant," Porter told friends, "and will make him do what he pleases."[5]

Butler and Porter were on such poor terms that even when their ships rendezvoused they had avoided meeting face to face, communicating only by dispatches. The general had been surprised to learn that Porter had already sent the powder boat toward the fort to be detonated right away. Butler had sent General Weitzel and Lieutenant Colonel Cyrus Comstock, one of Grant's aides who was serving as chief engineer of the expedition, over to protest this move. The wind had been rising and a gale might very well have been brewing, which would have prevented the troops from being landed right away, and that would have given the Rebels time to recover from the explosion before the army could have attacked. Butler had wanted to wait a day to see if the good weather would hold. So the admiral had reluctantly sent a fast tug to order the *Louisiana* returned.

By the next morning, the nineteenth, the wind had picked up, the calm sea had been replaced by light swells, and a storm had seemed likely. Porter had signaled to Butler that, since a landing was impractical, he was going to exercise his fleet by putting his ships through battle formations and rehearsing the plan of attack. In battle lines the naval ships had steamed to within five miles of the fort, close enough to be seen from it. By that evening the wind was blowing hard from the northeast, the sea rolling in whitecap waves, and experienced seamen had said a gale was coming and the landing would have to be postponed. The troop transports were low on drinking water and coal for the

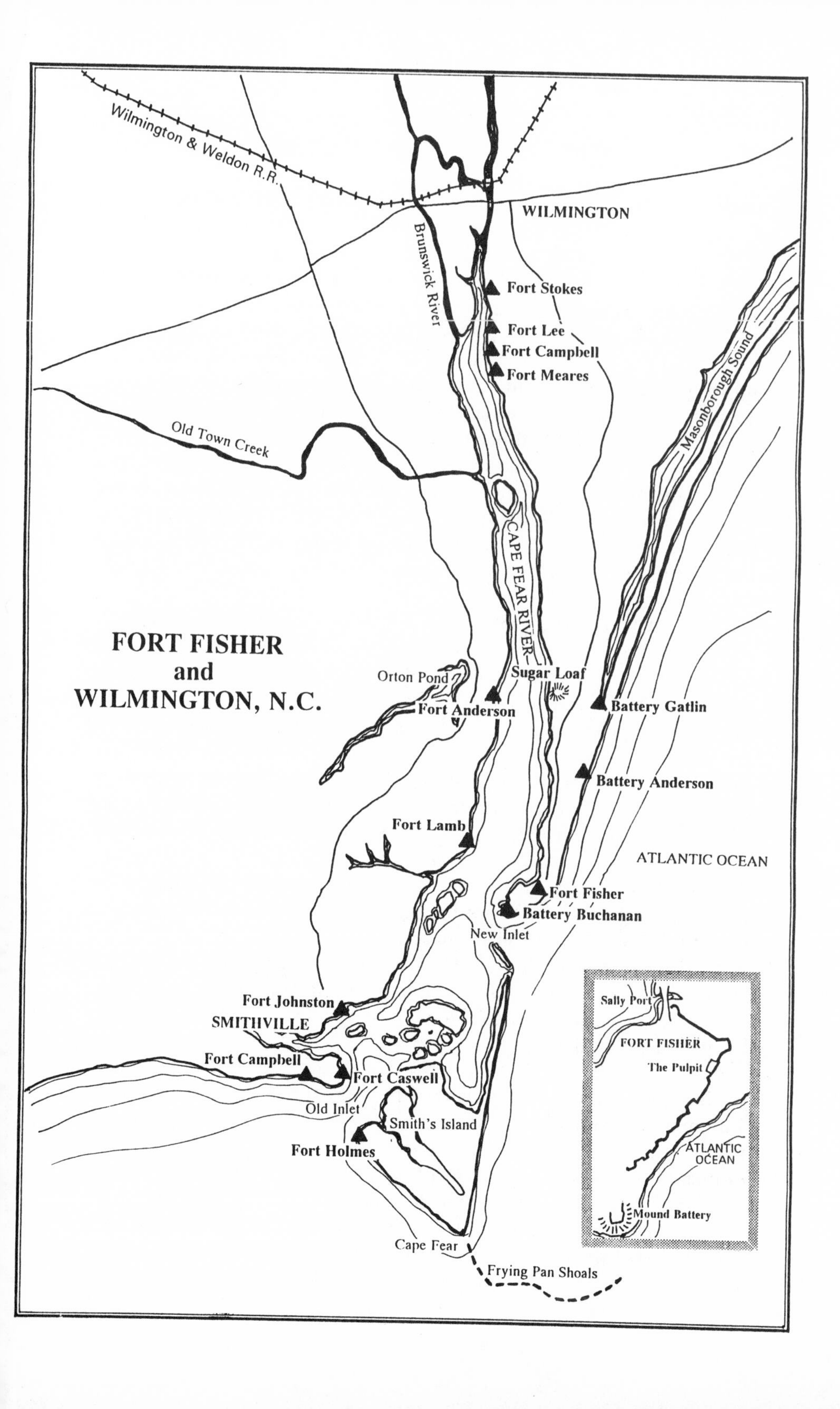

FORT FISHER
and
WILMINGTON, N.C.
Wilmington & Weldon R.R.
WILMINGTON
Brunswick River
Fort Stokes
Fort Lee
Fort Campbell
Fort Meares
Masonborough Sound
Old Town Creek
CAPE FEAR RIVER
Orton Pond
Sugar Loaf
Fort Anderson
Battery Gatlin
Battery Anderson
Fort Lamb
ATLANTIC OCEAN
Fort Fisher
Battery Buchanan
New Inlet
Fort Johnston
SMITHVILLE
Fort Campbell
Fort Caswell
Old Inlet
Smith's Island
Fort Holmes
Cape Fear
Frying Pan Shoals
Sally Port
FORT FISHER
The Pulpit
ATLANTIC
OCEAN
Mound Battery

engines by then anyway, so Butler had taken them into Beaufort to ride out the storm and stock up on supplies.

For security reasons, the soldiers had not been allowed to disembark at Beaufort, and when the two-day storm struck, most of them had soon become seasick. A chaplain recorded that the ocean "was covered with white foam and rolling waves, but still the wind increased, and higher did the billows roll until great mountains, towering apparently up to heaven, came dashing along in sublime vengeance.... Many, for a while, tried to laugh and shake off their fears, but about eight o'clock we ceased laughing. I had been praying all the time, and believe many others were. Now all began to feel serious and solemn. Even the crew looked and spoke apprehensively. Finally, an awful sea came and broke in our wheel-house. Still the raging waters and howling winds grew worse." One Federal sergeant was "amused at the sudden conversion of the boys by the storm. A night of prayer for once—quite an agreeable change from the usual swearing."[6]

Now, on the morning of Friday, 23 December, Butler sent an aide with a message for Admiral Porter saying that his transports would return to the rendezvous point the following night and the attack could take place on Christmas day. But Porter, whose ships had ridden out the storm in place, replied that the navy was not going to wait for the army and would attack right away. While the USS *Wilderness* towed the *Lousiana* toward Fort Fisher, Admiral Porter moved the rest of his ships twelve miles farther out to sea and ordered them to all release the steam from their boilers so they would not be ruptured by the explosion of the powder boat. The *Lousiana* would be exploded at 1 a.m. Then the fleet would open fire on the fort on the morning of the 24th. Butler was furious when this news was brought to him. "The Admiral supposed he would blow the fort all to pieces, and be able to land his marines and take possession of it," he later complained.[7] He ordered his headquarters ship, the *Ben De Ford*, to start immediately for Fort Fisher and for the transports to follow as soon as they finished coaling, but he knew he would arrive too late.

At 10:30 p.m. on 23 December 1864 the USS *Wilderness* began towing the *Louisiana* toward Fort Fisher. Aboard the powder boat were Commander Alexander C. Rhind, Lieutenant Samuel W. Preston, and twelve volunteer seamen. When the commander of the *Wilderness* estimated that he was 500 yards off the Federal Point peninsula a green lantern was flashed to the *Louisiana* three times, and the tow lines were cast off. The powder boat's own engines were then fired up and it moved slowly toward the beach. Rhind had wanted to take his craft to within 150 yards of Fort Fisher, but as the earthen walls of the fort began to loom up in the darkness he began to worry about being spotted by the Confederates. Just then another ship approached. It was a blockade runner, the *Little Hattie*, making for New Inlet in the dark. Rhind ordered his pilot to follow this ship, hoping that the Confederates would mistake the powder boat for another blockade runner. When Rhind judged that the *Louisiana* was within 300 yards of the fort's Northeast Bastion he killed the engines and dropped anchor. He had decided to settle for twice the distance that he had originally hoped for. What he did not realize was that he was really 600 yards out.

While the rest of his crew rowed for the *Wilderness*, Rhind, Lieutenant Preston, and engineer Anthony Mullin began setting the powder boat's ignition devices. Clockwork mechanisms were set up in the engine room and on the starboard and port bows, all set to activate at 1:18 a.m. Just in case these failed to function, two back-up systems were provided: candles cut to a timed length and a slow match. All of these devises were attached to a new invention known as a Gomez fuse, which was supposed to ignite all of the gunpowder simultaneously. These were lit and then, in accordance with Admiral Porter's orders, just before boarding his launch, Rhind set fire to a pile of "fat lighter" stacked beside the cabin. It was almost midnight as the three men rowed away, and as soon as they were taken on board the *Wilderness* this ship weighed anchor and steamed off at full speed, firing signal rockets to let the other ships know that the powder boat was set to explode.

It took 45 minutes for the *Wilderness* to reach the fleet, where Admiral Porter was steaming up and down the line in his flagship, the USS *Malvern*, signaling for the other ships to stand by for the explosion. Sailors lined the rails and crowded the rigging, gazing at the rosy glare in the western sky—a reflection of the fire Rhind had started on the *Louisiana*—and newspaper reporters whom Porter had brought along to record what he expected to be an historic occasion checked their watches. "I think that the concussion will tumble magazines," Porter had predicted, "and that the famous Mound will be among the things that were, and the guns buried beneath the ruins. I think that houses in Wilmington and Smithville will tumble to the ground and much demoralize the people, and I think if the rebels fight after the explosion they have more in them than I gave them credit for... I expect more good to our cause from a success in this instance than from an advance of all the armies in the field."[8]

The appointed hour of 1:18 a.m. came and went, and yet there was no explosion. Five minutes, ten, then twenty minutes passed. Finally, at 1:46 a.m., as one of Admiral Porter's aides wrote, "Suddenly a bright flash was observed and a stream of flames ascended to a great height and spread out in an immense sheet of fire, illuminating for an instant the whole horizon." This flash of light and flame was soon followed by a great boom that a *New York Times* correspondent said sounded like "the discharge of a 100-pounder." This was followed by an expanding wall of pale gray smoke that swept toward the fleet from the spot over the horizon where the *Louisiana* had been, spreading as it ascended like a giant waterspout. "In a very few minutes it passed us," the *Times* writer said, "filling the atmosphere with its sulphurous odor, as if a spirit from the infernal regions had swept by us." Commander Rhind turned to the officers lining the railing of the *Wilderness* with him and said, "There's a fizzle."[9] Then darkness and silence closed around the fleet once more.

The Federals had to wait until dawn to learn the results of their great experiment. Then the USS *Rhode Island* steamed toward shore. Aboard her was Major Thomas L. Casey, the officer who had prepared the *Louisiana* for her role. He studied the distant fort through his binoculars, looking for signs of damage. But he found none. "The edges and crests of the parapets remained as sharp and well-defined as ever," he reported. The log palisade, the wooden barracks inside the fort, even the rusted smokestack of a grounded blockade-runner nearby, gave no evidence that any explosion had ever occurred. Some Confederate Junior Reserves—teenagers too young for the real army—camped on the beach north of the fort had been severely frightened by the explosion, starting from their blankets "like popcorn from a popper," as one of them put it.[10] But the commander of Fort Fisher was unconcerned. He thought that a Union blockader had run aground, been abandoned and set afire, and its magazine had exploded. He did not learn that his fort was the object of the blast until after the war.

A number of problems had led to the failure of the powder boat: According to the original plan, the *Lousiana* was to carry 300 tons of gunpowder, half provided by the army and half by the navy, tightly packed and overlaid with normal and incendiary artillery shells, and the vessel was to be run onto the beach within 450 yards of the fort. The army actually provided 155 tons of powder, but the navy added only 60 tons, mainly because it was found that even with this total of only 215 tons the *Louisiana* was riding so low in the water that it was feared that she would sink without ever leaving her dock. The artillery shells were omitted for the same reason. What is more, this left a large empty space in the forward part of the ship. Evidently the Gomez fuse failed to function, which would explain why the explosion was almost a half-hour late. When it did come it was caused by the fire Rhind had set near the cabin. This, however, unlike the Gomez fuse, did not reach all of the powder simultaneously. In fact, only about 20 percent of the powder actually ignited, and that was the part near the top where it met no resistance from the empty compartments and blew straight up into the air. The other 80 percent was either scattered on the wind or sank with whatever remained of the ship. And, of course, Rhind had placed the ship 600 yards from the fort, not 450. Furthermore, Porter had ordered the ship anchored off the shore, not run onto the beach, fearing that either she would break up if run aground or that the Confederates might board her and cut the fuses or scuttle her. Because she was not grounded, the *Louisiana* drifted another 400 yards out to sea before the powder exploded.

Even had the explosion done all that had originally been expected of it there still remains room for doubting that Fort Fisher would have fallen as a result. For Porter had ignored the initial purpose of exploding the boat: to disable the fort's guns long enough for the army to assault and capture the place or for the navy to run ships through New Inlet and get in rear of the fort. No ships were prepared to run past the fort into the river because Porter had decided that, without a reliable pilot, the narrow, shallow channel could not be safely negotiated. And the soldiers were not only not ready to attack the fort but had not even been landed on the beach yet. And even if they had been ready, they could hardly have attacked in the middle of the night without being able to see what the explosion had done to the fort and the approaches to it. The Rebels would thus have been given hours to recover from the midnight explosion and to prepare for a morning attack.

When Porter learned that Fort Fisher was still standing he turned to the only option he had left, since he had already decided not to try to run past the fort through New Inlet. He would bombard the fort into submission. By 8 a.m. his fleet was under way. He soon ordered it to anchor again when the wind suddenly rose, but it quickly died down and the ships continued on to the west in tight formation. "The sunlight flashed on their numerous polished guns," one sailor wrote, "and the scene was very grand and imposing."[11] At 11:30 a.m. the ships' drummers beat "to quarters for action," and about an hour later the fleet came within range of the fort and prepared to open fire. The ships were organized into four lines. Three lines would bombard the fort while the fourth served as a reserve to replace any ships damaged by Confederate fire, to carry dispatches, and to cover the landing of Butler's soldiers.

When a Confederate lookout on the Pulpit Battery spotted the approach of the Union ships he sent for the fort's commander, Colonel

William Lamb, a 29-year-old former newspaper editor, son of a former mayor of Norfolk, Virginia, and a Phi Beta Kappa graduate of William and Mary College. As colonel of the 36th North Carolina Artillery, Lamb had been appointed to command Fort Fisher on the Fourth of July, 1862. "I determined at once to build a work of such magnitude that it could withstand the heaviest fire of any guns in the American Navy," he said.[12] And now, on Christmas Eve, 1864, he was about to find out if he had succeeded.

Word had come to Lamb from Richmond two months before that the Yankees were preparing an expedition against Fort Fisher, and the Union fleet had been spotted off the coast four days ago. Now Lamb ordered the fort's drummer to beat "the long roll" summoning his troops to battle stations. However, no gun was to fire until a 10-inch Columbiad in the Pulpit Battery gave the signal by firing one shot. Even after that, no gun was to be fired more than once each half-hour, because ammunition was in short supply, and only the long-range guns were to fire at all.

At 12:45 p.m. the first line of Federal ships, which included five ironclads—four monitors and a larger ship called the USS *New Ironsides*—opened fire from about three-quarters of a mile northeast of the fort. The first shot came from an 11-inch smoothbore shell gun on the *New Ironsides.* It just missed the fort's flagstaff and exploded behind the Pulpit Battery, where Colonel Lamb was still standing, and he ordered the Columbiad fired in reply. Its 10-inch solid shot ricocheted off the smooth sea and punched a hole through the smoke stack of the USS *Susquehanna* in the second line of ships, about a mile east of the fort. At this signal, the fort's other guns soon opened a slow and deliberate fire, but the fleet responded with a rapid and overwhelming storm of shells. Geysers of sand were thrown up all along the sloping earthen walls of the fort while bursting shells rained jagged iron slivers overhead. "What with the continuous roar of the firing," one Confederate remembered, "and the scarcely less frequent reports of bursting shells, the aggregate noise was not unlike that of a rolling, volleying, long-sustained thunderstorm. The hostile missiles which showered into the fort... were of all sorts and sizes, from the big XV-inch spherical shot or shell, and the 100-pounder rifled Parrott, down through the list, and the whiz or whistle of each variety seemed to strike a different and more vicious note." A Union sailor agreed that the noise was "one continual roar like the heaviest thunder—and the smoke so thick at times to completely hide the sun. I got so deaf after awhile as to be most entirely indifferent to it. My ears are singing yet. Oh! It was a sight never to be forgotten."[13]

The fort's garrison sheltered itself from the bombardment in the various bombproofs, only emerging occasionally to fire a few return shots. One gun crew disobeyed orders and kept firing at the USS *Powhatan* until they had found the range. They then put five shots into the ship in rapid succession. But the ship's crew merely shifted some of its guns to the other side so that their weight would keep the ship from listing and keep the holes in its side above water. A shot from another Confederate gun penetrated the hull of the USS *Pontoosuc*, just missed hitting its steam engine, tore through an iron bulkhead and a wall of mess lockers, splintered a heavy wooden beam, and exploded in the paymaster's storeroom, setting fire to the ship. The blaze was quickly extinguished, and no one was hurt. The USS *Osceola* was not so lucky. A shell punctured her hull, hit her boiler, and exploded. The escaping steam scalded six men and flooded the boiler room, and the ship pulled out of the fight, although a repair crew eventually managed to plug the huge hole in her side. Eight sailors and two marines were scalded when a shot from the Mound Battery exploded the boiler of the USS *Mackinaw*. Her commander also started to pull out of line, but Porter signaled from his flagship, "Remain where you are and fight."[14]

The fleet's fire was continuous but not concentrated, and in fact many of its shots fell harmlessly into the river behind the fort. Nevertheless, some damage was inflicted. One Union shell exploded among a group of Confederate sailors who manned one of the fort's batteries, blowing the left leg off Seaman J. F. Higgins. And a young courier carrying dispatches across the fort was horribly mangled by a splinter from an 11-inch shell. Gunners from a nearby battery braved the Union fire to dig him a hasty grave. Colonel Lamb's brick headquarters building, formerly the cottage of the keeper for the lighthouse on Federal Point, was pounded into rubble, and a small stable behind the seaface, where the officers' horses were kept, was set on fire. While the animals escaped from the blaze, they ran about the fort, maddened by the noise, until one by one they were all killed by the bombardment. The fort's wooden barracks also caught fire and the huge column of smoke billowing up from them brought a cheer from the Union sailors. After the *Mackinaw* was hit, three Union ships concentrated their fire on the Mound Battery and silenced it by driving its gunners to seek the permanent protection of their bombproof. But Federal gunners wasted numerous shells firing at Confederate flags flying over the Mound and Pulpit batteries.

One Confederate gun, an 8-inch Columbiad, was jarred off its carriage by the recoil of its first shot, and went spinning across the sand, scattering its crew in all directions. The fleet also suffered from self-inflicted damage. On the USS *Juanita* a navy lieutenant, a marine lieutenant, a seaman, a fireman, and a young powder monkey were killed and eight other men wounded when a 100-pounder Parrott rifle exploded. Parrotts had wrought-iron hoops reinforcing their breeches, and these had a nasty habit of occasionally bursting when the guns were fired, slinging iron fragments all about. The *Juanita* pulled out of line until Porter caught her. "My 100-pounder has exploded!" her captain shouted. "Then why in hell don't you go back and use your other guns?" the Admiral demanded.[15] Before the day was over, Parrott rifles had exploded on five ships, causing 37 casualties, and Porter ordered all of the 100-pounders to cease firing. The wounded were transferred to hospital ships anchored in the rear.

At about 4 p.m. a steamboat docked at the riverside wharf near Battery Buchanan to disembark Brigadier General William Henry Chase Whiting, Confederate commander of the District of Cape Fear. The general and three officers of his staff then made their way across the interior of the fort in spite of the bombardment and arrived at the Pulpit at about 4:30 p.m. Colonel Lamb offered to relinquish command of the fort to the general, but Whiting declined the offer, saying he had only come to observe and assist. Whiting was a brilliant engineer who had set a record of academic excellence at West Point that would stand until Douglas MacArthur finally broke it over sixty years later. He was not only Lamb's boss but his friend and his mentor, whose engineering talents had helped to make Fort Fisher, the key post in his district, so strong. He was beloved by his subordinates, including Lamb, but was distrusted and disliked by his superiors, especially Confederate president Jefferson Davis, one of whose pet projects Whiting had once had the temerity to criticize.

When the Confederates had gotten wind of Union designs on Wilmington, Davis, distrusting Whiting, had sent General Braxton Bragg to assume overall command in North Carolina. Bragg was just the opposite of Lamb, admired and trusted by Davis while distrusted and hated by his subordinates. As commander of the Army of Tennessee earlier in the war, he had become so unpopular with his officers and men, and the country as a whole, that Davis had finally been forced to remove him after his defeat by Grant at Chattanooga in November 1863. But Davis had then made him the titular general-in-chief of the Confederate Army. However, since Davis, a West Point graduate and Mexican War veteran himself, kept military matters tightly in his own hands, Bragg was actually little more than his chief of staff.

Throughout most of 1864, North Carolina had been part of the Confederate Department of Southern Virginia and North Carolina, commanded by General Pierre Gustave Toutant Beauregard. But that spring, when Butler had moved up the James River and threatened Richmond and Petersburg, Beauregard had concentrated most of his forces in southern Virginia for their defense. When Grant had brought the Army of the Potomac south of the James River to attack Petersburg, Lee's Army of Northern Virginia had been drawn partially into Beauregard's department, and soon Beauregard had become little more than a corps commander under Lee. Davis then had sent Beauregard to command a new Division of the West, consisting of Hood's Army of Tennessee and the adjacent Department of Alabama, Mississippi, and East Lousiana, commanded by Davis' brother-in-law, Lieutenant General Richard Taylor. This had left North Carolina without an overall commander, and, when the Confederates had gotten wind of Federal designs on Wilmington and Fort Fisher, Davis had sent Bragg to fill that void. Hardly had Bragg settled into place, however, when Sherman's march across Georgia had caused Davis to send him with most of the troops from North Carolina to defend Augusta, which Sherman had then promptly bypassed. Learning of Bragg's absence, Grant had ordered the expedition against Fort Fisher to get under way, but this had taken so long that Bragg had returned before the Federals got there, although without his troops. Other forces were on the way, however, from Lee's army. Major General Robert Hoke's division, composed mostly of troops Beauregard had taken from North Carolina in the spring to defend Richmond and Petersburg, was on its way via the rickety, worn-out Confederate railroad system, and Whiting now brought Lamb the welcome news that not only were two companies of reinforcements being ferried across the Cape Fear River from Fort Caswell to Battery Buchanan but the leading elements of Hoke's Division had reached Wilmington and were probably already being put in fortifications at a place called Sugar Loaf, some six miles upriver from Fort Fisher.

In fact, Brigadier General William W. Kirkland and the first 1,300 men of his brigade of Hoke's Division had reached Wilmington at midnight after a cold, tiring ride on the worn-out rails. They had marched all day through soft sand and had reached Sugar Loaf, on the western side of the Confederate Point peninsula, at about the same time that General Whiting had joined Colonel Lamb. Kirkland assumed command of the area north of Fort Fisher, stretched his forces, including some 1,200 old men and boys of the North Carolina reserves, on a line facing south across the peninsula from Sugar Loaf on the river to Battery Gatlin, a small earthwork on the ocean side holding one 32-pounder gun and a few field pieces. Then he watched the naval bombardment of Fort Fisher while waiting for the arrival of the rest of his men, or orders from General Bragg, or the landing of Union troops.

At 5:30 p.m. Admiral Porter gave the signal for the fleet to cease fire. As the ships slowly pulled back out of range of the fort acres of empty ammunition boxes that had been thrown overboard during the day followed them on the ebbing tide. General Butler, who had just arrived on the *Ben De Ford*, pulled alongside the flag ship and sent a staff officer over to inform the admiral that General Weitzel and Colonel Comstock would come aboard later to discuss arrangements for landing the troops the next day. Butler, who was furious that Porter had not only exploded the powder boat without him but had botched the job, was not about to see him in person. Porter, for his part, did not even want to see Weitzel and Comstock, but finally agreed to. He told them that if the fort's guns were not destroyed they were at least disabled by sand thrown into their muzzles by exploding Union shells. All the army would have to do was walk in and take possession of whatever remained.

The two army officers were not convinced. They had both had plenty of experience with earthworks, from the inside and the outside, and knew that the limited return fire during the day did not mean that the guns were damaged, just that the Confederates had been sensible enough to shelter in their bombproofs most of the time. But they would come out and fight when the Union army arrived. The two soldiers suggested that Porter run his ships past the fort through New Inlet into the river, while the army landed north of the fort and established a supply line for him across the peninsula. The fort would be cut off and starved out. But Porter said the channel was too shallow and probably full of Rebel torpedoes and obstructions. "Fine cooperation," Comstock sarcastically noted in his diary.[16]

When Butler and his officers conferred that night, the commanding general was ready to give up. His pet project had been spoiled by Porter and the element of surprise was gone. His staff and Weitzel agreed that they might as well return to the Richmond-Petersburg lines. Comstock, however, urged them to at least land part of the troops in the morning and reconnoiter. Then they could decide what to do after a closer look at the situation.

---

1. John Wilkinson, "Wilmington Is Turned Topsy-Turvy by the War," in *The Blue and the Gray, The Story of the Civil War as Told by Participants,* edited by Henry Steele Commager (New York, 1950), 867.
2. Noel Blakeman, "Noel Blakeman Recalls the Trials of Blockading," in *The Blue and the Gray,* 854.

3. Rod Gragg, *Confederate Goliath: The Battle of Fort Fisher* (New York, 1991), 21.
4. Ibid., 37.
5. Ibid., 44.
6. Ibid., 48-49.
7. Ibid., 49.
8. Ibid., 50.
9. Ibid., 52-53.
10. Ibid., 53.
11. Ibid., 63.
12. Ibid., 17.
13. Ibid., 65-66.
14. Ibid., 68.
15. Ibid., 69.
16. Ibid., 74.

CHAPTER THREE

We Did Not Enjoy Christmas

24 - 25 December 1864

John Wilkes Booth left Washington on 24 December to spend Christmas with relatives in New York.

Down in Virginia that day, Colonel Mayo's brigade, which had been pulled out of the Petersburg lines as a possible reinforcement for the forces sent to defend Gordonsville, was instead ordered to report on the 26th to Lieutenant General Richard Ewell, Commander of the Department of Richmond. It would be replaced by a small brigade of Tennessee regiments taken from that department. The purpose of this exchange of brigades appears to have been connected with the plot to capture President Lincoln. Mayo's brigade contained three Virginia regiments with men recruited from the area of the lower Potomac and Rappahannock rivers through which the captured Lincoln would be brought to Richmond. The Confederate government knew that the Federals kept a close watch on the location of Lee's various military units and might well discover the shift of any whole units to that area, but they needed to have some soldiers there to protect the kidnappers from any Union pursuit. Part of Lieutenant Colonel John S. Mosby's partisan cavalry unit was being shifted into that area, but to provide additional force, various units recruited from that area were being shifted into the Department of Richmond and placed under the command of Major General George Washington Custis Lee, eldest son of Robert E. Lee. From there numerous individuals in these units were sent home on "leave."[1]

In Savannah, Georgia, Major General William Tecumseh Sherman received a welcome Christmas present that day in the form of a letter from his old friend, General Grant, written on the eighteenth while the latter had been in Washington. It began with congratulations for Sherman's successful march across Georgia from Atlanta, which had just terminated in the capture of Savannah. "I never had a doubt of the result," Grant continued. "When apprehensions for your safety were expressed by the President, I assured him with the army you had, and you in command of it, there was no danger but you would *strike* bottom on salt-water some place; that I would not feel the same security—in fact, would not have intrusted the expedition to any other living commander.

"It has been very hard work to get Thomas to attack Hood. I gave him the most peremptory order, and had started to go there myself, before he got off. He has done magnificently, however, since he started. Up to last night, five thousand prisoners and forty-nine pieces of captured artillery, besides many wagons and innumerable small-arms, had been received in Nashville. This is exclusive of the enemy's loss at Franklin, which amounted to thirteen general officers, killed, wounded, and captured. The enemy probably lost five thousand men at Franklin, and ten thousand in the last three days' operations...."[2]

And then came the best part, so far as Sherman was concerned: "I did think the best thing to do was to bring the greater part of your army here and wipe out Lee. The turn affairs now seem to be taking has shaken me in that opinion. I doubt whether you may not accomplish more toward that result where you are than if brought here, especially as I am informed, since my arrival in the city, that it would take about two months to get you here with all the other calls there are for ocean transportation.

"I want to get your views about what ought to be done, and what can be done.... My own opinion is that Lee is averse to going out of Virginia, and if the cause of the South is lost he wants Richmond to be the last place surrendered. If he has such views, it may be well to indulge him until we get every thing else in our hands."[2]

Letters that had met Sherman near Savannah, written by Grant while Sherman's march had still been under way, had already ordered Sherman to prepare to have the bulk of his army transported to Virginia by sea, and he had not liked the idea much. In his reply to Grant's latest letter he said, "I am.... pleased that you have modified your former orders, for I feared that the transportation by sea would very much disturb the unity and *morale* of my army, now so perfect."[3] But there was more to it than that. He was more frank in a letter written that same day in reply to one from another old friend, Major General Henry W. Halleck, the army's chief of staff. "I am... very glad that General Grant has changed his mind about embarking my troops for James River, leaving me free to make the broad swath you describe through South and North Carolina... I have just finished a long letter to General Grant, and have explained to him that we are engaged in shifting our base from the Ogeechee to the Savannah River, dismantling all the forts made by the enemy to bear upon the salt-water channels, transferring the heavy ordnance, etc., to Fort Pulaski and Hilton Head, and in remodeling the enemy's interior lines to suit our future plans and purposes. I have also laid down the programme for a campaign which I can make this winter, and which will put me in the spring on the Roanoke, in direct communication with General Grant on James River."

He said he would threaten both Augusta, Georgia and Charleston, South Carolina, but would pass between them and break up the railroad that connected them. Then he would turn upon either Charleston or Wilmington to reestablish contact with the North by sea. "I rather prefer Wilmington, as a live place, over Charleston, which is dead and unimportant when its railroad communications are broken. I take it for granted that the present movement on Wilmington will fail." After that he would make for either Raleigh or Weldon, in North Carolina, "when Lee would be forced to come out of Richmond, or acknowledge himself beaten. He would, I think, by the use of the Danville Railroad, throw himself rapidly between me and Grant, leaving Richmond in the hands of the latter. This would not alarm me, for I have an army which I think can manoeuvre, and I would force him to attack me at a disadvantage, always under the supposition that Grant would be on his heels.... I think the time has come now when we should attempt the boldest moves, and my experience is, that they are easier of execution than more timid ones, because the enemy is disconcerted by them—as, for instance, my recent campaign.... I think our campaign of the last month, as well as every step I take from this point northward, is as much a direct attack upon Lee's army as though we were operating within the sound of his artillery....

"I attach more importance to these deep incisions into the enemy's country, because this war differs from European wars in this particular: we are not only fighting hostile armies, but a hostile people, and must make old and young, rich and poor, feel the hard hand of war, as well as their organized armies. I know that this recent movement of mine through Georgia has had a wonderful effect in this respect. Thousands who had been deceived by their lying newspapers to believe that we were being whipped all the time now realize the truth, and have no appetite for a repetition of the same experience. To be sure, Jeff. Davis has his people under pretty good discipline, but I think faith in him is much shaken in Georgia, and before we have done with her South Carolina will not be quite so tempetuous.... The truth is, the whole army is burning with an insatiable desire to wreak vengeance upon South Carolina. I almost tremble at her fate, but feel she deserves all that seems in store for her.

"Many and many a person in Georgia asked me why we did not go to South Carolina; and, when I answered that we were *en route* for that State, the invariable reply was, 'Well, if you will make those people feel the utmost severities of war, we will pardon you for your desolation of Georgia.'"[4]

"General Sherman is perfectly right," one of his staff officers, Major Henry Hitchcock, wrote—"the only possible way to end this unhappy conflict, in whose horrors, though he is Providentially a chief actor, no man is further from finding pleasure, is to make it *terrible beyond endurance*.... They may talk—the rebels and their friends—about 'the brute Sherman,' and to them while in arms against the Government they may be sure he will be nothing but a minister of wrath and vengeance, and of absolute destruction so far as the military power of the rebels and everything that is or can be used to maintain it is concerned. But as an individual and to individuals he is a straightforward, simple, kind-hearted, nay warm-hearted man, thoughtful and considerate of the feelings and scrupulously just and careful of the rights of others. I know this for I have already had unexpected opportunities of seeing it, in even trifling matters. His manner is off-hand, often almost blunt, but even in apparently harsh military measures there is often a reason not visible on the surface but founded in as much good feeling as good sense."[5]

This officer and the vast majority of Sherman's officers and men, were vastly proud of their commanding general and recognized in him a genuine and unique American genius. "He impresses me as a man of power more than any man I remember," Hitchcock said. "Not general intellectual power, not Websterian, but the sort of power which a flash of lightning suggests,—as clear, as intense, and as rapid."[6] A young naval officer who had recently met Sherman gave the classic description of the general, calling him "the most American looking man I ever saw, tall and lank, not very erect, with hair like a thatch, which he rubs up with his hands, a rusty beard trimmed close, a wrinked face, sharp, prominent red nose, small, bright eyes, course red hands; black felt hat slouched over his eyes... , dirty dickey with the points wilted down, black, old-fashioned stock, brown field officer's coat with high collar and no shoulder straps, muddy trowsers and one spur. He carries his hands in his pockets, is very awkward in his gait and motion, talks continually and with immense rapidity, and might sit to *Punch* for the portrait of an ideal Yankee."[7]

Benjamin Grierson's Union raiders continued to move southeastward into Mississippi on the 24th, getting as far as the town of Ripley. From there he sent two detachments on to the east for the purpose of cutting the Mobile & Ohio Railroad. A battalion of the large 2nd New Jersey Cavalry was to hit the line at Booneville, and the 4th Illinois Cavalry was to hit it farther south near Guntown.

In Tennessee, Wilson's cavalry took over the lead in the Union pursuit of Hood's retreating army at about 7 a.m. that day. Brigadier General John T. Croxton's 1st Brigade of the 1st Division of the Cavalry Corps was out in front, and it pushed rapidly ahead, encountering little opposition until about 4 p.m., when Forrest's entire cavalry command was found to be in position north of Richland Creek, with six pieces of artillery covering the turnpike. While Croxton's troopers dismounted to begin a cautious advance and Federal artillery was brought up to challenge the Rebel guns, Wilson sent Brigadier General Edward Hatch's 5th Division to the east in an attempt to bypass Forrest's line. This move was stopped by an unfordable stretch of Richland Creek, but Forrest soon withdrew after only a heavy skirmish with Croxton's men, during which one Union trooper captured the headquarters flag of Brigadier General James R. Chalmers' Confederate division and Forrest's other division commander, Brigadier General Abraham Buford, was wounded in the leg by a carbine bullet.

In Pulaski that night the Confederate rear guard, consisting of Forrest's cavalry and an ad hoc division of infantry commanded by Major General Edward C. Walthall, burned wagons full of abandoned ammunition and destroyed a locomotive and its five cars which could not go farther south because of destroyed bridges on the line. From

Pulaski the Rebels still had to traverse over forty miles of muddy roads to reach the Tennessee River at Bainbridge, Alabama. To buy time for the rest of the army to cover that distance, Forrest decided to set an ambush for the pursuing Federals.

On Christmas morning Wilson's troopers dashed into Pulaski, extinguished flames on the turnpike bridge over Richland Creek set by the retreating Rebels, and pushed on rapidly to the south in the rain. The roadside was strewn with weapons and equipment discarded by the Confederates as well as numerous abandoned wagons. At about 3 p.m. Colonel Thomas J. Harrison's 1st Brigade of the 6th Division, now in the lead, came to Anthony's Hill, about seven miles south of Pulaski. The road ascended the hill through a gorge lined with thick timber, so that it was difficult to see more than a few feet ahead. Here the Federals encountered stiff resistance from Rebel skirmishers, so Harrison ordered three of his regiments to dismount and attack.

They pushed forward rapidly until they were within a few yards of a barricade made of fence rails when suddenly they were fired on by two brigades of Walthall's infantry behind the barricade, two brigades of Forrest's cavalry on the flanks, and three pieces of artillery hidden in the trees. The sudden volley brought the Federals to a halt, and when the Rebels followed it with a charge, Harrison's men broke and ran. Their wild retreat broke up Brigadier General John H. Hammond's 1st Brigade of the 7th Division, which was just deploying to support them. Both brigades ran down the hill and past a single Union cannon that had been unlimbered in the valley below and continued on for half a mile, leaving the gun and many of their horses behind. The Confederates gathered these up but were soon pushed back into their barricade by the troopers of Hatch's division, who counterattacked on foot with their Spencer repeating carbines. Wilson, learning that he was up against Confederate infantry, sent back word for the Union infantry to come up and help him dislodge the enemy from their strong position, but it took an hour for the foot soldiers to reach the front. By then it was dark and the Rebels had slipped away.

General Thomas received a Christmas present that day in the form of a telegram from Secretary of War Stanton informing him that the president had sent his name to the Senate for promotion to the rank of major general in the regular army, a grade that he had held up until then only in the temporary volunteer force. "No commander has more justly earned promotion by devoted, disinterested, and valuable service to his country," Stanton told him.[8]

Hood's engineers spent a cold, rainy Christmas Day laying pontoon boats in the Tennessee River as rapidly as they arrived over the muddy roads. So many pontoons had been abandoned along the way that there would not have been enough to stretch across the swollen river, but fifteen boats, which had been captured when the Federals had withdrawn from Decatur, Alabama, during Hood's advance the previous month, had been floated down the river and over the flooded Muscle Shoals to arrive just in time. That was Hood's Christmas present.

Meanwhile his main column crossed Shoal Creek, two miles north of the river, and started digging entrenchments from which to protect the bridge. Many of the men were no-doubt comparing their present lot with the happier days of the previous spring down in Georgia under their favorite commander, Hood's predecessor, General Joseph E. Johnston. At some point on the road to Bainbridge that day Hood and his staff passed some of his men who were singing "The Yellow Rose of Texas," only they had added a new verse:

So now I'm marching southward;
My heart is full of woe.
I'm going back to Georgia
To see my Uncle Joe.
You may talk about your Beauregard
And sing of General Lee,
But the gallant Hood of Texas
Played Hell in Tennessee.[9]

Down in Mississippi on Christmas Day Grierson's Union raiders were rejoined by the 4th Illinois Cavalry, which had captured seven Rebels, burned two bridges on the Mobile & Ohio Railroad, and torn up about a quarter of a mile of track between Guntown and Baldwyn Station. The main column reached Old Town Creek that day, five miles north of Tupelo, and there learned that the Confederates had a camp for horseless cavalrymen and a large quantity of supplies at Verona, a few miles south of Tupelo. Grierson ordered Colonel Joseph Kargé to take his 1st Brigade to Verona by way of Harrisburg, an abandoned town west of Tupelo where A.J. Smith had defeated Forrest the previous summer. "Our movements thus far had been rapid," Grierson later reported, "and the indications were that the enemy had no knowledge of our presence, as our appearance was a complete surprise to the citizens on our line of march."[10] Kargé's brigade moved out at dark and then stopped to close up the column at Harrisburg. Two miles from Verona the leading regiment, the 7th Indiana, ran into a Rebel picket line and drove the two or three hundred defenders through the town. Then Kargé set details to work destroying the Confederate supplies, which included 950 rifles and carbines with 200 boxes of ammunition, a large amount

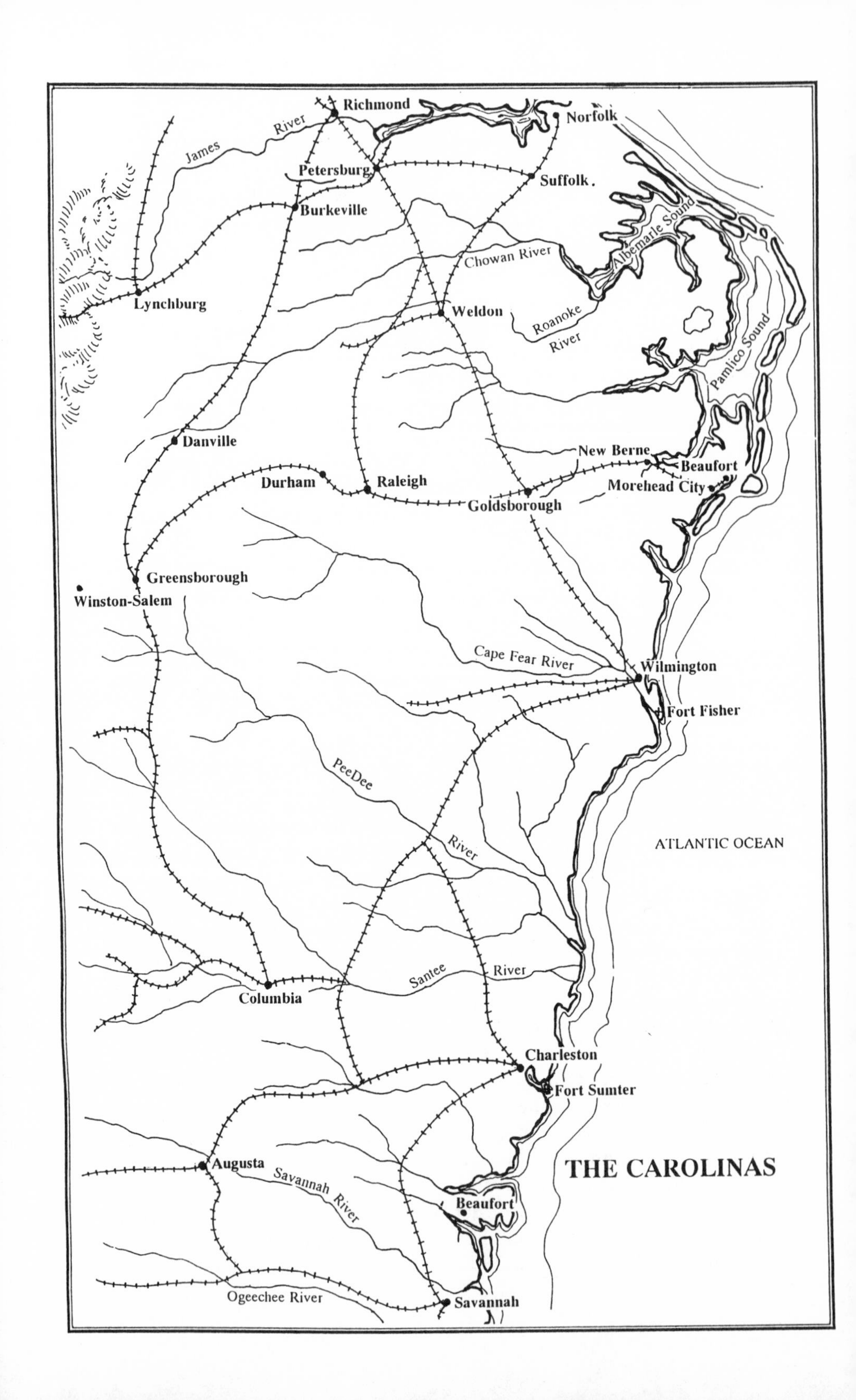

THE CAROLINAS
Richmond
Norfolk
James River
Petersburg
Suffolk
Burkeville
Albemarle Sound
Chowan River
Lynchburg
Weldon
Roanoke River
Pamlico Sound
Danville
New Berne
Beaufort
Durham
Raleigh
Morehead City
Goldsborough
Greensborough
Winston-Salem
Cape Fear River
Wilmington
Fort Fisher
PeeDee River
ATLANTIC OCEAN
Santee River
Columbia
Charleston
Fort Sumter
Augusta
Savannah River
Beaufort
Ogeechee River
Savannah

of artillery ammunition, 200 army wagons marked "U.S." that had been captured from Sturgis the previous summer, a train of 20 cars, a large quantity of saddles and quartermaster's and commissary supplies, and the eight large buildings used to house them all. The explosion of the ammunition, as Kargé reported, "commenced at 10 p.m. and did not cease until 5 o'clock the next morning."[11] Meanwhile, Grierson put the 11th Illinois Cavalry and his pioneer corps of fifty escaped slaves to work at tearing up the 900-foot bridge over Old Town Creek and a half mile of track of the Mobile & Ohio Railroad between there and Tupelo.

At 10:48 a.m. on Christmas Day, Admiral Porter's fleet began another bombardment of Fort Fisher with all the sound and fury of the day before. "Broadside followed broadside with great rapidity," wrote an army officer watching from one of the transports which were now on hand, "and the terrible discharges of the gunboats made it one continuous roar... heavy ordnance making the shores of the Old North State reverberate the deafening roar."[12] As on the day before, most of the fleet's shells landed inside the giant L of earthworks or in the river beyond. However, two of the four guns in Shepherd's battery on the landface were dismounted and ten of its gunners were wounded. When a shell exploded near the muzzle of a 10-inch Columbiad in a seaface battery it ignited the powder charge inside the gun and jarred it off its carriage. When an unexploded shell landed in the midst of another gun crew one man jumped on it and smothered the fuse and then another grabbed it and threw it out of the gun chamber. "I never saw shells fall so thick," a Confederate said. "They came down like hail. I thought every shell would get me. We did not enjoy Christmas."[13] Again the Rebels suffered self-inflicted damage when two of their big Brooke rifles exploded that afternoon.

At about 11 a.m. seventeen more Union ships opened fire on Battery Gatlin, well up the peninsula from Fort Fisher, and Battery Anderson, roughly halfway between the fort and Battery Gatlin. At first the gunners in these two smaller works, commanded by Lieutenant Colonel John P. Read, returned fire, but many of them were soon too intimidated by the incoming shells to man their guns. A shell fragment mangled Read's left arm and he was carried to the rear, after turning over command to the captain of a battery of field artillery that was just arriving as reinforcements. Then, in through the surf, came a line of navy launches loaded with Union soldiers from the transports.

The boats landed 400 yards north of Battery Anderson to the cheers of thousands of other Federals watching from the transports, and the first man to wade ashore was Brevet Brigadier General Newton M.

Curtis, 29-year-old commander of the 1st Brigade of the 2nd Division of the 24th Corps. He was followed by 500 men from his brigade, whom he deployed in a skirmish line behind some dunes. The cheers from the offshore transports increased and an army band aboard one of them struck up "Yankee Doodle" when Curtis's men unfurled the Stars and Stripes.

Then Curtis led part of his force down the beach to take Battery Anderson. He was still far from it, however, when the single company of Confederates manning the earthwork ran up a white flag. Seeing this, the Union ships that had been bombarding Battery Anderson ceased fire and four of them dispatched landing parties to accept the Rebels' surrender. The boats raced each other to be the first ashore, and when the soldiers saw what the navy was up to they too joined the race, breaking into a run in an effort to reach the battery before the sailors could land. Seamen from the USS *Britannia*, led by Acting Ensign William H. Bryant, won the race, accepted the surrender of the dejected North Carolinians, and ran up a U.S. flag over the captured works.

Curtis and his winded soldiers arrived too late to do more than watch the sailors row the captured Rebels out to their ships.

Seeing that his first wave had landed safely, Butler sent in the rest of Curtis's brigade and then the other two brigades of the division. And as more and more soldiers arrived, the Union skirmish line was expanded, sent up and down the peninsula, and into some woods to the west, where the first Confederate resistance was encountered in the form of some skirmishers from Kirkland's Brigade of Hoke's Division. The Federals fell back toward the beach, but the Rebels did not pursue them. Kirkland still had only a bit over one regiment of his brigade on hand and contented himself with holding a line running across the peninsula from Battery Gatlin on the beach to Sugar Loaf on the river. With the landing site now well defended, General Weitzel, who had come ashore with Curtis's brigade, ordered an advance southward toward Fort Fisher.

While the soldiers were being put ashore and the fleet continued to bombard the fort, Commander John Guest took nine warships to an anchorage near the south end of the peninsula, from which they opened fire on the Mound Battery and Battery Buchanan. The purpose of this operation was to provide cover for ten ships' boats that were sent to make soundings in New Inlet right under the Rebel guns. Leading this expedition was 22-year-old Lieutenant William B. Cushing, commander of Porter's flagship, who was a national hero after sinking the dreaded Confederate ironclad *Albemarle* two months before by steaming an open launch up the Roanoke River one night and shoving a spar torpedo up against the Rebel ship's hull under the waterline.

The fire of the Union ships failed to deter the Confederates in the Mound Battery and Battery Buchanan from manning their guns. But, in turn, their storm of grape shot and cannister failed to keep Cushing and his men from making their soundings. None of the Union sailors were hit—although near misses splashed so much water into their boats that they had to bail them out to keep from sinking—until about 3:30 p.m., when, his job completed, Cushing was preparing to withdraw. Then a shot from Battery Buchanan cut one of the launches in half, severing the leg of one seaman and hitting another with flying splinters. The other boats rescued the crew and returned to the ships, leaving the New Inlet channel marked. But Porter still considered it unnavigable for his deep-draft ships and refused to chance it.

General Whiting was inside Fort Fisher again this day, and when he saw Federal troops landed north of the fort and heading his way he began to bombard General Bragg, at Wilmington, with telegrams requesting reinforcements for the fort and an attack upon the enemy's rear. But Bragg seemed paralyzed with indecision, and one of his subordinates said that the general's hands were shaking. His only response to the crisis was to put his wife on a train heading out of the city. As Whiting had told another general a few weeks before, "Between Bragg and Lee, Sherman and Grant, old North Carolina is in a pretty fix."[14] At 4 p.m., just after Whiting had sent his last appeal to Bragg, the telegraph wire went dead.

Union skirmishers moving across the peninsula had found the telegraph line running between poles along the road to Wilmington less than a mile north of the fort, and General Curtis had ordered it cut. Curtis and General Weitzel then studied the fort through binoculars. They were impressed with its formidable-looking earthen walls and the wooden palisade and counted at least seventeen guns on the landface. The navy's bombardment did not seem to have done much damage. Curtis thought an attack on the fort would be costly but could be successful. Weitzel was not so sure. In the past, attacks on lesser works had proven disastrous. He told Curtis not to engage the Confederates without further orders and went back to the beach to get a launch to take him out to the ships to report to General Butler.

While Weitzel was gone, Curtis led his men to an abandoned line of old Confederate earthworks about 150 yards north of Fort Fisher and sent some of his skirmishers to within 75 yards of the fort, where they dug rifle pits in the sand near the river. Within minutes, a young Rebel courier came riding out of the fort and across the wooden bridge over the marsh near the gate. One of Curtis's skirmishers shot him out of the saddle and found that he was carrying a dispatch from Major William Saunders, the fort's chief of artillery, asking the force at Sugar Loaf to send him some field pieces. The soldier caught the Confederate's horse and took the message to Curtis.

That general had been studying the fort from his new, closer, position. Some of his men had worked their way forward for a really close look and could seen large gaps in the log palisade caused by naval gunfire. What's more, there was not a single Confederate manning the walls, not even a sentry, while the naval bombardment continued. While Curtis watched, one of his officers, Lieutenant William Walling of the 142nd New York, ran forward to seize a Confederate flag near the river that had been knocked down by a naval shell. Walling was momentarily stunned by the explosion of a Union shell nearby, but soon recovered, slipped through a gap in the palisade, grabbed the flag, and ran back to his unit. This brave act convinced Curtis that the fort could be taken, and he sent an orderly back to bring up reinforcements so that he would be ready when the attack order came.

While Curtis had been reconnoitering the land face of Fort Fisher with most of his brigade, one of his regiments, Colonel Rufus Daggett's 117th New York, moved across the peninsula to secure the road to Wilmington. Daggett had just put his men in position when one of them brought him a Confederate prisoner who identified himself as Major John M. Reece. The Rebel officer announced that he wanted to surrender his entire command, which consisted of over 200 17-year-old boys from the North Carolina Junior Reserves who had earlier been sent up the peninsula from the fort to relieve crowding in the bombproofs. One boy had been killed and several wounded by the Union navy's shellfire that morning as they had passed through the fort from Battery Buchanan to the landface, and now Reece was apparently determined that no more of them would suffer. Daggett was suspicious of Reece's offer to surrender but was convinced of the Confederate's sincerity by one of his own officers, Captain Arnold Stevens, who was a Mason, when Reece proved that he was also a member of that organization. Stevens volunteered to go with Reece to bring his boys in. As the two officers approached the Reserves' position near the river, they heard the sound of 200 muskets being cocked. Reece yelled a password and convinced his young soldiers not to shoot.

"Well boys, I've surrendered," he told them.

"Not by a damn sight," a young lieutenant replied.

"Yes, I have," Reece said. "We are surrounded and can't get away."

"We've got you, boys," Stevens told them. "You may as well give up."

"Are you a Yankee officer?" one of the boys asked, and they all gasped when Stevens confirmed that he was.

The beligerent young lieutenant and a few others slipped away upriver, but the rest surrendered quietly. "We can't be worse off," one of them told Stevens. "We have never received a cent of pay nor scarcely anything to eat except what we picked up."[15] The young soldiers were marched across the peninsula, put in boats, and rowed out to the troopships. Not until then did anyone think to tell them to hand over their loaded muskets.

Meanwhile, Weitzel reported to Butler that the navy had not seriously damaged the fort and that "it would be butchery to order an assault on that work under the circumstances."[16] He suggested giving the navy one more day to cause enough damage to the landface to make an assault feasible. But as far as Butler was concerned the expedition had been doomed to failure when Porter had improperly and prematurely detonated the powder boat, and the navy had already been bombarding the fort for two days without having done it any great damage. Grant had ordered him not to withdraw once his troops had been landed, but Butler had only put about 2,500 of his 6,500 men ashore so far, in what he considered to be merely a reconnaissance in force, not a permanent landing. What's more, interrogation of a Confederate deserter from Kirkland's Brigade revealed that Hoke's Division was arriving from Virginia to threaten the rear of his forces on the peninsula. To make matters even worse, another storm was brewing and the sea was already becoming rough. Soon it might be impossible to either land more men or take off those who were already ashore. A decision had to be made right away to do one or the other. Butler decided to return the landing force to the transports.

It was approaching 5 p.m. when General Curtis got tired of waiting for reinforcements and attack orders that never came. Soon it would be too dark to attack. He stomped through the sand up the peninsula to find out for himself what was going on. He found that more troops had been landed, but when he asked why none of them had been sent forward he was told that General Butler had decided to withdraw the troops. Curtis was stunned by this news and hastily scribbled a message to Butler: "Your order is held in abeyance that you may know the true condition of the fort. The garrison has offered no resistance; the flagstaff of the fort was cut by a naval shot and one of my officers brought from the rampart the garrison flag. Another cut the telegraph wire connecting the fort with Wilmington. My skirmishers are now at the parapet."[17] Curtis's division commander, Brigadier General Adelbert Ames, had not received the withdrawal order either, and he authorized Curtis to get his troops ready for an attack. Curtis returned to his front line and waited in the gathering dusk for the attack order, but still it did not come.

What did arrive was Lieutenant Colonel Cyrus Comstock, an aide on Grant's staff who was serving as chief engineer for this expedition. This 33-year-old officer knew about as much about fortifications as any man in the Union army. He had seen strong earthworks but never anything to match Fort Fisher. However, Curtis took him up to within a stone's throw of the landface and showed him that no Confederates were anywhere to be seen. Comstock knew that the Rebels could be huddling in their bombproofs ready to spring to the ramparts the moment the naval bombardment lifted, which it would have to do in order for the army to attack, but Curtis's enthusiasm and confidence convinced him that an attack could succeed and should be made. He so advised Curtis, but the young general wanted positive orders from General Butler before he would make it. Comstock offered to go back and try to convince Butler, but before he could depart the naval guns suddenly fell silent. Porter did not expect the army to attack until the next morning, and with darkness approaching he had ordered fire to cease. Almost immediately a Rebel yell rang out and the landface wall was soon filled with defenders, who sent a fusilade of artillery and small arms fire toward Curtis's Federals, and keeping it up until 7 p.m., well after dark. A successful attack in the face of such resistance would now take a force far larger than Curtis's lone brigade. But instead of reinforcements Curtis received definite orders to withdraw. Under the cover of darkness, he reluctantly marched his men up the peninsula, some of them cursing Ben Butler out loud.

The cursing increased when they reached the landing site and discovered that they were stranded. The other two brigades of Ames' division had been ferried out to the transports and part of Curtis's brigade was taken off, but the surf was soon too rough to allow any more boats to move through it, smashing some of the launches that tried. Now outnumbered by the enemy, without entrenching tools, blankets, adequate drinking water, food, or ammunition, Curtis's men were suddenly on their own. And, to add insult to injury, it began to rain. By 10 p.m. fog had settled in over the peninsula, the temperature had dropped, and the rain had turned to sleet. With planks torn from the smashed boats, discarded oars, tin plates, bayonets, and rifle butts, the cold, wet soldiers dug themselves in while ironclads began to lob shells through the darkness and fog over their heads into the woods to the west of them to discourage the Rebels from forming for an attack on the stranded Federals. Curtis doubted that it would be enough to save his 700 men if Hoke's entire division of veteran Confederates decided to attack before daylight made them visible to Porter's gunners.

Meanwhile, Colonel Lamb, unaware that most of the Union soldiers had been withdrawn, sent messages across the river where they could be telegraphed to Bragg at Wilmington. He was afraid that the Federals would carry the fort with an overwhelming assault unless they were pinned down by an attack on their rear by Kirkland. He also feared that the Union navy would enter New Inlet under the cover of darkness or of another bombardment and land troops to attack the fort from the open west or south sides. Bragg replied that he was forwarding the rest of Hoke's Division to reinforce Kirkland as fast as the units arrived from Virginia, told Whiting to bring more Junior Reserves over the river, and suggested that he consider an evacuation procedure in case the fort had to be abandoned.

---

1. A thorough development of the evidence for Confederate use of such methods to provide protection for the transportation of Lincoln through northern Virginia, as well as many other aspects of the plot, can be found in: William A. Tidwell, with James O. Hall and David Winfred Gaddy, *Come Retribution* (Jackson, Miss., 1988).
2. William Tecumseh Sherman, *Memoirs of General W. T. Sherman* (New York, 1886), Library of America edition, 700-701.
3. Ibid., 701.
4. Ibid., 703-705.
5. Henry Hitchcock, "The Sort of Power Which a Flash of Lightning Suggests," in *The Blue and the Gray: 926-927.*
6. Ibid., 926.
7. John Chipman Gray, "He Might Sit for a Portrait of an Ideal Yankee," in *The Blue and the Gray*, 925.
8. U.S. War Department, *The War of the Rebellion: A Compilation of the Official Records of the Union and Confederate Armies* (Washington, 1893), Series I, Vol. 45, Part II, 329.
9. Sword, *Embrace an Angry Wind*, 422.
10. *Official Records*, 45:I:845.
11. Ibid., 45:I:848.
12. Gragg, *Confederate Goliath*, 77.
13. Ibid., 78.
14. *Official Records*, 42:III:1264.
15. Gragg, *Confederate Goliath*, 91-92.
16. *Official Records*, 42:I:986.
17. Gragg, *Confederate Goliath*, 90.

CHAPTER FOUR

To See a Great Light

25 - 30 December 1864

On Christmas Day, President Lincoln received a message from General Sherman that had been sent up the coast by ship to Fort Monroe, at the tip of the Virginia Peninsula, and telegraphed to Washington from there: "I beg to present you, as a Christmas gift, the city of Savannah, with 150 heavy guns and plenty of ammunition, and also about 25,000 bales of cotton."[1] Sherman had been in contact with the Union fleet off Savannah on 13 December when his troops had captured Fort McAllister and opened the Ogeechee River for the receipt of supplies. But the city of Savannah had not fallen until the 22nd, when Sherman's message had been sent. Grant and Meade also learned on Christmas Day that Sherman had taken Savannah, and Meade ordered a 100-gun salute to be fired by the Army of the Potomac.

Grant's oldest son, Fred, came to spend Christmas with him at City Point. Fred soon decided to go duck hunting on the James River, borrowing a boat, an army rifle, and the general's servant, Bill. They paddled down the river but never got to do much hunting. The Union navy soon spotted them and arrested them as Confederate spies. Young Fred was dressed in the uniform of his school in New Jersey, which happened to be gray. It took him quite a while to convince the sailors that he was the son of the general-in-chief, and when he returned to his father's little cabin on the bluff overlooking the City Point wharves he had to put up with a good bit of teasing on the subject. Fred would return to school after the holidays, but Grant's wife, Julia, soon came to join her husband in his little cabin on the bluff and remained with him for as long as he stayed at City Point.

The day after Christmas, President Lincoln wrote a reply to General Sherman: "Many, many thanks for your Christmas-gift—the capture of Savannah. When you were about leaving Atlanta for the Atlantic coast, I was *anxious*, if not fearful; but feeling that you were the better judge, and remembering that 'nothing risked, nothing gained' I did not intervene. Now, the undertaking being a success, the honor is all yours; for I believe none of us went farther than to acquiesce. And, taking the work of Gen. Thomas into the count, as it should be taken, it is indeed a great success. Not only does it afford the obvious and immediate military advantages; but, in showing to the world that your army could be divided, putting the stronger part to an important new service, and yet leaving enough to vanquish the old opposing force of the whole—Hood's army—it brings those who sat in darkness, to see a great light. But what next? I suppose it will be safer if I leave Gen. Grant and yourself to decide. Please make my grateful acknowledgments to your whole army, officers and men."[2]

This letter was carried down to Savannah by Major General John A. Logan, an important War Democratic who had risen from colonel of an Illinois regiment to become one of the best corps commanders in Sherman's army. He had been back in Illinois campaigning for Lincoln's reelection when Sherman had started his march to the sea. Unable to rejoin his command until Sherman reached the coast, Logan had been visiting Grant at City Point when the latter had grown tired of trying to prod Thomas into attacking Hood. So Grant had sent Logan toward Nashville to take Thomas's place before deciding to go there himself. But Logan had made it only as far as Louisville, and Grant, Washington, when the news had come of Thomas's victory. Now Logan was on his way down the coast to resume command of the 15th Corps and he carried Lincoln's letter with him.

Down in Mississippi that day, the 26th, Grierson's raiding Union troopers, after having destroyed the Confederate base at Verona, marched on down the Mobile & Ohio Railroad, wrecking it thoroughly as they advanced. The colonel of the Third Iowa Cavalry described the part his regiment took in this work. "My officers and men labored with uncommon zeal," he said, "and by fire and force destroyed five bridges, one of them 100 yards long, another fifty, another forty, another thirty, and a small culvert bridge. This road is remarkably well constructed, and nothing but great power and invincible energy can affect it. We loosened the ties, and after displacing the rails on the bridges, piled over the different spans of the bridges rails (mostly carried from the nearest fence, half a mile distant), with such dry timber as could be gathered near at hand. After the bridges were fired and in full blaze, we proceeded nearer Shannon Station... and burned two large section houses. By their light, we also turned bottom up about one mile of the railroad track, and then piling fence upon it, liberally set fire to the whole at short intervals. Four hours were spent on this work, and I think the destruction was very thorough. Our way to camp was lighted for several miles by the fires we had made."[3]

The Rebels had concentrated a fairly large force at Okolona, but as the Federals approached the Confederates fell back to the village of Egypt. That evening the detached battalion of the 2nd New Jersey rejoined the main column after hitting the railroad up at Boonville. It had torn up a mile of track, burned two large houses filled with military supplies and a caboose full of arms, ammunition, and railroad implements, and destroyed eight or ten culverts and a 150-foot bridge.

Down on the Confederate Point peninsula of North Carolina, a Rebel sentry in Fort Fisher thought he saw Federals landing at about 3 a.m. on the 26th. The garrison poured a hail of small arms and artillery fire into the darkness of the early morning for several minutes until the Confederates finally discovered that nobody was out there. Later, in the light of a foggy morning, General Whiting and Colonel Lamb used a telescope to study the distant site of the Union landing, where Curtis's hungry men were still stranded by the heavy surf, and concluded that the Federals were still there, near the beach, and probably in the woods to the west. Kirkland's lone brigade continued to man a thin line across the peninsula north of the Union landing, waiting for the rest of Hoke's Division to arrive, and it did during the day. But it contained only 6,000 men, while a Union lieutenant from Curtis's force, captured by Kirkland's men, convinced the Confederates that they were facing up to 12,000 Federals, instead of 700. Bragg came down from Wilmington and took direct command of the Rebels north of Curtis's position, but did nothing.

There was also a fog that morning in Tennessee as Wilson's Union cavalry began crossing Sugar Creek at about 8:30 a.m. On the south side of the stream the troopers of Hammond's brigade dismounted and probed their way about 200 yards through the mist until they came to a barricade in a narrow ravine, where a Confederate volley exploded in their faces. This was followed by a bayonet charge by Walthall's Rebel infantry, and Hammond's troopers ran for their lives, wading the waist-high creek to escape. Wilson eventually brought up some artillery to blast the Confederates out of their barricade, but by then it was 4 p.m. and most of the Rebels had already slipped away to the south. For all practical purposes, the pursuit of Hood's army was over. Wilson's men were running out of ammunition and rations and had used up over 5,000 horses, while the Union infantry was lagging far behind. Only the 4th Corps had gone beyond Pulaski, and it was in camp only six miles south of that town, waiting for supply wagons which finally caught up with it that afternoon.

After working all night, Hood's exhausted engineers completed their bridge on about 80 pontoon boats over the Tennessee River on the morning of the 26th, and the first wagons began to cross about dawn. Union gunboats approached a few hours later and had a brief duel with some Confederate batteries just a few miles downstream. But in the fog, with the river falling and the Rebel guns in place, the Federals withdrew without reaching the bridge. About two-thirds of Hood's army crossed the river that day, and the rest, except for the rearguard, followed on the 27th. The Union gunboats came back again that day, but they were still unwilling to press on upstream in the face of Confederate guns and the falling water of the river. Forrest's cavalry crossed that night, leaving only Walthall's ad hoc infantry division north of the river.

Far to the east, Steedman's provisional Federal command, which had been sent down the Union-controlled railroad, recaptured Decatur, Alabama, that day, but far too late to go on from there and cut off Hood's retreat. Wilson's Union troopers rested in camp at Sugar Creek that day, except for about 500 men of the 12th Tennessee Cavalry sent on down the road to see what they could find.

Down in Mississippi on the 27th, Grierson's raiders continued down the Mobile & Ohio Railroad to Okolona and beyond, skirmishing along the way with some Confederate cavalry. By tapping into the Rebel telegraph line and questioning Confederate deserters the Federals learned that Rebel reinforcements were coming up the railroad from Mobile and other points but would probably not arrive until 11 a.m. the next day.

In Southern Virginia that day, Grant was writing to his old friend Sherman: "Your confidence in being able to march up and join this army pleases me, and I believe it can be done. The effect of such a campaign will be to disorganize the South, and prevent the organization of new armies from their broken fragments. Hood is now retreating, with his army broken and demoralized. His loss in men has probably not been far from 20,000, besides deserters. If time is given the fragments may be collected together and many of the deserters reassembled; if we can we should act to prevent this. Your spare army, as it were, moving as proposed, will do this.... I might bring A.J. Smith here with from 10,000 to 15,000 men. With this increase I could hold my lines and move out with a greater force than Lee has. It would compel Lee to retain all his present force in the defenses of Richmond, or abandon them entirely. This latter contingency is probably the only danger to the easy success of your expedition. In the event you should meet Lee's army, you would be compelled to beat it, or find the sea-coast. Of course I shall not let Lee's army escape if I can help it, and will not let it go without following to the best of my ability. Without waiting further directions, then, you may make preparations to start on your northern expedition without delay. Break up the railroads in South and North Carolina, and join the armies operating against Richmond as soon as you can. I will leave out all suggestions about the route you should take, knowing that your information, gained daily in the progress of events, will be better than any that can be obtained now. It may not be possible for you to march to the rear of Petersburg, but failing in this you could strike either of the sea-coast ports in North Carolina held by us; from there you could take shipping. It would be decidedly preferable, however, if you could march the whole distance. From the best information I have, you will find no difficulty in supplying your army until you cross the Roanoke. From there here is but a few days' march, and supplies could be collected south of the river to bring you through. I shall establish communication with you there by steam-boat and gun-boat. By this means your wants can be partially supplied."[4]

Up in the Shenandoah Valley, Torbert's cavalry returned to Sheridan's camps that day, the 27th, from its unsuccessful raid toward Gordonsville, having unknowingly passed on the return trip within a few miles of the house where badly wounded Lieutenant Colonel John S. Mosby, the famous Confederate guerrilla, lay recuperating from a dangerous wound. Sheridan also received that day a reply from the War Department to a request he had made on Christmas Day for the authority to issue government rations to needy civilians in his area. At the direction of Secretary of War Stanton, General Halleck replied that "while the men of Virginia are either serving in the rebel ranks, or as bushwhackers are waylaying or murdering our soldiers, our Government must decline to support their wives and children."[5]

Down on the North Carolina coast, their second night stranded on the beach north of Fort Fisher was even worse for Curtis's troops than the first had been. A heavy rain fell and the men were hungry, exhausted, and afraid. Their pickets sounded the alarm several times, causing the Federals to signal with torches to the fleet, which then blasted the nearby woods while the soldiers huddled in their trenches. But at dawn on the 27th they were cheered by the sight of a flotilla of launches braving the choppy seas to row in to the beach. "As soon as a boat came to them," a witness wrote, "five or six men grasped it on each side and turned its prow to the sea. Then throwing aboard their bundles, muskets and equipment, they waded out until breast deep in the water, where a final shove was given and all climbed in. Very often the boats swamped, but the boys came up laughing to renew their effort."[6]

After all the soldiers were safely on board the transports, the ships headed back to the James River, where Ben Butler had already preceded them. "I feel ashamed that men calling themselves soldiers should have left the place so ingloriously," Admiral Porter wrote to Secretary of the Navy Gideon Welles. "It was, however, nothing more than I expected when General Butler got himself mixed up in this expedition."[7] Curtis and his men felt about the same way. "Everybody is disgusted," one soldier wrote home. "Officers and men express that the fort was ours and that no one but Butler prevented them from taking it." Another said, "Curses enough have been heaped on Butler's head to sink him in the deepest hole of the bottomless pit."[8]

The next day, the 28th, Butler came to Grant's headquarters at City Point and tried to explain the failure of his expedition. "General Grant expressed himself very positively on the subject," one of his aides, Lieutenant Colonel Horace Porter, wrote. "He said he considered the whole affair a gross and culpable failure, and that he proposed to make it his business to ascertain who was to blame for the want of success. The delays from storms were, of course, unavoidable. The preparation of the powder-boat had caused a loss of several weeks. It was found that the written orders which General Grant had given to General Butler to govern the movements of the expedition had not been shown to Weitzel. An important part of these instructions provided that under certain contingencies the troops were expected to intrench and hold themselves in readiness to cooperate with the navy for the reduction of the fort, instead of reembarking on the transports. General Grant had not positively ordered an assault, and would not have censured the commander if the failure to assault had been the only error; but he was exceedingly disatisfied that the important part of his instructions as to gaining and holding an intrenched position had been disobeyed, and the troops withdrawn, and all further efforts abandoned."[9]

That day Lincoln wired Grant: "If there be no objection, please tell me what you now understand of the Wilmington expedition, present & prospective." Grant replied that same evening: "The Wilmington expedition has proven a gross and culpable failure. Many of the troops are now back here. Delays and free talk of the object of the expedition enabled the enemy to move troops to Wilmington to defeat it. After the expedition sailed from Fort Monroe three days of fine weather was squandered, during which the enemy was without a force to protect himself. Who is to blame I hope will be known."[10]

Snow covered the fields of Michigan as a train crossed the river that night from Canada to Detroit, and two New York City police detectives walked slowly through the cars looking for two Confederate agents that a telegram from other detectives in Canada had said would be on the train. But one of the Rebels, Lieutenant John T. Ashbrook, spotted them first, and while they were not looking he slipped out of a window and jumped into the snow. The other Confederate, however, Captain Robert Cobb Kennedy, was asleep. The two detectives were the first men off the train at the Detroit station, and they stood by a pillar and watched the other passengers as they stepped down.

Kennedy walked through the station and down the street, but then one of the detectives came up behind him and asked to see his passport. Kennedy handed him a Federal passport he had obtained in Canada.

"What's your name?" the detective asked without looking at the passport.

"Richard Cobb," the Rebel said. That was the name on the passport.

"Your name is Stanton," the detective replied.[11]

That was a name Kennedy had used in New York the month before when he and several other Confederate officers had tried to burn that city as retaliation for Union depredations in the Shenandoah Valley and in Georgia. Instantly he knew he was in trouble and he reached into his overcoat for a revolver he had stuck in his belt, but the other detective had quietly come up behind him and now grabbed him and pinned his arms. The two New Yorkers ignored his pleas to shoot it out with him at 10 paces and merely took his gun, handcuffed him, and took him to their hotel room to search him. In the lining of his jacket they found a Confederate $20 bill, an old receipt from a Southern quartermaster, and a statement intended to get him through Rebel lines in which he pledged his word of honor that he was a Confederate soldier. The detectives took him to the House of Correction, where he was placed in a cell to await transportation to New York.

Down in Mississippi on the morning of the 28th Grierson's Union raiders attacked the few hundred Confederates who had been collected at the village of Egypt to oppose them. Colonel Joseph Kargé had the lead with his 1st Brigade and he came upon the Rebels in a strong position about a half a mile from Egypt Station. The 2nd New Jersey Cavalry drove in their skirmishers with a charge, and then Kargé sent two smaller regiments to capture a train that was carrying a battery of field artillery whose guns were firing at his right flank from their flat cars. Just then Grierson himself rode up and took command of those two regiments. The train managed to escape with its guns by cutting loose several other cars to gain speed, and four or five miles south of Egypt it came upon another train bringing up about 500 Confederate infantrymen. These Rebels dismounted from the train and followed Grierson's two regiments as they fell back to the north, but they never got into the fight at Egypt.

Kargé, meanwhile, rode back to his left, where he found the 2nd New Jersey was driving the Rebels back to a stockade on the east side of the railroad. Three companies of dismounted troopers charged on the right and two mounted squadrons on the left, while the 4th Illinois Cavalry of Colonel Embury D. Osband's 3rd Brigade cut off the Confederates' retreat after chasing off their cavalry and seriously wounding its commander, Brigadier General Samuel Gholson. The 500 Confederates in the stockade soon surrendered. Grierson sent detachments ahead to secure the bridges over the Sookatanuchie and Houlka rivers while the 3rd Iowa was again put to the work of destruction. "Three-quarters of a mile of the track was turned over and burned," its colonel reported, "the depot buildings and five cars destroyed, with about 500 barrels of corn and 200 muskets."[12] Then Grierson turned to the west and put his men into camp that night near the town of Houston.

General Thomas was at Pulaski, Tennessee, on the 28th when the news reached him that his boss and old friend Sherman had captured Savannah a week before. He sent back orders to Nashville for the garrison to fire a 100-gun salute in celebration. Wilson and his cavalry were farther south at a little village that consisted of two or three log cabins. When they learned that Sherman had presented Savannah to the president as a Christmas gift, one of Wilson's staff officers suggested that for a New Year's present they could give Mr. Lincoln Pinhook, Tennessee.

Wilson also received less cheering news that day. The regiment he had sent on to the south while the rest of his men and horses rested from their exhausting pursuit brought him word that Hood's rearguard had crossed the Tennessee River. It was true. Walthall's ad hoc infantry division had crossed the pontoon bridge that day, and the pontoons had been taken up. Thomas finally received the same news the next day and formally called off the pursuit. His army would go into winter quarters and prepare to resume campaigning in the spring.

What was left of the Army of Tennessee had escaped, but not much of it was left. When President Lincoln learned of its escape he said it reminded him of a story from his youth on the Illinois frontier: "A certain rough, rude, and bullying man in our county had a bull-dog, which was as rude, rough, and bullying as his master. Dog and man were the terror of the neighborhood. Nobody dared to touch either for fear of the other. But a crafty neighbor laid a plan to dispose of the dog. Seeing Slocum and his dog plodding along the road one day, the dog a little ahead, this neighbor, who was prepared for the occasion, took from his pocket a junk of meat in which he had concealed a big charge of powder, to which was fastened a deadwood slow-match. This he lighted, and then threw into the road. The dog gave one gulp at it, and the whole thing disappeared down his throat. He trotted on a few steps, when there was a sort of smothered roar, and the dog blew up in fragments, a fore-quarter being lodged in a neighboring tree, a hind-quarter on the roof of a cabin, and the rest scattered along the dusty road. Slocum came up and viewed the remains. Then, more in sorrow than in anger, he said, 'Bill war a good dog; but, as a dog, I reckon his usefulness is over.'" With a twinkle in his eye, Lincoln added, "Hood's Army was a good army. We have been very much afraid of it. But, as an army, I reckon its usefulness is gone."[13]

In Mississippi on the 29th, Grierson sent detachments to the north, toward Pontotoc, and to the southeast, toward Starkville, but these were mere feints to confuse the Confederates while his main column marched to the southwest. On the 30th the Federals marched through Bellfontaine and rode on toward Grenada.

In Washington, Chief of Staff Halleck was writing to his friend Sherman on the 30th: "I take the liberty of calling your attention, in this private and friendly way, to a matter which may possibly hereafter be of more importance to you than either of us may now anticipate.

While almost every one is praising your great march through Georgia and the capture of Savannah, there is a certain class, having now great influence with the President, and very probably anticipating still more on a change of Cabinet, who are decidedly disposed to make a point aganst you—I mean in regard to 'Inevitable Sambo.' They say that you have manifested an almost *criminal* dislike to the negro, and that you are not willing to carry out the wishes of the Government in regard to him, but repulse him with contempt. They say you might have brought with you to Savannah more than 50,000, thus stripping Georgia of that number of laborers and opening a road by which as many more could have escaped from their masters; but that instead of this you drove them from your ranks, prevented them from following you by cutting the bridges in your rear, and thus caused the massacre of large numbers by Wheeler's cavalry.

"To those who know you as I do such accusations will pass as idle winds, for we presume that you discouraged the negroes from following you simply because you had not the means of supporting them and feared they might seriously embarrass your march. But there are others, and among them some in high authority, who think, or pretend to think, otherwise, and they are decidedly disposed to make a point against you."[14]

At City Point, Virginia, on Friday, the 30th, Grant received a telegram from Secretary of the Navy Gideon Welles: "The substance of dispatches and reports from Rear-Admiral Porter, off Wilmington, is briefly this: The ships can approach nearer to the enemy's works than was anticipated. Their fire can keep the enemy away from their guns. A landing can easily be effected upon the beach north of Fort Fisher, not only of troops, but all their supplies and artillery. This force can have its flanks protected by gun-boats.... The winter season is the most favorable for operations against Fort Fisher. The largest naval force ever assembled is ready to lend its co-operation. Rear Admiral Porter will remain off Fort Fisher, continuing a moderate fire to prevent new works from being erected, and the ironclads have proved that they can maintain themselves in spite of bad weather. Under all these circumstances, I invite you to such a military co-operation as will insure the fall of Fort Fisher, the importance of which has already received your careful consideration. This telegram is made at the suggestion of the President, and in hopes that you will be able at this time to give the troops which heretofore were required elsewhere. If it cannot be done, the fleet will have to disperse, whence it cannot again be brought to this coast."[15]

This came to Grant as being from Secretary of War Stanton, and he replied to him at 10:30 a.m.: "I will answer fully in a few hours. Troops have all returned and transports dispersed." At noon he said, "I have ordered the chief quartermaster to reassemble at Fortress Monroe all the transports used by Butler, and additional ones sufficient to carry 1,500 men, 8,000 in all, and to have them fueled and watered to their fullest capacity for carrying troops. He thinks it can be done by Monday morning. Not a person here knows the object of this but myself, chief of staff, and cipher operator, who has to know it, of course. It will not be known to another. When all is ready I will send troops and commander selected to Fortress Monroe and out to sea with sealed instructions not to be opened until they pass the Heads. I would advise that Admiral Porter simply be directed to hold on as he is until he receives further orders from the Department. You will understand why I would say no more. I am in hopes by secrecy the enemy may be lulled into such security as to induce him to send his Wilmington forces against Sherman, or bring them back here by the time we are ready to start. There will be no delay on the part of troops." By 2 p.m. Grant had discovered that the telegram had really come from the secretary of the navy and he wired Stanton to let him know. "It is all right, however," he added, "for I do not propose to correspond with the Navy Department about military operations except through you."[16]

Stanton replied at 9 p.m., "Your dispatch of 12 noon to-day just received, and I am rejoiced at its indications. No living man shall know anything upon the subject from me except the Secretary of the Navy. I would suggest an express from you to Porter to let him know at the earliest possible moment what to expect before he leaves." An hour later, he added, "Ingalls' requisition upon Meigs for the return of the transportation will, of course, set him and all the thousand and one guessers at work to nose out the object. You cannot count upon any secrecy in the Navy. Newspaper reporters have the run of that Department. Might it not throw them off to give out here confidentially that the troops are going to Sherman to enable him to march through the interior and garrison important points or else to attack Mobile?"[17]

Grant sent off a dispatch to Porter that night: "Please hold on where you are for a few days and I will endeavor to be back again with an increased force and without the former commander.... Your dispatch to the Secretary of the Navy, which informed me that you were still off Wilmington, and still thought the capture of that place practicable, was only received to-day.... The commander of the expedition will probably be Major-General Terry."[18]

Brevet Major General Alfred H. Terry was the temporary commander of the 24th Corps in Butler's Army of the James, in the absence of its regular commander, Major General E.O.C. Ord. Horace Porter. Grant's aide, recommended Terry for the command of the second Fort Fisher expedition. "We had served together in the Sherman-Dupont expedition which in 1861 took Hilton Head and captured Fort Pulaski and other points on the Atlantic coast," Porter wrote, "and I knew him to be the most experienced officer in the service in embarking and disembarking troops upon the sea-coast, looking after their welfare on transports, and intrenching rapidly on shore. General Grant had seldom come in contact with Terry personally, but had been much pleased at the manner in which he had handled his troops in the movements on the James River. A suggestion, too, was made that as Terry was a volunteer officer, and as the first expedition had failed under a volunteer, it would only be fair that another officer of that service, rather than one from the regular army, should be given a chance to redeem the disaster."[19]

Francis Preston Blair, Sr., had been a powerful figure in national politics for 35 years, although he had never held elected office. He had been a close friend of Andrew Jackson and the editor of the Washington *Globe* from 1830 to 1854. But he had broken with the Democratic party over the controversial Kansas/Nebraska Bill and had joined the new Republican party, backing the nomination of Lincoln and advising the latter on the selection of his cabinet. One of Blair's sons, Francis P. "Frank" Blair, Jr., was both a congressman from Missouri and corps commander in Sherman's army, while another, Montgomery Blair, had been postmaster general in Lincoln's cabinet until he had recently resigned as a concession to the Radical wing of the Republican party. The senior Blair's home in Silver Springs, Maryland, had been used as Confederate headquarters when Early's Army of the Valley had approached the outskirts of Washington the previous summer, and it had been burned when the Rebels retreated back to the Shenandoah Valley. Now Blair saw this occurrence as an excuse to serve as mediator between the warring sections of the country he loved. He obtained a pass from President Lincoln allowing him to go through Union lines and return.

Then, on 30 December, Blair wrote two letters to Jefferson Davis, former senator from Mississippi and currently president of the Confederate States. In one of them he said, "The loss of some papers of importance... which I suppose may have been taken by some persons who had access to my house when Genl Earlys army was in possession of my place induces me to ask the privilege of visiting Richmond &

beg the favor of you to facilitate my inquiries in regard to them." But in the other he hinted that the real reason for his proposed visit was to discuss some ideas he had for ending the war. "In candor I must say to you in advance," he added, "that I come to you wholly unaccredited except in so far as I may be by having permission to pass our lines & to offer to you my own suggestions."[20]

Jefferson Davis was writing that day to General Beauregard, who had been temporarily overseeing the defense of the Carolinas. Now Davis ordered him to resume command of his Division of the West, which consisted of Hood's Army of Tennessee and Lieutenant Richard Taylor's Department of Alabama, Mississippi and East Louisiana. Command in South Carolina reverted to Lieutenant General William J. Hardee, commander of the Department of South Carolina, Georgia and Florida.

That same day, John Wilkes Booth returned to Washington from his Christmas visit with his family.

---

1. *Official Records*, 44:783.
2. Roy P. Basler, editor, *The Collected Works of Abraham Lincoln* (New Brunswick, N.J., 1953-1955), 8:181-182.
3. *Official Records*, 45:I:853-854.
4. Ibid., 44:I:820-821.
5. Ibid., 43:II:831.
6. Gragg, *Confederate Goliath*, 97.
7. Ibid., 98.
8. Ibid., 97.
9. Horace Porter, *Campaigning With Grant* (New York, 1897), 362-363.
10. Basler, ed., *Collected Works of Abraham Lincoln*, 8:187 and *Official Records*, 42:III:1087.
11. Nat Brandt, *The Man Who Tried to Burn New York* (Syracuse, 1986), 150.
12. *Official Records*, 45:I:846.
13. Noah Brooks, *Washington in Lincoln's Time* (New York, 1958), 258-259.
14. *Official Records*, 44:836.
15. Ibid., 42:III:1091.
16. Ibid., 42:III:1098-1099.
17. Ibid., 42:III:1099.
18. Ibid., 42:III:1100-1101.
19. Porter, *Campaigning With Grant*, 368.
20. Basler, ed., *Collected Works of Abraham Lincoln*, 8:188.

CHAPTER FIVE

A Dead Cock in the Pit

31 December 1864 - 8 January 1865

On the last day of 1864 General Halleck telegraphed Thomas: "General Grant directs that all of your available forces, not essential to hold your communications, be collected on the Tennessee River, say at Eastport and Tuscumbia, and be made ready for such movements as may be ordered. It is supposed that a portion of the troops in Louisville and other parts of Kentucky and Tennessee can now be availed of for active operations elsewhere. They should be made ready for that purpose.... Please give us the earliest possible notice of Hood's line of retreat, so that orders may be given for a continuance of the campaign. General Grant does not intend that your army shall go into winter quarters; it must be ready for active operations in the field." Three hours later Halleck added: "General Dana telegraphs from Memphis on the 29th that his cavalry struck the railroad on the 26th, five miles south of

Corinth, and were destroying it as they went south. It is, therefore, important that your cavalry keep that of Forrest well employed, so that it will not be able to molest that destroying the railroad in Mississippi."[1]

That night Thomas replied: "I am watching Hood closely, to determine his line of retreat of which I will inform you as soon as ascertained. I have ordered the cavalry to Eastport, and also General A. J. Smith's command. The Fourth Army Corps has been ordered to Huntsville, Ala., as that place will be convenient to furnish the troops with supplies to refit. I had ordered the Twenty-third Army Corps to Dalton, but countermanded the order yesterday, upon a report that Hood was moving toward Corinth. I will now order the Twenty-third Corps to Eastport. I have received a communication from General Wilson to-day, dated the 29th instant, in which he represents his cavalry as very much fagged out and in need of rest, and asks that he may be allowed to assemble it at or near Eastport sufficiently to reorganize and recuperate, shoe up his horses, and organize his trains. His losses in horses have been very heavy since we left Nashville, owing principally to the intolerably bad weather, the almost impassable condition of the country, caused by constant and heavy rains and snow, and the great scarcity of forage along the route over which we pursued the enemy. The infantry, also, is very much exhausted, having been constantly on campaign duty since early last spring. To continue the campaign without any rest, I fear, will cost us very heavy losses from disease and exhaustion. The troops, however, will be assembled at Eastport and Huntsville as soon as possible, where we will await orders.... I had already taken steps, before receiving your telegram of to-day, to refit the troops under my command as soon as possible, so as to commence the campaign again at the earliest possible moment, and I do believe that it is much the best policy to get well prepared before starting on an important campaign."[2]

Part of Thomas's command was still pursuing Hood, however. After reoccupying Decatur, Alabama—on the south side of the Tennessee River where the Memphis & Charleston Railroad crossed and was joined by the line running south from Nashville and Pulaski—Major General James B. Steedman had sent a small force of cavalry westward to try to cut off Hood's escape. This small brigade of 600 men consisted of the 15th Pennsylvania Cavalry and detachments of several other regiments and was commanded by Colonel William J. Palmer of the 15th. Palmer's force had been pushing westward against light resistance from Brigadier General Philip Roddey's small division of Confederate cavalry when Palmer had learned that Hood's army had already crossed the Tennessee and was marching west toward Corinth, Mississippi, and that his pontoons had been taken up and were being transported overland to Columbus, Mississippi, with a comparatively small guard.

Palmer had received Steedman's permission to go after the pontoons or not, at his discretion, and before daylight on the 31st of December his troopers were on the road, following a trail that allowed them to bypass Brigadier General Frank Armstrong's brigade of Forrest's cavalry, which had been sent to reinforce Roddey. At about 1 p.m. the Federals passed through Russellville, Alabama, and began to run into opposition from part of Roddey's command, but they drove the Rebels off to the south and then continued on to the west. Other Confederates burned a bridge over Cedar Creek to block their path, but they found a ford and, as darkness fell, caught up with the rear of the wagon train carrying the pontoon boats ten miles beyond Russellville. "We met no resistance," Colonel Palmer reported, "and our advance guard rode through to the front of the train, which extended for five miles, and consisted of seventy-eight pontoon-boats and about 200 wagons, with all the necessary accouterments and material, egineering instruments, &c.; all the mules and oxen, except what the pontoniers and teamsters were able to cut loose and ride off, were standing hitched to the wagons. Three boats had been set fire to, but so carelessly that no damage had been done. We captured a few prisoners, and went into camp at about the center of the train, fed our horses, and I then started the entire command out in either direction to burn the train, which was done in the most thorough manner, and occupied till 3 a.m."[3]

Down in Mississippi Grierson's raiders came to Winona, on the Mississippi Central Railroad, that day, where a detachment of the 2nd New Jersey Cavalry destroyed the depot, two locomotives and several cars, tore up the track and cut the telegraph line. Meanwhile the head of the column pushed on to Middleton.

At Savannah, Georgia, Sherman was writing to Halleck and Grant on that final day of the year. "A mail leaves at 5 p.m. for Hilton Head and New York," he told Grant. "I have written a short official letter to General Halleck, amounting to nothing, simply because I suppose you want to hear from me at every opportunity. I have already reviewed my four corps, and wind up in a day or two with Kilpatrick's cavalry, which I keep out about nine miles. There is no doubt of it but this army is in fine condition and impatient to go ahead. I would like to have Foster re-enforced, if possible, so that I will not have to leave him a division to hold Savannah.... As soon as I can accumulate enough provisions and forage to fill my wagons, I will be ready for South Carolina, and if you want me to take Charleston I think I can do it, for I know the place well. I was stationed there from '42 to '46, and used to hunt a good deal all along the Cooper River.... I hope you will push Thomas up. Keep him going south anywhere. Let him make a track down into Alabama, or, if you think better, he can again come to Chattanooga and as far down as the Etowah, to which point I preserved the iron rails ready to be used again. I am fully aware of your friendly feeling toward me, and you may always depend on me as your steadfast supporter. Your wish is law and gospel to me, and such is the feeling that pervades my army."[4]

He told Halleck: "I propose at once to make lodgments in South Carolina, about Port Royal, opposite this city, and up about Sister's Ferry. When all is ready I can feign at one or more places and cross at the other, after which my movements will be governed by those of the enemy, and such instructions as I may receive from Lieutenant General Grant before starting. I do not think I can employ better strategy than I have hitherto done, namely, make a good ready and then move rapidly to my objective, avoiding a battle at points where I would be encumbered by wounded, but striking boldly and quickly when my objective is reached. I will give due heed and encouragement to all peace movements, but conduct war as though it could only terminate with the destruction of the enemy and the occupation of all his strategic points. The weather is fine, the air cool and bracing, and my experience in this latitude convinces me that I may safely depend on two good months for field-work. I await your and General Grant's answers to my proposed plan of operations before taking any steps indicative of future movements."[5]

Before the day was over, Sherman received a letter from Admiral Porter, which had been written two days before: "I send Captain Breese to communicate with you, and tell you about matters and things in this quarter. I congratulate you on your success, which I knew was sure when you started. I told the world you would be off Savannah on the 10th, and you were not far off on that day. I feel certain that you are in Savannah to-day, or will be there in a week. When you have caputured that place I invite you to add to your brow the laurels thrown away by General Butler after they were laid at his feet by the navy, and which neither he nor those with him had the courage to gather up. I felt sure that it would be so when we started on the expedition. We attacked Fort Fisher, silenced it, blew it up, burned it out, and knocked it to pieces.... Notwithstanding all this General Butler decided not to attack Fort Fisher, 'as the navy fire has not injured it as a defensive work!' Great heavens! what are we coming to? Well, I think that Providence intended it to be so; and it rests with you to add new honors to your name, already famous, notwithstanding the newspaper reporters. This is merely on your way to Richmond. Take this place and you take the 'creme de la creme' of the rebellion. I leave to Captain Breese to tell you all my views; and I do hope, my dear general, that you will second me here and let our people see the folly of employing such generals as Butler and Banks. I have tried them both, and God save me from further connection with such generals. With you I feel sure of success, and shall bless the day when I shall once more see your esteemed self in our midst. A host of old friends are here to welcome you, and show you the most magnificent naval fight you ever laid your eyes on."[6]

But Sherman replied: "Captain Breese has this moment arrived with your letter of December 29, and I assure you it does my heart good to feel that I am once more near you. I hope soon we will meet again in person. I have already submitted to Generals Halleck and Grant a plan for a campaign which will bring my whole army to Wilmington, which I know I can take as easily, if not more so, than Savannah. I do not think you can take those shore batteries with your gun-boats, or do more than drive the gunners to the cover of their bomb-proofs. I have examined carefully many of the forts about Savannah, and find them so well covered by traverses and bomb-proof shelters, that you might blaze away at them for a month from the direction of the sea channels without materially harming them. I have no doubt, however, from what you say, that Butler's men ought to have taken Fort Fisher in about three minutes, for its bomb-proofs cannot possibly shelter more than 200 men, who would be, as you say, crouching in a defenseless position as against an attacking force. But even after you have got Fisher, then comes Caswell, Fort Johnston, and, I suppose, a string of forts all the way back to Wilmington. Now, I propose to march my whole army through South Carolina, tearing up railroads and smashing things generally, feign on Charleston, and rapidly come down upon Wilmington from the rear, taking all their works in reverse.... It will take some time for me to reach Wilmington, but I am certain that mine is the only mode by which the place can be taken effectually.... I think when you come to consider my position, you will agree with me that my proposition is better than to undertake to reduce in detail the forts about Wilmington, and you can so maneuver as to hold a large portion of the enemy to the sea-coast, whilst I ravage the interior, and when I do make my appearance on the coast, we will make short work of them all. I have shown to Captain Breese my letters to Grant and Halleck, and will explain to him fully everything that will interest you, and as soon as I can hear from General Grant will send a steamer to you, advising you of the time of starting. I rather fear, however, that the

President's anxiety to take Charleston may induce Grant to order me to operate against Charleston, rather than Wilmington, though I much prefer the latter—Charleston being a dead cock in the pit altogether."[7]

Ben Butler was back at the head of his Army of the James, and although one of his pet projects, the powder boat, had failed, he had another one up his sleeve. Back in August he had come up with the idea of cutting a canal across a narrow neck of land, known as Dutch Gap, on the James River. This would cut almost five miles off river navigation and bypass some Confederate defenses along a stretch of the river known as Trent's Reach. Since August his engineers had been laboring faithfully on this project, which involved the removal of nearly 80,000 cubic feet of dirt. The Confederates had soon discovered what the Federals were up to and had put heavy guns and mortars in place to harass them but could not halt the work. On 31 December Butler notified Grant that the canal was almost finished and that the last barriers separating the excavation from the river would be blasted away the next day. Grant was invited to witness this culmination of the project, but he declined. The explosion took place as planned on the first day of 1865, but a great deal of debris remained in the canal and had to be removed by steam dredges. The canal was never of any service during the war, but it later formed the main channel of the James River.

General Halleck, in Washington, had not received Sherman's latest letter, of course, but he had received the one written on 24 December, and he wrote an answer on 1 January, saying that he was impressed with Sherman's prediction that Butler's attack on Fort Fisher would fail. "Your anticipations in regard to the Wilmington expedition have proved so correct," he said, "that your reputation as a prophet may soon equal that as a general. Thank God, I had nothing to do with it, except to express the opinion that Butler's torpedo ship would have about as much effect on the forts as if he should ——— at them." He fully approved of Sherman's plans for a campaign through the Carolinas and then turned to the state of things in Tennessee. "Thomas has done well against Hood, but he is too slow for an effective pursuit. Moreover, he will not live on the enemy. He himself is entirely opposed to a winter campaign, and is already speaking of recruiting his army for spring operations. I have, therefore, urged General Grant to send Schofield and A. J. Smith to re-enforce Canby at Mobile and move up the Alabama River to Selma and Montgomery, destroying all the enemy's manufactories and supplies on that line. Thomas, with the remainder of his forces, can easily defend Kentucky and Tennessee against any new raid that Jeff. Davis may plan in that direction. It is useless talking about putting any of our armies into winter quarters. It is not necessary, and the financial condition of the country will not permit it. Those troops not required for defense must move into the enemy's country and live on it. There is no alternative; it must be done."[8]

Down in Mississippi on 1 January, Grierson sent a detachment of 300 men north from Winona to follow the Mississippi Central tracks to Grenada and do as much damage to the railroad and Confederate property as possible. He also sent his 3rd Brigade along the tracks to the south for the same purpose, while his main column continued on to the southwest.

Over in northern Alabama, Colonel Palmer had learned from a slave of the Rebel captain who had commanded the pontoon train he had captured that a large train of supply wagons belonging to Hood's army was nearby. By 10 a.m. on 1 January his small brigade overtook this train, which consisted of 110 wagons and over 500 mules. About twenty of the teamsters were found to be former members of the U.S. Colored Troops who had been captured by the Confederates. A badly wounded Rebel colonel was found in one of the wagons, and Palmer left him behind with a tent, some supplies, and a Confederate soldier to look after him. "We burned the wagons," Palmer reported, "shot or sabered all the mules we could not lead off or use to mount prisoners, and started back."[9]

Only rumors had been reaching General Beauregard, still at Charleston, South Carolina, that Hood had been defeated and was retreating from Tennessee. On 1 January his headquarters at Montgomery, Alabama, sent a demand to Hood for a report of his recent operations, and Beauregard departed Charleston on the second, heading west, after having obtained permisssion from President Davis to replace Hood with Lieutenant General Richard Taylor, commander of the Department of Alabama, Mississippi and Louisiana, if necessary. This was a wise precaution. Hood was one of Davis's favorites, as Beauregard certainly was not, and might ordinarily be hard to displace, but Taylor was not only respected by all but was Davis's brother-in-law.

In Mississippi on 2 January, Colonel Embury D. Osband's 3rd Brigade of Grierson's cavalry division, which had been sent southward along the Mississippi Central Railroad, ran into a small division of Confederate cavalry commanded by Brigadier General Wirt Adams. A single regiment that led Adams' force up from Goodman was outflanked by the 3rd U.S. Colored Cavalry and driven back upon the main Rebel force. The Confederates then tried to turn both Federal flanks, but two Illinois regiments countered these moves and drove the Rebels across a creek. Both Osband and Adams then decided to withdraw, and the Union brigade moved to rejoin Grierson's main column, which reached Benton that night.

Over on the Georgia coast, Sherman received Grant's letter of 27 December that day and in reply sent him a detailed plan for the opening stages of his next campaign. Sherman also received a copy of a telegram Secretary of War Stanton had sent Grant on the 26th regarding captured cotton, which he answered that day. "I have already been approached by all the consuls and half the people of Savannah on this cotton question," he said, "and my invariable answer has been that all the cotton in Savannah was prize of war and belonged to the United States, and nobody should recover a bale of it with my consent, and that as cotton had been one of the chief causes of this war it should help to pay its expenses; that all cotton became tainted with treason from the hour the first act of hostility was committed against the United States, some time in December, 1860, and that no bill of sale subsequent to that date could convey title.... Mr. Barclay, former consul at New York, representing Mr. Molineux, former consul here but absent since a long time, called on me in person with refence to cotton claimed by English subjects. He seemed amazed when I told him I should pay no respect to consular certificates, and that in no event would I treat an English subject with more favor than one of our own deluded citizens, and that for my part I was unwilling to fight for cotton for the benefit of Englishmen openly engaged in smuggling arms and instruments of war to kill us; that on the contrary it would afford me great satisfaction to conduct my army to Nassau and wipe out that nest of pirates.... It appeared also that he owned a plantation on the line of investment of Savannah, which of course is destroyed, and for which he expected me to give him some certificate entitling him to indemnification, which I declined emphatically. I have adopted in Savannah rules concerning property, severe but just, founded upon the laws of nations and the practice of civilized governments; and am clearly of opinion that we should claim all the belligerent rights over conquered countries, that the people may realize the truth that war is no child's play."[10] He added that he was sending all the cotton he had captured to the quartermaster at New York, to be disposed of as Stanton wished.

Forrest's cavalry was only on loan to Hood and the Army of

Tennessee. It was actually a part of Richard Taylor's Department of Alabama, Mississippi and East Lousiana, into whose territory it and all of Hood's army had now retreated. From Corinth, Mississippi, Forrest sent a long letter to Taylor on 2 January. "I have just had an interview with General Hood," he reported, "and am informed by him that the Army of Tennessee is ordered to Augusta, and that I will be left to defend as well as can be done this section of the country. I regret to say that the means at my disposal are not adequate to the task devolving upon me. My command is greatly reduced in numbers and efficiency by losses in battle and in worn-down and unserviceable condition of animals. The Army of Tennessee was badly defeated and is greatly demoralized, and to save it during the retreat from Nashville I was compelled almost to sacrifice my command.... I shall remain in General Hood's rear until he moves off from here, and if the railroad can not supply me with forage in a short time will be compelled to leave a small force here and follow him down to the prairies and save my stock, if possible to do so."[11]

The next day, 3 January, one of Forrest's division commanders, Brigadier General James R. Chalmers, wrote him some unofficial advice. "To 'learn wisdom from your enemy' is one of the wisest maxims of history," he said. "At Nashville our enemy had a large force of cavalry, but instead of wasting its strength in the front, he kept it quietly in the rear of his infantry, resting and recruiting, until the time for action came, and then he moved it out fresh and vigorous with telling effect. We have now a good force of cavalry, and there is a rich country in our rear where we can rest and recruit it; here we cannot procure forage except by taking the bread from the mouths of a people who have already suffered greatly in this war, and even this can supply us but a day or two longer.... Under these circumstances, if we keep the main body of our cavalry here, we whip ourselves faster than the enemy could possibly do it, for every day that we remain here without forage we will be losing strength faster than if engaged in battle.... If we had time to reorganize, recruit, and fit up the command in a place where forage could be procured, we can whip the enemy's cavalry, and every man in your command is anxious that you should have a fair trial of strength with Major-General Wilson."[12]

Hood issued orders that day for his army to begin moving down to Tupelo, for after Grierson's raid the railroad was in no shape to supply it north of that point, nor was it in any shape to stay that close to the Federals, who might attack it again if they could reach it. He reported to Secretary of War James A. Seddon that day: "The army has recrossed the Tennessee River without material loss since the battle in front of

Nashville. It will be assembled in a few days in the vicinity of Tupelo, to be supplied with shoes and clothing, and to obtain forage for the animals."[13] In a separate message he asked for authority to furlough the 2,000 or so men in his army who came from the states west of the Mississippi in the hope that they would bring back recruits that would strengthen his army in the long run. How they were to twice get past the Union gunboats patrolling the Mississippi he did not say. He also notified Beauregard that he was "assembling the army at Tupelo" and asked him to visit the army before sending it elsewhere.[14] He asked Richard Taylor to meet him at Tupelo as well.

In Virginia that day, the third, Grant was writing to Admiral Porter again: "I send Maj. Gen. A.H. Terry, with the same troops General Butler had, with one brigade added, to renew the attempt on Fort Fisher. In addition to this I have ordered General Sheridan to send a division of infantry to Baltimore to be put on sea-going transports, so that they can go also if their services are found necessary.... General Terry will consult with you fully, and will be governed by your suggestions as far as his responsibility for the safety of his command will admit of."[15]

The next day, the fourth, as Terry's troops began to embark under the pretext of going to Savannah to reinforce Sherman, Assistant Secretary of the Navy Gustavus V. Fox wired Grant to, among other things, advise him that "Mr. Blair, sr., alone, will leave Washington Saturday, and arrive off City Point about noon, in the screw steamer Don.... As he goes by consent of the President, at the request of Mr. Davis, I ask for Mr. Blair that you will make arrangements to get him through comfortably as early as practicable, and as secretly." Speaking of secrecy, he also advised Grant that "I got the President to put into the old capitol [prison] the man who caused to be published the Wilmington expedition. Yesterday the Baltimore American sent me word that they had information that another expedition was fitting out. I sent them word that the Government would deal very summarily with the first party who published it. To-night Mr. Gobright, the agent of the Associated Press, informed me that he had such news from Hampton Roads, but had suppressed it." As a postscript, Fox added, "The country will not forgive us for another failure at Wilmington, and I have so informed Porter."[16]

With the election over, Butler's political pull would no longer protect him, and the Fort Fisher debacle gave Grant the perfect excuse for getting rid of him. There were also rumors that Butler had been allowing illegal trade with the enemy in return for a share of the profits. That same day Grant wrote a letter to Secretary Stanton: "I am constrained to request the removal of Maj. Gen. B.F. Butler from the command of the Department of Virginia and North Carolina. I do this with reluctance, but the good of the service requires it. In my absence General Butler necessarily commands, and there is a lack of confidence felt in his military ability, making him an unsafe commander for a large army. His administration of the affairs of his department is also objectionable."[17]

The next day, the fifth, Grant rode in the boat with Terry down the James River to Fort Monroe in order to give him his instructions. After they had gone some distance from City Point they sat down in the steamer's after cabin. "The object is to renew the attempt to capture Fort Fisher," Grant told Terry now for the first time, "and in case of success to take possession of Wilmington. It is of the greatest importance that there should be a complete understanding and harmony of action between you and Admiral Porter. I want you to consult the admiral fully, and to let there be no misunderstanding in regard to the plan of cooperation in all its details. I served with Admiral Porter on the Mississippi, and have a high appreciation of his courage and judgment. I want to urge upon you to land with all despatch, and intrench yourself in a position from which you can operate against Fort Fisher, and not to abandon it until the fort is captured or you receive further instructions from me."[18]

Secretary Stanton was writing to Grant that same day: "I think it would be useful if you would write to Sherman, urging him to give facilities to the organization of colored troops. He does not seem to appreciate the importance of this measure and appears indifferent if not hostile."[19]

President Lincoln was launching a scheme that day that would later bring him into conflict with Grant. He had frequently issued permits for Northerners to trade for Southern cotton and tobacco. And on Christmas eve an old friend, Orville H. Browning, former senator from Illinois, had asked the president to let a mutual acquaintance, "General" James W. Singleton, go to Richmond to swing a deal for millions of dollars worth of Southern goods. Singleton, who had gained his title of "General" in the 1846 expulsion of the Mormons from Illinois, was a Democrat and a Copperhead, and Lincoln called him "a miracle of meanness," but he was married to one of Mrs. Lincoln's numerous cousins.[20] And the president felt that Singleton could be useful.

Lincoln had recently explained the economic basis of trading with the enemy to Major General E.R.S. Canby, commander of the Military

Division of West Mississippi: "As to cotton. By the external blockade, the price is made certainly six time as great as it was. And yet the enemy gets through at least one sixth part as much in a given period, say a year, as if there were no blockade, and receives as much for it, as he would for a full crop in time of peace. The effect in substance is, that we give him six ordinary crops, without the trouble of producing any but the first; and at the same time leave his fields and his laborers free to produce provisions. You know how this keeps up his armies at home, and procures supplies from abroad. For other reasons we cannot give up the blockade, and hence it becomes immensely important to us to get the cotton away from him. Better give him *guns* for it, than let him, as now, get both guns and ammunition for it. But even this only presents part of the public interest to get out cotton. Our finances are greatly involved in the matter. The way cotton goes now carries so much gold out of the country as to leave us paper currency only, and that so far depreciated, as that for every hard dollar's worth of supplies we obtain, we contract to pay two and a half hard dollars hereafter. This is much to be regretted; and while I believe we can live through it at all events, it demands an earnest effort on the part of all to correct it. And if pecuniary greed can be made to aid us in such effort, let us be thankful that so much good can be got out of pecuniary greed."[21] So on 5 January 1865 Lincoln presented Browning with passes for Singleton to go South and to return "with any Southern products, and go to any of our trading posts, there to be subject to the Regulations of the Treasury Department."[22]

Down in Mississippi, Grierson's raid ended that day at Vicksburg, which Grant had captured eighteen months and one day before. Grierson had lost 27 men killed, 93 wounded, and 7 missing while bringing in 600 prisoners, 1,000 escaped slaves, and 800 head of captured live stock. Along their march of about 450 miles his men had destroyed: 20,000 feet of bridges and trestles, 10 miles of track, 20 miles of telegraph poles and wire, four serviceable locomotives and tenders and ten others in repair, 95 railroad cars, over 300 army wagons and two caissons, 30 warehouses filled with quartermaster, commissary, and ordnance stores, cloth and shoe factories, several tanneries and machine shops, seven railroad depots, 5,000 rifles and carbines, 500 bales of cotton marked C.S.A., 700 hogs, and large amounts of grain, wool, and leather.

At Savannah, Georgia, the next day, the sixth, Sherman was answering the letter that General Logan had brought him from Lincoln.

He said he thought that Lincoln's use of the motto "Nothing venture, nothing win," was most appropriate, "and should I venture too much and happen to lose I shall bespeak your charitable inference. I am ready for the 'great next' as soon as I can complete certain preliminaries and learn of General Grant his and your preferences of intermediate 'objectives.'"[23]

In the Shenandoah Valley of Virginia that day, the sixth, Brigadier General Cuvier Grover's 2nd Division of the 19th Corps boarded a train at Stephenson's Depot, just north of Sheridan's position at Winchester, for a ride to Baltimore, where ships were supposed to be waiting to take it to Fort Monroe.

Secretary of War Stanton was himself at Fort Monroe that afternoon, where he spent the night on his way down the coast to visit Sherman at Savannah. So Grant wired Lincoln that afternoon: "I wrote a letter to the Secretary of War, which was mailed yesterday, asking to have General Butler removed from command. Learning that the Secretary left Washington yesterday, I telegraph you asking that prompt action may be taken in the matter."[24] Action was indeed prompt, for in less than 24 hours Halleck wired back, "I send you by telgraph General Orders, No. 1, relieving General Butler from his command. It will not be entered on the files or published here till you have it delivered to him. Please answer by telegraph the date that General Butler is to be relieved."[25]

Grant wired Stanton on the morning of the seventh, before the latter left Fort Monroe: "Please say to General Sherman I do not regard the capture of Charleston as of any military importance. He can pass it by, unless in doing so he leaves a force in his rear which it will be dangerous to have there. It will be left entirely to his own discretion whether Charleston should be taken now."[26]

Grover's division reached Baltimore on the seventh only to find that the transport ships had not yet arrived, so he had to put his men into camp and wait for them.

On the morning of the eighth Grant sent lieutenant colonels Horace Porter and Orville Babcock of his staff to Butler's headquarters with the order to relieve him. The order was published that day, and Butler issued a farewell message to his troops in which he implied that he had been relieved because "I have refused to order the useless sacrifice of the lives of such soldiers."[27] He was immediately succeeded as commander of the Department of Virginia and North Carolina and the Army of the James by his senior corps commander, Major General E.O.C. Ord, who was one of Grant's favorite subordinates because of his aggressive spirit.

As Grant wrote to an old friend in the navy, "The failure at Fort Fisher was not without important and valuable results."[28]

---

1. *Official Records*, 45:II:441.
2. Ibid., 45:II:441-442.
3. Ibid., 45:I:643.
4. Ibid., 44:841.
5. Ibid., 44:842.
6. Ibid., 44:832.
7. Ibid., 44:842-843.
8. Ibid., 47:II:3-4.
9. Ibid., 45:I:643.
10. Ibid., 47:II:5-6.
11. Ibid., 45:II:756.
12. Ibid., 45:II:758-759.
13. Ibid., 45:II:757.
14. Ibid., 45:II:757-758.
15. Ibid., 46:II:19-20.
16. Ibid., 46:II:29.
17. Ibid.
18. Porter, *Campaigning with Grant*, 369.
19. *Official Records*, 47:II:16.
20. Philip Van Doren Stern, *An End to Valor: The Last Days of the Civil War* (Boston, 1958), 33.
21. Basler, ed., *Collected Works of Abraham Lincoln*, 8:163-164.
22. Ibid., 8:200.
23. *Official Records*, 47:II:18-19.
24. Ibid., 46:II:52.
25. Ibid., 46:II:60.
26. Ibid., 47:II:21.
27. Ibid., 46:II:71.
28. Bruce Catton, *Grant Takes Command* (Boston, 1968, 1969), 403.

CHAPTER SIX

A Fly Wheel Instead of a Mainspring

8 - 13 January

Admiral Porter was not pleased when he learned that Grant was sending him the same troops from the Army of the James, instead of Sherman. "The man Grant is going to send here, a volunteer general, is one of Butler's men who will likely white-wash Butler by doing just as he did," he complained to Assistant Secretary of the Navy Gustavus Fox. "Don't be surprised if I send him home with a flea in his ear." Nor did he appreciate the regiments of United States Colored Troops—composed of escaped slaves led by white officers—among the troops that Butler had brought and that were returning with Terry. "We want white men here—not niggers," he said.[1]

However, as the transport ships carrying Terry and his soldiers rendezvoused with Porter and his fleet in the harbor of Beaufort, North Carolina, on 8 January they were met by sustained cheering from the sailors aboard the warships, and the soldiers cheered the navy in return. Both soldiers and sailors were glad to see by the others' presence that they were going to make another try at Fort Fisher. Neither felt that they had been given a fair chance the first time.

Unlike Butler, Terry went aboard the *Malvern* to personally confer with Porter, and more cheering rang out across the bay when the two were seen to shake hands. Porter found the general "cold and formal" at first and lacking "the frankness of the true soldier." But he was soon won over by his lack of ostentation and by his common sense. "Terry had no staff, wore no spurs, and we do not think he owned a sword," Porter said later. But, he noted, "He had a well-formed head, full of sense, which served him in lieu of feathers, sword, boots, spurs and staff—of which a general can have too many." Terry, in turn, found the admiral to be "a frank, straightforward, courteous gentleman."[2]

Lieutenant Colonel Cyrus Comstock, one of Grant's aides, served as chief engineer on this expedition, as he had on the first, and he reported to Grant's chief of staff, Brigadier General John Rawlins, that day: "We arrived here this morning after a bad gale, which kept us knocking about off Hatteras, without making any headway. We have just been aboard the admiral's ship. He says there has not been a day fit for landing since the day we landed at Fort Fisher, December 25. He thinks a northeast gale is about to set in, and strongly urges that all our fleet be brought in to wait for good weather, as he thinks it impossible for them to stand a gale twenty-five miles out. General Terry will follow his advice, but will keep the transports away from here and out of sight as long as possible, giving them orders to run in at the last moment. The admiral thinks we will have good weather in four or five days at the change of the moon, and does not expect it before. General Terry is at once ordering ten days' additional coal and rations for our fleet. This bad weather is very unfortunate, but I don't see that we can do anything but trust to the admiral's judgment in that respect. He says the rebels abandoned Fort Fisher the night of the 25th, entirely."[3]

The Confederates had not, of course, abandoned Fort Fisher, but that very same day, 8 January, General Bragg ordered Hoke's Division withdrawn from the Confederate Point peninsula to Wilmington for a dress parade in honor of the defeat of Butler's expedition.

Grover's division, which Sheridan had sent from the Shenandoah Valley to Baltimore, was still waiting there for all of its transports to arrive. So Grover decided to start sending as many men as the ships on hand would carry and to load the others as they arrived. Meanwhile, another force would soon be reaching the Chesapeake Bay area, for that day Halleck telegraphed Thomas, at Nashville: "Lieutenant General Grant directs that, if you are assured of the departure of Hood south from Corinth, you will send General Schofield, with his corps, to Annapolis, Md., with as little delay as possible. The transportation will be left behind, and [wagon] trains will be furnished here. The two Departments of the Cumberland and Ohio will be united, under your command, as soon as General Schofield starts."[4] (Schofield was the commander of the Department of the Ohio, consisting of most of Kentucky and the eastern third of Tennessee, as well as the field force of his department, which was known both as the Army of the Ohio and the 23rd Corps.)

Even as the Federals were reestablishing their garrisons protecting the railroads in southern Tennessee and northern Alabama, a small force of Confederate cavalry appeared in their midst that day from an unexpected direction. Brigadier General Hylan B. Lyon, a former brigade commander under Forrest, had been put in command of the Department of Western Kentucky, given two small brigades of Kentucky mounted recruits, and sent across the lower Tennessee River into Kentucky just as Hood had started his campaign into Tennessee. But Thomas had sent two brigades of veteran cavalry after him, who had chased him out of the state. Lyon had avoided his pursuers by destroying bridges over the Green and Cumberland rivers behind him. Then he had crossed the state of Tennessee well to the east of Nashville, and on the evening of 8 January what was left of his force—over half of his men had deserted when they had learned of Hood's defeat at Nashville—attacked the small Union garrison at Scottsborough, Alabama.

This garrison consisted of 54 men and one officer in detachments from the 101st and 110th U.S. Colored Troops under the command of Lieutenant John H. Hull. These men were there to protect the railroad water tanks and miscellaneous government property. At 5:30 p.m. the Rebels attacked Hull's pickets, wounding one man. Hull sent the only other officer present, 2nd Lieutenant David Smart, with a detachment to bring the wounded man in. "After shooting him they stabbed him three times," Hull reported, "twice in the neck and once in the back."[5] Half an hour later the Confederates attacked in force. Hull thought there were about 1,500 of them, but in fact there were only about 350. However, they had a 12-pounder howitzer with them.

Three times the Rebels charged the depot building where the Federals were stationed, "coming up and laying hold of the muzzles of my men's guns, attempting to wrest them through the loop-holes," Hull reported. "They then fell back beyond the range of my muskets and opened on me with artillery, compelling me to abandon the depot." Hull withdrew his men about a mile and a quarter to the west, where they joined up with a larger force. Meanwhile Lyon's Confederates proceeded to the southeast toward Gunter's Landing (or Gunter's Ferry or Guntersville) where they hoped to cross the Tennessee River, and several Union forces were soon hot on their trail. "I take pleasure in saying," Hull reported, "that I find my men, though but little accustomed to the use of the musket, and not yet mustered into service, to be cool and determined and willing to obey my order; and at no time did I lose confidence in their willingness to fight to the last, though surrounded by a much larger force [that was] aided by artillery."[6] Hull reported his loss as six men wounded. Lyon did not even mention this fight in his report, but Hull claimed 1 Confederate colonel and 17 enlisted men killed and 40 wounded.

Confederate secretary of war Seddon wired Hood that day that "the proposition to furlough the Trans-Mississippi troops cannot be entertained; the suggestion is regarded as dangerous; compliance would probably be fatal; extinguish the thought in the troops, if practicable."[7] A similar message was sent to Beauregard, and when he received it the next day, the ninth, he was furious to learn that Hood had been corresponding directly with the War Department in Richmond instead of with himself or his headquarters. It was only one more instance of Hood trying to ignore the fact that Beauregard was officially his immediate boss. However, Richard Taylor, Beauregard's other principal subordinate, was also reporting directly to Richmond that day. "I have just returned from a visit to General Hood and his army," he wrote to President Davis. "The army needs rest, consolidation, and reorganization. Not a day should be lost in effecting these latter. If moved in its present condition, it will prove utterly worthless; this applies to both infantry and cavalry. Full powers should be immediately given to the commander."[8]

The Confederate congress passed a resolution that day urging the reappointment of General Joseph E. Johnston, Hood's predecessor, as commander of the Army of Tennessee. Meanwhile, a convention drawing up a new constitution for the Union-controlled state of Tennessee adopted an amendment abolishing slavery.

In Virginia that day Grant was already thinking up ways to make use of the aggressive spirit of the new commander of the Army of the James. He wrote a dispatch to Ord that afternoon that said, "I want you to have a thorough examination made of your Bermuda front, and report whether, in your judgment, we can go through by a surprise and by massing. I could give you an additional corps to hold what you got, and would give up all north of the James, except two or three important points, if it could be done."[9]

Down in Georgia that day, Sherman completed arrangements he had made with Confederate authorities to send them any civilians in Savannah who wanted to leave the Union-controlled city. In a final note to Major General Joseph Wheeler, commander of the cavalry corps that Hood had left behind to oppose Sherman's march to the sea, Sherman said, "I will send the families, as requested, to Charleston Harbor, and give public notice that a steamer will take them on board here on Wednesday, and suppose they can reach the anchorage off Charleston next day; but should any delay occur it will arise from the endless excuses made by ladies."[10]

By the tenth, Sherman had managed to complete the transfer of one of his four corps—the 17th, commanded by Major General Francis P. Blair, Jr., son of the man who was on his way to Richmond—to Union-controlled Beaufort Island, South Carolina (not to be confused with Beaufort, North Carolina, where Terry's transports and Porter's warships were waiting for calmer seas). And it began marching for Pocotaligo, 25 miles inland. This was the first step in Sherman's movement north from Savannah through the Carolinas, and it had been hampered by a lack of transports, no doubt because of the movement of Terry's and Grover's forces. "I was really amused at the effect this short sea-voyage had on our men," Sherman later wrote, "most of whom had never before looked upon the ocean. Of course, they were fit subjects for sea-sickness, and afterward they begged me never again to send them to sea, saying they would rather march a thousand miles on the worst roads of the South than to spend a single night on the ocean."[11]

On the eleventh, a revenue cutter arrived at Savannah and there deposited Quartermaster General Montgomery C. Meigs, Adjutant General Edward D. Townsend, Secretary of War Stanton, Simeon Draper, an agent of the Treasury Department, and a retinue of other civilians who had come to regulate the civil affairs of the city. "I was instructed by Mr. Stanton to transfer to Mr. Draper the custom-house, post-office, and such other public buildings as these civilians needed in the execution of their office, and to cause to be delivered into their custody the captured cotton... ," Sherman later wrote. "Up to this time all the cotton had been carefully guarded, with orders to General Easton to ship it by the return-vessels to New York, for the adjudication of the nearest prize court, accompanied with invoices and all evidence of title to ownership. Marks, numbers, and other figures, were carfully preserved on the bales, so that the court might know the history of each bale. But Mr. Stanton, who surely was an able lawyer, changed all this, and ordered the obliteration of all the marks; so that no man, friend or foe, could trace his identical cotton. I thought it strange at the time, and think it more so now; for I am assured that claims, real and fictitious, have been *proved up* against this identical cotton of three times the quantity actually captured, and that reclamations on the Treasury have been *allowed* for more than the actual quantity captured."[12]

"I saw a good deal of the secretary socially," Sherman said, "during the time of his visit to Savannah. He kept his quarters on the revenue-cutter with Simeon Draper, Esq., which cutter lay at a wharf in the river, but he came very often to my quarters at Mr. Green's house. Though appearing robust and strong, he complained a good deal of internal pains, which he said threatened his life, and would compel him soon to quit public office. He professed to have come from Washington purposely for rest and recreation, and he spoke unreservedly of the bickerings and jealousies at the national capital; of the interminable quarrels of the State Governors about their quotas, and more particularly of the financial troubles that threatened the very existence of the Government itself. He said that the price of every thing had so risen in comparison with the depreciated money, that there was danger of national bankruptcy, and he appealed to me, as a soldier and patriot, to hurry up matters so as to bring the war to a close."[13]

In Missouri that day, a constitutional convention adopted an ordinance abolishing slavery in that state.

In West Virginia that night Major General Thomas L. Rosser with 300 picked men of his Confederate cavalry division from the Shenandoah Valley, all wearing captured Union blue overcoats, took advantage of the deep snow and bitter cold weather to surprise regiments of Union cavalry and infantry at the town of Beverly and carried off 583 prisoners.

After riding out a gale in the harbor at Beaufort, North Carolina, for four days and nights, Porter's fleet and Terry's troop transports finally steamed south under clear blue winter skies on the morning of 12 January. The column of 21 army transports, carrying 8,897 officers and men, was flanked by 59 warships, bearing 627 guns, in two columns, and they were all followed by a collection of supply ships, coal carriers, tenders, and tugboats. "It was a grand and inspiring sight to see the long lines of vessels," one participant wrote. "The placid beauty of the sea and sky had banished our sea-sickness and raised our hopes—a grand display of naval beauty and symmetry and power."[14] The ships came to anchor five miles north of Fort Fisher at about 10 p.m., and Terry went over to the *Malvern* for another conference with the admiral. Because of the late hour they decided to let the troops rest over night and to begin landing them the first thing the next morning.

The lights of the Federal ships were soon spotted by the Rebels on shore, and inside Fort Fisher the long roll soon summoned the 700 members of the 36th North Carolina to their battle stations. However, the news did not reach General Bragg at Wilmington until after midnight due to the drunkenness of a Confederate telegraph operator. Bragg sent the news north to General Lee, suspended all leaves, called out the Senior Reserves, and, calling off his plans for an offensive against Union-held New Berne, ordered Hoke's Division back to Confederate Point with orders to make every effort to prevent a Federal landing.

Orders were issued that day, the twelfth, transferring the Union forces in North Carolina from Ord's department, which now became the Department of Virginia, to Major General John G. Foster's Department of the South. And Foster's command, which already included Union lodgements along the Atlantic coast in South Carolina, Georgia, and Florida, was subordinated temporarily to Sherman.

The first brigade of Grover's division from the Shenandoah Valley arrived at Fort Monroe that day after a two-day boat ride from Baltimore. The quartermaster there ordered it to be put ashore at nearby Newport News, Virginia, while the ships were replenished with rations and water. That afternoon Rawlins, Grant's chief of staff, sent orders to the quartermaster: "All troops arriving at Fort Monroe from General Sheridan's army will proceed, as fast as the vessels can get on coal, water, and rations, to Savannah, Ga., and report to Major-General Sherman for orders; and, in the event General Sherman should have departed from there, they will report to Maj. Gen. J.G. Foster for orders."[15] Grover's division, soon assigned to the Department of the South, would provide the garrison for Savannah so that Sherman would not have to leave any of his western veterans for that purpose.

Meanwhile, the Secretary of War's visit to that city continued. "Mr. Stanton staid in Savannah several days," Sherman later wrote, "and seemed very curious about matters and things in general. I walked with him through the city, especially the bivouacs of the several regiments that occupied the vacant squares, and he seemed particularly pleased at the ingenuity of the men in constructing their temporary huts. Four of the 'dog-tents,' or *tentes d'abri*, buttoned together, served for a roof, and the sides were made of clapboards, or rough boards brought from demolished houses or fences....

"He talked to me a great deal about the negroes, the former slaves, and I told him of many interesting incidents, illustrating their simple character and faith in our arms and progress. He inquired particularly about General Jeff. C. Davis [commander of the 14th Corps], who, he said, was a Democrat, and hostile to the negro. I assured him that General Davis was an excellent soldier, and I did not believe he had any hostility to the negro; that in our army we had no negro soldiers, and, as a rule, we preferred white soldiers, but that we employed a large force of them as servants, teamsters, and pioneers, who had rendered admirable service. He then showed me a newspaper account of General Davis taking up his pontoon-bridge across Ebenezer Creek, leaving sleeping negro men, women, and children, on the other side, to be slaughtered by Wheeler's cavalry. I had heard such a rumor, and advised Mr. Stanton, before becoming prejudiced, to allow me to send for General Davis, which he did, and General Davis explained the matter to his entire satisfaction.... General Jeff. C. Davis was strictly a soldier, and doubtless hated to have his wagons and columns encumbered by these poor negroes, for whom we all felt sympathy, but a sympathy of a different sort from that of Mr. Stanton, which was not of pure humanity, but of *politics*... "[16]

"Since Mr. Stanton got here," Sherman told his friend Halleck in a letter written that day, "we have talked over all matters freely, and I deeply regret that I am threatened with that curse to all peace and comfort—popularity; but I trust to bad luck enough in the future to cure that, for I know enough of 'the people' to feel that a single mistake made by some of my subordinates will tumble down my fame into infamy.... If it be insisted that I shall so conduct my operations that the negro alone is consulted, of course I will be defeated, and then where will be Sambo? Don't military success imply the safety of Sambo and vice versa? Of course that cock and bull story of my turning back negroes that Wheeler might kill them is all humbug. I turned nobody back. Jeff. C. Davis did at Ebenezer Creek forbid certain plantation slaves—old men, women, and children, to follow his column; but they would come along and he took up his pontoon bridge, not because he wanted to leave them, but because he wanted his bridge.... I profess to be the best kind of a friend to Sambo, and think that on such a question Sambo should be consulted. They gather round me in crowds, and I can't find out whether I am Moses or Aaron, or which of the prophets; but I rate as one of the congregation, and it is hard to tell in what sense I am most appreciated by Sambo—in saving him from his master, or the new master that threatens him with a new species of slavery. I mean State recruiting agents.... I do and will do the best I can for negroes, and feel sure that the problem is solving itself slowly and naturally. It needs nothing more than our fostering care. I thank you for the kind hint and will heed it so far as mere appearances go, but, not being dependent on votes, I can afford to act, as far as my influence goes, as a fly wheel instead of a mainspring."[17]

That evening twenty black ministers and church leaders were assembled at Sherman's headquarters at Stanton's request.

The secretary of war asked them several questions, which were taken down by an adjutant, along with the answers of their spokesman, 67-year-old Garrison Frazier, a retired Baptist minister who had bought his own freedom eight years before. First Stanton asked them if they understood the emancipation proclamation. "So far as I understand President Lincoln's proclamation to the rebellious States," Frazier replied, "it is, that if they would lay down their arms and submit to the laws of the United States before the 1st of January, 1863, all should be well, but if they did not, then all the slaves in the rebel States should be free, henceforth and forever."

After making sure they agreed on the definition of slavery, Stanton then asked them how they thought the former slaves could support themselves and assist the Federal government in maintaining their freedom. "The way we can best take care of ourselves," Frazier said, "is to have land, and turn in and till it by our labor—that is, by the labor of the women, and children, and old men—and we can soon maintain ourselves and have something to spare; and to assist the Government the young men should enlist in the service of the Government, and serve in such manner as they may be wanted.... We want to be placed on land until we are able to buy it and make it our own."

Stanton asked them whether they would rather live scattered among the whites or in colonies by themselves. One of them, James Lynch, a 26-year-old free-born preacher from Baltimore, thought they should live among the whites, but Frazier and the others thought they should be separated, "For there is a prejudice against us in the South that will take years to get over." But in reply to the next question, they said that the former slaves had enough intelligence to "maintain good and peaceable relations among [themselves] and with [their] neighbors."

The secretary then asked them how the black population of the South felt about the United States government and the causes and objects of the current war. "I think you will find there is thousands that are willing to make any sacrifice to assist the Government of the United States," he was told, "while there is also many that are not willing to take up arms. I do not suppose there is a dozen men that is opposed to the Government. I understand as to the war that the South is the aggressor. President Lincoln was elected President by a majority of the United States, which guaranteed him the right of holding the office and exercising that right over the whole United States. The South, without knowing what he would do, rebelled. The war was commenced by the rebels before he came into the office. The object of the war was not, at first, to give the slaves their freedom, but the sole object of the war was, at first, to bring the rebellious States back into the Union and their loyalty to the laws of the United States. Afterward, knowing the value that was set on the slaves by the rebels, the President thought that his proclamation would stimulate them to lay down their arms, reduce them to obedience, and help to bring back the rebel States, and their not doing so has now made the freedom of the slaves a part of the war. It is my opinion that there is not a man in this city that could be started to help the rebels one inch, for that would be suicide. There was two black men left with the rebels, because they had taken an active part for the rebels, and thought something might befall them if they staid behind, but there is not another man. If the prayers that have gone up for the Union army could be read out you would not get through them these two weeks."

Stanton asked them if the slaves would fight for the Confederacy if given the chance and was told, "I think they would fight as long as they were before the bayonet, and just as soon as they could get away they would desert." He asked them how they felt about enlisting in the Union army and what kind of service they preferred, and was told, "A large number have gone as soldiers to Port Royal to be drilled and put in the service, and I think there is thousands of young men that will enlist; there is something about them that, perhaps is wrong; they have suffered so long from the rebels that they want to meet and have a chance with them in the field. Some of them want to shoulder the musket, others want to go into the quartermaster or the commissary service."

When asked if they understood how blacks in the Rebel states were enlisted by agents from the northern states, Frazier said, "My understanding is that colored persons enlisted by State agents are elisted as substitutes, and give credit to the States, and do not swell the army, because every black man enlisted by a State agent leaves a white man at home; and also, that larger bounties are given or promised by the State agents than are given by the States. The great object should be to push through this rebellion the shortest way, and there seems to be something wanting in the enlistment by State agents, for it don't strengthen the army, but takes one away for every colored man enlisted."

Stanton then asked how they thought they should be enlisted. "I think, sir," Frazier said, "that all compulsory operations should be put a stop to. The ministers would talk to them, and the young men would enlist. It is my opinion that it would be far better for the State agents to stay at home, and the enlistments be made for the United States under the direction of General Sherman."

At this point, after more than an hour of questioning, Stanton asked Sherman to leave the room. And when he was gone he asked the blacks' opinion of the general, "and how far do they regard his sentiments and actions as friendly to their rights and interests, or otherwise." Lynch said that he was unwilling to express an opinion based on his limited acquaintance with the general, but the others agreed with Frazier, who said, "We looked upon General Sherman, prior to his arrival, as a man, in the providence of God, specially set apart to accomplish this work, and we unanimously felt inexpressible gratitude to him, looking upon him as a man that should be honored for the faithful performance of his duty. Some of us called upon him immediately upon his arrival, and it is probable he did not meet the Secretary with more courtesy than he met us. His conduct and deportment toward us characterized him as a friend and a gentleman. We have confidence in General Sherman, and think that what concerns us could not be under better hands. This is our opinion now from the short acquaintance and intercourse we have had."[18]

The blacks, Sherman later wrote, "understood their own interests far better than did the men in Washington, who tried to make political capital out of this negro question. The idea that such men should have been permitted to hang around Mr. Lincoln, to torture his life by suspicions of the officers who were toiling with the single purpose to bring the war to a successful end, and thereby to liberate *all* slaves, is a fair illustration of the influences that poison a political capital.

"My aim then was, to whip the rebels, to humble their pride, to follow them to their inmost recesses, and make them fear and dread us. 'Fear of the Lord is the beginning of wisdom.' I did not want them to cast in our teeth what General Hood had once done in Atlanta, that we had to call on *their* slaves to help us to subdue them. But, as regards kindness to the race, encouraging them to patience and forbearance, procuring them food and clothing, and providing them with land whereon to labor, I assert that no army ever did more for that race than the one I commanded in Savannah. When we reached Savannah, we were beset by ravenous State agents from Hilton Head, who enticed and carried away our servants, and the corps of pioneers which we had organized, and which had done such excellent service. On one occasion, my own aide-de-camp, Colonel Audenried, found at least a hundred poor negroes shut up in a house and pen, waiting for the night, to be conveyed stealthily to Hilton Head. They appealed to him for protection, alleging that they had been told that they *must be* soldiers, that 'Massa Lincoln' wanted them, etc. I never denied the slaves a full opportunity for voluntary enlistment, but I did prohibit force to be used, for I knew that the State agents were more influenced by the profit they derived from the large bounties then being paid than by any love of country or of the colored race."[19]

In Richmond that evening, Francis Blair, Sr., finally met with his old friend, Jefferson Davis, who greeted him with a hug. Alone with the Confederate president in his study, the elder Blair outlined his plan for ending the war. He proposed a cease fire, during which the two sides would unite to drive the French and their puppet, Emperor Maximilian, out of Mexico in defense of the Monroe Doctrine. It was his hope that after thus fighting on the same side against a common foe, and possibly under Davis's own command, the two sides would find it impossible to return to fighting each other. "He who expels the Bonaparte-Hapsburg dynasty from our southern flank... ," Blair said, "will ally his name with those of Washington and Jackson as a defender of the liberty of the country."[20] Davis did not think much of the idea, but he was under pressure from his own critics to show a willingness to end the war on reasonable terms—reasonable to Confederates at least—and he could not afford to ignore the fact that Lincoln had sent Blair to him, or at least had allowed him to come. Therefore he wrote a letter for Blair to take back to Washington with him, saying, in part, "Notwithstanding the rejection of our former offers, I would, if you could promise that a commission, minister, or other agent would be received, appoint one immediately, and renew the effort to enter into a conference with a view to secure peace to the two countries."[21]

Down in Mississippi, the last corps of Hood's Army of Tennessee reached Tupelo that day and went into camp. But there was such a shortage of food and supplies there that Hood began to issue furloughs in large numbers in order to ease the logistical problem. Most of the men sent home never returned to the army.

President Davis told Richard Taylor, in a message written that day: "Sherman's campaign has produced bad effect on our people. Success against his future operations is needful to reanimate public confidence. Hardee [commanding in South Carolina] requires more aid than Lee can give him, and Hood's army is the only source to which we can now look. If you can hold Thomas in check with the addition to your present force of Polk's old corps, restored to your department, and the cavalry of Hood's army, which cannot be profitably sent to the East, then, as fast as it can be done consistently with the efficiency of the troops, the rest of Hood's army should, I think, be sent to look after Sherman. The presence of those veterans will no doubt greatly increase the auxiliary force now with Hardee."[22] But the next day, the thirteenth, Beauregard, on his way to Tupelo, wired Davis from Meridian, Mississippi, Taylor's headquarters: "I regret to inform you that, from General Taylor's report of the disorganization and demoralization of the Army of Tennessee, and from the bad condition of the common roads and railroads hence to Augusta, no re-enforcements can be sent in time to General Hardee from that army, which does not now number 15,000 infantry."[23] Beauregard also telegraphed Hood: "I will leave here to-morrow morning. Meanwhile suspend movement of troops ordered until my arrival at Tupelo."[24] That same day, Hood, in order to forestall the axe that the hairs on the back of his neck must have told him was already descending, sent a one-sentence telegram to Secretary of War Seddon: "I respectfully request to be relieved from the command of this army."[25]

In northern Virginia that day, Friday the thirteenth, Private Lewis Powell of Lieutenant Colonel John S. Mosby's Confederate guerrilla command came into the Union camp at Fairfax Court House, near Washington, D.C., claiming to be a civilian named Lewis Paine. He applied to the provost marshal there to protect him as a civilian refugee and was sent to Federal headquarters at Alexandria, where he took the oath of allegiance and was released. In Washington that day John Surratt left his job with the Adams Express Company, which he had taken on 30 December, in order to devote his full attention to the plot to capture President Lincoln. He never bothered to go back to collect the pay due to him.

---

1. Gragg, *Confederate Goliath*, 108.
2. Ibid.
3. *Official Records*, 46:II:69.
4. Ibid., 45:II:540.
5. Ibid., 45:I:802.
6. Ibid., 45:I:803.
7. Ibid., 45:II:770.
8. Ibid., 45:II:772.
9. Ibid., 46:II:79.

10. Ibid., 47:II:29.
11. Sherman, *Memoirs*, 721.
12. Ibid., 723.
13. Ibid., 732-733.
14. Gragg, *Confederate Goliath*, 110.
15. *Official Records*, 46:II:106.
16. Sherman, *Memoirs*, 724-725.
17. *Official Records*, 47:II:36-37.
18. Ibid., 47:II:39-41.
19. Sherman, *Memoirs*, 729-730.
20. Noah Andre Trudeau, *The Last Citadel: Petersburg, Virginia, June 1864 - April 1865* (Boston, 1991), 303.
21. Shelby Foote, *The Civil War: A Narrative*, vol. 3 (New York, 1974), 771.
22. *Official Records*, 45:II:778-779.
23. Ibid., 45:II:780.
24. Ibid., 45:II:781.
25. Ibid.

CHAPTER SEVEN

You and Your Garrison Are to Be Sacrificed

13 - 14 January 1865

The eastern sky was beginning to grow light on the morning of 13 January as Admiral Porter's fleet got under way and steamed toward Fort Fisher. By 7 a.m. the ships were again forming into three lines and a reserve. At 7:19 a.m. the USS *Brooklyn* opened fire and soon other ships joined in. Their target was not the fort, however. For the first few hours they concentrated their fire on the scrub oaks and pines behind the area where the troops would be landed.

It was 8:30 a.m. by the time the five ironclads, led again by the USS *New Ironsides*, pulled into position in front of the first line, within 1200 yards of the fort. As soon as they dropped anchor, Confederate guns opened fire on them, but the ironclads did not respond at first. Commodore William Radford, captain of the *New Ironsides*, was counting the enemy guns and marking their range. Then he had each of his ship's guns fired one at a time and their shots watched carefully, while the four monitors followed suit. The second round fired by the number-one gun on the monitor *Mahopac* exploded prematurely, blowing away four feet of the gun's muzzle and wounding four members of the gun crew, but by some miracle no one was killed. Once the range was verified by hits on the fort, all five ironclads opened a sustained and accurate bombardment. This time the ships were under orders not to waste ammunition firing at flagstaffs. They were to concentrate their fire on the fort's guns.

"The day was bright and clear and cold and crisp," a watching Union soldier remembered, "which made the smoke light and the wind from the northwest quickly lifted the smoke so the flash of each gun could be seen clearly. To me it seemed like meteors were being fired out of a volcano.... I would watch the turrets of the monitors through my glass. They would turn their backs on the enemy to reload and I could distinctly see the big rammer staves come out of the ports. Then they would wheel around toward the fort. There would be two puffs of blue smoke, then I could see the big shells make a black streak through the air with a tail of white smoke behind them. Then would come over the water not the quick bark of the field gun, but a slow, quavering, overpowering roar, like an earthquake—then away among the Rebel traverses would be another huge ball of mingled smoke and flame as big as a meeting house."[1]

Terry put his troops ashore somewhat farther north than Butler and Weitzel had landed the first expedition. There a narrow body of water, Myrtle Sound, which divided the widening peninsula north of Battery Gatlin, would help to protect the northern flank of the Union forces. The Confederates had abandoned Battery Gatlin and nearby Battery Anderson, and there was no opposition to the landing, which began at 8:45 a.m. "The transports had hardly anchored," an army officer wrote, "when the water was covered with the small boats of the navy, varying in size from the small cutter to the huge launch, the former pulling six oars and the latter between twenty and thirty." These boats "pulled rapidly up to the transports and were quickly filled with the soldiers, who evidenced the utmost eagerness to reach the shore as soon as possible, more I fear to get on solid land once more than from their desire to meet the enemy." Sailors manned the oars, and, according to one soldier, "They jeered at us for land lubbers, but they gave us a helping hand where it was needed. A soldier astride a sailor's neck and being carried to land through the surf was a common sight."[2]

The first wave of men to reach shore ran across the beach and formed a skirmish line in the edge of the woods beyond, in order to cover the landing of subsequent waves of boats which soon began to fill two miles of beach with soldiers. Before long, driftwood fires were blazing to help dry the mens' wet uniforms, and, when the skirmishers discovered some 35 head of cattle nearby, steaks were soon grilling over those fires. The similarity to a giant picnic was enhanced by bands playing military airs and by soldiers playing in the sand and laughing at those who took particularly amusing dunkings on their way to shore. So many men found it impossible to get ashore without dunking themselves, their rifles, and their ammunition, in fact, that a naval officer ordered a line secured between a transport and a beached launch, thus providing a handhold for disembarking soldiers. They called it Tanner's Ferry in honor of the officer who divised it. By 3 p.m. almost 8,000 soldiers had been landed, and they were followed by 300,000 rounds of ammunition and enough rations to feed them all for six days.

Hoke's Confederates began to arrive at the northern end of the peninsula while the Federals were still coming ashore, but no effort was made to prevent or disrupt their landing. His skirmishers stayed under cover and watched the Yankee build-up. "We did nothing," one of them later complained, "just lay quiet... and let the enemy land. We could have repulsed them if we had fired on them as they landed, which we were anxious to do before they got a force together. We received no orders from our officers, just let [the Federals] assemble a force together, then they commenced firing on us."[3]

This firing was from Colonel Joseph C. Abbott's 2nd Brigade of the 1st Division of the 24th Corps, the brigade that had been added to the troops from Butler's original force to beef up this second expedition. Abbott had been ordered to probe the woods and see if the Confederates were up to anything in there, and before the watching Rebel skirmishers knew what was going on they were overrun by two regiments of Abbott's brigade and hustled off to the beach for interrogation by a group of Union officers, including General Terry himself. In this way Terry learned that Hoke's Division, which the Federals had thought had been sent to South Carolina to oppose Sherman, was now gathering just northwest of the landing site.

"We were soldiers of long acquaintance with the enemy's way of doing things," one Union officer wrote: "there we were on an open beach with the big fort on one side and a veteran division of Confederate soldiers on the other. We had learned in Virginia that Confederate soldiers could always be counted on to make trouble if there was an opportunity to do it, and we were not sure that an attack from Fort Fisher with one at the same time from the direction of Wilmington would not be tried."[4] Terry ordered Abbott's brigade to make a vigorous feint to the north in the hope of convincing the Rebels that the Federals were about to move toward Wilmington. Abbott's troops were also to dig entrenchments near the landing site for their own protection and build enough campfires to convice the Confederates that the entire Union force was encamped there. Meanwhile, as soon as it was dark, the rest of Terry's force would move down the peninsula toward the fort.

With Bragg in command of the Confederate forces, the Federals actually had no reason to fear a Rebel attack. Bragg was too afraid of the fleet's heavy guns to order one, and he mistakenly thought that Terry's force outnumbered Hoke's by two to one. Instead of attacking, Bragg began to order arms and ammunition relocated as if preparing to evacuate Wilmington. Whiting, meanwhile, was seething with frustration. He urged Bragg to order Hoke to attack before the Federals got organized and built defenses, but Bragg ignored him. Whiting even went so far as to telegraph the War Department about the defense of his district, or the lack of one, but Secretary Seddon replied, "Your superior in rank, General Bragg, is charged with the command and defense of Wilmington."[5] When Bragg began to trace on a map a line to fall back to when Fort Fisher fell, Whiting stormed out of headquarters and down to the docks on the Cape Fear River. There he commandeered a steamboat to take him and two young members of his staff downriver to the fort.

By the time the boat reached the wharf near Battery Buchanan the naval bombardment had reached its deadliest peak. The ships that had been covering the landing had now joined with the others. "In the midst of the bombardment," Colonel Lamb, the fort's commander, wrote, "General W.H.C. Whiting, the district commander, and his staff, arrived in the fort. They had walked up from Battery Buchanan. I did not know of their approach until the general came to me on the works and remarked, 'Lamb, my boy, I have come to share your fate. You and your garrison are to be sacrificed.' I replied, 'Don't say so, General; we shall certainly whip the enemy again.' He then told me that when he left Wilmington General Bragg was hastily removing his stores and ammunition, and was looking for a place to fall back upon. I offered him the command, although he came unarmed and without orders; but he refused, saying he would counsel with me, but would leave me to conduct the defense."[6]

Whiting moved about the fort amid the worst of the bombardment puffing calmly on his pipe as if he were taking a Sunday stroll and there was not an enemy gun within hundreds of miles. "I saw him stand with folded arms," a Confederate lieutenant wrote, "smiling upon a 400-pounder shell, as it stood smoking and spinning like a billiard ball on the sand not twenty feet away until it burst, and then move quietly away." His example was an inspiration to the men. "I saw him fight, and saw him pray," the lieutenant said, "and he was all that a general should be in battle."[7]

The underwater telegraph cable had been laid across the river since the first Union expedition had been cut by the bombardment, but Whiting sent a series of increasingly angry messages to Bragg by boat demanding that Hoke attack the Federals before they could attack the fort. Bragg sent the Senior Reserves to reinforce Hoke and called out the Home Guard to help protect Wilmington, and at about 2 p.m. he finally left for the front himself. However, it was almost dusk by the time he arrived at Sugar Loaf hill to confer with Hoke, who said he had deployed his division in a defensive line across the peninsula from the sea to the river to prevent any Union advance toward Wilmington and he had a detachment of South Carolina cavalry in the woods between the Federals and the fort to report any sign of an advance against the fort. Bragg approved of this and told Hoke to stay on the defensive unless the Yankees advanced from their entrenched landing site.

Somebody must have convinced Porter that the bombardment during the first expedition had not been as effective as he thought, for now the naval guns concentrated an accurate and destructive fire on the Confederate guns, especially those along the landface, since that was the part the army would have to attack. "I assure you it was the most terrible storm of iron and lead that I have ever seen during the war," one defender wrote, "exploding so fast that it would seem to be but one roaring sound—and the sand and water rising in great clouds—so that you could not see ten feet in any direction and the atmosphere was filled it seemed by sulfur." A Confederate sailor manning one of the guns wrote that he and his fellow gunners were nearly buried in sand several times. "This was caused by shells bursting in the sand," he said. "Whenever one would strike near us in the sand it would throw the sand over us by the cartload."[8]

At sundown most of the Union ships stopped firing, but the ironclads continued to shell the fort all night. Several guns on the landface had been damaged enough to prevent their use, the earthworks were severely cratered, and dozens of defenders had been killed or wounded. Sending out burial parties only resulted in more casualties, meals could not be cooked, and guns could not be manned. The Rebels could only huddle in their bombproofs and wait for the bombardment to end.

As the wooden ships retired, their crews could see, in the waning light, the Union soldiers forming for an advance on the fort. Abbott's brigade stayed behind as planned, and his extra campfires convinced not only Bragg and Hoke but Whiting and Lamb as well that the Federals were still camped where they had come ashore. But the rest of Terry's force marched through the darkness down the beach past Battery Anderson and across the peninsula toward the river, searching for a pond shown on the Union maps. However, the pond turned out to be only a low, swampy area of thick underbrush. So, led by Brigadier General Charles J. Paine's two brigades of U.S. Colored Troops from his 3rd Division of the 25th Corps, they pushed on through the brush to the riverbank and down the peninsula. After almost four hours of this, Paine's skirmishers emerged from the woods and a reconnoitering party soon reported a good position was not far beyond.

At about 2 a.m. 800 spades were issued to the Union troops and they began to dig a line of entrenchments across the peninsula facing the fort and about two miles north of it. Logs were placed along the southern rim of the trench and covered with dirt. "All night long the troops labored most vigorously, the tools passing from hand to hand," a Union officer wrote, "until by sunrise we had a line of breastworks across from the river to the sea, behind which our men could easily repel the attack of double their force."[9] While this was going on the 142nd New York of Curtis's brigade moved forward and established an advanced skirmish line within rifle range of the fort's landface.

Down in northern Alabama that night, the thirteenth, Colonel Palmer's 15th Pennsylvania Cavalry—the same regiment that had captured Hood's pontoons two weeks before—was in pursuit of Lyon's Kentucky Rebels, who had attacked the depot at Scottsborough five days before. The Union infantry had given up the chase when most of the Confederates had succeeded in crossing to the south side of the Tennessee River, but two shallow-draft gunboats ferried Palmer's horsemen across to continue the pursuit. At 4 a.m. on the fourteenth Palmer split his small regiment as it descended Sand Mountain, sending one battalion of fifty men under Lieutenant Colonel Charles B. Lamborn to take a back road where he knew that one of Lyon's regiments and his artillery was camped.

"With the other two battalions," Palmer reported, "I moved along the main road toward Warrenton, passing, when within one mile of Red Hill, a camp of about 150 of the enemy, who did not discover our presence until I had passed by them with one battalion. With this I pushed on to capture General Lyon, who was quartered with his staff and escort at the house of Tom Noble, half a mile beyond, leaving an orderly to direct the rear battalion to capture the enemy's camp. This was done; nearly all the horses and arms and most of the men being captured, the remainder of the men making their escape on foot in the dark. In the meantime my advance guard had reached General Lyon's headquarters, and captured him at the door of Noble's house, in his night clothes."

The general surrendered, as coincidence would have it, to a Union sergeant named Arthur P. Lyon, while Palmer's advance guard was charging the general's escort, which was camped in a barn lot 100 yards back of the house protected by fences and outbuildings. "The general begged permission to put on his pantaloons, coat, and boots," Palmer reported, "which Sergeant Lyon unfortunately granted, and went into the bedroom with him for that purpose. At that moment the escort fired a volley at the advance guard, when the sergeant said, 'Come, general, I can't allow you much more time.' The general then suddenly seized a pistol and shot the sergeant, killing him instantly, and made his escape through the back door in the dark, it being a half hour before daybreak. The escort fled at the same time through the woods, leaving all the headquarters horses, saddles, valises, &c. I left a detachment to gather these up, and pushed on toward Warrenton in the direction of other camp-fires which could be seen ahead on our left."

These fires proved to be at the camp that Lamborn's battalion was supposed to attack. But the Confederate regiment had already become alarmed by the firing on the main road, and had saddled up and moved out, taking the back valley road on which Lamborn was marching in the opposite direction. "Colonel Lamborn's advance had got astray in the dark," Palmer reported, "and he soon found his main column mixed up along the narrow road with the column of the advancing rebels, who anxiously inquired what that firing meant? The colonel then attacked them, taking a few prisoners, but the greater portion got off through the woods. He then proceeded to their camp and took possession of the piece of artillery, which proved to be a 12-pounder howitzer drawn by a yoke of oxen."

All together, Palmer's regiment took 95 prisoners and learned from them that Lyon had taken between 800 and 1000 men and two guns into Kentucky, had returned to Tennessee with only about 350 men and one gun, and had only been able to get about 250 men and the howitzer across the Tennessee River. That left Lyon only about 150 men after Palmer's attack. "I do not think," Palmer justly concluded, "Lyon's command will give much more trouble as an organization."[10]

John Wilkes Booth's friend John Surratt left Washington that day, the fourteenth, and traveled to Port Tobacco, Maryland, southeast of the capital. This tiny village, then the seat of Charles County, was a haven for Rebels and smugglers running contraband to Virginia in defiance of the blockade. There Surratt met Thomas Harbin, the Confederate agent that Dr. Mudd had introduced to Booth. With Harbin's help, Surratt purchased a large boat that could be used to ferry a captured Abraham Lincoln across the Potomac to Virginia. The boat was turned over to George Atzerodt, a Port Tobacco carriage painter and blockade runner whom Harbin and Surratt had recruited into their scheme. Atzerodt concealed the boat in Goose Creek and later in a tributary of Nanjemoy Creek in the care of two other blockade runners.

Over in Mississippi on the fourteenth, General Hood began to hedge on his request to be relieved of command of the Army of Tennessee in a message to Confederate secretary of war James Seddon. "General Beauregard will arrive here to-morrow," he said. "I will then communicate more fully in regard to my request contained in cipher telegram of yesterday morning. I have only [the] interest of my country at stake."[11] Meanwhile, he ordered a thorough inspection and a crackdown on desertion.

On the North Carolina coast during the night of 13-14 January, while Terry's main force was advancing from the landing site toward Fort Fisher, that fort was receiving reinforcements. One company of the 1st North Carolina Heavy Artillery, one company of the 10th North Carolina, four companies of the 40th North Carolina, and about 50 Confederate sailors and marines were ferried across the Cape Fear River from the smaller forts on the other side, bringing the garrison's strength up to about 1500 men. But General Whiting and Colonel Lamb knew that this was not enough. The fate of their fort still rested with Hoke's Division and with Braxton Bragg. Whiting took a steamer across the Cape Fear River to Smithville so that he could be in direct telegraph communication with Wilmington and sent a message to be forwarded to Bragg at Sugar Loaf that 76 Union ships had been counted off shore that morning in line of battle. "I must have a regiment to do duty at night," he said. "Men that fought their guns as mine did yesterday and will have to do to-day require some rest at night." Then Whiting learned that his subordinate in command of the small forts on the west side of the river had been ordered to send reinforcements to Hoke. So he telegraphed Bragg that he had already stripped those forts to obtain the reinforcements he had sent into Fort Fisher the night before and repeated his request for more men. "The best way to re-enforce Fisher is by land through the enemy," he said, "or by landing at Battery Buchanan."[12] He also advised Bragg that the Confederate gunboat *Chickamauga*, a converted British blockade runner armed with big Brooke rifles, was, on his advice, firing on the beach whenever the Federals showed themselves. At 11:45 a.m. he said, "Porter cannot come in now. The tide is turning. He cannot come in until at night. We hold Fisher. Sooner you attack the enemy the better."[13]

Bragg was acting with uncommon aggressiveness that morning. He ordered Hoke to send out a reconnaissance toward the fort and make contact with the 2nd South Carolina Cavalry, which had been left between the fort and the Federals. So Hoke personally led his skirmishers through the woods and down the peninsula until they stumbled into Terry's main force in its new position. Then Hoke sent back word of the Federals' new position to Bragg. How they had managed to get there without the cavalry having detected and reported their move he did not know. The horsemen must have been remiss in their duties. At noon Bragg's adjutant sent orders to Hoke: "On careful consideration the commanding general deems it of the highest importance to break the enemy line, if possible, and he hopes you may be able to do it by a judicious use of artillery, they having none. Once broken, we ought to be able to prevent their fortifying another line."[14]

Unknown to Bragg, the Federals did have artillery ashore. As soon as it was light Colonel Henry L. Abbot, Terry's chief of artillery, started landing his siege train, consisting of one company of engineers, two batteries of field artillery, and three companies of heavy artillerymen with twenty Coehorn mortars, twenty 30-pounder Parrott rifles, and four big 100-pounder Parrotts. There were also a number of caissons, and several teams of mules. The guns and caissons were taken apart and brought ashore in pieces, using Tanner's Ferry again, and by midday some of the field artillery was ready for action.

However, the mules were a bigger problem. They tangled their tow lines, bit, kicked, sat down on the transports and refused to budge, and generally refused to cooperate. One of the first mules that was successfully landed was tethered on the beach as a sort of decoy for the others, but he must not have been very popular among his peers, for they all ignored him. One kicked a hole in the launch that was towing him, almost sinking it, and then swam more than a mile out to sea before he was recaptured. It was Acting Master Zera Tanner, who had thought up Tanner's Ferry, who came up with the solution. The mules were blindfolded so that they could not see what was happening to them, and after that they were towed ashore with a minimum of resistance.

Curtis's 1st Brigade of the 2nd Division of the 24th Corps moved forward that morning and occupied Craig's Landing, a wharf on the river not far north of the fort, as well as the cottage where Colonel Lamb and his wife had lived before the Yankees came. Lamb ordered the surviving guns on the landface to open fire on Curtis's troops, but the naval bombardment soon drove his gunners back to the shelter of the bombproofs. Soon, as Lamb watched helplessly, a Confederate steamship loaded with ammunition and food for the fort came down the river and approached the landing, unaware that it was in Union hands. Lamb ordered gunners back to their post long enough to fire a warning shot that splashed in the river near the ship, but it came on anyway, pulled alongside the wharf, and tied up. As soon as it did so, Curtis's men swarmed aboard and captured her. They did not have much time to celebrate or examine their prize, however, for soon the Rebel gunboat *Chickamauga* came down and opened fire. The Federals scurried for cover, while the captured supply ship was holed and sunk in a matter of minutes. Lamb was relieved to see that the Federals had been deprived of the supply ship, but the fact that it had been sent to Craig's Landing showed that Braxton Bragg obviously did not understand the situation. Why the general did not just get on a boat and steam down to look for himself was more than Lamb could fathom.

At 1:30 p.m. Whiting, who had by then returned to the fort, sent a steamer upriver with a message: "The game of the enemy is very plain to me. They are now furiously bombarding my land front; they will continue to do that, in order, if posssible, to silence my guns until they are satisfied that their land force has securely established itself across the neck and rests on the river; then Porter will attempt to force a passage by to co-operate with the force that takes the river-bank. I have received dispatches from you stating that the enemy had extended to the river-bank. This they never should have been allowed to do; and if they are permitted to remain there the reduction of Fort Fisher is but a question of time. This has been notified heretofore frequently both to yourself and to the Department. I will hold this place till the last extremities; but unless you drive that land force from its position I cannot answer for the security of this harbor. The fire has been and continues to be exceedingly heavy, surpassing not so much in its volume as in its extraordinary condition even the fire of Christmas. The garrison is in good spirits and condition."[16]

Hoke does not seem to have thought much of Bragg's plan of attack, for at 2 p.m. another message to him from Bragg's adjutant said: "Your general views, as expressed in the note by Major Adams, will be adopted by the commanding general. He desires you will select a good line, as near the enemy as practicable, and intrench your position, taking care not to open your left flank to the enemy's view, and securing as strong a position on your left from which with artillery to cut the enemy's communication with his landing point. This will distress him, and if he is forced to land supplies, &c., as near as his right to Fisher, the heavy guns will destroy his boats. The general directs that 1,000 men of Hagood's brigade be sent by dusk to Gander Hall Landing for transportation to Fisher. Nearly 600 men are ordered to return from there, and will join you. We must keep the enemy in close to his lines, so as to observe his movements at all times, and by all means avoid another surprise to us."[16]

That afternoon, Terry, Curtis, and Comstock, Grant's aide who was also the expedition's chief engineer, studied the landface through binoculars from 500 yards away. Its traverses were pock-marked with craters, huge gaps had been torn in the log palisade, and only nine guns of the sixteen they had counted on the first expedition seemed to still be in place. They noted that an attack on the eastern half of the landface would have to cross a long expanse of high, open ground, which would expose the attackers to the fire of the defenders from all along the landface. But the ground sloped down to the river, so that an attack on the western end, along the road from Wilmington, would be less exposed. The swampy ground near the gate would be a problem, but even so the three officers agreed that this was the best area for an assault. Nevertheless, Terry wanted to give the navy time to inflict even more damage to the Confederate guns and defenses, so he decided that the next afternoon would be the best time to attack.

At 8:30 p.m., while Curtis's men dug more entrenchments along the advanced skirmish line, Terry had himself rowed out to the *Malvern* for another conference with Porter. The bombardment had ended again at sunset, although the ironclads continued to throw an occasional shell at the fort, just to keep the Confederates from getting any rest. Parrott rifles had exploded on three Union ships and two others had received some damage, but Porter estimated that his ships had already just about equaled the 20,271 projectiles they had fired at the fort back in December. Terry reported that their fire had done an impressive amount of damage, but more was needed. He wanted the rest of the guns on the landface silenced and the rest of the palisade blown apart so that it would not block the advance of his troops. Porter assured him that it would be done. The full bombardment would resume the next morning, and at noon he would throw in his reserves and step up the intensity with "every ship which could find a place to anchor and open upon the fort with every gun that could be brought to bear, firing as rapidly as was consistent with accuracy of aim."[17]

Army Signal Corps men would direct the fire from shore, shifting it to any point Terry wanted bombarded or calling for a cease fire if necessary. At 3 p.m., on Terry's signal, the fire would be shifted away from the land face and the attack would begin. Brigadier General Adelbert Ames' 2nd Division of the 24th Corps, led by Curtis's 1st Brigade, would assault the western end of the landface, while at the same time a naval "boarding party" would assault the eastern end. This force would consist of 2,000 volunteers drawn from the various ships of the fleet. Four hundred marines, armed with breechloading Sharps rifles and carbines, would provide covering fire, while 1600 sailors, armed only with cutlasses and revolvers, would charge the Northeast Bastion.

Inside Fort Fisher, more than 200 of the garrison's 1500 men were already casualties of the naval bombardment, as were all but three or four of the guns along the landface. The troops had had little to eat all day, and now the temperature was dropping to near the freezing point. But now that darkness had put an end to the bombardment, except for the occasional 11-inch or 15-inch shell from the ironclads, Colonel Lamb thought that Bragg surely would order Hoke to attack the Federals that night. Lamb ordered nine companies of infantry to stand by for action and took a tenth company out through the sally port and deployed it in a skirmish line from the beach to the river. Then he led it forward to probe the Union position. He found no Federals on the beach side, but drew fire from Federal pickets near the river. Having thus discovered the general position of the enemy, he waited for the sound of battle from the north that would indicate an attack by Hoke's Division. When it came, he would call his other nine companies forward and attack. Hour after hour he waited, but no firing was heard, and no word came from Bragg. Just before dawn the colonel and his weary men withdrew into the fort. There Lamb learned that only part of the 1,000 veteran troops Bragg had promised had actually arrived. Two of the three boats that had been carrying them down the river had repeatedly run aground.

---

1. Gragg, *Confederate Goliath*, 114.
2. Ibid., 115.
3. Ibid., 117.
4. Ibid., 118.
5. *Official Records*, 46:II:1046.
6. William Lamb, "The Defense of Fort Fisher," in *Battles and Leaders of the Civil War* edited by Robert Underwood Johnson and Clarence Clough Buel (New York, 1887), vol. 4, 647.
7. Gragg, *Confederate Goliath*, 122.
8. Ibid.
9. Ibid., 124.
10. *Official Records*, 45:I:799-800.
11. Ibid., 45:II:783.
12. Ibid., 46:II:1055.
13. Ibid., 46:II:1056.
14. Ibid., 46:II:1059.
15. Ibid., 46:II:1056.
16. Ibid., 46:II:1059-1060.
17. Gragg, *Confederate Goliath*, 133.

CHAPTER EIGHT

Come Aboard! Come Aboard!

15 January 1865

At 7:16 a.m. on Sunday, 15 January, the USS *New Ironsides* opened the third day of the bombardment of Fort Fisher, and she was promptly joined by the monitors. At 9:30 a.m. five wooden warships added their fire to that of the ironclads, and at 11:30 a.m. the entire fleet joined in. "A steady rain of great shells fell upon the fort," one Federal reported, "searching for every spot on its parapets and in its interiors. They came from every side except the west and they were falling and bursting faster than the ticking of a watch. The Confederate artillerists tried in vain to stand to their guns. One by one, these were broken or dismounted, and the garrison driven to their bombproofs."[1] By noon there was only one gun on the land face that was still serviceable. The log palisade was full of gaping holes, and the garrison was down to 1200 men fit for duty.

In Wilmington the services at St. James Episcopal Church were accompanied by the sound of the bombardment. "The thunder of the guns, distinctly audible and shaking the atmosphere like jelly, had been irregular until the Litany was read," one participant remembered. "Then from the beginning of that solemn service to its conclusion, almost simultaneously the responses of the congregation and the roar of the broadsides united. 'From battle and murder, and from sudden death,' read the minister. 'Good Lord, deliver us,' prayed the congregation, and, simultaneously 'Boom—boom—boom' answered the guns. The situation was almost intolerable."[2]

Late that morning the 2nd and 3rd brigades of Ames' division were sent forward to within supporting distance of Curtis's 1st Brigade, which had dug in near the skirmish line. A battery of field artillery was placed near the river to protect that flank from the *Chickamauga*, the two brigades of Paine's division were deployed to protect the rear from Hoke's Confederates, and Abbott's brigade was brought down from the landing site to provide support for whichever division needed it. Meanwhile, the naval landing party was assembling on the beach about two miles north of the fort. "The sailors as they landed from their boats were a heterogeneous assembly," one of their officers wrote, "companies of two hundred or more from each of the larger ships, down to small parties of twenty each from the gun-boats. They had been for months confined on shipboard, had never drilled together, and their arms, the old-fashioned cutlass and pistol, were hardly the weapons to cope with the rifles and bayonets of the enemy. Sailor-like, however, they looked upon the landing in the light of a lark, and few thought the sun would set with a loss of one-fifth of their number."[3]

They were commanded by 33-year-old Lieutenant Commander K. Randolph Breese, Porter's fleet captain and the officer he had sent to try to convince Sherman to make the attack on Fort Fisher. Breese sent a detachment of sailors with spades ahead under the command of Flag Lieutenant Samuel W. Preston, one of Porter's aides, to dig entrenchments. Breese also sent Lieutenant Louis E. Fagan with the first marines to come ashore to form a skirmish line in the first trench Preston's men dug, about 600 yards from the palisade. And, after conferring with several other officers, Breese divided his 1,600-man main force into three divisions, each about the size of a large army regiment. The first division would be commanded by Lieutenant Commander Charles H. Cushman of the USS *Wabash*, the second by

Lieutenant Commander James Parker of the USS *Minnesota*, who was actually senior in rank to Breese but conceded that Admiral Porter had put Breese in command, and the third division was commanded by Lieutenant Commander Thomas O. Selfridge, Jr., of the USS *Huron*. The marines would constitute a fourth division under the command of Captain Lucien L. Dawson, the senior Marine Corps officer ashore.

Dawson tried to organize his marines into platoons and companies, but it was taking too long and he finally had to give it up. With considerable difficulty the naval officers got the sailors formed into their three divisions, lined up one behind the other on the beach, and Breese read them Admiral Porter's orders for what he called a boarding operation. "From the constant noise and jar of the firing," one Federal officer wrote, "and the screaming of the flying shells, the volumes of gunpowder smoke, the movement of troops on the shore, it was evident that for better or worse, the mettle of Fort Fisher was to be put to a genuine test. But, though silent and sullen, the Rebel flag still fluttered, and the walls loomed huge and formidable through the smoke-clouds."[4]

On the river side of the peninsula, Ames' division was massed in the woods a half-mile north of the fort by 2 p.m., and Curtis's pickets had edged their rifle pits to within 250 yards of the landface. General Terry established his headquarters in some old abandoned Confederate earthworks near the river about 500 yards from the fort. From this position he watched Rebel ships steam past on the river, loaded with troops and headed for Fort Fisher. These were the ships that had run aground during the night. They were spotted by Porter's fleet, and shells from its big guns soon caused them to retreat across the river to Smithville.

The approximately 350 Confederates on the one boat that had made it downriver without running aground had been hustled into the bombproofs at Battery Buchanan and fed a small ration of wormy hardtack crackers. Then at 2 p.m. they were sent at the double-quick to reinforce the landface. They were ordered to move in single file, spread out, just behind the seaface, in order to minimize casualties from the naval bombardment, but even so it was a hazardous undertaking. "It was terrible, appalling," said Captain James F. Izlar, who led the way. "Shot hissed and shell bursted in every direction." They had a mile to go, and most of them did not make it. Many of these veterans of the defenses of Charleston and Petersburg could not face this fire and ducked into the seaface bombproofs, which they refused to leave. "The whole of this distance," Izlar said, "was covered and swept by the guns of the enemy. The scene was enough to terrify the stoutest heart."[5] Others were killed or wounded, including the senior officer, leaving

Captain Izlar in command. One private was slightly luckier. He was knocked down by an exploding shell and covered with so much sand that only one foot was left sticking out to show where he lay. But another soldier grabbed the foot and pulled him out, astonished to find him not only alive but unhurt. By the time the survivors reached the landface, so many had been killed, wounded, or scattered among the seaface bombproofs that Izlar had barely 100 men, all that was left of the 1,000 reinforcements Bragg had promised Whiting.

Whiting was sure the Federals would attack that day, probably preceded by some of Porter's ships trying to run past the fort through New Inlet—so sure that he had ignored an order Bragg had sent during the night for him to go upriver for a conference with him. Instead, he had sent a message across the river that morning: "Too late to do anything about obstructions [of the inlet]. I will try to confer to-day, but the chances are against it. Enemy still keeping heavy fire. They will try their passing this morning, unless you whip them off the land." But the fleet did not try to pass the fort, and Bragg was becoming increasingly irritated by the insubordinate tone of Whiting's messages, not to mention his failure to show up for the meeting the night before. At 1 p.m. his adjutant notified Whiting: "General Colquitt, assigned to the immediate command of Fort Fisher, will be down to-night. General Bragg directs you to report in person at these headquarters this evening for conference and instructions." Brigadier General Alfred H. Colquitt was one of Hoke's brigade commanders, who, evidently, Bragg thought would be less troublesome to deal with. This news was a hard blow to both Whiting's and Lamb's morale, but by the time Colquitt would arrive that night the fate of the fort might very well already be decided. For the message from Bragg arrived just as it was becoming obvious that the Federals were preparing for something. At 2:10 p.m. Whiting tried once more to get Bragg to order Hoke to attack the Union rear. "Is Fisher to be besieged, or you to attack?" he asked. "Should like to know."[6]

After reading Admiral Porter's orders to his assembled men, Lieutenant Commander Breese hiked across the peninsula to confer with General Terry. "Going into action as your men are now formed, you will get fearfully punished," an army officer told him.[7] But the attack was still set for 3 p.m., and that did not leave much time for changes. However, when Breese returned to the beach he conferred with his division commanders and decided to change the route the assault column would follow. By advancing closer to the ocean some cover would be provided by the sloping beach. Couriers hurried forward to tell Lieutenant Preston and Captain Dawson about the change in plan and have them dig new entrenchments and rifle pits to cover the new route of approach. By then Dawson had worked his skirmish line of marines to within 150 yards of the fort, ready to provide covering fire for the sailors' charge. Now, moving around to cover the new route meant starting all over again. He calculated that, on the new route, he would, at best, only be able to advance his rifle pits to within 600 yards of the fort. But he obediently hustled his marines over to the water's edge and had them start shoveling new holes. However, before they had time to do more than get started the whole 1600-man naval brigade came forward and lay down near his new line under the cover of the crest of the beach. Contrary to Admiral Porter's orders, the sailors unfurled their flags and began to wave them defiantly, which drew even more fire from the Confederates.

Colonel Curtis had developed the plan for the Union army's part in the assault. Under the cover of the fire of a detachment of sharpshooters, he would move his brigade as close to the fort as possible. Then, when he gave the command, his line would charge forward at an angle toward the western end of the landface. The other two brigades of Ames' division would then follow. General Terry approved this plan. Ames, who had a private feud going with Curtis, had asked the general not to put that brigade in the lead, but he had not only been overruled but was virtually ignored in the planning. At 2 p.m. the force of 100 sharpshooters—60 of them armed with Spencer repeating rifles—moved forward at a run and formed a line about 175 yards from the fort. Half of them had spades, and they began to dig rifle pits while covered by the fire of the other half. As soon as these sharpshooters showed themselves, Confederates rushed from their bombproofs to man the parapet, but the Federals' fire, "joined with the tremendous broadsides of the navy, which were at this time appalling beyond description," as a Union officer put it, "soon drove the garrison to their bombproofs again."[8]

From atop the Pulpit Battery, Colonel Lamb saw the Union army's skirmishers edging forward and could tell that a large formation was assembling in the edge of the distant woods. He could also see the marines and sailors digging trenches on the beach. Most visible of all was the dark mass of the main body of sailors, which he saw move forward and lie down just out of rifle range. It was obvious that the Federals were preparing an assault, so the colonel ordered the two heavy guns in the Mound Battery to turn and fire up the beach at the sailors, along with the one remaining heavy gun on the land face and some sharpshooters he put on top of the land face wall. To oppose the army's skirmishers, edging forward toward the fort, he sent two field pieces out of the sally port into the position prepared for them between the wall and the palisade, from which they blasted away with cannister ammunition—cans full of dozens of small iron balls that turned the cannon into oversized shotguns. In reply, the Union ships rained down a hail of concentrated fire upon these positions. However, Lamb knew that when the Union assault actually began the fleet would have to cease fire in order to avoid hitting its own men. When this happened he would bring 500 riflemen to the Northeast Bastion and the eastern end of the landface to meet what he took to be the Federals' main attack. At the same time he would send 250 men under Major James Reilly to defend the western end of the line, backed up by the two field pieces stationed at the riverside entrance to the fort.

At about 2:30 p.m. Curtis's veterans were ordered to fall in, but it was past 3 p.m. by the time their ranks were formed and they were ready to advance. Terry directed the opening moves himself, leaving Ames nothing to do but stand and watch as Curtis's men moved forward from the woods at the double-quick to within 400 yards of the fort. There they lay down and began to dig in with their bayonets, tin cups and plates, pocket knives, officers' swords, and anything else that they had with them. Again Confederates manned the parapets and started shooting at them, and their fire was joined by that of the field pieces at the sally port. But again the navy's bombardment soon drove the Rebels back to their bombproofs, and as soon as they were gone Curtis moved his brigade forward again, one regiment at a time. Again they started digging in, this time within 200 yards of the fort, while Colonel Galusha Pennypacker's 2nd Brigade advanced to the line Curtis had just vacated, and Colonel Louis Bell's 3rd Brigade moved up to the edge of the woods. The assault force was ready, General Terry decided. He consulted his watch and noted that it was 3:25 p.m. when he gave the order for the Signal Corps flags to pass the word to Admiral Porter just off shore on the *Malvern*. Then he turned to General Ames and said, "Your division is all ready to make the assault."[9]

Colonel Lamb was hurrying back to the Pulpit after going to meet Captain Izlar's reinforcements when a Confederate lookout called to him, "Colonel, the enemy are about to charge." Lamb turned to General Whiting and asked him to make one more appeal to Bragg. So Whiting hastily scribbled a message to be sent by courier to the signalmen at Battery Buchanan for relay across the river to the telegraph operator there. "The enemy are about to assault," he said; "they outnumber us heavily. Enemy on the beach in front of us in very heavy force, not more than 700 yards from us. Nearly all land guns disabled. Attack! Attack! It is all I can say, and all you can do."[10]

Lamb, meanwhile, ran to the sally port and down through the tunnel under the traverses and ordered the troops there to prepare to man the parapets as soon as the bombardment lifted. He sent more sharpshooters up to the landface wall immediately with orders to pick off the Union officers, and told the fort's electrician to allow the first wave of attackers to cross the minefield of subterranean torpedoes before setting them off. He wanted them to shatter and demoralize the supporting formations. The first wave would be dealt with by the rifles of the garrison.

Over on the beach, Breese, his officers and sailors, lying in the sand under an increasing Confederate fire, were waiting anxiously for the assault to get under way. The plan had set 3 p.m. for the hour of the attack, but 3 p.m. had come and gone. Finally, at 3:25 p.m. they could see some movement among the soldiers across the peninsula. Then the *Malvern* hoisted the signal for the fleet to cease fire. The original plan called for the sailors to wait until the soldiers had reached the parapet of the fort before charging, but for some reason—perhaps just the excitement of the moment, or maybe from a sense of rivalry—Breese either forgot or ignored this part of the plan. He turned to his men and yelled, "Charge!"[11]

Instantly the sailors were on their feet, cheering wildly and running down the beach toward the fort. Most of Captain Dawson's marines joined them, forgetting that they were supposed to stay in place and provide covering fire for the sailors. At almost the same instant the *Malvern* gave two long, shrill blasts on its steam whistle and the other ships soon followed suit. "The noise of the guns, whistles, cheers and yells of the sailors and marines was terrific," one Union witness remembered, "and made the most exciting and indescribable event."[12]

Colonel Lamb was starting back up to the Pulpit when he heard the unnerving screech of sixty ships' steam whistles drowning out all other sounds, including the bursting shells of the bombardment. He knew it must be the signal for the Union assault. When the whistles finally stopped, so did the bombardment. But before anyone could adjust to this strange and sudden silence the guns opened up again, this time concentrating their fire on the lower seaface. As soon as the bombardment lifted, the Rebels came pouring out of their bombproofs to man the landface and northeast bastion in accordance with Lamb's plan, but he ordered them to hold their fire, except for the artillery and sharpshooters. He also sent one of his aides to Captain Izlar with instructions to reinforce Major Reilly's defense of the western end of the line.

The sailors and marines were about 600 yards from the fort when men started to drop from Confederate fire. By then the three carefully separated divisions had merged into one great mass of men, and Breese had to run hard to stay in front of them. As their charge was the more obvious and immediate threat to the fort, they were drawing the fire of the sally port guns, the one remaining Columbiad on the landface, the Mound Battery, and the sharpshooters as well. But Lamb could see that, because they were following the beach, they would avoid the area where his torpedoes were buried. The defenders could see that they were badly outnumbered by the onrushing mob of sailors, but General Whiting reassured them by standing up on top of the sandbagged parapet of the Northeast Bastion shouting words of encouragement without getting hit by the few marines who had stayed where they belonged to provide covering fire. The sailors charged on down the beach toward the eastern end of the log palisade, but before they could reach it, at a range of about 150 yards, Lamb shouted the command, and the first Confederate volley flattened the entire mass of sailors, marines, and officers. Those who were not hit were tripped up by those who were, or just dove for cover. "The whole mass of men went down like a row of falling bricks," one survivor wrote. "In a second every man was flat on his stomach."[13]

For a minute they lay there while a thick cloud of white gunsmoke drifted from the fort's parapet out over the beach. Then Breese, Parker, Cushman, Selfridge and other officers were on their feet, waving their swords and calling for their men to get up and go on. The sailors rose up and charged over the bodies of their dead and wounded comrades, but as they did so the front rank of Confederate riflemen handed their weapons to the second rank to be reloaded and took their loaded rifles in return. At Lamb's command they fired another volley into the dense mass of Federals at a range of about 100 yards, and again the entire naval brigade hit the sand. But once more the officers were soon up and urging their men on, and again the sailors and marines stumbled over the bodies of those who were hit and ran on toward the fort.

There were no more volleys, for the Rebels now switched to individual fire, each man in the front rank firing as rapidly as he could get a loaded weapon from the second rank, creating what one Federal called "a perfect hail of lead, with men dropping in every direction. The officers were pulling their caps over their eyes, for it was almost impossible to look at the deadly flashing blue line on the parapet."[14] Lieutenant Benjamin H. Porter, a five-year veteran and commander of the *Malvern* at the age of 19, was out in front of the pack, carrying the admiral's flag. He was only 50 yards from the palisade when a bullet pierced his chest, killing him instantly. His friend, Lieutenant Preston, ran on a few yards more, until he was cut down by a bullet in the groin that severed the femoral artery, causing him to quickly bleed to death. And suddenly the charge ground to a halt less than 50 yards from the fort. "The rush of the sailors was over," Lieutenant Commander Selfridge wrote; "they were packed like sheep in a pen, while the enemy were crowding the ramparts not forty yards away, and shooting into them as fast as they could fire. There was nothing to reply with but *pistols*."[15]

Nevertheless, Breese and his senior officers were still on their feet, waving their swords and trying to get the men up and moving again. But fewer than 200 men got up, and instead of moving around the palisade most of these ran toward it to take cover behind it. Only a few small isolated groups charged on. Lieutenant Commander Parker led about a dozen men around the end of the palisade, but they soon realized they were too few and fell back to the comparative safety of its cover.

Acting Ensign Robley Evans, an 18-year-old Virginian whose brother was in the Confederate army, tried to lead the detail from the USS *Powhatan* through a hole in the fence, but only one man, Landsman Archibald Campbell, followed him. As they approached the fort's earthen wall Evans was hit in the knee by a bullet and Campbell was shot through the lungs. Another bullet kicked up sand near him as Evans tried to bandage his knee, and he looked up and saw a Rebel soldier taking aim at him. He heard the Confederate curse as again his bullet missed both Evans and Campbell and plowed into the sand nearby. Two more times the Rebel fired and missed, and then he hit the badly wounded Campbell in the foot, taking away a toe. Infuriated, Evans rolled over on his stomach, shouted a curse at the Confederate, took aim with his revolver, and shot him in the throat. The Rebel tumbled off the parapet to land near Evans. Campbell said he wanted to crawl over and shoot the Confederate again, but he died of his wound before he could do it. A marine private named Wasmuth, from Evans' ship, then dashed through a gap in the palisade, grabbed Evans under the arms, and dragged him to the shelter of a nearby shell crater and from there to another and another, ignoring Evans' pleas to leave him and save himself. They were in a crater near the palisade when Evans heard a peculiar thud and looked up to see blood spurting from Wasmuth's throat. The marine staggered down to the water's edge, fell into the surf, and died.

Only one Federal sailor reached the fort's parapet. He was a 5-foot-2 Englishman named James Tallentine who had joined the U.S. Navy three years earlier and had only three weeks left to go on his enlistment. As all the rest stopped, or turned back, or fell dead or wounded, Tallentine climbed on up the steep earthen wall, perhaps unaware that he was all alone. As he reached the top he was shot, fell over the parapet into the fort, and died among the enemies of his adopted country.

Most of the naval officers had raced to the front of the charging mass of sailors to be in the lead and were now separated from their proper commands. In their absence, the sailors and marines lay hugging the beach for what cover it could provide, confused and leaderless, while Confederate rifle and artillery fire continued to take its toll. "It would have been impossible for men made of tougher material than flesh to have withstood that firing. Neither would the palisades afford shelter for more than were already under them," one survivor reported. "Dead and wounded men were lying about in ghastly piles," another survivor remembered. "The scene on the beach was a pitiful one—dead and wounded officers and men as far as one could see. As a rule, they lay quiet on the sand and took their punishment like the brave lads they were, but occasionally... a sound wave would drift along, 'Water, water, water!'"[16] Two assistant surgeons moved among the wounded, carrying their instruments and tourniquets, but there were far too many victims for them to treat them all, and both were soon shot dead, leaving the wounded to take care of themselves.

Some of the sailors lying behind the palisade began to call for an officer to lead them foward again. When no one else responded, Acting Master's Mate Abraham Louch, the executive officer of the USS *Mackinaw*, jumped to his feet, drew his sword, and shouted for the men to get up and follow him. But none did. Louch lay down again and was promptly and painfully hit by a spent bullet.

Near the end of the palisade, Lieutenant Commander Cushman ran along behind that fence to where Parker and some of the other officers were huddled. They held a brief discussion on the subject of what to do next. Breese was too far away to join the conference, but they decided that they could not stay where they were and that Parker, as the senior officer present, should lead a renewed charge. So Parker stood up and shouted to the sailors for them to follow him around the end of the palisade and toward the wall of the fort, and several dozen men got up and followed Parker and the other officers along the palisade. Seeing this move, Breese stood up and shouted, "Rise, men, and charge!" But almost nobody moved. With bullets whizzing around him he pushed his way through the thick mass of men shouting repeatedly for them to get up and charge. Some men did get up, but instead of advancing they began to move back up the beach away from the fort. "Charge!"

Breese yelled to them. "Charge! Don't retreat!" Others sailors turned to watch Breese, straining to hear him over the noise of the firing, the surf, and the bombardment. "What did he say?" some asked. "Is it to retreat?" Someone else caught the key word. "Retreat!" he shouted. Soon a dozen voices took up the refrain: "Retreat! Retreat!"[17] The cry spread through the ranks, and more and more men got up and ran back up the beach the way they had come.

Parker and the other officers, hearing a commotion behind them just as they were approaching the end of the palisade, looked back to see the mass of men dissolve in a wave of panic. All the officers were at the front, so none were behind the men to stop them from running. "I could have cried when the blue jackets retreated," a lieutenant reported. "I shouted and waved my sword for the sailors to come back, but no, off they went down the beach."[18] Captain Dawson tried to get his marines to provide covering fire for the retreat, but most of them joined it instead. Breese finally gave up and followed the routing mob back up the beach, but at a walk despite the bullets buzzing around him. "It was certainly mortifying," Lieutenant Commander Selfridge wrote, "after charging for a mile, under a most galling fire, to the very foot of the fort, to have the whole force retreat down the beach."[19]

The delighted Confederates climbed up onto the parapet with General Whiting. "Come aboard!" they shouted to the retreating sailors, "Come aboard!"[20] But for the colonel the celebration was cut short when he looked to his left and saw Union battleflags atop the western end of the parapet.

---

1. Gragg, *Confederate Goliath*, 140.
2. Ibid., 189.
3. Thomas O. Selfridge, Jr., "The Navy at Fort Fisher" in *Battles and Leaders*, 4:659.
4. Gragg, *Confederate Goliath*, 146.
5. Ibid., 150.
6. *Official Records*, 46:II:1064.
7. Gragg, *Confederate Goliath*, 152.
8. Ibid., 171.
9. Ibid., 173.
10. Ibid., 151.
11. Ibid., 154.
12. Ibid., 155.
13. Ibid., 158.
14. Ibid., 159.

15. Selfridge, "The Navy at Fort Fisher," 660.
16. Gragg, *Confederate Goliath*, 165.
17. Ibid., 166-167.
18. Ibid., 167.
19. Selfridge, "The Navy at Fort Fisher," 660.
20. Gragg, *Confederate Goliath*, 168.

CHAPTER NINE

It Was Cold Steel or the Butt of a Gun

15 January 1865

When General Terry turned the direction of the attack over to Ames the latter immediately turned to Captain Albert G. Lawrence, one of his aides, and ordered him to not only give Curtis the order to advance but for him to lead the charge. Lawrence delivered the order to Curtis and asked to join the assault, but Curtis agreed only on the condition that Lawrence would not interfere with his brigade's movements. When Lawrence did not object, Curtis sent him to the far right of the brigade to report to Lieutenant Colonel Francis X. Meyer of the 117th New York. Then Curtis sent word up and down his line—stretched roughly from the river to a point opposite the fort's sally port—that when he waved his hat his men were to charge at a run and without a cheer, angling toward the riverside entrance to the fort. Among them were several pioneers carrying axes and battering rams for forcing a way through the palisade. When the ships all blew their whistles, Curtis stood up, waved his hat, and shouted, "Forward."[1]

With a flag in one hand and a sword in the other, Curtis ran toward the fort, and behind him the 1st Brigade arose as one man and followed him. The soldiers ignored the order not to cheer, however, and raised a loud hurrah as they stood up. This was answered by a volley of rifle fire from the western half of the fort, but it passed over the heads of the Union troops. However, the volume and accuracy of the fire improved rapidly, and men began to fall. Among the first to be hit was Colonel John F. Smith, popular commander of the 112th New York, some of whose men paused long enough to dig a shallow trench in the sand to shelter him until they could return for him. But most of the men ran on, too busy to be afraid. As one lieutenant put it, "My whole soul was wrapped up in the idea of taking that fort."[2]

Soon Curtis's men plunged waist-deep into the icy marsh near the river, except for a few who crowded onto the bridge, stepping from beam to beam where the planking had been removed. By this time the long line of men had become an unorganized mob and an easy target. "The garrison lined the ramparts," one witness wrote, "and poured tremendous volleys into the advancing column.... yet on they rushed until further advance was impossible unless the stockade could be removed or a passage forced through the gate."[3] Despite the holes blown in it by the naval bombardment, the palisade remained a formidible obstacle, but the pioneers attacked the big logs with their axes, while the sharpshooters, who had preceded the main line, laid down a covering fire. Captain Lawrence was the first man through the palisade, but when he looked back he saw the men were hesitating, so he reached for a flag with the intention of carrying it forward to inspire the men. However, as he did so a shell burst beside him, taking off his left arm and wounding him in the right arm and neck. He lived only long enough to dictate a letter to his father.

Singly or in small groups Curtis's men slipped through the holes in the palisade and advanced to a shallow depression at the foot of the fort's earthen walls, where sand had been dug with which to build the landface. There they could not be seen or shot by the Confederates on the parapet, and they took advantage of this respite to reform and rest a little. Then General Curtis started up the wall of sand, and with another chorus of hurrahs so did his men. "It was an exciting moment," one veteran remembered. "Regimental pride—nothing shows a soldier's spirit more strongly—animated the broken mass of men in the rough clamor up the slope; and a rush of color-bearers led the way, in the ambition to be the first on the parapet."[4]

The part of the fort they were scaling was known to the Confederates as Shepherd's Battery. It was the last gun chamber on the western end of the landface, but its two big guns had been put out of commission by the naval bombardment, and the mine field had proven to be useless. The bombardment had cut the ignition wires leading to the torpedoes. There were two field pieces guarding the gate, but the commander of those guns had obtained permission to keep his men in the bombproofs until the bombardment lifted. However, when it lifted only one artilleryman emerged, a corporal who went to his post manning one of the guns. Whiting and Lamb were busy beating off the naval attack on the Northeast Bastion, and no one knew where Major Reilly was. So the defense of the western end of the landface now depended upon Captain Kinchen Braddy and his company of the 36th North Carolina.

"A fierce outburst of musketry greeted the first heads that rose above the level of the fort," one Union soldier wrote, "and at least one flag and its bearer rolled down the slope into the ditch. But the fort wall once gained the assaulters were as much protected by it as the garrison, and so our men made some sort of foothold on the slope, and delivered over the parapet as fierce a fire as they received. They were thus burning powder close in each other's faces."[5]

At the gate through the palisade the lone artilleryman got off one round from one of the field pieces before he was killed, and then Captain Braddy sent some of his infantrymen to man the two guns. They fired off both pieces, but as they struggled to reload them they were cut down by the fire of Curtis's men. However, they were soon reinforced by men of the 1st North Carolina Heavy Artillery, who temporarily cleared the Wilmington road with a round of cannister from the 12-pounder Napoleon and a shell from the 10-pounder Parrott rifle that exploded on the bridge. Captain Braddy sent two messengers up the landface to ask for help, but no reinforcements came and his messengers did not return. Finally he decided to take a few men and go for help himself, but as he rounded the traverse into the next gun chamber the South Carolinians there mistook him and his men for Yankees and fired on them. They missed Braddy, but they hit some of his men. Braddy ran on toward the seaface, searching for Colonel Lamb, General Whiting, or anyone who could send him more men.

Reinforcements was also what the Federals had in mind. General Terry could see that some of Curtis's men were swarming over the first gun chamber but that others were stalled at the gate, while some were still floundering through the marsh or crowding onto the bridge. He turned to Ames and told him to send in the next brigade. When Curtis's men had begun their charge Pennypacker's 2nd Brigade had advanced and occupied the forward entrenchments they had just abandoned. Now the 2nd Brigade stood up and followed in the 1st Brigade's wake. And Ames went with it. But, as Pennypacker's men advanced, the two field pieces at the sally port battery, which had been firing on the sailors, turned and blasted the left-flank regiment with cannister, killing the entire color guard of the 47th New York. Other men picked up the flags and continued on. "In the crash and uproar of the battle, and the enthusiams of the advance," one of the Federals remembered, "the men shouldered their way forward with little regard to the regimental formation. The result was a crowd of men pouring through the log obstacles into the ditch, cheering and impetuous, but with no longer any visible military formation."[6]

Some of Pennypacker's men passed around the rear of Curtis's brigade, across the marsh and bridge, and headed for the riverside gate. The dwindling force of Confederate gunners there got off another round or two with the field pieces, killing and wounding a few more Federals, but there were far too many to stop them all. Soon the attackers forced their way through the gate, knocking aside the sandbags that blocked it, and overran the Rebel guns. Meanwhile, another part of the 2nd Brigade stormed up the earthen wall of Shepherd's Battery, carrying some of Curtis's men with it. This mixed force, which included both Curtis and Pennypacker, soon cleared the parapet of defenders and was firing on Confederates down in the gun chamber below when the Federals who had overrun the gate defenses turned to the east and attacked the Rebels from the rear. Some of the Confederates escaped up the landface or through the bombproof passageways, but over a hundred dropped their weapons and surrendered. The Federals pressed on, cheering wildly, and quickly captured the next gun chamber to the east, then climbed the next traverse and took a third gun emplacement. Colonel Galusha Pennypacker, a brigade commander and a good one at the age of twenty, led the way, carrying the colors of his old regiment, the 97th Pennsylvania. He was the first man to scale the third traverse, and he was just planting the flag at its top when he was shot. The bullet entered his right hip and came out of his lower back, just missing his spine. Some of his men carried the young colonel to the rear on a blanket. It was the fourteenth wound the young colonel had received in four years of war.

At 4 p.m. Braxton Bragg finally issued the order that General Whiting had been pleading for for days. He ordered Hoke to attack the Federal rear. Hoke's line, stretching across the peninsula, consisted of two brigades of North Carolinians, Brigadier General William W. Kirkland's and Brigadier General Thomas L. Clingman's. Colquitt's Brigade of Georgians was held in reserve. Opposing these Confederates were Abbott's brigade on the eastern side of the peninsula and Paine's two brigades of U.S. Colored Troops on the western side. Abbott's pickets quickly gave up their rifle pits and fell back to the cover of the main line, but Paine's men refused to yield. A brisk fight was developing in the woods when some of Porter's ships opened fire on the Rebels with an awesome display of firepower. It was what Bragg had been dreading. He considered it useless to sacrifice Hoke's men to the fleet's numerous big guns. He cancelled the attack.

The Confederate naval officers commanding Battery Buchanan, at the southern end of the peninsula, were drunk. They had seen the Union flags on the parapet of the landface and, assuming that the fort was captured, they decided to escape across the river. However, when their men were waist-deep in the cold water trying to get into their boats, the officers changed their minds and ordered them back to their guns. Soon the intoxicated officers and their cold, wet gunners were blasting the inside of the landface with their huge shells, killing friend and foe alike.

"Pull down those flags and drive the enemy from the works!" Whiting shouted when he, like Lamb, finally turned from watching the sailors and marines retreat up the beach to see that the Union army had planted its banners on the western end of the landface wall.[7] The general led the men who had repelled the naval brigade down the landface and was joined by artillerymen who no longer had serviceable guns to fire and by Captain Izlar's small band of reinforcements. They collided with the advancing Federals in the fourth gun chamber from the west end of the line. And it was a violent collision. Men from both sides fired their rifles into each other's faces or swung them like clubs at each other's heads. There were no tactics, no formations, no maneuvering, just killing and dying. "It was a soldier's fight now," a Confederate survivor recalled. "As a man would fall, another sprang up to take his place, our officers loading and firing with us... a hand-to-hand fight."[8]

Slowly the Rebels pushed the disorganized Federals back up the third traverse, the men of both sides trampling over the dead and wounded as they went, and many more joining them in the process. "You would constantly see them, by two's and three's, fall off and roll to the bottom," a Union officer remembered, "there weltering in their blood and gore." At the top of the traverse General Whiting reached for one of the Federal battleflags and was immediately confronted by several Union soldiers who demanded his surrender. "Go to hell, you Yankee bastards!" he replied.[9] Several Federals fired, and Whiting went down with a dangerous wound in the thigh. Some of his men dragged him down the traverse, and only as he was being carried away did Captain Braddy finally find him.

While Whiting led the counterattack, Colonel Lamb went out through the sally port to have a look at the situation outside the fort. "I doubt," he said later, "if ever before the commander of a work went outside of it and looked back upon the conflict for its possession; but from the peculiar construction of the works it was necessary to do so in order to see the exact position of affairs."[10] He went as far out as the palisade and could see Union troops still pouring into the western end of the land face. Two marines who had stayed behind when the naval brigade had retreated had been playing dead to avoid Rebel sharpshooters. Now they spotted Lamb and one of them raised up to take a shot at him, but a Confederate sharpshooter on the fort's parapet saw the marine move and picked him off before he could fire.

After making sure that the sally port field pieces were firing on the Federal soldiers still moving toward the gate, Lamb hurried back into the fort. There he learned that Whiting had been wounded and taken to the hospital bombproof beneath the Pulpit. Lamb could see the desperate fight still going on for the third traverse and saw Union soldiers massing behind Shepherd's Battery, threatening to outflank the landface positions. Quickly the colonel assembled Confederate riflemen in a line of light entrenchments behind the landface and had them open fire on this potential flanking force, blocking its advance. When Captain Braddy reported to Lamb, the colonel sent him to round up some more men to add to this force. "I want to drive those Yankees out of the fort," he said.[11] He also sent an aide down to Battery Buchanan to send another round-about message to Bragg urging him to attack the Federal rear, unaware that such an attack had already been ordered and cancelled.

But just as Lamb seemed to have stabilized the situation, Porter's fleet intervened. Huge shells from the naval guns began to burst among the Confederates in great profusion, directed by army signal flags. With impressive precision the barrage of shells moved along the landface wall, clearing the Rebel defenders off of it, to within a few yards of the Federals on the third traverse. Only the Confederates in actual hand-to-hand combat with the attackers were safe from the bombardment, and the rest fled to the safety of their bombproofs. The gunners of the sally port battery were also driven to cover, but shells striking the landface wall rolled down into the sally port and exploded there, killing or wounding many of the artillerymen.

From inside the fort General Ames sent word to Terry that he could take the fort if he had his 3rd Brigade. Terry agreed and sent one of his aides to give Colonel Bell the order to advance. By then some of Pennypacker's men had replaced the planking on the bridge, so Bell's brigade had an easier time getting over the marsh. But Bell himself never made it. He was hit in the chest just as he reached the bridge, and the bullet went clear through him. While some of his men carried him to the rear, Colonel Alonzo Alden of the 169th New York took command of the 3rd Brigade and led it into the fort. Part of the brigade joined the troops massing behind Shepherd's Battery and part scaled the fort's sloping outer wall.

Colonel Lamb could see that the Federals had been reinforced and knew that his own men must have help. So he ordered those in the inner line of entrenchments to hold their position at all costs and hurried across to the seaface. There he ordered all guns to be turned inward to fire across the interior of the fort at the invading Yankees. Actually only four guns were capable of being turned that far, two Columbiads and the two guns of the Mound Battery. But those immediately opened up, firing at the Federals over the heads of Lamb's men in the inner line. Then the colonel gathered up some soldiers not needed to man these guns, over 100 of them, and took them with him back to the interior earthworks. From there he could see that the fight was still raging on the third traverse, so he directed his men on the inner line to fire at the Union troops coming up the land face, forcing them to stay on the outside of the parapet. Other Federals, he could see, were lying shoulder to shoulder in a depression behind Shepherd's Battery. If he could only mount a counterattack, he felt, he might be able to drive the disorganized Yankees out of the fort. It would be dark soon and the Federals would not try again until the next morning, and by that time reinforcements might reach him from outside.

Again he left his inner line, this time to run to a bombproof to implore some of the South Carolina reinforcements Bragg had sent him to come out and help him save the fort. The said they would, but they were still in the bombproof when the colonel left it. He went to the sally port tunnel to instruct the battery there to fire on the Yankees along the outside of the land face wall, but the battery commander said he did not have enough men left to man his guns. Lamb told him to round up some replacements and then went on from bombproof to bombproof looking for manpower, even asking the sick and wounded to join him. He also sent a courier to Battery Buchanan asking for any help the Confederate Navy could send him and telling the battery commander there to hold his fire when he saw the Confederates counterattack.

Running back across the interior of his fort, Lamb was suddenly aware of the terrific damage it had suffered. Shell craters, dead men, and shattered artillery pieces were scattered all over the place. Back at his inner line with the few reinforcements he had scraped up he did what he could to prepare his men to attack. Then he sprang onto the breastwork, holding his sword aloft, and shouted, "Charge bayonets! Forward! Double-quick, march!"[12]

But as his men climbed over their earthworks they were immediately met by a heavy volley from the Federals, at less than 100 yards range. Most of the bullets passed over their heads, but some hit home. One slammed into Colonel Lamb's hip, and he dropped to his knees. One of his men pulled him out of the line of fire, and the rest of them, after a moment's hesitation, fell back to the safety of their entrenchments. Lamb turned command over to the senior officer present, a captain, and went off to the hospital. There he found both Whiting and Major Saunders, the chief of artillery, who had also been wounded. So he sent his adjutant off to find Major Reilly and tell him that he was now in command of the fort. Then he and Whiting, lying side by side in the hospital, agreed that they would not give up the fight, and Whiting sent off another message to be relayed to General Bragg: "The enemy are assaulting us by land and sea. Their infantry out-number us. Can't you help us? I am slightly wounded."[13]

Major James Reilly was a 42-year-old Irishman who had once served in the British army, deserted, immigrated to America and joined its army, fought in the Mexican War and against Indians in the West, resigned to join the Confederacy, and commanded a battery in Lee's Army of Northern Virginia before being sent to the District of Cape Fear over a year before. He soon appeared at the hospital and accepted command of the fort, promising to fight "as long as a man or a shot was left."[14] Then he hurried off to lead another counterattack.

Soon the fleet lifted its barrage to allow the Union infantry to advance, but when it did so more Confederates came out of the bombproofs to join the fight. However, when Reilly reached the inner line of entrenchments he found that many of the men Lamb had left there had joined the fight for the land face and others had retreated to the bombproofs, so that only about 150 remained in place. Reilly withdrew them to another line of earthworks near the fort's main ammunition magazine to regroup and prepare to charge. They formed around the battleflag of one of the South Carolina regiments among the reinforcements Captain Izlar had brought in, and then they advanced against the Federals massed in the rear of Shepherd's Battery. But as soon as this movement was detected it was met by a destructive rifle fire. The colorbearer was shot down, and Reilly's men began to waver and fall back. Some of them ran for the cover of the nearby bombproofs, and by the time Reilly had reassembled his force in the line near the magazine he had fewer than 60 men left.

The hand-to-hand fight on the third traverse was an awful, bloody meatgrinder, with the Confederates supported by the flanking fire of the Rebels along the inner line, and the Federals were taking heavy losses, especially in officers. In fact, there were so many dead and wounded men in the area that the living were having trouble climbing over them to get at their adversaries. But when Reilly took the troops from the inner line back to the magazine the flanking fire dwindled. The Federals made a concerted rush over the top of the third traverse and the Rebels fell back to the fourth. There the fighting was, if anything, worse than it had been on the third. Soldiers of the two armies massed on either side of the sloping earthen wall and fired their weapons over the crest into each other's faces. Casualties were unceremoniously dragged out of the way so that other men could take their places, only to fall and be dragged away in turn. There was, one survivor remembered, "an agonizing clamor from wounded men, who were writhing in the sand, beseeching, in heart-rending accents, those near them to end their suffering. The dead certainly, and perhaps the wounded, [did not] count for much on [this] battlefield. A colorbearer had fallen, and though choked by blood and sand, he murmured, 'I am gone. Take the flag.' An officer who had been shot through the heart retained nearly an erect position—he seemed to be leaning against a gun carriage. Some lay face downward, with their faces in the sand, and others who had been near each other when a shell exploded had fallen in a confused mass, forming a mingled heap of broken limbs and mangled bodies."[15]

But the weight of Union numbers told eventually, and the Confederates fell back to the fifth traverse. A handful of Union sailors who had been digging rifle pits when the naval brigade retreated had joined the army's charge, and now Curtis, who seemed to lead a charmed life as one of the few Union officers in the thick of the fight who had not been hit, sent one of them to ask General Terry to signal the fleet to bring its fire even closer to his men. Before long the navy did as requested, walking the barrage along the land face until one shell exploded among Curtis's own front line, leaving only four men on the traverse. Curtis scrambled up the sloping wall, grabbing up rifles dropped by the dead and wounded as he went, and fired them over the top in rapid succession to discourage a Rebel counterattack until more of his men could join him. And soon there were so many Federals on the traverse that they could not all bring their weapons to bear on the enemy. "Men unable to stand and fire their pieces handed up the guns of their dead and helpless comrades," one of them remembered, "and reloaded them again and again, exhibiting a frenzied zeal and unselfish devotion that seemingly nothing but death could chill."[16] Curtis himself remained at the top of the traverse firing guns loaded and handed up to him by soldiers in the gun chamber below. Several times he found when he turned to hand a rifle back to be reloaded that the men who had been loading for him were dead. "It surpassed all that I had ever seen or thought that men were capable of doing," Lieutenant William Ketcham wrote.[17]

Finally the Rebels were forced off the fifth traverse, and the Federals pushed on so rapidly and in such force that despite bloody hand-to-hand fighting they quickly took the sixth as well. "There they fought," Lieutenant Ketchum said, "from parapet to parapet, through traverse and bombproof, outside and in, the Navy in the meantime throwing shells just ahead of our soldiers. We could see them advance by the glorious old Stars and Stripes, which our people planted upon each successive parapet as they took them."[18] Lieutenant Colonel Samuel Zent said that the Federals' tactics were "to crawl near the crest of the traverse, then quickly elevating the guns above our heads with both hands, fire at random down the slope on the opposite side.... Even then some of my men were shot through their hands."[19]

The Federals who had collected behind Shepherd's Battery were a disorganized assortment from all three of Ames's brigades and they had been stopped by the fire of the Confederates Lamb had placed in the inner line of entrenchments. But when Reilly led those Rebels away, Lieutenant Colonel Jonas Lyman of the 203rd Pennsylvania led the Federals forward, paralleling the advance along the landface, until they were behind the seventh traverse, which Curtis and his men were struggling to capture. Lyman's men quickly dug in with shovels, plates, bayonets, and anything else they could find, and then he led part of them up the disputed traverse. Lyman was shot dead, but the Rebels fell back, giving up the seventh traverse.

The Federals were now approaching the sally port, in the center of the land face, and Lieutenant Ketcham went to Colonel Zent, his regimental commander, and asked permission to lead a detachment to take the sally port battery, which was still firing with murderous effect, although the crew had to take cover in the sally port tunnel from time to time when the fleet made things too hot for them. Zent told him to pick a dozen men and have at it. Ketcham organized a detail and led it rapidly along the front of the land face toward the sally port until they were within forty feet of the two Rebel guns. Just then the Confederate gunners left the cover of the tunnel to man their guns, but when they spotted Ketcham and his Federals they ducked back inside. Ketcham turned to urge his men on, only to discover that they too had taken cover, leaving him all alone. The lieutenant decided to follow suit and jumped into a nearby shell crater. Soon he heard voices and looked up, expecting to see his own men, but instead he saw the Rebels loading their two Napoleons. Like all members of his regiment, the 13th Indiana, Ketcham was armed with a Spencer repeating rifle. But when he checked his he found that it was clogged with sand. However, he soon had it clean enough to use, and with it he drove the Rebels away from their guns. Eventually some of his men joined him in his crater and he led them forward and took possession of the unmanned guns. Then they began pumping bullets into the tunnel and yelled for the Confederates to come out and give themselves up. One by one seventeen Rebel gunners emerged from the tunnel and surrendered. Then a white flag appeared at the other end of the tunnel and Captain John T. Melvin surrendered what was left of his own company and the sally port gunners to Curtis's men on that side of the land face.

When Major Reilly, still near the magazine, saw the white flag waving at the sally port tunnel he could not tell who was surrendering to whom. Some of his officers suggested that some of the Yankees might want to give up. So he ordered his men to cease fire and he sent Captain Braddy with a handkerchief stuck on the end of a sword to find out what was going on. Braddy had not gone very far when he saw Melvin's Confederates emerge from the sally port tunnel and surrender to the Federals. Then he saw hundreds of Yankees get to their feet and move forward. He turned and ran back toward Reilly, shouting for him to open fire. Reilly gave the order even before Braddy had reached cover, and the Confederates fired a well aimed volley that drove the Federals back to their rifle pits.

Meanwhile, from atop the newly captured traverse Curtis could see the one remaining heavy gun on the land face, which had been giving the Federals outside the fort wall a hard time. He ordered sharpshooters to pick off the cannoneers, and they soon silenced the big gun. With the sally port guns also out of commission there was now no opposition to an advance along the outside of the land face wall, so Curtis sent a man back to the west end of the fort to bring up reinforcements to make such a move. However, in a few minutes the man came back and told him that General Ames said that no more troops could be sent to Curtis and that spades would soon be sent up so that Curtis and his men could entrench and hold what they had gained. As far as Ames could see, his men were terribly disorganized, the Confederate resistance had not been broken, and it would soon be dark, forcing the navy to cease fire. The capture of the rest of the fort would have to wait until tomorrow.

Curtis sent his orderly back to explain the situation to Ames and to again ask for reinforcements, but the orderly soon returned with Ames's reiteration of his previous reply: The men were exhausted; dig in and hold on if possible. Curtis told the orderly to go back again, this time not to Ames but to find some subordinate officers and tell them to bring forward as many men as they could round up for another advance. A few minutes later the orderly was back again, not with troops but with an armload of spades that General Ames had given him, along with a repetition of his previous order.

Curtis exploded. He had just spent the two longest hours of his life taking part of the land face and he was not about to quit with the job half done. He grabbed the spades and threw them over the traverse onto the startled Confederates on the other side, yelling to them that he would be back soon and would fall on them just like those spades. Then, after sending the young naval officer who had earlier carried the message to Terry to go back to the general and tell him that Curtis believed the fort could be taken with a bold push if Terry could send him reinforcements, Curtis stormed off to the western end of the fort to round up more men himself. There he ran into Ames, who, over the noise of battle, repeated his order in person: "The men are exhausted and I will not order them to go forward."[20] Curtis, however, would not give up. He told Ames that if they did not take the fort now it would probably be reinforced during the night. Again Ames repeated his order. Curtis refused to obey. As far as he was concerned, General Terry had put him in charge of this attack and he was going to make another assault if he had to do it with only fifty men. Ames said nothing more and Curtis rounded up some volunteers. Then, leaving some junior officers to organize these troops and bring them forward, he went back to the fighting.

In his absence, the Federals had pushed on and taken the eighth traverse and were now hugging their side of the ninth, where they were trying to catch their breath. Not in the best of moods after his encounter with Ames, Curtis tore into Colonel Zent, the senior officer while he was gone, demanding to know why he had stopped. "Keep down," Zent replied calmly, "or you will find out why we don't advance."[21] Curtis ignored this advice, however, and peered over the traverse to look for a possible route for the assault he was planning. An exploding shell knocked him flat. One shell fragment destroyed his left eye and another ripped his face open, covering it in blood. His men carried his unconscious form out of the fort and across the bridge in search of medical aid.

At his headquarters in the old earthworks north of the fort, Terry contemplated his alternatives. Ames thought his division had accomplished all that it could for now and wanted to entrench for the night. Curtis had thought another push would finish the job now, but Curtis was wounded, probably mortally. Both had thought reinforcements necessary. Terry turned for advice to Lieutenant Colonel Cyrus Comstock, Grant's aide who was on loan to him as chief engineer of this expedition. Comstock said he should throw Abbott's brigade into the fight and Paine's division as well if necessary. Ignore the threat from Hoke, he said. He was sure the fort would fall to one more heavy blow.

Terry decided to risk Abbott's brigade at least. Earlier he had sent an aide, Captain George F. Towle, over to the naval brigade to ask it to reinforce Abbott's and Paine's rear line, but Towle had not been able to find Breese. Instead, he had found young Lieutenant Commander William B. Cushing, who had almost single-handedly sunk the Rebel ironclad *Albemarle* with a spar torpedo three months before, and Cushing had agreed to Terry's request. Now Terry sent the staff officer back to make sure the navy would really do it, and he sent an order to Abbott telling him to move his brigade into the fort. Towle found that the sailors and marines had indeed reinforced the rear line as promised, and after what seemed to Terry and Comstock a very long wait, Abbott's brigade finally moved forward.

The sun had set and darkness was almost upon them and still Terry and Comstock waited to hear the increased firing that would surely mark Abbott's attack, but nothing changed. Comstock urged the general to send in Paine's division. Terry was not willing to trust his army's rear to anything but the badly mauled and poorly armed naval brigade, but he did order Paine to send one of his strongest regiments into the fort. Paine sent Colonel Albert M. Blackman's 27th U.S. Colored Troops, and again Terry and Comstock waited for the results, but still there was no sign of a Union attack. Terry finally decided to go see what was going on for himself.

Inside the fort Terry found that instead of using the reinforcements for another attack Ames had sent one of Abbott's regiments to relieve the mixed bag of troops Curtis had been leading along the traverses, had kept the rest with the other troops behind the captured portion of the land face, and had ordered them all to dig in. When Blackman's regiment had showed up he had ordered it to dig another line of entrenchments outside the fort. In light of this situation, Terry considered bringing up the rest of Paine's division, but Comstock suggested that time was more important now than reinforcements. They had fresh troops on hand, why not use them? He suggested organizing Abbott's troops into 100-man detachments and throwing one detachment at a time at the next traverse, keeping the pressure on the defenders, who must be exhausted, until they broke. Terry agreed, and within an hour the first detachment was advancing along the land face.

"When they came against the enemy it was cold steel or the butt of a gun," a Union survivor wrote. "At other places the contending forces would blaze away in the darkness. They would throw themselves on the ground and then come alternately crawling or running for position. Hoarse voices were shouting orders, and from the huge round traverses, that looked like great sea-billows toppling over to engulf all before them, shadowy forms of friend and foe were seen in confused masses.... The outlines of the work could now and then be seen by the flash of exploding shells or blaze of musketry, but indistinct as the creation of some hideous dream."[21] Led by the 3rd New Hampshire, the Federals overran the ninth traverse and then the tenth and eleventh. There the exhausted Rebels, without a senior officer to lead them, but supported by the fire of Major Reilly's inner line near the magazine, managed to stall the Union advance one again.

Lamb's aide, Lieutenant John Kelly, waded through the dead and wounded in the Pulpit hospital around 8 p.m. to tell the colonel that the Yankees now held almost all of the land face and that the defenders were almost out of ammunition. Should they surrender? Lamb said no. Whiting agreed. General Lee had sent word that if the fort fell and the Confederacy lost its last port he could not keep his army in the field. Hoke might yet attack, or reinforcements might arrive from the river at any minute. Lamb had already sent the wounded Major Saunders down to Battery Buchanan to meet the rest of Hagood's Brigade, which he was sure must have arrived by now, and bring it up to the scene of the fighting. Lieutenant Kelly was sent back with orders to hold on until rescue arrived one way or the other. "Lamb," Whiting said, "when you die I will assume comand and I will not surrender the fort."[23]

But out on the traverses of the land face the Confederate fire slowly dwindled away to an occasional sputter as the last cartridges were fired. The dead and wounded had long since been stripped of ammunition and there was no other source available. Meanwhile Lieutenant Colonel Augustus W. Rollins led the 7th New Hampshire and the 6th Connecticut eastward between the land face and the palisade until they were opposite the last three traverses still held by the Rebels. Then they charged up the sloping outer wall and quickly overwhelmed the defenders who were busy holding off the Federals in their front. Rollins then turned his men about and seized the Northeast Bastion, key to the entire fort, from the rear. All Confederate resistance suddenly collapsed. It was almost 10 p.m., and for the first time that day it was quiet enough for Terry's men to hear the waves breaking on the nearby beach.

Major Reilly had already ordered stretcher bearers to carry General Whiting and Colonel Lamb down to Battery Buchanan despite their protests. He had also sent word to the battery's commander that if the fort fell he would fall back there with all the men he could muster. There, under cover of the battery's big guns, they could wait for reinforcements from across the river to help them retake the fort, or, if that failed, they could use the flotilla of small boats there to make their escape. Counting heads, Reilly found that he had 32 men left. They formed a column of fours and set off down the peninsula. But when they reached Battery Buchanan they discovered that not only had it been abandoned and its guns spiked but the boats were gone as well. There were several hundred survivors of the garrison there, but they were almost all unarmed. Unknown to Reilly, the wounded Major Saunders had been on his way back to report that the rest of Hagood's Brigade had not arrived when he had seen the Federals overrun the final traverses and the Northeast Bastion. Certain that all was lost, he had gone back to Battery Buchanan and advised its commander to spike his guns and retreat across the river. The commander had agreed and Saunders had joined them. They had pulled away in their boats just minutes before Lamb, Whiting, and Reilly had shown up.

A few more handfuls of Confederates made their way south in the darkness to escape capture, but most of the surviving Rebels were rounded up and taken prisoner. Some had retreated into the main magazine, where 13,000 pounds of gunpowder were stored. "Come out of there, Johnny Rebs," the Federals told them, "or we'll shoot into you." Lieutenant Henry Benton shouted back, "Shoot and be damned to you, and we'll all go to hell together."[24] The Federals did not shoot, but Benton and his men came out anyway.

At last it was over, and word raced through the Union ranks: They had won. "Victory!" one soldier wrote, "and we proclaimed it too, till sea and shore, and the tall, solemn pines echoed back wilder and heartier cheering than had ever before disturbed a midnight at Federal Point." Yes, it was Federal Point once again. Survivors overwhelmed with emotion danced and cavorted atop the traverses amid the bodies of the slain and mangled. "Never did I feel as I felt then," Lieutenant Frank Lay wrote home. He was the only officer left unhurt in the 117th New York. "Men grasped each other's hands and wept only as brave men can in the hour of victory."[25]

Two army Signal Corps officers were talking solemnly with the *Malvern*'s junior officers in that ship's wardroom about the naval officers who had been killed and wounded in the attack that afternoon when one of them was summoned to come to the bridge and interpret an army signal torch blinking on the shore. Letter by letter the young lieutenant spelled out the message: "THE FORT IS OUR... " Wild cheers broke out and spread all over the fleet before he could finish the message. "In a moment, the meaning of the signal was conveyed to the admiral," Porter's aide remembered. "He jumped on deck, and called all hands aft to the quarter deck. Every man and boy was soon around him, and in a loud, thrilling voice he directed them to give three cheers for the capture of Fort Fisher. The admiral never before gave an order which was as heartily obeyed. Everyone appeared to be wild with joy, all discipline was relaxed and the cheers of officers and sailors could be heard far and wide over the smooth water. Loud cheering could be heard in the fort and lights began to flash in all directions."[26] The ships finally ceased their fire on the seaface and instead fired off signal rockets of all colors and blew their steam whistles in celebration.

When things had calmed down sufficiently inside the fort, Terry had Colonel Abbott take the 7th New Hampshire and 6th Connecticut, supported by the 27th U.S. Colored Troops, and sweep down the inside of the sea face. And, leaving Ames in charge of the rest of troops in the fort, Terry and Comstock followed Abbott's advance. A few more Confederates were rounded up, but for the most part the sea face guns had been abandoned—even the formidable Mound Battery, where they found the garrison flag still flying. A captain hauled it down and gave it to Abbott, who presented it to Terry. Their new prisoners said that what was left of the garrison had retreated to Battery Buchanan, so the Federals pressed on down the peninsula.

There was one last brief moment of hope for the ever-optomistic Colonel Lamb when General Colquitt suddenly turned up at Battery Buchanan. But it died when he learned that the general had brought no troops. Only he and his staff had been rowed across the river by civilian oarsmen. Bragg had realized too late that the fort was in serious danger, and even when he had received an alarming report from Major Saunders after the latter had escaped across the river he had refused to believe the fort had fallen. Instead he had dispatched Colquitt to find out the true situation. Almost as soon as he landed, that general had encountered stragglers who said that the fort had already fallen, so he had left his staff to guard the boat and had walked on down to Battery Buchanan to find Whiting and Lamb. Lamb filled him in on the events of the day and asked him to evacuate General Whiting. However, one of Colquitt's men then showed up and urged him to get back to the boat, for the Yankees were coming. Colquitt took the man's advice, leaving the wounded Whiting and Lamb to their fate, and he made it back to his boat just in time to make his escape. While he was gone his staff had almost lost the boat to a drunken Confederate marine, and seconds after the general and his party rowed out into the river they saw Union troops march along the shore.

Major Reilly had already gone to meet the advancing Federals before Colquitt arrived, for he was worried that if they encountered the mob of Confederates at Battery Buchanan without realizing that they were unarmed they might fire into them. Holding a handkerchief aloft on the point of his sword he met a small force of Federals led by Captain Charles H. Graves, one of Terry's aides. Graves had set off down the river side of the peninsula with a small force of volunteers to keep the Confederates from escaping before they could be rounded up by Abbott's larger force, and now, to his surprise, he found this Rebel major who said he wanted to surrender the fort's garrison. He took Reilly across the peninsula where he surrendered his sword to a captain on Colonel Abbott's staff.

Abbott's three regiments pressed on down the peninsula to Battery Buchanan and there rounded up all that was left of the garrison of Fort Fisher. General Whiting, still lying on his stretcher, asked for the Union commander, and General Terry stepped forward and identified himself. "I surrender, sir, to you the forces under my command," Whiting said, "I care not what becomes of myself."[27]

---

1. Gragg, *Confederate Goliath*, 175.

2. Ibid., 176.
3. Ibid., 177.
4. Ibid., 178.
5. Ibid., 179.
6. Ibid., 185.
7. Lamb, "The Defense of Fort Fisher," 650.
8. Gragg, *Confederate Goliath*, 192.
9. William R. Trotter, *Ironclads and Columbiads: The Civil War in North Carolina: The Coast* (Winston-Salem, 1989), 397.
10. Lamb, "The Defense of Fort Fisher," 651.
11. Gragg, Confederate Goliath, 194.
12. Lamb, "The Defense of Fort Fisher," 652.
13. *Official Records*, 46:II:1064.
14. Lamb, "The Defense of Fort Fisher," 653.
15. Gragg, *Confederate Goliath*, 204-205.
16. Ibid., 205.
17. Ibid., 206.
18. Ibid.
19. Ibid.
20. Ibid., 211.
21. Ibid.
22. Ibid., 215.
23. Lamb, "The Defense of Fort Fisher," 653.
24. Gragg, *Confederate Goliath*, 220.
25. Ibid.
26. Ibid., 221.
27. Ibid., 228.

CHAPTER TEN

"But Their Enmity Will Remain"

15 - 20 January 1865

Up in southern Virginia that day Major General John Gibbon, commander of the 2nd Division of Humphreys' 2nd Corps in Meade's Army of the Potomac, was assigned to succeed Ord as the commander of the 24th Corps in the Army of the James, now that Ord had succeeded Butler in command of that army. And up in northern Virginia Sheridan departed the Shenandoah Valley that day to make an inspection of the Department of West Virginia.

The monitor USS *Patapsco* was sunk that day when it struck a torpedo off of Charleston, South Carolina, going down in 15 seconds with the loss of 62 hands. A little farther south, the 17th Corps of Major General Oliver O. Howard's Right Wing of Sherman's army reached Pocotaligo, South Carolina, that day and found the strong Confederate fort there abandoned. "All the country between Beaufort and Pocotaligo was low alluvial land," Sherman later wrote, "cut up by an infinite number of salt-water sloughs and fresh-water creeks, easily susceptible of defense by a small force; and why the enemy had allowed us to make a lodgement at Pocotaligo so easily I did not understand, unless it resulted from fear or ignorance. It seemed to me then that the terrible energy they had displayed in the earlier stages of the war was beginning to yield to the slower but more certain industry and discipline of our Northern men. It was to me manifest that the soldiers and people of the South entertained an undue fear of our Western men, and, like children, they had invented such ghostlike stories of our prowess in Georgia, that they were scared by their own inventions."[1] The 17th Corps marched on and made a lodgement on the railroad between Savannah and Charleston before the day was over.

Secretary Stanton left Savannah "about the 15th of January," Sherman wrote, "and promised to go North without delay, so as to hurry back to me the supplies I had called for, as indespensible for the prosecution of the next stage of the campaign. I was quite impatient to get off myself, for a city-life had become dull and tame, and we were all anxious to get into the pine-woods again, free from the importunities of rebel women asking for protection, and of the civilians from the North who were coming to Savannah for cotton and all sorts of profit."[2]

"During Mr. Stanton's stay in Savannah," Sherman said in his memoirs, "we discussed [the] negro question very fully; he asked me to draft an order on the subject, in accordance with my own views, that would meet the pressing necessities of the case, and I did so." All the sea islands from Charleston south, abandoned rice fields along the rivers for thirty miles inland, and all waterfront lands along the St. Johns River in northern Florida were set aside for the former slaves, and all whites, other than Union soldiers, were excluded from these areas. Each black family would be given up to forty acres of tillable land. Provision was also made for enlisting the blacks in the Union army, but the order specified that "by the laws of war, and orders of the President of the United States, the negro is free, and must be dealt with as such. He cannot be subjected to conscription, or forced military service, save by the written orders of the highest military authority in the department, under such regulations as the President or Congress may prescribe.... The bounties paid on enlistment may, with the consent of the recruit, go to assist his family and settlement in procuring agricultural implements, seed, tools, boots, clothing, and other articles necessary for their livelihood."[3]

"The secretary made some verbal modifications, when it was approved by him in all its details, I published it, and it went into operation at once...," Sherman wrote. "Of course, the military authorities at that day, when war prevailed, had a perfect right to grant the possession of any vacant land to which they could extend military protection, but we did not undertake to give a fee-simple title; and all that was designed by these special field orders was to make temporary provisions for the freedmen and their families during the rest of the war, or until Congress should take action in the premises. All that I now propose to assert is, that Mr. Stanton, Secretary of War, saw these orders in the rough, and approved every paragraph thereof, before they were made public."[4]

In Tennessee that day, Schofield's 23rd Corps began to embark at Clifton, on the Tennessee River, for the trip down that stream to Paducah, Kentucky, as the first leg of its transfer to the North Carolina coast.

Down in Mississippi that day, Beauregard arrived at Tupelo, Hood's headquarters. He found, according to one of his staff officers, that Hood's army was "a shattered debris of an army and needs careful yet vigorous handling to hold it together." The next day, the two generals conferred. Hood revealed that he had already asked to be relieved from command, and Beauregard found him, according to a staff officer, "so humiliated, so utterly crushed," that he "had not the heart virtually to disgrace him by ordering his immediate removal."[5] And Hood telegraphed President Davis that day as though he had not already requested to be relieved: "If allowed to remain in command of this army, I hope you will grant me authority to reorganize it and relieve all incompetent officers. If thought best to relieve me, I am ready to command a corps or division, or do anything that may be considered best for my country." He even managed to convince Beauregard to back his plan for granting extensive leaves. "To prevent disorder and dissertion in Army of Tennessee," Beauregard wired the War Department, "I have approved a judicious system of furlough."[6]

In Richmond that day, the sixteenth, President Davis received word of the fall of Fort Fisher, and he urged General Bragg to recapture it if possible. Also, the Confederate Senate passed a resolution that day that it was the judgment of Congress that General Robert E. Lee should be made general-in-chief of the Confederate Army—a position comparable to Grant's in the U.S. Army—that Beauregard should be put in command of the Department of South Carolina, Georgia and Florida, and that General Joseph E. Johnston should again be placed in command of the Army of Tennessee.

In Washington, that day, Francis Blair, Sr. met with President Lincoln to present to him the letter Jefferson Davis had given him and to report on his trip to Richmond. He also outlined for Lincoln the plan he had presented to Davis for the Union and Confederacy to declare a ceasefire and combine forces to drive the French out of Mexico. Lincoln showed little interest in the plan but was pleased to hear that a number of Blair's old acquaintances in Richmond had indicated that they were not sanguine about the Confederacy's military prospects.

That same day, "General" Singleton reached Richmond with his permit to bring out Southern cotton and tobacco.

A drizzling rain dampened the peninsula of Federal Point as the cool gray morning of 16 January dawned over Fort Fisher, revealing in its dim light the carnage of the day and night before. "Such a sight my eyes never beheld," one Union sailor wrote. "Dead lay in all directions and positions. It was a horrid sight to look at, some mangled terrible. The beach for 1,000 acres is covered with shot and broken shell." A sergeant in the 4th U.S. Colored Troops, who had already won a Congressional Medal of Honor in the fighting around Richmond, saw "scarcely a square foot of ground without some fragment or unexploded shell. Heavy guns bursted, others knocked to pieces as though made of pipe clay, heavy gun carriages knocked to splinters and dead bodies of rebels lying as they fell with wounds horrible enough to sicken the beholder. Some with half of their heads off, others cut in two, disembowled and every possible horrible wound that could be inflicted. Oh this terrible war!"[7]

Both inside and outside the walls of the captured fort thousands of exhausted Union soldiers, sailors, and marines lay huddled in their blankets on the sand wherever they had found room to lie down the night before. Many of them were allowed to sleep late, but others were up early, building campfires, boiling coffee, and visiting hastily dug latrines. Some of them prowled through the bombproofs, searching for abandoned valuables and souvenirs. One found the fort's logbook. Another found a Rebel pistol. Others found some medicinal whiskey in the hospital bombproof and got drunk. One member of a group of young officers found a lanyard dangling from one of the field pieces by the riverside gate and gave it a careless yank. The gun went off, its charge barely missing another group of Union soldiers.

Among those who were up early was Lieutenant Colonel Samuel Zent, commander of the 13th Indiana. General Ames had ordered him to post guards at all the bombproofs, and at first light he and the adjutant of the 169th New York went to make the rounds and check on his guard details. At about 7:30 a.m. Zent noticed some marines going into the fort's magazine and he realized that he had failed to post any guards there. He sent the adjutant to check on the magazine while he stepped into the sally port tunnel to give an order to the sentry there, when suddenly the magazine exploded. There were 13,000 pounds of gunpowder in that enclosed space. Or, there had been. "The entire structure, with a dull heavy sound that shook the surrounding country, went up into the air like an immense water-spout," one witness said, "with timbers, debris, and human forms flying against the sky."[8]

Many nearby soldiers were killed in their sleep. Everyone in the vicinity who was standing was knocked flat by a powerful shock wave. Some who survived the blast were buried alive by falling sand. Protected by the tunnel, Zent survived, although the sentry he was talking to was killed, as was the adjutant he had sent to check on the magazine. Thirty years later Zent was still blaming himself for the accident.

Most of the troops, however, blamed the Confederates. They knew that the Rebels had buried torpedoes outside the fort connected to a detonator by electrical wires, and someone found a wire leading to the magazine, or to the crater where the magazine had been. "Many were for killing all the rebel prisoners," an officer reported, "while others were for blowing them up."[9] Cooler heads prevailed, however, and General Whiting assured his captors that the suspicious wire was only a telegraph line. An official board of inquiry later concluded that the explosion was caused by drunken men going into the magazine with lights looking for loot. General Terry reported 130 men as killed, wounded or missing because of the explosion. Other officers said it was more like 200.

At 1:30 a.m. the next day, the seventeenth, the Federals were startled by the sound of another huge explosion—this time from the other side of the Cape Fear River—and it was soon followed by others. On General Bragg's orders, the Confederates were blowing up Fort Caswell and other fortifications downriver which would be cut off now that the Federal fleet had access to the river by way of New Inlet. The Confederates withdrew upstream to Fort Anderson, which was across the river from Hoke's position at Sugar Loaf.

In Washington, Ben Butler was testifying before Congress's powerful Joint Committee on the Conduct of the War. "This is the beginning of a war on Grant," General Meade predicted. "Grant undoubtedly has lost prestige," Meade told his wife, "owing to his failure to accomplish more, but as I know it has not been in his power to do more I cannot approve of unmerited censure, any more than I approved of the fulsome praise showered on him before the campaign commenced."[10] He had been relieved of command, Butler was telling the committee, because of his refusal to sacrifice his men in a vain attempt to capture Fort

Fisher. He had with him numerous reports from subordinates, maps, and charts to prove conclusively that the place could not possibly be taken by assault. However, he was soon interrupted by a commotion outside, where there were cheers and guns firing a salute and a newsboy crying, "Extra! Extra! Read all about it!" Someone asked the newsboy what all the fuss was about and learned that Fort Fisher had fallen after all. At first Butler insisted that there must be some mistake. It was impossible. The fort could not be taken. Yet there it was in black and white. Soon a wave of laughter surged across the room and Butler was swept up in it and eventually joined it himself. The committee adjourned, still chuckling, but before the members and spectators could file out Butler raised his hand and asked for silence. "Thank God for victory," he said.[11]

Grant responded to the news of the fort's capture with an order for a 100-gun salute. Cheers roared through the camps of the Army of the Potomac and the Army of the James and the news was shouted across the lines to the Confederates of Lee's army.

At the cabinet meeting that day Lincoln was unusually cheerful. Secretary of State William Seward kidded Secretary of the Navy Welles that his ships had nothing to do now that the Confederacy's last major port was sealed off. Postmaster General William Dennison said that he would like to have some of the faster ships to carry the mail. "The congratulations over the capture of Fort Fisher are hearty and earnest," Welles told his diary. "Some few whom I have met are a little out of humor. General Butler does not appear gladsome, and it is not in human nature that he should."[12]

Down in Mississippi on the seventeenth, Beauregard seemed to be completely won over to Hood's point of view. He telegraphed to President Davis: "I am fully satisfied the Army of Tennessee requires immediate reorganization and consolidation, removing at same time all inefficient and supernumerary officers. Generals Hood, Taylor, Forrest, and corps commanders agree fully with me in that opinion. Cannot necessary authority be granted me, at once, to that effect? The army cannot otherwise be made reliable for active operations." He even opposed the idea of sending any of Hood's forces to the Carolinas, for he added in a later wire: "To divide this small army at this juncture to re-enforce General Hardee would expose to capture Mobile, Demopolis, Selma, Montgomery, and all the rich valley of the Alabama River. Shall that risk be now incurred?"[13] However, before the day was over he received a telegram Secretary of War Seddon had sent two days before: "By telegraph of yesterday [thirteenth], General Hood requests to be relieved from command of Army of Tennessee. His request is granted, and you will place Lieutenant-General Taylor in command, he retaining command of his department as heretofore; and you, with such troops as may be spared, will return to Georgia and South Carolina."[14] The next day, the eighteenth, Beauregard ordered S.D. Lee's corps to be sent to Augusta. That same day, the last of the Union 23rd Corps embarked for its own trip east.

In North Carolina on the eighteenth, Lieutenant Commander William B. Cushing, the hero of the sinking of the *Albemarle*, led a naval landing party from the USS *Monticello* that raised the stars and stripes over the ruins of Fort Caswell. And later that day Admiral Porter sent gunboats through New Inlet into the lower Cape Fear River. General Terry then sent detachments of troops to occupy the defensive works downriver that the Rebels had abandoned.

In Washington on the eighteenth, John Wilkes Booth and his team of conspirators were preparing to capture President Lincoln at Ford's Theatre that night. Booth knew the theater well, and as a friend of the owners he had easy access to any part of it at just about any time. He also knew that Lincoln, a frequent visitor, was expected to attend that evening's performance. The plan, apparently, was for John Surratt to go under the stage, where, at a signal from Booth, he would turn off the master valve for all the gas lights in the building. This was intended to provide enough confusion in the audience and among the actors backstage to allow the kidnapping to take place unopposed while keeping anyone from discovering what was happening. Surratt was then to go up onto the darkened stage and wait.

Meanwhile, Booth would proceed to the presidential box—actually a combination of boxes 7 and 8 with the separating partition removed—where at gunpoint the actor would force Lincoln to submit to being bound and gagged. He would then lower the president's considerable bulk over the edge of the box to Surratt on the stage eleven feet below, and then follow the same route himself. Booth and Surratt would then hustle the bound president out the rear door and into a covered wagon waiting in the alley. They would drive eastward, passing into southern Maryland by way of the Navy Yard Bridge. Just beyond that point they would find the first of a series of relay teams of horses, provided by David Herold, a young admirer of Booth. These would allow the conspirators to keep ahead of any pursuit. Another of Booth's followers, the German-born carriage-maker and blockade runner from southern Maryland, George Atzerodt, had been sent ahead with the job of securing a flatboat large enough "to float ten or twelve people and a carriage."[15] At 7 p.m. the conspirators were in position and ready, but Lincoln did not show up at the theater that night.

Lincoln did meet with Blair again on the eighteenth and provided him with a letter in reply to the one Blair had obtained from Jefferson Davis: "You having shown me Mr. Davis' letter to you of the 12th. Inst., you may say to him that I have constantly been, am now, and shall continue, ready to receive any agent whom he, or any other influential person now resisting the national authority, may informally send to me, with the view of securing peace to the people of our one common country."[16] The final phrase, in obvious and presumably intentional contrast to Davis's phrase "the two countries," defined the obstacle to peace in a nutshell. Lincoln's sworn duty as president of the United States was to preserve, protect, and defend its constitution, its people, and its territory. Davis, as president of the Confederate States, had a similar commitment to a different constitution and to the government it had set up that claimed sovereignty over some of the same people and some of the same territory. To Davis the war involved two separate countries; to Lincoln, one common country. There could be no peace until this difference was resolved, but neither man could yield on this one essential point.

Down in Georgia on that eighteenth day of January, Sherman turned over the city of Savannah to Grover's division, formerly of the 19th Corps, which had just arrived from Baltimore and been assigned to Major General J.G. Foster's Department of the South. The next day Sherman issued orders for his army's move north. These were for Howard's Right Wing, or Army of the Tennessee, to mass at Pocotaligo and for Slocum's Left Wing, or Army of Georgia, plus Brigadier General Hugh Judson Kilpatrick's cavalry division, to assemble around Robertsville, South Carolina.

"Of course," Sherman later wrote, "I gave out with some ostentation, especially among the rebels, that we were going to Charleston or Augusta; but I had long before made up my mind to waste no time on either, further than to play off on their fears, thus to retain for their protection a force of the enemy which would otherwise concentrate in our front, and make the passage of some of the great rivers that crossed our route more difficult and bloody."[17]

Lincoln was writing to General Grant that day, the nineteenth, to ask for a personal favor: "Please read and answer this letter as though I was not President, but only a friend. My son, now in his twenty second year, having graduated at Harvard, wishes to see something of the war before it ends. I do not wish to put him in the ranks, nor yet to give him a commission, to which those who have already served long, are better entitled, and better qualified to hold. Could he, without embarrassment to you, or detriment to the service, go into your Military family with some nominal rank, I, and not the public, furnishing his necessary means? If no, say so without the least hesitation, because I am as anxious, and as deeply interested, that you shall not be encumbered as you can be yourself."[18]

General Lee was writing to his president, Jefferson Davis, that day, about the proposal to make him the general-in-chief of the Confederate Army. "I do not think," he said, "that while charged with my present command embracing Virginia & N.C. & the immediate controul of this army I could direct the operations of the armies in the S. Atlantic States. If I had the ability I would not have the time. The arrangement of the details of this army extended as it is, providing for its necessities & directing its operations engrosses all my time & still I am unable to accomplish what I desire & see to be necessary. I could not therefore propose to undertake more." He concluded by saying that he was "willing to undertake any service to which you think proper to assign me, but I do not wish you to be misled as to the extent of my capacity."[19]

Lee was also writing that day to William Porcher Miles, representative of the Charleston, South Carolina, district in the Confederate congress. He was replying to a letter that Miles had written to him the day before enclosing a telegram from the governor of South Carolina asking for troops to be sent to that state from Lee's army to defend against Sherman's advance. "As far as I know the views of the Government," Lee wrote, "no representations will be necessary to cause troops to be tranferred to South Carolina, if any could be obtained. I can only say I shall be most happy to do everything in my power to defend the State, but I do not know where to obtain the troops. Concurring in all you state with reference to the importance of preserving the port of Charleston, defeating the army of Sherman, and cheering the spirits of the people, I do not think that this would be accomplished by so weakening this army as to enable the enemy to disperse it, and achieve what he has been struggling to obtain the whole campaign. It seems to me it would only aggravate our disasters by adding the loss of Richmond to that of Charleston, should it fall.... It will be impossible for me to send sufficient troops from this army to oppose Sherman's and at the same time resist Grant. Sherman's army alone is equal to this, and I can see no benefit from inviting disaster at both places... but I need not tell you that the transfer of troops from this army to any part of the country does not depend upon me, but rests with the War Department. Any troops it may order I will cheerfully send."[20]

Some of Lee's men were indeed sent to South Carolina. In fact, a brigade of infantry had already been sent. And on that same day Major General Wade Hampton, commander of Lee's cavalry corps, issued orders for the transfer of his own old division, now commanded by Major General Matthew Butler and composed mostly of regiments from the Carolinas, to South Carolina. Hampton, a well known citizen of that state, would also be going along. In fact, the move had been his idea. A great many of the men of Butler's Division had lost their horses, and in the Confederate Army cavalrymen were responsible for furnishing their own mounts. Hampton's plan was to leave behind the few horses Butler's men still had and send the men down on the railroad to get more. While there they could help protect the Carolinas. He had presented this idea to Davis, and the president having approved it Lee had little choice but to go along with it, but did so on the condition that the men and the horses would be returned to him in time for the spring campaign in Virginia. "I think Hampton will be of service in mounting his men & arousing the spirit of & strength of the State & otherwise do good," Lee had told Davis.[21] Other Confederate troops were also on the way to oppose Sherman. S.D. Lee's corps of Hood's army left Tupelo that day on a roundabout railroad trip to Augusta, and Beauregard issued orders for Cheatham's Corps to follow, which it did the next day, the twentieth.

At Fort Lafayette in New York City on the twentieth, Acting Master's Mate John Yates Beall of the Confederate navy was brought to trial before a military commission. He was charged with seizing the steamer *Philo Parsons* on Lake Erie in an attempt to free Rebels from a prisoner of war camp near Sandusky, Ohio, and with being part of a group of Confederates who tried to derail a train in upstate New York for the purpose of freeing Rebel prisoners who were being transported from one prison to another. Chief witnesses against him were one of the owners of the *Philo Parsons* and one of the other Confederate agents working out of Canada who had been in the group that tried to derail the train. Beall was quickly found guilty of what the judge advocate said was a crime that "seems to assume that fiendish enormity which cries loudly for vengeance fo the outraged law. So dark a picture of guilt is revolting to all the instincts of humanity."[22]

Secretary of War Stanton had returned to Washington and reported to Lincoln that day on his trip down to Savannah and also on his stop at Fort Fisher on the way back. "His statements were not so full and comprehensive as I wished," Navy Secretary Welles told his diary, "nor did I get at the real object of his going, except that it was for his health, which seems improved. There is, he says, little or no loyalty in Savannah and the women are frenzied, senseless partisans.... I am apprehensive, from the statement of Stanton, and of others also, that the Rebels are not yet prepared to return to duty and become good citizens. They have not, it would seem, been humbled enough, but must be reduced to further submission. Their pride, self-conceit, and arrogance must be brought down.... How soon they will possess the sense and judgment to seek and have peace is a problem. Perhaps there must be a more thorough breakdown of the whole framework of society, a greater degradation, and a more effectual wiping out of family and sectional pride in order to eradicate the aristocratic folly which has brought the present calamities upon themselves and the country. If the fall of Savannah and Wilmington will not bring them to conciliatory measures and friendly relations, the capture of Richmond and Charleston will not effect it. They may submit to what they cannot help, but their enmity will remain."[23]

---

1. Sherman, *Memoirs*, 734.
2. Ibid., 733.
3. Ibid., 731.
4. Ibid., 730.
5. Sword, *Embrace an Angry Wind*, 429.
6. *Official Records*, 45:II:786.
7. Gragg, *Confederate Goliath*, 230-231.
8. Ibid., 233.
9. Ibid., 234.
10. Catton, *Grant Takes Command*, 408.
11. Foote, *The Civil War*, 3:740.
12. Howard K. Beale, editor, *Diary of Gideon Welles: Secretary of the Navy Under Lincoln and Johnson* (New York, 1960), Vol. 2, 227.
13. *Official Records*, 45:II:789.
14. Ibid., 45:II:784-785.
15. Jim Bishop, *The Day Lincoln Was Shot* (New York, 1955), 76.
16. Basler, ed., *The Collected Works of Abraham Lincoln*, 8:220-221.
17. Sherman, *Memoirs*, 733-734.
18. Basler, ed., *Collected Works of Abraham Lincoln*, 8:223.

19. Clifford Dowdey and Louis H. Manarin, editors, *The Wartime Papers of R. E. Lee* (New York, 1961), 884-885.
20. Ibid., 885-886.
21. Ibid., 881-882.
22. Brandt, *The Man Who Tried to Burn New York*, 166.
23. Beale, ed., *Diary of Gideon Welles*, 2:229-230.

PART TWO

PEACE FEELERS

Let nothing which is transpiring, change, hinder, or delay your military movements, or plans.

—President Abraham Lincoln to
Lieutenant General Ulysses S. Grant

CHAPTER ELEVEN

"Awaiting a More Favorable Change in the Weather"

21 - 26 January 1865

Before I again dive into the interior and disappear from view," Sherman wrote to General Thomas on the 21st, "I must give you, in general terms, such instructions as fall within my province as commander of the division. I take it for granted that you now reoccupy in strength the line of the Tennessee from Chattanooga to Eastport. I suppose Hood to be down about Tuscaloosa and Selma, and that Forrest is again scattered to get horses and men and to divert attention. You should have a small cavalry force of, say, 2,000 men to operate from Knoxville through the mountain pass along the French Broad into North Carolina, to keep up the belief that it is to be followed by a considerable force of infantry. Stoneman could do this, whilst Gillem merely watches up the Holston. At Chattanooga should be held a good reserve of provisions and forage, and in addition to its garrison a small force that could at short notice relay the railroad to Resaca, prepared to throw provisions down to Rome, or the Coosa. You remember I left the railroad track from Resaca to Kingston and Rome with such a view. Then with an army of 25,000 infantry and all the cavalry you can get, under Wilson, you should move from Decatur and Eastport to some point of concentration about Columbus, Miss., and thence march to Tuscaloosa and Selma, destroying former, gathering horses, mules (wagons to be burned), and doing all the damage possible; burning up Selma, that is the navy-yard, the railroad back toward the Tombigbee, and all iron foundries, mills, and factories. If no considerable army opposes you, you might reach Montgomery and deal with it in like manner, and then at leisure work back along the Selma and Rome road, via Talledega and Blue Mountain, to the Valley of Chattooga, to Rome or La Fayette. I believe such a raid perfectly practicable and easy, and that it will have an excellent effect. It is nonsense to suppose that the people of the South are enraged or united by such movements. They reason very differently. They see in them the sure and inevitable destruction of all their property. They realize that the Confederate armies cannot protect them, and they see in the repetition of such raids the inevitable result of starvation and misery. You should not go south of Selma and Montgomery, because south of that line the country is barren and unproductive. I would like to have Forrest hunted down and killed, but doubt if we can do that yet. Whilst you are thus employed I expect to pass through the center of South and North Carolina, and I suppose Canby will also keep all his forces active and busy."[1]

Thomas was, in turn, writing to Halleck from Eastport, Mississippi, that day: "A reconnaissance sent by me to Corinth on the 19th instant has returned to Iuka, the cavalry portion only having reached Corinth. The commanding officer reports only straggling parties of the rebels at Corinth, which ran away at his approach. I also have reports from scouts sent out in the direction of Columbus, Miss., that Hood's headquarters are at that place, and that Forrest's headquarters are at Tupelo, and also that they have furloughed most of their Mississippi, Alabama, and Tennessee troops until the 25th of this month, and that they were forced to resort to this measure on account of the destruction of their railroad communication. The above report of Hood's and Forrest's situation is confirmed by General Dana in a dispatch from Memphis. The commanding officer of the expedition to Corinth, as well as the scouts sent out, reports the roads in an impassable condition for wagons and artillery, and that it would be impossible to make a move of any magnitude until the weather becomes more favorable. Awaiting a more favorable change in the weather, I am doing everything possible to organize General Smith's command for a long march, and also equipping and mounting the cavalry as thoroughly as possible, which I am confident I shall be able to accomplish by the time the roads become passable, and shall then have a force which will be sufficient to overcome any resistance which the enemy may be able to bring against me. In this connection I respectfully request that you will order all horses required for the remount of the cavalry to be sent by steamers to this point, rather than to Louisville or Nashville. General Wilson has a fine location for thoroughly organizing and disciplining his command, which he can accomplish in a few weeks. He will then have a force which the enemy will be utterly unable to resist; and I earnestly recommend that I may be permitted to put my command in thorough shape before being again ordered to take the field. You may be assured I will not delay matters, but will be fully prepared before the roads are practicable, if sufficient horses can be furnished to remount the cavalry."[2]

Sherman also wrote to Grant that day, enclosing a copy of his letter to Thomas and informing him of his own progress, or lack of it. "The rains have so flooded the country," he said, "that we have been brought to a standstill; but I will persevere and get the army as soon as possible up to the line from Sister's Ferry to Pocotaligo, where we will have terra firma to work on." He also touched on other subjects: "I am rejoiced that Terry took Fisher, because it silences Butler, who was to you a dangerous man. His address to his troops on being relieved was a direct, mean, and malicious attack on you, and I amired the patience and skill by which you relieved yourself and the country of him.... I have been told that Congress meditates a bill to make another lieutenant-general for me. I have written to John Sherman [his brother, who was a senator from Ohio] to stop it, if it is designed for me. It would be mischievous, for there are enough rascals who would try to sow differences between us, whereas you and I now are in perfect understanding. I would rather have you in command than anybody else, for you are fair, honest, and have at heart the same purpose that should animate all. I should emphatically decline any commission calculated to bring us into rivalry, and I ask you to advise all your friends in Congress to this effect... I doubt if men in Congress fully realize that you and I are honest in our professions of want of ambition. I know I feel none, and to-day will gladly surrender my position and influence to any other who is better able to wield the power. The flurry attending my recent success will soon blow over, and give place to new developments."[3]

"Having accomplished all that seemed necessary," Sherman later wrote, "on the 21st of January, with my entire headquarters, officers, clerks, orderlies, etc., with wagons and horses, I embarked in a steamer for Beaufort, South Carolina, touching at Hilton Head, to see General Foster."[4]

Grant was on a short trip to Washington on the 21st to confer with Stanton and Halleck. Lincoln's letter about putting his oldest son on Grant's staff met him enroute and he replied from Annapolis Junction, Maryland, saying that he would be glad to have Robert Lincoln on his staff under the arrangement proposed and suggested giving him the nominal rank of captain. Grant had received letters from Sherman before leaving City Point, and he answered them from Washington that day. "Before your last request to have Thomas make a campaign into the heart of Alabama," he said, "I had ordered Schofield to Annapolis, Md., with his corps. The advance (six thousand) will reach the seaboard by the 23rd, the remainder following as rapidly as railroad transportation can be procured from Cincinnati. The corps numbers over twenty-one thousand men. I was induced to do this because I did not believe Thomas could possibly be got off before spring. His pursuit of Hood indicated a sluggishness that satisfied me that he would never do to conduct one of your campaigns. The command of the advance of the pursuit was left to subordinates, whilst Thomas followed far behind. When Hood had crossed the Tennessee, and those in pursuit had reached it, Thomas had not much more than half crossed the State, from whence he returned to Nashville to take steamer for Eastport. He is possessed of excellent judgment, great coolness and honesty, but he is not good on a pursuit. He also reported his troops fagged, and that it was necessary to equip up. This report and a determination to give the enemy no rest determined me to use his surplus troops elsewhere.

"Thomas is still left with a sufficient force surplus to go to Selma under an energetic leader. He has been telegraphed to, to know whether he could go, and, if so, which of the several routes he would select. No reply is yet received. Canby has been ordered to act offensively from the sea-coast to the interior, towards Montgomery and Selma. Thomas's forces will move from the north at an early day, or some of his troops will be sent to Canby. Without further reinforcements Canby will have a moving column of twenty thousand men.

"Fort Fisher, you are aware, has been captured. We have a force there of eight thousand effective. At New Bern about half that number.... If Wilmington is captured, Schofield will go there. If not, he will be sent to New Bern. In either event, all the surplus forces at the two points will move to the interior toward Goldsboro' in co-operation with your movements. From either point, railroad communications can be run out, there being here abundance of rolling-stock suited to the gauge of those roads.... All these troops are subject to your orders as you come in communication with them. They will be so instructed. From about Richmond I will watch Lee closely, and if he detaches much more, or attempts to evacuate, will pitch in. In the meantime, should you be brought to a halt anywhere, I can send two corps of thirty thousand effective men to your support, from the troops about Richmond."[5]

The next day, the 22nd, Francis Blair, Sr. returned to Richmond with Lincoln's answer to Jefferson Davis's letter. Davis read it over twice in Blair's presence. Blair remarked that the part about "our one common country" related to the part of Davis's letter about "the two countries," and Davis replied that he so understood it.

The day after that, the 23rd, the Confederates arrested Samuel Ruth, superintendent of the Richmond, Fredericksburg & Potomac Railroad. They had discovered that he was running a secret courier line between Richmond and Washington for Union spies. His activities were evidently discovered when the Federals tried to enlist the aid of Mrs. Frances Dade, a widow who lived east of Fredericksburg. She apparently tipped off Captain Thomas Nelson Conrad, who had a clandestine base near her home. Conrad had gone to Washington to spy on President Lincoln back in September and study the feasibility of capturing him, and he was evidently now in charge of covert operations in the area around Fredericksburg, through which a captured Lincoln would be brought to Richmond. To avoid attracting too much attention to their own operations in this area, the Confederates allowed Ruth to think that he had successfully bribed his way out of trouble.

Admiral Porter had withdrawn most of the naval vessels from the James River when he had made up his fleet for the Fort Fisher expedition. Only the double-turreted monitor *Onondaga* and a few light gunboats had been left behind. On the night of 23 January, at General Grant's suggestion, a naval officer was sent up the river to plant torpedoes at the obstructions at Trent's Reach to make sure that the Confederate ironclads at Richmond did not come down the river. But the officer soon discovered that the Rebel ironclads were already on their way. News of their approach was telegraphed to Grant's headquarters, and the general dispatched some of his aides to notify the naval vessels and to send them up to stop the Rebel warships, for if they got in position to bombard the transports and warehouses at City Point that supplied the Army of the Potomac and the Army of the James they could do a great deal of damage. Lieutenant Colonel Horace Porter was one of the officers sent, and when he returned to headquarters he found Grant with his wife, Julia, and Brigadier General Rufus Ingalls, chief quartermaster of the armies operating against Richmond who had been Grant's classmate at West Point.

"Well, now that we' ve got all ready for them," Ingalls said, "why don't their old gunboats come down?"

"Ingalls," Grant said, "you must have patience; perhaps they don't know that you 're in such a hurry for them, or they would move faster; you must give them time."

"Well, if they're going to postpone their movement indefinitely," Ingalls said, "I 'll go to bed."

Word soon arrived that it looked like the Rebel vessels would not be able to pass the obstructions at Trent's Reach, so Grant and his wife also turned in. But at about 1 a.m. on the 24th word came that at least some of the Confederates had gotten through the obstructions and were coming on. An aide knocked on the door that separated Grant's private quarters from his office and gave him the news. The general got up, put on his boots and uniform coat over his drawers, lit a cigar, and began to write hasty dispatches. "The puffs from the cigar," Horace Porter wrote, "were now as rapid as those of the engine of an express train at full speed."

Mrs. Grant, who had dressed and rejoined her husband, said, "Ulyss, will those gunboats shell the bluff?"

"Well," the general replied, "I think all their time will be occupied in fighting our naval vessels and the batteries ashore. The *Onondaga* ought to be able to sink them, but I don't know what they would do if they should get down this far." However, word arrived just then that the *Onondaga* had fled down the river. Grant, who had always received excellent cooperation from the navy, was astonished that her captain would retreat just when his ship was needed most. "Why, it was the great chance of his life to distinguish himself," he said.

"Mrs. Grant, who was one of the most composed of those present," Porter said, "now drew her chair a little nearer to the general, and with her mild voice inquired, 'Ulyss, what had I better do?' The general looked at her for a moment, and then replied in a half-serious and half-teasing way, 'Well, the fact is, Julia, you ought n't to be here.'"

An aide offered to drive Mrs. Grant away from the river in an ambulance wagon until she was out of range, but Grant said, "Oh, their gunboats are not down here yet; and they must be stopped at all hazards."

"Additional despatches were sent," Porter said, "and a fresh cigar was smoked, the puffs of which showed even an increased rapidity. In about two hours it was reported that only one of the enemy's boats was below the obstructions, and the rest were above, apparently aground. More guns had by this time been placed in the shore batteries, and the situation was greatly relieved."

"I tell you, I'm getting out of all patience," Ingalls grumped, "and I've about made up my mind that these boats never intended to come down here anyhow—that they 've just been playing it on us to keep us out of bed." He went off to catch up on his sleep and General and Mrs. Grant soon followed his example.

At daylight the *Onondaga* finally moved upriver and, supported by the shore batteries, opened fire on the Rebel flagship, the *Virginia II*, with her 15-inch smoothbores and 150-pounder Parrott rifles. At flood-tide the Confederates were able to get their grounded vessels afloat again and they withdrew up the river, except for the gunboat *Drewry* and a torpedo launch, both of which were destroyed by the Union guns. That night they came down again but were again driven back by the *Onondaga* and the shore batteries.

Breakfast was served late at headquarters on the 24th, as everyone tried to make up for the sleep lost the night before. When Grant lit his first cigar after the meal was over one of his staff officers kidded him about how hard he had been puffing on his cigars while writing dispatches to head off the Rebel ironclads. "No; when I come to think of it," the general said, "those cigars did n't last very long, did they?" He then related how he had been a pipe smoker until the capture of Fort Donelson three years before. But Flag Officer Andrew Foote, then commander of the gunboats on the western rivers, had presented him with a cigar on the morning that the Confederates had tried to break out of the fort and Grant had unconsciously carried the stump of it in his hand all during the battle. When the Rebels surrendered and the newspapers published reports of the general smoking a cigar in the midst of the conflict admirers were soon sending him thousands of the best cigars. "I gave away all I could get rid of," Grant said, "but having such a quantity on hand, I naturally smoked more than I would have done under ordinary circumstances, and I have continued the habit ever since."[6] Twenty years later he died of throat cancer.

Newspapers in both the North and the South were speculating on what Blair's visits to Richmond might mean, and Jefferson Davis was under political fire from two directions. There were those who criticized him for even receiving a man they considered a foreign enemy, and others, probably more numerous and influential, who feared that Davis had rejected a generous peace offer that would end the war on terms they would consider acceptable. But Davis had a plan for dealing with the latter. Vice President Alexander Stephens was one of Davis's strongest critics—so much so that Davis had not consulted with him for nearly four years. But he did so now. He called Stephens in for a consultation on the 24th and showed him the letter from Lincoln given to him by Blair, gave him the background, and asked his advice. Stephens said he thought the matter should be pursued, "at least so far as to obtain if possible a conference upon the subject."[7] Davis then asked for his recommendations for members of a commission to meet with the Federals.

Also on the 24th, the Confederate Congress offered to resume the exchange of prisoners on terms acceptable to the United States. The exchange had broken down the year before on two questions: the return to duty of the Confederates captured and paroled at Vicksburg and Port Hudson without proper exchange agreed to by the U. S. agent, and the Rebel policy of returning captured black soldiers to slavery rather than exchanging them.

General Thomas was writing to Halleck again on the 24th. He reported that scouts, refugees, and an officer sent under a flag of truce toward Columbus, Mississippi, all reported that the roads in that state and Alabama were still impractical for artillery and wagons. "I therefore think that it will be impossible to move from the Tennessee River upon Montgomery and Selma with a large force during the winter.... Should Lieutenant-General Grant determine upon a winter campaign from some point on the Gulf I could send General Canby Maj. Gen. A.J. Smith's command and all of the cavalry now here, except two divisions, feeling able to securely hold the line of the Tennessee and all the territory now held in East Tennessee with the Fourth Army Corps, the troops in East Tennessee, and two divisions of cavalry."[8]

Sherman was having similar problems with the weather. "The heavy winter rains had begun early in January," he wrote, "rendered the roads execrable, and the Savannah River became so swollen that it filled its many channels, overflowing the vast extent of rice-fields that lay on the east bank. This flood delayed our departure two weeks; for it swept away our pontoon-bridge at Savannah, and came near drowning John E. Smith's division of the Fifteenth Corps, with several heavy trains of wagons that were *en route* from Savannah to Pocotaligo by the old causeway.

"General Slocum had already ferried two of his divisions across the river, when Sister's Ferry, about forty miles above Savannah, was selected for the passage of the rest of his wing and of Kilpatrick's cavalry. The troops were in motion for that point before I quitted Savannah, and Captain S.B. Luce, United States Navy, had reported to me with a gunboat (the *Pontiac*) and a couple of transports, which I requested him to use in protecting Sister's Ferry during the passage of Slocum's wing, and to facilitate the passage of the troops all he could. The utmost activity prevailed at all points, but it was manifest we could not get off much before the 1st day of February; so I determined to go in person to Pocotaligo, and there act as though we were bound for Charleston. On the 24th of January I started from Beaufort with a part of my staff, leaving the rest to follow at leisure, rode across the island to a pontoon-bridge that spanned the channel between it and the main-land, and thence rode by Garden's Corners to a plantation not far from Pocotaligo, occupied by General Blair. There we found a house, with a majestic avenue of live-oaks, whose limbs had been cut away by the troops for firewood, and desolation marked one of those splendid South Carolina estates where the proprietors formerly had dispensed a hospitality that distinguished the old *regime* of that proud State. I slept on the floor of the house, but the night was so bitter cold that I got up by the fire several times, and when it burned low I rekindled it with an old mantel-clock and the wreck of a bedstead which stood in a corner of the room—the only act of vandalism that I recall done by myself personally during the war.

"The next morning I rode to Pocotaligo, and thence reconnoitered our entire line down to Coosawatchie. Pocotaligo Fort was on low, alluvial ground, and near it began the sandy pine-land which connected with the firm ground extending inland, constituting the chief reason for its capture at the very first stage of the campaign. Hatch's divison was ordered to that point from Coosawatchie, and the whole of Howard's right wing was brought near by, ready to start by the 1st of February. I also reconnoitered the point of the Salkiehatchie River, where the Charleston Railroad crossed it, found the bridge protected by a rebel battery on the farther side, and could see a few men about it; but the stream itself was absolutely impassable, for the whole bottom was overflowed by its swollen waters to the breadth of a full mile. Nevertheless, Force's and Mower's divisions of the Seventeenth Corps were kept active, seemingly with the intention to cross over in the direction of Charleston, and thus to keep up the delusion that that city was our immediate 'objective.' Meantime, I had reports from General Slocum of the terrible difficulties he had encountered about Sister's Ferry, where the Savannah River was reported nearly three miles wide, and it seemed for a time almost impossible for him to span it at all with his frail pontoons. About this time (January 25th), the weather cleared away bright and cold, and I inferred that the river would soon run down, and enable Slocum to pass the river before February 1st."[9]

Thomas's wire expressing willingness to send troops to reinforce Canby for operations on the Gulf coast had reached Washington, and Halleck wired to Grant, who was preparing to go down the coast for a look at Fort Fisher and the remaining defenses of Wilmington. "After reading General Thomas' telegram of 7.30 last evening," he wrote, "please give me your instructions before going South, if you wish to send troops to the Gulf, in order that I may order transports. After conversing with General Schofield, I am satisfied that no movement will be made from the Tennessee this winter."[10]

In Richmond on the 25th, Jefferson Davis assembled the three peace commissioners he had chosen after consulting with Vice President Stephens: Assistant Secretary of War John A. Campbell, a former justice of the United States Supreme Court; Robert M. T. Hunter, president pro tempore of the Confederate Senate and a former U. S. Senator; and Stephens himself. They were all influential politicians who had criticized Davis for not doing enough to negotiate a peace. He would let them see that such negotiations were not as easy as they looked. Stephens protested his own appointment but was overruled, and Davis handed the three commissioners their instructions, the original draft of which, written by Confederate secretary of state Judah P. Benjamin, had read: "In conformity with the letter of Mr Lincoln, of which the foregoing is a copy, you are requested to proceed to Washington City for conference with him upon the subject to which it relates." This, however, would have been a tacit acceptance of Lincoln's reference to their one common country. Davis, therefore, had revised it to read "... for an informal conference with him upon the issues involved in the existing war, and for the purpose of securing peace to the two countries."[11]

That same day, John Surratt left Washington, headed for Richmond to report to Secretary Benjamin, who was in charge of most Confederate clandestine operations.

A half a world away the Confederate commerce raider *Shenandoah* put into Melbourne, Australia, that day for coal and repairs. A sleek sail-and-steam ship with iron frame and wooden hull built in England and converted to a warship off Madeira, she had been in commission for three months and had already destroyed or ransomed more Union property than she had cost.

Grant replied to Halleck on the morning of the 26th: "You may order Thomas to send A.J. Smith's command to Canby with all dispatch. I do not think, however, it will do for Thomas to strip himself of cavalry as close as he proposes. If he will send one division of 3,000 or 4,000 it will be sufficient."[12] Halleck relayed these instructions to Thomas a couple of hours later but changed the amount of cavalry to be sent to 5,000.

---

1. Sherman, *Memoirs*, 621-622 and *Official Records*, 45:II:621-622.
2. *Official Records*, 45:II:621.
3. Ibid., 47:II:102-104.
4. Sherman, *Memoirs*, 734.
5. Ulysses S. Grant, *Personal Memoirs of U. S. Grant* (New York, 1886), vol. 2, 403-405.
6. Porter, *Campaigning With Grant*, 378-381.
7. Foote, *The Civil War*, 3:772.
8. *Official Records*, 45:II:627-628.
9. Sherman, *Memoirs*, 735-737.
10. *Official Records*, 49:I:581.
11. Foote, *The Civil War*, 3:773.
12. *Official Records*, 49:I:584.

CHAPTER TWELVE

"Hear All They May Choose to Say"

26 January - 4 February 1865

On the 26th, Jefferson Davis signed the act of the Confederate Congress creating the post of general-in-chief of the Confederate Army. He did not, however, yet nominate anybody to fill the position. The day after that, on the 27th, General Lee wrote to Confederate secretary of war James A. Seddon about the "alarming frequency of desertions" from his army. "You will perceive, from the accompanying papers," he said, "that fifty-six deserted from Hill's corps in three days. I have endeavored to ascertain the cause, and think that the insufficiency of food and non-payment of the troops have more to do with the dissatisfaction among the troops than anything else. All commanding officers concur in this opinion. I have no doubt that there is suffering for want of food. The ration is too small for men who have to undergo so much exposure and labor as ours.

"I know there are great difficulties in procuring supplies, but I cannot help thinking that with proper energy, intelligence, & experience on the part of the Commissary Department a great deal more could be accomplished. There is enough in the country, I believe, if it was properly sought for. I do not see why the supplies that are collected from day to day could not, by intelligent effort, be collected in such a manner as to have more on hand at a given time. The fact that they are collected at all is proof that they exist, and it must be possible to gather more in a given time than is now done. It will not answer to reduce the ration in order to make up for deficiencies in the Subsistence Department. The proper remedy is increased effort, greater experience in business, and intelligent management. It may be that all is done that can be, but I am not satisfied that we cannot do more. I think the efficiency of the army demands an increase of the ration, and I trust that no measure will be neglected that offers a chance of improvement."[1]

Lee did not mention them, but there were other reasons for the increasing desertions from his army, besides hunger and low pay. There was, for one thing, an increasing flood of letters coming to his men from their families telling them that they were needed at home. Their wives and children, their farms and businesses, were at the mercy of the invading Yankees because there was no Confederate force worthy of the name outside of the entrenchments around Richmond and Petersburg to protect them. "I heard it frequently remarked in our army," one of Lee's men said, "that scarcely a man had deserted but he could be proved to have been urged to it by his family at home. The very women began to fail us, those women who had blessed our banners when we went forth to battle; who had cheered us with their affection in all our toils; who had tended us when wounded and diseased; who had rewarded us with their favor when we acted well, and incited us to fresh exertion; who had made even death tolerable by the tenderness of their regret and by the sublimity of the self-denial with which they gave us to our country. The bloodshed had sickened them; their losses and their wants had become irritating to them. They began to complain, they lost heart, and, as a class, they finally sat down and left us to ourselves."[2]

Moreover, runaway inflation had made Confederate currency almost worthless. And life in the trenches had settled into a living hell. It was almost like one continuous battle lasting for months on end. It lacked the intensity of previous battles, and the casualties were spread out over a longer period of time, but the men of both sides were almost never free from the constant threat of the sniper's bullet and the plunging mortar shell. They lived in filth and were plagued by lice. The Federals, at least, could look forward to a satisfactory conclusion. They were winning the war, and they knew it. The Confederates, on the other hand, found it increasingly difficult to believe that their cause was anything but lost.

The next day, the 28th, Lieutenant General Jubal Early, Confederate commander of the Valley District, led Brigadier General Edward L. Thomas's brigade of infantry, Major General Thomas L. Rosser's cavalry brigade, and one battery of artillery westward from New Market, in the Shenandoah Valley, on a foraging raid into West Virginia. The next day they reached Moorefield and learned from scouts that a train of Union supply wagons was moving southward toward Petersburg, West Virginia. Early ordered Rosser to take his cavalry across Branch Mountain and intercept those wagons.

On the 29th, Sherman was again writing to Grant: "Captain Hudson has this moment arrived with your letter of January 21st, which I have read with interest.

"The capture of Fort Fisher has a most important bearing on my campaign, and I rejoice in it for many reasons, because of its intrinsic importance, and because it gives me another point of security on the seaboard. I hope General Terry will follow it up by the capture of Wilmington, although I do not look for it, from Admiral Porter's dispatch to me. I rejoice that Terry was not a West-Pointer, that he belonged to your army, and that he had the same troops with which Butler feared to make the attempt.

"Admiral Dahlgren, whose fleet is reenforced by some more ironclads, wants to make an assault *a la* Fisher on Fort Moultrie, but I withhold my consent, for the reason that the capture of all Sullivan's Island is not conclusive to Charleston; the capture of James Island would be, but all pronounce that impossible at this time. Therefore, I am moving (as hitherto designed) for the railroad west of Branchville, then will swing across to Orangeburg, which will interpose my army between Charleston and the interior. Contemperaneous with this, Foster will demonstrate up the Edisto, and afterward make a lodgment at Bull's Bay, and occupy the common road which leads from Mount Pleasant toward Georgetown. When I get to Columbia, I think I shall move straight for Goldsboro', *via* Fayetteville. By this circuit I cut all roads, and devastate the land; and the forces along the coast, commanded by

Foster, will follow my movement, taking any thing the enemy lets go, or so occupy his attention that he cannot detach all his forces against me. I feel sure of getting Wilmington, and may be Charleston, and being at Goldsboro', with its railroads finished back to Morehead City and Wilmington, I can easily take Raleigh, when it seems that Lee must come out. If Schofield comes to Beaufort, he should be pushed out to Kinston, on the Neuse, and may be Goldsboro' (or rather, a point on the Wilmington road, south of Goldsboro'). It is not necessary to storm Goldsboro', because it is in a distant region, of no importance in itself, and, if its garrison is forced to draw supplies from its north, it will be eating up the same stores on which Lee depends for his command.

"I have no doubt Hood will bring his army to Augusta. Canby and Thomas should penetrate Alabama as far as possible, to keep employed at least a part of Hood's army; or, what would accomplish the same thing, Thomas might reoccupy the railroad from Chattanooga forward to the Etowah, viz., Rome, Kingston, and Allatoona, thereby threatening Georgia. I know that the Georgia troops are disaffected. At Savannah I met delegates from several counties of the southwest, who manifested a decidedly hostile spirit to the Confederate cause. I nursed the feeling as far as possible, and instructed Grover to keep it up....

"You remember that we had fine weather last February for our Meridian trip, and my memory of the weather at Charleston is, that February is usually a fine month. Before the March storms come we should be within striking distance of the coast. The months of April and May will be the best for operations from Goldsboro' to Raleigh and the Roanoke. You may rest assured that I will keep my troops well in hand, and, if I get worsted, will aim to make the enemy pay so dearly that you will have less to do. I know that this trip is necessary; it must be made sooner or later; I am on time, and in the right position for it. My army is large enough for the purpose, and I ask no reenforcement, but simply wish the upmost activity to be kept up at all other points, so that concentration against me may not be universal.

"I expect that Jeff. Davis will move heaven and earth to catch me, for success to this column is fatal to his dream of empire. Richmond is not more vital to his cause than Columbia and the heart of South Carolina.... I think the 'poor white trash' of the South are falling out of their ranks by sickness, desertion, and every available means; but there is a large class of vindictive Southerners who will fight to the last. The squabbles in Richmond, the howls in Charleston, and the disintegration elsewhere, are all good omens for us; we must not relax one iota, but, on the contrary, pile up our efforts...

"I will issue instructions to General Foster, based on the

reinforcements of North Carolina; but if Schofield come, you had better relieve Foster, who cannot take the field, and needs an operation on his leg. Let Schofield take command, with his headquarters at Beaufort, North Carolina, and with orders to secure Goldsboro' (with its railroad communication back to Beaufort and Wilmington). If Lee lets us get that position, he is gone up.

"I will start with my Atlanta army (sixty thousand), supplied as before, depending on the country for all food in excess of thirty days. I will have less cattle on the hoof, but I hear of hogs, cows, and calves, in Barnwell and the Columbia districts. Even here we have found some forage. Of course, the enemy will carry off and destroy some forage, but I will burn the houses where the people burn their forage, and they will get tired of it."[3]

In a letter to his foster brother, Phil Ewing, written that same day, Sherman said, "I have been wanting to write you for a month but have let days & weeks pass by and now find myself on the edge of civilization about to cut loose to attempt another of those Grand Schemes of War that make me stand out as a Grand Innovator. Of course I know better, that I have done nothing wonderful or new, [taken] in our risks proportional to the ability to provide for them. The Dutch and Greek navigators clung to the land, but others struck out across the ocean depending on the compass, and now who clings to the land is deemed the less safe sailor. So in war. Who clings to a base or defends it is less at ease than one who makes his army strong and doesnt dissipate it by detachments. But let the world draw its own conclusions. I know my enemy and think I have made him feel effects of war that he did not expect. And he now learns how the Power of the United States can reach him in his innermost recesses."[4]

The three peace commissioners appointed by Jefferson Davis sent a note across the Union lines east of Petersburg that day, the 29th, under a flag of truce. Brevet Major General Orlando B. Willcox, temporarily in command of the 9th Corps, sent word to the headquarters of the Army of the Potomac: "Alexander H. Stephens, R.M.T. Hunter, and J.A. Campbell desire to cross my lines, in accordance with an understanding claimed to exist with Lieutenant-General Grant, on their way to Washington, as peace commissioners. Shall they be admitted? They desire an early answer, and to come through immediately; would like to reach City Point to-night. If they cannot do this they would like to come through at 10 o'clock to-morrow morning."[5]

Major General John G. Parke, normally the commander of the 9th Corps, was in temporary command of the Army of the Potomac, for

Meade was on leave, and he passed the buck to Ord, commander of the Army of the James, who was the senior officer in the area, since Grant was also away. Schofield had arrived ahead of his 23rd Corps, being shipped and railroaded from the Tennessee River to Washington, and Grant had taken him down the coast for a look at the defenses of Wilmington and a conference with Terry and Admiral Porter. Ord was also in the dark on the whole thing and sent a telegram to Secretary of War Stanton, meanwhile telling Parke, "Tell them to come to-morrow at 10; it is too late to-night." Stanton replied that night: "This Department has no knowledge of any understanding by General Grant to allow any persons to come within his lines as commissioners of any sort. You will therefore allow no one to come into your lines under such character or profession until you receive the President's instructions, to whom your telegram will be submitted for his directions."[6]

The next morning, 30 January, Stanton wired Ord: "By direction of the President you are instructed to inform the three gentlemen, Messrs Stephens, Hunter and Campbell, that a messenger will be dispatched to them at, or near where they now are, without unnecessary delay." Lincoln then put Major Thomas T. Eckert, superintendent of the military telegraph, on a boat for City Point with a letter addressed to the three Confederates written on the back of a copy of the letter Blair had taken to Jefferson Davis: "I am instructed by the President of the United States to place this paper in your hands with the information that if you pass through the U.S. Military lines it will be understood that you do so for the purpose of an informal conference, on the basis of the letter, a copy of which is on the reverse side of this sheet, and that if you choose to pass on such understanding, and so notify me in writing, I will procure the Commanding General to pass you through the lines, and to Fortress-Monroe, under such military precautions as he may deem prudent; and, at which place you will be met in due time by some person or persons for the purpose of such informal conference. And further that you shall have protection, safe-conduct, and safe return, in all events."[7] In effect, Lincoln was saying that the commissioners must acknowledge that they were negotiating a peace for the "one common country" before he would talk to them.

That same day "General" Singleton returned from Richmond. He told Browning that he had "brought back contracts for seven million dollars worth of Cotton, Tobacco, Rosin and Turpentine, which will make us rich if we can only get it out."[8]

Despite the attempt to negotiate a peace, which Jefferson Davis probably knew was doomed to failure, Confederate authorities continued to secretly build up strength in northern Virginia that day, presumably in preparation for conducting a captured Lincoln through that area to Richmond. The 24th Virginia Cavalry, many of whose men came from that area, was told that it would be sent home on furlough one-half at a time. The men in the first half, however, would take all the regiment's horses with them and the others would stay and fight on foot until their time came.

Rosser's Confederate cavalry left Moorefield, West Virginia that morning, 30 January, heading over Branch Mountain with the train of Union wagons as its objective. The Rebel horsemen found a regiment of Federal infantry blocking the pass, but the 12th Virginia Cavalry charged it and pushed it back in confusion to the town of Medley. There the Confederates found the wagons, guarded by four regiments of infantry and a detachment of cavalry. Rosser sent three of his regiments forward in a dismounted charge while the 12th Virginia circled around the Union flank. The initial attack was repulsed, but then Rosser sent the 35th Virginia Cavalry Battalion, better known as White's Comanches, forward in a mounted charge, supported by two dismounted regiments and one cannon, and this, coupled with the threat to their rear, broke the Federals' line, and they retreated in disorder, abandoning their 95 wagons full of supplies.

Out west of the Mississippi that day, Major General John Pope, famous for losing the second battle of Bull Run in August 1862, was assigned command of a new Military Division of the Missouri. It consisted of the Department of Missouri and the Department of Kansas.

In another command change, Schofield was put in charge of a new Department of North Carolina the next day, the 31st, although by then he was back with his 23rd Corps, or the leading elements of it, which were arriving at Washington and waiting for transports to take them south. Schofield would be subject to Sherman's orders when the latter came within reach of him, but until then Grant wanted to be able to direct Schofield's movements himself without having to go through Foster, to whose department Union troops in North Carolina had recently been transferred from Butler's old Department of Virginia and North Carolina.

In a Confederate command change on the 31st, Lee was finally appointed to fill the position of general-in-chief of the Confederate Army newly created by act of Congress.

The United States Congress passed a landmark piece of legislation itself that day. It approved and sent to the states for ratification an amendment to the Constitution abolishing slavery throughout the country.

In New York the trial of Captain Robert Cobb Kennedy began before the same military commission that was trying Acting Master Beall. Kennedy was charged with being one of the Confederate agents who had set fire to numerous hotels in New York back in November.

Grant returned to City Point on the morning of the 31st to find that the Confederate peace commissioners were still waiting for permission to cross the lines. He forwarded a copy of their request to President Lincoln by telegraph and added, "I have sent directions to receive these gentlemen and expect to have them at my quarters this evening awaiting your instructions." Lincoln replied that afternoon, "A messenger is coming to you on the business contained in your dispatch. Detain the gentlemen in comfortable quarters until he arrives, and then act upon the message he brings as far as applicable."[9]

Word had spread through the troops on both sides during the preceding two days that peace commissioners from the Confederate government were waiting to come through the lines. When a deputation of Union officers went out and conducted the three civilians across no-man's land, troops of both sides lined up to witness the event. "After a few minutes spent in the interchange of civilities," a *New York Times* reporter wrote, "the party came within our lines, at which moment the troops on both sides united in a simultaneous cheer, which seemed to give them greater confidence than they had before exhibited."[10]

It was nearly dark by the time the U.S. Military Railroad, which ran behind the Union lines, brought the three Confederates to Grant's headquarters. "As Grant had been instructed from Washington to keep them at City Point until further orders," Horace Porter wrote, "he conducted them in person to the headquarters steamer, the *Mary Martin*, which was lying at the wharf, made them his guests, and had them provided with well-furnished state-rooms and comfortable meals during their stay. They were treated with every possible courtesy; their movements were not restrained, and they passed part of the time upon the boat, and part of it at headquarters. Stephens was about five feet five inches in height; his complexion was sallow, and his skin seemed shriveled upon his bones. He possessed intellect enough, however, for the whole commission. Many pleasant conversations occurred with him at headquarters, and an officer once remarked, after the close of an interview: 'The Lord seems to have robbed that man's body of nearly all its flesh to make brains of them.'

"The commissioners twice endeavored to draw General Grant out as to his ideas touching the proper conditions of the proposed terms of peace; but as he considered himself purely a soldier, not intrusted with any diplomatic functions, and as the commissioners spoke of negotiations between the two governments, while the general was not willing to acknowledge even by an inference any government within our borders except that of the United States, he avoided the subject entirely, except to let it be known by his remarks that he would gladly welcome peace if it could be secured upon proper terms."[11]

That night Grant wired Stanton: "On my arrival here this morning I received a letter from Messrs. Stephens, Hunter, and Campbell, which I immediately telegraphed the contents of to the President, and sent at the same time a staff officer to receive the gentlemen and conduct them to my quarters to await the action of the President. The gentlemen have arrived, and since their arrival I have been put in possession of the telegraphic correspondence which had been going on for two days previous. Had I known of this correspondence in time these gentlemen would not have been received within our lines."[12] Grant then ordered Parke and Ord to have their armies ready to move on short notice, carrying six days rations, and he wired General Meade, at home in Philadelphia, to return from leave immediately. Lincoln, meanwhile, had sent Secretary of State William H. Seward to Fortress Monroe on Hampton Roads, where the James River flows into Chesapeake Bay, with instructions to "meet, and informally confer with Messrs. Stephens, Hunter, and Campbell, on the basis of my letter to F. P. Blair, Esq., of Jan. 18. 1865, a copy of which you have.

"You will make known to them that three things are indispensable, towit:

1. The restoration of the national authority throughout all the States.
2. No receding, by the Executive of the United States on the Slavery question, from the position assumed theron, in the late Annual Message to Congress, and on preceding documents.
3. No cessation of hostilities short of an end of the war, and the disbanding of all forces hostile to the government.

"You will inform them that all propositions of theirs not inconsistent with the above, will be considered and passed upon in a spirit of sincere liberality. You will hear all they may choose to say, and report it to me.

"You will not assume to definitely consummate anything."[13]

The next day, 1 February, Lincoln wired Grant: "Let nothing which is transpiring, change, hinder, or delay your Military movements, or plans."[14] Grant replied: "There will be no armistice in consequence of the presence of Mr. Stephens and others within our lines. The troops are kept in readiness to move at the shortest notice, if occasion should justify it."[15] Major Eckert arrived at City Point that afternoon and, after delivering Lincoln's letter to the commissioners and seeing their instructions from Jefferson Davis, announced that they could proceed no further. Their mission, to make peace between the "two countries," was not in keeping with Lincoln's letter. Grant then visited the commissioners, who complained that "We do not seem to get on very rapidly with Major Eckert. We are anxious to get to Washington and Mr. Lincoln has promised to see us there."

When Eckert learned that Grant was aboard the *Mary Martin*, he too returned to that boat, where the major remonstrated with the general-in-chief for getting involved in diplomatic matters outside his provence. "Grant was angry with me for years afterward," Eckert wrote, but the general gave in. However, before he left, Eckert did leave the door to peace slightly ajar. He told the commissioners that if they "concluded to accept the terms" they should "inform General Grant."[16] The major then tried to wire a report to Stanton but found that the telegraph was not working, so he proceeded down the James River to Fortress Monroe.

If the telegraph was really malfunctioning the problem did not last long, for Grant wired Stanton that night: "Now that the interview between Major Eckert, under his written instructions, and Mr. Stephens and party has ended, I will state confidentially, but not officially to become a matter of record, that I am convinced, upon conversation with Messrs. Stephens and Hunter, that their intentions are good and their desire sincere to restore peace and union. I have not felt myself at liberty to express even views of my own or to account for my reticency. This has placed me in an awkward position, which I could have avoided by not seeing them in the first instance. I fear now their going back without any expression from any one in authority will have a bad influence. At the same time I recognize the difficulties in the way of receiving these informal commissioners at this time, and do not know what to recommend. I am sorry, however, that Mr. Lincoln cannot have an interview with the two named in this dispatch, if not all three now within our lines. Their letter to me was all that the President's instructions contemplated, to secure their safe conduct, if they had used the same language to Major Eckert."[17]

Grant then returned to the *Mary Martin* and, as Stephens later wrote, with "an anxious disquietude upon his face," told the commissioners that, although Major Eckert was not satisified, he had determined to send them to Fortress Monroe, where they would find Secretary Seward, on his own responsibility.[18] In return, the commissioners gave him a letter, addressed to Eckert, side-stepping the issue of one country or two as best they could: "In reply to your verbal statement that your instructions did not allow you to alter the conditions upon which a passport could be given to us, we say that we are willing to proceed to Fortress Monroe and there to have an informal conference with any person or persons that President Lincoln may appoint on the basis of his letter to Francis P. Blair of the 18th of Jan'y ult. or upon any other terms, or conditions that he may hereafter propose not inconsistent with the essential principles of self government and popular rights upon which our institutions are founded.

"It is our earnest wish to ascertain after a free interchange of ideas and information, upon what principles and terms, if any, a just and honorable peace can be established without the further effusion of blood, and to contribute our utmost efforts to accomplish such a result.

"We think it better to add that in accepting your passport we are not to be understood as committing ourselves to anything, but to carry to this informal conference the views and feelings above expressed."[19]

Grant also wrote to Sherman that day, although there was a good chance that the latter would be out of reach by the time the letter made the trip down the coast. "Without much expectation of its reaching you in time to be of any service," he said, "I have mailed you copies of instructions to Schofield and Thomas...." Then after briefly outlining the verbal instructions he had given to Schofield and informing Sherman that peace commissioners had entered his lines, he said, "I have received your very kind letter in which you say you would decline, or are opposed to, promotion. No one would be more pleased at your advancement than I, and if you should be placed in my position, and I put subordinate, it would not change our relations in the least. I would make the same exertions to support you that you have ever done to support me, and I would do all in my power to make our cause win."[20]

Out in Tennessee on that first day of February, Andrew Johnson, military governor of that state and vice president-elect of the United States, was writing a letter of introduction for inclusion with a much longer letter to General Grant from Mr. J. J. Giers, of Alabama. Johnson described Giers as "a man of high character, standing, and integrity, and thoroughly loyal to the Federal Government. Any statement he may make can be relied upon with implicit confidence." Giers had visited his home state after Hood's retreat to check the political waters there. Among those he talked to was a Major McGaughy of the Confederate Army, who was a brother-in-law of Brigadier General Philip Roddey,

Rebel commander in northern Alabama. "He frankly admitted to me that the affairs of the Confederacy were in a hopeless condition, and that the people were anxious to know the best terms which could be given to Alabama in case of an immediate popular movement for reconstruction. He stated that there was a universal anxiety to have the war come to a close with or without Jeff. Davis' consent, if some reasonable terms could be extended to the people in the disposition of their slaves. If a plan of general emancipation, to be consummated, say within fifteen years, were adopted, he thought that it would be a satisfactory basis for adjustment." Giers said that under such terms the northern three-fourths of the state would be ready to return to the Union. "The chief difficulties in the way of reconstruction in Alabama," Giers said, "are the following: First, rebel soldiers; second, slavery. Minor obstructions, such as pride, perverted patriotism, sympathy for friends in the army, &c., it is believed have vanished before the victorious progress of our arms. There are but few rebel soldiers now in North Alabama, but a squad in a county is sufficient to check any popular movement outside the Federal lines." He said that the four northern tiers of counties had voted against secession in the first place and "the loss of our young men in the war, the destruction of property, the absence of mail facilities, presses, schools, commerce, the suspension of church service, scarcity of food, the falsification of rebel promises, have failed to convince men that secession was the rightful remedy." As for southern Alabama, "We have information through many channels that the feeling for reconstruction [there] is prevalent and strong, and, as some say, more intense than in the northern parts of the State. A wish to save their wealth from devastation and for their own use, heretofore untouched, added to the certainty that their day of security may soon pass away, renders the truth of these accounts in the highest degree probable." He said that the state government was still in the hands of the Rebels, but that "with some change in the policy of the Administration in regard to slavery, the Union men and former secessionists of Alabama believe that they can redeem Alabama and restore her as a valuable State to the Federal Union.... "[21]

Grant was sending his wife's brother, Lieutenant Colonel Frederick Dent, who had been his roommate at West Point and was now an aide on his staff, to Tennessee that day with a letter to Thomas. He also forwarded Sherman's letter to him of 21 January. "At the time of writing it," Grant told Thomas, "General Sherman was not informed of the depletion of your command by my orders. It will be impossible for you at present to move south as he contemplated with the force of infantry as indicated. General Sherman is advised before this of the changes made, and that for the winter you will be on the defensive. I think, however, an expedition from East Tennessee under General Stoneman might penetrate South Carolina well down toward Columbia, destroying the railroad and military resources of the country, thus visiting a portion of the State which will not be reached by Sherman's forces. He might also be able to return to East Tennessee by way of Salisbury, N.C., thus releasing some of our prisoners of war in rebel hands.... Three thousand cavalry would be sufficient force to take.... To save time I will send copy of this to General Stoneman, so that he can begin his preparations without loss of time, and can commence his correspondence with you as to these preparations."[22]

Sherman's forces began their advance into South Carolina on 1 February. He had about 60,000 men, including over 4,000 cavalry troopers, and 68 guns, as well as some 2,500 wagons and 600 ambulances. His immediate opponent was Lieutenant General William J. Hardee, commander of the Department of South Carolina, Georgia and Florida, with garrisons at Augusta, Georgia and Charleston, South Carolina. The Confederates expected Sherman's next objective to be one or the other of those two cities. Sherman considered these Rebels "capable of making a respectable if not successful defense, but utterly unable to meet our veteran columns in the open field." He therefore determined to bypass both cities and to move between them to tear up the railroad that connected them. He was opposed at first only by the cavalry corps of Major General Joseph Wheeler, which Hood had left in Georgia when he had marched toward defeat at Nashville, and these horsemen faded back, avoiding combat. Also present was the cavalry division of Matthew Butler that had come south with Wade Hampton from Lee's army to obtain more horses. However, "I knew full well at the time," Sherman later wrote, "that the broken fragments of Hood's army (which had escaped from Tennessee) were being hurried rapidly across Georgia, by Augusta, to make junction in my front; estimating them at the maximum twenty-five thousand men, and Hardee's, Wheeler's, and Hampton's forces at fifteen thousand, made forty thousand; which, if handled with spirit and energy, would constitute a formidable force, and might make the passage of such rivers as the Santee and Cape Fear a difficult undertaking. Therefore I took all possible precautions and arranged with Admiral Dahlgren and General Foster to watch our progress inland by all the means possible, and to provide for us points of security along the coast.... The question of supplies remained still the one of vital importance, and I reasoned that we might safely rely on the country for considerable quantity of forage and provisions, and that, if the worst came to the worst, we could live several months on the mules and horses of our trains. Nevertheless, time was equally material, and the moment I heard that General Slocum had finished his pontoon-bridge at Sister's Ferry, and that Kilpatrick's cavalry was over the [Savannah] river, I gave the general orders to march, and instructed the columns to aim for the South Carolina Railroad to the west of Branchville."[23]

Far to the north that day, at Patterson's Creek in West Virginia, Rosser's cavalry ended their raid by capturing 80 Federal soldiers, 1,200 cattle, and 500 sheep.

At Richmond, the Confederate secretary of war, James A. Seddon, resigned that day. The Virginia delegation in the Confederate Congress had recently threatened a vote of no confidence in the administration if President Davis did not replace all the members of his cabinet. Seddon was a Virginian himself, and he resigned in reaction to this insult from his home state despite Davis urging him to stay on.

That same day, John Surratt, John Wilkes Booth's accomplice, returned to Washington from his visit to Richmond.

Illinois became the first state to ratify the 13th Amendment, abolishing slavery, that day. And the next day, the second, Rhode Island and Michigan followed suit.

By 2 February Schofield's entire 23rd Corps was encamped on the banks of the Potomac River after completing its trip from the Tennessee. "The distance over which the corps was transfered was nearly fourteen hundred miles, about equally divided between land and water," wrote Assistant Secretary of War Charles A. Dana, the man in charge of the move. "The average time of transportation, from the embarkment on the Tennessee to the arrival on the banks of the Potomac, did not exceed eleven days; and what was still more important was the fact that during the whole movement not a single accident happened causing loss of life, limb, or property, except in a single instance where a soldier improperly jumped from the car, under apprehension of danger, and thus lost his life. Had he remained quiet, he would have been as safe as were his comrades in the same car."[24]

In Washington that morning, Lincoln received word from Seward that he was at Fortress Monroe but that the Confederate commissioners were not there. Major Eckert had tried to send word to Stanton from City Point the night before but the telegraph line from there had been temporarily out of order, so he had waited until he got to Fortress Monroe to send his report from there: "In reply to the letters delivered by me to Messrs. Stephens, Campbell, and Hunter," he said, "they give a copy of their instructions from Jefferson Davis, which I think is verbatim copy of that now in the President's possession. Am positive about the last two words, which differ from the ending of copy delivered by me, and to which the President called my particular attention. I notified them that they could not proceed further unless they complied with the terms expressed in my letter." Lincoln was about to recall both Eckert and Seward to Washington when Stanton brought him the wire that Grant had written the night before. At 9 a.m. Lincoln wired Seward: "Induced by a dispatch of General Grant, I join you at Fort Monroe so soon as I can come." To Grant he telegraphed: "Say to the gentlemen I will meet them personally at Fortress Monroe as soon as I can get there." At the very same hour, Grant was telegraphing Seward: "The gentlemen here have accepted the proposed terms and will start for Fort Monroe at 9.30 a.m."[25]

An aide of one of the Confederate commissioners stayed at City Point to discuss the exchange of prisoners of war, and Grant wired Secretary Stanton that day that he was "making arrangements to exchange about 3,000 prisoners per week. This is as fast and probably faster than they can be delivered to us." He said he wanted disabled Confederates and Rebels from Missouri, Kentucky, Arkansas, Tennessee, and Louisiana (all of which were completely or substantially behind Union lines) sent first "as but few of these will be got in the ranks again, and as we can count upon but little re-enforcement from the prisoners we get." He told the officer in charge of making the arrangements to expect "an exchange man for man until the party having the fewest prisoners is exhausted of all on hand."[26]

Lincoln steamed down the Potomac and Chesapeake Bay and reached Fortress Monroe about dark. There he saw for the first time the letter the commissioners had addressed to Major Eckert after he had left that had caused Grant to send them on to Fortress Monroe. Lincoln sent word over to the Confederates' boat that he would receive them the next morning on his own boat, the *River Queen.*

Shortly after breakfast on 3 February they came over and met with Lincoln and Seward. The diminutive, 90-pound Stephens, whom Lincoln had much admired when the two had been Whig Congressmen together two decades before, was wearing a huge overcoat, and Lincoln was amused when he took it off. He later asked Grant if he did not think, in corn-husking terms, that "it was the biggest shuck and the littlest ear that ever you did see?"[27] It was a friendly meeting. The

Confederates had all served at Washington before the war, and Hunter asked if the capitol's dome was finished. Seward described it for them.

After a few other pleasantries, Stephens got down to business. "Mr. President," he said, "is there no way of putting an end to the present trouble?"

"There is but one way," Lincoln replied, "and that is for those who are resisting the laws of the Union to cease that resistance."

"But is there no other question," Stephens asked, referring to Blair's proposed joint war to drive the French out of Mexico, "that might divert the attention of both parties for a time?"

"The restoration of the Union is a *sine qua non* with me," Lincoln said. All else had to follow that.

"A settlement of the Mexican question in this way would necessarily lead to a peaceful settlement of our own," Stephens insisted.

But Lincoln said he would make no agreement with men in arms against the government of the United States until the question of the restoration of the Union was resolved. Hunter then remarked that King Charles I had dealt with his Parliamentary foes during the English Civil War. "Upon questions of history I must refer you to Mr. Seward," Lincoln replied, "for he is posted in such things. My only distinct recollection of the matter is that Charles lost his head."

That put an end to that subject, but Campbell asked what the North had in mind to do, if the Union was restored, on such questions as Southern representation in Congress, the two Virginias, and the military confiscation of property, including slaves. Lincoln and Seward replied that West Virginia would remain a separate state, that only Congress could rule on who would be admitted to its seats, and that Congress would probably be lenient in its handling of property claims once the passions of war calmed down. But Lincoln said he had no intention of revoking the Emancipation Proclamation, which had not yet been tested in court. Then Seward broke the news to them that Congress had just passed a Constitutional amendment abolishing slavery. Lincoln said that he still favored some form of compensation by the government to the slave owners, but he doubted that Congress would vote the money for it. Seward, however, suggested that if the Southern states returned to the Union in time they might possibly be able to defeat the amendment, which required the approval of three-fourths of the states.

All of this came as quite a shock to the three Confederates. "Mr President," Hunter eventually said, "if we understand you correctly, you think that we of the Confederacy have committed treason; that we are traitors to your government; that we have forfeited our rights, and are proper subjects for the hangman. Is that not about what your words imply?"

There was a pause, and then Lincoln said, "Yes. You have stated the proposition better than I did. That is about the size of it."

The conference went on for about four hours, but the Confederates were bound by Davis's instructions insisting on independence, and Lincoln could give them no more than a few amusing stories and a promise of a liberal use of executive clemency, to the extent that Congress would allow it, once the Union was reestablished.

"Well, Mr Lincoln," Hunter finally said, "we have about concluded that we shall not be hanged as long as you are President: if we behave ourselves."

As the conference was breaking up with a round of handshaking, Lincoln said, "Well, Stephens, there has been nothing we could do for our country. Is there anything I can do for you personally?"

"Nothing," Stephens said. "Unless you can send me my nephew who has been for twenty months a prisoner on Johnson's Island."

"I'll be glad to do it," Lincoln said, his face lighting up. "Let me have his name."[28]

After the Confederates returned to the *Mary Martin*, Seward sent over a black servant in a rowboat with a basket of champagne for the commissioners. Through a boatswain's trumpet Seward told them, "Keep the champagne, but return the negro!"[29]

Maryland, West Virginia, and New York ratified the 13th Amendment on that third day of February. Down in South Carolina that day, the Right Wing of Sherman's army, Howard's Army of the Tennessee, crossed the Salkehatchie River, which was still over its banks due to the recent rains. "The enemy appeared in some force on the opposite bank," Sherman later wrote, "had cut away all the bridges which spanned the many deep channels of the swollen river, and the only available passage seemed to be along the narrow causeways which constituted the common roads."[30] However, two Union divisions were sent to wade across a marshy area known as Whippy Swamp.

"At the command," one witness wrote, "the troops plunge into the timber. So immense are the trees, and so thickly set, that the eye can not reach half pistol range.... the men force their way through the dense undergrowth, tearing their clothing, and scratching face and limbs.... Cypress-knees concealed beneath the water wound their feet at almost every step. Now the water grows deeper.... and the men take off their cartridge-boxes and suspend them from the muzzles of their guns.... Those who have watches, diaries or money place these within their hats.

Now the water reaches to the armpits and occasionally all that can be seen of a short man is his head sticking out of the water."[31] It took three hours for the Federals to reach dry ground on the other side, but when they did, they turned and flanked the Rebels defending the causeways out of their defenses.

General Beauregard reported to Jefferson Davis from Augusta that day: "Three points threatened by enemy are of greatest importance to hold at present: Charleston, Branchville, and Augusta. Sherman is now apparently moving on Branchville." Beauregard said he would like to concentrate all available forces to meet Sherman there, but since those forces (he calculated that they added up to 33,450 men) were scattered, and most of the Army of Tennessee would not even reach Augusta until the tenth, it seemed likely that Sherman would overwhelm any part of his forces that did manage to get to Branchville ahead of him. Beauregard therefore intended to concentrate at Columbia instead, and he urged the president to send him reinforcements there from North Carolina and Virginia. "Ten thousand or 12,000 additional men would insure the defeat of Sherman and the reopening of General Lee's communications with his base of supplies.... When railroad to Branchville shall have been tapped by enemy, General Lee's supplies will have to be sent via Washington, Ga., and Abbeville, S.C."[32]

Davis replied the next day, the fourth, that there were no reinforcements available to send him. "You will endeavor to obtain from Governor Magrath, of South Carolina, and Governor Brown, of Georgia," he said, "whatever auxiliary force they can add, and use all available means to restore absentees to the service. From these sources you should be able to obtain a greater number of men than that named in your dispatch as sufficient to enable you to defeat the enemy."[33]

Schofield, with Major General Jacob D. Cox's 3rd Division of the 23rd Corps, embarked on the fourth for the trip down the coast to Fort Fisher, where he would take command of his new Department of North Carolina.

Lee wrote to the Confederate adjutant and inspector general on the fourth: "I received your telegram of the 1st instant announcing my confirmation by the Senate as General-in-Chief of the Armies of the Confederate States. I am indebted alone to the kindness of His Excellency the President for my nomination to this high and arduous office, and wish I had the ability to fill it to advantage. As I have received no instructions as to my duties, I do not know what he desires me to undertake."[34]

The Confederate peace commissioners returned to Richmond by way of City Point, where they discussed the exchange of prisoners with General Grant. Horace Porter, Grant's aide, then accompanied them on part of their journey through the lines. He said that Stephens appeared to be greatly disappointed at the failure of their mission but was prudent enough not to say much about it. But he did open up on another subject: "We all form our preconceived ideas of men of whom we have heard a great deal," Stephens said, "and I had certain definite notions as to the appearance and character of General Grant; but I was never so completely surprised in all my life as when I met him and found him a person so entirely different from my idea of him. His spare figure, simple manners, lack of all ostentation, extreme politeness, and charm of conversation were a revelation to me, for I had pictured him as a man of a directly opposite type of character, and expected to find in him only the bluntness of the soldier. Notwithstanding the fact that he talks so well, it is plain that he has more brains than tongue.... He is one of the most remarkable men I ever met. He does not seem to be aware of his powers, but in the future he will undoubtedly exert a controlling influence in shaping the destinies of the country."[35] One country, not two; or, at least, so Porter remembered his words.

Grant reassured Secretary Stanton that day that "the appearance of Mr. Stephens and party within our lines has had no influence on military movements whatever. The swamps about Richmond and Petersburg are entirely impassable for artillery if I wanted to move by either flank. But I do not want to do anything to force the enemy from Richmond until Schofield carries out his programme. He is to take Wilmington and then push out to Goldsborough, or as near it as he can go, and build up the road after him. He will then be in a position to assist Sherman if Lee should leave Richmond with any considerable force, and the two together will be strong enough for all the enemy have to put against them.... I shall necessarily have to take the odium of apparent inactivity, but if it results, as I expect it will, in the discomfiture of Lee's army, I shall be entirely satisfied."[36]

However, Grant was not intending to allow his forces operating against Richmond and Petersburg to remain completely idle. Although the Army of the Potomac was solidly entrenched across the railroad that led south to Weldon, North Carolina, and had destroyed the track for a considerable distance to the south, the Federals were sure that the Confederates brought supplies up that line as far as they could and then transferred them to wagons that bypassed the Union lines. That same day, Grant told Meade to send his cavalry out the next morning to try to destroy or capture as many of those wagons as possible, backing up the horsemen with a sizable force of infantry to protect it from any counterattack by the Confederate infantry. Meade replied with an outline of a plan, but asked, "Are the objects to be attained commensurate with the disappointment which the public are sure to entertain if you make any movement and return without some striking result?"[37]

Meade knew that the bulk of any such criticism would fall on himself, not Grant. His relations with the press were never good, and now he was under fire from Congress's powerful Joint Committee on the Conduct of the War, which had just issued its report on the Battle of the Crater, an attempt to capture Petersburg the previous July by blowing a hole in the Confederate lines with gunpowder placed in a mine dug under their earthworks. The attempt had been badly bungled because of poor decisions made by Meade and by Major General Ambrose Burnside, who had then been the commander of the 9th Corps. But Burnside was a friend of influential Senator Ben Wade, chairman of the committee, and the committee had concentrated its criticism on Meade. "It is rather hard under these circumstances to be abused," Meade told his wife, "but I suppose I must make up my mind to be abused by this set, never mind what happens."[38]

"The objects to be attained are of importance," Grant replied that night. "I will telegraph to Secretary Stanton in advance, showing the object of the movement, the publication of which, with the reports of the operations, will satisfy the public."[39]

President Lincoln presented his cabinet with a plan for compensated emancipation on the fifth. He had written a message to be sent to both houses of Congress asking them to empower him to pay $400,000,000 to the slave states if "all resistance to the national authority shall be abandoned and cease, on or before the first day of April next." With this money, the states could recompense the slave owners for their financial losses. Once so empowered by Congress, Lincoln wanted to issue a proclamation offering this inducement and which would further say "that war will cease, and armies be reduced to a basis of peace; that all political offences will be pardoned; that all property, except slaves, liable to confiscation or forfeiture, will be released therefrom, except in cases of intervening interests of third parties; and that liberality will be recommended to congress upon all points not lying with executive control." To the president's surprise, his proposal met with universal opposition from his cabinet. Lincoln argued that another 100 days of war would cost more than what he proposed, not to mention the loss in lives. "But you are all opposed to me," he said with a deep sigh, "and I will not send the message."[40]

"The earnest desire of the President to conciliate and effect peace was manifest," Navy Secretary Welles told his diary, "but there may be such a thing as so overdoing as to cause a distrust or adverse feeling. In the present temper of Congress the proposed measure, if a wise one, could not be carried through successfully. I do not think the scheme could accomplish any good results. The Rebels would misconstrue it if the offer was made. If attempted and defeated it would do harm."[41]

---

1. Dowdey and Manarin, ed., *The Wartime Papers of R. E. Lee,* 886.
2. Richard Wheeler, *Witness to Appomattox* (New York, 1989), 6.
3. Sherman, *Memoirs,* 738-741.
4. Joseph H. Ewing, "The New Sherman Letters," *American Heritage* 38:5 (July-August 1987):40.
5. *Official Records,* 46:II:290.
6. Ibid., 46:II:292.
7. Basler, ed., *Collected Works of Abraham Lincoln,* 8:277-278.
8. Stern, *An End to Valor,* 36.
9. *Official Records,* 46:II:311.
10. Trudeau, *The Last Citadel,* 306-307.
11. Porter, *Campaigning With Grant,* 383.
12. *Official Records,* 46:II:311-312.
13. Basler, ed., *Collected Works of Abraham Lincoln,* 8:250-251.
14. Ibid., 8:252.
15. *Official Records,* 46:II:341.
16. William S. McFeely, *Grant: A Biography* (New York, 1981), 203.
17. *Official Records,* 46:II:342-343.
18. McFeely, *Grant,* 204.
19. *Official Records,* 47:II:193-194.
20. Ibid., 49:I:590-593.
21. Ibid., 49:I:616.
22. Sherman, *Memoirs,* 752-753.
23. Charles A. Dana, *Recollections of the Civil War* (Collier Books edition, New York, 1963), 221-222.
24. *Official Records,* Series II, 8:170.
25. Basler, ed., *Collected Works of Abraham Lincoln,* 8:284.
26. *Official Records,* 46:II:352.
27. Grant, *Memoirs,* 2:423.
28. Foote, *The Civil War,* 3:776-778.

29. Carl Sandburg, *Abraham Lincoln: The War Years*, 1864-1865 (New York, 1939), 754.
30. Sherman, *Memoirs*, 753.
31. Davis, *Sherman's March*, 146.
32. *Official Records*, 47:II:1083.
33. Ibid., 47:II:1090.
34. Dowdey and Manarin, eds., *The Wartime Papers of R. E. Lee*, 888-889.
35. Porter, *Campaigning With Grant*, 384-385.
36. *Official Records*, 46:II:365.
37. Ibid., 46:II:368.
38. Noah Andre Trudeau, *The Last Citadel: Petersburg, Virginia, June 1864-April 1865* (Boston, 1991), 313.
39. *Official Records*, 46:II:368.
40. Sandburg, *The War Years, 1864-1865*, 755.
41. Beale, ed., *Diary of Gideon Welles*, 2:237.

CHAPTER THIRTEEN

It Would Have Been a Terrible Blow

5 - 7 February 1865

At 3 a.m. on 5 February the cavalry division of Brigadier General David M. Gregg, "all that had been left of the Cavalry Corps of the Army of the Potomac when the rest of it had been sent to the Shenanadoah Valley the previous summer, started out on the raid on Confederate supply wagons that Grant had ordered the day before. The horsemen followed the Jerusalem Plank Road south from the Union lines to Ream's Station on the Weldon Railroad. Therethey turned west, heading toward Dinwiddie Court House, which was on the road the wagons were thought to use, "passing deserted Confederate camps *en route*," as one Federal wrote, "where the fires, like the Confederacy, were still burning, but very low."[1]

Dinwiddie Court House was some 10 miles southwest of the Union defenses, not counting the twists and turns or the ups and downs of the various country roads. So at 7 a.m. Meade sent out a sizable force of infantry along shorter routes to cover that ten-mile gap. Major

General Governeur K. Warren's 5th Corps was sent to protect the cavalry's right flank, and Major General Andrew A. Humphreys was sent with two divisions of his 2nd Corps to fill in between Warren and the western end of the Union defenses, which was manned by Humphrey's other division. Contrary to his practice on previous moves, Meade decided to lead this one in person.

Humphreys' column moved south along the Vaughn Road to its crossing of Hatcher's Run, which was found to be dammed and obstructed with fallen trees with a handful of Rebel infantry holding the other side. But by 9:30 a.m. a bridgehead had been secured on the south bank by one brigade of Brigadier General Gershom Mott's 3rd Division of the 2nd Corps. With considerable difficulty, a 100-foot bridge was thrown across the stream, a second brigade crossed over, and a battery of 12-pounder guns was put in position there. Brigadier General Thomas A. Smyth's 2nd Division of Humphreys' 2nd Corps, accompanied by a battery of rifled field guns, turned west up the north bank of Hatcher's Run and seized Armstrong's Mill, where the Duncan Road crossed that stream. By holding the two crossings, Humphreys protected a shortened line of communication between the western end of the Union defenses and Warren's 5th Corps.

Warren's column marched south on the Stage Road, between Humphreys and the cavalry, and eventually came to Monk's Neck Bridge over Rowanty Creek, just downstream from where that stream was formed by the confluence of Hatcher's Run and Gravelly Run. However, the bridge was no longer standing, and there were Confederates dug in on the other side to oppose the crossing. "Reaching the stream, we found it covered with ice, on which we hoped to cross," one Federal remembered. "One of the foremost boys stepped upon it, and it at once gave way, and let him into the water. Just the top of his head stuck out above the fragments of ice. He was fished out as expeditiously as possible, and the idea of crossing in that way was abandoned. Men came down with axes, and proceeded to fell trees across the run on which to cross.... Soon the trees were down, and part of the men crossed, while others kept careful watch on the rebels, and fired rapidly to keep them down. When enough had crossed, perhaps forty or fifty, then every body yelled, and those who had crossed charged the pits, and the rest came crowding over. Some of the rebels surrendered, and a few escaped."[2] By then it was 11 a.m., and it was 1 p.m. by the time a rough bridge was built for the corps' wagons and artillery. However, once across the Rowanty, Warren encountered very little opposition, and his three divisions pushed on to the west, following the Stage Road until it joined the Vaughn Road, which ran on to the southwest. Brigadier General

Charles Griffin's 1st Division proceeded to within two miles of Dinwiddie Court House, while Brigadier General Samuel Crawford's 3rd Division was left to guard the intersection of the Vaughn and Stage Roads and Brevet Major General Romeyn B. Ayres' 2nd Division held the intermediate junction of the Vaughn Road with the Quaker Road, which ran almost due north.

Meanwhile, Smyth's division of the 2nd Corps took position stretching from Hatcher's Run north and northeast to a marshy stream called Rocky Branch, facing, and within about a thousand yards of the southwestern end of the line of Confederate entrenchments. The remaining brigade of Mott's 3rd Division, Brigadier General Robert McAllister's 3rd Brigade, was sent to form on Smyth's right, facing north across the Vaughn Road with its right flank protected by another swamp. However, Humphreys soon discovered that there was still a large gap between Smyth's right and McAllister's left, in the very area most likely to be the target of any Confederate attack. He therefore sent an order to Brevet Major General Nelson Miles, commander of the 1st Division of the 2nd Corps, still holding the western end of the Union fortifications, to send out one of his brigades to take McAllister's place so that the latter could move to the left and connect with Smyth.

Meade, traveling with Humphreys' column, sent word to Grant at 2:30 p.m. via the portable field telegraph, that the 2nd Corps was in position but that he was worried about the four-mile gap between Humphreys and Warren, so he was sending for the 9th Corps' reserve division to fill that gap. It would take many hours, however, for it to arrive. However, it was the smaller gap between Smyth and McAllister that was the real danger spot. For Rebel scouts had spotted this weak point, and it was in close proximity to the main Confederate line. Finally, between 4 and 4:30 p.m., Brevet Brigadier General John Ramsey's 4th Brigade of Miles' 1st Division of the 2nd Corps started taking over McAllister's position. "My arrival, under the circumstances," Ramsey later reported, "was very portentous and opportune."[3] For before McAllister could move west to closeup on Smyth's right a large Confederate force launched an attack aimed right at the gap in the Union line.

"My right regiments were just filing in," McAllister said, "when the attack was made on the picket-line. I then ordered 'double-quick,' and we were moving in rapidly.... The pickets in my new front having come running in without firing a shot, left the enemy right on us before I had my line completed. Regiment after regiment opened on the rebels as fast as they wheeled into position, causing their line to halt and lie down. The left regiment, the Eighth New Jersey Volunteers, under command of Major Hartford, or the left wing of it, had no works, and were exposed to a terrible fire in this unprotected position, but they stood nobly and fought splendidly; not a man of this regiment, or indeed of the whole brigade, left for the rear."[4] Smyth sent three regiments of his own division toward the gap, but McAllister's brigade beat them to it. However, Smyth turned his attached battery and the right of his line to face the oncoming Rebels and add their fire to McAllister's.

The attacking force consisted of three brigades of Major General Henry Heth's division of Lieutenant General A.P. Hill's 3rd Corps of Lee's Army of Northern Virginia. And General Lee had ridden over from his headquarters to watch this attack go in. For ninety minutes the battle raged hot and heavy. Three times the Rebels advanced, three times they were driven back. Once they came within a hundred yards of the Union line and a few Federals started to waver, but the chaplain of the 120th New York started singing "The Battle Cry of Freedom." The song was taken up by the rest of the brigade, "And there is no doubt," one Federal wrote, "that as the strains of music rose above the battle's din many hearts resolved anew to 'rally 'round the flag' whenever danger menaced it."[5]

After the third repulse some new recruits among the Confederates broke and ran for the rear. General Lee rode over to try to rally these men himself, but one of the frightened Rebels cried, "Great God, old man; get out of the way! You don't know nothing!"[6] Brigadier General Clement Evans' division of Major General John B. Gordon's 2nd Corps was brought up on Heth's left, but by then it was too late in the short winter day to attack again. "It was about dark and the flash of the muskets was visible," a Union staff officer remembered. "The enemy's fire slackened, and it became apparent that his attack was ceasing."[7]

"All praise to my gallant brigade," McAllister wrote home to his wife, "and all are willing to award it to us; and well they may, for it saved our army. Had the Rebels succeeded, it would have been a terrible blow to us."[8]

At 6:45 p.m. Meade advised Grant by field telegraph: "The enemy at 5.15 attacked General Humphrey's right, and have been engaging him till this moment. General Humphreys has repulsed all their attacks. I have ordered up to his support not only a division from the Ninth Corps but one from the Sixth Corps. General Warren is in position at Hargrave's, about three miles and a half from here; has met no enemy. General Gregg reports that having occupied Dinwiddie Court-House and hearing nothing of any trains or the enemy, had returned to the crossing of Hatcher's Run by the Malone road. I have sent orders to

General Gregg to return to General Warren and report to that officer unless you send other orders for him. I think the enemy are trying to turn Humphreys' right and cut our communications with our line of works.... I shall leave Humphreys and Warren in their present positions, with directions to support each other. I do not think the cavalry will do anything in the way of destroying trains."[9]

Grant replied thirty minutes later: "Bring Warren and the cavalry back, and if you can follow the enemy up do it. If we can follow the enemy up, although it was not contemplated before, it may lead to getting the South Side [rail]road, or a position from which it can be reached. Change original instructions to give all advantages you can take of the enemy's acts." Meade replied at 8 p.m., "I have withdrawn Warren and the cavalry to this point, directing two divisions to remain on the other side of the run, one to cross to this side as a reserve for contingencies. Humphreys is instructed to await developments, and to attack, if advantageous, and drive the enemy into their works. The enemy have a strong line of works passing through the Clements house.... Unless we can carry this line we can hardly reach the Boydton plank road or South Side Railroad without a flank movement considerably to the left. I presume it was to stop this they attacked Humphreys' right."[10]

Leaving Humphreys in charge at the front, Meade returned to his headquarters, arriving at 10 p.m. There he found a dispatch that Gregg had sent to his chief of staff at 4:20 p.m.: "I arrived at Dinwiddie Court-House at about noon to-day. The Boydton plank road for ten days past has been very little used for wagoning; the only wagons I could hear of and could find by examination up and down the road I captured—eighteen in all.... Owing to the destruction of the bridge on the Boydton plank road and on the Weldon railroad but small amounts of stores are at Belfield. One regiment of cavalry opposed my advance. I have about fifty prisoners, including one colonel and three other commissioned officers."[11] Meade wired the contents of this note to Grant. "A staff officer who carried my last dispatch to General Warren," he added, "reports that, on leaving, three squadrons of Gregg's cavalry came in to Warren, saying the enemy's cavalry had attacked Gregg's rear guard and cut them off. I am a little apprehensive of the enemy's cavalry interposing between Gregg and Warren, and preventing the latter using the road he advanced on to withdraw his artillery and trains. I have, however, sent orders to Gregg to open this road, if possible, and escort back Warren's trains."[12]

Warren's infantry began pulling back at about 11 p.m. "The night was very cold and the troops suffered considerably, many having no blankets or overcoats," a newspaper reporter said. Troops in the 2nd Corps, not having to march, built fires. But the wood was so wet that they produced more smoke than heat. "Many of the boys," one soldier wrote, "went up on the hill above the smoke until they would get so cold they had to come back to the smoke and fire to get warm."[13] At 4 a.m. Gregg's exhausted cavalrymen caught up with Warren's infantry after retracing their steps, but at least they had not been cut off, as Meade had feared. "The cavalry then brought up the rear," Warren later reported, "skirmishing with the enemy and punishing him severely when he came close enough. The night was very cold and the roads were frozen hard before morning. The troops had little rest and no sleep."[14]

The Confederates had also suffered from the cold, and when the morning of the sixth brought nothing more serious than a few tentative probes by the Federals, Lee sent some of the troops who had been called to this flank back toward their camps in the Petersburg defenses. However, Brigadier General John Pegram's division of Gordon's 2nd Corps was ordered to reconnoiter a broad area south of Hatcher's Run. On the left, Walker's Brigade, under the temporary command of Colonel John S. Hoffman, followed the road that ran just south of the stream and passed Dabney's Mill, where the two armies had fought the previous October. The other two brigades advanced from farther to the southwest.

The tentative Union probes that morning were conducted only by the Federal 2nd Corps. However, Meade had meant for both Humphreys and Warren to "move out at once," as he informed Grant in a 7:15 a.m. wire from his headquarters, "to determine whether or not Hill's or any portion of the enemy's force is now outside of their line of works. In case any should be found they are to be driven in."[15] But Warren had thought he was only supposed to hold his corps in readiness to support Humphreys should the latter turn something up. Meade arrived at Warren's headquarters just after noon and straightened him out, and at 1:15 p.m. Warren issued instructions for Crawford's 3rd Division of the 5th Corps to "move out on the Vaughan road to where it turns off to Dabney's Mill, and then follow up that road toward the mill, drive back the enemy, and ascertain the position of his intrenched line said to be there."[16] He also ordered Ayres' 2nd Division to support Crawford and for Gregg's cavalry to push back down the Vaughan Road and across Gravelly Run.

The weary Federal troopers encountered and easily overcame outposts of Confederate cavalry, but then they ran into two brigades of Rebel infantry, part of Pegram's division advancing on a broad front.

The troopers fell back in considerable confusion, but a brigade of Ayres' Federal infantry came to their assistance. Neither side was interested in an all-out fight in this area, and by late afternoon the fighting there had ended. It was a different matter along the rough, back-country road that led past Dabney's Mill. There, just after 2 p.m., the gunfire swelled to a deep roar when Crawford's Division collided with Pegram's other brigade as both probed forward in search of their enemy. Two divisions of Confederate infantry that had been marching back to Petersburg were turned around and marched back at the double quick.

Crawford's three brigades easily drove Colonel Hoffman's one before them to the vicinity of Dabney's Mill, where it took cover in some temporary defenses. Then they drove the Rebels from these as well. The colorbearers of the 97th New York and the 16th Maine raced each other to be the first to reach what appeared to be a large fort in the works that Hoffman's men abandoned. The New Yorker won the race but was greatly disappointed to discover that it was not a fort at all, only a huge pile of sawdust from the mill.

However, the three brigades of Gordon's Division, now commanded by Brigadier General Clement A. Evans since, with Early still in the Shenandoah Valley, Gordon was in command of the whole corps, soon arrived and counterattacked, driving Crawford's men back and retaking the mill. Then Ayres' Union division, minus the brigade sent to bolster the cavalry, came up on Crawford's left and launched its own counterattack, and the mill changed hands again. "The musketry fire on both sides was for a time as terrible as any of the war," a newpaper correspondent wrote. Soon Crawford's brigades began to run short of ammunition, and, as one veteran said, the "best of men will not stand with empty muskets and be shot down."[17]

More Confederate reinforcements arrived—this time Mahone's Division of Hill's 3rd Corps under the temporary command of Brigadier General Joseph Finegan—and the Rebels attacked again. Once more the mill changed hands, although General Pegram was killed and Colonel Hoffman was mortally wounded in this attack. This time the Federal retreat turned into a rout, and part of Brevet Major General Frank Wheaton's 1st Division of the 6th Corps, just arriving from the Petersburg fortifications, was swept away before it ever got into the fight. But the rest of it and Griffin's 1st Division of the 5th Corps soon stabilized the situation, and the Federals established a line not far east of Dabney's Mill as darkness put an end to another day of fighting.

The weather that night was even worse than the night before. "It was bitterly cold," one Federal soldier complained, "and we were soaked with rain, which froze and stiffened our clothes under the influence of the wind. We built fires, but they were of little avail. The rain changed into snow and we finally rolled up in our blankets and slept the sleep of exhaustion, wet as we were." The Rebels had things no better. "During the evening the cooks brought to the men in line of battle a small pone of bread each," one of Finegan's men remembered, "the first morsel since early morning; then these hungry soldiers wrapped their shivering frames into wet blankets and slept as best they could under their brush shelters on the frozen ground, while the pickets paced their beats in front to watch the enemy."[18]

Lee assumed command of all Confederate forces that day—"at least two years too late," as a Confederate staff officer put it.[19] Also that day, Major General John C. Breckinridge, former vice president of the United States and the 1860 presidential candidate of the Southern wing of the Democratic Party, succeeded James Seddon as Confederate secretary of war. Also, the Confederate peace commissioners returned to Richmond that day and submitted their report to President Davis, who promptly forwarded it to Congress. "The enemy refused to enter into negotiations with the Confederate States, or with any of them separately," he said in his cover letter, "or to give to our people any other terms or guarantee than those which the conqueror may grant, or to permit us to have peace on any other basis than our unconditional submission to their rule, coupled with the acceptance of their recent legislation, including an amendment to the Constitution for the emancipation of all the negro slaves, and with the right on the part of the Federal Congress to legislate on the subject of the relations between the white and black population of each State. Such is, as I understand, the effect of the amendment to the Constitution which has been adopted by the Congress of the United States."[20] That night Davis appeared unannounced at a public meeting that had been hurriedly called at Metropolitan Hall to discuss the situation. He denounced Lincoln, calling him "His Majesty Abraham the First," and said that Lincoln and Seward might soon find that "they had been speaking to their masters" when they demanded unconditional surrender.[21]

On the morning of the seventh, Warren got his forces reorganized to suit him, and at 10 a.m. he ordered Crawford to "move out from our right near Armstrong's Mill and attack the enemy."[22] This advance was, as Meade later explained to Grant, "for the morale of the command," giving the troops a chance to redeem themselves for their rout of the day before.[23] "The enemy's pickets were found on the same intrenched lines as on the preceding day," Warren reported, "but in stronger force. General Baxter's brigade drove them out." Two brigades from Wheaton's division of the 6th Corps were then put in position to secure Crawford's flanks, and the latter advanced again about 6 p.m. and drove the Confederates back to Dabney's Mill, regaining part of the battlefield of the day before and burying the dead found there. "I did not think it proper to make more extensive operations in the severe storm which prevailed all day," Warren reported, "having instructions not to do so without I was confident of great advantages."[24]

Grant and Meade had already decided, before the fight of the previous afternoon, that the expedition had accomplished about all that it could. They did, however, decide to extend their permanent defenses down to Hatcher's Run at Armstrong's Mill. The cavalry would then picket the northeast bank of that stream to cover the army's flank and rear. "In view of the bad weather," Grant told Meade, "the troops had better be got back to the position you intend them to occupy." He also informed Meade that "I will go to Washington to-morrow, or as soon as you notify me the troops now out are in the new position they are to occupy. I was summoned some two weeks since to appear before the Committee on the Conduct of the War."[25]

---

1. Trudeau, *The Last Citadel,* 312.
2. Ibid., 312-313.
3. *Official Records,* 46:I:207.
4. Ibid., 46:I:238-239.
5. Trudeau, *The Last Citadel,* 316.
6. Douglas Southall Freeman, *R. E. Lee* (New York, 1934-1935), vol. 3, 535-536, n. 64.
7. Trudeau, *The Last Citadel,* 316.
8. Ibid.
9. *Official Records,* 46:II:389.
10. Ibid., 46:II:390.
11. Ibid., 46:II:409.
13. Trudeau, *The Last Citadel,* 317.
14. *Official Records,* 46:I:254.
15. Ibid., 46:II:417.
16. Ibid., 46:I:254.
17. Trudeau, *The Last Citadel,* 319.
18. Ibid., 320-321.
19. Henry Kyd Douglas, *I Rode With Stonewall* (Chapel Hill, 1940), 312.
20. *Official Records,* 46:II:446.

21. John B. Jones, *A Rebel War Clerk's Diary*, condensed edition, Earl Schenck Miers, editor (New York, 1958), 494.
22. *Official Records*, 46:I:256.
23. Ibid., 46:II:448.
24. Ibid., 46:I:256.
25. Ibid., 46:II:447-448.

CHAPTER FOURTEEN

Come Retribution

7 - 18 February 1865

Down in South Carolina, Sherman's army struggled its way through the swamps and over the swollen streams. By the seventh, in the midst of a rain storm, the Federals were approaching the railroad connecting Augusta with Charleston. General Howard was with Blair's 17th Corps as it approached the small town of Midway on the line, and five miles out he began to deploy the leading division in order to be ready for battle. "Sitting on his horse by the road-side," Sherman wrote, "he saw a man coming down the road, riding as hard as he could, and as he approached he recognized him as one of his own 'foragers,' mounted on a white horse, with a rope bridle and a blanket for a saddle. As he came near he called out, 'Hurry up, general; we have got the railroad!' So, while we, the generals, were proceeding deliberately to prepare for a serious battle, a parcel of our foragers, in search of plunder, had got ahead and actually captured the South Carolina Railroad, a line of vital importance to the rebel Government.

"As soon as we struck the railroad," Sherman said, "details of men were set to work to tear up the rails, to burn the ties and twist the bars. This was a most important railroad, and I proposed to destroy it completely for fifty miles, partly to prevent a possibility of its restoration and partly to utilize the time necessary for General Slocum to get up.

"The country thereabouts was very poor, but the inhabitants mostly remained at home. Indeed, they knew not where to go. The enemy's cavalry had retreated before us, but his infantry was reported in some strength at Branchville, on the farther side of the Edisto; yet on the appearance of a mere squad of our men they burned their own bridges—the very thing I wanted, for we had no use for them, and they had."[1]

General Howard received a message from Major General Joe Wheeler, commander of the Cavalry Corps of the Confederate Army of Tennessee, that day: "I have the honor to propose that if the troops of your army be required to discontinue burning the houses of our citizens I will discontinue burning cotton."[2]

Grant was also concerned with cotton that day. He sent a telegram to Secretary Stanton on the seventh in which he uncharacteristically let his temper show, but he won his point: "A.M. Laws is here with a steamer partially loaded with sugar and coffee, and a permit from the Treasury Department to go through into Virginia and North Carolina, and to bring out 10,000 bales of cotton. I have positively refused to adopt this mode of feeding the Southern army unless it is the direct order of the President." A few hours later Stanton replied: "The President directs that you will regard all trade permits, licenses, or privileges of every kind, by whomsoever signed and by whomsoever held, as subject to your authority and approval as commander of the U. S. forces in the field, and such permits as you deem prejudicial to the military service by feeding or supporting the rebel armies or persons in hostility to the Government you may disregard and annul, and if necessary to the public safety seize the property of the traders. In short, the President orders that you, 'as being responsible for military results, must be allowed to be judge and master on the subject of trade with the enemy.'"[3]

That same day "General" Singleton left Washington for New York to secure financing for all the Southern goods he had contracted for, while Lincoln was writing a note to Grant that would be passed on to Singleton's partners for him to carry to City Point. It said: "Gen. Singleton, who bears you this claims that, he already has arrangements made if you consent to bring a large amount of Southern produce through your lines. For its bearing on our finances I would be glad for this to be done if it can be without injuriously disturbing your military operations, or supplying the enemy. I wish you to be judge and master on these points. Please see and hear him fully, and decide whether anything, and if anything, what can be done in the premises."[4]

General Sheridan was writing to the adjutant general's office in Washington that day about a woman who had evidently asked permission to go to the relief of suffering families in the Shenandoah Valley: "A lady so easily deceived is safest at home," he said. "The worst case of distress in this Valley was the case of old Mr. Hupp, who lives near Strasburg. I issued to him thirty days' rations, and afterward found that he had six months' supplies buried; two sons in the rebel army; and at one time Mr. White, one of my scouts, found $10,000 in gold under his floor, and a sword that belonged to Stonewall Jackson. The gold was returned to him, and he has not since lost it, unless he sent it South."[5]

Maine and Kansas ratified the anti-slavery Thirteenth Amendment that day. Massachusetts and Pennsylvania did the same the next day, the eighth.

When it had become known that not only Secretary Seward but the president himself had gone to Hampton Roads to meet with Confederate commissioners, "The perturbation in Washington was something which cannot be readily described," as reporter Noah Brooks, a friend of Lincoln's, put it. "The Peace Democrats went about the corridors of the hotels and the Capitol, saying that Lincoln had at last come to their way of thinking.... The radicals were in a fury of rage. They bitterly complained that the President was about to give up the political fruits which had been already gathered from the long and exhausting military struggle." Some had even hinted at impeachment. "When the President and the Secretary of State returned to Washington... the tenseness of political feeling in Congress was slightly relaxed... ," Brooks said. "But with common consent everybody agreed that the President must at once enlighten Congress as to the doings of himself and Secretary Seward and the rebel commissioners."[6] A long and acrimonious debate in the Senate led, on 8 March, to a resolution calling on the president for information concerning the Hampton Roads conference. The House of Representatives passed a similar resolution the same day with far less ado.

General A.J. Smith telegraphed Secretary of War Stanton on the eighth from Cairo, Illinois. He and his so-called Detachment Army of the Tennessee were on their way down the Mississippi to New Orleans, where they would become part of Major General E.R.S. Canby's Military Division of West Mississippi. "I arrived at 1 p.m. with two divisions of my command," he said. "Will coal and take on board supplies and leave for my destination. My other command follows me. I am now without a heading or identity for my command. Unless I receive a number or a name for my command, I must style myself the Wandering Tribe of Israel. Please telegraph me immediately and give me a number." General Halleck answered that night: "Continue on in your exodus as the Wandering Tribe of Israel. On reaching the land of Canby you will have a number and a name."[7]

In New York on the eighth, Acting Master's Mate John Yates Beall was sentenced to death for espionage and violations of the laws of war.

From his headquarters near Petersburg that day, Lee was writing to the secretary of war: "All the disposable force of the right wing of the army has been operating against the enemy beyond Hatcher's Run since Sunday. Yesterday, the most inclement day of the winter, they had to be retained in line of battle, having been in the same condition the two previous days and nights. I regret to be obliged to state that under these circumstances, heightened by assaults and fire of the enemy, some of the men had been without meat for three days, and all were suffering from reduced rations and scant clothing, exposed to battle, cold, hail, and sleet. I have directed Colonel Cole, Chief Commissary, who reports that he has not a pound of meat at his disposal, to visit Richmond and see if nothing can be done. If some change is not made and the Commissary Department reorganized, I apprehend dire results. The physical strength of the men, if their courage survives, must fail under this treatment. Our cavalry has to be dispersed for want of forage. Fitz Lee's and Lomax's divisions are scattered because supplies cannot be transported where their services are required. I had to bring William H.F. Lee's division forty miles Sunday night to get him in position. Taking these facts in connection with the paucity of our numbers, you must not be surprised if calamity befalls us."[8] Jefferson Davis endorsed on this letter: "This is too sad to be patiently considered, and cannot have occurred without criminal neglect or gross incapacity."[9]

Down in South Carolina on the eighth, Sherman answered the note Wheeler had sent to Howard the day before: "I hope you will burn all cotton and save us the trouble. We don't want it, and it has proven a curse to our country. All you don't burn I will. As to private houses occupied by peaceful families, my orders are not to molest or disturb them, and I think my orders are obeyed. Vacant houses being of no use to anybody, I care little about, as the owners have thought them of no use to themselves. I don't want them destroyed, but do not take much care to preserve them."[10]

Also in South Carolina that day, Mary Boykin Chesnut, wife of Brigadier General James Chesnut, Jr., recorded in her diary that her husband, commander of the South Carolina reserves, received a coded message on the eighth using a new key phrase for the cypher. The old phrase, "Complete Victory," had been replaced by a new one. These key phrases were not only used to indicate which alphabet in a 26-alphabet matrix was used to encode the message but also served as a slogan, indicating the government's latest policy or attitude. The new phrase was, "Come Retribution."

It is probable that this new key phrase and slogan was connected with the Confederate plan to capture Lincoln, which seems to have moved into high gear after the failure of the peace commission made it evident to all that Lincoln would settle for nothing less than the total destruction of the Confederate government. Lieutenant Cornelius Hart Carlton was in the 24th Virginia Cavalry, the unit that had been told it would be sent on furlough a half at a time, and he was in the half that was sent home first. He recorded in his diary that on 9 February 1865, after only a week at home, he received orders from his captain to organize a five-man team to patrol the area south of the Rappahannock River for the next thirty days. This was an area through which a captured Lincoln would be brought to Richmond. Through the rest of February and into March men from the regiment, supposedly on furlough, were rotated into and out of the patrol.

A massive rally was held at the African Church in Richmond that day. The site was chosen because of its vast capacity. Beginning about noon, speaker after speaker sought to raise the patriotic fervor of the audience and, through the medium of newspaper coverage, of the Confederacy as a whole—"to reanimate the people for another carnival of blood" was how a war department clerk put it.[11] A Rebel cavalryman who attended said he "sat for hours under the spell of the eloquent and earnest addresses which were made, and was filled with renewed hope and determination." An artilleryman said, "Resolutions were passed pledging ourselves to a vigorous prosecution of the war, till our independence be won, be the cost what it may in time, treasure and blood." Secretary of State Judah Benjamin told the audience, "We know in our hearts that this people must conquer its freedom or die." As a means of strengthening the army for a fight to the death, the Davis administration proposed to enlist slaves. "Let us say to every negro who wishes to go into the ranks on the condition of being made free—'Go and fight, you are free,'" Benjamin said.[12] General Lee, Benjamin said, had indicated that he would have to abandon Richmond if he was not soon reinforced. The Confederate senate had just voted down, in secret session, a proposal to put 200,000 slaves in the army, but Davis was going over the senate's head to the people and the states. Virginia, Benjamin said, could send 20,000 slaves into the trenches within twenty days.

Ironically, the pro-Union shadow government of the state of Virginia, located at Alexandria, ratified the Thirteenth Amendment that same day.

In southern Virginia on the ninth, Brevet Major General David M. Gregg, the very capable commander of Meade's only cavalry division, turned over his command to his senior brigade commander. On the third, he had submitted his resignation of his commissions in both the volunteer and regular service—he was officially a captain in the 6th U.S. Cavalry—and word had arrived on the eighth that it had been accepted by the President. The reason for his resignation has never come to light.

Grant was writing to General Canby on the ninth: "I have ordered General Grierson to report to you to take chief command of your cavalry operating from Mobile Bay. I do not mean to fasten on you commanders against your judgment or wishes, but you applied for Averell, I supposed for that service. I have no faith in him, and cannot point to a single success of his except in his reports. Grierson, on the contrary, has been a most successful cavalry commander. He set the first example in making long raids by going through from Memphis to Baton Rouge. His raid this winter on to the Mobile and Ohio Railroad was most important in its results and most successfully executed. I do not think I could have sent you a better man than Grierson to command your cavalry on an expedition to the interior of Alabama. Unless you go yourself I am afraid your other troops will not be so well commanded. What is wanted is a commander who will not be afraid to cut loose from his base of supplies, and who will make the best use of the resources of the country. An army the size of the one you will have can always get to some place where they can be supplied, if they should fail to reach the point started for."[13]

The advance element of Schofield's 23rd Corps, Major General Jacob

Cox's 3rd Division, landed at Fort Fisher that day, after being delayed by a gale off Cape Hatteras, and Schofield assumed command of the new Department of North Carolina. "The fort still bore evidence of the extraordinary bombardment it had undergone," Cox noted, "and its broad sandy interior was thickly strewn with great shells rusted red in the weather, and resembling nothing so much as a farmer's field strewn with pumpkins."[14]

That same day, Major General Quincy Gillmore replaced Major General John G. Foster in command of the Department of the South, which was made up of the Union troops along the Atlantic coast of South Carolina, Georgia, and Florida. He had commanded the same department back in 1863, failing in his major objective: the capture of Charleston. He and most of his troops, the 10th Corps, had been transferred to Ben Butler's Army of the James in the spring of 1864, but he was too cautious and ineffectual even for Butler, who had relieved him. He had been at Washington when Early's Confederates had threatened the capital and had been severely injured in a fall from his horse while in temporary command of the 19th Corps. Now, with his injury healed and Foster suffering from an old one of his own, he was back on the South Carolina coast. But this time he was subject to the orders of William T. Sherman.

Another command change took place the next day, the tenth. Schofield's previous command, the Department of the Ohio, was discontinued. Its garrisons in eastern Tennessee became part of Thomas's Department of the Cumberland, while its District of Kentucky became the Department of Kentucky, with Major General J. M. Palmer in command. Both departments were part of Sherman's Military Division of the Mississippi, but the order making the change indicated that, in Sherman's absence, all the troops in both departments were subject to Thomas's orders, "except the posts on the east bank of the Mississippi River, which will be subject to Major-General Canby's orders in movements for protecting navigation of that river."[15]

Grant arrived at Washington on the tenth, where Congressman Elihu Washburne, his fellow townsman from Galena, Illinois, who was considered the watchdog of the Treasury, had been waiting to fill him in on the subject of cotton speculations.

President Lincoln was visited that day by Alexander Stephens' nephew, Lieutenant John A. Stephens, whom he had ordered released from the Johnson's Island prisoner of war camp. Lincoln gave him a pass through the Union lines and a photograph of himself. "You had better take that along," the President told him. "It is considered quite a curiosity down your way, I believe."[16] He also gave the lieutenant a note to deliver to his uncle, the Confederate vice president: "According to our agreement, your nephew, Lieut. Stephens, goes to you, bearing this note. Please, in return, to select and send to me, that officer of the same rank, imprisoned at Richmond, whose physical condition most urgently requires his release."[17]

That same day, in reply to the resolutions passed two days before, Lincoln sent a message to both houses of Congress forwarding copies of all the correspondence relating to the meeting with the Confederate commissioners. "The House, as seen from the reporter's gallery," Noah Brooks wrote, "when the President's message and accompanying documents relating to the Hampton Roads conference came in, was a curious and interesting study.... Instantly, by unanimous consent, all other business was suspended, and the communication from the President was ordered to be read. The reading began in absolute silence. Looking over the hall, one might say that the hundreds seated or standing within the limits of the great room had been suddenly turned to stone.... It is no exaggeration to say that for a little space at least no man so much as stirred his hand. Even the hurrying pages, who usually bustled about the aisles waiting upon the members, were struck silent and motionless. The preliminary paragraphs of the message recited the facts relating to F.P. Blair, Sr.'s, two journeys to Richmond, and, without the slightest appearance of argument, cleared the way for the departure of Secretary Seward to meet the commissioners at Fort Monroe. Then came the three indispensible terms given in the instructions to the Secretary.... When the clerk read the words at the close of the instructions to Seward, 'You will not assume to definitely consummate anything,' there ran a ripple of mirth throughout the great assembly of congressmen; and the tenseness with which men had listed to the reading was for the first time relaxed.... As the reading of the message and documents went on, the change which took place in the moral atmosphere of the hall of the House was obvious. The appearance of grave intentness passed away, and members smilingly exchanged glances as they began to appreciate Lincoln's sagacious plan for unmasking the craftiness of the rebel leaders; or they laughed gleefully at the occasional hard hits with which the wise President demolished the pretensions of those whose fine-spun logic he had so ruthlessly swept aside in the now famous interview.... When the reading was over, and the name of the writer at the end of the communication was read by the clerk with a certain grandiloquence, there was an instant and irrepressible storm of applause, begun by the members on the floor, and taken up by the people in the gallery.... It was like a burst of refreshing rain after a long and heartbreaking drought."[18]

Also that day, Ohio and Missouri ratified the Thirteenth Amendment.

Captain Thomas W.T. Richards led a small force of Mosby's rangers in a raid on Williamsburg that day. They chased the Union garrison into nearby Fort Magruder and captured a few horses. Early on the morning of the eleventh the Rebels attacked the fort's picket line but were driven off. Meanwhile, the Confederate troops north of the James River were on alert to move at short notice, probably in case Mosby's raiders stirred up a Union countermove. Evidently the Rebels were testing to see how sensitive the Federals were to any unusual activity in the area, as the plan to capture Lincoln and bring him to Richmond moved into high gear.

Down in South Carolina Sherman's forces were advancing again. "Having sufficiently damaged the railroad," he said, "and effected the junction of the entire army, the general march was resumed on the 11th, each corps crossing the South Edisto by separate bridges."[19] Kilpatrick's cavalry, meanwhile, had been sent to the left flank to keep up the pretention of threatening Augusta, where the Army of Tennessee was beginning to arrive, for as long as possible.

Up in North Carolina the next day, the twelfth, Schofield tried to outflank the Confederate defenses across the Federal Point peninsula north of Fort Fisher, even though the rest of his 23rd Corps had not yet arrived. Cox's division plus Ames's division of Terry's force marched up the beach that night while the navy carried some pontoons up the coast. When these were landed the Federals would use them to cross Myrtle Sound and get behind the Rebel line. However, the weather refused to cooperate. A northeaster blew up and the night was so stormy that the pontoons could not be landed, so the infantry marched back to camp before morning.

Sherman's forces crossed the main stream of the Edisto River on the twelfth and marched into Orangeburg, where a store and some cotton were already on fire when they arrived. "The railroad and depot were destroyed by order," Sherman wrote, "and no doubt a good deal of cotton was burned, for we all regarded cotton as hostile property, a thing to be destroyed." On the morning of the thirteenth Sherman personally joined John Logan's 15th Corps as it crossed the North Edisto and turned toward Columbia, the capital of South Carolina, "where it was supposed," Sherman later said, "the enemy had concentrated all the men they could from Charleston, Augusta, and even from Virginia." That night an officer of Sherman's staff fell in with a Confederate officer on the road who thought he was another Rebel. From him the Federals learned that the only opposition they would find at Columbia was Wade Hampton's cavalry. "The fact was," Sherman wrote, "that General Hardee, in Charleston, took it for granted that we were after Charleston; the rebel troops in Augusta supposed they were 'our objective;' so they abandoned poor Columbia to the care of Hampton's cavalry, which was confused by the rumors that poured in on it, so that both Beauregard and Wade Hampton, who were in Columbia, seem to have lost their heads."[20]

On the thirteenth, Grant, who was back at City Point, wired Halleck at Washington: "I wish every effort would be made to pay the army up to the 31st of December, 1864. There is much dissatisfaction felt by officers and men who have families partially or wholly dependent upon their pay for a support on account of delay in receiving their dues. Will you please submit this matter to the Secretaries of War and Treasury."[21]

Meanwhile, that same day, Halleck was writing a long letter to Grant about the problems he was having in getting the cavalry ready for the spring campaign. He calculated that during the previous year the cavalry of the Union army had used up 180,000 horses, as well as 93,394 carbines, 90,000 sabers and 71,000 pistols. "Expenses of cavalry in horses, pay, forage, rations, clothing, ordnance, equipments, and transportations, $125,000,000, is certainly a pretty large sum for keeping up our cavalry force for one year," he added. After passing over Meade's, Ord's, and Sheridan's cavalry, and noting that Sherman was keeping his cavalry mounted on horses captured from the enemy, he got down to cases: "In the Department of the Ohio (now Kentucky) there were issued to General Burbridge for his Saltville expedition 6,000 horses. On his return 4,000 were reported lost or unserviceable. When Hood commenced his march against Nashville General Thomas' immediate command had only about 5,000 effective cavalry, but between the 1st of October and 31st of December all horses purchased in the West were sent to his chief of cavalry, the issue amounting to 23,000, and including those sent to General Burbridge during the same period, 29,000, in three months to General Thomas' entire command. As Generals Wilson and Burbridge have made requisitions since that period for 14,000 additional horses, it is presumed that about the same number were lost or disabled during that period of three months. As soon as General Thomas determined to make no farther advance during the winter, and General Canby was directed to assume active operations in the field, orders were given to resume issues to his (Canby's) command in preference to all others. In General Canby's entire division there were about 30,000 effective cavalrymen, of which only about one-half were mounted. As, however, his cavalry force was so disproportionate to his infantry, his requisitions are for only 6,000 horses, which will soon be filled. Major-General Dodge has made a requisition for 1,000 horses to be sent to Fort Leavenworth to remount some regiments to be sent against the Indians on the Overland Mail Route.... Major-General Thomas has made a requisition for 3,000 cavalry horses to be sent to General Stoneman in East Tennessee. This requisition will be filled next after those of Generals Dodge and Canby. No issue of cavalry horses has been made to the Department of Arkansas for several months, and about one-half of the cavalry there are entirely dismounted.

"In regard to the enormous surplus of cavalry in the Western and Southwestern armies, as compared with infantry, I would remark that it has resulted in a great measure from the repeated requisitions of Generals Rosecrans, Banks, and others for increase of mounted forces, and their mounting infantry as cavalry. They were repeatedly informed that so large a cavalry force could not be supported, and experience has placed this question beyond doubt. Moreover, no general can command and efficiently employ, in our broken and wooded country, a body of cavalry of more than 10,000 or 12,000 men. In regard to the Department of North Carolina, which is nearly destitute of cavalry, I would respectfully suggest that some regiment, or a brigade, be sent there from General Sheridan's command. The mounted infantry and militia in Kentucky and Tennessee have destroyed a vast number of horses, without rendering any effective service in the field. The same remark is partly applicable to the mounted militia in Missouri. The terms of service of many of these will soon expire. There was with General Thomas' army on the 1st of January about 19,000 mounted men, about 16,000 of which were near Eastport. A part of Knipe's division was then dismounted at Louisville. It has since been remounted and sent to General Canby. This will leave General Thomas about 15,000. General Wilson wants 10,000 additional remounts for the spring campaign. It is certain that so large a number of remounts cannot be supplied to that army, even if we make no further issue to other cavalry troops supplied from the West. Neither will it be possible, in my opinion, for such a cavalry force to be subsisted in any operations against Selma or Montgomery. Like all extravagant undertakings, its very magnitude will defeat it; the horses will starve, the equipments be lost, and the men left on foot along the road. Moreover, I learn from the Quartermaster General that he is now some $180,000,000 in debt, and that unless more money is soon raised it will be very difficult to purchase supplies for the army.... It is also proper to determine when the purchase of remounts shall be resumed for Sheridan and the Armies of the Potomac and the James. Considering that the Quatermaster's Department cannot now supply forage to the animals we have on hand, I would not advise purchases to be commenced before the middle of March, and I doubt whether navigation will be sufficiently opened by that time to enable us to bring forward horses and supplies. The railroads of the North cannot do this."[22]

Grant wired Thomas, again headquartered at Nashville, on the fourteenth: "General Canby is preparing a movement from Mobile Bay against Mobile and the interior of Alabama. His forces will consist of about 20,000 men, besides A.J. Smith's command. The cavalry you have sent to Canby will be debarked at Vicksburg. It, with the available cavalry already in that section, will move from there eastward in co-operation. Hood's army has been terribly reduced by the severe punishment you gave it in Tennessee, by desertion consequent upon their defeat, and now by the withdrawal of many of them to oppose Sherman. I take it a large portion of the infantry has been so withdrawn. It is asserted in the Richmond papers, and a member of the rebel Congress said a few days since in a speech, that one-half of it had been brought to South Carolina to oppose Sherman. This being true, or even if it is not true, Canby's movement will attract all the attention of the enemy and leave an advance from your stand-point easy. It think advisable, therefore, that you prepare as much of a cavalry force as you can spare and hold it in readiness to go south. The object would be three-fold:

"First. To attack as much of the enemy's force as possible to insure success to Canby. Second. To destroy the enemy's line of communications and military resources. Third. To destroy or capture their forces brought into the field. Tuscaloosa and Selma probably would be the points to direct the expedition against. This, however, would not be so important as the mere fact of penetrating deep into Alabama. Discretion should be left with the officer commanding the expedition to go where, according to the information he may receive, he will best secure the objects named above. Now that your force has been so much depleted I do not know what number of men you can put into the field. If not more than 5,000 men, however, all cavalry, I think it will be sufficient. It is not desirable that you should start this expedition until the one leaving Vicksburg has been three or four days out, or even a week. I do not know when it will start, but will inform you by telegraph as soon as I learn. If you should hear through other sources before hearing from me you can act on the information received."

Thomas replied that night: "I can send on the expedition you propose about 10,000 men. They are fully equipped now, with a battery to each division composed of four guns, six caissons, and each carriage drawn by eight horses. I will have the command in readiness to move promptly upon receiving orders."[23]

Wilson, still camped along the Tennessee River at Gravelly Springs, Alabama, wrote to Thomas's chief of staff that day. "My scouts have just returned from about seventy miles south of here. They confirm original reports. Say all of Hood's infantry has gone [to] South Carolina, but that the country is full of Forrest's men hunting up the absent men from the furloughed Mississippi regiments.... The people do not estimate Forrest's whole force at more than 5,000 men, and only 3,000 of whom are reported mounted.... The people say the rebels are expecting an attack against Mobile, and that the rebel authorities are doing their utmost to reorganize the force in Mississippi and Alabama and put in the field a large number of negro troops. The enrollment is nearly completed, and they expect to have 200,000 under arms in sixty days."[24]

Stoneman, meanwhile, was in the midst of preparing for the raid from eastern Tennessee into the Carolinas. Mostly he needed more horses. And he was appointed on the fourteenth to the command of the District of East Tennessee, which had just been transfered from the now-defunct Department of the Ohio to Thomas's Department of the Cumberland.

Over on the North Carolina coast, Schofield tried again to outflank the Confederate line north of Fort Fisher on the night of the fourteenth. This time the pontoons were put on their wagons and the few horses and mules on hand were used to haul them along the beach. But again the movement failed. The sand, where dry, proved too deep and soft for the teams, and nearer the water the high tide and surf was too much for them. Before they reached their appointed position the moon rose and revealed the marching troops and the ships moving into position to provide cover to the Rebels, who shifted troops to meet this flanking movement.

Down in South Carolina on the fourteenth, Sherman was still traveling with Logan's 15th Corps of Howard's Army of the Tennessee. When the head of the column reached the Little Congaree River it found that the stream had overflowed to cover a number of cotton fields with slimy mud, the bridge was down, and there was a new-looking

Confederate fort on the other side. Sherman sent a brigade off to the left to cross higher upstream and drive off any Rebels on the other side. Then a working party repaired the bridge in less than an hour. Sherman himself crossed over and camped just beyond the Little Congaree that night.

The next day, the fifteenth, Halleck replied to Grant's telegraph about paying the troops in Meade's and Ord's armies: "These troops have been paid generally to a later period than those in the West and South. Some are unpaid for seven or eight months. The fault is not in the Pay Department, but a want of money in the Treasury. There will be a change of the head in a few days, but whether that will help us any remains to be seen.

"Officers and members of Congress have suggested that the money be given to the Pay Department in preference to the Quartermaster's, Commissary's, and other supply departments. You will readily perceive by doing this we would necessarily cut off the supplies of our army. I understand that the Quartermaster's Department is already some $180,000,000 in debt, and that until a part, at least, of this is paid it will be almost impossible to purchase and transport supplies. The manufacturers cannot furnish cloth, or the tailors make clothes, or the shoemakers make shoes, or the railroads transport troops and supplies, much longer, unless paid a part, at least, of their claims. Some of the Western roads cannot pay their employees, and threaten to stop running their trains if they cannot be paid what the Government owes them.... What is here said of the Quartermaster's Department also applies to the Commissary, Medical, Ordnance, and other departments.

"If we pay the troops to the exclusion of the other creditors of the Government supplies must stop, and our armies will be left without food, clothing, or ammunition. We must equalize and distribute the Government indebtedness in such a way as to keep the wheels going. I give you these views as the result of various consultations with the heads of departments. What we want is some more great victories to give more confidence in our currency and to convince financial men that the war is near its close. In money matters these are the darkest days we have yet had during the war, but I hope that relief is not very distant."[25]

Beauregard officially assumed command of all the Confederate troops operating in South Carolina the next day, 16 February. He had already asked General Lee, the new general-in-chief, to get Wade Hampton promoted, because Wheeler had seniority over him as a major general and he considered Hampton the better officer to command his cavalry.

And on the sixteenth President Davis personally telegraphed Hampton the news that he had been promoted to lieutenant general and confirmed by the Senate the day before. The Rebels had finally realized that Columbia was Sherman's objective and orders were flying about to try to move Wheeler's cavalry and Cheatham's Corps of the Army of Tennessee to that city, but they could not reach there in time. In all there were nine generals at Columbia, including Beauregard and Hampton, but only Matthew Butler's division of cavalry was in position to oppose the Federal advance.

Beauregard wired Lee that afternoon: "Our forces, about 20,000 effective infantry and artillery, more or less demoralized, occupy a circumference of about 240 miles from Charleston to Augusta. The enemy, well organized and disciplined, and flushed with success, numbering nearly double our force, is concentrated upon one point (Columbia) of that circumference. Unless I can concentrate rapidly here, or in my rear, all available troops, the result cannot be long doubtful. General Hardee still hesitates to abandon Charleston, notwithstanding I have repeatedly urged him to do so, thereby losing several days of vital importance to future operations."[26] Hardee, who had been sick in bed for two days, finally agreed that day to abandon Charleston, while Jefferson Davis wired Beauregard: "You can better judge of the necessity for evacuating Charleston than I can. Such full preparations had been made that I had hoped for other and better results, and the disappointment is to me extremely bitter. The re-enforcements calculated on from reserves and militia of Georgia and South Carolina, together with the troops ordered from Mississippi, must have fallen much short of estimate. What can be done with the naval squadron, the torpedo-boats, and your valuable heavy guns at Charleston? Do not allow cotton stored there to become prize of the enemy, as was the case at Savannah. From reverse, however sad, if you are sustained by unity and determination among the people, we can look hopefully forward."[27]

In response to Lee's letter complaining about the necessity for change in the Commissary Department, Jefferson Davis replaced the commissary general, Brigadier General Lucius Northrup, with Colonel Isaac M. St. John, the able chief of the Mining and Nitre Bureau, promoting him to brigadier general. Rumor had it that one condition Breckinridge had made for accepting the post of secretary of war was the removal of Northrup, who was notoriously inefficient.

"During the 16th of February," Sherman wrote, "the Fifteenth Corps reached the point opposite Columbia, and pushed on for the Saluda Factory three miles above, crossed that stream, and the head of column reached Broad River just in time to find its bridge in flames. Butler's cavalry having just passed over into Columbia. The head of Slocum's column also reached the point opposite Columbia the same morning, but the bulk of his army was back at Lexington. I reached this place early in the morning of the 16th, met General Slocum there, and explained to him the purport of General Order No. 26, which contemplated the passage of his army across Broad River at Alston, fifteen miles above Columbia. Riding down to the river bank, I saw the wreck of the large bridge which had been burned by the enemy, with its many stone piers still standing, but the superstructure gone. Across the Congaree River lay the city of Columbia, in plain, easy view. I could see the unfinished State-House, a handsome granite structure, and the ruins of the railroad depot, which were still smoldering. Occasionally a few citizens or cavalry could be seen running across the streets, and quite a number of negroes were seemingly busy in carrying off bags of grain or meal, which were piled up near the burned depot.

"Captain De Gres had a section of his twenty-pound Parrott guns unlimbered, firing into the town. I asked him what he was firing for; he said he could see some rebel cavalry occasionally at the intersections of the streets, and he had an idea that there was a large force of infantry concealed on the opposite bank, lying low, in case we should attempt to cross over directly into the town. I instructed him not to fire any more into the town, but consented to his bursting a few shells near the depot, to scare away the negroes who were appropriating the bags of corn and meal which we wanted, also to fire three shots at the unoccupied State-House. I stood by and saw these fired, and then all firing ceased....

"The night of the 16th I camped near an old prison bivouac opposite Columbia, known to our prisoners of war as 'Camp Sorghum,' where remained the mud-hovels and holes in the ground which our prisoners had made to shelter themselves from the winter's cold and the summer's heat. The Fifteenth Corps was then ahead, reaching to Broad River, about four miles above Columbia; the Seventeenth Corps was behind, on the river-bank opposite Columbia; and the left wing and cavalry had turned north toward Alston.

"The next morning, viz., February 17th, I rode to the head of General Howard's column, and found that during the night he had ferried Stone's brigade of Wood's division of the Fifteenth Corps across by rafts made of the pontoons, and that brigade was then deployed on the opposite bank to cover the construction of a pontoon-bridge nearly finished.

"I sat with General Howard on a log, watching the men lay this bridge; and about 9 or 10 A.M. a messenger came from Colonel Stone on the other side, saying that the Mayor of Columbia had come out of the city to surrender the place, and asking for orders. I simply remarked to General Howard that he had his orders, to let Colonel Stone go on into the city, and that we would follow as soon as the bridge was ready. By this same messenger I received a note in pencil from the Lady Superioress of a convent or school in Columbia, in which she claimed to have been a teacher in a convent in Brown County, Ohio, at the time my daughter Minnie was a pupil there, and therefore asking special protection. My recollection is, that I gave the note to my brother-in-law, Colonel Ewing, then inspector-general on my staff, with instructions to see this lady, and assure her that we contemplated no destruction of any private property in Columbia at all."[28]

The newly promoted Hampton had wanted to defend the capital of his home state house to house, but Beauregard knew that this would only result in the destruction of the city and put thousands of civilians in danger. So the Confederates fell back without a fight. Behind them they left the railroad depots aflame and numerous bales of cotton burning in the streets.

"As soon as the bridge was done," Sherman said, "I led my horse over it, followed by my whole staff. General Howard accompanied me with this, and General Logan was next in order, followed by General C. R. Woods, and the whole of the Fifteenth Corps. Ascending the hill, we soon emerged into a broad road leading into Columbia, between old fields of corn and cotton, and, entering the city, we found seemingly all its population, white and black, in the streets. A high and boisterous wind was prevailing from the north, and flakes of cotton were flying about in the air and lodging in the limbs of the trees, reminding us of a Northern snow-storm. Near the market-square we found Stones' brigade halted, with arms stacked, and a large detail of his men, along with some citizens, engaged with an old fire-engine, trying to put out the fire in a long pile of burning cotton-bales, which I was told had been fired by the rebel cavalry on withdrawing from the city that morning. I know that, to avoid this row of burning cotton-bales, I had to ride my horse on the sidewalk."[29]

Many other Federals remembered seeing the burning cotton. An Illinois lieutenant said that as his regiment approached the city he saw "small groups of rebels darting in and out, to and fro, carrying the torch—cotton burning in the streets." Private John Bell also remembered the burning cotton, but when he saw it "the cotton had been drenched and the street flooded with water and, to all appearances, the fire entirely subdued."[30]

Sherman passed through a large crowd in the market square, met the mayor, and rode down the street to the Charleston depot. "We found it and a large storehouse burned to the ground," Sherman remembered, "but there were, on the platform and ground near by, piles of cotton bags filled with corn and corn-meal, partially burned. A detachment of Stone's brigade was guarding this, and separating the good from the bad. We rode along the railroad-track, some three or four hundred yards, to a large foundery, when some man rode up and said the rebel cavalry were close by, and he warned us that we might get shot. We accordingly turned back to the market-square, and *en route* noticed that several of the men were evidently in liquor, when I called General Howard's attention to it."[31] Civilians, both black and white, standing along the street with pails full of whiskey had been ladling it out to the passing soldiers. Howard ordered up a fresh regiment to patrol the city.

Sherman again met the mayor and asked him where he could make his headquarters. He was directed to the home of Blanton Duncan, a Kentuckian who had been printing Confederate money under contract until departing with Hampton's cavalry. "I considered General Howard as in command of the place," Sherman said, "and referred the many applicants for guards and protection to him. Before our headquarter-wagons had got up, I strolled through the streets of Columbia, found sentinels posted in the principal intersections, and generally good order prevailing, but did not again return to the main street, because it was filled with a crowd of citizens watching the soldiers marching by."[32]

He visited a lady who had been a member of a family living near Charleston that he had fequently visited while stationed at Fort Moultrie as a young lieutenant. He was surprised to find the yard of her neat, well-furnished house full of chickens and ducks. He told her that he was glad to see that she had not been visited by his soldiers, knowing that the poultry, at least, would not have been safe. She said, however, that she had been visited, but that she had told the men that she was an old friend of their commander and had shown them a book that Sherman had given her years before with his signature on the flyleaf. "Boys that's so; that's Uncle Billy's writing," a large fellow who seemed to be their leader had said, "for I have seen it often before." He had not only stopped the others from pillaging but had left a man to watch over the house until the provost guard had posted a sentinel. Sherman asked her if the guard was causing her any problems. "She assured me that he was a very nice young man; that he had been telling her all about his family in Iowa; and that at that very instant of time he was in another room minding her baby."[33]

"Having walked over much of the suburbs of Columbia in the afternoon," Sherman said, "and being tired, I lay down on a bed in Blanton Duncan's house to rest. Soon after dark I became conscious that a bright light was shining on the walls; and, calling some one of my staff (Major Nichols, I think) to inquire the cause, he said there seemed to be a house on fire down about the market-house. The same high wind still prevailed, and, fearing the consequences, I bade him go in person to see if the provost-guard were doing its duty. He soon returned, and reported that the block of buildings directly opposite the burning cotton of that morning was on fire, and that it was spreading; but he had found General Woods on the ground, with plenty of men trying to put the fire out, or, at least, to prevent its extension."[34]

Private Bell, who had seen the cotton soaked with water, said that by afternoon "a high wind rose... and the smoldering fire in the cotton bales was fanned into flames unnoticed in the excitement and by dark the fire had reached the business houses lining the street.... "[35] But what really fanned the fires was liquor. The soldiers found a distillery and were soon passing whiskey around by the bucketful. Drunken soldiers were soon wreaking retribution on the capital of the state that had started the war. "Did you think of this," one soldier asked an old man whose store was on fire, "when you hurrahed for Secession? How do you like it, hey?"[36]

"Hundreds of houses were on fire at once," Bell said; "men swore and women and children screamed and cried with terror; drunken soldiers ran about the streets with blazing torches, the fire engines were manfully worked; soldiers and citizens heartily joined in the effort to subdue the flames as long as there was any hope of success, and long lines of sentries did all in their power to restrain their reckless and desperate comrades."[37] "We got all the fire Engines in town out to work," a Union captain said, "but it was no use for there was as many men setting fires as there was trying to put them out." Another Federal said, "The men were so excited, that discipline was at an end, & very little attention was paid to orders.[38]

"The fire continued to increase," Sherman wrote, "and the whole heavens became lurid. I dispatched messenger after messenger to Generals Howard, Logan, and Woods, and received from them repeated assurances that all was being done that could be done, but that the high wind was spreading the flames beyond all control. These general officers were on the ground all night, and Hazen's division had been brought into the city to assist Wood's division, already there. About eleven o'clock at night I went down-town myself, Colonel Dayton with me; we walked to Mr. Simon's house, from which I could see the flames rising high in the air, and could hear the roaring of the fire. I advised the ladies to move to my headquarters, had our own headquarter-wagons hitched up, and their effects carried there, as a place of greater safety. The whole air was full of sparks and of flying masses of cotton, shingles, etc., some of which were carried four or five blocks, and started new fires. The men seemed under good control, and certainly labored hard to girdle the fire, to prevent its spreading; but, so long as the high wind prevailed, it was simply beyond human possibility."[39]

Sherman might have thought the men were under good control, and doubtless many of them were, but not all. A Southern novelist who had taken refuge in the city after fleeing his home in Orangeburg said that groups of soldiers in the streets were "drinking, roaring, revelling, while the fiddle and accordion were playing their popular airs." A newspaper reporter agreed: "I trust I shall never witness such a scene again—drunken soldiers rushing from house to house, emptying them of their valuables and firing them; Negroes carrying off piles of booty… and exulting like so many demons; officers and men revelling on the wines and liquors until the burning houses buried them in their drunken orgies.… A troop of cavalry were left to patrol the streets, but I did not once see them interfering with the groups that rushed about to fire and pillage the houses. True, Generals Sherman, Howard and others were out giving instructions for putting out a fire in one place, while a hundred fires were lighting all around them."[40]

"Imagine night turning into noonday," a young woman who took refuge with her mother in their cellar wrote, "only with a blazing, scorching glare that was horrible—a copper-colored sky across which swept columns of black rolling smoke glittering with sparks and flying embers.… Everywhere the palpitating blaze walling the streets as far as the eye could reach—filling the air with its terrible roar… every instant came the crashing of timbers and the thunder of falling buildings. A quivering molten ocean seemed to fill the air and sky. The Library building opposite us seemed framed by the gushing flames and smoke, while through the windows gleamed the liquid fire."[41]

"Fortunately," Sherman wrote, "about 3 or 4 A.M., the wind moderated, and gradually the fire was got under control; but it had burned out the very heart of the city, embracing several churches, the old State-House, and the school or asylum of that very Sister of Charity who had appealed for my personal protection.… The morning sun of

February 18th rose bright and clear over a ruined city. About half of it was in ashes and in smouldering heaps. Many of the people were houseless, and gathered in groups in the suburbs, or in the open parks and spaces, around their scanty piles of furniture. General Howard, in concert with the mayor, did all that was possible to provide other houses for them; and by my authority he turned over to the Sisters of Charity the Methodist College, and to the mayor five hundred beef-cattle, to help feed the people; I also gave the mayor... one hundred muskets, with which to arm a guard to maintain order after we should leave the neighborhood."[42]

At about dawn fresh troops were ordered into the city to restore order. Two soldiers were killed, 30 were wounded, and 370 were arrested. A reporter who walked the streets at first light called it "a city of ruins.... The noble-looking trees that shaded the streets, the flower gardens that graced them, were blasted and withered by fire. The streets were full of rubbish, broken furniture and groups of crouching, desponding, weeping, helpless women and children." He said that "old and young moved about seemingly without a purpose. Some mournfully contemplated the piles of rubbish, the only remains of their late happy homesteads.... Some had piles of bedding and furniture which they had saved from the wreck.... Children were crying with fright and hunger; mothers were weeping; strong men, who could not help either them or themselves, sat bowed down with their heads buried between their hands.... Who is to blame... is a subject that will be long disputed. I know the Negroes and escaped prisoners were infuriated, and easily incited the inebriated soldiers to join them in their work of vandalism."[3]

"The Boys had long desired to See the City burned to ashes which we all had the pleasure of seeing that Night," one Union soldier wrote. "Our men had such a spite against the place," another said, "they swore they would burn the city, if they should enter it, and they did."[44] The reason for all this enmity is simple. Secession began at Columbia. "The Capital, where treason was cradled and reared a mighty raving monster, is a blackened ruin," one Federal exulted. "Columbia is nothing but a pile of ruins," another declared, "a warning to future generations to beware of treason."[45]

---

1. Sherman, *Memoirs*, 754-755.
2. *Official Records*, 47:II:330.
3. Ibid., 46:II:445.
4. Basler, ed., *Collected Works of Abraham Lincoln*, 8:267.
5. Ibid., 46:II:468.

6. Noah Brooks, *Washington in Lincoln's Time* (New York, 1958), 202-203.
7. *Official Records*, 49:I:669.
8. Dowdey and Manarin, ed., *Wartime Papers of R. E. Lee*, 890.
9. Foote, *The Civil War*, 3:761.
10. *Official Records*, 47:II:342.
11. Jones, *A Rebel War Clerk's Diary*, 495.
12. Trudeau, *The Last Citadel*, 324.
13. *Official Records*, 48:I:786.
14. Jacob D. Cox, *The March to the Sea, Franklin and Nashville* (New York, 1882), 148.
15. *Official Records*, 49:I:688.
16. Foote, *The Civil War*, 3:778.
17. Basler, ed., *Collected Works of Abraham Lincoln*, 8:287.
18. Brooks, *Washington in Lincoln's Time*, 205-207.
19. Sherman, *Memoirs*, 755.
20. Ibid., 756-757.
21. *Official Records*, 46:II:547-548.
22. Ibid., 46:II:546-547.
23. Ibid., 49:I:708-709.
24. Ibid., 49:I:711.
25. Ibid., 46:II:561-562.
26. Ibid., 47:II:1202.
27. Ibid., 47:II:1201.
28. Sherman, *Memoirs*, 758-760.
29. Ibid., 760.
30. Davis, *Sherman's March*, 164.
31. Sherman, *Memoirs*, 761.
32. Ibid., 762.
33. Ibid., 765.
34. Ibid., 766.
35. Davis, *Sherman's March*, 167.
36. Ibid., 168.
37. Ibid.
38. Joseph T. Glatthaar, *The March to the Sea and Beyond: Sherman's Troops in the Savannah and Carolinas Campaigns* (New York, 1986), 145.
39. Sherman, *Memoirs*, 766-767.
40. Davis, *Sherman's March*, 166.
41. Ibid., 172.
42. Sherman, *Memoirs*, 767-768.
43. Davis, *Sherman's March*, 178.
44. Glatthaar, *The March to the Sea and Beyond*, 144.
45. Ibid., 146.

CHAPTER FIFTEEN

The Idea Is Good, But the Means Are Lacking

18 – 24 February 1865

General Quincy Gillmore, the new commander of the Department of the South, sent a dispatch to Halleck on 18 February: "The city of Charleston and its defenses came into our possession this morning, with over 200 pieces of good artillery and a supply of fine ammunition. The enemy commenced evacuating all the works last night, and Mayor Macbeth surrendered the city to the troops of General Schimmelfennig at 9 o'clock this morning, at which time it was occupied by our forces. Our advance on the Edisto and from Bull's Bay hastened the retreat. The cotton warehouses, arsenal, quartermasters' stores, railroad bridges, and two iron-clad were burned by the enemy. Some vessels in the ship-yard were also burned. Nearly all the inhabitants remaining in the city belong to the poorer classes."[1] Grant, having heard through the Richmond papers that Sherman had captured Columbia, had already taken the fall of Charleston for granted. He told Halleck that same day, "With Charleston in our hands, which I now believe assured to us, Gillmore will be able to spare a large part of his force. Direct him the moment that takes place to garrison the seaport harbors he deems most important for us to hold, with minimum numbers, and send all surplus troops to Cape Fear River. If he should receive other instructions from Sherman he will be guided by them. He should send none but white troops out of his department."[2]

On the other side of the world, the CSS *Shenandoah* departed Melbourne, Australia, that day.

A.J. Smith's "wandering tribe of Israel" received its requested name and number that day. Orders were published designating his force as the 16th Corps. Most of his units had been part of the Right Wing of the old 16th Corps before it had been discontinued a few months before. In the same order, most of the other troops in Canby's Military Division of West Mississippi were designated the 13th Corps. The old 13th Corps had been another name for Grant's old Army of the Tennessee until it had been broken up into four corps. Then the 13th Corps had been one of those four, commanded by Major General John McClernand through most of the Vicksburg campaign. After that, commanded by Ord, it had been sent to the Department of the Gulf, which was later incorporated into Canby's command. The old 13th Corps had been redesignated the Reserve Corps back in June, but most of the units in the new 13th Corps had been in the old one. Thus most of Canby's field force was composed of veterans of the Vicksburg campaign. Major General Gordon Granger, commander of Union forces around Mobile Bay, was named commander of the new 13th Corps.

Lee, on the nineteenth, was contemplating the dangerous situation in the Carolinas and the possible necessity of abandoning Petersburg and Richmond. In a letter to John Breckinridge, the new secretary of war, he said: "The accounts received today from South & North Carolina are unfavorable. Genl Beauregard reports from Winnsboro that four corps of the enemy are advancing on that place, tearing up the Charlotte Railroad, & that they will probably reach Charlotte by the 24th & before he can concentrate his troops there. He states Genl Sherman will doubtless move thence on Greensboro, Danville, & Petersburg, or unite with Genl Schofield at Raleigh or Weldon.

"Genl Bragg reports that Genl Schofield is now preparing to advance from New Berne to Goldsboro, & that a strong expedition is moving against the Weldon Railroad at Rocky Mount. He says that little or no assistance can be received from the State of North Carolina. That exemptions & reorganizations under late laws have disbanded the State forces, & that they will not be ready for the field for some time.

"I do not see how Sherman can make the march anticipated by Genl Beauregard. But he seems to have everything his own way, which is calculated to cause apprehension. Genl Beauregard does not say what he proposes, or what he can do. I do not know where his troops are, or on what lines they are moving. His despatches only give movements of the enemy. He has a difficult task to perform under present circumstances, & one of his best officers, Genl Hardee, is incapacitated by sickness. I have also heard that his own health is indifferent, though he has never so stated. Should his strength give way, there is no one on duty in the department that could replace him, nor have I any one to send there. Genl J. E. Johnston is the only officer whom I know who has the confidence of the army & people, & if he was ordered to report to me I would place him there on duty. It is necessary to bring out all our strength, & I fear to unite our armies, as separately they do not seem able to make head against the enemy. Everything should be destroyed that cannot be removed out of the reach of Genls Sherman & Schofield. Provisions must be accumulated in Virginia, & every man in all the States must be brought out. I fear it may be necessary to abandon all our cities, & preparation should be made for this contingency."[3]

In a separate letter he said much the same thing to Jefferson Davis. But he added: "From this condition of things there is nothing to intercept Sherman's or Schofield's march through the country except the want of supplies, nor, unless our troops can be concentrated, anything to oppose them but this army which will be unable to cope with the armies of Genls Grant, Sherman, & Schofield. I however cannot believe that Genl Sherman can make the march anticipated by Genl Beauregard if our troops can do anything. They can at least destroy or remove all provisions in his route, which I have again directed Genl Beauregard to do, & requested the cooperation of Governor Vance. Everything on his route & Schofield's should be removed.... At the present rate of Beauregard's retreat, he will soon be within striking distance of the Roanoke, where from present appearances it seems is the first point at which the enemy can be brought to a stand. I fear Wilmington will have to be evacuated & Bragg fall back in the same direction, nor unless the enemy can be beaten, can Richmond be held.

I think it prudent that preparations be made at all these points in anticipation of what may be necessary to be done. The cotton & tobacco in Richmond & Petersburg not necessary should be quietly removed also.

"Genl Beauregard makes no mention of what he proposes or what he can do, or where his troops are. He does not appear from his despatches to be able to do much."[4]

On the North Carolina coast Schofield had given up on outflanking the Confederate line north of Fort Fisher on the east. He had decided to turn the inland flank instead. On the sixteenth, Cox's division and one brigade of Major General Darius Couch's 2nd Division of the 23rd Corps, which had just arrived, were landed on the west bank of the Cape Fear River. The seventeenth had been spent in closing up to the Rebel defenses, which were anchored by Fort Anderson on the river and extended west to Orton Pond, a lake several miles long. On the eighteenth, while ships from Admiral Porter's fleet engaged the fort, Cox entrenched two brigades to threaten the Confederate front and took his other two on a detour around Orton Pond. Ames' division of Terry's force was ordered to follow. After a march of about fifteen miles and sharp resistance from Rebel cavalry, it was almost night when Cox's column got into position.

During the night the Confederates abandoned their position, including Fort Anderson and ten pieces of heavy artillery, and fell back to Town Creek. The Rebel lines on the east bank of the river were also abandoned, and Hoke's division fell back to a position opposite the mouth of Town Creek, about halfway to Wilmington. Terry followed up this retreat on the nineteenth and Ames' division was sent back across the river to reinforce him, while Cox closed up on the Town Creek position.

"Town Creek," Cox wrote, "is a deep, unfordable stream, with marshy banks, which, near the river, had been dyked and cultivated as rice-fields. A strong line of earthworks had been built on the north bank of the stream before the evacuation of Fort Anderson."[5] The Confederates had removed the planking from the bridge over the creek, which had to be approached over a long causeway through marshy ground, and the north bank near the bridge was a bluff rising twenty or thirty feet about the stream. Covering the bridge and the causeway were two 12-pounder Napoleons and a Whitworth rifled cannon, and these guns were backed up by Brigadier General Johnson Hagood's brigade of Hoke's division reinforced by one other regiment.

East of the bridge, however, the ground fell off into a marsh and rice fields, which were hidden from the Rebels on the bluff by a bordering forest. A mile or two down the creek the Federals found a flat-bottomed boat used for transporting rice. Cox sent Brevet Brigadier General T. J. Henderson's 3rd Brigade forward to the south edge of the creek to keep the Confederates busy and spent the morning and half of the afternoon of the twentieth ferrying the rest of his troops, fifty at a time, across the creek on the rice boat. Henderson's sharpshooters kept the Rebels' heads down and Union artillery knocked out their Whitworth rifle while Cox marched his main force to the west and took position behind the Confederates. Colonel O.H. Moore's brigade, detached from Couch's division, was sent even farther west to block the road to Wilmington while Cox led his remaining two brigades in a charge against the rear of the Rebel position. Hagood's Confederates, now under the temporary command of their senior colonel, had learned of the Federals' presence behind them and, leaving a small force to hold the bridge, had faced about to the north. But they could not stop the charge of Cox's two brigades. The colonel commanding plus 375 of his men were captured, along with the two 12-pounders, and the rest fled toward Wilmington, getting away before Moore's brigade got in position to cut off their retreat.

Sheridan telegraphed to Grant on the twentieth, "It is the common talk that Richmond will be evacuated, Lee falling back to Danville. During January and February my scouting parties have had little brushes with guerrillas, capturing over 150 officers and men. These affairs have all been small and were not reported in detail. On the 18th instant one of my parties captured 40 of Mosby's men and about 100 horses, but in getting off with their plunder they were attacked and nearly all the prisoners recaptured, and some of our men were also taken. We never can tell how many, as they make their escape and come in. The snow is still on the ground here nearly a foot deep, and the weather has continued bad up to the present time."[6]

Meanwhile, Grant was telling Meade: "I believe, under the right sort of a commander, Gregg's cavalry could now push out, striking the South Side Railroad at some point between Petersburg and Burkeville, crossing the Danville road between the latter place and the Appomattox, and the South Side road again west of Burkeville; from thence they could push southwest, heading the streams in Virginia, until they reach North Carolina, when they could turn southwest and push on until it joins either Sherman or Schofield, whichever proves most practicable. They could destroy the railroads as they cross them, but should not stop in Virginia to do any extensive damage. In case you think of a general who can be intrusted with this, I could send you some of Ord's cavalry to do picket duty until a division could be brought from the Valley."

And Meade replied that night: "General Getty is, I expect, the best officer to intrust with the duty you propose. I will see him to-morrow. The roads at present are very bad, and the streams all full. The cavalry could not take any wagons, artillery, or pontoon trains; and if they do not stop to do any damage to the railroads it appears to me the effect of the movement will only be to re-enforce the army they join, except they will, undoubtedly, stir up the country through which they pass. How long will it take to get a division here to take their places? I am moderate in my cavalry wants, but do not like to be without any."[7]

But in the meantime, Grant had wired Sheridan that afternoon: "As soon as it is possible to travel I think you will have no difficulty about reaching Lynchburg with a cavalry force alone. From there you could destroy the railroad and canal in every direction, so as to be of no further use to the rebellion. Sufficient cavalry should be left behind to look after Mosby's gang. From Lynchburg, if information you might get there would justify it, you could strike south, heading the streams in Virginia to the westward of Danville, and push on and join Sherman. This additional raid—with one now about starting from East Tennessee under Stoneman, numbering 4,000 or 5,000 cavalry; one from Vicksburg, numbering 7,000 or 8,000 cavalry; one from Eastport, Miss., 10,000 cavalry; Canby from Mobile Bay, with about 38,000 mixed troops—these three latter pushing for Tuscaloosa, Selma, and Montgomery; and Sherman with a large army eating out the vitals of South Carolina—is all that will be wanted to leave nothing for the rebellion to stand upon. I would advise you to overcome great obstacles to accomplish this."[8]

The Confederate House of Representatives passed a bill on 20 February authorizing the use of slaves as soldiers, but the Senate had still not agreed. The question also remained whether or not the slaves would fight for the Confederacy, and even if they would, could enough be recruited in time to make any real difference?

Another attempt to end the war started that day. The politicians had tried and failed, and some thought that it was the generals' turn. Ord, commanding the Union Army of the James, and Longstreet, commanding the 1st Corps of Lee's army, were old friends, and that circumstance provided the opening wedge. "General Ord...sent me a note on the 20th of February," Longstreet wrote, "to say that the bartering between our troops on the picket lines was irregular; that he would be pleased to meet me and arrange to put a stop to such intimate intercourse. As a soldier he knew his orders would stop the business; it was evident, therefore, that there was other matter he would introduce when the meeting could be had. I wrote in reply, appointing a time and place between our lines.

"We met the next day, and presently he asked for a side interview. When he spoke of the purpose of the meeting, I mentioned a simple manner of correcting the matter, which he accepted without objection or amendment. Then he spoke of affairs military and political.

"Referring to the recent conference of the Confederates with President Lincoln at Hampton Roads, he said that the politicians of the North were afraid to touch the question of peace, and there was no way to open the subject except through officers of the armies. On his side they thought the war had gone on long enough; that we should come together as former comrades and friends and talk a little. He suggested that the work as belligerents should be suspended; that General Grant and General Lee should meet and have a talk; that my wife, who was an old acquaintance and friend of Mrs. Grant in their girlhood days, should go into the Union lines and visit Mrs. Grant with as many Confederate officers as might choose to be with her. Then Mrs. Grant would return the call under escort of Union officers and visit Richmond; that while General Lee and General Grant were arranging for better feelings between the armies, they could be aided by intercourse between the ladies and officers until terms honorable to both sides could be found.

"I told General Ord that I was not authorized to speak on the subject, but could report upon it to General Lee and the Confederate authorities, and would give notice in case a reply could be made.

"General Lee was called over to Richmond, and we met at night at the President's mansion. Secretary-of-War Breckinridge was there. The report was made, several hours were passed in discussing the matter, and finally it was agreed that favorable report should be made as soon as another meeting could be arranged with General Ord. Secretary Breckinridge expressed especial approval of the part assigned for the ladies.

"As we separated, I suggested to General Lee that he should name some irrelevant matter as the occasion of his call for the interview with General Grant, and that once they were together they could talk as they pleased. A telegram was sent my wife that night at Lynchburg calling her to Richmond."[9]

However, Grant was not as enthusiastic about the idea, especially the part to be played by the ladies. Mrs. Grant overheard her husband and

General Ord discussing the matter and got them to explain it to her. She was thrilled with the idea and begged to be allowed to go to Richmond, but Grant would not consent. "Besides," she later wrote, "he did not feel sure that he could trust me; with the desire I always had shown for having a voice in great affairs, he was afraid I might urge some policy that the President would not sanction." She continued to beg, however, and he finally told her, "No, you must not. It is simply absurd. The men have fought this war and the men will finish it."[10]

"During the 18th and 19th we remained in Columbia," Sherman wrote, "General Howard's troops engaged in tearing up and destroying the railroad, back toward the Wateree, while a strong detail...destroyed the State Arsenal, which was found to be well supplied with shot, shell, and ammunition....Having utterly ruined Columbia, the right wing began its march northward, toward Winnsboro', on the 20th, which we reached on the 21st, and found General Slocum, with the left wing, who had come by the way of Alston. Thence the right wing was turned eastward, toward Cheraw, and Fayetteville, North Carolina, to cross the Catawba River at Peay's Ferry. The cavalry was ordered to follow the railroad north as far as Chester, and then to turn east to Rocky Mount, the point indicated for the passage of the left wing."[11]

Lee had evidently been thinking more about the prospect of abandoning Richmond. He wrote to Secretary Breckinridge again on the 21st: "I have repeated the orders to the commanding officers to remove & destroy everything in enemy's route. In the event of the necessity of abandoning our position on the James River, I shall endeavour to unite the corps of the army about Burkeville (junction of South Side & Danville Railroads), so as to retain communication with the north & south as long as practicable, & also with the west. I should think Lynchburg, or some point west, the most advantageous place to which to remove stores from Richmond. This however is a most difficult point at this time to decide, & the place may have to be changed by circumstances.

"It was my intention in my former letter to apply for Genl J.E. Johnston, that I might assign him to duty, should circumstances permit. I have had no official report of the condition of Genl Beauregard's health. It is stated from many sources to be bad. If he should break entirely down, it might be fatal. In that event I should have no one with whom to supply his place. I therefore respectfully request Genl Johnston may be ordered to report to me & that I may be informed where he is."[12]

Beauregard was also thinking about the strategic situation and sent the following message to President Davis on the 21st: "Should enemy advance into North Carolina toward Charlotte and Salisbury, as is now almost certain, I earnestly urge a concentration in time of at least 35,000 infantry at latter point, if possible, to give him battle there, and crush him, then to concentrate all forces against Grant, and then to march on Washington to dictate a peace. Hardee and myself can collect about 15,000, exclusive of Cheatham and Stewart, not likely to reach in time. If Lee and Bragg could furnish 20,000 more the fate of the Confederacy would be secure."[13]

A party of some 60 to 70 Confederate guerrillas commanded by Lieutenant Jesse McNeil approached Cumberland, Maryland, on the upper Potomac River, at about 3 a.m. on 21 February. "They captured the picket and quietly rode into town," a Union staff officer reported, "went directly to the headquarters of Generals Crook and Kelley, sending a couple of men to each place to overpower the headquarters guard, when they went directly to the room of General Crook, and without disturbing anybody else in the house, ordered him to dress and took him down stairs and placed him upon a horse ready saddled and waiting. The same was done to General Kelley; Captain Melvin, assistant adjutant-general to General Kelley, was also taken.... It was done so quietly that others of us, who were sleeping in adjoining rooms to General Crook, were not disturbed." Major General George Crook was the commander of the Department of West Virginia in Sheridan's Middle Military Division, and Brigadier General Benjamin F. Kelley commanded the forces in Crook's department that were spread along the Baltimore & Ohio Railroad, supposedly protecting it from Confederate raids. "The alarm was given within ten minutes, by a darkey watchman at the hotel who escaped from them," the staff officer continued, "and within an hour we had a party of fifty cavalry after them. They tore up the telegraph lines, and it required almost an hour to get them in working order."[14] As soon as the telegraph was working again, troops were ordered out from several different points, even a detachment of picked men from Custer's division over in the Shenandoah Valley, but to no avail.

"The frequent surprises in Sheridan's command has excited a good deal of observation lately," Secretary Stanton complained to Grant that day. "Friday an entire detachment of 110 men were captured, of which I have seen no report from him. It was my design yesterday to recommend that Crook be ordered out of Cumberland to his front, but in the press of business it was not done. There has been negligence, I am afraid, along that whole line for months, and I have been in daily apprehension of disaster, so that Crook's misfortune is not unexpected. Can you excite more vigilence?"

In his reply, Grant neatly side stepped this criticism of Sheridan, one of his favorite subordinates, and changed the subject to the question of suitable replacements for Crook and Kelley: "General Warren or General Humphreys, either, would be good men to put in command of the Department of West Virginia. General Warren I would suggest. Brigadier General Carroll is a very active officer, and I think would do well to take the place of General Kelley. I will telegraph Sheridan to hold commanders on the Baltimore and Ohio road responsible for every disaster."

Stanton replied that night: "General Warren has a young wife in Baltimore, and of course family connections. I do not think he will suit for Crook's department. Humphreys will do better, but he would not be the right man. Can you not think of some one else? Ought not Crook and Kelley both be mustered out of service for gross negligence, and as an example, even if they should be afterward restored?"[15]

Grant sent the jist of all this to Sheridan, who replied that evening: "I would prefer Gibbon to either Humphreys or Warren if you can let me have him. If not, I prefer Humphreys to Warren. There is and has been an inexcusable carelessness on the part of the officers and troops in the Department of West Virginia. I have dismissed, subject to the approval of the President, in all cases. There is on the Baltimore and Ohio Railroad, or covering it from Martinsburg to Parkersburgh, 14,000 effective troops, and there was at Cumberland of this force between 3,500 and 4,000 men; still they have been asking for more."[16]

That same afternoon Meade returned to the subject of the proposed cavalry raid into North Carolina: "General Getty does not seem inclined to command the cavalry. I will see Crawford and Ayres; probably the latter is the best man. One difficulty is the evident separation from this army, with which those who have been identified desire to remain. How would it do to bring another division here and send it? Would this require too much time?"

Grant replied an hour later: "At the same time I telegraphed you on the subject of the proposed raid I telegraphed to General Sheridan as to the practicability of his starting from where he is, in person, to reach Sherman, going by way of Lynchburg. I do not want to send both. Sherman has but little over 4,000 cavalry, and Schofield none. The main object is to re-enforce Sherman in that arm of service. I may yet send the proposed re-enforcements to Wilmington. Going by Lynchburg would give us great advantages in cutting the Central road, Virginia and Tennessee road, the Danville road south of Danville, and the canal. If a division is sent from here it would have to be Gregg's to save time."[17]

In North Carolina on the 21st Cox followed up his success of the day before. About noon his troops came to Mill Creek and found the bridge over it had been burned. It took two hours to repair it, during which the troops had their lunch. Then the advance was resumed, headed for Brunswick Ferry, on the west bank of the Cape Fear River. Wilmington was on the east bank of the river, which was divided into two channels just there by Eagle Island. The western channel was known as the Brunswick River. The Confederates had burned the railroad bridge over the Brunswick River that morning, and it was still smoking when Cox's Federals reached it. "A pontoon bridge had been at the ferry," Cox wrote, "and in the hasty retreat the order to scuttle and destroy the boats had been so incompletely carried out that more than half of them were uninjured, and many of the rest could be quickly repaired. This work was immediately begun, while some of the boats were used to ferry a detachment over to the island, which was about a mile wide, but an almost unbroken marsh....A field battery of rifled guns was put in position, on a rise of ground on the west bank, to cover the detachment on the island, and the explosion of some of its shells in the city helped to hasten matters by showing that the town was within range. Meanwhile the work of repairing the pontoons was hurried, and reconnoissances made in the vicinity....Great columns of smoke soon began to ascend in the city, telling of the destruction of naval stores, and of preparation to evacuate the town."[18]

Hoke had not fallen back and even seemed to be preparing to attack, lending credence to a rumor that he had been reinforced. So Schofield ordered Cox back down the river to be ferried across to aid Terry. Cox, however, felt sure that the Rebels were about to abandon Wilmington, so he only sent one brigade as well as a report of the situation.

General Bragg returned to Wilmington that day from a trip to Greensborough and Richmond. "I find all our troops on this side Cape Fear," he wired the war department. "The enemy in force on the west, and our communications south cut. We are greatly outnumbered."[19] He then ordered the city to be abandoned and Hoke to fall back to avoid being cut off. Cotton, tobacco, military supplies, naval stores, and ships at the dock were burned that night to keep them from falling into the hands of the Yankees. The CSS *Chickamauga* was taken up the river and scuttled.

The next day, Washington's birthday, at about 10 a.m., the Federals marched in. "We entered the city with colors flying and music from the drum corps," one of them wrote, "and General Terry and staff rode at the head of the column....The sights we saw that day are seen but once in a lifetime, and then only by a few. One little Union flag particularly, a genuine stars and stripes, was seen timidly fluttering from the second-story window of a house, and was lustily cheered by the troops....The unbounded joy of the colored people could only be appreciated by being seen. It was expressed according to their different temperaments; some by sitting on the ground, rocking to and fro, lustily shouting, 'Bress de Lord! Bress de Lord! We knowed you's comin'! We knowed Massa Linkum's sojers would come!' Others were shouting and singing, dancing and hugging each other, and showing the gladness of their hearts."[20]

General Lee assigned J.E. Johnston to the command of both the Department of Tennessee and Georgia and the Department of South Carolina, Georgia and Florida that day with instructions to concentrate all available forces and drive Sherman back. Beauregard, who was subordinated to Johnston, wired Lee, "In the defense of our common country I will at all times be happy to serve with or under so gallant and patriotic a soldier as General Johnston."[21] Johnston himself replied to Lee, "It is too late to expect me to concentrate troops capable of driving back Sherman. The remnant of the Army of Tennessee is much divided. So are other troops."[22] He did not, however, decline the command.

In a letter to Lieutenant General James Longstreet, commander of his 1st Corps, Lee wrote that day: "I hope under the reorganization of the Commissary Department, if we can maintain possession of our communications, that the army will be better supplied than heretofore, and that we can accumulate some provisions ahead. As regards the concentration of our troops near the capital, the effect would be to produce a like concentration of the enemy, and an increase of our difficulties in obtaining food and forage. But this, whether for good or evil, is now being accomplished by the enemy, who seems to be forcing Genls Beauregard & Bragg in this direction. If Sherman marches his army to Richmond, as Genl Beauregard reports it is his intention to do, and Genl Schofield is able to unite with him, we shall have to abandon our position on the James River, as lamentable as it is on every account. The want of supplies alone would force us to withdraw when the enemy reaches the Roanoke. Our line is so long, extending nearly from the Chickahominy to the Nottoway, and the enemy is so close upon us that if we are obliged to withdraw, we cannot concentrate all our troops nearer than some point on the line of railroad between

Richmond and Danville. Should a necessity arise, I propose to concentrate at or near Burkeville....With the army concentrated at or near Burkeville, our communications north and south would be by that railroad and west by the South Side Railroad. We might also seize the opportunity of striking at Grant, should he pursue us rapidly, or at Sherman, before they could unite."[23]

Tennessee voters approved a new constitution that day that abolished slavery and repudiated all Confederate debts.

Meade told Grant that day, the 22nd: "Neither Ayres nor Crawford feels like taking the cavalry under existing circumtances. How would it do to transfer Kautz to this command? It seems to me this is the best and only arrangement we can make for immediate action."[24] That same day, Meade received word that his son had died the day before and obtained Grant's permission to go home for a day or two. The search for a replacement for Crook also continued, and Grant told Stanton that he really did not want to spare Humphreys anyway because he was turning out to be an excellent corps commander. He mentioned Terry for the job because where he was he was outranked by some of Schofield's division commanders.

Grant wired Sheridan that day about blockade running and trading with the enemy going on in the area of Fredericksburg, Virginia, halfway between Washington and Richmond, and the Northern Neck, which is the peninsula between the Potomac and Rappahannock rivers. "Many supplies have been collected in the Northern Neck and many more are smuggled in from Philadelphia and other places and taken to Richmond over this (Fredericksburg) [rail]road; 70,000 pounds of bacon alone have gone to Richmond the last week over that road. Cannot Augur send a force to break that trade up?"[25] Major General Christopher Colon Augur was the commander of the Department of Washington, which was part of Sheridan's Middle Military Division. That same day, "General" Singleton and a partner, Judge James Hughes, left Washington for City Point, on their way to Richmond with the trading permit Lincoln had given Orville Browning for them.

Robert Lincoln reported for duty as an assistant adjutant general on Grant's staff that day. Horace Porter said, "The new acquisition to the company at headquarters soon became exceedingly popular. He had inherited many of the genial traits of his father, and entered heartily into all the social pastimes at headquarters. He was always ready to perform his share of hard work, and never expected to be treated differently from any other officer on account of his being the son of the Chief Executive of the nation."[26]

That same day, John Wilkes Booth returned to Washington from New York, where he had gone after Lincoln's failure to appear at the theater when his group had planned to capture him had raised the possibility that the Federals suspected something.

Lee wrote to Jefferson Davis on the 23rd: "I have received the copy of Genl Beauregard's despatch of 21st instant, & wish it was in our power to carry out his plan. The idea is good, but the means are lacking. I have directed all the available troops in the Southern Department to be concentrated, with a view to embarrass if they cannot arrest Sherman's progress, & still hope that he cannot make the march contemplated by Genl Beauregard. I think it probable he may turn east by Camden towards the coast. It seems to me he ought not to be allowed to gather sufficient supplies for his journey, & indeed I do not know where they can be obtained. Our troops seem to be much scattered, but by diligence & boldness they can be united. I am much obliged to Your Excellency for ordering Genl Johnston to report to me. I have placed him in command of the army operating against Sherman, & directed him to assign Genl Beauregard to duty with him....I know of no one who had so much the confidence of the troops & people as Genl Johnston, & believe he has capacity for the command. I shall do all in my power to strengthen him, & should he be forced across the Roanoke, unite with him in a blow against Sherman before the latter can join Genl Grant. This will necessitate the abandonment of our position on James River, for which contingency every preparation should be made."[27]

Minnesota ratified the 13th Amendment that day.

Down at Gravelly Springs, Alabama, on 23 February, General Thomas arrived to review three divisions of Wilson's cavalry corps. Wilson had staged this review and invited Thomas in order to convince his superior to allow him to make the proposed cavalry raid into central and southern Alabama with his entire force, or at least as much of it as he could secure mounts for. Thomas was treated to the sight of thousands of men and horses moving with precision across a level valley a half-mile wide and two miles long and went away impressed enough to agree to Wilson's desire.

That night, one of Wilson's officers, with an escort of six troopers, met Confederate cavalry commander Nathan Bedford Forrest at his headquarters down in Mississippi under a flag of truce. The Federal officer found the Rebel general to be "a man fully six feet in height; rather waxen face; handsome; high, full forehead, and with a profusion of light gray hair thrown back from the forehead and growing down rather to a point in the middle of the same. The lines of thought and care, in an upward curve, receding, are distinctly marked and add much to the dignity of expression. The general effect is suggestive of notables of Revolutionary times." He was just as impressed with the Confederate's personality as his looks, saying that "there was about his talk and manner a certain soldierly simplicity and engaging frankness, and I was frequently lost in real admiration." He added that the general's speech "indicates a very limited education, but his impressive manner conceals many otherwise notable defects....His habitual expression seemed rather subdued and thoughtful, but when his face is lighted up with a smile, which ripples all over his features, the effect is really charming." In Wilson's name, the Union officer issued a challenge to battle to the Rebel, and recorded his answer as: "Jist tell General Wilson that I know the nicest little place down here...and whenever he is ready, I will fight with him with any number from one to ten thousand cavalry and abide the issue. Gin'ral Wilson may pick his men, and I'll pick mine. He may take his sabers and I'll take my six shooters. I dont want nary saber in my command—haven't got one....I ain't no graduate of West Point; never rubbed my back up agin any college, but Wilson may take his sabers and I'll use my six shooters and agree to whup the fight with any cavalry he can bring." It was during this meeting that Forrest issued his famous, if oft-misquoted, summation of his theory of strategy and tactics: "I always make it a rule to get there first with the most men."[28]

The 20th Corps of Slocum's wing of Sherman's forces crossed the Catawba River on the 23rd, but heavy rains begin to fall. Sherman wrote to General Howard, commanding the other wing: "I have just been down to the bridge. It will take all of to-day and to-morrow to get this wing across and out. You may go ahead, but keep communication with me. I expect Kilpatrick here this p.m. and will send him well to the left. He reports that two of his foraging parties were murdered by the enemy after capture and labeled, 'Death to all foragers.' Now it is clearly our war right to subsist our army on the enemy. Napoleon always did it, but could avail himself of the civil powers he found in existence to collect forage and provisions by regular impressments. We cannot do that here, and I contend if the enemy fails to defend his country we may rightfully appropriate what we want. If our foragers act under mine, yours, or other proper orders they must be protected. I have ordered Kilpatrick to select of his prisoners man for man, shoot them, and leave them by the roadside labeled, so that our enemy will see that for every man he executes he takes the life of one of his own. I want the foragers, however, to be kept within reasonable bounds for the sake of discipline. I will not protect them when they enter dwellings and commit wanton waste, such as woman's apparel, jewelry, and such things as not needed by our army; but they may destroy cotton or tobacco, because these are assumed by the rebel Government to belong to it, and are used as a valuable source of revenue. Nor will I consent to our enemy taking the lives of our men on their judgment. They have lost all title to property, and can lose nothing not already forfeited; but we should punish for a departure from our orders, and if the people resist our foragers I will not deem it wrong, but the Confederate army must not be supposed the champion of any people."[29]

He wrote much the same thing to Kilpatrick, and added: "It is petty nonsense for Wheeler and Beauregard and such vain heroes to talk of our warring against women and children. If they claim to be men they should defend their women and children and prevent us reaching their homes. Instead of maintaining their armies let them turn their attention to their families, or we will follow them to the death....For my part I want the people of the South to realize the fact that they shall not dictate laws of war or peace to us. If there is to be any dictation we want our full share."[30]

The next day Kilpatrick's cavalry division crossed the Catawba, and Sherman ordered it to move up to "make believe we were bound for Charlotte, to which point I heard that Beauregard had directed all his detachments, including a corps of Hood's old army, which had been marching parallel with us, but had failed to make junction with the forces immediately opposing us. Of course," Sherman added, "I had no purpose of going to Charlotte, for the right wing was already moving rapidly toward Fayetteville, North Carolina. The rain was so heavy and persistent that the Catawba River rose fast, and soon after I had crossed the pontoon-bridge at Rocky Mount it was carried away, leaving General Davis, with the Fourteenth Corps, on the west bank. The roads were infamous, so I halted the Twentieth Corps at Hanging Rock for some days, to allow time for the Fourteenth to get over."[31]

That day Sherman sent a letter through the lines to Wade Hampton complaining of the murder of his foragers in much the same terms he had written to Howard and Kilpatrick and informing him that a like number of Confederate prisoners would be executed. "Personally I regret the bitter feelings engendered by this war," he added, "but they were to be expected, and I simply allege that those who struck the first blow and made war inevitable ought not, in fairness, to reproach us for the natural consequences."[32]

General Joseph E. Johnston was writing to his old West Point classmate, Robert E. Lee, that day, the 24th: "The Federal army is within the triangle formed by the three bodies of our infantry. It can, therefore, prevent their concentration or compel them to unite in its rear by keeping on its way without loss of time. It is estimated at 40,000, and was at last accounts crossing the Wateree east of Winnsborough, as if moving upon Fayetteville. The available forces are Hardee's troops arriving at Cheraw by railroad and estimated by General Beauregard at 12,000. I believe that several thousand are South Carolina miltia and reserves, who will not go beyond Cheraw; Lee's corps, Army of Tennessee, near Charlotte, 3,500; Stewart's corps, Army of Tennessee, 1,200; Cheatham's corps, Army of Tennessee, 1,900. The two latter when last heard of were near Newberry. These troops, expect Hardee's, have only the means of transporting cooking utensils, and, therefore, cannot operate far from railroads. The cavalry, under Lieutenant-General Hampton, amounts to about 6,000. In my opinion these troops form an army too weak to cope with Sherman....If our troops and those of General Bragg could be united in time the progress of Sherman's army might be stopped, otherwise it may unite with that of Schofield. This junction of our forces might be made at Fayetteville."[33]

Comstock wired a report to Grant that day from Fortress Monroe, notifying him of the capture of Wilmington. Meanwhile, Schofield was writing to Grant from Wilmington that day: "I shall push forward as soon as I can get any means of transportation. Wagons are beginning to arrive, and I hope the delay will not be long. The rebel agent of exchange has informed me that he will deliver 10,000 of our prisoners at the point where the railroad crosses the Northeast River, and I have agreed to receive them at that point. I presume he will commence to deliver them to-day. I am making all possible provision for the care of the sick, which will no doubt be a large proportion of the whole number. I have sent General Ruger's division of the Twenty-third Corps to New Berne, and shall send either General Terry or General Cox there to command the troops operating from that point. I will go there or remain with the troops operating from this place, as may seem advisable. I will also keep transports enought for a short time to carry a division from one point to the other, if it becomes necessary....I have asked for the assignment of General Cox and General Terry to corps commands, both because the strength of my command renders it desirable and because it will enable me to leave either the one or the other in command of the column which I may not be with at any time. Moreover, it will make the organization of my army correspond with that of General Sherman's other grand divisions....I propose to repair both railroads toward Goldsborough as rapidly as possible. I shall also make such preparations as I can to send supplies to General Sherman by the river toward Fayetteville in case he should call for them."[34]

Lee, meanwhile, was writing to Secretary of War Breckinridge: "I regret to be obliged to call your attention to the alarming number of desertions that are now occuring in the army. Since the 12th instant they amount in two divisions of Hill's corps, those of Wilcox and Heth, to about four hundred. There are a good many from other commands. The desertions are chiefly from the North Carolina regiments, and especially those from the western part of that State. It seems that the men are influenced very much by the representations of their friends at home, who appear to have become very despondent as to our success. They think the cause desperate and write to the soldiers, advising them to take care of themselves, assuring them that if they will return home the bands of deserters so far outnumber the home guards that they will be in no danger of arrest. I do not know what can be done to prevent this evil, unless some change can be wrought in the state of public sentiment by the influence of prominent citizens of the State. The deserters generally take their arms with them. I shall do all in my power to remedy the evil by a stern enforcement of the law, but that alone will not suffice."[35]

At Fort Columbus, on Governor's Island, New York, John Yates Beall was hanged. "I've had more questions of life and death to settle in four years," President Lincoln said, "than all the other men who ever sat in this chair put together. No man knows the distress of my mind. The case of Beall on the Lakes—there had to be an example. They tried me every way. They wouldn't give up. But I had to stand firm. I even had to turn away his poor sister when she came and begged for his life, and let him be executed, and he was executed, and I can't get the distress out of my mind yet."[36]

---

1. *Official Records*, 47:II:483-484.
2. Ibid., 47:II:473.

3. Dowdey and Manarin, *Wartime Papers of R. E. Lee*, 904-905.
4. Ibid., 905-906.
5. Cox, *The March to the Sea, Franklin and Nashville*, 150.
6. *Official Records*, 46:II:605.
7. Ibid., 46:II:598.
8. Ibid., 46:II:605-606.
9. James Longstreet, *From Manassas to Appomattox: Memoirs of the Civil War in America* (Philadelphia, 1896), 583-585.
10. Julia Dent Grant, *The Personal Memoirs of Julia Dent Grant* (New York, 1975), 141.
11. Sherman, *Memoirs*, 768.
12. Dowdey and Manarin, *Wartime Papers of R. E. Lee*, 906.
13. *Official Records*, 47:II:1238.
14. Ibid., 46:II:621.
15. Ibid., 46:II:608.
16. Ibid., 46:II:619-620.
17. Ibid., 46:II:609.
18. Cox, *The March to the Sea, Franklin and Nashville*, 153-154.
19. *Official Records*, 47:II:1241.
20. Gragg, *Confederate Goliath*, 246.
21. *Official Records*, 47:II:1248.
22. Ibid., 47:II:1247.
23. Dowdey and Manarin, ed., *Wartime Papers of R.E. Lee*, 908.
24. *Official Records*, 46:II:630.
25. Ibid., 46:II:666.
26. Porter, *Campaigning With Grant*, 388-399. Porter gives the date as the 23rd. A wire from Grant to Lincoln on the 24th gives the date as either the 22nd or the 21st, depending on whether you believe Basler, ed., *Complete Works of Abraham Lincoln*, 8:314 n. 1 or *Official Records*, 46:II:668, respectively. I took the medium figure. The difference is hardly earth-shaking.
27. Dowdey and Manarin, ed., *Wartime Papers of R.E. Lee*,, 909-910.
28. James Pickett Jones, *Yankee Blitzkrieg: Wilson's Raid Through Alabama and Georgia* (Athens, Georgia, 1976), 24-25.
29. *Official Records*, 47:II:537.
30. Ibid., 47:II:544.
31. Sherman, *Memoirs*, 768-771.
32. *Official Records*, 47:II:546.
33. Ibid., 47:II:1271.
34. Ibid., 47:II:559.
35. Dowdey and Manarin, ed., *Wartime Papers of R. E. Lee*, 910.
36. Sandburg, *The War Years, 1864-1865*, 784.

CHAPTER SIXTEEN

I Feel a Great Anxiety to See Everything Pushed

24 February - 2 March 1865

On that same 24th day of February, Sergeant Benjamin Franklin Stringfellow, a reknowned Confederate cavalry scout who spent a great deal of time behind Union lines, wrote a letter to General Lee proposing to capture General Grant, much as Crook and Kelley had been captured at Cumberland.

Sheridan was writing to Grant the next day, Saturday the 25th, about the cavalry raid the latter wanted him to make, ending with riding south to join Sherman: "I could not get off to-day, as I expected in a previous dispatch to you, but will be off on Monday. I was delayed in getting the brigade from Loudoun County and the canvas pontoon bridge, which was necessary for me to have, as all the streams in the country are at present unfordable. Where is Sherman marching for? Can you give me any definite information as to the points he may be expected to move on this side of Charlotte? The cavalry officers say the cavalry never was in such good condition. I will leave behind about 2,000 men, which will increase to about 3,000 in a short time."

Grant replied that night: "General Sherman's movements will depend on the amount of opposition he meets with from the enemy. If strongly opposed he may possibly have to fall back to Georgetown, S.C., and fit out for a new start. I think, however, all danger of the necessity for going to that point has passed. I believe he has passed Charlotte. He may take Fayetteville on his way to Goldsborough. If you reach Lynchburg you will have to be guided in your after movements by the information you obtain. Before you could possibly reach Sherman I think you would find him moving from Goldsborough toward Raleigh, or engaging the enemy strongly posted at one or the other of these places, with railroad communications opened from his army to Wilmington or New Berne."[1]

Lincoln, who always kept a close eye on the military telegraph and who had had in the past many reasons to worry about the defense of the lower Shenandoah Valley, wired Grant: "General Sheridan's dispatch to you of to-day, in which he says he 'Will be off Monday,' and that he 'will leave behind about 2,000 men,' causes the Secretary of War and myself considerable anxiety. Have you well considered whether you do not again leave open the Shenandoah Valley entrance to Maryland and Pennsylvania, or at least to the Baltimore and Ohio Railroad?"[2]

Braxton Bragg, still commanding Confederate forces in North Carolina, wrote to Lee that day: "Sherman is reported to have turned east at Winnsborough, and crossed the Wateree River. This indicates Fayetteville and Raleigh by the old mail-stage road, and through a country not drained of supplies. Hardee is supposed to be in his front at Cheraw. By a union of my forces with General Beauregard at Fayetteville we might strike him before he forms a junction with Schofield or gets supplies up the Cape Fear. If we lose this opportunity we shall be again divided." He sent a similar dispatch to Beauregard and followed it with another: "A detachment is moving to the Cape

Fear to obstruct river and retard the enemy. His force is too large for me to meet him with success. He has two corps under Schofield. We have but a division."[3]

In Louisville, Kentucky, that day, at shortly after 6 p.m., Lieutenant John W. Headley, one of the officers who had participated in the Confederate attempt to burn New York City back in November, walked across the crowded lobby of the Louisville Hotel and climbed the stairs to the second floor. Peering through the open door of a suite of rooms he could see Andrew Johnson, vice president-elect of the United States and until recently military governor of Tennessee, bidding goodnight to several visitors. Lieutenant Colonel Robert Martin, who had commanded the raid on New York, was waiting for Headley out behind the hotel with a closed carriage. The two Rebel officers—in civilian clothes, of course—were working their way back to the Confederacy from Canada, where the New York raid, Beall's Great Lakes raid, and several other clandestine operations had been planned and financed by Confederate commissioners there, and while waiting in Louisville for the opportunity to slip through the Union lines they had learned that Governor Johnson was in town on his way to Washington, D.C., for the upcoming inauguration. They had quickly hatched a plot to capture him and take him to Richmond. (This might well indicate that they had acquired knowledge in Canada of John Wilkes Booth's longstanding plans to do the same with Lincoln. Martin is known to have said that he met Booth while in Canada.)

Lieutenant Headley hurried down the hotel's back stairway and out the ladies' entrance, noting that this escape route was clear, and found Martin pacing up and down under some trees. He had bad news. When the two had first learned of Johnson's presence in Louisville they had asked the pro-Confederate doctor who was making arrangements to slip them through Union lines whether he knew of any other Rebel soldiers hiding out in the city, and he had put them in touch with three young Rebel cavalry officers who had escaped from the Union prisoner of war camp at Johnson's Island, near Sandusky, Ohio. These three were to provide the extra manpower Martin and Headley felt they needed to accomplish their purpose. But now only one of the three had shown up at the hotel at the appointed time. The Federals had discovered the hiding place of the other two, forcing them to move to a new location. Martin and Headley therefore decided to put off their operation until the next evening.

Headley had met Johnson before the war and felt sure he would recognize him. He would therefore go to Johnson's room and pretend to seek his aid in obtaining a government job. While he was thus distracted, Martin would enter with his revolver drawn and say, "This doesn't mean any harm, Mr. Johnson. Just keep quiet a minute and I will tell you what it does mean, otherwise you will be killed in seconds." Headley later said, "We took it for granted that Johnson would have enough curiosity to listen rather than be killed."[4] Then they would tie him up, throw a coat over his shoulders to hide the ropes, and take him down the back stairs. If anyone asked what they were up to, they would say they were taking a sick friend to the nearby hospital. The other three officers would be waiting with the carriage and they would all spirit the vice president-elect out of town before anyone knew he was missing.

At 6 p.m. on the 26th the Rebels' carriage was again parked behind the hotel, this time with all three cavalry officers on hand, all armed and ready. Headley walked around the block and into the hotel's front door. The lobby was not as crowded as it had been the evening before, he noticed. He waited at the top of the stairs until Martin came in and ascended the stairs to join him. Then they walked down the hall to Johnson's room and found the door open a few inches. Headley looked up and down the stairs, making sure that no one was watching, and then entered while Martin remained on guard outside.

Headley found himself alone in a large living room, with a few cigar butts and empty glasses as the only signs of life. The door to the bedroom was closed, but Headley was just about to try it when he heard voices out in the corridor. Looking out the door he saw several Union officers and ladies talking and laughing in front of another door. Martin and Headley launched into an involved conversation about a fictitious cotton deal until the Federals finally went away, then they both went into Johnson's room with revolvers drawn. They crossed the living room and threw open the door to the bedroom, only to find it deserted, the bed unmade. With mingled feelings of disappointment and relief, they pocketed their weapons and went down to the lobby.

"Clerk, do you know if Governor Johnson is in?" Headley asked.

"Oh, no, sir," he was told. "He's not."

"Has he gone to dinner?" Headley asked.

Shaking his head, the clerk replied, "He left on the five o'clock boat for Cincinnati."

For some unknown reason, Johnson had decided to take the mailboat up the Ohio River instead of waiting for the train later that night. Had the Confederates known he would be traveling by steamboat, Headley later said, they would not have tried to kidnap him at the hotel. They would just have hijacked the entire boat.

Headley turned from the desk clerk to Martin and said, "I guess we missed him."[5]

Down in North Carolina that day, General Cox was detached from his division and sent to New Berne, a town on Pamlico Sound northeast of Wilmington that Union forces had held for the past three years. New Berne was also connected by railroad with Beaufort and Morehead City on the Atlantic coast, both of which were also in Federal hands. "Several things combined to make Newberne a more useful base of supply for Sherman than Wilmington," Cox later wrote. "The harbor at Morehead City and Fort Macon was a better one than that at the mouth of Cape Fear River, and would admit vessels of deeper draught. The railway, between the harbor and Newberne, some forty miles long, was in operation, with some locomotives and cars already there, while nothing of the kind was at Wilmington, the enemy having carefully removed all railway rolling stock on that line. From Newberne, much of the way to Kinston through the Dover Swamp, the iron was not so injured that it might not be used again, and the reconstruction of the railway by that route would be both easier and more economical. As, therefore, a safe base for Sherman was assured at Wilmington in case of need, Schofield turned his attention to the work of preparing a still better line of communication from Newbern to Goldsboro."[6]

Halleck wired Grant that afternoon: "General Augur, by direction of General Sheridan, is fitting out a cavalry expedition against the Rappahannock peninsula. To do this requires most of his cavalry, and General Sheridan has withdrawn his from the line of the Potomac. The Secretary of War thinks this will leave Alexandria and the Maryland line too much exposed to rebel raids. I have, therefore, directed General Augur to wait till I could hear from you as to the necessity of the Rappahannock expedition. Major-General Hancock has been assigned to the temporary command of West Virginia and the troops of the Middle Military Division not with General Sheridan in the field."[7] Major General Winfield Scott Hancock had been the commander of the 2nd Corps in Meade's Army of the Potomac until the previous November, when an old wound picked up at Gettysburg had forced him to leave the field. Since then he had been recruiting a new 1st Corps, to be formed entirely from reenlisting veterans. Grant thought so higly of him that he had once considered him to succeed Meade.

Grant replied to Halleck that night: "I approve of the assignment of Hancock to Sheridan's command during his absence.... I can send troops from here to break up traffic on the peninsula. Augur need not send out." He also replied to Lincoln's telegram of the day before: "Two thousand cavalry, and that to be increased to 3,000, besides all his infantry, is what Sheridan means. His movement is in the direction of the enemy, and the tendency will be to protect the Baltimore and Ohio road and to prevent any attempt to invade Maryland and Pennsylvania."[8] Lincoln replied the next day, the 27th: "Subsequent reflection, conference with General Halleck, your dispatch, and one from General Sheridan, have relieved my anxiety, and so I beg that you will dismiss any concern you may have on my account in the matter of my last dispatch."[9]

Grant also wrote a long letter that day to Canby about what he wanted the latter to do. He sent his aide Cyrus Comstock, now a Brevet Brigadier General for his part in the capture of Fort Fisher, to carry the letter and to serve with Canby temporarily. "Relieve him and order him back to these headquarters," Grant said, "as soon as you commence a movement to the interior from Mobile, should that city fall into your possession soon, or when it is clearly ascertained that you are to have a protracted siege. Until recently I supposed that Mobile would probably be surrendered without a struggle. Since, however, I have learned that orders have been given from Richmond to hold the place at all hazards. These orders are now but about a week old, and may have reached there too late. The great length of time that has elapsed since I have heard from you, however, makes it impossible for me to judge whether your campaign has progressed far enough to interfere with a compliance with this order. I am extremely anxious to hear of your forces getting to the interior of Alabama. I send Grierson, an experienced cavalry commander, to take command of your cavalry. At the time he received his orders I did not know that you were intending to send your cavalry from Vicksburg. He was, therefore, directed to report to you in person. I am afraid this will prevent his taking the command I intended, and interfere somewhat with the success of your cavalry. Forrest seems to be near Jackson, Miss., and, if he is, none but the best of our cavalry commanders will get by him. Thomas was directed to start a cavalry force from Eastport, Miss., as soon after the 20th of February as possible, to move on Selma, Ala., which would tend to ward Forrest off. He promised to start it by that day, but I know he did not, and I do not know that he has yet started it. It but rarely happens that a number of expeditions starting from various points to act upon a common center materially aid each other. They never do except when each acts with vigor, and either makes rapid marches or keeps confronting an enemy. Whilst one column is engaging anything like an equal force it is necessarily aiding the other by holding that force. With Grierson, I am satisfied you would either find him at the appointed place in time or you would find him holding an enemy, which would enable the otherclumn to get there. I think you will find the same true of Wilson, who I suppose will command the forces starting from Eastport. I directed that you should organize your forces in two corps, one under Steele and the other under A.J. Smith. Both these officers have had experience in subsisting off the country through which they are passing. I write this now, not to give any instructions not heretofore given, but because I feel a great anxiety to see the enemy entirely broken up in the West whilst I believe it will be an easy job. Time will enable the enemy to reorganize and collect in their deserters and get up a formidible force. By giving them no rest what they now have in their ranks will leave them. It is also important to get all the negro men we can before the enemy put them in their ranks.... I am not urging because of any even supposed delay, but because I feel a great anxiety to see everything pushed, and the time it takes to communicate leaves me in the dark as to the progress you are making."[10]

Thomas wrote to Grant that afternoon: "General Stoneman has not yet started, but informed by chief of staff, a few days since, at Louisville, that he would be ready to start about the 1st of March. I will notify you as soon as he gets off. He has been delayed for want of horses. I have just returned from Eastport, having completed the arrangements for the cavalry expedition from that point. Owing to the recent stormy and rainy weather, General Wilson will be delayed a few days for the roads to dry up. He will be able to start in a few days with at least 10,000 men."[11]

This crossed with a message Grant wrote to Thomas that morning: "General Stoneman being so late in making his start from East Tennessee, and Sherman having passed out of the State of South Carolina, I think now his course had better be changed. It is not impossible that in the event of the enemy being driven from Richmond they may fall back to Lynchburg with a part of their force and attempt a raid into East Tennessee. It will be better, therefore, to keep Stoneman between our garrisons in East Tennessee and the enemy. Direct him to repeat his raid of last fall, destroying the railroad as far toward Lynchburg as he can. Sheridan starts to-day from Winchester for Lynchburg. This will vastly favor Stoneman. Every effort should be made to collect all the surplus forage and provisions of East Tennessee at Knoxville, and to get there a large amount of stores besides. It is not impossible that we may have to use a very considerable force in that section the coming spring. Preparations should at once be made to meet such contingency."[12]

Thomas replied to that message that night: "I am sorry that the expedition under General Stoneman could not get off sooner than this, but he has not had time to prepare fully since I received your instructions. I will direct him to throw his forces into Southwestern Virginia, as you direct; and, in anticipation of probable operations in East Tennessee this spring, have already thrown into Knoxville over 2,000,000 rations, and have given orders to have the store-houses filled to their full capacity. Orders were also given, some weeks since, to accumulate forage at Knoxville, which order is now being complied with by the quartermaster's department. Unless you wish otherwise, I shall send General Stanley's entire [4th] corps to East Tennessee, as soon as a sufficient number of new regiments report to enable me to withdraw it from Huntsville, Ala. I shall also concentrate the surplus of new regiments at Chattanooga, as the most available point from which to re-enforce the troops in East Tennessee, if necessary."[13]

Down in South Carolina that day, Sherman's army was on the move again after the delay caused by the swollen streams. "General Jeff. C. Davis got across the Catawba during the 27th," he wrote, "and the general march was resumed on Cheraw. Kilpatrick remained near Lancaster, skirmishing with Wheeler's and Hampton's cavalry, keeping up the delusion that we proposed to move on Charlotte and Salisbury, but with orders to watch the progress of the Fourteenth Corps, and to act in concert with it, on its left rear."[14]

That same day, Sheridan started out on his raid. "On the 27th of February," he later wrote, "my cavalry entered upon the campaign which cleared the Shenandoah Valley of every remnant of organized Confederates. General Torbert being absent on leave at this time, I did not recall him, but appointed General Merritt Chief of Cavalry, for Torbert had disappointed me on two important occasions—in the Luray Valley during the battle of Fisher's Hill, and on the recent Gordonsville expedition—and I mistrusted his ability to conduct any operations requiring much self-reliance. The column was composed of Custer's and Devin's divisions of cavalry, and two sections of artillery, comprising in all about 10,000 officers and men. On wheels we had, to accompany this column, eight ambulances, sixteen ammunition wagons, a pontoon train for eight canvas boats, and a small supply-train, with fifteen days' rations of coffee, sugar, and salt, it being intended to depend on the country for the meat and bread ration, the men carrying in their haversacks nearly enough to subsist them till out of the exhausted valley.... The weather was cold, the valley and surrounding mountains being still covered with snow; but this was fast disappearing, however, under the heavy rain that was coming down as the column moved along up the Valley pike at a steady gait that took us to Woodstock the first day. The second day we crossed the North Fork of the Shenandoah on our pontoon-bridge, and by night-fall reached Lacy Springs, having seen nothing of the enemy as yet but a few partisans who hung on our flanks in the afternoon."[15]

Grant replied to Thomas's telegrams of the day before on 28 February: I think your precaution in sending the Fourth Corps to Knoxville a good one. I also approve of sending the new troops to Chattanooga. Eastport must be held, particularly whilst troops are operating in Alabama." Meanwhile, Thomas was wiring Grant: "Have just heard from General Canby that his cavalry will start from Vicksburg on the 5th of March. General Wilson is now ready, and I will give him instructions to start from Eastport about the same date as the cavalry from Vicksburg starts."[16]

Lee wired Bragg that day in reply to his proposal to unite with Hardee and Beauregard: "Keep advised of Johnston's route. Communicate with General Johnston at Charlotte. Unite with him as you propose for a blow on Sherman when practicable."[17]

In Richmond that day Jefferson Davis called Benjamin Stringfellow into his office. The sergeant's letter proposing to kidnap Grant had wound up on the Confederate president's desk. What the two men said that day is not known, but it is known that Stringfellow was promoted to lieutenant and given an undercover assignment that would take him to Washington, where he would use the name and papers of a Union soldier from Maryland who was in a Rebel prison, and he would become a student of dentistry to provide him an excuse for moving around. The new lieutenant left Richmond the next day. It is safe to say that Grant was not his target, for he, as the Confederates well knew, was at City Point.

Wisconsin ratified, but New Jersey rejected, the Thirteenth Amendment that first day of March.

Down in North Carolina on 1 March, Cox assumed command of the District of Beaufort, part of Schofield's department, which included the town of New Berne. He organized two divisions of infantry out of the Union troops in the area, including about 3,000 who belonged to the four corps with Sherman who had been left behind when the latter marched from Atlanta or who had been recruited for its regiments since then. These had recently been forwarded to the east coast by Thomas. These divisions were commanded by brigadier generals I.N. Palmer, who had been in charge of the New Berne area before Cox was assigned to it, and S.P. Carter. Cox's mission was to advance from New Berne to Goldsborough, so that the railroad between those two places could be repaired and ready to haul supplies to Sherman's forces when they got that far. An intermediate objective was the town of Kinston, on the Neuse River. "On March 1st," Cox wrote, "Classen's brigade, of Palmer's division, was sent to Core Creek, sixteen miles, to be followed next day by Carter's division, so that the mechanical work might begin at once. At that time only one Confederate brigade (Whitford's) was known to be in the vicinity; but the almost total lack of wagons made it necessary to limit operations to the covering of the railway work. The whole number of wagon-teams in the district was fifty, and the utmost these could do was to supply the divisions at points near the end of the completed railway."[18]

In the Shenandoah Valley that day Sheridan's column came to the North Fork of the Shenandoah River at the town of Mount Crawford and found the covered bridge there on fire. Tom Rosser had learned of the Federal advance and had managed to assemble part of his command, which had scattered during the winter in order to find forage for the horses. His force at Mount Crawford is variously estimated at from 200 to 600 men, and these were in rifle pits on a hill overlooking the bridge, backed up by some artillery. Brevet Major General George Armstrong Custer's 3rd Division was the first Union force to reach the burning bridge.

The 25-year-old "boy general" as he was sometimes called, quickly sized up the situation and sent two regiments from Colonel Henry Capehart's 3rd Brigade—composed of units that had only recently been transferred to the 3rd Division from the 2nd Division—a mile up the river to swim across the stream and take the Rebels in flank. Today Custer's name is synonymous with "defeat" because of his death, along with part of his 7th Cavalry Regiment, at the Battle of the Little Big Horn eleven years later. But in 1865 he was becoming increasingly known as the finest cavalry commander in the Union army. "I have seen him," Colonel Capehart later wrote, "under the most varying and critical circumstances, and never without ample resources of mind and body to meet the most trying contingency. He was counted by some rash; it was because he dared, while they dared not. There can be no doubt that he had a positive genius for war."[19]

"The river was deep and the water very cold," a captain in one of the flanking regiments wrote, "but the boys...were soon on the south side ready for work. They dismounted for a moment under the bank, to get rid of some of the water from their boots and clothing, and then formed line on the heights and began their advance. The enemy had not discovered the movement, and when our boys, with drawn sabres and ringing cheers, dashed upon them from the rear, they broke in confusion, and fled in wild disorder towards Staunton and Waynesboro."[20] Rosser escaped with the majority of his men, but he left behind, besides several killed, 30 prisoners and 20 wagons and ambulances. The fire was then extinguished and the bridge saved, so that the rest of the Union column could cross the frigid river without swimming.

Rosser's move had only been an attempt to buy time. Meanwhile, Lieutenant General Jubal Anderson Early, still the Confederate commander in the Valley despite several defeats by Sheridan, moved to block his opponent's latest move as best he could with his few remaining troops. He sent for Brigadier General John Echols' brigade of infantry, down in the southwestern corner of Virginia, to move toward Lynchburg and ordered Major General Lunsford Lomax's scattered cavalry division to concentrate at Pond Gap, protecting the road to that city. But with the troops closer to hand, Brigadier General Gabriel Wharton's two small brigades of infantry, a battalion of artillery, and Rosser's cavalry, he withdrew from Staunton to Waynesborough, near Rockfish Gap in the Blue Ridge. From there he would threaten the rear and flank of Sheridan's column if it continued up the Valley toward Lynchburg.

"I entered Staunton the morning of March 2," Sheridan later wrote, "and finding that Early had gone to Waynesboro' with his infantry and Rosser, the question at once arose whether I should continue my march to Lynchburg direct, leaving my adversary in my rear, or turn east and open the way through Rockfish Gap to the Virginia Central railroad and James River canal. I felt confidence of the success of the latter plan, for I knew that Early numbered there not more than two thousand men; so, influenced by this, and somewhat also by the fact that Early had left word in Staunton that he would fight at Waynesboro', I directed Merritt to move toward that place with Custer, to be closely followed by Devin, who was to detach one brigade to destroy supplies at Swoope's depot. The by-roads were miry beyond description, rain having fallen almost incessantly since we left Winchester, but notwithstanding the down-pour the column pushed on, men and horses growing almost unrecognizable from the mud covering them from head to foot."[21]

At 3 p.m. Custer came in sight of the little village of Waynesborough and found that Jubal Early was true to his word. Wharton's infantry and about eleven pieces of artillery were entrenched on a ridge west of the town with a clear line of fire covering the road along which the Federals were approaching. It was a formidible position to charge frontally, while Rosser's cavalry covered the Rebel right and the South River was to the left. However, Custer always had a quick appreciation for the advantages and disadvantages of terrain, and it served him well that day. He realized that there was a wide gap between Early's defenses and the South River. So he dismounted three regiments and sent them to move around the Rebel left under the cover of some woods near the stream. Meanwhile he sent forward a line of mounted skirmishers to pester the Confederates, posted some guns to shell the Rebel lines, and massed Capehart's 3rd Brigade for a mounted assault.

When all was ready, Custer's bugler sounded the charge and the flankers sprang from the trees onto the Confederate flank and rear with their Spencer repeating carbines blazing and the rest of his division charged up the slippery ridge straight for the Rebel entrenchments, "Custer's gleaming sabre and scarlet cravat being conspicuous among the foremost," as one of his officers put it.[22] The Confederate gunners stuck to their pieces, but Wharton's infantry broke and ran. Infantry could not outrun cavalry, however, even in the mud, and the mounted troopers rode right over the fleeing Rebels, then turned about and formed line, blocking their retreat. In less than three hours from the time that Custer had come within sight of Waynesborough the battle was over. One of Merritt's staff officers just riding up found Custer in what he called "a very high feather."

"Is General Sheridan over there, Sanford?" Custer asked.

"Yes," the staff officer answered, "he is just riding into the village."

"Well," the young general replied, "tell him I have got two thousand prisoners, seventeen battle flags and eleven pieces of artillery."[23]

Actually, only 1,600 Rebels were captured, but so were all 200 Confederate wagons and ambulances, as well as the guns and flags. Other than Rosser's cavalry, which had been stationed at the end of the line farthest from the flank attack and had horses on which to escape, only General Early, his staff, three other generals, and some 15 to 20 men escaped across the Blue Ridge. The Army of the Valley no longer existed.

---

1. *Official Records*, 46:II:701.
2. Ibid., 46:II:685.
3. Ibid., 47:II:1279.
4. James D. Horan, *Confederate Agent: A Discovery in History* (New York, 1954), 238.
5. Ibid., 240.
6. Cox, *The March to the Sea, Franklin and Nashville*, 154-155. As this paragraph shows, the spelling of New Berne was, during the Civil War, not particularly consistent.
7. *Official Records*, 46:II:704.
8. Ibid.
9. Ibid., 46:II:717.
10. Ibid., 49:I:780-781.
11. Ibid., 49:I:777
12. Ibid.
13. Ibid., 49:I:778.
14. Sherman, *Memoirs*, 771-772.
15. Philip Sheridan, *Civil War Memoirs* (New York, 1991), 293-294.
16. *Official Records*, 49:I:783.
17. Ibid., 47:II:1292.
18. Cox, *The March to the Sea, Franklin and Nashville*, 155-156.
19. Gregory J. W. Urwin, *Custer Victorious: The Civil War Battles of General George Armstrong Custer* (East Brunswick, N.J., 1983), 35.
20. Ibid., 226.
21. Sheridan, *Civil War Memoirs*, 294-295.
22. Urwin, *Custer Victorious*, 229.
23. Ibid., 230.

CHAPTER SEVENTEEN

With Malice Toward None

2 - 5 March 1865

"On the 2d of March we entered the village of Chesterfield," Sherman remembered, "skirmishing with Butler's cavalry, which gave ground rapidly. There I received a message from General Howard, who reported that he was already in Cheraw with the Seventeenth Corps, and that the Fifteenth was near at hand. General Hardee had retreated eastward across the Pedee, burning the bridge. I therefore directed the left wing to march for Sneedsboro', about ten miles above Cheraw, to cross the Pedee there, while I in person proposed to cross over and join the right wing in Cheraw. Early in the morning of the 3d of March I rode out of Chesterfield along with the Twentieth Corps, which filled the road, forded Thompson's Creek, and, at the top of the hill beyond, found a road branching off to the right, which corresponded with the one on my map leading to Cheraw. Seeing a negro standing by the road-side, looking at the troops passing, I inquired of him what road that was. 'Him lead to Cheraw, master!' 'Is it a good road, and how far?' 'A very good road, and eight or ten miles.' 'Any guerrillas?' 'Oh! no, master, dey is gone two days ago; you could have played cards on der coat-tails, dey was in sich a hurry!' I was on my Lexington horse, who was very handsome and restive, so I made signal to my staff to follow, as I proposed to go without escort. I turned my horse down the road, and the rest of the staff followed. General Barry took up the questions about the road, and asked the same negro what he was doing there. He answered, 'Dey say Massa Sherman will be along soon!' 'Why,' said General Barry, 'that was General Sherman you were talking to.' The poor negro, almost in the attitude of prayer, exclaimed: 'De great God! just look at his horse!' He ran up and trotted by my side for a mile or so, and gave me all the information he possessed, but he seemed to admire the horse more than the rider.

"We reached Cheraw in a couple of hours in a drizzling rain, and, while waiting for our wagons to come up, I staid with General Blair in a large house, the property of a blockade-runner, whose family remained. General Howard occupied another house farther down-town. He had already ordered his pontoon-bridge to be laid across the Pedee, there a large, deep, navigable stream, and Mower's division was already across, skirmishing with the enemy about two miles out. Cheraw was found to be full of stores which had been sent up from Charleston prior to its evacuation, and which could not be removed. I was satisfied, from inquiries, that General Hardee had with him only the Charleston garrison, that the enemy had not divined our movements, and that consequently they were still scattered from Charlotte around to Florence, then behind us. Having thus secured the passage of the Pedee, I felt no uneasiness about the future, because there remained no further great impediment between us and Cape Fear River, which I felt assured was by that time in possession of our friends."[1]

Up in Virginia on 3 March, Sheridan organized a force of some 1,200 officers and men, including those who had lost their horses or had the poorest horses plus the smallest regiments from each of his brigades. This force was to escort the Rebels and guns captured the day before back to Winchester. Meanwhile, the Reserve Brigade of the 1st Division blew up the iron bridge of the Virginia Central Railroad and destroyed the wagons, caissons, ammunition, weapons, and supplies captured the day before, and the rest of the column, still led by Custer's division, crossed the Blue Ridge and headed for Charlottesville. Mud continued to obstruct the Federals' progress and, as one regimental historian put it, "frequently a horse was abandoned through inability to extricate him." He added that "men and horses, teamsters and mules, wagons and negroes, were literally plastered from one end to the other, but the men were good natured, laughing and singing and joking, for the enemy was in the last ditch, the war was nearing its end, and home, sweet home, was almost in sight."[2] Another trooper remembered a stretch of road about 400 yards long in a deep cut where the wagons could not turn off the road and the dark reddish-brown mud had the consistency of soft mortar. The wheels of the wagons sunk into it until their beds rested on the surface of the road.

Custer reached Charlottesville late that afternoon, where he was met by the mayor and a delegation of prominent citizens who presented him with the keys to the city, literally, or at least to the courthouse, jail, several taverns and churches, and the University of Virginia. The latter, at least, proved useful, for the Federals slept that night in the school's dormitories.

At City Point, General Grant was just starting for the mess hut for dinner that evening when he was handed a note from General Lee that had been sent through the lines: "Lieutenant General Longstreet has informed me that in a recent conversation between himself and Major General Ord as to the possibility of arriving at a satisfactory adjustment of the present unhappy difficulties by means of a military convention, General Ord stated that if I desired to have an interview with you on the subject you would not decline, provided I had authority to act. Sincerely desiring to leave nothing untried which may put an end to the calamities of war, I propose to meet you at such convenient time and place as you may designate, with the hope that upon an interchange of views it may be found practicable to submit the subjects of controversy between the belligerents to a convention of the kind mentioned. In such event I am authorized to do whatever the result of the proposed interview may render necessary or advisable."[3] In addition, there was another note from Lee that raised some questions about the exchange of political prisoners and suggested that this subject could also be discussed at the proposed meeting. Longstreet, after seeing the first letter had suggested that Lee send a letter such as the second one instead, saying that "once they were together they could talk as they pleased."[4] For he correctly surmised that Grant could not comply with such a blatant invitation to meddle in political questions. But Lee had sent both letters.

Grant immediately telegraphed the contents of Lee's first letter to Secretary Stanton, saying, "General Ord met General Longstreet a few days since, at the request of the latter, to arrange for the exchange of citizen prisoners and prisoners of war improperly captured. He had my authority to do so, and to arrange it definitely for such as were confined in his department; arrangements for all others to be submitted for approval. A general conversation ensued on the subject of the war, and has induced the above letter. I have not returned any reply, but promised to do so at 12 m. to-morrow. I respectfully request instructions."

At midnight Stanton replied: "I send you a telegram written by the President himself in answer to yours of this evening, which I have signed by his order. I will add that General Ord's conduct in holding intercourse with General Longstreet upon political questions not committed to his charge is not approved....You will please in future instruct officers appointed to meet rebel officers to confine themselves to the matters specially committed to them." The telegram written by Lincoln but signed by Stanton said: "The President directs me to say to you that he wishes you to have no conference with General Lee, unless it be for the capitulation of General Lee's army or on some minor and purely military matter. He instructs me to say that you are not to decide, discuss, or confer upon any political question. Such questions the President holds in his own hands, and will submit them to no military conferences or conventions. Meantime you are to press to the utmost your military advantages."[5]

Late that night, Major General John B. Gordon was summoned to Lee's headquarters in the Turnbull house at Edge Hill on the outskirts of Petersburg. Gordon had been in command of Lee's 2nd Corps since it had left the Shenandoah Valley without Early several weeks before. It was about 3 a.m. and bitterly cold when the 33-year-old corps commander arrived. He found Lee all alone, gazing into the fire. "To me," Gordon wrote, "he had the appearance of one suffering from physical illness. In answer to my inquiry as to his health, he stated that he was well enough bodily...." Lee motioned him to a chair at a long table that was filled with depressing reports from the various commands of his army and told him to read them. "I was not prepared for the picture presented by these reports of extreme destitution—of the lack of shoes, of hats, of overcoats, and of blankets, as well as of food. Some of the officers had gone outside the formal official statement as to numbers of the sick, to tell in plain, terse, and forceful words of depleted strength, emaciation, and decreased power of endurance among those who appeared on the rolls as fit for duty...."

When Gordon had finished reading, Lee gave him his estimate of the situation. "Adding all the Union forces together, there would soon be in the seaboard states 280,000 Federal troops, to whom the Confederacy could oppose 65,000...." Lee wanted to know "what I thought under these conditions it was best to do—or what duty to the army and our people required of us...." Gordon told him he could only see three alternatives: "First, make terms with the enemy, the best we can get. Second, if that is not practicable, the best thing to do is to retreat—abandon Richmond and Petersburg, unite with General Johnston in North Carolina, and strike Sherman before Grant can join him; or lastly, we must fight, and without delay."[6] Lee said that he agreed fully. However, as a soldier he could not urge political action on the government. He made no mention of the letters already sent to Grant. He also explained the difficulties of retreating to North Carolina because his men and horses were in such poor condition. After a long discussion, Lee said that he had already planned to go to Richmond the next day to see President Davis.

The next day, 4 March, Lee and Davis were probably in conference when Grant's answer to Lee's letters was received: "Your two letters of the 2d instant were received yesterday. In regard to any apprehended misunderstanding in reference to the exchange of political prisoners, I think there need be none. General Ord and General Longstreet have probably misunderstood what I said to the former on the subject, or I may have failed to make myself understood, possibly....In regard to meeting you on the 6th instant, I would state that I have no authority to accede to your proposition for a conference on the subject proposed. Such authority is vested in the President of the United States alone. General Ord could only have meant that I would not refuse an interview on any subject on which I have a right to act, which, of course, would be such as are purely of a military character, and on the subject of exchanges which has been intrusted to me."[7]

He sent Stanton copies of Lee's letters and his own and told him: "I can assure you that no act of the enemy will prevent me from pressing all advantages gained to the utmost of my ability. Neither will I, under any circumstances, exceed my authority, or in any way embarrass the Government. It was because I had no right to meet General Lee on the subject proposed by him that I referred the matter for instructions."[8]

That same day, Grant wrote an order putting in motion a raid to break up trade with the Confederates in the Fredericksburg area. Before starting on his current raid, Sheridan had ordered General Augur, commanding at Washington to send a cavalry expedition to accomplish this object, but Grant had then decided to send an amphibious expedition from the James River instead. He chose the 3rd Brigade of the 3rd Division of Gibbon's 24th Corps in Ord's Army of the James, commanded by Colonel Samuel H. Roberts, reinforced with one regiment of cavalry, the 1st New York Mounted Rifles, commanded by Colonel E.V. Sumner, Jr. Grant's subordinates often commented on the clarity of his orders, which he almost always wrote with his own hand rather than by dictation. They always knew exactly what he wanted them to do. This order is a typical example: "With your brigade and the cavalry ordered to report to you, you will proceed up the Rappahannock River as far as you may deem it safe and expedient to go on transports. You will then debark and proceed by land as rapidly as possible to Fredericksburg, Va., and capture the place, if not too strongly defended. Two army and two navy gun-boats are ordered to accompany the expedition. They are authorized to assemble in the Rappahannock in advance of the expedition. You will ascertain at Fort Monroe, however, whether they have gone forward, and if they have not you will not proceed without them. In advancing up the river be careful that no transport precedes the leading convoy. When you leave the transports you will place a small guard on the river-bank for their protection in the absence of the expeditionary force. It is understood that a very considerable contraband trade is carried on across the Potomac by what is known as the Northern Neck and through Fredericksburg into Richmond. The object of your expedition is to break this up as far as possible. If you succeed in reaching Fredericksburg you will seize or destroy all property which you have good reason to believe is being used in barter for unauthorized articles of trade between the rebel armies and the Northern cities. You will also destroy the railroad depot and as much of the road back toward Richmond as you can. After having accomplished this you are authorized to go to any point where information you may receive may lead you to suppose goods can be found which are in transit either north or south. All such will be either seized or destroyed. You will also arrest and bring with you all persons you know to be engaged, directly or indirectly, in smuggling or trading between the North and South. You will not unnecessarily disturb peaceful and quiet citizens, but you will take from the country such supplies and forage as may be necessary for your command. You will also destroy all accumulation of supplies of whatever description as you may have reason to believe are being collected for the use of the enemy. Having accomplished the object of the expedition you are sent upon you will return with your command to the place of starting. If you find that it would be advantageous, after doing all you can from your first landing, to go elsewhere on the Potomac or tributaries, you are authorized to use your transports for that purpose."[9]

Out where Tennessee, Mississippi, and Alabama come together, Wilson had his cavalry all ready to start its raid, but the weather was not cooperating. Prolonged and heavy rain had turned the roads to quagmires and swollen the Tennessee River until it had overflowed its banks. "The river is four miles wide now…," one of his troopers wrote on 4 March. "I seen a boat out in a cornfield. The river is higher than it has been for forty years, so the citizens say." A large depot full of supplies at Eastport, Mississippi, was ruined by the rain and the rising water. What was even worse, from Wilson's standpoint, almost all of his men and horses were on the north side of the swollen stream. "The rain-storm just ended was the most violent of the season," Wilson wrote to Thomas, now back at Nashville, that evening. "The Tennessee is now higher than for many years and rising rapidly. It will be utterly impossible to get off to-morrow, though I shall use every possible effort to expedite the movement. My command is in splendid condition and will start at the earliest possible moment after it can cross the river. It is fair to presume this rain has been generally diffused and will delay General Canby's movements, those from Memphis and Vicksburg certainly, as much as mine."[10]

Lee sent J.E. Johnston a short telegram that day: "Assume command of all troops in Department of North Carolina, except those from this army arresting deserters. General Bragg informed."[11] With Sherman's forces nearing the North Carolina line and the Confederates in South Carolina doing their best to get in front of him, it made sense to put all the forces in the area under one commander, uniting Bragg's troops (mostly Hoke's Division) with Hardee's forces from Charleston and the remnants of the Army of Tennessee.

Sherman's troops were still at Cheraw that day. "There was an immense amount of stores in Cheraw," he wrote, "which were used or destroyed; among them twenty-four guns, two thousand muskets, and thirty-six hundred barrels of gunpowder. By the carelessness of a soldier, an immense pile of this powder was exploded, which shook the town badly, and killed and maimed several of our men."[12]

"When we made a fire to cook our coffee," one of Sherman's men explained, "there was a little flash of powder ran along the ground and one yelled, 'Look out for the magazine!' We did look out and ran for the river. The powder flashes ran in every direction.... Then there was a tremedous explosion.... The dirt and stones flew in every direction.... We made some pretty quick move." Six soldiers and several civilians were killed, and three houses were demolished. "Gen. Sherman was thoroughly aroused," another of his men recorded, "and was on the point of ordering the city reduced to ashes, and the Mayor and other city officials placed before a firing squad before it was found they weren't to blame."

Among the captured cannon was one that bore a brass plate identifying it as the first gun fired on Fort Sumter—the gun that had fired the first shot of the war. Sherman's men used these captured guns to fire a salute to celebrate the inauguration of President Lincoln's second term. Some of their barrels burst, but this failed to dampen the Federals' enthusiasm. A civilian whose home was being used as the headquarters for a regiment that Sherman visited asked the general where he planned to go next. Sherman smiled and said, "I have about 60,000 men out there, and I intend to go pretty much where I please."[13]

A presidential inauguration was then, as it is now, a public ceremony and celebration involving numerous dignitaries and organizations, foreign as well as domestic. Considerable coordination and timing are involved in bringing it off. But it had been raining in Washington for two days and had been coming down in torrents at daybreak. It let up about 10:30 a.m., and crowds of people ventured hopefully out onto the streets, but ten minutes later the rains started up again, sending them scurrying for cover. It was on again, off again after that.

Mud was almost as great an obstacle to the thousands of people who had descended on the capital city as it was to Sheridan's and Sherman's marching columns. "There is mud in Pennsylvania Avenue and all the other streets," a correspondent for the New York *Herald* reported. "There is also mud in the streets that cross Pennsylvania Avenue and all the other avenues....The streets are flooded and afloat with a vile yellow fluid, not thick enough to walk on nor thin enough to swim in. This yellow material added to the holiday appearance of the people, marking them with gay and festive spots from head to heel. All the backs were yellow with it, and all the horses, and all the little boys—all the world floundered about in it, and swore at it, and laughed at it. In Pennsylvania Avenue it was not so deep as in many other places, for as that street is paved, it was possible to touch bottom there. It was blacker there, however...and when it spattered on people it did not look so much like golden spangles."[14]

Nevertheless, at 11 a.m. the vehicles, floats, and marching bodies of men began to form up on the grounds around the White House and across the street in Lafayette Park for the procession up Pennsylvania Avenue to the Capitol. Mrs. Lincoln, in a closed carriage, became impatient at the delay and worried that she would be late for the swearing in, so she ordered the coachman to take her on ahead. With it went an escort of thirteen marshals and thirteen citizen aides as well as the President's Union Light Guard. The crowd that had gathered along the avenue cheered the carriage as it passed, assuming that the president was inside. Actually, however, he was already at the

Capitol, so busy signing bills before Congress adjourned that he had even forgotten to remove his stovepipe hat.

Mrs. Lincoln's hasty departure upset the carefully planned arrangements for the procession, but finally it got under way in a light drizzling rain and cold, gusty winds. Military bands played, the city's bells rang out, and on one of the floats sailors fired blank cartridges from the cannon in the turret of a miniature replica of the USS *Monitor*. Soldiers, marines, and Lincoln-and-Johnson club members marched, firemen from both Washington and Philadelphia drove their beautifully decorated and highly polished fire engines through the mud, and a float from the Washington *Daily Chronicle* carried a printing press in full operation, running off programs of the day's activities that were thrown to the crowd as they were printed.

The Senate of the outgoing 38th Congress was trying to wrap up its business when the doors to the gallery were opened at 11:30 a.m. and a crowd of ladies burst in, chattering like a flock of noisy birds as they took their seats, oblivious to the fact that the Senate was still in session. Senators protested that they could not hear what was being said, even though they were squeezed into half of their normal space to make room for the members of the House of Representatives, justices of the Supreme Court, and other dignitaries who would soon be joining them for the inauguration, and the presiding officer banged his gavel in vain.

The room was filling up rapidly when, shortly before noon, the outgoing vice president, Hannibal Hamlin, and his successor, Andrew Johnson, entered arm in arm. The latter had been suffering from a fever for weeks and had fortified himself with a sizable amount of brandy before entering the Senate chamber. Hamlin took the chair and delivered a short farewell to the Senate even as the cabinet and several of the Supreme Court justices arrived. Then Mrs. Lincoln and members of the diplomatic corps came in.

After completing his brief remarks, Hamlin turned to Johnson and asked if he was ready to take the oath of office. Johnson, red in the face from the brandy and the heat of the crowded room, stood up and said he was ready, but without waiting for Hamlin to administer the oath he launched into a long, loud, and rambling speech whose theme seemed to be that the powers of all the assembled dignataries, himself included, were derived from the people. The members of the House of Representatives began crowding in before anyone could stop him and finally President Lincoln came in, unobtrusively taking his seat at the end of the clerk's table. The unruly crowd, buzzing with each new arrival, eventually became aware that something was wrong and fell silent, causing Johnson's voice to ring abnormally loud in the sudden hush. Only seven minutes had been allotted for the vice president's speech, but Johnson rambled on and on, despite Hamlin nudging him, and embarrassed senators turning and twisting in their chairs.

Finally he stopped, and Hamlin tried to quickly administer the oath, but Johnson forced him to read it out a sentence at a time and, according to the New York *World*, Johnson "stumbled, stammered, [and] repeated portions of it several times over." Even that was not the end of the embarrassing incident. "The moment that he concluded this task," the *World* continued, "Mr. Johnson turned to the audience and commenced another speech, giving to those assembled his ideas of the oath which he had just taken. He had uttered but two or three sentences when some of the officials standing near him had the good sense to stop him."[15]

Hamlin adjourned the old Senate, Johnson called the new Senate to order, and the clerk read a proclamation convening an extraordinary session needed to confirm various civil and military appointments. Then eight new senators were called up to take their oaths of office. Johnson held out a Bible for them to touch and bow their heads, but then he dismissed them without giving them the oath. The clerk had to take over, call them back, and administer it. Then, to the relief of all, he announced that the procession to the east front of the Capitol should be formed. As Lincoln took his place a senator heard him tell a marshal, "Do not let Johnson speak outside."[16]

Capitol police held back the crowd of onlookers that had somehow gained access to the hallways in spite of orders to keep them out. But, after the president had passsed, a man broke through the police line and started toward the inauguration platform. A police lieutenant grabbed him, and after a scuffle the man was hustled off to the guardroom but soon released. Cranks were common enough in the national capitol, as were office-seekers. The lieutenant, and others who saw the man, later thought that he had been John Wilkes Booth, based on a photograph of the latter published in the papers after the assassination, but this is doubted by most historians. Booth did not need to break through the police lines to get near the president, having obtained a ticket to the dignitaries' platform from a senator's daughter who was infatuated with him. He later told an acquaintance that he had had an excellent chance to kill the president that day if he had wanted to. That, however, was not yet his goal, only capture, and anyway an escape would have been almost impossible.

A temporary platform had been constructed over the grand central staircase on the east front of the Capitol, between two groups of statuary symbolizing America's beginnings. Overhead was the recently completed dome, topped with Thomas Crawford's statue of Freedom. And beyond the platform a large crowd had gathered, in spite of the weather, which was improving at last. "Ladies, Senators, Negroes, Justices, secretaries, diplomats, and people generally, tumbled upon the platform pell-mell," the New York *Herald's* correspondent wrote. "As the ladies moved on to the north entrance there was a grand national display of ankles. Representative ankles were exhibited by the fair dames and lasses of every state in the Union. The variety of shape and size of hose was perfectly bewildering; but every foot was muddy and every skirt bedraggled....Colored persons innumerable flocked around, though none were admitted to the Capitol. Soldiers off duty were present in large numbers....Men, women, and children soaked about quietly, caught cold, and waited for something to see....The rain had taken all the starch out of them.

"Stanton and Seward retired to the left at some distance from the President and sat down together. They seemed very friendly. Stanton had his arm around Seward's neck and constantly whispered in his ear. Welles sat by himself, and Justice Chase sat erect and dignified, evidently reflecting that he ought to be in Lincoln's place. Senator Sumner stood prominently forward as if to attract attention....The President smiled to himself and seemed greatly to enjoy the sunshine which now streamed upon him. He was dressed in black, with a plain frock coat. In his hand he held a printed copy of his inaugural address. The marshals of the day were grouped around the President, swelling with pride, and often excluding him from sight. The planks of the platform were wet, and the airy position rather chilly. The bands played away most lustily, and their 'Hail to the Chief' could scarcely be stopped.

"From the platform nothing could be seen but a sea of faces below and a sea of mud beyond....In the Capitol all the windows were filled with ladies, and the steps and esplanade at the north wing presented the same dense crowd that the central steps did, while on the unfinished parts of the south wing, on all the scaffolding, hundreds of soldiers had clambored up and decorated all that part with the army blue....As the President came forward there was a cheer but not a great one, and at the same time the sun burst through the clouds, and, though pretty well to the south, lighted up the whole east face very brilliantly....Out by the colossal statue of Washington that faced the president with a monitory finger pointed to Heaven...the crowd was scattered thinly; but...toward the Capitol it grew denser at every step, until it became a packed mass impossible to penetrate. This mass surged in silence below. Above this was the central mass about the President...At about one o'clock...the President rose and stepped forward to the reading desk. He was greeted with very faint applause; indeed there was no enthusiasm throughout the address. It was not strictly an inaugural address, since it was read before Mr. Lincoln took the oath. It was more like a valedictory. The President read in a very loud, clear voice, and hundreds of the audience could hear it.... During the whole ceremony he looked unusually handsome. When delivering his speech his face glowed with enthusiasm, and he evidently felt every word that he uttered."[17]

"At this second appearing to take the oath of the presidential office," he began, "there is less occasion for an extended address than there was at the first. Then a statement, somewhat in detail, of a course to be pursued, seemed fitting and proper. Now, at the expiration of four years, during which public declarations have been constantly called forth on every point and phase of the great contest which still absorbs the attention, and engrosses the energies of the nation, little that is new could be presented. The progress of our arms, upon which all else chiefly depends, is as well known to the public as to myself; and it is, I trust, reasonably satisfactory and encouraging to all. With high hope for the future, no prediction in regard to it is ventured.

"On the occasion corresponding to this four years ago, all thoughts were anxiously directed to an impending civil-war. All dreaded it—all sought to avert it. While the inaugural address was being delivered from this place, devoted altogether to *saving* the Union without war, insurgent agents were in the city seeking to *destroy* it without war—seeking to dissolve the Union, and divide effects, by negotiation. Both parties deprecated war; but one of them would *make* war rather than let the nation survive; and the other would *accept* war rather than let it perish. And the war came.

"One eighth of the whole population were colored slaves, not distributed generally over the Union, but localized in the Southern part of it. These slaves constituted a peculiar and powerful interest. All knew that this interest was, somehow, the cause of the war. To strengthen, perpetuate, and extend this interest was the object for which the insurgents would rend the Union, even by war; while the government claimed no right to do more than to restrict the territorial enlargement of it. Neither party expected for the war, the magnitude, or the duration, which it has already attained. Neither anticipated that the *cause* of the conflict might cease with, or even before, the conflict itself should cease. Each looked for an easier triumph, and a result less fundamental and astounding. Both read the same Bible, and pray to the same God; and each invokes His aid against the other. It may seem strange that any man should dare to ask a just God's assistance in wringing their bread from the sweat of other men's faces; but let us judge not that we be not judged. The prayers of both could not be answered; that of neither has been answered fully. The Almighty has His own purposes. 'Woe unto the world because of offences! for it must needs be that offences come; but woe to that man by whom the offence cometh!' If we shall suppose that American Slavery is one of those offences which, in the providence of God, must needs come, but which, having continued through His appointed time, He now wills to remove, and that He gives to both North and South, this terrible war, as the woe due to those by whom the offence came, shall we discern therein any departure from those divine attributes which the believers in a Living God always ascribe to Him? Fondly do we hope—fervently do we pray—that this mighty scourge of war may speedily pass away. Yet, if God wills that it continue, until all the wealth piled by the bond-man's two hundred and fifty years of unrequited toil shall be sunk, and until every drop of blood drawn with the lash, shall be paid by another drawn with the sword, as was said three thousand years ago, so still it must be said, 'the judgments of the Lord, are true and righteous altogether.'

With malice toward none; with charity for all; with firmness in the right, as God gives us to see the right, let us strive on to finish the work we are in; to bind up the nation's wounds; to care for him who shall have borne the battle, and for his widow, and his orphan—to do all which may achieve and cherish a just, and a lasting peace, among ourselves, and with all nations."[18]

"During the delivery of the speech," the *Herald's* correspondent noted, "Stanton and Seward were remarkably attentive, rising and bending forward to listen. The crowd kept pushing nearer and nearer the platform. Sumner smiled superciliously at the frequent scriptural quotations. Negroes ejaculated 'Bress de Lord' in a low murmer at the end of almost every sentence. Beyond this there was no cheering of any consequence. Even the soldiers did not hurrah much....After a brief pause the President and Chief Justice rose together and the oath of office was administered. The voice of the Chief Justice was inaudible, but the workings of his countenance could be distinctly seen as he labored to be impressive. Then there was a cheer, and the President came forward and bowed and smiled....

"Cries for Andy Johnson next ensued. There was a momentary delay and then the Vice President presented himself and waved both hands. There were calls of 'Speech! Speech!' and some applause when Andy appeared. He rubbed his red face with his hands as if to clear up his ideas, but did not succeed and said nothing. A lane was then opened through the crowd on the platform, and the Presidential party retired into the Capitol amid the thunders of artillery in Capitol Square and the music of the bands."[19]

Lincoln was led to a carriage to return to the White House, and his 11-year-old son Tad climbed in and rode home with him. Walt Whitman, the poet, saw Lincoln on his return ride, escorted by the marshals and the motley retinue of the procession: "He was in his plain two-horse barouche, and looked very much worn and tired; the lines, indeed, of vast responsibilities, intricate questions, and demands of life and death, cut deeper than ever upon his dark brown face; yet all the goodness, tenderness, sadness, and canny shrewdness [showed] underneath the furrows."[20] Mrs. Lincoln and Captain Robert Lincoln followed in other carriages.

The senators returned to their chamber, more interested in discussing Johnson's embarrassing bahavior than the historic speech they had just heard. They waited for the new vice president to come and officially adjourn them, but he never came. Finally the senators gave up and left in ones and twos, more irked at Johnson than ever.

Lincoln and his wife took a drive that afternoon in their open barouche, enjoying the improved weather and stopping off at Willard's Hotel on Pennsylvania Avenue so that Mrs. Lincoln could see one of her friends. That night they had to undergo a public reception, at which anyone who was willing to wait in line could shake the president's hand as he stood in the receiving line. Cabinet members began arriving at the White House after dinner in order to beat the crowds, and when the gates were thrown open at 8 p.m. some 2,000 people rushed in, followed during the evening by many more. The front doors were only opened for a few minutes at a time in order to control the rate of entry, but even so, as one reporter noted, "Some of the more unfortunate females, who were caught in the surging mass, actually shrieked with pain while several fainted and were carried away."[21] The visitors had to carry their hats and coats because there was no provision for checking them.

Inside the East Room the Marine Band was playing and various dignitaries were clustered in little groups. "The President," one reporter noted, "in a plain black suit with white kid gloves, was in excellent spirits...and received all visitors cordially. It is estimated that he shook hands with between five and six thousand persons during the course of the evening. Mrs. Lincoln was also kept fully occupied."[22]

There was still a large crowd waiting to get in when the doors were closed at 11 p.m., and just before midnight the Marine Band struck up "Yankee Doodle," and the White House was cleared of guests before the clock struck twelve. It looked, according to one of the guards, "as if a regiment of rebel troops had been quartered there, with permission to forage. A great piece of red brocade, a yard square almost, was cut from the window-hangings of the East Room. Flowers from the floral design in the lace curtains were cut out. Some arrests were made, after the reception, of persons concerned in the disgraceful business." The president, the guard noted, was greatly distressed. "Why should they do it?" he asked. "How can they?"[23]

Outside, drunken celebrants were staggering through the streets, but one newspaper bragged that the night was the most orderly one to succeed a presidential inauguration since Andrew Jackson's first term. There were a few robberies, assaults, and riots, of course, but only a few.

The next morning, Lieutenant Stringfellow arrived in Washington on a secret mission for Jefferson Davis.

---

1. Sherman, *Memoirs*, 772-773.
2. Stephen Z. Starr, *The Union Cavalry in the Civil War*, volume 2 (Baton Rouge, 1981), 376.
3. Dowdey and Manarin, *Wartime Papers of R. E. Lee*, 911.
4. Longstreet, *From Manassas to Appomattox*, 585.
5. *Official Records*, 46:II:801-802.
6. Freeman, *R. E. Lee* 4:7-8 and Stern, *An End to Valor*, 67-69.
7. *Official Records*, 46:II:825.
8. Ibid., 46:II:824.
9. Ibid., 46:II:832.
10. Ibid., 49:I:825.
11. Ibid., 47:II:1320.
12. Sherman, *Memoirs*, 774.
13. Davis, *Sherman's March*, 203-204.
14. Stern, *An End to Valor*, 2-3.
15. Ibid., 12.
16. Sandburg, *The War Years*, 1864-1865, 770.
17. Ibid., 13-15.
18. Basler, ed. *Collected Works of Abraham Lincoln*, 8:332-333.
19. Stern, *An End to Valor*, 15-16.
20. Ibid., 17.
21. Ibid., 20.
22. Ibid., 21.
23. Sandburg, *The War Years, 1864-1865*, 774.

CHAPTER EIGHTEEN

Destroy... Everything Useful for Carrying on War

5 - 11 March 1865

The amphibious expedition to Fredericksburg left Fort Monroe at 5 p.m. on 5 March. It was commanded by Colonel Samuel H. Roberts and consisted of his five regiments of infantry, totalling 1,800 men, plus a detachment of 300 troopers from the 1st New York Mounted Rifles and was accompanied by three army gunboats. Fredericksburg is on the south bank of the Rappahannock River, about halfway between Washington and Richmond. "At the mouth of the Rappahannock

River," Roberts reported, "I met Commander Parker, of the Potomac flotilla, who strongly advised me to abandon my proposed route, and land at some point on the Potomac and march across to Fredericksburg, representing that it would take two days to reach the city by water, even if we escaped the torpedoes supposed to be planted in the channel. On signifying my determination to try the Rappahannock route, he furnished me with the gun-boats Yankee and Commodore Read, under Acting Volunteer Lieutenant Hooker, who gave me every assistance in his power."[1]

Led by one of the army gunboats, the expedition moved up the river. Opposite the town of Tappahannock one of the infantry transports ran aground, but after several hours of work it was got off, and meanwhile the rest of the expedition proceeded without it. At some obstructions six miles below Fredericksburg the same transport grounded again and one of the boats carrying the cavalry was unable to go any farther upriver. So the troops on both boats had to be ferried the rest of the way. "The advance reached the wharf at the city at dusk on the 6th," Colonel Roberts reported. "A squadron of cavalry, under Colonel Sumner, took possession of the town without opposition. Another body of cavalry, under Lieutenant-Colonel Patton, was at once dispatched to the railroad bridge on the Massaponax River, where they succeeded in capturing a train of 27 freight cars, 17 of which were loaded with tobacco and the others with vegetables and corn. A train of 14 army wagons, with 40 mules and sets of harness, was also taken near Hamilton's Cross-Roads. The railroad bridge, a structure 120 feet long and 75 feet high, was burned, and the depot and telegraph office destroyed. A picket of twenty-five men was left to insure the complete destruction of the bridge and to guard the tobacco. The wagons were brought in empty, since the roads were in a very bad state, and as much tobacco was known to be stored in the city as could be brought away on our transports."[2]

Sheridan's cavalry marched out of Charlottesville that day. During its stay there, waiting for the supply wagons to catch up, the Virginia Central Railroad had been destroyed in both directions, Custer's 3rd Division tearing up eight to ten miles of track to the northeast, toward Gordonsville, and the massive iron bridge over the Rivanna River, while part of Devin's 1st Division tore up three miles of track and two 50-foot bridges toward Lynchburg, to the southwest. Meanwhile the wagons were lightened, partly by issuing seven days' ration of coffee, sugar, and salt to the men, and captured horses were distributed to make sure that not a single trooper would be without a mount. Now, on the sixth, the

Federals moved in two columns. Sheridan, with Custer's division, followed the railroad toward Lynchburg, while Merritt took Devin's division due south to Scottsville, on the James River, where it was to follow the river to the southwest, destroying all the locks on the James River Canal as far as the town of New Market.

The inaugural ball was held Monday evening, 6 March, in the Hall of Patents in the Interior Department building, where thousands of patent models were stored in glass cases, as well as the Declaration of Independence, Ben Franklin's printing press, and mementos of Washington, Lafayette, Jefferson, Jackson, and other historic figures. Four second-story rooms, each about the size of a football field, were used for the ball, one as the grand entrance, one as a promenade, one as the main ballroom, and one for an elaborate midnight supper. Tickets sold for $10. Any proceeds left after covering expenses went to the aid of soldiers' families.

The north hall, the main ballroom, was "magnificently decorated with our glorious national emblem," according to the Washington *Morning Chronicle*, "large banners being festooned from the ceiling to the floor. Between the windows were artistically disposed guidons and corps insignia, bearing the marks of the various army corps, brigades, and regiments of the United States service, while miniature American flags were crossed and placed at intervals on the walls. Over the main entrance approaching from the east, on a balcony, was stationed a fine military band, and midway in the hall, on the southern side, upon another balcony, tastefully decorated, as was the former, with bunting, was placed the orchestra.…So, between the two bands, the music…was kept up continually. On a raised dias immediately opposite the latter balcony, and on the northern side of the hall, were placed handsome sofas of blue and gold adornment…as seats of honor for the President and his suite."[3]

The first guests began arriving a little before 9 p.m., and by midnight some four thousand people were on hand. The party actually began at 10 p.m., when the military band struck up a march that had been composed especially for the occasion. This was followed by a ceremonious grand promenade around the ballroom, and then the dancing began, with more enthusiasm than skill, according to the New York *World*. At 10:30 p.m. the military band struck up "Hail to the Chief," and the President entered with Congressman Shuyler Colfax, Speaker of the House of Representatives, followed by Mrs. Lincoln on the arm of Senator Charles Sumner. Sumner was the leader of the Radical Republicans who opposed the President's lenient plans for reconstruction of the seceded states, and this was Lincoln's way of demonstrating publicly that there was no personal enmity between them. The *Chronicle* described Mary Lincoln as "attired in faultless taste."[4]

During the festivities there was a brief fight in the temporary kitchen when one of the cooks threw a bowl of chicken salad at another. He was arrested, taken to court, and fined one dollar. Nevertheless there was plenty to eat—everything from oyster stew to leg of veal, to pheasant, to tongue englee, to pound cake, sponge cake, lady cake and fancy small cakes, to calfsfoot and wine jelly, to six flavors of ice cream and three flavors of fruit ices, to coffee, chocolate, and numerous other delicacies. The 250-foot table in the dining room was designed to seat 300 people at a time, and the presidential party was seated first, to be fed before the rest of the crowd. A large pedestal held numerous confectionary sculptures. The center ornament was a huge model of the Capitol made of pastry and icing. Others included a model of Fort Sumter surrounded by Union ironclads, a model of Farragut's flagship with the admiral lashed to the rigging as he was at Mobile Bay—the real admiral was among the guests—a Statue of Liberty, soldiers in camp and in battle, and eagles bearing mottoes.

As soon as the dining room doors were opened to admit the other guests there was a great rush for the food, as all four thousand of them seemed to be determined to eat at once. "The onset of the crowd upon the tables was frightful," the *Star* said, "and nothing but the immense reserves of eatables would have supplied the demand, or rather the waste. Numbers...with more audacity than good taste, could be seen snatching whole pates, chickens, legs of veal, halves of turkies, ornamental pyramids, &c., from the tables, and bearing them aloft over the heads of the shuddering crowd, (ladies especially, with greasy ruin to their dresses impending...).

"The floor of the supper room was soon sticky, pasty and oily with wasted confections, mashed cakes and debris of fowl and meat. The...appropriaters of eatables from the tables left their plates upon the floor...adding to the difficulty of locomotion; and gentlemen, in conscientiously giving a wide berth to a lady's skirt, not unfrequently steered clear of Scylla only to fall upon a Charybdis of greasy crockery. Finally everybody was satisfied, even those who felt bound to 'eat their ten dollars' worth'...the ball room again filled up, and the dance...was resumed."[5]

When the President and his party wished to leave, however, they found the mob still raiding the food tables blocking their exit. They had to make their way via an alcove between display cases, up a stairway to a balcony, and through little-used narrow passageways to an obscure side exit. Nobody seemed to miss them. The guests were too preoccupied with the food. Dawn was streaking the sky by the time the party finally broke up.

That same day, the Confederate senate, in secret session, passed a bill that the other house had already passed, establishing a Bureau of Special and Secret Service in the War Department. This bureau was to "examine, experiment with, and apply warlike inventions and to direct secret agencies."[6]

J.E. Johnston assumed command over the Confederate troops in North Carolina that day. His forces were required to supply themselves from the countryside and forbidden to draw supplies from the depots in the area because these were all needed for Lee's army in Virginia.

Meanwhile, Sherman's forces were on the move again. "We remained in or near Cheraw till the 6th of March," Sherman wrote, "by which time the army was mostly across the Pedee River, and was prepared to resume the march on Fayetteville. In a house where General Hardee had been, I found a late *New York Tribune*, of fully a month later date than any I had seen. It contained a mass of news of great interest to us, and one short paragraph which I thought extremely mischievous. I think it was an editorial, to the effect that at last the editor had the satisfaction to inform his readers that General Sherman would next be heard from about Goldsboro', because his supply-vessels from Savannah were known to be rendezvousing at Morehead City. Now, I knew that General Hardee had read that same paper, and that he would be perfectly able to draw his own inferences. Up to that moment I had endeavored so to feign to our left that we had completely misled our antagonists; but this was no longer possible, and I concluded that we must be ready for the concentration in our front of all the force subject to General Jos. Johnston's orders, for I was there also informed that he had been restored to the full command of the Confederate forces in South and North Carolina. On the 6th of March I crossed the Pedee, and all the army marched for Fayetteville."[7]

The next day, 7 March, it began crossing the border into North Carolina. For this new state, Sherman chose a new policy, as illustrated in a dispatch he sent that day to Kilpatrick: "In conversation with people evince a determination to maintain the Union, but treat all other matters as beneath a soldier's notice. Give us a whole country with a Government and leave details to the lawyers. Deal as moderately and fairly by the North Carolinians as possible, and fan the flame of discord already subsisting between them and their proud cousins of South Carolina. There never was much love between them. Touch upon the chivalry of running away, always leaving their families for us to feed and protect, and then on purpose accusing us of all sorts of rudeness."[8]

Meanwhile, J. E. Johnston was finally beginning to get the remnants of the Army of Tennessee around in front of Sherman's advancing columns. They were following a round-about route by railroad and assembling at Smithfield, west of Goldsborough and therefore within supporting distance, by rail, of Hoke's Division, which Bragg had placed at Kinston to block Schofield's advance from the coast. Johnston began thinking about exploiting his position between Schofield and Sherman to attack them one at a time. From Fayetteville, on the upper reaches of the Cape Fear River, he wired Bragg on the seventh: "I have instructed Major-General Hill, at Smithfield, to join you with his troops for a battle. At present they are S.D. Lee's corps, commanded by General Hill, and three brigades of Stewart's. Cheatham's corps, and the remainder of Stewart's, were to leave Chesterville by railroad on Sunday. When they come up Stewart will command, and the force be more than doubled. On the 5th Butler's cavalry was much to the north of the enemy's route, and Hampton's still farther from it, in the direction of Charlotte, the Federal army being then near Cheraw. General Hardee was to the north of Butler. There is, therefore, nothing to delay Sherman's march. I am anxious to concentrate all our troops in his front on this river, in the hope that the Federals may cross it at two points, and then give us an opportunity to fight to an advantage. It seems to me necessary under such circumstances that the Tennessee troops should remain at Smithfield until you have an opportunity to fight; then join you by railroad, and after action return in the same manner to be ready to meet General Hardee."[9]

A small event took place in Washington on 7 March that was to have large repercussions a few weeks later. Thomas Merrick, the day clerk at the National Hotel, arrived at Ford's Theatre with another gentleman and a lady at the start of the second act only to find that their seats had been taken. This was due to the fact that when ticket holders did not show up by the end of the first act, ushers were routinely authorized to allow patrons with less favorable seats to move to the unclaimed better seats. Merrick and his party were upset, but Thomas Raybold, the ticket seller, offered to show them to even better seats than the ones they had paid for. He led them up to the dress circle to Box Number 6, but they found that it was locked and he did not have the key. The dress circle usher would have it, but he was at home sick. Raybold then led them around to the other side of the theater and through a little white door to Box 7. It was also locked. So was Box 8. Angrily, Raybold pushed against the door to Box 8 with his shoulder. It bent inward but would not give. He tried again with the same result, so he raised his foot to the lock and kicked it open. Merrick and party happily took their seats, and Raybold went away. He never reported the fact that he had broken the lock on the presidential box.

Fifty miles or so south of Washington that day, at Fredericksburg, the Federal raiders burned the railroad cars they had captured and the pickets watching over the burned bridge were withdrawn. Thirteen Confederate soldiers were found hiding in the houses and cellars of the town, and fifty muskets were captured at the provost marshal's office. Half of those were British-made Enfield rifles in fine condition. A few rations were found at a quartermaster's office and these were issued to the poor of the area. Infantry pickets were established on both sides of the Rappahannock to protect the boats from any Rebels who might be lurking in the area and to keep unauthorized Union soldiers out of the town. Cavalry pickets were sent out on all the principal roads, and some of these captured two Confederate scouts. One of the Rebels was Sergeant George D. Shadburne, who had been instrumental in devising the Confederate capture of the Union army's cattle herd near the James River six months before. He offered the three Federals who were guarding the two scouts $3,000 each to let them go, but they refused this tempting bribe.

"The 7th of March was spent in loading tobacco from the store-houses," Colonel Roberts reported, "and in crowding on whatever other public property could be carried away. The mules were all brought off with their harnesses and eight of the wagons. The other wagons were burned. A small quantity of stores, collected for contraband traffic in the city, were also destroyed. Among these were several barrels of liquor (apple jack) and of tobacco. No private property was molested, and no depredations committed by the troops.

"As the water in the river was falling rapidly I did not deem it safe to remain after having accomplished what has already been reported. The force re-embarked at 4 p.m., and left the city, amid the openly expressed regrets of the crowd who witnessed our departure. I brought with me a citizen, Doctor Rose, the consignee of the tobacco which I had captured. I foward him to General Patrick [provost marshal general] for the purpose of explaining certain strange statements concerning this property; I would add that his statements were confirmed by common report in the city. Not a casualty occured in the command."[10] The strange statement that Dr. Rose had made was probably that Abraham Lincoln had signed a permit to allow the tobacco to be taken through Union lines.

Sheridan's cavalry continued its march to the southwest on the seventh, Custer's division destroying the Orange & Alexandria Railroad as far as Amherst Court House, sixteen miles from Lynchburg. But scouts brought Sheridan word that, in addition to the troops Early had ordered sent up from southwestern Virginia, that city was being reinforced from Richmond by part of Pickett's Division of Longstreet's 1st Corps plus Fitz Lee's cavalry division. Detachments from Devin's division were sent to seize bridges over the upper James River at Duguidsville and Hardwicksville, northeast of Lynchburg, but they were unsuccessful, for the Confederates had flamable materials already in place on the bridges and set them on fire as the Federals approached.

Out west, on the north bank of the swollen Tennessee River, General Wilson was worried about his inability to cross to the south side and start his long-planned raid into Alabama. He had once been an engineer on Grant's staff and knew that the general-in-chief must be chafing at his delay. He also knew how to bypass the chain of command and get an unofficial explanation of his delay to Grant's ear. He had recently received letters from his old friend Lieutenant Colonel Adam Badeau, Grant's military secretary. So on 7 March he wrote a reply: "Your letters of the 16th and 19th of February are just received. I am very sorry, however, they found me here instead of on the road to Dixie as the General expects and as I hoped. This is the only time in my life I was ever ordered to start by a certain time and could not do so. My command was all ready—everything in tip top order—but the extraordinary rains and rise in the Tennessee have stopped everything. My cantonments were located on this side of the river for many reasons, all good. My command, by its present condition, clearly proves my wisdom in the matter. The Tennessee is higher than ever before known, though thank heaven it has begun to fall rapidly, and unless it rains again in three or four days I shall be able to get to river banks and begin crossing.... Please explain this to the general and tell him I shall not lose a moment I can possibly avoid in getting away.... I am most anxious, lest my delay may not be sufficiently explained, but I venture to hope the General will not lose any of his confidence in my promptitude and determination."[11]

On the North Carolina coast, Cox resumed his advance toward Goldsborough that day. "About three miles below Kinston a considerable stream, known as Southwest Creek, crosses the railway and wagon-roads leading to Newbern," he wrote. "The upper course of this stream is nearly parallel to the Neuse River, and almost the whole country between the Neuse and Trent Rivers, thirty miles long, is a great marsh, called the Dover Swamp in the lower part, and Gum Swamp in the upper. It was important to get control of the position along Southwest Creek as soon as possible, for the slight ridge on the hither side of that stream was the only dry land in the vicinity, and upon it were the principal roads of the Neuse Valley. Information had been received that Hoke had reached Kinston with a large division, and rumors of still further reinforcements to the enemy were rife. It was also known that a Confederate iron-clad steamer was at Kinston, and it was desirable to get positions on the Neuse where batteries could be placed."[12]

At the risk, therefore, of being short of rations—for he was still very short of supply wagons—Cox advanced two divisions on 7 March to the upper margin of the swamp at Wise's Fork. Palmer's 1st Division was on the right, covering the railroad, and Carter's 2nd Division was on the left, covering the Dover Road, with an interval of nearly a mile between them.

"The Twelfth New York Cavalry, the only mounted men in the command," Cox said, "were used to patrol the roads to the left, and watch the crossings of Southwest Creek for five or six miles above, the stream being unfordable at this season. An old road, known as the British Road, ran parallel to the creek a mile in front of the position, and Colonel Upham, of Carter's division, was placed with two regiments at its intersection with the Dover Road, to cover approaches from the left. Some artillery fire had been drawn from the enemy on the other side of Southwest Creek in taking these positions, both at the railway crossing and at the Dover Road; but a chain of pickets was established along the stream, and the cavalry reported that they had dismantled all the bridges within the prescribed distance above, and had outposts at the crossings."[13]

Schofield had recently reinforced Cox with Brigadier General Thomas H. Ruger's 1st Division of the 23rd Corps—a unit which had been broken up during Sherman's Atlanta campaign and reformed since the battle of Nashville by transfers from the other two divisions and from garrisons in Thomas's department. "Ruger's division was marched to Gum Swamp, the end of the next section of railroad to be rebuilt," Cox said, "where it was about three miles from the lines of Carter and Palmer, and could support either in case of need."[14]

Schofield arrived at Newbern the same day, coming by sea from

Wilmington, and was in consultation with Cox at the railhead on the morning of the eighth, when a rapid artillery fire was heard at the left front. Ruger was ordered to march quickly to Carter's support while Cox rode ahead. He found that the Confederates had suddenly appeared on the flank of Colonel Upham's two regiments and attacked him without warning.

The Federals' advance had brought them within striking distance of the Confederate forces that were concentrating in the area, and Bragg called on Johnston for the loan of the advanced units of the Army of Tennessee at Smithfield under Major General D.H. Hill. Hill had been a division commander in Lee's army in 1862 and briefly a corps commander in the Army of Tennessee under Bragg in 1863, before quarreling with Jefferson Davis over the cancellation of his promotion to lieutenant general and going without a command throughout 1864. Bragg assigned Hill the task of holding the Federals in front while Hoke's Division moved to attack their left flank.

The Union cavalry had failed to warn Upham of the Confederate advance, and his two regiments, being composed mostly of new recruits, were easily overwhelmed by this sudden attack on their flank by a much larger force. Upham managed to extricate about a fourth of his men in reasonably good order, but the rest, 935, were captured. Hoke, however, thought he had routed the entire Union force and asked Bragg to send Hill in pursuit. "Carter's line was partially protected by a light intrenchment," Cox wrote, "and the division met, without flinching, the assault which quickly followed the rout of the advanced post. Palmer was ordered to send one brigade rapidly to the left, to support Carter, and with the rest of his division to make a vigorous demonstration of crossing the creek in his front.... Carter's division, at Wise's Forks, aided by the brigade sent from Palmer, maintained the fight till Ruger arrived, when his division filled the space between the two wings, and speedily making a barricade with fallen timber and other material at hand, a connected line of breastworks soon covered the whole front. The country was of tangled wood and swamp, which impeded movement and prevented either side from seeing far."[15]

When Bragg learned that the main Federal line had not been broken he adjusted his lines and ordered another attack, but it was easily repulsed. Schofield, learning that prisoners had been taken from at least three Confederate divisions, ordered Cox to stay on the defensive until the arrival in a day or two of the rest of the 23rd Corps, which was marching north from Wilmington, and personally returned to New Berne, where he would be in communication with his entire department.

That same day, Sherman sent two men with identical messages down the Cape Fear River to whomever was in command at Wilmington, which he was confident must be in Union hands by then: "We are marching for Fayetteville, will be there Saturday, Sunday, and Monday, and will then march for Goldsboro'. If possible, send a boat up the Cape Fear River, and have word conveyed to General Schofield that I expect to meet him about Goldsboro'. We are all well and have done finely. The rains make our roads difficult, and may delay us about Fayetteville, in which case I would like to have some bread, sugar, and coffee. We have abundance of all else. I expect to reach Goldsboro' by the 20th instant."[16]

Sheridan, with Custer's 3rd Division, joined Merritt and Devin's 1st Division that day at New Market, northeast of Lynchburg on the upper James River. But there was no way to cross that rain-swollen stream. "My eight pontoons would not reach half way across the river," Sheridan reported, "and my scouts from Lynchburg reported the enemy concentrating at that point from the west, together with a portion of General Pickett's division from Richmond and Fitz Lee's cavalry. It was here that I fully determined to join the armies of the lieutenant-general in front of Petersburg, instead of going back to Winchester, and also make a more complete destruction of the James River Canal and the Virginia Central and Fredericksburg railroads, connecting Richmond with Lynchburg and Gordonsville.

"I now had all the advantage, and by hurrying quickly down the canal, and destroying it as near Richmond as Goochland, or beyond, and then moving up to the railroad and destroying it as close up to the city as possible, in the same manner I did toward Lynchburg, I felt convinced I was striking a hard blow by destroying the means of supply to the rebel capital, and, to a certain extent, the Army of Northern Virginia, besides leaving the troops now concentrating at Lynchburg without anything to oppose them, and forcing them to return to Richmond. This conception was at once decided upon, and Colonel Fitzhugh's brigade was ordered to proceed to Goochland and beyond immediately, destroying every lock upon the canal, and cutting the banks wherever practicable."[17]

"Feeling that the war was nearing its end," he later wrote, "I desired my cavalry to be in at the death."[18]

Far to the north, in Montreal, Canada, Lieutenant Colonel James Gordon, CSA, checked into St. Lawrence Hall on that eighth day of March. That was the same hotel where Jacob Thompson, Confederate commissioner, was staying. Gordon had known Thompson in Mississippi before the war and was married to his niece. After serving in various Mississippi cavalry units, Gordon had been sent by Jefferson Davis to England to arrange the purchase of a ship for privateering. On his return trip he had contracted yellow fever at Bermuda, but had survived. He had reached Wilmington aboard a blockade-runner on the night of 24 January, unaware that the port had been captured by the Federals the week before. He had been taken to Fort Monroe, Virginia, but on 22 February he had been released after telling his captors that he was the son of the duke of Argyle fleeing from a scrape in Scotland. After a few days he had made his way to New York, where he was probably helped by John Potts Brown, a Confederate agent who ran a ship-chandlering business there. For when he arrived at Montreal, Gordon was accompanied by Brown's son, Robert, who was a Confederate lieutenant and married to a Rebel courier. After the war, Gordon often said that he had met John Wilkes Booth, though he did not say where. But, as a friend of Thompson, he was soon involved in a Confederate plot. "We knew," he told a magazine writer many years later, "that we were beaten, and there was a general fear among southern men that the North would impose terms so severe that the already shattered and impoverished South could not meet them. Many plans were discussed in this country and abroad looking to the reaching of a settlement on terms the South could endure. One plan which found favor was to capture Lincoln, take him into the Confederacy, and with him as a hostage, treat for peace. I was party to this plot and did some work to promote it and carry it to a successful conclusion. The venture needed desperate men and the exercise of great caution and skill as well. Somehow the men in the plot became impatient and finally a new conspiracy was hatched which contemplated the killing of Lincoln. With that conspiracy I had no part or sympathy."[19]

"General" Singleton's get-rich-quick scheme finally ran afoul of the general-in-chief on that eighth day of March. "I believe General Singleton should be ordered to return from Richmond," Grant wired Stanton that morning, "and all permits he may have should be revoked. Our friends in Richmond, and we have many of them there, send word that tobacco is being exchanged on the Potomac for bacon, and they believe Singleton to be at the bottom of it. I am also of the opinion that all permits issued to Judge Hughes should be canceled. I think the same of all other permits heretofore granted. But in the case of Singleton and Judge Hughes, I believe there is a deep laid plan for making millions, and they will sacrifice every interest of the country to succeed. I do not know Hughes personally, never having seen him but once, but the conviction here expressed is forced upon me."

A half-hour later he sent another telegraph saying that trade with the Rebels also seemed to be going on in the Blackwater River area, west of Union-occupied Norfolk. "They no doubt go on the Treasury permits heretofore given under the act of Congress regulating trade with States in insurrection. I would respectfully recommend that orders be sent to the Army and Navy everywhere to stop all supplies going to the interior, and annulling all permits for such trade heretofore given."[20]

Stanton replied that night: "In reply to your telegram in respect to trade with the enemy, I am unable to control the influences that procure permits, but I understand that the President's passes and permits are subject to your authority as commander-in-chief, and that, notwithstanding any permit given by the Secretary of the Treasury or President himself, you as commander may absolutely prohibit trade through your lines and may seize goods in their transit either way, and may also prohibit individuals crossing your lines. This, I understand, is the effect of the instruction given you by the President's order through me of February 7 and the President's letter of same date. Military necessity is paramount to every other consideration, and of that you, as commander of the forces in the field, are the absolute and paramount judge. This I believe to be the President's own view, and that every one who procures a trade permit or pass to go through the lines from him does it impliedly subject to your sanction. You are so instructed to act until further orders."[21]

A couple of hours later, Lincoln himself wired Grant: "Your two dispatches to the Secretary of War...have been laid before me by him. As to Singleton and Hughes, I think they are not in Richmond by any authority, unless it be from you. I remember nothing from me which could aid them in getting there except a letter to you...." And he quoted the note he had given to Orville Browning for Singleton on 7 February. "I believe I gave Hughes a card putting him with Singleton on the same letter. However this may be, I now authorize you to get Singleton and Huges away from Richmond if you choose and can. I also authorize you by an order, or in what form you choose, to suspend all operations on the Treasury trade permits in all places southeastward of the Alleghanies. If you make such orders, notify me of it, giving a copy, so that I can give corresponding direction to the Navy."[22]

Grant replied to Stanton the next day, the ninth: "My views about the operations of Mr. Singleton and Judge Hughes are merely suspicions, based upon what is said in Richmond of the object of Singleton's visit, and of the trade that is actually carried on. I recognize the importance of getting out Southern products if it can be done without furnishing anything that will aid in the support of the rebellion. I told Mr. Singleton that if the proposition was made I would agree that all Southern products should be brought to any of the ports held by us, the Government receiving one-third, and the balance should be stored and protected for the benefit of the owner at the end of the war; that under no circumstances would I approve of supplies of any kind going in payment. I was not certain but I might consent to part payment being made in United States currency, but before doing so I would have to think of the matter. Judge Hughes has not been south of our lines, and, if my suspicions are correct, it is not his interest to be there. I do not judge him to be worse than other men, but all who engage in trade promising such large rewards, and when the time it is likely to remain open to them is so limited, work themselves up to believe that the small assistance they can give to the rebellion will not be felt. I will make an order suspending the operations of all trade permits southeast of the Alleghenies, and submit it. I will also notify General Singleton that no agreement made by him would be regarded as binding upon military authorities without the approval of the President is obtained."[23]

Grant was doing all he could to cut off the Confederates' supplies, and not only did he have troubles with civilians trying to feed the Rebels in exchange for cotton and tobacco, but he could not seem to get any of his subordinate generals, except Sherman, to perform their parts in his plans. His temper boiled over in a message he wrote the next day, the ninth, to Canby, down on the Gulf coast: "I am in receipt of a dispatch from the Quartermaster-General informing me that you have made requisition for a construction corps and material to build seventy miles of railroad. I have directed that none be sent. General Thomas' army has been depleted to send a force to you, that they might be where they could act in the winter, and at least detain the forces the enemy had in the West. If there had been any idea of repairing railroads, it could have been done much better from the north, where we already had the troops. I expected your movements to have been co-operative with Sherman's last. This has now entirely failed. I wrote to you long ago urging you to push forward promptly and to live upon the country and destroy railroads, machine-shops, &c., not to build them. Take Mobile and hold it, and push your forces to the interior to Montgomery and Selma. Destroy railroads, rolling-stock, and everything useful for carrying on war, and when you have done this take such positions as can be supplied by water. By this means alone you can occupy positions from which the enemy's roads in the interior can be kept broken."[24]

Grant had no way of knowing it yet, but Sheridan, at least, was accomplishing something in the way of cutting off Confederate supplies. "On March 9," Sheridan wrote, "the main column started eastward down the James River, destroying locks, dams, and boats, having been preceded by Colonel Fitzhugh's brigade of Devin's division in a forced march for Goochland and Beaver Dam Creek, with orders to destroy everything below Columbia."[25]

Near Kinston, North Carolina, that day lively skirmishing continued between Cox's Federals and Bragg's Confederates, but there was no major attack by either side. The Rebels rebuilt the bridges over the creek behind them. They also tried to get around Palmer's flank to get between his division and the Neuse River, but they were unsuccessful in that.

Out west, Wilson was still unable to move. The weather turned very cold along the Tennessee River that day and it snowed there that afternoon.

The weather was also impeding Sherman's progress, but his columns did manage to keep moving. "On the 9th I was with the Fifteenth Corps," he wrote, "and toward evening reached a little church called Bethel, in the woods, in which we took refuge in a terrible storm of rain, which poured all night, making the roads awful. All the men were at work corduroying the roads, using fence-rails and split saplings, and every foot of the way had thus to be corduroyed to enable the artillery and wagons to pass."[26]

Kilpatrick's cavalry division, like the rest of Sherman's command, had not been involved in anything like a real battle since leaving the Savannah area. But it had been involved in an almost continuous series of skirmishes with Wheeler's and Hampton's Confederate troopers. One of Kilpatrick's sergeants said that all these fights followed the same pattern: "A crush of horses, a flashing of sword blades, five or ten minutes of blind confusion, and then those who have not been knocked out of their saddles by their neighbor's horses, and have not cut off their own horses' heads instead of their enemies', find themselves, they know not how, either running away or being run away from."[27] But things were about to heat up.

The Union cavalry was marching through the rain toward Fayetteville, North Carolina, on 9 March, occasionally skirmishing with Hardee's Confederate infantry, when Kilpatrick learned from prisoners that Hampton's cavalry, making a wide circuit from the direction of Charlotte to join Hardee, was behind him. He decided to set a trap for the Rebel horsemen and ordered each of his three brigades to camp that night blocking a different route that Hampton might follow. Kilpatrick himself spent the night in a small house near the center of his 3rd Brigade's camp, along with his staff and a "tall, handsome, well-dressed woman," Miss Marie Boozer, who had been with the general since Columbia.[28]

But in the rainy darkness of the night, as the 3rd Brigade's pickets rode south to take up position, they encountered Major General Matthew Butler and his escort riding north at the head of Hampton's column. The Federals did not realize they had encountered Rebels and tried to ride on past them to their assigned posts, when, at a word from Butler, the Confederate quickly drew revolvers and took them prisoner. Butler then conferred with Hampton while scouts moved on up the road and soon confirmed that a Union camp was not far ahead and unprotected by pickets.

"Before daylight," one of Hampton's men later remembered, "Butler's command was noiselessly formed in the road in column of fours, the portion to which was assigned the leading charge being advanced considerably beyond the others, and consequently close to the camp to be attacked, leaving a good interval between them and the troops behind, which admitted of the latter being promptly dismounted in case of a counterattack. The ground was soaked and steaming with exhalations, and the fog rendered it difficult to see, even after sunrise. When the proper moment arrived, the detachment intended to lead the charge was moved on a walk almost to the entrance to the camp, and there halted for a moment as Butler rode to their head. Removing his hat and waving it about his head, he spoke, in ringing tones: "'Troops from Virginia! Follow me! Forward, march!' and then 'Charge!'

"They thundered into the sleeping camp, and if all the foul fiends from the nether world had accompanied them the Federals could not have been more surprised or demoralized. The camp-guards, if there were any awake, had no time to give warning, and the men under the tent-flies were literally riden over; or, as they sprang out half-asleep, were sabred or ridden down before they knew what was doing. Undressed and unarmed, awakened out of a profound sleep to find their camp overrun, they fled in all directions, leaving accoutrements behind. It was a wild sight. When the Confederates had charged through the ground they wheeled and came rushing back, scattering and riding down what was left, and making prisoners. Meantime other detachments of the division had struck the position at different points, and were making themselves heard from most effectually."[29] Kilpatrick called it "the most formidable cavalry charge I ever have witnessed."[30]

A sizable group of Confederate prisoners broke free and rushed to meet their rescuers, but in the fog and smoke they were mistaken for a Union counterattack and two of them were killed before the charging Rebels realized who they were.

At least 170 Federals were captured and the rest of the 3rd Brigade ran for the cover of a nearby swamp, leaving their camp and a pair of artillery pieces in Rebel hands. Kilpatrick escaped in his drawers and nightshirt, leaving his staff, the brigade commander, and Marie Boozer beleaguered in the house that served as headquarters. Some Confederates wearing Federal uniforms rode up to him and, not recognizing him, asked where to find Kilpatrick's quarters. He directed them down the road about half a mile and then ran off to rally his men.

Meanwhile, some of the Rebels stopped to plunder the camp and others ran into a force of dismounted Federals armed with rifles and bayonets. They took these to be infantrymen coming to rescue the Union cavalry but actually they were members of a small ad hoc brigade of troopers who had lost their horses and were used to guard the division supply wagons. Kilpatrick reformed the routed troopers behind these train guards and then launched a counterattack that recaptured the two guns. These he used to drive the Confederates away from his headquarters, where his staff, the brigade commander, and Marie Boozer had barricaded themselves, and by the time his other two brigades and a brigade of real infantry arrived to help out the camp was recaptured and the battle was all over. The Rebels, however, had escaped his trap, retreating to the north, toward Fayetteville.

Near Kinston that day, the Confederates launched a serious attack on the front and left flank of Carter's Union division. "Anticipating this," Cox wrote, "Carter's line of breastworks had been extended a long distance on the left, recurving to the rear, and these had been occupied by a skirmish line. As soon as the attack came (which proved to be by Hoke's division) McQuiston's brigade, of Ruger's division, which had been placed in reserve, was ordered at double quick step to Carter's left. Hoke was met by a severe fire of canister and shrapnel from the artillery, as well as by a steadily sustained infantry fire, and after a vain but strenuous effort to carry the line he was forced to withdraw. McQuiston was ordered to charge after him from the flank and did so, capturing several hundred prisoners. But the advance of the enemy upon Ruger now came, and McQuiston was not allowed to follow Hoke far, but was quickly recalled to support the centre, where the line was very thin. Palmer was also called upon for several battalions from the right, and Ruger was made strong enough to repulse Hill's and Clayton's men in their turn."[31]

Johnston wired Bragg that morning: "Sherman may reach Fayetteville to-day. In your operations consider that all troops must be concentrated in his front, south of Raleigh and Goldsborough Railroad. We are not well informed. Want of pontoons keeps cavalry out of position." Bragg answered that afternoon: "The enemy is strongly intrenched in the position to which we drove him. Yesterday and to-day we have moved on his flanks, but without gaining any decided advantage. His line is extensive, and prisoners report large re-enforcements. Under these conditions I deem it best, with the information you give, to join you, which I shall proceed to do, unless otherwise directed."[32] That night his forces withdrew up the railroad toward Goldsborough.

Sheridan's cavalry continued its raid, and reached Columbia on the tenth, on the north bank of the James River about halfway between Lynchburg and Richmond. From there he sent a message to Grant reporting what he had done and his intention to join the armies before Richmond and Petersburg after doing as much damage as possible to the canal and railroads west and north of the Confederate capital. He asked Grant to send by boat rations for his men, forage for his horses, and more pontoons to White House plantation, on the lower Pamunkey River east of Richmond. He had used the same spot in similar fashion the previous spring when, as the commander of the cavalry corps of Meade's Army of the Potomac, he had gone on a raid to the outskirts of Richmond, but the Union supply base there had been removed long since.

"I regarded as too hazardous a march down the south bank of the Pamunkey," Sheridan wrote, "where the enemy, by sending troops out from Richmond, might fall upon my flank and rear. It was of the utmost importance that General Grant should receive these despatches without chance of failure, in order that I might depend absolutely on securing supplies at the White House; therefore I sent the message in duplicate, one copy overland direct to City Point by two scouts, Campbell and Rowan, and the other by Fannin and Moore, who were to go down the James River in a small boat to Richmond, join the troops in the trenches in front of Petersburg, and deserting to the Union lines, deliver their tidings into General Grant's hands."[33]

Lee was writing to President Davis that day: "I do not know whether the law authorizing the use of negro troops has received your sanction, but if it has, I respectfully recommend that measures be taken to carry it into effect as soon as practicable. It will probably be impossible to get a large force of this kind in condition to be of service during the present campaign, but I think no time should be lost in trying to collect all we can. I attach great importance to the result of the first experiment with these troops, and think that if it prove successful, it will greatly lessen the difficulty of putting the law into operation."[34]

Grant sent Stanton a copy of a proposed order that day that would cancel all permits to trade with the Confederates in Virginia, the Carolinas, and the Georgia coast. And Congressman Washburne and a dozen prominent ladies and gentlemen arrived at City Point. The purpose of the visit was to present the general with a medal that had been especially authorized by an act of Congress in recognition of his services. No doubt Grant and Washburne also discussed the order and the subject of trade permits in general. The next afternoon, the eleventh, Stanton replied to Grant's wire approving of his proposed order with the advice to not confine it to cancelling only Treasury Department permits but all permits regardless of the source. Grant took this advice and published the order that day.

That afternoon Grant and his guests paid a visit to the Army of the Potomac and reviewed some of the troops. Then at 8 p.m., in the main cabin of the steamer that had brought the visitors down from Washington, the medal was presented in the presence of Meade, his corps commanders, and numerous staff officers. "Mr. Washburne arose at the appointed hour," Colonel Horace Porter wrote, "and after delivering an exceedingly graceful speech eulogistic of the illustrious services for which Congress had awarded this testimonial of the nation's gratitude and appreciation, he took the medal from the handsome morocco case in which it was inclosed, and handed it to the general-in-chief."

Grant was always embarrassed by such moments and had absolutely no talent for speaking. "The general," Porter continued, "who had remained standing during the presentation speech, with his right hand clasping the lapel of his coat, received the medal, and expressed his appreciation of the gift in a few well-chosen words, but uttered with such modesty of manner, and in so low a tone of voice, that they were scarcely audible."

"A military band was in attendance," Porter wrote, "and at the suggestion of Mrs. Grant a dance was now improvised. The officers soon selected their partners from among the ladies present, and the evening's entertainment was continued to a late hour." Unfortunately for Grant, he was tone deaf and a terrible dancer. "The general was urged to indulge in a waltz, but from this he begged off. However, he finally agreed to compromise the matter by dancing a square dance. He went through the cotillion, not as gracefully as some of the beaux among the younger officers present, but did his part exceedingly well, barring the impossibility of his being able to keep exact time with the music."[35]

President Lincoln issued a proclamation on 11 March giving amnesty to all deserters if they would return to duty by 10 May.

That night, Lincoln had a visit from Orville Browning, "General" Singleton's lawyer. "Saw in the papers this morning," Browning told his diary that day, "the statement that 200,000 pounds of tobacco purchased by Genl Singleton in Richmond and sent to Fredericksburgh had been destroyed by our troops....Knowing...that Singleton had written authority from the President to go to Richmond & purchase and bring out produce....I was greatly surprised....Just at night I took Judge Hughes with me, and went to the Presidents....The President at once showed us despatches from Genl Grant...saying substantially that Genl Singleton and Judge Hughes were at Richmond engaged in a stupendous scheme to make millions...that they were willing to sacrifice the interests of the Country to the accomplishment of their purpose...This astonished me greatly. Hughes had not been in Richmond. All that Singleton had done had been open and above board....The President had not seen the paper Grant had given to Singleton authorising him to send products to Fredericksburg, and guarantying protection. I had a copy...which I showed to the President, and I think he was no less amazed at Grants subsequent conduct than I was. He seemed troubled and perplexed...and manifested a desire to keep faith, and save Singleton from ruin if he could, but at the same time gave me the impression that he was afraid to take the responsibility. I thought he was afraid of Secy Stanton, although he said Stanton had always been in favor of getting out products. I suggested that I would see, and converse, with Mr Stanton upon the subject, and he urged me to do so. He also thought that Judge Hughes ought to go down and see Grant, saying he would give him a pass to go, and also write a letter to Grant."[36]

Down in North Carolina, Sherman's forces continued to advance. "On the 11th I reached Fayetteville," Sherman wrote, "and found that General Hardee, followed by Wade Hampton's cavalry, had barely escaped across Cape Fear River, burning the bridge which I had hoped to save. On reaching Fayetteville I found General Slocum already in possession with the Fourteenth Corps, and all the rest of the army was near at hand...I took up my quarters at the old United States Arsenal, which was in fine order, and had been much enlarged by the

Confederate authorities, who never dreamed that an invading army would reach it from the west....During the 11th the whole army closed down upon Fayetteville, and immediate preparations were made to lay two pontoon-bridges, one near the burned bridge, and another about four miles lower down."[37]

While Sherman went off inspecting the town, a well-dressed civilian named Edward Monagan came to his headquarters to ask for guards to protect his house from looters. "General Sherman is an old and dear friend of mine," he told Adjutant S.H.M. Byers, an officer who had been liberated from the prisoner of war camp near Columbia, South Carolina. "We were at West Point together." While he waited for Sherman's return he regaled Byers with stories of their escapades as cadets. "I know he'll be pleased to see me," he said. "You just watch Sherman's face when we meet."

Byers dispatched a guard to Monagan's home even before the general came riding back from his tour. Monagan went toward his old friend with open arms, and Byers saw that "for a moment there was a ray of pleasure illuminating Sherman's face," but it soon disappeared.

"We were friends, weren't we?" Sherman asked.

"Oh, yes," Monagan agreed.

"You shared my friendship and my bread too, didn't you?" Sherman continued.

"That I did," the Southerner confirmed.

Sherman's face turned grim. "You have betrayed it all," he said. "Betrayed me, your friend, betrayed the country that educated you for its defense. And here you are—a traitor—asking me to be your friend once more, to protect your property. To risk the lives of brave men who were fired on from houses here today." After a pause he added, "Turn your back to me forever. I won't punish you. Only go your way. There is room in this world even for traitors."

Monagan hurried off and Sherman sat on the steps of the arsenal and ate his lunch with his staff, or tried to. "The corners of his mouth twitched...," Byers noted, "the hand that held the bread trembled and for a moment tears were in his eyes."[38]

---

1. *Official Records*, 46:I:542-543.
2. Ibid., 46:I:543.
3. Stern, *An End to Valor*, 23-24.
4. Ibid., 25.
5. Ibid., 28.
6. Tidwell, Hall and Gaddy, *Come Retribution*, 216.

7. Sherman, *Memoirs*, 774.
8. *Official Records*, 47:II:721.
9. Ibid., 47:II:1340.
10. Ibid., 46:I:543-544.
11. Jones, *Yankee Blitzkrieg*, 26-27.
12. Cox, *The March to the Sea, Franklin and Nashville*, 156.
13. Ibid., 156-158.
14. Ibid., 158.
15. Ibid., 158-159.
16. Sherman, *Memoirs*, 775.
17. *Official Records*, 46:I:478.
18. Sheridan, *Civil War Memoirs*, 297.
19. Tidwell, Hall and Gaddy, *Come Retribution*, 407-408.
20. *Official Records*, 46:II:886.
21. Ibid., 46:II:886-887.
22. Ibid., 46:II:885-886.
23. Ibid., 46:II:901-902.
24. Ibid., 49:I:875.
25. Sheridan, *Civil War Memoirs*, 297.
26. Sherman, *Memoirs*, 775.
27. Davis, *Sherman's March*, 151.
28. Starr, *The Union Cavalry in the Civil War*, 3:583.
29. Edward L. Wells, *Hampton and His Cavalry in '64* (Richmond, 1991), 403-405.
30. *Official Records*, 47:I:861.
31. Cox, *The March to the Sea, Franklin and Nashville*, 160.
32. *Official Records*, 47:II:1363-1364.
33. Sheridan, *Civil War Memoirs*, 297-298.
34. Dowdey and Manarin, ed., *Wartime Papers of R.E. Lee*, 914.
35. Porter, *Campaigning With Grant*, 393-394.
36. Basler, ed., *Collected Works of Abraham Lincoln*, 8:353, n. 1.
37. Sherman, *Memoirs*, 775-777.
38. Davis, *Sherman's March*, 217-218.

CHAPTER NINETEEN

It Was a Very Lively Skirmish

12 - 18 March 1865

"Sunday, March 12th, was a day of Sabbath stillness in Fayetteville," Sherman wrote. "The people generally attended their churches, for they were a very pious people, descended in a large measure from the old Scotch Covenanters, and our men too were resting from the toils and labors of six weeks of as hard marching as ever fell to the lot of soldiers. Shortly after noon was heard in the distance the shrill whistle of a steamboat, which came nearer and nearer, and soon a shout, long and continuous, was raised down by the river, which spread farther and farther, and we felt that it meant a messenger from home. The effect was electric, and no one can realize the feeling unless, like us, he has been for months cut off from all communication with friends, and compelled to listen to the croakings and prognostications of open enemies. But in a very few minutes came up through the town to the arsenal on the plateau behind [it] a group of officers, among whom was a large, florid seafaring man, named Ainsworth, bearing a small mail-bag from General Terry, at Wilmington, having left at 2 p.m. the day before. Our couriers had got through safe...and this was the prompt reply.

"As in the case of our former march from Atlanta, intense anxiety had been felt for our safety, and General Terry had been prompt to open communication. After a few minutes' conference with Captain Ainsworth about the capacity of his boat, and the state of facts along the river, I instructed him to be ready to start back at 6 p.m., and ordered Captain Byers to get ready to carry dispatches to Washington."[1]

One letter Sherman sent by that means was addressed to Secretary Stanton: "I know you will be pleased to hear that my army has reached this point and have opened communication with Wilmington....I have written to General Grant a letter, the substance of which he will doubtless communicate, and it must suffice for me to tell you what I know will give you pleasure, that I have done all I proposed and the fruits seem to me ample for the time employed. Charleston, Georgetown, and Wilmington are incidents, whilst the utter demolition of the railroad system of South Carolina, and the utter destruction of the enemy's arsenals at Columbia, Cheraw, and Fayetteville are the principles of the movement. These points were regarded as inaccessible to us, and now no place in the Confederacy is safe against the Army of the West. Let Lee hold on to Richmond and we will destroy his country, and then of what use is Richmond? he must come out and fight us on open ground, and for that we must ever be ready. Let him stick behind his parapets and he will perish. I remember what you once asked me, and think I am on the right road, though a long one."[2]

In his letter to Grant he recounted his route and accomplishments in more detail. "At Columbia we destroyed immense arsenals and railroad establishments," he added, "among which were forty-three cannon. At Cheraw we found also machinery and material of war from Charleston, among which 25 guns and 3,600 barrels of gunpowder, and here we find about twenty guns and a magnificent U.S. arsenal. We cannot afford to leave detachments, and I shall, therefore, destroy this valuable arsenal, for the enemy shall not have its use, and the United States should never again confide such valuable property to a people who have betrayed a trust. I could leave here to-morrow, but want to clean my columns of the vast crowd of refugees and negroes that encumber me. Some I will send down the river in boats, and the balance will send to Wilmington by land under small escort as soon as we are across Cape Fear River....If I can now add Goldsborough without too much cost, I will be in position to aid you materially in the spring campaign. Joe Johnston may try to interpose between me here and Schofield about New Berne, but I think he will not try that, but concentrate his scattered armies at Raleigh, and I will go straight at him as soon as I get my men reclothed and our wagons reloaded. Keep everybody busy and let Stoneman push toward Greensborough or Charlotte from Knoxville. Even a feint in that quarter will be most important. The railroad from Charlotte to Danville is all that is left to the enemy, and it won't do for me to go there on account of the 'red clay' hills, that are impassable to wheels in wet weather. I expect to make a junction with General Schofield in ten days."[3]

To Schofield he wrote: "We reached here yesterday and will be delayed until Tuesday or Wednesday putting down pontoons. I will destroy utterly the arsenal and other public property, and I hope to get up some shoes and small stores from Wilmington before we leave. I will then march in compact order straight for the bridge across Neuse River, south of Goldsborough. I expect to make junction with you thereabouts. If I don't find you there I will feel toward Kinston and New Berne. I will need clothing and provisions. We have gathered plenty of cattle and bacon and a good deal of corn meal and molasses. We have also found plenty of corn and fodder, and my animals are all in good order. I will have trains enough for you. I have plenty of wagons and mules for 100,000 men, so you need not bring any from the North. On making junction with you, I want you to make your command 25,000, and will call it the Center, thus restoring our old Atlanta organization....If I find that holding Savannah, Charleston, and Wilmington will cost us too many men I would not hesitate to destroy them and use the garrisons in the field. It will be time enough to build up the country when war is over....Hardee crossed here with a force represented as 20,000, but I don't see the 'signs' of that many....I suppose Johnston may have up about Greensborough now moving to Raleigh 10,000, and I estimate Hoke's command at 8,000. All told, he may concentrate at Raleigh 40,000 to 45,000 men. I can whip that number with my present force, and with yours and Terry's added we can go wherever we can live. We can live where the people do, and if anybody has to suffer let them suffer....We will need an immense supply of clothing, for we have been working from knee to waist deep in water for 400 miles....We have had so much bad weather in February and March that I hope we now may count on a change for the better."[4]

Colonel Roberts' amphibious Union raiders struck again on the morning of the twelfth when they landed on the Northern Neck peninsula east of Fredericksburg. "The rebel cavalry, under Lieutenant-Colonel Chapman, of Mosby's command, were constantly hovering about our column," Roberts reported, "and being splendidly mounted and familiar with the roads, were able to avoid collision with anything more than our advance and rear guard....At every crossroads the enemy would separate, each squad taking a different path, until our cavalry found themselves pursuing only three men. These were captured and sent back toward the main column, but were retaken, together with a portion of their guard, on the way....At the point where the skirmish commenced there was a blacksmith's shop and quite an extensive wheelwright's establishment. These, with a granary containing 500 bushels of wheat, were burned. I now decided to return. I could have marched through in any direction, but it seemed unwise to continue the risk of occasionally losing a few men when the damage inflicted on the enemy was so trifling and the results secured so unsubstantial. Four small store-houses, filled with grain, tobacco, and bacon, were destroyed, and twenty-six head of cattle and fifty sheep were driven before us on our march back to Kinsale....By 3 o'clock all were on board, and we dropped down to the mouth of the river, the army gun-boats throwing a few shells as a farewell present to the rebels, who were concealed in the background of woods."[5]

"On Sunday evening, March 12," Colonel Horace Porter of Grant's staff wrote, "the members of the mess sat down to dinner about dark. Mrs. Grant and Mrs. Rawlins, who was also visiting headquarters, were at the table. Toward the end of the meal the conversation turned upon Sheridan, and all present expressed the hope that we might soon hear something from him in regard to the progress of his movements. Just then a colored waiter stepped rapidly into the mess-room, and said to the general: 'Thah 's a man outside dat say he want to see you right away, and he don't 'pear to want to see nobody else.' 'What kind of looking man is he?' asked the general. 'Why,' said the servant, 'he 's de mos' dreffle-lookin' bein' I ebber laid eyes on; he 'pears to me like he was a' outcast.' With the general's consent, I left the table and went to see who the person was. I found a man outside who was about to sink to the ground from exhaustion, and who had scarcely strength enough to reply to my questions. He had on a pair of soldier's trousers three or four inches too short, and a blouse three sizes too large; he was without a hat, and his appearance was grotesque in the exteme. With him was another man in about the same condition. After giving them some whiskey they gathered strength enough to state that they were scouts sent by Sheridan from Columbia on the James River, had passed through the enemy lines, bringing with them a long and important despatch from their commander, had ridden hard for two days, and had had a particularly rough experience in getting through our lines. Their names were J.A. Campbell and A.H. Rowan, Jr. As Campbell had the despatch in his possession, I told him to step into the mess-room with me, and hand it to the general in person, so as to comply literally with his instructions, knowing the general's anxiety to have the news at once. The message was written on tissue-paper and inclosed in a ball of tin-foil, which the scout had carried in his mouth. The general glanced over it, and then read it aloud to the party at the dinner-table.... The general proceeded to interrogate Campbell, but the ladies, who had now become intensely interested in the scout, also began to ply him with questions, which were directed at him so thick and fast that he soon found himself in the situation of the outstretched human figure in the almanac, fired at with arrows from every sign of the zodiac. The general soon rose from his seat, and said good-naturedly: 'Well, I will never get the information I want from this scout as long as you ladies have him under cross-examination, and I think I had better take him over to my quarters, and see if I cannot have him to myself for a little while.'... Campbell and Rowan started on horseback from Columbia on the evening of the 10th, following the roads on the north side of Richmond. They were twice overhauled by parties of the enemy, but they represented themselves as belonging to Imboden's cavalry, and being in Confederate uniforms and skilled in the Southern dialect, they escaped without detection. When they approached the Chickahominy they were met by two men and a boy, with whom they fell into conversation, and were told by them that they had better not cross the river, as there were Yankee troops on the other side. Before the scouts were out of earshot they heard one of the men say to the other, 'I believe those fellows are d—d Yankees,' and soon they found that the alarm had been given, and the Confederate cavalry were pursuing them. They rode forward to the Chickahominy as rapidly as they could proceed in the jaded condition of their horses, and when they reached the stream they took off everything except their undershirts, tied their clothes on the pommels of their saddles, and swam their horses across the river.... As the horses could not struggle out, the men abandoned them, and got into a canoe which providentially happened to be floating past, and by this means got ashore. The Confederates by this time had opened fire on them from the opposite bank. The scouts made their way on foot for eleven miles, in their almost naked condition, to Harrison's Landing on the James River, where they met a detachment of our troops. The soldiers supplied them with trousers and blouses such as they could spare, and took them by boat to City Point.... The scouts were given a meal of the best food of which the headquarters mess could boast, and put into a comfortable hut, where they lost no time in making up for lost sleep....Campbell was only nineteen years of age."[6]

That evening Grant wrote an order to Colonel Roberts, directing him to proceed with his brigade and the gunboats up the York and Pamunkey rivers to White House plantation and to hold it until Sheridan arrived there. He sent Lieutenant Colonel Orville Babcock of his staff to deliver this order. He also ordered 100,000 rations sent to White House, and Babcock, after delivering the order to Roberts, was to make sure that the supplies were delivered and to stay at White House until he could see Sheridan and find out if there was anything else he needed. Grant also directed Ord to send his cavalry division north to the Chickahominy River, to distract the Confederates from Sheridan and to be in a position to possibly provide him help if needed. And he sent a message to Sheridan, to be waiting for him at White House, in which, besides informing him of all this, he said: "The importance of your success can scarcely be estimated. I congratulate you and the command with you upon the skill and endurance displayed."[7]

At Washington that night Orville Browning, "General" Singleton's lawyer, had a long talk with Stanton and learned, to his consternation, that the secretary of war was violently opposed to the idea of trading for Confederate cotton and tobacco. Stanton, Browning told his diary, "said every man who went thro the lines to buy cotton ought to be shot—that it was trading in the blood of our soldiers, and sacrificing the interests of the Country to enable mercenary scoundrels to amass large fortunes &c, and that he had rather every pound of tobacco, and every pound of cotton in Richmond should be burnt, than that we should buy it, and pay for it in Green backs....I showed him the paper Grant had given to Singleton. He expressed his surprise at it—said with great emphasis that if he had given such a guaranty he would never have destroyed the produce afterwards—that the letter needed explanation, and asked me if I had any objection to giving him a copy of it....Although he occasionally became very much excited on the subject he was perfectly kind and courteous to me."[8]

The next day, the thirteenth, Lincoln again wrote to Grant: "I think it will tend to remove some injurious misunderstanding for you to have another interview with Judge Hughes. I do not wish to modify anything I have heretofore said, as to you having entire control whether anything in the way of trade shall pass either way through your lines. I do say, however, that having known Judge Hughes intimately during the whole rebellion, I do not believe he would knowingly betray any interest of the country and attempt to deceive you in the slightest degree. Please see him again."[9]

Also on the thirteenth, the Confederate congress finally passed the measure providing for enlisting slaves in the army, and President Davis signed it immediately.

That same day, John Wilkes Booth telegraphed his old friend Michael O'Laughlen in Baltimore asking him and another friend, Samuel B. Arnold, to come to Washington. Both men had been recruited back in August into the plot to kidnap President Lincoln, and both had been Confederate soldiers prior to that. "Don't fear to neglect your business," Booth told them. "You had better come at once."[10] The two men took the train to Washington the next day. On that day, the fourteenth, John Surratt sent a wire to a Baltimore china dealer asking for Lewis Powell to be sent to Washington. Powell was the member of Mosby's command who had entered Union lines back in January claiming to be a civilian refugee named Lewis Paine. Powell had been in Baltimore since then, and Surratt had visited him there shortly after his arrival. When the message arrived, Powell was in jail for beating up a black maid at Branson's boarding house two days before, but he managed to talk his way out, again taking the oath of allegiance to the Union as Lewis Paine.

Their intended target, Lincoln, fell ill that day and had to stay in bed for a day or two. No one but cabinet members and his family was allowed to see him. The halls of the White House continued to be filled with throngs of office-seekers nevertheless. One of the White House guards, William H. Crook, described Lincoln's bedroom as "handsomely furnished; the bedstead, bureau, and wash-stand were of heavy mahogany, the bureau and washstand with marble tops; the chairs were of rosewood. Like all the other chambers, it was covered with a carpet....All night I walked up and down the long corridor which...divided the second story of the White House in half....When in my patrol I came near to the door of the President's room I could hear his deep breathing. Sometimes, after a day of unusual anxiety, I have heard him moan in his sleep. It gave me a curious sensation. While the expression of Mr. Lincoln's face was always sad when he was quiet, it gave one the assurance of calm. He never seemed to doubt the wisdom of an action when he had once decided on it. And so when he was in a way defenceless in his sleep it made me feel the pity that would have been almost an impertinence when he was awake. I would stand there and listen until a sort of panic stole over me. If he felt the weight of things so heavily, how much worse the situation of the country must be than any of us realized! At last I would walk softly away, feeling as if I had been listening at a keyhole."[11]

Perhaps, however, by that fourteenth day of March, it was Jefferson Davis who moaned in his sleep over the situation of his country. Lee wrote to him that day, quoting a message he had received from Joe Johnston two days before, asking, "Is it so important to prevent the interruption of the road by Raleigh, by which you are supplied, as to make it proper to fight with the chance of winning against us? I would not fight Sherman's united army unless your situation makes it necessary." Lee told Davis that he had replied on the same day, "I fear I cannot hold my position if road by Raleigh is interrupted. Should you be forced back in this direction both armies would certainly starve. You must judge what the probability will be of arresting Sherman by a battle. If there is a reasonable probability I would recommend it. A bold & unexpected attack might relieve us." Now he told his president, "I do not think more specific instructions can be given. A defeat would not improve our condition, & the officer on the spot can alone judge as to the propriety of delivering battle. The army under Genl Johnston is about being united at Raleigh. It is inferior in number to the enemy, & I fear its tone is not yet restored. It is in great part without field transportation, & labours under other disadvantages. I think it would be better at this time if practicable to avoid a general engagement & endeavour to strike the enemy in detail. This is Genl Johnston's plan, in which I hope he may succeed, & he may then recover all the ground he may be obliged to relinquish in accomplishing it. The greatest calamity that can befall us is the destruction of our armies. If they can be maintained, we may recover from our reverses, but if lost we have no resource."[12]

Grant told Meade that day: "From this time forward keep your command in condition to be moved on the very shortest possible notice in case the enemy should evacuate, or partially evacuate, Petersburg, taking with you the maximum amount of supplies your trains are capable of carrying. It will not be necessary to keep wagons loaded, as they can be loaded in a few hours at any time."[13]

He also sent another message to White House plantation for Sheridan that day: "Information just received from Richmond indicates that every thing was being sent from there to Lynchburg, and that the place would have been cleared out but for your interference. I am disposed now to bring your cavalry over here and to unite it with what we have and see if the Danville and South Side [rail]roads cannot be cut....Troops can be thrown out from the Army of the James to protect you in crossing, and a bridge for the Chickahominy can be sent from here if you are not sufficiently provided. Write to me how soon you feel you could start and what assistance you would want from here. Do not start, however, until you hear from me again....When you start I want no halt made until you make the intended raid, unless rest is necessary; in that case take it before crossing the James."[14]

Grant also wired Thomas that day: "Has Stoneman started on his raid? Have you commenced moving troops to Knoxville and Cumberland Gap?" Thomas replied that evening: "General Stoneman has not started yet. I am now on my way to Knoxville to get him off. The heavy rains have delayed him up to this time. One division of infantry is now on its way to Bull's Gap. The others will follow as soon as we get the transportation."[15]

Cox's Federals occupied Kinston, North Carolina, that day, and a large number of them were put to work repairing the railroad bridge over the Neuse River and helping the engineers to repair the railroad to that point. They also built a wagon bridge over the river there, while Schofield ordered Terry to advance from Wilmington toward Goldsborough. Sherman spent the thirteenth and fourteenth getting his forces across the Cape Fear River and on the latter date his last division completely leveled the arsenal at Fayetteville and then set the rubble on fire. "On the 14th," Sherman wrote, "the tug Davidson again arrived from Wilmington, with [Brigadier] General [George S.] Dodge, quartermaster, on board, reporting that there was no clothing to be had at Wilmington; but he brought up some sugar and coffee, which were most welcome, and some oats. He was followed by a couple of gunboats, under command of Captain Young, United States Navy, who reached Fayetteville after I had left, and undertook to patrol the river as long as the stage of water would permit; and General Dodge also promised to use the captured steamboats for a like purpose. Meantime, also, I had sent orders to General Schofield, at Newbern, and to General Terry, at Wilmington, to move with their effective forces straight for Goldsboro', where I expected to meet them by the 20th of March."[16]

In Virginia, Sheridan's cavalry continued its destruction of the canal and railroads. "I halted for one day at Columbia," Sheridan wrote, "to let my trains catch up, for it was still raining and the mud greatly delayed the teams, fatiguing and wearing the mules so much that I believe we should have been forced to abandon most of the wagons except for the invaluable help given by some two thousand negroes who had attached themselves to the column: they literally lifted the wagons out of the mud. From Columbia Merritt, with Devin's division, marched to Louisa Court House and destroyed the Virginia Central to Frederick's Hall. Meanwhile Custer was performing similar work from Frederick's Hall to Beaver Dam Station, and also pursued for a time General Early, who, it was learned from despatches captured in the telegraph officer at Frederick's Hall, was in the neighborhood with a couple of hundred men."[17] Custer charged these Rebels with two regiments, and when they scattered he shouted that he would give a thirty-day furlough to the man who captured Jubal Early. They chased him some twelve miles, but could not catch him, although they did capture two of his staff officers and several other Rebels.

The next morning, the fifteenth, a messenger sent out from White House reached Sheridan at the railroad bridge over the South Anna River, a tributary of the Pamunkey, informing him of the situation there. That afternoon he sent a reply to Grant: "After sending my dispatch to you from Columbia, Colonel Fitzhugh's brigade was advanced as far as Goochland, destroying the canal to that point. We then marched up to the Virginia Central Railroad at Tolersville, and destroyed it down to Beaver Dam Station, totally destroying fifteen miles of the railroad. General Custer was then sent to Ashland and General Devin to the South Anna bridges, all of which have been destroyed. There is not a bridge on the railroad from the South Anna to Lynchburg. This morning two [Confederate] divisions of infantry came out to near Ashland (Pickett's and Corse's), and I have concluded to cross the North Anna and go to the White House, on the north side. I think this force too large to fight, and it may attempt to prevent my crossing over from the White House, unless you can draw them back. They know that if this cavalry force can join you it will be bad for Richmond. The amount of public property destroyed on our march is enormous. The enemy attempted to prevent our burning the Central railroad bridge over the South Anna, but the Fifth U.S. Cavalry charged up to the bridge, and about thirty men dashed across on foot, driving off the enemy and capturing three pieces of artillery—20-pounder Parrotts."[18]

"Reasoning that Longstreet could interpose effectually only by getting to the White House ahead of me," Sheridan later wrote, "I pushed one column under Custer across the South Anna, by way of Ground Squirrel bridge, to Ashland, where it united with Merritt, who had meanwhile marched through Hanover Junction. Our appearance at Ashland drew the Confederates out in that direction, as was hoped, so, leaving Colonel Pennington's brigade there to amuse them, the united command retraced its route to Mount Carmel church to cross the North Anna. After dark Pennington came away, and all the troops reached the church by midnight of the 15th."[19]

Out along the Tennessee River the waters had finally receded enough that Wilson's cavalry, now concentrated at Waterloo, Alabama, began crossing to the south bank that day, ferried by a few steamboats. Of course, the boats could have crossed the river at any time. The problem had been the flooded areas on both banks which were too shallow for the boats and too deep for anything else. Not until the waters had gone down could the men and horses get to the boats or the boats get to a place on the other side where they could be landed. It would take three days, however, to get the entire force across by this method.

John Surratt took Lewis Powell—still using the name Paine—to Ford's Theatre in Washington that evening so that he would be familiar with its layout. Surratt and Paine escorted Miss Honora Fitzpatrick, 19, and Miss Mary Appolonia Dean, 10, to see a performance of "Jane Shore," and they occupied the same box the president always used when he came to Ford's. Paine wore a military cape he had borrowed from Louis Weichmann. During the play John Wilkes Booth stopped by their box and talked excitedly with the two men. After the final curtain, Surratt and Paine took the young ladies home, and then they met Booth at Gautier's Restaurant on Pennsylvania Avenue.

There Booth had engaged a private room where he assembled his co-conspirators. Besides Booth, Surratt, and Paine, four other men were present. Michael O'Laughlin and Samuel Arnold were there from Baltimore, and David Herold and George Atzerodt from Washington. Herold, who was unemployed, was 23 but looked 17 and had the intellect of an 11-year-old. His main value to the group was his complete devotion to Booth. Atzerodt was a German-born carriage-maker from Port Tobacco, Maryland, a town southeast of Washington on or near the route by which Booth planned to take the captured president to Richmond. He was a dirty-looking cowardly little man with a drooping mustache and a thirst for whiskey. His war-time occupation was ferrying blockade runners and Confederate agents across the lower Potomac River. Surratt, one of the agents he ferried, had brought him into the conspiracy because he would be needed to get them—and the president—to Virginia.

Now Booth introduced each man to the assembled group while everybody helped themselves to the food, champagne, and whiskey that Booth had paid for. Booth then outlined his plan of action: The president was fond of the theater and often came to Ford's. The next time he did, they would take him. According to Sam Arnold, Booth and Paine would make the actual capture, screened from the audience by the folding drapes of the presidential box, and handcuff Lincoln. At their signal, Sam Arnold would walk onstage with his gun drawn and help them to lower the president to the stage while O'Laughlin and Herold would turn off all the gas jets from a central control, so that no one would see what was going on. Herold would drive the carriage, and Arnold would ride inside with Lincoln, while Booth and Paine, mounted on horses, would cover the escape of the carriage with drawn revolvers. Surratt and Atzerodt would wait on the far side of the Navy Yard bridge at the eastern edge of Washington to lead the party to the flatboat that they would use to cross the Potomac.

Sam Arnold said he was opposed to the whole proceeding and that it could not be accomplished. Even if they did get Lincoln out of the box and to the Navy Yard bridge—which he considered an impossiblity—they would be stopped by the sentinel at the bridge.

"Shoot the sentinel," Booth said.

Arnold said that would not do, for if an alarm was given there the whole plan would collapse. He wanted at least some chance for success and escape. O'Laughlin agreed with him.

"You find fault with everything concerned about it," Booth said.

Arnold said, no, he just wanted to have a chance. Booth could be the leader of the party but not his executioner.

"Do you know," Booth demanded in a stern, commanding voice, "that you are liable to be shot? Remember your oath."

Arnold said the plan had been changed; that a compact broken on the part of one was broken by all. If Booth wanted to shoot him, there he was, but he would defend himself. "Gentlemen," he said, "if this is not accomplished this week, I forever withdraw from it."[20]

According to John Surratt, the argument was over whether or not to abandon the whole project. He had learned that the government was building a stockade and gates at the Navy Yard bridge, which was their escape route for either plan. This caused him to worry that the government might be onto them. He thought that everyone but Booth had agreed with him.

Booth said, according to Surratt, "Well, gentlemen, if the worst comes to the worst, I shall know what to do."

Surratt said that he and three others then stood up, and one of them said, "If I understand you to intimate anything more than the capture of Mr. Lincoln I for one will bid you goodbye."[21] Everyone agreed and started putting on their hats.

Booth, realizing that he had gone too far, apologized, saying he had drunk too much champagne. A general discussion then followed in which they decided to return to the original plan of trying to capture Lincoln when he rode out alone, or nearly so, to such places as the Soldiers Home. It was 5 a.m. by the time the meeting broke up.

"On the 15th of March," Sherman wrote, "the whole army was across Cape Fear River, and at once began its march for Goldsboro'; the Seventeenth Corps still on the right, the Fifteenth next in order, then the Fourteenth and Twentieth on the extreme left; the cavalry acting in close concert with the left flank. With almost a certainty of being attacked on this flank, I had instructed General Slocum to send his corps-trains under strong escort by an interior road, holding four divisions ready for immediate battle. General Howard was in like manner ordered to keep his trains well to his right, and to have four divisions unencumbered, about six miles ahead of General Slocum, within easy support.

"In the mean time, I had dispatched by land to Wilmington a [wagon]train of refugees who had followed the army all the way from Columbia, South Carolina, under an escort of two hundred men…, so that we were disencumbered, and prepared for instant battle on our left and exposed flank.

"In person I accompanied General Slocum, and during the night of March 15th was thirteen miles out on the Raleigh road. This flank followed substantially a road along Cape Fear River north, encountered pretty stubborn resistance by Hardee's infantry, artillery, and cavalry, and the ground favored our enemy; for the deep river, Cape Fear, was on his right, and North River on his left, forcing us to attack him square in the front. I proposed to drive Hardee well beyond Averysboro', and then to turn to the right by Bentonville for Goldsboro'. During the day it rained very hard, and I had taken refuge in an old cooper-shop, where a prisoner of war was brought to me (sent back from the skirmish-line by General Kilpatrick), who proved to be Colonel Albert Rhett, former commander of Fort Sumter. He was a tall, slender, and handsome young man, dressed in the most approved rebel uniform, with high jack-boots beautifully stitched, and was dreadfully mortified to find himself a prisoner in our hands. General Frank Blair happened to be with me at the moment, and we were much amused at Rhett's outspoken disgust at having been captured without a fight. He said he was a brigade commander, and that his brigade that day was Hardee's rear-guard; that his command was composed mostly of the recent garrisons of the batteries of Charleston Harbor, and had little experience in woodcraft; that he was giving ground to us as fast as Hardee's army to his rear moved back, and during this operation he was with a single aide in the woods, and was captured by two men of Kilpatrick's skirmish-line that was following up his retrograde movement. These men called on him to surrender, and ordered him, in language more forcible than polite, to turn and ride back. He first supposed these men to be of Hampton's cavalry, and threatened to report them to General Hampton for disrespectful language; but he was soon undeceived, and was conducted to Kilpatrick, who sent him back to General Slocum's guard.

"The rain was falling heavily, and, our wagons coming up, we went into camp there, and had Rhett and General Blair to take supper with us, and our conversation was full and quite interesting. In due time, however, Rhett was passed over by General Slocum to his provost-guard, with orders to be treated with due respect, and was furnished with a horse to ride.

"The next day (the 16th) the opposition continued stubborn, and near Averysboro' Hardee had taken up a strong position, before which General Slocum deployed Jackson's division (of the Twentieth Corps), with part of Ward's. Kilpatrick was on his right front. Coming up, I advised that a brigade should make a wide circuit by the left, and, if possible, catch this line in flank. The movement was completely successful, the first line of the enemy was swept away, and we captured the larger part of Rhett's brigade, two hundred and seventeen men, including Captain Macbeth's battery of three guns, and buried one hundred and eight dead."[22] One member of the flanking brigade described the attack in a letter home: "As soon as we got in behind them we started with a yell on the double quick and I tell you I was never so pleased in my life as I was to see the rebs get up and try to get out of the way, but I tell you what thare was a good many of them bit the dust. I never saw the dead so thick on the field before."[23]

"The deployed lines (Ward's and Jackson's) pressed on," Sherman wrote, "and found Hardee again intrenched; but the next morning he was gone, in full retreat toward Smithfield....In person I visited [a] house while the surgeons were at work, with arms and legs lying around loose, in the yard and on the porch; and in a room on a bed lay a pale, handsome young fellow, whose left arm had just been cut off near the shoulder. Some one used my name, when he asked, in a feeble voice, if I were General Sherman. He then announced himself as Captain Macbeth, whose battery had just been captured; and said that he remembered me when I used to visit his father's house, in Charleston. I inquired about his family, and enabled him to write a note to his mother, which was sent her afterward from Goldsboro'....

"While the battle of Averysboro' was in progress, and I was sitting on my horse, I was approached by a man on foot, without shoes or coat, and his head bandaged by a handkerchief. He announced himself as...Captain Duncan who had been captured by Wade Hampton in Fayetteville, but had escaped; and, on my inquiring how he happened to be in that plight, he explained that when he was a prisoner Wade Hampton's men had made him 'get out of his coat, hat, and shoes,' which they appropriated to themselves. He said Wade Hampton had seen them do it, and he had appealed to him personally for protection, as an officer, but Hampton answered him with a curse. I sent Duncan to General Kilpatrick, and heard afterward that Kilpatrick had appealed to General Slocum for his prisoner, Colonel Rhett, whom he made march on foot the rest of the way to Goldsboro', in retaliation. There was a story afloat that Kilpatrick made him 'get out' of those fine boots, but restored them because none of his own officers had feet delicate enough to wear them."[24]

For the first time since Sherman's army had crossed the Savannah River the Confederates had shown some willingness to stand and fight. "Averasboro is not put down in history as a battle," one of Sherman's sergeants wrote, "but simply a skirmish. We will say, however, it was a very lively skirmish."[25] Howard's Army of the Tennessee had marched on ahead during the sixteenth, while Slocum's Army of Georgia was fighting Hardee. Now Howard slowed his pace on the seventeenth to allow Slocum to catch up, but the latter was delayed by swampy ground that day and the two wings remained widely separated.

Canby's campaign against Mobile finally got under way on that seventeenth day of March. His main force, under his immediate command, consisted of A.J. Smith's 16th Corps, most of Granger's 13th Corps, and some odds and ends of cavalry and engineers, and was based on Mobile Point and Dauphin Island at the entrance to Mobile Bay. Two brigades of the 13th Corps, a division of U.S. Colored Troops, and a brigade of cavalry, all under Major General Frederick Steele, were based at Pensacola, Florida. "The general plan of operations," Canby later reported, "embraced the reduction of the enemy's works on the east side of Mobile Bay, the opening of the Tensas and Alabama Rivers, turning the strong works erected for the defense of Mobile, and forcing the surrender or evacuation of the city; or if this was found to involve too great a delay, a direct movement upon Montgomery, shifting for the subsequent operations of the army the base of supplies from Mobile to Pensacola Bay, and using the railroad from Pensacola to Montgomery for that purpose. In carrying out the first part of this plan the main army, moving by land and water, was to establish itself on firm ground on the east side of Mobile Bay. Steele, with a sufficient force to meet any opposition that could be sent against him, was to move from Pensacola, threatening Montgomery and Selma, and covering the operations of the cavalry in disabling the railroads. This accomplished, he was to turn to the left and join the main force on Mobile Bay in season for the operations against Spanish Fort and Blakely. Minor operations for the purpose of distracting the enemy's attention were to be undertaken at the same time from Memphis, Vicksburg, Baton Rouge, and the west side of Mobile Bay, and it was expected that Wilson's raid would give full employment to Forrest's rebel cavalry."[26] On the seventeenth, Granger's 13th Corps began marching up the east side of Mobile Bay. That same day, a brigade of the 16th Corps was landed at Cedar Point on the west side of the bay with instructions to occupy Mon Louis Island with as much display of force as possible.

The American consulate in London sent a message to Secretary of State Seward that day saying that a secret agent in Paris had uncovered a Confederate plot to assassinate General Sherman and Seward himself. Two men had allegedly been sent to America with the promise of $5,000 each if they succeeded in eliminating their intended victims. The man assigned to get Sherman was supposedly a Texan named Clark, and a detailed description of him was sent. He was supposed to join Sherman's army and then, under the cover of battle, shoot him. All that was known about the other man was that his name was Johnston and that he had come to Paris from Canada by way of Liverpool, England. He was supposed to go to Washington and kill Seward as soon as possible.

In Washington that day, an actor named John Matthews walked into his room across the street from Ford's Theatre with a couple of other actors and found his old friend John Wilkes Booth lying on his bed, studying the part of Marc Antony in *Julius Caesar*. It was the same room in which President Lincoln was to die a few weeks later. From Matthews and his friends Booth learned that they were giving a matinee performance of *Still Waters Run Deep* that day for the sick and wounded soldiers at a hospital near the Soldiers Home. Lincoln, now over his illness, was expected to attend.

Hastily Booth got word to his team that an ideal opportunity had arisen to capture the president. He sent David Herold in a buggy to deliver a cache of weapons—two Spencer repeating carbines, two double-barrelled shotguns, one pistol, some ammunition, a sword, a dirk, a rope, and a monkey wrench—to the Surratt Tavern, which was in southern Maryland about ten miles south of the Navy Yard bridge. The other members of the team assembled at a restaurant near the hospital. "The report only reached us about three quarters of an hour before the time appointed," John Surratt later said, "but so perfect was our communication that we were instantly in our saddles on the way to the hospital. This was between one and two o'clock in the afternoon. It was our intention to seize the carriage, which was drawn by a splendid pair of horses, and to have one of our men mount the box and drive direct for southern Maryland via Benning's bridge. We felt confident that all the cavalry in the city could never overhaul us. We were all mounted on swift horses, besides having a thorough knowledge of the country, it being determined to abandon the carriage after passing the city limits. Upon the suddenness of the blow and the celerity of our movements we depended for success. By the time the alarm could have been given and horses saddled, we would have been on our way through southern Maryland towards the Potomac river."[27]

Leaving the others at the restaurant, Booth rode on to the hospital. There he learned from one of the actors he had seen that afternoon that Lincoln had not shown up. Booth returned to the restaurant with this news. They were all very alarmed, again fearing that their plot had been discovered.

At the Surratt boarding house that evening, Louis Weichmann was surprised that neither Surratt nor Paine was there. A servant told him he had seen them ride off with Booth, Atzerodt, Herold and others about 2 p.m. On the way to dinner, Weichmann met Mrs. Surratt, John's mother, in the hall. She was crying bitterly and told Weichmann to go down and make the best dinner he could. She had none. "John is gone away," she said, "John is gone away." During dinner, Mrs. Surratt's daughter Anna said, "Mr. Weichmann, do you know that if anything were to happen to my brother John through his acquaintance with Booth, I would kill him?" After dinner, Weichmann returned to his room, where he was reading Dickens' *Pickwick*. At about 6:30 p.m. John Surratt excitedly burst in. He was wearing spurs, had his pants tucked into his boots, and was brandishing a small four-barreled pistol.

"Weichmann," he said, "my prospects are gone; my hopes are blasted; I want something to do; can you get me a clerkship?"

"You are foolish," Weichmann replied; "why don't you settle down and be a sensible man?"

About ten minutes later Paine came in. He said nothing, but he too was excited, and his face was very flushed. When he pulled up his vest to adjust his suspenders, Weichmann saw that he had a big revolver on his hip. To his increasing suprise, Booth then came in. He was wearing dark clothes and carrying a riding whip. He walked excitedly around the room two or three times before he noticed Weichmann.

"Hallo, you here?" he said. "I did not see you."[28]

At a signal from Booth, all three went upstairs to the little back attic where Paine slept. After conferring for half an hour they all left without saying anything to Weichmann.

Had Booth only stayed at home in the National Hotel that day he would have seen Lincoln. For the president appeared there that afternoon to speak at a ceremony accompanying the presentation to the governor of Indiana of a Confederate flag that had been captured by a regiment from that state. After a few introductory remarks, he said: "There are but few aspects of this great war on which I have not already expressed my views by speaking or writing. There is one—the recent effort of our erring brethren, sometimes so-called, to employ the slaves in their armies. The great question with them has been: 'will the negro fight for them?' They ought to know better than we; and, doubtless, do know better than we. I may incidentally remark, however, that having, in my life, heard many arguments,—or strings of words meant to pass for arguments,—intended to show that the negro ought to be a slave, that if he shall now really fight to keep himself a slave, it will be a far better argument why [he] should remain a slave than I have ever before heard. He, perhaps, ought to be a slave, if he desires it ardently enough to fight for it. Or, if one out of four will, for his own freedom, fight to keep the other three in slavery, he ought to be a slave for his selfish meanness. I have always thought that all men should be free; but if any should be slaves it should be first those who desire it for *themselves*, and secondly those who *desire* it for *others*. Whenever [I] hear any one, arguing for slavery I feel a strong impulse to see it tried on him personally.

"There is one thing about the negroes fighting for the rebels which we can know as well [as] they can; and that is that they can not, at [the] same time fight in their armies, and stay at home and make bread for them. And this being known and remembered we can have but little concern whether they become soldiers or not. I am rather in favor of the measure; and would at any time if I could, have loaned them a vote to carry it. We have to reach the bottom of the insurgent resources; and that they employ, or seriously think of employing, the slaves as soldiers, gives us glimpses of the bottom. Therefore I am glad of what we learn on the subject."[29]

The next day, the eighteenth, John Surratt and Atzerodt met Herold at Surratt's Tavern. There Surratt showed John M. Lloyd, an alcoholic who leased the tavern from John's mother, a bundle containing the weapons Herold had brought and asked the tavernkeeper to hide it for him. Lloyd said he wanted nothing to do with it, for Union patrols were searching homes in the area looking for arms and contraband. If he was found with this small arsenal he could be in real trouble. However, Surratt told him that he knew of a hiding place where they would not be found. Lloyd doubted the existence of such a place, but Surratt showed him a tiny room over the kitchen that Lloyd had never known existed, and the bundle was hidden there. "We'll pick it up in a few days," Surratt told him.[30]

That night, Booth gave what turned out to be his final performance on the stage when he appeared in "The Apostate" at Ford's Theatre. "The part that Booth took in the play was that of Pescara, the infamous Duke of Alva," Louis Weichmann, who was in the audience with John Surratt, remembered. "In one of the scenes, a female was dragged on the stage by Pescara and subjected to torture on the wheel. Never in my life did I witness a man play with so much intensity and passion as did Booth on that occasion. The hideous, malevolent expression of his distorted countenance, the fierce glare and ugly roll of his eyes, which seemed ready to burst from their sockets as he seized his victim by the hair and, placing her on the wheel, exclaimed, 'Now behold Pescara's masterpiece!' are yet present with me. I cannot use language forcible enough to describe Booth's actions on that night."[31]

---

1. Sherman, *Memoirs*, 777.
2. *Official Records*, 47:II:793.
3. Ibid., 47:II:794-795.
4. Ibid., 47:II:799-800.
5. Ibid., 46:I:549.
6. Porter, *Campaigning With Grant*, 396-399.
7. *Official Records*, 46:II:940.
8. Stern, *An End to Valor*, 44-45.
9. Basler, ed., *Collected Works of Abraham Lincoln*, 8:353.
10. Tidwell, Hall, and Gaddy, *Come Retribution*, 413.
11. Stern, *An End to Valor*, 40-41.
12. Dowdey and Manarin, ed., *Wartime Papers of R. E. Lee*, 915.
13. *Official Records*, 46:II:962.
14. Ibid., 46:II:980.
15. Ibid., 49:I:916.
16. Sherman, *Memoirs*, 781-782.
17. Sheridan, *Civil War Memoirs*, 298.
18. *Official Records*, 46:II:993-994.
19. Sheridan, *Civil War Memoirs*, 298-299.

20. Weichmann, *A True History of the Assassination of Abraham Lincoln and the Conspiracy of 1865*, 383.
21. Ibid., 431-432.
22. Sherman, *Memoirs*, 782-783.
23. Glatthaar, *The March to the Sea and Beyond*, 167.
24. Sherman, *Memoirs*, 784-785.
25. Davis, *Sherman's March*, 229.
26. *Official Records*, 49:I:92-93.
27. Weichmann, *A True History of the Assassination of Abraham Lincoln and of the Conspiracy of 1865*, 432.
28. Ibid., 102.
29. Basler, ed., *Collected Works of Abraham Lincoln*, 8:360-361.
30. Bishop, *The Day Lincoln Was Shot*, 87. This source places this incident a few days before the attempt to capture Lincoln, but it also places that attempt on 20 March. Weichmann places the attempt on 16 March, but Arnold said it was 17 March. The latter is confirmed by two newspaper articles mentioned in the editor's notes to Weichmann's book, both of which said the play *Still Waters Run Deep* was presented at Campbell Hospital on 17 March. Tidwell, Hall, and Gaddy, in *Come Retribution*, place the attempt on the 17th and Surratt's conversation with Lloyd on the 18th (p. 425, n. 25). *The Collected Works of Abraham Lincoln* gives 17 March as the date of Lincoln's speech. And, while the version quoted here is taken from Lincoln's draft, Basler also gives a version taken from the New York *Herald* of 18 March, which precludes 20 March as the date of that speech.
31. Weichmann, *A True History of the Assassination of Abraham Lincoln and of the Conspiracy of 1865*, 119.

CHAPTER TWENTY

They Don't Drive Worth a Damn

18 - 21 March 1865

The Confederate Congress adjourned on 18 March, never to meet again, leaving many badly-needed military measures unresolved. It had spent its last few days arguing with President Davis about who was responsible for some of the difficulties the Confederacy now faced.

Down in North Carolina that day, Sherman's forces continued to advance. "From Averysboro' the left wing turned east," he wrote, "the Fourteenth Corps leading. I remained with this wing until the night of the 18th, when we were within twenty-seven miles of Goldsboro' and five from Bentonville."[1] But several miles still separated Slocum's Army of Georgia from Howard's Army of the Tennessee. Both of Slocum's corps were following the same road, and the troops were strung out, with those further back slowed by the way those ahead of them churned up the mud. The train of supply wagons was stretched out for miles and impeded by small bridges that repeatedly had to be repaired and the necessity of corduroying the roads.

Joe Johnston learned from Wade Hampton early that morning that Sherman was making for Goldsborough and that the two Federal wings were widely separated. This provided him the only chance he might ever get to attack the larger Union force in detail and he quickly seized it. He ordered all of his available forces to concentrate on a spot chosen by Hampton two miles south of Bentonville, and the resistence of the Rebel cavalry began to stiffen in order to provide time for the infantry to get into position.

Sheridan's cavalry reached the vicinity of White House on 18 March and crossed to the south side of the Pamunkey River on the railroad bridge the next day. The plantation belonged to Robert E. Lee's second son, Major General W. H. F. "Rooney" Lee, who had inherited it from his maternal grandfather, George Washington Parke Custis, George Washington's adopted son. "We here found supplies in abundance," Sheridan reported.[2]

Grant, who had ordered Ord's cavalry back from the Chickahominy, wrote to Sheridan from City Point that day: "Start for this place as soon as you conviently can, but let me know as early as possible when you will start. I will send cavalry and infantry to Chickahominy to meet you when you do start....When you start out from here you will be re-enforced with about 6,000 cavalry. I will also move out by the left at least 50,000 infantry and demonstrate on the enemy's right, and probably remain out. Your problem will be to destroy the South Side and Danville [rail]roads, and then either return to this army or go on to Sherman, as you may deem most practicable."[3]

Grant also wired Thomas on the nineteenth: "If Stoneman has not got off on his expedition, start him at once with whatever force you can give him. He will not meet with opposition now that cannot be overcome with 1,500 men. If I am not much mistaken, he will be able to come within fifty miles of Lynchburg."[4]

Down in North Carolina on the nineteenth, Schofield's advancing forces skirmished with Confederates at the bridge over the Neuse River near Goldsborough. The day dawned bright and clear over Sherman's two widely separated wings, heading for the same point, with a feeling of spring in the air. Apple and peach trees were in blossom and the countryside was touched with green. Two divisions of Davis's 14th Corps had camped the night before within about eight miles of Bentonville, which was a village on the southeast side of Mill Creek, a small tributary of the Neuse River. Two divisions of Brevet Major General Alpheus S. Williams' 20th Corps were eight miles back on the same road, and Kilpatrick's cavalry was to the left and rear of Williams. One division from each corps was marching with the wagon trains far to the rear, while Howard's Right Wing, or Army of the Tennessee, was following roads several miles farther south.

Brigadier General William Carlin's 1st Division of the 14th Corps was to lead Slocum's column that day, and despite his inability to convince his superiors that the Rebels were gathering nearby he still felt that a battle was brewing. He put on his best uniform that morning and ordered his wagons and mules to the rear. When his division took up the march at 7 a.m. it immediately ran into Confederate skirmishers. His own skirmishers sent back word that "they don't drive worth a damn."[5]

Meanwhile, Sherman decided to leave Slocum's column. "Supposing that all danger was over," he wrote, "I crossed over to join Howard's column, to the right, so as to be nearer to Generals Schofield and Terry, known to be approaching Goldsboro'. I overtook General Howard at Falling-Creek Church, and found his column well drawn out, by reason of the bad roads."[6]

While the Rebel cavalry fought to delay Slocum's advance, the infantry began to file into position a couple of miles south of Bentonville. Bragg, with Hoke's Division and a brigade of North Carolina Junior Reserves, was the first to arrive, and they took cover, with their left in a tangle of blackjack oaks, blocking the east-west road the Federals were following. Johnston's plan was for Hardee's two divisions from South Carolina to form on Bragg's right, facing southwest so as to take Slocum's column in flank when it ran into Bragg, with the troops from the Army of Tennessee, under Lieutenant General A.P. Stewart, even farther to the right, facing south. However, Hardee's corps, having the farthest to march, arrived late, and there was still a gap between Bragg's corps and Stewart's, which Hampton filled with two batteries of horse artillery, when the battle began.

Slocum had deployed Colonel Harrison Hobart's 1st Brigade of Carlin's division, backed up by a battery of artillery moving along the road, in order to push the Confederate cavalry back, but it was nearly noon by the time these Federals encountered Hoke's Rebels behind hastily constructed breastworks blocking their advance. Davis, commander of the 14th Corps, sent Colonel George P. Buell's 2nd Brigade of Carlin's division on a detour to the left to get around the Confederate flank and deployed Lieutenant Colonel David Miles' 3rd Brigade on Hobart's right. Carlin then advanced with Hobart's and Miles' brigade, but they were driven back by heavy rifle fire. A few prisoners were taken, however, and among them were three Union soldiers who had previously been captured by the Rebels and had joined the Confederate Army in order to avoid prison camp with the intention of deserting at their first opportunity. The collision of the two armies had given them their opportunity, and they now informed the Federals that Johnston's entire army was lying in ambush. Slocum dismissed their information as coming from an unreliable source until one of his staff officers vouched for the reliability of one of the men, who was an old friend of his. Convinced at last, Slocum sent off a messenger to inform Sherman at about 2 p.m. and sent Davis's chief of staff, Lieutenant Colonel Alexander McClurg, to hurry the 20th Corps forward. Then he brought up Brigadier General James D. Morgan's 2nd Division of Davis' 14th Corps and placed it on Carlin's right, in a swampy pine woods, with two brigades on line and one in support.

While a heavy line of skirmishers engaged the Rebels, the rest of the troops began to throw up a line of breastworks. "It was surprising," an onlooking Union surgeon wrote, "to see the rapidity with which men will intrench themselves under fire—a few rails piled up in a twinkling, then dirt thrown upon them with numberless tools, bayonets, frying pans, bits of board, bare hands, anything to move dirt and it is not long before a protecting mound rises sufficiently to cover men lying behind it and as the digging proceeds, the ditch deepens as fast as the mound rises until in an almost incredible space of time an intrenchment has been thrown up sufficient to protect from cannon shot as well as rifle balls."[7]

Carlin's attack on his right and Morgan's arrival threatening his left caused Bragg to ask for reenforcements, and Johnston reluctantly sent him Major General Lafayette McLaw's division, the first half of Hardee's corps to reach the field. Hardee's other division, commanded by Major General William B. Taliaferro, was sent to the Confederate far right flank, beyond the remnants of Cheatham's Corps of the Army of Tennessee, commanded by Major General William B. Bate. Buell's Union brigade, which had been sent to take the Rebels in flank, had been slowly making its way through swamps and thickets until it was struck at about 3:15 p.m. by a crash of musketry, attacked in front and flank by Bate and Taliaferro, and driven to the rear in confusion. The Confederate attack was then taken up by the rest of Stewart's forces, which swept across the fields of a plantation and hit Carlin's other two brigades in the flank and rear. Hobart's brigade was forced back a regiment at a time until it was pushed back a mile. Then a rush by the Rebels captured the battery in the road, and Carlin's division began to fall apart. A Union lieutenant said that he and his men led the way with "some of the best running ever did."[8]

Colonel McClurg, who had been sent to hurry the 20th Corps forward, returned in time to witness this retreat. "Almost immediately I met masses of men slowly and doggedly falling back along the road...retreating, and evidently with good cause...," he said, "but they were not demoralized. Minie balls were whizzing in every direction." An artillery officer retreating with a pair of guns warned him not to proceed any farther: "For God's sake, don't go down there! I'm the last man of the command. Everything in front of you is gone." McClurg did not believe him until he saw the long Confederate line "stretching across the fields to the left as far as the eye could reach, advancing rapidly, and firing as they came....the onward sweep of the rebel lines was like the waves of the ocean, resistless."[9] After the pursuit had gone about a mile, General Hardee, who had led the attack on horseback, called a halt to reform his ragged line. Davis sent Morgan's reserve brigade, Colonel Benjamin Fearing's 3rd, to counterattack, and it struck Hardee's flank and drove the Rebels back in confusion.

The leading unit of the 20th Corps, Brigadier General James Robinson's 3rd Brigade of the 1st Division, then came up and formed on Fearing's left. Carlin's men were rallied and put in line on Robinson's left, and the artillery of the 20th Corps, as it arrived, was put in position on high ground nearby. Bate attacked this position several times but was repulsed every time and withdrew when Fearing routed the Confederate center. At about 4 p.m. another brigade of the 20th Corps arrived and was placed on Fearing's right, but there was still a gap between it and Morgan's main position.

At 4:30 p.m. Bragg's troops attacked Morgan's front, and what followed was one of the hottest fights of the war. "Seldom have I seen such continuous and remorseless roll of musketry," Colonel McClurg said. "It seemed more than men could bear....Soldiers in the command who have passed through scores of battles...never saw anything like the fighting at Bentonville."[10] A Union countercharge captured the colors of the 40th North Carolina. The battle raged until the rifles become too hot to hold or load, and beyond. When ammunition began to run low, some of Morgan's men were sent to gather some from the dead and wounded. "I came upon a rebel who was fatally wounded," a Union sergeant wrote. "He cried out, 'Is there no help for a widow's son?' I told him he was beyond help, and that I had no time to give to his wants, but that, as he had no further use for the cartridges in his box nor for the Yankee knapsack on his back, I would relieve him of both."[11] When Confederates found the gap between Morgan's main line and the 20th Corps brigade next to Fearing, some of them got behind Morgan's line. The Federals jumped over their breastworks and fought on from the other side. "If Morgan's troops can stand this, all is right," General Davis told a staff officer; "if not the day is lost. There is no reserve—not a regiment to move—they must fight it out."[12] A counterattack drove the Rebels off, capturing the battleflag of the 54th Virginia. Near dark, Johnston moved McLaws' Division around to his right to reinforce Bate, but he arrived too late to attack, and the Confederates withdrew to their original position.

"I had heard some cannonading over about Slocum's head of column," Sherman wrote, "and supposed it to indicate about the same measure of opposition by Hardee's troops and Hampton's cavalry before experienced; but during the day a messenger overtook me, and notified me that near Bentonville General Slocum had run up against *Johnston's whole army.*

"I sent back orders for him to fight defensively to save time, and that I would come up with reenforcements from the direction of Cox's Bridge, by the road which we had reached near Falling-Creek Church. The country was very obscure, and the maps extremely defective.

"By this movement I hoped General Slocum would hold Johnston's army facing west, while I would come on his rear from the east. The Fifteenth Corps, less one division (Hazen's), still well to the rear, was turned at once toward Bentonsville; Hazen's division was ordered to Slocum's flank, and orders were also sent for General Blair, with the Seventeenth Corps, to come to the same destination. Meantime the sound of cannon came from the direction of Bentonsville.

"The night of the 19th caught us near Falling-Creek Church; but early the next morning the Fifteenth Corps, General C.R. Woods's division leading, closed down on Bentonsville, near which it was brought up by encountering a line of fresh parapet, crossing the road and extending north, toward Mill Creek. After deploying, I ordered General Howard to proceed with caution, using skirmishers alone, till he had made junction with General Slocum, on his left. These deployments occupied all day, during which two divisions of the Seventeenth Corps also got up. At that time General Johnston's army occupied the form of a V, the angle reaching the road leading from Averysboro' to Goldsboro', and the flanks resting on Mill Creek, his lines embracing the village of Bentonsville.

"General Slocum's wing faced one of these lines and General Howard's the other; and, in the uncertainty of General Johnston's strength, I did not feel disposed to invite a general battle, for we had been out from Savannah since the latter part of January, and our wagon-trains contained but little food. I had also received messages during the day from General Schofield, at Kinston, and General Terry, at Faison's Depot, approaching Goldsboro', both expecting to reach it by March 21st. During the 20th we simply held our ground and started our trains back to Kinston for provisions, which would be needed in the event of being forced to fight a general battle at Bentonsville."[13]

As Howard's divisions reached the field they ran into Bragg's troops, and some fierce skirmishing took place but no major assaults were made. Sherman did not want to fight and did not understand why Johnston did not retreat now that most of the Union army was on hand. "Johnston hoped to overcome your wing before I could come to your relief," he told Slocum in a dispatch written that night. "Having failed in that, I cannot see why he remains and still think he will avail himself of night to get back to Smithfield. I would rather avoid a general battle if possible, but if he insists on it, we must accommodate him." Slocum replied, "I can, at any time, move this wing to the Goldsborough road without a fight. Johnston was too slow; he allowed me to discover his strength before he made any strong efforts, and then found my men behind a very strong line of works."[14]

In New York that day, Captain Robert Cobb Kennedy was found guilty of spying and of taking part in the burning of parts of that city.

Major General George Stoneman's raid finally got under way on the twentieth. He rode out of Knoxville with the cavalry division of his District of East Tennessee, commanded by Brigadier General Alvan C. Gillem, consisting of three brigades of cavalry and one battery of horse artillery. Down in Alabama, Wilson had hoped to get his raid into that state moving that day, but scouts reported that the first eighty miles of his route would be devoid of any forage for his horses, so he had to wait for boats to ferry forage across the Tennessee River to take with him. "I hope we shall be off in time to do good service," he wrote to his friend Adam Badeau, Grant's military secretary, that day. "My command is certainly in a magnificent condition, well armed, spendidly mounted, perfectly clad and equipped, and will turn out a heavier fighting force than ever before started on a similar expedition in this country."[15] He knew the general-in-chief would be disappointed at the delay but felt it was unavoidable. "Isn't it unfortunate that the rain cannot be controlled by General Grant," he asked.[16]

There was one thing, however, that, as it turned out, Grant could influence. "While I was at headquarters in March, 1865," his wife Julia wrote, "the papers daily announced the exhausted appearance of the President. On more than one occasion, I petitioned the General with hospitable intent to invite Mr. and Mrs. Lincoln down to visit the army; so many people were coming, and the weather was simply delightful. The General would always reply to my request: 'If President Lincoln wishes to come down, he will not wait to be asked. It is not my place to invite him.' 'Yes,' I urged, 'it is. You know all that has been said about his interference with army movements, and he will never come for fear of appearing to meddle with army affairs.' But the general did not invite them. One day, Captain Robert Lincoln, in reply to my inquiries about his father's health and my asking why his father and mother did not come down on a visit, said: 'I suppose they would, if they were sure they would not be intruding.'"[17] That day Grant telegraphed Lincoln: "Can you not visit City Point for a day or two? I would like very much to see you, and I think the rest would do you good." Lincoln replied that evening: "Your kind invitation received. Had already thought of going immediately after the next rain. Will go sooner if any reason for it. Mrs. L and a few others will probably accompany me. Will notify you of exact time, once it shall be fixed upon."[18]

Brigadier General Ranald Mackenzie was put in command of the cavalry division of Ord's Army of the James that day. His predecessor, Brigadier General August V. Kautz, was given command of the 1st Division of the 25th Corps. The records do not reveal why this change was made, but Grant was the one who selected Mackenzie, who was only 24 years old. Just three years before he had been a cadet at West Point, graduating at the top of the class of 1862. He had served as an engineer officer for two years, then as the colonel of the 2nd Connecticut Heavy Artillery and a brigade commander in the 6th Corps. "I regarded Mackenzie as the most promising young officer in the army," Grant said.[19] He would have been given the cavalry division of the Army of the Potomac, but the commander of one of its brigades had seniority on the list of brigadier generals. So Grant decided to give the job to Crook, who had just been exchanged. He wired Stanton, who had just returned from a visit to City Point, about it the next afternoon, the 21st, and Stanton replied that night that he had issued an order relieving Crook from the command of his department and appointing him to that command. Crook had been Sheridan's roommate at West Point and had served under Grant in the regular army.

Grant also wrote to Sheridan again that day: "I do not wish to hurry you, and besides fully appreciate the necessity of both having your horses well shod and well rested before starting again on another long march. But there is now such a possibility, if not probability, of Lee and

Johnston attempting to unite that I feel extremely desirous not only of cutting the lines of communication between them, but of having a large and properly commanded cavalry force ready to act with in case such an attempt is made. I think that by Saturday next you had better start, even if you have to stop here to finish shoeing up."[20] In his memoirs, Grant said, "One of the most anxious periods of my experience during the rebellion was the last few weeks before Petersburg. I felt that the situation of the Confederate army was such that they would try to make an escape at the earliest practicable moment, and I was afraid, every morning, that I would awake from my sleep to hear that Lee had gone, and that nothing was left but a picket line. I knew he could move much more lightly and more rapidly than I, and that, if he got the start, he would leave me behind so that we would have the same army to fight again farther south—and the war might be prolonged another year."[21]

At Washington that day, Orville Browning, "General" Singleton's lawyer, saw Secretary of War Stanton, just back from City Point, and walked with him from the War Department on his way to a cabinet meeting at the White House. Stanton took Browning's arm and laughed. "That was not Singleton's tobacco that was seized at Fredericksburg after all," he said. "Strange what stories get in circulation!" That did not mean, however, that it might not be seized eventually. Browning said that Singleton's activities were legitimate and aboveboard and it would be a shame to see him ruined. "We'll not ruin him bad," Stanton replied grimly.[22]

A reporter was at the White House that day to gather material for a story to be titled "A Day at the White House" for the Baltimore *American.* "A gentleman," he wrote, "largely engaged in bringing out cotton, etc. from the rebel states, inquired of the President whether it was his intention to sustain the recent order issued by General Grant putting a stop to the whole business. The President replied that in no case would he interfere with the wishes of General Grant. He held him responsible for inflicting the hardest blows possible on the enemy, and as desirable as it was to possess the cotton, if he thought that bacon was of more importance to the enemy at this moment than cotton to us, why we must do without the cotton."[23]

John Wilkes Booth left Washington that day for Baltimore and New York.

Down in North Carolina it began to rain again on the 21st. Schofield's troops marched into Goldsborough that day and Terry's reached Cox's Bridge on the Neuse River west of there. Meanwhile Johnston's Confederates were still in place at Bentonville and countinued to face Sherman's Federals across their respective breastworks. Things remained quiet there until around noon. Then Major General Joseph Mower, commander of the 1st Division of Blair's 17th Corps and one of Sherman's favorite subordinates, took it upon himself to break the stalemate. His division held the far right of Howard's line, and thus of the entire Union army, and he found a road running through a swamp that seemed to lead around the Rebels' left flank. He took two of his brigades and exploited this opening, chasing off some skirmishers, and came within rifle range of the bridge over Mill Creek that was Johnston's only line of retreat. His skirmishers came within 200 yards of Johnston's headquarters. Wheeler, Hampton, and Hardee all rushed troops to the threatened flank—among them Hardee's 16-year-old son who was killed riding with the 8th Texas Cavalry—and brought Mower's advance to a halt. Mower sent a request for reinforcements, and Howard ordered Blair to support Mower's breakthrough, but word soon arrived from Sherman to withdraw Mower instead and for the skirmishers along the rest of the line to keep the Rebels in their front too busy to concentrate on Mower.

"I think I made a mistake there," Sherman wrote in his memoirs, "and should rapidly have followed Mower's lead with the whole of the right wing, which would have brought on a general battle, and it could not have resulted otherwise than successfully to us, by reason of our vastly superior numbers; but at the moment, for the reasons given, I preferred to make junction with Generals Terry and Schofield, before engaging Johnston's army, the strength of which was utterly unknown."[24] Sherman was always more interested in winning campaigns with marches than with battles. General Howard later said of his commander, "Strategy was his strongest point. Take him in battle and he did not seem to be the equal of Thomas or Grant." Someone asked Sherman what he thought Johnston would do next. "Joe Johnston and I aren't on speaking terms," he said.[25]

That night Johnston quietly withdrew his army to the north side of Mill Creek.

---

1. Sherman, *Memoirs*, 785.
2. *Official Records*, 46:I:480.
3. Ibid., 46:III:46.
4. Ibid., 49:II:28.
5. Davis, *Sherman's March*, 233.

6. Sherman, *Memoirs*, 785.
7. Glatthaar, *The March to the Sea and Beyond*, 158.
8. Davis, *Sherman's March*, 235.
9. Ibid.
10. Ibid., 237.
11. Ibid., 236.
12. Ibid.
13. Sherman, *Memoirs*, 785-786.
14. *Official Records*, 47:II:919-920.
15. Jones, *Yankee Blitzkrieg*, 28.
16. Ibid., 1.
17. John Y. Simon, ed., *The Personal Memoirs of Julia Dent Grant*, 141-142.
18. *Official Records*, 46:III:50.
19. Grant, *Memoirs*, 2:541.
20. *Official Records*, 46:III:67.
21. Grant, *Memoirs*, 2:424-425.
22. Stern, *An End to Valor*, 45-46.
23. Ibid., 53-54.
24. Sherman, *Memoirs*, 786.
25. Davis, *Sherman's March*, 239-240.

PART THREE

RICHMOND

We are coming back into the Union, boys, we are coming back into the Union.

— Confederate soldiers captured at Five Forks

CHAPTER TWENTY-ONE

Look Out; We Are Coming

22 - 25 March 1865

Peach and plum trees were in blossom, the sky was clear, and the weather warm as Brevet Major General James Harrison Wilson finally led his Cavalry Corps of the Military Division of the Mississippi southward from the Tennessee River on the morning of 22 March 1865. Actually, he was taking only three of his corps' six divisions with him. The 3rd Division, Kilpatrick's, was with Sherman, the 6th Division was left behind to guard middle Tennessee, and there were not enough horses to mount the 5th, which was left in the camps north of the Tennessee River. Wilson later said that he should have brought the 5th Division along on foot and mounted it on some of the numerous horses he found along the way, but he did not. Nevertheless, the force he did take with him consisted of almost 14,000 men, including about 1,500 without horses who guarded the wagon train, 211 members of the battalion of pontoniers, and 334 in Wilson's escort, the 4th U.S. Cavalry. All but a few hundred of these cavalry troopers were armed with Spencer repeating carbines, and even the few who did not possess this superb weapon were armed with single-shot breechloaders that, like the Spencer, used metallic cartridges.

Each of the three divisions going on the raid consisted of two brigades plus a battery of horse artillery, and each, at first, followed a different road south. "The entire valley of the Tennessee," Wilson reported, "having been devastated by two years of warfare, was quite as destitute of army supplies as the hill country south of it. In all directions for 120 miles there was almost absolute destitution. It was, therefore, necessary to scatter the troops over a wide extent of country and march as rapidly as circumstances would permit. This was rendered safe by the fact that Forrest's forces were at that time near West Point, Miss., 150 miles southwest of Eastport, while Roddey's occupied Montevallo, on the Alabama and Tennessee River Railroad, nearly the same distance to the southeast. By starting on diverging roads the enemy was left in doubt as to our real object, and compelled to watch equally Columbus, Tuscaloosa, and Selma."[1]

In North Carolina the 22nd of March came in clear and mild, although windy. Sherman was neither surprised nor unhappy to find that Johnston's Confederates had retreated across Mill Creek during the night. He marched his own troops on toward Goldsborough, passing Terry's two divisions at Cox's Bridge on the way. "Ain't that a hard-looking set, man?" one of Terry's soldiers asked as he watched them go past.[2] In a letter Sherman wrote to Grant on the 22nd he described the battles at Averysborough and Bentonville and the progress of his columns. "Our combinations were such," he bragged, "that Schofeild entered Goldsborough from New Berne, Terry got Cox's Bridge with pontoons laid and a brigade across intrenched, and we whipped Joe Johnston, all on the same day."[3]

At City Point, Grant was writing to Sherman that same day: "I congratulate you and the army on what may be regarded as the successful termination of the third campaign since leaving the Tennessee River less than one year ago. Since Sheridan's very successful raid north of the James the enemy are left dependent on the South Side and Danville roads for all their supplies. These I hope to cut next week. Sheridan is at White House shoeing up and resting his cavalry. He will make no halt with the armies operating here, but will be joined by a division of cavalry 5,500 strong from the Army of the Potomac, and will proceed directly to the South Side and Danville roads. His instructions will be to strike the South Side road as near Petersburg as he can and destroy it so that it cannot be repaired for three or four days, and push on to the Danville road as near to the Appomattox as he can get. Then I want him to destroy the road toward Burkeville as far as he can, then push on to the South Side road west of Burkeville and destroy it effectually. From that point I shall probably leave it to his discretion either to return to this army, crossing the Danville road south of Burkeville, or go and join you, passing between Danville and Greensborough. When this movement commences I shall move out by my left with all the force I can, holding present intrenched lines. I shall start with no distinct view further than holding Lee's forces from following Sheridan, but I shall be along myself and will take advantage of anything that turns up. If Lee detaches I will attack, or if he comes out of his lines I will endeavor to repulse him and follow it up to the best advantage."[4]

Sherman reached Goldsborough on the morning of the 23rd, and Slocum's wing of his army soon followed, linking up with Schofield's force from the coast. Sherman wrote Grant another letter from there that day in which he said: "At all events we have now made a junction of all the armies, and if we can maintain them will in a short time be in position to march against Raleigh, or Gaston, or Weldon, or even Richmond, as you may determine. If I get the troops all well placed, and the supplies working well, I might run up to see you for a day or two before diving again into the bowels of the country."[5]

Down on the Gulf coast, General Canby was answering Grant's angry letter of the ninth, which he had just received, on the 23rd: "Estimates for railroad material and construction had no reference to immediate operations, but was made with a view to the future, if we should not be able to open navigation of the Alabama. You cannot regret more than I do the delays that have attended this movement. We have been embarrassed and delayed by rain and wind storms that have not been paralleled in the last forty years. The floods have been general, and embraced the whole section of the Southwest. It was impossible to bridge streams in order to move by land, because the overflow was so great that their banks could not be reached, and the weather on the Gulf has been so tempetuous that our transports could not be used more than half the time, and the services of several have been lost by being driven ashore. We have had now two consecutive bright days, the only two in a month, and a footing upon fair ground. If the Thirteenth Corps gets up to-night, as I hope it will, we will move in the morning for Blakely and will endeavor to open way for the gunboats into the Alabama."[6]

From the telegraph office at the St. Nicholas Hotel in New York City that day, John Wilkes Booth sent a brief telegram to Louis Weichmann at Mrs. Surratt's boardinghouse: "Tell John to telegraph number and street at once."[7] Another boarder took the message to Weichmann where he worked at the office of the commissary general of prisoners, but it made no sense to him. He later showed it to John Surratt, who knew just what it meant, although he did not tell Weichmann. Booth wanted the address of a boarding house in Washington where Lewis Paine (Powell) was to stay. Evidently Booth, after talking with Confederate agents in New York, was ready to try again.

However, President Lincoln left Washington that same day. After receiving Grant's invitation to visit City Point he had quickly made arrangements to do just that. Mrs. Lincoln and their youngest son, Tad, went along. A strong wind stirred up waves on the Potomac River as the civilian steamer *River Queen* cast off at 1 p.m., escorted by a fast, heavily armed navy gunboat called the *Bat.* By 2 p.m. the wind had risen to gale force, tearing the roof off a foundry in Washington, killing a man and his horse and sinking a schooner at the wharf. But then it died down again to occasional gusts. That evening the Lincolns were entertained by the *River Queen*'s captain, who told them stories about the Rebel spies and blockade runners who regularly crossed this stretch of the river under the cover of darkness. Little did they know that some of those same Confederate agents hoped to capture Lincoln and smuggle him to Richmond via that very route and that the fact that he was on that boat instead of back in Washington might be the only thing saving him from such a fate.

At 8:30 p.m. the two steamers dropped anchor for the night in St. Mary's River, a small tributary on the Northern Neck just short of the point where the Potomac flows into Chesapeake Bay. At 5:15 a.m. on the 24th they started off again, with a strong west wind and high waves that caused the *River Queen* to roll heavily. The president got seasick shortly before noon, and the two boats stopped near Fort Monroe so a boat could be sent ashore to bring his some fresh drinking water. At 2 p.m. they got under way again and turned into the James River. The *Bat* developed engine trouble and had to stop at Harrison's Landing on the north bank, where there was a Union garrison, at 8:25 p.m. But the *River Queen* went on alone and joined the 100 or so other vessels at the City Point wharfs at 9 p.m. Grant and some of his staff, including Captain Robert Lincoln, went down the bluff from his headquarters cabin to greet the new arrivals.

It was a day of family reunions for Robert Lincoln. Earlier that day he had accidentally run into his aunt. His mother's half-sister was the widow of Confederate brigadier general Ben Hardin Helm, who had been mortally wounded at Chickamauga. Mrs. Helm had come down from Richmond on the flag-of-truce boat carrying exchanged prisoners. She was accompanied by "General" James Singleton, who still hoped to bring out Mrs. Helm's 600 bales of cotton.

Grant issued orders for the coming campaign to Meade, Ord, and Sheridan that day, the 24th: "On the 29th instant the armies operating against Richmond will be moved by our left, for the double purposes of turning the enemy out of his present position around Petersburg and to insure the success of the cavalry under General Sheridan, which will start at the same time, in its efforts to reach and destroy the South Side and Danville railroads. Two corps of the Army of the Potomac will be moved at first in two columns...both moving toward Dinwiddie Court-House.

"The cavalry under General Sheridan, joined by the division now under General Davies, will...then move independently, under, other instructions which will be given him. All dismounted cavalry...not needed for guarding property belonging to their arm of service, will...be added to the defenses of City Point. Major-General Parke will be left in command of all the army left for holding the lines about Petersburg and City Point. The Ninth Army Corps will be left intact to hold the present line of works so long as the whole line now occupied by us is held. All troops to the left of the Ninth Corps will be held in readiness to move at the shortest notice by such route as may be designated when the order is given.

"General Ord will detach three divisions, two white and one colored...and hold his present lines and march for the present left of the Army of the Potomac. During the movement Major-General Weitzel will be left in command of all the forces remaining behind from the Army of the James.

"The movement of troops from the Army of the James will commence on the night of the 27th instant. General Ord will leave behind the minimum number of cavalry necessary for picket duty, in the absence of the main army. A cavalry expedition from General Ord's command will also be started from Suffolk, to leave there on Saturday, the 1st of April, under Colonel Sumner, for the purpose of cutting the railroad about Hicksford. This, if accomplished, will have to be a surprise, and therefore from 300 to 500 men will be sufficient. They should, however, be supported by all the infantry that can be spared from Norfolk and Portsmouth, as far out as to where the cavalry crosses the Blackwater. All the troops will move with four days' ration in haversacks and eight days' in wagons. Sixty rounds of ammunition per man will be taken in wagons, and as much grain as the transportation on hand will carry. The densely wooded country in which the army has to operate making the use of much artillery impracticable, the amount taken with the army will be reduced to six or eight guns to each division.

"All necessary preparations for carrying these directions into operation may be commenced at once. The reserves of the Ninth Corps should be massed as much as possible. While I would not now order an unconditional attack on the enemy's line by them, they should be ready, and should make the attack if the enemy weakens his line in their front, without waiting for orders. In case they carry the line, then the whole of the Ninth Corps could follow up, so as to join or co-operate with the balance of the army. To prepare for this the Ninth Corps will have rations issued to them, same as the balance of the army. General Weitzel will keep vigilant watch upon his front, and if found at all practicable to break through at any point, he will do so. A success north of the James should be followed up with great promptness. An attack will not be feasible unless it is found that the enemy are relying upon their local reserves, principally, for the defense of Richmond. Preparations may be made for abandoning all the line north of the James, except inclosed works—only to be abandoned, however, after a break is made in the lines of the enemy.

"By these instructions a large part of the armies operating against Richmond is left behind. The enemy, knowing this, may, as an only chance, strip their lines to the merest skeleton, in the hope of advantage not being taken of it, while they hurl everything against the moving column, and return. It cannot be impressed too strongly upon commanders of troops left in the trenches not to allow this to occur without taking advantage of it. The very fact of the enemy coming out to attack, if he does so, might be regarded as almost conclusive evidence of such a weakening of his lines. I would have it particularly enjoined upon corps commanders that, in case of an attack from the enemy, those not attacked are not to wait for orders from the commanding officer of the army to which they belong, but that they will move promptly, and notify the commander of their action. I would also enjoin the same action on the part of division commanders when other parts of their corps are engaged. In like manner, I would urge the importance of following up a repulse of the enemy."[8]

In far off Europe that day the most fearsome Confederate commerce raider yet commissioned steamed out of Ferrol, Spain. The CSS *Stonewall* was a seagoing ironclad built by the French at Bordeaux. Her armor reportedly made her unsinkable, her prow had an underwater beak said to be capable of sinking any ship, wooden or iron, by ramming, and she carried a huge 300-pounder Armstrong rifles in her bow. She had set off down the coast in mid-January with instructions to cross the Atlantic and break the blockade at Wilmington, but she had been damaged by rough weather and put into Ferrol for repairs. That allowed time for two Union wooden frigates to take station outside the harbor, but when she steamed out on the 24th of March they stood aside and let her go. One Federal captain said, "The odds in her favor were too great and too certain, in my humble judgment, to admit of the slightest hope of being able to inflict upon her even the most trifling injury."[9] He might well have been correct, but the Union commander was court-martialed anyway for not at least trying to stop her.

In New York City the next day, 25 March, Confederate captain Robert Cobb Kennedy was hanged for "crimes, which outrage and shock the moral sense by their atrocity."[10]

Down on the Gulf on the 25th, Canby's main army finally began advancing along the eastern shore of Mobile Bay toward the defenses of the city. On the same day, Steele's column struggling northward from Pensacola over muddy roads first ran into sizable opposition. Brigadier General Thomas J. Lucas's brigade of cavalry in the lead, drove about a hundred Rebels from a line of log defenses stretching across a narrow ridge over which the road passed. Steele ordered Lucas to push on and get possession of the bridge over the Big Escambia River, but at Bluff Springs he found two regiments of Confederate cavalry drawn up in line of battle, mostly dismounted, on the north bank of Canoe Creek. Lucas's leading regiment, the 1st Louisiana (Union) Cavalry, charged. The Confederates broke and ran, and the Federals pursued them for four miles to the Escambia River, where they found that the bridge had already been destroyed. Some of the Rebels, in their haste to get away, dived, horse and all, off the end of the broken bridge and were drowned. Many others escaped through the swamps and woods on both flanks. Confederate artillery opened fire from the other side of the river, but Lucas brought up his own guns and drove the Rebels away, then sent a detachment across to hold a bridgehead until the infantry caught up. The Confederate brigade commander, Brigadier General J.H. Clanton, was captured, along with 18 other officers, 111 enlisted men, and the battleflag of the 6th Alabama Cavalry.

Sheridan's cavalry left White House plantation that day, crossed the Chickahominy River, and marched to Harrison's Landing on the north bank of the James.

On the Union lines east of Petersburg in the pre-dawn darkness of 25 March a captain in the 9th Corps noticed something unusual. "Desultory firing was kept up that night until about 1 o'clock," he said, "when everything became suddenly still and the unusual silence along the line to the left seemed to me very suspicious and I ordered a shot from each of the six posts every three minutes as near as could be judged." Before long "one of the men came in and reported that he had heard a noise in front which sounded as if someone was removing an obstruction, but a thorough investigation failed to reveal any cause for alarm." Not far away a private in another Union regiment was on picket duty when he saw eight Rebels coming his way with their rifles reversed as a sign that they were deserters. It was a common sight. The Federal army paid $10 to every deserter who brought his rifle with him. "Our videt received them," the private remembered, "and escorted them to the inner post, but as soon as they reached it they turned their rifles and ordered all to surrender."[11] The Union pickets were quietly hurried across the broken no-man's-land between the lines and into captivity.

After his late-night talk with Gordon three weeks earlier and Grant's refusal to meet him, Lee had instructed Gordon to plan an attack on the Federal lines as a preliminary to the withdrawal of Lee's army from Richmond. A Confederate staff officer explained that Lee now had little choice but to retreat. "But this now seemed difficult, if not impossible. General Grant had a powerful force not far from the main roads over which Lee must move; and, unless a diversion of some description were made, it seemed barely possible that the Southern army could extricate itself."[12]

As Lee later explained it to President Davis, "I have been unwilling to hazard any portion of the troops in an assault upon fortified positions, preferring to reserve their strength for the struggle which must soon commence, but I was induced to assume the offensive from the belief that the point assailed could be carried without much loss, and the hope that by the seizure of the redoubts in the rear of the enemy's main line, I could sweep along his entrenchments to the south, so that if I could not cause their abandonment, Genl Grant would at least be obliged so to curtail his lines, that upon the approach of Genl Sherman, I might be able to hold our position with a portion of the troops, and with a select body unite with Genl Johnston and give him battle. If successful, I would then be able to return to my position, and if unsuccessful I should be in no worse condition, as I should be compelled to withdraw from James River if I quietly awaited his approach."[13]

Gordon had chosen an enclosed redoubt on the Union line called Fort Stedman as the target of the attack. It was in the Ninth Corps sector near the right, or northern, end of the Union defenses, where the opposing trench lines were closest together. Only about 150 yards separated Fort Stedman from a Confederate redoubt called Colquitt's Salient. The two works occupied opposite ends of a small plateau. Stedman contained four Union guns, and there were other Federal batteries north and south of it in smaller earthworks. On high ground beyond Fort Stedman, Gordon thought he could see three more Union forts. If these could be taken it should be possible for the Rebels to successfully defend their breakthrough from counterattacks.

Gordon had worked out an intricate plan. Special squads were appointed to go out between the lines in the dark and remove the Rebels' own obstacles beyond their trenches, which had been placed there long ago to slow and break up any Union attack. Next, other men would sneak up on the Federal picket posts, capture them, and open paths through the outer obstructions in front of the Union entrenchments. After that, fifty men with axes would be sent forward to cut openings in the final obstructions in front of Fort Stedman and the nearby batteries. Behind these fifty would come three separate groups of a hundred men each. One was to rush forward and capture Fort Stedman, another to capture Battery No. 10 just north of it, and the last to capture batteries 11 and 12 just south of Stedman. "For hours Mrs. Gordon sat in her room in Petersburg," the general wrote, "tearing up strips of white cloth to tie across the breasts of the leading detachments, that they might recognize each other in the darkness and in the hand-to-hand battle expected at the Federal breastworks and inside the fort."[14] These men were promised, if they accomplished their tasks, a thirty-day furlough and a silver medal each.

As soon as other troops came up to defend what they had captured, the 100-man detachments were to pass through the captured fort and batteries and seize the forts on the high ground beyond. In an effort to get by any Federal challenge, the officers in charge of these detachments were each to assume the name of a Union officer known to be assigned to units in the area and they were to pretend to be retreating Federals. Meanwhile, the bulk of Gordon's three divisions was to widen the breach by sweeping along the trenches to the north and south, and, finally, a division of cavalry would pass through the captured lines to attack the Union rear, cut lines of communication and, if possible, capture General

Grant himself. Two brigades from Anderson's 4th Corps were available for support, and four brigades from Hill's 3rd Corps were on call. Pickett's Division of Longstreet's 1st Corps was on its way from the north side of the James to serve as a reinforcement but it had not yet arrived when the hour for the attack, 4 a.m., arrived.

At that hour, still well before dawn, Gordon was standing on top of the Confederate earthworks with, as he wrote, "no one at my side except a single private soldier with rifle in hand, who was to fire the signal shot for the headlong rush. This night charge on the fort was to be across the intervening space covered with ditches, in one of which stood the watchful Federal pickets. There still remained near my works some of the debris of our obstructions, which had not been completely removed and which I feared might retard the rapid exit of my men; and I ordered it cleared away. The noise made by this removal, though slight, attracted the attention of a Union picket who stood on guard only a few rods from me, and he called out, 'What are you doing there, Johnny? What is that noise? Answer quick or I'll shoot.'

"The pickets of the two armies were so close together at this point that there was an understanding between them, either expressed or implied, that they would not shoot each other down except when necessary. The call of this Union picket filled me with apprehension. I expected him to fire and start the entire picket line to firing, thus giving the alarm to the fort, the capture of which depended largely upon the secrecy of my movement. The quick mother-wit of the private soldier at my side came to my relief. In an instant he replied, 'Never mind, Yank. Lie down and go to sleep. We are just gathering a little corn. You know rations are mighty short over here.' There was a narrow strip of corn which the bullets had not shot away still standing between the lines. The Union picket promptly answered, 'All right, Johnny; go ahead and get your corn. I'll not shoot at you while you are drawing your rations.'"

The last obstructions were removed from Gordon's front and he ordered the private to fire the signal. "He pointed his rifle upward, with his finger on the trigger, but hesitated. His conscience seemed to get hold of him. He was going into the fearful charge, and he evidently did not feel disposed to go into eternity with the lie on his lips, although it might be a permissible war lie, by which he had thrown the Union picket off his guard. He evidently felt that it was hardly fair to take advantage of the generosity and soldierly sympathy of his foe, who had so magnanimously assured him that he would not be shot while drawing his rations from the little field of corn.

"His hesitation surprised me, and I again ordered, 'Fire your gun, sir.' He at once called to his kindhearted foe and said, 'Hello, Yank! Wake up; we are going to shell the woods. Look out; we are coming.' And with this effort to satisfy his conscience and even up accounts with the Yankee picket, he fired the shot and rushed forward in the darkness."[15]

A private in Grimes's Division of Gordon's corps remembered how the storming party "with unloaded muskets and a profound silence, leaped over our breastworks, [and] dashed across the open space in front." Brigadier General James Walker, commanding a division, said, "The cool, frosty morning made every sound distinct and clear, and the only sound heard was the tramp! tramp! of the men as they kept step as regularly as if on drill." In spite of all Gordon's precautions at least one Union picket raised the alarm. Walker heard him shouting, "The Rebels are coming! The Rebels are coming!"[16]

Federal artillerymen in Battery 10, some ninety yards northwest of Fort Stedman, heard the picket's cry and quickly sprang to their guns. Their two 3-inch rifles were kept loaded for just such emergencies, and both were fired off within seconds. But before they could be reloaded one of the 100-man Confederate storming parties began clambering over their parapet. "Small-arms were brought into use," a Federal officer reported, "and for a short time the enemy were held in check by a hand-to-hand confict."[17] But in the darkness their aim was bad, and the Rebels quickly overwhelmed them.

The Union artillerymen in Fort Stedman were alerted by the sound of the attack on Battery No. 10 and they immediately fired their four 12-pounders, which were kept loaded with canister. Their captain ordered one of the pieces manhandled around to face Battery No. 10. and meanwhile the other three guns managed to get off about a dozen rounds in the direction of the Rebel lines. "At the flash of their guns darkness disappeared," the Confederate commander in charge of the detachment detailed to capture the fort remembered, "and at intervals, as the guns were discharged, it was as light as day. We struck the middle line of brush, climbing, falling, and rolling over into the open ground beyond. Then the wind from the cannon and flying balls was so strong that we could not keep our hats on, while the frightful roar of the guns drowned every other sound. We went the balance of the way with hats and guns in hand till we reached the last line of obstructions. In a few minutes we were in the moat. We had struck the fort about the middle. The infantry in the fort was...firing straight down upon us. We were in the dark, while the enemy above us were faintly outlined against the sky. I shouted to the men to shoot every man who showed himself. They began firing at once, and in a few moments the works were cleared.

It was but thirteen feet up, and my men were sharpshooters. Word was quietly passed from the right of our line that a low place had been found. We filed along until the place was reached and scrambled into the fort. Forming my line, we struck the enemy at right angles, and they in a few minutes surrendered."[18]

The Confederates turned the captured guns and opened fire on adjoining Union positions. Battery No. 11, south of Fort Stedman, was captured before its defenders ever got off a shot. Then the Rebels overran the camps of a pair of Union infantry regiments just behind the front lines. "It was a complete surprise," one Confederate said. "Many were killed coming out of their tents by our men, using their guns as clubs." The Rebel attack was more disrupted by the Federals' supplies than by their resistance. "We were soon in possession," one Confederate wrote, "and our half-starved men busy searching the bomb proofs and covered ways for rations."[19]

The commander of the Union brigade whose front was being attacked was Brevet Brigadier General Napoleon Bonaparte McLaughlen. When the sound of firing woke him that morning he quickly dressed and rode to Fort Haskell, south of Fort Stedman, and found the troops there "on the alert and ready to resist an attack." He continued moving to the north and found infantrymen manning the trenches and the artillery still holding Battery No. 12, between the two forts, but he soon learned that Battery No. 11 had been captured. He ordered the mortars in Battery 12 to fire on Battery 11 and sent for his reserve regiment, the 59th Massachusetts. "On the arrival of the Fifty-ninth," he reported, "I put them into the work with fixed bayonets and recaptured it at once. Supposing that I had restored the only break in the line, I crossed the parapet into Fort Stedman on the right, and meeting some men coming over the curtains, whom in the darkness I supposed to be a part of the picket, I established them inside the work, giving directions with regard to position and firing, all of which were instantly obeyed. In a few minutes I saw a man crossing the parapet, whose uniform in the dawning light I recognized to be the enemy's, and I halted him, asking his regiment. This called attention to myself, and the next moment I was surrounded by the rebels, whom I had supposed to be my men, and sent to the rear, where I found General Gordon, to whom I delivered my sword, and was sent by him to Petersburg. While standing by General Gordon four brigades moved forward toward our works, their commanders reporting to him."[20] Even though two other regiments joined the 59th Massachusetts to form a line facing north anchored on Battery 11 the Confederates soon outflanked this new line and retook the battery.

Not long after meeting with the captured McLaughlen, Gordon moved into Fort Stedman himself. "Up to this point," he wrote, "the success had exceeded my most sanguine expectations. We had taken Fort Stedman and a long line of breastworks on either side. We had captured nine heavy cannon, eleven mortars, nearly 1,000 prisoners, including General McLaughlen, with the loss of less than half a dozen men. From the fort I sent word to General Lee, who was on a hill in the rear, that we were in the works and that the 300 were on their way to the lines in the rear. Soon I received a message from one of these three officers...that he had passed the line of Federal infantry without trouble by representing himself as Colonel——of the 100th Pennsylvania, but that he could not find his fort. I soon received a similar message from the other two, and so notified General Lee."[21] There were no Union forts on the high ground behind Stedman. What Gordon had seen from a distance were merely the remains of some badly worn Confederate earthworks that the Federals had overrun back in June 1864.

Fort Haskell, south of Battery No. 12, became the rallying point for retreating Federals and the next target of the Confederates sweeping south along the lines. The defenders could hear the Rebels approaching under the cover of darkness. "A breath seemed an age," one Federal remembered, "for we knew nothing of the numbers before us. Finally, the Confederate leaders called out, 'Steady! We'll have their works. Steady, my men!' Our nerves rebelled, and like a flash the thought passed along the parapet, 'Now!' Not a word was spoken, but in perfect concert the cannon and muskets were discharged upon the hapless band. It must have been a surprise for the surprisers, though fortunately for them we had been too hasty, and, as they were moving by the flank along our front, only the head of their column received the fire. But this repulse did not end it; the survivors closed up and tried it again. Then they divided into squads and moved on the flanks, keeping up the by-play until there were none left. Daylight soon gave us perfect aim, and their game was useless."[22] One Federal, arriving with a regiment of reinforcements, said, "As daylight approached a slight air movement made a rift in the pall of smoke over Fort Haskell, and we could see Old Glory waving from its ramparts. It looked good, and oh, how we did cheer!"[23]

But another column of Rebels approached from Fort Stedman, and with the growing light Confederate artillery in their own lines and some of the captured guns in Fort Stedman began to bombard Fort Haskell. "The air was full of shells," one defender said, "and on glancing up one saw, as it were, a flock of blackbirds with blazing tails beating about in a gale. At first the shells did not explode. Their fuses were too long, so they fell intact, and the fires went out. Sometimes they rolled about like foot-balls, or bounded along the parapet and landed in the watery ditch. But when at last the Confederate gunners got the range, their shots became murderous."[24]

North of the Confederate breakthrough a Union lieutenant commanding a pair of 3-inch guns in Battery No. 9 peered over his parapet in the growing light. "I could just see in the gray dawn (it was then about 5:15 a.m.) a line of battle drawn up, moving toward me," he wrote, "their right being inside of our works; this line extended along the ravine between Battery No. 9 and Fort Stedman, their left resting near the rebel lines. I immediately ordered my section to open on them with spherical case; they were in easy range, about 400 yards, maybe a little more. As soon as I opened a heavy fire was in a few minutes concentrated on Battery No. 9."[25]

But the Federals had the preponderance of artillery, including a number of reserve guns that were brought up, and as soon as it grew light their shells began to rain down on the captured positions from every direction except west. "Their fire completely enfiladed our position," one Rebel remembered, with "shrapnel from our right beyond Fort Stedman and minnies from the fort near the river on our left, and with shell from the bluffs in our front, our position was made, in the opinion of our commanders, untenable."[26] A captured Union officer who was sheltered in a bombproof with some of his Confederate captors said the Federal fire "was most accurate and destructive. Rebel officers came in and reported the effect to be terrible, and stated that their lines could not be held at any point. The wounded were brought in in great numbers; I noticed among them a large proportion of officers. The number of stragglers and skulkers was astonishingly large; and I saw several instances where the authority of the officers who urged them on was set at defiance."[27]

Grant's headquarters was notified of the Confederate attack at about 6 a.m., but soon thereafter the telegraph line went dead. The general was still in bed, but he was soon up and dressed and consulting with Meade and Ord, both of whom had spent the night at City Point. "Meade was greatly nettled by the fact that he was absent from his command at such a time," Horace Porter said, "and was pacing up and down with great strides, and dictating orders to his chief of staff, General Webb, who was with him, in tones which showed very forcibly the intensity of his feelings. The President, who was aboard his boat anchored out in the river, soon heard of the attack, and he was kept informed of the events which were taking place by his son Robert, who carried the news to him."[28] Grant telegraphed Gibbon, commanding north of the James in Ord's absence: "The enemy have attacked on General Parke's front and broken through his line. This may be a signal for leaving. Be ready to take advantage of it."[29]

In Meade's absence his chief of artillery, Brevet Major General Henry Hunt, alerted all the corps commanders and sent batteries of reserve artillery to the threatened sector. The other corps commanders then reported to Parke, the senior among them, until Meade was back in communication. The 6th Corps sent one division toward the threatened sector and most of the 5th Corps, farther to the left, began marching in that direction.

Brigadier General John Hartranft's 3rd Division constituted the general reserve of the 9th Corps. It consisted entirely of newly raised Pennsylvania regiments, but many of its men were veterans who had reenlisted in these new outfits after their old regiments had gone home. When Hartranft had been alerted he had put his troops under arms and had ridden to the headquarters of Brigadier General Orlando Willcox, whose 1st Division included the sector under attack. Just as the two commanders had finished consulting, Hartranft saw a Confederate battle line with skirmishers out front advancing from Fort Stedman toward the military railroad at Meade's Station, which was the depot for the 9th Corps. He raced to bring up one of his large new regiments and ordered it to drive back the approaching Rebels. It advanced bravely, only to be driven back by a very heavy fire from the Confederate infantry and the captured guns in Fort Stedman. But the Pennsylvanians rallied on some old earthworks, attacked again, and gained what Hartranft considered a very good position, which it held for some twenty minutes despite heavy losses. This gave Hartranft time to patch together a line enclosing the Rebels on the south, east, and north.

By the time his other brigade finally arrived from farther off, Hartranft was thinking about counterattacking. By 7:45 a.m. he had five regiments and detachments, totaling almost 4,000 men, ready to charge. Just as the attack was getting started Hartranft received an order from Parke, his corps commander, to wait for a division being sent over from the 6th Corps, but he decided it was too late to stop all of his units, and anyway he could see the Confederates starting to waver. The 211th Pennsylvania was sent forward to draw the Rebels' attention and fire and to cover the advance of the rest of the force. "This ruse was a complete success," he reported. "The enemy, seeing the advance of this regiment, numbering about 600 muskets, in such handsome manner, commenced to waver, when the balance of the division charged with a will, in the most gallant style, and in a moment Stedman, Batteries 11 and 12, and the entire line which had been lost, was recaptured with a large number of prisoners, battleflags, and small arms."[30] One of Hartranft's men who grabbed a Confederate flag began to wave it around for everyone to see. "In two seconds several lively shells from one of our batteries well toward a mile in the rear crashed on us," a Federal said. "Needless to say we ceased to wave that rebel battle flag then and there."[31]

At 8 a.m., just before Hartranft's counterattack, Lee sent word to Gordon to bring his men back to Colquitt's salient, as the assault was obviously stalled and attempting to hold the captured positions would only increase the length of the casualty lists. But getting back across the open area of no-man's land under the bombardment of the Union artillery and the attack of Hartranft's infantry was easier to order than to accomplish. The Rebels suffered far more casualties in their retreat than they had in attacking and defending. Many of them refused to go, preferring to stay put and surrender than to run the gauntlet of fire. A Federal soldier in Fort Haskell felt pity for the men who a few minutes before had been trying to kill or capture him: "My mind sickens at the memory of it—a real tragedy in war—for the victims had ceased fighting, and were now struggling between imprisonment on the one hand, and death or home on the other."[32]

The 9th Corps took 1,949 prisoners and captured nine battleflags, while losing 1,017 men killed, wounded, and missing. Gordon blamed the failure of his plan on the failure of Pickett's Division to arrive in time and "Grant's...overwhelming forces," but he did not even use the troops from the 3rd Corps who were assigned to him and, other than a few batteries of artillery, the only Union forces he faced were Willcox's 1st and Hartranft's 3rd divisions of the 9th Corps.[33] The division sent over by the 6th Corps did not arrive until after the Confederates had been driven back to their own lines, and the 5th Corps did not get close to the action. However, after it was known that the captured positions had been retaken, the 6th Corps and 2nd Corps attacked and captured the Rebels' entrenched picket lines in their own fronts, taking several hundred more prisoners. Altogether the day's losses amounted to about 2,000 men for the Federals and about 5,000 for the Confederates.

"The shifting scenes and threatening demonstrations on my front," Gordon wrote, "and in front of A.P. Hill on my right, kept me on horseback until my tired limbs and aching joints made a constant appeal for rest. The coming of night brought little or no cessation of the perplexing and fatiguing activities. Troops were marching, heavy guns were roaring, picket lines were driven in and had to be reestablished; and the great mortars from both Union and Confederate works were hurling high in the air their ponderous shells, which crossed each other's paths and, with burning fuses like tails of flying comets, descended in meteoric showers on the opposing entrenchments...

"At a point near where the left of A.P. Hill's corps touched the right of mine, a threatened attack brought together for counsel a number of officers from each of these commands. After this conference as to the proper disposition of troops for resisting the expected assault, we withdrew into a small log hut standing near, and united in prayer to Almighty God for His guidance. As we assembled, one of our generals was riding within hailing distance, and General Harry Heth of Hill's corps stepped to the door of the log cabin and called to him to come in and unite with us in prayer. The officer did not understand the nature of General Heth's invitation, and replied, 'No thank you, general; no more at present; I've just had some.'"[34]

According to Horace Porter, "General Grant proposed to the President that forenoon that he should accompany him on a trip to the Petersburg front. The invitation was promptly accepted, and several hours were spent in visiting the troops, who cheered the President enthusiastically. He was greatly interested in looking at the prisoners who had been captured that morning."[35] General Meade greeted the president by saying, "I have just now a despatch from General Parke to show you." But Lincoln pointed to the captured Rebels and said, "Ah, *there* is the best despatch you can show me from General Parke!"[36] Colonel Theodore Lyman of Meade's staff thought the Rebel prisoners were a disheveled lot. "They grew rougher and rougher," he said. "These looked brown and athletic, but had the most matted hair, tangled beards, and slouched hats, and the most astounding carpets, horse-sheets and transmogrified shelter-tents for blankets." Lyman also turned a critical eye on Lincoln. "The President is, I think, the ugliest man I ever put my eyes on," he said. "On the other hand, he has the look of sense and wonderful shrewdness, while the heavy eyelids give him a mark almost of genius. He strikes me, too, as a very honest and kindly man; and, with all his vulgarity, I see no trace of low passions in his face. On the whole, he is such a mixture of all sorts, as only America brings forth. He is as much like a highly intellectual and benevolent satyr as anything I can think of. I never wish to see him again, but, as humanity runs, I am well content to have him at the head of affairs."[37]

The president and the generals then reviewed part of the 5th Corps. After leaving the military railroad at Meade's Station the men proceeded on horseback, but an ambulance wagon was provided for Mrs. Lincoln and Mrs. Grant. Lieutenant Colonel Adam Badeau, Grant's military secretary, rode with them. "I chanced to mention," he later wrote, "that all the wives of officers at the army front had been ordered to the rear—a sure sign that active operations were in contemplation. I said not a lady had been allowed to remain, except Mrs. Griffin, the wife of General Charles Griffin, who had obtained a special permit from the President. At this Mrs. Lincoln was up in arms, 'What do you mean by that, sir?' she exclaimed. 'Do you mean to say that she saw the President alone?' She was absolutely jealous of poor, ugly Abraham Lincoln.

"I tried to pacify her and to palliate my remark, but she was fairly boiling over with rage. 'That's a very equivocal smile, sir,' she exclaimed: 'Let me out of this carriage at once. I will ask the President if he saw that woman alone.' Mrs. Griffin, afterward the Countess Esterhazy, was one of the best known and most elegant women in Washington, a Carroll, and a personal acquaintance of Mrs. Grant, who strove to mollify the excited spouse, but all in vain. Mrs. Lincoln again bade me stop the driver, and when I hesitated to obey, she thrust her arms past me to the front of the carriage and held the driver fast. But Mrs. Grant finally prevailed upon her to wait till the whole party alighted, and then General Meade came up to pay his respects to the wife of the President. I had intended to offer Mrs. Lincoln my arm, and endeavor to prevent a scene, but Meade, of course, as my superior, had the right to escort her, and I had no chance to warn him. I saw them go off together, and remained in fear...for what might occur. But General Meade was very adroit, and when they returned Mrs. Lincoln looked at me significantly and said: 'General Meade is a gentleman, sir. He says it was not the President who gave Mrs. Griffin the permit, but the Secretary of War.' Meade was the son of a diplomatist, and had evidently inherited some of his father's skills."[38]

After the review the presidential party went to Fort Wadsworth, near where the Union lines crossed the Weldon Railroad, and for two hours they watched some of the fighting for the Confederate picket line. When they returned to the military railroad the depot was filled with dead and wounded men. Lincoln told one of the officers with him that "he had seen enough of the horrors of war, that he hoped this was the beginning of the end, and that there would be no more bloodshed or ruin of homes."[39]

"Upon the return to headquarters at City Point," Horace Porter said, "[Lincoln] sat for a while by the camp-fire; and as the smoke curled about his head during certain shiftings of the wind, and he brushed it away from time to time by waving his right hand in front of his face, he entertained the general-in-chief and several members of the staff by talking in a most interesting manner about public affairs, and illustrating the subjects mentioned with his incomparable anecdotes. At first his manner was grave and his language much more serious than usual. He spoke of the appalling difficulties encountered by the administration, the losses in the field, the perplexing financial problems, and the foreign complications; but said they had all been overcome by the unswerving patriotism of the people, the devotion of the loyal North, and the superb fighting qualities of the troops." General Grant asked: "Mr. President, did you at any time doubt the final success of the cause?" "Never for a moment," was the prompt and emphatic reply.[40]

---

1. *Official Records*, 49:I:356.
2. Davis, *Sherman's March*, 240.
3. *Official Records*, 47:II:950.
4. Ibid., 47:II:948.
5. Ibid., 47:II:969.
6. Ibid., 49:II:66.
7. Tidwell, Hall and Gaddy, *Come Retribution*, 415.
8. *Official Records*, 46:I:50-51.
9. Foote, *The Civil War*, 3:1028.
10. Brandt, *The Man Who Tried to Burn New York*, 229.
11. Trudeau, *The Last Citadel*, 332.
12. Richard Wheeler, *Witness to Appomattox*, 41.
13. Dowdey and Manarin, ed., *Wartime Papers of R. E. Lee*, 917.
14. Wheeler, *Witness to Appomattox*, 42.
15. Ibid., 44-46.
16. Trudeau, *The Last Citadel*, 338-339.
17. Ibid., 339.
18. Stern, *An End to Valor*, 76-77.
19. Trudeau, *The Last Citadel*, 340.
20. *Official Records*, 46:I:331-332.
21. Wheeler, *Witness to Appomattox*, 46-47.
22. Trudeau, *The Last Citadel*, 346.
23. George L. Kilmer, "Gordon's Attack at Fort Stedman," in *Battle and Leaders*, 4:580-581.
24. Ibid., 582.
25. *Official Records*, 46:I:190-191.
26. Trudeau, *The Last Citadel*, 345.
27. Ibid., 347.
28. Porter, *Campaigning With Grant*, 404.
29. *Official Records*, 46:III:162.
30. Ibid., 46:I:348.

31. Trudeau, *The Last Citadel*, 350.
32. Kilmer, "Gordon's Attack at Fort Stedman," 583.
33. Wheeler, *Witness to Appomattox*, 47.
34. Ibid., 54-56.
35. Porter, *Campaigning With Grant*, 406.
36. Trudeau, *The Last Citadel*, 352.
37. Burke Davis, *To Appomattox: Nine April Days, 1865* (New York, 1959), 28-29.
38. Stern, *An End to Valor*, 87-88.
39. Trudeau, *The Last Citadel*, 353.
40. Porter, *Campaigning With Grant*, 406-408.

CHAPTER TWENTY-TWO

The Last Evening of the Old Dispensation

25 - 28 March 1865

John Wilkes Booth returned to the National Hotel in Washington on the 25th, after a stop in Baltimore on his way from New York. The next day, with George Atzerodt, he called on Mary Surratt at her boarding house and learned that John Surratt had gone to Richmond again. This time he was escorting Confederate courier Sarah Slater, alias Kate Thompson, who was carrying dispatches from Montreal to the Rebel capital. Her regular escort, Confederate agent Augustus Howell, had been arrested at the Surratt tavern on the 24th.

That day, the 26th, General Crook, Sheridan's old friend, took command of the one cavalry division that had remained with the Army of the Potomac during Sheridan's months in the Shenandoah Valley.

Sheridan's cavalry crossed the James River on a pontoon bridge that day, but Sheridan himself went ahead by boat to City Point. In his memoirs he said that the first person he met at army headquarters was Brigadier General John A. Rawlins, Grant's chief of staff. "Rawlins was a man of strong likes and dislikes," Sheridan said, "and positive always both in speech and action, exhibiting marked feelings when greeting any one, and on this occasion met me with much warmth. His demonstrations of welcome over, we held a few minutes' conversation about the coming campaign, he taking strong ground against a part of the plan of operations adopted, namely, that which contemplated my joining General Sherman's army. His language was unequivocal and vehement, and when he was through talking, he conducted me to General Grant's quarters, but he himself did not enter.

"General Grant was never impulsive, and always met his officers in an unceremonious way, with a quiet 'How are you?' soon putting one at his ease, since the pleasant tone in which he spoke gave assurance of welcome, although his manner was otherwise impassive. When the ordinary greeting was over, he usually waited for his visitor to open the conversation, so on this occasion I began by giving him the details of my march from Winchester, my reasons for not joining Sherman, as contemplated in my instructions, and the motives which had influenced me to march to the White House. Commenting on this recital of my doings, the General referred only to the tortuous course of my march from Waynesboro' down, our sore trials, and the valuable services of the scouts who had brought him tidings of me, closing with the remark that it was rare a department commander voluntarily deprived himself of independence, and added that I should not suffer for it. Then turning to the business for which he had called me to City Point, he outlined what he expected me to do; saying that I was to cut loose from the Army of the Potomac by passing its left flank to the southward along the line of the Danville railroad, and after crossing the Roanoke River, join General Sherman. While speaking he handed me a copy of a general letter of instructions that had been drawn up for the army on the 24th....

"When I had gone over the entire letter I showed plainly that I was dissatisfied with it, for, coupled with what the General had outlined orally, which I supposed was the 'other instructions,' I believed it foreshadowed my junction with General Sherman. Rawlins thought so too, as his vigorous language had left no room to doubt, so I immediately began to offer my objections to the programme. These were, that it would be bad policy to send me down to the Carolinas with a part of the Army of the Potomac, to come back to crush Lee after the destruction of General Johnston's army; such a course would give rise to the charge that his own forces around Petersburg were not equal to the task, and would seriously affect public opinion in the North; that in fact my cavalry belonged to the Army of the Potomac, which army was able unaided to destroy Lee, and I could not but oppose any dispersion of its strength.

"All this was said in a somewhat emphatic manner, and when I had finished he quietly told me that the portion of my instructions from which I so strongly dissented was intended as a 'blind' to cover any check the army in its general move to the left might meet with, and prevent that element in the North which held that the war could be ended only through negotiation, from charging defeat. The fact that my cavalry was not to ultimately join Sherman was a great relief to me, and after expressing the utmost confidence in the plans unfolded for closing the war by directing every effort to the annihilation of Lee's army, I left him to go to General Ingalls's quarters....

"Toward noon General Grant sent for me to accompany him up the river. When I joined the General he informed me that the President was on board the boat....We steamed up to where my cavalry was crossing on the pontoon-bridge below the mouth of the Dutch Gap canal, and for a little while watched the column as it was passing over the river, the bright sunshine presaging good weather, but only to delude, as was proved by the torrents of rain brought by the succeeding days of March. On the trip the President was not very cheerful. In fact, he was dejected, giving no indication of his usual means of diversion, by which (his quaint stories) I had often heard he could find relief from his cares. He spoke to me of the impending operations and asked many questions, laying stress upon the one, 'What would be the result when the army moved out to the left, if the enemy should come down and capture City Point?' the question being prompted, doubtless, by the bold assault on our lines and capture of Fort Stedman...by General Gordon. I answered that I did not think it at all probable that General Lee would undertake such a desperate measure to relieve the strait he was in; that General Hartranft's successful check of Gordon had ended, I thought, attacks of such a character; and in any event General Grant would give Lee all he could attend to on the left."[1]

After watching Sheridan's troopers for a while, the boat steamed past several naval vessels and came along side Admiral Porter's flagship, where a grand luncheon was waiting for the important visitors. After lunch the party returned to the *River Queen* and steamed back to Aiken's

Landing and rode off to review part of the Army of the James. "The division was drawn up in a wide field at 'parade rest' and had been so for several hours," remembered Lieutenant Commander John S. Barnes, commander of the *Bat*, who had been invited along on this excursion. "After hurried conferences with the commanding officer General Ord reported to General Grant, who referred to the President with the statement that the soldiers' dinner time was long past, and asked whether the review should await the coming of Mrs. Lincoln and Mrs. Grant....Mr. Lincoln exclaimed against such postponement, and in a few moments the review began." Mrs. Ord accompanied the cavalcade until the ambulance finally arrived over the bumpy corduroyed road with Mrs. Lincoln and Mrs. Grant, escorted by Horace Porter and Adam Badeau. Then she and Barnes rode to meet them. "Our reception was not cordial," Barnes said; "it was evident that some unpleasantness had occured. Porter and Badeau looked unhappy, and Mrs. Grant was silent and embarrassed. It was a painful situation, from which the only escape was to retire."[2]

"Mrs. Ord accompanied her husband..." Badeau explained. She was mounted, and as the ambulance was full, she remained on her horse and rode for a while by the side of the President....As soon as Mrs. Lincoln discovered this her rage was beyond all bounds. 'What does the woman mean,' she exclaimed, 'by riding by the side of the President? and ahead of me? Does she suppose that *he* wants *her* by the side of *him*?' She was in a frenzy of excitement, and language and action both became more extravagant every moment. Mrs. Grant again endeavored to pacify her, but then Mrs. Lincoln got angry with Mrs. Grant; and all that Porter and I could do was to see that nothing worse than words occurred....When there was a halt Major Seward, a nephew of the Secretary of State, and an officer of General Ord's staff, rode up, and tried to say something jocular. 'The President's horse is very gallant, Mrs. Lincoln,' he remarked; 'he insists on riding by the side of Mrs. Ord.' This of course added fuel to the flame. 'What do you mean by that, sir?' she cried. Seward discovered that he had made a huge mistake, and his horse at once developed a peculiarity that compelled him to ride behind, to get out of the way of the storm.

"Finally the party arrived at its destination and Mrs. Ord came up to the ambulance. Then Mrs. Lincoln positively insulted her, called her vile names in the presence of a crowd of officers, and asked what she meant by following up the President. The poor woman burst into tears and inquired what she had done, but Mrs. Lincoln refused to be appeased, and stormed till she was tired. Mrs. Grant still tried to stand by her friend, and everybody was shocked and horrified. But all things come to an end, and after a while we returned to City Point.

"That night the President and Mrs. Lincoln entertained General and Mrs. Grant and the General's staff at dinner on the steamer, and before us all Mrs. Lincoln berated General Ord to the President, and urged that he should be removed. He was unfit for his place, she said, to say nothing of his wife. General Grant sat next and defended his officer bravely....During all this visit similar scenes were occurring. Mrs. Lincoln repeatedly attacked her husband in the presence of officers because of Mrs. Griffin and Mrs. Ord....He bore it as Christ might have done; with an expression of pain and sadness that cut one to the heart, but with supreme calmness and dignity. He called her 'mother,' with his old-time plainness; he pleaded with eyes and tones, and endeavored to explain or palliate the offenses of others, till she turned on him like a tigress; and then he walked away, hiding that noble, ugly face that we might not catch the full expression of his misery."[3]

Horace Porter did not go into such detail in his account of the incident. He just said that "Mrs. Grant enjoyed the day with great zest, but Mrs. Lincoln had suffered so much from the fatigue and annoyances of her overland trip that she was not in a mood to derive much pleasure from the occasion. I made up my mind that ambulances, viewed as vehicles for driving distinguished ladies to military reviews, were not a stupendous success, and that thereafter they had better be confined to their legitimate uses of transporting the wounded and attending funerals."[4]

For weeks Nathan Forrest, now a Confederate lieutenant general commanding all of the cavalry in Richard Taylor's Department of Alabama, Mississippi and Louisiana, had been trying to get ready for the spring campaign that he knew would be starting soon. He had reorganized his three divisions to incorporate units that were now subject to his orders and had begun to edge more of these units from Mississippi over into Alabama, which he felt would be the scene of the next Union move. Then had come news of Steele's movement northward from Pensacola, and some of his units had been diverted to meet it. Only on the 26th, as the head of Forrest's main column reached Tuscaloosa and was cheered by the University of Alabama's corps of cadets, did he learn that Wilson had started south from the Tennessee River four days before. The next day Forrest sent word for his scattered units to converge on Montevallo, Alabama, roughly in the center of the state.

On that same day, 27 March, Wilson's three divisions, having separately traversed the sparsely-settled hill country, came together at the town of Jasper, only 60 miles northwest of Montevallo. There Wilson learned that Forrest was on the move from Mississippi to Tuscaloosa and beyond. He determined to press on rapidly before Forrest could get in front of him, even though it meant leaving his wagon train behind when his men and horses swam two rapidly flowing forks of the Black Warrior River. He did take his artillery and a string of pack animals with him.

Down on the Gulf coast on the 27th, Canby's main column invested the Confederate defenses at Spanish Fort, an outwork that protected the eastern approaches to Mobile. But the Union lines were from 1,000 to 1,200 yards from the Rebel lines.

Orders were published that day by the Federal war department naming General Cox as commander of the 23rd Corps in Schofield's Department of North Carolina and designating all other troops in that department the 10th Corps, with General Terry as its commander.

Somehow, on Monday, 27 May, John Wilkes Booth learned that Mrs. Lincoln had made plans to see Verdi's opera "Ernani" at Ford's Theatre on the 29th with her husband and Senator Charles Sumner. He telegraphed O'Laughlen in Baltimore, "Get word to Sam. Come on, with or without him, Wednesday morning. We sell that day sure. Don't fail."[5] Lewis Paine returned to Washington from Baltimore that day and occupied a room at the Herndon House that John Surratt had reserved for him, but neither Arnold nor O'Laughlen came.

Word was telegraphed to Grant at City Point that day that Sherman had reached Fort Monroe and was on his way up the James River. Grant sent off telegrams to several of his officers to meet Sherman at headquarters that evening. "Late in the afternoon," Horace Porter said, "the *Russia*, a captured steamer, arrived with Sherman aboard, and General Grant and two or three of us who were with him at the time started down to the wharf to greet the Western commander. Before we reached the foot of the steps, Sherman had jumped ashore and was hurrying foward with long strides to meet his chief. As they approached Grant cried out, 'How d'you do, Sherman!" 'How are you, Grant!' exclaimed Sherman; and in a moment they stood upon the steps, with their hands locked in a cordial grasp, uttering earnest words of familiar greeting. Their encounter was more like that of two school-boys coming together after a vacation than the meeting of the chief actors in a great war tragedy. Sherman walked up with the general-in-chief to headquarters, where Mrs. Grant extended to the illustrious visitor a cordial greeting. Sherman then seated himself with the others by the camp-fire, and gave a most graphic description of the stirring events of his march through Georgia. The story was the more charming from the fact that it was related without the manifestation of the slightest egotism....Never were listeners more enthusiastic; never was a speaker more eloquent. The story, told as he alone could tell it, was a grand epic related with Homeric power. At times he became humorous, and in a nervous, offhand, rattling manner recounted a number of amusing incidents of the famous march."

One of Sherman's favorite topics was his "bummers," and Porter recorded the general's words: "They are not stragglers or mere self-constituted foragers, as many have been led to suppose, but they are organized for a very useful purpose from the adventurous spirits who are always found in the ranks. They serve as 'feelers' who keep in advance and on the flanks of the main columns, spy out the land, and discover where the best supplies are to be found. They are indispensable in feeding troops when compelled, like my army, to live off the country, and in destroying the enemy's communications. The bummers are, in fact, a regular institution."

Then Sherman recounted what one of Schofield's officers had told him at Goldsborough about one of his bummers: "He said Schofield's army was maintaining a telegraph-line to keep up communication with the sea-coast, and that one of my men, who was a little more 'previous' than the rest, and was far in advance of my army, was seen up a telegraph-pole hacking away at the wires with a hatchet. The officer yelled out to him: 'What are you doing there? You're destroying one of our own telegraph-lines.' The man cast an indignant look at his questioner, and said, as he continued his work of destruction: 'I'm one o' Billy Sherman's bummers; and the last thing he said to us when we started out on this hunt was: "Be sure and cut all the telegraph-wires you come across, and don't go to foolin' away time askin' who they belong to."[6]

"After I had been with him an hour or so," Sherman wrote, "[Grant] remarked that the President, Mr. Lincoln, was then on board the steamer *River Queen*, lying at the wharf, and he proposed that we should call and see him. We walked down to the wharf, went on board, and found Mr. Lincoln alone, in the after-cabin. He remembered me perfectly, and at once engaged in a most interesting conversation. He was full of curiosity about the many incidents of our great march, which had reached him officially and through the newspapers, and seemed to enjoy very much the more ludicrous parts—about the 'bummers,' and their devices to collect food and forage when the outside world supposed us to be starving; but at the same time he expressed a good deal of anxiety lest some accident might happen to the army in North Carolina during my absence. I explained to him that that army was snug and comfortable, in good camps, at Goldsboro'; that it would require some days to collect forage and food for another march; and that General Schofield was fully competent to command it in my absence. Having made a good, long, social visit, we took our leave and returned to General Grant's quarters, where Mrs. Grant had provided tea. While at the table, Mrs. Grant inquired if we had seen *Mrs.* Lincoln. 'No,' said the general, 'I did not ask for her;' and I added that I did not even know that she was on board. Mrs. Grant exclaimed, 'Well, you are a pretty pair!' and added that our neglect was unpardonable; when the general said we would call again the next day, and make amends for the unintended slight."[7]

Then Sherman suggested that they discuss the future movements of his army.

"Perhaps you don't want me here listening to all your secrets," Mrs. Grant said.

"Do you think we can trust her?" Sherman asked, casting a sly glance her way.

"I'm not so sure about that, Sherman," Grant said.

So Sherman proceeded to playfully quiz Mrs. Grant about the geography of Virginia and North Carolina to "tell whether you are likely to understand our plans well enough to betray them to the enemy."

"Mrs. Grant caught the true essence of the humor," Horace Porter said, "and gave replies which were the perfection of drollery. When asked where a particular river in the South was, she would locate it a thousand miles away, and describe it as running up stream instead of down; and when questioned about a Southern mountain she would place it somewhere in the region of the north pole."

"Well, Grant, I think we can trust her," was Sherman's final verdict. "Never mind, Mrs. Grant; perhaps some day the women will vote and control affairs, and then they will take us men in hand and subject us to worse cross-examinations than that."[8]

Sheridan, who had been busy getting his cavalry ready for its part in the upcoming campaign, was one of the officers to receive a telegram from Grant informing him that Sherman would be at headquarters that night and asking him to come to see him. He said: "Sherman's coming was a surprise —at least to me it was—this despatch being my first intimation of his expected arrival. Well knowing the zeal and emphasis with which General Sherman would present his views, there again came into my mind many misgivings with reference to the movement of the cavalry, and I made haste to start for Grant's headquarters. I got off a little after 7 o'clock, taking the rickety military railroad, the rails of which were laid on the natural surface of the ground, with grading only here and there at points of absolute necessity, and had not gone far when the locomotive jumped the track. This delayed my arrival at City Point till near midnight, but on repairing to the little cabin that sheltered the general-in-chief, I found him and Sherman still up talking over the problem whose solution was near at hand.

"My entrance into the shanty suspended the conversation for a moment only, and then General Sherman, without prelude, rehearsed his plans for moving his army, pointing out with every detail how he would come up through the Carolinas to join the troops besieging Petersburg and Richmond, and intimating that my cavalry, after striking the Southside and Danville railroads, could join him with ease. I made no comments on the projects for moving of his own troops, but as soon as opportunity offered, dissented emphatically from the proposition to have me join the Army of the Tennessee, repeating in substance what I had previously expressed to General Grant. My uneasiness made me somewhat too earnest, I fear, but General Grant soon mollified me, and smoothed matters over by practically repeating what he had told me in regard to this point at the close of our interview the day before, so I pursued the subject no further. In a little while the conference ended, and I again sought lodging at the hospitable quarters of Ingalls. Very early the next morning, while I was still in bed, General Sherman came to me and renewed the subject of my joining him, but when he saw that I was unalterably opposed to it the conversation turned to other channels, and after we had chatted awhile he withdrew."[9]

That morning, the 28th, a correspondent for the Boston *Journal* saw Lincoln, Grant, Sherman, Meade, and Sheridan all walking together and described them for his readers: "Lincoln, tall, round-shouldered, loose-jointed, large-featured, deep-eyed, with a smile upon his face. He is dressed in black, and wears a fashionable silk hat. Grant is at Lincoln's right, shorter, stouter, more compact; wears a military hat with a stiff, broad brim, had his hands in his pantaloons' pockets, and is puffing away at a cigar while listening to Sherman. Sherman, tall, with high, commanding forehead, is almost as loosely built as Lincoln; has sandy whiskers, closely cropped, and sharp, twinkling eyes, long arms and legs, shabby coat, slouch hat, his pants tucked into his boots. He is talking hurriedly, gesticulating now to Lincoln, now to Grant, his eyes wandering everywhere. Meade, also tall, with thin, sharp features, a gray beard, and spectacles, is a little stooping in his gait. Sheridan, the shortest of all, quick and energetic in all his movements, with a face bronzed by sun and wind; courteous, affable, a thorough soldier."[10]

Sheridan went back to his cavalry and Meade to his army, but their place was soon taken by Admiral Porter, who had served with Grant and Sherman on the Mississippi River during the Vicksburg campaign of 1863. "When you were in the region of those swamps and overflowed rivers, coming through the Carolinas," he asked Sherman, "didn't you wish you had my gunboats with you?"

"Yes," Sherman answered; "for those swamps were very much like that Western fellow's Fourth of July oration, of which a newspaper said, 'It was only knee-deep, but spread out over all creation.' One day, on the march, while my men were wading a river which was surrounded for miles by swamps on each side, after they had been in the water for about an hour, with not much prospect of reaching the other side, one of them cried out to his chum: 'Say, Tommy, I'm blowed if I don't believe we' ve struck this river lengthways!"[11]

Porter, Sherman, and Grant soon went off to see Lincoln on the *River Queen.* This time Grant made sure to inquire after Mrs. Lincoln, and the president went to her state-room but came back and begged that she be excused as she was not feeling well. Then the president, the two generals, and the admiral sat down in the after cabin for an informal conference. Grant left no written account of this meeting, but upon returning to his headquarters he described it to some of his staff. "It began," Horace Porter wrote, "by his explaining to the President the military situation and prospects, saying that the crisis of the war was now at hand, as he expected to move at once around the enemy's left and cut him off from the Carolinas, and that his only apprehension was that Lee might move out before him and evacuate Petersburg and Richmond, but that if he did there would be a hot pursuit. Sherman assured the President that in such a contingency his army, by acting on the defensive, could resist both Johnston and Lee till Grant could reach him, and that then the enemy would be caught in a vise and have his life promptly crushed out. Mr. Lincoln asked if it would not be possible to end the matter without a pitched battle, with the attendant losses and suffering; but was informed that that was a matter not within the control of our commanders, and must rest necessarily with the enemy.... Sherman related many interesting incidents which occurred in his campaign. Grant talked less than any one present."[12]

"In this crisis," Adam Badeau wrote, "[Grant] asked no advice on military matters from the President, who offered none; and he listened to Sherman's eager and restless eloquence, suggestive and advisory, yet deferential and subordinate, but said nothing in return more definite than he had already written. If there was a man living whose advice in such matters he would have sought, that man was certainly Sherman; and, as he had written and said, if Sherman had been his superior Grant would have obeyed absolutely, but it was never his nature to seek advice; he sought only information, and without vanity or self-assertion, he came to his own conclusions. He did this always. He did so now."[13]

"Mr. Lincoln more than once expressed uneasiness that I was not with my army at Goldsboro'," Sherman remembered, "when I again assured him that General Schofield was fully competent to command in my absence; that I was going to start back that very day, and that Admiral Porter had kindly provided for me the steamer *Bat*, which he said was much swifter than my own vessel, the *Russia*. During this interview I inquired of the President if he was all ready for the end of the war. What was to be done with the rebel armies when defeated? And what should be done with the political leaders, such as Jeff. Davis, etc.? Should we allow them to escape, etc.? He said he was all ready; all he wanted of us was to defeat the opposing armies, and to get the men composing the Confederate armies back to their homes, at work on their farms and in their shops. As to Jeff. Davis, he was hardly at liberty to speak his mind fully, but intimated that he ought to clear out, 'escape the country,' only it would not do for him to say so openly. As usual, he illustrated his meaning with a story: 'A man once had taken the total-abstinence pledge. When visiting a friend, he was invited to take a drink, but declined, on the score of his pledge; when his friend suggested lemonade, which was accepted. In preparing the lemonade, the friend pointed to the brandy-bottle, and said the lemonade would be more palatable if he were to pour in a little brandy; when his guest said, if he could do so "unbeknown" to him, he would not object.' From which illustration I inferred that Mr. Lincoln wanted Davis to escape, 'unbeknown' to him."[14]

"My opinion is," Admiral Porter wrote, "that Mr. Lincoln came down to City Point with the most liberal views toward the rebels. He felt confident that we would be successful, and was willing that the enemy should capitulate on the most favorable terms. I don't know what the President would have done had he been left to himself, and had our army been unsuccessful, but he was then wrought up to a high state of excitement. He wanted peace on almost any terms, and there is no knowing what proposals he might have been willing to listen to. His heart was all tenderness throughout, and, as long as the rebels laid down their arms, he did not care how it was done."[15]

"Mr. Lincoln was full and frank in his conversation," Sherman said, "assuring me that in his mind he was all ready for the civil reorganization of affairs at the South as soon as the war was over; and he distinctly authorized me to assure Governor Vance and the people of North Carolina that, as soon as the rebel armies laid down their arms, and resumed their civil pursuits, they would at once be guaranteed all their rights as citizens of a common country; and that to avoid anarchy the State governments then in existence, with their civil functionaries, would be recognized by him as the government *de facto* till Congress could provide others.

"I know, when I left him, that I was more than ever impressed by his kindly nature, his deep and earnest sympathy with the afflictions of the whole people, resulting from the war, and by the march of hostile armies through the South; and that his earnest desire seemed to be to end the war speedily, without more bloodshed or devastation, and to restore all the men of both sections to their homes. In the language of his second inaugural address, he seemed to have 'charity for all, malice toward none,' and, above all, an absolute faith in the courage, manliness, and integrity of the armies in the field. When at rest or listening, his legs and arms seemed to hang almost lifeless, and his face was care-worn and haggard; but, the moment he began to talk, his face lightened up, his tall form, as it were, unfolded, and he was the very impersonation of good-humor and fellowship. The last words I recall as addressed to me were that he would feel better when I was back at Goldsboro'. We parted at the gangway of the River Queen, about noon of March 28th, and I never saw him again. Of all the men I ever met, he seemed to possess more of the elements of greatness, combined with goodness, than any other."[16]

"As soon as possible," Sherman said, "I arranged with General Grant for certain changes in the organization of my army; and the general also undertook to send to North Carolina some tug-boats and barges to carry stores from Newbern up as far as Kinston, whence they could be hauled in wagons to our camps, thus relieving our railroads to that extent. I undertook to be ready to march north by April 10th, and then embarked on the steamer Bat, Captain Barnes, for North Carolina. We steamed down James River, and at Old Point Comfort took on board my brother, Senator [John] Sherman, and Mr. Edwin Stanton, son of the Secretary of War, and proceeded at once to our destination. On our way down the river, Captain Barnes expressed himself extremely obliged to me for taking his vessel, as it had relieved him of a most painful dilemma. He explained that he had been detailed by Admiral Porter to escort the President's unarmed boat, the *River Queen*, in which capacity it became his special duty to look after Mrs. Lincoln.... This made

Barnes's position very unpleasant, so that he felt much relieved when he was sent with me to North Carolina."[17]

In far-off Europe on the 28th, the powerful French-built CSS *Stonewall* set out across the Atlantic after filling with coal at Lisbon, Portugal. No one challenged her.

By the 28th the Confederates were aware that Sheridan's cavalry had crossed the James River, and it was not hard to predict that this move presaged another move around their right, either to cut their supply lines or to join Sherman in North Carolina. The cavalry division commanded by Major General Fitzhugh Lee, nephew of the commanding general, began moving from the army's far left, north of the James, to the far right that day, leaving some 390 men without horses to reinforce the cavalry brigade of Brigadier General M.W. Gary, from the Department of Richmond, which was staying behind to guard that flank. Lieutenant General James Longstreet, commander of the 1st Corps and in charge of all Confederate forces north of the James River, suggested to Lee that Pickett's Division, his only mobile reserve, be sent with Fitz Lee's cavalry, since he feared that the latter was not strong enough to handle Sheridan alone. "I do not think that we can well spare the division," Longstreet told Lee, "but I think that we would choose a lesser risk by sparing it in case Sheridan's cavalry makes either of these moves contemplated than we would by holding him here to await the result of these operations. The enemy seems now to count upon taking Richmond by raiding upon our lines of communication and not by attacking our lines of work. I think, therefore, that we should endeavor to put a force in the field that can contend against that of the enemy. If Grant sends off his cavalry he can hardly intend to make any general move of his main army until its return. In every aspect of affairs, so far as I am advised, I think that the greater danger is from keeping too close within our trenches."[18] Lee agreed with this assessment, and Pickett's brigades, which were somewhat scattered at the time, were alerted to be ready to move. But the actual march order was not yet given.

Although the Confederates had learned that Sheridan's cavalry had crossed the James, they had not detected Ord's movement with half of his Army of the James in the same direction. An 18-year-old girl whose family lived within the Union lines had gotten through the Federal pickets to bring word of this movement, but Longstreet's scouts could not find any evidence to confirm it. Ord left Major General Godfrey Weitzel, commander of the 25th Corps, in command north of the James with one of his own divisions, one from the 24th Corps, and a division-sized force holding the Bermuda Hundred line between the James and the Appomattox. As directed by Ord, Weitzel used extra tents to make it look like the camps of the departed troops were still occupied, had campfires lit there each night, and had musicians playing in the old camps at the usual times.

By 7:40 a.m. on the 28th, the last troops of Ord's moving column had crossed to the south side of the James River. This consisted of Gibbon with two divisions of his 24th Corps plus Brigadier General William Birney's 2nd Division of the 25th, which, like all of that corps, was composed entirely of regiments of United States Colored Troops. It was hours later before all of Ord's wagons were across, and his cavalry division, now under Mackenzie, did not leave its camps north of the James until that evening and it took all night to get across the broad river. But by dark Ord's infantry had gone into camp behind Humphrey's 2nd Corps.

Grant was preparing to leave City Point the next day and move closer to the scene of the coming action. He pointed to a chest that always stood in the corner of his office and told Captain Joe Bowers, one of his staff officers, "Bowers, I want that chest of papers taken up to headquarters."

Mrs. Grant, who happened to be present, said, "Why not leave it here with me?"

"Oh," Grant said, "you cannot remain here, Julia."

"No! then where?" she asked. She had been meaning to ask earlier but the general had been so busy she had not found the chance.

"I have thought of that," Grant now told her, "and decided that you and Mrs. Rawlins had better remain on the dispatch boat for the present, and if all my plans turn out as I hope and expect they will, I will then return with you to Washington. But if Lee should escape me—and I am desperately afraid he will move now before I am ready—and make his way to the mountains, there is no telling when this war will end, and in that case you would have to go home alone."[19]

Meade and his corps commanders issued detailed orders that day for the movement that would begin the next morning. "When the instructions for this campaign reached us," wrote Brigadier General Joshua Lawrence Chamberlain, commander of a brigade in the 5th Corps, "all were animated with confidence of quick success. If Lee's lines before Petersburg were held in place, it would be easy work to cut his communications, turn his right, and roll him back upon Petersburg or Richmond; if, on the other hand, his main lines were stripped to resist our attack, our comrades in the old lines would make short work of

Lee's intrenchments and his army."[20] Chamberlain called the order "thrilling" and said it "woke new courage and inspired confidence. Its very style and manner was new. It seemed to take us all into confidential relations with the commander; the whole object and plan set forth in a manner clear, circumstantial, and complete, so that each subordinate knew the part he was expected to take....

"So when on the last evening of the old dispensation we prepared to break camp before the dawn, silently and unseen, without blast of bugle or blow of axe, or sight of fire to betray unusual movements to the ever watchful foe so near, and each one who could dashed off his little farewell message home, there was in his heart a strange mingling of emotion, the vision of a great joy, in which, perhaps, he was to lie silent and apart, a little shadow on the earth, but overhead a great light filling the sky. This lifted him to the surpassing joy that, however it should be with him, his work and worth had entered into the country's life and honor.

"Now the solemn notes of the last tattoo rang 'Lights out!' through the deepening shades, echoed from point to point of wooded hill and earth-piled parapet, floating away northward over the awful powers lying hushed beneath the twilight semblance of peace,—northward, toward the homes our hearts reached after, the lingering echoes sweeping the heartstrings as they died away. But the same heart told that the evening bugle would not sound 'Lights out!' again till the nights of the tremendous tragedy were over; that whatever of him or his should be of the returning, never would return that awful, long repeated scene: two armies, battered, broken, blood-bathed from brow to foot, but still face to face in unconquerable resolve. No, but in the far sky another vision: calm in triumph, thinking not of mastery over man, but of right for all; and in God's heaven the old flag redeemed from shame and scorn, standing for a regenerated people and a new covenant of brotherly love for the world's hereafter."[21]

---

1. Sheridan, *Civil War Memoirs*, 301-304.
2. Stern, *An End to Valor*, 93.
3. Ibid., 94-95.
4. Porter, *Campaigning With Grant*, 414.
5. Tidwell, Hall, and Gaddy, *Come Retribution*, 416.
6. Porter, *Campaigning With Grant*, 417-419.
7. Sherman, *Memoirs*, 810-811.
8. Porter, *Campaigning With Grant*, 420-421.
9. Sheridan, *Civil War Memoirs*, 305-306.

10. Wheeler, *Witness to Appomattox*, 63.
11. Porter, *Campaigning With Grant*, 422.
12. Ibid.,423-424.
13. Stern, *An End to Valor*, 103.
14. Sherman, *Memoirs*, 812.
15. Ibid., 814-815. Porter furnished Sherman with an account of the meeting, which he wrote in 1866, and Sherman included it in his own memoirs to back his contention that the controversial terms he later granted J. E. Johnston were based on Lincoln's wishes as expressed at this meeting.
16. Ibid., 813.
17. Ibid., 817-818.
18. *Official Records*, 46:III:1360.
19. Simon, ed., *The Personal Memoirs of Julia Dent Grant*, 148-149.
20. Joshua Lawrence Chamberlain, *The Passing of the Armies: An Account of the Final Campaign of the Army of the Potomac, Based Upon Personal Reminiscences of the Fifth Army Corps* (New York, 1915; Bantom Books paperback edition 1993), 32.
21. Ibid., 25-26.

CHAPTER TWENTY-THREE

It Was Thunder and Lightning and Earthquake

29 - 30 March 1865

John Surratt arrived in Richmond the next day, 29 March, still escorting Confederate courier Sarah Slater.

* * *

The Union troops in the lines near Petersburg began to move before dawn on 29 March. "The ground about to be traversed by us is flat and swampy," Joshua Chamberlain wrote, "and cut up by sluggish streams which, after every rain, become nearly impassable. The soil is a mixture of clay and sand, quite apt in wet weather to take the character of sticky mire or of quicksands. The principal roads for heavy travel have to be corduroyed or overlaid with plank. The streams for the most part find their way southeasterly into the tributaries of the Chowan River. Some, however, flow northeasterly into the waters of the Appomattox. Our available route was along the divide of these waters.

"The principal road leading out westerly from Petersburg is the Boydton Plank Road, for the first ten miles nearly parallel with the Appomattox, and distant from it from three to six miles. The Southside Railroad is between the Boydton Road and the river. South of the Boydton is the Vaughan Road; the first section lying in rear of our main entrenchments, but from our extreme left at Hatcher's Run inclining towards the Boydton Road, being only two miles distant from it at Dinwiddie Court House. Five miles east of this place the Quaker Road, called by persons of another mood, the 'Military Road,' crosses the Vaughan and leads northerly into the Boydton Road midway between Hatcher's Run and Gravelly Run, which at [their] junction became Rowanty Creek.

"A mile above the intersection of the Quaker Road with the Boydton is the White Oak Road, leading off from the Boydton at right angles westerly, following the ridges between the small streams and branches forming the headwaters of Hatcher's and Gravelly Runs, through and beyond the 'Five Forks.' This is a meeting-place of roads, the principal of which, called the Ford Road, crosses the White Oak at a right angle, leading from a station on the Southside Railroad, three miles north, to Dinwiddie Court House, six miles south.

"The enemy's main line of entrenchments west from Petersburg covered the important Boydton Plank Road, but only so far as Hatcher's Run, where at Burgess' Mill their entrenchments leave this and follow the White Oak Road for some two miles, and then cross it, turning to the north and following the Claiburne Road, which leads to Sutherland's Station on the Southside Railroad ten miles distant from Petersburg, covering this road till it strikes Hatcher's Run about a mile higher up. This 'return' northerly forms the extreme right of the enemy's entrenched line."[1]

The beginnings of the Federals' movement was very similar to the expedition of the month before that went in search of Confederate supply wagons coming up through Dinwiddie Court House, with the cavalry heading for the latter place and two corps of infantry filling in the gap between it and the left flank of the Union defenses. The 5th Corps moved south before daylight to Monk's Neck Bridge over Rowanty Creek. A few Confederate skirmishers on the other side fired a few shots and faded away as troops of Ayres' 2nd Division scrambled across the ruins of the bridge. Once a bridgehead was established, engineers laid a new bridge on canvas pontoons. Warren himself then crossed over and ordered Ayres to follow the Old Stage Road west to its intersection with the Vaughan Road, then follow the Vaughan Road on west to its intersection with the Quaker Road. The other two divisions were deployed to cover the left flank.

At 10:20 a.m. a staff officer brought Warren a dispatch from Webb, Meade's chief of staff, telling him to move northward up the Quaker Road to its crossing of Gravelly Run. Warren replied that he thought his skirmishers had gone that far already but he would make sure that they did. An hour later Webb wrote another message informing Warren that he had misunderstood the previous message. Meade wanted his entire corps, not just a few skirmishers, to move up the Quaker Road, cross to the northeast side of Gravelly Run, take position facing north and connect his right with the left of Humphrey's 2nd Corps. Not long after Warren received this message and got Griffin's 1st Division moving in compliance, General Meade rode up, and both he and Warren accompanied Griffin's advance.

At 6:30 a.m. the 2nd Corps had begun marching southwestward down the Vaughan Road while Gibbon's 24th Corps took its place at the left end of the Union defenses, with one division in the trenches and one held in reserve. Birney's division of the 25th Corps remained in place at Humphreys' Station on the military railroad. The advance of the 2nd Corps crossed Hatcher's Run without opposition and deployed just beyond it, forming a line about a half-mile north of the Vaughan Road facing north. A battery was brought up and emplaced where its four 12-pounder guns could be trained up the road toward the Rebel outpost at Dabney's Mill. While the infantry began to construct breastworks, skirmishers and patrols were sent out.

Sheridan's cavalry also marched south early that morning to Ream's Station on the Weldon Railroad, then turned toward Dinwiddie Court House. "Our general direction was westward," Sheridan wrote, "over such routes as could be found, provided they did not embarrass the march of the infantry. The roads, from the winter's frosts and rains, were in a frightful state, and when it was sought to avoid a spot which the head of the column had proved almost bottomless, the bogs and quicksands of the adjoining fields demostrated that to make a detour

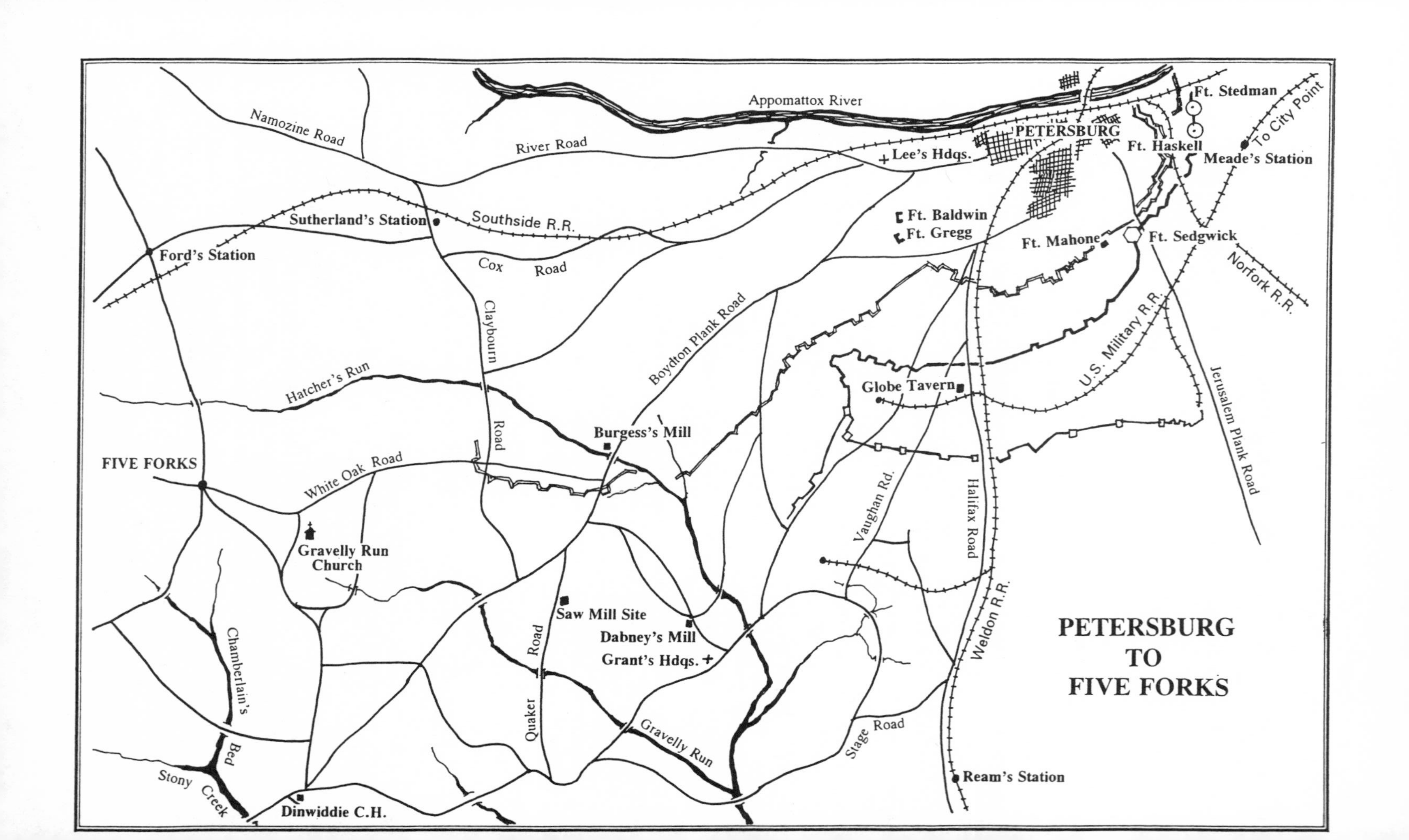
PETERSBURG
TO
FIVE FORKS
Appomattox River
PETERSBURG
Ft. Stedman
Ft. Haskell
To City Point
Meade's Station
Lee's Hdqs.
Namozine Road
River Road
Southside R.R.
Sutherland's Station
Ford's Station
Cox Road
Claybourn Road
Ft. Baldwin
Ft. Gregg
Ft. Mahone
Ft. Sedgwick
Norfolk R.R.
U.S. Military R.R.
Jerusalem Plank Road
Boydton Plank Road
Hatcher's Run
Globe Tavern
Burgess's Mill
FIVE FORKS
White Oak Road
Vaughan Rd.
Halifax Road
Weldon R.R.
Gravelly Run Church
Saw Mill Site
Dabney's Mill
Grant's Hdqs.
Quaker Road
Chamberlain's Bed
Gravelly Run
Stage Road
Stony Creek
Dinwiddie C.H.
Ream's Station

was to go from bad to worse. In the face of these discouragements we floundered on, however, crossing on the way a series of small streams swollen to their banks."[2]

Sometime that morning, Lee learned that Union infantry and cavalry had crossed Rowanty Creek at Monk's Neck Bridge, but their objective was uncertain. He immediately pulled one brigade out of the lines east of Hatcher's Run, spreading the rest of Wilcox's Division of Hill's 3rd Corps to cover its position, and sent it westward beyond Burgess's Mill. He then sent orders to Pickett to collect the three brigades of his division that were south of the James River and take them by rail to Sutherland's Station on the Southside Railroad ten miles west of Petersburg. Pickett's other brigade, commanded by Brigadier General Eppa Hunton, was still north of the James. It was to cross the river to the Richmond suburb of Manchester and be ready to either follow the rest of the division or to be transported down the Richmond and Danville Railroad to protect Burkeville should Sheridan's cavalry head in that direction. Meanwhile, Fitz Lee's cavalry division rode into Petersburg from the north and was directed to proceed westward to Five Forks, thus interposing between Dinwiddie Court House and the Southside Railroad. Rooney Lee, the commander's son and Fitz Lee's cousin, was bringing his own division and what was left of Rosser's up from Stony Creek Depot on the Weldon Railroad, where the horsemen had been stationed in order to draw forage for their mounts from North Carolina. As the senior cavalry commander in the absence of Wade Hampton, Fitz Lee was to take charge of all the cavalry south of the James. Lee also sent word to Longstreet that he might need him to bring another division south of the James and asked him to find out what Union troops were presently confronting him on the north side. Weitzel's deceptions were still working, however, for Longstreet replied, "The usual force is in our front, so far as we can learn. Our scouts are in from enemy's line this morning, and report affairs as usual. If Field's division is taken away from this side all of the Locals must be put in his place as will be the Cadets."[3]

Lieutenant General Richard H. Anderson's corps (technically the 4th but always referred to in Confederate reports merely as Anderson's Corps) held the extreme right end of Lee's defenses, in the area around Burgess's Mill. Since the departure of Hoke's Division for North Carolina, this corps consisted only of Major General Bushrod Johnson's division of infantry and several artillery units. Around noon, Johnson learned from scouts that a strong Union force was coming up the Quaker Road toward his entrenchments and he passed the information on to Anderson. The corps commander told Johnson to drive the Federals back to the Vaughan Road.

Meanwhile, Joshua Chamberlain's 1st Brigade was leading Griffin's division up the Quaker (or Military) Road until it came to Gravelly Run. "We soon found this road better entitled to its military than its Quaker appellation," he said. "A spirited advanced line of the enemy had destroyed the bridge over Gravelly Run and were placed behind some defenses on the north bank intending to give serious check to our advance. Evidently there was something nearby which they deemed it important to cover; and which accordingly we felt an interest to uncover."[4] With the support of Brevet Brigadier General Edgar M. Gregory's 2nd Brigade on the left, Chamberlain would take the bridge.

Chamberlain's brigade consisted of only two regiments, but they were both new and large. One of them, the 198th Pennsylvania, consisted of fourteen companies instead of the usual ten. Its colonel, Horatio G. Sickel, was a brevet brigadier general and had once been a brigade commander in the Department of West Virginia. The other regiment was the 185th New York, "A noble body of men of high capability and character," Chamberlain said, "and a well-disciplined regiment now commanded by Colonel Gustave Sniper, an able man and thorough soldier."[5] "I placed General Sickel with eight companies on the right below the ruined bridge," Chamberlain wrote, "with instructions to pour a hot fire upon the enemy opposite when with the rest of the brigade I would ford the stream waist-deep above the bridge and strike the enemy's right flank obliquely. This led to a hand-to-hand encounter. The attack was impetuous; the musketry hot. Major Glenn with his six companies in skirmishing order dashed through the stream and struck the enemy's breastworks front and flank. In a moment everything started loose. The entire brigade forded the stream and rolled forward, closing upon Glenn right and left, and the whole command swept onward like a wave, carrying all before it a mile or more up the road, to the buildings of the Lewis Farm. The enemy now re-enforced made a decided stand, and the fight became sharp. But our enveloping line pressed them so severely that they fell back after each struggle to the edge of a thick wood, where a large body had gathered behind a substantial breastwork of logs and earth."[6]

Switching into the present tense, Chamberlain continued his narrative: "A withering volley breaks our line into groups. Courage and resolution are great, but some other sentiment mightier for the moment controls our men; a backward movement begins, but the men retire slowly, bearing their wounded with them, and even some of their dead. The enemy, seeing this recoil, pour out of their shelter and make a dash upon our broken groups, but only to be dashed back in turn hand to hand in eddying whirls. And seized by our desperate fellows, so many are dragged along as prisoners in the receding tide that it is not easy to tell which side is the winning one. Much of the enemy's aim is unsteady, for the flame and murk of their thickening fire in the heavy moist air are blown back into their eyes by the freshening south wind. But reinforcements are coming in, deepening and broadening their line beyond both our flanks. Now roar and tumult of motion for a fierce pulse of time, then again a quivering halt. At length one vigorous dash drives the assailants into the woods again with heavy loss. We had cleared the field, and thought it best to be content with that for the present. We reform our lines each side the buildings of the Lewis Farm, and take account of the situation. We had about a hundred prisoners from Wise's and Wallace's Brigades, who said nearly all Anderson's Division were with them, and that more were coming, and they were bound to hold this outpost covering the junction of two roads which are main arteries of their vital hold,—the White Oak and the Boydton Plank."[7]

Gregory's brigade, on his left, had not been able to cross Gravelly Run, but once Chamberlain's brigade had crossed the stream Warren had directed Griffin's pioneers to build a bridge across the stream. Meade rode back to his forward command post, and Griffin rode forward and told Chamberlain to resume his advance. "So we were in for it again," the latter wrote, "and almost in cavalry fashion. Giving the right of the line to General Sickel and the left to Colonel Sniper on each side of the road, I took Major Glenn with his six companies for a straight dash up the Quaker Road, our objective point being a heap of sawdust where a portable mill had stood, now the center of the enemy's strong advanced line. We received a hot fire which we did not halt to return as that would expose us to heavy loss, but advanced at the double quick to go over the enemy's works with the bayonet. At close quarters the sharp-shooters in the tree-tops cut us up badly, but we still pressed on, only now and then, here and there, delivering fire ourselves."[8]

As he neared the pile of sawdust, Chamberlain realized that he was getting too far out in front of his men, so he suddenly checked his horse, which caused the animal to throw up its head. "Just at that instant a heavy blow struck me on the left breast just below the heart," Chamberlain wrote. "I fell forward on my horse's neck and lost all consciousness. The bullet at close range had been aimed at my breast, but the horse had lifted his head just in time to catch it, so that, passing through the big muscle of his neck (and also I may say through a leather case of field orders and a brass-mounted hand-mirror in my breast-pocket—we didn't carry towels in this campaign), demolished the pistol in the belt of my aide Lieutenant Vogel, and knocked him out of the saddle....The bullet had riddled my sleeve to the elbow and bruised and battered my bridle arm so that it was useless, and the obstructions it met had slightly deflected it so that, instead of striking the point of my heart, it had followed around two ribs so as to come out at the back seam of my coat."[9]

As Chamberlain came to, he heard General Griffin say, "My dear General, you are gone." Chamberlain was still in the saddle but covered with blood. However, it was his horse's blood, not his own. Just then, Chamberlain heard a wild Rebel yell and turned his head to see the right of his line broken and Sickel's men running for the rear. "Yes, General, I am," he said, meaning his brigade was "gone," however, not his life.[10] And he rode to intercept his routing troops.

"In the shock my cap had fallen to the ground," he said, "and I must have been a queer spectacle as I rose in the saddle tattered and battered, bare-headed and blood-smeared. I swung the rein against my horse's wounded neck and lightly touching his flank with my heel, we made a dash for the rally of our right. Pushing in among our broken ranks of our 198th Pennsylvania, the men might well have thought me a messenger from the other world. That rally was sharp work—and costly. Down at the extreme right, in the maddened whirl, I found the brave Sickel, his face aflame, rallying his men with an appeal none could resist. In a moment after he fell by my side with a shattered arm." A young major was also shot trying to stop the rout. "So passed a noble spirit," Chamberlain wrote, "a sweet soul, only son of his proud father and last of his race on earth. By such appeal and offering this gallant regiment, forced back by overpowering onset, straightened up into line again, and with a thrilling, almost appalling cheer, turned the tide of battle, and rolled it fairly back inside the enemy's works." This accomplished, Chamberlain returned to the center of his line, near the pile of sawdust. "I was astonished at the greeting of cheers which marked my course," he said. "Strangest of all was that when I emerged to the sight of the enemy, they also took up the cheering. I hardly knew what world I was in.

"By the time I got back to the center the loss of blood had exhausted the strength of my horse, and his nose came to earth. I had to send him back and become a foot soldier. It was a critical time there, with much confusion. Glenn was having a hard time at the sawdust pile, and I worked myself forward in the crowd to get at the state of things in front." Suddenly Chamberlain found himself surrounded by Rebels who demanded his surrender. "The old coat was dingy almost to gray," he wrote; "I was bare-headed, and rather a doubtful character anyway....To their exhortation I replied: 'Surrender? What's the matter with you? What do you take me for? Don't you see these Yanks right onto us? Come along with me and let us break 'em.' I still had my right arm and my light sword, and I gave a slight flourish indicating my wish and their direction. They did follow me like brave fellows,—most of them too far; for they were a long time getting back."[11]

Soon there was a lull in the fighting as Chamberlain found himself surrounded by friends again. Among them was Colonel Ellis Spear of Griffin's staff and a former member of the 20th Maine, Chamberlain's own former regiment which was now part of the 3rd Brigade. "With a mysterious and impressive look, as if about to present a brevet commission," Spear offered Chamberlain a swallow from a flask of choice wine. But the term "swallow" was, as Chamberlain put it, "a very indeterminate and flighty term." He took a "swallow" that made him "glad the Colonel was not on my staff then, and I did not have to meet him at evening...."[12]

"A hoarse yell rose through the tumult on the left, where the impetuous Sniper had tried to carry the breastworks in the woods, and now, badly cut up, his regiment was slowly falling back, closely followed by the enemy pouring out from their works. They were soon pressed back to a line perpendicular to their proper front, and the fight was fierce. Meantime, I scarcely know how, nor by whom helped, I found myself mounted on the back of a strange, dull-looking white horse, that had been bespattered by the trodden earth, and as I rode down among my fine New Yorkers, I must have looked more than ever like a figure from the Apocalypse.

"There I found the calm, cold-steel face of Sniper, who had snatched his regimental colors from the dead hands of the third color-bearer that had gone down under them in the last half-hour, and was still holding his shattered ranks facing the storm; himself tossing on the crest of every wave, rolling and rocking like a ship laying to in the teeth of a gale. I dispatched a staff officer for Gregory to attack where I supposed him to be, in position to enfilade the enemy's newly gained alignment. In response up rode Griffin, anxious and pale, his voice ringing with a strange tone, as of mingled command and entreaty: 'If you can hold on there ten minutes, I will give you a battery.' That was a great tonic: Griffin's confidence and his guns. There was quite an eminence a little to our rear, behind which I was intending to reform my line should it be driven from the field. I changed my plan. Pushing through to Sniper,

I shouted in his ear in a voice the men should hear: 'Once more! Try the steel! Hell for ten minutes and we are out of it!'

"I had no idea we could carry the woods, or hold them if we did. My real objective was that knoll in the rear. I wanted to keep the enemy from pressing over it before we could get our guns up. A desperate resort was necessary.

"While a spirit as it were superhuman took possession of minds and bodies; energies of will, contradicting all laws of dynamics, reversed the direction of the surging wave, and dashed it back upon the woods and breastworks with them. Having the enemy now on the defensive, I took occasion to let Sniper know my purpose and plan, and to instruct his men accordingly: to demoralize the enemy by a smashing artillery fire, and then charge the woods by similar bolt-like blast of men. They took this in with calm intelligence, and braced assent. I knew they would do all possible to man. All the while I was straining my eyes and prayers for a sight of the guns."[13]

The guns Griffin was sending were four 12-pounder smoothbores belonging to a crack outfit, Battery B of the 4th U.S. Artillery Regiment. John Gibbon had been its commander in the early days of the war before he had been promoted to command the famous Iron Brigade, beginning his climb to corps commander. Now the battery was commanded by Lieutenant John Mitchell. "And now they come...," Chamberlain wrote, "Mitchell leading with headlong speed, horses smoking, battery thundering with jolt and rattle, wheeling into action front, on the hillock I had been saving for them, while the earth flew beneath the wheels,—magnificent, the shining, terrible Napoleons. I rode out to meet them, pointing out the ground. Mitchell's answering look had a mixed expression, suggestive of a smile. I did not see anything in the situation to smile at, but he evidently did. I should have remembered my remarkable personal appearance. He did not smile long...."

"Mitchell, do you think you can put solid shot or percussion into those woods close over the rebels' heads, without hurting my men?" Chamberlain asked.

"Yes, Sir!" Mitchell replied, "if they will keep where they are."

"Well then," Chamberlain said, "give it to them the best you know. But stop quick at my signal, and fire clear of my men when they charge."[14]

Mitchell's guns opened fire. "It was splendid and terrible," Chamberlain wrote: "the swift-served, bellowing, leaping big guns; the thrashing of the solid shot into the woods; the flying splinters and branches and tree-tops coming down upon the astonished heads; shouts changing into shrieks at the savage work of these unaccustomed missiles;

then answering back the burst of fire oblique upon the left front of the battery, where there was a desperate attempt to carry it by flank attack; repulsed by Sniper drawing to the left, and thus also leaving clear range for closer cutting projectiles, when now case shot and shell, now a blast of cannister, poured into the swarming, swirling foe.

"My right wing was holding itself in the line of woods they had carried, reversing the breastworks there. The strain was on the left now. I was at the guns, where danger of disaster centered, so closely were they pressed upon at times. Mitchell, bravely handling his imperilled battery,—I had just seen him mounting a gun carriage as it recoiled, to observe the effect of its shot,—went down grievously wounded. It was thunder and lightning and earthquake; but it was necessary to hold things steady. Now, thank Heaven! comes up Griffin, anxious and troubled. I dare say I too looked something the worse for wear...."

Griffin brought with him one large regiment from Gregory's 2nd Brigade and three old regiments from Brigadier General Joseph Bartlett's 3rd Brigade. Meanwhile, Warren had sent Crawford's 3rd Division along a side road that his mounted escort company had discovered ran to the Boydton Plank Road beyond the Confederate flank. "It is soon over," Chamberlain wrote. "Woods and works are cleared, and the enemy sent flying up the road towards their main entrenchments....Gregory takes the advance line, and soon Bartlett comes up and presses up the road to near the junction of the Boydton and White Oak, reminded of the enemy's neighborhood by a few cannon shots from their entrenchments near Burgess' Mill bridgehead. At about this time word comes that the Second Corps is on our right, not far away."[15]

At about 4 p.m. a dispatch from Meade's headquarters had informed Humphreys that Warren's 5th Corps was advancing up the Quaker Road to the left of his 2nd Corps. He was ordered to advance his corps and connect his left flank with Warren's right. Reconnaissance patrols that had already been sent out had learned that only a small force of Rebel pickets was in front of the 2nd Corps, and it advanced against only token resistance. Brigadier General Nelson A. Miles' 1st Division of the 2nd Corps soon made contact with Warren's right, but the dense woods and underbrush in the 2nd Corps' front made it difficult to maintain the connection and slowed Humphreys' advance. Not long after the roar of battle was first heard from the direction of the Quaker Road Humphreys received orders to send Miles' division to support Griffin. Humphreys gave the necessary directions to Miles and personally rode ahead to see what was happening, but by the time he arrived the Confederates had fallen back. Then Humphreys received a dispatch from army headquarters informing him that Warren had been ordered to advance again at 6 p.m., only a few minutes away, and if Miles' division could be spared it should support Warren. In fact, if he thought it worthwhile he was to advance his entire corps. However, Griffin's pursuit of the retreating Confederates had found them firmly ensconced behind earthworks beyond an open field and supported by artillery, and the heavy woods had prevented Crawford's and Miles' divisions from catching up before darkness had covered the battlefield. Warren called off the advance.

Chamberlain's brigade had been left behind when the rest of Griffin's division advanced. After seeing to his wounded horse, he walked out to examine the field of his battle as night and rain both began to fall. There were 150 dead Confederates strewn over the field, and many of the 167 of his own men who were killed or wounded—about ten percent of his brigade. He learned that he had been fighting Johnson's entire division of about 6,000 men. The nearby Quaker meeting house, which gave the road its name, became a field hospital and was soon filled and overflowing with wounded men of both sides, and burial parties were already at work disposing of the dead. "Never to be forgotten,—that night of March twenty-ninth, on the Quaker Road," he said. "All night the dismal rain swept down the darkness, deep answering deep, soaking the fields and roads, and drenching the men stretched on the ground, sore with overstrain and wounds,—living, dead, and dying all shrouded in ghastly gloom. Before morning the roads were impassable for artillery and army-wagons, and nearly so for the ambulances, of our Corps and the Second, that crept up ghostlike through the shuddering mist."[16]

Sheridan's cavalry had spent the entire day trudging over the muddy roads. "Crook and Devin reached the county-seat of Dinwiddie about 5 o'clock in the evening," Sheridan wrote, "having encountered only a small picket, that at once gave way to our advance. Merritt left Custer at Malon's crossing of Rowanty Creek to care for the trains containing our subsistence and the reserve ammunition, these being stuck in the mire at intervals all the way back to the Jerusalem plank-road; and to make any headway at all with the trains, Custer's men often had to unload the wagons and lift them out of the boggy places.

"Crook and Devin camped near Dinwiddie Court House in such manner as to cover the Vaughan, Flatfoot, Boydton, and Five Forks roads; for, as these all intersected at Dinwiddie, they offered a chance for the enemy's approach toward the rear of the Fifth Corps, as Warren extended to the left across the Boydton road. Any of these routes leading to the south or west might also be the one on which, in conformity with one part of my instructions, I was expected to get out toward the Danville and Southside railroads, and the Five Forks road would lead directly to General Lee's right flank, in case opportunity was found to comply with the other part. The place was, therefore, of great strategic value, and getting it without cost repaid us for floundering through the mud.

"Dinwiddie Court House, though a most important point in the campaign, was far from attractive in feature, being made up of a half-dozen unsightly houses, a ramshackle tavern propped up on two sides with pine poles, and the weather-beaten building that gave official name to the crossroads. We had no tents—there were none in the command—so I took possession of the tavern for shelter for myself and staff, and just as we had finished looking over its primitive interior a rainstorm set in.

"The wagon containing my mess equipment was back somewhere on the road, hopelessly stuck in the mud, and hence we had nothing to eat except some coffee which two young women living at the tavern kindly made for us; a small quantity of the berry being furnished from the haversacks of my escort. By the time we got the coffee, rain was falling in sheets, and the evening bade fair to be a most dismal one; but songs and choruses set up by some of my staff—the two young women playing accompaniments on a battered piano—relieved the situation and enlivened us a little. However the dreary night brought me one great comfort; for General Grant, who that day had moved out to Gravelly Run, sent me instructions to abandon all idea of the contemplated raid, and directed me to act in concert with the infantry under his immediate command, to turn, if possible, the right flank of Lee's army."[17]

Grant's message to Sheridan, after briefly summarizing the infantry's day for him, said, "I now feel like ending the matter if it is possible to do so before going back. I do not want you, therefore, to cut loose and go after the enemy's roads at present. In the morning push round the enemy if you can and get onto his right rear. The movements of the enemy's cavalry may, of course, modify your action. We will act together as one army here until it is seen what can be done with the enemy."[18]

That morning Grant and most of his staff had boarded a train on the military railroad to take them to the left flank of the Army of the Potomac. At about 8:30 a.m. President Lincoln came ashore to say goodbye. "We had the satisfaction of hearing one good story from him before parting," Horace Porter wrote. Grant was telling the president about the numerous impractical suggestions for destroying the enemy that he received almost daily: "The last plan proposed was to supply our men with bayonets just a foot longer than those of the enemy, and then charge them. When they met, our bayonets would go clear through the enemy, while theirs would not reach far enough to touch our men, and the war would be ended."

"Well," Lincoln laughed, "there is a good deal of terror in cold steel. I had a chance to test it once myself. When I was a young man, I was walking along a back street in Louisville one night about twelve o'clock, when a very tough-looking citizen sprang out of an alleyway, reached up to the back of his neck, pulled out a bowie-knife that seemed to my stimulated imagination about three feet long, and planted himself square across my path. For two or three minutes he flourished his weapon in front of my face, appearing to try to see just how near he could come to cutting my nose off without quite doing it. He could see in the moonlight that I was taking a good deal of interest in the proceeding, and finally he yelled out, as he steadied the knife close to my throat: 'Stranger, kin you lend me five dollars on that?' I never reached in my pocket and got out money so fast in all my life. I handed him a bank-note, and said: 'There's ten, neighbor; now put up your scythe.'"

"The general soon after bade an affectionate good-by to Mrs. Grant," Porter wrote, "kissing her repeatedly as she stood at the front door of his quarters. She bore the parting bravely, although her pale face and sorrowful look told of the sadness that was in her heart. The party, accompanied by the President, then walked down to the railroad-station. Mr. Lincoln looked more serious than at any other time since he had visited headquarters. The lines in his face seemed deeper, and the rings under his eyes were of a darker hue. It was plain that the weight of responsibility was oppressing him.... Five minutes' walk brought the party to the train. There the President gave the general and each member of the staff a cordial shake of the hand, and then stood near the rear end of the car while we mounted the platform. As the train was about to start we all raised our hats respectfully. The salute was returned by the President, and he said in a voice broken by an emotion he could ill conceal: 'Good-by, gentlemen. God bless you all! Remember, your success is my success.' The signal was given to start; the train moved off; Grant's last campaign had begun.

"The general sat down near the end of the car, drew from his pocket the flint and slow-match that he always carried, struck a light, and was soon wreathed in the smoke of the inevitable cigar. I took a seat near him, with several other officers of the staff, and he at once began to talk over his plans. Referring to Mr. Lincoln, he said: 'The President is one of the few visitors I have had who have not attempted to extract from me a knowledge of my movements, although he is the only one who has a right to know them. He intends to remain at City Point for the present, and he will be the most anxious man in the country to hear from us, his heart is so wrapped up in our success; but I think we can send him some good news in a day or two.' I never knew the general to be more sanguine of victory than in starting out on this campaign. When we reached the end of the railroad, we mounted our horses, started down the Vaughan road, and went into camp for the night in an old corn-field just south of that road, close to Gravelly Run.... The weather had now become cloudy, and toward evening rain began to fall."[19]

Jefferson Davis's family was leaving Richmond that night as the rains came again. "The deepest depression had settled upon the whole city," his wife, Varina, wrote; "the streets were almost deserted." The Confederate president was sending Varina and their children away because he expected the capital to fall soon. He told her that his headquarters "must be in the field, and our presence would only embarrass and grieve, instead of conforting him." Varina had argued and pleaded to be allowed to stay with him, but he would not give in. "If I live you can come to me when the struggle is ended," he told her, "but I do not expect to survive the destruction of constitutional liberty." Except for one $5 gold piece, he gave Varina all of his gold, but he would not let her take several barrels of flour that she had saved. "The people want it," he told her, "and you must leave it here." He also gave her a pistol and showed her how to load, aim, and fire it. "He was very apprehensive of our falling into the hands of the disorganized bands of troops roving about the country," Varina wrote. Davis told her, "You can at least, if reduced to the last extremity, force your assailants to kill you, but I charge you solemnly to leave when you hear the enemy are approaching." He did not want her to fall into Federal hands. "If you cannot remain undisturbed in our country," he told her, "make for the Florida coast and take a ship there for a foreign country."

That evening Varina took a carriage to the railroad station. With her went her younger sister, her four children, the oldest of whom was nine, two daughters of the secretary of the treasury, and Colonel Burton N. Harrison, President Davis's private secretary. "With hearts bowed down by despair," she wrote, "we left Richmond. Mr. Davis almost gave way, when our little Jeff begged to remain with him, and Maggie clung to him convulsively, for it was evident he thought he was looking his last upon us."[20] The rickety train ground to a halt not far south of the capital and was stuck there all night. With considerable trouble some crackers and milk were found for the children, at a cost of $100 in Confederate money. The next day, the thirtieth, Davis had all the food in the Confederate White House sent to the hospitals and then hurried to his office in the Treasury building, where he started packing all his papers into boxes.

The rain that had begun as Davis's family left for the railroad station continued to fall. "It descended in torrents all night," Horace Porter wrote, "and continued with but little interruption during the next day. The country was densely wooded, and the ground swampy, and by the evening of the 30th whole fields had become beds of quicksand, in which the troops waded in mud above their ankles, horses sank to their bellies, and wagons threatened to disappear altogether.... The buoyancy of the day before was giving place to gloom; men lost their tempers, and those who employed profanity on such occasions as a means of mental relaxation wanted to set up a mark and go to swearing at it. Some began to apprehend that the whole movement was premature. This led to an animated debate at headquarters. General Rawlins expressed the opinion around the camp-fire, on the morning of the 30th, that no forage could be hauled out to our cavalry; that Joe Johnston might come up in our rear if we remained long in our present position; that the success of turning Lee's right depended on our celerity; that now he had been given time to make his dispositions to thwart us; and that it might be better to fall back, and make a fresh start later on. General Grant replied by saying that if Johnston could move rapidly enough in such weather to reach us, he (Grant) would turn upon him with his whole command, crush him, and then go after Lee; and that as soon as the weather cleared up the roads would dry rapidly, and the men's spirits would recover all their former buoyancy."[21]

At daylight on the 30th Sheridan made his dispositions in accordance with Grant's new instructions. He told Merritt to push Devin's 1st Division to make a reconnaissance toward Five Forks with the support of one brigade of Crook's 2nd Division. Crook was to use another of his brigades to hold the crossing of the Boydton Plank Road over Stony Creek and to keep his other brigade in reserve near Dinwiddie Court House. "The rain that had been falling all night gave no sign of stopping," Sheridan wrote, "but kept pouring down all day long, and the swamps and quicksands mired the horses, whether they marched in the roads or across the adjacent fields. Undismayed, nevertheless, each column set out for its appointed duty, but shortly after the troops began to move I received from General Grant [a] despatch, which put a new phase on matters."[22]

"The heavy rain of to day will make it impossible for us to do much until it dries up a little," Grant's dispatch said, "or we get roads around our rear repaired. You may therefore leave what cavalry you deem necessary to protect the left and hold such positions as you deem necessary for that purpose, and send the remainder back to Humphreys' Station, where they can get hay and grain."[23]

"When I had read and pondered this," Sheridan wrote, "I determined to ride over to General Grant's headquarters on Gravelly Run, and get a clear idea of what it was proposed to do, for it seemed to me that a suspension of operations would be a serious mistake."[24] Sheridan mounted a big grey horse he had captured from a Rebel officer in the Shenandoah campaign and with one staff officer and an escort of a dozen troopers rode off to find Grant, his horse's powerful legs driving themselves knee-deep into the mud with every step. He found the general-in-chief's camp and "dismounted near a camp-fire, apparently a general one, for all the staff-officers were standing around it on boards and rails placed here and there to keep them from sinking into the mire."[25]

"As soon as Sheridan dismounted," Horace Porter said, "he was asked with much eagerness about the situation on the extreme left. He took a decidedly cheerful view of matters, and entered upon an animated discussion of the coming movements. He said: 'I can drive in the whole cavalry force of the enemy with ease, and if an infantry force is added to my command, I can strike out for Lee's right, and either crush it or force him to so weaken his entrenched lines that our troops in front of them can break through and march into Petersburg.' He warmed up with the subject as he proceeded, threw the whole energy of his nature into the discussion, and his cheery voice, beaming countenance, and impassioned language showed the earnestness of his convictions.

"'How do you expect to supply your command with forage if this weather lasts?' he was asked by one of the group. 'Forage!' said Sheridan. 'I'll get up all the forage I want. I'll haul it out, if I have to set every man in the command to corduroying roads, and corduroy every mile of them from the railroad to Dinwiddie. I tell you, I'm ready to strike out to-morrow and go to smashing things'; and, pacing up and down, he chafed like a hound in the leash. We told him that this was the kind of talk we liked to hear, and that while General Grant felt no apprehension, it would do his heart good to listen to such words as had just been spoken. Sheridan, however, objected to obtruding his views unbidden upon the generall-in-chief. Then we resorted to a stratagem. One of us went into the general's tent, and told him Sheridan had just come in from the left and had been telling us some matters of much interest, and suggested that he be invited in and asked to state them.

This was assented to, and Sheridan was told that the general wanted to hear what he had to say. Sheridan then went in, and found Grant and Rawlins still discussing the situation."[26]

Sheridan's account indicates that it was Grant who wanted to suspend operations and Rawlins who wanted to press on, while Porter says it was the other way around. Also, Sheridan omits any mention of discussing the matter with Grant's staff officers first: "Going directly to General Grant's tent, I found him and Rawlins talking over the question of suspending operations till the weather should improve. No orders about the matter had been issued yet, except the despatch to me; and Rawlins, being strongly opposed to the proposition, was frankly expostulating with General Grant, who, after greeting me, remarked, in his quiet way: 'Well, Rawlins, I think you had better take command.' Seeing that there was a difference up between Rawlins and his chief, I made the excuse of being wet and cold, and went outside to the fire. Here General Ingalls met me and took me to his tent, where I was much more comfortable than when standing outside, and where a few minutes later we were joined by General Grant. Ingalls then retired, and General Grant began talking of our fearful plight, resulting from the rains and mud, and saying that because of this it seemed necessary to suspend operations. I at once begged him not to do so, telling him that my cavalry was already on the move in spite of the difficulties, and that although a suspension of operations would not be fatal, yet it would give rise to the very charge of disaster to which he had referred at City Point, and, moreover, that we would surely be ridiculed, just as General Burnside's army was after the mud march of 1863. His better judgment was against suspending operations, but the proposition had been suggested by all sorts of complaints as to the impossibility of moving the trains and the like, so it needed little argument to convince him, and without further discussion he said, in that manner which with him meant a firmness of purpose that could not be changed by further complainings, 'We will go on.' I then told him that I believed I could break the enemy's right if he would let me have the Sixth Corps; but saying that the condition of the roads would prevent the movement of infantry, he replied that I would have to seize Five Forks with the cavalry alone.

"On my way back to Dinwiddie I stopped at the headquarters of General Warren, but the General being asleep, I went to the tent of one of his staff-officers, Colonel William T. Gentry, an old personal friend with whom I had served in Oregon. In a few minutes Warren came in, and we had a short conversation, he speaking rather despondently of the outlook, being influenced no doubt by the depressing weather."[27]

Warren's 5th Corps had spent the night fortifying the position Chamberlain had gained the day before. Bartlett's brigade dug in near the home of a J. Stroud, which was the most advanced position gained the day before, and Griffin's other two brigades camped behind Bartlett's. Crawford's 3rd Division connected with Griffin's left and extended down the Boydton Plank Road to Gravelly Run. Ayres' 2nd Division advanced cautiously toward the White Oak Road on the 30th, but when it made contact with some of Johnson's Confederates it halted and settled in for the night. Humphreys 2nd Corps connected with Warren's right, advanced during the day until it contacted the Confederate main line, and extended the Union line to Hatcher's Run, where it connected with Ord's forces holding the left of the old defensive line. Other than a bit of skirmishing, there was no fighting on the infantry's front that day. A confused series of messages flashed back and forth over the field telegraph—which was functioning erratically because of the heavy rain—between Warren and Meade and Meade and Grant. Warren proposed that if Humphreys could extend more to the left and take over Griffin's position, that division could be used to reinforce Ayres and the next day these two divisions could be used to get across the White Oak Road beyond the Confederate right flank, which would keep the Rebels from moving west to interfere with a move by Sheridan toward the Southside Railroad. This idea was eventually approved, but the Federals did not realize that a Confederate force had by then already moved farther west, to Five Forks.

Lee spent the day scraping up forces to counter the threat to his right flank and the Southside Railroad. Because they had to detour around Sheridan's position at Dinwiddie Court House, it took all day for Rooney Lee and Rosser to bring their two small cavalry divisions up to Five Forks from Stony Creek. Meanwhile Pickett was sent with three brigades of his own division and two brigades of Johnson's Division to rendezvous with the cavalry at Five Forks and take overall command in that area.

After his visit to Grant and Warren, Sheridan returned to Dinwiddie Court House to try to get all of his troops up to that point. Meanwhile, Merritt probed to the north up the road from Dinwiddie Court House to Five Forks against slight resistance from Fitz Lee's cavalry. But then Pickett's Confederate infantry drove the Union troopers back and took possession of the crossroads. At 7 p.m. Sheridan sent word to Grant that Pickett's division was deployed along the White Oak road with its right at Five Forks.

This Confederate force threatened Warren's left flank, and he was cautioned to be ready to receive an attack the next morning. Humphreys was ordered to extend farther to his left so that Warren could move Griffin and Crawford to support Ayres. To allow Humphreys to make this move, Ord was directed to move one division across Hatcher's Run. For a while, Grant considered ordering the troops still manning the main line of defenses—Parke's 9th Corps, Wright's 6th Corps, and Ord's three divisions—to attack the Rebels' main line, but later he changed his mind. In a dispatch to Sheridan, Grant said: "If your situation in the morning is such as to justify the belief that you can turn the enemy's right with the assistance of a corps of infantry, entirely detached from the balance of the army, I will so detach the Fifth Corps, and place the whole under your command for the operation. Let me know as early in the morning as you can your judgment in the matter, and I will make the necessary orders. Orders have been given Ord, Wright, and Parke to be ready to assault at daylight to-morrow morning. They will not make the assault, however, without further directions. The giving of this order will depend upon receiving confirmation of the withdrawal of a part of the enemy's forces on their front."[27]

That night Grant wired Lieutenant Colonel T. S. Bowers of his staff, who had been left back at City Point: "The rain of to-day has made the roads horrible, and our operations have been confined to advancing our lines closer to the enemy and in making corduroy roads. There has been some skirmishing all along the lines, resulting in a few casualties on both sides. We have captured and also lost a few men by capture. To-night the enemy seem to be concentrating a force on our left, and I do not think an attack upon us there in the morning improbable. All the orders I can give to prepare for it have been given."[29]

---

1. Chamberlain, *The Passing of the Armies*, 31-32.
2. Sheridan, *Civil War Memoirs*, 310.
3. *Official Records*, 46:III:1363.
4. Chamberlain, *The Passing of the Armies*, 33.
5. Ibid., 31.
6. Ibid., 33.
7. Ibid., 33-34.
8. Ibid., 34-35.
9. Ibid., 35-36.
10. Ibid., 35.
11. Ibid., 36-37.
12. Ibid., 37-38.
13. Ibid., 38-39.
14. Ibid., 39.

15. Ibid., 39-41.
16. Ibid., 46.
17. Sheridan, *Civil War Memoirs*, 310-311.
18. *Official Records*, 46:III:266.
19. Porter, *Campaigning With Grant*, 424-427.
20. A.A. and Mary Hoehling, *The Last Days of the Confederacy* (New York, 1981), 69-70.
21. Porter, *Campaigning With Grant*, 427-28.
22. Sheridan, *Civil War Memoirs*, 312-313.
23. *Official Records*, 46:III:325.
24. Sheridan, *Civil War Memoirs*, 313.
25. Ibid., 314.
26. Porter, *Campaigning With Grant*, 428-429.
27. Sheridan, *Civil War Memoirs*, 314-315.
28. *Official Records*, 46:III:325.
29. Ibid., 46:III:281-282.

CHAPTER TWENTY-FOUR

One of the Most Gallant Things I Had Ever Seen

30 - 31 March 1865

On the morning of 30 March, General Sherman arrived off the coast of North Carolina on his way back from his conference with Grant and Lincoln. Because of some mechanical problems on the *Bat* he had to be taken the final seven miles up the Neuse River to New Berne in Commander Barnes's barge. "As soon as we arrived at Newbern," Sherman wrote, "I telegraphed up to General Schofield at Goldsboro' the fact of my return, and that I had arranged with General Grant for the changes made necessary in the reorganization of the army, and for the boats necessary to carry up the provisions and stores we needed, prior to the renewal of our march northward.

"These changes amounted to constituting the left wing a distinct army, under the title of 'the Army of Georgia,' under command of General Slocum, with his two corps commanded by General Jeff. C. Davis and General Joseph A. Mower; the Tenth and Twenty-third Corps already constituted another army, 'of the Ohio,' under the command of Major-General Schofield, and his two corps were commanded by Generals J.D. Cox and A.H. Terry. These changes were necessary, because army commanders only could order courts-martial, grant discharges, and perform many other matters of discipline and administration which were indispensable; but my chief purpose was to prepare the whole army for what seemed among the probabilities of the time—to fight both Lee's and Johnston's armies combined, in case their junction could be formed before General Grant could possibly follow Lee to North Carolina.

"General George H. Thomas, who still remained at Nashville, was not pleased with these changes, for the two corps with General Slocum, viz., the Fourteenth and Twentieth, up to that time, had remained technically a part of his 'Army of the Cumberland;' but he was so far away, that I had to act to the best advantage with the troops and general officers actually present. I had specially asked for General Mower to command the Twentieth Corps, because I regarded him as one of the boldest and best fighting generals in the whole army. His predecessor, General A.S. Williams, the senior division commander present, had commanded the corps well from Atlanta to Goldsboro', and it may have seemed unjust to replace him at that precise moment; but I was resolved to be prepared for a most desperate and, as then expected, a final battle, should it fall on me.

"I returned to Goldsboro' from Newbern by rail the evening of March 30th, and at once addressed myself to the task of reorganization and replenishment of stores, so as to be ready to march by April 10th, the day agreed on with General Grant."[1]

Down in Alabama on 30 March, Wilson's three divisions of cavalry came together at Elyton, in the center of an iron-producing region in the middle of the state. It was, as Wilson called it, "a poor insignificant

Southern village" of 3,000 inhabitants, but after the war it grew into the city of Birmingham.[2] The iron production facilities were destroyed, as was a flour mill north of the town. And here Wilson detached Brigadier General John T. Croxton's 1st Brigade of Brigadier General Edward McCook's 1st Division and sent it westward toward Tuscaloosa with orders to "destroy the bridge, factories, mills, university (military school), and whatever else may be of benefit to the rebel cause."[3] Brigadier General Emory Upton's 4th Division led Wilson's main column on to the south that day, crossing the Cahaba River and entering "a region abounding in forage, corn, bacon, chickens, turkeys and other comforts for hungry soldiers."[4] Eight miles north of the town of Montevallo Upton's vanguard ran into Rebel troopers of Brigadier General Philip Roddey's brigade but easily pushed the Confederates beyond Montevallo. This was a "pretty little town" on the Alabama & Tennessee River Railroad with its own iron production facilities. There and in the surrounding area the Federals destroyed many foundries, mills, and collieries.

The next day, 31 March, Roddey, who had brought up the rest of his brigade, formed a dismounted skirmish line along a ridge two miles south of Montevallo, backed up by the remainder of his command. Upton's scouts discovered the Confederates there, and the division commander was deploying his forces when Wilson joined him at about 1 p.m. One of Upton's brigades charged, supported by the other, broke up the Rebel skirmish line and with flashing sabers cut its way through Roddey's main force. The Confederates fell back about three miles to the south side of a creek, where they were reinforced by about 500 Kentuckians from Colonel Edward Crossland's brigade and a small force of infantry under Brigadier General Daniel W. Adams.

The Rebels counterattacked and drove back the 10th Missouri Cavalry, commanded by Lieutenant Colonel Frederick W. Benteen, who eleven years later would play a controversial part in the Battle of the Little Big Horn. But the 3rd Iowa charged Crossland's Rebels and drove them back in turn, while Upton's battery of horse artillery opened up on the Confederates along the creek. Several of Crossland's men were captured, and the rest, along with the other Rebels, were driven in confusion to the town of Randolph, sixteen miles south of Montevallo. This time it had been the Federals who got there first with the most men and, as Wilson said, had "the bulge on Forrest and held it to the end... fairly turning his own rules of war against himself."[5]

Forrest himself and his escort happened to reach the Montevallo-Randolph road on their ride from the west in time to charge the rear of part of Upton's force. From wounded Confederates and captured Federals the Rebel general learned enough to understand the situation and he soon circled around to the east to join his forces at Randolph that night. He hoped to use Roddey's, Crossland's, and Adams' men to delay Wilson long enough to combine them with Brigadier General James R. Chalmers' division, coming up from the south, and Brigadier General William H. Jackson's division, which was still working its way southeast from Tuscaloosa. That night his aide wrote to Jackson: "The lieutenant-general commanding directs me to say that the enemy are moving right on down the railroad with their wagon train and artillery. He directs that you follow down after them, taking the road behind them from Montevallo down. He further directs me to say that he does not wish you to bring on a general engagement, as he thinks their force is much stronger than yours; and an engagement should be avoided unless you find the balance of our forces in supporting distance of you."[6]

But Jackson had problems of his own. Croxton, as he advanced toward Tuscaloosa that afternoon, learned that Jackson's Division had recently passed through the area headed south, and he decided to follow. He did not know it, but his brigade interposed between Jackson's cavalry and his artillery and wagons. When Jackson discovered the Federals in his rear he turned back to attack them. "I am closing around them with the view of attacking at daylight in the morning," he wrote to Forrest.[7] But Croxton soon learned of the danger he was in and slipped off westward under the cover of darkness. Jackson did manage to catch up with him, however. He overran his camp, cut off part of the 8th Iowa—which wandered across Alabama for several days—and drove the main force for several miles. But each mile traveled was taking Jackson farther away from Forrest. He was also driving the Federals directly toward his own guns and wagons.

Sam Arnold and Michael O'Laughlen finally came down to Washington from Baltimore on Friday, 31 March, to see John Wilkes Booth. The fact that they came two days later than Booth had wanted them did not matter because Lincoln was still down at City Point and thus had not appeared at the theater on the 29th after all. Anyway, Booth's two friends now refused any further participation in the plan to capture Lincoln, and, as Arnold understood it anyway, the plan was abandoned.

In southeastern Virginia the rain had stopped on the afternoon of the 30th, but it started again at about 3 a.m. on the 31st. "Owing to the heavy rain this morning," Grant wired Meade at 7:40 a.m., "the troops will remain substantially as they now are, but the Fifth Corps should to day draw three days' more rations."[8] Meade suggested that the 2nd Corps should also draw three days' rations and the wagons thus emptied could be sent back to the railroad terminus to be refilled, and Grant promptly approved. The order for the assault on the Petersburg lines was not given, and Grant's thoughts continued to turn away from the idea of turning the Confederate right between Hatcher's Run and Gravelly Run and toward reinforcing Sheridan for an attack on Five Forks.

That morning Sheridan received Grant's offer of the 5th Corps written the night before. He replied: "My scouts report the enemy busy all last night in constructing breast-works at Five Forks, and as far as one mile west of that point. There was great activity on the railroad; trains all going west. If the ground would permit I believe I could, with the Sixth Corps, turn the enemy's left or break through his lines, but I would not like the Fifth Corps to make such an attempt." The 6th Corps had been part of Sheridan's Army of the Shenandoah—along with the cavalry the very heart of that army—until being sent back to the Army of the Potomac only recently. He knew it and trusted it. He did not know, or did not trust, the 5th Corps, or, more likely, Warren, who was cautious and methodical while Sheridan was bold and impulsive. Grant replied, "It will be impossible to give you the Sixth Corps for the operation by our left. It is in the center of our line between Hatcher's Run and the Appomattox. Besides, Wright thinks he can go through the line where he is, and it is advisable to have troops and a commander there who feels so, to co-operate with you when you get around. I could relieve the Second with the Fifth Corps and give you that. If this is done it will be necessary to give the orders soon to have the troops ready for to-morrow morning."[9]

By dawn the 2nd Corps had finally completed its shift to the left and the three divisions of the 5th Corps were just beginning their separate concentrations, all facing north one behind the other, with Ayres' 2nd Division in front, Crawford's 3rd Division behind it, and Griffin's 1st Division farther back. Each division straddled a country road that ran northwest from the Boydton Plank Road. This road was in terrible condition and crossed a swollen branch of Gravelly Run which Warren's pioneers were working hard to bridge, but for the time being it was impassable to wheeled vehicles, including artillery. Warren then decided that Ayres should drive in the Confederate pickets opposite him to give his own pickets more room. Meade, when informed of this, told Warren that if Ayres found it possible to block the White Oak Road west of the Rebel defenses he should do so.

Therefore, at about 10:30 a.m. Ayres sent one brigade forward, but when the Federals were within ten or fifteen yards of that vital artery they ran into three Confederate brigades advancing against them.

Lee had learned that morning that Ayres' flank was unprotected and he had immediately begun forming an ad hoc force with which to attack the Union left, just as Grant had predicted the night before. Bushrod Johnson was put in immediate command of the attack, with one brigade of his own division, Hunton's brigade of Pickett's Division, and one brigade from the 3rd Corps. Another brigade of Johnson's Division, commanded by Brigadier General Henry A. Wise, was held in reserve, connecting Johnson's left with the troops holding the Confederate defenses. Wise was an eccentric political general who had been governor of Virginia at the time John Brown had attacked the Harper's Ferry arsenal in an attempt to start a slave revolt before the war.

Johnson's plan was that the brigade on the right of his line, Brigadier General Samuel McGowan's brigade of Major General Cadmus Wilcox's division of the 3rd Corps, was to hit the Federals in the flank and drive them across in front of his other two brigades, who would then attack and complete their rout. But before this plan could be put into effect a lieutenant in Hunton's Brigade, seeing Brevet Brigadier General Frederick Winthrop's 1st Brigade of Ayres' division closing in on their position in the woods, jumped up with his sword in his hand and yelled, "Boys, they will capture our skirmishers; charge them."[10] His whole regiment charged forward, the rest of his brigade followed, and so did the other two.

"Without further orders," wrote Sam Paulette, a member of Hunton's Brigade, "the boys raised the old yell, and at them we went on the run, with guns at the trail. Nearing them we opened fire, but continued to advance. The boys in blue stood it for a while, but finding that we were closing in for a hand-to-hand fight, they broke and ran, we at their heels yelling like devils, and burning powder for all we were worth. Running them into a large body of woods, we found another line formed to meet us. We did not stop, but charged...and broke this line also, and continued to advance. About a quarter-mile from this point we discovered their third line. By this time we were all broken up, and orders came to halt and reform the line, which we did in a few minutes although under fire. Orders now came to charge the third line, which we did in fine style, breaking it up in short order. We now had three lines of battle of the enemy, running in our front, we following on the run, yelling, shooting and killing all we could. This was all very nice, and we enjoyed it, but the Yanks' time was now to come."[11]

Winthrop's brigade, hit in the flank and the front simultaneously by three Rebel brigades, fell back in increasing disorder. The second line the Confederates encountered consisted of the rest of Ayres' division, reinforced by one brigade of Crawford's division. But these units were somewhat disordered and demoralized by Winthrop's retreat and were also flanked as well as attacked in front. They too gave way. The third line the Rebels encountered consisted of Crawford's other two brigades, who just barely had time to deploy before they too were hit by retreating Federals and charging Confederates. Colonel John A. Kellogg's 1st Brigade, on the left, consisted of only three regiments, but two of them were the crack 6th and 7th Wisconsin regiments, former members of the old Iron Brigade. They stopped the Rebels in their tracks for a while, but the other brigade was soon driven back, exposing their right flank, and they too finally had to fall back. All of the retreating Federals of Ayres' and Crawford's divisions fell back across the branch of Gravelly Run almost a mile south of the White Oak Road. On a hill south of that natural moat Griffin's 1st Division of the 5th Corps was rapidly taking position.

"It was a good position," wrote Private Theodore Gerrish, a member of the 20th Maine in Bartlett's brigade. "The rebels must descend a hill in our front, cross Gravelly Run, and then climb the hill upon which our line would be formed. Our colonel gave the order, 'By battalion, into line!' and we quickly formed upon the crest of the hill. It was an exciting moment. The rebel line was advancing, in plain view, down the hill on the other side of the stream. Artillery had gone into position and was throwing shells over our head; the bands played; the cannons roared; our muskets crashed with awful force; the hill itself shivered as if with fear. The rebel line came to the stream, but could come no further, and was thrown back."[12]

Gregory's brigade held Griffin's left and was subordinated to Chamberlain, whose brigade held the center. "I was apprehensive of an attempt to take us in flank on the left in Gregory's front and was about giving my attention to this," Chamberlain wrote, "when General Warren and General Griffin came down at full speed, both out of breath, with their efforts to rally the panic-stricken men whose honor was their own, and evidently under great stress of feeling."

"General Chamberlain, the Fifth Corps is eternally damned," Griffin said. Chamberlain tried to make a pleasant reply, but Griffin went right on. "I tell Warren you will wipe out this disgrace, and that's what we're here for."

"General Chamberlain," Warren added in a strangely compressed tone, "will you save the honor of the Fifth Corps? That's all there is about it."

Chamberlain was still worried about his left and all too conscious of the beating his brigade had taken two days before. He asked why they did not use Bartlett's brigade, which was much larger than his own and had not seen much fighting lately.

"We have come to see you; you know what that means," he was told. So Chamberlain had no choice but to agree to try.

"I will have a bridge ready here in less than an hour," Warren said. "You can't get men through this swamp in any kind of order."

"It may do to come back on, General," Chamberlain replied; "it will not do to stop for that now. My men will go straight through."[13]

So while one battalion of the 198th Pennsylvania provided covering fire the other battalion waded across the swollen stream, holding their cartridge boxes on their bayonets to keep their ammunition dry. Once the Pennsylvanians had formed a skirmish line on the north bank the rest of the brigade followed, and then Gregory's brigade. "The enemy fell back without much resistance," Chamberlain wrote, "until finding supports on broken strong ground they made stand after stand. Griffin followed with Bartlett's Brigade, in reserve. In due time Ayres' troops got across and followed up on our left rear, while Crawford was somewhere to our right and rear, but out of sight or reach after we had once cleared the bank of the stream."[14]

Warren, meanwhile, had asked Humphrey for help, and at about 12:30 p.m. the latter sent two brigades of Miles's division to attack the Rebel flank. One of these brigades fell behind, however, and the other one ran into Wise's Virginia brigade, which Lee had sent forward to cover Johnson's left from a slight ridge. The lone Union brigade was driven back, but it rallied behind the stream and then tried again. While this brigade attacked Wise's front, Miles, with the other brigade, hit his flank. The Virginians were driven back in confusion, and the Federals captured 100 men and a battleflag. Covered by a strong rear guard, Johnson's entire task force now fell back. "Our boys, having already broken three lines of battle," Confederate Sam Paulette said, "were very much scattered, and before we could line them up, the Yanks charged. It was impossible in our condition, to successfully resist this counter-charge, and the boys began to fall back; slowly at first. The Yanks, seeing how few we were, began to crowd us, and we broke into a run, and made back to our starting point, and, this being the Yanks' time, they gave us 'hail Columbia' before we reached the White Oak...Road."[15] The Confederates did not actually go quite all the way back to their starting place but occupied the rifle pits Ayres's men had dug the night before. To their own left, or east, was the main line of defenses running along the White Oak Road and then turning to the north along the Claiborne Road to anchor its flank on Hatcher's Run.

Meanwhile, Humphreys sent two more brigades to join Miles, and these Federals soon attacked the Rebel skirmishers covering this main line along White Oak Road and captured another 100 Confederates and another battleflag. Other units of the 2nd Corps farther east also made threatening moves against the Rebels' main line to prevent these sections from being thinned in order to send help to Johnson.

Chamberlain's two brigades followed Johnson's retreating Rebels. "Taking advantage of the slight shelter of a crest in the open field I was preparing for a final charge," he wrote, "when I received an order purporting to be Warren's, to halt my command and hold my position until he could reconnoitre conditions in my front. I did not like this much. It was a hard place to stay in. The staff officer who brought me the order had his horse shot under him as he delivered it. I rode back to see what the order meant. I found General Griffin and General Warren in the edge of the woods overlooking the field, and reported my plans.... It was evident that things could not remain as they were. The enemy would soon attack and drive me back. And it would cost many men even to try to withdraw from such a position. The enemy's main works were directly on my right flank, and how the intervening woods might be utilized to cover an assault on that flank none of us knew. I proposed to put Gregory's Brigade into those woods... [to] take in flank and reverse...any attacks on my right. When Gregory should be well advanced I would charge the works across the field with my own brigade."[16]

Chamberlain's plan was approved, and he rode to Gregory to give him his instructions: "The moment he struck any opposition to open at once with full volleys and make all the demonstration he could, and I would seize that moment to make a dash at the works in my front. Had I known of the fact that General Lee himself was personally directing affairs in our front, I might not have been so rash, or thought myself so cool." He informed the officers of his own brigade of the plan, and "soon the roar of Gregory's guns rose in the woods like a whirlwind. We sounded bugles 'Forward!' and that way we go; mounted officers leading their commands, pieces at the right shoulder until at close quarters.... What we had to do could not be done by firing. This was foot-and-hand business. We went with a rush, not minding ranks nor alignments, but with open front to lessen loss from the long-range rifles. Within effective range, about three hundred yards, the sharp, cutting fire made us reel and shiver. Now, quick or never! On and over!

The impetuous 185th New York rolls over the enemy's right, and seems to swallow it up; the 198th Pennsylvania, with its fourteen companies, half veterans, half soldiers 'born so,' swing in upon their left, striking Hunton's Brigade in front, and for a few minutes there is a seething wave of countercurrents, then rolling back, leaving a fringe of wrecks,—and all is over. We pour over the works, swing to the right and drive the enemy into their entrenchments along the Claiborne Road, and then establish ourselves across the White Oak Road facing northeast, and take breath."[17]

"The Federal line wavered under the fire very decidedly," General Hunton later remembered, "and a portion of it broke and ran. The balance of the line re-formed under my fire, advanced, and drove us back. I thought it was one of the most gallant things I had ever seen."[18] "Only for a moment," the historian of the 198th Pennsylvania wrote, "did the sudden and terrible blast of death cause the right of the line to waver. On they dashed, every color flying, officers leading, right in among the enemy, leaping the breastworks,—a confused struggle of firing, cutting, thrusting, a tremendous surge of force, both moral and physical, on the enemy's breaking lines,—and the works were carried."[19]

Most of the surviving Confederates were driven into their main line of defenses. The entire 56th Virginia was captured, and McGowan's brigade was cut off and had to swing far to the north to get back around to the main line. By then it was 3:40 p.m. Warren had definitely cut the road that directly connected the right flank of the main Rebel line with Pickett's forces about Five Forks. According to what Warren and his officers still thought was the overall Union plan, Sheridan was now supposed to come up on Warren's left and sweep around behind the Confederate right. "But another, and by far minor, objective interposed," Chamberlain wrote. "Instead of the cavalry coming to help us complete our victories at the front, we were to go to the rescue of Sheridan at the rear."[20]

At around 10 o'clock that morning the bulk of Pickett's Confederate task force had marched out of Five Forks heading south with the intention of taking the offensive against Sheridan's Union cavalry. In the column were Rosser's and Rooney Lee's cavalry divisions, with Fitz Lee in overall command of them, and all of Pickett's infantry—three of his own brigades and two from Johnson's Division. Only Fitz Lee's own division, under the temporary command of its senior brigade commander, Brigadier General Thomas Munford, was left behind to guard Five Forks. Further, it was to confront the Union troopers out on the roads leading into that crossroads from the east and southeast.

Pickett's column followed the Scott Road south to another intersection known as Little Five Forks and turned to the east along the Ford Station Road. Soon the Confederates approached a swampy little stream called Chamberlain's Bed, which ran south from the White Oak Road about a half-mile east of Five Forks and flowed into Stony Creek about a mile west of Dinwiddie Court House.

There were two main crossings of Chamberlain's Bed west of Dinwiddie Court House. The Ford Station Road crossed the stream at Fitzgerald's Ford, and a side road crossed it about a mile farther north at Danse's Ford. Fitz Lee, with Rooney Lee's and Rosser's cavalry divisions, was to cross at Fitzgerald's Ford, and Pickett, with the five infantry brigades, would cross at Danse's Ford. When Munford heard the noise of battle from the main column, he was to attack down the Dinwiddie Court House Road, which should have bought him in on Pickett's left.

It was a good plan, but Sheridan's patrols discovered the Rebel column marching down the Scott Road, and the Union commander quickly realized that it intended to turn left at Little Five Forks, cross Chamberlain's Bed, and attack Dinwiddie Court House. Therefore he sent Brigadier General Henry E. Davies' 1st Brigade of Crook's 2nd Division to defend the crossing at Danse's Ford and Brevet Brigadier General Charles H. Smith's 3rd Brigade of the same division to hold Fitzgerald's Ford. Crook's other brigade, Brevet Brigadier General J. Irvin Gregg's 2nd, was placed in reserve a mile or more east of Davies, where the road leading from Danse's Ford intersected the road leading north from Dinwiddie Court House to Five Forks. Devin's three brigades of the 1st Division were farther north and northwest, confronting Munford and probing the area between Five Forks and the area of Warren's fight with Bushrod Johnson. Custer's 3rd Division was still guarding the cavalry's supply wagons, which were still floundering through the mud toward Dinwiddie Court House.

It was almost 2 p.m. by the time the Confederates launched their attack, and then Fitz Lee's cavalry jumped the gun, attacking Smith's brigade at Fitzgerald's Ford before Pickett's infantry was ready to make its own attack at Danse's Ford. Rosser's Rebel division attacked the 2nd New York Mounted Rifles, which was picketing the west bank of Chamberlain's Bed, and drove it across the swampy stream. On the east bank the New Yorkers dismounted and were joined by the 6th Ohio Cavalry, and with their repeating carbines they drove back the Confederate attack. General Smith then sent a battalion of the 1st Maine Cavalry across to the west side of the stream, but it soon ran into a powerful Rebel battle line and was driven back in confusion. The

Confederate troopers followed this Federal retreat with such reckless abandon that some of them were drowned trying to cross the creek. The Rebels then drove back the New Yorkers and Ohioans, but Smith brought up his remaining units, the 13th Ohio and the other two battalions of the 1st Maine. These launched a dismounted counterattack which was soon joined by the re-formed regiments from the first line, and this time it was the Confederates who broke and ran, scrambling back to the west bank of the stream.

When General Crook learned that Smith's brigade had been attacked he sent Irvin Gregg's reserve brigade to its support. And, since Davies' brigade at Danse's Ford had not yet been attacked, he sent the bulk of Davies' force to lend Smith a hand as well. Only two battalions of the 1st New Jersey Cavalry were left to watch Danse's Ford, one forming a picket line and the other in the defenses. Davies rode ahead to check the situation, however, and learned that Smith had already repulsed the Confederates on his own, so he turned his own column around, and when firing broke out at Danse's Ford his men, who were dismounted, were ordered to double quick. The battalion left in the defenses had repulsed the first Confederate attack, by one brigade of Pickett's infantry, but then some of the Rebels managed to get across the stream farther upstream and threatened the flank of the New Jersey troopers while most of the Confederate brigade attacked them in front again. The Federals held their ground until the Rebels were within fifteen yards of their position, but then their commander ordered them to fall back.

As the Rebels were crossing the creek the head of Davies' column reached the scene. He put the 10th New York Cavalry in a dismounted line blocking the road east, and some of the New Jersey troopers rallied beside it. However, the New Yorkers broke and ran after delivering only two or three volleys, and the New Jersey troopers were left on their own again. The brigade's horses just barely managed to escape capture, but they remained separated from the rest of the brigade for the rest of the day. Once the crossing had been secured, Pickett's other brigades were rapidly pushed across, and Davies had to fall back to the Dinwiddie Court House-Five Forks road in the face of such a large force.

The colonel of the 1st New Jersey had called on Devin's division, to the north and northeast of the Danse's Ford position, for help, and Devin had ordered his 1st Brigade—Colonel Peter Stagg's Michigan Brigade—to send one regiment to his support. Then Devin decided to ride along with it to see what was going on. He soon came upon Davies' disorganized brigade and deployed his regiment to help the New Jersey troopers cover its retreat. Finding that Davies' men could not be rallied, he sent his adjutant to bring up Colonel Charles Fitzhugh's 2nd Brigade of his 1st Division. Fitzhugh left the 6th New York Cavalry to hold its roadblock on the Dinwiddie-Five Forks road and brought the rest of his brigade to the road leading east from Danse's Ford. When his troops were deployed, the New Jersey troopers rejoined Davies' retreating brigade and the Michigan regiment that Devin had brought over was returned to his 1st Brigade. Pickett's leading infantry brigade soon ran into Fitzhugh's dismounted troopers and was checked.

However, just then Munford sent one of his brigades of cavalry forward in a dismounted attack that rolled over the 6th New York back on the Dinwiddie-Five Forks road. Colonel Stagg rushed part of one of his Michigan regiments over to help out and, together with the New Yorkers, it managed to hold off Munford's attack for a while. But the Confederate troopers regrouped and tried again, and this time the Federal line collapsed. Meanwhile, Pickett deployed a second brigade of his infantry, extending his line beyond Fitzhugh's right, and Devin ordered the latter to fall back while calling for Stagg to bring up the rest of his brigade. As the two brigades came together they exchanged roles, with Fitzhugh on the right facing Munford and Stagg on the left facing Pickett. Fitzhugh fought off Munford's first attack but was forced back by a second effort, and the two brigades again fell back, this time to J. Boisseau's farm east of the Crump Road, a lane that diverged from a nearby bend of the Dinwiddie-Five Forks Road and ran due north to the White Oak Road. Davies' brigade had already retreated to the same point.

Merritt deployed the three brigades at J. Boisseau's farm in the hope of holding the intersection of the Crump and Dinwiddie roads, but patrols he sent out to open communications with Dinwiddie Court House soon reported that Pickett's infantry was blocking the Dinwiddie Road. Merritt ordered Devin to take his two brigades farther east to the Boydton Plank Road, where he would protect the flank of the Union infantry farther east and threaten the flank of the Confederates if they turned south toward Dinwiddie Court House. Davies' brigade soon followed.

The move to the Boydton Plank Road had been Sheridan's idea. He still was not sure whether Pickett's objective was Dinwiddie Court House or Warren's flank. In case it was the former, he posted Devin's other brigade, Brigadier General Alfred Gibbs' Reserve Brigade, at the junction of the Dinwiddie Road and the Brock Road, which was an eastern extention of the road Pickett had followed from Danse's Ford. Gibbs' job was to delay any Confederate move down the road toward Dinwiddie Court House. Sheridan sent a staff officer to Custer with orders to leave one of his brigades to protect the wagons and to bring the other two to Dinwiddie Court House. Meanwhile, Irvin Gregg's brigade was ordered to leave its position in support of Smith at Fitzgerald's Ford and attack the Rebels in the flank and rear.

Gregg moved his brigade toward the sound of firing, but after proceeding about a mile without encountering the Rebels he stopped and dismounted three of his regiments and deployed them in a line of battle. With a strong skirmish line out front Gregg worked his way forward and soon his right flank established contact with Gibbs' left while Pickett's infantry was soon spotted moving south in a powerful battle line. He was heading toward Dinwiddie Court House after all. Gregg continued to advance and drove in Pickett's skirmishers and captured a number of prisoners, then took position beside Gibbs' brigade. With the help of a battery of horse artillery, the dismounted troopers of the two brigades managed to hold off Pickett's five brigades of infantry and Munford's Confederate cavalry for two hours, then, covered by a strong rear guard, they fell back.

It was 5:30 p.m. when Smith's brigade finally had to abandon its position at Fitzgerald's Ford because Fitz Lee had brought up some horse artillery and the retreat of Gregg and Gibbs left his flank and rear vulnerable to Pickett's advancing infantry. But by that time Custer had arrived with two of his brigades. Colonel Alexander Pennington's 1st Brigade took position on Gregg's left, about a half-mile north of Dinwiddie Court House and east of the road to Five Forks, with Colonel Henry Capehart's 3rd Brigade on Pennington's left, west of the road. Smith's brigade fell in on Capehart's left. Custer also had a battery of four 3-inch rifles with him. Gibbs' brigade reformed near Dinwiddie Court House, where it found Devin's other two brigades and Davies' brigade. When these three units had reached the Boydton Plank Road, Davies, as the senior officer, had taken command and led them down that road back to the county seat.

Pennington's brigade was the last to take position and was posted somewhat in advance of the other Federals. As Pennington's men formed up in front of Pickett's massive battle line they began screeching like a war party of wild Indians. One of Pennington's regiments, the 2nd Ohio Cavalry, had served out in Indian Territory with pro-Union Indians a couple of years before and had learned their war whoop. The rest of Pennington's regiments took it up, but, as one Ohioan noted, "They never got to be more than about HALF BREEDS."[21] The Confederates answered with a volley and a Rebel yell and charged forward. Pennington's men fell back to the edge of some trees, where Custer had them throw up breastworks of fence rails. Finally, just before dark,

Pickett launched one last attack with all of his infantry, while Fitz Lee's two divisions were to hit the Union left, and Munford's division was to cover the Confederate left.

"Accompanied by Generals Merritt and Custer and my staff," Sheridan wrote, "I now rode along the barricades to encourage the men. Our enthusiastic reception showed that they were determined to stay. The cavalcade drew the enemy's fire, which emptied several of the saddles—among others Mr. Theodore Wilson, correspondent of the New York *Herald*, being wounded. In reply our horse-artillery opened on the advancing Confederates, but the men behind the barricades lay still till Pickett's troops were within short range. Then they opened, Custer's repeating rifles pouring out such a shower of lead that nothing could stand up against it. The repulse was very quick, and as the gray lines retired to the woods from which but a few minutes before they had so confidently advanced, all danger of their taking Dinwiddie or marching to the left and rear of our infantry line was over, at least for the night."[22]

Sheridan's cavalry could now settle into camp for the night, but not Warren's infantry. "Just as we had got settled in our position on the White Oak Road," Joshua Chamberlain wrote, "heavy firing was heard from the direction of Sheridan's supposed position. This attracted eager attention on our part as, with that open flank, Sheridan's movements were all important to us. At my headquarters we had dismounted, but had not ventured yet to slacken girths. I was standing on a little eminence, wrapped in thoughts of the declining day and of these heavy waves of sound, which doubtless had some message for us, soon or sometime, when Warren came up with anxious earnestness of manner, and asked me what I thought of this firing,—whether it was nearing or receding. I believed it was receding towards Dinwiddie; that was what had deepened my thoughts. Testing the opinion by all tokens known to us, Warren came to the same conclusion. He then for a few minutes discussed the situation and the question of possible duty for us in the absence of orders. I expressed the opinion that Grant was looking out for Sheridan, and if help were needed, he would be more likely to send Miles than us, as he well knew we were at a critical point, and one important for his further plans as we understood them, especially as Lee was known to be personally directing affairs in our front. However, I thought it quite probable that we should be blamed for not going to the support of Sheridan even without orders, when we believed the enemy had got the advantage of him."

"Well, will you go?" Warren asked.

"Certainly, General," Chamberlain replied, "if you think it best; but surely you do not want to abandon this position."

"At this point," Chamberlain said, "General Griffin came up and Warren asked him to send Bartlett's Brigade at once to threaten the rear of the enemy then pressing upon Sheridan. That took away our best brigade. Bartlett was an experienced and capable officer, and the hazardous and trying task he had in hand would be well done.

"Just after sunset Warren came out again, and we crept on our hands and knees out to our extreme picket within two hundred yards of the enemy's works, near the angle of the Claiborne Road. There was some stir on our picket line, and the enemy opened with musketry and artillery, which gave us all the information we wanted. That salient was well fortified. The artillery was protected by embrasures and little lunettes, so that they could get a slant- and cross-fire on any movement we should make within their range.

"I then began to put my troops into bivouac for the night, and extended my picket around my left and rear to the White Oak Road, where it joined the right of Ayres' picket line. It was an anxious night along that front. The darkness that deepened around and over us was not much heavier than that which shrouded our minds, and to some degree shadowed our spirits. We did not know what was to come, or go."[23]

---

1. Sherman, *Memoirs*, 818-819.
2. Jones, *Yankee Blitzkrieg*, 58.
3. *Official Records*, 49:II:135.
4. Jones, *Yankee Blitzkrieg*, 63.
5. Robert Henry Selph, *"First with the Most" Forrest* (New York, 1991), 429.
6. *Official Records*, 49:II:1182.
7. Ibid., 49:II:174.
8. Ibid., 46:III:334.
9. Ibid., 46:III:380.
10. Chris Calkins, "The Battle of Five Forks: Final Push for the South Side," *Blue and Gray Magazine*, April 1992, 12.
11. Ibid.
12. Wheeler, *Witness to Appomattox*, 71.
13. Chamberlain, *The Passing of the Armies*, 56-57.
14. Ibid., 57.
15. Calkins, "The Battle of Five Forks," 13.
16. Chamberlain, *The Passing of the Armies*, 58.
17. Ibid., 58-59.

18. Ed Bearss and Chris Calkins, *The Battle of Five Forks* (Lynchburg, Va. 1985), 71.
19. Chamberlain, *The Passing of the Armies*, 59.
20. Ibid., 63.
21. Urwin, *Custer Victorious, 237.*
22. Sheridan, *Civil War Memoirs*, 320.
23. Chamberlain, *The Passing of the Armies*, 66-68.

CHAPTER TWENTY-FIVE

Why Did You Not Come Before?

31 March - 1 April 1865

On the evening of 31 March, after the 5th Corps had regained its honor in the battle of the White Oak Road, Grant sent Colonel Horace Porter down to Dinwiddie Court House to inform Sheridan of events on the infantry's front. "I rode rapidly down the Boydton plank-road," he wrote, "and soon came to Gravelly Run. The bridge was destroyed, but my horse was able to ford the stream, notwithstanding the high water caused by the recent rains. Hearing heavy firing in the direction of the Five Forks road, I hurried on in that direction by way of the Brooks road, and soon saw a portion of our cavalry moving eastward, pressed by a superior force of the enemy, while another portion was compelled to fall back southward toward Dinwiddie. I turned the corner of the Brooks cross-roads and the Five Forks road just as the rear of the latter body of cavalry was passing it, and found one of Sheridan's bands with his rear-guard playing 'Nellie Bly' as cheerfully as if furnishing music for a country picnic. Sheridan always made an effective use of his bands. They were usually mounted on gray horses, and instead of being relegated to the usual duty of carrying off the wounded and assisting the surgeons, they were brought out to the front and made to play the liveliest airs in their repertory, which produced excellent results in buoying up the spirits of the men. After having several of their instruments pierced by bullets, however, and the drums crushed by shells, as often happened, it must be admitted that the music, viewed purely in the light of an artistic performance, was open to adverse criticism.

"I found Sheridan a little north of Dinwiddie Court-house, and gave him an account of matters on the left of the Army of the Potomac. He said he had had one of the liveliest days in his experience, fighting infantry and cavalry with only cavalry, but that he would hold his position at Dinwiddie at all hazards. He did not stop there, but declared his belief that with the corps of infantry which he expected to be put under his command, he could take the initiative the next morning, and cut off the whole of the force which Lee had detached."

"This force is in more danger than I am," Sheridan exclaimed. "If I am cut off from the Army of the Potomac, it is cut off from Lee's army, and not a man of it ought ever be allowed to get back to Lee. We at last have drawn the enemy's infantry out of its fortifications, and this is our chance to attack it."

"He begged me to go to General Grant at once," Porter wrote, "and urge him to send him Wright's corps, because it had been under his command in the valley of Virginia, and was familiar with his way of fighting. I told him, as had been stated to him before, that Wright's corps was next to our extreme right, and that the only corps which could reach him by daylight was Warren's. I returned soon after to headquarters at Dabney's Mill, a distance of about eight miles, reaching there at 7 p.m., and gave the general a full description of Sheridan's expedition. He took in the situation in an instant, and at once telegraphed the substance of my report to Meade, and preparations soon began looking to the sending of Warren's corps and Mackenzie's small division of cavalry to report to Sheridan."[1]

In reality, the process of sending Warren to reinforce Sheridan was not nearly so simple and straightforward as that. Warren had already sent Bartlett's brigade of Griffin's division west along the White Oak Road. Actually, Bartlett only had with him part of his large brigade—which was the consolidated remains of an entire division. Three of his regiments had been left under Brevet Brigadier General Alfred Pearson, colonel of the 155th Pennsylvania, on the Boydton Plank Road south of the rest of the corps, where they were guarding the artillery that had been left there because the mud prevented moving it to the front. Bartlett did not follow the White Oak Road for very long, however, but soon turned off onto a country lane that bent increasingly toward the southwest. It ended near the home of Dr. James Boisseau, which was on the Crump Road about a mile south of the White Oak Road and a half-mile north of the J. Boisseau house where Devin's brigades had congregated earlier in the day and where numerous Confederates were then camped. Between the two Boisseau homes was a branch of Gravelly Run.

"The narrow road along which we marched was lined on either hand with a dense growth of pine trees," remembered Theodore Gerrish of the 20th Maine in Bartlett's column. "The sun was sinking from view, and the tall trees cast their lengthening shadows across our pathway. It was to us a time of thrilling interest, as we all understood the situation. Our brigade…was marching through the great forest to meet an enemy of whose strength and location we knew nothing. The sounds of battle in our front died away. The darkness became so intense that it was not prudent to proceed further, especially as nothing was to be gained by such a course. The pickets were sent out, and we lay down to sleep and rest."[2]

It was a night filled with a great deal of message-writing, countermarching, and confusion as information filtered up the chain of command through Warren and Meade to Grant and back down again. Sheridan and Ord reported directly to Grant and sometimes what they said got passed on to Meade and sometimes it did not. "This proved to be one of the busiest nights of the whole campaign," Horace Porter said. "Generals were writing despatches and telegraphing from dark to daylight. Staff-officers were rushing from one headquarters to another, wading through swamps, penetrating forests, and galloping over corduroy roads, carrying instructions, getting information, and making extraordinary efforts to hurry up the movement of the troops."[3]

At 5:50 p.m. Warren reported to Brevet Major General Alexander Webb, Meade's chief of staff, that he had sent Bartlett's brigade toward Sheridan. Webb replied that one of Merritt's staff officers had reported that the Rebels had penetrated between Sheridan and Warren and added, "Let the force ordered to move out the White Oak road move down the Boydton plank road as promptly as possible." At 6:30 p.m. Warren replied, "I have ordered General Pearson, with three regiments that are now on the plank road, right down toward Dinwiddie Court House. I will let Bartlett work and report result, as it is too late to stop him."[4]

At 6:35 p.m. Meade passed on to Grant what Merritt's staff officer had said about Confederate brigades being between Warren and Sheridan and added, "I have directed Warren to send a force down Boydton plank road to try and open communication with Sheridan. Under the present state of affairs it was impossible to send down the White Oak road, as first ordered. Please let me know in regard to Sheridan's report as soon as convenient; my disposition against these brigades should be made shortly." By the time Grant replied, Horace Porter had reached him and reported on the situation on Sheridan's front. Grant gave Meade a very brief summary of that situation and added, "The effort has been to get our cavalry onto the White Oak road west of Dabney's house. So far this has failed, and there is no assurance that it will succeed. This will make it necessary for Warren to watch his left all round. The cavalry being where it is will probably make the enemy very careful about coming round much in his rear, but he cannot be too much on his guard." Grant also forwarded to Meade a copy of a message Sheridan had sent at 2:30 p.m. in which the latter mistakenly reported that Hoke's Division was in his front, and Grant told Meade to have prisoners questioned about whether any troops had reinforced Lee from North Carolina. At 7:10 p.m. Meade replied that he had not heard anything to indicate that Confederate troops had been sent up from North Carolina but that it was not impossible. "If Hoke or any considerable force of infantry is in Sheridan's front it opens the rear of our army.... General Sheridan will be pressed to-morrow. He will either have to come in or support must be sent to him. My line is so extended and flank in air that I don't see how I can detach for this purpose, unless I contract my lines, when I shall have troops to spare. Let me hear as soon as possible what you desire done."[5]

At 7:30 p.m. Meade wrote to Warren: "Dispatches from General Sheridan say he was forced back to Dinwiddie Court-House by a strong force of cavalry supported by infantry. This leaves your rear and that of the Second Corps on the Boydton plank open and will require great vigilance on your part. If you have sent the brigade down the Boydton plank it should not go farther than Gravelly Run, as I don't think it will render any service but to protect your rear." It was 8 p.m. by the time Warren received this, and the three regiments under Pearson had to stop at Gravelly Run anyway, because the bridge was down at that point, and, unlike Horace Porter, who had been mounted, they could not ford it. At 8:20 p.m. Warren replied: "I sent General Bartlett out on the road running south from the White Oak road and left him there. He is nearly down to the crossing of Gravelly Run. This will prevent the enemy communicating by that road to-night.…It seems to me the enemy cannot remain between me and Dinwiddie if Sheridan keeps fighting them, and I believe they will have to fall back to the Five Forks. If I have to move to-night I shall leave a good many men who have lost their way. Does General Sheridan still hold Dinwiddie Court-House?" Only ten minutes later Webb wrote a note to Warren marked "Confidential" that confirmed Warren's fears: "The probability is that we will have to contract our lines to-night. You will be required to hold, if possible, the Boydton plank road and to Gravelly Run; Humphreys and Ord along the run. Be prepared to do this upon short notice."[6]

"I regretted exceedingly to see this step foreshadowed," Warren later reported, "for I feared it would have the morale of giving a failure to our whole movement, as similar orders had done on previous occasions. It would besides relieve the enemy in front of Sheridan from the threatening attitude my position gave me."[7] So Warren replied at 8:40: "The line along the plank road is very strong. One division, with my artillery, I think can hold it if we are not threatened south of Gravelly Run, east of the plank road. General Humphreys and my batteries, I think, could hold this securely, and let me move down and attack the enemy at Dinwiddie on one side and Sheridan on the other. From Bartlett's position they will have to make a considerable detour to re-enforce their troops at that point from the north. Unless Sheridan has been too badly handled, I think we have a chance for an open field fight that should be made use of."[8]

At 8:45 p.m. Grant told Meade, "Let Warren draw back at once to his position on Boydton road and send a division of infantry to Sheridan's relief. The troops to Sheridan should start at once and go down Boydton road."[9] Despite the fact that Horace Porter and other staff officers knew from first hand experience that the Boydton Plank Road bridge over Gravelly Run was down, Grant and Meade seemed to be unaware of it. At 9:17 p.m. Warren received a message that Webb wrote at 9 p.m.: "You will, by the direction of the major-general commanding, draw back at once to your position within the Boydton plank road and send a division down to Dinwiddie Court-House to report to General Sheridan. The division will go down the Boydton plank road. Send Griffin's division." This was followed twenty minutes later by another message: "The division to be sent to Sheridan will start at once. You are to be held free to act within the Boydton plank road. General Humphreys will hold to the road and the return." At 9:40 p.m. Webb wrote again: "Since your dispatch of 8.20 this p.m. the general commanding finds that it is impossible for Bartlett to join Griffin in time to move with any promptitude down the Boydton plank road. He therefore directs that you send another good brigade to join Griffin in the place of Bartlett for this movement." But Warren had already answered Webb at 10 p.m.: "I had already sent out my orders, of which I send you a copy. You asked General Griffin to be sent to General Sheridan at once. It will take so much time to get his command together that I withdraw the other divisions first, they being unengaged, but this will not retard General Griffin. The bridge it broken on the plank road, and will take I hardly know how long to make passable for infantry. I sent an officer to examine it as soon as your first order was received. He now reports it not fordable for infantry....Nevertheless, I will use everything I can get to make it passable by the time General Griffin's division reaches it."[10] For some reason this dispatch was not received by Webb until much later, and higher headquarters remained ignorant of the fact that the Boydton Plank Road crossing of Gravelly Run was impassable for infantry.

But soon the plan changed again. At 9:45 p.m. Meade wrote to Grant: "Would it not be well for Warren to go down with his whole corps and smash up the force in front of Sherdan? Humphreys can hold the line to the Boydton plank road and the refusal along it. Bartlett's brigade is now on the road from J. Boisseau's running north, where it crosses Gravelly Run, he having gone there down the White Oak road. Warren could move at once that way and take the force threatening Sheridan in rear, or he could send one division to support Sheridan at Dinwiddie and move on the enemy's rear with the other two." Grant replied at 10:15 p.m.: "Let Warren move in the way you propose and urge him not to stop for anything. Let Griffin go on as he was first directed."[11]

Meade himself, rather than Webb, immediately wrote directly to Warren: "Send Griffin promptly, as ordered, by the Boydton plank road, but move the balance of your command by the road Bartlett is on, and strike the enemy in rear, who is between him and Dinwiddie....You must be very prompt in this movement....The enemy will probably retire toward Five Forks, that being the direction of their main attack this day. Don't encumber yourself with anything that will impede your progress or prevent your moving in any direction across country." Warren received this order at 10:48 and replied at 10:55: "I issued my orders on General Webb's first dispatch to fall back, which made the divisions retire in the order Ayres, Crawford, and Griffin, which was the order they could most rapidly move in. I cannot change them to-night without producing confusion that will render all my operations nugatory. I will now send General Ayres to General Sheridan, and take

General Griffin and General Crawford to move against the enemy, as this last dispatch directs I should. I cannot accomplish the apparent objects of the orders I have received."[12]

Meanwhile, at 10:45 p.m., Grant wrote to Sheridan: "The Fifth Corps has been ordered to your support. Two divisions will go by J. Boisseau's and one down the Boydton road. In addition to this I have sent Mackenzie's cavalry, which will reach you by the Vaughan road. All these forces except the cavalry should reach you by 12 to-night. You will assume command of the whole force sent to operate with you and use it to the best of your ability to destroy the force which your command has fought so gallantly to-day."[13] It cannot be imagined where Grant got the idea that Warren could possibly reach Sheridan by any route by midnight. Even if the bridge over Gravelly Run had been in place, the roads in perfect shape, no enemy in the way, and Warren's men already formed up on the road ready to march they could not have reached Dinwiddie Court House or Sheridan lines near there in so little time. And yet none of those conditions existed. Moreover, Warren had not been ordered to send all three of his divisions to Sheridan, only one. With the other two he was supposed to attack the rear of the Confederates who were threatening Dinwiddie Court House. However, Sheridan had no way of knowing any of this and could only take Grant's estimate as reasonable, if approximate.

For Warren to have followed in Bartlett's wake would have taken even longer, it being a less direct route, and the Confederates were definitely between Bartlett and Sheridan. Moreover, Bartlett's brigade was soon withdrawn from its advanced position. "At midnight," Private Theodore Gerrish wrote, "we were aroused with the information that our pickets had discovered the enemy, who was in great force in our immediate front, so near that they could easily listen to the conversation of their pickets, and also of the soldiers behind their breastworks. Silently we fell into line, and, retracing our steps along the way we came for several miles, encamped for the remainder of the night."[14]

As if the Union high command did not already have enough trouble, problems with the field telegraph also intervened. At 12:30 a.m., now 1 April, Warren discovered that his dispatch to Meade of 10:55 p.m. had not been sent because of a break in the telegraph line, so he forwarded it with the comment: "I believe it impossible efficiently to change the directions I have given before daybreak."[15] At 1 a.m. Warren received a message Meade had written at 11:45 p.m.: "A dispatch, partially transmitted, is received, indicating the bridge over Gravelly Run is destroyed, and time will be required to rebuild it. If this is the case, would not time be gained by sending the troops by the Quaker road? Time is of the utmost importance. Sheridan cannot maintain himself at Dinwiddie without re-enforcments, and yours are the only ones that can be sent. Use every exertion to get the troops to him as soon as possible. If necessary, send troops by both roads and give up the rear attack." Meade also added a postscript that said, "If Sheridan is not re-enforced in time and compelled to fall back he will retire by the Vaughan road."[16]

"On receiving this dispatch showing so much solicitude for General Sheridan's position and the necessity of re-enforcing him directly," Warren later reported, "even if I had to countermand the previous order and forego entirely the rear attack, and which also left the question for me [to] determine, I felt much anxiety about what to do. The night was far advanced. The distance to Dinwiddie Court-House by the Quaker road from the location of my troops was over ten miles. It was impossible for them to reach there by that road before 8 a.m. By that time they could be of no use in holding Dinwiddie Court-House."[17] Moreover, it seemed to Warren that if Sheridan was on the verge of retreating by the Vaughan Road that it would make more sense for Warren to make his two-division attack on the Confederate rear down the Boydton Plank Road, which was closer to Sheridan's position. This would also allow him to make a more powerful attack, because, since Ayres' division was already headed down that road, it could be added to the attack as well. However, he hedged his bet. "I therefore determined that it was best to abide the movements already begun," he said, "and keep the two divisions—Griffin's and Crawford's—where they were, till I could hear that General Ayres had certainly re-enforced General Sheridan. The men of the two divisions were gaining, while waiting the result, a little of that rest they stood so much in need of on this their fourth night of almost continual deprivation of it, and we had but a short distance to move before reaching the enemy near J. Bouisseau's."[18]

At 1:20 a.m. Warren advised Meade: "I think we will have an infantry bridge over Gravelly Run sooner than I could send troops around by the Quaker road, but if I find any failure I will send that way....I am sending to General Sheridan my most available force." And at 2:05 he added, "The bridge over Gravelly Run [is] now practicable for infantry, and General Ayres' division advancing across it toward Dinwiddie Court House. I have given General Ayres orders to report to General Sheridan."[19] There was no reply.

"The orders which came to General Warren that night were to an amazing degree confused and conflicting," Joshua Chamberlain later wrote. "This is charging no blame on any particular person. We will call it, if you please, the fault of circumstances. But of course many evil effects of such conditions must naturally fall upon the officer receiving them. Although the responsibility according to military usage and ethics rests upon the officer originating the order, yet the practical effects are apt to fall upon the officer trying to execute it. And when he is not allowed to use his judgment as to the details of his own command, it makes it very hard for him sometimes. Indeed it is not very pleasant to be a subordinate officer, especially if one is also at the same time a commanding officer.... The frictions, mischances, and misunderstandings of all these circumstances falling across Warren's path, might well have bewildered the brightest mind, and rendered nugatory the most faithful intentions.

"Meantime, it may well be conceived we who held that extreme front line had an anxious night. Griffin was with me most of the time, and in investigating the state of things in front of our picket lines some time after midnight, we discovered that the enemy were carefully putting out their fires all along their own visible front. Griffin regards this as evidence of a contemplated movement on us, and he sends this information and suggestion to headquarters, and thus adds a new element to the already well-shaken mixture of uncertainty and seeming cross-purposes. But with us, the chief result was an anxiety that forbade a moment's relaxation from intense vigilance."[20] Meanwhile, Ayres' division was finally on the move, pausing to receive a small installment of rations from a pack train of mules on the way, arriving at the bridge over Gravelly Run just as it was ready at about two a.m. Since all of the available pontoons were already in use, Warren's engineers had pulled down a nearby barn to obtain timber to build a forty-foot span. Then Ayres pushed on down the Plank Road toward Sheridan.

By 3 a.m. Sheridan had received Grant's dispatch saying that Warren's three divisions would reach him by midnight, but he had not heard anything from Warren, let alone seen any of his units, so he sent him a message: "I am holding in front of Dinwiddie Court-House, on the road leading to Five Forks, for three-quarters of a mile, with General Custer's division. The enemy are in his immediate front, lying so as to cover the road just this side of A. Adams' house, which leads out across Chamberlain's bed or run. I understand you have a division at J. Boisseau's; if so, you are in rear of the enemy's line and almost on his flank. I will hold on here. Possibly they may attack Custer at daylight; if so, have this division attack instantly and in full force. Attack at daylight anyway, and I will make an effort to get the road this side of Adams' house, and if I do you can capture the whole of them. Any force moving down the road I am holding, or on the White Oak road, will be in the enemy's rear, and in all probability get any force that may escape you by a flank attack. Do not fear my leaving here. If the enemy remain I shall fight at daylight."[21] But Warren did not receive this message until 4:50 a.m., and even at that hour only Ayres' division had left its camps.

"At three o'clock," Joshua Chamberlain wrote, "I had got in my pickets, which were replaced by Crawford's and let my men rest as quietly as possible, knowing there would be heavy burdens laid on them in the morning. For, while dividing the sporadic mule-rations, word came to us that the Fifth Corps, as an organization, was to report to Sheridan at once and be placed under his orders. We kept our heads and hearts as well as we could; for we thought both would be needed. It was near daylight when my command—all there was of Griffin's Division then left on the front—drew out from the White Oak Road; Crawford's Division replacing us, to be brought off carefully under Warren's eye. We shortly picked up Bartlett's returning brigade, halted, way-worn and jaded with marching and countermarching, and struck off in the direction of the Bousseau houses and the Crump Road, following their heavy tracks in the mud and mire marking a way where before there was none; one of those recommended 'directions across country,' which this veteran brigade found itself thus compelled to travel for the third time in lieu of rest or rations, churning the sloughs and quicksands with emotions and expressions that could be conjectured only by a veteran of the Old Testament dispensation."[22]

"I remained with General Crawford's division," Warren later reported, "which we formed to retire in line of battle to meet the enemy should he pursue us from his breast-works, as I confidently expected he would as soon as he discovered our movements. I also deployed my escort to retire toward the plank road to take back any men or supplies which might be coming to that point through ignorance of the change that had been made in the night."[23]

Dawn came in cold and foggy on 1 April, and still the impatient Sheridan had neither seen nor heard anything of Warren's infantry. The fog soon began to lift, and as it did so Sheridan, Merritt, Custer, and their respective staffs rode forward to see what could be seen in their front, Warren's Federals or Pickett's Rebels. Men could be seen moving about in the distance, with a few mounted officers among them, but nobody could tell in the mist and the dim light whether they were wearing Union blue or Confederate gray. So one of Custer's officers rode forward to investigate. "We heard a 'Halt!'" one of Sheridan's officers wrote, "a question, and an answer...then the sharp report of a pistol, and Custer's officer came galloping back through the muddy field, and was able to report positively that the line was gray—a very gray gentlemen having shot at him and called him some highly improper names."[24]

The Rebels soon began to fall back, however, and Sheridan sent Merritt with Custer's and Devin's divisions to follow them. During the night the Confederates had captured two of Bartlett's men and learned that the 5th Corps—or so they thought—was closing in on their left rear. So at 2 a.m. Pickett had sent all of his wagons back toward Five Forks, and at 4 a.m. his infantry began to follow. Munford's cavalry formed a rear guard for the infantry, while Rosser's and Rooney Lee's divisions withdrew to the west the way they had come, across Chamberlain's bed and then up to Five Forks. Merritt, with Devin's and Custer's divisions, followed the Rebels, and when his men came to the Brock Road some of them followed it to the east far enough to see at its other end Ayres' division marching along the Boydton Plank Road. A staff officer was sent to turn Ayres' column into the Brock Road, and its approach helped to hasten the Confederates' withdrawal. Sheridan had hopes that Warren, with his other two divisions coming down the Crump Road, would come in on the Rebels' rear or left flank but he did not. When the Confederates had retreated beyond the junction of that road with the Dinwiddie-Five Forks road, Sheridan rode up it in search of the infantry.

Joshua Chamberlain's brigade was at the head of Warren's column. "I moved with much caution in approaching doubtful vicinities," he wrote, "throwing forward an advance guard which, as we expected to encounter the enemy in force, I held immediately in my own hand. Griffin followed at the head of my leading brigade, ready for whatever should happen. Arrived at the banks of the south branch of Gravelly Run, where Bartlett had made his dispositions the night before, from a mile in our front the glitter of advancing cavalry caught my eye, saber-scabbards and belt-brasses flashing back the level rays of the rising sun. Believing this to be nothing else than the rebel cavalry we expected to find somewhere before us, we made dispositions for instant attack. But the steady on-coming soon revealed the blue of our own cavalry, with Sheridan's weird battle-flag in the van. I reduce my front, get into the road again, and hardly less anxious than before move forward to meet Sheridan."

Chamberlain saluted and said, "I report to you, General, with the head of Griffin's Division."

Sheridan returned the salute and asked, more charge than question: "Why did you not come before? Where is Warren?"

"He is at the rear of the column, sir."

"That is where I expected to find him. What is he doing there?"

"General, we are withdrawing from the White Oak Road, where we fought all day," Chamberlain explained. "General Warren is bringing off his last division, expecting an attack."

"Griffin comes up," Chamberlain wrote. "My responsibility is at an end. I feel better. I am directed to mass my troops by the roadside. We are not sorry for that. Ayres soon comes up on the Brooks Road. Crawford arrives at length, and masses his troops also, near the J. Boisseau house, at the junction of the Five Forks Road. We were on the ground the enemy had occupied the evening before. It was Bartlett's outstretched line in the rear, magnified by the magic lens of night into the semblance of the whole Fifth Corps right upon them, which induced them to withdraw from Sheridan's front and fall back upon Five Forks. So after all Bartlett had as good as fought a successful battle, by a movement which might have been praised as Napoleonic had other fortunes favored."[25]

At about 9 a.m. Grant told Horace Porter, "I wish you would spend the day with Sheridan's command, and send me a bulletin every half-hour or so, advising me fully as to the progress made. You know my views, and I want you to give them to Sheridan fully. Tell him the contemplated movement is left entirely in his hands, and he must be responsible for its execution. I have every confidence in his judgment and ability. I hope that there may now be an opportunity of fighting the enemy's infantry outside of their fortifications."

"I set out," Porter wrote, "with half a dozen mounted orderlies to act as couriers in transmitting field bulletins, and met Sheridan about 10 a.m. on the Five Forks road not far from J. Boisseau's house. Ayres had his division on this road having arrived about daylight; and Griffin had reached J. Boisseau's between 7 and 8 a.m. I had a full conference with Sheridan, in which he told me that the force in front of him had fallen back early in the morning; that he had pursued with his cavalry, had had several brushes with the enemy, and was driving him steadily back; that he had had his patience sorely tried by the delays which had occurred in getting the infantry to him, but that he was going to make every effort to strike a heavy blow with all the infantry and cavalry as soon as he could get them into position, provided the enemy should make a stand behind his intrenchments at Five Forks, which seemed likely. While we were talking, General Warren, who had accompanied Crawford's division rode up and reported in person to Sheridan. It was then eleven o'clock.

"About an hour after Porter had left Grant, another aide had told that general, erroneously, that Warren's infantry was still waiting to cross Gravelly Run. Angrily, Grant declared that he had wanted to fire Warren the year before, at Spotsylvania, but Meade had talked him out of it. Now he was sorry he had given in. He sent for another aide, Lieutenant Colonel Orville Babcock.

"A few minutes before noon," Porter wrote, "Colonel Babcock came over from headquarters, and said to Sheridan: 'General Grant directs me to say to you that if, in your judgment, the Fifth Corps would do better under one of its division commanders, you are authorized to relieve General Warren and order him to report to him [General Grant] at headquarters.' General Sheridan replied in effect that he hoped such a step as that might not become necessary, and then went on to speak of his plan of battle. We all rode on farther to the front, and soon met General Devin of the cavalry, who was considerably elated by his successes of the morning, and loudly demanded to be permitted to make a general attack on the enemy. Sheridan told him he didn't believe he had ammunition enough. Said Devin: 'I guess I 've got enough to give 'em one surge more.' Colonel Babcock now left us to return to headquarters. About one o'clock it was reported by the cavalry that the enemy was retiring to his intrenched position at Five Forks, which was just north of the White Oak road and parallel to it, his earthworks running from a point about three quarters of a mile east of Five Forks to a point a mile west, with an angle or 'crochet,' about one hundred yards long, thrown back at right angles to the left of his line to protect that flank. Orders were at once given to Warren's corps to move up the Gravelly Run Church road to the open ground near the church, and form in order of battle, with Ayres on the left, Crawford on his right, and Griffin in rear as a reserve. The cavalry, principally dismounted, was to deploy in front of the enemy's line and engage his attention, and as soon as it heard the firing of our infantry to make a vigorous assault upon his works."[26]

Pickett deployed his troops behind breastworks at Five Forks and sent a telegram to Lee informing him that he had found it necessary to fall back from Dinwiddie Court House and asking for help. His supply wagons were sent north to safety across Hatcher's Run, which there ran from east to west about a mile and a quarter north of the White Oak Road. With his infantry in the breastworks, he placed Rooney Lee's cavalry to cover his right and one regiment of Munford's division to cover his left. The rest of Munford's division was used to guard the Ford Road, which ran north to Hatcher's Run, and Rosser's small division was placed north of that stream to protect the wagons. Covering the stretch of roughly three miles of woods along the White Oak Road between Munford's regiment and Anderson's position on the right of Lee's main defenses there was nothing but a small brigade of cavalry commanded by Brigadier General William P. Roberts.

Pickett wanted to fall back behind Hatcher's Run with his entire force, but he received a telegram from Lee telling him to hold Five Forks at all hazards so as to prevent the Federals from moving westward down the White Oak Road to the Southside Railroad. In a note written that day, Lee told Jefferson Davis, "The movement of Genl Grant to Dinwiddie Court House seriously threatens our position, and diminishes our ability to maintain our present lines in front of Richmond and Petersburg. In the first place it cuts us off from our depot at Stony Creek at which point forage for the cavalry was delivered by the Weldon Railroad and upon which we relied to maintain it. It also renders it more difficult to withdraw from our position, cuts us off from the White Oak road, and gives the enemy an advantageous point on our right and rear. From this point I fear he can readily cut both the South Side & the Danville Railroads being far superior to us in cavalry. This in my opinion obliged us to prepare for the necessity of evacuating our position on James River at once, and also to consider the best means of accomplishing it, and our future course."[27]

Nevertheless, despite Lee's concern, the knowledge that at least part of the 5th Corps was between them and Anderson, and the fact that Sheridan's cavalry had eagerly followed them all the way from Dinwiddie Court House, the Confederates did not seem to be worried about a Union attack. "When we moved towards Five Forks," Fitz Lee later said, "hearing nothing more of the [Federal] infantry's move which we had heard of the night before, I thought that the movements just there, for the time being, were suspended, and we were not expecting any attack that afternoon, so far as I know. Our throwing up works and taking position were simply general matters of military precaution."[28]

Both Pickett and Fitz Lee had something more interesting on their minds just then than the possibility of an attack by the Federals. Just before coming to join the concentration of Rebel cavalry about Five Forks two days before, Tom Rosser had spent a day on the Nottoway River, south of Dinwiddie Court House, where the shad had been running. Shad, which belong to the herring family, ascend far up the rivers along the Atlantic coast once a year to spawn and are easily caught in nets or seines. The young general had caught a large number of them and had brought them along with him in his headquarters ambulance wagon to Five Forks. Now that his division was resting north of Hatcher's Run with no prospects of an immediate battle he ordered the fish to be cleaned and roasted on sticks and invited Pickett and Fitz Lee to join him in what was traditionally known as a shad bake.

Sometime between noon and 1 p.m. Fitz Lee was just mounting up to start off for Rosser's headquarters when Tom Munford rode up and handed him a dispatch from the regiment detailed to maintain contact with Roberts' brigade, the unit that was covering the three-mile gap between Five Forks and the main Confederate lines. It said that Roberts had been attacked by a large force of Union cavalry and split in two, half falling back toward Anderson's position on the main line and half falling back toward Five Forks. If true this would mean that Pickett's task force was cut off from direct communication with Anderson and from any possibilty of help coming from that direction. Fitz, however, was not very concerned. "Well, Munford," he said, I wish you would go over in person at once and see what this means and, if necessary, order up your Division and let me hear from you."[29] Then he and and Pickett rode northward together to join Rosser for the shad bake. Their departure left Fitz's cousin Rooney the senior officer in the command, but he was far off on the right of the position with his own division and was not even aware that Cousin Fitz and Pickett had left the front, nor were any of Pickett's brigade commanders informed.

---

1. Porter, *Campaigning with Grant*, 431-432.
2. Wheeler, *Witness to Appomattox*, 72.
3. Porter, *Campaigning with Grant*, 432-433.
4. *Official Records*, 46:III:364.
5. Ibid., 46:III:338-339.
6. Ibid., 46:III:364-365.
7. Ibid., 46:I:818.
8. Ibid., 46:III:365.
9. Ibid., 46:III:340.
10. Ibid., 46:III:365-366.
11. Ibid., 46:III:341-342.
12. Ibid., 46:III:367.
13. Ibid., 46:III:380.
14. Wheeler, *Witness to Appomattox*, 72.
15. *Official Records*, 46:III:417.
16. Ibid., 46:III:367.
17. Ibid., 46:I:823.
18. Ibid., 46:I:824.
19. Ibid., 46:III:417-418.
20. Chamberlain, *The Passing of the Armies*, 74-79.

21. *Official Records*, 46:III:419-420.
22. Chamberlain, *The Passing of the Armies*, 79.
23. *Official Records*, 46:III:824-825.
24. Stern, *An End to Valor*, 129-130.
25. Chamberlain, *The Passing of the Armies*, 79-80.
26. Porter, *Campaigning with Grant*, 434-435.
27. Dowdey and Manarin, ed., *Wartime Papers of R. E. Lee*, 922.
28. Douglas Southall Freeman, *Lee's Lieutenants: A Study in Command* (New York, 1944), Vol. 3, 664.
29. Ibid., 3:667.

CHAPTER TWENTY-SIX

We Flanked Them Gloriously!

1 April 1865

The force of Union horsemen that attacked Roberts' brigade of Confederate cavalry was Ranald Mackenzie's small division (about 1,000 men) from the Army of the James. It had reached Dinwiddie Court House that morning and had been allowed to rest just north of there for a while. However, Sheridan later learned that Meade had, in the absence of the 5th Corps, pulled his left back from the White Oak Road to the Boydton Plank Road. This move opened the White Oak Road for the Rebels in their main line of defenses to communicate with Pickett at Five Forks and to send out reinforcements that might hit Sheridan's attack in the flank or rear. Therefore, in order to protect against such an event, he sent Mackenzie to block the White Oak Road.

This was Mackenzie's first chance for a major fight since taking command of his division, and he made the most of it. Advancing up the Crump Road he drove in Roberts' pickets and discovered the main force posted, dismounted, in a line of rifle pits in the edge of some woods along the White Oak Road with an open field in their front. He used two companies of dismounted troopers to keep the Rebels' heads down with their repeating carbines and then led a battalion in a mounted charge that swept over the Confederate defenses and scattered Roberts' men in confusion. When Sheridan learned of this success he told Mackenzie to leave a small force to block the White Oak Road and to follow that road westward with the rest of his command and join Sheridan's main force. But by the time it got to the area defended by Pickett's force Warren's infantry had intervened between it and Merritt's divisions.

While Mackenzie rode off to block the White Oak Road, and Merritt's cavalry followed the Rebels and reconnoitered their position, Warren's infantry had been allowed to get a little rest and to draw rations and ammunitions from whatever supply wagons had been able to keep up with them. "The troops," Joshua Chamberlain said, "had enjoyed about four hours of this unwonted rest when, the cavalry having completed its reconnoissance, we were ordered forward. We turned off on a narrow road said to lead pretty nearly to the left of the enemy's defenses at Five Forks on the White Oak Road. Crawford led, followed by Griffin and Ayres....The road had been much cut up by repeated scurries of both the contending parties, and was even yet obstructed by cavalry led horses, and other obstacles, which it would seem strange had not been got off the track during all this halt. We who were trying to follow closely were brought to frequent standstill. This was vexatious,—our men being hurried to their feet in heavy marching order, carrying on their backs perhaps three days' life for themselves and a pretty heavy installment of death for their antagonists, and now compelled every few minutes to come to a huddled halt in the muddy road, 'marking time' and marking place also with deep discontent."[1]

Sheridan was impatiently waiting for Warren's infantry to get into position. "But the movement was slow," Horace Porter wrote, "the required formation seemed to drag, and Sheridan, chafing with impatience and consumed with anxiety, became as restive as a racer struggling to make the start. He made every possible appeal for promptness, dismounted from his horse, paced up and down, struck the clenched fist of one hand against the palm of the other, and fretted like a caged tiger. He exclaimed at one time: 'This battle must be fought and won before the sun goes down. All the conditions may be changed in the morning. We have but a few hours of daylight left us. My cavalry are rapidly exhausting their ammunition, and if the attack is delayed much longer they may have none left.' And then another batch of staff-officers was sent out to gallop through the mud and hurry up the columns."[2]

"In about two hours we get up where Sheridan wants us," Joshua Chamberlain wrote, "in some open ground and thin woods near the Gravelly Run Church, and form as we arrive, by brigades in column of regiments.... It is now about four o'clock. Near the church is a group of restless forms and grim visages, expressing their different tempers and temperaments in full tone. First of all the chiefs: Sheridan, dark and tense, walking up and down the earth, seeking—well, we will say—some adequate vehicle or projectile of expression at the prospect of the sun's going down on nothing but his wrath; evidently having availed himself of some incidental instrumentalities to this end, more or less explicit or expletive. Warren is sitting there like a caged eagle or rather like a man making desperate effort to command himself when he has to obey unwelcome orders,—all his moral energies compressed into the nerve centers somewhere behind his eyes and masked pale cheek and compressed lip. Griffin is alert and independent, sincere to the core, at his ease, ready for anything.... Bartlett, with drawn face, like a Turkish scimetar, sharp, springy, curved outward, damascened by various experience and various emotion; Crawford, a conscious gentleman, having the entree at all headquarters, somewhat lofty of manner, not of the iron fiber, nor spring of steel, but punctilious in a way, obeying orders in a certain literal fashion that saved him the censure of superiors,—a pet of his State, and likewise, we thought, of Meade and Warren, judging from the attention they always gave him—possibly not quite fairly estimated by his colleagues as a military man, but the ranking division commander of the corps.... Ayres comes up after a little, ahead of his troops, bluff and gruff at questions about the lateness of his column; twitching his mustache in lieu of words, the sniff of his nostrils smelling the battle not very much afar; sound of heart, solid of force, all the manly and military qualities ready in reserve,—the typical old soldier.

"During this impatient waiting for the seemingly slow preparatory formation, our spiritual wheels were lubricated by the flow of discussion and explanation about the plan of attack. Sheridan took a saber or scabbard and described it graphically on the light earth. The plan in general was for the cavalry to occupy the enemy's attention by a brisk demonstration along the right front of their works, while the Fifth Corps should fall upon their left and rear, by a sort of surprise if possible, and scoop them out of their works along the White Oak Road, and capture or disorganize them. The report of the cavalry reconnoissance, as it came to us, was that the enemy had fortified this road for nearly a mile westward, and about three-quarters of a mile eastward from Five Forks, and at the extreme left made a return northerly for perhaps one hundred and fifty yards, to cover that flank. As I understood it, the formation and advance were to be such that Ayres should strike the angle of the 'return,' and Crawford and Griffin sweep around Ayres's right, flanking their 'return' and enfilading their main line. This was perfectly clear, and struck us all as a splendid piece of tactics, cyclone- and Sheridan-like, promising that our success was to be quick and certain. Our somewhat jaded faculties were roused to their full force....

"The corps formation was: Ayres on the left, west of the Church Road, the division in double brigade front in two lines, and Winthrop with the First Brigade in reserve, in rear of his center; Crawford on the right, east of the road, in similar formation; Griffin in rear of Crawford, with Bartlett's Brigade in double column of regiments, three lines deep; my own brigade next, somewhat in echelon to the right, with three battalion lines in close order, while Gregory at first was held massed in my rear." Griffin knew that Mackenzie's cavalry had been sent to block the White Oak Road, but he had not heard of his success, so he was still worried about his right flank, so Chamberlain had Gregory "throw out a small battalion as skirmishers and flankers, and march another regiment by the flank on our right, ready to face outwards, and let his other regiment follow in my brigade column.

"At four o'clock we moved down the Gravelly Run Church Road, our lines as we supposed nearly parallel to the White Oak Road, with Ayres directed on the angle of the enemy's works. Just as we started there came from General Warren a copy of a diagram of the proposed movement. I was surprised at this. It showed our front of movement to be quite oblique to the White Oak Road,—as much as half a right angle,—with the center of Crawford's Division directed upon the angle, and Ayres, of course, thrown far to the left, so as to strike the enemy's works halfway to Five Forks. Griffin was shown as following Crawford; but the whole direction was such that all of us would strike the enemy's main line before any of us could touch the White Oak Road. The diagram, far from clearing my mind, added confusion to surprise....

"Ill at ease in such uncertainty I rode over to General Griffin, who with General Warren was close on my left at this early stage of the movement, and asked for an explanation. Griffin answers quickly: 'We will not worry ourselves about diagrams. We are to follow Crawford. Circumstances will soon develop our duty.' In the meantime we were moving right square down the Church Road, and not oblique to it as the diagram indicated. However, I quieted my mind with the reflection that the earth certainly was a known quantity, and the enemy susceptible to discovery, whatever might be true of roads, diagrams, or understandings.

"Crawford crossed the White Oak Road, his line nearly parallel to it, without encountering the expected angle. This road, it is to be remarked, made a considerable bend northerly at the crossing of the Church Road, so that Ayres had not reached it when Crawford and even Griffin were across. We naturally supposed the angle was still ahead. Crawford immediately ran into a sharp fire on his right front, which might mean the crisis. I had been riding with Griffin on the left of my front line, but now hastened over to the right, where I found Gregory earnestly carrying out my instructions to guard that flank. I caught a glimpse of some cavalry in the woods on our right, which I judged to be Roberts' North Carolina Brigade, that had been picketing the White Oak Road, and so kept Gregory on the alert. The influence of the sharp skirmish fire on Crawford's right tended to draw the men towards it; but I used all my efforts to shorten step on the pivot and press the wheeling flank, in order to be ready for the 'swing' to the left. Still, the firing ahead kept me dubious. It might mean Fitzhugh Lee's cavalry making a demonstration there; but from the persistence of it was more likely to mean infantry reinforcements sent the enemy from the ...entrenchments where we had left them the day before....

"It was, in fact, Fitzhugh Lee's cavalry, commanded now by the experienced and able Munford who had dismounted his men and posted them at the junction of the Church Road and the White Oak Road, behind some light rail defenses which they had hastily thrown up. From this they were being slowly driven by Crawford's advance. We crossed the White Oak Road without hearing anything from Ayres, a circumstance which troubled me very much, as our division was supposed to be in supporting distance of both Crawford and Ayres. It was now apparent that the road-crossing Crawford had struck was not at the angle of the enemy's entrenched line, but at least a gunshot to the east of this,—in fact it was a thousand yards away....My orders were in general to follow Crawford.

"I had managed, however, to gain towards the left until we had fairly got past Crawford's left rear. Some firing we had heard in the supposed direction of our cavalry, but it did not seem heavier than that in Crawford's front. We were moving rapidly, and had been out about twenty minutes from the church, and perhaps nearly a mile distant, when a sudden burst of fire exactly on our left roused very definite thoughts. This could only be from Ayres' attack."[3]

Horace Porter witnessed what happened to Ayres' division. "I rode to the front, in company with Sheridan and Warren," he wrote, "with the head of Ayres's division, which was on the left. Ayres threw out a skirmish-line and advanced across an open field which sloped down gradually toward the dense woods just north of the White Oak road. He soon met with a fire from the edge of these woods, a number of men fell, and the skirmish-line halted and seemed to waiver. Sheridan now began to exhibit those traits which always made him a tower of strength in the presence of an enemy. He put spurs to his horse, and dashed along in front of the line of battle from left to right, shouting words of encouragement, and having something cheery to say to every regiment."

"Come on, men," Sheridan cried; "go at 'em with a will! Move on at a clean jump, or you 'll not catch one of 'em. They're all getting ready to run now, and if you don't get on to them in five minutes they 'll every one get away from you! Now go for them!"

"Just then," Porter wrote, "a man on the skirmish-line was struck in the neck; the blood spurted as if the jugular vein had been cut."

"I'm killed!" the man cried, and dropped to the ground. "You're not hurt a bit!" Sheridan cried. "Pick up your gun, man, and move right on to the front."

"Such was the electric effect of his words," Porter wrote, "that the poor fellow snatched up his musket, and rushed forward a dozen paces before he fell, never to rise again. The line of battle of weather-beaten veterans was now moving right along down the slope toward the woods with a steady swing that boded no good for Pickett's command, earthworks or no earthworks....

"Soon Ayres men met with a heavy fire on their left flank, and had to change directions by facing more toward the west. As the troops entered the woods, and moved forward over the boggy ground, and struggled through the dense undergrowth, they were staggered by a heavy fire from the angle, and fell back in some confusion. Sheridan now rushed into the midst of the broken lines, and cried out; 'Where is my battle-flag?' As the sergeant who carried it rode up, Sheridan seized the crimson-and-white standard, waved it above his head, cheered on the men, and made heroic efforts to close up the ranks. Bullets were now humming like a swarm of bees about our heads, and shells were crashing through the ranks. A musket-ball pierced the battle-flag; another killed the sergeant who had carried it; another wounded an aide...in the side; others struck two or three of the staff-officers' horses. All this time Sheridan was dashing from one point of the line to another, waving his flag, shaking his fist, encouraging, entreating, threatening, praying, swearing, the true personification of chivalry, the very incarnation of battle. It would be a sorry soldier who could help following such a leader. Ayres and his officers were equally exposing themselves at all points in rallying their men; and soon the line was steadied, for such troops could suffer but a momentary check. Ayres, with drawn saber, rushed forward once more with his veterans, who now behaved as if they had fallen back only to get a 'good ready,' and with fixed bayonets and a rousing cheer dashed over the earthworks, sweeping everything before them, and killing or capturing every man in their immediate front whose legs had not saved him. Sheridan spurred 'Rienzi' up to the angle, and with a bound the animal carried his rider over the earthworks, and landed among a line of prisoners who had thrown down their arms and were crouching close under the breastworks. Some of them called out: 'Wha' do you want us all to go to?' Then Sheridan's rage turned to humor, and he had a running talk with the 'Johnnies' as they filed past. 'Go right over there,' he said to them, pointing to the rear. 'Get right along, now. Oh, drop your guns; you'll never need them any more. You'll all be safe over there. Are there any more of you? We want every one of you fellows.' Nearly 1500 were captured at the angle."[4]

Brevet Brigadier General Charles Wainwright, chief of artillery for the 5th Corps, saw the Rebel prisoners being led to the rear. "These men all moved along cheerfully," he wrote, "without one particle of that sullenness which formerly characterized them under similar circumstances. They joked with our men along the line and I repeatedly heard them say, 'We are coming back into the Union, boys, we are coming back into the Union.' It was a joyful and an exciting sight, seeming to say that the war was about over, the great rebellion nearly quelled."[5]

Ayres' division had overrun two Confederate brigades at the angle where Pickett's line bent back to the north. Those Rebels who had not been captured fled westward, and many of them joined three regiments of reinforcements that had been sent from farther down the line. These arrived just in time to form a new north-south line just northwest of the lost return.

Joshua Chamberlain had meanwhile entered the gap between Ayres and Crawford. "I was anxious about my duty," he said. "My superiors were not in sight. Bartlett had closely followed Crawford, away to my right. But I could see the corps flag in the Sydnor field, moving towards Crawford, and on the other side, in a ravine half-way to Ayres, I saw the division flag. There was Ayres fighting alone, and that was not in the program. There was Griffin down there; that was order enough for me, and I took the responsibility of looking out for the left instead of the right, where my last orders committed me. I pulled my brigade out of the woods by the left flank, telling Gregory to follow; and, sending to Bartlett to let him know what I was doing, pushed across a muddy stream and up a rough ravine towards Ayres. Half-way up, Griffin came to meet me,—never more welcome. He gave the look I wanted, and without coming near enough for words waved me to follow up to the head of the ravine and to attack on my right, along the bank where, hidden by brush and scrub, the enemy had a line perpendicular to their main one on the White Oak Road, and were commencing a slant fire in Ayres' direction. Griffin rode past me towards Warren and Bartlett.

"At the head of the gully all we had to do was to front into line of battle, and scramble up the rough brambly steep. The moment we showed our heads, we were at close quarters with the enemy. We exchanged volleys with good will, and then came the rush. Our lines struck each other obliquely, like shutting jaws. It was rather an awkward movement; for we had to make a series of right half-wheels by battalion to meet the fire, and all the while gain to the left. Thus we stopped that cross-fire on Ayres, who was now lost from sight by intervening scrubby woods. The brunt of this first fell on my stalwart 185th New York, Colonel Sniper; but Gregory soon coming in by echelon on their right took the edge off that enfilading fire. Ayres' fitful fire was approaching, and I rode over towards it. Somewhere near the angle of the 'return' I met Sheridan. He had probably seen me putting my men in, and hence I escaped censure for appearing. Indeed his criticism seemed to be that there were not more of me, rather than less."

"By God, that's what I want to see!" was Sheridan's greeting, "general officers at the front. Where are your general officers?"

Chamberlain replied that he had seen General Warren's flag in the big field to the north, and that seeing Ayres in a tight place he had come to help him, by General Griffin's order.

"Then," cried Sheridan, "you take command of all the infantry round here, and break this dam...."

"I didn't wait to hear any more," Chamberlain wrote. "That made good grammar as it stood. I didn't stand for anything, but spurred back to some scattered groups of men, demoralized by being so far in the rear, and not far enough to do them any good, yet too brave to go back. Captain Laughlin of Griffin's staff came along, and I took him with me down among these men to get them up. I found one stalwart fellow on his hands and knees behind a stump, answering with whimsical grimaces to the bullets coming pretty thick and near."

"Look here, my good fellow," Chamberlain called down to him, "don't you know you'll be killed here in less than two minutes? This is no place for you. Go forward!"

"But what can I do?" the man asked. "I can't stand up against all this alone!"

"No, that's just it," Chamberlain replied. "We're forming here. I want you for guide center. Up, and forward!"

"Up and out he came like a hero," Chamberlain wrote. "I formed those 'reserves' on him as guide, and the whole queer line—two hundred of them—went in right up to the front and the thick of it. My poor fellow only wanted a token of confidence and appreciation to get possession of himself. He was proud of what he did, and so I was for him. I let the staff officers take these men in, for I had caught sight of Ayres' Third Brigade coming out of the woods right behind me, and standing in the further edge of the scrubby field. The men were much excited, but were making a good line. [Brevet Brigadier] General [James] Gwyn was riding up and down their front in a demonstrative manner, but giving no sign of forward movement. I thought this strange for him and bad for us all, in the pinch things then were at, and with the warrant Sheridan had given me galloped down to him and asked him if he was acting under any particular orders from General Ayres."

"No, General," Gwyn answered. "I have lost Ayres. I have no orders. I don't know what to do."

"Then come with me," Chamberlain said; "I will take the responsibility. You shall have all credit. Let me take your brigade for a moment!"

"His men gave me good greetings as I rode down their front," Chamberlain wrote, "and gave the order, 'Forward, right oblique!' On they came, and in they went, gallantly, gladly, just when and where they were needed, with my own brigade fighting the 'return,' and ready to take touch with Ayres. His fire was advancing rapidly on my left, and I rode over to meet him. Sheridan was by my side in a moment, very angry."

"You are firing into my cavalry!" Sheridan exclaimed. ("His face darkening with a checked expletive," Chamberlain wrote.)

"Then the cavalry have got into the rebels' place," Chamberlain answered. "One of us will have to get out of the way. What will you have us do, General?"

"Don't you fire into my cavalry, I tell you!" Sheridan yelled.

"I felt a little left out in the cold," Chamberlain wrote, "by General Sheridan's calling them 'my cavalry,' as if we were aliens and did not belong to him also; but, whosesoever they were, I could not see what business they had up here at the 'angle.' This was our part of the field.

The plan of the battle put them at the enemy's right and center, a mile away on the Dinwiddie Road and beyond. Fortunately for me, Ayres comes up, his troops right upon the angle—the Maryland Brigade on the 'return'—brave Bowerman down—and Winthrop's Brigade—gallant Winthrop gone—reaching beyond, across the White Oak Road, driving a crowd before them. I have only time to say to Ayres, 'Gwyn is in on the right'; for Sheridan takes him in hand."

"I tell you again, General Ayres," Sheridan said, "you are firing into my cavalry!"

"We are firing at the people who are firing at us!" was Ayres' retort. "These are not carbine shot. They are minie-balls. I ought to know."

"But I felt the point of Sheridan's rebuke," Chamberlain wrote. "As my oblique fire across the 'return' was now so near the enemy's main line on the White Oak Road, it was not unlikely that if any of the cavalry were up here on their front, I might be firing into them and they into me. There was a worse thing yet: if we continued advancing in that direction, in another minute we should be catching Ayres' fire on our left flank. He was already in, with his men. Griffin, coming up, detains me a moment. Sheridan greets him well. 'We flanked them gloriously!' Sheridan exclaims with a smile. After a minute's crisp remark, Griffin wheels away to the right, and I am left with Sheridan. He was sitting right in the focus of the fire, on his horse 'Rienzi,'—both about the color of the atmosphere, his demon pennon, good or ill, as it might bode, red and white, two-starred, aloft just behind him. The stream of bullets was pouring so thick it crossed my mind that what had been to me a poet's phrase—'darkening the air'—was founded on dead-level fact. I was troubled for Sheridan. We could not afford to lose him. I made bold to tell him so, and begged him not to stay there;—the rest of us would try to take care of things, and from that place he could be spared. He gave me a comical look, and answered with a peculiar twist in the toss of his head, that seemed to say he didn't care much for himself, or perhaps for me."

"Yes, I think I'll go!" Sheridan said.

"And away he dashed," Chamberlain wrote, "right down through Ayres' left, down the White Oak Road, into that triple cross-fire we had been quarreling about. I afterwards learned that Sheridan did order his cavalry to cease firing in the direction of our advancing infantry.

"I plunged into my business, to make up for this minute's lost time. My men were still facing too much across Ayres' front and getting into the range of his fire. We had got to change that, and swing to the right, down the rear of the enemy's main works. It was a whirl. Every way was front, and every way was flank. The fighting was hand to hand. I was trying to get the three angles of the triangle into something like two right angles, and had swung my left well forward, opening quite a gap in that direction, when a large body of the enemy came rushing in upon that flank and rear. They were in line formation, with arms at something like a 'ready,' which looked like 'business.' I thought it was our turn to be caught between two fires, and that these men were likely to cut their way through us. Rushing into the ranks of my left battalion I shouted the order, 'Prepare to fire by the rear rank!' My men faced about at once, disregarding the enemy in front; but at this juncture our portentous visitors threw down their muskets, and with hands and faces up cried out, 'We surrender,' running right in upon us and almost over us. I was very glad of it, though more astonished, for they outnumbered us largely. I was a little afraid of them, too, lest they might find occasion to take arms again and revoke the 'consent of the governed.' They were pretty solid commodities, but I was very willing to exchange them for paper token of indebtedness in the form of a provost-marshal's receipt. So getting my own line into shape again, I took these well-mannered men, who had been standing us so stiff a fight a few minutes before, with a small escort out over the 'return,' into the open field in rear, and turned them over to one of Sheridan's staff, with a request for a receipt when they were counted.

"In the field I find Ayres, who is turning over a great lot of prisoners. The 'angle' and the whole 'return' are now carried, but beyond them the routed enemy are stubbornly resisting. I have time for a word with Ayres now, and to explain my taking up Gwyn so sharply. He is not in the mood to blame me for anything....General Bartlett now came appealing for assistance. Two of his regiments had gone off with Crawford, and Bartlett had more than he could do to make head against a stout resistance the enemy were making on a second line turned back near the Ford Road. I helped him pick up a lot of stragglers and asked Gregory to give him the 188th New York for assistance."[6]

Bartlett had had more trouble with surrendering Rebels than had Chamberlain and Ayres. "Having marched for some two or three miles," wrote Private Theodore Gerrish of the 20th Maine, "the lines were so changed while we were marching, that we soon found we were in the front line. Our regiment and the 1st Michigan were under the command of Colonel Walter G. Morrill, and in all our previous experience we had never been led by a braver or more skillful commander.

"We climbed a hill, looked down through the trees, and saw the breastworks but a short distance in our front. We had advanced so quietly that the enemy was not aware of our presence. Our lines were reformed, and then with a yell we charged. Before the enemy had time to recover from their surprise, we were upon them, so that they threw down their guns without firing a shot and surrendered. The number of prisoners embarrassed us, and we sent them to the rear as fast as we could....

"They soon discovered the superiority of their numbers and the mistake they had made in surrendering. A large portion of our men had gone to the rear with prisoners when a rebel officer came dashing down the line, calling upon them to rally. A rebel who had surrendered was standing near Colonel Morrill, and, catching up from the ground a loaded rifle, yelled with an oath, 'We can whip you yet,' and deliberately shot a captain of the 1st Michigan Regiment who stood beside him. At the same moment a private of Company D in our regiment thrust his bayonet through the breast of the treacherous rebel, who fell dead at his feet.

"In a moment's time the battle was raging all along our line. It was hot work, and in many places it was a hand-to-hand fight. Men deliberately pointed their rifles in each other's faces and fired. Clubbed muskets came crushing down in deadly force upon human skulls. Men were bayoneted in cold blood. Feats of individual bravery were performed on that afternoon which, if recorded, would fill a volume....The rebels would climb up on one side of the breastworks, and our men on the other side would knock them back. We heard bugles in our front, and out from a piece of woods some eighty rods away came dashing squadrons of cavalry. With a cheer our men sprang over the works and upon the rebels, who reeled and staggered before us."[7]

Pickett, Fitz Lee, and Rosser, savoring their roasted shad, first became aware of the Union attack when they heard a great burst of firing off to the south. Pickett borrowed a courier from Rosser to send a message to the front, but before the man had ridden out of sight they saw him captured just south of Hatcher's Run by a line of Federals crossing the road. This was either Crawford's infantry or Mackenzie's cavalry. Pickett galloped across the stream until he found Tom Munford with a line of his troopers facing eastward along the Ford Road. "Do hold them back till I can pass to Five Forks," Pickett said.[8] A young captain, overhearing the request, led his men in a dash straight at the oncoming Union line. The captain was killed, but Pickett was able to dash down the road during this brief charge, clinging to the far side of his horse's neck. Fitz Lee tried to get through the same way but was driven back. He then took command of Rosser's troopers and tried to lead them down the Ford Road, but this move was also easily repulsed.

"Meanwhile," Joshua Chamberlain wrote, "Warren, searching for

Crawford, had come upon his First Brigade, Kellogg's, and had faced it southerly towards the White Oak Road, as a guide for a new point of direction for that division, and had then gone off in search of the rest of the troops to bring them in on the line. Thereupon one of Sheridan's staff officers came across Kellogg standing there, and naturally ordered him to go forward into the 'fight.' Kellogg questioned his authority, and warm words took the place of other action, till at length Kellogg concluded it best to obey Sheridan's representative, and moved promptly forward, striking somewhere beyond the left of the enemy's refused new flank. It seems also that Crawford's Third Brigade, Coulter's, which was in his rear line, had anticipated orders or got Warren's, and moved by the shortest line in the direction Kellogg was taking. So Crawford himself was on the extreme wheeling flank, with only Baxter's Brigade and two regiments of Bartlett's of the First Division immediately in hand.... Our commands were queerly mixed; men of every division of the corps came within my jurisdiction, and something like this was probably the case with several other commanders. But that made no difference; men and officers were good friends. There was no jealousy among us subordinate commanders. We had eaten salt together when we had not much else. This liveliness of mutual interest and support, I may remark, is sometimes of great importance in the developments of a battle.

"The hardest hold-up was in front of my left center, the First Battalion of the 198th Pennsylvania. I rode up to the gallant Glenn, commanding it, and said, 'Major Glenn, if you will break that line you shall have a colonel's commission!' It was a hasty utterance, and the promise unmilitary, perhaps; but my every energy was focused on that moment's issue. Nor did the earnest soldier need a personal inducement; he was already carrying out the general order to press the enemy before him, with as much effect as we could reasonably expect. But it was deep in my mind how richly he already deserved this promotion, and I resolved that he should get it now.... Glenn sprung among his men, calling out, 'Boys, will you follow me?' wheeled his horse and dashed forward, without turning to see who followed. Nor did he need.... On the brave fellows go with a cheer into the hurricane of fire. Their beautiful flag sways gracefully aloft with the spring of the brave youth bearing it, lighting the battle-smoke; three times it goes down to earth covered in darkening eddies, but rises ever again passing from hand to hand of dauntless young heroes. Then bullet-torn and blood-blazoned it hovers for a moment above a breastwork, while the regiment goes over like a wave.... The sight so wrought upon me that I snatched time to ride over and congratulate Glenn and his regiment. As I passed into a deeper shadow of the woods, I met two men bearing his body, the dripping blood marking their path..."

"By this time Warren had found Crawford," Chamberlain wrote, "who with Baxter's Brigade had been pursuing Munford's dismounted cavalry all the way from where we had crossed the White Oak Road, by a wide detour reaching almost to Hatcher's Run, until he had crossed the Ford Road, quite in rear of the breaking lines which [the Confederate brigade commanders] were trying to hold together. Hence he was in position to do them much damage, both by cutting off their retreat by the Ford Road and taking many prisoners, and also by completing the enemy's envelopment. To meet this, the enemy, instead of giving up the battle as they would have been justified in doing, stripped still more their main works in front of our cavalry by detaching nearly the entire brigade of General Terry, now commanded by Colonel Mayo, and facing it quite to its rear pushed it down the Ford Road and across the fields to resist the advance of Warren with Crawford.

"We, too, were pressing hard on the Ford Road from the east, so that all were crowded into that whirlpool of the fight. Just as I reached it, Captain Brinton of Griffin's staff dashed up at headlong speed and asked if I knew that Griffin was in command of the corps. I was astonished at first, and incredulous afterwards. I had heard nothing from General Warren since I saw his flag away in the Sydnor field when I was breaking out from the column of march to go to Ayres' support. My first thought was that he was killed. I asked Brinton what he meant. He told me the story. General Warren, when he got to the rear of the Ford Road, sent an enthusiastic message by Colonel Locke, his chief of staff, to Sheridan, saying that he was in the enemy's rear, cutting off his retreat, and had many prisoners. This message met scant courtesy. Sheridan's patience was exhausted."

"By God, sir, tell General Warren he wasn't in the fight!" Sheridan had exclaimed.

"Must I tell General Warren that, sir?" the thunderstruck Locke had replied.

"Tell him that, sir!" Sheridan had said.

"I would not like to take a verbal message like that to General Warren," Locke had said. "May I take it down in writing?"

"Take it down, sir; tell him, by God, he was not at the front!"

"Locke," Chamberlain wrote, "the old and only adjutant-general of the Fifth Corps, himself just back from a severe wound in the face on some desperate front with Warren, never felt a blow like that. Soon thereafter Sheridan came upon General Griffin, and, without preface or index, told the astonished Griffin, 'I place you in command of the

Fifth Corps!' This was Brinton's story; dramatic enough, surely; pathetic, too. I hardly knew how to take it. I thought it possible Sheridan had told every general officer he met, as he had told me, to take command of all the men he could find on the field and push them in. I could not think of Warren being so wide-off an exception.

"Pressing down towards the Forks, some of Ayres' men mingled with my own, I saw on emerging into a little clearing, Sheridan riding beside me like an apparition. Yet he was pretty certain flesh and blood. I felt a little nervous, not in the region of my conscience, nor with any misgiving of the day's business, but because I was alone with Sheridan. His expression was at its utmost bent; intent and content, incarnate will. But he greeted me kindly, and spoke freely of the way things had been going. We were riding down inside the works in the woods covering the Forks and Ford Road, now the new focus of the fight. Just then an officer rode flightily up from that direction, exclaiming to General Sheridan, 'We are on the enemy's rear, and have got three of their guns.'"

"I don't care a damn for their guns, or you either, sir!" Sheridan replied. "What are you here for? Go back to your business, where you belong! What I want is that Southside Road."

"The officer seemed to appreciate the force of the suggestion," Chamberlain wrote, "and the distant attraction of the Southside Road. I looked to see what would happen to me. There were many men gathered round, or rather we had ridden into the midst of them, as they stood amazed, at the episode. The sun was just in the tree-tops; it might be the evening chill that was creeping over us."

Then Sheridan rose in his stirrups, waving his hat in his hand above his head, and roared out, "I want you men to understand we have a record to make, before that sun goes down, that will make hell tremble!—I want you there!"

"I guess they were ready to go," Chamberlain wrote; "to that place or any other where death would find them quickest; and the sooner they got there, the safer for them....As [the Confederates'] reinforced but wasting lines had fallen back before us along the north and east side of their works, our cavalry kept up sharp attacks upon their right across the works, which by masterly courage and skill they managed to repel, replacing as best they could the great gaps made in their defenses by the withdrawal of so many of [the Rebels] to form the other sides of their retreating 'hollow square.' Driven in upon themselves, and over much 'concentrated,' they were so penned in there was not a fair chance to fight. Just as Ayres' and Griffin's men struck the brave fellows holding on around the guns at the Forks, from which Pegram, the gifted young commander, had been borne away mortally wounded,—and spirits as well as bodies were falling,—two brigades of our cavalry, Fitzhugh's and Pennington's of Devins' and Custer's commands, seizing the favorable moment, made a splendid dash...."[9]

Custer himself rode out in front of the 2nd Ohio and told his men, "We are going to take those works, and we will not come back again until we get them!" The dismounted Federal troopers swept forward through the woods, but halfway to the Rebel defenses Custer could see that the Confederates were about to fire. Quickly he ordered his bugler to sound a little-used call, "Down." He men recognized the call in time and hit the dirt. "We all hugged America," one of the cavalrymen recounted. "As we did so, a most terrible fire went over us, from both Infantry and Artillery."[10]

The bugler, however, paid for his part in saving the others. He was hit, as were one of Custer's orderlies and the man who carried his personal battleflag, which always marked Custer's location on the battlefield. Custer leaned down from the saddle without dismounting and snatched up his fallen guidon like a circus rider—it was a brand new flag that he had just received from his wife the day before—and swinging it over his head he raced right up to the Rebel line. His horse leaped over the breastworks, and the 2nd Ohio, whooping like Indians, chased after him, as did the rest of the brigade. At the earthworks the Federals blasted the Confederates with their repeating carbines and then scrambled over the works, capturing several Rebels and chasing the rest away. The 1st Connecticut overran some guns, and Custer's artillerymen left their own cannon in the woods and rushed forward to turn the captured pieces against their former owners.

"Bartlett, also, with some of Crawford's men following," Chamberlain wrote, "came down nearly at the same time from the north of the Ford Road. All, therefore, centered on the three guns there; so that for a moment there was a queer colloquy over the silent guns." In short, there was an argument over who deserved the credit for capturing them. Chamberlain's conclusion was that they, "with due acknowledgments of individual valor, were taken by all the troops who closed in around them, front, flank, and rear; by the whole movement, indeed, from the brain of the brilliant commander who planned, to the least man who pressed forward to fulfill his high resolve.

"We had pushed the enemy a mile from the left of their works—the angle, their tactical center—and were now past the Forks. Something remained to be done, according to Sheridan's biblical intimation. But the enemy made no more resolute, general stand. Only little groups, held back and held together by individual character, or the magnetism of some superior officer, made front and gave check. For a moment, after the deafening din and roar, the woods seemed almost given back to nature, save for the clinging smoke and broken bodies and breaking moans which betokened man's intervention.

"Our commands were much mixed, but the men well moving on, when in this slackening of the strain, Griffin and Ayres, who were now riding with me, spoke regretfully, sympathizingly, of Warren. They thought he had sacrificed himself for Crawford, who had not proved equal to the demands of the situation. 'Poor Warren, how he will suffer for this!' they said with many variations of the theme. Griffin did not say a word about his being placed in command of the corps. He was a keen observer, a sharp critic, able and prompt to use a tactical advantage, but he was not the man to take pleasure which cost another's pain, or profit from another's loss. It was high promotion, gratifying to a soldier's ambition; it was special preferment, for he was junior to Crawford. But he took it all modestly, like the soldier and man he was, thinking more of duty and service than of self."

Then Sheridan rode up again. "Get together all the men you can," he said, "and drive on while you can see your hand before you!"

"The men were widely scattered from the proper commanders," Chamberlain wrote. "Griffin told me to gather the men of the First Division and bring them to the White Oak Road. Riding along the ground of the wide pursuit, I kept my bugler sounding the brigade calls of the division. This brought our officers and men to the left. Among others, General Warren came riding slowly from the right. I took pains to greet him cheerfully, and explained to him why I was sounding all the bugle calls."

"You are doing just right," Warren told him, "but I am no longer in command of the corps."

"That was the first authoritative word I had heard spoken to this effect," Chambelain wrote. "I told him I had heard so, but that General Sheridan had been putting us all in command of everything we could get in hand, and perhaps after the battle was over we would all get back where we belonged. I told him I was now moving forward under Sheridan's and Griffin's order, and rode away from him towards the left with my gathered troops, shadowed in spirit for Warren's sake. I could not be sorry for the corps, nor that Griffin was in command of it—he had the confidence of the whole corps. And however sharp was Griffin's satire, he had the generosity which enables one to be truly just, and never made his subordinates vicarious victims of his own interior irritations."[11]

After leading Pennington's brigade over the Rebels' works near the

Five Forks intersection, Custer took his other two brigades in a move to get around the Confederate right. But there he ran into Rooney Lee's division, which held him off, buying time for Pickett's infantry to get away, until the Federals sweeping westward along the Rebel defenses approached its flank while Warren and Crawford closed in from the rear. "We had now come to the edge of a wide field across the road and the works on the enemy's right, known as the Gilliam field," Chamberlain wrote. "Here I came to Sheridan and Griffin, my troops all up, and well in hand. A sharp cavalry fight was going on, in which some of Ayres' men and my own had taken part. On the right, along the White Oak Road, were portions of Crawford's infantry that had swung around so quickly as to get ahead of us and they were the ones now principally engaged.

"Here Warren took his leave of the corps, himself under a shadow as somber as the scene and with a flash as lurid as the red light of the battle-edge rolling away into the darkness and distance of the deep woods. When our line was checked at this last angle, Griffin had ordered one of Crawford's colonels to advance. The colonel, a brave and well-balanced man, replied that where soldiers as good as Griffin's men had failed, he did not feel warranted in going in without proper orders. 'Very well I order you in!' says Griffin, without adding that he did it as commander of the corps. The gallant colonel bows,—it is Richardson, of the 7th Wisconsin,—grasps his regimental colors in his own hand, significant of the need and his resolution in face of it, and rides forward in advance of his men. What can they do but follow such example? General Warren, with intensity of feeling that is now desperation, snatches his corps flag from the hands of its bearer, and dashes to Richardson's side. And so the two leaders ride, the corps commander and his last visible colonel,—colors aloft, reckless of the growing distance between them and their followers, straight for the smoking line, straight for the flaming edge; not hesitating at the breastworks, over they go....Over the breastworks, down among the astonished foe, one of whom, instinct overmastering admiration, aims at the foremost a deadly blow, which the noble youth rushes forward to parry, and shielding with his own the breast of his uncaring commander, falls to earth, bathing his colors with his blood....One crested wave sweeps on; another, broken, rolls away. All is lost; and all is won. Slowly Warren returns over the somber field. At its forsaken edge a staff officer hands him a crude field order. Partly by the lurid flashes of the last guns, partly by light of the dying day, he reads: 'Major-General Warren, commanding the Fifth Army Corps, is relieved from duty and will at once report for orders to Lieutenant-General Grant, commanding

Armies of the United States. By command of Major-General Sheridan.' With almost the agony of death upon his face, Warren approaches Sheridan and asks him if he cannot reconsider the order."

"Reconsider," Sheridan snorted. "Hell! I don't reconsider my decisions. Obey the order!"[12]

"The sun was low in the western sky," wrote Theodore Gerrish of the 20th Maine, "but there was no rest. Sheridan, like a madman, dashed here and there, urging on his men. The cavalry followed the retreating foe, capturing prisoners by hundreds, while the infantry pressed on after them, and so we soon reached the desired point.... Our bugles sounded the recall, and we were to march back to the battlefield and reform our lines. Slowly we retraced our steps, joyous over the great victory won, but sorrowful over the loss of our brave men."[13]

"After nightfall the corps was drawn in around Five Forks, for a brief respite," Chamberain wrote. "We were all so worn out that our sinking bodies took our spirits with them. We had reasons to rejoice so far as victory gives reasons; but there was a strange weight on the hearts of us all... It was not wholly because Warren had gone, although in the sundering of old ties there is always a strain, and Warren had been part of the best history of the Fifth Corps from the beginning. Even victory is not for itself; it looks to a cause and an end.... We grouped ourselves around Griffin at the Forks, center of the whirling struggle.... Suddenly emerged from the shadows a compact form, with vigorous stride unlike the measure and mood of ours and a voice that would itself have thrilled us had not the import of it thrilled us more."

It was Sheridan. "Gentlemen," he said, as they started to rise, "I have come over to see you. I may have spoken harshly to some of you to-day; but I would not have it hurt you. You know how it is: we had to carry this place, and I was fretted all day till it was done. You must forgive me. I know it is hard for the men, too; but we must push. There is more for us to do together. I appreciate and thank you all."

"And this is Phil Sheridan!" Chamberlain wrote. "A new view of him, surely, and amazing. All the repressed feeling of our hearts sprang out towards him. We were ready to blame ourselves if we had been in any way the cause of his trouble. But we thought we had borne a better part than that. We had had a taste of his style of fighting, and we liked it.... We went at things with dogged resolution; not much show; not much flare; not much accompaniment of brass instruments. But we could give credit to more brilliant things. We could see how this voice and vision, this swing and color, this vivid impression on the senses, carried the pulse and will of men.... We had a habit, perhaps, drawn from dire experience, and for which we had also Grant's quite recent sanction, when we had carried a vital point or had to hold one, to entrench. But Sheridan does not entrench. He pushes on, carrying his flank and rear with him,—rushing, flashing, smashing. He transfuses into his subordinates the vitality and energy of his purpose; transforms them into part of his own mind and will. He shows the power of a commander,—inspiring both confidence and fear."[14]

"Sheridan had that day fought one of the most interesting tactical battles of the war," Horace Porter wrote, "admirable in conception, brilliant in execution, strikingly dramatic in its incidents, and productive of immensely important results.

"I said to him: 'It seems to me that you have exposed yourself to-day in a manner hardly justifiable on the part of a commander of such an important movement.' His reply gave what seems to be the true key to his uniform success on the field: 'I have never in my life taken a command into battle, and had the slightest desire to come out alive unless I won.' "About half-past seven o'clock I started for general headquarters. The roads in many places were corduroyed with captured muskets; ammunition-trains and ambulances were still struggling forward; teamsters, prisoners, stragglers, and wounded were choking the roadway; the 'coffee-boilers' had kindled their fires in the woods; cheers were resounding on all sides, and everybody was riotous over the victory. A horseman had to pick his way through this jubilant condition of things as best he could, as he did not have a clear right of way by any means. As I galloped past a group of men on the Boydton plank-road, my orderly called out to them the news of the victory. The only response he got was from one of them, who raised his open hand to his face, put his thumb to his nose, and yelled: 'No, you don't—April fool!' I then realized that it was the 1st of April. I had ridden so rapidly that I reached headquarters at Dabney's Mill before the arrival of the last courier I had despatched. General Grant was sitting, with most of the staff about him, before a blazing camp-fire. He wore his blue cavalry overcoat, and the ever-present cigar was in his mouth. I began shouting the good news as soon as I got in sight, and in a moment all but the imperturbable general-in-chief were on their feet giving vent to boisterous demonstrations of joy. For some minutes there was a bewildering state of excitement, and officers fell to grasping hands, shouting, and hugging each other like school-boys. The news meant the beginning of the end, the reaching of the 'last ditch.' It pointed to peace and home. Dignity was thrown to the winds, and every man at that moment was in a fitting mood to dig his elbows into the ribs of the Archbishop of Canterbury, or to challenge the Chief Justice of the

Supreme Court to a game of leap-frog. The proprieties of army etiquette were so far forgotten in the enthusiasm of the occasion that as soon as I had thrown myself from my horse I found myself rushing up to the general-in-chief and clapping him on the back with my hand, to his no little astonishment, and to the evident amusement of those about him. The general, as might have been expected; asked his usual question: 'How many prisoners have been taken?' I was happy to report that the prisoners this time were estimated at over five thousand, and this was the only part of my recital that seemed to call forth a responsive expression from his impassive features. After having listened attentively to the description of Sheridan's day's work, the general, with scarcely a word of comment, walked into his tent, and by the light of a flickering candle took up his 'manifold writer,' and after finishing several despatches handed them to an orderly to be sent over the field wires, came out and joined our group at the camp-fire, and said as coolly as if remarkingpon the state of the weather: 'I have ordered a general assault along the lines.'"[15]

---

1. Chamberlain, *The Passing of the Armies*, 92-93.
2. Porter, *Campaigning with Grant*, 436.
3. Chamberlain, *The Passing of the Armies*, 93-98.
4. Porter, *Campaigning with Grant*, 437-440.
5. Wainwright, Charles S., *A Diary of Battle: The Personal Journals of Colonel Charles S. Wainwright*, 1861-1865 (New York, 1962), 512.
6. Chamberlain, *The Passing of the Armies*, 98-104.
7. Wheeler, *Witness to Appomattox*, 73-76.
8. Freeman, *Lee's Lieutenants*, 3:669.
9. Chamberlain, *The Passing of the Armies*, 104-109.
10. Urwin, *Custer Victorious*, 241.
11. Chamberlain, *The Passing of the Armies*, 109-112.
12. Ibid., 112-114.
13. Wheeler, *Witness to Appomattox*, 78.
14. Chamberlain, *The Passing of the Armies*, 114-116.
15. Porter, *Campaigning with Grant*, 441-443.

CHAPTER TWENTY-SEVEN

I Should Have the Game Entirely in My Hands

1 - 2 April 1865

Halfway around the world from Southside Virginia, at Ponape in the Caroline Island in the middle of the wide Pacific Ocean, the CSS *Shenandoah* took four Yankee whalers on 1 April. And the Rebel sailors captured charts from these ships that marked the traditional American whaling grounds. "With such charts in my possession," her captain wrote, "I not only held a key to the navigation of all the Pacific Islands, the Okhotsk and Bering Seas, and the Arctic Ocean, but the most probable localities for finding the great Arctic whaling fleet of New England, without a tiresome search."[1]

A small team of Confederates, including an explosives expert named Thomas F. Harney, left Richmond that day with orders for Mosby to smuggle them into Washington. Their mission was evidently nothing less than to blow up the White House.

That same day, Lieutenant Ben Stringfellow (the Rebel scout who had proposed to kidnap Grant but had been sent to Washington instead) left the Union capital, heading down through southern Maryland. "Leaving the City of Washington," as he wrote to Jefferson Davis after the war, "by the aid of a person whose name is linked in the history of these last dark days...." Stringfellow had been staying at the Kirkwood House, where Vice President Johnson lived, and he told Davis he had been "in constant communication with an officer occupying an important position about Mr. Lincoln." He added that he made this officer a "proposition." He told Davis that he "went some twelve miles the first evening."[2] That was almost exactly the distance from downtown Washington to the Surratt tavern in Prince George's County, Maryland. John Wilkes Booth left the capital that same day, taking the afternoon train for New York. He told George Atzerodt that he was on his way to Canada. John Surratt also left for Canada that day, from Richmond, serving as a courier for Confederate Secretary of State Benjamin.

Down in Alabama on the first day of April, Wilson's Union cavalry captured a Confederate courier carrying dispatches from Forrest. By this means he learned that Jackson's Division of Forrest's Rebel cavalry had turned back toward Tuscaloosa to chase Croxton's Union brigade that had appeared in its rear and therefore had not yet crossed the Cahaba River. He also learned that Chalmers' Confederate division was at least twenty miles south of the rest of Forrest's corps. Wilson thus knew, as he later wrote, "if I would force the marching and the fighting with sufficient rapidity and vigor, I should have the game entirely in my hands."[3]

First, he sent Brigadier General Edward McCook, Croxton's division commander, to attack Jackson's rear with his other brigade, Colonel Oscar H. LaGrange's 2nd, and to link up with Croxton. Part of the 1st Wisconsin cavalry was sent racing ahead to seize the bridge over the Cahaba at Centerville. It covered the fifteen miles in two hours, captured fifteen men from a small Rebel force guarding the crossing, routed the rest, and blockaded the Tuscaloosa Road on the north side of the bridge. By noon, McCook had arrived with the rest of his brigade.

He left a small force to guard the bridge and rode on to Scottsville, where he bivouacked for the night. Meanwhile, Jackson pursued Croxton northward along the Mud Creek Road until he learned that other Union troops had captured the bridge at Centerville, toward which he had been marching until Croxton had appeared behind him. Then he broke off the pursuit and turned back toward Centerville. That night, some of his men, foraging through the woods around Scottsville, ran into some of McCook's Federals who were on a similar mission. The two sides agreed "to a truce while they shared such good things as the farmer had to contribute."[4] Croxton's brigade wound up that night at Johnson's Ferry, on the Black Warrior River forty miles north of Tuscaloosa. After consulting with the commanders of his four regiments about their next move, Croxton decided to cross the river and turn south on the other side for a surprise attack on Tuscaloosa from an unexpected direction.

Having sent McCook to secure his flank and rear, Wilson felt that "it remained only to hurl my two splendid divisions with all possible speed against the enemy in my front, which I knew they outnumbered."[5] At daylight his main column took the road south again. Brigadier General Eli Long's 2nd Division followed the main road toward Randolph, while Upton's 4th Division moved a few miles farther east to Maplesville before turning to the southwest to rejoin Long's route. Wilson's escort, the 4th U.S. Cavalry, was detailed to destroy all bridges on the Alabama & Tennessee River Railroad, which paralleled Long's line of march.

After pushing a Rebel delaying force ahead of it all day, by 4 p.m. Long's column had encountered skirmishers covering Forrest's main force, which was drawn up behind hastily built breastworks of fence rails and dirt near Ebenezer Church. Here Adams' state troops held the Confederate right, which was anchored on Mulberry Creek, Roddey's Alabama cavalry held the center, and Crossland's Kentuckian's held the left, on a wooded ridge. Four batteries covered the roads leading in from Randolph and Maplesville. Chalmer's Division had taken a wrong road before Forrest could get it straightened out, and only part of Brigadier General Frank Armstrong's brigade had arrived that afternoon.

Long took the Rebel skirmishers to be just one more delaying force, and while his advance guard, the 72nd Indiana Mounted Infantry, laid down a covering fire with their repeating carbines, he sent four mounted companies of the 17th Indiana Mounted Infantry forward in a saber-swinging charge. The Hoosiers chased the skirmishers into the main line and captured and disabled one cannon there but soon found themselves involved in a furious hand-to-hand melee with a large

Confederate force. Captain James D. Taylor found himself up against Forrest himself and managed to wound the Rebel general with his saber before the latter killed him with his revolver. "If that boy had known enough to give me the point of his saber instead of the edge," Forrest later told Wilson, "I should not have been here to tell you about it."[6]

The surviving Federals retreated, but Long sent the rest of Colonel Abram Miller's Lightning Brigade forward dismounted to probe the Confederate position, and soon Upton's leading brigade rode up on the Maplesville road, attracted by the sound of firing. It too was sent forward dismounted, and it struck the Rebel right, where Adams' state troops gave way. Upton then sent in the 3rd and 4th Iowa from his other brigade in a mounted charge, and the entire Confederate right fell apart. The center and left were forced to retreat or be surrounded, and Forrest's entire force fled across Bogler's Creek and on to Selma. Three hundred Rebels and three of their guns were captured.

After his twelve dead had been buried and his 58 wounded cared for, Wilson moved on to Plantersville, camping that night amid the plenty of Alabama's fertile black belt. There a cotton warehouse and railroad depot were burned.

Farther south, the Union siege of Spanish Fort, on the eastern approaches to Mobile, continued. "Every day was full of incident," one Confederate defender said, "and it soon got so that we had no rest day or night....Artillery duels became of daily occurence, our 'head logs' were constantly knocked down upon us, bruising and crippling us; squads of sharpshooters devoted their especial attention to our port holes or embrasures and poured a steady stream of bullets through them from early morn till dewy eve."[7]

General Steele's Union column from Pensacola, after feinting toward Montgomery and then suddenly turning west, approached another key component of the defenses of Mobile that day, Fort Blakely. A 100-man Confederate outpost of the 46th Mississippi was the first to see the Federals' advance guard of two regiments of cavalry. They watched as one regiment dismounted and closed in on foot, backed up by the other regiment, still mounted and with sabers drawn. The Rebels fell back slowly for over a mile, taking advantage of every obstruction to make a brief stand, until suddenly the mounted regiment charged and routed them. Three officers, 71 men, and the regimental battleflag were captured, and the few remaining Confederates were pursued almost to the trenches of Fort Blakely before rifle and artillery fire from the defenses turned the Federals back.

The Confederate commander at Blakely, Brigadier General St. John

R. Liddell, expected Steele to try to storm his defenses that very day, but when no attack developed, he sent out skirmishers to try to drive in the Union cavalry pickets the next morning, the second. Brigadier General John P. Hawkins, commander of the 1st Division, U.S. Colored Troops, promptly formed his men into line of battle with a strong line of skirmishers out front, and drove the Rebels back into their entrenchments. Then, at a distance of about half a mile from the Confederate defenses, the Federals began to dig in. Soon Steele's other division came up on Hawkin's left and also began entrenching. And so began the siege of another Rebel fort.

Up at Scottsville on the morning of the second, McCook sent the 4th Indiana Cavalry Regiment and the 2nd Indiana Cavalry Battalion up the road toward Tuscaloosa, but about four miles out of Scottsville these Hoosiers ran into Brigadier General Tyree Bell's brigade of Jackson's Confederate division, behind a barricade. The Federals charged, but Bell's Tennesseans had a strong position and easily repulsed them. McCook realized that he could not push an entire division out of the way to link up with Croxton, so he abandoned Scottsville and retired across the Cahaba River, destroying the bridge behind him, as well as all boats found along the river, leaving Jackson cut off from Forrest.

Meanwhile, Croxton's brigade spent the night and morning ferrying across the Black Warrior River on a flatboat and a "few miserable dugouts." It was, a trooper in the 2nd Michigan Cavalry said, a "very hazardous undertaking but very laborious and exciting."[8] Croxton let his men rest that afternoon and night and planned to move south toward Tuscaloosa early on the third.

At 6 a.m. on 2 April, Wilson's main column broke camp and headed down the road toward Selma, only nineteen miles to the south. Selma was one of the few industrial cities of the South, a beautiful town with broad streets lying on the north bank of the Alabama River. One Union soldier called it "a place of great wealth."[9] Selma, along with Richmond, Virginia, and Columbus, Georgia, was among the Confederacy's few remaining cities capable of producing the armaments needed to keep its armies supplied. Approximately 10,000 workers, black and white, male and female, were employed in Selma's factories. During the final two years of the war, half of the cannon and two-thirds of the fixed ammunition used by the Rebel armies came from the Selma area. It also produced knapsacks, uniforms, swords, bayonets, shovels, and gear for wagons and horses, and it was a production and repair center for locomotives and railroad cars. The Confederate Subsistence Department headquartered in the area gathered meat, grain, and fodder from throughout the fertile black-soil region of Alabama and shipped it to Rebel forces throughout the Confederacy by way of the Alabama River and the two railroads that connected the city with the rest of the South.

In 1863 Confederate authorities had used slave labor to construct a semicircle of defenses around Selma, with the Alabama River covering the southern approaches. West, east, and northeast of the city the defenses consisted only of rifle pits, but these areas were also covered by creeks that flowed into the river on each side of town. The works facing the north and northwest consisted of parapets from six to eight feet tall and eight feet thick at their base, with a ditch in front that was five feet wide and five feet deep. But this three-and-one-half-mile circuit of works was too extensive for Forrest's small command to man adequately, so as soon as he arrived that morning the Confederate general ordered a second, shorter, line to be constructed closer to the city. Chalmers had still not arrived with his other brigade, and of course Jackson was still beyond the Cahaba and blocked by McCook. Large numbers of civilians were pressed into hastily formed local defense battalions and armed with whatever weapons came to hand, but they would be of little value against Wilson's well-armed veteran troopers.

Wilson's scouts approached the city at 2 p.m. on that beautiful spring Sunday and got their first look at the city, where, as one of them said, the sun was "dancing in diamond flashes on the distant river winding away to the south-west. Bodies of troops in motion, with clouds of dust pierced by flashes of light from glistening bayonets, indicating the state of busy preparation within the works."[10] By 3 p.m. Long's 2nd Division had arrived. A few miles north of Selma it had swung to the west and now approached the city along the Summerfield Road that led to the northwestern face of the defenses. The night before, an Englishman named Millington, who had helped to build the earthworks, had voluntarily surrendered to the Federals and had drawn a sketch of the defenses for his captors. Wilson had decided to feint with Long's division on the Summerfield Road and then to make the real attack with part of Upton's division just west of where the road from Plantersville entered the works, while the rest of his division demonstrated east of the road.

Long sent a dismounted skirmish line forward to engage the Confederate pickets in his front while he formed the rest of his force in a single dismounted line of battle behind a low ridge that shielded it from view. Two regiments were detached to protect the rear of his division, and his battery of horse artillery unlimbered just east of the Summerfield Road and began to exchange shots with the Confederate defenders while the dismounted cavalrymen lay down to await the signal to advance. Veterans among Long's troopers said that Selma's defenses looked more formidable than those encountered at Vicksburg and Atlanta. Forrest, Armstrong, and several other Rebel officers watched the artillery duel and all of them thought that it would be all the fighting that would take place that day. "None...thought the enemy would assault the works," a Confederate officer wrote, "exposed as they would be on the open field for some hundreds of yards."[11]

At about 4 p.m. Upton's 4th Division arrived and he dismounted his two leading regiments in the cover of some trees and deployed them on both sides of the road. The rest of his troops, except for a detachment sent to block the road leading eastward out of the city, remained in column and were allowed to make coffee and rest while waiting for the signal to attack. Wilson, after checking the accuracy of Millington's map of the defenses as best he could by long-range personal reconnaissance, found no reason to change his plan. He notified his commanders that the signal to charge would be the firing of a single cannon from Upton's battery just after dark. However, this plan, like most, did not long survive contact with the enemy. While the Federals were waiting for darkness to fall, the two regiments that were guarding the rear of Long's division were attacked by a small force of Rebels—part of the long-lost remainder of Chalmers' Division. The attack was beaten off, and a countercharge routed the Confederates, but Long decided on his own initiative that he could not afford to put off his attack on the defenses any longer, for fear that more Rebels would soon attack his rear again.

When the order was given, about 1,500 dismounted troopers in Long's main line slowly moved forward over the crest of the slight ridge that had been sheltering them toward the formidable line of defenses some 600 yards away across an open field. Confederate artillery and rifle fire took its toll as the troopers advanced, at times enfilading their entire line. The Federals fired their Spencers as they marched steadily forward until within 150 yards of the works, when the command to charge was given, and with a cheer they started for the works on a run, sweeping forward in a solid line over fences, ravines, and a 5-foot stockade, and charged up the smoke-enshrouded parapet. An eerie quiet suddenly descended as the defenders held their fire waiting for the first attackers to reach the top. Their volley soon ended the brief silence but failed to stop the onrushing Federals, and after a short, violent melee, the Rebels retreated toward the city in great disorder. "I doubt," Wilson wrote in his official report, "if the history of this or any other war will show another instance in which a line of works as strongly constructed and as well defended as this by musketry and artillery has been stormed and carried by a single line of men without support."[12]

Union fire from the captured portion of the defenses then enfiladed the rest of the Confederate line, and the entire Rebel force soon fell back to the cover of some heavy timber behind the breastworks. But Long's troopers again advanced, and the Confederates fell back to the partially completed inner line in what the Columbus, Georgia, *Daily Sun* called "a disgraceful stampede." Lieutenant Colonel Frank Montgomery of the 1st Mississippi Cavalry was captured, along with many of his men. The Union sergeant who captured him demanded not only the Rebel's sidearm but his wallet as well, but he returned the latter when he discovered that it contained only Confederate money. "This," said Montgomery, "was the 'unkindest cut of all.'"[13]

The ground outside the Rebel works was covered with dead and wounded Federal troopers, and many of the senior Union officers, who led their men on horseback, had been hit. Long himself had been wounded in the head and was unable to speak or think clearly for two weeks. The commander of his 1st Brigade, Colonel Abram Miller, was hit in the leg, as was the colonel of the 7th Pennsylvania. The commander of the 4th Ohio was killed, and the commander of the 123rd Illinois Mounted Infantry was severely wounded in the chest. Colonel Robert Minty, commander of the 2nd Brigade, succeeded to command of the division.

Wilson rode forward and helped get the 2nd Division reorganized after its loss of so many senior officers. With him came that division's battery of artillery, which deployed inside the outer defenses, and his escort regiment, the 4th U.S. He sent orders for Upton to charge as well, but Upton had seen Long's assault himself and had already ordered his two dismounted regiments to advance. As they went forward several officers galloped up. "Go in boys, give them hell, we have the city, we are all right, give them hell," one of them yelled. "From that moment," an officer in one of the regiments wrote, "there was no holding back. The men picked up the double quick."[14] The defenses in their front were only lightly held, and they easily seized those works.

Wilson now decided that it was taking too long to get the 2nd Division ready for another advance, so, hoping that a quick strike at Forrest's inner line would catch the Rebels before they were ready, he led the 4th U.S. forward alone in a saber-swinging mounted charge. One of the dismounted troopers of the 2nd Division thought the charging regulars "looked grand" as they thundered past, but a sergeant in the 4th thought that sabers were rather useless against an enemy "firing furiously into our column from behind the embankment."[15] Wilson's horse was shot out from under him, and the charge was repulsed. So he brought up two regiments from the 2nd Division to reinforce his escort and tried again as darkness fell. Dismounted this time, and with a shout, the Federals went right over the center of the inner line, and the Rebels broke and ran. Those on the flanks and in support soon joined the rout.

Upton's division pursued the Confederates right into the city and captured many of them, especially from the militia, along with 31 field pieces and a 30-pounder Parrott rifle. But Adams, Armstrong, and Roddey, with small remnants of their brigades, and Forrest with his escort company, cut their way out in the confusion and darkness. Part of Upton's division pursued them and captured many prisoners and four guns. Some Rebels tried to escape by swimming across the Alabama River. A few were successful, while others drowned. All together, Wilson captured some 2,700 Rebels at Selma, probably about half of the Confederate soldiers present. They were confined in a stockade that had once held Union prisoners, who had been forced to build it in the first place. At the huge arsenal on the river bank the Federals found 15 siege guns, 10 carriages for heavy guns, 10 field pieces, 60 field carriages, 10 caissons, 60,000 rounds of artillery ammunition, and a million rounds of small arms ammunition. At the nearby naval foundry they found 29 unfinished siege guns and the machinery to produce many more. The Confederates had also thrown several cannon in the river as the Federals approached. Wilson lost 46 men killed, about 300 wounded, and 13 missing.

The Confederates had set fire to the Central Commercial Warehouse, and this blaze spread to at least one adjacent business. Altogether they burned 35,000 bales of cotton to keep it from falling into Federal hands. The fire, possibly helped along by either Union or Rebel incendiaries, spread during the night and burned down two blocks of one street and three of another. Among the buildings burned were the Episcopal church, several businesses, and quite a few homes.

"Of all the nights of my experience," one of Wilson's men wrote, "this is the most like the horrors of war—a captured city burning at night, a victorious army advancing, and a demoralized one retreating."[16] Far to the northeast, similar scenes were enacted that night at Petersburg and Richmond.

---

1. William M. Fowler, Jr., *Under Two Flags: The American Navy in the Civil War* (New York, 1990), 296.

2. Tidwell, Hall and Gady, *Come Retribution*, 412.
3. Jones, *Yankee Blitzkrieg*, 67.
4. Ibid., 68.
5. Ibid., 70.
6. Henry, *"First with the Most" Forrest*, 431.
7. Bergeron, *Confederate Mobile*, 178.
8. Jones, *Yankee Blitzkrieg*, 146-147.
9. Ibid., 75.
9. Ibid., 83-84.
10. Ibid., 86.
11. *Official Records*, 49:I:361.
12. Jones, *Yankee Blitzkrieg*, 87.
13. Ibid., 88-89.
14. Ibid., 89.
15. Ibid., 95.

CHAPTER TWENTY-EIGHT

Your Last Chance for a Fight

1 - 2 April 1865

The chief of the *New York Herald's* newsmen at Petersburg was Sylvanus Cadwallader, who had attached himself to Grant's headquarters. After Horace Porter brought word of Sheridan's success at Five Forks, Grant asked Cadwallader to take the news and some captured Rebel flags to City Point. Mrs. Lincoln was on her way back to Washington, but the president had stayed on. By the time Cadwallader got there over the crowded, muddy roads, Lincoln had gone to bed, but he got up to see the reporter, hear his news, and look at the flags.

"Here is something material—something I can see, feel, and understand," the president said. "This means victory. This *is* victory."

Soon the sound of artillery fire could be heard all along the front, and the president knew a full-scale assault would follow by dawn. "Mr. Lincoln would not go to his room," his bodyguard, William Crook, remembered. "Almost all night he walked up and down the deck, pausing now and then to listen or to look out into the darkness to see if he could see anything. I have never seen such suffering in the face of any man as was in his that night."[1]

"Grant was anxious to have the different commands move against the enemy's lines at once," Horace Porter wrote, "to prevent Lee from withdrawing troops and sending them against Sheridan. Meade was all activity, and so alive to the situation, and so anxious to carry out the orders of the general-in-chief, that he sent word that he was going to have the troops make a dash at the works without waiting to form assaulting columns. Grant at 9:30 p.m. sent a message that he did not mean to have the corps attack without assaulting columns, but to let the batteries open at once, and to feel out with skirmishers, and if the enemy was found to be leaving to let the troops attack in their own way."[2]

Major General John Parke, commander of the 9th Corps, had been ready to attack the Confederate defenses in his front ever since the night of March 30, when Meade had told him to attack at 4 a.m. on the 31st. But that attack had been called off. Parke had decided to make the attack, as soon as authorized, in the sector between Fort Sedgwick, on the Union line, and Fort Mahone, on the Confederate line—known colloquially by the troops as Fort Hell and Fort Damnation. But as soon as the order came down from Meade, one of Parke's brigade commanders, thinking that an immediate attack all along the line was intended, rushed the Rebel picket line between forts Hays and Howard, capturing 8 officers and 241 enlisted men. The Federals also started bombarding the Confederate main line with all their artillery. One Union soldier recorded the result: "About ten o'clock on the ever-to-be-remembered Saturday night, the 1st of April, 1865, a tremendous fire is opened all along the lines. It seems as though bedlam was let loose, and such was the fact, for Fort Hell opened with her neighboring forts and poured the shot and shell into the enemy's lines as quick as Uncle Sam's powder monkeys could load and fire."[3]

When Grant's order was passed on to Major General Horatio Wright, commander of the 6th Corps, he told his chief of artillery "to open fire on the enemy's lines with all the batteries."[4] The firing quickly spread along the lines of both armies, and the infantry soon added rifle fire to the bombardment. "The noise was terrific," Lieutenant Colonel Elisha Hunt Rhodes in the 6th Corps wrote, "and the shriek of the shot and shell gave us an idea of what we might expect in the morning."[5] The sound and fury were too much for a West Virginia soldier in Gibbon's 24th Corps who "became a raving maniac on the instant," as another Federal wrote, "from the great and unexpected shock to his nervous system caused by the tremendous and sudden roar of cannon and outpour of musketry on that memorable morning."[6]

A Confederate officer stationed far out on the western end of Lee's defenses recorded his impressions: "The night was extremely dark and still, so that we could see the flashes of musketry for a great distance, and could hear the roar that rang along the line for miles....Several miles on our left, and rather more than halfway to Petersburg, the volleys of musketry were furiously fast and concentrated. They were not continuous like our own slow fire, but they would break out in an instant, with a fierce roar of small arms accompanied by a rapid discharge of artillery, then melt away almost to a complete calm, then reopen with the former violence."[7] He and his fellow veterans were convinced by what they could hear and see that the Yankees were charging the Rebel lines farther east, but that was not to come until morning.

"The corps commanders reported that it would be impracticable to make a successful assault until morning," Horace Porter wrote, "but sent back replies full of enthusiasm, and having in them a ring of the true soldierly metal. Ord said he would go into the enemy's works 'as a hot knife goes into butter.' Wright sent word that when he started in he would 'make the fur fly,' and said: 'If the corps does half as well as I expect, we will have broken through the rebel lines in fifteen minutes from the word "go."' Grant was highly pleased with the spirit evinced in these messages, and said: 'I like the way Wright talks; it argues success. I heartily approve.' The hour for the general assault was fixed at four o'clock the next morning. Miles was ordered to march with his division at midnight to reinforce Sheridan and enable him to make a stand against Lee in case he should move westward in the night. A little after midnight the general tucked himself into his camp-bed, and was soon sleeping as peacefully as if the next day was to be devoted to a picnic instead of a decisive battle."[8]

Lee, meanwhile, when he learned that Pickett had been defeated, pulled Bushrod Johnson's two remaining brigades, and Hunton's Brigade of Pickett's Division, out of the defenses and sent them under Anderson and Johnson to cover the Southside Railroad by moving north of Hatcher's Run before turning to the west to Church Crossing. One regiment and a battalion of sharpshooters from the 3rd Corps were sent to hold Johnson's old line during the night. Lee also sent orders for a brigade to be sent south from Major General William Mahone's division of the 3rd Corps, holding the defenses across the Bermuda Hundred peninsula between Petersburg and Richmond and for Longstreet to bring Major General Charles Field's Division of his 1st Corps from north of the James. Longstreet arranged for it to be transported on the railroad that connected Richmond with Petersburg. Then he and his staff started riding south so as to join his troops on the south side without taking up space on the trains needed for the men. Longstreet's departure left Lieutenant General Richard Ewell, commander of the Department of Richmond, in charge of all Confederate troops north of the James. Ewell sent officers to call out the local reserves, composed of soldiers and civilians who worked for the various goverment agencies in Richmond, to take the place of Field's veterans.

Earlier, when Grant had learned that Sheridan was about to attack Pickett at Five Forks, he had ordered Miles' 1st Division of the 2nd Corps to advance and block the White Oak Road so that Lee could not use it to send troops to help Pickett or attack Sheridan's rear. After he had learned of Sheridan's success, Grant had ordered Humphreys to feel for a vulnerable point in the Rebel defenses in his front but if none was found by midnight he was to send Miles' division to reinforce Sheridan. Humphreys drove in the Confederate pickets but felt that the main line was too strongly held, so shortly after midnight Miles' division marched west along the White Oak Road to join Sheridan. It arrived at around 1 a.m., only to find that it was not particularly needed. Miles let his weary men catch a few hours of rest.

At about that same hour, the artillery duel along the main front east and southeast of Petersburg died down, and the troops of the 6th and 9th corps began to quietly form up under cover of the darkness for the 4 a.m. assault. On the 9th Corps front, Hartranft's 3rd Division took position along the right side of the Jerusalem Plank Road, facing northwest, in front of Fort Sedgwick (Fort Hell). Brevet Major General Robert B. Potter's 2nd Division formed on the left of the road, and Colonel Samuel Harriman's 1st Brigade of Willcox's 1st Division took position on Hartranft's right. Willcox's other two brigades were left to hold the corps' defenses. In the 6th Corps sector, Wright formed his troops into a huge wedge. Brevet Major General George W. Getty's 2nd Division formed the center of the wedge, with Brigadier General Lewis A. Grant's crack Vermont Brigade at the point. Brevet Major General Frank Wheaton's 1st Division took position to the right and rear of Getty, and Brigadier General Truman Seymour's 3rd Division formed on Getty's left rear. All three divisions were accompanied by pioneers with axes for hacking paths through the obstructions in the front of the Confederate defenses.

The men left their knapsacks behind and arranged their canteens so that they would not bump against their bayonet scabbards and make noise. "In the dark and damp of the early morning," one of Wright's men remembered, "the powder smoke which hung like huge clouds near the ground deepened the obscurity and made our movements somewhat slow." One of Seymour's brigade commanders said, "The night added to the solemnity of the preparation for the bloody work." As soon as the men were in their proper places they were allowed to lie down.

Rebel pickets soon realized that something was going on out there in the darkness but were not aware of the magnitude of it. Some of them opened fire, but the Federals were under orders not to shoot back. "Every once in a while some one would get hit with a ball," one Federal remembered, "and we could hear his cry of anguish as the lead tore through." One of those hit was General Lewis Grant, who was wounded. "This was a tough place to stay," a Union soldier wrote, "with nothing to do but lie there and take our medicine." Some Federals could not resist the urge to return fire, but Union officers got their men under control before the Confederates realized how many of them there were out there, and as the Federals stopped firing, so did the Rebels. "The silence of the men became painful and almost unendurable," a Pennsylvanian remembered. "Would that signal gun never sound! Would daylight never come!" an officer wrote.[9]

There was still no daylight when 4 a.m. finally came, but Willcox's two brigades holding the 9th Corps lines began a noisy demonstration at that hour to divert Confederate attention from the sector the rest of the corps would soon attack. The artillery of both sides stirred to life again. "From countless muzzles on either side," a Union gunner wrote, "there seemed to flow a constant stream of living fire as the shells, with burning fuzes, screamed and hissed through the night in a semicircle of lurid flame." An infantryman gave a less elaborate description. "The deafening roar and crash were simply appalling," he said.

At 4:30 a.m. dawn was just breaking and, as one witness said, "a considerable mist hung over the fields, so that objects were quite indistinct at a very short distance and not visible at all a few hundred yards away." The cry "Forward" finally rippled through the regiments massed for the 9th Corps' attack. "Go in, boys. It's your last chance for a fight," Colonel Harriman shouted. "We raised as one man and rushed towards the rebel works," a Federal wrote.[10]

The men surged over their own picket line and then the Confederate picket line and right up to the entanglements in front of the main Rebel defenses. A Union sergeant in Hartranft's division saw the primer flash on a Confederate cannon in front of him and he hit the dirt. He said the "air was full of cannister" and he "could hear the thud as it hit men, their cries of agony, curses and cheers, and by the flash of bursting mortar shells could see men falling all about in the rear; then the roll of musketry from the main line of works." But Union sharpshooters soon pinned down the Rebel gunners while the pioneers cut openings through the obstacles, and then Hartranft's men swarmed through, up over the breastworks, and captured Battery No. 27 on the Confederate line. To their right, Harriman's brigade clawed its way up the parapet of Battery No. 25, where Rebel artillerymen were hurriedly reloading their guns. "If you discharge that piece," a Union captain shouted to one Confederate, "you are a dead Johnny."[11] The Rebel surrendered, and that fort, too, was captured.

On the left, Brigadier General Simon Griffin's 2nd Brigade of Potter's division had to get across a water-filled ditch in front of Battery No. 28, and "some of the men," one of them wrote, "fell in as they rushed ahead to climb the high, slanting ascent and were unable to get out and were drowned." But most of Griffin's men scrambled up the parapet, clubbed the defenders with their rifle butts, and turned the Confederate cannon against their former owners. Potter's other brigade, Brevet Brigadier General John Curtin's 1st, veered farther to the left, heading straight for Fort Mahone (Fort Damnation). Curtin's men swept away the Confederate pickets and crossed the ditch, heedless of the Rebel fire. Small portions of the 39th New Jersey twice fought their way into the three-sided earthwork, only to be driven out by heavy fire from the Confederate inner lines, a few hundred yards away. On the third try they gained a foothold, but the Rebels on the 9th Corps front, belonging to John Gordon's 2nd Corps of Lee's army, were recovering from the initial surprise and shock of the attack and blocked all Union attempts to widen the breach they had made. From both flanks, as well as from an inner line of defenses, they put up a stubborn resistance. "The fighting here was most stubborn and desperate," one Confederate remembered, "being at close range, almost hand to hand."[12] Parke had captured a 400-yard stretch of the Rebels' main line and 12 guns, but there was a second line behind that, and he could make no further progress.

To the left of the 9th Corps, Wright waited until 4:40 a.m.—ten minutes longer than Parke—before giving the order to fire the gun signaling the 6th Corps' attack. No one in the Vermont Brigade, at the point of the corps' wedge formation, heard the signal, however, because of the heavy firing already going on in the 9th Corps sector. The order had to be passed to it by other means. "While waiting for the signal," wrote Lieutenant Colonel Elisha Hunt Rhodes, "a mule belonging to the Brigade Pioneer Corps and loaded with picks and shovels broke loose and made for the front. The entrenching tools rattled at such a rate that the Rebels thought that something was up and opened a terrible fire. But for this accident I think the surprise would have been complete. When the signal sounded the entire Corps, notwithstanding the orders to keep silent, sent up a mighty cheer and then dashed forward into the fog."[13]

There was more than one reason for yelling at a time like this. It could do wonders for the men's morale. "When I started on that charge," one Union soldier remembered, "I was not feeling very well; there was something the matter with my throat. I thought my heart would jump clear out of my mouth. The boys were yelling and charging all around me. I think I went more than half way across before I yelled, and then I felt so much better that I was sorry I had not yelled when I started. I was much surprised at the great change in my feelings. After that whoop I think I could have tackled the whole so-called Southern Confederacy."[14]

The Vermont Brigade, as one of its officers said, "immediately moved forward over the works of the skirmish line and pressed on steadily and silently until they had very nearly reached the first line of the enemy's intrenchments, when they were discovered by their skirmishers, who delivered a weak and scattering volley and then fled." Another member of the brigade described what happened when the Vermonters reached the obstacles in front of the main Confederate line: "Their works were impregnable with big ditches and staked, but they had a small opening through where their pickets passed out and into their front. We broke through this little roadway, driving the rebels before us, and then commenced a run for our lives."[15]

Echeloned behind and to the right of the Vermont Brigade was Colonel Thomas Hyde's 2nd Brigade of Getty's 2nd Division. "I remember ordering a lot of rebels to the rear as we crossed their picket pits," Hyde remembered, "for then the black darkness was becoming gray in the coming dawn, and the shot and shell from the enemy's forts were like so many rockets fired horizontally, and they were mostly a few feet over our heads." Behind and to the right of Hyde came Colonel James Warner's 1st Brigade. Its first two regiments bogged down in front of the main Confederate line, but the 93rd Pennsylvania, divided into two battalions, passed on through them. "The first Battalion of the Regiment reached the abatis," one Pennsylvanian said, "and in an instant the second Battalion was mixed up with it and assisted in the work of making an opening through the abatis, and with a cheer leaped over the breastworks."[16]

To the right rear of Getty's division came Wheaton's 1st Division, with Colonel Oliver Edwards' 3rd Brigade in the lead. Lieutenant Colonel Elisha Hunt Rhodes' 2nd Rhode Island Volunteer Regiment was in that brigade's second line, but, as Rhodes wrote, "I could not see my position very well and so moved to the right. The 2nd R.I. Vols. first struck the Rebel picket line who fired in our faces, and we went over them without firing a shot. In fact as my men had no caps on their guns we could not fire.... The Rebels in the rifle pits threw down their guns and surrendered. They shouted, 'Don't fire, Yanks!' and I ordered them to go to the rear, which they did on the run. I hastily reformed my line in the rifle pits when Corporal Maurice O. Hearn called for 'Three cheers for Colonel Rhodes!' and they were given before I could interfere. The cheering gave the enemy an idea of our position, and they opened four guns from a redoubt on my left and two guns from one on my right. I shouted 'Forward!' and on we went in between the two redoubts. As we struck the enemy's abatis I happened to be on the right flank of the Regiment, and discovering an opening left for wagons to go through the wood I gave the proper commands which caused the Regiment to go through by the flank and then come into line in front of the two gun Batteries. The first I knew I fell into the ditch with a number of my men after me. The Rebels fired their cannon and muskets over our heads, and then we crawled up the rope and onto the parapet of their works, stepping right among their muskets as they were aimed over the work. It was done so quick that the Rebels had no chance to fire again but dropped their guns and ran."[17]

The Federals went wild with excitement at their success in carrying the formidable defenses they had confronted for so many months. "Then, and there," a man in another of Wheaton's brigades remembered, "the long tried and ever faithful soldiers of the Republic saw DAYLIGHT!—and such a shout as tore the concave of that morning sky, it were worth dying to hear."[18]

"As the 2nd R.I. reached the parapet," Colonel Rhodes said, "I gave the order to prime and then fire, and we sent a volley into their huts which were in rear of the line of works.... The Rebels ran one gun out of the rear of the fort, but we were upon them so quick that they left it. [We] then turned the gun upon the enemy and fired several rounds into their works. As they rallied to charge upon it Corporal William Railton put in a cartridge, but not having a shot filled the gun to the muzzle with stones and fired it right in the faces of the Rebels who were charging upon us. The gun burst but did not hurt any of my men, but broke up the Rebels who retreated."[19]

Seymour's division, on the corps' left, seems to have had the least trouble in reaching the Confederate works. "We rushed through like a hurricane," one member of that division said. "Not even a temporary check was experienced," another wrote, "in passing through and over the double line of abatis, ditch and high, strong earthworks. A hand-to-hand fight ensued within the main works in which many gallant officers and men fell killed and wounded."[20]

By 5 a.m., while the 9th Corps was still engaged in heavy fighting, the 6th Corps had torn a large hole in the Rebel lines. While Parke's attack was opposed by most of Gordon's 2nd Corps of Lee's army, the Confederate lines opposite Wright's 6th Corps was manned by only about half of Lee's 3rd Corps, and the actual assault fell mostly on one Rebel brigade, commanded by Brigadier General James Lane. "My line was pierced by the enemy in strong force," Lane said.[21]

"In the ardor of the movement," Wright later reported, "it was quite impossible to check the advance of the troops at once, and parties from each division soon reached the Boydton plank road and the South Side Railroad, breaking up the latter somewhat and cutting the telegraph wire of the enemy. As promptly as possible the lines were reformed, wheeled to the left, and moved, with the left of line guiding on the rebel intrenchments, toward Hatcher's Run. At first the enemy attempted resistance, but he was soon broken, and the entire rebel line from the point of attack to Hatcher's Run, with all his artillery and a large number of prisoners, was in our possession. In making this movement the Second Brigade, First Division, was left at the point of assault to hold what we had gained and to resist any force the enemy might send from Petersburg. Portions of this brigade and a part of the Second Division picket-line gained a considerable extent of the enemy's line of works to the right of the point of attack."[22] A member of the brigade left behind remembered how he and his fellows "fired into the running Rebs, and also into some wagons which were passing. We also twisted off the telgraph wires with our bayonets, continuing our firing at everything in sight."[23]

Not far behind Lane's front line was Lee's headquarters, in the Turnbull house. Longstreet had reached there at about 4 a.m., having arrived ahead of his troops even though they were coming by train and he and his staff had ridden from north of the James on horseback. (After four years of war, the railroads of the Confederacy were in terrible condition.) Longstreet was in conference with Lee, who was still in bed, and had just received instructions to "march to support the broken forces about Five Forks," when Colonel Charles Venable of Lee's staff interrupted to say that frightened teamsters were rushing past and the nearby line had evidently been broken. Lee got up to have a look for himself. "Drawing his wrapper about him," Longstreet said, "he walked with me to the front door and saw, as far as they eye could cover the field, a line of skirmishers in quiet march towards us. It was hardly light enough to distinguish the blue from the gray....General Lee appealed to have me interpose and stop the march, but not a man of my command was there, nor had we notice that any of them had reached the station at Petersburg. All staff-officers mounted and rode to find the parts of Heth's and Wilcox's divisions that had been forced from their lines. The display of officers riding in many directions seemed to admonish the skirmishers to delay under cover of an intervening swale."[24]

Lieutenant General A.P. Hill, commander of the 3rd Corps of Lee's army, had been concerned by all the firing going on during the night and had also ridden over to consult with Lee that morning. When Colonel Venable announced that the line had been broken, Hill rushed out of the house and rode off with such a reckless air that Lee sent Venable to caution him not to expose himself to danger. Hill had grown increasingly ill during the war. Historians have variously estimated his trouble to be psychosomatic, or ulcers, or syphilis, or malaria. Whatever his problem was, he had been on sick leave for a few weeks until the day before, when reports of the Federal moves around the Confederate right had caused him to return to duty. When Venable caught up with him and reported Lee's concern, Hill said he must join his men on the right. The two officers, along with two of Hill's couriers, rode on and soon encountered a pair of Union soldiers. The two couriers quickly got the drop on the Federals and captured them, and Hill sent one courier back to Lee's headquarters with the prisoners. Riding on, the other three Confederates soon spotted Union troops milling around among the huts of the Rebels' winter quarters. Before long the small party came upon a battalion of Confederate artillery. Hill sent Venable to move those guns to where they could bear upon the enemy soldiers they had seen and rode on with the remaining courier, Sergeant George Tucker.

"Please excuse me, General," Tucker said, "but where are you going?"

"Sergeant," Hill replied, "I must go to the right as quickly as possible. We will go up this side of the branch to the woods, which will cover us until reaching the field in rear of General Heth's quarters. I hope to find the road clear at General Heth's."

Still carrying his Colt revolver since helping to capture the two Federals, Tucker now rode slightly ahead of his general. They crossed the Boydton Plank Road and followed the edge of a woods for about a mile without seeing anyone from either side. "Sergeant," Hill said, "should anything happen to me, you must go back to General Lee and report it."[25]

They entered a field, and in a road beyond it they could see a mass of men. Hill examined them with his field glasses and determined that they were Federals. The Confederates turned toward the woods that paralleled the Boydton Plank Road, but as they approached the trees Tucker saw six or eight Union soldiers among them. The two Federals nearest to the field that Tucker and Hill were crossing ran to a large tree and took cover behind its trunk.

The two Federals were members of the 138th Pennsylvania in Seymour's division, Corporal John Mauk and Private Daniel Wolford. In the confusion, during which about 500 of Seymour's men had gone as far north as the Southside Railroad, the two had become completely separated from their regiment and had wandered about on their own. After using some crowbars they had found on the rails of the Southside's track, they had turned back toward the Boydton Plank Road, where they had found some Union stragglers boiling coffee. The two had been moving to join them when they saw "two men on horseback coming from the direction of Petersburg, who had the appearance of officers."[26] After taking cover behind the same large tree, both Federals leveled their rifles, one under the other, at the two Rebels.

"We must take them," Hill told Tucker as he drew his own revolver.

"Stay there!" the sergeant told the general. "I'll take them." He shouted to the two Yankees, who were not more than twenty yards away, "If you fire, you'll be swept to hell! Our men are here—surrender."

"Surrender," Hill echoed, riding up beside Tucker.

Private Wolford started to lower his rifle, but Corporal Mauk said, "I can't see it. Let us shoot them."[27]

Both men fired. Wolford missed, but Wauk's shot took off Hill's left thumb, pierced his heart, and came out his back. With their guns empty, the two Federals hurried south to rejoin their unit without knowing who they had just killed. Tucker rode back to Lee's headquarters to tell the commanding general what had happened to Hill. "He is at rest now," Lee said, "and we who are left are the ones to suffer."[28]

Because the terrain in their front was particularly difficult, the troops with Ord, on Wright's left, were not ordered to attack at dawn, but to be ready to attack the Confederates in their front if the situation looked favorable or to support Wright if he needed help. "At daylight on the 2d," wrote General Gibbon, commander of the 24th Corps, "all our preparations were made for assault, two brigades each of Turner's and Foster's divisions being massed in rear of our line. At 6.50 a.m. an order was received from Major-General Ord directing me to send all my available force to the support of the Sixth Corps, which had broken through the enemy's line near Fort Welch. I at once ordered the whole of Foster's division and two of Turner's brigades to move to the right, and almost immediately afterward Harris' brigade, of Turner's division, carried the enemy's line in front of them, and pushing forward Birney's division, we occupied the enemy's line and met the Sixth Corps coming down from the right, sweeping everything before them."[29] Almost an entire brigade of Hill's corps, commanded by Brigadier General Joseph R. Davis, nephew of the Confederate president, was captured near Hatcher's Run, as was part of another brigade.

Beyond Ord's sector was Humphreys' 2nd Corps. It had originally been scheduled to attack a Confederate work near its right known as the Crow House Redoubt, but after Miles division had been sent to join Sheridan the order had been rescinded. At 4 a.m., Humphreys' two remaining division's, Brigadier General William Hays' 2nd and Brevet Major General Gershom Mott's 3rd, began harrassing the Rebel picket line in their front. "About 6 a.m.," Humphreys later reported, "having been informed by General Webb that both General Wright and General Parke had carried and held portions of the enemy's lines, I directed General Hays to try and carry the Crow-house redoubt and General Mott to strain every effort in his front. About 7:30 a.m. General McAllister captured the enemy's intrenched picket-line in his front, under the fire of their artillery as well as musketry, and about 8 a.m. General Hays carried the Crow-house redoubt and the work adjoining it on the enemy's right, capturing three pieces of artillery and a large part of the garrisons."[30]

Hays's men had "expected a desperate resistance and great loss," as one of them wrote...."But a sudden change came over us, for as we gazed at the point we were to attack, a sight met our eyes that nearly unmanned us. Where two minutes before the Stars and Bars had flown, now floated the glorious old Stars and Stripes. Never before have we thought it so beautiful, and a cheer went up that could have been heard in Petersburg." The four brigades of Rebels in Humphreys' front, between the west side of Hatcher's Run and the Claiburne Road, were commanded by Major General Henry Heth, a division commander in the 3rd Corps. "As soon as I found that the enemy had possession of the Boydton Plank Road," Heth wrote, "and that he was moving down this road—my position being no longer tenable—I gave orders to withdraw to Sutherlands Station on the S&S Rail Road, crossing Hatcher's Run at Watkins Bridge."[31]

At 8:30 a.m. Mott reported to Humphreys that the Confederates were withdrawing their artillery and moving to the west behind their works, and at 9 a.m. Humphreys learned that Miles was returning to him along the White Oak Road. He ordered his two divisions to take the Claiburne Road and pursue the Rebels toward Sutherland Station.

By then Grant had ridden to the front to sort out the confusion of intermingling and overlapping corps commands. "He urged his horse over the works which Wright's corps had captured," Horace Porter wrote, "and suddenly came upon a body of 3000 prisoners marching to our rear. His whole attention was for some time riveted upon them, and we knew that he was enjoying his usual satisfaction in seeing so large a capture. Some of the guards told the prisoners who the general was, and they manifested great curiosity to get a good look at him. Next he came up with a division of Wright's corps, flushed with success, and rushing forward with a dash that was inspiriting beyond description."[32]

"As soon as the soldiers saw the Lieutenant General...," one of them wrote, "the men cheered him with the wildest enthusiasm; he rode with head uncovered, and bowed his thanks for the soldiers' hearty greeting." A correspondent for the *New York Herald* wrote that Grant's "strongly marked and sun-browned face lighted up with stern pleasure as he rode along through the rebel works. On seeing Generals Wright, Getty, Seymour, Wheaton and other Sixth Corps officers, he shook hands with great heartiness."[33]

"The general galloped along toward the right," Horace Porter said, "and soon met Meade, with whom he had been in constant communication, and who had been urging on the Army of the Potomac with all vigor. Congratulations were rapidly exchanged, and both went to pushing forward the good work. Grant, after taking in the situation, directed both Meade and Ord to face their commands more toward the east, and close up toward the inner lines which covered Petersburg."[34] At about 9 a.m., Wright's 6th Corps turned back from Hatcher's Run toward the inner Confederate line around Petersburg, and Ord's troops soon began to pass through the hole the 6th Corps had punched in the outer line.

"General Grant dismounted near a farm-house which stood on a knoll," Porter wrote, "from which he could get a good view of the field of operations. He seated himself on the ground at the foot of a tree, and was soon busy receiving despatches and writing orders to officers conducting the advance. The position was under fire, and as soon as the group of staff-officers was seen, the enemy's guns began paying their respects to the party. This lasted for about a quarter of an hour, and as the fire became hotter and hotter, several of the officers, apprehensive for the general's safety, urged him to move to some less conspicuous position; but he kept on writing and talking, without the least interruption from the shots falling around him, and apparently not noticing what a target the place was becoming, or paying any heed to the gentle reminders to 'move on.' After he had finished his despatches he got up, took a view of the situation, and as he started toward the other side of the farm-house said with a quizzical look at the group around him: 'Well, they do seem to have the range on us.'"[35]

It was 10 a.m. by the time that the 6th Corps began to close up to the inner defenses of Petersburg, which formed a rough semi-circle from the Appomattox below the city to the same river above it. By then Brigadier General Nathaniel Harris's brigade of Mahone's Division of Hill's 3rd Corps had arrived from the Confederate defenses covering the Bermuda Hundred peninsula between Petersburg and Richmond. When Harris's Mississippians topped a rise near the point where the 6th Corps had originally broken through the line they saw Gibbon's two divisions of the 24th Corps moving through that gap. "They seemed to be in no hurry," one Rebel noted, "but very deliberately dressed their line and then moved forward. It was a grand but awful sight, the Federals moving with the same precision as though on parade."[36]

The line that Wright had broken that morning was merely a long extention that hooked into the inner line near its southwestern-most point and ran in that direction all the way to the Clairborne Road to cover the Southside Railroad. Near the point where the inner line connected with the abandoned extention there were two earthworks, not part of either line, facing west or southwest. They were called, among other things, Fort Gregg and Fort Whitworth. Nathaniel Harris received orders from Major General Cadmus Wilcox, a division commander in Hill's 3rd Corps who commanded the area where Wright had originally broken through, "not to suffer himself to be cut off, but to hold the enemy in check as long as possible, and when compelled to retire to fall back slowly and to throw two regiments into Battery Gregg and two regiments into Battery Whitworth."[37]

General Lee's headquarters at the Turnbull house was outside of the inner line, and as his troops were pushed back it became necessary for him to abandon it. Sometime around 10 a.m. he dictated a telegram to be sent to Secretary of War Breckinridge: "I see no prospect of doing more than holding our position here till night. I am not certain that I can do that. If I can I shall withdraw to-night north of the Appomattox, and, if possible, it will be better to withdraw the whole line to-night from James River. The brigades on Hatcher's Run are cut off from us;

enemy have broken through our lines and intercepted between us and them, and there is no bridge over which they can cross the Appomattox this side of Goode's or Beaver's, which are not very far from the Danville railroad. Our only chance, then, of concentrating our forces, is to do so near Danville railroad, which I shall endeavor to do at once. I advise that all preparation be made for leaving Richmond to-night. I will advise you later, according to circumstances."[38]

"Standing on the lawn in front of his headquarters," John Esten Cooke, a Confederate staff officer wrote, "General Lee now saw, approaching rapidly, a heavy column of Federal infantry.... The spectacle was picturesque and striking. Across the extensive fields, houses set on fire by shell were sending aloft huge clouds of smoke and tongues of flame; at every instant was seen the quick glare of the Federal artillery, firing from every knoll; and in front came on the charging column, moving at a double-quick, with burnished gun barrels and bayonets flashing in the April sunshine. General Lee watched with attention, but with perfect composure, this determined advance of the enemy; and, although he must have realized that his army was on the verge of destruction, it was impossible to discern in his features any evidences of emotion. He was in full uniform and had buckled on his dress sword, which he seldom wore—having, on this morning declared, it is said, that if he were compelled to surrender he would do so in full harness."[39]

Lee's telegrapher was in the Turnbull house in the middle of sending the message to Richmond when the Federals approached. As soon as he finished he galloped away with the headquarters band. When a Union artillery shell burst under his horse he was sent sprawling, but he got up and escaped on foot. "He quickly gathered his instrument together," one of Lee's staff officers said, "and the last I saw of him he was making very good time for the city." Union shells soon set the Turnbull house on fire. "I am afraid it was burned because they knew I had been there," Lee said. "I should not occupy a private house."[40]

Soon Field's Division of Longstreet's corps began to arrive. "Not venturing to hope," Longstreet said, "I looked towards Petersburg and saw General Benning, with his Rock brigade, winding in rapid march around the near hill. He had but six hundred of his men. I asked for two hundred, and led them off to the canal on our right, which was a weak point, threatened by a small body of skirmishers, and ordered the balance of his troops deployed as skirmishers in front of the enemy's main force. I rode then to Benning's line of skirmishers, and at the middle point turned and rode at a walk to the top of the hill, took out my glasses, and had a careful view of the enemy's formidable masses. I thought I recognized General Gibbon, and raised my hat, but he was busy and did not see me."[41]

Among the Union troops approaching Lee and Longstreet was Colonel Thomas W. Hyde's 3rd Brigade of Getty's 2nd Division of the 6th Corps. "As we advanced in a handsome line of battle over rolling and open country," Hyde wrote, "our batteries galloped to the front and opened fire in a most spirited manner. But soon a rebel battery opened on our left....Several times, as it was forced to change position by the fire of the 1st Maine, we noticed each time a fine-looking old officer on a gray horse, who seemed to be directing its movements.

"At length the guns went into battery again on a hill near a large house, and their audible presence became more annoying than ever. By common consent the three brigades attempted to charge the hill, but the cannister fire was so hot and the division now so small and wearied, the first attack was a failure. While our men were getting in shape to charge again, I sent Lieutenant Nichols with fifty men of the 1st Maine off to the left and around the hill with orders to shoot the battery horses, as we knew we could get on their flank, and they were probably standing hitched to the caissons and would be a fine mark from that side.

"As soon as he had disappeared in a piece of woods, on we started again, this time through a swamp where many sank to the waist, and where shot was splashing the mud and water in every direction. Here I saw two color sergeants of the 1st Maine fall, but the colors were picked up promptly, and everyone struggled over as best he could; but the wounded, as well as the dead, had to stay there for a time. The first five hundred men across made a run for the battery, and, as we went up the hill amid the roar of guns and whir of cannister, amid Yankee cheers and rebel yells, I detected the crack of Nichols' rifles and knew the guns could not be got away.

"The din was terrible! Brass Napoleons were never better served, but they were doomed. I saw Sergeant Highill of my brigade and two Vermont colors go between the guns at the same time, so neither brigade could claim the sole honor. Riding through the guns, I could not see the road beyond where the enemy were retreating, for dust, and most of the battery horses lay in their tracks."

Hyde asked a mortally wounded Confederate artillery officer what battery it was. "Captain Williams' North Carolina, of Poague's Battalion," the Rebel answered.

"And who was the officer on the gray horse?" Hyde asked.

"General Robert E. Lee, sir," The Confederate replied, almost exhausted by the effort, "and he was the last man to leave these guns."

"What a prize we had missed!" Hyde lamented. "This gallant old man, struggling like a Titan against defeat. He...had done all one brave man could do to save his fortunes from the wreck. They told us the house had been his headquarters during the Siege of Petersburg."[42]

John Esten Cooke said that Lee "slowly rode back, accompanied by a number of officers, toward his inner line. He still remained entirely composed, and only said to one of his staff, in his habitual tone, 'This is a bad business, colonel.'...He said afterward to another officer, 'It has happened as I told them it would at Richmond. The line has been stretched until it has broken.'

"The Federal column was now pressing along the Cox Road toward Petersburg, and General Lee continued to ride slowly back in the direction of the city. He was probably recognized by officers of the Federal artillery, for his cortege drew their fire. The group was furiously shelled, and one of the shells burst a few feet in rear of him, killing the horse of an officer near him, cutting the bridle-reins of others, and tearing up the ground in his immediate vicinity. This incident seemed to arouse in General Lee his fighting blood. He turned his head over his right shoulder, his cheeks became flushed, and a sudden flash of the eye showed with what reluctance he retired before the fire directed upon him.

"No other course was left him, however, and he continued to ride slowly toward his inner line—a low earthwork in the suburbs of the city—where a small force was drawn up, ardent, hopeful, defiant, and saluting the shell, now bursting above them, with cheers and laughter. It was plain that the fighting spirit of the ragged troops remained unbroken; and the shout of welcome with which they received Lee indicated their unwavering confidence in him, despite the untoward condition of affairs."[43]

The troops of Gordon's 2nd Corps were certainly still full of fight. At 11 a.m. Major General Bryan Grimes, a division commander in that corps, launched a counterattack against Parke's 9th Corps troops that managed, as he put it, "gradually to gain traverse after traverse of our captured works." The combat resembled that at Fort Fisher two months earlier. "The fight was from traverse to traverse as we slowly drove them back," one of Grimes' men wrote. "The Yankees would get on top of them and shoot down at our men, and as we would re-take them our men did the same thing."[44]

The second day of April was a bright and beautiful spring Sunday in Virginia. One Richmond resident, writing to her cousin, said it was "one of those unusually lovely days that the Spring sometimes brings...when delicate silks that look too fine at other times, seem just to suit; when invalids and convalescents venture out in the sunshine; when the churches are crowded as never before. So it was this Sunday. I have never seen a calmer or more peaceful Sabbath morning."[45] In Richmond that morning Postmaster General John Reagan was at the War Department at 10:40 a.m. when Lee's telegram to Secretary of War Breckinridge arrived. He hurried toward the Confederate White House and met President Davis, who was on his way to church with Francis R. Lubbock, an aide to the president and a former governor of Texas, Reagan's home state. Reagan reported the substance of Lee's message and was surprised that the president, who appeared oddly distracted, did not seem to understand the gravity of the situation. Davis and Reagan were not close. The president considered the Texan unpolished and uncouth, and he may not have paid much attention to his information. War Department messages were not the business of the Postmaster General. Anyway, Davis and Lubbock continued on to St. Paul's Episcopal Church for the 11 a.m. services.

Most of the worshipers there that morning were women, many of them wearing black in mourning for a husband, brother, father, or son fallen in the Confederate service. Secretary of the Navy Stephen Mallory was there, and he noticed that Davis wore his usual cold, stern expression. The service had begun and the worshipers were praying when a young man in civilian clothes came in. He whispered to the elderly sexton that he had to see President Davis. The sexton refused to interrupt the prayer, and the young man waited impatiently. Finally he pulled a pencil and some paper from his pocket and hastily scribbled a note to the president: "General Lee telegraphs that he can hold his position no longer. Come to the office immediately. Breckinridge."[46] The sexton tiptoed down the aisle and delivered the message to Davis, who glanced at it, turned pale, and got up and left the church. Soon the sexton returned and began tapping various officers and officials on the shoulder. They too quietly got up and left. "But when the sexton appeared the fourth time," a boy in the gallery noted, "all restraint of place and occasion yielded, and the vast congregation rose en masse and rushed towards the door. I sat still for a moment, wondering and withal listening to the preacher's earnest appeal to the people to remember where they were and be still…[H]e might just as well have tried to turn back the waters of Niagara Falls."[47] Similar scenes were enacted at other churches in the city. Word quickly spread that Lee's lines had been broken. "Suddenly, as if by magic," the Richmond *Whig* said, "the streets became filled with men, walking as though for a wager, and behind them excited Negroes with trunks, bundles and baggage of every description. All over the city it was the same—wagons, trunks, band-boxes and their owners, a mass of hurrying fugitives."[48]

President Davis, members of the cabinet, and other officials converged on the War Department through the growing pandemonium in the streets of Richmond. "The Secretary of War has shown me your dispatch," Davis wired to Lee. "To move to-night will involve the loss of many valuables, both for want of time to pack and of transportation. Arrangements are progressing, and unless you otherwise advise the start will be made."[49] When Lee received this telegram he crumpled it up and then tore it to pieces. "I am sure," he was heard to say, "I gave him sufficient notice."[50]

---

1. Trudeau, Noah Andre, *Out of the Storm: The End of the Civil War, April - June 1865* (Boston, 1994), 47.
2. Porter, *Campaigning with Grant*, 444.
3. Wheeler, *Witness to Appomattox*, 83-84.
4. Trudeau, *The Last Citadel*, 367.
5. Robert Hunt Rhodes, editor, *All for the Union: The Civil War Diary and Letters of Elisha Hunt Rhodes* (New York, 1985), 225.
6. Trudeau, *The Last Citadel*, 379.
7. Wheeler, *Witness to Appomattox*, 84.
8. Porter, *Campaigning with Grant*, 444-445.
9. Trudeau, *The Last Citadel*, 367-369.
10. Ibid., 360.
11. Ibid., 361.
12. Ibid., 361-362.
13. Rhodes, *All for the Union*, 225.
14. Trudeau, *The Last Citadel*, 371.
15. Ibid., 370.
16. Ibid., 370-371.
17. Rhodes, *All for the Union*, 225-226.
18. Trudeau, *The Last Citadel*, 373.
19. Rhodes, *All for the Union*, 226.
20. Trudeau, *The Last Citadel*, 371.
21. Ibid., 372.
22. *Official Records*, 46:I:903-904.
23. Trudeau, *The Last Citadel*, 373.
24. Longstreet, *From Manassass to Appomattox*, 604-605.
25. Freeman, *Lee's Lieutenants*, 3:678.
26. Trudeau, *The Last Citadel*, 374.
27. Freeman, *Lee's Lieutenants*, 3:679.

28. William Woods Hassler, *A.P. Hill: Lee's Forgotten General* (Richmond, 1962), 242.
29. *Official Records*, 46:I:1174.
30. Ibid., 46:I:679.
31. Trudeau, *The Last Citadel*, 392.
32. Porter, *Campaigning with Grant*, 446.
33. Trudeau, *The Last Citadel*, 377.
34. Porter, *Campaigning with Grant*, 446-447.
35. Ibid., 447.
36. Trudeau, *The Last Citadel*, 381.
37. Ibid., 381-382.
38. *Official Records*, 46:III:1378.
39. Wheeler, *Witness to Appomattox*, 86.
40. Burke Davis, *The Long Surrender* (New York, 1985), 17.
41. Longstreet, *From Manassass to Appomattox*, 606.
42. Wheeler, *Witness to Appomattox*, 86-87.
43. Ibid., 87-88.
44. Trudeau, *The Last Citadel*, 362-363.
45. A. A. Hoehling and Mary Hoehling, *The Last Days of the Confederacy* (New York, 1981), 104.
46. Davis, *To Appomattox*, 88.
47. Hoehling and Hoehling, *The Last Days of the Confederacy*, 112.
48. Davis, *The Long Surrender*, 23.
49. *Official Records*, 46:III:1378.
50. Trudeau, *The Last Citadel*, 385.

CHAPTER TWENTY-NINE

The Rebellion Has Gone Up!

2 - 3 April 1865

As he traveled through southern Maryland, Lieutenant Ben Stringfellow, the Confederate agent who had been in Washington, was captured on the second day of April by a patrol of the 238th Provisional Cavalry, Veteran Reserve Corps.

In southern Virginia that morning, Sheridan sent Merritt's cavalry to the west, and by 10 a.m. his troopers reached Ford's Station on the Southside Railroad. Very few Rebels were seen on the way, but a slave told the Federals that the Confederates had been at the station until about two hours before. There was a small train on the track with some medical supplies on it and a dozen wounded Rebels. Eventually a few

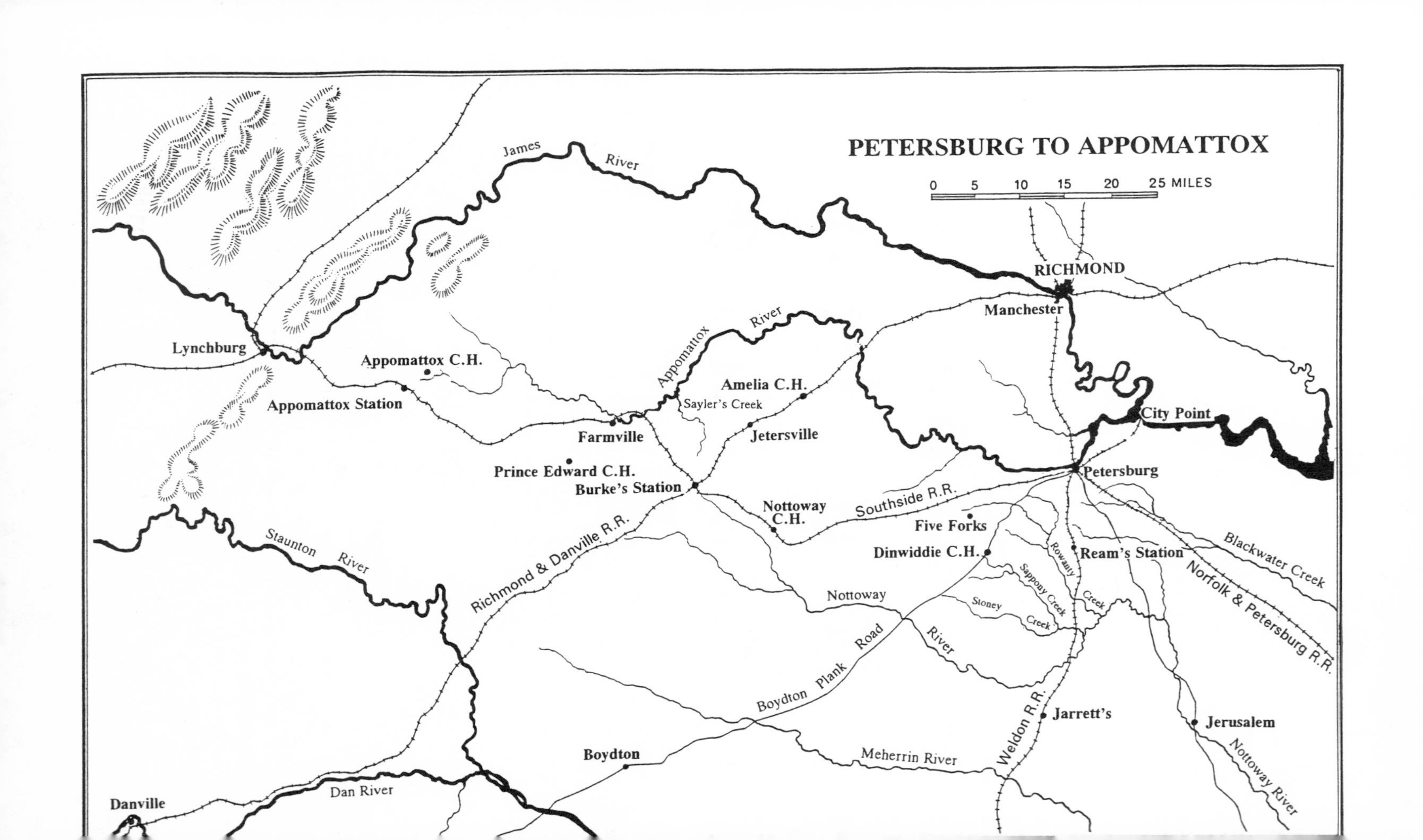
PETERSBURG TO APPOMATTOX
0 5 10 15 20 25 MILES
James River
Richmond
Manchester
City Point
Petersburg
Appomattox River
Lynchburg
Appomattox C.H.
Appomattox Station
Amelia C.H.
Sayler's Creek
Jetersville
Farmville
Prince Edward C.H.
Burke's Station
Nottoway C.H.
Southside R.R.
Five Forks
Dinwiddie C.H.
Ream's Station
Rowanty Creek
Sappony Creek
Stoney Creek
Blackwater Creek
Norfolk & Petersburg R.R.
Staunton River
Richmond & Danville R.R.
Nottoway River
Boydton Plank Road
Weldon R.R.
Jarrett's
Jerusalem
Nottoway River
Meherrin River
Boydton
Danville
Dan River

unwounded Confederates came down from the upper story and surrendered. Merritt pushed on to the north.

At 7:30 a.m. Sheridan sent Miles' division of the 2nd Corps back up the White Oak Road to attack the Rebels on the far right end of the Confederate line near the Claiborne Road and took Ayres' and Crawford's divisions of the 5th Corps in support. Griffin's division, now under Bartlett, was left near Five Forks. At about 9 a.m., Miles found that the Rebel lines at the White Oak-Clairborne intersection had been abandoned but he soon discovered Heth's Confederates retreating northward up the Claiborne Road toward Sutherland Station. Under orders from Humphreys, Miles followed. Rebel sharpshooters repulsed the Union pursuit where the road crossed Hatcher's Run, but the Federals came on again, better organized this time, and forced a crossing. "We threw out first one regiment and then another as skirmishers," a Confederate remembered, "to retard the enemy, who was pressing us hard."[1]

As he rode north with his retreating command, Major General Henry Heth was met by a courier sent by Lee to inform him of Hill's death. Heth, the senior division commander in the 3rd Corps, was to take command of it and to report in person to Lee as soon as possible. Heth rode on to Sutherland Station, where he found a train of supply wagons preparing for a general retreat. There Heth turned over command of the four brigades that were with him, two from his own division and two from Wilcox's, to Brigadier General John Cooke. Before riding away Heth told Cooke to follow the wagons as soon as they withdrew and to avoid a battle if possible. At about 11 a.m., Cooke formed the four brigades in line of battle to protect the station and the wagons. "We... selected a position," one Confederate wrote, "on the brow of a slight hill in an open field and rapidly fortified our line as well as we could, with bayonets used to break the earth, and such other means as were at command."[2]

Humphreys originally ordered his other two divisions to follow Miles up the Claiborne Road, but Meade soon told him to take them instead up the Boydton Plank Road toward Petersburg to reinforce Wright's 6th Corps. Meade also wanted Miles' division to turn right once it crossed Hatcher's Run and join the rest of the corps. Humphreys rode off to see Miles and instead found Phil Sheridan. What resulted was a serious confusion of purposes that might have led to a serious problem for the Union forces if they had not already dealt the Confederates a knock-out blow that day. No order had been published clarifying Sheridan's exact status in relation to the Army of the Potomac and the Army of the James. He was not an officer of either army but the commander of a collection of distant departments which he had ridden off and left. In addition to the two cavalry divisions that belonged to his own command he now commanded several forces that had been detached from the armies of the Potomac and the James, Crook's division, Mackenzie's division, the 5th Corps, and Miles' division. It was not clear how long those forces were to remain under his command nor under what cirmcumstances they would revert to their proper armies. Especially it was unclear who Miles' division belonged to.

In his subsequent report of his part in the campaign, Humphreys said, "Upon learning from [Sheridan] that he had not intended to return General Miles' division to my command, I declined to assume further command of it, and left it to carry out General Sheridan's instructions, whatever they may be."[3] Sheridan, however, in his report, said, "Miles... pursued with great zeal, pushing [Heth] across Hatcher's Run and following him up on the road to Sutherland's Depot. On the north side of the run I overtook Miles, who was anxious to attack, and had a very fine and spirited division. I gave him permission, but about this time General Humphreys came up, and receiving notice from General Meade that General Humphreys would take command of Miles' division, I relinquished it at once."[4] A message from Meade to Sheridan seems to have been part of the problem. Sent at 10 a.m. by courier, it said, "The enemy has abandoned his line opposite Humphreys, and is falling back to his own left and said to be forming line beyond Hatcher's Run. Humphreys is moving out on the Boydton road and Miles on the Claiborne. General Humphreys has assumed command of Miles. Fifth Corps is left to you....We presume you to be on Cox and River roads. If General Humphreys hears you engaged he will move toward you. If you hear him engaged you are requested to move toward him."[5]

Anyway, both Sheridan and Humphreys, thinking that they had turned over command of Miles' division to the other, rode off and left it on its own. Further, Sheridan seems to have received the impression that he was in the wrong place with the 5th Corps. In his memoirs he said, "On this request I relinquished command of the division, when, supported by the Fifth Corps it could have broken in the enemy's right at a vital point; and I have always since regretted that I did so, for the message Humphreys conveyed was without authority from General Grant, by whom Miles had been sent to me, but thinking good feeling a desideratum just then, and wishing to avoid wrangles, I faced the Fifth Corps about and marched it down to Five Forks, and out the Ford road to the crossing of Hatcher's Run."[6]

"Sheridan having returned from the Claiborne Road with the rest of the Fifth Corps," Joshua Chamberlain wrote, "at about noon our column moved out, my own command in the advance, down the Ford Road. At Hatcher's Run a vigorous demonstration of the enemy's skirmishers to prevent our crossing was soon dislodged by a gallant attack by Colonel Sniper with the 185th New York. Throwing forward a strong skirmish line, in command of Colonel Cunningham of the 32d Massachusetts, we pressed on for the Southside Railroad. Hearing the noise of an approaching train from the direction of Petersburg, I pushed forward our skirmishers to catch it. A wild, shriek of the steam-whistle brought our main line up at the double-quick. There we find the train held up, Cunningham mounted on the engine pulling the whistle-valve wide open to announce the arrival at a premature station of the last train that tried to run the gauntlet out of Petersburg under the Confederate flag. This train was crowded with quite a mixed company as to color, character, and capacity, but united in the single aim of forming a personally-conducted southern tour. The officers and soldiers we were obliged to regard as prisoners of war: the rest we let go in peace, if they could find it."[7]

At about 1 p.m. the 5th Corps advance resumed with Chamberlain's command still in the lead. When he reached the east-west Cox Road he ran into opposition from Fitz Lee's cavalry, but, deploying his troops, he pushed the Rebels back and moved eastward along that road. "Anticipating the burden of the retreat from the direction of Petersburg to fall this way," he said, "I prepared to hold this road against all comers, in the meantime pushing forward to the bank of a branch of Hatcher's Run a mile short of Sutherland's. Here my command was held in line and on the alert while the rest of the Fifth Corps were engaged in tearing up the Southside Railroad between us and Cox's Station in our rear. We were on the flank and rear of the enemy fighting Miles, but the stress of that fire died away as we approached."[8]

As soon as Miles came upon Heth's, now Cooke's, brigades, entrenched on their hill just south of Sutherland's Station, he ordered two of his brigades to charge them. "They advanced promptly to the attack," he reported, "but owing to the natural strength of the position and the difficult nature of the ground intervening the assault was unsuccessful."[9] The commander of the 3rd Brigade was severely wounded in this attack. After the Federals fell back, some of the Confederates rushed forward with a wild, derisive yell, and gathered up many of the wounded. One Union soldier, badly hurt, begged the Rebels to shoot him. He had vowed never to be taken alive. When they refused, he took out his pocket knife and slit his own throat.

At 12:30 p.m. the 3rd Brigade, under a new commander, attacked again, this time with the support of some artillery that had come up.

"This attack was also repulsed," Miles reported, "the enemy being able to concentrate his force opposite any threatened point." The new brigade commander was wounded in this attack. "The brigade was withdrawn to its former position—a crest about 800 yards from that occupied by the enemy. I now determined to carry the position by an attack on the enemy's flank. A strong skirmish line was pushed forward upon the extreme right flank of the enemy, overlapping it and threatening the railroad. Indeed, a portion of this skirmish line was on the railroad at 1.10 o'clock. The attention of the enemy being thus diverted from his left flank, the Fourth Brigade (Brevet Brigadier-General Ramsey) was moved rapidly around it through a ravine and wood, and massed in the woods without being discovered by the enemy."[10]

At about 1 p.m. on the main front, east of Petersburg, the Confederates launched another counterattack against Parke's 9th Corps, trying to dislodge it from their front line. But this attack, like the previous one, was eventually beaten off. Also at about the same hour, the Federals attacked forts Gregg and Whitworth. John Gibbon was in charge of this operation. It was his first chance to lead his new 24th Corps in battle, and he was determined to make the most it, especially since it might also be his last chance. He selected Foster's 1st Division to assault Fort Gregg, the more southerly and more formidable of the two works, supported by two brigades of Turner's Independent Division. Turner's other brigade, Brigadier General Thomas M. Harris's 3rd, was given the task of threatening Fort Whitworth while Gregg was being stormed. Once Gregg fell, Whitworth would easily follow.

Another Harris was inside Fort Whitworth. This was Brigadier General Nathaniel ("Nate") Harris, who had brought his brigade from Mahone's Division that morning. Harris and his brigade had been instrumental in preventing the Union breakthrough at Spotsylvania the previous May from doing even more damage to Lee's army than it had done. Now the fate of that army again depended on his ability to hold strong earthworks against overwhelming odds. He had two of his Mississippi regiments with him inside Whitworth and two others inside Fort Gregg under Lieutenant Colonel James H. Duncan. Also inside Gregg were remnants of Lane's and Thomas's brigades of Wilcox's Division of the 3rd Corps and a detachment of artillerymen with two guns.

It was just about 1 p.m. when Colonel Thomas Osborn's 1st Brigade, on the right of Foster's line, began to cross the 800 yards that separated it from Fort Gregg. "I moved my command forward about half the distance, in quick time, at right shoulder shift arms," Osborn later reported, "and having passed a deep and difficult slough, gave the command charge, when the brigade, with cheers, swept up the ascent at the double-quick, under a terrible fire of grape, canister, and minie-balls tearing through the ranks."[11] The Federals got almost as far as the ditch in front of the fort's parapet. As one of Osborn's men put it, "A few feet from the ditch, which was deep and broad, the withering fire of the fort became too hot for even the most desperate men, and the whole column recoiled."[12] The Federals fell back a short distance, reformed, and came on again, this time reinforced by two regiments from the 3rd Brigade. Again the Confederate fire broke their momentum, but this time a few of the men actually got into the ditch, and the colors of two regiments were planted on the fort's earthen walls. Other Federals soon plunged into the breast-high water of the ditch along the front and side walls of the fort. Yet others made their way around behind the fort, looking for a way in. "But it was found to be an inclosed fort," Colonel Osborn wrote, "admirably constructed for defense."[13]

The men in the ditch tried to climb up the earthen walls of the fort, but it was no easy task. "The excitement which now prevailed beggars description," one of them wrote. "The men were nearly frantic in their attempts to gain the top of the works." Another said, "The steepness and slippery nature of the sides of the fort for a time rendered futile all our efforts to scale them." A third said that "only by digging with swords and bayonets could footholds be secured on the slippery ascent." Colonel Osborn, who was boosting soldiers up the wall as fast as possible, shouted, "Men, we must take this fort before the enemy receives reinforcement."[14]

The Federals along the north face of Fort Gregg were being blasted by cannon fire from nearby Fort Whitworth, so Gibbon ordered Thomas Harris's brigade to charge that work and the other two brigades of Turner's division to join the assault on Fort Gregg. The 3rd Corps's chief of artillery soon ordered the guns withdrawn from Fort Whitworth to prevent their capture. Of this second wave of attackers, one of Fort Gregg's defenders said the Rebels "gave them the same warm welcome that we gave the first, and more of it." But on the Federals came, and, together with men from Foster's division, they were soon scrambling up the slippery earthen walls. One Confederate said "the battle flags of the enemy made almost a solid line of bunting around the fort." Another Rebel said, "The noise outside was fearful, frightful and indescribable. The curses and groaning of frenzied men could be heard over and above the din of our musketry. Savage men, ravenous beasts!" The Confederate artillerymen inside Fort Gregg, their guns disabled, turned their shells into hand grenades. "I was down behind the breastworks," one of them remembered, "& lit the fuse of the shells & these men rolled them to the Yankees....I had a block of Confederate matches...& I struck the match on the shell. The sulphur burned blue and the powder s-s-s-s & away she went."[15]

Eventually a few Federals reached the top of the parapet. One of the first to get there threw dirt in the eyes of the nearest Rebels to give himself time to pull some of his fellows up to join him. "Soon the Stars and Stripes could be seen floating by the side of the Rebel flag," a Union officer wrote. "Cheer after cheer rent the air—the Rebels fighting with the desperation of madmen, and shouting to each other, 'Never surrender! Never surrender!' For twenty-seven minutes we hung upon the works, knowing we could not retreat if we wished to. One more rush, and we were inside the fort, and for a minute or two there was a hand-to-hand contest. The works were ours, *and* the garrison—dead and alive."[16]

A lieutenant from the 12th West Virginia was one of the first to get inside the fort. He "was shot dead by a Confederate who was immediately bayoneted by one of our men," a Union soldier wrote. "When we rushed over the top," another officer said, "the sight was truly terrific—dead men and the dying lay strewn all about, and it was with the greatest difficulty that we could prevent our infuriated solders from shooting down and braining all who survived of the stubborn foe." One Rebel said, "'Tis true that when they rushed into the fort upon us, they were yelling, cursing and shooting with all the frenzy and rage of a horde of merciless barbarians." Another said, "More of our men were killed after the Yankees got into the fort than during the fighting." When the fighting stopped, it was found that, out of the approximately 300 defenders, 56 had been killed and about 200 wounded. One Federal said, "The interior of the fort was a pool of blood, a sight which can never be shut from memory. The rebels had recklessly fought to the last."[17]

Over at Fort Whitworth, "Gen. Harris mounted the parapet," one of its defenders wrote, "and waved the flag over our heads, and shouted 'Give 'em hell, boys.'" But as the Union attack closed in on his fort Harris received orders "from General Lee to evacuate Whitworth, as time had been gained for Longstreet to arrive...and an inner line formed." The Confederates escaped from the rear of the fort just as the Federals charged over its front. One of Nate Harris's men noted that the general "did not relish the 'home stretch,' and soon became tired. The run exhausted him, and while catching his breath he said to me, 'I'll be d——d if I run any more.'" However, when the Federals opened fire on the retreating Rebels, "the volley stimulated [us] to renewed exertions," the Confederate said, "so much so that I believe that we led the boys into the last ditch of Petersburg, spitting into spray the placid waters of Old Town Creek." On the east side of that stream, all of Field's division was now in position and digging in. Some of Gibbons' men pushed on to take what one of them called "a skirmishing position on Indian Town Creek where they remained for some time, anxiously looking for an advancing Union column, and fully determined to head it, and if possible be the first armed Yankees to enter the Cockade City."[18] But no such column appeared.

"Any further resistance on the part of General Lee seemed now impossible," staff officer John Esten Cooke wrote, "and nothing appeared to be left to him but to surrender his army. This course he does not seem, however, to have contemplated. It was still possible that he might be able to maintain his position on an inner line near the city until night; and, if he could do so, the friendly hours of darkness might enable him to make good his retreat...and shape his course toward North Carolina where General Johnston awaited him. If the movements of the Federal forces, however, were so prompt as to defeat his march in that direction, he might still be able to reach Lynchburg, beyond which point the defiles of the Alleghenies promised him protection against the utmost efforts of his enemy."[19]

By this time it was nearly 2:30 p.m. At about that same hour, Humphreys reached the Petersburg front with his two divisions. But by then Meade had learned that Miles had been left on his own and was facing a large Confederate force, so he ordered Humphreys to take one of his divisions back and rejoin Miles, leaving the other to reinforce Wright's 6th Corps. "Mott's division was going into position," Humphreys reported, "and was left. Taking the Second Division, I moved rapidly as possible by the Cox road toward Sutherland's Station, expecting, if the enemy were still in front of Miles, to take them in flank."[20] However, before he reached Miles, his help was no longer needed. Miles' one-brigade flank attack was ready to go in.

"At 2.45 p.m. the brigade advanced at double quick, with a hearty cheer and in magnificent order," Miles reported.[21] A Confederate sharpshooter said, "Our line opened fire in full chorus at long range, and as the enemy closed upon us the vigor of our defense increased, until the entire line was enveloped in one living cloud of blue coats." Brigadier General Samuel McGowan's brigade was the first to be overrun. Brigadier General William MacRae's brigade was next. "When McGowan...gave way in confusion," MacRae said, "I ordered up my sharpshooters to the support of his left, but they arrived too late to effect anything. In a few moments Scales' Brigade on my right gave way, leaving me alone to confront the enemy with 280 men."[22] MacRae's Brigade was also swept away. Only Cooke's Brigade, on the opposite end of the Rebel line, managed to fall back in reasonable order. "Never shall I forget," Miles later wrote, "the exultation that thrilled my very soul as our troops swept over the line of fortifications...on that memorable day of April 2, 1865."[23]

"Now was the most disorderly movement I ever saw among Confederate troops," one of McGowan's officers, Lieutenant J.F.J. Caldwell, wrote. "We had to pass from 200 to 300 yards through a clear field under the fire of infantry from flank and rear, and under artillery. The whole air shrieked with missiles, the whole earth trembled. We fled for the cover of woods and distance." A Rebel major said, "Officers and men, mixed together in the wildest confusion, fled before the withering fire until the point of danger was passed, when they came together, were assorted out and formed into some sort of organization and continued the retreat." Caldwell added that "a weary, mortified, angry stream of men poured through the fields and roads, some pushing toward Amelia Courthouse, some making direct for the [Appomattox] river."[24] Many of them had thrown away their weapons in order to facilitate their escape. In this attack the Federals captured one battleflag, two guns, and 600 men.

Humphreys arrived not long after the Confederates retreated, and soon he, along with most of Miles' division were countermarching again, back to the east toward Petersburg, in case they might be needed there. By then Sheridan and the 5th Corps were not far from Sutherland Station, along the Cox Road to the west. "Our cavalry shortly afterwards coming up in our rear," Joshua Chamberlain wrote, "Sheridan with them pursued the fugitives along their retreat, now northwesterly, our rear division, Crawford's joining in a skirmish about dusk."[25] Sheridan said, "Crawford and Merritt engaged the enemy lightly just before night, but his main column, retreating along the river road south of the Appomattox, had got across Namozine Creek, and the darkness prevented our doing more than to pick up some stragglers."[26]

"We wandered," Lieutenant Caldwell said, "strung out along the river bank for miles, floundering in the beds of small streams or in mudholes filled by the recent heavy rains, pressing forward to some point undetermined in our own minds. Night fell upon us, but even that brought no repose until, at a late hour, we collected a little band and lay down by the roadside in utter exhaustion and almost despair. Some of us were so worn that we slept like the dead; others so anxious that we could not sleep at all. I never saw more haggard countenances in my life. I, for one, felt years older than I had that morning."[27]

At about 3 p.m.—just about the time Miles' attack was routing Cooke's Confederates at Sutherland Station—the Rebels hit Parke's 9th Corps again, trying to drive him out of the toe hold he had gained on the outer line. This time, while a skirmish line advanced against the Union front, two brigades hit each flank. One of the skirmishers remembered that "shells burst over our heads, or rolled and spun and darted and hissed about our feet in a dreadfully demoralizing way. Then, too, the wounded men, pale-faced and bloody, some borne on litters, others limping and trotting, and passing us in crowds, had no tendency to enliven our spirits." But the attack made some headway as the Federals began to give ground. "Every few steps we came upon a dead man," another Confederate said, "nearly always shot through the head." Again the fighting centered around the traverses in the Rebel line. "The ends of the traverses next to the works," one Confederate said, "were roughly fitted, leaving many holes and openings. Through these holes some of the men fired away at light-blue legs while the bulk of the command fired over the traverses at dark-blue heads."[28]

But just as Parke's men, weary and low on ammunition, were in danger of losing all that they had gained, they were reinforced by the Independent Brigade, normally posted at City Point to guard the headquarters and supply depots. It included a crack zouave outfit, the 114th Pennsylvania, whose former colonel now commanded the brigade. These Federals were met by a withering fire as they crossed no-man's land toward Fort Mahone. "The fire which rained on the ground and around this fort," a newspaper reporter watching from Fort Sedgwick wrote, "was of the most terrible and fearful character, and to stand and see our men advance on a run through the very thickest of it, many of them being torn to pieces and lost to sight before they crossed half the distance was a sight not soon to be forgotten." A soldier in the 9th Corps said, "The thought was, 'Can they stand it?'—will they make it?'" And make it they did. With this fresh support, Parke's men held their ground and fought off this final Confederate attack. General Gordon was busily preparing another when he received orders from Lee to stop. "In the face of the almost complete crushing of every command defending the entire length of our lines on my right," Gordon wrote, "the restoration of the remaining breach in my front could contribute nothing toward the rescue of Lee's army." Here too darkness soon put an end to the fighting. "I never was so glad to see the sun go down," one of Parke's men declared.[29]

Also at about 3 p.m. Lee began dictating the orders for the withdrawal of his army from Petersburg and Richmond. The movement was to begin as soon as darkness fell. In four columns, his forces were to converge on Amelia Court House, which was on the Richmond and Danville Railroad almost due west of Petersburg and just to the west of a north-south stretch of the Appomattox River. There they were to be met by supplies brought by rail. One column, commanded by Anderson, consisted of Johnson's Division of his 4th Corps, Pickett's Division of the 1st Corps, all three of Fitz Lee's cavalry divisions, and whatever remained of the brigades under Cooke that had been routed by Miles. These troops were to continue moving west along the south bank of the Appomattox. Lee himself would lead another column, consisting of the troops at Petersburg, along the north bank. These included Field's Division of the 1st Corps and remnants from the 3rd Corps, both under Longstreet, plus Gordon's 2nd Corps. Mahone's Division of the 3rd Corps, manning the lines blocking the Bermuda Hundred peninsula, would take a parallel route slightly farther north and constitute part of Longstreet's command. Ewell, commander of the Department of Richmond, would bring his own forces, primarily a division commanded by Lee's oldest son, Custis, and a brigade of cavalry, plus Kershaw's Division of the 1st Corps, from north of the James and be joined by naval gunners and marines who were manning the defenses at Drewry's Bluff on the south bank of that river. After the orders were all written and sent out, Colonel Walter Taylor of Lee's staff, who had done most of the actual writing, obtained permission to go to Richmond and marry his sweetheart before he had to ride off and leave her for an unknown future.

At 4:40 p.m. Grant sent a message over the field telegraph to Colonel Bowers back at City Point. "We are now up," he said, "and have a continuous line of troops, and in a few hours will be intrenched from the Appomattox, below Petersburg, to the river above." After giving a brief description of the position of the troops, he added, "The whole captures since the army started out gunning will not amount to less than 12,000 men, and probably 50 pieces of artillery. I do not know the number of men, and guns accurately, however....All seems well with us, and everything quiet just now. I think the President might come out and pay us a visit to-morrow." Lincoln, who had been relaying Grant's dispatches to Stanton back at Washington ever since the general-in-chief had left City Point, soon replied to Grant: "Allow me to tender to you and all with you the nation's grateful thanks for this additional and magnificent success. At your kind suggestion I think I will meet you to-morrow."[30]

"Prominent officers," Horace Porter wrote, "now urged the general to make an assault on the inner lines, and capture Petersburg that afternoon; but he was firm in his resolve not to sacrifice the lives necessary to accomplish such a result. He said the city would undoubtedly be evacuated during the night, and he would dispose the troops for a parallel march westward, and try to head off the escaping army."[31]

"Dusk came," a citizen of Petersburg wrote, "and with it began the evacuation. Noiselessly from the lines they had so gallantly defended, the Confederates withdrew; and the long, dark columns passed through the streets unattacked, unpursued. We were spared the horror of a fight through the streets, which had been feared. Now began the wild farewells and long embraces with which mothers sent forth their sons to unknown fates, and perchance endless partings." General Lee watched his army march for the Appomattox bridge. "He had stationed himself at the mouth of the Hickory Road," John Esten Cook wrote, "and, standing with the bridle of his horse in his hand, gave his orders. His bearing still remained entirely composed, and his voice had lost none of its grave strength of intonation. When the rear was well closed up, Lee mounted his horse, rode on slowly with his men; and, in the midst of the glare and thunder of the exploding magazines at Petersburg, the small remnant of the Army of Northern Virginia...went on its way through the darkness."[32]

In the Union army, almost everybody, from the general-in-chief to the lowliest private, felt that the war was all but won. "After dark," Lieutenant Colonel Rhodes of the 2nd Rhode Island wrote, "the officers assembled and we joined with grateful hearts in singing 'Praise God from Whom All Blessings Flow.' Hurrah for the Union! It will soon be restored, thank God."[33] Colonel Theodore Lyman of Meade's staff put it succinctly, if colloquially, in a letter he wrote to his wife that night: "My dear Mimi: THE REBELLION HAS GONE UP!"[34]

In Richmond that afternoon, indications that the city was being abandoned by the Confederate government became, as one resident put it, "obvious to even the most incredulous. Wagons were driven furiously through the streets to the different departments, where they received as freight the archives...and carred them to the Danville Depot, to be there conveyed away by railroad. Thousands of citizens determined to evacuate the city with the government. Vehicles commanded any price....The streets were filled with excited crowds hurrying to the different avenues for transportation, intermingled with porters carrying huge loads, and wagons piled up with incongruous heaps of baggage of all sorts and descriptions. The banks were all open, and depositors were busily and anxiously collecting their species deposits, and directors were as busily engaged in getting off their bullion. Millions of dollars of paper money, both State and Confederate, were carried to the Capitol Square and burned."[35]

President Davis was among those trying to use the banks that afternoon. Before sending off his wife he had auctioned off her furniture and silver, and now he sent the treasurer of the Confederacy off to cash the check he had received for $28,400, specifying that he wanted it in United States coins. The treasurer came back with the check, saying the bank refused to cash it. Davis could only hope that it could be cashed at Danville, which would be the first stop on the government's flight. That evening Davis and most of his cabinet gathered at the train station, but he delayed their departure hoping to receive word from Lee that the situation had improved and they would not have to leave. The treasury itself was loaded onto another train that was to follow the president's. It consisted of U.S. double eagle gold pieces, Mexican silver dollars, copper coins, silver bricks, and gold ingots and nuggets—in all valued at about $500,000. It was joined by the reserves of several Richmond banks and guarded by sixty midshipmen from the Confederate naval academy, some of whom were no more than twelve years old. They were brought up from their training ship on the James River.

As word spread that the army and government were evacuating, order in the city began to melt away. Some people were frantic to get out before the Yankees came, others merely saw an opportunity for plunder. "The disorder," a newspaper editor wrote, "increased each hour.... Pale women and little shoeless children struggled in the crowd. Oaths and blasphemous shouts smote the ear.... Outside, the mass of hurrying fugitives, there were collected here and there mean-visaged crowds, generally around the commissary depots. They had already scented prey. They were of that brutal and riotous element that revenges itself on all communities in a time of great public misfortune."[36]

"About dusk," according to the *Richmond Times*, "the government commissaries begun the destruction of their immense quantities of stores." Among the supplies being destroyed were large amount of whiskey, which was poured in the gutters. "Several hundred soldiers and citizens gathered in front of the building, and contrived to catch most of the liquor in pitchers, bottles and basins, that was poured out. This liquor was not slow in manifesting itself. The crowd became a mob and began to howl. Soon other crowds had collected in front of other government warehouses. At some, attempts were made to distribute supplies, but so frenzied had the mob become, that the officers in charge, in many cases, had to flee for their lives. All through the night, crowds of men, women and children traversed the streets, rushing from one store-house to another, loading themselves with all kinds of supplies.... This work went on fast and furious until after midnight, about which time large numbers of straggling soldiers made their appearance on the streets and immediately set about robbing the principal stores on Main Street. Drunk with vile liquor, the soldiers roamed from store to store, followed by a reckless crowd, drunk as they."[37]

Fires soon broke out, adding to the city's problems. "O, the horrors of that night!" a Richmond woman who watched the looting from her windows wrote. "The rolling of vehicles, excited cries of the men, women and children as they passed loaded with such goods as they could snatch from the burning factories and stores that were being looted by the frenzied crowds; for to such straits had many been brought that the looting was not confined to the 'poor white' or rabble. Delicately reared ladies were seen with sheets and shawls filled with goods, provisions, etc., even to boxes of tobacco."[38]

President Davis kept the train that was to carry himself and most of his cabinet waiting at the station for three hours. He and Secretary of War Breckinridge lingered in the station's office hoping to hear of some reversal of fortune that would make it unnecessary to flee the capital. "Mr. Davis was calm, dignified as usual," wrote Captain William H. Parker, the naval officer in command of the midshipmen guarding the treasury, "and Gen. Breckinridge...was as cool and gallant as ever—but the others, I thought, had the air, as the French say, of wishing to be off."[39] They were worried that Sheridan's cavalry would cut the railroad before they could get through, and most of them expected to be hanged if caught by the Yankees, with or without trial.

Both the presidential train and that carrying the treasury, which would follow, were packed with refugees, Captain Parker said, "not only inside, but on top, on the platforms, on the engine—everywhere, in fact, where standing-room could be found; and those who could not get that 'hung on by their eyelids.' I placed sentinels at the doors of the depot finally, and would not let another soul enter."[40]

At last Davis gave up hope and took his place aboard his train. Breckinridge stayed behind to supervise the evacuation. The engine soon pulled out and crossed the long bridge over the James River, heading south. "Why Jeff Davis should have preferred to be kicked out of Richmond," a Rebel colonel riding west with the retreating troops speculated, "to evacuating it in a dignified manner I suppose he himself does not know. It was the egotistical, bull-headed obstinacy of the man no doubt."[41]

Abraham Lincoln had stayed at army headquarters at City Point, waiting beside the telegraph key for news, until after dark. Then he returned to Admiral David Porter's flagship. He was staying on board the *Malvern* since the *River Queen* had returned to Washington with Mrs. Lincoln. The admiral had offered to yield his own bed to the president, but Lincoln had elected to sleep in a small stateroom, only six feet long by four and a half wide. "When the President retired for his first night on board," Porter wrote, "he put his shoes and socks outside the state-room door. I am sorry to say the President's socks had holes in them; but they were washed and darned, his boots cleaned, and the whole placed at his door." That had been the night of 1-2 April. At breakfast on the second, the president had said, "A miracle happened to me last night. When I went to bed I had two large holes in my socks, and this morning there are no holes in them. That never happened to me before; it must be a miracle!"

"How did you sleep?" the admiral had asked.

"I slept well," Lincoln had answered, "but you can't put a long blade in a short scabbard. I was too long for that berth."

"Then I remembered," Admiral Porter wrote, "he was over six feet four inches, while the berth was only six feet."[42] That day, while Lincoln and Porter were off the ship, carpenters were put to work and the state-room was taken down and increased in size to eight feet by six and a half feet. The mattress was widened to suit a berth four feet wide, and the entire state-room was remodeled.

Now, on the night of 2-3 April, Lincoln watched from the deck of the *Malvern* as the Union army's heavy artillery tried to hit the railroad bridge over the Appomattox in the dark. Grant had ordered it, knowing that Lee's troops must be using that bridge to evacuate Petersburg. One lucky hit might bring down the bridge. Lincoln knew that momentuous events were taking place that night and seemed to be anxious to contribute.

"Can't the navy do something at this particular moment to make history?" he asked Porter.

The Navy's doing its best," the admiral said, "holding the enemy's four ironclads in uselessness up there in the river. If those boats could reach City Point they would cause havoc. They came near it once."

"Can't we make a noise, then?" Lincoln asked.

"Yes," Porter said, "and if you desire it, we will commence."[43]

The admiral sent a message to the commander of the gunboats up the river to open fire on the Confederate forts that guarded the river and to keep it up until ordered to stop.

Rear Admiral Raphael Semmes, who had been captain of the commerce raider *Alabama* until it had been sunk off Cherbourg, France, the year before, had recently been appointed to command the Confederacy's James River gunboats. He set fire to his four ironclads at about 2 a.m. to keep them from falling into Union hands. "My little squadron of wooden boats," Semmes remembered, "now moved off up the river by the glare of the burning ironclads. They had not proceeded far, before an explosion like the shock of an earthquake took place, and the air was filled with missiles...." It was the Confederate flagship. "The spectacle was grand beyond description," Semmes said. "Her shell rooms had been full of loaded shells. The explosion of the magazine threw all these shells, with their fuses lighted, into the air. The fuses were of different lengths, and as the shells exploded by twos and threes, and by the dozen, the pyrotechnic effect was very fine. The explosion shook the houses in Richmond, and must have waked the echoes of the night for miles around."[44]

That was putting it mildly. One Richmond woman said the noise was "like that of a hundred cannon at one time. The very foundations of the city were shaken; windows were shattered more than two miles from where the gunboats were exploded, and the frightened inhabitants imagined that the place was being furiously bombarded." A Union officer in Weitzel's command east of the city said the concussion was so terrific that "the earth shook where we were, and there flashed out a glare of light as of noonday, while the fragments of the vessel, pieces of timber and other stuff, fell among my pickets."[45]

A Confederate officer commanding a battalion that was retreating from the defenses of Richmond said, "The explosions began just as we got across the river. When the magazines at Chaffin's and Drewry's Bluffs went off, the solid earth shuddered convulsively; but as the ironclads—one after another—exploded, it seemed as if the very dome of heaven would be shattered down upon us. Earth and air and the black sky glared in the lurid light. Columns and towers and pinnacles of flame shot upward to an amazing height, from which, on all sides, the ignited shells flew on arcs of fire and burst as if bombarding heaven....I walked in rear of the battalion to prevent straggling, and as the successive flashes illumed the darkness the blanched faces and staring eyes turned backward upon me spoke volumes of nervous demoralization. I felt that a hare might shatter the column."[46]

Downstream, Lincoln and Porter heard the great explosion. "I hope to heaven one of our vessels hasn't exploded," the president said.

"No. It's farther upstream," the admiral replied. "Doubtless the Rebels, blowing up the ironclads." When other explosions followed he added, "That's all of them. No doubt the forts have fallen. Tomorrow you can go up to Richmond."[47]

In that city, an argument was soon in progress between officers of General Ewell's staff and representatives of Mayor Joseph Mayo. Around midnight the mayor learned that Ewell had ordered the burning of four huge warehouses full of tobacco in order to keep it out of Federal hands. One of the mayor's men called it a "reckless military order which plainly put in jeopardy the whole business portion of Richmond." A major from the War Department called the civilians' protest "a cowardly pretext on the part of the citizens, trumped up to endeavor to save their property for the Yankees." The civilians failed to change the soldiers' minds, and around 2 a.m. fires were set at the warehouses, and a nearby flour mill. The soldiers were also, as one civilian noted, "putting the torch to every armory, machine shop and storehouse belonging to the government" until "one lurid glare shot upward...then another, and another." La Salle Pickett, wife of the recently defeated general, said, "A fresh breeze was blowing from the south; the fire swept on in its haste and fury over a great area in an almost incredibly short time."[48]

General Ewell blamed the burning of Richmond on the plundering civilians. "A mob of both sexes and all colors soon collected," he wrote, "and about 3 a.m. set fire to some buildings on Cary Street, and began to plunder the city. The convalescents then stationed in the Square were ordered to surpress the riot, but their commander shortly reported himself unable to do so, his force being inadequate. I then ordered all my staff and couriers who could be spared to scour the streets, so as to intimidate the mob by a show of force, and sent word to General Kershaw who was coming up from the lines, to hurry his leading regiment into town."[49]

Many rioters were shot, but that did not stop what La Salle Pickett called the "saturnalia." Whatever their cause, the flames were spreading, and, as she put it, "on the wings of the wind...were carried to the next building and the next...[and] leaped from house to house in mad revel.

"They stretched out burning arms on all sides and embraced in deadly clasp the stately mansions which had stood in lofty grandeur from the olden days of colonial pride. Soon they became towering masses of fire, fluttering immense flame-banners against the wind, and fell, sending up myriads of fiery points into the air, sparkling like blazing stars against the dark curtain that shut out the sky.

"A stormy sea of smoke surged over the town—here a billow of blackness of suffocating density—there a brilliant cloud, shot through with crimson arrows. The wind swept on and the ocean of smoke and flame rolled before it in surges of destruction over the once fair city of Richmond.

"The terrified cries of women and children arose in agony above the roaring of the flames, the crashing of falling buildings, and the trampling of countless feet.

"Piles of furniture and wares lay in the streets as if the city had struck one great moving day, when everything was taken into the highways and left there to be trampled to pieces and buried in the mud....

"The sea of darkness rolled over the town, the crowds of men, women and children went about the streets laden with what plunder they could rescue from the flames. The drunken rabble shattered the plate-glass windows of the stores and wrecked everything upon which they could seize. The populace had become a frenzied mob, and the kingdom of Satan seemed to have been transferred to the streets of Richmond.

"The fire revealed many things which I should like never to have seen, and, having seen, would fain forget.

"The most revolting revelation was the amount of provisions, shoes and clothing which had been accumulated by the speculators who hovered like vultures over the scene of death and desolation. Taking advantage of their possession of money and lack of both patriotism and humanity, they had, by an early corner in the market and by successful blockade running, bought up all the available supplies with an eye to future gain, while our soldiers and women and children were absolutely in rags, barefoot and starving."[50]

At 3 a.m. Jefferson Davis's train stopped briefly at the little town of Clover Station, Virginia, some eighty miles southwest of Richmond. Eighteen-year-old lieutenant John Wise, who was stationed there, saw "physical and mental exhaustion" in the president's expression and manner. The lieutenant was the son of Brigadier General Henry A. Wise, a former governor of Virginia who was no great supporter of Davis. The train soon moved on again, but it was followed by the Treasury Department train, guarded by Captain Parker and his young midshipmen, and then others carrying the archives and employees of the Post Office Department and the Bureau of War. "I saw the government on wheels...," the young officer realized, "the marvelous and incongruous debris of the wreck of the Confederate capital...indescriminate cargoes of men and things. In one car was a cage with an African parrot, and a box of tame squirrels, and a hunchback."

As the last train pulled out of the little town, a man standing at the rear of the last car shouted to the people watching from the station. "Richmond's burning," he told them. "Gone. All gone."[51]

---

1. Trudeau, *The Last Citadel*, 393.
2. Ibid.
3. *Official Records*, 46:I:679.
4. Ibid., 46:I:1106.
5. Ibid., 46:III:489.
6. Sheridan, *Civil War Memoirs*, 333.
7. Chamberlain, *The Passing of the Armies*, 143.
8. Ibid., 146.
9. *Official Records*, 46:I:711.
10. Ibid.
11. Ibid., 46:I:1186.
12. Trudeau, *The Last Citadel*, 384.
13. *Official Records*, 46:I:1186.
14. Trudeau, *The Last Citadel*, 385.
15. Ibid., 386-387.
15. Ibid., 387-388.
16. Wheeler, *Witness to Appomattox*, 88.
17. Ibid., 387-389.
18. Ibid., 388.
19. Wheeler, *Witness to Appomattox*, 88-89.
20. *Official Records*, 46:I:679.
21. Ibid., 46:I:711.
22. Trudeau, *The Last Citadel*, 396-397.
23. Ibid., 397.
24. Davis, *To Appomattox*, 74-75.
25. Chamberlain, *The Passing of the Armies*, 146.
26. Sheridan, *Civil War Memoirs*, 333-334.
27. Davis, *To Appomattox*, 75.
28. Trudeau, *The Last Citadel*, 364.
29. Ibid., 365.
30. *Official Records*, 46:III:449.
31. Porter, *Campaigning with Grant*, 448.
32. Wheeler, *Witness to Appomattox*, 96-97.
33. Rhodes, *All For the Union*, 226-227.
34. Trudeau, *The Last Citadel*, 398.
35. Ibid., 93.
36. Ibid.

37. A. J. Hanna, *Flight Into Oblivion* (New York, 1938), 11-12.
38. Hoehling and Hoehling, *The Last Days of the Confederacy,* 158.
39. Davis, *The Long Surrender*, 31.
40. Hoehling and Hoehling, *The Last Days of the Confederacy,* 144.
41. Davis, *The Long Surrender*, 39.
42. Stern, *An End to Valor*, 150.
43. Davis, *To Appomattox*, 85.
44. Hoehling and Hoehling, *The Last Days of the Confederacy,* 168.
45. Ibid., 168-169.
46. Wheeler, *Witness to Appomattox*, 99.
47. Davis, *To Appomattox*, 85.
48. Hoehling and Hoehling, *The Last Days of the Confederacy,* 166-167.
49. Ibid., 171.
50. Ibid., 171-173.
51. Davis, *The Long Surrender*, 52.

CHAPTER THIRTY

Babylon Has Fallen!

3 April 1865

Confederate deserters alerted the Federals in the lines about Petersburg to the withdrawal of Lee's army, and pickets confirmed that the Rebel lines were unusually quiet. Anyone with ears could hear the rumble of explosions in Petersburg, and they could see flames rising from various points in the town, as government installations and tobacco warehouses there were destroyed, as they were in Richmond. Union pickets began to investigate and found the Confederate defenses deserted. Soon whole regiments were moving into them, and some moved on to the outskirts of the city.

At 3:10 a.m. Brevet Colonel Ralph Ely, commanding the 2nd Brigade of Willcox's 1st Division of the 9th Corps, sent two of his regiments, the 1st Michigan Sharpshooters and the 2nd Michigan, up the City Point Road toward Petersburg. As they were reforming their ranks after passing through the Rebel lines a race developed between their color guards to be the first to get into the city. A delegation from the Petersburg Common Council tried to surrender to the leading Federals, the group from the 1st Michigan, but Major Clement Lounsberry brushed them aside, saying that he "could listen to no proposition until the 'old flag' was floating from the highest point of the court-house steeple and proper pickets had been established in the vicinity." A color sergeant remembered that "it was yet dark when we made our way into the courthouse and up the winding stairs into the clock tower. For want of a better place to display our colors we opened the door of the clock face and thrust them out through it, and there, for the first time in years, floated the dear old flag....Our hearts were too full for utterance, so we clasped hands and shed tears of joy, for we knew that the beginning of the end had come." Colonel Ely checked his watch and saw that it was 4:28 a.m.[1]

The delegation that Major Lounsberry met was only one of several sent out by the Petersburg Common Council in search of Federals to surrender to. Another, composed of Mayor W.W. Townes and a councilman, carrying a white handkerchief on a stick, had just reached Old Town Creek west of the city as dawn was breaking when they heard a signal gun fired somewhere to their left. "Instantaneously," the councilman wrote, "there sprang forth, as from the bowels of the earth, it seemed to me, a mighty host of Federal soldiers, and there followed such a shout of victory as seemed to shake the very ground on which we stood."[2] The civilians tried to get the soldiers' attention, but the Federals rushed right past them into the Confederate defenses and the city. Eventually someone escorted the pair to Colonel Oliver Edwards, commander of the 3rd Brigade of the 1st Division of the 6th Corps, who accepted their surrender of the city.

A reporter for the *New York Herald* rode into Petersburg behind some of the troops. "The streets at first seemed deserted," he wrote, "but the cheers of the excited soldiers, as they marched through the town, soon brought out swarms of negroes—men, women and children—who manifested their gladness by every conceivable demonstration." The reporter, being one of the few mounted men among the Federals, received quite a bit of this attention. "It was somewhat embarrassing, as well as a little annoying," he said, "to be compelled to explain at every street corner that I was no very great personality after all."[3]

However, two genuinely great personalities were also on hand. "General Meade and I entered Petersburg on the morning of the 3d," Grant wrote in his memoirs, "and took a position under cover of a house which protected us from the enemies musketry which was flying thick and fast there. As we would occasionally look around the corner we could see the streets and the Appomattox bottom, presumably near the bridge, packed with the Confederate army. I did not have artillery brought up, because I was sure Lee was trying to make his escape, and I wanted to push immediately in pursuit. At all events I had not the heart to turn the artillery upon such a mass of defeated and fleeing men, and I hoped to capture them soon.

"Soon after the enemy had entirely evacuated Petersburg, a man came in who represented himself to be an engineer of the Army of Northern Virginia. He said that Lee had for some time been at work preparing a strong enclosed intrenchment, into which he would throw himself when forced out of Petersburg, and fight his final battle there; that he was actually at that time drawing his troops from Richmond, and falling back into this prepared work....I had already given orders for the movement up the south side of the Appomattox for the purpose of heading off Lee; but Meade was so much impressed by this man's story that he thought we ought to cross the Appomattox there at once and move against Lee in his new position. I knew that Lee was no fool, as he would have been to have put himself and his army between two formidable streams like the James and Appomattox rivers, and between two such armies as those of the Potomac and the James. Then these streams coming together as they did to the east of him, it would be only necessary to close up in the west to have him thoroughly cut off from all supplies or possibility of reinforcement. It would only have been a question of days, and not many of them, if he had taken the position assigned to him by the so-called engineer, when he would have been obliged to surrender his army. Such is one of the ruses resorted to in war to deceive your antagonist. My judgment was that Lee would necessarily have to evacuate Richmond, and that the only course for him to pursue would be to follow the Danville Road. Accordingly my object was to secure a point on that road south of Lee, and I told Meade this. He suggested that if Lee was going that way we would follow him. My reply was that we did not want to follow him; we wanted to get ahead of him and cut him off....

"I had held most of the command aloof from the intrenchments, so as to start them out on the Danville Road early in the morning, supposing that Lee would be gone during the night. During the night I strengthened Sheridan by sending him Humphreys's corps...and directed him to move out on the Danville Railroad to the south side of the Appomattox River as speedily as possible. He replied that he already had some of his command nine miles out. I then ordered the rest of the Army of the Potomac under Meade to follow the same road in the morning....

"I telegraphed Mr. Lincoln asking him to ride out there and see me, while I would await his arrival. I had started all the troops out early in the morning, so that after the National army left Petersburg there was not a soul to be seen, not even an animal in the streets. There was absolutely no one there, except my staff officers and, possibly, a small escort of cavalry. We had selected the piazza of a deserted house, and occupied it until the President arrived."[4]

Lincoln had slept on the *Malvern* again the night before. No one had mentioned the alteration of his state room to him before he had gone to bed. But this morning he had emerged with a smile. "A greater miracle than ever happened last night," he told Admiral Porter; "I shrank six inches in length and about a foot sideways. I got somebody else's big pillow, and slept in a better bed than I did on the *River Queen*."[5] The president then resumed his self-appointed post in the telegraph office at City Point. At 8:30 a.m. he wired Stanton, back at Washington: "This morning General Grant reports Petersburg evacuated, and he is confident Richmond also is. He is pushing forward to cut off, if possible, the retreating army. I start to him in a few minutes."[6]

The president, with his young son Tad and the admiral, took the military railroad as far as they could and were met by Lincoln's oldest son, Robert, who had brought horses for his father and his little brother but had none for Porter. However, Robert had a small cavalry escort with him, and from one of the troopers the admiral borrowed a mount which he called a "raw-boned white horse, a hard trotter and a terrible stumbler. How the Government became possessed of such an animal the Lord only knows." The horse ran away with the admiral several times, which was, Porter said, "the only way by which I could keep up with the President, who was splendidly mounted." When they reached Grant's headquarters the admiral told one of the general's staff officers that he wanted buy the horse. Lincoln tried to dissuade him, pointing out the animal's many faults.

"He's fourteen years old if he's a day," the president said; "his hoofs will cover half an acre. He's spavined, and only has one eye. What do you want with him?"

"I want to buy it and shoot it," the admiral said, "so that no one else will ever ride it again."[7]

Colonel Horace Porter witnessed Lincoln's arrival: "He dismounted in the street and came in through the front gate with long and rapid strides, his face beaming with delight. He seized General Grant's hand as the general stepped forward to greet him, and stood shaking it for some time, and pouring out his thanks and congratulations with all the fervor of a heart which seemed overflowing with its fullness of joy. I doubt whether Mr. Lincoln ever experienced a happier moment in his life."

"Do you know, general," the president said, "I had a sort of sneaking idea all along that you intended to do something like this; but I thought some time ago that you would so maneuver as to have Sherman come up and be near enough to cooperate with you."

"Yes," Grant replied, "I thought at one time that Sherman's army might advance far enough to be in supporting distance of the Eastern armies when the spring campaign against Lee opened; but I had a feeling that it would be better to let Lee's old antagonists give his army the final blow, and finish up the job. If the Western troops were even to put in an appearance against Lee's army, it might give some of our politicians a chance to stir up sectional feeling in claiming everything for the troops from their own section of the country. The Western armies have been very successful in their campaigns, and it is due to the Eastern armies to let them vanquish their old enemy single-handed."

"I see, I see," Lincoln said, "but I never thought of it in that light. In fact, my anxiety has been so great that I didn't care where the help came from so that the work was perfectly done."

"The general hoped," Horace Porter wrote, "that before he parted with Mr. Lincoln he would hear that Richmond was in our possession; but after waiting about an hour and a half, he said he must ride on to the front and join Ord's column, and took leave of the President, who shook his hand cordially, and with great warmth of feeling wished him God-speed and every success."[8]

Lincoln and Admiral Porter rode about the captured city for a while before returning to the military railroad. "The streets," the admiral said, "were alive with Negroes who were crazy to see their savior, as they called the President." Porter's horse was cutting all sorts of capers again, but he managed to stay aboard.

"Admiral," the president said, "you mistook your profession; you ought to have been a circus rider."

"Several regiments passed us en route," Porter later wrote, "and they all seemed to recognize the President at once. 'Three cheers for Uncle Abe!' passed along among them, and the cheers were given with a vim which showed the estimation in which he was held by the soldiers."[9]

"We'll get 'em, Abe, where the boy had the hen," one soldier shouted to Lincoln. "You go home and sleep sound tonight. We boys will put you through!"[10]

When he got back to City Point, the president found a message from Stanton waiting for him: "I congratulate you and the nation on the glorious news in your telegram just received. Allow me respectfully to ask you to consider whether you ought to expose the nation to the consequence of any disaster to yourself in the pursuit of a treacherous and dangerous enemy like the rebel army. If it was a question concerning you only I should not presume to say a word. Commanding generals are in the line of their duty in running such risks; but is the political head of a nation in the same condition?"

"Thanks for your caution," Lincoln replied, "but I have already been to Petersburg. Staid with General Grant an hour and a half and returned here. It is certain now that Richmond is in our hands, and I think I will go there to-morrow. I will take care of myself."[11]

Grant and his staff had ridden as far as Sutherland's Station when a dispatch from Weitzel overtook him: "We took Richmond at 8.15 this morning. I captured many guns. The enemy left in great haste. The city is on fire in two places. Am making every effort to put it out. The people received us with enthusiastic expressions of joy."[12]

Just before dawn, Richmond had been rocked by yet another explosion, even louder than all that had gone before, when the arsenal behind the Alms House went up in a roaring tower of flames. The noise, one Richmond resident said, "might almost have awakened the dead. The earth seemed fairly to writhe as if in agony, the house rocked like a ship at sea, while stupendous thunders roared around." Another said the explosion was "perfectly awful, and lasted I suppose about two minutes...I thought the house would be jarred to the ground. It broke the windows and I declare it sounded as if a shell had bursted in the house; three times as loud as any thunder I ever heard in my life."[13]

Soon thereafter the sun rose, and, as one Richmond resident said, "shone with fiery redness through a dense blackness, which at first we took to be heavy clouds, but soon saw was in reality a great volume of smoke passing over the city from south to north."[14] Admiral Semmes, with a different view from aboard one of his wooden gunboats in the James River, watched "a glorious unclouded sun, as if to mock our misfortunes, now rising over Richmond. Some windows, which fronted to the east, were all aglow with his rays, mimicking the real fires that were already breaking out in various parts of the city. In the lower part of the city, the schoolship *Patrick Henry* was burning, and some of the houses near the Navy Yard were on fire....

"But higher up was the principal scene of the conflagration. Entire blocks were on fire here, and a dense canopy of smoke, rising high in the still morning air, was covering the city as with a pall. The rear-guard of our army had just crossed, as I landed my fleet at Manchester, and the bridges were burning in their rear. The Tredegar Iron Works were on fire, and continual explosions of loaded shells stored there were taking place....

"The population was in a great state of alarm. Hundreds of men and women had sought refuge on the Manchester side, in the hope of getting away, by some means or other, they knew not how. I was, myself, about the most helpless man in the whole crowd. I had just tumbled on shore, with their bags and baggage, 500 sailors, incapable of marching a dozen miles without becoming foot-sore, and without any means, whatever, of transportation being provided for them." To underscore the sailors' plight, just then a body of Rebel cavalry rode by. "It was every man for himself and devil take the hindmost," Semmes said. "Some of the young cavalry rascals—lads of eighteen or twenty—as they passed, jibed and joked with my old salts, asking them how they liked navigating the land, and whether they did not expect to anchor in Fort Warren pretty soon? The spectacle presented by my men was, indeed, rather a ludicrous one; loaded down, as they were, with pots, and pans, and mess-kettles, bags of bread, and chunks of salted pork, sugar, tea, tobacco, and pipes. It was as much as they could do to stagger under their loads—marching any distance seemed out of the question."[15]

Semmes was under orders to join General Lee in the field, but he knew neither where Lee was nor how to join him. "Blinded by the dust kicked up by those vagabonds on horseback," the sailors marched as best they could into the town of Manchester, on the south side of the James opposite Richmond. "When we came in sight of the railroad depot," Semmes said, "I halted, and inquired of some of the fugitives who were rushing by, about the trains." He was told that the last train had departed at daylight, filled with civil officers of the Confederate government, but he decided to have a look for himself. He found a crowd of people crammed into and on top of a few decrepit passenger cars that were not attached to any engine "in seeming expectation that someone was to come, in due time, and take them off." But the railroad men had all fled.

However, he also found a small engine on the track, although there was no fire in its furnace. "I resolved to set up railroading on my own account," he said. "Having a dozen and more steam-engineers along with me, from my late fleet...." He forced the civilians to get off of the cars, put his sailors on them, sent his marines to chop up the nearest picket fence to provide firewood, detailed an engineer and a firemen to run the locomotive, got it fired up, and attached it to the cars. Then he invited the civilians back on board. "With the triumphant air of a man who had overcome a great difficulty and who felt as if he might snap his fingers at the Yankees once more, I gave the order to 'go ahead!'" The little engine started off at a crawl and came to "a dead halt" just outside the station.[16] He soon found another engine, however, which was also hitched to the cars, and soon the train was chugging off at five or six miles an hour. Looking across the river to Richmond, the admiral saw, "amid flames and smoke and tumult and disorder, the enemy's hosts were pouring into the streets of the proud old capital. Long lines of cavalry and artillery and infantry could be seen, moving like a huge serpent through the streets, and winding their way to State-House Square."[17]

Like their counterparts in the Union lines around Petersburg, Weitzel's Federals on the north side of the James learned during the night that the Confederate defenses were being evacuated, and near dawn various units started moving toward Richmond. Lieutenant R. B. Prescott led a small detachment of pickets that was among the first. "Every moment the light we had seen over Richmond on starting became more and more brilliant," he wrote. "Above it hung great clouds of heavy smoke, and as we drew nearer there arose a confused murmur now swelling into a loud roar and then subsiding, and again swelling into a great tumult of excited voices, while at frequent intervals short, sharp explosions were heard as of the discharge of field artillery. Weary, breathless, hungry, begrimed with dust and perspiration, but eager and excited, we pushed on, and at half-past six o'clock in the morning I stood with about two-thirds of my men on the summit of a hill and looked down upon the grandest and most appalling sight that my eyes ever beheld. Richmond was literally a sea of flame, out of which the church steeples could be seen protruding here and there, while over all hung a canopy of dense black smoke, lighted up now and then by the bursting shells from the numerous arsenals scattered throughout the city."

Prescott and his detachment of infantry were soon stopped by a couple of cavalrymen sent by General Weitzel to keep anyone from crossing a bridge over a small creek into Richmond before the general arrived. While they were waiting the infantrymen saw a Confederate ship in the nearby James River explode "with a terrific crash," as Prescott said, "scattering fragments of iron and timbers all about us, but fortunately no one was hurt. In a few minutes more a carriage appeared coming from the city, and stopped directly before us. Beckoning me to approach, the occupant asked if I was in command of the men lying about, and on being answered in the affirmative, he said that he was the mayor of Richmond, and that he wished to make a formal surrender of the city. At the same time he placed in my hands a large package, containing, I presume, official papers, the city seal, keys and other property. I told him that General Weitzel, commanding the department, would be present in a short time and that he would be a proper person to treat with. Even while we were speaking the general and his staff appeared at the top of the hill, and the mayor rode forward to meet him. The whole party shortly returned, and General Weitzel ordered me to follow him into the city."

Prescott's detachment soon lost sight of the general in the thick smoke, however. But coming to Main Street they turned into it in hope of finding the capitol grounds. "The scene that met our eyes here almost baffles description," Prescott said. "Pandemonium reigned supreme. Two large iron-clads near by in the river exploded with a deafening crash, the concussion sweeping numbers of people off their feet. The street we were in was one compact mass of frenzied people, and it was only with the greatest difficulty that we were able to force our way along. Had they been hostile our lives would not have been worth a moment's purchase.

"But the poor colored people hailed our appearance with the most extravagant expressions of joy. They crowded into the ranks and besought permission to carry the soldiers' knapsacks and muskets. They clapped them on the back, hung about their necks, and 'God bless you,' and 'Thank God, the Yankees have come,' resounded on every side...One woman, I distinctly remember, with three little pale, starved girls clinging about her, herself barefoot, bareheaded, thinly and miserably clad, seized my arm with a vise-like grip, and begged for the love of God, for just a morsel for her starving children. They had tasted nothing since Sunday morning, and then only a spoonful of dry meal. I gave her the contents of my haversack, and one man in the ranks, a great, rough, swearing fellow, poured into her lap his entire three days' rations of pork and hard bread, thrust a ten dollar greenback, all the money he possessed, into her hand, swearing like a pirate all the while as a means of relief to his overcharged feelings, their intensity being abundantly evident by the tears which coursed rapidly down his cheeks....

"The gutters literally ran whiskey....The poisonous flood rolled like a river of death rapidly on into the sewers, while the atmosphere fairly reeked with its unsavory odor. The rougher element of the population, white and black alike, were dipping up the vile stuff with their hands, and pouring it down their throats....Bands of thieves and rascals of every degree, broken loose from the penitentiary, were entering the stores on either side the street and stealing whatever they could lay their hands upon, while the entire black population seemed out of doors and crazy with delight. Tumult, violence, riot, pillage, everywhere prevailed, and as if these were not enough to illustrate the horrors of war, the roar of the flames, the clanging of bells, and general uproar and confusion were sufficient to appall the stoutest heart....

"At length the heat became so great that we could proceed no further. Our hair and beards were scorched, our clothing smoked, the air we breathed was like a furnace blast, and many of the men, weighed down as they were with musket, knapsacks, blanket, ammunition, and other accoutrements, were well-nigh exhausted. Three fire engines were burning in the street immediately before us. On the side walk near by lay the bodies of three young girls burnt to a crisp. People jumped from the windows of burning buildings; others with wildly waving arms shrieked for help, not daring to take the fatal leap...."

Finally Prescott found Capitol Square, where the Virginia state capitol building had served the same function for the Confederacy. "The spacious capitol grounds afforded the only spot of refuge," Prescott wrote, "and these were crowded with women and children, bearing in their arms and upon their heads their most cherished possessions. Piles of furniture lay scattered in every direction, and about them clustered the hungry and destitute family groups, clinging to each other with the energy of despair. One of the most touching sights amid these accumulated horrors, was that of a little girl—a toddling infant—holding her kitten tightly under her arm, a dilapidated rag doll in one hand and grasping her mother's gown with the other, as they sought shelter from showers of cinders, under the capitol steps."[18]

Several units, black and white, infantry, cavalry, and artillery, had raced to be the first Union soldiers into Richmond and raise the first Union flag over the Confederate capital. Lieutenant Livingston de Peyster of Weitzel's staff, who was carrying a flag that had previously flown over captured New Orleans, was among the first. "Arriving at the Capitol," he wrote in a letter home, "I sprang from my horse, first unbuckling the Stars and Stripes, a large flag I had on the front of my saddle. With Captain Langdon, Chief of Artillery, I rushed up to the roof. Together we hoisted the first large flag over Richmond and on the peak of the roof drank to its success....I found two small guidons, took them down, and returned them to the Fourth Massachusetts Cavalry where they belong." Onlooking soldiers, slaves, and even some Southern whites, cheered the sight of de Peyster's flag. "The excitement was intense; old men gray and scarred by many battles, acted the part of boys, shouting and yelling at the top of their voices."[19]

However, even the cavalry guidons were probably not the first Union flags hoisted over Richmond. A few blocks away Elizabeth Van Lew, a Union-sympathizer and Federal spy, sent a servant to the roof of her house shortly after dawn to unfurl a big flag she had been hiding for just this occasion.

More troops were brought into the city, and General Weitzel soon set them to work to put out the fires and reestablish order. "The few fire-engines in order were sought out," a Union officer said, "and placed in the hands of our boys in blue, who worked as earnestly to save the city of Richmond from destruction as if performing a like duty for their native towns. A police was organized, and within an hour every street was under the protection of a Union sentinel. The printing presses were brought into action, and by noon circulars had been prepared and distributed announcing the rules deemed necessary for the temporary government of the inhabitants. Not a soldier was allowed to come within the city limits except those detailed for its special protection. The men seemed to understand that they were called upon to uphold the name of the American soldier in a new sphere of duty, and right nobly did they perform it."[20]

A staff officer was sent to free the Union prisoners of war from the infamous Libby Prison, but he found it empty. By nightfall it and the equally infamous Castle Thunder were full of looters and Confederate deserters. Other staff officers spent the day furiously writing lists of looted property that had been confiscated. Guards were provided for the homes of any women who asked for protection. A corporal and two men of the 9th Vermont were posted at the home of Robert E. Lee to protect his wife and daughter. They were replaced later in the day by a cavalry sentry, but when Mrs. Lee saw that he was a black man she sent a servent to the Union provost marshal with an indignant message protesting this insult.

"About ten o'clock on the morning of April third," wrote reporter Noah Brooks, "word was received in Washington from President Lincoln at City Point that [Petersburg] had been evacuated, and that our Army was pushing into it, sweeping around it, and pursuing the flying squadrons of Lee. At a quarter to eleven in that forenoon came a despatch to the War Department from General Weitzel, dated at Richmond, announcing the fall of the Confederate capital. It was not many minutes before the news spread like wildfire through Washington, and the intelligence, at first doubted, was speedily made certain by the circulation of thousands of newspaper 'extras' containing the news in bulletins issued from the War Department. In a moment of time the city was ablaze with excitement the like of which was never seen before; and everybody who had a piece of bunting spread it to the breeze; from one end of Pennsylvania Avenue to the other the air seemed to burn with the bright hues of the flag. The sky was shaken by a grand salute of eight hundred guns, fired by order of the Secretary of War—three hundred for Petersburg and five hundred for Richmond. Almost by magic the streets were crowded with hosts of people, talking, laughing, hurrahing, and shouting in the fullness of their joy. Men embraced one another, 'treated' one another, made up old quarrels, renewed old friendships, marched through the streets arm in arm, singing and chatting in that happy sort of abandon which characterizes our people when under the influence of a great and universal happiness. The atmosphere was full of the intoxication of joy. The departments of the Government and many stores and private offices were closed for the day, and hosts of hard-worked clerks had their full share of the general holiday. Bands of music, apparently without any special direction or formal call, paraded the streets, and boomed and blared from every public place, until the air was resonant with the expression of the popular jubilation in all the national airs....

"Wherever any man was found who could make a speech, or who thought he could make a speech, there a speech was made; and a great many men who had never before made one found themselves thrust upon a crowd of enthusiastic sovereigns who demanded of them something by way of jubilant oratory....The day of jubilee did not end with the day, but rejoicing and cheering were prolonged far into the night. Many illuminated their houses, and bands were still playing, and leading men and public officials were serenaded all over the city. There are always hosts of people who drown their joys effectually in the flowing bowl, and Washington on April third was full of them. Thousands besieged the drinking-saloons, champagne popped everywhere, and a more liquorish crowd was never seen in Washington than on that night. Many and many a man of years of habitual sobriety seemed to think it a patriotic duty to 'get full' on that eventful night, and not only so, but to advertise the fact of fullness as widely as possible. I saw one big, sedate Vermonter, chief of an executive bureau, standing on the corner of F and Fourteenth streets, with owlish gravity giving away fifty-cent 'shin plasters' (fractional currency) to every colored person who came past him, brokenly saying with each gift, 'Babylon has fallen!'"[21]

John T. Holahan, a tombstone carver who lived at the Surratt boarding house, was in bed at 9 that night, despite all the celebrating in the city. He was not yet asleep, though, when he heard a soft knock at his door. He got up and put on his trousers over his nightshirt and opened the door to find John Surratt there, just home from Richmond. He wanted to borrow some money, which Holahan agreed to. Surratt asked for $50 and then upped it to $60, which Holahan gave him in greenbacks. In return, Surratt unexpectedly gave him two $20 gold pieces. That night, Surratt left Washington by train, heading for Canada on a mission for the Confederate government. He had been assured before leaving Richmond that no matter what happened, the Confederacy would not surrender.

At about the same hour, "J.W. Booth & Lady" checked into the Aquidneck Hotel in New York City.

With a head start of several hours, Lee's main column from Petersburg marched in good order all through that day. John Esten Cooke saw Lee that morning. "His expression," he noted, "was animated and buoyant, his seat in the saddle erect and commanding, and he seemed to look forward to assured success." The general told his staff, "I have got the army safe out of the breastworks. In order to follow me, Grant must leave his lines, and he'll get no more benefit from railroads or the James River." The men were also glad to be on the road, out of the trenches. "A sense of relief seemed to pervade the ranks," said a Confederate officer, "at their release from the lines where they had watched and worked for more than nine weary months. Once more in the open field, they were invigorated with hope, and felt better able to cope with their powerful adversary."[22]

There were three bridges over the north-south stretch of the Appomattox River that the Confederates had to cross to reach Amelia Court House. Lee's main column was heading for the most southerly of the three, known as Bevill's Bridge, 25 miles west and slightly north of Petersburg, until he received word that the river was so high that the approaches to that bridge were covered with water. Late that afternoon he also learned that the engineers had failed to send, as ordered, pontoons to the site of the northern-most bridge, whose condition was unknown. Ewell's forces from north of the James were scheduled to cross there. Because of these difficulties, all columns north of the Appomattox had to be rerouted to the middle crossing, Goode's Bridge. By nightfall, Longstreet had Field's and Wilcox's divisions across, ready to cover the passage of the artillery and wagons. Gordon's 2nd Corps remained on the east side, and Mahone's Division was still farther back.

Meanwhile, Pickett and Anderson, along with the remnants of the force from Sutherland's Station, finally came together that night near the west side of Bevill's Bridge after marching up the south side of the river. "We set out soon after daylight," Lieutenant Caldwell of McGowan's Brigade wrote, "pursuing the general direction of the Appomattox. There was an attempt made to organize the various commands; but it proved, in the main, abortive. According to the inelegant, but to us expressive, phraseology of the army, the Confederacy was considered as 'gone up'; and every man felt it his duty, as well as his privilege, to save himself. I do not mean to say that there was any insubordination whatever; but the whole left of the army was so crushed by the defeats of the last few days that it straggled along without strength, and almost without thought. So we moved on in disorder, keeping no regular column, no regular pace. When a soldier became weary, he fell out, ate his scanty rations—if, indeed, he had any to eat—rested, rose, and resumed the march when his inclination dictated."[23]

Sheridan's cavalry had moved out that morning, heading west along the south side of the Appomattox River. Custer's division had the lead and easily outflanked a small Confederate rear guard entrenched behind Namozine Creek. A running fight then developed with Rooney and Fitz Lee's cavalry divisions, during which Custer's younger brother and aide, Captain Tom Custer, won a Congressional Medal of Honor by capturing a battleflag, three officers, and eleven enlisted men. "The roads in places were horrible," a cavalry sergeant wrote, "the terrible rain of Thursday & Friday before having covered the level land & the road was badly cut up by the enemy's train; in many of the low bad places the enemy had been obliged to abandon wagon, caisson, forges, &c., while the roadside was thickly strewn by ammunition of every kind and sort.... We moved rapidly forward, having now the Appomattox River on our right, distant half a mile to a mile, at one place we could distinguish a large wagon train going west."

Early that afternoon an officer came galloping along the Union cavalry column, shouting something over and over. "As he came near," the same sergeant said, "we could catch what he was repeating, 'Hurrah! Richmond is taken, Grant has taken Richmond! hurrah' in a moment we were as wild as he was, yelling & cheering long after he was past, hunger, hardship & danger all were overlooked, it was a proud moment."[24]

"The roads are strewn with burning and broken-down caissons, ambulances, wagons, and debris of all descriptions," Sheridan reported to Grant at 4:10 p.m. "Up to this hour we have taken about 1,200 prisoners, mostly of A. P. Hill's corps, and all accounts report the woods filled with deserters and stragglers, principally of this corps. One of our men, recaptured, reports that not more than one in five of the rebels have arms in their hands."[25]

"As we pressed our adversaries," Sheridan wrote in his memoirs, "hundreds and hundreds of prisoners, armed and unarmed, fell into our hands, together with many wagons and five pieces of artillery. At

Deep Creek the rear-guard turned on us, and a severe skirmish took place. Merritt, finding the enemy very strong, was directed to await the arrival of Crook and for the rear division of the Fifth Corps; but by the time they reached the creek, darkness had again come to protect the Confederates, and we had to be content with meagre results at that point."[26]

"The cavalry ahead were pressing on the enemy's rear all day," Joshua Chamberlain said, "and just at dusk of the evening came upon a strong line of Lee's cavalry with Hunton's and Wise's infantry brigades boldly confronting us at the crossing of Deep Creek. The cavalry had forced them away in a sharp engagement before we got up to share in it. We could not help admiring the courage and pluck of these poor fellows, now so broken and hopeless, both for their cause and for themselves. A long and hard road was before them, whatever fate should be at the end of it. We had a certain pride in their manliness, and a strong 'fellow-feeling,' however determined we were to destroy the political pretension which they accepted as their cause."[27]

Humphreys, with his reunited 2nd Corps, followed the 5th Corps and camped that night with the rear of its column near Namozine Creek, where the cavalry had started that morning, and the head of the column about three miles farther west. Wright's 6th Corps got only as far as Sutherland's Station that day, as did Parke with two divisions of the 9th Corps. Willcox's 1st Division of that corps was left behind to hold Petersburg and the surrounding defenses. Warren was put in charge of all the forces left behind at Petersburg and City Point. Ord's corps-sized command was between the 2nd and 6th Corps.

"We had still time to march as much farther," Grant later wrote, "and time was an object; but the roads were bad and the trains belonging to the advance corps had blocked up the road so that it was impossible to get on. Then, again, our cavalry had struck some of the enemy and were pursuing them; and the orders were that the roads should be given up to the cavalry whenever they appeared. This caused further delay.

"General Wright...thought to gain time by letting his men go into bivouac and trying to get up some rations for them, and clearing out the road, so that when they did start they would be uninterrupted. Humphreys, who was far ahead, was also out of rations. They did not succeed in getting them up through the night; but the Army of the Potomac, officers and men, were so elated by the reflection that at last they were following up a victory to its end, that they preferred marching without rations to running a possible risk of letting the enemy elude them."[28]

Lieutenant Colonel Elisha Hunt Rhodes, commander of the 2nd

Rhode Island in the 6th Corps, would have agreed with that statement. "We heard today," he told his diary, "that Richmond has been evacuated and is in flames. Well, let it burn, we do not want it. We are after Lee, and we are going to have him."[29]

Grant took time that evening to write to his old friend Sherman: "The movements of which I spoke to you when you were here commenced on the 28th, and, notwithstanding two days of rain which followed, rendering roads almost impassable even for cavalry, terminated in the fall of both Richmond and Petersburg this morning. The mass of Lee's army was whipped badly south of Petersburg, and to save the remnant he was forced to evacuate Richmond. We have about 12,000 prisoners, and stragglers are being picked up in large numbers. From all causes I do not estimate his loss at less than 25,000....The troops from Petersburg, as well as those from Richmond, retreated between the two rivers, and there is every indication that they will endeavor to secure Burkeville and Danville. I am pursuing with five corps and the cavalry and hope to capture or disperse a large number more. It is also my intention to take Burkeville and hold it until it is seen whether it is a part of Lee's plan to hold Lynchburg and Danville. The railroad from Petersburg up can soon be put in condition to supply an army at that place. If Lee goes beyond Danville you will have to take care of him with the force you have for a while....Should Lee go to Lynchburg with his whole force and I get Burkeville there will be no special use in you going any farther into the interior of North Carolina. There is no contingency that I can see except my failure to secure Burkeville that will make it necessary for you to move on to the Roanoke as proposed when you were here. In that case it might be necessary for you to operate on the enemy's lines of communication between Danville and Burkeville, whilst I would act on them from Richmond between the latter place and Lynchburg. This army has now won a most decisive victory and followed the enemy. This is all it ever wanted to make it as good an army as ever fought a battle."[30]

---

1. Trudeau, *The Last Citadel*, 405.
2. Ibid., 406.
3. Ibid.
4. Grant, *Personal Memoirs*, 2:454-459.
5. Stern, *An End to Valor*, 150.
6. *Official Records*, 46:III:508.
7. Wheeler, *Witness to Appomattox*, 125-126.
8. Porter, *Campaigning with Grant*, 450-452.

9. Wheeler, *Witness to Appomattox*, 127.
10. Davis, *To Appomattox*, 143.
11. *Official Records*, 46:III:509.
12. Ibid., 46:III:509.
13. Hoehling and Hoehling, *The Last Days of the Confederacy*, 182.
14. Ibid., 184.
15. Ibid., 173-174.
16. Ibid., 188-190.
17. Ibid., 193-194.
18. R.B. Prescott, "The Poor Colored People Thanked God That Their Sufferings Were Ended," in *The Blue and Gray*, 1129-1132.
19. Hoehling and Hoehling, *The Last Days of the Confederacy*, 199.
20. Wheeler, *Witness to Appomattox*, 110.
21. Brooks, *Washington in Lincoln's Time*, 218-222.
22. Davis, *To Appomattox*, 146.
23. Wheeler, *Witness to Appomattox*, 143.
24. Starr, *The Union Cavalry in the Civil War*, 2:460.
25. *Official Records*, 46:III:529.
26. Sheridan, *Civil War Memoirs*, 334.
27. Chamberlain, *The Passing of the Armies*, 148.
28. Grant, *Personal Memoirs*, 2:463-464.
29. Rhodes, *All for the Union*, 227.
30. *Official Records*, 46:III:510.

PART FOUR

APPOMATTOX

If I were in your place, I'd let 'em up easy.

—Abraham Lincoln

CHAPTER THIRTY-ONE

I See No Escape for Lee

3 - 5 April 1865

The train bearing Jefferson Davis and the Confederate cabinet reached Danville, Virginia at 4 p.m. on 3 April, having covered the 140 miles from Richmond in eighteen hours. "Nothing," Davis said, "could have exceeded the kindness and hospitality of the patriotic citizens. They cordially gave us an 'Old Virginia welcome.'"[1] Danville's hospitality did not extend, however, to Davis's check drawn on a Richmond bank for the proceeds of the sale of his wife's furniture and silver. It was declared non-negotiable. Davis asked for news of Lee, but was told there was none. Then he put soldiers and slaves to work digging new defenses around the town and gathering supplies for Lee's army.

Stoneman, with Gillem's division of Union cavalry from his District of East Tennessee, after riding northeastward from Knoxville almost to the Virginia line, had crossed the mountains into the northwestern part of North Carolina. Then they had turned north, and on the third they reached Hillsville, Virginia, capturing a train of seventeen Confederate supply wagons filled with forage along the way. They kept the horses, fed the forage to their mounts, and burned the wagons. Then Colonel John Miller, commanding the 3rd Brigade, was ordered to take 500 picked men to Wytheville and destroy the depot of supplies there and two nearby bridges on the Virginia & Tennessee Railroad. At sunset the rest of the division resumed its northward march and kept on until midnight, when it camped by a hay depot belonging to the Confederate government.

Down in Alabama on that third day of April, Wilson sent Upton's division out from Selma to search for Croxton's brigade and McCook, who had gone with his other brigade to try to connect with Croxton. Wilson also wanted to make sure that all Rebel forces retreated to the west side of the Cahaba River. Forrest's retreating Confederates reached Plantersville, north of Selma, that day and turned to the west. About a mile beyond the town the Rebels ran into the advance of McCook's Federals, who were returning from their expedition against the Centerville bridge. Forrest charged forward, and then, while McCook formed his men in line of battle, the Rebels withdrew into the woods and continued their retreat to the west.

Croxton's brigade followed the Watermelon Road south from Johnson's Ferry toward Tuscaloosa that day. To prevent word of his move from reaching Rebel ears, he sent out a few men in advance to capture everyone, soldiers or civilians, found along the road. Among those who were picked up was a Confederate scout, who provided the Federals with vital information about the position of Rebel patrols and the vital bridge over the Black Warrior River connecting Tuscaloosa with Northport on the northwest side.

At around 9 p.m. the advance of the Union column approached Northport. Croxton hid most of his troops in a cedar grove and took 150 men of the 2nd Michigan Cavalry, guided by friendly slaves, quietly forward on foot to the river. There they discovered that a small force of Rebel troops was ripping up the wooden flooring of the bridge. Croxton sent the detachment racing toward the Confederates, and the Rebels fled across the river where they joined another small group behind a barricade of cotton bales. The Federals followed them across and routed them with their repeating carbines. Then, while part of the detachment rounded up a couple of 6-pounder cannon kept in a nearby stable, the remainder repaired the damage the Rebels had done to the bridge. The rest of the brigade was then brought across the river.

Meanwhile, news of the Union attack was carried to Dr. Landon C.

Garland, president of the University of Alabama, and Colonel James Murfree, commandant of the school's military cadets. The long roll was sounded, and the cadets quickly formed ranks. Then Garland and Murfree led them to River Hill, overlooking the Union position. While the main body opened fire on the Federals, a small detachment was sent to fetch the two cannon but soon returned with word that both guns had been captured. Information received from civilians convinced Garland that his students were greatly outnumbered, so he returned them to the campus, where they stocked up on rations and ammunition, and then marched them out of town to keep them from being either slaughtered or captured. At 1 a.m. on 4 April, the mayor and a Confederate captain jointly surrendered the city of Tuscaloosa to General Croxton.

Forrest's Rebels crossed to the west side of the Cahaba River on the fourth, and by midmorning they reached Marion, where they found the supply train, the artillery, Jackson's division and Chalmers with his other brigade. But, although his force was now united, Forrest made no move to take on Wilson's Federals again, not even Croxton's lost brigade.

At daylight on the fourth, Stoneman's main column resumed its march and reached Jacksonville, Virginia at 10 a.m., where another government depot of hay and corn furnished ample supplies for its horses. From there 250 picked men of the 15th Pennsylvania Cavalry were detached with orders to proceed to Salem, Virginia and destroy the railroad bridges as far east of there as possible. At 2 p.m. the main column resumed its march, and it arrived at Christiansburg, on the railroad about halfway between Wytheville and Salem, about midnight.

General Lee reached Goode's Bridge at about 7 a.m. on the fourth and by 8:30 a.m. he came to the railroad station at Amelia Court House. There he discovered that none of the 350,000 rations that he had ordered to be sent here by rail had arrived, although there were hundreds of boxes of ammunition and harness for artillery horses. John Esten Cooke saw Lee's reaction: "No face wore a heavier shadow than that of General Lee. The failure of the supply of rations completely paralyzed him. An anxious and haggard expression came to his face."[2] The ammunition was of no use, as it could not be carried, and was destroyed that afternoon.

A drizzling rain was falling as Lee sent several regiments to forage for food. He also issued a proclamation to the people of Amelia County asking for contributions and sent messages to Danville and Lynchburg asking that rations be sent by railroad from those places. The dispatches had to be carried on horseback seven miles down the line to Jetersville in search of an intact telegraph line. During the day, all of Anderson's and Longstreet's columns came in and made camp around the little town of Amelia Court House. Gordon's 2nd Corps was across Goode's Bridge but bivouacked about halfway between it and the town. Mahone's Division was still farther back. At 9 p.m. word reached Lee that Ewell's column would soon cross the Appomattox River farther north, where some of his men were laying planks over the railroad trestle at Mattoax Bridge. It was after midnight when those troops finally made camp on the west side of the river.

The Union troops, still marching far ahead of their supply wagons, continued to parallel Lee's column to the south, making for the Richmond & Danville Railroad in order to cut Lee off from North Carolina. Sheridan's cavalry continued to lead the way, with the 5th Corps, still under his orders, right behind. Private Theodore Gerrish of the 20th Maine in the 5th Corps saw Sheridan that day and left a classic description of the cavalry general: "This is how he appeared on the field: a short, [slight] man with very short legs, his broad shoulders a little stooping as he sat upon his horse, having a very large head with hair clipped close, a short, thick mustache; his uniform being usually the worse for wear and spotted with mud; wearing a soft felt hat at least two sizes too small, and, for safekeeping, usually pressed down upon... the back of his head. He rode a splendid horse, usually went at a round gallop, and rolled and bounced upon the back of his steed much as an old salt does when walking up the aisle of a church after four years' cruise at sea.

"Some of his surroundings were also of a singular character. At his side usually rode a party of a dozen scouts clad in the neat gray uniform of rebel officers, and ranking from captains to colonels. They were evidently brave, jolly, reckless fellows, and theirs was a most dangerous occupation—one that required skill, tact, and cool, deliberate daring. Entering the rebel lines and making themselves familiar with all their movements, dashing from one brigade to another, they would claim to be on one general's staff, and then on that of another, to suit the situation. They would give orders that purported to come from rebel commanders, to colonels, quartermasters, and officers in charge of wagon trains; and, these being obeyed, would add to the confusion of the rebel army and hastened its destruction.... Success made these scouts reckless, and quite a number were captured, and some, I believe, were executed.... Another singular feature in Sheridan's procession was at least twenty captured battle flags, which were borne unfurled as trophies of the campaign. His staff officers and body guard were all as rash and daring as Sheridan himself, and whenever they went dashing past us it would stir the boys up to the wildest enthusiasm.... They would cheer as if a pandemonium had broken loose."[3]

Sheridan's scouts, commanded by Major Henry K. Young, outdid themselves that day. Some Union officers spotted a road filled with Confederate stragglers and noticed that occasionally a mounted Rebel officer would emerge from some nearby woods and join the column. But as the Federal officers drew closer they saw these mounted Confederates making covert signals to them to keep away. Finally two of the Rebels rode to meet them and identified themselves as Major Young's scouts. They were leading the Confederates into a trap and wanted the Federals to stay back until the job was completed. Soon the Union officers came upon Major Young himself. In the brush below a railroad embankment he had about a dozen of his scouts with him, and they were holding a whole regiment of Rebels at gunpoint. And, even as the officers watched, a new stream of prisoners was brought in and added to the catch. Among the Confederates thus captured was a brigade commander in Rooney Lee's cavalry.

Meade, with the 2nd and 6th Corps, followed in Sheridan's wake as best he could, while Grant, with Ord's force, took a more southerly route leading directly for Burkeville, where the Richmond & Danville Railroad crossed the Southside Railroad, which led to Lynchburg. Meade was sick now, apparently with a nervous stomach, and had to ride in an ambulance. Parke's two divisions of the 9th Corps were left behind to repair and guard the Southside Railroad so that it could serve as a line of supply for the Union forces. Ord also dropped off Birney's division of the 25th Corps at the village called Blacks and Whites for the same purpose.

The Federals, like their Confederate counterparts, were happy to be out of the trenches. "The balmy air and invigoration of sun and cheerful fields of the Virginia spring," one of Ord's men wrote, "stirred the physical man; and the very beasts of burden, escaped from plodding through the winter's mud, seemed to catch the contagion of the march. We were like so many schoolboys on a holiday. Sick of the restraints of the earthworks' narrow limits, of the monotonous routine of camp, of shelling and being shelled.... But no form of words can describe our exultation, partly physical from pure animal excitement, but chiefly moral from the consciousness of the speedy triumph of the good cause for which we had fought so desperately and so long."[4]

An artilleryman in the 5th Corps column was very impressed with the infantry's dedication and determination: "It was only once in a lifetime—and comparatively few lifetimes at that—when one could see in flesh and blood and nerve and pluck and manhood [the likes of] that immortal old 5th Corps on its way to Appomattox! On its way, keeping step and step with Sheridan's cavalry, to get across the path of Lee's army! During these terrible forced marches of the 5th Corps, General Griffin's wonderful power in dealing with soldiers, and his marvellous tact in cheering men on to incredible exertions, became manifest. If that noble man had a fault, it was his apparent incapacity to understand that there was a limit to human endurance."

"What's the matter with you fellows?" Griffin would ask when he came upon a dozen stragglers.

"Clean tuckered out, General; can't march another step."

"Look here boys," Griffin would say, "don't you know that we have got old Lee on the run, and our corps and the cavalry are trying to head him off? If he escapes from us, old Sherman and his bummers will catch him and get all the glory, and we won't have anything to show for our four years' fighting! Try it once more!"

The general's bit of psychology always worked, the artilleryman said. "It made no difference how tired or faint or sore an Army of the Potomac man might be," he wrote, "he couldn't endure the thought of letting Lee's army get away, so that those Western fellows would catch him and get the glory of winding the thing up. When I was riding along... I used to wish that I could dismount and give up my horse to every one of those poor, exhausted, but brave and determined infantry comrades, who were actually 'falling by the wayside,' but who, when their pride was stirred by the thought that Sherman's army might usurp the fruits of their toils and sufferings of four long years, took a new lease on life and strength, and staggered on once more.... No one who did not see them can form the faintest idea of what they did and dared and suffered! And General Griffin was a whole provost guard all by himself."[5]

"Our Second and Sixth Corps had been trying to follow the Fifth all the morning of the 4th," Joshua Chamberlain wrote, "but had been stopped a long way back by one of those common, and therefore presumably necessary, but unspeakably vexatious, incidents of a forced march,—somebody else cutting in on the road, claiming to have the right of way. The cavalry had come in on them from one of the river-crossings where they had been heading off Lee from his nearest road to Amelia Court House, and precedence being given the cavalry in order, our infantry corps had to mass up and wait till they could get the road. The fields were in such condition that troops could not march over them, and the roads were not much better for the rear of a column, with all its artillery and wagons. These delayed corps were not allowed to get rheumatism by resting on the damp ground, but were favored with the well-proved prophylactic of lively work corduroying roads, so that they could have something substantial to set foot on."[6]

"From the beginning," Sheridan later wrote, "it was apparent that Lee, in his retreat, was making for Amelia Court House, where his columns north and south of the Appomattox River could join, and where, no doubt, he expected to meet supplies, so Crook was ordered to march early on April 4 to strike the Danville railroad, between Jettersville and Burkeville, and then move south along the railroad toward Jettersville, Merritt to move toward Amelia Court House, and the Fifth Corps to Jettersville itself.

"The Fifth Corps got to Jettersville about 5 in the afternoon, and I immediately intrenched it across the Burkeville road with the determination to stay there till the main army could come up, for I hoped we could force Lee to surrender at Amelia Court House, since a firm hold on Jettersville would cut him off from his line of retreat toward Burkeville.

"Accompanied only by my escort—the First United States Cavalry, about two hundred strong—I reached Jettersville some little time before the Fifth Corps, and having nothing else at hand I at once deployed this handful of men to cover the crossroads till the arrival of the corps. Just as the troopers were deploying, a man on a mule, heading for Burkeville, rode into my pickets. He was arrested, of course, and being searched there was found in his boots this telegram in duplicate, signed by Lee's Commissary General. 'The army is at Amelia Court House, short of provisions. Send 300,000 rations quickly to Burkeville Junction.' One copy was addressed to the supply department at Danville, and the other to that at Lynchburg. I surmised that the telegraph lines north of Burkeville had been broken by Crook after the despatches were written, which would account for their being transmitted by message. There was thus revealed to me not only the important fact that Lee was concentrating at Amelia Court House, but also a trustworthy basis for estimating his troops, so I sent word to Crook to strike up the railroad toward me, and to Merritt—who, as I have said, had followed on the heels of the enemy—to leave Mackenzie there and himself close in on Jettersville. Staff-officers were also despatched to hurry up Griffin with the Fifth Corps, and his tired men redoubled their strides.

"My troops too were hard up for rations, for in the pursuit we could not wait for our trains, so I concluded to secure if possible these provisions intended for Lee. To this end I directed Young to send four of his best scouts to Burkeville Junction. There they were to separate, two taking the railroad toward Lynchburg and two toward Danville, and as soon as a telegraph station was reached the telegram was to be transmitted as it had been written and the provisions thus hurried forward."[7]

In southern Maryland on the fourth, Lieutenant Ben Stringfellow, who had been on some secret mission to Washington, escaped from the Union troopers who had captured him two days before. He eventually made his way to Canada, where he stayed for over a year, until he was sure that it was safe to return to the United States.

By 8 a.m. on the fourth, the James River between City Point and Richmond had been cleared of obstructions, and naval parties in small boats began sweeping it for floating torpedoes. When the channel was reported to be clear, Admiral Porter, on the *Malvern,* started up the river, followed by President Lincoln and Tad on the *River Queen*, which had returned after taking Mrs. Lincoln to Washington. Other boats were also on their way to the former Confederate capital. "Every vessel," Admiral Porter said, "that got through the obstructions wished to be the first one up, and pushed ahead with all steam; but they grounded, one after another, the *Malvern* passing them all until she also took the ground. Not to be delayed, I took the President in my barge, and, [pulled by] a tug… with a file of marines on board, we continued on up to the city.

"There was a large bridge across the James about a mile below the landing, and under this a party in a small steamer were caught and held by the current, with no prospect of release without assistance. These people begged me to extricate them from their perilous position, so I ordered the tug to cast off and help them, leaving us in the barge to go on alone."[8]

The barge carrying the president and the admiral was rowed on by a detachment of sailors against the current and finally landed near a party of some forty or fifty newly liberated slaves, who were working for the Union army on the bank of a nearby canal. A Northern newspaper reporter was on hand, and pointed out the president to the freedmen. They immediately dropped their work and crowded around the author of the Emancipation Proclamation. "They pressed round the President," the reported wrote, "ran ahead, and hovered upon the flanks and rear of the little company. Men, women, and children joined the constantly increasing throng. They came from all the streets, running in breathless haste, shouting and hallooing, and dancing with delight. The men threw up their hats, the women waved their bonnets and handkerchiefs, clapped their hands and shouted, 'Glory to God! Glory! Glory! Glory!'—rendering all the praise to God, who had given them freedom, after long years of weary waiting, and had permitted them thus unexpectedly to meet their great benefactor....

"No carriage was to be had, so the President, leading his son, walked [toward] General Weitzel's headquarters—Jeff Davis's mansion. Six sailors, wearing their round blue caps and short jackets and baggy pants, with navy carbines, formed the guard. Next came the President and Admiral Porter, flanked by the officers accompanying him, and the writer, then six more sailors with carbines—twenty of us in all.

"The walk was long, and the President halted a moment to rest. 'May de good Lord bless you, President Linkum!' said an old Negro, removing his hat and bowing, with tears of joy rolling down his cheeks. The President removed his own hat, and bowed in silence. It was a bow which upset the forms, laws, customs, and ceremonies of centuries of slavery. It was... a mortal blow to caste."[9]

The crowd continued to grow, with a number of poor whites joining the throng, and the progress of the small party slowed to less than one mile an hour. "We were nearly half an hour getting from abreast of Libby Prison to the edge of the city," Admiral Porter said. "The President stopped a moment to look on the horrid bastille where so many Union soldiers had dragged out a dreadful existence.... 'We will pull it down,' cried the crowd, seeing where his look fell. 'No,' he said, 'leave it as a monument.' He did not say a monument to what, but he meant, I am sure, to leave it as a monument to the loyalty of our soldiers, who would bear all the horrors of Libby sooner than desert their flag and cause.

"We struggled on, the great crowd preceding us, and an equally dense crowd of blacks following on behind.... It was not a model style for the President of the United States to enter the capital of a conquered country, yet there was a moral in it all which had more effect than if he had come surrounded with great armies and heralded by the booming of cannon. He came, armed with the majesty of the law, to put his seal to the act which had been established by the bayonets of the Union soldiers—the establishment of peace and good will between the North and the South, and liberty to all mankind who dwell upon our shores.

"We forced our way onward slowly, and, as we reached the edge of the city, the sidewalks were lined on both sides of the streets with black and white alike—all looking with curious eager faces at the man who held their destiny in his hand.... It was a warm day, and the streets were dusty, owing to the immense gathering which covered every part of them, kicking up the dirt. The atmosphere was suffocating, but Mr.

Lincoln could be plainly seen by every man, woman, and child, towering head and shoulders about that crowd.... He carried his hat in his hand, fanning his face, from which the perspiration was pouring....

"We were brought to a halt by the dense jam before we had gone a square into the city, which was still on fire near the Tredegar Works and in the structures thereabout, and the smoke, setting our way, almost choked us. I had not seen a soldier whom I could send to General Weitzel to ask for an escort....

"While we were stopped... a white man in his shirt sleeves rushed from the sidewalk toward the President. His looks were so eager that I questioned his friendship, and prepared to receive him on the point of my sword; but when he got within ten feet of us he suddenly stopped short, took off his hat, and cried out, 'Abraham Lincoln, God bless you! You are the poor man's friend!' Then he tried to force his way to the President to shake hands with him. He would not take 'no' for an answer until I had to treat him rather roughly, when he stood off, with his arms folded, and looked intently after us. The last I saw of him he was throwing his hat into the air.

"Just after this a beautiful girl came from the sidewalk with a large bouquet of roses in her hand, and advanced, struggling through the crowd toward the President. The mass of people endeavored to open to let her pass, but she had a hard time in reaching him. Her clothes were very much disarranged in making the journey across the street. I reached out and helped her within the circle of the sailors' bayonets, where, although nearly stifled with the dust, she gracefully presented her bouquet to the President and made a neat little speech, while he held her hand. The beauty and youth of the girl—for she was only about seventeen—made the presentation very touching.

"There was a card on the bouquet with these simple words: 'From Eva to the Liberator of the Slaves.' She remained no longer than to deliver her present; then two of the sailors were sent to escort her back to the sidewalk. There was no cheering at this, nor yet was any disapprobation shown; but it was evidently a matter of great interest, for the girl was surrounded and plied with questions.... At length I got hold of a cavalryman. He was sitting his horse near the sidewalk, blocked in by the people, and looking on with the same expression of interest as the others...."

"Go to the general," the admiral told the trooper, "and tell him to send a military escort here to guard the President and get him through this crowd!"

"Is that Old Abe?" the soldier asked, his eyes growing as big as saucers.

"The sight of the President was as strange to him," Porter said, "as to the inhabitants; but off he went as fast as the crowd would allow him, and, some twenty minutes later, I heard the clatter of horses' hoofs over the stones as a troop of cavalry came galloping and clearing the street, which they did, however, as mildly as if for a parade.

"For the first time since starting from the landing we were able to walk uninteruptedly. In a short time we reached the mansion of Mr. Davis, President of the Confederacy, occupied after the evacuation as the headquarters of Generals Weitzel and Shepley."[10]

Captain Thomas Graves, one of Weitzel's aides, who wa ust leaving the headquarters, "saw a crowd coming, headed by Presic it Lincoln, who was walking with his usual long, careless stride, and lc oking about with an interested air and taking in everything.... He was shown into the reception-room, with the remark that the housekeeper had said that that room was President Davis's office. As he seated himself, he remarked, 'This must have been President Davis's chair,' and, crossing his legs, he looked far off with a serious, dreamy expression. At length he asked me if the housekeeper was in the house. Upon learning that she had left, he jumped up and said, with a boyish manner, 'Come, let's look at the house!' We went pretty much over it. I related all that the housekeeper had told me, and he seemed interested in everything. As we came down the staircase General Weitzel came, in breathless haste, and at once President Lincoln's face lost its boyish expression as he realized that *duty* must be resumed."[11]

Soon Judge Campbell, who had been one of the peace commissioners Lincoln had met with at Hampton Roads a few weeks before, and General Joseph Anderson, director of the Tredegar iron works, came to see Lincoln. After lunch had been served, Lincoln talked with the Confederates in the parlor. Campbell told the president that he had no commission to speak for the Confederate government. He had asked Secretary of War Breckinridge for some such authority but had received none. "I then told the President," Campbell wrote, "that the war was over, and all that remained to be done was to compose the country.... I told him that he should talk to the public men, and get Virginia back into the Union."[12] Lincoln asked him who he had in mind, and Campbell named several, including General Lee. Lincoln told him he would think it over and talk with him again.

The president, Tad, Weitzel, and Admiral Porter then took a tour of Richmond in a carriage provided by the army, escorted by a squadron of cavalry and a crowd of thousands of freed slaves. He had a look at the burned-out section of the city and Capitol Square. He also stopped to see Sally Pickett, wife of the Confederate general whose appointment to West Point he had helped to secure when he had been in law practice with Pickett's uncle. The uncle had wanted young George, then 17, to become a lawyer, like him, but George was more inclined to be a soldier and Lincoln had come to his rescue.

"With my baby on my arm," Mrs. Pickett said, "I answered the knock, opened the door, and looked up at a tall, gaunt, sad-faced man in ill-fitting clothes, who, with the accent of the North, asked, 'Is this George Pickett's place?'"

"Yes, sir," she answered, "but he is not here."

"I know that, ma'am," he replied, "but I just wanted to see the place. I am Abraham Lincoln."

"'The President!" Sally gasped.

"No, ma'am; no, ma'am; just Abraham Lincoln; George's old friend."

"I am George Pickett's wife and this is his baby," Sally said.

"I had never seen Mr. Lincoln," she wrote, "but remembered the intense love and reverence with which my Soldier always spoke of him. My baby pushed away from me and reached out his hands to Mr. Lincoln, who took him in his arms. As he did so, an expression of rapt, almost divine, tenderness and love lighted up the sad face.... My baby opened his mouth wide and insisted upon giving his father's friend a dewy infantile kiss. As Mr. Lincoln gave the little one back to me, shaking his finger at him playfully, he said, 'Tell your father, the rascal, that I forgive him for the sake of that kiss and those bright eyes.' He turned and went down the steps, talking to himself, and passed out of my sight forever."[13]

At first Lincoln had intended to spend the night in Richmond, but Admiral Porter and others talked him into returning to the *Malvern*. On the way back to the ship he stopped for a closer look at Libby Prison and Castle Thunder, where looters and Confederate deserters were being held. There General Weitzel asked the president what he should do about the captives and how he should treat the people of Richmond. "President Lincoln replied that he did not wish to give any orders on that subject," Captain Graves remembered, "but, as he expressed it, 'If I were in your place, I'd let 'em up easy, let 'em up easy.'"[14]

"I was oppressed with uneasiness," Admiral Porter wrote, "until we got on board and stood on deck with the President safe; then there was not a happier man anywhere than myself."[15] On the way back down the river they saw dozens of torpedoes—what we call "mines" today—that had been taken from the river lying on the bank "like so many queer fish basking in the sun," as Porter put it.[16] After dark, the *Malvern* was hailed from the shore by someone claiming to have dispatches for the president. The admiral sent a boat with orders to bring the messages but not the courier. But the boat returned with word that the messenger insisted on delivering the dispatches himself. Porter sent the boat back to fetch the man, but with orders to watch him. However, when the boat then reached shore the messenger was gone. Shortly afterwards, the *Malvern* was hailed from the bank again, this time by a man claiming to be a sailor from the *Saugus* who asked to be brought aboard. There was no such vessel in the fleet. Porter sent a boat to investigate, but it found no one. Lincoln did not object when the admiral placed a marine outside his stateroom door that night.

Colonel Edward H. Ripley, commander of the 1st Brigade of the 3rd Division of the 24th Corps, was in immediate charge of Richmond. A Rebel soldier came to Ripley's office that day and begged for an interview on a "very important subject." The man's name was Snyder, and he was an enlisted man in Brigadier General Gabriel Rains' Torpedo Bureau of the Confederate War Department. He impressed Ripley as being "more than usually intelligent and a fine-appearing man in uniform." Snyder said that he felt that the war was over and he was worried about the safety of President Lincoln, whom he had seen walking through the streets of the city that day almost unguarded. "He knew," Ripley later wrote, "that a party had just been dispatched from Raine's torpedo bureau on a secret mission, which vaguely he understood was aimed at the head of the Yankee government, and he wished to put Mr. Lincoln on his guard and have impressed upon him that just at this moment he believed him to be in great danger of violence and he should take greater care of himself. He could give no names or facts, as the work of his department was secret, and no man knew what his comrade was sent to do, that the President of the United States was in great danger."[17]

Ripley sent a note to Lincoln aboard the *Malvern* asking for a conference with him, and one was arranged for 9 a.m. the next day, the fifth, by which time the *Malvern* had come up the river to Richmond. Ripley took Snyder with him, but the Confederate was not allowed to enter Lincoln's cabin. Ripley read to the president a statement that his adjutant had taken down and Snyder had sworn to and urged Lincoln to talk with Snyder. But the president refused and ended the meeting by saying, "I must go on as I have begun in the course laid out for me, for I cannot bring myself to believe that any human being lives who would do me any harm."[18]

At 10 a.m., Judge Campbell arrived at the *Malvern* for the second meeting that the president had promised him. With him were a prominent Richmond lawyer, Gustavus Myers, who was a member of the Virginia legislature, and General Weitzel. They were closeted with the president for an hour or more, and Admiral Porter, who saw their parting, said they "seemed to enjoy themselves very much, to judge from their laughter."[19] Weitzel later wrote that "Mr Campbell and the other gentleman assured Mr Lincoln that if he would allow the Virginia Legislature to meet, it would at once repeal the ordinance of secession, and that then General Robert E. Lee and every other Virginian would submit; that this would amount to virtual destruction of the Army of Northern Virginia, and eventually to the surrender of all the other rebel armies, and would assure perfect peace in the shortest possible time."[20] Lincoln gave the two Confederates written permission to convene the legislature, but when Admiral Porter learned what he had done he pointed out that Richmond was under martial law and General Grant should be consulted. General Weitzel and the two Virginians had already departed, but Lincoln sent a message to Weitzel canceling permission for the legislature to meet until further notice.

Assistant Secretary of War Charles Dana had just arrived at Richmond that day to report on the situation there. He wired Stanton that afternoon: "Judge Campbell and Mr. Meyer had an interview with the President here this morning to consider how Virginia can be brought back to the Union. All they ask is an amnesty and a military convention, to cover appearances. Slavery they admit to be defunct. General Weitzel, who was present, tells me that the President did not promise the amnesty, but told them he had the pardoning power, and would save any repentant sinner from hanging. They propose to send for Hunter, and are sure if amnesty could be offered the rebel army would dissolve and all the States return."[21]

Not long afterward, the *Malvern* steamed down the James toward City Point. As Lincoln and Porter were going ashore a transport carrying Confederate prisoners went by. "They seemed perfectly content," the admiral wrote; "every man had a hunk of meat and a piece of bread in his hand, and was doing his best to dispose of it." They recognized "Old Abe" and called friendly greetings to him. Porter thought they were good-natured and kindly and no different from Federal soldiers except that they were leaner and wore more ragged clothes. "They will never shoulder a musket in anger again," Lincoln observed. "And if Grant is wise he will leave them their guns to shoot crows with, and their horses to plow with. It would do no harm."[22]

Mary Lincoln departed Washington that day, on her way back down Chesapeake Bay to rejoin her husband. She took a party of friends along who wanted to see Richmond. Not long after she left, Secretary of State Seward was out riding in his carriage in Washington when his horses ran away with him, cutting a corner too sharply. The front right wheel was smashed, and Seward was thrown out of the carriage. He suffered a broken jaw, a broken arm, multiple contusions of the head and face, and a concussion of the brain.

At Amelia Court House on the morning of the fifth, the wagons Lee had sent out the day before to collect supplies returned. They were almost empty. The farms of the area had already been stripped by the Confederate commissary department in previous weeks. Lee's hungry soldiers would stay hungry for yet another day. There was still the hope that trains of supplies would meet them as they marched down the railroad toward Jetersville, Burkeville, and Danville. The day before, Lee had ordered all surplus wagons and artillery weeded out, with the best of the horses transferred to the wagons and guns that would stay with the troops. It was hoped that the unneeded guns could be sent to safety by rail once they met a train. Meanwhile, they and the extra wagons were started that morning on a roundabout road leading to the west before turning south toward Danville, leaving the direct road uncluttered for the troops. The wagons that were staying with the army also moved west before turning south on a road that would take them between the troops and the surplus wagons. Brigadier General Martin Gary's cavalry brigade from Ewell's Department of Richmond was assigned to guard the wagons. Rooney Lee's cavalry division took the lead as the army started following the railroad to the southwest at about 1 p.m., followed by Longstreet's infantry, then Anderson's, then Ewell's. Gordon's 2nd Corps covered the rear. Fitzhugh Lee, with his own and Rosser's divisions of cavalry, did not arrive until the army was on the road. He was sent to help Gary, for by then reports were coming in that Union cavalry was attacking the wagons.

While the 5th Corps and most of his cavalry blocked the railroad at Jetersville, Sheridan sent Davies' brigade of Crook's division to the northwest. These troopers soon came upon Lee's undefended wagons and surplus artillery near a town called Paineville and promptly attacked this tempting target. Major Edward Boykin of the 7th South Carolina Cavalry in Gary's Brigade, hastening to protect this column, described the Federals' technique. "Their plan of operation seemed to be to strike the train, which was several miles long, at a given point, fire as many wagons as their number admitted of doing at once, then making a circuit and striking it again.... We did not suppose the troops actually engaged in the firing exceeded three or four hundred well-mounted men, but had a large body of cavalry moving parallel with them in easy supporting distance. This was a very effectual mode of throwing the march of the wagon train into confusion, independent of the absolute destruction they caused."[23]

As Gary's Brigade came up, the Federals withdrew. The Confederates pursued until they came upon Davies' main force dismounted behind defenses hastily constructed of fence rails. Gary's men took shelter in a nearby ravine, and the two forces faced off against each other until Fitz Lee arrived with his two divisions of cavalry. Finding themselves outnumbered and outflanked, the Federals withdrew again, this time to the protection of the rest of Crook's division. The Rebels, Major Boykin said, "moved on slowly after them—the sun being nearly down—to Amelia Springs, some two miles off, crossed the creek, and... were politely requested (everybody knows what a military request is) by General Lee to move down the road until we could see the Yankee pickets, put the brigade into camp, post pickets, and make the best of it—all of which we did."[24] Davies reported the capture of five guns, eleven flags, 320 soldiers, an equal number of black teamsters, and over 400 animals, in addition to the destruction of 200 wagons, caissons, and ambulances. He had also cost the Confederate wagon train six precious hours during which it was unable to move.

Meanwhile, Rooney Lee, at the head of Lee's main column, encountered increasing resistance from Merritt's cavalry as he advanced down the railroad. Soon the Confederates found their path blocked by Griffin's 5th Corps, dug in across the railroad just south of Jetersville. In a drizzling rain, Longstreet's infantry deployed to support Rooney's cavalry, and Lee rode forward to discuss the situation with his son. More Union infantry was known to be heading this way from the east, Rooney said, and others directly toward Burkeville. Lee consulted local farmers about the terrain and the roads in the area but learned little of importance. He studied the enemy position through his field glasses, and finally decided that it was too strong to risk an attack. Instead he ordered the army to detour west 23 miles to Farmville, where it would turn to the south again in an attempt to bypass this Union force.

"We had all expected a great battle at Jetersville," Joshua Chamberlain wrote. "A sonorous name is not necessary for a famous field.... Sheridan thought Lee missed his great opportunity in not attacking us here before any reinforcements got up. We shall not censure Lee. If he had doubts about the issue of a fight with the Fifth Corps we willingly accord him the benefit of his doubt."[25]

Meade reached Jetersville about 2 p.m., ahead of his troops. He was so sick that he asked Sheridan to put his men in position as they came up. The 2nd Corps arrived at about 3 p.m. "It being plain," Sheridan later wrote, "that Lee would attempt to escape as soon as his trains were out of the way, I was most anxious to attack him when the Second Corps began to arrive, for I felt certain that unless we did so he would succeed in passing by our left flank, and would thus again make our pursuit a stern chase; but General Meade, whose plan of attack was to advance his right flank on Amelia Court House, objected to assailing before all his troops were up." Stymied by Meade, who was his senior in rank, Sheridan sent off a dispatch to Grant explaining what Davies had done and informing him that the 2nd Corps was arriving. "I wish you were here yourself," he said. "I feel confident of capturing the Army of Northern Virginia if we exert ourselves. I see no escape for Lee. I will put all my cavalry out on our left flank except Mackenzie, who is now on the right."[26] Sheridan deployed the 2nd Corps between the cavalry and the 5th Corps, and the 6th Corps, when it arrived, on the right of the 5th.

Grant was still riding with Ord's column, taking the direct road for Burkeville. A Union surgeon who saw him about noon at Nottoway Court House described him as a "sturdy, thoughtful, but cheerful-looking man.... His voice, as caught, was low, but clear and gentle. There appeared in his manner, or in that of his companions, nothing to excite remark, certainly nothing to inspire awe; and, above all, there was not the least token of... 'fuss and feathers,' no glitter and dash such as the heroes of the books are often invested with. The most timid child would not have hesitated to ask a favor of that cigar-smoking, tawny-bearded, kindly-looking man."[27]

Grant and Ord were there for a while, studying maps and discussing the situation on the porch of an old tavern. While they were there a young staff officer rode up and excitedly asked, "Is this a way station?"

With great deliberation, Ord dryly replied, "This is Nott-a-way Station."[28]

It was nearly dark by the time Sheridan's message reached Grant. He had separated from Ord and was riding with his staff along a wagon road about halfway between Nottoway Court House and Burkeville. "A commotion suddenly arose among the headquarters escort," Horace Porter remembered, "and on looking round, I saw some of our men dashing up to a horseman in full Confederate uniform, who had emerged like an apparition from the woods, and in the act of seizing him as a prisoner. I recognized him at once as the scout who had brought the important despatch sent by Sheridan from Columbia to City Point. I said to him, 'How do you do, Campbell?' and told our men he was all right, and was one of our people. He said he had had a hard ride from Sheridan's camp, and had brought a despatch for General Grant. By this time the general had also recognized him, and had ridden up to him and halted in the road to see what he had brought. Campbell took from his mouth a small pellet of tin-foil, opened it, and pulled out a sheet of tissue paper, on which was written the famous despatch... in which Sheridan described the situation at Jetersville, and added, 'I wish you were here yourself.'"

Grant decided to go at once to Jetersville, twenty miles away, and, after changing to a fresh horse and writing a quick note to Ord to let him know where he was going, he started north through the woods with Porter, three other staff officers, the scout, and an escort of fourteen cavalrymen. "About half-past ten o'clock," Porter wrote, "we struck Sheridan's pickets. They could hardly be made to understand that the general-in-chief was wandering about at that hour with so small an escort, and so near to the enemy's lines. The cavalry were sleeping on their arms, and as our little party picked its way through their ranks, and the troopers woke up and recognized the general in the moonlight, their remarks were highly characteristic of the men. One said: 'Why, there's the old man. Boys, this means business'; and another: 'Great Scott! the old chief's out here himself. The rebs are going to get bu'sted to-morrow, certain'; and a third: 'Uncle Sam's joined the cavalry sure enough. You can bet there'll be lively times here in the morning.' Sheridan was awaiting us, feeling sure that the general would come after getting his despatch."[29]

They had a late supper and Sheridan, with great enthusiasm and not a little profanity, briefed Grant on the situation and proposed moving against Lee that night. Grant was "brimming over with quiet enjoyment" of Sheridan's tirade, a newspaper reporter observed.

"Lee's surely in a bad fix," Grant said. "He'll have to give up his line of retreat through here. But if I were in his place I think I could get away with part of the army. I suppose Lee will."

"He'll not take off a single regiment if we move," Sheridan said.

"We've done very well," Grant replied. "Everything's in our favor now. Don't expect too much at once. We'll do all in our power."[30]

After talking with Sheridan, Grant sent another message to Ord: "In the absence of further orders move west at 8 a.m. to-morrow and take position to watch the roads running south between Burkeville and Farmville. I am strongly of the opinion Lee will leave Amelia to-night to go south. He will be pursued at 6 a.m. from here if he leaves. Otherwise an advance will be made upon him where he is."[31] Then Grant and Sheridan went over to Meade's camp, reaching there about midnight. "I explained to Meade," Grant later wrote, "that we did not want to follow the enemy; we wanted to get ahead of him, and that his orders would allow the enemy to escape, and besides that, I had no doubt that Lee was moving right then. Meade changed his orders at once. They were now given for an advance on Amelia Court House, at an early hour in the morning, as the army then lay; that is, the infantry being across the railroad, most of it to the west of the road, with the cavalry swung out still farther to the left."[32]

A few Confederate troops reached Danville by rail that day, including Admiral Semmes and his sailors from the James River gunboats. Jefferson Davis put Semmes in charge of the troops and defenses of the city and immediately commissioned him a brigadier general in the army. Semmes pointed out that this was lower than his naval rank of rear admiral, but said, with a grin, "I will waive my rights pending further discussion."

"That's the spirit," Davis said with a rare smile.[33]

The telegraph line to Jetersville was working that morning, but during the day it went dead. Brigadier General Henry H. Walker, in charge of the defense of the railroads south of Petersburg, was studying a map of the area in the little depot at Clover Station when he heard about this. President Davis had been pestering Walker for news of Lee's army, and when he replied that the wire was down between him and Jetersville, Davis asked Walker if he could send a trustworthy man on an engine to Burkeville to communicate with Lee and bring back word to Davis of his position and plans. For lack of any older, more experienced officer, Walker sent Lieutenant John Wise, with an order from Davis authorizing him to impress any men, horses, or food that he might need.

After a meeting of his cabinet, Davis issued a proclamation that day, written by Secretary of State Benjamin, exhorting the people of the Confederacy to further exertions and sacrifices. "We have now entered upon a new phase of the struggle," he said. "Relieved from the necessity of guarding particular points, our army will be free to move from point to point to strike the enemy.... Let us but will it, and we are free.... I will never consent to abandon to the enemy one foot of the soil of any of the states of the Confederacy."[34]

---

1. Davis, *The Long Surrender,* 52.
2. Davis, *To Appomattox,* 171.
3. Wheeler, *Witness to Appomattox,* 151-152.
4. Ibid., 149-150.
5. Ibid., 150-151.
6. Chamberlain, *The Passing of the Armies,* 149-150.
7. Sheridan, *Civil War Memoirs,* 334-335.
8. Wheeler, *Witness to Appomattox,* 128-129.

9. Ibid., 130.
10. Ibid., 130-133.
11. Thomas Thatcher Graves, "The Occupation," in *Battles and Leaders,* 4:727-728.
12. Davis, *To Appomattox,* 168.
13. Wheeler, *Witness to Appomattox,* 135-137.
14. Graves, "The Occupation," 728.
15. Wheeler, *Witness to Appomattox,* 137.
16. Davis, *To Appomattox,* 169.
17. Tidwell, Hall, and Gaddy, *Come Retribution,* 420-421.
18. Stern, *An End to Valor,* 208.
19. Davis, *To Appomattox,* 188.
20. Foote, *The Civil War,* 3:901.
21. *Official Records,* 46:III:575.
22. Davis, *To Appomattox,* 191.
23. Wheeler, *Witness to Appomattox,* 156.
24. Ibid., 158.
25. Chamberlain, *The Passing of the Armies,* 149.
26. *Official Records,* 46:III:582.
27. Wheeler, *Witness to Appomattox,* 160.
28. Porter, *Campaigning with Grant,* 453.
29. Ibid., 454-456.
30. Davis, *To Appomattox,* 210-211.
31. *Official Records,* 46:III:583.
32. Grant, *Personal Memoirs,* 2:469.
33. Davis, *The Long Surrender,* 54.
34. Ibid.

CHAPTER THIRTY-TWO

The Day Long Foreseen Has Arrived

5 - 6 April 1865

On that same fifth day of April, Stoneman, at Christiansburg, Virginia, on the Virginia & Tennessee Railroad well to the west of Lynchburg, set one brigade of Gillem's division to work tearing up track west of the town and another on the east. He also sent the 11th Kentucky Cavalry to take possession of the railroad bridge and ferries over New River and the 10th Michigan Cavalry to destroy the bridges over the Roanoke River. The Federal raiders thus held at least ninety miles of railroad that day, from Wytheville on the southwest to Salem on the northeast.

Down in Alabama that day, Croxton's brigade of Wilson's Union cavalry left Tuscaloosa after destroying everything that might help the

Confederacy sustain its armies. It did not, however, head southeast toward Wilson's main force, still at Selma, but southwest. Croxton did not yet know that Wilson had twice defeated Forrest and captured Selma. But he did know that Jackson's Rebel cavalry was still between him and Wilson. However, when Wilson had sent Croxton off on his detached raid he had told him to break up the Alabama & Mississippi Railroad west of Selma if taking Tuscaloosa looked too difficult. He had taken Tuscaloosa, but now, with nothing better to do next, he led his 1,500 troopers to the southwest, aiming for the railroad somewhere between Demopolis, Alabama and Meridian, Mississippi. His four regiments recrossed the Black Warrior River that day and burned the bridge between Tuscaloosa and Northport behind them. That night they bivouacked 25 miles down the road, while a detachment from the 6th Kentucky Cavalry scouted ahead.

The next morning, the sixth, just as his main column was nearing the Sipsey River at Lanier's Mill, Croxton heard that there was a force of 3,000 Confederate cavalry not far away at Pickensville on the Tombigbee River. He also received definite word that Wilson was at Selma, but that Forrest's main force had fled west from there and was now squarely between Wilson and Croxton at Marion, Alabama. He also learned that Jackson's Division was somewhere between Tuscaloosa and Centerville. His brigade was therefore almost surrounded by three larger Rebel forces, so, after burning Lanier's Mill, he turned his column around and started back toward Tuscaloosa.

There actually was a force of Confederate cavalry at Pickensville. However, it numbered only about 1,500 men instead of the 3,000 that Croxton had been told. This was Brigadier General Wirt Adams' brigade, which Richard Taylor had sent eastward the day before from Columbus, Mississippi. It had been guarding the north-south Mobile & Ohio Railroad, but now it was on its way to join Forrest. As he crossed the Tombigbee, Adams, older brother of the Daniel Adams who was already with Forrest, learned of Croxton's position and decided to give chase.

At about 10 a.m. Croxton halted his column to feed his men and horses. They were just renewing their march at noon when Adams' advance slammed into Croxton's rearguard, the 6th Kentucky. Caught unprepared, the Kentuckians were easily routed, and their retreat uncovered the Union wagon train. Several wagons were captured, including Croxton's ambulance wagon carrying his personal effects. The major commanding the 6th Kentucky was cut off from his regiment and was eventually captured, as were a number of his men.

Both the retreating Federals and the pursuing Confederates were soon strung out over miles of road. But Croxton dismounted the 2nd Michigan Cavalry and positioned it across the road behind fence rails, trees, and mounds of plunder taken from Lanier's Mill. The fleeing Kentuckians were allowed to pass through a gap in the 2nd Michigan's line, which was then rapidly closed, and when the Rebels came up they were greeted by a fusilade from the Federals' Spencer repeating carbines.

After that, the Federals were able to retreat in good order, Adams following through a heavy downpour but unable to catch them or harry their march. That night both forces camped in the rain near Romulus, not far from Northport. The scouting force from the 6th Kentucky, which had originally been out in front of the Union column as it moved southwest, was cut off by Adams' advance and, unknown to Croxton, eventually made its way northward to the safety of Federal positions along the Tennessee River.

Upton's division and McCook with his remaining brigade rejoined Wilson at Selma that day, bringing in the Union supply wagons as well. But neither had been able to learn anything of Croxton's fate.

Stoneman's raiders spent the day of the sixth tearing up the Virginia & Tennessee Railroad. By 4 p.m. the bridge over New River had been disabled and the rails and ties had been destroyed for twenty miles to the east, as well as numerous bridges on the Roanoke River. Colonel Miller, the commander of the 3rd Brigade, reported that he had destroyed at Wytheville a large depot of commissary, quartermaster and ordnance supplies, including 10,000 pounds of gunpowder, and two nearby bridges. He had repulsed a Confederate attack and recrossed the New River. He was directed to return to Hillsville and then go on to Taylorsville, Virginia, and at 8 p.m. Stoneman's main column also resumed its march. It too headed back to the south, making for Jacksonville again.

Far to the north, John Surratt arrived in Montreal, Canada on that sixth day of April with dispatches from Secretary of State Benjamin for Brigadier General Edwin G. Lee, Robert E. Lee's cousin, who was now in charge of Confederate operations in and from Canada.

In southern Virginia on the night of 5-6 April Lee's army continued its march westward from Amelia Court House. Many of his men had marched all day and now had to march all night. "If all our marchings, sufferings, hardships, privations and sacrifices for all the preceding years of the war were summed up," a Confederate sergeant said, "shaken together and pressed down, they would not equal those we were now undergoing on this tramp." A major on Ewell's staff said, "I saw men apparently fast asleep in ranks, standing up, & walking enough to move on a few yards at a time as the wagons & troops in front gave us a little space. During the whole night our command could not have made three or four miles."[1]

A Confederate scout brought two men to General Gordon, commander of Lee's 2nd Corps, that night. They were wearing Rebel uniforms, and they claimed to belong to Fitz Lee's cavalry, but he thought they were Yankee spies. Gordon questioned the two men but could find nothing wrong with them. The Rebel scout insisted on searching them, however, and in one suspect's boot he found Grant's message to Ord about guarding the roads leading south between Burkeville and Farmville. After that they confessed that they were two of Sheridan's scouts. Gordon told the two men that they would be shot at sunrise. "We knew what we were doing, General," replied the older of the two, who was all of nineteen. "You have the right to shoot us, but it would do you no good. The war can't last much longer."[2] Gordon sent them away and hurried the captured dispatch to Lee.

Colonel T.M.R. Talcott, a Confederate engineer, was with Lee at the crossing of Flat Creek when the message was brought to the general at about 3 a.m. "The country road bridge over the stream had given away," Talcott wrote, "so that neither artillery nor wagons could cross it. General Lee… considered the situation critical enough to require his personal attention… and did not leave until he was assured that material for a new bridge was close at hand."[3] The captured dispatch revealed that Union infantry would be blocking Lee's intended route around the Jetersville roadblock. His only option now was to follow the Southside Railroad westward toward Lynchburg. Unfortunately for him, this meant that his troops and his wagons would soon be sharing the same road again.

At 4 a.m. Lee wrote instructions to Gordon, whose corps still formed the army's rearguard: "I have seen the dispatches (intercepted) you sent me. It was from my expectation of an attack being made from Jetersville that I was anxious that the rear of the column should reach Deatonsville as soon as possible. I hope the rear will get out of harm's way, and I rely greatly upon your exertions and good judgment for its safety. I know that men and animals are much exhausted, but it is necessary to tax their strength. I wish after the cavalry crosses the bridge at Flat Creek that it be thoroughly destroyed so as to prevent pursuit in that direction…. I see no way of relieving the column of the wagons, and they must be brought along. You must, of course, keep everything ahead of you, wagons, stragglers, etc. I will try to get the head of the column on and to get provisions at Rice's Station or Farmville."[4]

As Gordon's aide prepared to carry this message back to his commander, he asked Lee what should be done with the two Union scouts. After pondering the question, Lee said, "Tell the General the lives of so many of our men are at stake that all my thoughts now must be given to disposing of them. Let him keep the prisoners until he hears further from me."[5]

Lee was soon joined by Commissary General St. John, who had been one of the last Confederates out of Richmond and had been shepherding a train of wagons loaded with supplies from there. Some of these wagons had been captured by pursuing Federals. But St. John also brought the welcome news that 80,000 rations were waiting nearby. These supplies had been on the way to the army by rail when the Southside Railroad had been cut at Burkeville, so they had been brought back up that line to Farmville.

Meade advanced the 2nd, 5th, and 6th Corps up the railroad from Jetersville toward Amelia Court House at 6 a.m. on the sixth, but the Confederates had been marching all night and were all gone from there by then, as Sheridan and Grant had expected. "Satisfied that this would be the case," Sheridan later wrote, "I did not permit the cavalry to participate in Meade's useless advance, but shifted it out toward the left to the road running from Deatonsville to Rice's station, Crook leading and Merritt close up. Before long the enemy's trains were discovered on this road, but Crook could make but little impression on them, they were so strongly guarded; so, leaving Stagg's brigade and Miller's battery about three miles southwest of Deatonsville... to harass the retreating column and find a vulnerable point, I again shifted the rest of the cavalry toward the left, across-country, but still keeping parallel to the enemy's line of march."[6]

Sheridan had returned command of the 5th Corps to Meade for the latter's advance on Amelia Court House, but now Grant ordered Wright's 6th Corps, which Sheridan had originally requested before the battle of Five Forks, to move across from Meade's right flank to the left and to take its place under Sheridan's command. For once, however, he failed to make his intention clear to Meade, who continued to consider the 6th Corps subject to his own orders.

At 6:30 a.m. Humphreys visited his 2nd Division to see how it was doing, only to discover that it was not doing anything. "At General Hays' headquarters," he reported, "I found every one sound asleep. Upon proceeding to General Smyth's brigade, which I was informed... was the leading brigade, I learned from General Smyth that no order of precedence had been given to the brigade, and in consequence no one was moving. I ordered him to lead and move at once. I have relieved General Hays from the command of the Second Division and assigned General Smyth to it."[7] Before the day was over, Brevet Major General Francis Barlow was assigned to the command of that division. He had just returned to the army after a long leave of absence. Humphreys' troops soon found the tail of the Confederate column and followed directly on Lee's heels, repairing the bridge over Flat Creek for his guns and wagons, while Griffin's 5th Corps moved on farther to the north before turning west to join the pursuit on Humphreys' right. Humphreys' leading division, Mott's 3rd, caught up with Gordon's rearguard at about 9 a.m., beginning a day-long running battle. Mott was soon wounded and was succeeded by his senior brigade commander, Brigadier General Philip Regis de Trobriand, a very capable French soldier of fortune.

Ord, with Gibbon's two divisions of the 24th Corps, reached Burkeville at about 10 a.m. "As Lee appeared to be aiming for either Danville or Lynchburg," Ord reported, "Lieutenant-General Grant directed me to cut the bridges in his front and wait orders at Burkeville, which it was important to hold. To cut the high bridge near [Farmville] I dispatched two small regiments of infantry and all my headquarters escort, the only cavalry I had, under Colonel [Francis] Washburn, [4th] Massachusetts Cavalry, before daylight in the morning, with orders to push as rapidly as the exhausted condition of men and horses would permit, for the bridge, make a reconnaissance when near there, and, if not too well guarded, to burn it, returning at once with great caution.

"After they had left..., about 9 or 10 a.m., I received a dispatch by courier from General Sheridan, that Lee's army had broken away from him and were making, apparently, direct for me, at Burke's Junction. My command was immediately put in position to meet them, but it seems they turned off and took the road toward Farmville. Apprehending that my bridge-burning party might meet a force of Lee's cavalry sent southward to hold this bridge I had, before receiving Sheridan's dispatch, sent [Brigadier] General Theodore Read, my chief of staff, and the most gallant and reliable officer I had at hand, to conduct the party, cautioning him to reconnoiter the country well before he moved up to the Farmville bridge; and after I received General Sheridan's dispatch I sent the next best staff officer I had to caution Read that Lee's army was in his rear, and he must return by pressing on, crossing the Appomattox and going around by Prince Edward Court-House. The last officer was driven back by Lee's cavalry."[8]

Read's detachment consisted of Colonel Washburn's 83 officers and men from the 4th Massachusetts Cavalry plus the 54th Pennsylvania and the 123rd Ohio infantry regiments, from two different brigades of Turner's Independent Division of the 24th Corps, totaling about 700 men. Other than the cavalry, they were hardly crack troops, having recently been transfered from the Department of West Virginia, where they had often been defeated. The bridge Read and Washburn had been sent to destroy crossed the Appomattox east of Farmville and almost due north of Rice Station. It was a trestle 2,400 feet long and 126 feet high, consisting of 21 stone arches, aptly named the High Bridge. It had two levels, the upper one for the railroad and the lower for foot and wagon traffic.

"At Sailor's Creek," General Longstreet later wrote, "the road 'forks,'—one road to the High Bridge crossing of Appomattox River, the other by Rice's Station to Farmville. We had information of Ord's column moving towards Rice's Station, and I was ordered to that point to meet it, the other columns to follow the trains over the bridge. At Rice's Station the command was prepared for action,—Field's division across the road of Ord's march, Wilcox on Field's right; both ordered to intrench, artillery in battery. Heth's division was put in support of Wilcox, Mahone to support Field. Just then I learned that Ord's detachment of bridge-burners had passed out of sight when the head of my command arrived. I had no cavalry, and the head of Ord's command was approaching in sight; but directly General Rosser reported with his division of cavalry. He was ordered to follow after the bridge-burners and capture or destroy the detachment, *if it took the last man of his command to do it.* General Ord came on and drove in my line of skirmishers, but I rode to meet them, marched them back to the line, with orders to hold it till *called in.* Ord's force proved to be the head of his column, and he was not prepared to press for general engagement.

"General T.T. Munford reported with his cavalry and was ordered to follow Rosser, with similar directions. Gary's cavalry came and reported to me. High Bridge was a vital point, for over it the trains were to pass, and I was under the impression that General Lee was there, passing with the rest of his army, but hearing our troops engaged at Rice's Station, he had ridden to us and was waiting near Mahone's division. Ord's command was not up till near night, and he only engaged with desultory fire of skirmishers and occasional exchange of battery practice, arranging to make his attack the next morning."[9]

Longstreet's forces at Rice's Station were now between Read's Union raiders and Ord's main force. Read took the cavalry almost to Farmville but was prevented from entering the town by increasing resistance from

Rebel cavalry. "We skirmished with them for half an hour or more," a Union lieutenant reported, "when they opened on us with artillery, and we gradually fell back, hearing our infantry firing quite rapidly in our rear." Rosser's division was attacking the two Union infantry regiments.

"The fight took place at about noon," the lieutenant said, "in a small strip of woodland nearly a mile from the bridge, the country adjacent being very rough and hilly, so that it was impossible for cavalry to work to any advantage. When we reached the scene of action the infantry were deployed and holding a fence just inside the woods, while a few rods beyond was a brigade of dismounted rebel cavalry engaging our infantry at short range. Immediately on our arrival Colonel Washburn held a consultation with General Read, and at once determined to charge the enemy. Forming the squadron on the brow of the hill we moved forward in column of fours, at a trot, until beyond the right flank of our infantry, and then, wheeling to the left, by fours we charged into the woods. This charge was eminently successful, the enemy scattering in every direction, and we captured a number of them. The squadron was then reformed and we charged back into the woods, meeting a large force of rebel cavalry who had come up during our first charge. The men fought desperately hand to hand, but the conflict only lasted a few minutes, for, overpowered by numbers and all the officers being disabled or captured, many of our men surrendered. Some tried to cut their way out, but it was useless. The guidons of Companies I, L, and M were captured, but the regimental flag was burned by Color-Sergeant Hickey when he found that escape was impossible."[10]

Colonel Washburn, who briefly crossed swords with Brigadier General James Dearing, commander of Rosser's Laurel Brigade, was knocked unconscious when he ran into a low-hanging tree limb. "I have been, many a day, in hot fights," Rosser told one of Washburn's men after the war. "I never saw anything approaching that at High Bridge. While your Colonel kept the saddle, everything went down before him."[11] When Washburn came to, a Rebel trooper was rifling his pockets. Because he objected, the Confederate hit him with a saber, fracturing his skull, and he died after being sent home to Massachusetts.

Dearing fought with Read as well, and wounded him with a blow from his sword but was then shot by Read's orderly. Both generals died of their wounds. All the officers in the Union cavalry detachment were killed or wounded, leaving their men leaderless. On the Confederate side, Rosser was wounded slightly and, in addition to Dearing, also lost the colonel of one of his regiments and two majors, among others. "As the end was so near," Rosser later declared, "it would have been better to have allowed the enemy to have captured us all and burnt all the bridges in the country than to have thrown away such lives as [these], for they died to no purpose—the cause was already lost!"[12] The surviving Federals were soon surrounded and forced to surrender, but their battle may have served some useful purpose. "Reed's fight was as gallant and skilful as a soldier could make," Longstreet said, "and its noise in rear of Sailor's Creek may have served to increase the confusion there."[13]

And there certainly was confusion along Sayler's Creek. Throughout the morning Sheridan's cavalry had been nipping at the southern flank of the moving Confederate column, while Humphreys' 2nd Corps pressed its rearguard with increasing success. "Twenty-eight wagons and five guns had already fallen into our hands," General de Trobriand wrote. "At each capture the ardor of the chase increased. The men no longer halted even to load. When an obstacle presented itself, behind which the enemy made a pretense of standing, the skirmishers ran upon them with cheers. The regiments nearest dashed forward, and the position was carried even before the rest of the column knew what was going on."[14]

Having to share the road with the wagons and protect them from the Federals made the march even harder for the Rebels than it otherwise would have been. By 11 a.m., Anderson and Ewell, in the middle of the column between Longstreet and Gordon, were forced to bring their men to a halt in order to let the wagons get farther ahead. In the confusion of the repeated slashing Federal attacks, Anderson forgot to notify Mahone, at the tail of Longstreet's column, that they were stopping. Mahone, and the rest of Longstreet's command, marched on to take position at Rice's Station, and an increasingly long gap began to open in the Confederate column in which there was almost nothing but wagons.

Into this gap rode George Armstrong Custer. His leading brigade, Pennington's, "took off through the fields... on the gallop," one of his sergeants wrote, "gradually making for the train, yelling like Indians... we soon flanked the train guard, who had been hastily drawn up in line to oppose us. This done we came on the wagon train where there was not a single guard, or, indeed, often a man, for most of the drivers jumped off & ran away on our approach or ran toward us swinging their hats in token of surrender."[15] This attack captured, burned, or overturned at least 300 wagons and 10 guns, including a battery that had been in the process of deploying to protect the wagons. What was even more important, Custer's division, soon joined by Devin's and Crook's, now stood across the road blocking Anderson's column.

Gordon, hard pressed by Humphreys and unaware of Custer's

position, now sent a message to Anderson urging him to move on so that Ewell and then his own command could advance. At about 2 p.m. Anderson's corps resumed its march and almost immediately discovered Custer's Federal troopers in the way. Brigadier General Henry Wise launched an immediate attack with his brigade alone without consulting his division commander, Bushrod Johnson, whom he despised. His attack briefly shook Custer's cavalrymen, but failed for lack of support. Anderson evidently did not even know the attack had been made, for he had ridden back to consult with Ewell, who was the senior Confederate in the column now that it was cut off from Lee and Longstreet.

Ewell, meanwhile, informed by Fitz Lee that Anderson's path was blocked by Union cavalry, added to the confusion by ordering the remaining wagons to turn off on a road to the northwest to get them to safety and out of the way. This was a sound move, but he neglected to inform Gordon of what he had done. When the wagons began to move again, Gordon followed them, as he had been doing all day, without realizing that the wagons were no longer following the rest of the army.

At the same time, Anderson conferred with Ewell. "General Anderson informed me," Ewell wrote, "that at least two divisions of cavalry were in his front, and suggested two modes of escape—either to unite our forces and break through, or to move to the right through the woods and try to strike a road which ran toward Farmville. I recommended the latter alternative, but as he knew the ground and I did not, and had no one who did, I left the dispositions up to him."[16]

In this statement, Ewell revealed his habitual weakness as a commander: In the absense of orders from his superiors he avoided making a decision on his own but deferred to the judgment of others. The truth was that Anderson had no better knowledge of the terrain than Ewell did. Actually their two small corps were between Sayler's Creek on the west and Little Sayler's Creek on the east, while Gordon and the wagons followed a road that took them across the former stream just to the north of where it was joined by the latter. Both streams were fairly shallow but boggy and were separated by substantial ridges. As Fitz Lee later wrote, either of Anderson's options would have worked if undertaken when his march was first interrupted, but hesitation and indecision led to disaster. When Gordon turned off to the north, Humphreys' Federals followed him, but as Gordon moved out of the way, Ewell's own rear became liable to attack, and Wright's 6th Corps soon approached.

Elisha Rhodes' 2nd Rhode Island happened to be at the head of the

6th Corps column that day. "In the afternoon as we came out of the woods into an opening," Rhodes wrote, "I heard firing off to our right and front. I saw Gen. Sheridan, Gen. Wright, Gen. Wheaton and Gen. Edwards sitting on horses and talking earnestly.... I rode up and saluted and was told that in our front was a small stream called Sailor's Creek and that on the opposite side Gen. Ewell's Rebel Corps was guarding Lee's wagon train, and that our Cavalry had cut them off and we were to attack."[17]

"Before any [dispositions] were made," Ewell reported, "the enemy appeared in rear of my column in large force preparing to attack. General Anderson informed me that he would make the attack in front if I would hold in check those in rear.... I had no artillery, all being with the train. My line ran across a little ravine which leads nearly at right angles toward Sailor's Creek. General G.W.C. Lee was on the left, with the Naval Battalion, under Commodore Tucker, behind his right. Kershaw's division was on the right. All of Lee's and part of Kershaw's division were posted behind a rising ground that afforded some shelter from artillery. The creek was perhaps 300 yards in their front, with brush pines between and a cleared field beyond it. In this the enemy's artillery took a commanding position, and finding we had none to reply, soon approached within 800 yards and opened a terrible fire. After nearly half an hour of this, their infantry advanced, crossing the creek above and below us at the same time."[18]

Major Robert Stiles was commander of a Confederate battalion of heavy artillerymen from the defenses of Richmond now serving as infantrymen in Custis Lee's division on Ewell's left. "My men were lying down and were ordered not to expose themselves," he said. "I was walking backward and forward just back of the line, talking to them whenever that was practicable, and keeping my eye upon everything.... A good many men had been wounded and several killed, when a twenty-pounder Parrott shell struck immediately in my front, on the line, nearly severing a man in twain, and hurling him bodily over my head, his arms hanging down and his hands almost slapping me in the face as they passed....

"In a few moments the artillery fire ceased and I had time to glance about me and note results a little more carefully. I had seldom seen a fire more accurate, nor one that had been more deadly... in so brief a time. The expression of the men's faces indicated clearly enough its effect upon them. They did not appear to be hopelessly demoralized, but they did look blanched and haggard and awe-struck."[19]

While his artillery pounded the Confederates, General Wright deployed Seymour's 3rd Division on his right, overlapping Ewell's left, and Wheaton's 1st Division on his left. Elisha Rhodes' 2nd Rhode Island was in Wheaton's division. "The line moved down a hill," Rhodes said, "and seeing a river in front I dismounted and sent my horse to the rear behind a barn. The Rebels opened upon us soon as we reached the river, but we jumped in with the water up to our waists and soon reached the opposite side. Here we formed and advanced up a slight hill towards a piece of wood, the Rebels retreating from our front."[20]

Among the Rebels at the top of that hill was Major Stiles' Confederate battalion, supported by the Naval Battalion, made up of sailors and marines from the batteries that had guarded the river approaches to Richmond. "The Federal infantry had crossed the creek and were now coming up the slope in two lines of battle," Stiles wrote. "I stepped in front of my line and passed from end to end, impressing upon my men that no one must fire his musket until I so ordered; that when I said *'ready'* they must all rise, kneeling on the right knee; that when I said *'aim'* they must all aim about the knees of the advancing line; that when I said *'fire'* they must all fire together, and that it was all-important they should follow these directions exactly, and obey, implicitly and instantly, any other instructions or orders I might give.

"The enemy was coming on, and everything was still as the grave. My battalion was formed upon and around a swell of the hill, which threw it further to the front than any other command in the division, so that I was compelled to shape my own course, as I had received no special orders. The Federal officers, knowing, as I suppose, that we were surrounded, and appreciating the fearful havoc their artillery fire had wrought, evidently expected us to surrender, and had their white handkerchiefs in their hands, waving them toward us as if suggesting this course....

"The enemy showed no disposition to break into the charge, but continued to advance in the same deliberate and even hesitating manner, and I allowed them to approach very close... before retiring behind my men. I had continued to walk along their front for the very purpose of preventing them from opening fire; but now I stepped through the line, and, stationing myself about the middle of it, called out my orders deliberately, the enemy, I am satisfied, hearing every word. 'Ready!' To my great delight the men rose, all together, like a piece of mechanism, kneeling on their right knees, and their faces set with an expression that meant everything. 'Aim!' The musket barrels fell to an almost perfect horizontal line leveled about the knees of the advancing front line. 'Fire!'

"I have never seen such an effect, physical and moral, produced by the utterance of one word. The enemy seemed to have been totally unprepared for it, and, as the sequel showed, my own men scarcely less so. The earth appeared to have swallowed up the first line of the Federal force in our front. There was a rattling supplement to [our] volley, and the second line wavered and broke.... On the instant every man in my battalion sprang to his feet and, without orders, rushed bareheaded and with unloaded muskets down the slope after the retreating Federals. I tried to stop them, but in vain, although I actually got ahead of a good many of them. They simply bore me on with the flood."[21]

Colonel Rhodes' Rhode Islanders were evidently among the Federals struck by Stiles' volleys and countercharge. "When within about fifty yards of the woods," he said, "a Rebel officer stepped out and shouted: 'Rise up, fire!' A long line of Rebels fired right into our faces and then charged through our line and getting between us and the river."[22] In his official report, General Wright said, "I was never more astonished. These [Confederate] troops were surrounded—the First and Third Divisions of this corps were on either flank, my artillery and a fresh division in their front, and some three divisions of Major-General Sheridan's cavalry in their rear. Looking upon them as already our prisoners, I had ordered the artillery to cease firing as a dictate to humanity; my surprise therefore was extreme when this force charged upon our front."[23] Wright promptly ordered his six batteries of artillery to resume firing.

"The standard-bearer was dashing by me," Major Stiles wrote, "colors in hand, when I managed to catch his roll of blankets and jerk him violently back, demanding what he meant, advancing the battalion colors without orders. As I was speaking, the artillery opened fire again and he was hurled to the earth.... I stooped to pick up the flag, when his brother, a lieutenant, a fine officer and a splendid-looking fellow, stepped over the body, saying, 'Those colors belong to me, Major!' at the same time taking hold of the staff. He was shot through the brain and fell backward. One of the color guard sprang forward, saying, 'Give them to me, Major!' But by the time his hand reached the staff he was down.

"There were at least five men dead and wounded lying close about me, and I did not see why I should continue to make a target of myself. I therefore jammed the color staff down through a thick bush, which supported it in an upright position, and turned my attention to my battalion, which was scattered over the face of the hill firing irregularly at the Federals, who seemed to be reforming to renew the attack. I managed to get my men into some sort of formation and their guns loaded, and then charged the Federal line, driving it back across the creek, and forming my command behind a little ridge, which protected it somewhat."[24]

Colonel Rhodes was also having problems with his flag. "I found that the Rebels had our state color," he said, "but quickly faced the Regiment to the rear, and we charged them and breaking their line recrossed the stream. Gen. Edwards had become separated from the Brigade, and I, being the senior officer present, was ordered by General Wheaton to take command and recross. I sent for my horse and after reforming the line, we again crossed the stream and drove the enemy from the woods capturing the wagon train."[25]

"I ran back up the hill," Major Stiles said, "and had a brief conversation with General Custis Lee, commanding the division (our brigade commander having been killed), explaining to him that I had not ordered the advance and that we would be cut off if we remained long where we were, but that I was satisfied I could bring the battalion back through a ravine, which would protect them largely from the fire of the enemy's artillery, and reform them on the old line.... He expressed his doubts as to this, but I told him I believed my battalion would follow me anywhere, and with his permission I would try it.

"I ran down the hill again and explained to my men that when I got to the left of the line and shouted to them they were to get up and follow me, on a run and without special formation, through a ravine that led back to the top of the hill. Just because these simple-hearted fellows knew only enough to trust me, and because the enemy was not so far recovered as to take advantage of our exposure while executing the movement to the rear and reforming, we were back in the original lines in a few moments—that is, all who were left of us.

"It was of no avail. By the time we had well settled into our old position we were attacked simultaneously, front and rear, by overwhelming numbers, and, quicker than I can tell it, the battle degenerated into a butchery and a confused melee of brutal personal conflicts. I saw numbers of men kill each other with bayonets and the butts of muskets, and even bite each other's throats and ears and noses, rolling on the ground like wild beasts. I saw one of my officers and a Federal officer fighting with swords over the battalion colors, which we had brought back with us, each having his left hand upon the staff. I could not get to them, but my man was a very athletic, powerful seaman, and soon I saw the Federal officer fall.

"I had cautioned my men against wearing Yankee overcoats, especially in battle, but had not been able to enforce the order perfectly, and almost at my side I saw a young fellow of one of my companies jam the muzzle of his musket against the back of the head of his most intimate friend, clad in a Yankee overcoat, and blow his brains out."[26]

While the unexpected Confederate countercharge was achieving temporary success near the center of the line, Ewell's flanks were being turned by Seymour's division and by Custer's and one brigade of Devin's cavalry. At the same time, Anderson, with the remnants of Pickett's and Johnson's divisions, was launching his own attack against Crook's and the rest of Devin's cavalry. "The command forward was given," Bushrod Johnson said, "when General Pickett rode up and asked me to halt until he connected with my left flank. At this moment the enemy appeared in rear of my left, having passed between my command and that of General Pickett's, and my troops broke and moved rapidly on to the west and gained the road in rear, which connected with the right or advanced portion of our army."[27] As Anderson put it, "The troops seemed to be wholly broken down and disheartened. After a feeble effort to advance they gave way in confusion."[28]

Two brigades of Johnson's Division were about all of Anderson's corps that escaped. One was Henry Wise's brigade. "We pressed up a hill in our front," Wise said, "halted behind a worm fence on the crest, fired three volleys to the rear... poured three volleys obliquely to the left and front, broke the enemy and got out."[29] And Wise claimed that when his men fired a volley into a nearby woods Brigadier General William Wallace's brigade of South Carolinians came out under a white flag and he put them in front of his own Virginians and hurried the lot off toward Farmville and temporary safety.

With Anderson's troops out of the way, the Union cavalry began to close in on the rear of Kershaw's right flank brigade, commanded by Brigadier General J.P. Simms. "That officer attempted to extricate his command," Kershaw reported, "but found it impossible to do so without confusion, as he was attacked on all sides. This condition of things being discovered by the other troops, all fell back toward the rear and left. I kept up something of a skirmish as the command retreated; but after moving some 400 yards I discovered that all who had preceded me had been taken by the Yankee cavalry, who were in line of battle across the road. I then directed the men about me and the members of my staff to make their escape in any way possible. I discovered afterward that but one had succeeded, as the enemy had completed the circle around our position when General Anderson's line was broken."[30]

General Ewell had been with Anderson. "I had ridden up near his lines with him to see the result," Ewell wrote, "when a staff officer, who had followed his troops in their charge, brought him word of its failure. General Anderson rode rapidly toward his command. I returned to mine to see if it were yet too late to try the other plan of escape. On riding past my left I came suddenly upon a strong line of the enemy's skirmishers advancing upon my left rear. This closed the only avenue of escape, as shells and even bullets were crossing each other from front and rear over my troops, and my right was completely enveloped. I surrendered myself and staff to a cavalry officer who came in by the same road General Anderson had gone out on. At my request he sent a messenger to General G.W.C. Lee, who was nearest, with a note from me telling him he was surrounded, General Anderson's attack had failed, I had surrendered, and he had better do so too, to prevent useless loss of life, though I gave no orders, being a prisoner. Before the messenger reached him General Lee had been captured, as had General Kershaw, and the whole of my command."[31]

"I don't think," Major Stiles wrote, "I ever suffered more than during the few moments after I saw that nothing could possibly effect or change the result of the battle." His men began to surrender, but he tried to escape. "I had always considered it likely I should be killed, but had never anticipated or contemplated capture.... Selecting the direction which seemed to be most free from Federal soldiers... I started first at a walk and then broke into a run; but in a short distance ran into a fresh Federal force, and it seemed the most natural and easy thing in the world to be simply arrested and taken in."[32]

General Pickett was more fortunate. "A squadron of the enemy's cavalry was riding down upon us," he wrote, "two of my staff and myself, when a small squad of my men recognized me and, risking their own lives, rallied to our assistance and suddenly delivered a last volley into the faces of the pursuing horsemen, checking them but for a moment. But in that one moment we, by the speed of our horses, made our escape."[33]

While Anderson and Ewell were brought to bay, Humphreys' 2nd Corps of the Army of the Potomac continued to snap at the heels of Gordon's 2nd Corps of the Army of Northern Virginia. The slow crossing of the Confederate wagons over Sayler's Creek a couple of miles north of the other battlefield delayed the Rebels enough for the head of the Union column, Brigadier General Bryon R. Pierce's 2nd Brigade of de Trobriand's 3rd Division, to catch up with Gordon as the sun was going down. A Confederate remembered hearing Pierce's skirmishers calling, "Come along, boys. Here are the damned rebel wagons! Damn 'em; shoot 'em down!"

Come along they did. "In a few moments," the same Rebel said, "their line of battle, in beautiful order, stepped out of the woods with colors flying, and for a moment halted. In front of the center of that portion of the line which was visible—probably a full regimental front—marched the colors and color guard." A squad of Rebels rose and fired. "The colorbearer pitched forward and fell, with his colors, heavily to the ground. The guard of two men on either side shared the same fate, or else feigned it. Immediately the line of battle broke into disorder and came swarming down the hill, firing, yelling, and cursing as they came."[34]

The Federals broke Gordon's line, drove him across the creek, and captured 3 guns, 13 battleflags, several hundred prisoners, and a large portion of the wagons, bringing the 2nd Corps total for the day to 4 guns, 13 flags, 1,700 prisoners, and over 300 wagons and ambulances. Gordon tried to form another line on the high ground beyond the creek but fell back as the Federals crossed the stream. However, darkness soon put an end to the fighting and the pursuit for the day, here as well as on the field of Ewell's and Anderson's defeat. Gordon's column continued on to High Bridge during the night.

Among the Confederates captured that evening was an intelligent young sergeant with whom General de Trobriand had a talk. "General," the young Rebel told him, "I can tell you nothing which you do not well know. The Army of Northern Virginia no longer exists. What remains cannot escape you. It must end in that manner, and, since it cannot be otherwise, we do not regret that the day long foreseen has arrived. On the contrary, we are all rejoiced that the war is finished. If we had been consulted, it would have ended many months ago, but the government chose to hold out to the end.

"I was taken by the conscription.... Of those who volunteered at the beginning of the war, very few now remain. For six or eight months back, our men have deserted by thousands. Those who remain have been held by a sentiment of honor only. They did not wish to disgrace themselves by deserting their flag. They have done their duty to the best of their ability. As to the Southern Confederacy, although they would have liked to have seen it triumph, they lost all hope of it long since.

"Personally, I care little for slavery, and it is all the same to me whether the Negroes be free or not. I belong to a family of farmers who sometimes hired black labor, but who owned no slaves. Now, when we employ them, we will pay *them* instead of their masters; that is all the difference. As to politics, I have never taken any part. I know very well that the war was brought on principally for the benefit of the planters; but what could we do? When one is on board of a ship, he must do what he can to keep it afloat. The Confederacy has ruined the South by the war; our hope is now that the Union will raise her out of her ruin by peace."[35]

General Lee had been with Longstreet's command that morning and then had ridden to the Appomattox River at the point where Sayler's Creek joins it. There he found a brigade of his son Rooney's cavalry, which was watching the running fight between Gordon's Confederates and Humphreys' Federals coming their way. Lee wondered what had become of Anderson's and Ewell's troops, who were supposed to be ahead of Gordon's corps. He dismounted and studied the distant fields with his binoculars, spotting a mass of indistinct white objects.

"Are those sheep or not?" he asked a young officer.

"No, General," was the answer, "they are Yankee wagons."

"You are right," Lee said; "but what are they doing there?"[36]

Lee rode toward the area through which Anderson and Ewell's column should be moving but saw no sign of them. Eventually he came to Mahone's Division as it was taking place on the left of Longsteet's line near Rice's Station. He was talking with Mahone when Colonel Venable of his staff rode up and asked if Lee had received his message. When Lee replied that he had not, Venable told him that the Federals had captured the wagon train at Sayler's Creek.

"Where is Anderson? Where is Ewell?" Lee asked rhetorically. "It is strange I can't hear from them." Then he turned to Mahone. "General Mahone, I have no other troops, will you take your division to Sailor's Creek?"

"I promptly gave the order by the left flank," Mahone later wrote, "and off we were for Sailor's Creek, where the disaster had occurred. General Lee rode with me, Colonel Venable a little in the rear. On reaching the south crest of the high ground at the crossing of the river road overlooking Sailor's Creek, the disaster which had overtaken our army was in full view, and the scene beggars description,—hurrying teamsters with their teams and dangling traces (no wagons), retreating infantry without guns, many without hats, a harmless mob, with the massive columns of the enemy moving orderly on. At this spectacle General Lee straightened himself in his saddle, and looking more the soldier than ever, exclaimed, as if talking to himself, 'My God, has the army dissolved?' As quickly as I could control my own voice I replied, 'No, general, here are troops ready to do their duty'; when, in a mellow voice, he replied, 'Yes, general, there are some true men left. Will you please keep those people back?' As I was placing my division in position to 'keep those people back,' the retiring herd... crowded around General Lee while he sat on his horse with a Confederate battle flag in his hand. I rode up and requested him to give me the flag, which he did.

"It was near dusk, and he wanted to know of me how to get away. I replied, 'Let General Longstreet move by the river road to Farmville, and cross the river there, and I will go through the woods to the High Bridge... and cross there.' To this he assented. I asked him then, after crossing at the High Bridge, what I should do, and his reply was, to exercise my judgment. I wanted to know what should be done with the bridge after crossing it. He said, 'Set fire to it,' and I replied that the destruction of a span would as well retard the enemy as the destruction of the whole half mile of bridge, and asked him to call up Colonel Talcott, of the Engineers Regiment, and personally direct him in the matter, which he did."[37]

As the Federals settled into camp that night, Sheridan sent Colonel Redwood Price to Grant with news of his successes: "I have the honor to report that the enemy made a stand at the intersection of the Burke's Station road with the road upon which they were retreating. I attacked them with two divisions of the Sixth Army Corps and routed them handsomely, making a connection with the cavalry. I am still pressing on with both cavalry and infantry. Up to the present time we have captured Generals Ewell, Kershaw, Barton, Corse, De Foe [Du Bose], and Custis Lee, several thousand prisoners, 14 pieces of artillery, with caissons, and a large number of wagons. If the thing is pressed I think that Lee will surrender."[38]

On his way to Grant, Colonel Price stopped by Meade's headquarters, where the news was received with astonishment and Sheridan's report with dismay. Colonel Theodore Lyman of Meade's staff noted in his diary, "There comes a staff officer with a dispatch. '*I* attacked with two divisions of the 6th Corps. *I* captured many thousand prisoners, etc. P.H. Sheridan.'"

"Oh," said Meade, "so General Wright wan't there?"

"Oh, yes," Price said ["as if speaking of some worthy man who had commanded a battalion," Lyman said], "General Wright *was* there."

"Meade turned on his heel without a word," Lyman wrote, "and Cavalry Sheridan's dispatch proceeded—to the newspapers!"[39]

"Price gave the story of the battle," Sheridan wrote in his memoirs, "and General Meade, realizing its importance, sent directions immediately to General Wright to make his report of the engagement to the headquarters of the Army of the Potomac, assuming that Wright was operating independently of me in the face of Grant's despatch of 2 o'clock, which said that Wright was following the cavalry and would 'go in with a vim' wherever I dictated. Wright could not do else than comply with Meade's orders in the case, and I, being then in ignorance of Meade's reasons for the assumption, could say nothing."[40]

Sheridan had several Confederate guests in his camp that night. "He is lying on the broad of his back on a blanket," wrote one of his staff officers, "with his feet to the fire, in a condition of sleepy wakefulness which can only be attained through excessive fatigue and a sense of responsibility. Clustered about are blue uniforms and gray in equal numbers, and immediately around his campfire are most of the Confederate generals who have just been captured. General Ewell is the principal figure in the group, and attracts, though he seems to avoid, attention. He has plainly admitted that there is no hope now for General Lee, and has begged General Sheridan to send him a flag of truce and demand his surrender, in order to save any further sacrifice, but the general has made no further response to this than to urge General Grant to push on faster. Ewell is sitting on the ground hugging his knees, his face bent down between his arms, and if anything could add force to his words, the utter despondency of his air would do it. The others are mostly staid, middle-aged men, tired to death nearly, and in no humor for a chat; and so the party is rather a quiet one, for our fellows are about done over, too, and half starved. To this sprawling party enter Sandy Forsyth, *aide-de-camp,* to announce that he has established headquarters in a lovely orchard, where tents are up and supper is cooking.... We carried the Confederate generals with us and shared our suppers and blankets with them."[41]

General Kershaw was a guest of Custer. During the day he had ordered his men to concentrate their fire on Custer's personal battleflag in an unsuccessful effort to bring him down, but now they met on friendly terms. Years later he sent an account of that night to Custer's widow: Custer met his guest with a smile and shook his hand.

"Why General," he said, "I am glad to see you here. I feel as if I ought to know about you."

"Yes, General," Kershaw replied, "we have met very often but not under circumstances favorable to cultivating an acquaintance."

"This little passage of pleasantry," Kershaw told Mrs. Custer, "made us quite at home immediately, and very soon the conversation became free, general and kindly around the camp fire. With a soldier's hospitality, we were made to feel welcome by our host, and notwithstanding our misfortunes, enjoyed not a little the camp luxuries of coffee, sugar, condensed milk, hard-tack, broiled ham, etc., spread before us upon the tent fly converted into a table cloth around which we all sat upon the ground. Custer and his Rebel guests. After supper we smoked and talked over many subjects of interest to all of us dwelling, however, almost wholly upon the past. The future to us, was not inviting, and our host with true delicacy of feeling avoided the subject. We slept beneath the stars, Custer sharing his blankets with me."[42]

That night, after a long, eventful trip from Clover Station, young

Lieutenant John Wise found General Lee standing by a campfire in a field near Rice's Station. Wise's special train had reached Burkeville early that morning, where he had found Union cavalrymen at work on the Southside Railroad, moving rails to widen the gauge to fit their rolling stock. When the Federals had charged his train, Wise had found it necessary to draw his revolver to make the engineer reverse his engine rather than surrender. They had backed the engine to Meherrin Station, where the lieutenant, using his authorization from Jefferson Davis, had taken a horse from a Rebel cavalryman on furlough and ridden off in search of Lee. He had heard the fight at Sayler's Creek, had outrun a couple of Union cavalry detachments, had almost been ambushed by Rebel scouts, and had ridden all the way up to Farmville before finally finding Lee. The general was dictating dispatches to Colonel Charles Marshall, who was sitting in a headquarters wagon with a lap desk. Young Wise informed Lee that he had been sent at the behest of President Davis to learn of Lee's situation and plans.

"I hardly think it necessary to prepare written dispatches," the general told him. "They may be captured. You may say to Mr. Davis that, as he knows, my original purpose was to adhere to the line of the Danville road. I have been unable to do so, and am now trying to hold the Southside road as I retire toward Lynchburg."

Before going back to Farmville to find his father's brigade and get a night's rest, the lieutenant asked Lee if he had chosen a place to make a stand.

"No," the general replied, "I'll have to wait for developments. A few more Sayler's Creeks and it will be all over."[43]

---

1. Burleigh Cushing Rodick, *Appomattox: The Last Campaign* (New York, 1965), 57.
2. Davis, *To Appomattox,* 217.
3. Ibid.
4. *Official Records,* 46:III:1387.
5. Freeman, *R. E. Lee,* 4:79.
6. Sheridan, *Civil War Memoirs,* 337.
7. *Official Records,* 46:III:597-598.
8. Ibid., 46:I:1161.
9. Longstreet, *From Manassas to Appomattox,* 611-612.
10. *Official Records,* 46:I:1169.
11. Rodick, *Appomattox,* 74.
12. Ibid., 72.
13. Longstreet, *From Manassas to Appomattox,* 616.

14. Wheeler, *Witness to Appomattox,* 170.
15. Starr, *The Union Cavalry in the Civil War,* 2:469.
16. *Official Records,* 46:I:1294.
17. Rhodes, *All for the Union,* 227.
18. *Official Records,* 46:I:1294-1295.
19. Wheeler, *Witness to Appomattox,* 173.
20. Rhodes, *All for the Union,* 228-229.
21. Wheeler, *Witness to Appomattox,* 175.
22. Rhodes, *All for the Union,* 229.
23. *Official Records,* 46:I:906.
24. Wheeler, *Witness to Appomattox,* 176.
25. Rhodes, *All for the Union,* 229.
26. Wheeler, *Witness to Appomattox,* 176-178.
27. *Official Records,* 46:I:1290.
28. Freeman, *Lee's Lieutenants,* 3:706.
29. Davis, *To Appomattox,* 229.
30. *Official Records,* 46:I:1284.
31. Ibid., 46:I:1295.
32. Wheeler, *Witness to Appomattox,* 180.
33. Ibid.
34. Ibid., 185.
35. Ibid., 188.
36. Freeman, *R. E. Lee,* 4:84.
37. Longstreet, *From Manassas to Appomattox,* 614-615.
38. *Official Records,* 46:III:610.
39. Davis, *To Appomattox,* 240-241.
40. Sheridan, *Civil War Memoirs,* 340-341.
41. Stern, *An End to Valor,* 228-229.
42. Urwin, *Custer Victorious,* 248.
43. Davis, *To Appomattox,* 235.

CHAPTER THIRTY-THREE

Let the Thing Be Pressed

6 - 7 April 1865

Mary Lincoln returned to City Point at about noon on the sixth with a boatload of friends who wanted to see captured Richmond. These included Senator Charles Sumner, the radical Republican leader; James H. Harlan, the new secretary of the interior, with his wife and daughter as well as an undersecretary—the daughter would marry Robert Lincoln after the war—Elizabeth Keckley, a free black woman who had been Varina Davis's seamstress when the latter's husband had been a U.S. senator and who now held the same position with Mary Lincoln; and a liberal young French nobleman, the Marquis de Chambrun. Harlan, a former senator from Iowa and an old friend of Lincoln's, was amazed at the change a few days away from Washington had wrought in the president: "His whole appearance, pose and bearing had marvellously changed. He was, in fact, transfigured. That indescribable sadness, which had previously seemed to be an adamantine element of his very being, had been suddenly changed for an equally indescribable expression of serene joy, as if conscious that the great purpose of his life had been achieved."[1]

Mrs. Lincoln and her friends went on up the James to Richmond that afternoon on the *River Queen,* while the president returned to his little cabin aboard the *Malvern.* Sometime during the day Vice President Johnson and his friend Preston King, a former senator from New York, showed up, but Lincoln refused to see them. He continued to hang around the headquarters telegraph and forward reports to Stanton at Washington. He had already wired Grant: "Secretary Seward was thrown from his carriage yesterday and seriously injured. This, with other matters, will take me to Washington soon. I was at Richmond yesterday and the day before, when and where Judge Campbell, who was with Messers. Hunter and Stephens in February, called on me and made such representations as induced me to put in his hands an informal paper, repeating the propositions in my letter of instructions to Mr. Seward, which you remember, and adding that if the war be now further persisted in by the rebels confiscated property shall, at the least, bear the additional cost; and that confiscations shall be remitted to the people of any State which will now, promptly and in good faith, withdraw its troops and other support from resistance to the Government. Judge Campbell thought it not impossible that the rebel legislature of Virginia would do the latter if permitted, and accordingly I addressed a private letter to General Weitzel, with permission for Judge Campbell to see it, telling him (General W.), that if they attempt this to permit and protect them, unless they attempt something hostile to the United States, in which case to give them notice and time to leave and to arrest any remaining after such time.

"I do not think it very probable that anything will come of this, but I have thought best to notify you so that if you should see signs you may understand them. From your recent dispatches it seems that you are pretty effectually withdrawing the Virginia troops from opposition to the Government. Nothing I have done, or probably shall do, is to delay, hinder, or interfere with you in your work."[2]

The next morning, the seventh, Lincoln received a report from Grant that included Sheridan's dispatch of the sixth, and the president replied: "Gen. Sheridan says 'If the thing is pressed I think that Lee will surrender.' Let the *thing* be pressed."[3]

Assistant Secretary Dana wired Stanton that evening: "Meeting of five members of the Virginia legislature held here to-day upon the President's propositions to Judge Campbell. The President showed me the papers confidentially to-day. They are two in number, one without address, the other letter to General Weitzel. The one states *sine qua non* of reunion, and does not differ essentially from previous statements. The second authorizes Weitzel to allow members of the body claiming to be legislature of Virginia to meet here for purpose of recalling Virginia soldiers from rebel armies, with safe conduct to them, so long as they do and say nothing hostile to the United States. Judge Campbell laid these papers before the five men, who met twice, but I am not advised that they took any action. The President told me this morning that Sheridan seemed to be getting Virginia soldiers out of the war faster than this legislature could think."[4]

John Wilkes Booth arrived in New York from Boston that day, the seventh. He was drinking hard and talking too loud when, according to Samuel Chester, an actor friend, he thumped the table and exclaimed, "What a splendid chance I had to kill the president on the 4th of March."[5] Back in December or January, Booth had unsuccessfully tried to recruit Chester into the plot to capture Lincoln. He had wanted to get Chester a job at Ford's Theatre so Chester would be in position to open the back door at a signal, thus aiding the getaway. Booth had told him then that there were parties on the "other side" (of the Potomac, presumably) ready to cooperate with him. Chester had presumed he meant the Confederate authorities. "He said there were from fifty to one hundred persons in the conspiracy," Chester said.[6]

Reconstructed Tennessee ratified the 13th Amendment and inaugurated an abolitionist governor on the seventh. And the U.S. State Department opened discussions with the British that day concerning compensation for damages caused by the CSS *Alabama* and other Confederate commerce raiders that had been built in England.

In Alabama on the seventh, Wirt Adams' Confederates turned away from pursuing Croxton's lost brigade of Wilson's cavalry. Rebel scouts brought Adams word that the Federals were moving west toward Columbus, Mississippi and the Mobile & Ohio Railroad. The Confederates turned back to Mississippi to protect their base and the railroad. In fact, however, Croxton's Federals returned to Northport, across the river from Tuscaloosa, that night, where they camped for four days, hoping the missing Kentucky scouts would come in.

The night of 6-7 April turned so cold in southside Virginia that snow flurries were seen in Burkeville, and with morning came rain. Sheridan's troopers were up and on the road as soon as it was light enough to see, too full of enthusiasm to mind the rain. He and his officers soon parted from their Confederate guests. "After a sleep of hardly an hour," a staff officer said, "[we] took breakfast in their company and then parted... as we followed the general's swallow-tailed flag down the road."[7]

Kershaw's letter to Libby Custer told of memories of her husband that morning: "While at breakfast, one after another some 30 troopers rode up within a few rods, each dismounting and aligning himself, holding his horse by the bridle. Each also carried a *Confederate battleflag,* except my captor of the previous day whom I recognized in the ranks, and he bore two of our flags. He also, as he caught my eye and bowed, pointed to my own sabre worn with an air of pride and pleasure.

"My curiousity was greatly excited by this group and I asked General Custer what it meant. 'That,' said he, 'is my escort for the day. It is my custom after a battle to select for my escort a sort of *garde de honeur* those men of each regiment who most distinguished themselves in action, bearing for the time, the trophies which they have taken from the enemy. These men are selected as the captors of the flags which they bear.'

"I counted them. There were 31 captured banners representing 31 of our regiments killed, captured or dispersed the day before. It was not comforting to think of.

"He shook my hand, mounted a magnificent charger and rode proudly away followed at a gallop by his splendid escort bearing the fallen flags. As he neared his conquering legions cheer after cheer greated his approach, bugles sounded and sabres flashed as they saluted. The proud cavalcade filed through the open ranks and moved to the front, leading that magnificent column in splendid array."[8]

While the Union cavalry prepared to ride, the thousands of Rebel soldiers captured the day before were marched away in the opposite direction, escorted by a regiment from Custer's division. "They marched past Division headquarters," one Federal wrote, "in immense ranks.... They had some spirit in them, notwithstanding all the hardships they had gone thro'. The Division Bands were playing as... they marched; when they played 'Yankee Doodle,' 'Hail Columbia' & kindred tunes, they would groan, but as... they struck up 'Dixie,' this called out rousing cheers from them... it was a noble sight [as] they moved off, with the manner & tread of trained soldiers, & it was impossible not to accord them respect as brave men. Often enough had we met them to prove this."[9]

Merritt's two divisions, plus Mackenzie's, were sent some twenty miles westward to Prince Edward Court House, which they reached about 3 p.m., to prevent Lee from working around the Federals and going on to Danville and North Carolina. Crook's division was sent to follow Longstreet's Rebels to Farmville. As Crook's men took to the road they found the infantrymen of the 6th Corps, as one trooper wrote, "already on the move, singing, laughing, joking and apparently happy as they marched along, though a little inclined to growl at being obliged to let the cavalry have the road, while they took the rougher, harder-to-march-over ground at the side. Along the side were evidences of the rapid retreat of the enemy—all sorts of munitions of war laying around in loose profusion,—a dead rebel soldier lying on the road where he halted his last time, with every appearance of having died from hunger and exhaustion,—dead horses, the infallible army guideboards, lying where they dropped, and others abandoned because unable longer to carry their riders,—all informed the men that the men ahead of them were in a great hurry, and had an exhilarating effect upon their spirits."[10]

After seeing young Lieutenant John Wise, Lee rode north to Farmville, where he had a few hours' rest at a friendly home and a cup of tea—a rarity in the blockaded South—for breakfast. He saw to it that the quartermasters were beginning to issue the rations that, as promised, were waiting for them here, and then he rode across one of the two bridges in the town to the north side of the Appomattox to meet the troops who were crossing the river farther east at High Bridge. The remnants of Anderson's and Ewell's commands came along first, and Lee soon met Bushrod Johnson, who reported that his division had been destroyed. This was a slight exaggeration, as was soon proven when, about daybreak, General Henry Wise marched up at the head of his troops.

Wise had lost his horse, was wrapped in an old blanket, and had red mud all over his face from having washed in a puddle, but he was as pugnacious as ever. He marched up to the commanding general and demanded that his men be given something to eat. Lee told him to take his men to the top of a nearby hill where they would soon be fed. He also told him to take command of all the stragglers and remnants of units in the area. Wise protested that he did not even have a horse. Lee told him to get one and to make all the stragglers fall into his ranks. Wise protested that it would ruin his brigade to take in such demoralized troops, but Lee insisted. Finally, casting a glance toward Johnson, whom he detested, he said, "Do you mean to say, General Lee, that I must take command *of all men of all ranks?"* Lee turned his head to conceal a smile and only said, "Do your duty, sir."[11] Wise led his men up the hill, saw that they got something to eat and let them have an hour or so of rest. After a while his son finally found him. "The troops were lying there more like dead men than live ones," the lieutenant remembered. "They did not move, and they had no sentries out. The sun was shining upon them as they slept. I did not recognize them. Dismounting, and shaking an officer, I awoke him with difficulty." The officer directed young Wise to his father. "Nearly sixty years old, he lay, like a common soldier, sleeping on the ground among his men."

But the general was soon awake, and his son had to explain the errand that had brought him there. At his mention of General Lee, his father said he wanted to see Lee again, so they soon went off together looking for him. "The roads and fields were filled with stragglers," the younger man wrote. "They moved looking behind them, as if they expected to be attacked.... Demoralization, panic, abandonment of all hope, appeared on every hand. Wagons were rolling along without any clear order or system. Caissons and limber-chests, without commanding officers, seemed to be floating aimlessly upon a tide of disorganization. Rising to his full height, casting a glance around him like that of an eagle, and sweeping the horizon with his long arm and bony forefinger, my father exclaimed, 'This is the end!' It is impossible to convey an idea of the agony and the bitterness of his words and gestures."[12]

They found Lee on the back porch of a house in Farmville, and the elder Wise began to profanely denounce Bushrod Johnson. Sternly Lee asked him if he was aware that he could be court-martialed and executed for insubordination. Undaunted, Wise replied that Lee could not afford to shoot the men who fought for cursing those who ran away. And that anyway if Lee did not shoot him some Yankee probably would within the next 24 hours. Perhaps to change the subject, Lee asked what he thought of their military situation, and Wise boldly told him that the army was already whipped and that the blood of every man who was killed from then on would be on Lee's head. He should send the men home before it was too late for spring plowing. Lee asked what the country would think of him if he did anything like that. Wise replied that there was no country—had been none for a year or more—that Lee himself was the only cause the men were fighting for now. Lee looked away and made no reply, studying the distant fields. Then he wrote a brief message to President Davis for the lieutenant to carry, saying only that he had talked with the young man, who would deliver his message verbally. Not long after the Wises, father and son, departed, Lee conferred with Secretary of War Breckinridge, who would also be reporting soon to President Davis. Lee told him that the retreat across the Appomattox was only a temporary expedient and that he still hoped to get around the Federals and escape to North Carolina.

Soon the head of Longstreet's column reached Farmville and crossed to the north side of the Appomattox on the two bridges there. The men were issued two days' rations from the trains that had met the army there, and then fell out and began to cook them. Lieutenant J.F.J. Caldwell, in Wilcox's Division of the 3rd Corps, was near the tail of Longstreet's column. "The enemy were already pressing upon our rear...," he said. "Our cavalry now lined the high hills, in order of battle. The skirmishing grew closer and more rapid in our rear.... Scales' brigade of our division was left behind as rearguard of our column. The rest of the division marched into Farmville.

"Farmville is beautifully situated, occupying a table-ground inclosed by a circumference of lofty hills. The Appomattox flows along the northern and eastern side of the town. Upon the hills on the northern bank of the stream we could see hundreds of wagons quietly lying in park, and, from the numerous columns of smoke that curled among them, it seemed that there were rations being cooked and repose enjoyed after the long-continued labors and perils."[13]

After the remnants of Anderson's and Ewell's commands had crossed the Appomattox over the High Bridge, Gordon's corps had followed, and then Mahone's Division. "What strange sensations the men had as they marched slowly across the High Bridge," one of Gordon's men remembered. "They knew its great height, but the night was so dark that they could not see the abyss on either side. Arrived on the other side, the worn-out soldiers fell to the ground and slept, more dead than alive. Some had slept as they marched across the bridge, and declared that they had no distinct recollection of when they left it, or how long they were upon it."[14]

By dawn Gordon's men were marching west and Mahone's men were crossing the double-decker bridge. Confederate engineers were standing by to burn the bridge once the troops were across, but there was some confusion about whether they needed Mahone's permission to set the fire. By the time it was obtained, Humphreys' 2nd Corps of the Army of the Potomac was approaching.

"In the rapidity of the march," said Regis de Trobriand, "I passed a crossroad I should have taken, and soon, having some suspicion on the subject, I halted while my aides sought for information. A general, followed by some staff officers and an escort of cavalry, came up by the road near which I had halted. Those around me said, 'It is Sheridan!' which excited my curiosity. I had seen the general once or twice only, but without ever having had an opportunity to exchange a word with him....

"He halted near me, saluting me, calling me by my name as if we had been old acquaintances, and, as soon as I had made known to him my doubt as to which road I ought to take, in a few words he put before me very clearly my line of march.... At such an hour we would reach High Bridge.... My brigade... should take the road that I had passed, and which would bring me out at such a crossroad, where I would meet such and such troops. All this was told so clearly that I could not doubt the perfect accuracy of his information. The general had in his head not only the general character of the movements of the army, but also the details. I left him immediately, in order to repair the delay of some minutes, and at the hour announced we reached High Bridge.

"This is a magnificent viaduct of twenty-one arches, crossing the valley of the Appomattox from one hill to the other. It is designed both for the Lynchburg Railroad and for the inhabitants who wish to cross on foot or in carriage from one side to the other. When we presented ourselves at one end, the enemy... was setting fire to the other. We had to throw a pontoon bridge across the river. General Humphreys determined to... save the viaduct, the second arch of which was already on fire. A strong detachment, armed with axes borrowed from the different regiments, hurried to the fire under the direction of some engineer officers. The upper bridge, on which was the railroad, was saved by the sacrifice of a third span, and the lower bridge was open for our [wagon] trains after some slight repairs. The 2nd division crossed over first."[15]

"A considerable force of the enemy was drawn up in a strong position on the heights of the opposite bank to oppose our passage," Humphreys reported, "a position the strength of which the redoubts on the opposite side increased. Their skirmishers attempted to hold the bridge, but were quickly driven from it, and the troops crossed over, General Barlow's division leading. Artillery was rapidly put in position to cover our attack, but the enemy moved off without waiting for it. The redoubt forming the bridge-head on the south bank was blown up as we approached and eight pieces of artillery in it abandoned to us, as were ten pieces in the works on the north side.... A strong column of the enemy moved off along the railroad in the direction of Farmville, while another moved in a northwest direction. Believing that General Lee was moving toward Lynchburg by the old stage road, pushing through Appomattox Court-House, north of the Appomattox River, I moved, with Miles and de Trobriand, on the road running northwest and intersecting the stage road at a point about four miles from Farmville and four or five miles from High Bridge; but, lest I might be mistaken in the route Lee was following, I sent General Barlow's (Second) division to Farmville by the railroad, about three miles distant. Artillery could not accompany him."[16]

When Lee learned that the High Bridge had not been destroyed and that the Federals were across the river already he exploded with anger. He had retreated across the Appomattox in order to break contact with the enemy and to gain a days' march on Grant. Now, because somebody had bungled their assignment, all that had been lost. He soon regained his temper, however, and set to work to salvage what he could from the situation. He called for Brigadier General E.P. Alexander, chief of artillery of Longstreet's 1st Corps. He told him what had happened and showed him on the map a place three miles up the road where the Federals could strike his column. Alexander was to take his artillery to the vulnerable spot to cover the retreat, and he was also to be responsible for burning the bridges at Farmville. He was to be sure that they were not destroyed before the Confederate cavalry got across them, but to be sure that the Federals could not extinguish the flames and make use of the bridges, as they had done at the High Bridge.

Meanwhile, the rest of Longstreet's column crossed at Farmville. "We entered the town," Lieutenant Caldwell said, "and proceeded to draw rations of meat. But before the distribution was completed the skirmishing in our rear increased, and we were ordered back. Cavalry now thronged the streets, and the citizens began hurrying to and fro. We moved just outside of the southeastern limits, but were suddenly ordered to the right about, and carried through the town almost at the double-quick. Two columns of infantry marched abreast along the streets, and cavalry came pressing among us in confusion.

"When we reached the bridge, we discovered it to be on fire at the other end—the work of excited pioneers placed there for its destruction. At the same moment, the enemy, having driven in our rearguard of cavalry to the town, ran out artillery and opened on the road which led from the opposite end of the bridge. The cavalry... rushed forward into the closed bridge with us, and the whole mass of men and horses crowded and pushed through in horrible disorder. Fortunately... we... received no injuries from either flames or horses in the bridge; but, when we passed it, a great danger presented itself in the shells plumping into the middle of the road, and either ricocheting far up the hillsides or bursting and hurling fragments in every direction. Lane's brigade moved straight up the ridge, and lost men in doing so. We followed the hollow for some distance before taking the ascent, so that we escaped with an insignificant loss....

"We formed on attaining the crest of the ridge north of the Appomattox. Some Confederate guns now replied to the enemy, but with little effect. The last of our rearguard now quitted Farmville. The enemy's cavalry charged furiously after them down the long, steep hills approaching the southern bank of the Appomattox, firing and hurrahing loudly; but almost all the Confederates escaped across to us. Here the advance of that portion of the Federals ceased; but an attack upon the rear and left flank of the column which had crossed at the High Bridge now became audible."[17]

"We had not heard of the disasters on the other route and the hasty retreat," Longstreet wrote, "and were looking for a little quiet to prepare breakfast, when General Lee rode up and said that the bridges had been fired before his cavalry crossed, that part of that command was cut off and lost, and that the troops should hurry on to position at Cumberland Church. I reminded him that there were fords over which his cavalry could cross, and that they knew of or surely would find them. Everything except the food was ordered back to the wagons and dumped in. Meanwhile, the alarm had spread, and our teamsters, frightened by reports of cavalry trouble and approaching fire of artillery, joined in the panic, put whips to their teams as quick as the camp-kettles were tumbled over the tail-boards of the wagons, and rushed through the woods to find a road somewhere in front of them. The command was ordered under arms and put in quick march, but General Lee urged double-quick."[18]

"General Barlow found Farmville in possession of a strong force of the enemy," Humphreys reported, "who were burning the bridges there and covering a wagon train moving toward Lynchburg. The bridges were burned and the troops on the south side prevented from crossing, as the river was not fordable for infantry and scarcely for cavalry. General Barlow attacked, and the enemy soon abandoned the town, burned about 130 wagons, and joined the main body of Lee's army."[19]

About two-and-half miles north of Farmville, Lee and Longstreet's column came upon the Confederate cavalry, which had indeed found a ford over the Appomattox, as Longstreet had predicted, and crossed safely to the north side. While the cavalry escorted the wagons, Lee sent Mahone's Division to the position occupied by Alexander's artillery, four or five miles north of Farmville, covering the stage and plank road to Lynchburg and protecting the passage of the wagons and the rest of the army.

Humphrey's corps approached Mahone's position at about 1 p.m. "Upon approaching the vicinity of the Lynchburg stage road our skirmishers suddenly came in contact with those of the enemy and drove them back," Humphreys reported. "The artillery of the enemy opened upon us as we approached with some effect. Our troops and artillery were quickly formed for attack, the skirmishers were advanced, and developed the position of the enemy. It was too strong naturally and too well intrenched to admit of a front attack, the ground being open and sloping up gradually to a crest, about 1,000 yards distant, which was crowned with their intrenchments and batteries. An effort was made to take it in flank, but their flanks were found to extend beyond ours. Our skirmishers were kept pressed against those of the enemy, and an attack with my whole force threatened."[20]

Humphreys sent for Barlow to rejoin him from Farmville, and, not yet aware that the bridges had been destroyed, asked Meade to send reinforcements across there. But it would be dark before a pontoon bridge was finished at Farmville. Meanwhile, the 2nd Corps and Crook's cavalry had the tiger by the tail. Fortunately for them, Lee was unaware that he was facing only one corps of Union infantry and one division of cavalry and did not launch a major counterattack. He did, however, use most of his infantry to reinforce Mahone as the Federals probed his position. At about 4:30 p.m. Humphreys noticed the Confederates shortening their line, and, even though Barlow had not yet rejoined him, he heard firing from the direction of Farmville, indicating that perhaps reinforcements were coming, so he extended his right in an attempt to outflank the Rebels. Miles attacked with three regiments across difficult ground and was repulsed, losing the flag of the 5th New Hampshire. "From the extent and solidity of the enemy's line," de Trobriand said, "it became evident that we had before us all that remained of Lee's army.... We had to do with too strong a force. All the remainder of the army was some distance away, on the other side of the Appomattox. The cavalry and the 5th Corps were on the road via Prince Edward Court House. The 6th Corps and the 24th were still at Farmville, where the bridge was not rebuilt.... We were thus compelled to put off the renewal of the attack."[21]

The firing Humphreys had heard had been caused by a brief attack and repulse of Crook's cavalry. This division had found the same ford the Rebel troopers had used to cross to the north side of the river. Crook's leading brigade, J. Irving Gregg's, was charging toward some Confederate wagons when, topping a rise of ground, it was ambushed by a battalion of Rebel artillery that had wheeled into position upon the Federals' appoach. "With shell cut for close range, and canister, our twelve guns were let loose," the artillery commander wrote, "and such a scattering I never saw before." Some Rebel infantry came up and then Munford's cavalry charged Gregg's front while Rosser's division struck its flank, and his troopers fled for the protection of Davies' supporting brigade. Gregg and two of his staff officers were among the 300 or so Federals captured. "The general was quite chagrined," the Confederate artillery officer noted, "and said he had thought he would have had an easy time of it destroying our moving trains, and had not expected to run into the jaws of a whole park of artillery. It was fortunate that we were there just in the nick of time, for had Gregg obtained possession of the road, he stood a good chance of cutting off General Lee and staff and capturing them."[22] Lee's morale was lifted by this success and he told his son, Rooney, "Keep your command together and in good spirits, General—don't let them think of surrender—I will get you out of this."[23]

Barlow's division finally caught up with the rest of Humphreys' corps about sunset, but it was dark before it could be put into position. Crook's cavalry withdrew across the river under cover of the darkness. "When Crook sent word of [his] fight," Sheridan said, "it was clear that Lee had abandoned all effort to escape to the southwest by way of Danville. Lynchburg was undoubtedly his objective point now; so, resolving to throw my cavalry again across his path, and hold him till the infantry could overtake him, I directed everything on Appomattox depot, recalling Crook the night of the 7th to Prospect Station, while Merritt camped at Buffalo Creek, and Mackenzie made a reconnaissance along the Lynchburg railroad."[24]

"A little before noon on April 7, 1865," Horace Porter wrote, "General Grant, with his staff, rode into the little village of Farmville, on the south side of the Appomattox River.... He drew up in front of the village hotel, a comfortable brick building, dismounted, and established headquarters on its broad piazza." That afternoon, Porter was sent to check on the situation north of the river. "On my return... that evening," he said, "Wright's corps was ordered to cross the river and move rapidly to the support of our troops there. Notwithstanding their long march that day, the men sprang to their feet with a spirit that made every one marvel at their pluck, and came swinging through the main street of the village with a step that seemed as elastic as on the first day of their toilsome tramp. It was now dark, but they spied the general-in-chief watching them with evident pride from the piazza of the hotel as they marched past. Then was witnessed one of the most inspiring scenes of the campaign. Bonfires were lighted on the sides of the streets; the men seized straw and pine-knots, and improvised torches; cheers arose from their throats, already hoarse with shouts of victory; bands played, banners waved, and muskets were swung in the air. A regiment now broke forth with the song of 'John Brown's body,' and soon a whole division was shouting the swelling chorus of that popular air, which had risen to the dignity of a national anthem. The night march had become a grand review, with Grant as the reviewing officer.

"Ord and Gibbon had visited the general at the hotel, and he had spoken with them, as well as with Wright, about sending some communication to Lee that might pave the way to the stopping of further bloodshed. Dr. Smith, formerly of the regular army, a native of Virginia and a relative of General Ewell, now one of our prisoners, had told General Grant the night before that Ewell had said... that their cause was lost when they crossed the James River, and he considered that it was the duty of the authorities to negotiate for peace then, while they still had a right to claim concessions, adding that now they were not in condition to claim anything. He said that for every man killed after this somebody would be responsible, and it would be little better than murder. He could not tell what Lee would do, but he hoped that he would at once surrender his army. This statement, together with the news that had been received from Sheridan, saying that he had heard that General Lee's trains of provisions, which had come by rail, were at Appomattox, and that he expected to capture them before Lee could reach them, induced the general to write" a letter to Lee:[25] "General: The result of the last week must convince you of the hopelessness of further resistance on the part of the Army of Northern Virginia in this struggle. I feel that it is so, and regard it as my duty to shift from myself the responsibility of any further effusion of blood by asking of you the surrender of that portion of the C.S. Army known as the Army of Northern Virginia."[26]

Grant entrusted the delivery of this note to Brevet Major General Seth Williams, his inspector general, who rode to Humphreys' position north of the river and then, under a flag of truce, toward the Confederate lines. His party was fired upon, and one of his orderlies was hit, but he finally was able to present Grant's letter to a Rebel colonel at about 9 p.m. "After I had introduced myself," the colonel wrote, "he felt in his side pocket for documents, as I thought, but the document was a very nice-looking silver flask.... He remarked that he hoped I would not think it was unsoldierly if he offered me some very fine brandy. I will own up... that I wanted that drink awfully.... But I raised myself about an inch higher, if possible, bowed, and refused politely, trying to produce the ridiculous appearance of having feasted on champagne and pound-cake not ten minutes before.... He was a true gentleman, begged pardon, and placed the flask in his pocket again without touching the contents in my presence. If he had taken a drink, and my Confederate olfactories had obtained a whif of the odor of it, it is possible that I should have 'caved.' The truth is, I had not eaten two ounces in two days, and I had my coattail then full of corn, waiting to parch it as soon as an opportunity might present itself."[27]

The letter was soon carried to Lee, who had stopped for the evening at a cottage near Cumberland Church. "I was sitting at his side when the note was delivered," Longstreet wrote. "He read it and handed it to me without referring to its contents. After reading it I gave it back, saying, *'Not yet.'*"[28]

---

1. Davis, *To Appomattox,* 243.
2. *Official Records,* 46:III:593.
3. Basler, ed., *The Collected Works of Abraham Lincoln,* 8:392.
4. *Official Records,* 46:III:619.
5. Tidwell, Hall, and Gaddy, *Come Retribution,* 408.
6. Louis J. Weichmann, *A True History of the Assassination of Abraham Lincoln and of the Conspiracy of 1865,* 58.
7. Stern, *An End to Valor,* 229.
8. Urwin, *Custer Victorious,* 249-250.
9. Starr, *The Union Cavalry in the Civil War,* 2:474.
10. Ibid., 2:475.
11. Freeman, *R.E. Lee,* 4:96-97.
12. Davis, *To Appomattox,* 250.
13. Wheeler, *Witness to Appomattox,* 194.
14. Ibid., 191.
15. Ibid., 191-192.
16. *Official Records,* 46:I:683.
17. Wheeler, *Witness to Appomattox,* 194-195.
18. Longstreet, *From Manassas to Appomattox,* 616.
19. *Official Records,* 46:I:683.
20. Ibid., 46:I:683-684.
21. Wheeler, *Witness to Appomattox,* 198.
22. Ibid., 196.
23. Freeman, *R.E. Lee,* 4:101.
24. Sheridan, *Civil War Memoirs,* 343.
25. Porter, *Campaigning with Grant,* 458-459.
26. *Official Records,* 46:III:619.
27. Wheeler, *Witness to Appomattox,* 201-202.
28. Longstreet, *From Manassas to Appomattox,* 619.

CHAPTER THIRTY-FOUR

Like Hounds... Coming Upon Their Quarry

8 April 1865

By midnight, the tail of Lee's column was on the march again, this time with Gordon leading and Longstreet, with the cavalry's help, serving as rearguard. "We passed abandoned wagons in flames," Longstreet wrote, "and limbers and caissons of artillery burning sometimes in the middle of the road. One of my battery commanders reported his horses too weak to haul his guns. He was ordered to bury the guns and cover their burial-place with old leaves and brushwood.

Many weary soldiers were picked up, and many came to the column from the woodlands, some with, many without, arms,—all asking for food."[1] "Our march," one Confederate wrote, "is lighted by the fires of burning wagons.... The constant marching and fighting without sleep or food are rapidly thinning the ranks of this grand old army. Men who have stood by their flags since the beginning of the war now fall out of ranks... simply because it is beyond their power of physical endurance to go any farther."[2]

Lee's reply to Grant's note reached the Union commander at Farmville by midnight: "General: I have received your note of this date. Though not entertaining the opinion you express of the hopelessness of further resistance on the part of the Army of Northern Virginia, I reciprocate your desire to avoid useless effusion of blood, and therefore, before considering your proposition, ask the terms you will offer on condition of its surrender."[3] Grant answered the next morning: "Your note of last evening, in reply to mine of same date, asking the conditions on which I will accept the surrender of the Army of Northern Virginia, is just received. In reply I would say that, peace being my great desire, there is but one condition I would insist upon, viz, that the men and officers surrendered shall be disqualified for taking up arms again against the Government of the United States until properly exchanged. I will meet you, or will designate officers to meet any officers you may name for the same purpose, at any point agreeable to you, for the purpose of arranging definitely the terms upon which the surrender of the Army of Northern Virginia will be received."[4]

"There turned up at this time," Horace Porter wrote, "a rather hungry-looking gentleman in gray, wearing the uniform of a colonel, who proclaimed himself the proprietor of the hotel. He gave us to understand that his regiment had crumbled to pieces; that he was about the only portion of it that had succeeded in holding together, and he thought he might as well 'stop off' at home and look after his property. It is safe to say that his hotel had never before had so many guests in it, nor at such reduced rates. His story was significant as indicating the disintegrating process which was going on in the ranks of the enemy.

"General Grant had been marching most of the way with the columns which were pushing along south of Lee's line of retreat; but expecting that a reply to his last letter would soon be received, and wanting to keep within easy communication with Lee, he decided to march this day with the portion of the Army of the Potomac that was pressing Lee's rear-guard. After issuing some further instructions to Ord and Sheridan, he started from Farmville, crossed to the north side of the

Appomattox, conferred in person with Meade, and rode with his columns."[5]

Humphreys' 2nd Corps continued to lead the column that snapped at Lee's heels on 8 April, followed by Wright's 6th Corps. Regis de Trobriand said the Confederate army "was breaking up more and more, leaving its stragglers in the woods, in the fields, and along the roadside.... The wagons were left in the ruts; the cannon abandoned in the thickets or buried in holes, hurriedly dug, that the Negroes hasted to point out to us.... We pushed forward, 'on a hot trail' like hounds who are coming upon their quarry. As for men, we captured them everywhere.... Whenever they met our detachments, they surrendered with eagerness rather than repugnance. They had had enough of the war, and henceforth were less rebels than the Virginia sheep." The sheep, on the other hand, the hungry Federals found, had to be shot "when they refused to surrender."[6]

Brigadier General W.N. Pendleton, Lee's chief of artillery and a former clergyman, was riding up and down the Confederate column that day discussing the situation with various officers. The night before, he had been chosen by a group of prominent officers to inform Lee that they felt that further resistance was useless and that negotiations should be opened with Grant. That morning he came to Longstreet to get his feelings on the subject. That general asked Pendleton if he was aware that, according to the articles of war, they could be shot for suggesting surrender to their commander and added, "If General Lee doesn't know when to surrender until I tell him, he will never know."[7] Nevertheless, Pendleton went to see Lee, whom he found resting alone at the base of a large pine tree. When he heard what Pendleton had to say, Lee replied, "I trust that it has not come to that! We certainly have too many brave men to think of laying down our arms. They still fight with great spirit, whereas the enemy does not. And, besides, if I were to intimate to General Grant that I would listen to terms, he would at once regard it as such an evidence of weakness that he would demand unconditional surrender—and sooner than that I am resolved to die. Indeed, we must all determine to die at our posts."[8] At about 1 p.m. Fitzhugh Lee informed his uncle that only Union infantry was following the Confederate column. This could only mean that Sheridan's cavalry was again moving along parallel roads to the south to head them off.

"At break of day, April 8," Sheridan wrote, "Merritt and Mackenzie united with Crook at Prospect Station, and the cavalry all moved then toward Appomattox depot. Hardly had it started when one of the scouts—Sergeant White—informed me that there were four trains of cars at the depot loaded with supplies for Lee's army; these had been sent from Lynchburg, in compliance with the telegram of Lee's commissary-general, which message, it will be remembered, was captured and transmitted to Lynchburg by two of Young's scouts on the 4th. Sergeant White, who had been on the lookout for the trains ever since sending the dispatch, found them several miles west of Appomattox depot, feeling their way along, in ignorance of Lee's exact position. As he had the original despatch with him, and took pains to dwell upon the pitiable condition of Lee's army, he had little difficulty in persuading the men in charge of the trains to bring them east of Appomattox Station, but fearing that the true state of affairs would be learned before long, and the trains be returned to Lynchburg, he was painfully anxious to have them cut off by breaking the track west of the station.

"The intelligence as to the trains was immediately despatched to Crook, and I pushed on to join him with Merritt's command. Custer having the advance, moved rapidly, and on nearing the station detailed two regiments to make a detour southward to strike the railroad, some distance beyond and break the track. These regiments set off at a gallop, and in short order broke up the railroad enough to prevent the escape of the trains, Custer meanwhile taking possession of the station, but none too soon, for almost at the moment he did so the advance-guard of Lee's army appeared, bent on securing the trains. Without halting to look after the cars further, Custer attacked this advance-guard and had a spirited fight, in which he drove the Confederates away from the station, captured twenty-five pieces of artillery, a hospital train, and a large park of wagons, which, in the hope that they would reach Lynchburg next day, were being pushed ahead of Lee's main body.

"Devin coming up a little before dusk, was put in on the right of Custer, and one of Crook's brigades was sent to our left and the other two held in reserve. I then forced the enemy back on the Appomattox road to the vicinity of the Court House, and that the Confederates might have no rest, gave orders to continue the skirmishing throughout the night. Meanwhile, the captured trains had been taken charge of by locomotive engineers, soldiers of the command, who were delighted evidently to get back at their old calling. They amused themselves by running the trains to and fro, creating much confusion, and keeping up such an unearthly screeching with the whistles that I was on the point of ordering the cars burned. They finally wearied of their fun, however, and ran the trains off to the east toward General Ord's column."[9]

"For the second time during the pursuit," General Devin wrote,

"General Sheridan had overtaken the retreating army, and, placing the force at his disposal directly in the front, stood as a bar to further progress. During the night he felt assured that his position could be held, but knew that after daylight his force would be insufficient to withstand the desperate assault he must expect from an enemy whose last and only hope remained in forcing a passage to the west. Everything depended upon the arrival of additional troops in time to resist the attack that would surely be made the following morning, and courier after courier was sent back to urge greater speed upon the commanders of the infantry, still far in the rear."[10]

"For our part," Joshua Chamberlain wrote, "on the morning of the 8th the Fifth Corps moved out at six o'clock, pressing with all our powers to outflank Lee's march.... This driving pursuit, this relentless 'forward,' was altogether new experience for our much-enduring, much-abused old Army of the Potomac.... Now we realized the effects of Grant's permission to 'push things,'—some of these things being ourselves. But the manifest results on others helped our spirits to sustain the wear and tear of body. The constantly diminishing ratio of the strength of Lee's army compared with ours made it clear that we should soon overcome that resistance and relieve Virginia of the burden of being the head of the Confederacy, and from that must follow the downfall of the Confederacy itself.

"In this race, the 8th of April found the Fifth Corps at Prospect Station on the Southside Railroad, nearly abreast of Lee's hurrying column, ten miles north of us at New Store, across the Appomattox,—Meade with his two corps close upon his rear. We had been now a week in hot pursuit, fighting and marching by sharp turns, on a long road. At noon of this day we halted to give opportunity for General Ord of the Army of the James to have the advance of us upon the road.... The Fifth Corps was under Sheridan's immediate orders but General Ord being the senior officer present was by army regulations commander of our whole flanking column. He was very courteous to us all and we greeted him heartily. The preference of his corps to ours on the road was but natural considering his rank, and I am sure no one thought of taking offense at it. But we could not resist the thought that it was for some reasons other than military...

"These men of the Army of the James had been doing splendid work,—especially in getting up to us. But the hard march to overtake us had pretty nearly used them up. A marching column under such circumstances cannot help stretching. This was the case before us now. When we pulled out to follow their column we found it dragging and lagging before us, the rear moving at a rate ever slower than the head. This made it very hard on our men. We had managed hitherto to keep in pretty close touch with the cavalry, but this constant checking up was a far worse trial. It fretted our men almost to mutiny.... The head of our column seemed more like a mob than our patient well-disciplined soldiers. The headquarters wagons and pack mules which made the bulk of that real rabble ahead got unceremoniously helped along. Whoever blocked the way was served with a writ of ejection in quite primitive fashion. After dark the belated artillery obstructing the way was treated without much reverence. Even the much suffering horses were held responsible, and prodded and belabored by men who wanted to put two legs in the place of four.... We tried to drown the tumult, if we could not pacify the spirits of our exasperated men, by bringing the bands to the head of the column to administer the unction of the 'Girl I left behind me.' However, this seemed to make them want to 'get there' all the more.

"Commanding officers could not exercise 'discretion' about moving. We could not bring our men to a halt when there was the kind of obstacle before us, impassable as if it were a wall or a bog, and let them rest until the way could be cleared, as would have been reasonable. For some roving staff officer would happen along just then, and without inquiring into the case, would report to headquarters that such an officer was not moving according to orders, but was absolutely halting on the road. Then back would come an unjust reprimand, or perhaps the stultification of an 'arrest,'—of which there was quite too much already. So officers had to seem like incapables, and the men, poor fellows, had to keep on their feet, creeping at a snail's pace, or standing like tripods, on two legs and a musket-butt; weighed down with burdens of 'heavy-marching order,' which the mere momentum of marching, the changing play of muscles, would have helped to bear; all knowing full well that they would have to make up for this weary work by running themselves fever-wild for hours at the end."[11]

"The sun sunk from view," Private Theodore Gerrish of the 20th Maine wrote, "but there were no indications of halting. Our regiment chanced that day to be marching in the rear of our whole division, a position which... is the hardest in the whole line. Just at dark we entered a forest, through which was a single road, narrow and crooked. The road was filled with artillery, cavalry, infantry, baggage wagons, all pushing for the front.... The artillery, each gun and caisson drawn by six horses, crashed and thundered along the narrow road, and, by the right of superior strength, claimed the right of way. We marched as best we could, tired, hungry, and mad. If the artillery horses came too near, we would hammer them over their heads with our guns. This, of course, would enrage their riders, and, in the midst of all the uproar, there was a fierce warfare of words and oaths and threats. We were descending a hill when a gun came crashing down upon us. It was almost a case of life or death. One of ours boys brought the heavy stock of his rifle down upon the head of one of the leading horses, and the animal staggered and fell. The sergeant who had command of the gun rode up to a lieutenant commanding a company and ordered the man's arrest. The officer chanced to have a rifle in his hands that he was carrying for one of his men, and with a half-muttered exclamation he dealt the sergeant's horse such a blow that horse and rider went down together, and we rushed on our way."[12]

Grant stopped for the night at a large white farmhouse at Curdsville and, still being far ahead of his headquarters wagons, had dinner with Meade. "General Grant had been suffering all the afternoon from a severe headache," Horace Porter said, "the result of fatigue, anxiety, scant fare, and loss of sleep, and by night he grew much worse. He was induced to bathe his feet in hot water and mustard, and appy mustard-plasters to his wrists and the back of his neck; but these remedies afforded little relief.... About midnight we were aroused by Colonel Charles A. Whittier of Humphreys's staff, who brought the expected letter from Lee. Rawlins took it, and stepped across the hall to the door of General Grant's room. He hesitated to knock, not wishing to awake the commander if he were asleep, and opened the door softly and listened a moment...."

"Come in," Grant said; "I am awake. I am suffering too much to get any sleep."

Porter brought in a candle, and the general sat up to read what Lee had to say: "General: I received at a late hour your note of to-day. In mine of yesterday I did not intend to propose the surrender of the Army of Northern Virginia, but to ask the terms of your proposition. To be frank, I do not think the emergency has arisen to call for the surrender of this army; but as the restoration of peace should be the sole object of all, I desired to know whether your proposals would lead to that end. I cannot, therefore, meet you with a view to surrender the Army of Northern Virginia; but as far as your proposal may affect the C.S. forces under my command, and tend to the restoration of peace, I should be pleased to meet you at 10 a.m. to-morrow, on the old stage road to Richmond, between the picket-lines of the two armies."

Grant shook his head in disappointment. "It looks as if Lee still means to fight," he said.[13]

Rawlins, Grant's chief of staff and self-appointed conscience, was indignant at Lee's change of tack. "He did not propose to surrender!" Rawlins scoffed. "Diplomatic, but not true. He did propose, in his heart, to surrender... he now wants to entrap us into making a treaty of peace. You said nothing about that. You asked him to surrender. He replied by asking what terms you would give. You answered by stating the terms. Now he wants to arrange for peace—something beyond and above the surrender of his army; something to embrace the whole Confederacy, if possible. No, sir. No, sir. Why, it is a positive insult—an attempt, in an underhanded way, to change the whole terms of the correspondence."

"It amounts to the same thing, Rawlins," Grant replied. "He is only trying to be let down easy. I could meet him as requested, in the morning, and settle the whole business in an hour."

But Rawlins would not hear of it. He insisted that Lee had changed the subject to gain time and better terms. "He don't think 'the emergency has arisen'! That's cool, but another falsehood. That emergency has been staring him in the face for forty-eight hours. If he hasn't seen it yet, we will soon bring it to his comprehension! He has to surrender. He shall surrender. By the eternal, it shall be surrender or nothing else."

Grant tried to defend Lee's position, pointing out that the Confederate was "compelled to defer somewhat to the wishes of his government.... But it all means precisely the same thing. If I meet Lee he will surrender before I leave."

But Rawlins, a lawyer, was more concerned about deferfing to the wishes of their own government than Lee's. "You have no right to meet Lee," he pointed out, "or anyone else, to arrange terms of peace. That is the prerogative of the President, or the Senate. Your business is to capture or destroy Lee's army."

That point carried the argument, but Grant wanted to think about how to answer Lee's note. "I will reply in the morning," he said.[14]

Lee had also become separated from his headquarters wagon, so he camped in the open about two miles east of Appomattox Court House. To his campfire that night came his senior officers: Longstreet, Gordon and Fitz Lee. That afternoon Anderson, Johnson and Pickett had all been relieved of their almost-nonexistant commands and their few remaining troops attached to Gordon's and Longstreet's commands. Lee read to these corps commanders his correspondence with Grant and asked for their advice. The ensuing discussion ranged from the future of the Southern people to the tactics of the next battle. Eventually it was decided that in the morning the advance would be resumed. If the Federals across their path at Appomattox Station proved to be only cavalry then Fitz Lee would attack them, supported by Gordon, and drive them out of the way. Longstreet would again bring up the rear. Only two battalions of artillery would remain with the troops, and all excess guns and wagons would head for Lynchburg, only some twenty miles or so to the west. The movement would begin at 1 a.m.

After the meeting broke up, Gordon sent a staff officer back to ask what his objective should be for the next day's march. "Tell General Gordon," Lee replied facetiously, "I should be glad for him to halt just beyond the Tennessee line."[15] That objective was a mere 175 miles away.

Jefferson Davis was meeting with his cabinet in the dining room of the Sutherlin family at Danville that night when Lieutenant Wise arrived with his verbal message from Lee. When Davis asked the young messenger if Lee might escape, Wise replied, "I regret to say, no. From what I saw and heard I am satisfied that General Lee must surrender. It may be that he has done so today." The men about the table seemed shocked by this statement, and Wise noticed that they shifted uneasily when he added, "It is a question of only a few days at most."[16] The exhausted lieutenant was given something to eat and then quoted Lee's exact words from memory. Davis sat quietly for a moment, peering into the gloom outside, and then entrusted young Wise with instructions to Lee urging him to keep his army together.

Down on the gulf coast of Alabama the siege of Spanish Fort, defending the eastward approaches to Mobile, was approaching a climax. The Confederate commander, Brigadier General Randall L. Gibson, noticing unusually heavy activity in the Union lines that day, ordered his sharpshooters to keep up a steady fire on parties of Federals working to advance their trenches even closer to the Rebel lines. That afternoon he ordered some of his artillery to bombard those working parties, but it received in reply such concentrated fire from Union guns that it soon had to cease firing. One Confederate gun was disabled by this return fire and an ammunition chest exploded. Nevertheless, Gibson was so worried about Union activity that he ordered his batteries to open fire at sunset. Unknown to him, Canby had planned a bombardment of the fort for his own guns to begin at sundown. The Rebel guns opened fire first, at about 5:30 p.m., but they were almost immediately silenced by the Union artillery. The Confederates could not even find safety in their bombproofs, for shells from the Federals' huge 15-inch mortars could penetrate six feet of solid earth before exploding. Musketry from the Union infantry and the dense clouds of gunsmoke generated by the bombardment added to the confusion. One Rebel said, "It was though the mouth of the pit had yawned and the uproar of the damned was about us. And it was not taking away from this infernal picture to see men, as I did, hopping about, 'raving, distracted mad,' the blood bursting from eyes and ears and mouth, driven stark crazy by concussion or some other cause."[17]

With the bombardment still going on, the 8th Iowa, from A.J. Smith's 16th Corps, advanced through a swamp as darkness fell and drove a brigade of Texans from its position on the Confederate left flank. Part of the 14th Texas Dismounted Cavalry counterattacked but was beaten off. Several hundred Rebels were captured by the Iowans, as well as about 300 yards of trenches. Another counterattack was launched by Gibson's 100-man provost guard. It was also driven back, but it stopped the Union advance. The Federals dug in and waited to see what would happen next.

Gibson decided that he could not hold the fort much longer, so, rather than risk the loss of his men as well, he ordered them to evacuate. After spiking their guns, the Rebels and several slave laborers assembled on the beach behind the fort. There they removed their shoes and boots and quietly crossed a wooden treadway across a marsh to a point on the Apalachee River where, under the cover of darkness, steamboats picked them up and conveyed them to Blakely, farther north, which was also being bombarded by the Federals. After a short rest there, the steamers carried them on to Mobile.

Farther north, at the town of Cahaba, Wilson and Forrest met face to face under a flag of truce. Wilson had suggested the meeting to discuss arrangements for parolling and exchanging prisoners, but his primary purpose was to see if he could find out what had happened to Croxton's brigade.

"Well, General," Forrest told the young Federal, "you have beaten me badly, and for the first time I am compelled to make such an acknowledgement."

"Our victory was not without cost," Wilson replied. "You put up a stout fight."

"If I had captured your entire force twice over," Forrest answered, "it would not compensate us for the blow you've inficted upon us."

Forrest carried one arm in a sling due to the saber wound he had received, and he seemed depressed, one witness said. Wilson said his counterpart "did not impress me as I expected—neither as large, dignified nor striking as I expected—seemed embarrassed." A Union captain said that he thought he saw in the Rebel general "all the brutal intincts of the slave driver."[18]

After a sumptuous dinner the two generals, treating each other like old acquaintances, retired to the parlor to discuss the exchange of prisoners. As Wilson had hoped, Forrest innocently let slip that Croxton's missing Federals were still in good shape and operating somewhere north and west of the Black Warrior River.

The trip to Petersburg that President Lincoln had arranged for himself and his guests to take that day involved a ride on the Military Railroad. "Our car was an ordinary American car," the Marquis de Chambrun wrote, "and we took seats in its centre, grouping ourselves around Mr. Lincoln. In spite of the car's being devoted to Mr. Lincoln's special use, several officers also took their places in it without attracting any remark. Curiosity, it seems, also had induced the negro waiters of the *River Queen* to accompany us. The President, who was blinded by no prejudices against race or color, and who had not what can be termed false dignity, allowed them to sit quietly with us."

After leaving the train, they passed through the Union and Confederate lines of entrenchments around the city, mostly abandoned now, though guns still stood on their mountings in some places. The town seemed deserted except for the crowds of former slaves who gathered to cheer Lincoln when they learned of his presence. "Every now and then a white man could be seen hastening to take refuge in some house, in order to escape the sight of his conqueror." They visited military headquarters in a "pretty house, around which the vegetation of spring was already luxuriantly developing in this Southern climate." On the way back, Lincoln stopped the carriage to admire a very tall and beautiful tree, saying it reminded him of great oaks of the western forests where he had spent his youth and tried to make the others understand "the distinctive character of these different types." De Chambrun thought the president's dissertation revealed "a remarkable precision of mind."

Eventually the party came to the vast field hospitals, where each Federal corps had its own area. "This consisted of a large rectangle of ground divided by open corridors placed at equal distances from one another. Between these corridors stood a row of tents or of frame huts, each of which was capable of containing about twenty wounded. One side of these corridors was given up to officers, the other to privates. At the centre.... was located a pharmacy, a kitchen, and that which Americans consider as always essential—a post office.... A Bible and newspapers were to be found on nearly every bed....

"Our visit began with the hospitals of the Fifth Corps. Mr. Lincoln went from one bed to another, saying a friendly word to each wounded man, or at least giving him a handshake. .... Following Mr. Lincoln.... we reached a bed on which lay a dying man; he was a captain, aged twenty-four years, who had been noticed for his bravery. Two of his friends were near him; one held his hand, while the other read a passage from the Bible in a low voice. Mr. Lincoln walked over to him and took hold of his other hand, which rested on the bed. We formed a circle around him, and every one of us remained silent. Presently the dying man half-opened his eyes; a faint smile passed over his lips. It was then that his pulse ceased beating."[19]

The party returned to City Point by train and dined that evening aboard the *River Queen.* Mary Lincoln's jealousy of her husband caused another scene that night. "One of the guests was a young officer attached to the Sanitary Commission," Elizabeth Keckley said. "He was seated near Mrs. Lincoln, and, by way of a pleasantry, remarked: 'Mrs. Lincoln, you should have seen the President the other day on his triumphal entry into Richmond. He was the cynosure of all eyes. The ladies kissed their hands to him and greeted him with a waving of handkerchiefs. He is quite a hero when surrounded by pretty young ladies.' The young officer suddenly paused with a look of embarrassment. Mrs. Lincoln turned to him with flashing eyes, with the remark that his familiarity was offensive to her. Quite a scene followed, and I do not think that the Captain, who incurred Mrs. Lincoln's displeasure, will ever forget that memorable evening."[20] That night the *River Queen,* and the Lincolns, started down the river on the way back to Washington.

A force of 150 men from Mosby's battalion of Confederate rangers left Upperville, Virginia, near the Blue Ridge, that day, also headed for Washington. Among these Rebels was a recently promoted lieutenant who had served in Lieutenant Walter Bowie's abortive attempt to kidnap the governor of Maryland six months before and Sergeant Harney, the explosives expert who had been sent north from Richmond shortly before that city was evacuated.

And John Wilkes Booth returned to Washington that day from New York. George Atzerodt, the German-born ferryman of Confederate spies who belonged to Booth's circle of conspirators, made a statement after his arrest that connected these two events: "Booth said he had met a party in New York who would get the prest. certain. They were going to mine the end of the pres. House near the War Dept. They knew an entrance to accomplish it through. Spoke about getting friends of the prest. to get up an entertainment & they would mix in it, have a serenade & thus get at the prest. & party. These were understood to be projects. Booth said if he did not get him quick the New York crowd would. Booth knew the New York party apparently by a sign. He [Atzerodt] saw Booth give some kind of sign to two parties on the [Pennsylvania] Avenue who he said were from New York."[21]

---

1. Longstreet, *From Manassas to Appomattox,* 620.
2. Wheeler, *Witness to Appomattox,* 203-204.
3. *Official Records,* 46:III:619.
4. *Official Records,* 46:III:641.
5. Porter, *Campaigning with Grant,* 461.
6. Wheeler, *Witness to Appomattox,* 206.
7. Longstreet, *From Manassas to Appomattox,* 620.
8. Freeman, *R.E. Lee,* 4:109-110.
9. Sheridan, *Civil War Memoirs,* 343-344.
10. Wheeler, *Witness to Appomattox,* 208.
11. Chamberlain, *The Passing of the Armies,* 167-171.
12. Wheeler, *Witness to Appomattox,* 210.
13. Porter, *Campaigning with Grant,* 462-463.
14. Foote, *The Civil War,* 3:936-937.
15. Freeman, *R.E. Lee,* 4:116.
16. Davis, *The Long Surrender,* 57.
17. Bergeron, *Confederate Mobile,* 181.
18. Jones, *Yankee Blitzkrieg,* 99.
19. Stern, *An End to Valor,* 292-294.
20. Ibid., 294.
21. Tidwell, Hall and Gaddy, *Come Retribution,* 418.

CHAPTER THIRTY-FIVE

I Would Rather Die a Thousand Deaths

9 April 1865

The darkest hours before the dawn of April 9, 1865," Joshua Chamberlain wrote, "shrouded the Fifth Corps sunk in feverish sleep by the roadside six miles away from Appomattox Station on the Southside Railroad. Scarcely is the first broken dream begun when a cavalryman comes splashing down the road and vigorously dismounts, pulling from his jacket-front a crumpled note. The sentinel standing watch by his commander, worn in body but alert in every sense, touches your shoulder. 'Orders, sir, I think.' You rise on elbow, strike a match, and with smarting, streaming eyes read the brief, thrilling note, sent back by Sheridan to us infantry commanders. Like this, as I remember: 'I have cut across the enemy at Appomattox Station, and captured three of his trains. If you can possibly push your infantry up here to-night, we will have great results in the morning.' Ah, sleep no more. The startling bugle notes ring out.... Word is sent for the men to take a bite of such as they have for food: the promised rations will not be up till noon, and by that time we shall be perhaps too far away for such greeting.... You eat and drink at a swallow; mount, and away to get to the head of the column before you sound the 'Forward.' They are there—the men: shivering to their senses as if risen out of the earth, but something in them not of it. Now sounds the 'Forward,' for the last time in our long-drawn strife. And they move—these men—sleepless, supperless, breakfastless, sore-footed, stiff-jointed, sense-benumbed, but with flushed faces pressing for the front."[1]

If the Union infantry had little sleep that night, the cavalry had even less. "I did not sleep at all," Sheridan wrote, "nor did anybody else, the entire command being up all night long; indeed, there had been little rest in the cavalry for the past eight days. The necessity of getting Ord's column up was so obvious now that staff-officer after staff-officer was sent to him and to General Grant requesting that the infantry be pushed on, for if it could get to the front, all knew that the rebellion would be ended on the morrow. Merritt, Crook, Custer, and Devin were present at frequent intervals during the night, and everybody was overjoyed at the prospect that our weary work was about to end so happily. Before sun-up General Ord arrived, and informed me of the approach of his column, it having been marching the whole night. As he ranked me, of course I could give him no orders, so after a hasty consultation as to where his troops should be placed we separated, I riding to the front to overlook my line near Appomattox Court House, while he went back to urge along his weary troops."[2]

Sleep was also hard to come by at the farm house at Curdsville, where Grant and his staff were staying. At about 4 a.m. Horace Porter crossed the hall to see how the general was feeling. "I found his room empty," Porter wrote, "and upon going out of the front door, saw him pacing up and down in the yard, holding both hands to his head." Despite this obvious evidence, Porter asked the general how he felt, and Grant replied that he was still suffering from an excruciating headache and had had very little sleep.

"Well," Porter observed, "there is one consolation in all this, general: I never knew you to be ill that you did not receive some good news before the day passed. I have become a little superstitious regarding these coincidences, and I should not be surprised if some good fortune were to overtake you before night."

Grant smiled and said, "The best thing that could happen to me to-day would be to get rid of the pain I am suffering."

They were soon joined by some of the other staff officers, and together they walked over to Meade's nearby headquarters to get some coffee. Feeling a little better then, Grant wrote an answer to Lee: "General: Your note of yesterday is received. As I have no authority to treat on the subject of peace, the meeting proposed for 10 a.m. to-day could lead to no good. I will state, however, general, that I am equally anxious for peace with yourself, and the whole North entertains the same feeling. The terms upon which peace can be had are well understood. By the South laying down their arms they will hasten that most desirable event, save thousands of human lives, and hundreds of millions of property not yet destroyed. Sincerely hoping that all our difficulties may be settled without the loss of another life, I subscribe myself, etc. U.S. Grant, Lieutenant-general."[3]

"The night before General Lee had held a council with his principal generals," Sheridan wrote, "when it was arranged that in the morning General Gordon should undertake to break through my cavalry, and when I neared my troops this movement was beginning, a heavy line of infantry bearing down on us fron the direction of the village. In front of Crook and Mackenzie firing had already begun, so riding to a slight elevation where a good view of the Confederates could be had, I there came to the conclusion that it would be unwise to offer more resistance than that necessary to give Ord time to form, so I directed Merritt to fall back, and in retiring to shift Devin and Custer to the right so as to make room for Ord, now in the woods to my rear. Crook, who with his own and Mackenzie's divisions was on my extreme left covering some by-roads, was ordered to hold his ground as long as practicable without sacrificing his men, and, if forced to retire, to contest with obstinancy the enemy's advance."[4]

The infantry was now approaching to back up Sheridan's troopers. "By sunrise," Chamberlain remembered, "we have reached Appomattox Station, where Sheridan has left the captured trains. A staff officer is here to turn us square to the right, to the Appomattox River, cutting across Lee's retreat. Already we hear the sharp ring of the horse-artillery, answered ever and anon by heavier field guns; and drawing nearer, the crack of cavalry carbines; and unmistakably, too, the graver roll of musketry of opposing infantry. There is no mistake. Sheridan is square across the enemy's front, and with that glorious cavalry alone is holding at bay all that is left of the proudest army of the Confederacy. It has come at last,—the supreme hour. No thought of human wants or weakness now: all for the front; all for the flag, for the final stroke to make its meaning real—these men of the Potomac and the James, side by side, at the double in time and column, now one and now the other in the road or the fields beside. One striking feature I can never forget,—Birney's black men abreast with us, pressing forward to save the white man's country."[5]

"As already stated," Sheridan wrote, "I could not direct General Ord's course, he being my senior, but hastily galloping back to where he was, at the edge of the timber, I explained to him what was taking place at the front. Merritt's withdrawal inspired the Confederates, who forthwith began to press Crook, their line of battle advancing with confidence till it reached the crest whence I had reconnoitered them. From this ground they could see Ord's men emerging from the woods, and the hopelessness of a further attack being plain, the gray lines instinctively halted, and then began to retire toward a ridge immediately fronting Appomattox Court House, while Ord, joined on his right by the Fifth Corps, advanced on them over the ground that Merritt had abandoned."[6]

"Heavy firing was heard in our front, not over half a mile distant," remembered Private Theodore Gerrish of the 20th Maine in the 5th Corps. "Orders were given to double-quick. We dashed through a thick belt of woods, and met cavalrymen riding back, badly broken up and demoralized. They told us they had been fighting all night and holding the rebels in check until we should arrive, and this explained why we had marched all night. We passed through the woods and came out into a field some forty rods in width. For a fourth of a mile in our front there was flat and level ground, and then a ridge of land on whose crest there was a house, barn, and numerous outbuildings. The field on either side, up to this hill, was bordered with a forest, while beyond there was—we knew not what.

"In that field we halted. A group of Union generals were sitting upon their horses near us—Sheridan, Griffin, Chamberlain, and others. Sheridan was evidently much excited, and was talking rapidly, and adding emphasis to his words by bringing his clenched right hand down on the open palm of his left. It was evident to all that some enterprise of importance was on foot."[7]

Joshua Chamberlain did not remember his encounter with Sheridan in quite the same way: "Pushing through the woods at cavalry speed, we come out right upon Sheridan's battle flag gleaming amidst the smoke of his batteries in the edge of the open field. Weird-looking flag it is: fork-tailed, red and white, the two bands that composed it each charged with a star of the contrasting color; two eyes sternly glaring through the cannon-cloud. Beneath it, that storm-center spirit, that form of condensed energies, mounted on the grim charger, Rienzi, that turned the battle of the Shenandoah,—both, rider and steed, of an unearthly shade of darkness, terrible to look upon, as if masking some unknown powers.

"Right before us, our cavalry, Devin's division, gallantly stemming the surges of the old Stonewall brigade, desperate to beat its way through. I ride straight to Sheridan. A dark smile and impetuous gesture are my only orders. Forward into double lines of battle, past Sheridan, his guns, his cavalry, and on for the quivering crest! For a moment it is a glorious sight: every arm of the service in full play,—cavalry, artillery, infantry; then a sudden shifting scene as the cavalry, disengaged by successive squadrons, rally under their bugle-calls with beautiful precision and promptitude, and sweep like a storm-cloud beyond our right to close in on the enemy's left and complete the fateful envelopement."[8] "I now directed my steps toward Merritt," Sheridan said, "who, having mounted his troopers, had moved them off to the right, and by the time I reached his headquarters flag he was ready for work, so a move on the enemy's left was ordered, and every guidon was bent to the front."[9]

"Ord's troops," Chamberlain wrote, "are now square across the Lynchburg Pike. Ayres and Bartlett have joined them on their right, and all are in for it sharp. In this new front we take up the battle. Gregory follows in on my left. It is a formidable front we make.... In truth, the Stonewall men hardly show their well-proved mettle. They seem astonished to see before them these familiar flags of their old antagonists, not having thought it possible that we could match our cavalry and march around and across their pressing columns.

"Their last hope is gone,—to break through our cavalry before our infantry can get up. Neither to Danville nor to Lynchburg can they cut their way; and close upon their rear, five miles away, are pressing the Second and Sixth Corps of the Army of the Potomac. It is the end! They are now giving way, but keep good front, by force of old habit. Halfway up the slope they make a stand.... behind a stone wall. I try a little artillery on them, which directs their thoughts towards the crest behind them, and stiffen my lines for a rush, anxious for that crest myself."

Griffin, a former artilleryman, rode up and accused Chamberlain of mistaking a peach tree for a Rebel flag with his bombardment. It was Griffin's way of calming his subordinate down. Chamberlain apologized. "I was a little nearsighted," he said, "and hadn't been experienced in long-range fighting." In a few minutes Griffin was back, this time in a different mood. He wanted Chamberlain to go back and take over

Crawford's division. "He is acting in the same old fashion that got Warren into trouble at Five Forks. He should have been up here long ago. We need him desperately. He deserves to be relieved of his command." Chamberlain talked him out of it, and Crawford caught up before long.

Before he did, Ord rode up and told Chamberlain not to advance to the crest in his front. "The enemy have massed their guns to give it a raking fire the moment you set foot there." Chamberlain did not like this order either. He was given no chance to protest, however, "I thought I saw a qualifying look as he turned away. But left alone, youth struggled with prudence. My troops were in a bad position down here. I did not like to be 'the under dog.' It was much better to be on top and at least know what there was beyond. So I thought of Grant and his permission to 'push things' when we got them going; and of Sheridan and his last words as he rode away with his cavalry, smiting his hands together—'Now smash 'em, I tell you; smash 'em!' So we took this for orders, and on the crest we stood. One booming cannon-shot passed close along our front, and in the next moment all was still."

What he saw beyond the crest was worth the risk he took. "For there burst upon our vision a mighty scene, fit cadence of the story of tumultuous years. Encompassed by the cordon of steel that crowned the heights about the Court House, on the slopes of the valley formed by the sources of the Appomattox, lay the remnants of that far-famed counterpart and companion of our own in momentous history,—the Army of Northern Virginia—Lee's army!.... It was hilly, broken ground, in effect a vast amphitheater, stretching a mile perhaps from crest to crest. On the several confronting slopes before us dusky masses of infantry suddenly resting in place; blocks of artillery, standing fast in column or mechanically swung into park; clouds of cavalry small and great, slowly moving, in simple restlessness;—all without apparent attempt at offense or defense, or even military order.

"In the hollow is the Appomattox,—which we had made the dead-line for our baffled foe, for its whole length, a hundred miles; here but a rivulet that might almost be stepped over dry-shod, and at the road crossing not thought worth while to bridge. Around its edges, now trodden to mire, swarms an indescribable crowd; worn-out soldier struggling to the front; demoralized citizen and denizen, white, black, and all shades between,—following Lee' army, or flying before these suddenly confronted terrible Yankees pictured to them as demon-shaped and bent; animals, too, of all forms and grades; vehicles of every description and nondescription,.... heading and moving in every direction, a swarming mass of chaotic confusion.

"All this within sight of every eye on our bristling crest. Had one the heart to strike at beings so helpless, the Appomattox would quickly become a surpassing Red Sea horror. But the very spectacle brings every foot to an instinctive halt. We seem the possession of a dream. We are lost in a vision of human tragedy. But our light-twelve Napoleon guns come rattling up behind us to go into battery; we catch the glitter of the cavalry blades and brasses beneath the oak groves away to our right, and the ominous closing in on the fated foe."[10]

"As the cavalry marched along parallel with the Confederate line," Sheridan wrote, "and in toward its left, a heavy fire of artillery opened on us, but this could not check us at such a time, and we soon reached some high ground about half a mile from the Court House, and from here I could see in the low valley beyond the village the bivouac undoubtedly of Lee's army. The troops did not seem to be disposed in battle order, but on the other side of the bivouac was a line of battle—a heavy rear-guard—confronting, presumably, General Meade."[11]

The Federal forces were not only closing in on the Rebels from several directions but Sheridan's cavalry was threatening to get in between Gordon's troops facing Ord and Longstreet's facing Meade. "While the Confederate infantry and cavalry were thus fighting at the front," General Gordon wrote, "and the artillery was checking the development of Federal forces around my right and rear, Longstreet was [threatened] by other portions of the Federal army. He.... could not join, as contemplated, in the effort to break the cordon of men and metal around us. At this critical juncture a column of Union cavalry appeared on the hills to my left, headed for the broad space between Longstreet's command and mine. In a few minutes that body of Federal cavalry would not only have seized the trains but cut off all communication between the two wings of Lee's army and rendered its capture inevitable. I therefore detached a brigade to double-quick and intercept this Federal force."[12]

Colonel Venable of Lee's staff had ridden forward to see how Gordon's advance was faring. "Tell General Lee," Gordon said, "I have fought my corps to a frazzle, and I fear I can do nothing unless I am heavily supported by Longstreet's corps." Lee was not far away. He had put on his best uniform and sword that morning. "I have probably to be General Grant's prisoner," he told General Pendleton, "and thought I must make my best appearance." When he heard Venable's report of Gordon's words, Lee said, as if oblivious of those around him, "Then there is nothing left me to do but to go and see General Grant, and I would rather die a thousand deaths." Death tempted him. "How easily I could be rid of this," he said, "and be at rest! I have only to ride along the line and all will be over! But it is our duty to live," he said with a deep sigh. "What will become of the women and children of the South if we are not here to protect them?"[13]

Lee sent for Longstreet, his "old warhorse," as he called him, who was the next ranking officer in his army. "He was dressed in a suit of new uniform," Longstreet noticed, "sword and sash, a handsomely embroidered belt, boots, and a pair of gold spurs. At first approach his compact figure appeared as a man in the flush vigor of forty summers, but as I drew near, the handsome apparel and brave bearing failed to conceal his profound depression. He stood near the embers of some burned rails, received me with graceful salutation, and spoke at once of affairs in front and the loss of his subsistence stores. He remarked that the advanced columns stood against a very formidable force, which he could not break through, while General Meade was at my rear ready to call for all the work that the rear-guard could do, and, closing with the expression that it was not possible for him to get along, requested my view. I asked if the bloody sacrifice of his army could in any way help the cause in other quarters. He thought not. Then, I said, your situation speaks for itself."[14]

Lee then consulted Mahone, who was stirring up the embers of the fire and took pains to explain to his commander that he was shivering from cold, not from fear. After asking several questions, Mahone said he thought it was time for Lee to see General Grant. Alexander, Longstreet's chief of artillery, appeared, and Lee consulted him as well.

"Well, we have come to the junction," Lee said, "and they seem to be here ahead of us. What have we got to do today?"

Alexander replied that the 1st Corps was still in good condition and ready to do its part if Lee wanted to try to cut his way out.

"I have only two divisions," Lee replied, "Field's and Mahone's, sufficiently organized to be relied upon. All the rest have been broken and routed and can do little good. Those divisions are now scarcely 4000 apiece, and that is far too little to meet the force now in our front."

Alexander then proposed that the men scatter through the woods with orders to report to the governors of their respective states with their weapons.

"What would you hope to accomplish with that?" Lee asked.

Alexander said it might prevent the surrender of the other Confederate armies, which otherwise would surely follow the surrender of his own; it would prevent the humiliation of an unconditional surrender, for which Grant was famous for demanding of other forces he had cornered; and it might allow the states to make an honorable peace.

"If I should take your advice," Lee asked, "how many men do you suppose would get away?"

"Two-thirds of us," Alexander replied. "We would be like rabbits and partridges in the bushes and they could not scatter to follow us."

"I have not over 15,000 muskets left," Lee said. "Two-thirds of them divided among the states, even if all could be collected, would be too small a force to accomplish anything. All could not be collected. Their homes have been overrun, and many would go to look after their families. Then, General, you and I as Christian men have no right to consider only how this would affect us. We must consider its effect on the country as a whole. Already it is demoralized by the four years of war. If I took your advice, the men would be without rations and under no control of officers. They would be compelled to rob and steal in order to live. They would become mere bands of marauders, and the enemy's cavalry would pursue them and overrun many sections they may never have occasion to visit. We would bring on a state of affairs it would take the country years to recover from. And, as for myself, you young fellows might go to bushwhacking, but the only dignified course for me would be to go to General Grant and surrender myself and take the consequences of my acts."

After a pause he added, "But I can tell you one thing for your comfort. Grant will not demand an unconditional surrender. He will give us as good terms as this army has the right to demand, and I am going to meet him in the rear at 10 a.m. and surrender the army on the condition of not fight again until exchanged."

"I had not a single word to say in reply," Alexander wrote. "He had answered my suggestion from a plane so far above it, that I was ashamed of having made it."[15]

At about 8:30 a.m. Lee mounted his famous horse Traveller and, accompanied by Colonels Taylor and Marshall of his staff and Sergeant Tucker, chief courier of the 3rd Corps, rode through Longstreet's lines toward the pursuing Federals of Meade's column for the 10 a.m. meeting that he had proposed to Grant in his message of the night before. Tucker carried a white flag. They had gone about a half-mile and had just rounded a bend in the road when they saw a line of Union skirmishers approaching. Colonel Marshall rode ahead, expecting to see Grant and his staff at any minute. Instead, Lieutenant Colonel Charles Whittier of Humphreys' staff soon appeared bearing Grant's reply written that morning saying that he could not meet Lee for the purpose of negotiating a peace. Lee was dictating a reply to Marshall when a

Confederate staff officer came galloping around the bend behind them so hard that he was a hundred yards beyond the general before he could turn his lathered horse around.

"Oh, why did you do it?" Lee cried. "You have killed your beautiful horse."

The officer replied that Longstreet had sent him and told him to kill his mount if necessary. Fitz Lee had just reported that he had found a road by which the army might escape. But Lee had already decided on his course. He finished dictating his reply to Grant and signed it as the sound of firing grew behind him. It said: "I received your note of this morning on the picket line whither I had come to meet you and ascertain definitely what terms were embraced in your proposal of yesterday with reference to the surrender of this army. I now request an interview in accordance with the offer contained in your letter of yesterday for that purpose."[16]

Colonel Marshall delivered the letter to Whittier, and, seeing that the Union skirmishers were again advancing, he explained the nature of the message to the Federal officer and said he hoped hostilities could be suspended until it could reach General Grant. Whittier promised to bring an answer from his commander and hurried off with Lee's letter.

Meanwhile, another message came to Lee from his nephew, Fitz Lee, saying that he had been mistaken. There was no escape route after all. Lee sent this messenger back to notify Gordon and Longstreet of what was going on and to tell them to ask the Federals on Gordon's front for a truce pending his meeting with Grant.

"Hey! What!" Meade exclaimed when he was informed of the Confederate request for a suspension of hostilities. "I have no sort of authority to grant such suspension. General Lee has already refused the terms of General Grant. Advance your skirmishers, Humphreys, and bring up your troops! We will pitch into them at once!"[17] Colonel Whittier returned and informed Marshall that an attack had been ordered and that his commander had no discretion but to obey. Lee's letter, he explained, could not reach Grant in time to forestall the attack. Marshall asked Whittier to have his commander read Lee's letter to Grant and maybe then he would feel justified in suspending the attack and avoid any useless killing. Whittier went away, and the Confederates waited, but soon the Union skirmishers began to advance again, and a Federal messenger came to tell them to withdraw as the attack was about to begin. Lee quickly dictated another note to Grant: "I ask a suspension of hostilities pending the adjustment of the terms of surrender of this army, in the interview requested in my former communication today."[18]

This message was given to the Union courier, but the Federals continued to advance.

The head of their column was visible about 100 yards away when another warning arrived that the attack could not be stopped. Reluctantly, Lee and his companions turned and rode back within Longstreet's lines. But just as the Union attack was about to be launched, sometime after 11 a.m., Whittier returned with a note from Meade agreeing to an informal truce on his front for one hour and suggesting that Lee might be able to communicate with Grant more quickly in the other direction. In response, Lee dictated another note to Colonel Marshall: "General, I sent a communication to you today from the picket line whither I had gone in hopes of meeting you in pursuance of the request contained in my letter of yesterday. Maj. Gen. Meade informs me that it would probably expedite matters to send a duplicate through some other part of your lines. I therefore request an interview at such time and place as you may designate, to discuss the terms of the surrender of this army in accord with your offer to have such an interview contained in your letter of yesterday."[19] This was sent to the Federals in front of Gordon's corps.

"My troops," Gordon wrote, "were still fighting, furiously fighting, in nearly every direction, when the final note from General Lee reached me.... I called Colonel Green Peyton of my staff, and directed him to take a flag of truce... to General Ord, who commanded, as I supposed, the Union infantry in my front. I ordered him to say to the Union commander this, and nothing more: 'General Gordon has received a notice from General Lee of a flag of truce, stopping the battle.' Colonel Peyton soon informed me that we had no flag of truce."

"Well," Gordon said, "take your handkerchief and tie that on a stick, and go."

Peyton felt in his pockets and said, "General, I have no handkerchief."

"Then tear your shirt, sir," Gordon replied, "and tie that to a stick."

Peyton looked at his own shirt and then at Gordon's and said, "General, I have on a flannel shirt, and I see you have. I don't believe there is a white shirt in the army."

"Get something, sir," Gordon ordered. "Get something and go!"[20]

---

1. Chamberlain, *The Passing of the Armies,* 172-173.
2. Sheridan, *Civil War Memoirs,* 344-345.
3. Porter, *Campaigning with Grant,* 464.
4. Sheridan, *Civil War Memoirs,* 345.
5. Chamberlain, *The Passing of the Armies,* 173.

6. Sheridan, *Civil War Memoirs,* 345-346.
7. Wheeler, *Witness to Appomattox,* 216.
8. Chamberlain, *The Passing of the Armies,* 175.
9. Sheridan, *Civil War Memoirs,* 346.
10. Chamberlain, *The Passing of the Armies,* 175-178.
11. Sheridan, *Civil War Memoirs,* 346.
12. Wheeler, *Witness to Appomattox,* 216.
13. Freeman, *R.E. Lee,* 4:118-121.
14. Longstreet, *From Mannassas to Appomattox,* 624-625.
15. Freeman, *R.E. Lee,* 4:122-123.
16. Ibid., 4:126-127.
17. Catton, *Grant Takes Command,* 463.
18. Freeman, *R.E. Lee,* 4:128.
19. Ibid., 4:129-130.
20. Wheeler, *Witness to Appomattox,* 218.

CHAPTER THIRTY-SIX

This Will Have the Best Possible Effect

9 April 1865

The 20th Maine was preparing to attack a formidable-looking Confederate position when, according to Theodore Gerrish, "We saw a white object flutter in an orchard up in the rear of their line of battle. 'A signal for their infantry to open fire,' growled the boys as they saw it. Then we expected to see their line of battle mantled in fire and smoke as they poured volleys of death upon us. But a moment passed, and not a gun had been fired. We looked again. We saw the object we had supposed to be a signal flag, but it had changed its position. It was advancing.... down to their line of battle. It continued to advance, and passed their battle line. Three men accompanied it. What could it mean? It was a white flag! We could not believe our eyes. At a brisk gallop the officers rode to within twenty rods of our line, then turned down to our right where Sheridan had disappeared."[1]

Joshua Chamberlain was still worried about his right and hoping that the cavalry would protect his flank. He could see the squadrons forming up over there. "Watching intently," he wrote, "my eye was caught by the figure of a horseman riding out between those lines, soon joined by another, and taking a direction across the cavalry front towards our position. They were nearly a mile away, and I curiously watched them till lost from sight in the nearer broken ground and copses between.

"Suddenly rose to sight another form, close in our own front,—a soldierly young figure, a Confederate staff officer undoubtedly. Now I see the white flag earnestly borne, and its possible purport sweeps before my inner vision like a wraith of morning mist. He comes steadily on, the mysterious form in gray, my mood so whimsically sensitive that I could even smile at the material of the flag,—wondering where in either army was found a towel, and one so white.... The messenger draws near, dismounts; with graceful salutation and hardly suppressed emotion delivers his message: 'Sir, I am from General Gordon. General Lee desires a cessation of hostilities until he can hear from General Grant as to the proposed surrender.'"[2]

Sheridan had already ordered Merritt's two divisions to charge down the slope into the Confederate camps along the Appomattox. "Custer was soon ready," Sheridan said, "but Devin's division being in rear its formation took longer, since he had to shift further to the right; Devin's preparations were, therefore, but partially completed when an aide-de-camp galloped up to me with the word from Custer, 'Lee has surrendered; do not charge; the white flag is up.' The enemy perceiving that Custer was forming for attack, had sent the flag out to his front and stopped the charge just in time."[3]

The Confederate officer who came to Custer was a captain on Longstreet's staff, but he too was carrying a white towel attached to a pole. "Go with this officer," Custer told his chief of staff, "and say for me to General Lee that I cannot stop this charge unless he announces an unconditional surrender, as I am not in sole command on this field." Then he sent an aide to Sheridan with the note quoted above. A strange silence fell upon the two armies, but it was soon shattered by a wild celebration among Custer's men when they learned from a staff officer that "Lee has surrendered!"[4]

The infantry too was soon celebrating. Chamberlain had sent the Confederate request for a truce up the chain of command and back down it the response returned. "Shortly comes the order, in due form, to cease firing and to halt," he wrote. "There was not much firing to cease from; but 'halt,' then and there? It is beyond human power to stop the men." First the soldiers pressed on from eagerness to finish the fight and the war, then, as the implications of what was going sank in, from curiosity. "The more the captains cry, 'Halt! the rebels want to surrender,' the more the men want to be there and see it," Chamberlain said. The soldiers were beyond control. "To the top of fences, and haystacks, and chimneys they clamber, to toss their old caps higher in the air, and leave the earth as far below them as they can....

"'Your legs have done it, my men,' shouts the gallant, gray-haired Ord, galloping up cap in hand, generously forgiving our disobedience of orders, and rash 'exposure' on the dubious crest. True enough, their legs had done it.... But other things too had 'done it'; the blood was still fresh upon the Quaker Road, the White Oak Ridge, Five Forks, Farmville, High Bridge, and Sailor's Creek.... A truce is agreed upon until one o'clock—it is now ten.... Six or eight officers from each side meet between the lines, near the Court House, waiting Lee's answer to Grant's summons to surrender. There is lively chat here on this unaccustomed opportunity for exchange of notes and queries. The first greetings are not all so dramatic as might be thought, for so grave an occasion."

"Well Billy, old boy, how goes it?" a Federal officer asked an old West Point classmate.

"Bad, bad, Charlie, bad I tell you; but have you got any whiskey?"[5]

"I at once sent word of the truce to General Ord," Sheridan wrote, "and hearing nothing more from Custer himself, I supposed he had gone down to the Court House to join a mounted group of Confederates that I could see near there, so I, too, went toward them, galloping down a narrow ridge, staff and orderlies following."[6] This cavalcade of mounted Federals, which Gordon called "almost as large as one of Fitz Lee's regiments," soon drew fire from Rebel infantry, and had to detour through a ravine before emerging near the court house.[7] Here some Rebels again leveled their rifles at the Union general. "Their officers kept their men from firing, however," Sheridan said, "but meanwhile a single-handed contest had begun behind me, for on looking back I heard a Confederate soldier demanding my battle-flag from the color-bearer, thinking, no doubt, that we were coming in as prisoners. The sergeant had drawn his sabre and was about to cut the man down, but at a word from me he desisted and carried the flag back to my staff, his assailant quickly realizing that the boot was on the other leg."[8]

As Gordon remembered it, Sheridan came over under a white flag. "Sheridan was mounted on an enormous horse," he said, "a very handsome animal. He rode in front of the escort, and an orderly carrying the flag rode beside him. Around me at the time were my faithful sharpshooters, and as General Sheridan and his escort came within easy range of the rifles, a half-witted fellow raised his gun as if to fire. I ordered him to lower his gun, and explained that he must not fire on a flag of truce. He did not obey my order cheerfully, but held his rifle in position to be quickly thrown to his shoulder. In fact, he was again in the act of raising his gun to fire at Sheridan when I caught the gun and said to him, with emphasis, that he must not shoot men under flag of truce. He at once protested, 'Well, general, let him stay on his own side.'"[9]

No sooner had Sheridan and Gordon come together than they heard firing break out in front of Merritt's cavalry. "General," Sheridan told the Confederate, "your men fired on me as I was coming over here, and undoubtedly they are treating Merritt and Custer the same way. We might as well let them fight it out."

"There must be some mistake," Gordon replied.

"Why not send a staff-officer," Sheridan asked, "and have your people cease firing; they are violating the flag."

"I have no staff-officer to send," Gordon confessed.

So Sheridan lent the Confederate one of his own officers, who was sent to carry Gordon's order to Gary's cavalry brigade. "I do not care for white flags," Gary told the Federal lieutenant; South Carolinians never surrender." However, by then Merritt's patience had been exhausted, and the advance of the Michigan Brigade of Devin's division soon changed Gary's mind.

When quiet was restored, Gordon told Sheridan, "General Lee asks for a suspension of hostilities pending the negotiations which he is having with General Grant."

"I have been constantly informed of the progress of the negotiations," Sheridan replied, "and think it singular that while such discussions are going on, General Lee should have continued his march and attempted to break through my lines this morning. I will entertain no terms except that General Lee shall surrender to General Grant on this arrival here. If these terms are not accepted we will renew hostilities."

According to Sheridan, Gordon said, "General Lee's army is exhausted. There is no doubt of his surrender to General Grant."[10] According to Gordon, "Upon my exhibiting to [Sheridan] the note from

Lee, he at once proposed that the firing cease and that our respective lines be withdrawn to certain positions while we waited further intelligence from the commanders of the two armies."[11]

"It was then that General Ord joined us," Sheridan wrote, "and after shaking hands all around, I related the situation to him, and Gordon went away agreeing to meet us again in half an hour. When the time was up he came back accompanied by General Longstreet, who brought with him a despatch, the duplicate of one that had been sent General Grant through General Meade's lines back on the road over which Lee had been retreating.

"General Longstreet renewed the assurances that already had been given by Gordon, and I sent Colonel Newhall with the despatch to find General Grant and bring him to the front. When Newhall started, everything on our side of the Appomattox Court House was quiet, for inevitable surrender was at hand, but Longstreet feared that Meade, in ignorance of the new conditions on my front might attack the Confederate rear-guard. To prevent this I offered to send Colonel J. W. Forsyth through the enemy's lines to let Meade know of my agreement, for he too was suspicious that by a renewed correspondence Lee was endeavoring to gain time for escape. My offer being accepted, Forsyth set out accompanied by Colonel Fairfax, of Longstreet's staff, and had no difficulty in accomplishing his mission."[12]

Because of the headache that was still tormenting him, Grant's staff tried to get him to ride in an ambulance wagon that day, like Meade. But he insisted on mounting his big bay, Cincinnati, and rode west from Curdsville to New Store. There, having heard the distant sound of firing on Ord's front, he turned to the south, crossed the Appomattox, and turned onto the road running from Farmville to Appomattox Court House. Nine miles east of that soon-to-be-famous village, a lieutenant from Meade's staff caught up with him bearing the first note Lee had written that morning. "When the officer reached me," Grant said, "I was still suffering with the sick headache; but the instant I saw the contents of the note I was cured."[13]

Without expression, Grant handed the note to Rawlins and asked him to read it out loud for the benefit of the staff. Although it meant victory and peace and going home, there was little celebrating. Most throats were too constricted to speak, let alone cheer.

"How will that do, Rawlins?" Grant asked with a smile.

"I think *that* will do," Rawlins said.[14]

Then Grant dismounted, sat down on the grass next to the road, and wrote a reply: "Your note of this date is but this moment (11.50 a.m.)

received. In consequence of my having passed from the Richmond and Lynchburg road to the Farmville and Lynchburg road I am at this writing about four miles west of Walker's Church, and will push forward to the front for the purpose of meeting you. Notice sent to me on this road where you wish the interview to take place will meet me."[15] He gave this note to Lieutenant Colonel Orville Babcock of his staff, who, after changing to a fresh horse, hurried on ahead with one other officer. Grant and the rest of the staff followed at a trot.

Three or four miles farther down the road they were met by Sheridan's Colonel Newhall carrying Lee's second note. After stopping to read it, they pressed on. Newhall led them on a short cut, but it took them almost into the Rebel lines. "It looked for a moment," Horace Porter wrote, "as if a very awkward condition of things might possibly arise, and Grant become a prisoner in Lee's lines instead of Lee in his. Such a circumstance would have given rise to an important cross-entry in the system of campaign bookkeeping."[16] So, despite Grant's lifelong aversion to retracing his steps, there was no choice but to go back to the main road.

When Babcock reached Sheridan's front he found the truce still in effect and the fiesty cavalry commander restlessly pacing up and down. "Damn them," Sheridan said, "I wish they had held out an hour longer and I would have whipped hell out of them." Babcock went on through the lines to deliver Grant's message to Lee, but soon one of Grant's military secretaries, Adam Badeau, arrived after having also ridden ahead of his commander. "What do you think?" Sheridan asked him. "What do you know? Is it a trick? Is he negotiating with Grant?" Brandishing a fist he added, "I've got 'em—I've got 'em like that!"[17]

Reclining on some fence rails laid under an apple tree while waiting for Grant's answer to his messages of the morning, Lee told Longstreet that he was worried that his refusal to meet the Federal commander's first proposition might cause him to now demand harsher terms. "I assured him," said Longstreet, who was related to Grant's wife, "that I knew General Grant well enough to say that the terms would be such as he would demand under similar circumstances, but he yet had doubts. The conversation continued in broken sentences until the bearer of the return despatch approached."[18]

"General," Longstreet said as he saw Babcock ride up, "unless he offers us honorable terms, come back and let us fight it out."[19]

"The thought of another round seemed to brace him," Longstreet wrote, "and he rode with Colonel Marshall, of his staff, to meet the Union commander."[20] Sergeant Tucker again accompanied them, and the three Confederates rode with Babcock toward the village of Appomattox Court House until Lee remembered that Grant had left it up to him to select the place for them to meet. He waited with Babcock while Marshall and Tucker went ahead to find a suitable site. Why the court house itself could not have been used has never been explained. Tucker soon returned to lead them to the house on the edge of town that Marshall had selected: the home of Wilmer McLean, who, oddly enough, had owned a farm over which the battles of Bull Run had raged early in the war. To avoid further visits from contending armies he had moved to this more southerly clime, but the armies had now caught up with him again.

At the front, the truce was about to expire. "One o'clock comes; no answer from Lee," Joshua Chamberlain wrote. "Nothing for us but to shake hands and take arms to resume hostilities. As I turned to go, General Griffin said to me in a low voice, 'Prepare to make, or receive, an attack in ten minutes!' It was a sudden change of tone in our relations, and brought a queer sensation.... It did not seem like war we were to recommence, but wilful murder. But the order was only to 'prepare,' and that we did.... I had mounted, and sat looking at the scene before me, thinking of all that was impending and depending, when I felt coming in upon me a strange sense of some presence invisible but powerful—like those unearthly visitants told of in ancient story, charged with supernatural message. Disquieted, I turned about, and there behind me, riding in between my two lines, appeared a commanding form, superbly mounted, richly accoutred, of imposing bearing, noble countenance, with expression of deep sadness overmastered by deeper strength. It is no other than Robert E. Lee! And seen by me for the first time within my own lines. I sat immovable, with a certain awe and admiration. He was coming with a single staff officer, for the great appointed meeting which was to determine momentous issues."[21] As Lee rode by, a Federal band struck up "Auld Lang Syne."

"About one o'clock," Horace Porter wrote, "the little village of Appomattox Court-house, with its half-dozen houses, came in sight, and soon we were entering its single street.... We saw a group of officers who had dismounted and were standing at the edge of the town, and at their head we soon recognized the features of Sheridan..... "

"How are you, Sheridan?" Grant asked.

"First-rate, thank you," the little cavalryman happily replied; "how are you?"

"Is Lee over there?"

"Yes; he is in that brick house, waiting to surrender to you."

"Well, then," Grant said, "we'll go over."[22]

Sheridan, Ord, and their staff officers mounted and followed Grant and his staff to McLean's house. Chamberlain saw the general-in-chief ride by, "Plain, unassuming, simple, and familiar to our eyes, but to the thought as much inspiring awe as Lee in his splendor and his sadness.... slouched hat without cord; common soldier's blouse, unbuttoned, on which, however, the [three] stars; high boots, mud-splashed to the top; trousers tucked inside; no sword, but the sword-hand deep in the pocket; sitting his saddle with the ease of a born master, taking no notice of anything, all his faculties gathered into intense thought and mighty calm. He seemed greater than I had ever seen him,—a look as of another world about him. No wonder I forgot altogether to salute him. Anything like that would have been too little."[23]

Grant and his generals and staff officers rode up the street and turned into Wilmer McLean's yard and dismounted. Grant climbed the steps and entered the house. As he stepped into the hall, Babcock opened the door of the room where he had been sitting with Lee and Marshall. The general passed in, and as Lee arose and stepped forward, Grant extended his hand, saying, "General Lee," and the two shook hands cordially.

"What General Lee's feelings were I do not know," Grant later wrote. "As he was a man of much dignity, with an impassible face, it was impossible to say whether he felt inwardly glad that the end had finally come, or felt sad over the result, and was too manly to show it. Whatever his feelings, they were entirely concealed from my observation; but my own feelings, which had been quite jubilant on the receipt of his letter, were sad and depressed. I felt like anything rather than rejoicing at the downfall of a foe who had fought so long and valiantly, and had suffered so much for a cause, though that cause was, I believe, one of the worst for which a people ever fought, and one for which there was the least excuse."[24]

Grant's staff plus Sheridan, Ord and a few other generals remained in McLean's yard, but in a few minutes Babcock came to the front door, and, making a motion with his hat toward the sitting-room, said, "The general says come in."

"We entered," Horace Porter wrote, "and found General Grant seated in an old office arm chair in the center of the room, and Lee sitting in a plain arm-chair with a cane seat beside a square, marble-topped table near the front window, in the corner opposite the door by which we entered, and facing General Grant. Colonel Marshall was standing at his left, with his right elbow resting upon the mantlepiece. We walked in softly, and ranged ourselves quietly about the sides of the room, very much as people enter a sick-chamber when they expect to find the patient dangerously ill. Some found seats on the sofa standing against the wall between the two doors and on the few plain chairs which constituted the furniture, but most of the party stood.

"The contrast between the two commanders was singularly striking, and could not fail to attract marked attention as they sat, six or eight feet apart, facing each other. General Grant, then nearly forty-three years of age, was five feet eight inches in height, with shoulders slightly stooped. His hair and full beard were nut-brown, without a trace of gray in them. He had on his single-breasted blouse of dark-blue flannel, unbuttoned in front and showing a waistcoat underneath. He wore an ordinary pair of top-boots, with his trousers inside, and was without spurs. The boots and portions of his clothes were spattered with mud. He had worn a pair of thread gloves of a dark-yellow color, which he had taken off on entering the room. His felt 'sugar loaf,' stiff-brimmed hat was resting on his lap. He had no sword or sash, and a pair of shoulder-straps was all there was about him to designate his rank. In fact, aside from these, his uniform was that of a private soldier.

"Lee, on the other hand, was six feet and one inch in height, and erect for one of his age, for he was Grant's senior by sixteen years. His hair and full beard were a silvery-gray, and thick, except the hair had become a little thin in front. He wore a new uniform of Confederate gray, buttoned to the throat, and a handsome sword and sash. The sword was of exceedingly fine workmanship, and the hilt was studded with jewels. It had been presented to him by some ladies in England who sympathized with the cause he represented. His top-boots were comparatively new, and had on them near the top some ornamental stitching of red silk. Like his uniform, they were clean. On the boots were handsome spurs with large rowels. A felt hat which in color matched pretty closely that of his uniform, and a pair of long, gray buckskin gauntlets, lay beside him on the table."

Grant said, "I met you once before, General Lee, while we were serving in Mexico, when you came over from General Scott's headquarters to visit Garland's brigade, to which I then belonged. I have always remembered your appearance, and I think I should have recognized you anywhere."

"Yes," Lee replied; "I know I met you on that occasion, and I have often thought of it, and tried to recollect how you looked, but I have never been able to recall a single feature."

After a little more talk about Mexico, Lee said, "I suppose, General Grant, that the object of our present meeting is fully understood. I asked to see you to ascertain upon what terms you would receive the surrender of my army." Grant replied, "The terms I propose are those stated substantially in my letter of yesterday; that is, the officers and men surrendered to be paroled and disqualified from taking up arms again until properly exchanged, and all arms, ammunition, and supplies to be delivered up as captured property."

Lee nodded an assent and said, "Those are about the conditions which I expected would be proposed."

"Yes," Grant went on; "I think our correspondence indicated pretty clearly the action that would be taken at our meeting, and I hope it may lead to a general suspension of hostilities, and be the means of preventing any further loss of life."

"Lee inclined his head," Porter wrote, "indicating his accord with this wish, and General Grant then went on to talk at some length in a very pleasant vein about the prospects of peace. Lee was evidently anxious to proceed to the formal work of the surrender, and he brought the subject up again...."

"I presume, General Grant, we have both carefully considered the proper steps to be taken, and I would suggest that you commit to writing the terms you have proposed, so that they may be formally acted upon."

"Very well," Grant replied; "I will write them out."

He called for his order book, opened it, laid it on a small oval wooden table that Lieutenant Colonel Ely Parker, his military secretary, brought to him, and wrote rapidly:

"General: In accordance with the substance of my letter to you of the 8th inst., I propose to receive the surrender of the Army of Northern Virginia on the following terms, to wit: Rolls of all the officers and men to be made in duplicate, one copy to be given to an officer to be designated by me, the other to be retained by such officer or officers as you may designate. The officers to give their individual paroles not to take up arms against the Government of the United States until properly [exchanged], and each company or regimental commander to sign a like parole for the men of their commands. The arms, artillery, and public property to be parked and stacked and turned over to the officers appointed by me to receive them.... ."

Then he looked toward Lee," Porter said, "and his eyes seemed to be resting on the handsome sword that hung at that officer's side. He said afterward that this set him to thinking that it would be an unnecessary humiliation to require the officers to surrender their swords, and a great hardship to deprive them of their personal baggage and horses; and after a short pause.... " he continued writing:

"This will not embrace the side-arms of the officers.., nor their private horses or baggage. This done, each officer and man will be allowed to return to his home, not to be disturbed by the United States authorities so long as they observe their paroles and the laws in force where they may reside."

The final sentence was probably inspired by the talks Grant had had with Lincoln, for it made it impossible for the Radical Republicans of Congress to prosecute Lee or any of his officers for treason.

"When he had finished the letter," Porter said, "he called Colonel Parker to his side, and looked it over with him, and directed him as they went along to interline six or seven words, and to strike out the word 'their,' which had been repeated. When this had been done the general took the manifold writer in his right hand, extended his arm toward Lee, and started to rise from his chair to hand the book to him. As I was standing equally distant from them, with my back to the front window, I stepped forward, took the book, and passed it to General Lee....

"Lee pushed aside some books and two brass candlesticks which were on the table, then took the book and laid it down before him, while he drew from his pocket a pair of steel-rimmed spectacles, and wiped the glasses carefully with his handkerchief. He crossed his legs, adjusted the spectacles very slowly and deliberately, took up the draft of the terms, and proceeded to read them attentively. They consisted of two pages. When he reached the top of the second page, he looked up, and said to General Grant: 'After the words "until properly" the word "exchanged" seems to be omitted. You doubtless intended to use that word.'"

"Why, yes," Grant said; "I thought I had put in the word 'exchanged.'"

"I presumed it had been omitted inadvertently," continued Lee; "and, with your permission, I will mark where it should be inserted."

"Certainly," Grant replied.

"Lee felt in his pocket as if searching for a pencil," Porter wrote, "but he did not seem to be able to find one. Seeing this, I handed him my lead-pencil. During the rest of the interview he kept twirling this pencil in his fingers and occasionally tapping the top of the table with it. When he handed it back, it was carefully treasured by me as a memento of the occasion. When Lee came to the sentence about the officers' side-arms, private horses, and baggage, he showed for the first time during the reading of the letter a slight change of countenance, and was evidently touched by this act of generosity."

He looked up at Grant as he finished reading and said with some warmth, "This will have a very happy effect upon my army."

"Unless you have some suggestions to make in regard to the form in which I have stated the terms," Grant said, "I will have a copy of the letter made in ink, and sign it."

Lee paused and said, "There is one thing I should like to mention. The cavalrymen and artillerists own their own horses in our army. Its organization in this respect differs from that of the United States. I should like to understand whether these men will be permitted to retain their horses."

"'You will find that the terms as written do not allow this," Grant replied; "only the officers are permitted to take their private property."

Lee read over the second page of the letter again, and said, "No, I see the terms do not allow it; that is clear." "His face showed plainly that he was quite anxious to have this concession made," Porter noticed; "and Grant said very promptly, and without giving Lee time to make a direct request: 'Well, the subject is quite new to me. Of course I did not know that any private soldiers owned their animals; but I think we have fought the last battle of the war,—I sincerely hope so,—and that the surrender of this army will be followed soon by that of all the others; and I take it that most of the men in the ranks are small farmers, and as the country has been so raided by the two armies, it is doubtful whether they will be able to put in a crop to carry themselves and their families through the next winter without the aid of the horses they are now riding, and I will arrange it in this way: I will not change the terms as now written, but I will instruct the officers I shall appoint to receive the paroles to let all the men who claim to own a horse or mule take the animals home with them to work their little farms.'....

"Lee now looked greatly relieved," Porter said, "and though anything but a demonstrative man, he gave every evidence of his appreciation of this concession, and said: 'This will have the best possible effect upon the men. It will be very gratifying, and will do much toward conciliating our people.'"

Lee handed the draft of the terms back to General Grant, who told Colonel T. S. Bowers of his staff to copy it in ink. Bowers was nervous and turned the job over to Parker, who had the best handwriting on the staff. Then it was discovered that McLean's inkstand was dry. Marshall came to the rescue, loaning Parker a small wooden inkstand he carried in his pocket. When the terms had been copied, Lee had his own military secretary draw up a letter of acceptance for his signature. Marshall wrote out a formal-sounding draft and Lee read it over very carefully, directing that the formal expressions be stricken out and the letter shortened. He then went over it again and changed a few words and told the colonel to make a final copy in ink. At that point it was found that the Federals had the only supply of paper.

The letter when completed said: "General: I have received your letter of this date containing the terms of the surrender of the Army of Northern Virginia as proposed by you. As they are substantially the same as those expressed in you letter of the 8th inst., they are accepted. I will proceed to designate the proper officers to carry the stipulations into effect."

"While the letters were being copied," Porter said, "General Grant introduced the general officers who had entered, and each member of the staff, to General Lee. The general shook hands with General Seth Williams, who had been his adjutant when Lee was superintendent at West Point some years before the war, and gave his hand to some of the other officers who had extended theirs; but to most of those who were introduced he merely bowed in a dignified and formal manner. He did not exhibit the slightest change of features during this ceremony until Colonel Parker of our staff was presented to him. Parker being a full-blooded Indian, when Lee saw his swarthy features he looked at him with evident surprise, and his eyes rested on him for several seconds. What was passing in his mind no one knew, but the natural surmise was that he at first mistook Parker for a negro, and was struck with astonishment to find that the commander of the Union armies had one of that race on his personal staff.

"Lee did not utter a word while the introductions were going on, except to Seth Williams, with whom he talked cordially. Willams at one time referred in a rather jocose manner to a circumstance which had occurred during their former service together, as if he wished to say something in a good-natured way to thaw the frigidity of the conversation; but Lee was in no mood for pleasantries, and he did not unbend, or even relax the fixed sterness of his features. His only response to the remark was a slight inclination of the head. General Lee now took the initiative again in leading the conversation back into business channels."

"I have," he said, "a thousand or more of your men as prisoners, General Grant, a number of them officers, whom we have required to march along with us for several days. I shall be glad to send them into your lines as soon as it can be arranged, for I have no provisions for them. I have, indeed, nothing for my own men. They have been living for the last few days principally upon parched corn, and we are badly in need of both rations and forage. I telegraphed to Lynchburg, directing several train-loads of rations to be sent on by rail from there, and when they arrive I should be glad to have the present wants of my men supplied from them."

"At this remark," Porter wrote, "all eyes turned toward Sheridan, for he had captured these trains with his cavalry the night before near Appomattox Station."

"I should like to have our men sent within our lines as soon as possible," Grant said. "I will take steps at once to have your army supplied with rations, but I am sorry we have no forage for the animals. We have had to depend upon the country for our supply of forage. Of about how many men does your present force consist?"

After a slight pause, Lee said, "Indeed, I am not able to say. My losses in killed and wounded have been exceedingly heavy, and, besides, there have been many stragglers and some deserters. All my reports and public papers, and indeed some of my own private letters, had to be destroyed on the march to prevent them from falling into the hands of your people. Many companies are entirely without officers, and I have not seen any returns for several days, so that I have no means of ascertaining our present strength."

Grant always had a daily estimate made of the enemy's forces. "Suppose I send over 25,000 rations," he asked, "do you think that will be sufficient supply?"

"I think it will be ample," Lee replied, adding earnestly, "and it will be a great relief, I assure you."

Grant's eye now returned Lee's sword. "I started out from my camp several days ago without my sword," he explained, "and as I have not seen my headquarters baggage since, I have been riding about without any side-arms. I have generally worn a sword, however, as little as possible—only during the active operations of a campaign."

"I am in the habit of wearing mine most of the time." Lee said, "when I am among my troops moving about through the army."

Sheridan now stepped up to General Lee and said that when he had discovered some of the Confederate troops moving during the truce he had sent Lee a couple of notes protesting against this act, and since he had not had time to copy them he would like to have them long enough to make copies for his records. Lee took the notes out of his breast pocket and handed them to Sheridan, expressing regret and saying that it must have been the result of some misunderstanding.

After a little general conversation, the two letters were signed. Grant signed the terms and Lee signed his letter of acceptance. Parker folded up the terms, and gave them to Marshall, who handed Lee's acceptance to Parker. Lee then asked Grant to notify Meade of the surrender, fearing that fighting might otherwise break out on that front. Two Union officers were sent through the Rebel lines on the shortest route to Meade, and some of Lee's officers went with them.

"A little before four o'clock General Lee shook hands with General

Grant, bowed to the other officers, and with Colonel Marshall left the room," Porter wrote. "One after another we followed, and passed out to the porch. Lee signaled to his orderly to bring up his horse, and while the animal was being bridled the general stood on the lowest step, and gazed sadly in the direction of the valley beyond, where his army lay—now an army of prisoners. He thrice smote the palm of his left hand slowly with his right fist in an absent sort of way, seemed not to see the group of Union officers in the yard, who rose respectfully at his approach, and appeared unaware of everything about him. All appreciated the sadness that overwhelmed him, and he had the personal sympathy of every one who beheld him at this supreme moment of trial. The approach of his horse seemed to recall him from his reverie, and he at once mounted. General Grant now stepped down from the porch, moving toward him, and saluted him by raising his hat. He was followed in this act of courtesy by all our officers present. Lee raised his hat respectfully, and rode off at a slow trot to break the sad news to the brave fellows whom he had so long commanded."[25]

Sheridan thrust $20 in gold upon the unwilling Wilmer McLean and carried off the table upon which Grant had written out the terms of surrender. He gave it to Custer as a present for his wife in appreciation of all her husband had done to secure the victory. Ord paid $40 for the table at which Lee had sat, and other officers bought other mementos, including the chairs, the empty inkstand, the brass candlesticks, and even a child's doll that was found in the room, a silent witness to history. McLean did not want to sell these items, and he is said to have thown the Federal money down on his porch. It was a bad day for this civilian. He told General Alexander, the Confederate artilleryman, to whom he was related by marriage, "These armies tore my place on Bull Run all to pieces, and kept running over it backward and forward till no man could live there, so I just sold out and came here, two hundred miles away, hoping I should never see a soldier again. And now just look around you! Not a fence rail is left on the place, the last guns trampled down all my crops, and Lee surrenders to Grant in my house."[26]

Before Grant had ridden very far from McLean's place, he was reminded that he had not announced the important news to the government. So he dismounted by the roadside, sat down on a large rock, and wrote a short telegram to Secretary of War Stanton: "General Lee surrendered the Army of Northern Virginia this afternoon on terms proposed by myself. The accompanying additional correspondence will show the conditions fully."[27]

Not long afterwards the general finally came together with his headquarters tent once again. "Upon reaching camp," Porter said, "he seated himself in front of his tent, notwithstanding the light shower which was then falling, and we all gathered about him, curious to hear what his first comments would be upon the crowning event of his life. But our expectations were doomed to disappointment, for he appeared to have already dismissed the whole subject from his mind." Instead, he was more interested in pursuing the memories of the Mexican war that had been stirred up by his conversation with Lee. He turned to his chief quartermaster and said, "Ingalls, do you remember that old white mule that So-and-so used to ride when we were in the city of Mexico?"[28]

The time for the truce had elapsed on Meade's front, and Humphreys was preparing to attack before word finally arrived from Grant. "All at once a tempest of hurrahs shook the air along the front of our line," General de Trobriand said. "General Meade is coming at a gallop from Appomattox Court House. He has raised his cap and uttered a few words: LEE HAS SURRENDERED!.... Mad hurrahs fill the air like the rolling of thunder, in the fields, in the woods, along the roads, and are prolonged in echo....

"General Meade leaves the road and passes through my division. The men swarm out to meet him, surrounding his horse. Hurrah for General Meade! Again, Hurrah! And on all sides, Hurrah! The enthusiasm gains the officers of his staff, who cry out like all the rest, waving their hats. Caps fly in the air; the colors are waved in salute.... glorious rags in the breeze; all the musicians fill the air with the joyous notes of 'Yankee Doodle' and the sonorous strains of 'Hail, Columbia.'

".... All the hopes of four years at last realized; all the fears dissipated, all perils disappeared; all the privations, all the sufferings, all the misery ended; the intoxication of triumph; the joy at the near return to the domestic hearth—for all this, one single burst of enthusiasm did not suffice. So the hurrahs and cries of joy were prolonged."[29]

Similar scenes were enacted on the other front as well, where Ord and Sheridan commanded. "Staff officers are flying," Joshua Chamberlain wrote, "crying 'Lee surrenders!' Ah, there was some kind of strength left among those worn and famished men belting the hills around the springs of the Appomattox, who rent the air with shouting and uproar, as if earth and sea had joined the song!"[30] The artillery started firing a salute, but Grant ordered it stopped.

The men eventually settled down, and although orders had been issued to keep the two armies apart they did not prevent a certain amount of mingling. Lee was annoyed by visits from several Union officers, some of whom had known him before the war and others who just wanted to meet him. Various Federal officers also played host to Confederate friends. Even the enlisted men refused to stay put. "Now large numbers of the rebel soldiers came over to us," Theodore Gerrish said. "We were glad to see them. They had fought bravely, and were as glad as we that the war was over. They told us of the fearful condition General Lee's army was in, and we only wondered that they endured the hardships so long as they did. We received them kindly, and exchanged pocket knives and sundry trinkets, that each could have something to carry home as a reminiscence of the great event."[31]

Grant designated Gibbon, Griffin and Merritt to parole the Confederates, and Lee named Longstreet, Gordon and Pendleton to work with them. "Late that night I was summoned to headquarters," Chamberlain said, "where General Griffin informed me that I was to command the parade on the occasion of the formal surrender of the arms and colors of Lee's army. He said the Confederates had begged hard to be allowed to stack their arms on the ground where they were, and let us go and pick them up after they had gone; but that Grant did not think this quite respectful enough to anybody, including the United States of America; and while he would have all private property respected, and would permit officers to retain their side-arms, he insisted that the surrendering army as such should march out in due order, and lay down all tokens of Confederate authority and organized hostility to the United States, in immediate presence of some representative portion of the Union Army. Griffin added in a significant tone that Grant wished the ceremony to be as simple as possible, and that nothing should be done to humiliate the manhood of the Southern soldiers.

"I appreciated the honor of this appointment, although I did not take it much to myself. There were other things to think of. I only asked General Griffin to give me again my old Third Brigade, which I had commanded after Gettysburg, and with which I had been closely associated in the great battles of the first two years. Not for private reasons, however, was this request made, but because this was to be a crowing incident of history, and I thought these veterans deserved this recognition. I was therefore transferred from the First Brigade, of which I had been so proud, to the Third, representing the veterans of the Fifth Corps."[32]

As usual, Grant sat up late that night, talking with Colonel Adam Badeau of his staff, for he never could get to sleep early. "This night we spoke of the terms he had granted Lee," Badeau said. "There were some of his officers who disliked the idea of paroles, and thought at least the highest of the rebels should have been differently dealt with—held for trial. This was not my feeling, and I spoke of the effect his magnaminity was sure to have upon the country and the world. He was not averse to listen."

"I'll keep the terms," Grant said quietly, "no matter who's opposed. But Lincoln is sure to be on my side."[33]

At last the momentuous day drew to a close. "The fires are burning low," one Union soldier wrote, "and only here and there can we see a man with clasped knees still looking into the failing blaze. Hark! the first bugle is sounding 'taps,' and.... if you have never heard it blown on the field, you will not realize the depth of its moving tones; that call, to be at its best, must be heard on the edge of a battlefield and in the presence of the enemy. Then the night-enveloped neighboring fields and woods, and the vaulted skies seem to lend each note some of their own subdued, sweetly-lamenting loneliness. One by one, camp after camp, battery after battery, is sounding the call, and now the last one—oh, trumpeter, you nor any other will ever blow its like again—is dying away, dying over the field of Appomattox—its last note lingers as if reluctant to go, it is fading, it is gone."[34]

When the last bugle had sounded the final note, rain started to fall gently on the two weary armies. A band somewhere in Sheridan's cavalry camp began to softly play "Home Sweet Home."

---

1. Wheeler, *Witness to Appomattox,* 219-221.
2. Chamberlain, *The Passing of the Armies,* 179-180.
3. Sheridan, *Civil War Memoirs,* 346.
4. Urwin, *Custer Victorious,* 254-255.
5. Chamberlain, *The Passing of the Armies,* 181-182.
6. Sheridan, *Civil War Memoirs,* 346.
7. Wheeler, *Witness to Appomattox,* 221.
8. Sheridan, *Civil War Memoirs,* 347.
9. Wheeler, *Witness to Appomattox,* 221.
10. Sheridan, *Civil War Memoirs,* 348.
11. Wheeler, *Witness to Appomattox,* 222.
12. Sheridan, *Civil War Memoirs,* 348-349.
13. Grant, *Personal Memoirs,* 2:485.
14. Foote, *The Civil War,* 3:939.
15. *Official Records,* 46:III:665.
16. Porter, *Campaigning with Grant,* 468.
17. Catton, *Grant Takes Command,* 462.
18. Longstreet, *From Manassas to Appomattox,* 627-628.

19. Freeman, *R.E. Lee,* 4:132.
20. Longstreet, *From Manassas to Appomattox,* 628.
21. Chamberlain, *The Passing of the Armies,* 183-184.
22. Porter, *Campaigning with Grant,* 468-470.
23. Chamberlain, *The Passing of the Armies,* 184.
24. Grant, *Personal Memoirs,* 2:489.
25. Porter, *Campaigning with Grant,* 472-486.
26. Rodick, *Appomattox,* 152.
27. *Official Records,* 46:III:663.
28. Porter, *Campaigning with Grant,* 488-489.
29. Wheeler, *Witness to Appomattox,* 231.
30. Chamberlain, *The Passing of the Armies,* 186.
31. Wheeler, *Witness to Appomattox,* 231.
32. Chamberlain, *The Passing of the Armies,* 186-187.
33. Davis, *To Appomattox,* 355.
34. Stern, *An End to Valor,* 278-279.

CHAPTER THIRTY-SEVEN

Now Father Will Come Home

9 - 12 April 1865

Down on the Gulf coast of Alabama on that fateful Palm Sunday, the ninth of April, 1865, Canby's Federals continued their bombardment of Fort Blakely that had begun the day before, dismounting two Rebel guns. At 5:30 p.m. four Union divisions simultaneously advanced with a shout against the two miles of Confederate entrenchments. They clambered over the obstructions of slashed timber, abatis, telegraph wire and buried torpedoes under a heavy fire of artillery and musketry and carried the Rebel works in about twenty minutes. They captured large supplies of food and ammunition, forty guns, and about 3,200 prisoners, including three Rebel brigadier generals. With the fall of Spanish Fort and Blakely, the Confederates could not hold Mobile, and preparations for its evacuation were started immediately. Neither side, of course, was yet aware that Lee had surrendered earlier that day.

The Lincolns and their guests were still aboard the *River Queen* that day, steaming up Chesapeake Bay on their way back to Washington. The Marquis de Chambrun remembered that the President read to them from Shakespeare for hours, especially from "Macbeth," lingering over Macbeth's speech after the murder of Duncan. "Now and then he paused," the French nobleman said, "to expatiate on how exact a picture Shakespeare here gives of a murderer's mind when, the dark deed achieved, its perpetrator already envies his victim's calm sleep. He read the scene twice." Both de Chambrun and Senator Sumner noticed that Lincoln repeated, with obvious familiarity, the lines:

Duncan is in his grave;
After life's fitful fever he sleeps well;
Treason has done his worst: nor steel, nor poison,
Malice domestic, foreign levy, nothing
Can touch him further.

It was still daylight when the *River Queen* passed George Washington's famous plantation, Mount Vernon, on its hill overlooking the lower Potomac River. De Chambrun told the president that someday his home in Springfield, Illinois would be equally honored. "Springfield!" Lincoln replied, as if awaking from a trance, "How glad I'll be to get back there—peace and tranquility."

Not long afterward the boat arrived at the dock in Washington, putting an end to the Lincolns' only vacation in four years. "That city is full of enemies," Mary Lincoln said, dreading the return to the national capital.

"Enemies!" Lincoln replied with an impatient gesture, "Never again must we repeat that word."[1]

Through the night and the rain after dropping Mary and Tad at the White House, Lincoln drove to Seward's home on Lafayette Square. He found the injured secretary of state in bed upstairs with his bruised and swollen face swathed in bandages and his jaw wired shut. Then the lanky president stretched out on the bed beside the injured man and told him all about his trip to the front. After a half-hour he silently slipped out, signaling to Seward's son that the secretary had fallen asleep.

At 9 p.m. Grant's message reached Secretary Stanton, who was dozing on a couch at his home. After reading it twice the secretary of war went to his desk and wrote a reply: "Thanks be to Almighty God for the great victory with which he has this day crowned you and the gallant army under your command. The thanks of this Department and of the Government, and of the people of the United States, their reverence and honor, have been deserved and will be rendered to you and the brave and gallant officers and soldiers of your army for all time."[2] Then Stanton dressed and hurried over to the White House. He found the Lincolns and a few friends in the Red Room. His news was met with a stunned silence. That night, or sometime near it, Stanton tried to resign. He was tired out. Lincoln read the paper Stanton handed him and slowly tore it up. "You cannot go," he said.[3]

"Most people were sleeping soundly in their beds," reporter Noah Brooks wrote, "when, at daylight on the rainy morning of April 10, 1865, a great boom startled the misty air of Washington, shaking the very earth, and breaking the windows of houses about Lafayette Square, and moving the inhabitants of that aristocratic locality to say once more that they would be glad when Union victories were done with, or should be celebrated elsewhere. Boom! boom! went the guns, until five hundred were fired. A few people got up in the chill twilight of the morning, and raced about in the mud to learn what the good news might be, while others formed a procession and resumed their parades,—no dampness, no fatigue, being sufficient to depress their ardor. But many placidly lay abed, well knowing that only one military event could cause all this mighty pother in the air of Washington; and if their nap in the gray dawn was disturbed with dreams of guns and of terms of armies surrendered to Grant by Lee, they awoke later to read of these in the daily papers; for this was Secretary Stanton's way of telling the people that the Army of Northern Virginia had at last laid down its arms, and that peace had come again.... .

"When the capital was broad awake, and had taken in the full value of the news, the fever-heat that had fired the city on the day after the fall of Richmond did not return. Popular feeling had culminated then, and after that great event there was nothing that could surprise us, not even if 'Jeff' Davis himself had come to Washington to surrender. The streets were shockingly muddy, but were all alive with people singing and cheering, carrying flags, and saluting everybody, hungering and thirsting for speeches. General Butler was called out, among others, and he made a speech full of surprising liberality and generosity toward the enemy. The departments gave another holiday to their clerks; so did many business firms; and the Treasury employees assembled in the great corridor of their building and sang 'Old Hundredth' with thrilling, even tear-compelling effect. Then they marched in a body across the grounds to the White House, where the President was at breakfast, and serenaded him with 'The Star-Spangled Banner.'

"As the forenoon wore on, an impromptu procession came up from the Navy Yard, dragging six boat-howitzers, which were fired through the streets as they rolled on. This crowd, reinforced by the hurrahing legions along the route, speedily swelled to enormous proportions, and filled the whole area in front of the White House, where guns were fired and bands played while the multitude waited for a speech. The young hope of the house of Lincoln—Tad—made his appearance at the well-known window from which the President always spoke, and was received with great shouts of applause, whereupon he waved a captured rebel flag, to the uproarious delight of the sovereign people below. When Lincoln came to the window shortly after, the scene before him was one of the wildest confusion. It seemed impossible for men adequately to express their feelings. They fairly yelled with delight, threw their hats again and again, or threw up one another's hats, and screamed like mad. From the windows of the White House the surface of that crowd looked like an agitated sea of hats, faces, and arms. Quiet being restored, the President briefly congratulated the people on the occasion which called out such unrestrained enthusiasm, and said that, as arrangements were being made for a more formal celebration, he would defer his remarks until that occasion; 'for,' said he, 'I shall have nothing to say then if it is all dribbled out of me now.' He said that as the good old tune of 'Dixie' had been captured on the ninth of April, he had submitted the question of its ownership to the Attorney-General, who had decided that that tune was now our lawful property; and he asked that the band should play it, which was done with a will, 'Yankee Doodle' following. Then the President proposed three cheers for General Grant and the officers and men under him, then three cheers for the navy, all of which were given heartily, the President leading off, waving his hand; and the laughing, joyous crowd dispersed."[4]

All the Union troops at Appomattox Court House marched for Burkeville on the tenth except the 5th and 24th corps, which were to stay at Appomattox Court House until after the surrender ceremony planned for the twelfth. At about 9 a.m. that day, Grant and his staff rode over toward the Confederate camps. He wanted to see Lee again before he left. Satisfied that the war was all but over, he wanted to get to Washington as soon as possible to start cutting back on the enormously expensive procurement of supplies and equipment, so he would not be staying for the surrender ceremony. The Confederate pickets politely refused to allow the Federals to pass until they could get instructions from General Lee. "As soon as Lee heard that his distinguished opponent was approaching," Horace Porter wrote, "he was prompt to correct the misunderstanding at the picket-line, and rode out at a gallop to receive him. They met on a knoll that overlooked the lines of the two armies, and saluted respectfully by each raising his hat.

The officers present gave a similar salute, and then withdrew out of ear-shot, and grouped themselves about the two chieftains in a semi-circle."[5]

"We had there between the lines, sitting on horseback," Grant remembered, "a very pleasant conversation of over half an hour, in the course of which Lee said to me that the South was a big country and that we might have to march over it three or four times before the war entirely ended, but that we would now be able to do it as they could no longer resist us. He expressed it as his earnest hope, however, that we would not be called upon to cause more loss and sacrifice of life; but he could not foretell the result. I then suggested to General Lee that there was not a man in the Confederacy whose influence with the soldiery and the whole people was as great as his, and that if he would now advise the surrender of all the armies I had no doubt his advice would be followed with alacrity. But Lee said, that he could not do that without consulting the President [Davis] first. I knew there was no use to urge him to do anything against his ideas of what was right."[6]

As Lee rode back to his camp he met a group of Federals, one of whom greeted him with a cheery "good morning, General." Lee did not recognize the Union officer until he identified himself as George Meade, whom Lee had known in the regular army before the war, when they had both looked a lot younger.

After a closer look, Lee recognized him. "But what are you doing with all that gray in your beard?" he asked.

"You have to answer for most of it!" Meade told him.[7]

Grant spent the rest of the morning sitting on Wilmer McLean's front porch. McLean's house was being used by the Union and Confederate commissioners to arrange the parole of Lee's troops. Sheridan, Ingalls, and Seth Williams went to visit old friends in the Confederate camp and soon brought some visitors to see Grant. Among them were Longstreet and Wilcox, both of whom had attended his wedding long before the war when they were all young officers in the regular army. Pickett and Heth and a number of others came as well. Grant slapped Longstreet on the shoulder, suggested a game of brag to bring back the old days, and gave him a cigar.

A Rebel soldier who saw Grant there recorded his impressions: "General Grant impressed me at the time as a self-contained, self-reliant man—with massive, solid head and a square jaw. His entire face, from the low brow to the square chin, from the calm clear eye to the inflexible lips—bore a look of intelligent, steadfast purpose; and yet it was a manly, kindly face withal.... His face was one a man with a just cause would appeal to with confidence for justice and kind, but ineffusive sympathy.

His bearing was that of a modest unasssuming man—wearing no air of a proud conqueror, no smile of satisfaction, no look of exultation. His air was that of a man too full of a great purpose brought to a successful issue to think of his own part in it. I examined him narrowly—partly because his actual appearance was in no respect in accord with the idea I had formed of him."[8]

At about noon, Grant shook hands with all those present who were not going with him, mounted his horse, and rode off with his staff for Burkeville, where he could take the newly repaired railroad back to City Point and then go on to Washington by steamboat. "No man could have behaved better than General Grant did under the circumstances," Lee told a friend when he got back to Richmond. "He did not touch my sword; the usual custom is for the sword to be received when tendered, and then handed back, but he did not touch mine." His nephew Fitz Lee added that "neither did the Union chief enter the Southern lines to show himself or to parade his victory, or go to Richmond or Petersburg to exult over a fallen people, but mounted his horse and with his staff started for Washington. Washington at Yorktown, was not as considerate and thoughtful of the feelings of Cornwallis or his men."[9]

Down at Danville, Jefferson Davis was in conference with some of his advisors when a Confederate captain brought him word of Lee's surrender. "This news," Secretary of the Navy Mallory said, "fell upon the ears of all like a fire bell in the night.... They carefully scanned the message as it passed from hand to hand, looked at each other gravely and mutely, and for some moments a silence more eloquent of great disaster than words could have been, prevailed."[10] Then, as they struggled to recover from this blow to their hopes, they were told that Stoneman's Union cavalry was approaching from the west. Government documents were repacked and hauled to the railroad station while Davis telegraphed the news to General Johnston, asking him to meet the cabinet in Greensborough, North Carolina. The treasury train had already been sent even farther south, to Charlotte.

It was 10 p.m. by the time the official party gathered at the station and boarded its train. "Much rain had fallen," Secretary Mallory wrote, "and the depot could be reached only through mud knee deep. With the utter darkness, the crowding of quartermasters' wagons, the yells of their contending drivers, the curses, loud and deep, of soldiers, organized and disorganized, determined to get upon the train in defiance of the guard, the mutual shouts of inquiry and response as to missing individuals or baggage, the want of baggage arrangements, and the insufficient and dangerous provision made for getting horses into their cars, the crushing of the crowd, and the determination to get transportation at any hazard, together with the absense of any recognized authority, all seasoned by *sub rosa* rumors that the enemy had already cut the Greensboro road, created a confusion such as it was never before the fortune of old Danville to witness."[11]

It was nearly 11 p.m. when Davis finally arrived with his aides and the train got under way. The engineer inched along, afraid that if the Yankees had really cut the line they would run off the rails in the dark. The car where Davis and his cabinet were riding was soon filled with smoke from its stove. A squad of Confederate soldiers riding its roof had piled blankets over the stove's chimney in order to stay warm by keeping all the heat from escaping into the night.

Stoneman's raiders were indeed not far away. They reached Germantown, North Carolina about noon, and from there Stoneman sent several hundred escaped slaves, who had been following his column, toward Tennessee with a small detachment to guard them. Palmer's 1st Brigade was sent from Germantown to Salem to destroy some large factories there that were manufacturing Confederate uniforms. From there Palmer was to send out detachments to destroy the railroad south of Greensborough and one to cut the line between Danville and Greensborough. The road was, in fact, cut that night but shortly after the presidential train passed by. Meanwhile, the rest of Stoneman's force resumed its march southward at 4 p.m.

To the east, Sherman's army, now including Schofield's two corps, began marching that morning from Goldsborough toward Smithfield, or, as Sherman put it, "straight against Joe Johnston wherever he may be." Sherman said his men, who had been issued new uniforms at last, were "as proud as young chicken cocks, with their clean faces and bright blue clothes.... new clothing, with soap and water, has made a wonderful change in our appearance."[12]

In Alabama, Wilson's raiders were on the move again. With considerable difficulty, the Federals had bridged and crossed the Alabama River, and on the tenth they rode off to the east, headed for Montgomery, the state capital where the Confederacy had been founded four years before. With them went three ad hoc regiments formed from escaped slaves who had joined them. One regiment was assigned to each division, serving as foragers, train guards, pioneers and teamsters.

The head of the column, LaGrange's brigade of McCook's division, encountered two regiments of Alabama cavalry drawn up on a ridge near the town of Benton, but the 7th Kentucky dismounted and pushed them back, and a mounted charge by a battalion of the 2nd Indiana soon scattered them. The 1st Wisconsin then gave chase, while the rest of the Union column marched on unmolested through what Wilson considered the richest planting district of the South.

In northern Virginia that day, the detachment from Mosby's rangers heading for Washington was surprised by a detachment of the 8th Illinois Cavalry just fifteen miles from the city. After a brief fight the Confederates retreated and most of them got away. But among the five Rebels captured was Lieutenant Harney, the explosives expert from the Torpedo Bureau. This skirmish, therefore, inadvertantly put an end to the Confederate plan to blow up the White House.

Grant had sent word to City Point that he expected to arrive there on the night of the tenth, and his wife had prepared the best dinner her river boat's staff could provide for her returning hero. But the railroad from Burkeville had been only hastily repaired, and the trip took longer than expected. Julia waited up with Mrs. Rawlins and the wife of another staff officer, whiling away the hours by playing the piano and singing as well as discussing what little they knew of Lee's surrender. But just before dawn the ladies went to their beds. "Soon after," Horace Porter wrote, "our tired and hungry party arrived. The general went hurriedly aboard the boat, and ran at once up the stairs to Mrs. Grant's state-room. She was somewhat chagrined that she had not remained up to receive her husband, now more than ever her 'Victor'; but she had merely thrown herself upon the berth without undressing, and soon joined us all in the cabin, and extended to us enthusiastic greetings and congratulations. The belated dinner now served in good stead as a breakfast for our famished party."[13]

"About fifty generals and other officers of high rank breakfasted with us that morning," Julia Grant wrote. "I shall never forget how happy and satisfied they were—the grand, noble fellows!"

"General," someone asked, "of course you will go up to Richmond, will you not?"

"No," Grant said sternly, "I will go at once to Washington."

When his wife urged him to reconsider, he leaned toward her and said, "Hush, Julia. Do not say another word on this subject. I would not distress these people. They are feeling their defeat bitterly, and you would not add to it by witnessing their dispair, would you?"[14]

Washington officially celebrated Lee's surrender on the eleventh. That night all of the government buildings were illuminated. So were most of the people of the city, according to reporter Noah Brooks. "The night was misty," Brooks wrote, "and the exhibition was a splendid one. The

him, being seconded in this by another listener. Mr. Lincoln hesitated, but at length commenced very deliberately, his brow overcast with a shade of melancholy."

"About ten days ago," Lincoln said, "I retired very late. I had been up waiting for important dispatches from the front. I could not have been long in bed when I fell into a slumber, for I was weary. I soon began to dream. There seemed to be a death-like stillness about me. Then I heard subdued sobs, as if a number of people were weeping. I thought I left my bed and wandered downstairs. There the silence was broken by the same pitiful sobbing, but the mourners were invisible. I went from room to room; no living person was in sight, bu the same mournful sounds of distress met me as I passed along. It was light in all the rooms; every object was familiar to me; but where were all the people who were grieving as if their hearts would break? I was puzzled and alarmed. What could be the meaning of this? Determined to find the cause of a state of things so mysterious and so shocking, I kept on until I arrived at the East Room, which I entered. There I met with a sickening surprise. Before me was a catafalque, on which rested a corpse wrapped in funeral vestments. Around it were stationed soldiers who were acting as guards; and there was a throng of people, some gazing mournfully upon the corpse, whose face was covered, others weeping pitifully. 'Who is dead in the White House?' I demanded of one of the soldiers. 'The President,' was his answer; 'he was killed by an assassin!' Then came a loud burst of grief from the crowd, which awoke me from my dream. I slept no more that night; and although it was only a dream, I have been strangely annoyed by it ever since."[17]

John Wilkes Booth and Lewis Paine had been somewhere in that sea of faces beneath Lincoln's window. Booth had urged Paine to shoot Lincoln then and there, but Paine had refused. It was too risky. Afterwards, as the two conspirators walked around Lafayette Square, Booth said, "That is the last speech he will ever make." Capturing the president and taking him to Richmond was no longer possible, for the simple reason that Richmond had been lost, and so had Lee' army. "For six months we had worked to capture," Booth wrote in his diary, "but our cause being almost lost, something decisive and great must be done."[18]

In Alabama that day, Croxton finally gave up on his lost Kentucky scouts, pulled his brigade out of its camps at Northport and began marching back toward Elyton in the hope of getting back into contact with Wilson. Meanwhile, Wilson, marching east from Selma, learned from a Montgomery newspaper that Richmond had fallen on the second, and he had the news announced to his men. He felt sure that the war was almost over, and he issued new, more stringent, orders against looting. He had a trooper who was charged with stealing flogged that day and displayed to the entire corps as it rode on to the east.

The train carrying Jefferson Davis and his cabinet reached Greensborough that day, the eleventh, but their greeting was much different than it had been in Danville the week before. North Carolina had been the last and most reluctant state to seceed back in 1861, and Guilford County had voted heavily against secession. Only a few months before Davis's train arrived a mass meeting at Greensborough had declared that the war was lost and that the South should sue for peace. Residents of the area also feared the damage the Federals would wreak upon them when they came after the Confederate leaders. Davis could only find a tiny upstairs room in a modest home, and his landlord complained that he might as well burn down the place himself, for the Yankees surely would when they appeared. Most of the cabinet members had to use their railroad car for quarters and office, and their meals were cooked over an open fire built beside the tracks by a young slave.

Far to the east, Sherman's armies reached Smithfield that day and found that Johnston's Confederates were gone. The Rebels had retreated in haste to Raleigh, burning the bridges behind them. "The day was a warm and bright spring day," Jacob Cox remembered; "the columns had halted for the usual rest at the end of each hour's march; the men were sitting or lying upon the grass on either side the road, near Smithfield, when a staff officer was seen riding from the front, galloping and gesticulating in great excitement, the men cheering and cutting strange antics as he passed. When he came nearer he was heard to shout, 'Lee has surrendered!' The soldiers screamed out their delight; they flung their hats at him as he rode; they shouted, 'You're the man we've been looking for these three years!' They turned somersaults like over-excited children. They knew the long Civil War was virtually over."

The news was also welcomed in another way, Cox noted. "A Southern woman had come to the gate with her children, to ask of a corps commander the usual protection for her family while the column was passing, and as she caught the meaning of the wild shout, she looked down upon the wondering little ones, while tears streamed down her cheeks, saying to them only, 'Now father will come home.'"[19]

To the west, Stoneman's raiders reached Shallow Ford on the Yadkin River. A detachment of Rebels there was taken by surprise and routed, leaving a hundred muskets behind. Another party of Confederates was met farther south, near Mocksville. The Union advance guard charged them and dispersed them. At 8 p.m. the Federals bivouacked in the road twelve miles north of Salisbury, and at 12:30 a.m. on the twelfth the column was again in motion. Three miles down the road it came to the South Yadkin, a deep and rapid stream with only a few fords, but these were not disputed. There were a few Rebels on the north side of the stream, but they crossed over without meeting any resistance.

A quarter of a mile beyond the river the road forked. Both branches led to Salisbury. One battalion of the 12th Kentucky Cavalry followed the older eastern road while the rest of the division followed the other. Day was dawning when the head of the main column came upon Confederate pickets, and these were pushed back to a crossing of Grant's Creek, two miles from Salisbury. Rebel infantry and artillery was found to be stationed on the far side of the stream, and the flooring had been removed from the bridge. Trains could be heard leaving Salisbury on both railroads that ran through the town, one going down to South Carolina and the other west to Morganton.

Detachments were sent up and down stream to get on the Rebels' flank. As soon as the rattle of their carbines was heard across the stream, Miller's brigade advanced. The flooring of the bridge was found and soon put back in place and Miller charged across, followed shortly by Brown's brigade. The Confederates fell back, and their retreat soon turned into a rout. The Federals pursued until the remaining Rebels scattered and hid in the woods. Over 1,200 Confederates were captured out of about 3,000, as well as all 18 of their guns. Palmer's brigade rejoined the column from Salem that afternoon after destroying two large factories, 7,000 bales of cotton, cutting the railroad on both sides of Greensborough and capturing 400 Rebels. Now Palmer was ordered to destroy the railroad between Salisbury and Charlotte.

In Alabama that day, the twelfth, the mayor of Montgomery and nine prominent citizens rode out of the city at 3 a.m. under a flag of truce, and five miles to the west they came to Wilson's cavalry, camped along Catoma Creek. The Union commander was pleasantly surprised to learn that the Rebels were not going to defend the state capital and that these civilians had come to formally surrender the city. General Dan Adams and one of Forrest's division commanders, Brigadier General Abraham Buford, had planned to defend the city with a small force augmented with home guards, but Richard Taylor, the department commander, had told them not to. Before leaving, the Confederates had set fire to over 80,000 bales of cotton, but when the flames threatened to get out of hand the Rebels were soon fighting to put them out. An east wind finally came to their rescue, blowing the flames away from town. One witness said it was a "miracle that the city was not utterly destroyed."[20]

Wilson sent his escort, the 4th U.S. Cavalry, into Montgomery ahead of his corps. They established a provost guard headquarters at the capitol and formed a line in front of the building. Then, after again being admonished against straggling and looting, the main force rode in. "We put on all the style possible," one Federal wrote, "and marched according to regulations." A Montgomery teacher was suitably impressed. From behind her front yard fence she saw "host upon host of blue coats—looking brilliant with buttons and *'accouterments'*.... fine looking men—handsomely dressed—gleaming linen.... brass buttons, brilliant epaulets, sabres drawn and clashing, they made their entrance at full gallop. Generals Wilson and McCook at the head."[21]

Far to the south, General Granger and two Union divisions crossed Mobile Bay and at 10:30 a.m. on the twelfth landed at Catfish Point, about five miles below the city of Mobile. At noon the mayor and several citizens rode out in a carriage, using a large sheet as a flag of truce, and formally surrendered the city. That afternoon, Granger sent a regiment into town, and the stars and stripes were raised over the customhouse. But about sunset a small force of Rebels dashed in and captured several Union soldiers. So Granger sent in an entire brigade to occupy the entrenchments around the city. The main force of the Confederates from Mobile reached Meridian, Mississippi that day. "I had tried for more than two years," Grant later wrote, "to have an expedition sent against Mobile when its possession by us would have been of great advantage. It finally cost lives to take it when its possession was of no importance, and when, if left alone, it would within a few days have fallen into our hands without any bloodshed whatever."[22]

On the evening of the twelfth, Lincoln sent a telegram to General Weitzel at Richmond: "I have just seen Judge Campbell's letter to you of the 7th. He assumes as appears to me that I have called the insurgent Legislature of Virginia together, as the rightful Legislature of the State, to settle all differences with the United States. I have done no such thing. I spoke of them not as a Legislature, but as 'the gentlemen who have *acted* as the Legislature of Virginia in support of the rebellion.' I did this on purpose to exclude the assumption that I was recognizing them as a *rightful* body. I dealt with them as men having power *de facto* to do a specific thing, towit, 'to withdraw the Virginia troops, and other support from resistance to the General Government,' for which in the paper handed Judge Campbell I promised a specific equivalent, to wit, a remission to the people of the State, except in certain cases, the confiscation of their property. I meant this and no more. In as much however as Judge Campbell misconstrues this, and is still pressing for an armistice, contrary to the explicit statement of the paper I gave him; and particulary as Gen. Grant has since captured the Virginia troops, so that giving a consideration for their withdrawal is no longer applicable, let my letter to you, and the paper to Judge Campbell both be withdrawn or, countermanded, and he be notified of it. Do not now allow them to assemble; but if any have come, allow them safe-return to their homes."[23]

At Appomattox Court House, the morning of the twelfth brought the formal ceremony of surrender. With considerable labor the parole papers had all been made out and signed over the past two days. Joshua Chamberlain was in command of the Union forces who would receive the surrender. At his request he had been transferred to the command of the 3rd Brigade of the 1st Division of the 5th Corps, which contained most of the surviving veteran regiments of that corps, for he thought these men most deserved the honor of receiving the surrender. But perhaps he felt a little guilty for thus abandoning the two brigades he had been leading, for he had obtained permission from Griffin to include them as well. He formed the 3rd Brigade along the principal street of the little village from the bank of the Appomattox nearly to the court house, placed the 1st Brigade in line behind the 3rd and the 2nd across the street facing them.

"It was a chill gray morning," Chamberlain said, "depressing to the senses. But our hearts made warmth." In the nearby Confederate camps the Rebels could be seen taking down their tents and slowly forming ranks. "On they come, with the old swinging route step and swaying battle-flags. In the van, the proud Confederate ensign—the great field of white with canton of star-strewn cross of blue on a field of red, the regimental battle-flags with the same escutcheon following on, crowded so thick, by thinning out of men, that the whole column seemed crowned with red.... Instructions had been given; and when the head of each division column comes opposite our group, our bugle sounds the signal and instantly our whole line from right to left, regiment by regiment in succession, gives the soldier's salutation, from the 'order arms' to the old 'carry'—the marching salute. Gordon at the head of the column, riding with heavy spirit and downcast face, catches the sound of shifting arms, looks up, and, taking the meaning, wheels superbly, making with himself and his horse one uplifted figure, with profound salutation as he drops the point of his sword to the boot toe; then facing to his own command, gives word for his successive brigades to pass us with the same position of the manual,—honor answering honor. On our part not a sound of trumpet more, nor roll of drum; not a cheer, nor word nor whisper of vain-glorying, nor motion of man standing again at the order, but an awed stillness rather, and breath-holding, as if it were the passing of the dead!

"As each successive division masks our own, it halts, the men face inward towards us across the road, twelve feet away; then carefully 'dress' their line, each captain taking pains for the good appearance of his company, worn and half starved as they were. The field and staff take their positions in the intervals of regiments; generals in rear of their commands. They fix bayonets, stack arms; then, hesitatingly, remove cartridge-boxes and lay them down. Lastly,—reluctantly, with agony of expression,—they tenderly fold their flags, battle-worn and torn, blood-stained, heart-holding colors, and lay them down; some frenziedly rushing from the ranks, kneeling over them, clinging to them, pressing them to their lips with burning tears. And only the Flag of the Union greets the sky!.... "Thus, all day long, division after division comes and goes, surrendered arms being removed by our wagons in the intervals, the cartridge-boxes emptied in the street when the ammunition was found unservicable, our men meanwhile resting in place."[24]

Major Henry Kyd Douglas commanded the final Confederate brigade to surrender. He had asked Gordon for the honor of that position on the grounds that his brigade had fired the last shot before the truce that had led to the surrender. Even so, his time soon came. "A heavy line of Union soldiers stood opposite us in absolute silence," he later wrote. "As my decimated and ragged band with their bullet-torn banner marched to its place, someone in the blue line broke the silence and called for three cheers for the last brigade to surrender. It was taken up all about him by those who knew what it meant. But for us this soldierly generosity was more than we could bear. Many of the grizzled veterans wept like women, and my own eyes were as blind as my voice was dumb. Years have passed since then and time mellows memories, and now I almost forget the keen agony of that bitter day when I recall how that line of blue broke its respectful silence to pay such tribute, at Appomattox, to the little line in grey that had fought them to the finish and only surrendered because it was destroyed."[25]

Chamberlain spoke with several Confederate generals that day. "Their bearing was, of course, serious," he wrote, "their spirits sad. What various misgivings mingled in their mood we could not but conjecture. Levying war against the United States was serious business. But one certain impression was received from them all; they were ready to accept for themselves and for the Confederacy any fate our Government should dictate. Lincoln's magnanimity, as Grant's thoughtfulness, had already impressed them much. They spoke like brave men who mean to stand upon their honor and accept the situation."

"General," an unnamed corps commander told him, "this is deeply humiliating; but I console myself with the thought that the whole country will rejoice at this day's business."

"You astonish us," another said, "by your honorable and generous conduct. I fear we should not have done the same by you had the case been reversed."

"I will go home," a North Carolinian said, "and tell Joe Johnston we can't fight such men as you. I will advise him to surrender."

"I went into that cause," another unnamed Confederate officer said, "and I meant it. We had our choice of weapons and of ground, and we have lost. Now that is my flag," he said, pointing to the stars and stripes, "and I will prove myself as worthy as any of you."[26]

There was one, however, who remained a stubborn Rebel to the last. It was old Henry Wise. He was reprimanding his men in harsh and profane language for not properly responding to his orders. They replied that he was closer to the Yankees now than he'd ever been during a battle. He was causing such a fuss that the Federals asked the Confederates who he was, and when they learned that he had been the governor of Virginia when John Brown was hanged they began to heckle him with cries of "Who hanged John Brown?" and "shoot him, shoot him." One witness said, "As he sat on his horse, with his grey hair and beard, and tobacco juice trickling from his mouth, he resembled a withered old crab-apple tree."[27]

"I saw him moving restlessly about," Chamberlain said, "scolding his men and being answered back by them instead of ordering them. He seemed so disturbed in mind that I rode down the line to see if I could not give him a word of cheer."

"This promises well for our coming good will," Chamberlain told him; "brave men may become good friends."

"You're mistaken, sir," Wise turned and said. "You may forgive us but we won't be forgiven. There is a rancor in our hearts which you little dream of. We hate you, sir."

"Oh, we don't mind much about dreams," Chamberlain quietly replied, "nor about hates either. Those two lines of business are closed."

Perhaps a little sorry for his remarks, Wise noticed a pair of holes in the breast of Chamberlain's coat. "Those were ugly shots, General," he said in a milder tone. "Where did you get these?"

Chamberlain told him how he got them at the Quaker Road on the opening day of the final campaign.

"I suppose you think you did great things there," Wise broke in. "I was ordered to attack you and check your advance; and I did it too with a vim, till I found I was fighting three army corps, when I thought it prudent to retire."

Chamberlain informed him that there was no more than a single division present on the Union side that day.

"I know better," Wise replied; "I saws the flags myself."

"You saw the flags of three regiments," Chamberlain said; "steady eyes could see no more."

One of Wise's staff officers confirmed this, and for a moment the old Rebel subsided. But then he started up again on a new subject. "It's a pity you have no lawyers in your army," he said. "You don't know how to make out paroles. Who ever heard of paroles being signed by any but the parties paroled?"

"I tried to explain to him," Chamberlain wrote, "that this was a matter of mercy and humanity, for if we should keep all their men there till every individual could sign his parole, half of them would be dead of starvation before their turn came."

"Nonsense," Wise replied; "all that is *spargere voces;* every lawyer knows such a parole as this is a mere *brutum fulmen.*"

Chamberlain was no lawyer, but he was a scholar who knew his Latin. "Sir," he said, "if by brute thunderbolts you mean a pledged word to keep the peace accepted and adopted by the recipient of the favor, I don't believe your people need any lawyer to instruct them as to the word of honor."

Chamberlain started to turn away, and Wise called after him, "You go home, you take these fellows home. That's what will end the war."

"Don't worry about the end of the war," Chamberlain told him. "We are going home pretty soon, but not till we see you home."

"Home!" Wise exclaimed. "We haven't any. You have destroyed them. You have invaded Virginia, and ruined her. Her curse is on you."

"You shouldn't have invited us down here then," Chamberlain shot back. "We expected somebody was going to get hurt when we took up your challenge. Didn't you? People who don't want to get hurt, General, had better not force a fight on unwilling Yankees."

"By this time the thing grew comic," Chamberlain wrote. "The staff officers both in blue and gray laughed outright; and even his men looked around from their somber service and smiled as if they enjoyed the joke.

He turned away also to launch his 'brute thunderbolts,' not waiting to receive my thanks for instruction in Law and Latin....

"When all is over, in the dusk of evening, the long lines of scattered cartridges are set on fire, and the lurid flames wreathing the blackness of earthly shadows give an unearthly border to our parting.

"Then, stripped of every token of enmity or instrument of power to hurt, they march off to give their word of honor never to lift arms against the old flag again till its holders release them from their promise. Then, their ranks broken, the bonds that bound them fused away by forces stronger than fire, they are free at last to go where they will; to find their homes, now most likely stricken, despoiled by war."[28]

---

1. Foote, *The Civil War*, 3:906-907.
2. *Official Records*, 46:III:663-664.
3. Bishop, *The Day Lincoln Was Shot*, 50.
4. Brooks, *Washington in Lincoln's Time*, 223-225.
5. Porter, *Campaigning with Grant*, 490.
6. Grant, *Personal Memoirs*, 2:497.
7. Freeman, *R.E. Lee*, 4:152.
8. Rodick, *Appomattox*, 167.
9. Fitzhugh Lee, *General Lee* (New York, 1894), Fawcett 1961 paperback edition, 379.
10. Hanna, *Flight into Oblivion*, 20.
11. Ibid., 21-22.
12. Davis, *Sherman's March*, 247.
13. Porter, *Campaigning with Grant*, 493.
14. Grant, *The Personal Memoirs of Julia Dent Grant*, 153.
15. Brooks, *Washington in Lincoln's Time*, 225-227.
16. Bishop, *The Day Lincoln Was Shot*, 53-54.
17. Paul M. Angle, editor, *The Lincoln Reader* (New Brunswick, N.J., 1947), 520-522.
18. Tidwell, Hall and Gaddy, *Come Retribution*, 421.
19. Cox, *The March to the Sea, Franklin and Nashville*, 213- 214.
20. Jones, *Yankee Blitzkrieg*, 111.
21. Ibid., 112-113.
22. Grant, *Personal Memoirs*, 2:519.
23. Basler, ed., *The Collected Works of Abraham Lincoln*, 8:406-407.
24. Chamberlain, *The Passing of the Armies*, 194-200.
25. Henry Kyd Douglas, *I Rode With Stonewall*, 318-319.

26. Chamberlain, *The Passing of the Armies,* 200-201.
27. Rodick, *Appomattox,* 181-182.
28. Chamberlain, *The Passing of the Armies,* 201-203.

PART FIVE

ASSASSINATION AND FLIGHT

I am afraid all this rejoicing will be turned into mourning, and all this glory into sadness.

— Mary Surratt

CHAPTER THIRTY-EIGHT

Towards an Indefinite Shore

12 - 14 April 1865

Jefferson Davis and his cabinet met with generals Joe Johnston and Beauregard at Greensborough on the twelfth. Davis did not like either general very much, and the feeling was mutual. He seemed to be more interested in dispensing than obtaining information or assessments and opened the meeting with talk of raising a new army. They could round up deserters, conscript more men.

"It would be the greatest of human crimes," Johnston said stiffly, "for us to attempt to continue the war; for, having neither money nor credit, nor arms but those in the hands of our soldiers, nor ammunition but that in the cartridge-boxes, nor shops for repairing arms or fixing ammunition, the effect of our keeping the field would be, not to harm the enemy, but to complete the devastation of our country and ruin of its people."[1] He proposed that he open negotiations with Sherman.

Davis replied that he had already tried to negotiate a peace. Such an effort was bound to fail, for the Federals would insist on unconditional surrender. And its failure would have a demoralizing effect on both the soldiers and the people, neither of whom, he said, "had shown any disposition to surrender, or had any reason to suppose that their government contemplated abandoning its trust."[2] Secretary of War Breckinridge was expected to arrive soon, so Davis decided to adjourn the meeting until the next day.

Not long after the meeting broke up, young Captain Robert E. Lee, Jr., arrived. He had escaped from the Federal trap at Appomattox before the surrender. While he was with Davis a message for the president came from his father giving definite information on the surrender of his army. "He seemed quite broken at the moment," young Lee later remembered, "by this tangible evidence of the loss of his army and the misfortunes of its General. All of us, respecting his great grief, withdrew, leaving him with Captain Wood." John Taylor Wood, nephew of Davis's first wife and grandson of Zachary Taylor, was equally stunned. "I can hardly realize this overwhelming disaster," he wrote that night. "It crushes the hopes of nearly all."[3]

Breckinridge arrived late that night, conferred with Beauregard and Johnston, and agreed with them that further resistance was useless. The next day, the thirteenth, the cabinet met in Davis's tiny upstairs room, and Breckinridge presented his report on Lee's surrender. Postmaster General John Reagan described the conference as "most solemnly funereal."[4] Everyone except Davis and Secretary of State Benjamin seemed convinced that their cause was lost.

As soon as Johnston and Beauregard were admitted to the room, Davis began another exposition of his views. "Our late disasters are terrible," he said, "but I do not think we should regard them as fatal. I think we can whip the enemy yet, if our people will turn out. We must look at matters calmly, however, and see what is left to do. We haven't a day to lose." This statement was met by silence, so he turned to his senior commander. "We should like to hear your views, General Johnston."

"My views are, sir," Johnston said almost spitefully, "that our people are tired of the war, feel themselves whipped, and will not fight. Our country is overrun, its military resources greatly diminished.... My small force is melting away like snow before the sun and I am hopeless of recruiting it. We may, perhaps, obtain terms which we ought to accept."

Davis listened without change of expression, his eyes focused on a small piece of paper that he kept folding and unfolding over and over. "What do you say, General Beauregard?" he asked without looking up.

"I concur in all General Johnston has said," Beauregard replied quietly.

Still folding and refolding his piece of paper, Davis reminded them that he had made several attempts at negotiating terms but had been offered nothing but unconditional surrender.

"I think Sherman will offer terms," Johnston said. "I recommend that you exercise at once the only function of government still in your hands, and open negotiations."[5] He offered to ask Sherman for an interview. Everybody except Benjamin agreed that this was the thing to do.

"Well, sir," you can adopt this course," Davis conceded, "though I am not sanguine as to ultimate results."[6]

At Johnston's insistence, Davis outlined the terms he was willing to accept. Johnston could offer to disband the Confederate forces and Federal authority would be recognized, but only on the condition that the existing state governments be retained, that all political and property rights be respected and that there would be no punishment for having engaged in rebellion. No specific mention was made of slavery. Presumably that was what Davis meant by property rights.

Sherman's forces occupied Raleigh, the capital of North Carolina, that day. As they had approached the day before they had been met by a locomotive bringing four gentlemen under a flag of truce with a letter from Governor Zebulan Vance to Sherman asking for a personal interview to discuss peace terms. Now he sent them back "to assure the Governor and the people that the war was substantially over, and that I wanted the civil authorities to remain in the execution of their office till the pleasure of the President could be ascertained."[7] On the way back into Raleigh the peace commissioners saw smoke rising from the depot. Wheeler's Rebel cavalry had looted and burned it. "If God Almighty had yet in store another plague worse than all the others," Vance had said, "I am sure that it must have been a regiment of half-armed, half-disciplined Confederate cavalry."

One of the commissioners, a former governor of the state, pleaded with a dozen Rebel troopers they found looting shops along Fayetteville Street. "I've just come from Sherman," he said. "If there's no plundering and we don't resist him, he'll spare the city. Please go with your command. Stop this at once."

"Damn Sherman and the town, too," one Rebel replied. "We don't care a damn for either one."

The mayor of Raleigh, two councilmen, and a doctor met Kilpatrick's cavalry as it approached the city and asked the Federals to spare property and lives. After some bluster, Kilpatrick agreed. The first Union troopers to enter the town scared off all the looters except one. A lieutenant from Texas calmly sat his horse until the Federals were within a hundred yards, then shouted, "God damn you!" and emptied his revolver at them.[8] He failed to hit anyone, but scattered the leading files, then he wheeled and galloped away with a half-dozen Federals giving chase. He might have gotten away if his horse had not fallen at a corner. He got up and remounted but was caught and brought to Capitol Square. Kilpatrick had him hanged immediately in the back yard of a nearby house, without even giving him five minutes to write his wife.

When Sherman entered the city that morning he found that Governor Vance had fled in fear of arrest and imprisonment. He did find newspapers in Raleigh that gave him his first information about Stoneman's and Wilson's raids. He hoped that Sheridan would yet join him with his cavalry, which he needed to keep Johnston from slipping away from him. Meanwhile, he gave orders for the railroad to be repaired from the coast to Raleigh.

Grant, his wife and staff arrived at Washington on the morning of the thirteenth and took up residence at Willard's Hotel on Pennsylvania Avenue. Word soon spread through the city that the hero of the war was in town and dense crowds soon gathered outside the hotel. A short trip to the war department that morning proved a difficult undertaking. "His appearance in the street," Horace Porter wrote, "was a signal for an improvised reception, in which shouts of welcome rent the air, and the populace joined in a demonstration which was thrilling in its earnestness. He had the greatest difficulty in making his way over even the short distance between the hotel and the department. At one time it was thought he would have to take to a carriage as a means of refuge, but by the interposition of the police he finally reached his destination."[9] Quartermaster General Montgomery Meigs noted that Grant "was welcomed and thanked by the Secretary with much emotion."[10] The general and Stanton spent the afternoon conferring and then announced an end to the draft and all recruiting, curtailed the purchase of supplies, reduced the number of officers, and eased the restrictions on commerce with the South.

These indications of the imminent return of peace set off another round of celebrations in the capital that night. "Bands were everywhere heard playing triumphal strains," Porter wrote, "and crowds traversed the streets, shouting approval and singing patriotic airs. The general was the hero of the hour and the idol of the people; his name was on every lip; congratulations poured in upon him, and blessings were heaped upon him by all."[11]

During the afternoon Grant and Stanton were visited by Lincoln, and Grant received an invitation to take a drive around the city that evening with the Lincolns to view the many illuminations. The invitation made no mention of Mrs. Grant. He didn't want to go without her and probably knew that she wouldn't want to go with Mary Lincoln. But he was unsure of how to get out of it, so he consulted Stanton. The secretary was familiar with such problems. His wife also avoided Mrs. Lincoln whenever possible. He suggested the general plead the press of urgent business. Grant did work late that night, and when Stanton stopped to see him on his way home at about 6 p.m. the general told him he had succeeded in getting out of the invitation. However, now the President wanted him to go to the theater with him the next night. Stanton urged him not to go and to use his influence to keep Lincoln from going either. He said that he made it a personal rule to turn down all such invitations and that he and other cabinet members had often warned the president about these public appearances. They were not safe.

After Grant finished his work, he and Julia were entertained at the Stanton home that night. A band serenaded the party. Soldiers standing guard outside soon let curious citizens know that General Grant was inside, and before long a crowd gathered and clamored for a speech. Stanton said a few words from his steps, but the general, who hated speaking in public, only waved to the crowd. A drunk, who claimed to know Stanton, tried to mingle with the party, but he was sent away. He was later identified—perhaps mistakenly—as John Wilkes Booth's friend Michael O'Laughlin. The party broke up early so Stanton could work on a plan for the military government of the South that he wanted to present to the cabinet meeting the next day.

Booth had been depressed by the steady stream of bad news for the Confederate cause over the past few weeks, but his spirits suddenly soared when he learned that Grant was in town. He evidently surmised that the Lincolns were bound to do something to honor the hero of the hour, and he knew that Mrs. Lincoln was fond of theater parties on such occasions, since Congress objected to the expense of state dinners, fancy dress balls and the like. If Lincoln came to the theater in the next day or two, the young actor might still be able to reverse the fortunes of war. Booth probably reasoned that the dignitaries were far more likely to go to Grover's Theatre, which was staging the dramatic new *Aladdin, or the Wonderful Lamp,* than to Ford's, which had a mediocre old comedy, *Our American Cousin.* He visited Grover's that day and learned from the manager that the Lincolns would be invited to attend the next night, the fourteenth. That would be the fourth anniversary of the fall of Fort Sumter, and in addition to the play there would be a special celebration honoring the return of the Stars and Stripes to the remains of that historic fort in Charleston harbor that same day. There would be fireworks out front, a "Grand Oriental Spectacle," and a reading of a new poem, "The Flag of Sumter." It would be a great evening. Booth asked the manager to reserve a box for him.

He spent the cool, starry evening of the 13th riding around Washington on a rented horse to alert David Herold, Lewis Paine, George Atzerodt and perhaps others. He ordered Atzerodt to move out of the four-or-more-men-to-a-room Pennsylvania House and take a room at the much better Kirkwood House, where Vice President Johnson had a two-room suite.

Booth hoped to completely decapitate the Federal government. When Lincoln and Grant came to the theater, Booth would kill them. There is some evidence that John Surratt was to get Grant. Meanwhile, Atzerodt was to attack Johnson, and Herold, evidently, was initially assigned to assist him. With the president and vice president both dead, the president pro tempore of the Senate would act as president until the electoral college could choose a new one, but Congress was not in session. It would be the secretary of state's job to get this process going. Therefore, Paine was assigned to finish off the already injured Seward. Since Paine always got hopelessly lost in the urban complexity of Washington, Herold would have to act as his guide. If all went according to plan, the Union would have neither a president nor a general-in-chief for weeks.

Whether the Confederate government, or any part of it, knew that Booth was changing the plan from capturing to killing Lincoln is not known. Nor is it known for certain that the change was Booth's idea. But, except for that one change, the plot had almost certainly originated in Richmond. And even in an attempt to capture the president and others there was always a very great chance that the victim(s) would put up an fight and be killed in the struggle.

Down at Charleston harbor at noon the next day, Good Friday, 14 April 1865, several shiploads of Union dignitaries looked on as Brigadier General Robert Anderson raised over what little was left of Fort Sumter the very same flag he had hauled down from there exactly four years before, when he had been a major in the regular army and commander of its garrison. "I thank God that I have lived to see this day," he said before hauling on the lanyards to hoist the banner. "It went up slowly," a young woman who was present remembered long afterwards, "and hung limp against the staff, a weather-beaten, frayed, and shell-torn old flag, not fit for much more work, but when it had crept clear of the shelter of the walls a sudden breath of wind caught it, and it shook its folds and flew straight out above us, while every soldier and sailor instinctively saluted.

"I don't know just what we did next, but I remember looking on either side of me and seeing my father's eyelids brimming over and that Admiral Dahlgren's lips were trembling. I think we stood up, somebody started 'The Star-Spangled Banner,' and we sang the first verse, which is all that most people know. But it did not make much difference, for a great gun was fired close to us from the fort itself, followed, in obedience to the President's order, 'by a national salute from every fort and battery that fired upon Fort Sumter.' The measured, solemn booming came from Fort Moultrie, from the batteries on Sullivan and Folly Islands, and from Fort Wagner.... When the forts were done it was the turn of the fleet, and all our warships from the largest.... down to the smallest monitor, fired and fired in regular order until the air was thick and black with smoke and one's ears ached with the overlapping vibrations."[12]

Wilson's Union cavalry departed Montgomery, Alabama on the fourteenth, heading eastward toward Georgia. During their two days at Montgomery, the Federals had destroyed a niter works, some foundries and small shops, a locomotive and twenty cars, the depots of two railroads, three steamboats loaded with food, and an arsenal containing 20,000 small arms. In a letter written to Canby the night before, to be carried to Mobile by a sergeant from his escort, he explained: "My orders were to make a demonstration toward Selma and Tuscaloosa, and then to act as I might think best. Having destroyed those places and everything of value between here and the Tennessee River, and in consideration of General Grant's great victory and the capture of Richmond, as well as of your capacity to effectually dispose of the rebels in this State, I have determined to move at once and rapidly toward Columbus and Macon. If I can destroy the arsenals at those places the rebel armies must fall to pieces for want of munitions. There are but few troops to resist my march. My command is in splendid condition—every man mounted, plenty of ammunition, and in splendid spirits."[13] The Federals covered about forty miles that day, driving a small force of Rebels before them. Each time the Confederates tried to make a stand the 1st Wisconsin Cavalry routed them. About a hundred Rebels had been captured by the end of the day.

In North Carolina, Sherman's forces continued to advance on the fourteenth, although he personally remained at Raleigh. Kilpatrick reported by telegraph that morning from Durham's Station, 26 miles up the railroad, that the Rebels had, under a flag of truce, presented him with a message from Joe Johnston addressed to Sherman. It reached him later that day and said: "The results of the recent campaign in Virginia have changed the relative military condition of the belligerents. I am therefore induced to address you in this form in the inquiry, whether, in order to stop the further effusion of blood and devastation of property, you are willing to make a temporary suspension of active operations, and to communicate to Lieutenant-General Grant, commanding the Armies of the United States, the request that he will take like action in regard to other armies; the object being to permit the civil authorities to enter into the needful arrangements to terminate the existing war."[14]

Sherman sent an aide up to Durham's Station with his answer, which turned the subject from negotiation between civil authorities to the surrender of one army to the other: "I have this moment received your communication of this date. I am fully empowered to arrange with you any terms for the suspension of hostilities as between the armies commanded by you and those commanded by myself, and will be willing to confer with you to that end. I will limit the advance of my main column to-morrow to Morrisville, and the cavalry to the University, and expect that you will also maintain the present position of your forces until each has notice of a failure to agree. That a basis of action may be had, I undertake to abide by the same terms and conditions as were made by Generals Grant and Lee at Appomattox Court-House, on the 9th instant, relative to our two armies; and, furthermore, to obtain from General Grant an order to suspend the movement of any troops from the direction of Virginia. General Stoneman is under my command, and my order to suspend any devastation or destruction contemplated by him. I will add that I really desire to save the people of North Carolina the damage they would sustain by the march of this army through the central or western parts of the State."[15]

At the White House on 14 April, President Lincoln worked in his office until 8 a.m., then had breakfast with his son Robert, who gave him a personal account of Grant's pursuit of Lee and the latter's surrender. William H. Crook, Lincoln's bodyguard, came on duty at 8 a.m. and relieved the night guard, who was stationed in a chair in the hall outside the Lincolns' bedroom. Crook stashed the chair in a closet and turned off the gas jets in the corridor. He was feeling less uneasy about the president's safety now that the war was all but over, but he went downstairs and made sure the military guards were at their stations at the front gate, the front door, and the door leading to the president's office. By then the night man was standing on the front portico and laughing at the antics of some of the drunken celebrants beyond the fence. Crook joined him and later wrote, "Everybody is celebrating. The kind of celebration depends on the kind of person. It is merely a question of whether the intoxication is mental or physical. A stream of callers comes in to congratulate the President, to tell how loyal they have been, and how they have always been sure that he would be victorious."[16]

One of the first of Lincoln's visitors that day was Schuyler Colfax, speaker of the House of Representatives, who had ambitions to join Lincoln's cabinet. Whether he came to discuss his chances—it was common knowledge that Stanton wanted to quit—or to ask Lincoln not to try to decide on a policy for reconstructing the Southern states without calling Congress into special session is not known; perhaps both. But it was noticed that Colfax left with a spring in his step, a smile on his face, and a pleasant greeting for those still waiting to see the president.

Another visitor was John P. Hale, former senator from New Hampshire and newly appointed ambassador to Spain. Hale, who had been critical of the administration in the past, had recently been defeated for reelection, and he was doubly grateful for the job. He had recently told friends that he was glad to be leaving the country, if only to get his daughter away from a young actor she was infatuated with, named John Wilkes Booth.

After Hale, came John Cresswell, the man generally credited with keeping Maryland from seceding back in 1861. Lincoln seemed genuinely glad to see him and met him with a warm handclasp.

"Cresswell, old fellow," he said, "everything is bright this morning. The war is over. It has been a tough time, but we have lived it out—or some of us have," he added, dropping his voice. However, the gloomy thought of all those who had died to make victory possible soon passed. "But it is over," he said. "We are going to have good times now, and a united country."

After further small talk, Cresswell finally came to the point of his visit. A friend of his had gone south and joined the Confederate army and was now a prisoner of war. From his pocket, Cresswell produced affidavits attesting to the friend's good character. "I know he acted like a fool," the Marylander said, "but he is my friend and a good fellow. Let him out, give him to me, and I will be responsible for him."

Lincoln studied one of the affidavits soberly and said, "Cresswell, you make me think of a lot of young folks who once started out Maying. To reach their destination, they had to cross a shallow stream, and did so by means of an old flat boat. When they came to return, they found to their dismay that the old scow had disappeared.

"They were in sore trouble and thought over all manner of devices for getting over the water, but without avail. After a time, one of the boys proposed that each fellow should pick up the girl he liked best and wade over with her. The masterly proposition was carried out, until all that were left upon the island was a little short chap and a great, long, gothic-built elderly lady. Now, Cresswell, you are trying to leave me in the same predicament. You fellows are all getting your own friends out of this scrape, and you will succeed in carrying off one after another until nobody but Jeff Davis and myself will be left on the island, and then I won't know what to do. How should I feel? How should I look lugging him over? I guess the way to avoid such an embarrassing situation it to let them all out at once."[17]

Several more visitors came in after Cresswell. When two Southerners sent word in that they would like to have passes to go to Richmond, Lincoln sent a note out to them: "No pass is necessary now to authorize anyone to go to & return from Richmond. People go & return just as they did before the war."[18]

During a short lull, he sent a messenger over to Ford's Theatre on Tenth Street to tell the management there that he would like to have the state box for that evening's performance and to inform them that General Grant would be in the party. The messenger reached the theater at 10:30 a.m., and James Ford, the business manager, was very glad to receive the news. His older brother John, the owner, had gone to Richmond to look after some relatives and left him in charge. This was Good Friday, which was traditionally the worst night of the year for show business, and Grover's Theatre would be drawing away even more customers than usual with its special celebrations. So Ford was expecting an almost empty house for the final performance of *Our American Cousin.* The attendance of the president would be a boost to sales at any time, but having General Grant, the hero of the hour, come on such a night, that was a real coup. After passing the news to his younger brother, Harry, and the actors who were rehearsing, he hurried over to the Treasury building to get some flags for decorating the state box.

Not long after he left, John Wilkes Booth came in to pick up his mail, which he always had sent to him at Ford's. Booth was chatting with young Harry Clay Ford when the stage carpenter came in to see what Ford wanted him for. Harry told him that Lincoln and Grant were coming that night and asked him to have the stage hands remove the partition between boxes 7 and 8, converting them into the state box. Booth concealed his surprise and went out and sat down on the big granite step in front of the theater and opened his mail. A passerby noticed him laughing heartily at something he was reading. As he was returning from the Treasury building with his flags, James Ford met Booth near the corner of Tenth and E Street. He stopped his buggy and the two men chatted a while. Booth said he would try to attend that night's performance but could not promise. Ford went on to the theater, where he wrote a special notice for the newspapers announcing the presence of Lincoln and Grant as honored guests at that evening's performance.

As soon as Grant awoke that morning, his wife asked him if they could go home to Burlington, New Jersey that day and see the other children. (Their son Jesse was with them in Washington.) The general promised to try, but he had work to do. For one thing, he was supposed to attend a cabinet meeting that day. Soon a note arrived from Lincoln putting off the meeting from 9 a.m. to 11, and Grant said this postponement would make it even harder for him to leave Washington that day, but he would try his best. Then he went off to work at the War Department.

About noon, there was a knock at the door of the Grants' hotel room. Julia opened the door and found a man there wearing a light-colored corduroy coat and trousers and a rather shabby hat of the same color. Julia was startled by his appearance, for she had expected it would be the bellboy with cards from potential visitors.

"What do you want?" she asked.

The man blushed and bowed. "This is Mrs. Grant?" he asked.

She bowed in assent.

"Mrs. Lincoln sends me, Madam, with her compliments," he said, "to say she will call for you at exactly eight o'clock to go to the theater."

Julia did not like either the looks of the messenger or the content of his message. "The former savored of discourtesy and the latter seemed like a command," she later wrote.

"You may return to Mrs. Lincoln with my compliments," she said with some feeling, "and say I regret that as General Grant and I intend leaving the city this afternoon, we will not, therefore, be here to accompany the President and Mrs. Lincoln to the theater."

The man hesitated, then said, "Madam, the papers announce that General Grant will be with the President tonight at the theater."

"You deliver my message to Mrs. Lincoln as I have given it to you," Julia told him. "You may go now."

He smiled and turned away.

"I have thought since," she later wrote, "that this man was one of the band of conspirators in that night's sad tragedy, and that he was not sent by Mrs. Lincoln at all. I am perfectly sure that he, with three others, one of them Booth himself, sat opposite me and my party at luncheon that day."[19]

At the White House, the cabinet members began to gather for the 11 a.m. meeting, and Lincoln met them with jovial greetings. He stood to shake hands with Grant when the general came in, and the cabinet ministers broke into applause. The president and the general sat near a window, where the sunlight streamed in, and chatted while they waited for the late-comers to arrive. When young Frederick Seward came in he informed the president that his father was improving slowly. When Attorney General James Speed arrived, Lincoln asked everyone to take their places around the cabinet table. They were all there but Stanton, who was often late.

The president sat sideways at the head of the table so he could cross his long legs, and asked Grant if there was any news from Sherman. The general answered softly that there had been none when he left the War Department. Lincoln said he thought there would be news soon, favorable news, for he had had a dream the night before; the same dream that he had often had preceding important events. Navy Secretary Welles asked him what this remarkable dream could be and was told that it concerned his own element, the water, and "that he seemed to be in some singular, indescribable vessel, and that he was moving with great rapidity towards an indefinite shore; that he had this dream preceding Sumter, Bull Run, Antietam, Gettysburg, Stone River, Vicksburg, Wilmington, etc. General Grant said that Stone River was certainly no victory, and he knew of no great results which followed from it. The President said however that might be, his dream preceded that fight."

"I had this strange dream again last night," Lincoln continued, "and we shall, judging from the past, have great news very soon. I think it must be from Sherman. My thoughts are in that direction, as are most of yours."[20]

The subject then turned to reconstruction of the South. Frederick Seward said he had talked over the subject with his father before leaving home that morning, and, while it was still painful for the secretary to talk, he had made a number of suggestions, which the young assistant now passed on. Mainly they concerned the various Federal departments resuming their normal functions in the Southern states, including the appointment of judges and opening of Federal courts, and he emphasized that care should be taken not to molest private citizens or interfere with local authorities. Others had suggestions, and Lincoln listened, making comments from time to time. Stanton read the plan he had been working on and then promised to have copies made for all of them for criticism and suggestions, and Lincoln asked them to consider the subject carefully.

They also discussed what to do with the Confederate leaders, if they were caught. Postmaster General Dennison said he supposed that Lincoln would not be sorry for them to escape the country. The president agreed but added that they should be closely followed to make sure of their going. It was providential, he said, the rebellion was crushed just as Congress has adjourned, and there were none of the disturbing elements of that body to hinder and embarrass them. If they were wise and discreet they could reanimate the states and get their governments in successful operation, with order prevailing and the Union reestablished, before Congress reconvened in December. He said he hoped there would be no persecution of the Confederate leaders. "No one need expect [me] to take any part in hanging or killing these men, even the worst of them," Welles remembered him saying. "Frighten them out of the country, open the gates," he said, throwing up his arms in a shooing motion, "let down the bars, scare them off, enough lives have been sacrificed; we must extinguish our resentments if we expect harmony and union."[21]

Therein lay one of the difficulities for the Union cause: In their efforts to separate the two sections, the Confederate leaders could be as violent and vindictive as their consciences would allow; but in their efforts to reunite the country the Union leaders had to both overcome the Confederacy's military resistance and yet win, to some degree, the loyalty of the Southern people. For, even if they did not want to be, they were citizens of the one common country. Lincoln had seen this from the start. Many other Union leaders never did see it. Lincoln put it very well in a note written to Stanton the year before: "In using the strong hand, as now compelled to do, the government has a difficult duty to perform. At the very best, it will by turns do both too little and too much. It can properly have no motive of revenge, no purpose to punish merely for punishment's sake. While we must, by all available means, prevent the overthrow of the government, we should avoid planting and cultivating too many thorns in the bosom of society."[22]

The meeting eventually drew to a close, and Grant walked over to the president and thanked him for letting him attend. Then, with evident embarrassment, he brought up the subject of the invitation to attend the theater. He said that Mrs. Grant would be greatly disappointed if they did not leave that evening to go home and see the children. Lincoln replied that there would be plenty of time for that, but the public would dearly love to get a first-hand look at the man who had won the war. Just then, Horace Porter brought the general a note that Julia had written after receiving Mrs. Lincoln's invitation. It said she hoped the general would not delay their departure on the 6 p.m. train. That was just what Grant needed to get out of an embarrassing situation. He showed the note to Lincoln and said he really could not dissappoint Julia. The president went off for a late lunch with his wife and no-doubt informed her of Grant's decision.

Grant sent word to Julia to have her trunks ready and for her and Jesse to have their lunch. He would complete his work at the War Department, and if possible they would take the late train to Philadelphia. "It was in obedience to this that I was at late luncheon with Mrs. Rawlins and her little girl and my Jesse," Julia wrote, "when these men came in and sat opposite to us. They all four came in together. I thought I recognized in one of them the messenger of the morning, and one, a dark, pale man, played with his soup spoon, sometimes filling it and holding it half-lifted to his mouth, but never tasting it. This occurred many times. He also seemed very intent on what we and the children were saying. I thought he was crazy."

Julia turned to Mrs. Rawlins and said, "Be careful, but observe the men opposite to us and tell me what you think."

"Since you call my attention," she answered after a couple of minutes, "I believe there is something peculiar about them."

"I believe they are part of Mosby's guerrillas," Julia said, "and they have been listening to every word we have said. Do you know, I believe there will be an outbreak tonight or soon. I just feel it, and am glad I am going away tonight."[23]

Booth visited the Surratt boarding house that afternoon and left a pair of French field glasses with Mary Surratt, John's mother. She was instructed to deliver them to John Lloyd at the Surratt tavern at Surrattsville in southern Maryland right away and to tell Lloyd to have the weapons that were concealed at the tavern ready to be picked up that night. Louis Weichmann, who had been given the afternoon off from his War Department job because it was Good Friday, hired a buggy and drove her down. She told him she was going to see a man about some money he owed her. Weichmann was curious about the package she carried, but she did not tell him what was in it. About halfway to the tavern, they saw some Union cavalrymen resting beside the road. Mrs. Surratt hailed an old man and asked him what those soldiers were doing there.

"They are pickets," he replied.

She asked him if they stayed out all night, and he said they were usually called in about 8 p.m.

"I'm glad to know that," she said.[24]

President Lincoln left the White House for a brief visit to the War Department building next door that afternoon, leaving word for Mrs. Lincoln that when he returned he would be ready to take a drive with her. Crook, the bodyguard, walked with him, and out on Pennsylvania Avenue he had to clear a path through some rowdy, drunken celebrants. After they were past them, Lincoln said, "Crook, do you know, I believe there are men who want to take my life. And I have no doubt they will do it."

Crook was surprised. Lincoln had always deprecated the idea when others brought it up. "Why do you think so, Mr. President?" he asked.

"Other men have been assassinated," he said, his voice trailing off.

"I hope you are mistaken, Mr. President," Crook said.

"I have perfect confidence," Lincoln said, "in those who are around me—in every one of you men. I know no one could do it and escape alive. But if it is to be done, it is impossible to prevent it."[25]

At the War Department, Lincoln asked Stanton if there was any news from Sherman. Stanton shook his head. He too was waiting impatiently to hear from North Carolina. Lincoln then said he was looking for someone to go to the theater with him that night. Since neither Grant nor Stanton would go, he wanted to take Major Eckert, the supervisor of military telegraphs, a big man who looked like a policeman. Stanton said he had important work for Eckert to do that night. Lincoln said he thought highly of Eckert as a bodyguard. Once he had seen him demonstrate the poor quality of a shipment of iron pokers by breaking them over his arm one after another. Stanton insisted that Eckert could not be spared and counseled the president against going to the theater at all. Things were still too unsettled. The president gave up on Eckert but not on going himself. He said he would find someone else.

On the way back to the White House, Lincoln talked to Crook about the theater party. "It has been advertised that we will be there, and I cannot disappoint the people," he said. "Otherwise I would not go. I do not want to go." Crook thought that was strange, knowing how much Lincoln usually enjoyed going to the theater. At the White House door, the president turned to face him and said, "Good-bye, Crook."

Always before, the guard remembered, it had been, "Good-night, Crook."[26]

Assistant Secretary of War Charles Dana, who had returned to Washington with General Grant, received a telegram from the provost marshal in Portland, Maine that afternoon that said, "I have positive information that Jacob Thompson will pass through Portland to-night, in order to take a steamer for England. What are your orders?" One of Dana's duties was to receive reports from officers of the secret service throughout the country. Jacob Thompson had been the secretary of the interior in the Buchanan administration and an ardent secessionist. For several months he had been one of the senior Confederate agents in Canada and had organized several clandestine operations, including the raid on St. Albans, Vermont back in September and the attempt to burn New York City in November. He probably had a hand in Booth's plan to capture Lincoln and might even have known that the plan had been changed from kidnapping to assassination. Dana took the telegram and read it to Stanton.

"Arrest him!" was the secretary's immediate response. But as Dana was going out the door he added, "No, wait; better go over and see the President."

It was 4 p.m. by then, and Lincoln's work was done for the day. Dana went to the president's office but there did not seem to be anyone there. As he was turning to leave, Lincoln called to him from a little side room, where he was washing his hands: "Halloo, Dana! What is it? What's up?"

Dana read him the telegram.

"What does Stanton say?" the president asked. "He says arrest him, but that I should refer the question to you."

"Well," Lincoln said slowly, as he dried his hands, "no, I rather think not. When you have got an elephant by the hind leg, and trying to run away, it's best to let him go."

Dana returned to the War Department and repeated the president's words to Stanton.

"Oh, stuff!" the secretary said.[27]

John Wilkes Booth rented a spirited mare from Pumphrey's stable near the Mall and rode her up Pennsylvania Avenue to Grover's Theatre, hitched her to a post, and went inside. No one was in the manager's office, so he walked upstairs to Deery's tavern for a drink. When he returned, the manager was still out, so he sat at his desk, took some paper, and wrote a letter to the editor of the *National Intelligencer* justifying his crime in advance. He signed it, put it in his pocket, and left. According to the only other person who ever read the letter, he signed it "J. W. Booth—Paine—Atzerodt —Herold."[28]

Riding up Pennsylvania Avenue, Booth headed back toward Ford's Theatre, waving and tipping his hat to friends along the way. At 14th Street he saw John Matthews, an actor whom he had once tried to enlist in his plot. Although he had called Matthews a coward for refusing, he stopped now to shake his hand and talk a minute. He dismounted, slapped some dust off his black suit, and asked Matthews to do him a favor. He took the letter out of his pocket and asked if he would deliver it for him. He would do it himself but he expected to be out of town the next day. Matthews said he could do it right now if Booth wanted, but Booth said no, it must be delivered tomorrow, before noon if possible. Matthews said to consider it done and asked what was so important about it. Booth wasn't listening. He was watching a bedraggled set of men marching up Pennsylvania Avenue.

"Who are those men?" he asked.

"They look like officers of Lee's army," Matthews said. Booth mounted his mare. "Good God!" he said as he turned to ride away. "Matthews, I have no country left!"[29]

Booth rode up to 15th Street but turned and started back slowly as a carriage pulled away from Willard's Hotel with two cavalrymen riding behind it. The outriders were a dead give away that the carriage held somebody important.

The wife of Brigadier General Daniel Rucker, commander of the quartermaster's depot in Washington, had brought her carriage to take the Grants to the train station. Mrs. Rucker and Julia, in their voluminous dresses, took up the back seat, so the general sat up front with the driver. Booth galloped past them and peered into the carriage.

"That is the same man who sat down at the lunch-table near me," Julia told Grant. "I don't like his looks."[30]

Booth went on for about twenty yards and then turned and rode back past the carriage again, this time at a walk, and examined Grant so closely as to cause him to draw back.

"General," Mrs. Rucker said after Booth passed, "everyone wants to see you."

"Yes," Grant replied, "but I do not care for such glances. These are not friendly at least."[31]

Around 5 p.m., after talking with a few more visitors, the president left the White House again for a carriage ride with Mrs. Lincoln. She had asked if he wanted to take someone else along, but he said he preferred they go by themselves. Of course, there was the driver sitting up front, and two cavalrymen rode along behind.

The president was in a good mood, and passers-by heard Mrs. Lincoln laughing. "Dear husband," she said. "You almost startle me by your great cheerfulness."

"And well may I feel so," Lincoln replied. "Mother, I consider that this day the war has come to a close." He patted her hand and added, "We must both be cheerful in the future. Between the war, and the loss of our darling Willie, we have both been very miserable."

Mary Lincoln stopped laughing. The death of their middle son was still a very touchy subject with her. They rode in silence for a while, past the capitol building, past marching soldiers and Confederate prisoners. But soon they regained their buoyant mood. He talked about what they might do after his second term ended: maybe a trip to Europe, then perhaps return to Springfield and resume his law practice. It would be nice, he thought, to have a prairie farm along the Sangamon River.

"I never felt so happy in my life," he told her.

"Don't you remember feeling just so before our little boy died?" she asked.[32]

Mary Surratt and Louis Weichmann arrived at the tavern at Surrattsville only to find that the man who owed her money was not there. She asked Weichmann to write a letter to him for her. Although she claimed that the purpose of her trip to Surrattsville was to see this man, who lived farther south, there is no evidence that he was ever told to meet her there. And she could have written to him from Washington.

John Lloyd, who rented the tavern from Mrs. Surratt, was not there either, but she waited for him, and at 5:30 p.m. he returned from a day at court and a card game. Evidently he was drunk, which apparently was his usual state. He staggered as he carried a bag of oysters to the tavern and said he felt sick. Mrs. Surratt gave him the package containing Booth's field glasses and told him, according to Lloyd's later testimony "to have those shooting-irons ready; there will be parties here to-night who will call for them."[33] Weichmann did not hear this conversation. According to Mrs. Surratt, she only told Lloyd to have those "things" ready, and claimed not to know the things in question were guns. The difference between the two terms would cost Mary Surratt her life.

In Washington, Booth went back to Ford's Theatre about 6 p.m., approaching it from the alley, and asked Ned Spangler, a friendly stagehand who had once worked for his father, to take care of his mare.

This done, he took Spangler and two other stagehands, the only men in the theater at that hour except the ticket-seller out front, across the alley to Taltavul's tavern for a drink. There Booth learned that Davy Herold had been looking for him. He bought a bottle of whiskey for the three stagehands and told them to drink up; he had an errand to do.

Booth went back through the alley and an underground passage up onto the stage, where he picked up a pine board that had held a music stand. He carried this upstairs to the dress circle and around to where there was a cane chair beside a white door that opened inward onto a small hallway leading to the state box. He tried to brace the board between the inside of the door and the rear wall of the box but found the board was about half an inch too long. So he gouged plaster from the wall to make a niche that would fit the board. That night, after he entered, he could place the board in the niche and it would hold the door shut, so that nobody could follow him in. He put the board in a dark corner nearby and then drilled a small peephole in the thin inner door to the state box. After cleaning up the shavings from the door and the plaster from the wall, he went back downstairs and out the back, got his mare, and rode to the National Hotel for dinner and some rest.

At about 6:30 p.m., Davy Herold came to George Atzerodt's room at the Kirkwood House just as the latter was about to leave. Herold left a pistol, a knife, and a black coat in the room, and later the two men went to the Herndon House, at the corner of 9th and F streets, where Lewis Paine had a room.

William Crook, Lincoln's bodyguard, had gone off duty at 4 p.m., but it was 7 p.m. before his relief showed up. This was John F. Parker, another member of the Washington police department, who, unlike Crook, was undependable, lazy, and constantly in trouble with his superiors. Crook held his temper and did not bawl the man out for being three hours late, but merely briefed him on the events of the day. After supper he had walked the president over to the War Department again. Stanton and Major Eckert had gone home by then, but telegrapher David Bates and newspaperman Noah Brooks had been there, and they had said there was still no news from Sherman. Now Crook informed Parker that the president and Mrs. Lincoln were going to the theater at 8 p.m. They had arranged to take a young couple with them, an army major and his fiancee, so there would be no room for Parker in the carriage. Crook suggested that he precede the president by about fifteen minutes and wait for him at the theater. He asked Parker if he was armed, and the man patted his pocket. About then,

Lincoln appeared at his office door, and Crook said, "Good night, Mr. President."

Again Lincoln said, "Good-by, Crook."[34]

On the way back to Washington from Surrattsville, Louis Weichmann made some remark to Mrs. Surratt about Booth appearing to be out of work and asked when he would act again.

"Booth is done acting," she replied, and "is going to New York very soon, never to return." She turned and added, "Yes, and Booth is crazy on the subject, and I am going to give him a good scolding the next time I see him."

Weichmann later remembered that she was very anxious to be home by 9 p.m., saying that she had an appointment to meet some gentleman at that hour. He asked if it was Booth, but she made no reply. When they topped a hill about a mile from the city they could see it all swimming in light down below.

"I am afraid all this rejoicing will be turned into mourning," she said, "and all this glory into sadness."

Weichmann asked her what she meant, "and she replied that after sunshine there was always a storm, and that the people were too proud and licentious, and that God would punish them."[35]

As they drove past the Capitol they heard music in the distance and then saw a procession of arsenal employees turn from 7th Street into Pennsylvania Avenue and parade up toward the White House. They got back to the boarding house about 8:30 p.m., and Weichmann returned the rented horse and buggy to the stable. Then, over a late supper, Mrs. Surratt showed him a letter she had received from her son, John. It was dated Montreal, 12 April 1865. It had not been delivered by mail but by a young schoolteacher who was a friend of the family. There was nothing special in the letter except for one odd reference. "I believe," Weichmann later wrote, "it was purposely shown to me at that time. A queer circumstance connected with it was that the writer referred to me having driven his mother into the country on the previous Tuesday, April 11. This he did in a jesting manner. Now, the hotel register of St. Lawrence Hall showed that John Harrison Surratt, under the assumed name of John Harrison, arrived there on the 6th of April 1865, left on the 12th for the United States, and returned on the 18th. Now, how could he in Canada on the 12th of April know about the drive to Surrattsville on the 11th unless he had been informed to that effect by telegraph?"[36]

While they were still eating, someone came to the front door and rang the bell. Since there was no servant in the house at the time,

Weichmann offered to answer it, but Mrs. Surratt insisted on going herself. Her 9 p.m. appointment had arrived. Weichmann heard the door open and footsteps move into the front parlor and then heard the visitor leave, but he never saw him. He later became convinced that it was Booth, checking to make sure that the guns and field glasses had been delivered to the tavern and to learn if the road was clear for his escape.

After finishing his supper, Weichmann went into the parlor. He was surprised to find that Mrs. Surratt was no longer cheerful. He thought she seemed agitated and restless, so he asked her what was the matter. She replied that she was nervous and did not feel well. Then she asked him which way the torchlight procession was going that they had seen on Pennsylvania Avenue. He told her it was going toward the White House, presumably to serenade the president.

"She said," Weichmann later remembered, "she would like to know, as she was very much interested in it. She had a pair of prayer beads in her hands and once she asked me to pray for her intentions. I answered her by saying that I did not know what her intentions were. She then said to pray for them anyhow."[37]

---

1. Hanna, *Flight to Oblivion,* 36.
2. Foote, *The Civil War,* 3:967.
3. Davis, *The Long Surrender,* 68.
4. Foote, *The Civil War,* 3:968.
5. Davis, *The Long Surrender,* 70-71.
6. Foote, *The Civil War,* 3:969.
7. Sherman, *Memoirs,* 833.
8. Davis, *Sherman's March,* 255.
9. Porter, *Campaigning with Grant,* 496.
10. Benjamin P. Thomas and Harold M. Hyman, *Stanton: The Life and Times of Lincoln's Secretary of War* (New York, 1962), 356.
11. Porter, *Campaigning with Grant,* 496.
12. Mary Cadwalader Jones, "The Stars and Stripes Are Raised Over Fort Sumter," in *The Blue and the Gray,* 1149.
13. *Official Records,* 49:II:347.
14. Ibid., 47:III:206-207.
15. Ibid., 47:III:207.
16. Bishop, *The Day Lincoln Was Shot,* 108.
17. Ibid., 115-116.
18. Basler, ed., *The Collected Works of Abraham Lincoln,* 8:410.
19. Grant, *The Personal Memoirs of Julia Dent Grant,* 155.

20. Welles, *Diary of Gideon Welles,* 2:282-283.
21. John G. Nicolay and John Hay, *Abraham Lincoln: A History* (New York, 1890), 10:283-284.
22. Basler, ed., *The Collected Works of Abraham Lincoln,* 7:255.
23. Grant, *The Personal Memoirs of Julia Dent Grant,* 155-156.
24. Weichmann, *The True History of the Assassination of Abraham Lincoln and of the Conspiracy of 1865,* 166.
25. Sandburg, *Abraham Lincoln,* 3:835-836.
26. Ibid., 3:836.
27. Dana, *Recollections of the Civil War,* 237-238.
28. Bishop, *The Day Lincoln Was Shot,* 160.
29. Ibid., 166.
30. Porter, *Campaigning with Grant,* 498-499.
31. Grant, *The Personal Memoirs of Julia Dent Grant,* 156.
32. Bishop, *The Day Lincoln Was Shot,* 164-165.
33. Weichmann, *A True History of the Assassination of Abraham Lincoln and the Conspiracy of 1865,* 171.
34. Bishop, *The Day Lincoln Was Shot,* 181. According to a footnote in Trudeau's *Out of the Storm,* recent research indicates Parker was not at Ford's Theatre that night and that the bodyguard on duty was probably Charles Forbes, a White House messenger.
35. Weichmann, *A True History of the Assassination of Abraham Lincoln and the Conspiracy of 1865,* 172.
36. Ibid., 173.
37. Ibid., 175.

CHAPTER THIRTY-NINE

Now He Belongs to the Ages

14 - 15 April 1865

At about 8 p.m., Herold, Atzerodt, Booth and Paine met in the latter's room at the Herndon House. According to Atzerodt, Booth told them that he had just seen John Surratt a few minutes before and that Surratt and others would help him at the theater. Atzerodt later claimed that this was the first time he knew that the plan had been changed from capturing Lincoln and the others to killing them and that he refused to participate. However, Booth told him that if he backed out the rest would do it anyway and that he would be implicated, so he might as well go through with it. Herold said he had a letter to Johnson from a printer and that he would use that as an excuse to see the vice president. He asked Atzerodt for the key to his room, but according to the latter he refused to give it.

"All the parties seemed to be engaged at something that night," Atzerodt later said, "and were not together. Booth appointed me and Harold (sic) to kill Johnson; in going down the street I told Booth we could not do it. Booth said Harold had more courage, and he would do it. Harold and I were on Pennsylvania Avenue together. I told him I would not do it, and should not go to my room for fear he would disturb Mr. Johnson. He left me to go for Booth."[1] Atzerodt claimed that he went to a bar called the Oyster Bay on Pennsylvania Avenue near 12th Street and that while he was there Herold came in and said Booth wanted to see him; that he got his horse and went to see Booth (he did not say where) and again refused to murder Andrew Johnson. However, if this was really true, it seems logical that Booth would have sent Herold or Paine or both to kill Johnson, since eliminating the vice president would have been much more important than attacking Seward, who was already disabled by his accident. Booth was paying for Atzerodt's room, and if he had really wanted Herold to get his weapons from it, Booth could have demanded the key, at gunpoint if necessary.

The first act was well under way when, at 8:25 p.m., the Lincolns' carriage drew up in front of Ford's Theatre. The two cavalrymen who had followed from the White House turned and rode back, but a policeman stood in front of the main entrance for crowd control, and John Parker was leaning against the front wall of the theater. As Crook had suggested, Parker had walked ahead, and he had checked out the state box. Everything had seemed in order. Evidently he failed to notice, or understand, the niche carved in the wall by the outer door or the peephole drilled in the inner door. Now he led the presidential party inside.

Patrons in the dress circle stood and applauded as the president approached, and onstage the actors stopped. Laura Keene, the star and producer who had performed in this play over a thousand times, applauded vigorously, and the entire audience stood. The scene that had been interrupted had involved a play on words, with mentions of a window draft, a draught of medicine, a draft on a bank and a game of draughts (checkers). Now she ad libbed, "The draft has been suspended."[2] The band struck up "Hail to the Chief," and the members of the presidential party took their places in the state box, and Parker took the cane chair outside the little white door. After prolonged applause everyone resumed their seats, and when quiet had returned the play continued.

The young lady with the Lincolns was Clara Harris. She was the daughter of Senator Ira Harris of New York. Her fiance, Henry R. Rathbone, was the senator's stepson. He was a major in the army, but he was not in uniform that night. These two occupied a sofa near the end of the box. The First Lady sat on another sofa to their left. The president sat next to her in a large upholstered rocking chair provided especially for him. When the president saw the young couple holding hands during the first act, he took Mary's hand in his own.

Shortly before 9 p.m., Parker got up and walked out of the theater. He was bored. He found Lincoln's driver dozing in the carriage and suggested they go to Taltavul's for some ale. On their way they were joined by Lincoln's footman. Soon thereafter, the first act ended and the lights went up. Many of the 1,675 members of the audience took advantage of this chance to study the presidential box, some hoping that General Grant might have arrived while they were engrossed in the play. A lady in the audience wrote a letter to her father during the intermission. "Cousin Julia has just told me," she said, "that the President is in yonder upper right hand private box so handsomely decked with silken flags festooned over a picture of George Washington. The young and lovely daughter of Senator Harris is the only one of his party we see as the flags hide the rest. But we know Father Abraham is there like a Father watching what interests his children."[3]

Booth rode up to the back door of the theater and called for Spangler. The stagehand came out and told the actor he couldn't take care of his horse right now, he was needed to handle the scenery. He sent another man to do it. As Booth stepped into the rear of the theater, he was heard to say, "Ned, you will help me all you can, won't you?"

"Oh, yes," Spangler replied.[4]

Booth went in and watched the play from the wings and tried to see into the state box, but the glare of the lights kept him from seeing much. Just then Lincoln told his wife he felt a chill. He stood up and put on a black overcoat. Booth went down through the passage under the stage and went out through the side alley to the front of the theater. He studied the playbills for a while and then went into Taltavul's tavern, where he asked for a bottle of whiskey and some water, although brandy was his usual drink. Down the bar, Parker, the coachman and the footman were having a few more drinks.

A drunk lifted his glass to Booth and said, "You'll never be the actor your father was." Booth smiled and nodded. "When I leave the stage," he said, "I will be the most famous man in America."[5]

Once, when a boy, Booth had told a friend that he did not want to be a great actor like his father; he wanted to be a name in history. He said that if the Colossus of Rhodes were still standing he would pull it down, even at the cost of his own life, and thus for thousands of years, whenever anyone read about the great statue his own name would be remembered as well.

George Atzerodt claimed that after being sent for by Booth he returned to the Oyster Bay and stayed there until nearly 10 p.m., then got his horse and rode about town without ever going back to his room at the Kirkwood House, where he was supposed to kill Andy Johnson. Others, however, say that he did come there about 10 p.m. but that once inside the hotel he went, not to Johnson's room, nor his own, but to the bar.

At 10:10 p.m., Lewis Paine and David Herold reached Madison Place, across the street from the White House, and stopped in front of Secretary Seward's home. A sentry was posted three doors away, at the home of Major General Christopher Augur, commander of the Department of Washington, but there was none in front of Seward's door. Herold stayed with the horses while Paine went up to the front door, carrying a small bottle, and gave the knocker a loud rap. There was a light on inside, but no one answered. Paine knocked again, and a young black man in a white coat opened the door. Paine told him he had medicine from Dr. Verdi, whom the plotters had learned was Seward's physician. The servant, whose name was William Bell, reached for the bottle, but Paine said he had to deliver it personally and, despite Bell's protests, pushed past him and went up the stairs.

Frederick Seward had been in bed on the top floor when he heard the commotion at the front door. He put on a dressing robe and went to see what was going on, and he found Paine just reaching the top of the stairs. An angry whispered argument ensued, with Paine insisting that he had to put the medicine in the secretary's own hand. Young Seward finally agreed to go and see if his father was awake, but he came back and said he was not. After further argument, Paine agreed to leave, but when he turned to face the stairs he pulled his revolver, wheeled about, and tried to fire it at Seward. The weapon only clicked. Before Seward could react, Paine brought the gun down on his head. Seward fell, and Paine bent over him, striking again and again at his head and neck until his revolver broke. The servant, Bell, who had followed halfway up the stairs, turned and ran back down, crying "Murder! Murder!" He ran outside, still yelling the same word over and over, and that was enough for Davy Herold. He quickly dismounted, tied Paine's horse to a tree, got back on his horse, and galloped off.

Upstairs, Paine threw his broken weapon at his victim, drew a knife, and hurried to the room he had seen Seward go to when he went to check on his father. He pushed against the door but found that someone was leaning against it on the other side. He stepped back and hit the door hard. It flew open and he fell into the dark room. He saw a moving figure and slashed at it with his knife. A man screamed, and Paine jumped onto the bed, where he found the helpless secretary of state. He struck the injured man repeatedly with his knife and heard him moan. When he lifted his weapon high to strike again, someone grabbed his arm. Two people tried to pull him off the bed, and while he was busy with them the secretary rolled away, fell off the bed onto the floor against the wall, and landed on his broken arm. Paine slashed about him with his knife, and when his opponents let go of him he got up and ran out, crying, "I'm mad! I'm mad!" In the hall he saw a young woman in a nightdress and a well-dressed man. Paine let the man, a State Department messenger, approach him, and then he thrust the knife into his chest up to the hilt. The man fell without uttering a word, and Paine hurried down the stairs and out into the street.

He found that Herold had deserted him, so he untied his horse, mounted, and rode north at a walk. William Bell saw him and followed, again crying "Murder!" Soldiers came running from General Augur's house but rushed past both Paine and the servant and ran up the steps of Seward's house to see what was going on. Bell followed Paine for a block and a half before turning and hurrying back to the Seward home. He found another of Seward's sons, Major Augustus Seward, standing in the door with a huge pistol in his hand. Augustus was injured but not bleeding. His sister Fanny was unconscious on the floor of her father's bedroom. It was she who had been leaning against the bedroom door when Paine burst in. A male nurse, who was a sergeant in the army, was badly hurt and bleeding. Frederick Seward was lying curled on his side at the top of the stairs, in a coma. The messenger was bleeding badly and gagging on his own blood. The injured nurse found the secretary lying in a pool of blood. His eyes were open, but the nurse could not find a pulse. Miss Fanny, who was awake by then, threw the front window open and cried, "Murder! Murder!" Meanwhile, the nurse tore Seward's nightshirt open, listened for a heartbeat, and found a strong one. Then he heard the secretary whisper:

"I am not dead. Send for a surgeon. Send for the police. Close the house."[6]

The sergeant lifted the secretary and placed him back on the bed, telling him not to talk and wrapping the bedclothes about him. With a cloth, he wiped the blood from Seward's face and found there was a large pulsing wound on each cheek. But the leather-covered iron brace around the secretary's neck and jaw had protected his throat and saved his life.

Without Herold to guide him, Paine soon became lost in Washington's maze of streets. Somewhere east of the Capitol, he abandoned his horse, perhaps after a fall. It was the one-eyed pacer

Booth had bought at Bryantown, Maryland. A soldier found it about 1 a.m., lame, lathered, and exhausted. A search by cavalry failed to find the rider, who was hiding in a nearby cemetery.

After leaving Taltuval's, Booth stood outside Ford's for a while, talking with a few acquaintances. A soldier waiting outside the theater later testified that one of these other men was John Surratt, who was nervously calling out the time to Booth. But others said they were a carpenter, an actor, and a costumer, all connected with Ford's Theatre, and that the costumer had been giving the time to the actor, who was soon due to go on stage.

When Booth entered the theater it was 10:07 p.m. A member of the audience saw the famous actor come in. At almost the same moment, he saw President Lincoln lean forward with his left hand on the ledge of the box, looking down at the people below. Booth went up to the dress circle, and when Booth approached the door to the little hallway that led to the state box he must have been pleasantly surprised to find the cane chair beside it empty. When a wave of laughter swept over the crowd, Booth quietly opened the door, closed it behind him, and placed the pine board in its niche to hold the door closed. With his eye to the peephole he had carved in the inner door that afternoon, he could see that his intended victim was intent on the play. He could hear the actors on the stage as he quietly turned the nob and slipped into the box:

"I am aware, Mr. Trenchard," the outraged Mrs. Mountchessington declaimed in icy tones, "that you are not used to the manners of good society, and that alone will excuse the impertinence of which you have been guilty." She bustled offstage, leaving Harry Hawks, who played Trenchard, alone in the footlights.

"Don't know the manners of good society, eh?" Trenchard replied to her disappearing back. "Well, I guess I know enough to turn you inside out, old gal—you sockdologizing old man trap!"[7]

As Hawks spoke these lines, Booth slipped a single-shot pistol from his pocket, cocked it, placed it behind the president's head, and pulled the trigger. The loud report was partially masked by the laughter that had followed Hawks' soliloquy. Some people heard it; some did not. An actor off stage heard it and looked up to see "Mr. Lincoln lean back in his rocking chair, his head coming to rest against the wall which stood between him and the audience.... well inside the curtains."[8] Major Rathbone, Clara Harris and Mrs. Lincoln turned in the middle of laughing at the play to see Booth standing behind the president in a cloud of blue smoke.

"Sic Semper tyrannis!" the actor cried: thus ever to tyrants. It is the motto of the state of Virginia, whose seal shows a triumphant Liberty standing over the body of a fallen Tyranny.

Mary Lincoln stared at the handsome young man without comprehension. As Booth forced his way between her and her dying husband, Major Rathbone tried to grab him. Booth dropped his derringer, pulled out a knife, and slashed at him. Rathbone threw up his left arm to block the blow, and the knife cut him to the bone. The major tried to catch Booth with his other hand as the latter moved to the ledge of the box, but the actor shoved him and cried, "Revenge for the South!"[9] Then he lowered himself over the ledge of the box and dropped twelve feet to the stage, turning slightly as he fell. The spur on his right foot caught the Treasury Department flag, and it ripped and fell with him to the stage.

Booth landed with all his weight on his left leg, and his shin bone snapped just above the instep. He fell onto his hands, got up, and ran past the dumbfounded Harry Hawks toward the wings. He fell again, got up, and limped offstage. He brushed past Laura Keene, slashed at the orchestra leader who had gone backstage to confer about a special patriotic song that was to be presented after the play, and made his way to the back door. It was later claimed that the orchestra leader's unexpected presence had prevented Ned Spangler from turning out the lights in the theater because the musician was sitting on the box where the controls were.

The audience was unsure what to make of what had happened. Was it part of the play? Then came a piercing scream from the state box. Mary Lincoln had finally discovered that something was terribly wrong with her husband. Clara Harris stood up, looked down at the audience and called for water. Major Rathbone cried, "Stop that man!"[10]

Major A.C. Richards, superintendent of police for the District of Columbia, was sitting in the dress circle when the shot was fired. He rushed down the stairs, through the crowd in the orchestra circle, and onto the stage. Major Joseph B. Stewart, who had been sitting in the front row, got there first. Together they searched through the scenery and found the door to the alley. Richards later claimed the door slammed closed before he reached it and that he saw a man who looked like Spangler lurking nearby, the only person around who seemed to be calm and collected. Outside, Stewart and Richards found the stagehand who had been holding Booth's horse but who claimed not to have recognized the rider. They could hear the rattling of the mare's hooves moving rapidly down the alley, but they could see neither horse nor rider. Booth rode through the alley to 9th Street, then turned onto Pennsylvania Avenue and galloped toward the Capitol.

A scenery-shifter had gone out the back door just ahead of Stewart and Richards. As he came back in, Ned Spangler struck him in the face with the back of his hand and said, "Don't say which way he went." The man asked Spangler why he had done that and was told, "For God's sake, shut up."[11]

Inside the theater, the audience was buzzing with questions, but nobody had any answers. Rathbone's cry, "Stop that man!" was soon followed by another scream from the box, and a chill swept over the audience, bringing most of it to its feet.

"For God's sake," a man called from the orchestra, "what is it? What happened?"

Rathbone yelled back, "He has shot the President!"

Pandemonium struck the audience. The aisles and stairs were instantly jammed with people trying to move in all directions. Some rushed out into the street, carrying word that the president had been shot. Their ranks were soon swelled by people coming from E and F streets. Some tried to force their way inside even as others were struggling to get out. When someone on the street was heard to say he was glad it happened he was immediately attacked, and it took three policmen with drawn revolvers to keep the crowd from lynching him then and there.

"Water!" "Water," Clara Harris called again from the box.[15] The cry was echoed from several places in the audience, where women had fainted. Someone turned up the gas lights, revealing hundreds of faces with their various expressions of confusion, fright and outrage. In the center of the stage, Harry Hawks stood alone and wept.

Up on the dress circle, several men tried repeatedly to force open the outer door that led to the box, but Booth's pine board held it firmly shut. Major Rathbone, covered with blood from his slashed arm, yelled for the men on the outside of the door to stop pushing on it, and when he finally made them understand, he pulled the pine board from its niche and opened the door. He asked that only doctors come inside, and a small man near the back of the crowd, Charles Leale, 23, assistant surgeon of volunteers, was pushed forward through the mob and through the door. Rathbone told him he was afraid he was bleeding to death. The young surgeon lifted the major's chin, looked into his eyes, and walked past him into the box.

Miss Harris was hysterically begging everyone to help the president. When Dr. Leale pulled Mary Lincoln away from her husband she grabbed his hand and pleaded pitifully for the doctor to help him. He told her he would do what he could and signalled the men who had crowded in behind him to take her away. They led her to one of the sofas in the box, and Clara Harris sat beside her and patted her hand. Laura Keene soon came into the box and sat with them.

Leale called for a lamp, asked for someone to hold matches so he could see until the lamp came, and ordered the door closed and no one admitted but doctors of medicine. At first he thought Lincoln was dead, but when he opened the president's clothing he could find no wound. However, when he looked into Lincoln's eyes and saw evidence of brain injury, he ran his hands through the president's hair until he found matted blood. After he loosened a clot, shallow breathing began, and Leale found a faint pulse. A probe of the wound revealed that the bullet had entered behind the left ear, traveled diagonally through the brain, and lodged behind the right eye. Two other doctors came to Leale's assistance, and together they administered artificial respiration. The president's breathing strengthened to a snore, but the doctors agreed that the wound was fatal. While they discussed moving him to the White House, Laura Keene, with Leale's permission, sat on the floor and held Lincoln's head in her lap.

When the doctors concluded that the president could not survive a move to the White House, an army officer was sent to find a place nearby to take him. Four artillerymen were called upon to help the three doctors carry Lincoln's limp body. Other soldiers were ordered to clear a passage. They got him down the stairs and outside, only to find the street blocked by a sea of humanity made almost frantic by the sight of their stricken president. A captain of infantry put together a make-shift guard. "Surgeon," he told Leale, "give me your commands and I will see that they are obeyed." He was told to clear a path to the nearest house across the street. The captain drew his sword and yelled, "Out of the way you sons of bitches."[13]

People began to move, and a barrier of soldiers formed to hold a pathway open. Slowly the limp body was carried through it. Several times they stopped so that Leale could removed a fresh clot from the wound and relieve pressure on the brain. The first house they tried was found to be locked, but Leale could see a man with a lighted candle standing in the doorway next door motioning to him. So they carried the stricken president over there, up the steps, and down a narrow hall to a small bedroom on the first floor. It was a room rented by a soldier on leave, who picked up his gear and departed. The bed was too small for Lincoln's long legs, but they pulled it away from the wall and laid him on it diagonally. Then they undressed him, covered him with mustard plasters, and placed him between the sheets and under a comforter. Soldiers were sent to summon the surgeon general, Lincoln's personal physician, his pastor, and Captain Robert Lincoln.

Major Richards, superintendent of Washington police, was among those who helped carry Lincoln out of the state box, and while he was there someone handed him the assassin's pistol, which had been picked up from the floor. Laura Keene informed him that the man who had jumped from the box was John Wilkes Booth. Richards tried to find Parker, who worked for him, but when he was unsuccessful, he went back to police headquarters and sent out his night crew of detectives to round up witnesses.

Surgeon General Joseph Barnes was in a carriage just passing Willard's Hotel on Pennsylvania Avenue when a cavalryman found him, told him Lincoln had been shot, and advised him to go to Ford's Theatre at once. The doctor, however, wanted his instruments, so he had his driver take him to his office first. There another soldier found him and told him Secretary Seward had been stabbed and needed him. Barnes felt that the first soldier must have gotten the story all wrong, so he hurried over to Seward's home. He was there dressing Frederick Seward's wounds when a hack driver found him and begged him to come to the theater at once. The president was dying.

Robert Lincoln had just returned to the White House and was talking with members of his father's staff when the news reached him. He and John Hay, one of the president's secretaries, raced up Pennsylvania Avenue in a carriage. A block and a half from the theater they found the street so full of people they had to proceed on foot to the house across from the theater. When Robert found his mother in the parlor he burst into tears.

Vice President Andrew Johnson was half asleep in his room at the Kirkwood House when he heard a pounding at the door. Since it wouldn't stop, he got up. From outside his door came the voice of Leonard Farwell, former governor of Wisconsin, who had visited him earlier, before going off to Ford's Theatre for an evening's entertainment. Johnson invited him in, and Farwell whispered the news that Lincoln had been shot at the theater. Johnson did not believe it at first, but when he turned up the lamp and saw Farwell's agonized expression he had to. Farwell went to the door and peered out. All seemed normal. Nevertheless he rang for servants and asked for guards. When some were provided he stationed a man inside the door with orders to admit no one. When somebody knocked, Farwell refused to open the door until he recognized the voice of a congressman, who told him there were 500 people in the lobby. Johnson, meanwhile, had dressed, and now he sent Farwell back to the theater to check on Lincoln's condition. He soon returned with Major James O'Beirne, the provost marshal of the District of Columbia, and found Johnson's two rooms filled with excited people. Farwell assured them that the president was dying and that Seward was dead. He said it was part of a plot to eliminate the president, vice president, and all the ministers of the cabinet. Johnson wanted to go to the dying Lincoln, but O'Beirne talked him into waiting, at least, until the excitement in the streets had died down.

George Atzerodt's opportunity to attack the vice president was gone, although it is doubtful that he ever intended to try it. Whether his reluctance was due to timidity or scruples will never be known, possibly both. Booth, however, seems to have been relying on him to get the job done. After a few drinks at the bar in the Kirkwood House, Atzerodt evidently rode up toward Ford's Theatre. Frightened by the frenzied mob there, he rode aimlessly about for a while, stopping once for another drink. He was afraid to go back to his room at the Kirkwood House. At about 11 p.m. he returned his rented horse to Keleher's stable and caught a horse car heading toward the Navy Yard. On the car were a couple of men he knew. He asked one of them if he could sleep on the floor of his store that night but was refused. So he rode the car back uptown and got a bed at the Pennsylvania House.

John Matthews' part as the lawyer in *Our American Cousin* was completed before the play was done, and he was in a small saloon a block from Ford's Theatre when he heard the news that John Wilkes Booth had shot the president. Suddenly he knew what was so important about the letter Booth had given him to deliver the next morning. Frightened that he might be implicated, he went back to his room, where he read it and burned it. He did not even reveal its existence until years later.

Secretary Welles of the Navy was just getting to sleep when he heard someone shouting to his son, whose room was just above the front door. Welles raised a window and found it was his own messenger. He doubted the man's story that both Lincoln and Seward had been attacked, for he knew they were at different places that night. But the messenger said that he had gone by Seward's first and could confirm that much of the story at least. Welles got dressed and hurried across the square to Seward's house. He found the lower hall and office full of people, including most of the foreign legations. Upstairs he found Dr. Verdi ministering to the twice-injured secretary, and while he was there, Stanton came in. In the next room they found another doctor attending Frederick Seward, whom he said was hurt more dangerously than his father.

Stanton confirmed the story of Lincoln being shot. He had talked to a man who had been in the theater at the time. They both decided that they should go to the president. Back downstairs they met General Meigs, who begged them not to go to the theater. The streets were full of all sorts of people, and it could be dangerous. But they were determined to go and invited Meigs to go with them. David Cartter, the chief justice of the District of Columbia court of appeals, climbed up beside the driver, and Meigs ordered a couple of soldiers to go along on each side of the carriage. They found the streets full of people, mostly hurrying toward the theater, as they were. They, too, had to proceed on foot. Finally they reached the house where Lincoln had been taken and found at least half a dozen doctors in attendance. One of them told Welles there was no hope; the president might live a few hours, but he could never recover.

"The giant sufferer lay extended diagonally across the bed," Welles noted, "which was not long enough for him. His large arms, which were occasionally exposed, were of a size which one would scarce have expected from his spare appearance. His slow, full respiration lifted the clothes with each breath that he took. His features were calm and striking. I had never seen them appear to better advantage than for the first hour, perhaps, that I was there. After that, his right eye began to swell and that part of his face became discolored."[14]

Corporal James Tanner, a clerk in the Ordnance Bureau, had gone to Grover's Theatre that night, and he returned to his room on the second floor of the house next door to the one where Lincoln lay to find both the room and his tiny balcony filled with fellow boarders. He had just managed to fight his way out onto the balcony when General Augur came out on the stoop next door, waved his hands for quiet, and asked the throng of people in the street if anyone there knew shorthand. Someone volunteered Tanner, so he worked his way back inside, picked up a pad of paper, a couple of pencils, and his military cap and, with the help of other soldiers, worked his way through the mob to the house next door. In the back parlor he found Secretary Stanton and Justice Cartter interviewing witnesses. Taking down their statements in longhand had proved impossible, so he was put to work recording their testimony in shorthand. "In fifteen minutes," Tanner said, "I had testimony enough to hang Wilkes Booth, the assassin, higher than ever Haman hung." He added, however, that although everyone thought it was Booth, no one wanted to say so positively. "It was evident that the horror of the crime held them back. They seemed to hate to think that one they had known at all could be guilty of such an awful crime."[15]

Assistant Secretary of War Dana was awakened from a sound sleep, given the news, and told that Stanton needed him. He arrived to find the president still alive and all the members of the cabinet, except Seward, gathered in the parlor. All but Stanton seemed stunned into inactivity. "Sit down here," Stanton told him; "I want you."

"Then he began and dictated orders," Dana remembered, "one after another, which I wrote out and sent swiftly to the telegraph. All these orders were designed to keep the business of the Government in full motion until the crisis should be over. It seemed as if Mr. Stanton thought of everything, and there was a great deal to be thought of that night. The extent of the conspiracy was, of course, unknown, and the horrible beginning which had been made naturally led us to suspect the worst. The safety of Washington must be looked after. Commanders all over the country had to be ordered to take extra precautions. The people must be notified of the tragedy. The assassins must be captured. The coolness and clearheadedness of Mr. Stanton under these circumstances were most remarkable."[16]

Stanton ordered guards for the homes of all cabinet members and ranking officials, ordered the confiscation of Ford's Theatre and the arrest of all its employees, and sent orders to the chief engineer of the Washington fire brigade to have his apparatus ready in case the Rebels tried to burn the city, as they had tried with New York four months before. Stanton had no doubt that the assassins were in the employ of the Confederacy, and he feared that hundreds of Rebel terrorists might be in the capital that night. Orders were sent to various military commanders in and around Washington to stop all men trying to leave the city, but they were far too late to catch Booth and Herold. At Stanton's instigation, Welles ordered navy steamers to patrol the lower Potomac in search of fugitives. The commander at Point Lookout, where the river empties into Chesapeake Bay, was ordered to stop all boats coming downriver and hold all persons found on board. Nobody bothered to send any information or orders to the men at the Navy Yard bridge, at the southwestern edge of town, because it would have been closed more than an hour before the attacks.

John Fletcher was foreman at Naylor's livery stable, and he was worried about the horse he had rented to David Herold. He had warned the young man to have the horse back by 9 p.m., and he was standing in front of Willards' Hotel well after 10 p.m. when he saw Herold and the missing roan approaching. He ran out in the street and shouted for Herold to get off that horse, but the youngster pulled away from him and turned up 14th Street. Certain that Herold intended to steal the horse, Fletcher ran back to the stable, saddled another horse, and rode in search of him. He reasoned that a horse thief would most likely head for the Navy Yard bridge and southern Maryland. As he rode past the south side of the Capitol he met a horseman coming the other way and asked him if he'd seen a rider ahead of him. The man said he'd seen two men, both going very fast.

Although the Navy Yard bridge over the east branch of the Potomac—also called Anacostia Creek—was officially closed every night at 9 p.m., with the war all but over the rule was not strictly enforced. It was about 10:45 p.m. when Sergeant Silas T. Cobb saw Booth approach. The assassin gave his right name and said he was going home to Charles County, Maryland. He said he did not know the bridge closed at 9 p.m. and that he had waited for the moon to rise to give him light to ride by. The sergeant let him cross. A few minutes later, Davy Herold rode up. He gave his name as Smith and said he lived in White Plains. Cobb let him cross as well. Then Fletcher rode up, and before Cobb could question him, he asked if a man on a roan horse with an English saddle had crossed a few minutes ago. He was told one had. He asked if he could also cross and was told he could, but he couldn't come back. At that, he turned back to the city. There he learned that Lincoln and Seward had been attacked, but he was not very interested. He put up his mount, and about midnight he walked up to police headquarters to report a stolen horse.

Detective Charles Stone informed Fletcher that a horse had been found by the army, and he took him down to General Augur's headquarters. Augur was not terribly interested in Fletcher's story. He was too busy making sure the defenders of the city were ready for any further Rebel mischief. Fletcher's description of Davy Herold did not match those he had of Booth, whom Stanton and Augur at that point suspected of making both attacks. But the general showed him the saddle and bridle taken from Paine's horse and asked him if he knew anything about it. Fletcher recognized it; it had white leather trim. He had seen it on the one-eyed horse ridden by a friend of Herold's, which he had stabled for him not long ago. Fletcher could not remember the rider's name, but he and Detective Stone went back to his stable, where he checked the records. The name of Herold's friend was George Atzerodt. None of this interested Augur, however, who could see no connection with the assassination.

Captain D.H.L. Gleason came to Augur's headquarters and asked for permission to lead a mounted squad after the assassins and capture them. Augur said no and told the captain to stay at headquarters; he might be needed. Gleason was the officer Louis Weichmann had told about the plotting going on at the Surratt boarding house. The captain knew that Booth and his fellow conspirators met there and also at the tavern in Surrattsville, but nobody asked him why he thought he could capture the assassins, and since he had been denied his chance for glory he did not volunteer the information.

Sometime before midnight Major Richards of the Washington police telegraphed the police chiefs of Baltimore, Philadelphia, New York and Alexandria that "J. Wilkes Booth the tragedian is the person who shot the President this evening at Ford's Theatre. He made off on horseback probably toward Baltimore."[17] But when he learned, probably from Fletcher through Detective Stone, that two men had crossed the Navy Yard bridge into southern Maryland, he sent an officer to the War Department to ask for about a dozen horses to mount a squad of policemen to follow them. His man got the run around for a couple of hours but was finally told that the horses would be sent right away. However, it was actually 11 a.m. the next day before they were delivered. This fact has been used by some writers as evidence that Stanton was in on the plot to kill Lincoln, but a more logical explanation is that Stanton—who was not at the War Department but at the house where Lincoln was dying—and his entire department were already swamped with things to do. It might have made more sense for Richards to ask Augur for horses, or, even better, for some cavalry. Or, why not rent or even commandeer some horses from the numerous livery stables in the city? That's where the conspirators got most of theirs.

Major O'Beirne, provost marshal of the city, was one of the first to get any kind of investigation started. After hearing from several people that Booth was the assassin, he asked some theater people where the actor lived and was told the National Hotel. He sent a detective there to see what he could find. The detective soon returned with word that nobody at the hotel had seen Booth since early evening, but he also brought with him a trunk and some papers he had found in Booth's room. These were turned over to an army lieutenant, who examined them. Among the papers was a letter from Sam Arnold hinting at the plot and the involvement of Richmond. In the trunk was found a paper containing a secret cipher. Major Eckert recognized it as matching one that Assistant Secretary Dana had found in Richmond.

"The secret cipher key," Dana wrote, "was a model consisting of a cylinder, six inches in length and two and one half in diameter, fixed in a frame, the cylinder having the printed key pasted over it. By shifting the pointers fixed over the cylinder on the upper portion of the frame, according to a certain arrangement previously agreed upon, the cipher letter or dispatch could be deciphered readily."[18] Dispatches were found in Booth's trunk that were written in the cipher and sent from Canada to the Confederacy. "By the key which I had found," Dana wrote, "these dispatches could be read. These dispatches indicated plots against the leaders of our Government, though whether Booth had sent them or not was, of course, never known."[19]

Secretary Stanton sent one of O'Beirne's men, John Lee, to protect Vice President Johnson. While looking over the building at the Kirkwood House, Lee was told by a customer in the bar about a suspicious man who had taken a room the day before and had been asking a lot of questions about Johnson. Lee then asked the night manager to point out the names of anyone on the register that he couldn't vouch for as regular customers. He was given the name G. Atzerodt. He was told Atzerodt was not in, so he took the manager with him and went to Atzerodt's room.

The room was locked, no one answered, and the lodger had the only key. With the owner's permission, Lee and the manager broke in. Under the pillow on the bed they found a large revolver. Lee went downstairs and found Major O'Beirne, who had just delivered official notice from the cabinet to the vice president that Lincoln was dying and to be ready to take the oath of office. Beirne told Lee to continue his search. In David Herold's black coat that he found hanging on the door was a banknote from Canada made out to J. Wilkes Booth for $455, a large-scale map of Virginia, a handkerchief marked "Mary R. E. Booth" (John Wilkes' mother), another marked "F.M. Nelson" (Herold's cousin), and a third marked with the letter "H." A large Bowie knife was found between the mattress and the bottom sheet.

The Grants rode northward in the private car of the president of the Baltimore & Ohio Railroad. The conductor locked the doors of the car as the train had pulled out of the station. Sometime before the train reached Baltimore, a man tried to get in, but he was chased off by the train crew. At Philadelphia, the Grants had to leave the train, drive through the city, take a ferry, and change to a different line. Since the general had not had anything to eat since 9 a.m., they stopped at a hotel for a late supper. But before the food was ready, a telegram from Major Eckert arrived bringing the news of the attacks on Lincoln and Seward and Stanton's desire for the general to return to Washington. A special train was ordered for the return trip. While it was being prepared, Grant took Julia on to Burlington and then returned to Philadelphia.

"It would be impossible for me to describe the feeling that overcame me at the news of these assassinations," Grant wrote, "more especially the assassination of the President. I knew his goodness of heart, his generosity, his yielding disposition, his desire to have everybody happy, and above all his desire to see all the people of the United States enter again upon the full privileges of citizenship with equality among all. I knew also the feeling that Mr. Johnson had expressed in speeches and conversation against the Southern people, and I feared that his course towards them would be such as to repel, and make then unwilling citizens; and if they became such they would remain so for a long while. I felt that reconstruction had been set back, no telling how far."[20]

On the road southeast of Washington, Booth stopped a man riding toward the city and learned from him that there was no rider ahead of him going south. Soon he heard hoofbeats on the road behind him. He hid in a stand of trees until the rider went by, and he saw that it was Davy Herold. The two then rode on together to Surrattsville, exchanging stories on their nights' work. Booth's leg was causing him pain, and the mare's bouncing gait made it worse, so the two swapped mounts.

A few minutes after midnight, they came to Surrattsville and stopped in front of the tavern. Herold dismounted and went inside, where he found John Lloyd asleep on a couch. He was drunk. At Herold's insistence, Lloyd got up and fetched the two carbines, a box of cartridges, the field glasses, and a quart of whiskey. Booth took the binoculars but told Herold to leave the carbines; they would just slow them up. Herold kept one of them anyway and a few cartridges. Booth took two deep drinks of the whiskey and returned the bottle to Herold. Booth asked if there was a doctor nearby. Lloyd said there was one about a half-mile down the road, but he did not practice anymore. Booth announced that they had killed the president and Seward, but Lloyd was too drunk to be either impressed or surprised. Herold gave the man a silver dollar, and the two rode away. But Booth's leg was causing him too much pain for them to follow their intended escape route along the Confederate clandestine courier line. He would have to detour to the home of Dr. Samuel Mudd, near Bryantown, to get his leg treated.

Fletcher's visit to Augur's headquarters evidently got the general to thinking about horses and stables. Booth rode off on a horse. Where did he stable it? Augur wanted to talk to any stableman who had seen Booth. By 2 a.m. he had one who had seen Booth on a small roan mare and knew that he owned a large one-eyed gelding. What's more, the stableman informed the general that Booth often loaned or borrowed horses from a man named John Surratt, and those two sometimes loaned horses to a couple of other men: George Atzerodt and David Herold.

Someone at Augur's headquarters recognized the name Surratt from the report Wiechmann had made the month before.

But Major Richards, superintendent of the Washington police, was way ahead of Augur. Richards discovered from a saloon keeper the connection of Booth with Herold, Paine and Atzerodt, and then discovered the connection of this group with John Surratt and that Booth had often visited the Surratt boarding house. "Those facts," he later wrote, "led me to pay that house a visit that night at about one o'clock.

When I reached the house and had rung the door bell, Mrs. Surratt answered it very promptly. The house was dark so far as I could discover but there was no unusual delay in the response of Mrs. S. to the bell. She appeared dressed as a lady of her station might be expected to dress of an evening. Her hair was not disarranged. She had not time to dress and smooth her hair between the ringing of the bell and her appearance at the door. She had not retired for the night, but was evidently, waiting in a dark house for some one to call. When I informed her why I had called after informing her of the assassination she expressed no surprise or regret. In fact she only answered such questions as I asked her in the briefest possible terms—gave me no information in regard to Booth, his visits or the visits of others of the assassins to her house. She seemed entirely self-possessed and did not seem in the least affected when I said to her that President Lincoln had just been assassinated and that Booth and her son were suspected of being implicated in the crime."[21]

At about 2 a.m., a group of Richards' detectives came to the boarding house to search the place. This time, it was Louis Weichmann who answered the door bell.

"Who is there?" he asked.

"Detectives," he was told, "come to search the house for John Wilkes Booth and John Surratt."

"They are not here," Weichmann told them, not aware of why detectives should be looking for either one.

"Let us in anyhow," they said, "we want to search the house."

Weichmann went to Mrs. Surratt's door, knocked, and told her that detectives had come to search the house.

"For God's sake!" she replied, "Let them come in. I expected the house to be searched."

While others watched the house from outside, four detectives came in and, as Weichmann put it, "explored the house from top to bottom, going even into the rooms occupied by the young ladies and looking to see who they were." When he asked them why, they told him that

Booth had shot the president and John Surratt had attacked the secretary of state. Weichmann threw up his hands. "My God, I see it all," he said.

"In that instant," he later wrote, "the facts of Booth's continued friendship for Mrs. Surratt and her son, his frequent visits to the house, and on the very day of the murder, flashed across my mind, and I realized that every person living in that house would be subjected to a rigid examination in the investigation that would surely be made by the Government."

He told the detectives that Surratt could not possibly have been the man who attacked Seward, because he was in Canada. He had seen a letter from him that very night. One of the detectives asked Mrs. Surratt for the letter but it could not be found. "There was a purpose in witholding it," Weichmann later concluded. "Had that letter and envelope been produced it would have settled the fact as to whether it was written by Surratt in Canada on the 12th of April, or elsewhere, and dated back."[26] Weichmann told the detectives he would see them early in the morning and would do all he could to assist their investigation.

At about that same hour of 2 a.m., Vice President Johnson decided that it was time for him to go to the dying Lincoln. Governor Farwell and Major O'Beirne tried to talk him out of it, but his mind was made up. O'Beirne said he would summon a guard, but Johnson declined. He did not want a carriage, either. So, flanked, by Farwell and O'Beirne, he walked up to 10th Street in the cool damp night. By then, only a few civilians remained in the street outside the house where the stricken president lay, and a pair of soldiers were stationed out front. Cavalrymen waited nearby to carry dispatches from Stanton to the War Department, where they were telegraphed to their various destinations. Johnson was shown into the bedroom and stood with his hat in his hand, saying nothing, showing no emotion, his eyes fixed on the tall figure in the bed. He took Robert Lincoln's hand and whispered a few words to him, went into the back parlor and spoke briefly to Stanton, passed through the front room, where he took the hand of the whimpering Mrs. Lincoln, and walked back to his hotel.

At about 4 a.m., Booth and Herold reached the home of Dr. Samuel Mudd, who examined Booth's leg and found that he had fractured the fibula just above the ankle. He made cardboard splints and set the leg, cutting away the boot in the process, and had one of his employees make a pair of crutches for Booth. It is quite possible that Mudd and Herold had never met, but at his trial Mudd claimed not to have recognized Booth either, saying the actor wore a false beard. This seems unlikely. Up to now, Booth had made no effort to disguise himself. And the two conspirators stayed with Mudd for about thirteen hours. In 1877, Mudd told Samuel Cox, Jr. that he actually had recognized Booth but that the latter had not revealed that he had shot the president.

This sounds more plausible, but if Booth had bragged about the deed to Lloyd, whom he did not know, why hide it from Mudd, whom he knew to be a fellow secessionist?

In the early hours of the morning, Stanton's mind turned from keeping the government running and protecting it against further attacks to pursuit of the culprits. He sent out orders to find and arrest Booth. He also sent dispatches to Major General John A. Dix in New York announcing the attacks. Dix was the normal outlet for announcements from the War Department, which he passed on to the news services. Since the letter from Sam Arnold found in Booth's room came from the Baltimore, Maryland area, Stanton sent orders there to find and arrest Arnold. Someone was sent to Ford's to find a photograph of Booth. Through some error, they came back with a picture of his brother, Edwin, but except for not having a mustache, it bore a close resemblence to John Wilkes. An examination of the map, and the fact that the one-eyed horse had been found in the eastern part of town, suggested that the assassin might have fled into southern Maryland. A troop of cavalry, commanded by Lieutenant David A. Dana, younger brother of the assistant secretary of war, was sent to patrol the area around Piscataway, Maryland, not far south of Washington.

At about 6 a.m., George Atzerodt left the Pennsylvania House and began to walk westward across Washington to Georgetown.

Detective John Parker, Lincoln's missing bodyguard, walked into the police station about then with a drunken prostitute he had arrested. The booking sergeant turned her loose with orders to get out of town. Parker did not say where he had been all night, and no one asked him. Nor did he file any report. The sergeant told him to go home and get some sleep. Parker remained on the force for another three years and was never charged with neglecting his duties that night.

With the approach of morning, the crowd outside the house where Lincoln lay was growing again. Secretary Welles went out for a brief walk at about 6 a.m. After sitting in the small room with the dying man and too many live ones for seven hours he felt the need for fresh air and exercise. "It was a dark and gloomy morning," he later told his diary, "and rain set in before I returned to the house, some fifteen minutes later. Large groups of people were gathered every few rods, all anxious and solicitous. Some one or more from each group stepped forward as I passed, to inquire into the condition of the President, and to ask if there was no hope. Intense grief was on every countenance when I replied that the President could survive but a short time. The colored people especially—and there were at this time more of them, perhaps, than of whites—were overwhelmed with grief."[23]

Throughout the long night, Mary Lincoln sat in the front parlor with Clara Harris and Laura Keene. About once an hour she went into the bedroom but was soon overcome by emotion and returned to the parlor. On her last visit she fainted, and Stanton ordered her taken out and kept out. Major Rathbone had fainted from loss of blood shortly after reaching the house and was taken home. Robert Lincoln divided his time between watching over his father in the bedroom and comforting his mother in the parlor.

Dr. Leale sat by the president's side and held his hand most of the night, frequently checking his pulse and repeatedly breaking up the clots that formed in the wound to keep pressure from building up on the brain. The surgeon general and Lincoln's personal physician were both on hand, as were several other doctors, but for the most part they deferred to Leale, who had been first on the scene. They probed the wound with some hope of removing the bullet but found it blocked, probably by a piece of bone from the back of the skull.

As dawn arrived, the stricken giant's pulse began to fail and the unconscious moans he had been emitting for some while ceased. Surgeon General Barnes, sensing that the end was at hand, asked an officer to bring Mrs. Lincoln back into the bedroom. She came in, looked at her husband, heard Robert sob and looked at him, and was led back out again. Welles returned, and Stanton came in and stood beside the bed. The tiny room was filled with doctors and officials of the government. At 7:22 a.m., Leale saw the president's chest heave upward, hold there, and then relax. It was his final breath. Barnes looked into one of Lincoln's eyes and then bent down to listen to the chest. When he straightened up he took two silver coins from his vest pocket and placed them on the president's eyelids.

"Now he belongs to the ages," Stanton said.[24]

---

1. Weichmann, *A True History of the Assassination of Abraham Lincoln and the Conspiracy of 1865,* 387.
2. Bishop, *The Day Lincoln Was Shot,* 194.
3. Sandburg, *Abraham Lincoln,* 3:843.
4. Weichmann, *A True History of the Assassination of Abraham Lincoln and of the Conspiracy of 1865*, 149-150.

5. Bishop, *The Day Lincoln Was Shot,* 203.
6. Ibid., 221-225.
7. Ibid., 130.
8. Sandburg, *Abraham Lincoln,* 3:844.
9. Bishop, *The Day Lincoln Was Shot,* 209.
10. Ibid., 210-212.
11. Weichmann, *A True History of the Assassination of Abraham Lincoln and of the Conspiracy of 1865,* 155. In his testimony, Stewart claimed to have recognized Booth and to have come very close to catching him, but Richards flatly counterdicted this in a letter written to Weichmann given on page 418 of the work cited here.
12. Bishop, *The Day Lincoln Was Shot,* 212.
13. Ibid., 217.
14. Welles, *Diary of Gideon Welles,* 2:286-287.
15. Thomas Reed Turner, *Beware the People Weeping: Public Opinion and the Assassination of Abraham Lincoln* (Baton Rouge, 1982), 56.
16. Dana, *Recollections of the Civil War,* 238-239.
17. Turner, *Beware the People Weeping,* 105.
18. Dana, *Recollections of the Civil War,* 243, n. 1.
19. Ibid., 244.
20. Grant, *Personal Memoirs,* 2:508-509.
21. Weichmann, *The True History of the Assassination of Abraham Lincoln and the Conspiracy of 1865,* 411-412.
22. Ibid., 175-178.
23. Welles, *Diary of Gideon Welles,* 2:287-288.
24. Nicolay and Hay, *Abraham Lincoln,* 10:302.

CHAPTER FORTY

Who Killed My Father?

15 - 17 April 1865

Jefferson Davis and the Confederate cabinet left Greensborough, North Carolina on the fifteenth, heading south. They had to go by carriage and wagon because Stoneman's Union raiders had cut the railroad. The only horses and vehicles available were in poor condition, and recent rains had turned the roads to mud, so they made only about ten miles that first day. With them went several boxes of presidential papers and two heavy containers holding $35,000 in coins left for the use of the president and cabinet when the rest of the treasury had preceded them to the south. They were escorted by a few squadrons of Tennessee cavalry under Brigadier General George Dibrell, while about a dozen Kentucky troopers served as scouts and couriers. "Mr. Davis was very moody and unhappy," Secretary Mallory noted, "and this was the first day on which I had noticed in him a thorough surrender & abandonment of the cause of Southern independence."[1] The party spent the night at the home of a hospitable farmer, where, according to one of them, they had their first good meal since leaving Danville.

Down in Alabama, the advance of Wilson's cavalry, LaGrange's brigade of McCook's division, outflanked some Rebel opposition early on the fifteenth and rode into Tuskegee. LaGrange then pushed on to the northeast along the Montgomery & West Point Railroad, and, after spending much of the afternoon tearing up track, reached Auburn that night. The Chattahoochee River, swollen by recent rains, lay ahead of the Federals along the border between Alabama and Georgia. Wilson did not know which bridges he might find still intact. So he sent LaGrange to check on the bridge at West Point, Georgia while he led the rest of his force due east to Columbus. The main column rode out of Tuskegee at about 5 p.m. in the midst of thunder, lightning and drizzling rain. A Union officer noticed three white women "standing in the rain waving their handkerchiefs and *hurraying for Lincoln.* This is the first time that this happened to us. The boys cheered them."[2]

A cold rain was falling on Washington that Saturday morning, in keeping with the city's mood, as Louis Weichmann left Mary's Surratt's boarding house to buy a newspaper. "Eagerly I read Stanton's dispatches," he later remembered. "Booth had indeed murdered the President, but who was the man who had assaulted Mr. Seward?" He rejoiced when he read the description of the man, for it did not match his old schoolmate John Surratt at all. "I felt grateful for so much," he wrote, "and a heavy weight was rolled from my heart." He went back to the boarding house for breakfast, and during the meal he made some remark deploring the assassination. Mrs. Surratt's daughter, Anna, said that the death of Lincoln was "no worse than that of the meanest nigger in the army."[3] He told her he thought she would soon learn otherwise.

Noah Brooks, the reporter, noted that "with incredible swiftness Washington went into deep, universal mourning. All shops, Government departments, and private offices were closed, and everywhere, on the most pretentious residences and on the humblest hovels, were the black badges of grief. Nature seemed to sympathize in the general lamentation, and tears of rain fell from the moist and somber sky. The wind sighed mournfully through streets crowded with sad-faced people, and broad folds of funeral drapery flapped heavily in the wind over the decorations of the day before. Wandering aimlessly up F street toward Ford's Theatre, we met a tragical procession. It was headed by a group of army officers walking bareheaded, and behind them, carried tenderly by a company of soldiers, was the bier of the dead President, covered with the flag of the Union, and accompanied by an escort of soldiers who had been on duty at the house where Lincoln died. As the little cortege passed down the street to the White House every head was uncovered, and the profound silence which prevailed was broken only by sobs and by the sound of the measured tread of those who bore the martyred President back to the home which he had so lately quitted full of life, hope, and cheer."[4]

Louis Weichmann and John Holahan, another boarder at the Surratt house, went over to police headquarters after breakfast. As they turned into 10th Street they too saw the soldiers carry the body of Abraham Lincoln from the house across from Ford's Theatre out into the street. At police headquarters, Weichmann met Major Richards, and after some consultation he went with a group of detectives to the government stables on 19th Street. There they ran into John Fletcher, from whom they got David Herold's name as the man who had taken his horse. Weichmann knew where Herold's family lived, near the Navy Yard, so, after a stop at the boarding house to get a photo of John Surratt, they went there. They discovered that Herold's mother, who was in tears, had not seen him since Friday evening. They got a picture of Herold from the family album and took both it and Surratt's photo to the government authorities, who made copies of them that, with one of Booth, were distributed all over the country. After that, Weichmann and the detectives finally crossed the Navy Yard Bridge and rode into southern Maryland. They scoured the countryside all day, but for some reason they never went to Surrattsville. That night, Weichmann slept on the floor of the police station.

After going home for breakfast Saturday morning, Secretary Welles went to the executive mansion. "There was a cheerless cold rain," he remembered, "and everything seemed gloomy. On the Avenue in front of the White House were several hundred colored people, mostly women and children, weeping and wailing their loss. This crowd did not appear to diminish through the whole of that cold, wet day; they seemed not to know what was to be their fate since their great benefactor was dead, and their hopeless grief affected me more than almost anything else, though strong and brave men wept when I met them.

"At the White House all was silent and sad. Mrs. W[elles] was with Mrs. L[incoln] and came to meet me in the library. Speed came in, and we soon left together. As we were descending the stairs, 'Tad,' who was looking from the window at the foot, turned and, seeing us, cried aloud in his tears, 'Oh, Mr. Welles, who killed my father?' Neither Speed nor myself could restrain our tears, nor give the poor boy any satisfactory answer."[5]

Andrew Johnson was sworn in that day as the seventeenth president of the United States. But, since Mrs. Lincoln still occupied the White House, he was an executive without an office. Secretary Stanton was, by default, running the government. Grant returned that morning to help. "Stanton's grief was uncontrollable," Horace Porter remembered, "and at the mention of Mr. Lincoln's name he would break down and weep bitterly. General Grant and the Secretary of War busied themselves day and night in pushing a relentless pursuit of the conspirators...."[6]

Grant was in a grim mood. "I did not know what it meant," he later said. "Here was the Rebellion put down in the field, and starting up in the gutters; we had fought it as war, now we had to fight it as assassination."[7] Some time that day he must have seen a message received the day before from Ord for Lincoln. The president had already left for the theater and never saw it. Ord, who was in Richmond, had sent word that Judge Campbell and R.M.T. Hunter, who had been two of the three Confederate peace commissioners who met with Lincoln at Hampton Roads, had requested permission to come to Washington to see the president. Grant wired Ord at 4 p.m.: "Arrest J.A. Campbell, Mayor Mayo, and the members of the old council of Richmond, who have not yet taken the oath of allegiance, and put them in Libby Prison. Hold them guarded beyond the possibility of escape until further orders. Also arrest all paroled officers and surgeons until they can be sent beyond our lines, unless they take the oath of allegiance. The oath need not be received from any one who you have not good reason to believe will observe it, and from none who are excluded by the President's proclamation, without authority of the President to do so. Extreme rigor will have to be observed whilst assassination remains the order of the day with the rebels."

Ord, well beyond the fear and hysteria of Washington, was appalled and had the courage to speak out against such orders. He replied: "Cipher dispatch directing certain parties to be arrested is received. The two citizens I have seen. They are old, nearly helpless, and I think incapable of harm. Lee and staff are in town among the paroled prisoners. Should I arrest them under the circumstances I think the rebellion here would be reopened. I will risk my life that the present paroles will be kept, and if you will allow me to do so trust the people here who, I believe, are ignorant of the assassination, done, I think, by some insane Brutus with but few accomplices. Mr. Campbell and Hunter pressed me earnestly yesterday to send them to Washington to see the President. Would they have done so if guilty? Please answer."

At 8 p.m. Grant replied: "On reflection I will withdraw my dispatch of this date directing the arrest of Campbell, Mayo, and others so far as it may be regarded as an order, and leave it in the light of a suggestion, to be executed only so far as you may judge the good of the service demands."[8]

Assistant Secretary Dana had gone home about 3 a.m., while Lincoln was still alive. At about 8 a.m. he was awakened by a colonel from the adjutant general's office rapping on his window.

"Mr. Dana, the President is dead," the officer told him, "and Mr. Stanton directs you to arrest Jacob Thompson."[9]

Dana sent the order to Portland, but Thompson never showed up there. However, as soon as Dana had recovered from the shock of Lincoln's death, he remembered that back in November General Dix in New York sent him a pair of letters that had been found on a street car there. They referred to a plan to assassinate the president. Dana had taken them to the president, who had looked at them but had not seemed to place much importance on them. "I now reminded Mr. Stanton of this circumstance," Dana wrote, "and he asked me to go immediately to the White House and see if I could find the letters. I thought it rather doubtful, for I knew the President received a great many communications of a similar nature. However, I went over, and made a thorough search through his private desk. He seemed to have attached more importance to these papers than to others of the kind, for I found them inclosed in an envelope marked in his own handwriting, 'Assassination.'"[10]

Mrs. Hudspeth, the woman who had turned in the letters, later testified at the trial of Booth's accomplices. On 11 November 1864 she had overheard a curious conversation between two men on a 3rd Avenue street car. "She had observed," Dana wrote, "when a jolt of the car pushed the hat of one of the men forward, that he wore false whiskers. She had noticed that his hand was very beautiful; that he carried a pistol in his belt; that, judging from his conversation, he was a young man of education; she heard him say that he was going to Washington that day. The young men left the car before she did, and after they had gone her daughter, who was with her, had picked up a letter from the floor. Mrs. Hudspeth, thinking it belonged to her, had carried it from the car.... When a photograph of Booth was shown to Mrs. Hudspeth, she swore that it was the man in disguise whom she had seen in the car."[11] She also had noticed a scar on the man's neck, which matched one Booth had.

There were actually two letters, found together. One was dated St. Louis, 21 October 1864, and was signed "Leenea." It was a pitiful appeal of a woman to her husband, Louis, to come home. The other was addressed to Louis: "The time has at last come that we have all so wished for, and upon you everything depends. As it was decided before you left, we were to cast lots. Accordingly we did so, and you are to be the Charlotte Corday of the nineteenth century. When you remember the fearful, solemn vow that was taken by us, you will feel there is no drawback—Abe must die, and now. You can choose your weapons. The cup, the knife, the bullet. The cup failed us once, and might again. Johnson, who will give this, has been like an enraged demon since the meeting, because it has not fallen upon him to rid the world of the monster. He says the blood of his gray-haired father and his noble mother call upon him for revenge, and revenge he will have; if he can not wreak it upon the fountain-head, he will upon some of the blood-thirsty generals. Butler would suit him. As our plans were all concocted and well arranged, we separated, and as I am writing—on my way to Detroit—I will only say that all rests upon you. You know where to find your friends. Your disguises are so perfect and complete that without one knew your face no police telegraphic dispatch would catch you. The English gentleman 'Harcourt' must not act hastily. Remember he has ten days. Strike for your home, strike for your country; bide your time, but strike sure. Get introduced, congratulate him, listen to his stories—not many more will the brute tell to earthly friends. Do anything but fail, and meet us at the appointed place within the fortnight. Inclose this note, together with one of poor Leenea. I will give the reason for this when we meet. Return by Johnson. I wish I could go to you, but duty calls me to the West; you will probably hear from me in Washington. Sanders is doing us no good in Canada. Believe me, your brother in love, Charles Selby."[12] (George Sanders was one of the Confederate commissioners in Canada.)

Booth was in New York on the date the letters were found and had gone from there to Washington, as Mrs. Hudspeth heard the man on the street car say he would do. A handwriting expert testified at John Surratt's trial that this letter was written by Booth.

The phrase "the cup failed us once" could be connected with an inscription found cut with a diamond into a window of the McHenry House in Meadville, Pennsylvania: "Abe Lincoln Departed This Life August 13th 1864 By The Effects of Poison."[13] Nobody knew who had inscribed it or when. According to the hotel clerk, Booth had been registered at that hotel on 10 June and 29 June 1864, but he had not occupied the room with the inscribed window. Of course, that doesn't mean he might not have been in that room. Someone else involved in the plot might have occupied it. Nor does the difference in dates matter. The inscription was, no doubt, a prediction, or a hope. It might be significant that David Herold was employed as a clerk at a drug store at 15th Street and Pennsylvania Avenue, where the Lincoln family usually bought its medicines, and he delivered some to the White House on at least one occasion.

Julia Grant got no sleep on the night of the fourteenth-fifteenth. "Crowds of people came thronging into our cottage," she wrote, "to learn if the terrible news were true.... The first mail that sad morning brought a letter to General Grant. He having directed me to open all telegrams and letters, I read the following letter: 'General Grant, thank God, as I do, that you still live. It was your life that fell to my lot, and I followed you on the cars. Your car door was locked, and thus you escaped me, thank God!'"[14]

General Grant later mentioned this letter but said it came a few days later.

John Surratt might have been the would-be assassin of Grant, but witnesses placed him at Elmira, New York early on the morning of the fifteenth. He later claimed to have been sent there by the Confederate commissioners in Canada to examine the feasibility of a raid to free Rebel prisoners of war being held there. It does not seem impossible for him to have been on Grant's train out of Washington on the night of the fourteenth and still have reached Elmira the next morning. When Surratt was tried in 1867 there was conflicting testimony about whether he had been in Washington or Elmira on the thirteenth and fourteenth. The question of whether he was on Grant's train was not considered. At the conspiracy trial, Michael O'Laughlin was accused of trying to kill Grant, but he was acquitted. He was seen in Washington on the fourteenth and was known to have visited Booth's hotel room that day. Before noon on the fifteenth, the provost marshal of Maryland knew of Booth's close association with O'Laughlin and Sam Arnold, and a search for them was started.

George Atzerodt walked across Washington on the rainy morning of the fifteenth and reached Georgetown by 8 a.m. There he borrowed $10 from an acquaintance who was manager of a grocery store, leaving a revolver as security for the loan. From there he took a stagecoach for Rockville, Maryland. When the stage was stopped behind a line of wagons at a military checkpoint near Tennallytown, he got off, went up to the roadblock and bought the sergeant in charge a drink of cider from a nearby sutler's store. Then he hitched a ride on one of the wagons, which let him off at a tavern about three miles north of Rockville. After a visit to the tavern, he walked to a mill on Great Seneca Creek, where the miller, another acquaintance, put him up for the night.

After lunch on the fifteenth, Dr. Mudd and David Herold went to the home of Mudd's father, where they hoped to borrow a carriage, since Booth's broken leg made it difficult for him to ride. However, no carriage was available, so the two went on toward Bryantown. But Herold soon changed his mind and turned back to Mudd's house, leaving the doctor to go on alone to mail some letters that had been smuggled across the Potomac from the South. Mudd later said he learned from a Union soldier at Bryantown that Booth had assassinated Lincoln. He did not report the presence of two strangers—if such they were—at his home.

Booth and Herold left Mudd's place at about 5 p.m., skirted the swamp behind it, and made a circuit that took them east of Bryantown. They were trying to reach the secluded farm of William Bertle, near St. Mary's Catholic Church, which was sometimes used to shelter Confederate agents. They got lost and had to stop for directions twice. Their second stop, at 9 p.m., was at the home of Oswell Swann, a black tobacco farmer who lived about three miles southeast of Bryantown. Swann gave them some bread and whiskey, and they offered him two dollars to guide them to Bertle's farm, which was less than two miles away. But on the way they changed their minds and offered him another five dollars to take them to the home of Samuel Cox, which they reached at around midnight. Cox and his young servant girl later claimed that he turned Booth and Herold away at the door, but Swann said they went in and remained there for three or four hours. When they came out, Swann claimed he heard one of them say, "I thought Cox was a man of Southern feeling."[15] Swann helped Booth mount and then left for home without knowing where the two went next.

Cox was almost certainly a member of the clandestine Rebel organization in southern Maryland. He had already learned of the assassination from a steamer in the nearby river. Now Booth identified himself as the assassin and showed Cox the initials JWB tattooed on his wrist. Cox had his overseer hide the two men in a pine thicket about a mile from his house, and the next morning, the sixteenth, he sent someone to get his foster brother, Thomas A. Jones, who was also an agent on the clandestine Confederate mail line through southern Maryland. In an 1895 interview, Jones said, "I was given instructions how to reach them without being shot—certain signs by whistling, etc. Upon reaching the dense pines I met Herold, to whom I explained that I was sent by Cox. I was then piloted to where Booth was. He lay on the ground wrapped in a pile of blankets, and his face bore traces of pain. Booth asked many questions as to what people thought of the assassination. He appeared to be proud of what he had done. I at the time thought he had done a good act, but, Great God, I soon saw that it was the worst blow that ever struck the south! I did best I could for the poor fellow. I carried him papers to read and something to eat and tried to keep him in good spirits until I got a chance to get him across the river."[16]

While hiding near Cox's, Booth wrote in his memorandum book: "April 13, 14, Friday, the Ides. Until today nothing was ever thought of sacrificing to our country's wrongs. For six months we have worked to capture. But our cause being almost lost, something decisive and great must be done. But its failure was owing to others who did not strike for their country with a heart. I struck boldly, and not as the papers say. I walked with a firm step through a thousand of his friends; was stopped but pushed on. A colonel was at his side. I shouted Sic Semper before I fired. In jumping I broke my leg. I passed all his pickets. Rode sixty miles that night, with the bone of my leg tearing the flesh at every jump.

"I can never repent it, though we hated to kill. Our country owed all our troubles to him, and God simply made me the instrument of his punishment.

"The country is not what it was. This forced Union is not what I have loved. I care not what becomes of me. I have no desire to out live my country. This night (before the deed) I wrote a long article and left it for one of the editors of the *National Intelligencer* in which I fully set forth our reasons for our proceedings. He or the gov'r—"[17] The entry was never finished. No doubt he was going to say that either the editor or the government must have supressed his letter. He did not know that John Matthews had burned it.

Thomas Harbin, an agent of the Confederate Secret Service, and his partner, Joseph Baden, were rowed across the Potomac that morning, probably carrying word of Booth's deed and possibly his location to Rebels in Virginia who had been involved in the plan to capture Lincoln and transport him to Richmond.

After early mass that Easter Sunday morning, Louis Weichmann, John Holahan, and Detective James A. McDevitt went to Baltimore, following some clue regarding George Atzerodt. They called on the provost marshal of the city, but did not learn much and returned to Washington.

Meanwhile, Atzerodt left the mill where he had spent the night, heading for the farm of a cousin, near Germantown, Maryland. He had lived there as a boy and had visited it frequently since. Most people in the area knew Atzerodt as Andrew Atwood. Along the way, he stopped at the farm of Hezekiah Metz, where he was invited to stay for Sunday dinner. There were two other guests as well, a pair of brothers, at least one of whom had known Atzerodt/Atwood since boyhood. News of the assassination of Lincoln and the attack on Seward had reached the area, but few details were known. When Atzerodt mentioned that he had just come from Washington the others pressed him for information. Some of his answers later aroused the suspicions of those around the table, especially when Metz said he had heard a rumor that Grant had been shot on the train and asked Atzerodt if this was true. Atzerodt said, "If the man that was to follow him followed him, it is likely to be so."[18]

As word of the assassination spread across the country, public outrage frequently flared into violence. Members of Booth's family were suspected of complicity. A mob of over 500 gathered outside the hotel in Cincinnati where Booth's brother Junius Brutus Booth was staying, and it was four or five days later before he was able to get away. He later found himself in the Old Capitol Prison in Washington until the government's suspicions were allayed. Actors in general, and those at Ford's Theatre in particular, were also under suspicion. And anyone who looked like Booth was definitely in danger.

This fact almost spelled the end of one of the Confederacy's top secret agents. Captain Thomas Hines was in charge of military raids conducted out of Canada and efforts to instigate armed rebellion by the Copperheads of the North. He had been forming a new unit in his home state of Kentucky when he heard of the fall of Richmond and Lee's surrender. He had disbanded his men and headed back to Canada. When he reached Detroit on Sunday, the sixteenth, tired and unshaven, he went into a saloon for a drink and some dinner. But as he sat down at a table a man at the bar pointed to him and shouted, "That's John Wilkes Booth, I saw him many times in Baltimore and New York!"[19]

The place was instantly in an uproar. Hines stood up and drew a revolver as the men in the saloon tried to mob him. He clubbed the first man to reach for him and kicked another in the stomach and backed out of the building menacing them with his Colt. He then made his way across back fences to the wharf on the Detroit River where the ferry to Windsor, Canada had just arrived. He waited until the wagons and passengers from the other side had disembarked, then went on board and made his way to the boat's bridge. There he pulled his revolver again and forced the captain to immediately depart for the Canadian side. Once across, he gave the captain five dollars and apologized for the inconvenience before disappearing into the darkness. For some time it was feared by Federal authorities that Booth had escaped to Canada.

The War Department issued orders that day sending Halleck to command the Department of Virginia instead of Ord, who replaced Gillmore in command of the Department of the South.

Grant received a message that day from General Ewell, who, having been captured at Sayler's Creek before Lee's surrender, was confined with other Confederate generals at Fort Warren: "You will appreciate, I am sure, the sentiment which prompts me to drop you these lines. Of all the misfortunes which could befall the Southern people, or any Southern man, by far the greatest, in my judgment, would be the prevalence of the idea that they could entertain any other than feelings of unqualified abhorrance and indignation for the assassination of the President of the United States, and the attempt to assassinate the Secretary of State. No language can adequately express the shock produced upon myself, in common with all the other general officers confined here with me, by the occurrence of this appalling crime, and by the seeming tendency in the public mind to connect the South and Southern men with it. Need we say that we are not assassins, nor the allies of assassins, be they from the North or from the South, and that coming as we do from most of the States of the South we would be ashamed of our own people, were we not assured that they will reprobate this crime. Under the cirmcumstances I could not refrain from some expression of my feelings. I thus utter them to a soldier who will comprehend them. The following officers, Maj. Gens. Ed. Johnson, of Virginia, and Kershaw, of South Carolina; Brigadier-Generals Barton, Corse, Hunton, and Jones, of Virginia; Du Bose, Simms, and H.R. Jackson, of Georgia; Frazer, of Alabama; Smith and Gordon, of Tennessee; Cabell, of Arkansas, and Marmaduke of Missouri, and Commodore Tucker, of Virginia, all heartily concur with me in what I have said."[20]

Down in Alabama, at first light on the sixteenth LaGrange's brigade of Wilson's cavalry broke camp at Auburn and continued to follow the Montgomery & West Point Railroad to the northeast. By midmorning the head of the column came in sight of Fort Tyler, on the western side of the Chattahoochee River. Inside the fort, a small but formidible earthwork, was a scratch force of about 200 Rebels commanded by Brigadier General Robert C. Tyler, who was still recuperating from a wound received in the battles around Chattanooga seventeen months before. There were also three guns in the fort, two 12-pounders and a 32-pounder siege gun, that covered the railroad and wagon bridges over the Chattahoochee.

LaGrange's battery of horse artillery drove the Confederate

skirmishers into the fort, and three regiments of dismounted troopers worked their way to within fifty yards of the Rebel work, some of them carrying boards ripped from nearby houses to bridge the fort's ditch. Sharpshooters crawled even closer to snipe at the Confederate artillerymen. At LaGrange's signal, the three regiments charged the fort while the 4th Indiana galloped for the wagon bridge. The Hoosiers spurred their horses over a gap where the planking of the bridge had been taken up and drove off a few Rebels who had been stationed on the Georgia side with cotton and turpentine for burning it.

LaGrange then hurried back to the Alabama side, where some of his men had reached the ditch outside the fort. He ordered his battery to concentrate on the Rebel guns and it soon silenced them. Then he ordered his troopers forward again. General Tyler was dead, and his successor, Colonel James H. Fannin, surrendered. Since Alabama and Georgia had not agreed on a common gauge for their railroads, goods moving between the two states had to be transhipped at West Point. The Federals found the railyards there filled with rations, ordnance and clothing that had not been transferred in time. They destroyed 19 locomotives and 340 cars.

Thirty-five miles to the south, Wilson's main force approached Girard, Alabama that afternoon, just across the river from Columbus. The Rebels had between two and three thousand men to defend Columbus. These included one cavalry regiment and one battery of veterans and the two regiments of the Georgia state line, which had some drill and experience. But the rest were county reserves and workers from the numerous war industries of the city. In overall command was Major General Howell Cobb of the Georgia Militia. Because of a lack of men, the Confederates abandoned an outer line of defenses on the outskirts of Girard and instead manned an inner line on some hills covering a railroad bridge and footbridge across the Chattahoochee. Two other bridges farther south were rendered unusable. Forts along this line of works contained 21 pieces of artillery.

The first Union regiment to arrive, the 1st Ohio Cavalry of Upton's division, tried to capture one of the southern bridges, but the Rebels managed to set in on fire from the Georgia side before the Federals could replace the missing planking. Wilson then decided to attack the works defending the northern bridges with Winslow's brigade of Upton's division, but there was some confusion about what road Winslow was on, and by the time he was found it was almost dark. However, darkness had served the Federals well at Selma, and now Wilson decided to use it again. In conferring with Upton he spoke of attacking at 8 p.m. "Do you mean it?" Upton asked. "It will be dark as midnight by that hour and that will be a night attack indeed!"[21] Wilson left the tactical details to Upton, who made a study of such things. An infantry assault he had led the year before at Spotsylvania had been a model for attacking earthworks.

During the afternoon Wilson sent part of Benteen's 10th Missouri to try a bridge north of town, but it was also found to be partially destroyed and unusable. However, a local citizen was found who was able to draw Wilson a fairly accurate sketch of the Rebel defenses.

At 8 p.m. about half of the 3rd Iowa advanced dismounted, following a road that ran southeast toward the Confederate line. The night was dark but clear and was soon lit up by the fire of the Rebel artillery and infantry. Like most inexperienced troops, they fired too high and did little damage. "The whole country seemed to be alive with demons….," said Captain Charles Hinricks of the 10th Missouri, "the next second brought the balls of the enemy by thousands over our heads and the shells hurried their way in every direction, leaving a fiery streak behind them. This was the first time I ever saw shelling during night time, it is a beautiful but awful spectacle."

When the dismounted troopers crossed the abatis and drove the defenders from some outer rifle pits, Winslow and Upton thought that they had taken the main line. Upton ordered the 10th Missouri to charge for the bridge in column of fours. "A sweet thing I can tell you," Captain Hinricks wrote, "to charge the enemy's works, when it is dark as pitch and you don't know where they are. Particularly sweet when every second your eyes are blinded by the blue light of the shells exploding all around you and passing within four or five feet of the ground across the road you have to travel, not speaking of the grape, cannister and small bullets which however likely you cannot see, but only hear whistling by, or striking trees, or something else."[22] Two companies of the 10th Missouri found their way through the Confederate defenses, where they were either unnoticed or mistaken for retreating Rebels. They passed within a few feet of General Cobb and briefly held a footbridge across the river before a counterattack drove them off.

While this was going on, the Confederate fire outlined the Rebel strongpoints enough for Wilson, Upton and Winslow to direct the rest of the brigade to the proper places. The Federals had to cross a ravine and charge through thick woods, which broke up their formations, but they reformed and came on. The poorly trained Confederates were also disorganized by fear and confusion and unable to see what the Yankees were up to. Their line quickly dissolved, and their officers told them to save themselves. The men of both sides raced for the bridge, which was soon jammed with men, horses, wagons and ambulances. Part of the 4th Iowa passed some of the Rebels without knowing it, crossed the bridge, struck down a defender who was about to set it on fire, had a sharp little fight with a Confederate battery, and scattered the defenders in all directions. Over a thousand Rebels were captured. Firing had ceased by 11 p.m., when Wilson personally crossed the bridge. Many civilians joined in the rout when they learned that the defense had collapsed. According to one witness, "The women and children were running through the streets like people deranged, and men, with mules and wagons, driving in every direction."[23]

In North Carolina that day, the sixteenth, Jefferson Davis and his cabinet were on the road south again. Their host of the night before presented the Confederate president with a handsome filly. After toiling over a poor road all day, they failed to find another such friendly host and had to camp in the open for the night. Secretary Mallory was surprised to find that this change of venue seemed to relax Davis and bring him new vigor. "He decidedly preferred the bivouac to the bedroom," Mallory said. To the cabinet's amazement they found the usually stern president had become pleasant and talkative, as he lay smoking a cigar by the campfire with his saddle for a pillow.

Governor Vance of North Carolina caught up with Davis at Lexington. He had come, he said, to find out what Davis wanted him to do. Davis launched into a long and solemn review of the Confederacy's situation, insisting that an army could be rallied to fight in the trans-Mississippi West and intimating that Vance should raise troops from his state to join it. This speech was met by a sad silence. Secretary of War Breckinridge broke it by saying he did not think the president had answered the governor's question. Davis asked him how he would advise the governor.

"My advice would be," he said, turning to Vance, "that you return to your responsibilities and do the best you can for your people and share their fate, whatever it might be."

"Well," Davis sighed, "perhaps you are right."[24]

Sherman received a reply from General Johnston that day to his letter offering the same terms Grant had given to Lee.

Johnston asked to meet the Union commander the next day somewhere between their lines. "I ordered a car and locomotive to be prepared," Sherman wrote, "to convey me up to Durham's at eight o'clock of the morning of April 17th. Just as we were entering the car, the telegraph-operator, whose office was up-stairs in the depot-building, ran down to me and said that he was at that instant of time receiving a most important dispatch in cipher from Morehead City, which I ought to see. I held the train for nearly half an hour, when he returned with the message translated and written out. It was from Mr. Stanton announcing the assassination of Mr. Lincoln, the attempt on the life of Mr. Seward and son, and a suspicion that a like fate was designed for General Grant and all the principal officers of the Government. Dreading the effect of such a message at that critical instant of time, I asked the operator if any one besides himself had seen it; he answered no. I then bade him not to reveal the contents by word or look till I came back, which I proposed to do the same afternoon."[25]

Sherman did not mention it in his memoirs, but another message was sent to him at the same time, from General Halleck: "It has been stated that when an assassin was chosen to kill Mr. Seward one also was sworn to murder you. His name was said to be Clark. He is about five feet nine inches high, rather slender, high cheek bones, low forehead, eyes dark and sunken, very quiet, seldom or never speaks in company unless spoken to, has a large dark-brown mustache and large long goatee, hair much darker than whiskers, complexion rather sallow; while in Paris, March 12, wore dark-gray clothes, a wide-awake slouched hat. He is a Texan by birth, and has a very determined look. He had a confederate, whose name was Johnson, but no description of him is given."[26] The Johnson mentioned here might have been the same one mentioned in the letter found by Mrs. Hudspeth.

Sherman reached Durham at about 10 a.m., where Kilpatrick had horses for him and his staff and a squadron of cavalry waiting to escort him. They rode toward Hillsborough with a man carrying a white flag before them, and four or five miles up the road they met a similar party of Confederates, including Joe Johnston and Wade Hampton. "We shook hands," Sherman wrote, "and introduced our respective attendants. I asked if there was a place convenient where we could be private, and General Johnston said he had passed a small farm-house a short distance back, when we rode back to it together side by side, our staff-officers and escorts following. We had never met before, though we had been in the regular army together for thirteen years.... He was some twelve or more years my senior; but we knew each other to be well acquainted at once. We soon reached the house of a Mr. Bennett, dismounted, and left our horses with orderlies in the road. Our officers, on foot, passed into the yard, and General Johnston and I entered the small frame-house. We asked the farmer if we could have the use of his house for a few minutes, and he and his wife withdrew into a smaller log-house, which stood close by."[27]

While the two generals went inside alone, the officers left outside sized each other up. "Sherman is hard-featured and ill-favored," a Rebel colonel wrote. "What shall I say of Kilpatrick? His looks and his deeds favor each other." A Union major thought even less of Wade Hampton's "vulgar insolence," saying he was "a man of polished manners, scarcely veiling the arrogance and utter selfishness which marks his class, and which I hate with a perfect hatred."[28]

"As soon as we were alone together," Sherman wrote, "I showed him the dispatch announcing Mr. Lincoln's assassination, and watched him closely. The perspiration came out in large drops on his forehead, and he did not attempt to conceal his distress. He denounced the act as a disgrace to the age, and hoped I did not charge it to the Confederate Government. I told him I could not believe that he or General Lee, or the officers of the Confederate army, could possibly be privy to acts of assassination; but I would not say as much for Jeff. Davis, George Sanders, and men of that stripe. We talked about the effect of this act on the country at large and on the armies, and he realized that it made my situation extremely delicate. I explained to him that I had not yet revealed the news to my own personal staff or to the army, and that I dreaded the effect when made known in Raleigh. Mr. Lincoln was peculiarly endeared to the soldiers, and I feared that some foolish woman or man in Raleigh might say something or do something that would madden our men, and that a fate worse than that of Columbia would befall the place.

"I then told Johnston that he must be convinced that he could not oppose my army, and that, since Lee had surrendered, he could do the same with honor and propriety. He plainly and repeatedly admitted this, and added that any further fighting would be '*murder*;' but he thought that, instead of surrendering piecemeal, we might arrange terms that would embrace *all* the Confederate armies. I asked him if he could control other armies than his own; he said, not then, but intimated that he could procure authority from Mr. Davis. I then told him that I had recently had an interview with General Grant and President Lincoln, and that I was possessed of their views; that with them and the people of the North there seemed to be no vindictive feeling against the Confederate armies, but there was against Davis and his political adherents; and that the terms that General Grant had given to General Lee's army were certainly most generous and liberal. All this he admitted, but always recurred to the idea of a universal surrender, embracing his own army, that of Dick Taylor.... and of Maury, Forrest, and others.... "

Johnston interrupted the conference long enough to step outside and send a message to Secretary of War Breckinridge asking him to join the negotiations the next day. "Our conversation was very general and extremely cordial," Sherman said, "satisfying me that it could have but one result, and that which we all desired, viz., to end the war as quickly as possible; and, being anxious to return to Raleigh before the news of Mr. Lincoln's assassination could be divulged, on General Johnston's saying that he thought that, during the night, he could procure authority to act in the name of all the Confederate armies in existence, we agreed to meet again the next day at noon at the same place, and parted, he for Hillsboro' and I for Raleigh.

"We rode back to Durham's Station in the order we had come, and then I showed the dispatch announcing Mr. Lincoln's death. I cautioned the officers to watch the soldiers closely, to prevent any violent retaliation by them, leaving that to the Government in Washington; and on our way back to Raleigh in the cars I showed the same dispatch to General Logan and to several of the officers of the Fifteenth Corps that were posted at Morrisville and Jones's Station, all of whom were deeply impressed by it; but all gave their opinion that this sad news should not change our general course of action.

"As soon as I reached Raleigh I published.... orders to the army, announcing the assassination of the President, and I doubt if, in the whole land, there were more sincere mourners over his sad fate than were then in and about Raleigh. I watched the effect closely, and was gratified that there was no single act of retaliation; though I saw and felt that one single word by me would have laid the city in ashes, and turned its whole population houseless upon the country, if not worse."[29]

His fears were not groundless. Logan had to draw his sword to turn back some of his men who were bent on destroying Raleigh. There was a riot in Washington that day when a crowd somehow got the idea that Booth was among a group of Confederate prisoners being marched through the streets. Several people were wounded, including some of the soldiers guarding the prisoners, before the mob was satisfied that Booth was not there.

Louis Weichmann, John Holahan and Detective James McDevitt left Washington on the morning of the seventeenth for New York and Canada to see if they could find John Surratt. "I went with the kindest intentions in my heart towards him," Weichmann later wrote, "I began to realize that his mother and himself were in the greatest possible danger, and I felt that he owed it to her and to his own good name that he should return to the United States, surrender himself to the authorities, and clear himself of all connection with this great crime."[30]

The first arrests of Booth's conspirators were made that day, the seventeenth. The letter from Sam Arnold found in Booth's trunk was the key. Arnold was traced to Fort Monroe, Virginia, where he had been working for a sutler since 1 April. He readily admitted the plot to capture Lincoln but denied any part in any plan to kill him. He named the other conspirators as Booth, O'Laughlin, Atzerodt, Surratt, a man he knew as Mosby (Paine), and a small man (Herold) whose name he could not remember. That same day O'Laughlin was arrested in Baltimore. After an initial denial he refused to talk.

Also that day, the Navy's Potomac River Squadron captured Captain Thomas Nelson Conrad, a Confederate officer who had once spied on Lincoln's activities to see if capturing him was feasible and who had broken up the secret Union courier line from Richmond. The same ship then sent a landing party to arrest Mrs. Frances Dade, who had revealed the Union line to Conrad.

Federal soldiers came to the Surratt boarding house near midnight that night and informed Mrs. Surratt that they were there to arrest her and everyone in the house and take them to General Augur's headquarters for questioning. Four officers entered the house and arrested Mrs. Surratt, her daughter Anna, her cousin Miss Olivia Jenkins, and Miss Honora Fitzpatrick. Before the women could be rounded up and marched away, the doorbell rang. Two captains opened the door, and Lewis Paine walked in. He had lost his hat in his fight at Seward's house, and he was now wearing a stocking cap made from a sleeve of his undershirt. His clothes were muddy, and on his shoulder he carried a pickaxe he had found in the cemetery where he had hidden without food or drink for three days.

"I guess I am mistaken," he said, seeing the officers.

"Whom do you want to see?" one of them asked.

"Mrs. Surratt," he replied.

"You are right, walk in," the captain said.

Paine took a seat in the hall, and the captain, taking his pick from him, asked him why he was there.

"To dig a gutter," he said.

"When?"

"In the morning," he said.

He gave his name as Lewis Paine from Fauquier County, Virginia and produced his copy of the oath of allegiance he had taken in Baltimore on 14 March. He said he had come north in order to stay out of the Confederate army and that he made a meager living digging ditches.

The major in charge of the arresting party brought Mrs. Surratt into the hall. "Do you know this man," he asked, "and did you hire him to come and dig a gutter for you?"

Mary Surratt looked at the young man who had been one of her boarders, raised her right hand and said, "Before God, I do not know this man and have never seen him before, and I did not hire him to dig a gutter for me."

Paine and the women were taken to General Augur's headquarters. After questioning, the women were sent to Carrol Prison. Mrs. Surratt's room was searched and a bullet mold was found there. And beneath a picture representing morning, noon, and night was concealed a photo of John Wilkes Booth. On another wall was the coat of arms of the state of Virginia with the motto "Sic Semper Tyrannis."

The next day, William Bell, the servant at the Seward home, was brought to a room containing twenty or thirty people and asked if there was anyone there who looked like Mr. Seward's assailant. He said, "No." Then Paine and several others were brought in. Bell walked up, put his finger in Paine's face, and said, "I know you, you are the man."[31]

---

1. Davis, *The Long Surrender,* 80.
2. Jones, *Yankee Blitzkrieg,* 121.
3. Weichmann, *A True History of the Assassination of Abraham Lincoln and of the Conspiracy of 1865,* 179.
4. Brooks, *Washington in Lincoln's Time,* 231-232.
5. Welles, *The Diary of Gideon Welles,* 2:290.
6. Porter, *Campaigning with Grant,* 501.
7. Catton, *Grant Takes Command,* 476.
8. *Official Records,* 46:III:762.
9. Dana, *Recollections of the Civil War,* 239.
10. Ibid., 241.
11. Ibid., 242.
12. Ibid., 240.
13. Tidwell, Hall and Gaddy, *Come Retribution,* 262.
14. Grant, *The Personal Memoirs of Julia Dent Grant,* 156-157.
15. Tidwell, Hall and Gaddy, *Come Retribution,* 446-447.
16. Weichmann, *A True History of the Assassination of Abraham Lincoln and of the Conspiracy of 1865,* 195.
17. Tidwell, Hall and Gaddy, *Come Retribution,* 450.
18. Ibid., 434.

19. James D. Horan, *Confederate Agent: A Discovery in History* (New York, 1954), 261. A comparison of photographs shows only a superficial resemblance between Booth and Hine.
20. *Official Records,* 46:III:787.
21. Jones, *Yankee Blitzkrieg,* 135.
22. Ibid., 136-137.
23. Ibid., 139.
24. Davis, *The Long Surrender,* 82-83.
25. Sherman, *Memoirs,* 835-836.
26. *Official Records,* 47:III:221.
27. Sherman, *Memoirs,* 836-837.
28. Davis, *Sherman's March,* 259-261.
29. Sherman, *Memoirs,* 837-839.
30. Weichmann, *A True History of the Assassination of Abraham Lincoln and of the Conspiracy of 1865,* 220.
31. Ibid., 185-187.

CHAPTER FORTY-ONE

These Terms Are Too Generous

17 - 22 April 1865

Wilson's Union raiders, unaware of developments in Virginia and North Carolina, put numerous war industries in Columbus, Georgia to the torch on the seventeenth. By that evening much of the city lay in ashes, while exploding magazines of ammunition still occasionally rocked the earth for miles around. The fires at Selma had been small, one Union trooper said, compared to the vast columns of black, sulphurous smoke rising from Columbus. Among the items destroyed were a gunboat, an arsenal, the Confederate Naval Iron Works, the quartermaster's depot, a paper mill, several textile mills and flour mills, 15 locomotives, about 200 railroad cars, 5,000 rounds of ammunition, 74 cannon, and 50-100,000 bales of cotton. Wilson's next step would be to move another hundred miles to the east and take Macon, Georgia. To do so, his corps would have to cross the Flint River. So, late on the seventeenth, he ordered two regiments to ride all night and seize the crossing at a place called Double Bridges, where an island split the stream and bridges connected it to both banks.Jefferson Davis and most of his cabinet reached Salisbury, North Carolina on that seventeenth day of April. The ruins of the prison and the railroad depot were still smoldering as a result of Stoneman's raid. Davis and several others stayed with the rector of St. Luke's Church. A telegram from General Johnston had caused Postmaster General Reagan and Secretary of War Breckinridge to retrace their steps in order to join in the negotiations with Sherman.

Sherman returned to the Bennett house that day at noon, but it was nearly 2 p.m. by the time Johnston showed up. "General Johnston then assured me that he had authority over all the Confederate armies, so that they would obey his orders to surrender on the same terms with his own, but he argued that, to obtain so cheaply this desirable result, I ought to give his men and officers some assurance of their political rights after their surrender. I explained to him that Mr. Lincoln's proclamation of amnesty, of December 8, 1863, still in force, enabled every Confederate soldier and officer, below the rank of colonel, to obtain an absolute pardon, by simply laying down his arms, and taking the common oath of allegiance, and that General Grant, in accepting the surrender of General Lee's army, had extended the same principle to *all* the officers, General Lee included; such a pardon, I understood, would restore to them all their rights of citizenship."[1]

Johnston insisted that his officers and men were very worried about the subject. He said that Breckinridge was not far off and he would like him to join them. Sherman objected that he could not negotiate with a member of Davis's cabinet, but Johnston pointed out that Breckinridge was also a major general in the Confederate army and he could attend on that basis. Sherman consented, and Breckinridge was sent for. Johnston remembered that the Kentuckian was suffering from an involuntary lack of alcohol in his system that day and was trying to compensate with a big plug of tobacco. But, fortunately for him, when he appeared Sherman produced a bottle of medicinal whiskey from his saddlebags and invited the two Confederates to join him in a drink before they got down to business. "The expression of Breckinridge at this announcement... was beatific," Johnston remembered. "Tossing his quid into the fire, he rinsed his mouth, and when the bottle and the glass were passed to him, he poured out a tremendous drink, which he swallowed with great satisfaction. With an air of content, he stroked his mustache and took a fresh chew of tobacco."

Thus fortified, Breckinridge launched into a brilliant discussion in which he cited every rule and maxim of international and constitutional law and the laws of war that was so eloquent that Sherman said, "See here, gentlemen, who is doing this surrendering anyhow? If this thing goes on, you'll have me sending a letter of apology to Jeff Davis."

A messenger brought in a parcel of papers that Johnston said were from Postmaster General Reagan. The two Confederate generals looked them over and after a brief conversation handed one to Sherman. It was a draft of an agreement. However, Sherman considered it too general and verbose, so he sat down at a table and wrote out terms that he thought were in keeping with the conversation he had had with Lincoln at City Point.

"Sherman sat for some time absorbed in deep thought," Johnston remembered. "Then he arose, went to the saddlebags, and fumbled for the bottle. Breckinridge saw the movement. Again he took his quid from his mouth and tossed it into the fireplace. His eye brightened, and he gave every evidence of intense interest in what Sherman seemed about to do.

"The latter, preoccupied, perhaps unconscious of his action, poured out some liquor, shoved the bottle back into the saddlepocket, walked to the window, and stood there, looking out abstractedly, while he sipped his grog.

"From pleasant hope and expectation the expression on Breckinridge's face changed successively to uncertainty, disgust, and deep depression. At last his hand sought the plug of tobacco, and, with an injured, sorrowful look, he cut off another chew. Upon this he ruminated during the remainder of the interview taking little part in what was said."[2]

The terms that Sherman offered went considerably beyond the mere surrender of all Confederate forces: The rebel armies would disband and deposit their arms and public property at their respective state arsenals, to be reported to Washington and to be used only to maintain peace and order; each officer and man would sign an agreement to cease from acts of war; the president would recognize the existing state governments when their officers and legislators took the oaths prescribed by the federal constitution, with the legitimacy of rival governments being submitted to the Supreme Court; federal courts would be reestablished; the people would be guaranteed their political rights and franchises and their rights of person and property as defined by the constitution of the United States and of the states; the federal government would not punish anyone as long as they lived in peace, abstained from armed hostility, and obeyed the laws where they lived. Sherman was well aware that these terms were beyond his power to grant. Therefore the first proviso was for an armistice during which the forces of neither side would move until they had given the other side

48 hours notice. During this armistice, Sherman would submit the terms to the new president. "I cared little," he later said, "whether they were approved, modified, or disapproved *in toto*; only I wanted instructions."[3]

"These terms are too generous," Sherman told the two Rebels, "but I must hurry away before you make me sign a capitulation. I will submit them to the authorities at Washington, and let you hear how they are received." Then he told them goodbye, took his saddlebags, and left.

"Sherman is a bright man," Breckinridge told Johnston, "and a man of great force, but" he added with a look of great intensity, raising his voice, "General Johnston, General Sherman is a hog. Yes, sir, a *hog.* Did you see him take that drink by himself? No Kentucky gentleman would ever have taken away that bottle. He knew we needed it, and needed it badly."[4]

The next day, the eighteenth, Sherman dispatched a message to Stoneman, although he did not know the raider's position, informing him of the armistice with Johnston and ordering him to join Sherman's army at Durham's Station or Chapel Hill.

At noon on the eighteenth, Colonel John S. Mosby appeared at the hotel in Millwood, south of Winchester, Virginia. Hancock, still commanding the Middle Military Division in Sheridan's absence, had written to him offering the same terms that Grant had given Lee. Mosby had asked for a truce while he consulted his superiors. Hancock had agreed and had arranged to have one of his officers, Brigadier General George H. Chapman, meet Mosby to discuss it. But at this meeting Mosby said that he still had not heard from Johnston's army, and since his own command was not in immediate danger he would not yet surrender it. He did say that if Johnston surrendered or was defeated he would probably disband his battalion of rangers. He also expressed his regret at the assassination of President Lincoln. It was agreed to extend the truce two more days and, if Hancock agreed, ten more beyond that.

In Philadelphia on that eighteenth day of April, John Wilkes Booth's brother-in-law, John S. Clarke, a well known comic actor, opened an envelope that Booth had left in his safe back in November. It contained $4,000 in bonds, documents assigning his stock in the Pennsylvania oil fields to a brother and a sister, an undated letter to his mother, and a long letter addressed "to whom it may concern." The last was a justification of his plan to capture Lincoln, claiming that the South was justified in seceding and claiming the abolitionists were the real traitors.

It was signed "A Confederate, at present doing duty upon his own responsibility."[5] The words "at present" had been crossed out, probably when Booth had visited the Clarkes in February. Evidently he signed it at that time, also. The envelope had also contained another document which his sister, Asia Booth Clarke, destroyed.

Union officers came to Dr. Mudd's home that day, having tracked Booth and Herold that far. Mudd not only denied knowing Booth but said he had never heard of him, although he had heard of his brother Edwin, who was a more famous actor. He did say that two men he did not know had come to his house and that one of them had a broken leg. He claimed that the latter also had a long beard.

In southern Maryland on the eighteenth, Major O'Beirne's detectives were making a house-to-house search of the Banks O'Dee area in Charles County. Richard Clagett told them his son had seen men in a boat out on the river early Sunday morning, the sixteenth, heading toward Virginia. He did not say, and probably did not know that the men seen had probably been Thomas Harbin and Joseph Baden, but this information would eventually lead the Federals to John Wilkes Booth.

Lincoln's body lay in state in the East Room of the White House all that day. The great room was draped with crepe and black cloth, relieved only occasionally by white flowers and green leaves. The casket lay upon a fifteen-foot-high catafalque that was covered with a dome of black cloth. The custom of sending flowers to funerals was not yet common in those days, but this funeral was remarkable in its day for the abundance and beauty of the floral displays sent by various organizations and individuals. All day and night the body was watched over by a guard of honor consisting of four navy and eight army officers, including two generals.

The funeral ceremonies were conducted the next day, the nineteenth. Four clergymen officiated at the services. An inclined platform had been erected in the East Room and covered with black cloth, and on it stood numerous senators, congressmen, generals and admirals, and few prominent civilians, all of whom were pall-bearers. There were also representatives of the New York Chamber of Commerce and New York Associated Merchants, as well as many governors of states, and opposite the main entrance stood President Andrew Johnson, his friend Preston King, and Hannibal Hamlin, who had been vice president during Lincoln's first term. Behind them stood the justices of the Supreme Court and the cabinet officers with their wives. Also present were other members of the House and Senate and members of the diplomatic corps, their brilliant court costumes standing out strangely in the otherwise somber assemblage. At the foot of the catafalque was a small semi-circle of chairs for members of the family, but Robert was the only one there. His mother was unable to leave her room, and she kept Tad with her. At the head of the catafalque stood General Grant, separated from the other pall-bearers, his eyes filled with tears.

Long before the services ended, the streets outside were blocked by crowds of people who gathered to watch the procession that would carry the body to the Capitol, where it would again lie in state. Amid the tolling of bells and the booming of minute guns the procession left the White House at exactly 2 p.m. The sun shone brightly through a cloudless sky, picking out the colors in the uniforms of infantry, cavalry, artillery, and marines, the marching societies and associations, and the flags draped in black. There were several mounted generals with their staffs and hundreds of other army and naval officers on foot and on horseback. The pall-bearers rode in carriages, followed by the funeral carriage, a large canopied structure covered with black cloth, not unlike the catafalque that had stood in the East Room; it was surrounded by an honor guard of mounted non-commissioned officers of light artillery.

"One noticeable feature of the procession," reporter Noah Brooks said, "was the appearance of the colored societies which brought up the rear, humbly, as was their wont; but just before the procession began to move, the Twenty-Second United States Colored Infantry (organized in Pennsylvania), landed from Petersburg and marched up to a position on the avenue, and when the head of the column came up, played a dirge, and headed the procession to the Capitol."[6] The coffin was carried from the funeral car and put on a catafalque in the rotunda of the Capitol, which had been darkened and draped in mourning. There thousands of people passed to gaze on the face of the dead president.

The War Department published orders that day revoking the order that replaced Ord with Halleck and Gillmore with Ord. Instead, the new order combined the Department of Virginia, such parts of North Carolina not occupied by Sherman's forces, and the Army of the Potomac into a new Military Division of the James. Halleck was appointed to command it.

Jefferson Davis and the Confederate cabinet had spent the night of the eighteenth at Concord, North Carolina. On the nineteenth they came to Charlotte, where they would stop for a while. Fear of retaliation by Stoneman's cavalry made most of the town's resident's reluctant to take Davis in. The only one daring enough was a bachelor of Northern birth and poor reputation named Lewis F. Bates, who was suspected by some of being a Yankee spy. Davis was about to give a speech to a column of cavalry from Bates' porch when he was handed a telegram from Secretary of War Breckinridge informing him of the assassination of Abraham Lincoln. Accounts of Davis's reaction vary. One version is that after reading the telegram twice he handed it to a prominent civilian, saying, "Here is a very extraordinary communication. It is sad news."[7] Bates later testified at the trial of Booth's conspirators that the Confederate president had said, "If it were to be done, it were better it were well done." Davis said that Bates was not even present at the time. Bates also testified that a day or two later when Breckinridge, who had rejoined the president by then, remarked that he regretted the assassination, Davis made the same remark and added "if the same had been done to Andy Johnson, the beast, and to Secretary Stanton, the job would then be complete."[8]

Early on the nineteenth, Sherman sent Major Henry Hitchcock of his staff by rail to Morehead City, on the coast, bearing the agreement signed the day before with Johnston and Breckinridge. He also telegraphed ahead to have a steamer ready to take Hitchcock to Washington. Besides the agreement, the major carried letters to Halleck and Grant.

To Halleck, Sherman said, "I received your dispatch describing the man Clark, detailed to assassinate me. He had better be in a hurry, or he will be too late.

"The news of Mr. Lincoln's death produced a most intense effect on our troops. At first I feared it would lead to excesses; but now it has softened down, and can easily be guided. None evinced more feeling than General Johnston, who admitted that the act was calculated to stain his cause with a dark hue; and he contended that the loss was most serious to the South, who had begun to realize that Mr. Lincoln was the best friend they had.

"I cannot believe that even Mr. Davis was privy to the diabolical plot, but think it the emanation of a set of young men of the South, who are very devils. I want to throw upon the South the care of this class of men, who will soon be as obnoxious to their industrial classes as to us.

"Had I pushed Johnston's army to an extremity, it would have dispersed, and done infinite mischief. Johnston informed me that

General Stoneman had been at Salisbury, and was now at Statesville. I have sent him orders to come to me.

"General Johnston also informed me that General Wilson was at Columbus, Georgia, and he wanted me to arrest his progress. I leave that to you.

"Indeed, if the President sanctions my agreement with Johnston, our interest is to cease all destruction.

"Please give all orders necessary according to the views the Executive may take, and influence him, if possible, not to vary the terms at all, for I have considered every thing, and believe that, the Confederate armies once dispersed, we can adjust all else fairly and well."

The letter to Grant was to cover the copy of the agreement. After a brief introduction, he said, "You will observe that it is an absolute submission of the enemy to the lawful authority of the United States, and disperses his armies absolutely; and the point to which I attach most importance is, that the dispersion and disbandment of these armies is done in such a manner as to prevent their breaking up into guerrilla bands. On the other hand, we can retain just as much of an army as we please. I agreed to the mode and manner of the surrender of arms set forth, as it gives the States the means of repressing guerrillas, which we could not expect them to do if we stripped them of all arms.

"Both Generals Johnston and Breckinridge admitted that slavery was dead, and I could not insist on embracing it in such a paper, because it can be made with the States in detail. I know that all the men of substance South sincerely want peace, and I do not believe they will resort to war again during this century. I have no doubt they will in the future be perfectly subordinate to the laws of the United States. The moment my action is approved, I can spare five corps, and will ask for orders to leave General Schofield here with the Tenth Corps, and to march myself with the [rest] via Burkesville and Gordonsville to Frederick or Hagerstown, Maryland, there to be paid and mustered out.

"The question of finance is now the chief one, and every soldier and officer not needed should be got home at work. I would like to be able to begin the march north by May 1st.

"I urge on the part of the President, speedy action, as it is important to get the Confederate armies to their homes as well as our own."

Major Hitchcock got off on the morning of the 20th," Sherman later wrote, "and I reckoned that it would take him four or five days to go to Washington and back. During that time the repairs on all the railroads and telegraph-lines were pushed with energy, and we also got possession of the railroad and telegraph from Raleigh to Weldon, in the direction of Norfolk.... On the 20th I reviewed the Tenth Corps, and was much pleased at the appearance of General Paine's division of black troops, the first I had ever seen as a part of an organized army.... "[9]

In Maryland on the nineteenth, Hezekiah Metz, who had invited George Atzerodt to Sunday dinner three days before, met Nathan Page, a neighbor. While they were discussing the assassination of President Lincoln, Metz told Page some of the suspicious things that had been said by the man he knew as Andrew Atwood. Page knew James W. Purdum, a strong supporter of the Lincoln administration who had close ties with the Union garrison at Monocacy Junction. That afternoon Page visited Purdum at his home north of Germantown and repeated to him what Metz had told him. Purdum rode toward Monocacy Junction to report it, but on his way ran into a Union private he knew and asked him to take the message for him. The private told a sergeant, who in turn told a captain. This officer was skeptical because Purdum had sent him worthless information before. He reported it to the major commanding the post, but did not think it was worth bothering about. The major agreed at first, but by 9 p.m. he had changed his mind. He told the captain to send a detail of men to arrest the man who had made the suspicious remarks.

The detail consisted of six troopers of the 1st Delaware Cavalry and Sergeant Zachariah Gemmill. By the time the story got to Gemmill he thought he was after a man named Lockwood, thought to be on the Richter farm near Germantown. The Federals got lost on the back roads, so it was past midnight when they found Purdum's place and got him out of bed. At about 4 a.m. on the twentieth they reached the Richter farm. When Richter came to the door, Gemmill asked him if Lockwood was there. Richter said his cousin had gone to Frederick, but the sergeant searched the house and found three men in an upper bedroom. Two were farmhands named Nichols, brothers. The other said his name was Atwood. To Gemmill, that was close enough. He took him to the Solomon Leaman home in Germantown where he was identified as Atwood. Gemmill went back and arrested Richter and by noon delivered both prisoners to Monocacy Junction. There is was quickly established that Atwood was George Atzerodt, who was wanted in connection with the assassination. By 11:30 p.m. both prisoners were under guard aboard the USS *Saugus,* a monitor anchored at the Washington Navy Yard.

Louis Weichmann, Holahan, and Detective McDevitt reached Montreal on the twentieth. "How can I ever forget that trip to Canada!" Weichmann wrote. "Black everywhere. The railway coaches were all heavily draped in mo[u]rning. Along the lines of travel where a house could be seen, there hung some sable emblem as a mute witness of the great and universal grief under which the land rested. The great cities of Baltimore, Philadelphia, New York, Albany, and Troy, through which we passed, were one mass of swaying crepe. The heart of the nation was almost ready to burst in its mighty agony; yet, amidst all this woe, strange as it may now appear, there were people who actually rejoiced in the assassination, and were glad that Abraham Lincoln was no more."[10] Weichmann went to St. Lawrence Hall and examined the hotel register. He found that John Surratt, under the name John Harrison, had arrived there on 6 April, had left for the states on 12 April, had returned on the eighteenth, and had left again on the same evening without saying where he was going.

The War Department offered a reward, on the twentieth, of $50,000 for the murderer of President Lincoln. A $25,000 reward was offered for John H. Surratt, and the same amount for David E. Herold. Notice was also given that "all persons harboring or secreting the said persons, or either of them, or aiding or assisting their concealment or escape, will be treated as accomplices in the murder of the President and the attempted assassination of the Secretary of State, and shall be subject to trial before a military commission and the punishment of death."[11]

The legislature of Union-occuppied Arkansas ratified the 13th Amendment on the twentieth, and Robert E. Lee wrote a letter to Jefferson Davis from his home at Richmond. He had already sent Davis a long formal report before leaving Appomattox Court House, but this letter was more like an appeal for the Confederate president to make peace. He told Davis that "the operations which occurred while the troops were in the entrenchments in front of Richmond and Petersburg were not marked by the boldness and decision which formerly characterized them. Except in particular instances, they were feeble; and a want of confidence seemed to possess officers and men. This condition, I think, was produced by the state of feeling in the country, and the communications received by the men from their homes, urging their return and the abandonment of the field." After giving a brief description of how his army disintegrated on the road to Appomattox, he said, "I have given these details that Your Excellency might know the state of feeling which existed in the army, and judge of that in the country. From what I have seen and learned, I believe an army cannot be organized or supported in Virginia, and as far as I know the condition of affairs, the country east of the Mississippi is morally and physically unable to maintain the contest unaided with any hope of ultimate success. A partisan war may be continued, and hostilities protracted, causing individual suffering and the devastation of the country, but I see no prospect by that means of achieving a separate independence. It is for Your Excellency to decide, should you agree with me in opinion, what is proper to be done. To save useless effusion of blood, I would recommend measures be taken for suspension of hostilities and the restoration of peace."[12]

Lee learned of Lincoln's assassination that same day and viewed it as bad news for the South. He said he had surrendered as much to the president's "goodness as to Grant's artillery."[13] Although Lee did not mention it, Sheridan's cavalry had had even more to do with it.

At Macon, Georgia, capital of the state since Sherman had marched through Milledgeville five months before, General Howell Cobb had gathered some 2,500 men from the Georgia Militia, reserves, new recruits, and veterans separated from their own units. But on the afternoon of 20 April he received an unexpected message from Beauregard: "Inform General commanding enemy's forces in your front that a truce for the purpose of a final settlement was agreed upon yesterday between Generals Johnston and Sherman, applicable to all forces under their commands. A message to that effect from General Sherman will be sent to him as soon as practicable. The contending forces are to occupy their present position, forty-eight hours warning being given in the event of the resumption of hostilities."[14] Cobb sent Brigadier General Felix Robertson, who had been a West Point classmate of Wilson's, to meet the advancing Federals under a flag of truce and deliver this message. Meanwhile, Cobb began to evacuate the fortifications of Macon and started sending his militia home.

As Wilson's troopers had advanced the day before, they had begun to encounter individual Confederate soldiers from Lee's army, making their way home from Appomattox. Rumors soon spread through the Union column that Lee had surrendered, but not everyone was convinced until a train was captured on which they found newspapers that confirmed the rumors. The 17th Indiana Mounted Infantry led Wilson's main column on the twentieth, driving small bodies of Rebels before it. About thirteen miles west of Macon the Hoosiers came upon General Robertson's flag of truce. The commander of the 17th sent the message he carried to his division commander, Minty, who sent it on to Wilson. Meanwhile, Minty told the Hoosiers to give Robertson's party five minutes to either surrender or clear the road. The Confederate refused to surrender and retired toward Macon.

After waiting five minutes, the 17th charged and chased the Rebels across Rocky Creek and into the defenses of Macon. No resistance was offered, so the Federals rode right on into the city, where they soon met another truce party sent out by Cobb. The 17th's commander was told that, under the terms of the truce, he should withdraw to the point where Robertson had first presented him the news of the armistice. The Federal said he could not receive orders through Confederate officers and demanded the immediate surrender of all Rebel forces in Macon. Cobb was angry but had little choice, so at 6 p.m. he surrendered, under protest. The lone Union regiment thus captured 2,000 Rebels, including five generals, 3,000 small arms, 60 pieces of artillery, and a large amount of supplies.

When Wilson received Robertson's message he rode forward, but by the time he reached the head of the column, Cobb had already surrendered. The Confederate reiterated his demand that the Federals fall back to the point where they had received word of the truce, but Wilson upheld his subordinate's actions and said he could only be bound by prior orders until he received others directly from Sherman.

The next day, the 21st, Wilson established contact with Sherman via the Confederate telegraph, verified the armistice and received orders to abstain from acts of war and devastation and to start paying for supplies. He was also informed by Sherman of the assassination of Lincoln. His officers watched the men closely for, as one put it, "distressing results might have followed any indiscreet word or act on the part of a Southerner."[15]

Sherman also sent a letter to Wilson through Johnston, telling the latter, "He may distrust the telegraph, therefore better send the original, for he cannot mistake my handwriting.... He seems to have his blood up and will be hard to hold." He also told Johnston, "I shall look for Major Hitchcock back from Washington on Wednesday and shall promptly notify you of the result. By the action of General Weitzel, in relation to the Virginia Legislature, I feel certain we will have no trouble on the score of recognizing existing State governments. It may be the lawyers will want us to define more minutely what is meant by the guaranty of rights of person and property. It may be construed into a compact for us to undo the past as to the rights of slaves and 'leases of plantations' on the Mississippi, of 'vacant and abandoned' plantations. I wish you would talk to the best men you have on these points and if possible let us in the final convention make these points so clear as to leave no room for angry controversy. I believe, if the South would simply and publicly declare what we all feel, that slavery is dead, that you would inaugurate an era of peace and prosperity that would soon efface the ravages of the past four years of war. Negroes would remain in the South and afford you abundance of cheap labor which otherwise will be driven away, and it will save the country the senseless discussions which have kept us all in hot water for fifty years. Although strictly speaking this is no subject of a military convention, yet I am honestly convinced that our simple declaration of a result will be accepted as good law everywhere. Of course I have not a single word from Washington on this or any other point of our agreement, but I know the effect of such a step by us will be universally accepted."[16]

Colonel Mosby returned to Millwood on the twentieth to meet with General Chapman again. Hancock had referred Mosby's request to extend the truce another ten days to Halleck and had received an answer from Grant telling him, "If Mosby does not avail himself of the present truce end it and hunt him and his men down. Guerrillas.... will not be entitled to quarter."[17] Mosby was suspected of being involved in the killing of Lincoln and the attack on Seward, he had been offered a chance to surrender on the same terms as Lee, and Union patience with him was wearing thin.

Mosby said he was not prepared to surrender, although part of his command had already disbanded. The Federals said that the truce was ended and that, if he did not surrender, Hancock would use his 40,000 men, who had nothing else to do, to dismantle the area of northern Virginia known as "Mosby's Confederacy" and turn it into a desert.

Mosby was stunned. "Tell General Hancock he is able to do it," he said.[18]

One of Mosby's men, who had been amusing himself with horse races with the Federal escort while the officers met, rushed in just then to say that he had seen a thousand Yankee troops hiding in the bushes and claimed that the Rebels had been tricked. Mosby drew his revolver, and he and his officers backed out of the room. "Had a single pistol been discharged by accident," one Confederate wrote, "or had Mosby given the word, not one Yankee officer in the room would have lived a minute." Once outside the Rebels quickly mounted their horses. "We galloped rapidly from Millwood to the Shenandoah River," the same officer said, "closely followed by a cloud of Yankee cavalry."[19]

Mosby gathered his men at Salem, east of the Blue Ridge, the next day, the 21st. He assembled them in an open field, and then his adjutant, who was also his brother, read them a message from the colonel disbanding the battalion forever.

That same day, as Abraham Lincoln's body started a long train ride home to Springfield, Illinois by way of various Northern cities, Major Hitchcock reached Washington and delivered Sherman's letter to Grant and the peace terms he and Johnston had agreed to. When he read them, Grant knew Sherman had made a big mistake. Quickly he dashed off a note to Secretary Stanton, who was at home having dinner: "I have received and just completed reading the dispatches brought by special messenger from General Sherman. They are of such importance that I think immediate action should be taken on them and that it should be done by the President in council with his whole cabinet. I would respectfully suggest whether the President should not be notified and all his cabinet, and the meeting take place to-night."

Stanton hurried back to the War Department, read Sherman's dispatches, and took Grant to see President Johnson. By 8 p.m. the cabinet was assembled. "Stanton briefly mentioned that General Grant had important communications from General Sherman," Secretary Welles recorded, "and requested that he would read them, which he did. It stated he had made a peace, if satisfactory, with the Rebels, etc., etc. This and everything related to it will be spread before the world. Among the Cabinet and all present there was but one mind on this subject. The plan was rejected, and Sherman's arrangement dissapproved. Stanton and Speed were emphatic in their condemnation, though the latter expressed personal friendship for Sherman. General Grant, I was pleased to see, while disapproving what Sherman had done, and decidedly opposed to it, was tender to sensitiveness of his brother officer and abstained from censure. Stanton came charged with specific objections, four in number, counting them off on his fingers. Some of his argument was apt and well, some of it not in good taste nor precisely pertinent."[20]

The secretary of war then put the results of the meeting in writing for Grant: "The memorandum or basis agreed upon between General Sherman and General Johnston having been submitted to the President, they are disapproved. You will give notice of the disapproval to General Sherman and direct him to resume hostilities at the earliest moment. The instructions given to you by the late President Abraham Lincoln of the 3d of March by my telegraph of that date, addressed to you, express substantially the views of President Johnson and will be observed by General Sherman. A copy is herewith appended. The President desires that you proceed immediately to the headquarters of General Sherman and direct operations against the enemy." The telegram from Lincoln referred to was the one in which the late president told Grant to "have no conference with General Lee, unless it be for the capitulation of General Lee's army or on some minor and purely military matter.... you are not to decide, discuss, or confer upon any political question."[21]

By then it was 11 p.m., and Grant dashed off a quick note to Julia to let her know that he would not be coming home to see her soon, as he had hoped, but instead had to go to North Carolina. He was finding that the end of combat had not made his job any easier. "I find my duties, anxieties and the necessities for having all my wits about me increasing instead of diminishing," he told her. "I have a Hurculean task to perform and shall endeavor to do it, not to please anyone but for the interest of our great country that is now beginning to loom above all other countries, modern and ancient."[22]

Union officers returned to the home of Dr. Samuel Mudd in southern Maryland on the 21st to arrest him and search his house. Mudd's alarmed wife then produced the boot that the doctor said he had cut off the man with the broken leg six days before. One of the Federals turned down the top of the boot and found the name "J. Wilkes" written inside it. Mudd then admitted that he had been introduced to Booth the previous fall, and the doctor was taken to Washington for further questioning. The Union authorities had now traced Booth as far as Mudd's house, but they still had no idea what had happened to him since he left there on the fifteenth.

That same day, Thomas Jones learned that most of the Union troops had left the area in the immediate vicinity of Booth's hiding place. After dark he went and got Booth and Herold and, with Booth mounted on a horse, set out for his home, three miles away. There he fed them, and then he led them down a creek to where he had a 14-foot boat. The creek flowed through a deep ravine into the lower Potomac River. Booth had a box compass, and Jones gave him the heading for Machodoc Creek on the Virginia side of the river, which was almost two miles wide at that point. Once across, the two conspirators were to contact Confederate agents Thomas Harbin and Joseph Baden.

At about 10 p.m. the boat was pushed out onto the broad river. But about fifteen minutes later the USS *Juniper,* a gunboat of the Potomac River Flotilla, came to anchor off Persimmon Point. An hour and a half later, the USS *Heliotrope* passed the *Juniper* on its way upstream, and at about the same time the wind began to blow from the south. The combination of unfavorable winds and patrolling gunboats forced Booth and Herold to return to the Maryland side of the river. They came ashore over four miles upstream from their starting point, on the bank of Nanjemoy Creek near the home of another Confederate sympathizer, John J. Hughes, who fed them and treated them kindly.

"After being hunted like a dog through swamps, woods, and last night being chased by gunboats till I was forced to return wet, cold and starving," Booth recorded in his makeshift diary, "I am here in despair. And why? For doing what Brutus was honored for—What made Tell a hero. And yet I, for striking down a greater tyrant than they ever knew am looked upon as a common cut-throat.... Tonight I will once more try the river with the intent to cross. Though I have a greater desire and almost a mind to return to Washington, and in a measure clear my name—which I feel I can do. I do not repent the blow I struck. I may before my God but not to man."[23]

---

1. Sherman, *Memoirs,* 840.
2. Stern, *An End to Valor,* 326-327.
3. Sherman, *Memoirs,* 842.
4. Stern, *An End to Valor,* 327-328.
5. Tidwell, Hall and Gaddy, *Come Retribution,* 405.
6. Brooks, *Washington in Lincoln's Time,* 235.
7. Davis, *The Long Surrender,* 85.
8. Weichmann, *A True History of the Assassination of Abraham Lincoln and of the Conspiracy of 1865,* 272.
9. Sherman, *Memoirs,* 842-845.
10. Weichmann, *A True History of the Assassination of Abraham Lincoln and of the Conspiracy of 1865,* 220-221.
11. *Official Records,* 46:III:847.
12. Dowdey and Manarin, ed., *The Wartime Papers of R.E. Lee,* 938-939.
13. Stern, *An End to Valor,* 330.
14. Jones, *Yankee Blitzkrieg,* 165.
15. Ibid., 168.
16. *Official Records,* 47:III:265-266.
17. Ibid., 46:III:839.
18. Kevin H. Siepel, *Rebel: The Life and Times of John Singleton Mosby* (New York, 1983), 152.
19. Virgil Carrington Jones, *Ranger Mosby* (Chapel Hill, 1944), 268-269.
20. Welles, *The Diary of Gideon Welles,* 2:294-295.
21. *Official Records,* 47:III:263.
22. Catton, *Grant Takes Command,* 484.
23. Trudeau, *Out of the Storm,* 232.

CHAPTER FORTY-TWO

The Matter Was Surely At an End

22 - 27 April 1865

The train bearing President Lincoln's body reached Philadelphia on 22 April. "Thousands of the plain people whom Lincoln loved," reporter Noah Brooks wrote, "came out from their homes to stand bareheaded and reverent as the funeral train swept by, while bells were tolled and the westward progress through the night was marked by campfires built along the course by which the great emancipator was borne at last to his dreamless sleep."[1] Thirty thousand people had come out in a heavy rain to see the coffin at Harrisburg, the state capital. Half a million were on hand at Philadelphia when the train arrived at noon. A young child was said to have been killed in the crush of the crowd, and a young lady's arm was broken.

Halleck took up his new duties that day as commander of the Military Division of the James, and he wired Stanton that morning from Richmond: "It is stated by respectable parties that the amount of specie taken South by Jeff. Davis and his partisans is very large, including not only the plunder of the Richmond banks, but previous accumulations. They hope, it is said, to make terms with General Sherman or some other Southern commander by which they will be permitted with their effects, including this gold plunder, to go to Mexico or Europe. Johnston's negotiations look to that end. Would it not be well to put Sherman and all other commanding generals on their guard in this respect."

Stanton replied that afternoon: "Your telegram of this morning indicates that Sherman's agreement with Johnston was not known to you. His action is disapproved, and he is ordered to resume hostilities immediately, as his order to Stoneman will allow Jeff. Davis to escape with his plunder. I will write you the details."

Grant, on his way to North Carolina, wired Halleck from Fort Monroe that afternoon: "The truce entered into by Sherman will be ended as soon as I can reach Raleigh. Move Sheridan with his cavalry toward Greensborough, N.C., as soon as possible. I think it will be well to send one corps of infantry also, the whole under Sheridan. The infantry need not go farther than Danville unless they receive orders hereafter to do so."[2] The infantry corps chosen was Sheridan's favorite, the 6th.

Stanton sent a long dispatch to General Dix in New York that day for release to the press. It announced the receipt of Sherman's agreement with Johnston and its unanimous disapproval by the president, the cabinet and General Grant. It also said that Sherman had been instructed to resume hostilities and that Johnson had approved and reiterated the message Lincoln had sent to Grant on 3 March, and it gave the impression that Sherman should have been aware of that message. He also said, "The orders of General Sherman to General Stoneman to withdraw from Salisbury and join him will probably open the way for Davis to escape to Mexico or Europe with his plunder, which is reported to be very large.... " and went on to quote Halleck's dispatch on the subject. He also revealed that Grant had started for North Carolina "to direct operations against Johnston's army."[3]

Stanton ordered Hancock to move the headquarters of the Middle Military Division to Washington that day, and Hancock reported that night that "Nearly all of Mosby's command has surrendered, including nearly or quite all of the officers except Mosby himself, who has probably fled. His next in rank, Lieutenant-Colonel Chapman, surrendered with the command. He is as important as Mosby, and from conversation had with him I think he will be valuable to the Government hereafter. Some of Mosby's own men are in pursuit of him for a reward of $2,000 offered by me. As near as I can tell about 380 of Mosby's men are paroled."[4]

Brigadier General John P. Slough, military governor of Alexandria, Virginia, reported to Augur's headquarters that day that "Rebel soldiers of the Army of Northern Virginia report that this side of the Rappahannock River there are large numbers of men of that army without paroles; some say many hundreds."[5] Many of those unparoled Rebels must have been members of the force secretly put in place to provide security for bringing a captured Lincoln to Richmond. When the Confederate capital had been hastily abandoned, there had not been time to recall them to their units.

Booth and Herold again tried crossing the Potomac to Virginia that day, and this time they made it. About sundown they crossed the mouth of Nanjemoy Creek. Their easiest route would have been directly across the river, but instead they rowed downstream, heading for the area that Jones had pointed them toward the night before, where they were supposed to contact Confederate agent Tom Harbin. The tide was against them much of the way, but a northwest wind aided them until they neared the mouth of Machodoc Creek on the Virginia side. They finally had to land a bit farther north, near the mouth of Gambo Creek. There they were over a mile from their objective, the Cottage, home of Elizabeth Quesenberry, on Machodoc Creek.

Leaving Booth behind, Herold walked across the fields and reached the widow Quesenberry's place at about 1 p.m. on the 23rd. She wasn't home but soon returned. She later claimed that she refused to help the two fugitives, other than to give them food. But she sent for Harbin and Baden, which means almost certainly that she had been expecting them and knew who they were. Harbin took the promised food to Gambo Creek. He later said that Booth complained about his broken leg and asked to be taken to Dr. Richard H. Stuart. Herold was sent to get horses from a nearby farmer, William Bryant, and Harbin then sent the two with Bryant to Stuart's, which they reached about 8 p.m.

According to Stuart's later statement, Herold did all the talking and asked him to put them up for the night. Herold said they were Marylanders and that his brother had a broken leg that had been set by Dr. Mudd, who had referred them to Stuart for further medical help. Stuart claimed to have refused to help them, saying he was a physician not a surgeon, he did not know Dr. Mudd, and his house was too full to accommodate the two men. He did, however let them come in for something to eat. They said they wanted to "go to Mosby" and needed transportation to Fredericksburg. "Mosby has surrendered," Stuart told them, and added, ".... you will have to get your paroles."[6] Actually, Mosby himself had not surrendered, but was making his way with a few followers toward Richmond, seeking information about Johnston's army in North Carolina. But many of his men were making their way to various Union units to give their parole under the terms Grant had given Lee. Stuart also said his neighbor, William Lucas, a free black man, had a wagon they might be able to hire. Booth and Herold rode over to Lucas's one-room cabin and took it over for the night. They threatened Lucas with a knife and put his family outside. Down at Charlotte, North Carolina on that Sunday, the 23rd, Jefferson Davis, his aides, part of his cabinet, and a few Confederate congressmen attended services at St. Peter's Episcopal Church and heard an impassioned sermon on the murder of Abraham Lincoln, which the rector described as "unjustifiable at any time, but occuring just now, renders it obligatory upon every Christian to set his face against it—to express his abhorrence of a deed fraught with consequences to society everywhere, and more especially to Southern society." Davis left the church with a smile on his face and said, "I think the preacher directed his remarks at me; and he really seems to fancy I had something to do with the assassination."[7] It did not seem to occur to him that many others, including the Federal authorities, shared that opinion, nor to heed the pastor's advice to speak out against it.

Sherman, still at Raleigh, sent Joe Johnston a bundle of newspapers he had just received from the North giving news of the North's reaction to the assassination of Lincoln. "Young Fred. Seward is alive," he said, "having been subjected to the trepan, and may possibly recover. There appears no doubt the murder of Mr. Lincoln was done by Booth, and the attempt on Mr. Seward by Surratt, who is in custody." Evidently, Paine was thought to be Surratt at first. "The feeling North on this subject is more intense than anything that ever occurred before," Sherman went on. "General Ord, at Richmond, has recalled the permission given for the Virginia Legislature, and I fear much the assassination of the President will give such a bias to the popular mind which, in connection with the desire of our politicians, may thwart our purpose of recognizing 'existing local governments.' But it does seem to me there must be good sense enough left on this continent to give order and shape to the now disjointed elements of government. I believe this assassination of Mr. Lincoln will do the cause of the South more harm than any event of the war, both at home and abroad, and I doubt if the Confederate military authorities had any more complicity with it than I had. I am thus frank with you and have asserted as much to the War Department. But I dare not say as much for Mr. Davis or some of the civil functionaries, for it seems the plot was fixed for March 4, but delayed, awaiting some instructions from Richmond. You will find in the newspapers I send you all the information I have on this point. Major Hitchcock should be back to morrow, and if any delay occurs it will result from the changed feeling about Washington arising from this new and unforeseen complication."[8] In anticipation of the need to discuss the situation with Washington, Sherman urged that day that the telegraph lines be repaired between Weldon, North Carolina and Petersburg, Virginia.

Down in the southwestern part of North Carolina Stoneman's raiders were heading back to Tennessee, playing havoc with small Confederate units along the way. Stoneman himself had left the column on the seventeenth to return to Tennessee, leaving Gillem in command. At daylight on the 23rd the advance of the division entered Hendersonville, and Gillem learned that Rebels had been there the day before with four pieces of artillery. They had been looking for the Federals, but failing to find them had returned toward Asheville. Gillem sent the 11th Kentucky Cavalry to pursue, attack, and capture those guns at all hazards. The 11th Michigan was sent in support. At noon the commander of the Kentucky regiment reported he had overtaken the artillery twelve miles from Hendersonville, charged and captured them and 70 of their supporting infantry.

Gillem heard from one of his brigade commanders, who had been ordered to move to Rutherford, that he had been informed by Brigadier General John Echols of the Confederate army of the existence of a truce and therefore had not moved. Gillem told him to get to Rutherford anyway. "I regarded the possession of one of the gaps of the Blue Ridge as being absolutely necessary to the safety of my command," Gillem explained. At noon Gillem left Hendersonville with the intention of attacking Asheville, but at 3 p.m. he received a flag of truce from the Rebels there saying they had official notice of the armistice. That night Gillem received direct word of it himself. "General Sherman's order to General Stoneman to come to the railroad at Durham's Station or Hillsborough was received at 11 p.m.," Gillem later reported. "Being thoroughly convinced that the order had been given by General Sherman in the belief that the Cavalry Division was at or near Salisbury, when in fact it would have required a march of 200 miles to have reached Durham's Station, and but sixty to our base at Greeneville, Tenn., after mature consideration I determined to march to the latter place."[9]

Because of the tip about men rowing across the Potomac on the sixteenth, Major O'Beirne, his detectives, and some cavalry had conducted a search into King George County, Virginia on the 22nd but found no sign of the assassins. On the morning of the 24th O'Beirne met Samuel Beckwith, General Grant's telegrapher and cipher operator, at Port Tobacco, Maryland. Beckwith was there with two detectives who worked for Colonel Lafayette C. Baker, Stanton's top counter-espionage agent. O'Beirne happened to mention to Beckwith the men who had been seen crossing the Potomac on the sixteenth, and Beckwith thought this sounded important. He tapped into the telegraph line and wired the information to Major Eckert at the War Department. Colonel Baker happened to be in Eckert's office when the deciphered message was delivered at 11 a.m., and he jumped to the conclusion that the men seen had been Booth and Herold. He went immediately to Secretary Stanton and asked for 25 cavalrymen, a commissioned officer to lead them, and a vessel to take them downriver to King George County, along with two of his detectives, Everton Conger and Luther Baker. The latter was Colonel Baker's cousin; both detectives had until recently been officers in the 1st District of Columbia Cavalry.

That morning Booth threatened to take Lucas's wagon and team, but Herold intervened, and it was finally agreed that for $10 Lucas's son Charley would drive them to Port Conway on the north bank of the Rappahannock River. They left about 7 a.m. and reached Port Conway about noon. This had once been a small village, but now it was almost deserted. William Rollins lived in a rundown old building that had once been a store and made a precarious living by farming and fishing. He also forwarded dispatches for the Confederate Signal Corps between Richmond and the Potomac River. Herold asked him to take him and Booth to Orange Court House, but Rollins said he did not know the way. Herold then asked him to take them to Bowling Green, about fifteen miles away. Rollins said he would do it for ten dollars. Herold asked him to at least row them across the Rappahannock to Port Royal, but nothing definite had been decided when Rollins and his helper went out to tend their fishing nets. When Rollins came back, the wagon was gone, and he saw Booth and Herold talking with some Confederate soldiers.

These were some of Mosby's men who had been late for the Partisans' final meeting three days before. One of them, Lieutenant Mortimer B. Ruggles, son and former aide of Brigadier General Daniel Ruggles, had been second in command of Captain Thomas Conrad's spy group. The others were Private Absalom Bainbridge, Ruggles' cousin and a former member of the 3rd Virginia Infantry Regiment, and Private William S. Jett, who had belonged to the 9th Virginia Cavalry. All three had only recently joined Mosby's Rangers. Jett later said, "I heard on the day of the disorganization of Mosby's command that the President had been assassinated."[10] The chances are that Mosby or one of his officers, or possibly someone else among the Confederates who had been positioned to aid in bringing a captured Lincoln south, had sent these three to find Booth. Whether or not the Rebels approved of the assassination, it would not do to have Booth captured and reveal the Confederate involvement in the plot.

At first, Herold told the three Rebels that his name was Boyd, and that his brother was on crutches because of a war wound. But he soon revealed their true names and said they were the "assassinators of the President."[11] The Confederates quickly agreed to help them. They got the ferryman to bring his scow over from Port Royal and they all crossed, Booth sitting on Ruggles horse, which belonged to Captain Conrad. With them went Enoch Mason, a member of the consolidated 5th/15th Virginia Cavalry, which was also part of the Rebel security force stationed to cover a captured Lincoln. Mason, who served as a courier, had been the only member of his regiment to be parolled at Appomattox. He had probably been caught with the army while delivering messages to it. He was a nephew of Charles Mason, who was involved in the operations of the Confederate Signal Corps in the area. The younger Mason later claimed to have been on a trip to buy a wagon that day, but it's more likely that his job was to carry word of Booth's location to units of the security force, such as elements of the 9th Virginia Cavalry at Milford Station, on the Richmond, Fredericksburg & Potomac Railroad southwest of Bowling Green.

Lieutenant Ruggles needed a place to stash Booth until he could be passed on to someone who knew what to do with him. Jett suggested the home of the Peyton sisters in Port Royal. The sisters agreed at first, but then changed their minds because their brother was away that day. So, again at Jett's suggestion, they went to the home of Richard Garrett, a hospitable farmer who lived three miles down the road toward Bowling Green. Garrett agreed to take in the crippled man, who gave his name as James W. Boyd, until his friends could come back for him in a day or two.

With Herold riding double behind one of the soldiers, the other four went on to Bowling Green, where Jett was courting the daughter of the man who kept the Star Hotel. They stopped for a drink on the way at a disreputable tavern called the Trap, run by a Mrs. Carter and her four daughters. Ruggles and Jett spent the night at the Star, while Bainbridge and Herold stayed at the home of Elizabeth Clarke, a widow whose son had ridden with Jett and Bainbridge in Mosby's battalion.

At 10 p.m. a steamer pulled into the wharf at Belle Plaine, on the Virginia side of the great bend of the lower Potomac, not far north of Fredericksburg. During the fighting around Spotsylvania eleven months before, Belle Plaine had been a supply depot for the Army of the Potomac, but now it was abandoned. After men and horses were unloaded, the Federals skirted a swamp and rode south for three miles to the Rappahannock River, striking it about twelve miles upstream from Port Conway. They turned to the southeast and headed downstream along the River Side Road, waking up sleeping farmers along the way. Sometimes they pretended to be Confederates searching for a couple of lost companions, one of them crippled, and sometimes they just barged in, poking into back rooms and looking under beds.

At Newark, New Jersey, the train carrying Lincoln's body moved slowly through a square mile of people that morning, and there was a similar scene at Jersey City. A ferry boat carried the coffin to New York, and the 7th New York National Guard escorted it to City Hall, where it lay in state for 24 hours.

At Charlotte, North Carolina that day, the 24th, Breckinridge brought Jefferson Davis the terms Sherman had offered Joe Johnston. Davis agreed that the terms were liberal. In fact, they were so liberal he was sure Stanton and Andy Johnson would repudiate them. Davis called the cabinet together and asked for each man to give his opinion in writing of the choices facing the Confederate government. They all urged Davis to sign the agreement, but if it was rejected by the Washington authorities they should continue the struggle as best they could. Davis signed.

"The issue is one which it is very painful for me to meet," he later wrote his wife, who had gone on ahead of him to Abbeville, South Carolina. "On one hand is the long night of repression which will follow the return of our people to the 'Union'; on the other, the suffering of the women and children, and the carnage among the few brave patriots who.... would struggle but to die in vain." He told Varina to sail for Europe or Texas. His own plans were uncertain. "It may be that a devoted band of cavalry will cling to me, and that I can force my way across the Mississippi, and if nothing can be done there.... I can go to Mexico and have the world from which to choose a location."[12]

Grant arrived at Raleigh near dawn that day, a complete surprise to Sherman and his officers but not unwelcome. "All is well," Slocum wrote. "Grant is here. He has come to save his friend Sherman from himself."[13] Sherman was still in his night clothes when he greeted his old friend. Grant gave him a letter he had written to Sherman on the night of the 21st. Instead of sending it ahead, he had decided to bring it with him: "The basis of agreement entered into between yourself and General J.E. Johnston for the disbandment of the Southern army and the extension of the authority of the General Government over all the territory belonging to it, sent for the approval of the President, is received. I read it carefully myself before submitting it to the President and Secretary of War and felt satisfied that it could not possibly be approved. My reasons for these views I will give you at another time in a more extended letter. Your agreement touches upon questions of such vital importance that as soon as read I addressed a note to the Secretary of War notifying him of their receipt and the importance of immediate action by the President, and suggested in view of their importance that the entire cabinet be called together that all might give an expression of their opinions upon the matter. The result was disapproval by the President of the basis laid down, a disapproval of the negotiations altogether, except for the surrender of the army commanded by General Johnston, and directions to me to notify you of this decision. I cannot do so better than by sending you the inclosed copy of a dispatch (penned by the late President, though signed by the Secretary of War) in answer to me on sending a letter received from General Lee proposing to meet me for the purpose of submitting the question of peace to a convention of officers. Please notify General Johnston immediately on receipt of this of the termination of the truce and resume hostilities against his army at the earliest moment you can, acting in good faith. The rebels know well the terms on which they can have peace and just when negotiations can commence, namely, when they lay down their arms and submit to the laws of the United States. Mr. Lincoln gave the full assurances of what he would do, I believe, in his conference with commissioners met in Hampton Roads."[14]

Grant also gave Sherman a copy of the written instructions he had received from Stanton and of the 3 March dispatch from Lincoln, "which dispatch," Sherman later wrote, "if sent me at the same time (as should have been done), would have saved a world of trouble." Sherman took it all well. "I did not understand that General Grant had come down to supercede me in command," he said, "nor did he intimate it, nor did I receive these communications as a serious reproof, but promptly acted on them."[15] He immediately telegraphed Kilpatrick at Durham's Station to have a courier ready to take messages to Johnston, and he wrote two notes to the Confederate and sent them to Kilpatrick by railroad. The first was a simple one-sentence notice that the truce would end 48 hours after receipt of that notice. In the second, he said,

"I have replies from Washington to my communications of April 18. I am instructed to limit my operations to your immediate command, and not to attempt civil negotiations. I therefore demand the surrender of your army on the same terms as were given to General Lee at Appomattox, April 9 instant, purely and simply."[16] Grant, of course, was shown and approved both dispatches before they were sent. Sherman also sent orders to all parts of his army to be ready to resume operations on the expiration of the 48 hours. Gillmore, in South Carolina, was sent a message to the same effect, with instructions to get word to Wilson.

Grant wired Stanton at 9 a.m.: "I reached here this morning, and delivered to General Sherman the reply to his negotiations with Johnson. He was not surprised, but rather expected their rejection. Word was immediately sent to Johnston terminating the truce, and information that civil matters could not be entertained in any convention between army commanders. General Sherman has been guided in his negotiations with Johnston entirely by what he thought was precedent authorized by the President. He had before him the terms given by me to Lee's army and the call of the rebel legislature of Virginia, authorized by General Weitzel, as he supposed with the sanction of the President and myself. At the time of the agreement General Sherman did not know of the withdrawal of authority for the meeting of that legislature. The moment he learned through the papers that authority for the meeting had been withdrawn he communicated the fact to Johnston as having bearing on the negotiations had."[17]

At 6:30 p.m. Joe Johnston wired Breckinridge: "I have just received dipatches from General Sherman informing me that instructions from Washington direct him to limit his negotiations to my command, demanding its surrender on the terms granted to General Lee, and notifying me of the termination of the truce in forty-eight hours from noon to-day. Have you instructions? We had better disband this small force to prevent devastation to the country." Breckinridge replied: "Does not your suggestion about disbanding refer to the infantry and most of the artillery? If it be necessary to disband these they might still save their small-arms and find their way to some appointed rendezvous. Can you not bring off the cavalry and all of the men you can mount from transportation and other animals, with some light field pieces? Such a force could march away from Sherman and be strong enough to encounter anything between us and the Southwest. If this course be possible, carry it out and telegraph your intended route."[17]

The next day Johnston replied: "We have to save the people, spare the blood of the army, and save the high civil functionaries. Your plan,

I think, can only do the last. We ought to prevent invasion, make terms for our troops, and give an escort of cavalry to the President, who ought to move without loss of a moment. Commanders believe the troops will not fight again. We think you plan impracticable.... Wilson has captured Macon.... Federal papers announce the capture of Mobile with 3,000 prisoners."[18]

That day, the 25th, Sherman sent a message to Stanton: "I have been furnished a copy of your letter of April 21 to General Grant, signifying your disapproval of the terms on which General Johnston proposed to disarm and disperse the insurgents on condition of amnesty, &c. I admit my folly in embracing in a military convention any civil matters, but unfortunately such is the nature of our situation that they seem inextricably united, and I understood from you at Savannah that the financial state of the country demanded military success, and would warrant a little bending to policy. When I had my conference with General Johnston I had the public examples before me of General Grant's terms to Lee's army and General Weitzel's invitation to the Virginia Legislature to assemble. I still believe the Government of the United States has made a mistake, but that is none of my business; mine is a different task, and I had flattered myself that by four years' patient, unremitting, and successful labor I deserved no reminder such as is contained in the last paragraph of your letter to General Grant. You may assure the President I heed his suggestion."[19]

He also gave a written reply to Grant in which he said much the same thing and added: "I have not the least desire to interfere in the civil policy of our Government, but would shun it as something not to my liking; but occasions do arise when a prompt seizure of results is forced on military commanders not in immediate communication with the proper authority.

"It is probable that the terms signed by General Johnston and myself were not clear enough on the point well understood between us; that our negotiations did not apply to any parties outside the officers and men of the Confederate armies, which would have been easily remedied. No surrender of an army not actually at the mercy of an antagonist was ever made without 'terms,' and these always define the military status of the surrendered. Thus you stipulated that the officers and men of Lee's army should not be molested at their homes so long as they obeyed the laws at the place of their residence. I do not wish to discuss the points involved in our recognition of the State governments in actual existence, but merely state my conclusions to await the solution of the future.

"Such action on our part in no manner recognizes for a moment the so-called Confederate Government, or makes us liable for its debts or acts. The laws and acts done by the several States during the period of rebellion are void because done without the oath prescribed by the Constitution of the United States, which is a 'condition precedent.' We have a right to use any sort of machinery to produce military results, and it is the commonest thing for military commanders to use the civil Government in actual existence as a means to an end. I do believe we could and can use the present State governments lawfully, constitutionally, and as the very best possible means to produce the object desired, viz, entire and complete submission to the lawful authority of the United States.

"As to punishment for past crimes, that is for the judiciary, and can in no manner of way be disturbed by our acts, and so far as I can I will use my influence that rebels shall suffer all the personal punishment prescribed by law, as also the civil liabilities arising from their past acts. What we now want is the mere forms of law by which common men may regain the positions of industry so long disturbed by the war. I now apprehend that the rebel armies will disperse, and instead of dealing with six or seven States we will have to deal with numberless bands of desperadoes, headed by such men as Mosby, Forrest, Red Jackson, and others, who know not and care not for danger and its consequences."[20]

That evening, Sherman received a message from Joe Johnston: "Your dispatch of yesterday received. I propose a modification of the terms you offered, such terms for the army as you wrote on the 18th; they also modified according to change of circumstances, and a further armistice to arrange details and meeting for that purpose." Sherman replied, "I will meet you at the same place as before, to-morrow at 12 o'clock noon."[21]

Sherman also sent off a dispatch to Admiral Dahlgren at Charleston: "I expect Johnston will surrender his army to-morrow. We have had much negotiation, and things are settling down to the terms of General Lee's army. Jeff. Davis and cabinet, with considerable specie, are making their way toward Cuba. He passed Charlotte going south on the 23rd, and I think he will try to reach Florida coast, either Cedar Keys or lower down. It would be well to catch him. Can't you watch the east coast and send word round to the west coast?"[22]

Lincoln's body left New York City that day, the 25th. At noon a huge procession of nearly 100,000 people took it from City Hall to the Hudson River Railroad depot. About a million others lined the streets to watch. Among the spectators was six-year-old Theodore Roosevelt, who watched from an upper window with his younger brother Elliott, the future father of Eleanor Roosevelt.

In Virginia, the Federals who had landed at Belle Plaine the evening before came to the home of Dr. Horace Ashton near King George Court House just after dawn on the 25th. Ashton courteously provided breakfast for the troopers and feed for their horses, and about the time breakfast was over a Confederate captain named Murray F. Taylor rode up. He had been an aide to A.P. Hill, and when Conger, one of Colonel Baker's detectives, questioned him he produced his Appomattox parole. Conger arrested him anyway, but Thomas H. Williamson was sent for to vouch for Taylor. Williamson had been staying at the nearby home of John Temple Taylor. He was a close friend of General Daniel Ruggles, father of Lieutenant Mortimer Ruggles, who was helping Booth. A lieutenant colonel of militia not on active duty, Williamson had arrived at the Taylor home from Richmond five or six days before and had very probably been sent there to watch for Booth. Williamson, an engineer, knew King George County well, for in the early days of the war he had made a strategic survey of the area for the state of Virginia. He was a professor of engineering at the Virginia Military Institute, where his host, John Temple Taylor, had been a cadet, although Taylor was now a private in the 9th Virginia Cavalry. In addition to Williamson, Major General Charles Field, a division commander in Longstreet's 1st Corps who had been parolled at Appomattox, also soon showed up. He was staying with relatives of his wife while on his way home to Maryland. Between the two of them, Williamson and Fields managed to get Captain Taylor out of arrest.

From Dr. Ashton's the Federals split up in order to cover more ground. The two detectives took a corporal and four troopers and moved along the Rappahannock toward Port Conway, while Lieutenant Edward Doherty, the only commissioned officer in the party, took the rest to King George Court House before turning toward Port Conway. Early that afternoon they came together again near the ferry. While the troops were having lunch and Conger had a nap, the other detective, Luther Baker, and Lieutenant Doherty met the black man who helped William Rollins with his fishing. From him the two Federals learned that two men matching the descriptions of Booth and Herold had crossed over to Port Royal the day before. Baker and Doherty found Rollins, and he confirmed the story. They showed him pictures of Booth and Herold and he recognized them, although, he said, the man on crutches did not have a mustache. He said they had crossed about 1 p.m. the day before with three Confederate soldiers, one of whom he recognized as Willie Jett.

Doherty sent for Conger and put three troopers in Rollins' boat with orders to bring the ferry from the other side of the Rappahannock. When Conger joined them he also questioned Rollins and his wife, and the latter identified the other two Rebel soldiers as Ruggles and Bainbridge. She also added that Jett was courting a girl at the hotel in Bowling Green, so he might be found there. By 6 p.m. the entire command had been ferried to the south bank of the Rappahannock. Conger took Rollins along, under highly visible arrest to protect him from reprisals in case someone thought he was being too cooperative with the Yankees. Beyond Port Royal, on the road to Bowling Green, Doherty and Baker thought they saw two or three horsemen watching them from high ground ahead.

Herold and Bainbridge returned to the Star Hotel from Mrs. Clarke's before noon, where they met Ruggles and Jett. Jett stayed at the hotel, where his girlfriend was, but early that afternoon the rest of them decided to go back to Garrett's farm and leave Herold with Booth. On the way they stopped again at the Trap for drinks and to see the Carter girls. At Garrett's, Booth probably told them he had arranged for Garrett to take them to Orange Court House the next morning. Ruggles and Bainbridge left Herold and rode off toward Port Royal. At the top of a hill overlooking the town they met another of Ruggles' men, who told them that the town was full of Union soldiers looking for Booth. They quickly rode back the three miles to Garrett's to warn Booth and Herold and then took off for Essex County, to the east. Booth and Herold hid in the woods behind Garrett's barn, but Herold soon came back to ask the farmer if he thought the Yankees were really crossing at the ferry. Garrett thought it was doubtful, but a passing black man confirmed that the Federals were in Port Royal when he left. While the three were talking, the cavalry passed along the road not far from the farm, heading toward Bowling Green.

It was dark when the search party stopped at the Trap. Conger, Baker, and later Doherty, went in. At first they received no cooperation, just a loud clamor from the Carter women. But when they said they were looking for a man who had committed an outrage on a girl they were told that four men on three horses had come by the day before. One of them was Willie Jett, but none of them was lame. Three of them had been back that day, without Jett. The Federals had lost track of Booth, but they decided to go on to Bowling Green and find Jett. They arrived there between 11 p.m. and midnight. Leaving half the men on the outskirts of town, they surrounded the hotel with the rest, and Doherty pounded on the door. The owner's wife let them in and told them her husband was away. There was no one there but herself, her children, and Willie Jett. Jett was brought down and questioned. Badly frightened, he soon told Conger that Booth had been left at Garrett's farm and that Ruggles and Bainbridge had taken Herold back there to join him. The Federals arrested him and took him along as a guide as they headed for Garrett's at about 1 a.m. on the 26th.

The Garretts became suspicious of their guests when they showed so much concern about the Federal cavalry. The two men were obviously on the run, and they might not be above stealing some of the Garretts' horses to make a getaway. Booth and Herold were talked into spending the night in the tobacco barn, and after they entered William Garrett locked the door behind them. William and his brother John decided to sleep in a nearby corncrib as a precaution. At around 2 a.m. their dogs began to bark.

When the Federals came to the gate at the entrance to the lane that led to the Garrett house they left Rollins and Jett there under guard and quietly surrounded the house. Conger banged on the door, and when Richard Garrett opened it the detective stuck his revolver in the man's face and demanded to know where his two visitors were. Garrett had a slight speech defect. Some thought he said they were gone, others that they were out in the woods. He was dragged out into the yard and told he would be hanged if he did not start talking.

John Garrett, out in the corncrib, heard the commotion and started for the house. One of the cavalrymen almost shot him before he could identify himself, but as soon as he was brought to the detectives he told them the men they were after were in the barn. That building was quickly surrounded, and John Garrett was persuaded to go in and ask Booth and Herold to give themselves up. Booth refused the offer and threatened to shoot Garrett if he came back again. A long parley between Booth and Baker followed, and finally Conger threatened to set the barn on fire. At this, Herold agreed to surrender. He came out and was taken away, but Booth still refused to come out unless promised a fair fight. Conger lost his patience, made a torch out of some hay, and at about 3 a.m. he set fire to the barn in three places. Loose hay in the barn quickly ignited, illuminating the interior. Through four-inch gaps between the planks of the barn, Conger saw Booth approach the fire but back off. Booth dropped the carbine he had been carrying and had turned toward the front of the barn, when a shot was fired and Booth fell forward. There was much confusion about what had happened. Some thought that Booth had committed suicide. Detective Baker thought that Conger had shot him. But one of the troopers, Sergeant Boston Corbett, something of a religious fanatic, said he had done it, because God had told him to.

Booth was carried to the front porch of the Garrett house, while the barn was left to burn to the ground. The bullet had struck his spine, and he was paralyzed from the neck down. When he seemed to revive slightly, Conger sent for a doctor, and within an hour one arrived from Port Conway. He examined Booth and said the wound would prove mortal.

Conger said that Booth whispered, "Tell mother I died for my country." And when he saw Jett he asked, "Did that man betray me?"[23] At sunrise he asked to have his paralyzed hands raised so he could see them. "Useless, useless," he muttered.[24] A few minutes after 7 a.m. he died.

David Herold and Booth's body were both taken to Washington and placed aboard a monitor anchored in the Potomac. Sergeant Corbett was arrested at first, for having shot Booth in spite of orders to the soldiers that the fugitives should be taken alive, but he soon became something of a hero to the North and was never punished.

Sherman and Johnston met at the Bennett house again that day, although Johnston's arrival was delayed by an accident on the railroad. This time Sherman took Howard, Schofield and Blair with him. Grant remained at Raleigh, for he wanted his friend to have the credit he deserved for obtaining the surrender. Sherman and Johnston conferred alone for an hour or more, but then Schofield was called in. Sherman planned to march away with his other forces as soon as the Rebels surrendered, leaving Schofield in command since North Carolina was his department. So he was consulted.

"We can't agree," Sherman told him.

Johnston said that since Lee's surrender his men were wandering through the countryside stealing from farmers on their way home, and that if he accepted the same terms his men would also be loosed upon the civilians. Sherman said Washington would accept no other terms.

"I'll be in command here," Schofield said, "and I'll handle any problems that arise." He said his forces could cope with any marauding Confederate veterans, and he offered to write out terms of surrender.

"I think Schofield can fix it," Johnston said. When Schofield handed him what he had written, Johnston said, "I believe this is the best we can do."

He handed the paper to Sherman, who approved it at once, and when copies had been made, Sherman and Johnston signed it:

1. All acts of war on the part of the troops under General Johnston's command to cease from this date.

2. All arms and public property to be deposited at Greensborough, and delivered to an ordnance officer of the United States Army.
3. Rolls of all the officers and men to be made in duplicate; one copy to be retained by the commander of the troops, and the other to be given to an officer to be designated by General Sherman, each officer and man to give his individual obligation in writing not to take up arms against the Government of the United States, until properly released from this obligation.
4. The side arms of officers and their private horses and baggage to be retained by them.
5. This being done, all the officers and men will be permitted to return to their homes, not to be disturbed by the United States authorities, so long as they observe their obligation and the laws in force where they may reside.[25]

"I returned to Raleigh the same evening," Sherman later wrote, "and, at my request, General Grant wrote on these terms his approval, and then I thought the matter was surely at an end."[26]

---

1. Brooks, *Washington in Lincoln's Time,* 236.
2. *Official Records,* 46:III:887-888.
3. Ibid., 47:III:285-286.
4. Ibid., 46:III:897.
5. Ibid., 46:III:899.
6. Tidwell, Hall and Gaddy, *Come Retribution,* 460.
7. Davis, *The Long Surrender,* 88.
8. *Official Records,* 47:III:287.
9. Ibid., 49:I:335.
10. Tidwell, Hall and Gaddy, *Come Retribution,* 462.
11. Ibid., 465.
12. Davis, *The Long Surrender,* 92.
13. Davis, *Sherman's March,* 273.
14. *Official Records,* 47:III:263-264.
15. Sherman, *Memoirs,* 847.
16. *Official Records,* 47:III:294.
17. Ibid., 47:III:293.
18. Ibid., 47:III:835-836.
19. Ibid., 47:III:302.
20. Ibid., 47:III:302-303.
21. Ibid., 47:III:303-304.

22. Ibid., 47:III:310.
23. Tidwell, Hall and Gaddy, *Come Retribution,* 477.
24. Foote, *The Civil War,* 3:997.
25. *Official Records,* 47:III:313.
26. Sherman, *Memoirs,* 852.

CHAPTER FORTY-THREE

He Had Come to a Great Victory

27 April - 4 May 1865

Jefferson Davis and the Confederate cabinet left Charlotte, North Carolina that day, the 26th, and crossed into South Carolina. Three small brigades of cavalry had joined the escort, bringing its strength up to 2,000 men, all under the command of Breckinridge. Not far south of the state line they were met by a bevy of ladies who emerged from a handsome mansion at the small town of Fort Mill to strew flowers in their path and insist that the party go no farther that day. That night the president and secretaries Benjamin, Breckinridge and Reagan forgot their cares by getting down on their knees for an animated game of marbles with two boys of the house.

From Richmond that day, Halleck bombarded Stanton with telegrams. In one of them he said: "Generals Meade, Sheridan, and Wright are acting under orders to pay no regard to any truce or orders of General Sherman suspending hostilities, on the ground that

Sherman's agreements could bind his own command only and no other. They are directed to push forward, regardless of orders from anyone except General Grant, and cut off Johnston's retreat. Beauregard has telegraphed to Danville that a new arrangement had been made with Sherman, and that the advance of the Sixth Corps was to be suspended till further orders. I have telegraphed back to obey no orders of General Sherman, but to push forward as rapidly as possible. The bankers here have information to-day that Jeff. Davis' specie is moving south from Goldsborough in wagons as fast as possible. I suggest that orders be telegraphed through General Thomas that Wilson will obey no orders of Sherman, and notifying him and General Canby and all commanders on the Mississippi River to take measures to intercept the rebel chiefs and their plunder. The specie taken with them is estimated here at from six to thirteen millions."[1]

Stanton took this advice and also ordered Thomas to spare no exertion to catch Davis and his presumed treasure. Thomas passed the order on to Stoneman, who had recently returned to Knoxville. Stoneman in turn passed the job of chasing Davis to Brevet Brigadier William J. Palmer, who had succeeded to command of the cavalry from east Tennessee when Gillem had gone on leave two days before. Palmer was the officer who had captured Hood's pontoon train before becoming one of Gillem's brigade commanders. His quarry, Jefferson Davis, left Fort Mill, South Carolina that day, crossed the Catawba River on a ferry, and stopped that night at the village of Yorkville.

That night, Grant wired Halleck from Raleigh: "General Johnston surrendered the forces under his command, embracing all from here to the Chattahoochee, to General Sherman, on the basis agreed upon between General Lee and myself for the Army of Virginia. Please order Sheridan back to Petersburg at once. If you think proper a sufficient force may go on to Danville to take possession of all munitions of war that may be stored there. Send copy of this to the Secretary of War."[2] However, this message was not received by Halleck until the morning of the 28th. On the 27th, after a last conference with Sherman, Grant left for Washington.

The train bearing Lincoln's body passed through Rochester and Buffalo, New York on the 27th. Millard Fillamore, the former president, attended the ceremony at Buffalo, as did future president Grover Cleveland. There were reports that the face in the coffin was starting to shrink and decay, but an embalmer who rode the train had been able to make improvements. An old friend of Lincoln's, David R. Locke, whose humor, written under the name Petroleum V. Nasby, had so often helped to ease the late president's burden, wrote, "I saw him, or what was mortal of him in his coffin. The face had an expression of absolute content, or relief, at throwing off a burden such as few men have been called upon to bear—a burden which few men could have borne. I had seen the same expression on his living face only a few times, when, after a great calamity, he had come to a great victory."[3]

George Trenholm resigned as the Confederate secretary of the treasury that day. He was ill and had been riding in an ambulance as the cabinet made its way south, but the pain of bouncing along in the little wagon day after day was becoming unbearable, and he wanted to go home. Davis named Postmaster General Reagan to succeed him. Reagan protested against this extra burden, but Davis said, "There's not that much for the Secretary of Treasury to do. There's but little money left for him to steal."[4]

Out on the Mississippi River before dawn that morning a boiler exploded on the steamboat *Sultana* as it was heading upriver from Memphis. The boat was not supposed to carry more than 376 passengers, but that day it was carrying about 2,400 Union soldiers who had made their way to Vicksburg from Andersonville, Salisbury, and other Confederate prison camps, as well as over 100 other passengers, 80 crewmen and about 100 mules and horses. A ship's clerk told one soldier that there were more people on board than had ever been carried on one Mississippi River boat before. The government was paying the boat owners by the head to take the soldiers north, and evidently somebody had been bribed to cram as many as possible onto the *Sultana* despite the fact that she had a bad boiler that had been hastily patched. Many of the men were in bad physical condition, and they were all in a desperate hurry to get home. They lay so thick all over the boat that one soldier said it was impossible to see the deck. Another said that the boat was so top-heavy with passengers that she listed from one side to the other as she fought her way up the rain-swollen river.

The *Sultana* pulled out of Memphis at about 1 a.m. on the 27th with all her lights aglow and was about eight miles upstream when, a little past 2 a.m., her patched and over-worked boiler exploded without warning. "Not more than three feet from where I was lying," one soldier said, "was a hole clear through the boat. It seemed as if the explosion of the boilers had torn everything out from top to bottom." Another said, "Everywhere steam was escaping, women were screaming, soldiers and crew cursing and swearing, horses neighing, mules braying, splinters flying—the once magnificent *Sultana* [was] a wreck." The force of the explosion had torn through everything above it and demolished the pilot house at the very top of the boat. "Men were lying everywhere," recalled a cavalryman on his way home. "The hurricane deck was crowded. The chimneys fell, killing and crippling many, and fire started from the wreckage in the furnace pit." In less than twenty minutes the midsection of the boat was engulfed in flames that were working their way toward the stern, for everyone was in too much of a panic to fight the fire. The same cavalryman said, "three or four men with buckets could have kept the wreck from burning."

One soldier remembered rushing toward the stern only to find men and women there were leaping into the water on top of each other, "hundreds drowning together." Hundreds more were burned alive as more and more of the boat collapsed into the flames. A few soldiers began to throw badly wounded men into the water, sure, as one man put it, that it was "better that they should take their chances drowning than be left to burn up, which they would do if left on the boat."

When the wheelhouses on each side of the boat were consumed by the fire, the boat spun around 180 degrees and the fire moved toward the bow, where about 500 people were still on board. "I saw men," one soldier wrote, "while attempting to escape, pitch down through the hatchway that was full of blue curling flames, or rush wildly from the vessel to death and destruction in the turbid waters below." The water was cold, and many people, laden with heavy clothes and shoes, could not swim. "I heard a lady crying for help," another cavalryman remembered, "asking her husband to rescue her.... I also saw the husband, with a little child on his back, struggling in the water for a moment, then sinking." Another soldier said he saw about twenty people drown together. "As fast as one would feel he was drowning he would clutch at the nearest," he said, "and I believe many a bold swimmer was drowned that night who could have saved himself if alone."[5]

As people along the shore realized that a steamboat was sinking, the river began to fill with small boats snatching victims from the water. Then other steamboats came to the rescue. One survivor said he and about a dozen others were saved by a farmer in a skiff. The exact number of people killed was never known—some of the bodies were never recovered—but around 1,800 may have died, more than later went down with the *Titanic*. Only four battles in the entire war killed more Union soldiers than were lost on that one boat. The Chicago *Tribune* complained that "more lives were sacrificed to a patched boiler and a captain's criminal cupidity than it cost us ... to capture Lee's army and terminate the rebellion."[6] The captain was among the victims. The river was filled with bodies for weeks, some floating as far downstream as Helena, Arkansas, almost ninety miles away.

Lincoln's train reached Cleveland, Ohio on the 28th, where more than 50,000 people viewed the coffin and over 1,000,000 from throughout northern Ohio came to pay homage to the fallen president.

Confederate agents Thomas Harbin and Joseph Baden were among the 73 Rebels paroled at Ashland, in Hanover County, Virginia, north of Richmond, that day. Harbin was paroled as a member of Company B, 1st Maryland Cavalry, but there is no evidence that he ever belonged to that unit. He just needed a parole to give him cover. He then disappeared for five years before turning up as a clerk at the National Hotel in Washington, the very place where Booth had lived. He later said that he had gone to Cuba and then to England.

The hotel and resort at Ashland was evidently the place to which Lincoln would have been brought had he been captured before Richmond fell. And it was to Ashland that many members of the security force for that operation went to give their paroles. Over 900 Confederates were paroled there between 21 April and 3 May, inclusive, with over half of them appearing on 24, 25, 26, and 27 April.[7]

Sometime on the 28th, Sherman finally saw newspapers from the North containing Stanton's first bulletin on the original Sherman-Johnston agreement. "The publication of this bulletin by authority was an outrage on me," Sherman later wrote, "for Mr. Stanton had failed to communicate to me in advance, as was his duty, the purpose of the Administration to limit our negotiations to purely military matters; but, on the contrary, at Savannah he had authorized me to control all matters, *civil* and military. By this bulletin, he implied that I had previously been furnished with a copy of his dispatch of March 3d to General Grant, which was not so; and he gave warrant to the impression, which was sown broadcast, that I might be bribed by banker's gold to permit Davis to escape."[8]

Sherman wrote Grant a long letter on the 28th airing his grievance in the matter. "Mr. Stanton," he said, in addition to many other things, "in stating my orders to General Stoneman were likely to result in the escape of 'Mr. Davis to Mexico or Europe,' is in deep error. General Stoneman was not at 'Salisbury,' but had gone back to 'Statesville.' Davis was between us, and therefore Stoneman was beyond him. By turning toward me he was approaching Davis, and, had he joined me as ordered, I would have had a mounted force greatly needed for Davis's capture, and for other purposes. Even now I don't know that Mr. Stanton wants Davis caught, and as my official papers, deemed sacred, are hastily published to the world, it will be imprudent for me to state what has been done in that regard.

"As the editor of the *Times* has (it may be) logically and fairly drawn from this singular document the conclusion that I am insubordinate, I can only deny the intention.

"I have never in my life questioned or disobeyed an order, though many and many a time have I risked my life, health, and reputation, in obeying orders, or even hints to execute plans and purposes, not to my liking. It is not fair to withhold from me the plans and policy of Government (if any there be), and expect me to guess at them; for facts and events appear quite different from different stand-points. For four years I have been in camp dealing with soldiers, and I can assure you that the conclusion at which the cabinet arrived with such singular unanimity differs from mine. I conferred freely with the best officers in this army as to the points involved in this controversy, and, strange to say, they were singularly unanimous in the other conclusion. They will learn with pain and amazement that I am deemed insubordinate, and wanting in common-sense; that I, who for four years have labored day and night, winter and summer, who have brought an army of seventy thousand men in magnificent condition across a country hitherto deemed impassable, and placed it just where it was wanted, on the day appointed, have brought discredit on our Government! I do not wish to boast of this, but I do say that it entitled me to the courtesy of being consulted, before publishing to the world a proposition rightfully submitted to higher authority for adjudication, and then accompanied by statements which invited the dogs of the press to be let loose upon me. It is true that non-combatants, men who sleep in comfort and security while we watch on the distant lines, are better able to judge than we poor soldiers, who rarely see a newspaper, hardly hear from our families, or stop long enough to draw our pay. I envy not the task of 'reconstruction,' and am delighted that the Secretary of War has relieved me of it.

"As you did not undertake to assume management of the affairs of this army, I infer that, on personal inspection, your mind arrived at a different conclusion from that of the Secretary of War. I will therefore go on to execute your orders to the conclusion, and, when done, will with intense satisfaction leave to the civil authorities the execution of the task of which they seem so jealous. But, as an honest man and soldier, I invite them to go back to Nashville and follow my path, for they will see some things and hear some things that may disturb their philosophy."

He added a postscript: "As Mr. Stanton's most singular paper has been published, I demand that this also be made public, though I am in no manner responsible to the press, but to the law, and my proper, superiors."[9]

Sherman summoned his army and corps commanders to meet with him at his quarters in the governor's mansion in Raleigh that day and explained the situation to them and made plans for the future. Kilpatrick's cavalry division would be transferred to Schofield's department, Schofield would return to Savannah the two brigades of the 19th Corps that had been brought up from there, and Slocum's and Howard's armies would, in a few days, march north to Richmond. The next day, the 29th, Sherman left to go down to Savannah, to check on things there and try to establish reliable communiction with Wilson.

In Georgia that day, Croxton's lost brigade rode into Wilson's camps around Macon, almost two months since separating from the rest of the cavalry corps. Since leaving Tuscumbia, it had marched across central Alabama and Georgia trying to find the main column, occasionally colliding with small Confederate forces and destroying some cotton factories and other facilities. "Held in an open trap," one of Croxton's men wrote, "this small resolute band of seasoned troops, known to history as the Lost Brigade, fought a superior force by day, marched all night, swam swollen streams.... The boys called the campaign, 'Croxton's Naval Expedition'.... How we ever did succeed in holding out until the final surrender.... is yet an enigma to those of us who went through it."[10] Wilson learned that day that Jefferson Davis had left Charlotte, North Carolina, heading south, so he began to spread his cavalry in a net across Georgia, from Marietta on the north to Jacksonville, Florida on the south, while McCook was sent with about 500 men to occupy Tallahassee and receive the surrender of the Confederates in Florida.

General Palmer was near the old Revolutionary War battlefied of Cowpens in South Carolina with his brigade of cavalry when he received Stoneman's order to pursue Jefferson Davis that day. "I had already ascertained that Davis and the money, with an escort of four brigades of cavalry.... which had evaded the terms of surrender of Johnston to Sherman, were moving from Yorkville, S.C., and had crossed Smith's Ford, of Broad River, toward Unionville and Abbeville, S.C., with the intention of going through to the Trans-Mississippi Department."[11]

The train carrying Lincoln's remains came to Columbus, Ohio on the 29th in a driving rain. The body lay in state in the rotunda of the state capitol, where 8,000 people an hour filed past the coffin.

Louis Weichmann and John Holahan returned to Washington that day, the 29th, without having found John Surratt in Canada, and were discharged as Federal special agents by Brevet Brigadier General Henry L. Burnett of the Bureau of Military Justice, who was in charge of gathering the evidence against the conspirators. But when Burnett returned to the War Department that night he ran into a colonel who told him, "Stanton is in a rage over your actions in discharging Weichmann and Holahan. He is furious, and won't accept any excuses." Burnett went to the secretary's office at once and tried to explain that he had only been following Stanton's own orders, but the latter would not listen. He told Burnett that if the two were not back by morning to consider himself out of the service. Burnett sent orders to all the military camps and stations around Washington not to let anyone answering the two men's descriptions pass their lines, and Holahan was found with his family and taken into custody.

Weichmann spent the night at a boarding house about a half-block from the War Department and had breakfast at Willard's Hotel the next morning, the thirtieth, at the same table with young Ulysses S. Grant, Jr. He was taking a walk along Pennsylvania Avenue with a friend when Burnett found him. The general took Weichmann to the War Department and then went to see Stanton, told him Weichmann was in the building, and tendered his resignation. With tears in his eyes and reference to the pressure on him to see justice served in this case, Stanton talked the general into staying on. Then he sent for Weichmann.

"I found him," Weichmann said, "to be a sturdy, heavy-set man, about five feet ten inches in height, with iron-gray whiskers. He wore gold-rimmed spectacles. A glance revealed to me at once the man I had to deal with. Bidding me 'Good morning,' he at once began questioning me. He desired to know all about my antecedents; who my parents were and where they lived; in fact, all possible information I could give in relation to them and myself."

"Mr. Weichmann," Stanton said, "I believe you are a clerk in my department; for a year and a half you have had your support and clothing from the Government."

Weichmann said that was so and that he was glad of the opportunity.

"That being so," Stanton continued, "how in the name of common sense did you come to make your home with that disloyal Surratt family?"

Weichmann told him he had known John Surratt at college, which had led him to board at Surratt's mother's house. He said he knew they were Southern sympathizers, but had no evidence of any disloyal act on their part. Stanton asked him if he knew Booth, and if so, how did they meet, and the young man related to the secretary of war how he had met John Wilkes Booth through John Surratt and Dr. Mudd.

"Did you say Dr. Mudd?" Stanton asked.

"Yes, sir."

Half rising from his desk and banging a fist on the table, Stanton exclaimed, "By God, put that down, Burnett; it is damned important."

Weichmann did not know until then that Booth and Herold had stopped at Mudd's house in southern Maryland after the assassination and that Mudd had denied knowing them. Stanton then informed Weichmann that he would be held until the conspiracy could be throroughly investigated. "Before leaving his presence," Weichmann later wrote, "I made a plea in behalf of Mrs. Surratt, and begged him to be lenient and gentle with her. To this, as I recollect, he answered that he was sorry that she was in such a plight, but that the law must take its course, and that justice must be done."

Weichmann was put in the custody of Lafayette Baker (who had been brevetted a brigadier general as of the day Booth was killed) and was taken to Carroll Prison, behind the Capitol. There he was put in a room with twenty or thirty others, some of whom he afterwards learned were detectives placed there to report on all that was said and done. "The time of my arrival in this place was about eleven o'clock in the morning," he wrote. "At noon, a bell was rung, and then all the persons who were in the different rooms of the building descended to the prison yard, and I went along with the crowd. The very first man I saw whom I knew was Dr. Samuel A. Mudd. Never did a man's face change its color more quickly than his. It became almost deathlike in its expression, and of a frightful pallor. No attempt at recognition was made, but he gave me a quick, sharp glance which satisfied me that he knew me."

Others that Weichmann saw at Carroll Prison included John Ford, owner of the theater, and his two brothers; Booth's brother, Junius Brutus Booth, and brother-in-law, John S. Clark; and Mrs. Surratt's brother. He also saw, seated at a window of the nearby Old Capitol prison, Mrs. Surratt, her daughter, and another young woman who had boarded with her.

That afternoon General Baker came to the front of Carroll Prison in a two-seat buggy. "I could see him from the window where I was," Weichmann said. "He entered the prison, and in a short time returned accompanied by Dr. Mudd, who now took a seat in the buggy alongside the great detective. Baker was one of the most impassable and imperturbable men I ever saw, and as cool as an iceberg. And it was now evident to all who witnessed this affair that the Government had concluded to hold Dr. Mudd as one of the guilty parties."[12]

Jefferson Davis, his cabinet and escort passed through Unionville, South Carolina on the thirtieth and stopped for the night in the southern part of Union County.

Rain was falling in Indianapolis that day as Lincoln's body lay in state at the Indiana capitol.

Down in Alabama on that last day of April, General Canby met with his Confederate counterpart, Richard Taylor, twelve miles up the railroad from Mobile. They had learned of the original agreement between Sherman and Johnston and now met to extend it to their own commands. Canby had a full brigade of troops drawn up as a guard of honor, as well as a brass band and all his staff officers in their best uniforms, when the Rebel general and one aide, both in weathered gray uniforms, arrived from Meridian on a handcar pumped by two slaves. Taylor later said that "the appearance of the two parties contrasted the fortunes of our respective causes." Canby and Taylor withdrew to a nearby house, where they quickly agreed to observe a truce while waiting to hear of the ratification of the agreement between Sherman and Johnston. Then they had lunch out in the yard, complete with champagne. When the band struck up "Hail Columbia," Canby had them change to "Dixie," but Taylor suggested that they continue with the original tune, for the time had come for them all to "Hail Columbia" together once again.[13]

Sherman's armies began marching north that day. There had been no surrender ceremony in North Carolina like the one Joshua Chamberlain had presided over at Appomattox. "According to immemorial custom," one Union soldier wrote, "Sherman's victorious legions should have been drawn up in line with sounding trumpet and waving plume, while the captives should in that imposing presence furl their flags and ground their arms. But instead of this triumphant pageant, the rebel army was permitted to furl its ill-starred banners and lay down its arms in the seclusion of its own camp, and there was neither blare of band nor peal of cannon heard in the quarters of the Federal army."[14]

Only a few miles north of Raleigh Sherman's columns began to encounter veterans of Lee's army making their way home. The Federals invited them to share their bivouac and their rations. They sat up most of the night swapping war stories and parted the best of friends the next morning. On the second day out, the first of May, they came upon an old man with a heavy beard and long flowing hair standing beneath the stars and stripes. "When they fired on Fort Sumter," he told the passing soldiers, "I vowed I'd never shave nor cut my hair 'til this flag waved again over the whole country."[15] Each regiment gave him a cheer as it marched past.

Thousands of slaves greeted the marching column, staring in wonder at the first Union soldiers they had seen. One Federal stopped to talk to an old man and his wife who were working in a field. He asked them if they got paid for their work, and when they said no, he tried to explain the Emancipation Proclamation to them and tell them that the Rebel armies were defeated. "Lincoln might have freed us," they said, "but we're still in slavery."[16] And they turned back to their work as the soldiers marched out of sight.

On that first day of May, Lincoln's body reached Chicago, where a procession of 50,000 people, watched by 100,000 more, escorted the coffin to the courthouse in a drizzling rain through streets of slippery mud.

General Baker returned to Carroll Prison that day and took Mrs. Surratt away in his buggy. President Johnson named officers to a military commission on that day to try the suspects for the assassination of Lincoln. Those charged were: David E. Herold, George A. Atzerodt, Lewis Paine, Michael O'Laughlin, Samuel Arnold, Mary E. Surratt, Samuel A. Mudd, and Edward Spangler. Named as co-conspirators were John H. Surratt, who had not been found, and John Wilkes Booth, deceased, and all were said to have been incited and encouraged by Confederate officials Jefferson Davis, George N. Sanders, Beverly Tucker, Jacob Thompson, William C. Cleary, Clement C. Clay, George Harper, George Young and others unknown. Johnson had referred the question of whether to try the suspects in a civil court or by military commission to Attorney General James Speed, who, because the war was not yet over when Lincoln had been killed, because Lincoln had been the commander-in-chief of the armed forces, the killing had taken place within the military lines of the Department of Washington, and the assassination was thought to be a plot of the Confederate government, chose a military commission.

Down in Alabama, Canby notified Taylor that the agreement between Sherman and Johnston—the first one; he had not yet learned of the second one—had been disapproved by Washington, and that he would therefore resume hostilities in 48 hours unless Taylor agreed to the same terms Grant had given Lee.

Jefferson Davis's party crossed the muddy Saluda River on 1 May and spent the night at Cokesbury, South Carolina. It was joined that day by General Braxton Bragg.

Sherman himself reached Savannah that day, where he was met by an officer sent there by Wilson bearing letters giving a brief summary of operations for him and for Grant. Sherman sent a captured steamer loaded with supplies up the Savannah River to Augusta with a small detachment of troops to occupy the arsenal there and open communication with Wilson at Macon. The next day, 2 May, he sent up another boat loaded with clothing, sugar, coffee, and bread with a stronger guard. And then he started back up the coast.

Canby heard from Taylor that day, the second, that he would surrender on the terms offered him. And in Washington that day President Johnson issued a proclamation stating that "it appears from evidence in the Bureau of Military Justice that the atrocious murder of the late President Abraham Lincoln, and the attempted assassination of.... Seward.... were incited, concerted, and procured by and between Jefferson Davis, late of Richmond, Va., and Jacob Thompson, Clement C. Clay, Beverly Tucker, George N. Sanders, William C. Cleary, and other rebels and traitors against the Government of the United States harbored in Canada."[17] He therefore offered a reward of $100,000 for Davis, $10,000 for Cleary, who was Clay's clerk, and $25,000 for each of the others.

Since the capture of Vicksburg, Mississippi and Port Hudson, Louisiana in the summer of 1863, the Union had been in complete control of the Mississippi River. From that time, the Confederate forces west of that river had been cut off from those east of it and from the government at Richmond. All Rebel forces west of the river belonged to the Trans-Mississippi Department, commanded by General Edmund Kirby Smith, who had found it necessary to assume some civil functions in addition to his military duties. Now he was extending into the diplomatic sphere by sending a representative to Maximilian, the Austrian prince who had been installed as the emperor of Mexico by France's Napoleon III while the United States had been too busy to enforce the Monroe Doctrine.

In his instruction to his representative, written on 2 May, Smith said: "As the military commander of this department, I have no authority to appoint diplomatic agents or to initiate negotiations with foreign powers. Yet in the present condition of our national affairs I deem it highly important, in a military point of view at least, to place myself in communication with the Government of Mexico. While, therefore, you will expressly disclaim any authority from the Confederate Government to act in a diplomatic capacity, you may give assurance that there is every possibility that our Government will be willing to enter into a liberal agreement with the authorities of the Mexican Empire, based upon the principle of mutual protection from their common enemy. It cannot be disguised that recent reverses of the most serious character have befallen the Confederate arms. Nor can it be denied that there is a probability of still further losses to us. It may even be that it is the inscrutable design of Him who rules the destinies of nations that the day of our ultimate redemption should be postponed. If then, final catastrophe should overwhelm our just cause, the contiguity of Mexico to us and the future designs of the United States must naturally be a subject of the deepest solicitude to His Imperial Majesty." He went on to hint that the United States was hostile to the emperor's government and had territorial ambitions regarding Mexico. "If such be the ultimate purpose of the Federal Government, it cannot fail to strike his Imperial Highness that in the Confederate States, and more especially in the department adjoining his dominions, and over which I have the honor to preside as military chief, that there are many trained soldiers inured to the hardships of the field, and inspired by a bitter hatred of the Federals, whose services might be tendered to him against the North." He said that out of his force of 60,000 men that at least 19,000 "would gladly rally around any flag that promises to lead them to battle against their former foe." In summary, he said, "If I am not mistaken in my conclusions as to the future policy of the United States, the propriety of an understanding between the Emperor and the Confederate States Government for their mutual defense will be apparent to His Majesty. The services of our troops would be of inestimable value to him."[18]

Jefferson Davis and his cabinet hurried out of Cokesbury, South Carolina on the morning of the second. Scouts had brought word that Union cavalry was nearby. This was Palmer's brigade of what had been Gillem's division, which Stoneman had led out of east Tennessee. But Palmer did not attempt to follow Davis, since he assumed the Confederates would burn bridges and ferry boats on the Savannah River to elude pursuit. Instead, the Federals skirted the headwaters of the Savannah. Palmer figured the fugitive Rebels were heading for Athens, Georgia, and he moved to cut them off.

The Confederates came to Abbeville, South Carolina that day. Davis and Postmaster General Reagan were riding ahead of the rest of the column, and they stopped at a roadside cabin to ask a woman for a drink of water. While they were having their drink a baby crawled across the porch and down the steps.

"Ain't you President Davis?" the woman asked.

"Yes, I am," he said.

"He's named for you," she said, nodding at the child. Davis took a gold piece from his pocket and gave it to her, saying "Please keep this for him, and tell him about it when he's old enough to understand."

After they rode on, Davis told Reagan, "That's the last coin I have to my name. I wouldn't have had that but for the fact I've never seen one like it, and kept it for luck. My home is a wreck, Benjamin's and Breckinridge's are in Federal hands. Mallory's at Pensacola has been burned by the enemy, your house in Texas has been wrecked.... " He pulled a sheaf of Confederate paper money from his pocketbook and said, "That is my entire estate at the moment."[19] Davis stayed that night in the same room his wife, now only a few days ahead of him, had recently occupied.

Davis and the cabinet were rejoined by Captain Parker, his midshipmen, and the wandering treasury that day. They had been heading for Macon, then, after a brief halt at Washington, Georgia, they went instead to Augusta. But Confederate officials there refused to share the responsibility for the treasury, fearing lawless, penniless Rebel troops even more than the Federals. So Parker had brought it to Abbeville. It was being readied for a train ride to Newberry when the president and his party rode into town. Parker turned the money over to acting Secretary of the Treasury Reagan, made his final report to President Davis, and disbanded the midshipmen, whose conduct he praised highly.

The party was also joined near Abbeville by a Union lieutenant and twenty Federal cavalry, disguised as Rebels. They were a detachment of Wilson's cavalry sent out to find Davis and keep track of him.

When word was received that Federals had raided a town only thirty miles away, Davis convened what he called a council of war with his senior remaining officers. "It was a historic scene," one witness remembered. "Mr. Davis presided, with General Bragg, who had become by the surrender of Lee, Johnston, Beauregard and Cooper, the senior general of the Confederacy, on his right hand, and General Breckinridge, Secretary of War and Major General, on the other side. Next came Brigadier General S.W. Ferguson, a gallant and enterprising South Carolinian, a West Pointer, a pet of Beauregard's and a favorite of Davis; next came Gen. George G. Dibrell, a plain, practical, sensible, middle-aged Tennessee clerk and merchant, who was beloved by his men and had justly won his spurs by long, hard, skillful, devoted service;

next, on a little sofa, sat two young men—Brig. Gen. Basil W. Duke and Col. William C.P. Breckinridge—well known among the troops from Kentucky in the Confederate Army; and then, near General Bragg, sat General J.C. Vaughn of East Tennessee, a brave soldier and an earnest man."[20]

"It is time we adopt some definite plan upon which the further prosecution of our struggle shall be conducted," Davis told them. "I have summoned you for consultation. I feel that I ought to do nothing now without the advice of my military chiefs."

"He smiled rather archly as he used this expression," General Duke remembered, "and we could not help thinking that such a term addressed to a handful of brigadiers, commanding altogether barely three thousand men, by one who so recently had been the master of legions was a pleasantry, yet he said it in a way that made it a compliment."

Each brigade commander gave a report on the condition of his command and the state of its equipment, and then Davis proceeded to declare his conviction that the Confederate cause was not lost and that energy, courage and constancy might yet save all. "Even," he said, "if the troops now with me be all that I can for the present rely on, three thousand brave men are enough for a nucleus around which the whole people will rally when the panic which now affticts them has passed away." Then he asked for suggestions regarding the future conduct of the war.

"We looked at each other in amazement and with a feeling a little akin to trepidation," Duke said, "for we hardly knew how we should give expression to views diametrically opposed to those he had uttered. Our respect for Mr. Davis approached veneration, and notwithstanding the total dissent we felt, and were obliged to announce, to the programme he had indicated, that respect was rather increased than diminished by what he had said.

"I do not remember who spoke first, but we all expressed the same opinion. We told him frankly that the events of the last few days had removed from our minds all idea or hope that a prolongation of the contest was possible. The people were not panic-stricken, but broken down and worn out. We said that an attempt to continue the war, after all means of supporting warfare were gone, would be a cruel injustice to the people of the South. We would be compelled to live on a country already impoverished, and would invite its further devastation. We urged that we would be doing a wrong to our men if we persuaded them to such a course; for if they persisted in a conflict so hopeless they would be treated as brigands, and would forfeit all chance of returning to their homes.

"He asked why then we were still in the field. We answered that we were desirous of affording him an opportunity of escaping the degradation of capture, and perhaps a fate which would be direr to the people than even to himself, in still more embittering the feeling between the North and South. We said that we would ask our men to follow us until his safety was assured, and would risk them in battle for that purpose, but would not fire another shot in an effort to continue hostilities.

"He declared, abruptly, that he would listen to no suggestion which regarded only his own safety. He appealed eloquently to every sentiment and reminiscence that might be supposed to move a Southern soldier, and urged us to accept his views. We remained silent, for our convictions were unshaken; we felt responsible for the future welfare of the men who had so heroically followed us; and the painful point had been reached, when to speak again in opposition to all that he urged would have approached altercation. For some minutes not a word was spoken. Then Mr. Davis rose and ejaculated bitterly that all was indeed lost. He had become very pallid, and he walked so feebly as he proceeded to leave the room that General Breckinridge stepped hastily up and offered his arm."[21]

Breckingridge and Bragg said nothing throughout the entire discussion. Not being in immediate command of the troops, they could not know the men's sentiments as well as the brigade commanders, but after Davis left they assured the junior officers that they heartily approved of their position. They promised to urge Davis to get out of the country without further delay, in order to avoid further complications that would be produced by his capture, imprisonment, and perhaps execution.

It was cold and raining at midnight when Davis, the cabinet, Bragg, and a small escort left Abbeville. A number of important papers were left at a private home there, and many others were destroyed. By riding briskly, the party reached the Savannah River by dawn on 3 May, crossed on a pontoon bridge below Vienna, South Carolina and reached Washington, Georgia that evening.

Secretary of State Benjamin separated from the party before it reached Washington, with the understanding that he would rejoin Davis in Texas. He bought a buggy from a farmer, disguised himself as a Frenchman, and, with one companion, the owner of the house where the state papers had been left, set out over back roads for the interior of Florida. "With goggles on, his beard grown, a hat well over his face, and a large cloak hiding his figure, no one would have recognized him as the late Secretary of State of the Confederacy," John Taylor Wood wrote.[22]

Mallory resigned as secretary of the navy that day, saying he needed to look after his family, now refugees in Georgia. He offered to stay with the president long enough to guide him along the Florida coast, which he knew well, but Davis would not hear of it. Mallory made his way to a railroad that was still running and took a train to Atlanta, from which he could ride down to the village of La Grange, Georgia, where his wife and children awaited him. "I regarded all designs.... for continuing the war as wrong," he later said.[23]

Breckinridge followed Davis's advance party with the main escort and the treasury, but he was soon faced with a near-mutiny among the troops. Many of them wanted to go find the Federals and surrender, and some of them threatened to seize the Confederate treasury before the Federals could capture it. The Rebels had not been paid for months, and they felt they had first claim on the Confederacy's remaining assets. Every time the wagons that carried the money stopped they attracted a crowd that greatly outnumbered the few guards. Breckinridge, who was ill, appealed to the men as soldiers and Southern gentlemen and promised to pay them when they reached Washington. The men refused to wait; they might never get the wagons safely to Washington. Finally Breckinridge gave in. Near the crossing of the Savannah River he had the wagons drawn up across the road and broke open the boxes of coins.

"Nothing can be done with the bulk of this command," he wrote to Davis. "It has been with difficulty that anything has been kept in shape. I am having the silver paid to the troops, and will in any event save the gold and have it brought forward in the morning when I hope Judge Reagan will take it. Many of the men have thrown away their arms. Most of them have resolved to remain here under Vaughn and Dibrell, and will make terms. A few hundred men will move on and may be depended on for the object we spoke of yesterday."[24] According to the official account, each man was given about $26. Basil Duke said that his officers and men received $32 each. A staff officer said the division of the treasury among the men was not so orderly. "They were impatient," he said, "and helped themselves as soon as they discovered where to get it. The result was an inequitable distribution—many got too much, many got nothing; and 'dust hunters' pikced up a good deal the following day—a good deal that was trampled under foot during the contemptible scramble."[25]

Breckinridge gave most of the men an honorable discharge from the army and urged them to surrender to the Federal authorities right away.

Only a few hundred troopers remained with him after receiving their share of the silver, and most of them were sent off in various directions to decoy the Federals away from President Davis.

In Alabama that day, 3 May, General Forrest attended a conference of Rebel leaders and heard them outline a plan to cross the Mississippi and join Kirby Smith's forces. "Men," Forrest told them, getting up to leave, "you may all do as you damn please, but I'm a-going home." Somebody reminded Forrest that he still commanded troops in the field. "Any man," the general said, "who is in favor of a further prosecution of this war is a fit subject for a lunatic asylum, and ought to be sent there immediately."[26]

After being viewed by 125,000 people in Chicago on the first and second of May, Lincoln's body came home at last to Springfield, Illinois on the third. All that day and night an unbroken line of 75,000 people viewed the casket in the state capitol. The next day, the fourth, a procession accompanied the body to Oak Ridge Cemetery, where it was laid in a vault, and a crowd of thousands sang hymns, heard the second inaugural address read, heard prayers, and heard Bishop Matthew Simpson's oration. "There are moments which involve in themselves eternities," he said. "There are instants which seem to contain germs which shall develop and bloom forever. Such a moment came in the tide of time to our land when a question must be settled, affecting all the powers of the earth. The contest was for human freedom. Not for this republic merely, not for the Union simply, but to decide whether the people, as a people, in their entire majesty, were destined to be the Governments or whether they were to be subject to tyrants or aristocrats, or to class rule of any kind. This is the great question for which we have been fighting, and its decision is at hand, and the result of this contest will affect the ages to come. If successful, republics will spread in spite of monarchs all over this earth."[27]

---

1. *Official Records,* 46:III:953-954.
2. Ibid., 46:III:954.
3. Sanburg, *Lincoln,* 3:891.
4. Davis, *The Long Surrender,* 103.
5. Trudeau, *Out of the Storm,* 270-273.
6. Stern, *An End to Valor,* 331.
7. Tidwell, Hall and Gaddy, *Come Retribution,* 482. Much supporting

evidence for the security force and the use of Ashland is given in this excellent work.

8. Sherman, *Memoirs,* 853-854.
9. Ibid., 855-856.
10. Jones, *Yankee Blitzkrieg,* 159.
11. *Official Records,* 49:I:547.
12. Weichmann, *A True History of the Assassination of Abraham Lincoln and of the Conspiracy of 1865,* 224-227.
13. Foote, *The Civil War,* 3:999.
14. Trudeau, *Out of the Storm,* 242.
15. Davis, *Sherman's March,* 279.
16. Ibid.
17. *Official Records,* 49:II:566.
18. Ibid., 48:II:1292-1293.
19. Davis, *The Long Surrender,* 112-113.
20. Hanna, *Flight into Oblivion,* 63-65.
21. Basil W. Duke, "Last Days of the Confederacy," in *Battles and Leaders,* 4:764-765.
22. Davis, *The Long Surrender,* 125.
23. Ibid., 122.
24. Hanna, *Flight into Oblivion,* 6.
25. Davis, *The Long Surrender,* 123, note.
26. Trudeau, *Out of the Storm,* 261.
27. Sandburg, *Lincoln,* 3:895.

CHAPTER FORTY-FOUR

The Opportunity Had Been Lost

4 - 10 May 1865

Taylor and Canby met again on the fourth, this time at Citronelle, Alabama, some twenty miles north of where they had met four days before. There, as Taylor put it, "I delivered the epilogue of the great drama in which I had played a humble part."[1] He surrendered his Department of Alabama, Mississippi and East Louisiana on the same terms as had been given to Lee and Johnston, leaving only the Trans-Mississippi Department still at war.

Sherman returned from Savannah to Morehead City, North Carolina on the fourth, where he found the revenue-cutter *Wayanda,* which had brought Chief Justice Salmon Chase down from Washington. Chase was on a tour of the South to investigate the question of giving the vote to the former slaves. Chase, however, was off on a visit to Newbern that day. Sherman contacted Schofield by telegraph and learned that the latter had made great progress in paroling Johnston's men, but in order to facilitate returning the Rebels to their homes Schofield and Johnston had signed some supplemental terms:

1. The field tranportation to be loaned to the troops for their march to their homes, and for subsequent use in their industrial pursuits. Artillery-horses may be used in field-transportation, if necessary.
2. Each brigade or separate body to retain a number of arms equal to one-seventh of its effective strength, which, when the troops reach the capitals of their States, will be disposed of as the general commanding the department may direct.
3. Private horses, and other private property of both officers and men, to be retained by them.
4. The commanding general of the Military Division of West Mississippi, Major-General Canby, will be requested to give transportation by water, from Mobile or New Orleans, to the troops from Arkansas and Texas.
5. The obligations of officers and soldiers to be signed by their immediate commanders.
6. Naval forces within the limits of General Johnston's command to be included in the terms of this convention.[2]

From Canada that day, Confederate commissioners George Sanders and Beverly Tucker wrote to President Andrew Johnson offering to enter the United States at Rouse's Point, New York, and clear themselves of any complicity in the assassination plot by trial by a court-martial of nine generals to be chosen from a list of 25 top-ranking officers of the Union army. No attention was paid to their offer. Both men had already publicly accused Johnson of being behind the assassination.

Down in Georgia, Palmer's cavalry, the entire division now united, occupied Athens that day, in an effort to head off Jefferson Davis. He sent out detachments to guard the fords and ferries of the Broad River and others to cut the railroads and watch other roads, and one to communicate with Wilson at Macon.

Davis held a meeting with Reagan, who was all that was left of his cabinet, and several army officers in a bank at Washington, Georgia that day. He still spoke hopefully of uniting scattered forces and re-establishing the Confederate government west of the Mississippi. He appointed Captain M.H. Clark as acting treasurer of the Confederacy and asked him to take charge of his personal baggage, including what was left of the $35,000 of government funds he had with him. He asked each man present to give their written views on what to do next, and they said that the government could no longer function and that its members should scatter. Davis had learned that Upton had occupied Augusta, so he decided he would ride ahead with his staff and an escort of one officer and ten picked men from the Kentucky cavalry and that Reagan and Clark would follow with what was left of the treasure that Breckinridge was bringing in. But he lingered behind to say goodbye to many friends after his aides left with the three wagons of his advanced party and finally left at 10 a.m.

Not long after he left, Breckinridge arrived, and Captain Clark took charge of the remaining treasury. He entrusted $86,000 in gold to a naval officer, who was to hide it in the false bottom of a carriage and take it to Charleston or Savannah and ship it to the Bahamas, Bermuda, or England whence Davis and Reagan, if they reached the Trans-Mississippi, could draw on it for purchasing supplies to run the blockade into Texas. A major was given $40,000 in silver to feed impoverished Confederate soldiers returning to their homes. Breckinridge was given $10,000 to pay the troops still under his command, as well as the quartermaster department there at Washington, and to carry $1,000 across the Mississippi. Bragg was given $2,000 to take there, and most of the rest, about $5,000 was given to Senator Robert Toombs, who lived there at Washington. The funds of the Richmond banks were deposited temporarily in a local bank, and Reagan burned millions of dollars in Confederate paper money and bonds. After Reagan and Clark left to follow Davis, Breckinridge sent the remaining troops off in another direction to confuse the Federals and then took his own route south.

The next day, the fifth, as Connecticut ratified the 13th Amendment, Sherman, still at Morehead City, North Carolina, received a dispatch from Schofield at Raleigh: "When General Grant was here, as you doubtless recollect, he said the lines (for trade and intercourse) had been extended to embrace this and other States south. The order, it seems, has been modified so as to include only Virginia and Tennessee. I think it would be an act of wisdom to open this State to trade at once.

"I hope the Government will make known its policy as to the organs of State government without delay. Affairs must necessarily be in a very unsettled state until that is done. The people are now in a mood to accept almost any thing which promises a definite settlement. 'What is to be done with the freedmen?' is the question of all, and it is the all-important question. It requires prompt and wise action to prevent the negroes from becoming a huge elephant on our hands. If I am to govern this State, it is important for me to know it at once. If another is to be sent here, it cannot be done too soon, for he probably will undo the most that I shall have done."[3]

"I was utterly without instructions from any source on the points of General Schofield's inquiry," Sherman later wrote, "and under the existing state of facts could not even advise him, for by this time I was in possession of the second bulletin of Mr. Stanton, published in all the Northern papers, with comments that assumed that I was a common traitor and a public enemy; and high officials had even instructed my own subordinates to disobey my lawful orders.... General Halleck's measures to capture General Johnston's army, actually surrendered to me at the time, at Greensboro', on the 26th of April, simply excited my contempt for a judgment such as he was supposed to possess. The assertion that Jeff. Davis's specie-train, of six to thirteen million dollars, was reported to be moving south from Goldsboro' in wagons as fast as possible, found plenty of willing ears, though my army of eighty thousand men had been at Goldsboro' from March 22d to the date of his dispatch, April 26th; and such a train would have been composed of from fifteen to thirty-two six-mule teams to have hauled this specie, even if it all were in gold.... To say I was merely angry at the tone and substance of these published bulletins of the War Department, would hardly express the state of my feelings. I was outraged beyond measure, and was resolved to resent the insult, cost what it might. I went to the Wayanda and showed them to Mr. Chase, with whom I had a long and frank conversation, during which he explained to me the confusion caused in Washington by the assassination of Mr. Lincoln, the sudden accession to power of Mr. Johnson, who was then supposed to be bitter and vindictive in his feelings toward the South, and the wild pressure of every class of politicians to enforce on the new President their pet schemes. He showed me a letter of his own, which was in print, dated Baltimore, April 11th, and another of April 12th, addressed to the President, urging him to recognize the freedmen as equal in all respects to the whites. He was the first man, of any authority or station, who ever informed me that the Government of the United States would insist on extending to the former slaves of the South the elective franchise, and he gave as a reason the fact that the slaves, grateful for their freedom, for which they were indebted to the armies and Government of the North, would, by their votes, offset the disaffected and rebel element of the white population of the South.... Always claiming that the South had herself freed all her slaves by rebellion, and that Mr. Lincoln's proclamation of freedom (of September 22, 1862) was binding on all officers of the General Government, I doubted the wisdom of at once clothing them with the elective franchise, without some previous preparation and qualification; and then realized the national loss in the death at that critical moment of Mr. Lincoln, who had long pondered over the difficult questions involved, who, at all events, would have been honest and frank, and would not have withheld from his army commanders at least a hint that would have been to them a guide. It was plain to me, therefore, that the manner of his assassination had stampeded the civil authorities in Washington, had unnerved them, and that they were then undecided as to the measures indispensably necessary to prevent anarchy at the South."[4]

The powerful French-built ironclad, the CSS *Stonewall,* finally completed its trip across the Atlantic on 6 May, when it reached Nassau in the Bahamas. She had found it necessary to stop at the Canary Islands for coal, and yet her bunkers were now empty again. "You must not expect too much of me," her captain wrote to his superiors; "I fear the power and effect of this vessel have been much exaggerated."[5]

Word that Taylor had surrendered to Canby reached Forrest at Gainesville, Alabama on the sixth. Forrest's cavalry was, of course, included in the surrender, since it was part of Taylor's department. A colonel noted that the "younger element revolted against surrender," nor was Forrest himself fully reconciled to it. Talk of going to Mexico soon filled the air. Taking a staff officer with him, Forrest rode through the night, thinking about it. When they came to a fork in the road, the officer asked which way they should go. "Either," the general said. "If one road led to hell and the other to Mexico, I would be indifferent as to which to take."

They talked and argued for a while, and when the younger man mentioned the general's duty to his men, Forrest said, "That settles it."[6] He rode back to camp and told his men to forget about Mexico.

In Georgia that day, Wilson learned that the scouts he had sent out in Confederate uniforms had lost track of Jefferson Davis, but they knew he had been in the town of Washington. Convinced that Davis and his party would head for the pine forests of southwest Georgia, he ordered Croxton and Minty to each send their best regiment in that direction. Croxton chose the 1st Wisconsin Cavalry, and Minty sent the 4th Michigan. The commander of the Wisconsin troops was told that if there was a fight and Davis should get hurt General Wilson would not feel very bad about it.

Captain Clark and the wagons carrying the baggage and remaining Confederate treasury caught up with Davis near Sandersville that day. But after Clark had distributed some $10,000 more of the gold, Davis again separated from the wagons, heading south toward Florida with Reagan, four aides, one servant, the ten Kentuckians and their captain. He hoped to get a ship and reach Texas by sea.

That evening they were preparing their camp on the bank of the Oconee River when they learned that a large wagon train had passed that way a few hours earlier and that it was being followed by a group of soldiers who planned to rob it during the night. Davis became alarmed because the wagon train was almost certainly the one carrying his wife, led by his secretary, Colonel Burton Harrison. All thought of his own escape and safety was forgotten. Although he had just completed a hard ride, he climbed back into the saddle. "I'll probably be captured or killed for this," he told his aides. "I don't feel that you're bound to go with me, but I must protect my family."[7] The entire party followed him, but after several hours of hard riding, the escorting Kentuckians had to stop and give their horses a rest but Davis pressed on with his four aides, one servant, and Reagan. They rode on through the night, covering some sixty miles. In the early light of dawn they found Varina's camp. The expected attack did not come, and the two parties rode together on the seventh and camped together that night.

Lieutenant Colonel Henry Harnden, with about 120 men of the 1st Wisconsin Cavalry reached Dublin, Georgia at about 5 p.m. and camped near a ferry across the Oconee River after riding some 55 miles. A large party of paroled men from Johnston's army was in the area, so Harnden was not too impressed when some former slaves told him that a train of wagons and ambulances had crossed by ferry that day, especially when citizens of Dublin denied all knowledge of it. But later another slave told him Jeff Davis and his wife were with the wagons. Harnden left a lieutenant with 45 men to watch the ferry and patrol the roads and started at daylight with the rest, in pursuit of the wagons.

In response to Varina's plea that he hurry on his way, Davis, his aides and escort rode ahead after breakfast that morning, the eighth, leaving her with the slower wagons. At nightfall they took shelter in an abandoned house near the village of Abbeville, Georgia. Davis sent word back to Varina that Federal cavalry were on their trail and reported to be only 25 miles away. Then he fell asleep, despite a severe thunderstorm raging outside.

Harnden's Wisconsin cavalry had trouble following Davis's trail that day, but he impressed a guide who led them to the place the Rebel party had camped the night before. After feeding the horses and finding another guide the Federals pressed on across streams and through swamps until darkness and the storm made it impossible to follow the trail. They had ridden 40 miles that day.

A storm had kept Sherman's ship in port at Morehead City, North Carolina until the seventh, when he had started up the coast. He reached Fort Monroe on the eighth, where he found a message from Halleck waiting for him: "When you arrive here come directly to my headquarters. I have a room for you, and will have rooms elsewhere for your staff." But Sherman replied, "After your dispatch to the Secretary of War of April 26 I cannot have any friendly intercourse with you. I will come to City Point to-morrow and march with my troops, and I prefer we should not meet."[8]

Sherman took the railroad from City Point on the ninth to Petersburg and on to Manchester, across the James from Richmond, where he found his troops just going into camp. "I found that General Halleck had ordered General Davis's corps (the Fourteenth) for review by himself," Sherman wrote. "This I forbade. All the army knew of the insult that had been made me by the Secretary of War and General Halleck, and watched me closely to see if I would tamely submit."[9]

In the report he wrote that day he made no effort to hide his contempt for Stanton and Halleck. "As to Davis and his stolen treasure," he wrote, among other things, "did General Halleck, as chief of staff or commanding officer of the neighboring military division, notify me of the facts contained in his dispatch to the Secretary? No, he did not. If the Secretary of War wanted Davis caught, why not order it, instead of, by publishing in the newspapers, putting him on his guard to hide away and escape? No orders or instructions to catch Davis or his stolen treasure ever came to me; but, on the contrary, I was led to believe that the Secretary of War rather preferred he should effect an escape from the country if made 'unkown' to him.... but I don't believe a word of the treasure story; it is absurd on its face, and General Halleck, or anybody, has my full permission to chase Jeff. Davis and Cabinet, with their stolen treasure, through any part of the country occupied by my command.

"The last and most obnoxious feature of General Halleck's dispatch is wherein he goes out of his way and advises that my subordinates, Generals Thomas, Stoneman, and Wilson, should be instructed not to obey 'Sherman's' commands.

"This is too much, and I turn from the subject with feelings too strong for words, and merely record my belief that so much mischief was never before embraced in so small a space as in the newspaper paragraph headed 'Sherman's truce disregarded,' authenticated as 'official' by Mr. Secretary Stanton, and published in the New York papers of April 28." He added that he had left Schofield and Gillmore with plenty of men in their departments and that "I shall henceforth cease to give them any orders at all, for the occasion that made them subordinate to me is past, and I shall confine my attention to the army composed of the Fifteenth and Seventeenth, the Fourteenth and Twentieth Corps, unless the commanding general of the Armies of the United States orders otherwise."[10]

A Union officer, Lieutenant Colonel John T. Sprague, chief of staff to Major General John Pope, commander of the Military Division of the Missouri, had reached Shreveport, Louisiana, headquarters of Kirby Smith, on the eighth with a request for the latter to surrender his Trans-Mississippi Department on terms similar to those given to Lee. On the ninth, Smith responded with a letter to Pope, in which he said, "Your propositions for the surrender of the troops under my command are not such that my sense of duty and honor will permit me to accept." However, Smith invited the governors of Louisiana, Texas, Arkansas and Missouri to meet with him, telling them: "It is impossible to confer with the President so as to meet the exigencies of the times, and questions of grave political importance beyond any military authority may arise and require prompt decision. Intending to uphold the authority of the Confederate Government by arms to the utmost, I yet feel that I should carefully avoid any appearance of usurping functions not intrusted to my discretion. Under these circumstances I esteem it my duty to consult you, in the absence of the President, as the chief magistrates of the States within this department, touching such important matters as are not embraced in my powers as commanding general and as may conduce to the common defense and welfare."[11] Colonel Sprague was invited to stay and await the deliberations of the governors.

The trial of the conspirators began at Washington that day, the ninth, at an arsenal building on the banks of the Potomac. Brevet Brigadier General Cyrus Comstock and Colonel Horace Porter, both on Grant's staff, were originally members of the commission. "The defense, however, raised the objection," Porter wrote, "that I was a member of General Grant's military family, and as it was claimed that he was one of the high officials who was an intended victim of the assassins, I was disqualified from sitting in judgment upon them. The court very properly sustained the objection, and I was relieved, and another officer was substituted." The same was true of Comstock. "However," Porter said, "I sat one day at the trial, which was interesting from the fact that it afforded an opportunity of seeing the assassins and watching their actions before the court. The prisoners, heavily manacled, were marched into the court-room in solemn procession, an armed sentinel accompanying each of them. The men's heads were covered with thickly padded hoods with openings for the mouth and nose. The hoods had been placed upon them in consequence of Powell, *alias* Payne, having attempted to cheat the gallows by dashing his brains out against a beam on a gunboat on which he had been confined. The prisoners, whose eyes were thus bandaged, were led to their seats, the sentinels were posted behind them, and the hoods were then removed. As the light struck their eyes, which for several days had been unaccustomed to its brilliancy, the sudden glare gave them great discomfort. Payne had a wild look in his wandering eyes, and his general appearance stamped him as the typical reckless desperado. Mrs. Surratt was placed in a chair at a little distance from the men. She sat most of the time leaning back, with her feet stretched forward. She kept up a piteous moaning, and frequently called for water, which was given her. The other prisoners had a stolid look, and seemed crushed by the situation."[12]

As finally constituted, the commission consisted of: Major General David Hunter, hated in the South as one of the first Union officers to recruit former slaves and for his devastation of the Shenandoah Valley in the summer of 1864; Major General Lewis Wallace, commander of the Middle Department, who later wrote the novel *Ben Hur*; Brevet Major General August V. Kautz, a division commander in the 25th Corps; Brigadier General Albion P. Howe, commander of the Light Artillery Depot and Camp of Instruction in the Department of Washington; Brigadier General Robert S. Foster, a division commander in the 24th Corps; Brevet Brigadier General James A. Ekin, chief quartermaster of the Cavalry Corps; Brigadier General Thomas M. Harris, another division commander in the 24th Corps; Brevet Colonel Charles H. Tompkins; and Lieutenant Colonel David R. Clendenin of the 8th Illinois Cavalry; with Brigadier General Joseph Holt as judge advocate and recorder. Holt was assisted by General Burnett and John A. Bingham, a civilian. Brevet Major General John F. Hartranft, the hero of Fort Stedman, served as special provost marshal general.

"The appearance and demeanor of the court, it must be admitted," said reporter Noah Brooks, "were neither solemn nor impressive. The members of the commission sat about in various negligent attitudes, and a general appearance of disorder was evident. Many ladies were present, and their irrepressible whispering was a continual nuisance to the reporters, who desired to keep track of the evidence. The witnesses were first examined by the Judge-Advocate, the members of the court putting in a question now and then, and the counsel for the prisoners taking up the cross-examination, each counselor attending only to the witness whose testimony affected his own client. The witnesses were brought in without regard to any particular criminal, all being tried at once. Occasionally an attorney for one prisoner would 'develop' the witness under examination in such a manner as to injure the cause of another of the defendants, and then a petty quarrel would ensue between the different counsel."[13]

Varina Davis's party struggled through the muddy bottom lands bordering the Ocmulgee River on the night of 8/9 May and made a cold, wet camp, but Colonel Harrison decided to move on again after midnight, and they struggled on to Abbeville, where they found President Davis. The latter told them to go on; he and his party would follow as soon as their horses were rested. Harrison had been suffering from dysentery and fever for four days, but he, Varina, and the children pressed on through the darkness and the storm. Sometimes their teamsters had to wait for a flash of lightning in order to find their way. After several hours, Davis and his escort overtook the wagons, and they road together for about twenty miles before stopping for breakfast and a bath. Then they took to the rode again, until about 5 p.m. on the ninth, when they went into camp beside a stream just north of Irwinville, Georgia, still some 65 miles from the Florida line. Colonel Preston Johnston, one of Davis's aides, rode into town to buy some eggs.

Burton Harrison and others urged Davis to leave his family behind and ride on for Florida at once. Davis promised to leave after supper and ride another ten miles at least, but Colonel Johnston soon returned with his eggs and the now-familiar rumor that Rebel soldiers planned to attack the camp during the night. Davis decided to delay his departure a couple of hours in case it was true, and after supper he complained of a bilious feeling and fell asleep on a cot in Varina's tent. Harrison, still sick, also went to sleep, without providing for the security of the camp as he usually did.

Colonel Harnden's Wisconsin troopers were in the saddle at 3 a.m. that day and rode to Sugar Creek, Cypress Creek, and then the Ocmulgee River, which they followed through a dense swamp to Brown's Ferry. An accident to the ferry boat while they were crossing the river delayed them a couple of hours, but Harnden learned there that Davis and his family were definitely with the wagons he was following. At Abbeville the troopers fed their horses, and Harnden learned that the wagons had left there at 10 a.m., heading toward Irwinville. He also learned that the 4th Michigan was nearby. While his men rode on toward Irwinville, Harnden went to confer with Lieutenant Colonel Benjamin Pritchard, commander of that regiment. The latter said he had been ordered to Abbeville, or so Harnden understood him, but he offered to loan Harnden some men. Harnden declined, however, since he thought his force was large enough for the job, and he was having enough trouble feeding the men and horses he had.

Harnden caught up with his men, and about ten miles south of Abbeville they found the camp Varina's party had made the night before. It had been abandoned so recently that the campfires had not yet burned out. The Federals rode on until 9 p.m., when they stopped to let their horses graze. Harnden was sure he was close to the Confederate fugitives, but he was afraid that if he came upon them in the dark that Davis and others might escape, so he decided to wait for daylight.

After conferring with Harnden, Colonel Pritchard sent one company of his 4th Michigan Cavalry to take possession of Brown's Ferry and continued on down a road that followed the Ocmulgee River with the rest of his regiment. A slave who was guarding a broken-down wagon for his master gave the Federals enough information on the party that had crossed by ferry the night before to convice Pritchard that either Davis or some other very important Confederates were with the wagons Harnden was following. The slave also informed them that there was another road to Irwinville beside the one the 1st Wisconsin was following and that it connected with the road the 4th Michigan was on at a place called Wilcox's Mills. Pritchard decided to take that road in case the Rebels used it to get away from Harnden. He selected about 150 officers and men whose horses were in the best condition and led them forward at about 4 p.m., leaving the rest under a captain to picket the river.

They reached Wilcox's Mills at sunset, where they stopped for an hour to feed and rest the horses. From there they followed a blind road through an almost unbroken pine forest for eighteen miles and came to Irwinville at about 1 a.m. on the tenth without seeing any signs of the Confederates or of the 1st Wisconsin. Pritchard sent out men to examine all the roads and then, posing as a Rebel officer, made inquiries in the town. He soon learned that a party had camped at sunset about a mile or so out of town on the Abbeville road and that some men from the camp had come into town during the evening. At first he thought this might be the 1st Wisconsin, but when he learned that the camp included tents and wagons he knew it was not, for Harnden's men had neither. Pritchard moved his command to within about a half-mile of the camp, deployed it quietly behind the cover of a small hill, and sent a dismounted detachment of 25 men under a lieutenant to slip around behind the camp and cut off all chance of escape in that direction. By then it was 2 a.m. Pritchard, like Harnden, feared that Davis would escape if approached in the dark, so he decided to wait for daylight before charging the camp.

At earliest dawn, around 3:30 a.m., Pritchard put his men in motion. Some of them ran into one of the Confederates, Colonel Charles E. Thorburn, who was riding ahead to the Indian River in Florida, where he had arranged for a small boat to await Davis's party. The Federals opened fired and some of them gave chase, thinking he was Davis. Thorburn shot the leading pursuer out of the saddle and outran the rest. Not long after that, Pritchard's men dashed into the Rebel camp, meeting no resistance. But within minutes firing was heard in the direction of the detail sent to cut off retreat.

Harnden's 1st Wisconsin had left its bivouac about a mile north of Davis's camp at 3 a.m., but its advance party, a sergeant and six men, soon encountered Pritchard's flanking force. In the dark, both groups thought the other was the rebels, and a brief fire fight broke out in which the 1st Wisconsin lost three men severely wounded, several lightly wounded, and two horses killed. The 4th Michigan had two men killed and one officer wounded. Pritchard hastened to where the firing was taking place with most of his detachment, leaving only a few men to capture the Confederate camp. The Federals soon learned that they were firing on friends, and Pritchard and Harnden entered the Rebel camp together.

The sound of firing awakened the Confederates. Davis thought it was the expected attack of Rebel marauders. "Those men have attacked us at last," he told Varina. "I'll go and see if I can't stop the firing. Surely I'll have some authority with the Confederates." But when he raised the tent flap he saw Union soldiers in the camp. "Federal cavalry!" he cried.[14]

Colonel John Taylor Wood ran up and told Davis he should escape in the confusion of the awakening camp. Varina screamed for him to flee. Davis called to his servant to take his horse into the swamp. In the dark tent he reached for his sleeveless raincoat but grabbed Varina's, which was similar, instead. When he could not find his hat, Varina threw her shawl over his head and shoulders. There was only one Union soldier near Davis's tent, and Colonel Harrison was able to lead him into the road a few yards away while Davis walked off into the woods to the east. Varina sent her maid after him with a bucket, hoping any Federals who saw them would think they were just a couple of servants going for water.

But Davis had gone no more than twenty yards when Private Andrew Bee rode up and ordered him to stop. "Anybody who think Sheff Davis a coward should have seen him," Bee, a Norwegian immigrant, later said. "He turned right square around and came towards me fast."[15]

"I gave a defiant answer," Davis later wrote, "and dropping the shawl and raglan from my shoulders, advanced toward him; he leveled his carbine at me, but I expected, if he fired, he would miss me, and my intention was in that event to put my hand under his foot, tumble him off on the other side, spring into the saddle, and attempt to escape. My wife, who had been watching, ran forward and threw her arms around me. Success depended on instantaneous action, and, recognizing that the opportunity had been lost, I turned back, and, the morning being damp and chilly, passed on to a fire beyond the tent."[16] When he met Pritchard he asked that his family and his aides be turned loose.

"My orders are to take eveyone to Macon," Pritchard replied.

"God's will be done," Davis said.[17]

---

1. Foote, *The Civil War,* 3:999.
2. Sherman, *Memoirs,* 858-859.
3. Ibid., 859-860.
4. Ibid., 860-862.
5. Foote, *The Civil War,* 3:1028.
6. Henry, *"First with the Most" Forrest,* 437.
7. Davis, *The Long Surrender,* 137.
8. *Official Records,* 47:III:435.
9. Sherman, *Memoirs,* 863.
10. *Official Records,* 47:I:37-40.
11. Ibid., 48:I:189-190.
12. Porter, *Campaigning with Grant,* 501-502.
13. Brooks, *Washington in Lincoln's Time,* 240-241.
14. Davis, *The Long Surrender,* 143.
15. Ibid., 145.
16. Hanna, *Flight into Oblivion,* 101.
17. Davis, *The Long Surrender,* 146.

CHAPTER FORTY-FIVE

That Winds Up the War

10 - 22 May 1865

By the time Jefferson Davis was captured, the war was almost over. The small Confederate forces in Florida surrendered on that same tenth day of May. Up in Kentucky Captain William Clarke Quantrill, the famous Rebel guerrilla leader, was mortally wounded in a brief fight with Union troops. The Trans-Mississippi Department was the only sizable Confederate force still holding out, and its fall was only a matter of the time the Federals needed to bring more forces against it. Already Canby and others were preparing to do just that.

While the shooting war was all but over, the war of words between Sherman on one side and Stanton and Halleck on the other was still white hot. Halleck had sent Sherman a message trying to patch things up, but Sherman replied that day: "I received your cipher dispatch last evening, and have revolved it in my mind all night in connection with that telegraphic message of April 26 to Secretary Stanton, and by him rushed with such indecent haste before an excited public. I cannot possibly reconcile the friendly expressions of the former with the deadly malignity of the latter, and cannot consent to the renewal of a friendship I had prized so highly till I can see deeper into the diabolical plot than I now do. When you advised me of the assassin Clark being on my track I little dreamed he would turn up in the direction and guise he did, but thank God I have become so blase to the dangers to life and reputation by the many vicissitudes of cruel war, which some people are resolved shall never be over, that nothing surprises me. I will march my army through Richmond quietly and in good order, without attacting attention, and I beg you to keep slightly perdu, for if noticed by some of my old command I cannot undertake to maintain a model behavior, for their feelings have become aroused by what the world adjudges an insult to at least an honest commander. If loss of life or violence result from this you must attribute it to the true cause—a public insult to a brother officer when he was far away on public service, perfectly innocent of the malignant purpose and design."[1]

"Tomorrow I march through Richmond with colors flying and drums beating," Sherman wrote his wife, "as a matter of right and not by Halleck's favor, and no notice will be taken of him personally or officially. I dare him to oppose my march. He will think twice before he again undertakes to stand between me and my subordinates....

"Stanton wants to kill me because I do not favor the scheme of declaring the Negroes of the south, now free, to be loyal voters, whereby politicians may manufacture just so much more pliable electioneering material. The Negroes don't want to vote. They want to work and enjoy property, and they are not friends of the Negro who seek to complicate him with new prejudices."[2]

To his old friend Grant he wrote, "I will treat Mr. Stanton with like scorn & contempt, unless you have reasons otherwise, for I regard my military career as ended, save and except so far as necessary to put my army in your hands. Mr. Stanton can give me no orders of himself. He may, in the name of the President, and those shall be obeyed to the letter; but I deny his right to command an army.... Subordination to authority is one thing, to insult another."[3]

Slocum's wing, the Army of Georgia, marched through Richmond the next day, the eleventh, and nothing more violent occurred than some mutual name-calling between his troops and some of the Eastern soldiers. Although Halleck watched from his portico as Slocum's men passed his headquarters, they did not salute him or acknowledge him in any way. There was a guard out front wearing a neat, clean uniform, however, and one scruffy Westerner made a point of squirting tobacco juice on the sentry's polished boots.

The CSS *Stonewall* reached Havana, Cuba on the eleventh. News of the capture of Jefferson Davis the day before had not, of course, reached that Spanish colony yet, but word of Lee's surrender and Johnston's had, leaving her captain in a quandry about what to do next.

Clement C. Clay, who had been one of the Confederate commissioners to Canada and was among those accused of inciting Lincoln's assassination, surrendered himself to troops of the 4th Iowa Cavalry at La Grange, Georgia on the eleventh. That regiment made a real haul of Confederate dignitaries. It also arrested Vice President Alexander Stephens at his plantation near Crawfordville, as well as Secretary of the Navy Mallory at La Grange.

Colonel (soon to be brevet brigadier general) Pritchard herded his prisoners toward Macon on the eleventh. Colonel John Taylor Wood and a lieutenant had escaped at the Irwinville camp by hiding in the woods, but the rest of Davis's party plodded north in two columns with their Union captors. When the procession passed some Confederate soldiers on their way home, one Federal called to them, "Hey, boys, we've got your old boss back here in the ambulance—we've got Jeff Davis and his whole band of rebels and are taking them to Macon."

"Hang him! Shoot him!" the Rebels replied,".... We've got no use for him. The damned Mississippi Mule got us into this scrape. Hope you'll hang every man in Mississippi and South Carolina."[4]

Pritchard sent a dispatch to Minty, his division commander, from Abbeville that day telling him that Davis had been caught. The message reached Macon the next day, the twelfth, and Minty broke into Wilson's quarters with the news.

"We've captured Jeff Davis," he exclaimed, "and by jingo, we got him in his wife's clothes."

Afraid of a hoax, Wilson said, "I trust there is no mistake about it."

"It's all right, General; here is Pritchard's dispatch by a special courier."[5]

Wilson immediately telegraphed the news to Stanton, Grant, and Thomas. Neither Pritchard's dispatch nor Wilson's telegrams said anything about Davis being caught in his wife's clothes, but such an accusation, perhaps first brought by Pritchard's courier, soon spread across the North and was exaggerated with each telling. He was, of course, literally caught in Varina's clothing, that is, her shawl and raincoat, but political cartoonists soon pictured him in a dress and bonnet. The adjutant of the 4th Michigan claimed that Varina's maid had begged him to "Please let me and my grandmother go to the brook and wash ourselves." But Captain James H. Parker, who claimed to have recognized Davis immediately, said, "I defy any person to find a single officer or soldier who was present at the capture.... who will say upon honour that he was disguised in women's clothes.... His wife.... behaved like a lady, and he as a gentleman, though manifestly chagrined at being taken into custody." Parker added that "I am a Yankee, full of Yankee prejudices, but I think it wicked to lie about it."[6]

As they continued marching north that day, Pritchard and his men learned for the first time when they stopped near a Union camp that there was a $100,000 reward for Jefferson Davis. They whooped and hollered, and a band struck up "Yankee Doodle." When Pritchard showed him the reward notice, Davis saw that it was signed by Andrew Johnson. "The miserable scoundrel.... knows that it is false," he said. "Of course, the accusation will fail—but now these people will be willing to assassinate me." Davis was not assassinated, however, although some of the Federals were evidently less than polite to the Confederates, for which Varina never forgave them, though she did eventually forgive Pritchard, whom she said tried to cause them "as little unnecessary pain" as possible.[7]

A Union colonel out in Louisiana reported that same day that Davis had already reached the Trans-Mississippi. "Reports say," one wrote, "that Davis is over the river. One statement is that he went from Florida to Cuba, thence to Texas. Another that he crossed the Mississippi River. I conversed with a Confederate soldier, who said he knew General Hood had crossed." Another Federal colonel reported that "Jeff. Davis, Breckinridge, Benjamin, Trenholm, and other prominent officers of the Confederate Government crossed the river one week ago to-day.... Lieutenant General Longstreet accompanies them."[8]

The right wing of Sherman's force, the Army of the Tennessee, marched through Richmond on the twelfth. But it had lost its commander, for Howard was appointed that day to be the commissioner of the Freedman's Bureau, an organization recently established in the War Department to oversee the welfare of the former slaves. It obtained labor contracts for them, helped them find homes, settled their disputes, found them jobs. During its existence it founded over 100 hospitals, gave medical aid to half a million patients, distributed over 20,000,000 rations to whites as well as blacks, settled freedmen on abandoned or confiscated land, and established over 4,000 schools. But the bureau became a political football during reconstruction, and many of its functionaries were more interested in lining their own pockets than in helping the former slaves. Major General John A. Logan, commander of the 15th Corps, was Howard's obvious successor. Logan had briefly succeeded to command of the army when Major General James B. McPherson had been killed during the battle of Atlanta, but Sherman had moved Howard, a West Pointer, over from the 4th Corps in Thomas's Army of the Cumberland, distrusting the ability of Logan, a hard-fighting political general, to handle the complexity of army command. Logan had been very disappointed, but now, with the war all but over, there could be no such objection. The appointment was not made for a few days, but it was made.

In Georgia, the 4th Michigan Cavalry reached Macon on the afternoon of the thirteenth with Jefferson Davis, his family, and followers. They were greeted by shouts from Union soldiers in language Varina considered "unfit for women's ears." Evidently she did not take it calmly, for one Federal officer found her "haughty & insulting, as any woman I ever saw—if she is a lady I failed to discover it."[9] Davis was taken to the Lanier House, where Wilson had his headquarters, entering the hotel between files of cavalrymen who presented arms as he passed.

The Davises were given a spacious room, where a sumptuous meal was brought to them. Afterwards, Davis and Wilson talked for about an hour. Davis found the young general courteous and obliging. Wilson said that Davis "looked bronzed and somewhat careworn, but hardy and vigorous, and during the conversation behaved with perfect self-possession and dignity." They talked about West Point, which they had both attended, although 32 years separated their classes, and discussed various generals on both sides. Davis critized Johnston for "timidity and insubordination," Beauregard for "military pedantry," and Hood for "heroic rashness," but he praised Taylor, Hardee and Bragg and "spoke feelingly of Lee's character and deeds." On the Union side, he praised Thomas and Sherman and expressed surprise at Grant's "skill and persistency."[10]

Davis spoke of Lincoln's death in terms of respect and kindness, and of Johnson's proclamation charging him with inspiring the assassination he said, "There's one man who knows it is false—the man who signed it. Johnson knows I preferred Lincoln to himself."[11] That, of course, ignored the fact that Johnson had also been a target of the assassins. "I have no doubt, General, the Government of the United States will bring a much more serious charge against me," he added, meaning treason.[12]

At 5 p.m. Davis and his party were put on a train for Augusta. At Davis's own request, Colonel Pritchard was put in charge of his guards. Just before the train pulled out of Macon, two more prisoners were brought on board, Clement Clay and his wife, Virginia.

The last battle of the war took place on that thirteenth day of May.

A Union colonel, supposedly looking for horses with which to mount a small force of Union-loyal Texas cavalry, had crossed a couple of regiments from the island of Brazos Santiago over to the Texas mainland near the mouth of the Rio Grande the day before, the twelfth, and had marched up the river to Palmito Ranch, capturing three Rebels, two horses and four head of cattle, and then marched back again. Now, on the thirteenth, the Federals marched back up the river with no clear objective in mind. The Confederates, meanwhile, alerted by the advance of the day before, assembled their scattered force of cavalry that had been picketing the river and advanced to confront the invaders.

The Federals tried to set up an ambush, but someone fired too soon, and a hidden unit revealed itself prematurely. The Union force, consisting of the 34th Indiana Infantry, the 62nd U.S. Colored Troops, and a small detachment of unmounted Texas cavalry, fell back and started preparing its supper. Before the Federals knew it, the Rebels, all mounted, started moving around their flank, threatening to cut them off, and opened on them with four pieces of artillery. The Union commander, having neither cannon nor mounted cavalry, sent out two companies from the Indiana regiment as skirmishers, backed up by the unmounted cavalrymen, while the rest of the force hastily fell back to avoid being cut off from the coast.

The Federals managed to avoid being trapped, but the 34th Indiana lost both of its battleflags when the colorbearers couldn't keep up, and most of the skirmishers and about half of the Texans were captured. Only one Union soldier was killed in the fighting, Private Jefferson Williams of the 34th Indiana, the last Union battle fatality of the war. The Federals crossed some tide-covered mud flats on a narrow levee and then turned to fire a few last volleys at the Rebels before the latter broke off their pursuit. As the echoes of the final shots died away, the commander of the 62nd U.S. Colored Troops turned to one of his company commanders. "That winds up the war," he said.[13]

Near the opposite end of Texas, at the town of Marshall in the northeast part of the state, the Confederate governors of Louisiana, Arkansas and Missouri, and a representative of the governor of Texas, who was ill, met that day and wrote a recommendation to Kirby Smith that he surrender to the Federals, provided that neither soldiers nor civilians would be prosecuted for any offenses committed against the United States during the war, that the present state governments be recognized until conventions could be called to finally settle any and all conflicts between the states, that each state be allowed to retain a few men as guards to preserve good order, and that time be given to state officers and others to leave the country if they wanted to.

While the governors were meeting, so too were most of Smith's senior officers. Brigadier General Jo Shelby, commander of a division of Missouri Cavalry, made a speech suggesting that they concentrate all their forces behind the Brazos River in Texas and if necessary retreat into Mexico, where they could ally themselves with either the Emperor Maximilian or the rebels under Benito Juarez. He also suggested that they needed a leader in whom they had more confidence than Smith and suggested Lieutenant General Simon Bolivar Buckner, commander of the District of Arkansas and West Louisiana as well as Smith's chief of staff. The assembled generals, including Buckner, agreed. (Lieutenant General John B. Magruder, commanding in Texas, who was senior to Buckner, was not present.) Shelby then volunteered to present their decision to Smith, who acquiesced, signed a paper resigning his military duties in favor of Buckner but retaining his de facto civilian powers, and then went right on issuing orders as if the whole thing had never happened.

As for surrendering to Pope, "An officer can honorably surrender his command," Smith told Colonel Sprague on the fifteenth, "when he has resisted to the utmost of his power and no hopes rest upon his further efforts. It cannot be said that the duty imposed upon me has been fulfilled to the extent required by the laws of honorable warfare. To have conceded to the terms demanded would, therefore, have dishonored the commander who submitted to them."[14] He then proposed to surrender on terms similar to those recommended by the governors, except that he did not mention the recognition of the state governments.

When Jefferson Davis, his family and his fellow prisoners arrived at Augusta, they were joined by Vice President Alexander Stephens, still wearing the bulky overcoat that had amused Lincoln, and Major General Joseph Wheeler, who had been captured a few days before just east of Atlanta while trying to make his way to the Trans-Mississippi Department. As the party was driven through the streets of Augusta, 9-year-old Woodrow Wilson watched from the window of the Presbyterian minister's manse. It was a scene he would remember years later when he was president of the United States. Such a large crowd of civilians and paroled Confederates gathered that the Union guards were worried. "It was an anxious moment," one Federal remembered, "for that little squad of blue-coats that were nearly surrounded by their bitterest foes, and outnumbered by more than fifty to one.... The silence which had thus far prevailed was broken, not by cheers for their chieftain, but by cries from the Confederates on both sides of the street:

'Got any of that gold with you, Jeff?'—'We want our pay!'.... And amid such cries of derision from his own troops, the carriages moved on to the landing."[15] Then the prisoners were put on a steamboat and taken down the river to Savannah. From there they went to nearby Port Royal, South Carolina, where they were put on the *Clyde,* a seagoing sidewheel steamer, to take them up the Atlantic coast.

Before learning what Kirby Smith's answer would be to Pope's call for the Confederate's surrender, Grant was laying plans to invade Smith's department, in case he insisted on holding out. For this job he turned to the able and aggressive Sheridan. That officer reached Washington on 16 May, well ahead of his cavalry, which was making its way overland from Richmond ahead of Sherman's armies. The next day he received new orders and a letter from Grant. The orders abolished Canby's Military Division of West Mississippi, reduced that officer to command of the Department of the Gulf, now to consist of the states of Louisiana, Mississippi, Alabama and Florida, relieved Sheridan from command of the Middle Military Division, and assigned him to "the general command west of the Mississippi River, south of the Arkansas River."

Grant's letter told him to "proceed without delay to the West to arrange all preliminaries for your new field of duties. Your duty is to restore Texas and that part of Louisiana held by the enemy to the Union in the shortest practicable time, in a way most effectual for securing permanent peace. To do this you will be given all the troops that can be spared by Major General Canby, probably 25,000 men of all arms; the troops with Maj. Gen. J.J. Reynolds in Arkansas, say 12,000, Reynolds to command; the Fourth Army Corps now at Nashville, Tenn., awaiting orders, and the Twenty-fifth Army Corps, now at City Point, Va., ready to embark. I do not wish to trammel you with instructions. I will state, however, that if Smith holds out without even an ostensible government to receive orders from or to report to, he and his men are not entitled to the considerations due to an acknowledged belligerent. Theirs are the conditions of outlaws, making war against the only Government having an existence over the territory where war is now being waged. You may notify the rebel commander west of the Mississippi, holding intercourse with him in person or through such officers of the rank of major-general as you may select, that he will be allowed to surrender all his forces on the same terms as were accorded to Lee and Johnston. If he accedes, proceed to garrison the Red River as high up as Shreveport, the seaboard at Galveston, Matagorda Bay, Corpus Christi, and mouth of the Rio Grande. Place a strong force on the Rio Grande, holding it at least to a point opposite Camargo and above that, if supplies can be procured. In case of an active campaign (a hostile one), I think a heavy force should be put on the Rio Grande as a first preliminary. Troops for this might be started at once. The Twenty-fifth Corps is now available, and to it should be added a force of white troops, say those now under Major-General Steele. To be clear on this last point I think the Rio Grande should be strongly held, whether the forces in Texas surrender or not, and that no time should be lost in getting troops there. If war is to be made, they will be in the right place; if Kirby Smith surrenders they will be on the line which is to be strongly garrisoned. Should any force be necessary other than those designated, they can be had by calling for them on Army headquarters."[16]

Sheridan went at once to see Grant. Plans were under way for a grand review of the Army of the Potomac, Sheridan's cavalry, and Sherman's two armies on the 23rd and 24th of that month, and Sheridan hoped to be able to delay this new assignment long enough to lead his command on that occasion. "But the General told me that it was absolutely necessary to go at once," he later wrote, "to force the surrender of the Confederates under Kirby Smith. He also told me that the States lately in rebellion would be embraced in two or three military departments, the commanders of which would control civil affairs until Congress took action about restoring them to the Union, since that course would not only be economical and simple, but would give the Southern people confidence, and encourage them to go to work, instead of distracting them with politics.

"At this same interview he informed me that there was an additional motive in sending me to the new command, a motive not explained by the instructions themselves, and went on to say that, as a matter of fact, he looked upon the invasion of Mexico by Maximilian as a part of the rebellion itself, because of the encouragement that invasion had received from the Confederacy, and that our success in putting down secession would never be complete till the French and Austrian invaders were compelled to quit the territory of our sister republic. With regard to this matter, though, he said it would be necessary for me to act with great circumspection, since the Secretary of State, Mr. Seward, was much opposed to the use of our troops along the border in any active way that would be likely to involve us in a war with European powers."[17]

In fact, it seemed far more likely that Sheridan would have to fight the French in Mexico than the Rebels in Texas. That same day, General Pope was writing to Grant from St. Louis. He had not yet heard from Colonel Sprague, who had gone to see Kirby Smith, but he had heard from J.J. Reynolds, who commanded the Department of Arkansas.

Reynolds had sent a scout to Camden, in the southern part of that state, which had been the headquarters of the Confederates in the area. The scout reported that there were about 300 Rebel cavalrymen there and two batteries of artillery that were kept there for want of horses to haul them to Marshall, Texas, where most of Kirby Smith's troops were assembling. "Rebel officers are making great efforts to persuade the men to go to Mexico and establish a colony," Reynolds had reported, "but the men are opposed to it, and are willing to return to their allegiance on any terms."[18]

In forwarding this report to Grant, Pope said, "I do not of course know what course Kirby Smith will adopt, but I think there is not much doubt that a campaign into Texas will be unnecessary. I presume that Kirby Smith is delaying Sprague until he receives further news of the rebels east of the Mississippi; and as every day will render it more and more clear that the rebellion and the rebel Government are at an end, I think he will very shortly agree to the terms without the necessity of assembling an army to march against him. His men are altogether demoralized, and will leave him in large numbers. Information from several sources confirms General Reynolds' dispatch.... A very few days will, I am sure, decide the matter.... General M. Jeff. Thompson surrendered with his forces. How many he has, or can collect, it would be difficult to say. He claims to have from 5,000 to 10,000, and his vanity will prompt him to collect as many as he can to be paroled on the 29th of this month. The terms of surrender are the same as those granted to General Lee."[19]

Two days later, in Havana, Cuba, the captain of the Rebel cruiser CSS *Stonewall* made his decision. News had reached him that Richard Taylor had surrendered, ending all Confederate resistance east of the Mississippi. Moreover, since his ship's arrival eight days before, Federal warships of all kinds had converged on Havana, including two powerful monitors, the *Canonicus* and the *Monadnock,* both veterans of the Fort Fisher expedition. The *Stonewall* was powerful, but no match for the monitors. "*Canonicus* would have crushed her," the commander of the Union flotilla said, "and the *Monadnock* could have taken her beyond doubt."[20] Between the two of them, with the help of lesser ships, the *Stonewall* had little chance. Her captain chose not to risk it. He turned his ship over to the Spanish authorities.

The ship carrying Jefferson Davis and his fellow prisoners entered Chesapeake Bay on the nineteenth but did not steam on up the bay to the Potomac and Washington as they expected. Instead, she came to anchor in Hampton Roads, near Fort Monroe.

Sherman reached Alexandria, Virginia that same afternoon at the head of his two armies. On the way up from Richmond he and many of his men got a look at some of the famous battlefields of the Army of the Potomac: Hanover Court House, Spotsylvania Court House, Chancellorsville, Fredericksburg, and Manassas, where Sherman had been a brigade commander at the first battle of Bull Run. He sent a message to President Johnson notifying him of his arrival and another to Rawlins, Grant's chief of staff. "Send me all orders and letter you may have for me," he told the latter, "and let some newspaper know that the vandal Sherman is encamped near the canal bridge half way between the Long Bridge and Alexandria to the west of the road, where his friends, if any, can find him. Though in disgrace he is untamed and unconquered."[21]

"The next day (by invitation)," he wrote, "I went over to Washington and met many friends—among them General Grant and President Johnson. The latter occupied rooms in the house on the corner of Fifteenth and H Streets, belonging to Mr. Hooper. He was extremely cordial to me, and knowing that I was chafing under the censures of the War Department, especially of the two war bulletins of Mr. Stanton, he volunteered to say that he knew of neither of them till seen in the newspapers, and that Mr. Stanton had shown neither to him nor to any of his associates in the cabinet till they were published. Nearly all the members of the cabinet made similar assurances to me afterward, and, as Mr. Stanton made no friendly advances, and offered no word of explanation or apology, I declined General Grant's friendly offices for a reconciliation, but, on the contrary, resolved to resent what I considered an insult, as publicly as it was made."[22]

Down in Hampton Roads on the twentieth, Alexander Stephens and John Reagan were transferred from the ship that still carried Jefferson Davis to a warship that would take them to Fort Warren in Boston Harbor. The day after that, General Joseph Wheeler, Colonel Preston Johnston and Colonel Francis Lubbock were also taken away, headed for Fort Delaware, near Philadelphia. On the 22nd, Davis finally learned his own destination. He was given ten minutes to say goodbye to his wife and children, and then he and Clay were taken into Fort Monroe by Brevet Major General Nelson A. Miles, former commander of the 1st Division of the 2nd Corps, who had just been appointed commander of the Military District of Fort Monroe the day before. Also on hand was Assistant Secretary of War Charles Dana. Stanton had told Dana that he was worried that Davis would commit suicide. Stanton said he would himself, if he were in similar circumstances. Dana wrote a report to Stanton that afternoon:

"The two prisoners have just been placed in their respective casemates. The sentries are stationed both within and without their doors. The bars and locks are fastened, and the regular routine of their imprisonment has begun. At precisely one o'clock General Miles left with a tug and a guard from the garrison to go for Davis and Clay. At half past one the tug left the Clyde for the fortress. She landed at the engineers' wharf, and the procession, led by the cavalrymen of Colonel Pritchard's command, moved through the water battery on the east front of the fortress and entered by a postern leading from the battery. The cavalrymen were followed by General Miles, holding Davis by the right arm. Next came half a dozen soldiers, and then Colonel Pritchard with Clay, and last the guard which Miles took out with him. The arrangements were excellent and successful, and not a single curious spectator was any where in sight.

"Davis bore himself with a haughty attitude. His face was somewhat flushed, but his features were composed and his step firm. In Clay's manner there was less expression of bravado and dramatic determination. Both were dressed in gray, with drab slouched hats. Davis wore a thin dark overcoat. His hair and beard are not so gray as has been reported, and he seems very much less worn and broken by anxiety and labor than Mr. Blair reported him when he returned from Richmond last winter. The parties were not informed that they were not to be removed to the fortress until General Miles went on board the Clyde, but they had before learned generally what was their destination.

"From his staff officers Davis parted yesterday, shedding tears at the separation. The same scene has just been renewed at his parting from Harrison, his private secretary, who left at one o'clock for Washington. In leaving his wife and children he exhibited no great emotion, though she was violently affected. He told her she would be allowed to see him in the course of the day. Clay took leave of his wife in private, and he was not seen by the officers. Both asked to see General Halleck, but he will not see them.

"The arrangements for the security of the prisoners seem to me as complete as could be desired. Each one occupies the inner room of a casemate; the window is heavily barred. A sentry stands within, before each of the doors leading into the outer room. These doors are to be grated, but are now secured by bars fastened on the outside. Two other sentries stand outside of these doors. An officer is also constantly on duty in the outer room, whose duty is to see his prisoners every fifteen minutes. The outer door of all is locked on the outside, and the key is kept exclusively by the general officer of the guard. Two sentries are also stationed without that door, and a strong line of sentries cuts off all access to the vicinity of the casemates. Another line is stationed on the top of the parapet overhead, and a third line is posted across the moats on the counterscarps opposite the places of confinement. The casemates on each side and between these occupied by the prisoners are used as guard rooms, and soldiers are always there. A lamp is constantly kept burning in each of the rooms. The furniture of each prisoner is a hospital bed, with iron bedstead, chair and table, and a movable stool closet. A Bible is allowed to each. I have not given orders to have them placed in irons, as General Halleck seemed opposed to it, but General Miles is instructed to have fetters ready if he thinks them necessary. The prisoners are to be supplied with soldiers' rations, cooked by the guard. Their linen will be issued to them in the same way."[23]

The North was no mood to be lenient with the man it felt was more responsible than any other for the four long years of civil war the country had just endured, not to mention the assassination of Abraham Lincoln. "Jefferson Davis must be tried for treason," *Harper's Weekly* said a few days later. "If convicted he must be sentenced. If sentenced he must be executed.... Can any lesson be so permanently impressive as the final proof by the solemn sanction of the supreme authority that treason against the United States is not a political difference of opinion, but a crime whose enormity will not remit the legal penalty?"[24]

---

1. *Official Records,* 47:III:454-455.
2. Davis, *Sherman's March,* 282.
3. Thomas and Hyman, *Stanton,* 414-415.
4. Davis, *The Long Surrender,* 149.
5. Jones, *Yankee Blitzkrieg,* 177.
6. Davis, *The Long Surrender,* 145.
7. Ibid., 150-151.
8. *Official Records,* 48:II:416.
9. Davis, *The Long Surrender,* 151.
10. Jones, *Yankee Blitzkrieg,* 178.
11. Trudeau, *Out of the Storm,* 310.
12. Davis, *The Long Surrender,* 152.
13. Jones, *Yankee Blitzkrieg,* 179.
14. *Official Records,* 48:I:192.
15. Trudeau, *Out of the Storm,* 296.
16. *Official Records,* 48:II:476.

17. Sheridan, *Civil War Memoirs,* 355-356.
18. *Official Records,* 48:II:417.
19. Ibid., 48:II:481.
20. Foote, *The Civil War,* 3:1028.
21. *Official Records,* 47:III:531.
22. Sherman, *Memoirs,* 864.
23. Dana, *Recollections of the Civil War,* 246-247.
24. Hanna, *Flight into Oblivion,* 103.

CHAPTER FORTY-SIX

Clothed With Power, Crowned With Glory

22 - 26 May 1865

Mary Lincoln finally moved out of the White House on the 22nd, and Sherman testified before Congress's Joint Committee on the Conduct of the War that day. He told the committee that the terms he had offered Johnston were based roughly on what Lincoln had said about the need for a quick and humane peace, and he pointed out that he had made the agreement subject to the approval of the government, but his main concern had been to keep Johnston's army from breaking up into guerrilla bands. When asked why slavery had not been covered by that agreement, he said Lincoln had already freed the slaves in the Emancipation Proclamation. "For me to have renewed the question when that decision was made would have involved the absurdity of an inferior undertaking to qualify the work of his superior." As for Stanton's criticisms published in the newspapers, "I did feel indignant—I do feel indignant. As to my own honor, I can protect it."[1]

The next day, 23 May, while the doors to the casemate where Jefferson Davis was held were being replaced with heavier, grated ones, General Miles ordered wrought-iron shackles put on Davis's ankles. Davis resisted what he regarded as a degradation, but four soldiers held him down while a blacksmith riveted a shackle on one ankle and fastened the other with a brass lock. The two shackles were linked by a heavy chain.

The grand review of the Army of the Potomac was held on the 23rd, with Sherman's armies due to follow the next day. "During the preceding five days Washington had been given over to elaborate preparations for the coming pageant," Horace Porter wrote. "The public buildings were decked with a tasteful array of bunting; flags were unfurled from private dwellings; arches and transparencies with patriotic mottos were displayed in every quarter; and the spring flowers were fashioned into garlands, and played their part. The whole city was ready for the most imposing fete-day in its history. Vast crowds of citizens had gathered from neighboring States. During the review they filled the stands, lined the sidewalks, packed the porches, and covered even the housetops."[2]

"For some weeks," reporter Noah Brooks wrote, "there had been so vast a volume of applications for accommodations at the hotels and boarding-houses that every available nook and corner had been taken. Governors and other state functionaries, congressmen, and private citizens from even distant cities desired to look at last upon the grand armies now about to dissolve. So great was the number of visitors that many were obliged to spend the night in the open air, sleeping on park benches, or walking the streets. The mild summer weather of Washington softened these discomforts to the houseless and determined patriots.

"Along the route of the great march stands were built by the Government or by the District authorities, and in some instances by private individuals; so that, from the Capitol to the White House, Pennsylvania Avenue presented a well-nigh unbroken mass of seats, rising rank above rank along the line of march, decorated with the national colors, and filled with joyful and enthusiastic crowds of men, women, and children. The city had ordered a closing of the schools for these two days, and one of the charming features of the great occasion was the massing of the children, in gay attire, on the steps and platforms of the massive porticos and terraces of the northern end of the Capitol....

"The main point of attraction was the part of Pennsylvania Avenue which is nearest the White House. There were built several covered stands for the comfortable accomodation of some ten or fifteen thousand people; the central space being designed for the President of the United States, members of his cabinet, heads of departments, military officers of the highest rank, and the diplomatic corps. On the opposite side of the avenue were stands for use of congressmen, the Federal judiciary, the press, and invited guests. A commodious stand had been built near here, too, by a public-spirited Bostonian, at his own expense, for the exclusive use of crippled and convalescent soldiers. These disabled heroes filled the structure, and it was impossible to regard without emotion the continual exchange of cheers between the scarred veterans and their returning comrades.

"The weather was absolutely perfect on both the days of the grand review; all the conditions, barring the painful memories which even this inspiring sight recalled to many minds, were complete for the full enjoyment of the people's holiday. Two days of rain had cooled the air and laid the dust; and the streets of Washington, not always clean, were pleasant to march through. The air was bright, clear, and invigorating; as far as the eye could reach along the wide avenues through which the armed hosts moved with measured tread there was a blaze of color. Flags, banners, streamers, and all imaginable forms of patriotic device were lavishly spread to the air. The homecoming of the armies had been the signal for the removal of the somber badges of mourning that for more than a month had marked the grief of the city over the death of the beloved Lincoln. Looking over the canopy of the reviewing stand opposite that in which I sat, one could see that the flag on the White House, for the first time since the fifteenth of April, was no longer at half-mast.

"In the center of the reviewing stand nearest the White House grounds was seated President Andrew Johnson; on his right were Secretary Stanton, General Grant, and Attorney-General Speed; and on his left were General Meade, Secretary Welles, Postmaster-General Dennison, and Generals Sherman, Barnard, and Meigs. Behind these were Secretary McCulluch, Secretary Harlan, and a group of military notables. On the higher platform behind were the members of the diplomatic corps in full ceremonial costume, and in the stands at the right and left of that occupied by the President and other dignitaries were military, naval, and civil functionaries by the hundreds. Among these one noted the fine figure and handsome face of General W.S. Hancock; he was often recognized and cheered by the passing soldiery, as well as by civilian spectators. As each Army corps passed the President's stand, the commander of the corps took his seat by the side of President Johnson."[3]

"General Grant, accompanied by the principal members of his staff, was one of the earliest arrivals," Horace Porter wrote. "With his customary simplicity and dislike of ostentation, he had come on foot through the White House grounds from the headquarters of the army at the corner of 17th and F streets. Grant's appearance was, as usual, the signal for a boisterous demonstration. Sherman arrived a few minutes later, and his reception was scarcely less enthusiastic.

"At nine o'clock the signal-gun was fired, and the legions took up their march. They started from the Capitol, and moved along Pennsylvania Avenue toward Georgetown. The width and location of that street made it an ideal thoroughfare for such a purpose. Martial music from scores of bands filled the air, and when familiar war-songs were played the spectators along the route joined in shouting the chorus.... At the head of the column rode Meade, crowned with the laurels of four years of warfare. The plaudits of the multitude followed him along the entire line of march; flowers were strewn in his path, and garlands decked his person and his horse. He dismounted after having passed the reviewing-stand, stepped upon the platform, and was enthusiastically greeted by all present."[4]

The Cavalry Corps led the parade the first day. Wesley Merritt was at its head, since Sheridan had already headed west to take up his new command. Marching behind that many horses must have been hard on the infantry's shoes, if nothing else. "The cavalry, a mighty cavalcade, occupied a full hour in passing," Noah Brooks wrote. "The clatter of hoofs, the clank of sabers, and the shrill call of bugles resounding on the air invested this favorite arm of the service with something of that romance with which our people usually regard it.... Suddenly dashed upon the scene, while the pavement was clear and the spectators were watching for the first appearance of General Wesley Merritt's forces, a splendid blooded charger, covered with foam, wildly plunging and galloping, and ridden by a young major-general. His stirrups were loose, his empty scabbard clattered behind him, his long yellow curls were flying in the wind, but his saber was gallantly carried at salute as he fled by. This was the dashing Custer, whose horse, frightened at a tremendous wreath of flowers flung over his head by some indiscreet admirer, was for a few minutes beyond the control of his rider. There was an irrepressible burst of cheers from the spectators as the scared steed flashed past, and 'Custer!' 'Custer!' 'Custer!' 'Custer!' flew from lip to lip. Shortly, curbing his horse, the gallant young cavalryman rode back again—a beautiful figure, lithe, graceful, and every inch a soldier, saluting again as he repassed the President and took his place at the head of his division, which now came up and passed in review."

After the cavalry came nine batteries of regular horse artillery. "The glitter of their equipments," Brooks said, "the gleam of their polished cannon, the champing and tramping of their fine horses, and the soldierly appearance of the men, made this an impressive feature of the great parade." Then came the provost marshal general's brigade, two regiments of cavalry plus two of regular infantry, the signal corps detachment, and the Engineer Brigade, which Brooks said "was a corps that roused the enthusiasm and gratified the curiosity of the multitudes as it marched past, with pioneers bearing the implements of their branch of the service, and hauling with them the pontoons, boats, and other appliances required on the march to battle, but seldom seen in a holiday military show."

The infantry followed the engineers, with Parke's 9th Corps leading. Attached to it was the division of the 19th Corps that had been left in the Shenandoah Valley when the other had been sent to Savannah. Both it and the 9th Corps had been brought to Washington right after the assassination in order to beef up the defenses of the capital. "This corps was one of the most splendidly equipped and best drilled in the first day's parade," Brooks wrote; "the regiments appeared in fine order, marching 'company front,' with arms at right-shoulder-shift until just before reaching the President's stand, when they were brought to shoulder-arms with a military precision that evoked a great roar of applause from the admiring thousands who looked on. Each brigade of infantry was accompanied by six ambulances, three abreast, and the rear of the corps was brought up by a brigade of artillery. Almost no break occurred in the line of march, and the passing troops were halted but once, and that for a brief moment in front of the main reviewing stand."[5]

Next came the 5th Corps, with Griffin in command. Right behind him came Joshua Chamberlain, now commanding the 1st Division of that corps, which he said had swollen from 5,000 men when it left Appomattox to 10,000, so many detachments, detailed men, and convalescent wounded had showed up for the review. Unlike some other units, his officers and men did not dress up for the occasion. "Perhaps we thought," Chamberlain wrote, "we could not look equal to what we deemed our worth and possibly our reputation; so we resolved to do nothing for show, but to look just what we were, and be judged by what we wore, letting our plainness tell its own story. The men brought themselves up to regulation field inspection; themselves, their dress and accouterments clean and bright, but all of every-day identity. And for officers no useless trappings, rider or horse.... ; light marching order, just as in the field, but clean and trim. No doubt this might make us somewhat conspicuous, as things were; but homeliness was a character we thought we could maintain, even 'before company.'"[6]

Not long after he turned into Pennsylvania Avenue, a girl tried to hand Chamberlain a wreath of flowers. His horse, however, like Custer's, refused to cooperate. Every time she lifted the garland to the general the horse reared in alarm. The general finally delegated an aide to take the flowers from the young lady, and he said that he did not see the aide again for some time. He added that his horse was shy of girls from that time on. But his division marched on. "All the way up the Avenue a tumult of sound and motion," he wrote. "Around Griffin is a whirlpool, and far behind swells and rolls the generous acclaim. At the rise of ground near the Treasury a backward glance takes in the mighty spectacle: the broad Avenue for more than a mile solid full, and more, from wall to wall, from door to roof, with straining forms and outwelling hearts. In the midst, on-pressing that darker stream, with arms and colors resplendent in the noon-day sun, an army of tested manhood, clothed with power, crowned with glory, marching to its dissolution!

"At this turn of the Avenue, our bugle rings out the signal: 'Prepare for Review!' The bands strike the cadenced march; the troops take up the step; the lines straighten; the column rectifies distances; the company fronts take perfect 'dress,' guide left, towards the side of the reviewing stand ahead, arms at the ceremonial 'carry.'

"All is steadiness, dignity, order now. We are to pass in final review. The culminating point is near; the end for us nearing; a far-borne vision broods upon our eyes; world-wide and years-long thought,—deep, silent, higher than joy!" Chamberlain took his place on the reviewing stand among all the brass and the dignitaries, whom he noticed stood up for each brigade if not continually, even though it had already taken three hours just to get to his division. But he paid little attention to them. "For me," he said, "while this division was passing, no other thing could lure my eyes away, whether looking on or through. These were my men, and those who followed were familiar and dear. They belonged to me, and I to them, by bonds birth cannot create nor death sever. More were passing here than the personages on the stand could see. But to me so seeing, what a review, how great, how far, how near! It was as the morning of the resurrection!"[7]

"A vivid bit of color," Noah Brooks noted, "giving a pictorial effect to the show, was the appearance of four regiments of Zouaves in the First Brigade, Second Division, of this corps.... They were splendid in appearance; their marching was perfect, and the men were all well formed and muscular; their gay uniforms and unique dress gave a pleasant relief in the general monotony of color that pervaded the ranks of the marching armies."

Humphreys' 2nd Corps brought up the rear of the marching column. The 6th Corps was still down in Virginia. A unit of the 2nd Corps that caught Brooks's eye was the Irish Brigade. "Every soldier and every officer wore a sprig of green in his hat," he noted, "and the regimental colors had the emerald-green ground, the sunburst, and the harp of Erin. These emblems and the men who bore them were loudly cheered all along the line; we could hear the great roar of the people long before the regiments reached us. Generally speaking, it was noticeable that the applause and the cheering were less frequent at the grand stands where the dignitaries were assembled than at other places along the line where the multitude was enjoying itself in its own free-and-easy fashion.

"On the stand where I sat it was entertaining to watch the movements of many Governors of States, who made it their business to 'rally' whenever a regiment from their own prideful community came marching by.... It was noticeable that the commanders of divisions and corps were not, for the most part, men of an elderly appearance. Meade, Benham, and Humphreys were the only exceptions to this rule; almost all the other general officers being youthful of look. Another notable feature of the parade was the fewness of the field officers; companies were commanded by lieutenants who had taken the places of captains temporarily commanding regiments; and colonels led brigades. This was an expressive reminder of the sorrowful mortality that had laid low so many gallant officers leading their men in desperate charges on the field of battle.

"There were many inquiries why there were no colored troops in line; at that time the Negro troops were being massed at City Point, Virginia, preparatory to being sent to Sheridan's new command in the Southwest. Those troops would doubtless have had a rousing welcome in Washington; for in those days men recognized in the tardily enlisted freedmen something very like the last hope of the distraught and long-harrassed republic."[8]

"The men preserved their alignment and distances with an ease which showed their years of training in the field," Horace Porter wrote. "Their movements were unfettered, their step was elastic, and the swaying of their bodies and the swinging of their arms were as measured as the vibrations of a pendulum. Their muskets shone like a wall of steel. The cannon rumbled peacefully over the paved street, banks of flowers almost concealing them.

"Nothing touched the hearts of the spectators so deeply as the sight of the old war-flags as they were carried by—those precious standards, bullet-riddled, battle-stained, many of them but remnants, often with not enough left of them to show the names of the battles they had seen. Some were decked with ribbons, and some festooned with garlands. Everybody was thrilled by the sight; eyes were dimmed with tears of gladness, and many of the people broke through all restraint, rushed into the street, and pressed their lips upon the folds of the standards....

"For nearly seven hours the pageant was watched with unabated interest; and when it had faded from view the spectators were eager for the night to pass, so that on the morrow the scene might be renewed in the marching of the mighty Army of the West."[9]

On the reviewing stand, Sherman turned to Meade and said, "I'm afraid my poor tatterdemalion corps will make a poor appearance tomorrow when contrasted with yours."

"The people in Washington are so fond of the army that they will make allowances," Meade reassured him. "You needn't be afraid."

But Sherman was being disingenuous. He had noticed how Meade's troops "turned their eyes around like country gawks to look at the big people on the stand." He told his officers, "Be careful about your intervals tomorrow. Don't let your men look back over their shoulders. I'll give you plenty of time to go to the Capitol and see everything afterward, but let them keep their eyes fifteen feet to the front and march by in the old customary way." General Augur offered to loan Sherman his two concert bands for the next day's march, but Sherman said he would rely on his own regimental bands. In fact, although he did not tell them, he thought Meade's soldiers would have marched better without the "pampered and well-fed bands taught to play the very latest operas."[10]

"The next day," Horace Porter wrote, "the same persons, with a few exceptions, assembled upon the reviewing-stand. At nine o'clock Sherman's veterans started."[11] The 9th Illinois Mounted Infantry led the way, followed by Sherman and his staff. Howard, no longer the commander of the Army of the Tennessee, rode with him. As the head of the column rounded the Capitol, the soldiers broke into spontaneous cheers at the sight of the all the banners, the bunting, and the sea of people lining the street all the way to the Treasury building, where they would make a jog to the right and then back to the left to pass the reviewing stand in front of the White House. "The band at once struck up a beautiful march," one soldier wrote, "the column moved.... like one footfall—Rap! rap! rap! down Pennsylvania Avenue. The pavements are lined with spectators; boys as thick as locusts; windows crowded with ladies; roofs of the houses are jammed full of people. Everybody is looking on with astonishment and awe as the Army of the Tennessee, formed into a monster column, closed in mass, full company front, moved down the avenue. The earth shakes under our feet.... The air is bristling with bayonets."[12]

"Sherman, unknown by sight to most of the people in the East, was eagerly watched for," Porter said, "and his appearance awoke great enthusiasm. His tall, spare figure, war-worn face, and martial bearing made him all that the people had pictured him. He had ridden but a little way before his body was decorated with flowery wreaths, and his horse enveloped in garlands."[13] But his horse, like Custer's and Chamberlain's, did not like the flowers or the crowds. "Sherman was a skilful horseman," Noah Brooks said, "but his spirited steed, a powerful beast, gave him all he could do to manage him."[14]

"Down the avenue poured the shining river of steel," wrote Joshua Chamberlain, who, like many other officers of the Army of the Potomac, had come to watch the Western armies march, "gay with colors and rippling with cascades of mounted staff and burnished cannon. At the head proud, stern Sherman, who with thoughtful kindness had brought brave Howard, now ordered to other important duty, to ride by his side in this pageant. Following next is swarthy John Logan, leading the Army of the Tennessee, and Hazen with the Fifteenth Corps. Each division is preceded by its corps of black pioneers, shining like polished ebony, armed with pick and spade, proud of their perfect alignment, keeping step to the music with inborn stress. Significant frontispiece. Almost equally interesting was the corps of foragers, familiarly known as Sherman's 'bummers,' following each brigade. These were characteristic representatives of the career of that army, and they tried to appear as nearly as possible like what they were in that peculiar kind of service. Their dress, and free and easy bearing, as well as their packmules and horses with rope bridles, laden with such stores as they had gathered from the country through which they passed, was a remarkable feature in a military review."[15]

"When I reached the Treasury-building," Sherman wrote, "and looked back, the sight was simply magnificent. The column was compact, and the glittering muskets looked like a solid mass of steel, moving with the regularity of a pendulum."[16] He later remembered that sight as "the happiest and most satisfactory moment of my life."[17]

"We passed the Treasury-building," he said, "in front of which and of the White House was an immense throng of people, for whom extensive stands had been prepared on both sides of the avenue. As I neared the brick-house opposite the lower corner of Lafayette Square, some one asked me to notice Mr. Seward, who, still feeble and bandaged for his wounds, had been removed there that he might behold the troops. I moved in that direction and took off my hat to Mr. Seward, who sat at an upper window. He recognized the salute, returned it, and then we rode on steadily past the President, saluting with our swords."[18]

"As he approached the reviewing-stand," Porter wrote, "the bands struck up 'Marching through Georgia,' and played that stirring air with a will. This was the signal for renewed demonstrations of delight."[19] "There was something almost fierce," Brooks said, "in the fever of enthusiasm roused by the sight of Sherman. Volleys of cheers, prolonged and loud, rose from the crowd; a multitude of small flags waved from the reviewing stands, and wreaths and bouquets of flowers flew thick and fast through the air."[20]

"When he had passed," Porter said, "he turned his horse into the White House grounds, dismounted, and strode rapidly to the platform. He advanced to where the President was standing, and the two shook hands. The members of the cabinet then stepped up to greet him. He took their extended hands, and had a few pleasant words to say to each of them, until Stanton reached out his hand. Then Sherman's whole manner changed in an instant; a cloud of anger overspread his features, and, smarting under the wrong the Secretary had done him in his published bulletins after the conditional treaty with Johnston, turned abruptly away. This rebuff became the sensation of the day."[21]

"In the group of notable men on the grand stand," Brooks wrote, "Sherman was certainly the most notable in appearance. His head was high and narrow, his hair and whiskers were sandy in hue, his moustache stiff and bristling, and his eyes keen and piercing. He was very tall, walked with an immense stride, talked rapidly and nervously, and would be picked out in any assemblage as a man of distinction. All eyes were fastened upon his striking countenance, the vast multitude gazing with a certain rapture at the famous man whom they now saw for the first time."[22]

"Sherman's active mind was crowded with the remembrance of past events," Porter wrote, "and he spent all the day in pointing out the different subdivisions of his army as they moved by, and recalling in his pithy and graphic way many of the incidents of the stirring campaigns through which they had passed."[23]

"There was, of course," Brooks said, "a great deal of popular curiosity to see the Western soldiers who had marched from Atlanta to the sea, and through the Carolinas and Virginia to Washington.... Comparisons between the Eastern and the Western men were made at once. It was observed that the Western men wore a more free-and-easy uniform, generally adopting the loose blue blouse and the sugar-loaf-shaped felt hat, rather than the close-fitting coat and natty French *kepi* of the Eastern soldiers who had marched before us in the Army of the Potomac. But nothing could be more perfect than their marching order, each rank stepping out as one man. As a rule, the Westerners were of larger build than their brothers in the Army of the Potomac; and they were so allotted in the ranks that each company front presented a line of uniform height, the tallest men in the front."[24]

"Logan, 'Black Jack,' came riding at the head of the Army of the Tennessee," Porter said, "his swarthy features and long, coal-black hair giving him the air of a native Indian chief. The army corps which led the column was the Fifteenth, commanded by Hazen; then came the Seventeenth, under Frank P. Blair. Now Slocum appeared at the head of the Army of Georgia, consisting of the Twentieth Corps, headed by the gallant Mower, with his bushy whiskers covering his face, and looking the picture of a hard fighter, and the Fourteenth Corps, headed by Jefferson C. Davis."[25]

"It was, in my judgment," Sherman wrote, "the most magnificent army in existence—sixty-five thousand men, in splendid *physique,* who had just completed a march of nearly two thousand miles in a hostile country, in good drill, and who realized that they were being closely scrutinized by thousands of their fellow-countrymen and by foreigners."[26]

At least one of the foreigners agreed with Sherman. As the 15th Corps passed, the German ambassador was heard to say, "An army like that could whip all Europe." When the 20th Corps had gone by, he said, "An army like that could whip the world." By the time the 14th Corps had passed, he said, "An army like that could whip the devil."[27]

"The steadiness and firmness of the tread," Sherman wrote, "the carefull dress on the guides, the uniform intervals between the companies, all eyes directly to the front, and the tattered and bullet-riven flags, festooned with flowers, all attracted universal notice. Many good people, up to that time, had looked upon our Western army as a sort of mob; but the world then saw, and recognized the fact, that it was an army in the proper sense, well organized, well commanded and disciplined; and there was no wonder that it had swept through the South like a tornado."[28]

"Comparisons were naturally instituted between the Eastern and

Western armies," Porter said. "The difference was much less than has been represented. The Army of the Potomac presented a somewhat neater appearance in dress, and was a little more precise in its movements. Sherman's army showed, perhaps, more of a rough-and-ready aspect and a devil-may-care spirit. Both were in the highest degree soldierly, and typical representatives of the terrible realism of relentless war."[29]

"Now on every pennon, flag, and guidon fluttered a black streamer," Brooks noted; "the hilt of every victorious saber wore a band of crape. These were the tokens of that national mourning over the last illustrious martyr, whose death left a pang of sorrow, even in this hour of jubilation, in every patriot's heart. Nor could the thoughtful spectator restrain a sigh for the thousands who should have marched with these triumphal cohorts, but who fell, a sacrifice for the cause of the Union for whose defense they had risked and lost their lives. They were not forgotten in that hour of triumph—they who had fallen out of the ranks now marching past, although they slept their last sleep in the bayous and marshes of the Southwest and had made the South all billowy with graves. One could almost imagine, as the glittering, cheered, and cheering columns passed by, redundant with life and vigor, that another host, spectral and shadowy, but as numerous and as vividly characterized and marked, moved with and over them with silent tread in the viewless air—two armies, one living and one dead."[30]

"For six hours and a half," Sherman wrote, "that strong tread of the Army of the West resounded along Pennsylvania Avenue; not a soul of that vast crowd of spectators left his place; and, when the rear of the column had passed by, thousands of the spectators still lingered to express their sense of confidence in the strength of a Government which could claim such an army."[31]

That same day, the 6th Corps marched through Richmond on its way to Washington. Halleck had part of the 24th Corps turned out to salute it as it passed in review before him. "The people looked on with indifference," Colonel Elisha Hunt Rhodes recorded, "but a party of colored children sang 'John Brown' to us as we marched along."[32]

The next day, 25 May, tons of captured Confederate gunpowder accidentally exploded at Mobile, Alabama. Union soldiers who had been loading more munitions into a warehouse were seen to be tossing it about carelessly, despite warnings from others who knew the risks they were taking. At about 2:15 p.m. there was a terrific double explosion at the warehouse, two blasts less than a second apart. People all over town were splattered with wood and flying pieces of glass from shattered windows, and the northeast part of the city was covered by a great column of smoke that one witness said "mounted up in a dark, thick mass and then spread out like an immense umbrella or mushroom, and through it could be seen broken timbers and *debris* of all kinds flying in every direction." Brigadier General James Totten, chief of artillery in Canby's Military Division of West Mississippi, said he saw "an immense mass of shot and shell and fragments flying up vertically as high as five hundred feet in the air, as if a mass of the ammunition had been lifted by the ammunition or powder below it." Where the warehouse had stood was a smoking 10-foot-deep crater 57 feet wide by 254 feet long. Eight square blocks of surrounding buildings were destroyed.

"Immediately following the explosion, the buildings began to burn," said Brigadier General James Slack. "A great many persons underneath the rubbish, unable to get out, were roasted alive. Shells were constantly exploding, men crying most piteously for help, the fire approaching them, and no helping hand could save them." Some firefighters were frightened off by the shells that continued to explode, but soldiers with fixed bayonets drove them back to their work and held them to it. Other soldiers, along with sailors from the ships in Mobile Bay, combed the wreckage for survivors. The rescue and cleanup work continued for several days. It was eventually calculated that between 200 and 300 people had been killed and another 200 seriously injured. Sixty-eight buildings had been damaged, tearing the heart out of the city's commercial district; two steamers were destroyed; and from 8,000 to 10,000 bales of cotton had been burned. A court of inquiry said it was "impossible to render an opinion as to the immediate cause of the explosion, as so far as is known, no person at or in the building survived the explosion." It concluded, however, that there had been "gross and culpable carelessness on the part of the fatique party in handling the fixed ammunition." A *New York Times* editorial thought that was beside the point, for "some one must be terribly to blame for allowing a quantity of explosive material sufficient to blow up eight squares of buildings to remain stored in the heart of a large city."[33]

That same day, General Canby reached New Orleans from Mobile and found Buckner there, Kirby Smith's chief of staff. Smith had learned that Jefferson Davis had been captured. The next day, the 26th, Buckner signed an agreement with Canby's chief of staff, Major General Peter J. Osterhaus, surrendering the Trans-Mississippi Department on terms similar to those given to Lee, Johnston and Taylor.

A few days later Kirby Smith wrote to Colonel Sprague from Houston to explain what had happened: "When I gave you, at Shreveport, a memorandum which I hoped might be the basis of negotiations with the United States Government, I commanded an army of over 50,000 men and a department rich in resources. I am now without either. The army in Texas disbanded before my arrival here. From one extremity of the department to the other the troops, with unexampled unanimity of action, have dissolved all military organization, seized the public property, and scattered to their homes. Abandoned and mortified, left without either men or material, I feel powerless to do good for my country and humiliated by the acts of the people I was striving to benefit. The department is now open to occupation by your Government. The citizen and soldier alike, weary of war, are ready to accept the authority and yield obedience to the laws of the United States."[34]

---

1. John F. Marszalek, *Sherman: A Soldier's Passion for Order* (New York, 1993), 354.
2. Porter, *Campaigning with Grant,* 505-506.
3. Brooks, *Washington in Lincoln's Time,* 272-274.
4. Porter, *Campaigning with Grant,* 506-507.
5. Brooks, *Washington in Lincoln's Time,* 274-275.
6. Chamberlain, *The Passing of the Armies,* 250.
7. Ibid., 257-260.
8. Brooks, *Washington in Lincoln's Time,* 277.
9. Porter, *Campaigning with Grant,* 507-509.
10. Davis, *Sherman's March,* 288.
11. Porter, *Campaigning with Grant,* 509.
12. Davis, *Sherman's March,* 290.
13. Porter, *Campaigning with Grant,* 509.
14. Brooks, *Washington in Lincoln's Time,* 279.
15. Chamberlain, *The Passing of the Armies,* 277.
16. Sherman, *Memoirs,* 865.
17. Davis, *Sherman's March,* 293.
18. Sherman, *Memoirs,* 865-866.
19. Porter, *Campaigning with Grant,* 509.
20. Brooks, *Washington in Lincoln's Time,* 279-280.
21. Porter, *Campaigning with Grant,* 509-510.
22. Brooks, *Washington in Lincoln's Time,* 280.
23. Porter, *Campaigning with Grant,* 510.
24. Brooks, *Washington in Lincoln's Time,* 280.
25. Porter, *Campaigning with Grant,* 510.

26. Sherman, *Memoirs,* 866.
27. Davis, *Sherman's March,* 294.
28. Sherman, *Memoirs,* 866.
29. Porter, *Campaigning with Grant,* 512.
30. Brooks, *Washington in Lincoln's Time,* 283.
31. Sherman, *Memoirs,* 866.
32. Rhodes, *All for the Union,* 241.
33. Trudeau, *Out of the Storm,* 330-333.
34. *Official Records,* 48:I:193-194.

Epilogue
28 May 1865 - ?

On the 28th of May the leg irons were removed from Jefferson Davis, five days after they had been put on him. Word of this severe treatment had reached the press, and public opinion in the North had forced their removal.

The day after that, Andrew Johnson issued a proclamation granting amnesty and pardon to almost all persons participating in "the existing rebellion." Those excepted were those who had taxable property of over $20,000, civil and diplomatic officers of the Confederacy, governors of Rebel states, generals of the Confederate Army, Confederate naval officers above the rank of lieutenant, those who had left United States judicial posts or the U.S. Congress to join the Confederacy, all officers who had resigned from the U.S. Army or Navy "to evade duty in resisting the rebellion," all who had been educated at the U.S. military and naval academies, those who had violated oaths, those who had come from states that had not seceded, those who had engaged in raiding commerce, and those who had mistreated prisoners of war. However, members of any of these groups could apply to the president for an individual pardon, and "such clemency will be liberally extended as may be consistent with the facts of the case and the peace and dignity of the United States."[1]

Four days later, as Kirby Smith officially accepted the surrender terms signed by his chief of staff, Johnson lifted military restrictions on trade with the South, except for contraband of war. Britain withdrew its recognition of belligerent rights from the Confederacy on that same second day of June. On 23 June, Johnson declared the blockade of Southern ports at an end, and that same day Brigadier General Stand Watie surrendered his unit of Confederate Cherokees, Creeks, Seminoles, and Osage Indians.

On the last day of June the military commission found guilty all eight persons charged in relation to the assassination of Lincoln. David Herold, Lewis Paine (alias Powell), George Atzerodt, and Mary Surratt were sentenced to be hanged. Dr. Mudd, Sam Arnold and Michael O'Laughlin were sentenced to life in prison. Edward Spangler was given six years. The idea of hanging a woman was very repugnant to the ideals of the Victorian age, and several efforts were made to get her sentenced changed or get her pardoned. But all four death penalties were carried out on 7 July.

Historians have been critical of the trial ever since. The main complaint is that they were tried by a military commission, instead of a civil court, where their rights would have received more protection. There is some validity to this argument, but the standards of justice even in the civil courts of that day were considerably lower than they are now. Efforts are still being made today to clear the names of Dr. Mudd and Mrs. Surratt.

"A painful and depressing feature of this tragical business," reporter Noah Brooks wrote, "was the ease with which many well-meaning but unreasonable people not only appeared to forget the awfulness of the crime committed, but made objection to the findings of the court as well. Judge John A. Bingham, who assisted the judge-advocate in the trial, was unjustly, even wickedly, pursued by some of these wrong-headed persons for the part he took in the conviction of Mrs. Surratt. All the evidence in her case pointed unerringly to her guilt as an intelligent accomplice of the assassins. And the fact that Paine sought her house as a place of refuge after his murderous assault upon Seward, was only one of many more conclusive evidences of her active share in the great conspiracy. Her sex appears to have confused the judgment of many who did not follow the trial with attentiveness."[2]

Confederate commissioners E.G. Lee and Beverly Tucker arranged passage to England from Quebec for John Surratt on 16 September. He later went to Italy and joined the Papal Zouaves under the name John Watson. But he was recognized by another zouave who had known him in Maryland before the war. Surratt was eventually arrested, escaped, and was arrested again in Egypt. He was tried in Washington in June of 1867 for complicity in the assassination, but the trial ended in a hung jury and he was released.

The CSS *Shenandoah* continued to sink Union ships in the Pacific Ocean until it learned on 2 August that the war was over. Rather than surrender to American authorities, she sailed back to Britain, where on 6 November she surrendered.

On 2 April 1866, Johnson declared the insurrection over except for Texas. On 20 August 1866, Johnson declared the insurrection over in Texas and the United States at peace.

On 10 May 67, two years to the day since he was captured, Jefferson Davis was released from imprisonment at Fort Monroe on a writ of habeus corpus. Stanton and Johnson had finally given up on the idea of trying him for treason or for complicity in the assassination of Lincoln. Although he had been rather unpopular in the South by the end of the war and blamed for the Confederacy's decline, his imprisonment without trial had made him a hero in the South. It also won him a great deal of sympathy in the North, and many prominent Northerners were involved in securing his release.

By then Andrew Johnson was increasingly involved in a dispute with Congress over reconstruction of the Southern states. Johnson did not have Lincoln's patience or talent for dealing with those who disagreed with him. Most of the opposition to his policies came from the Radical Republicans who thought he was being too lenient with the Rebels. He was impeached and came within one vote of being removed from office. Grant was elected president in 1868 and served two terms, which are known today mostly for the extreme corruption rampant among his appointees. Although honest himself, he lacked Lincoln's knowledge of politics and human nature.

The shore towards which the war pushed the country remained as indefinite as in Lincoln's dream. The war settled for all time that the United States is one nation, not a collection of independent states. The great underlying cause of the war had been slavery, and that was eliminated. But the underlying cause of slavery had been racial prejudice, and that was hardly touched by the war, either in the South or the North. The considerable contribution of black troops to the Union war effort was quickly forgotten. The former slaves were given the right to vote by the 14th Amendment, but a divided North soon tired of trying to enforce political equality on the unwilling South. The Federal troops were withdrawn in the 1870s, and it was another hundred years before equality became anything like a reality.

They say that the winners write the history books, and this is usually true. However, the American Civil War has proven to be a notable exception. In writing about the war the victors were constrained by the need to avoid stirring up or prolonging sectional hatreds. The assassination of Lincoln has received much the same treatment. Despite considerable evidence and testimony that Booth had been working for the Confederate government in his plan to capture Lincoln, this connection was downplayed and almost forgotten. Historians have preferred to believe that Booth was crazy and had cooked up the entire plot on his own, recruiting a few weak-minded friends to help him. Corollaries to this theorum were that Mrs. Surratt and Dr. Mudd, at least, were innocent of the conspiracy and convicted by the military commission at the instance of a malignant Stanton. Those who wanted to believe in wider conspiracies have usually sought to blame Stanton himself for the assassination. Only recently has the team of William A. Tidwell, James O. Hall and David Winfred Gaddy, in their book *Come Retribution,* thoroughly explored the Confederate involvement in the conspiracy, and I highly recommend that work to anyone interested in examining the evidence in more detail.

Although the war itself was a popular subject in books and magazines for those who had fought in it, mostly for reasons of nostalgia, as that generation passed away the subject was increasingly neglected in the North. In the South, however, almost as soon as the shooting stopped the arguments began about why the Confederacy lost. George Pickett's quip that the Yankees might have had something to do with it was ignored. The myth of the Lost Cause insisted that the Southern soldiers and generals had been superior to their Northern counterparts and that the Confederacy had been overwhelmed by sheer numbers of men and weapons. This was viewed as somehow unfair, or at least ungentlemanly, as if the war had been some knightly tournament and not the life-or-death struggle of a nation.

In the numerous Western movies of the 1940s and '50s that touched on the Civil War, the Southerners were almost always depicted as noble heroes and gentlemen and the Northerners as mean, selfish boors. The Southern version of history, which came to be the dominant one, even denied that the war had anything to do with slavery. It said the war had been about states' rights, although it was a little vague about exactly what rights were involved, if not the right to own slaves. And, while admitting that it was best that the country had been reunited, this version lamented that the good old days of the idyllic plantation society were gone with the wind.

One corollary of this theorum was that the trans-Allegheny West, where the North won most of the battles, was unimportant compared to Virginia, where the Rebels had a better record. By the time I was growing up, this theory had come to dominate the popular view of the war, and it still does among those who have never studied the subject, despite numerous books to the contrary written during and since the war's centennial.

Another corollary was that Lee was a noble man and a great general while Grant was a drunkard and a butcher whose only strategy was to wear down Lee's army by attrition. This remains the popular view of those who get their history from Hollywood. It was not the view of Grant's contemporaries. James Harrison Wilson, who had served on the staffs of Hunter, McClellan and Grant before becoming a general himself, once wrote to his friend Adam Badeau, "With General Grant nothing is done from improper motives, everything is for the good of the service." And he added: "Grant is *sui generis,* has no equal, no successful imitator among his lieutenants in unselfish, true-hearted devotion to duty. He excels them all in magnanimity and truthfulness. You must not look for the same virtues everywhere."[3]

Sheridan said this of Grant: "The assignment of General Grant to the command of the Union armies in the winter of 1863-64 gave presage of success from the start, for his eminent abilities had already been proved, and besides, he was a tower of strength to the Government, because he had the confidence of the people. They knew that henceforth systematic direction would be given to our armies in every section of the vast territory over which active operations were being prosecuted, and further, that this confidence, this harmony of plan, was the one thing needed to end the war, for in the three preceding years there had been illustrated most lamentable effects of the absence of system. From the moment he set our armies in motion simultaneously, in the spring of 1864, it could be seen that we should be victorious ultimately, for though on different lines we were checked now and then, yet we were harassing the Confederacy at so many vital points that plainly it must yield to our blows. Against Lee's army, the forefront of the Confederacy, Grant pitted himself; and it may be said that the Confederate commander was now, for the first time, overmatched, for against all his devices—the products of a mind fertile in defense—General Grant brought to bear not only the wealth of expedient which had hitherto distinguished him, but also an inperturbable tenacity, particularly in the Wilderness and on the march to the James, without which the almost insurmountable obstacles of that campaign could not have been overcome. During it and in the siege of Petersburg he met with many disappointments—on several occasions the shortcomings of generals, when at the point of success, leading to wretched failures. But so far as he was concerned, the only apparent effect of these discomfitures was to make him all the more determined to discharge successfully the stupendous trust committed to his care, and to bring into play the manifold resources of his well-ordered military mind. He guided every subordinate then, and in the last days of the rebellion, with a fund of common sense and superiority of intellect, which have left an impress so distinct as to exhibit his great personality. When his military history is analyzed after the lapse of years, it will show, even more clearly than now, that during these as well as in his previous campaigns he was the steadfast centre about and on which everything else turned."[4]

---

1. Long with Long, *The Civil War Day by Day*, 691.
2. Brooks, *Washington in Lincoln's Time*, 241-242.
3. Jones, *Yankee Blitzkrieg*, 191, n. 19.
4. Sheridan, *Civil War Memoirs*, 351-353.

Appendix A

Cast of Characters

The principal characters mentioned in this book are listed here alphabetically, with a brief description of their places in the scheme of events. Those who have only minor roles in the text, and are not likely to be confused with others, are not listed.

Abbreviations used below:

CSA—Confederate States Army
CSN—Confederate States Navy
USA—United States Army
USMA—United States Military Academy (given with class)
USMC—United States Marine Corps
USN—United States Navy
USNA—United States Naval Academy (given with class)
USV—United States Volunteers

ABBOTT, Joseph C.—Colonel, USV. Commander of the 2nd Brigade of Terry's 1st Division of the 24th Corps in Butler's, later Ord's, Army of the James (Department of Virginia). His brigade was part of Terry's provisional corps that captured Fort Fisher, which later became the reconstituted 10th Corps.

ADAMS, Daniel W.—Brigadier General, CSA. Commander of the District of Central Alabama in Taylor's Department of Alabama, Mississippi and East Louisiana.

ADAMS, Wirt—Brigadier General, CSA. Commander of a small division of cavalry in Taylor's Department of Alabama, Mississippi and East Louisiana in Beauregard's Division of the West. His division was later reorganized as a brigade in Armstrong's Division of Forrest's cavalry corps of Taylor's department. Brother of Daniel W. Adams.

ALEXANDER, E. Porter—Brigadier General, CSA (USMA 1857). Chief of artillery of Longstreet's 1st Corps of Lee's Army of Northern Virginia.

AMES, Adelbert—Brigadier General, USV (USMA May 1861). Commander of the 2nd Division of Ord's (later Gibbon's) 24th Corps in Butler's (later Ord's) Army of the James.

ANDERSON, Richard H. ("Dick")—Lieutenant General, CSA (USMA 1842). Commander of the 4th Corps of Lee's Army of Northern Virginia.

ARMSTRONG, Frank C.—Brigadier General, CSA. Commander of a brigade of cavalry in Jackson's Division of Forrest's cavalry corps of Taylor's Department of Alabama, Mississippi and East Louisiana in Beauregard's Division of the West.

ATZERODT, George (alias Andrew Atwood)—A German-born carriage maker from Port Tobacco, Maryland, who had engaged in ferrying Confederate agents across the lower Potomac before becoming a member of John Wilkes Booth's group.

AUGUR, Christopher Colon—Major General, USV (USMA 1843). Commander of the Department of Washington in Sheridan's (temporarily Hancock's) Middle Military Division.

AYRES, Romeyn B.—Brevet Major General, USV (USMA 1847). Commander of the 2nd Division of Warren's 5th Corps in Meade's Army of the Potomac.

BABCOCK, Orville—Lieutenant Colonel, USV (USMA 1861). Aide on Grant's staff.

BADEAU, Adam—Lieutenant Colonel, USV. One of Grant's military secretaries.

BAKER, Lafayette C.—Colonel (later Brigadier General), USV. Commander of the 1st District of Columbia Cavalry Regiment and head of the Secret Service of the United States War Department. Put in charge of the search for Booth and his accomplices.

BAKER, Luther—A detective in the Secret Service of the Union War Department. Former lieutenant of the 1st District of Columbia Cavalry.

BARLOW, Francis—Brevet Major General, USV. Returned from leave to take command of the 2nd Division of Humphreys' 2nd Corps in Meade's Army of the Potomac on 6 April 1865.

BARNES, John S.—Lieutenant Commander, USN. Captain of the USS *Bat.*

BARTLETT, Joseph J.—Brigadier General, USV. Commander of the 3rd Brigade of Griffin's 1st Division of Warren's 5th Corps in Meade's Army of the Potomac.

BATE, William B.—Major General, CSA. Commander of a division in Cheatham's Corps of the Army of Tennessee. Commanded the corps at Bentonville.

BEALL (pronounced bell), John Yates—Acting Master of Privateers, CSN. Confederate agent working out of Canada who seized ships on Lake Erie in an attempt to liberate prisoners of war from Johnson's Island and was part of a group of agents who attempted to derail a train in upstate New York to free Confederate prisoners of war being transported from one camp to another.

BEAUREGARD, Pierre Gustave Toutant—General, CSA (USMA 1838). Commander of the Western Division, which contained Hood's Army of Tennessee and Taylor's Department of Alabama, Mississippi and East Louisiana. Former commander of the Department of Southern Virginia and North Carolina.

BELL, Louis—Colonel, USV. Commander of the 3rd Brigade of Ames's 2nd Division of the 24th Corps in Butler's, later Ord's, Army of the James (Department of Virginia). Mortally wounded at Fort Fisher.

BELL, Tyree H.—Colonel, CSA. Commander of a brigade in Jackson's Division of Forrest's Cavalry Corps of Taylor's Department of Alabama, Mississippi and East Louisiana.

BENHAM, Henry W.—Brigadier General, USV (USMA 1837). Commander of the Volunteer Engineer Brigade of Meade's Army of the Potomac and of the defenses of Grant's headquarters at City Point.

BENJAMIN, Judah P.—Confederate Secretary of State. In charge of many Confederate clandestine activities.

BLAIR, Francis Preston, Sr.—Influential Northern politician who tried to arrange peace with Jefferson Davis.

BLAIR, Francis P. ("Frank"), Jr.—Major General, USV. Commander of the 17th Corps in Howard's Army of the Tennessee in Sherman's

Military Division of the Mississippi. Simultaneously a member of Congress. Brother of Montgomery Blair.

BLAIR, Montgomery—Former postmaster general in Lincoln's cabinet. Brother of Frank Blair.

BOOTH, John Wilkes—Well known actor on the American stage. Involved in a Confederate plot to capture President Lincoln, possibly for the purpose of exchanging him for a large number of Confederate prisoners of war.

BRAGG, Braxton—General, CSA (USMA 1837). Nominal general-in-chief of the Confederate army and temporary commander of the Department of North Carolina. Former commander of the Army of Tennessee.

BRECKINRIDGE, John C.—Major General, CSA. Last secretary of war in Jefferson Davis's cabinet. Former vice president of the United States. Presidential candidate of the Southern wing of the Democratic Party in 1860.

BREESE, K. Randolph—Lieutenant Commander, USN. Fleet captain of Porter's North Atlantic Blockading Squadron and the commander of the naval brigade that assaulted Fort Fisher.

BROOKS, Noah—Newspaper reporter on friendly terms with President Lincoln.

BUCKNER, Simon Bolivar—Lieutenant General, CSA (USMA 1844). Commander of the District of Arkansas and West Louisiana and chief of staff in Kirby Smith's Trans-Mississippi Department.

BUELL, George P.—Colonel, USV. Commander of the 2nd Brigade of Carlin's 1st Division of Davis's 14th Corps in Slocum's Army of Georgia in Sherman's Military Division of the Mississippi.

BUFORD, Abraham—Brigadier General, CSA (USMA 1841). Commander of a division in Forrest's Cavalry Corps of Taylor's Department of Alabama, Mississippi and East Louisiana.

BURNETT, Henry L.—Brevet Brigadier General, USV. Judge advocate with the Bureau of Military Justice in the War Department. Gathered most of the evidence against Booth's accomplices.

BUTLER, Benjamin Franklin—Major General, USV. Commander of the Department of Virginia and North Carolina and its main field force, the Army of the James. Relieved for the total failure of the first expedition against Fort Fisher.

BUTLER, Matthew C.—Major General, CSA. Commander of the 1st

Division of Hampton's Cavalry Corps of Lee's Army of Northern Virginia, which, with Hampton, was sent to the Carolinas to obtain horses and became attached to the forces opposing Sherman's advance from Savannah.

CAMPBELL, John A.—Confederate Assistant Secretary of War. A former justice of the United States Supreme Court. One of the three peace commissioners who met with Lincoln near Fortress Monroe.

CANBY, Edward R.S.—Major General, USV (USMA 1839). Commander of the Military Division of West Mississippi, consisting of the Department of Arkansas, the Department of the Gulf, the Department of the Mississippi, and, briefly, the Department of Missouri.

CAPEHART, Henry—Colonel, USV. Commander of the 3rd Brigade of Custer's 3rd Division of Merritt's Cavalry Corps of Sheridan's Army of the Shenandoah.

CARLIN, William—Brigadier General, USV. Commander of the 1st Division of Davis's 14th Corps in Slocum's Army of Georgia in Sherman's Military Division of the Mississippi.

CARTER, Samuel P.—Brigadier General, USV (USNA 1846). Commander of the 2nd Division of Cox's District of Beaufort in Schofield's Department of North Carolina.

CHALMERS, James R.—Brigadier General, CSA. Commander of a division in Forrest's Cavalry Corps of Taylor's Department of Alabama, Mississippi and East Louisiana.

CHAMBERLAIN, Joshua Lawrence—Brigadier General, USV. Commander of the 1st Brigade of Griffin's 1st Division of Warren's 5th Corps in Meade's Army of the Potomac.

CHASE, Salmon P.—Former Secretary of the Treasury in Lincoln's cabinet. Named by Lincoln to succeed Taney as the Chief Justice of the Supreme Court.

CHEATHAM, Benjamin Franklin—Major General, CSA. Commander of a corps in Hood's Army of Tennessee.

CLARK, M.H.—Captain, CSA. Appointed temporary treasurer of the Confederate States during Jefferson's Davis's flight through Georgia.

CLAY, Clement C.—Confederate commissioner to Canada.

CLINGMAN, Thomas L.—Brigadier General, CSA. Commander of a brigade in Hoke's Division of Anderson's 4th Corps of Lee's Army of Northern Virginia, sent to help defend Wilmington, North

Carolina, and later to oppose Sherman's march through the Carolinas.

COLQUITT, Alfred H.—Brigadier General, CSA. Commander of a brigade in Hoke's Division of Anderson's 4th Corps of Lee's Army of Northern Virginia, sent to help defend Wilmington, North Carolina, and later to oppose Sherman's march through the Carolinas. Intended by Bragg as a temporary commander of Fort Fisher but arrived after the fort had already fallen.

COMSTOCK, Cyrus B.—Lieutenant Colonel, USV (USMA 1855). Aide on Grant's staff and chief engineer of the Fort Fisher expeditions and of Canby's Mobile campaign.

CONGER, Everton—Detective in the Secret Service of the Union War Department. Former lieutenant colonel of the 1st District of Columbia Cavalry.

COOKE, John R.—Brigadier General, CSA. Commander of a brigade in Heth's Division of Hill's 3rd Corps of Lee's Army of Northern Virginia.

COUCH, Darius N.—Major General, USV (USMA 1846). Commander of the 2nd Division of the 23rd Corps in Schofield's Army of the Ohio (Department of North Carolina).

COX, Jacob D.—Brigadier General, USV. Commander of the 3rd Division of the 23rd Corps in Schofield's Army of the Ohio. Later commander of the corps when Schofield's army was transferred to North Carolina and expanded to include Terry's reconstituted 10th Corps.

CRAWFORD, Samuel W.—Commander of the 3rd Division of Warren's (later Griffin's) 5th Corps in Meade's Army of the Potomac.

CROOK, George—Major General, USV (USMA 1852). Commander of the Department of West Virginia in Sheridan's Middle Military Division. After captured and exchanged, commanded the 2nd Cavalry Division of Meade's Army of the Potomac.

CROOK, William H.—One of President Lincoln's bodyguards.

CROSSLAND, Edward—Colonel, CSA. Commander of a brigade of Kentucky troops in Buford's division of Forrest's cavalry corps in Taylor's Department of Alabama, Mississippi and East Louisiana.

CROXTON, John T.—Brigadier General, USV. Commander of the 1st Brigade of McCook's 1st Division of Wilson's Cavalry Corps of Sherman's Military Division of the Mississippi.

CURTIN, John I.—Brevet Brigadier General, USV. Commander of the 1st Brigade of Potter's 2nd Division of Parke's 9th Corps in Meade's Army of the Potomac.

CURTIS, Newton M.—Brevet Brigadier General, USV. Commander of the 1st Brigade in Ames's 2nd Division of Ord's (later Gibbon's) 24th Corps in Butler's (later Ord's) Army of the James.

CUSHING, William B.—Lieutenant Commander, USN. Commander of the successful attack upon the CSS *Albemarle* with a spar torpedo in October 1864. In charge of sounding New Inlet during the bombardment of Fort Fisher.

CUSHMAN, Charles H.—Lieutenant Commander, USN. Commander of the first division of Breese's naval brigade in the attack on Fort Fisher.

CUSTER, George Armstrong—Brevet Major General, USV (USMA June 1861). Commander of the 3rd Division of Merritt's Cavalry Corps in Sheridan's Army of the Shenandoah (Middle Military Division).

DAHLGREN, John A. B.—Rear Admiral, USN. Commander of the South Atlantic Blockading Squadron.

DANA, Charles A.—Union Assistant Secretary of War.

DANA, Napoleon Jackson Tecumseh—Major General, USV. Commander of the Department of the Mississippi in Canby's Military Division of West Mississippi.

DAVIES, Henry E.—Brigadier General, USV. Commander of the 1st Brigade of Gregg's (later Crook's) 2nd Division of cavalry in Meade's Army of the Potomac. Temporarily commanded the division after Gregg resigned until Crook was appointed.

DAVIS, Jefferson—(USMA 1828). First and only president of the Confederate States of America.

DAVIS, Jefferson C.—Brevet Major General, USV. Commander of the 14th Corps in Slocum's Army of Georgia in Sherman's Military Division of the Mississippi.

DAVIS, Joseph R.—Brigadier General, CSA. Commander of a brigade in Heth's Division of Hill's 3rd Corps of Lee's Army of Northern Virginia. Nephew of President Jefferson Davis.

DAVIS, Varina—Wife of President Jefferson Davis.

DAWSON, Lucien L.—Captain, USMC. Senior marine officer in

Breese's naval brigade, and therefore commander of the fourth division, in the attack on Fort Fisher.

DEARING, James—Brigadier General, CSA (USMA ex-1862). Commander of the Laurel Brigade in Rosser's division of Fitz Lee's Cavalry Corps of Lee's Army of Northern Virginia.

DENNISON, William—Postmaster General in Lincoln's cabinet.

DENT, Frederick T.—Lieutenant Colonel, USV (USMA 1843). Aide on Grant's staff. Also Grant's brother-in-law.

DE TROBRIAND, Philip Regis D.—Brigadier General, USV. Commander of the 1st Brigade of Mott's 3rd Division of Humphreys' 2nd Corps in Meade's Army of the Potomac. Succeeded to command of the division on 6 April 1865.

DEVIN, Thomas C.—Brigadier General, USV. Commander of the 1st Division of Merritt's Cavalry Corps in Sheridan's Army of the Shenandoah (Middle Military Division).

DIBRELL, George G.—Brigadier General, CSA. Commander of one of the brigades of cavalry that escorted Jefferson Davis through the Carolinas.

DIX, John Adams—Major General, USV. Commander of the Department of the East, with headquarters at New York City.

DUKE, Basil W.—Brigadier General, CSA. Commander of one of the cavalry brigades that escorted Jefferson Davis through the Carolinas.

EARLY, Jubal Anderson—Lieutenant General, CSA (USMA 1837). Commander of the Army of the Valley, also known as the Valley District, and of the 2nd Corps of Lee's Army and Department of Northern Virginia.

ECKERT, Thomas T.—Major, USV. Supervisor of Military Telegraphs in the Union War Department.

ELY, Ralph—Brevet Colonel, USV. Commander of the 2nd Brigade of Willcox's 1st Division of Parke's 9th Corps in Meade's Army of the Potomac.

EVANS, Clement A.—Brigadier General, CSA. Temporary commander of Gordon's Division of Gordon's 2nd Corps of Lee's Army of Northern Virginia.

EWELL, Richard S. ("Dick")—Lieutenant General, CSA (USMA 1840). Commander of the Department of Richmond.

FARRAGUT, David Glasgow—Rear Admiral, USN. The captor of New

Orleans and hero of the battle of Mobile Bay.

FEARING, Benjamin—Colonel, USV—Commander of the 3rd Brigade of Morgan's 2nd Division of Davis's 14th Corps in Slocum's Army of Georgia in Sherman's Military Division of the Mississippi.

FERGUSON, Samuel W.—Brigadier General, CSA (USMA 1857). Commander of one of the small brigades of cavalry that escorted Jefferson Davis through the Carolinas.

FIELD, Charles W.—Major General, CSA (USMA 1849). Commander of a division in Longstreet's 1st Corps of Lee's Army of Northern Virginia.

FINEGAN, Joseph—Brigadier General, CSA. Temporary commander of Mahone's Division of Hill's 3rd Corps of Lee's Army of Northern Virginia.

FITZHUGH, Charles—Colonel, USV (USMA ex-1863). Commander of the 2nd Brigade of Devin's 1st Division in Merritt's Cavalry Corps of Sheridan's Army of the Shenandoah.

FORREST, Nathan Bedford—Major General (later Lieutenant General), CSA. Commander of a district and cavalry corps in Taylor's Department of Alabama, Mississippi and East Louisiana, temporarily attached to Hood's Army of Tennessee for the Nashville campaign.

FOSTER, John G.—Major General, USV (USMA 1846). Commander of the Department of the South, which included Union lodgments along the coast of South Carolina, Georgia, and Florida.

FOSTER, Robert S.—Brigadier General, USV. Commander of the 1st Division of Gibbon's 24th Corps in Ord's Army of the James (Department of Virginia). Member of the military commission that tried Booth's conspirators.

FOX, Gustavus V.—Union Assistant Secretary of the Navy.

GARY, Martin W.—Brigadier General, CSA. Commander of the Cavalry Brigade of Ewell's Department of Richmond.

GERRISH, Theodore—Private, USV. Member of the 20th Maine Volunteer Infantry Regiment in Bartlett's 3rd Brigade of Griffin's 1st Division of Warren's (later Griffin's) 5th Corps in Meade's Army of the Potomac.

GETTY, George Washington—Brigadier General, USV (USMA 1840). Commander of the 2nd Division of Wright's 6th Corps in Sheridan's Army of the Shenandoah (Middle Military Division).

GIBBON, John—Major General, USV (USMA 1847). Commander of

the 24th Corps in Ord's Army of the James (Department of Virginia).

GIBBS, Alfred—Brigadier General, USV (USMA 1846). Commander of the Reserve Brigade of Devin's 1st Division of Merritt's Cavalry Corps of Sheridan's Army of the Shenandoah.

GIBSON, Randall L.—Brigadier General, CSA. Commander of the defenders of Spanish Fort, in the landward defenses of Mobile, Alabama, which included his brigade from the Army of Tennessee.

GILLEM, Alvan C.—Brigadier General, USV (USMA 1851). Commander of the Cavalry Division of Stoneman's District of East Tennessee in Thomas's Department of the Cumberland in Sherman's Military Division of the Mississippi.

GILLMORE, Quincy Adams—Major General, USV (USMA 1849). Commander of the Department of the South.

GORDON, John B.—Major General, CSA. Temporary commander of Early's 2nd Corps of Lee's Army of Northern Virginia.

GRANGER, Gordon—Major General, USV (USMA 1845). Commander of the 13th Corps in Bank's Department of the Gulf in Canby's Military Division of West Mississippi.

GRANT, Julia Dent. Wife of Ulysses S. Grant.

GRANT, Lewis A.—Brigadier General, USV. Commander of the 2nd (Vermont) Brigade of Getty's 2nd Division of Wright's 6th Corps in Meade's Army of the Potomac.

GRANT, Ulysses Simpson—Lieutenant General, USA (USMA 1843). General-in-chief of the United States Army.

GREGG, David McMurtrie—Brigadier General (Brevet Major General), USV (USMA 1855). Commander of the 2nd Division of the Cavalry Corps of Meade's Army of the Potomac, which was the only division of that corps left behind when the rest of it was transferred to Sheridan's Army of the Shenandoah (Middle Military Division).

GREGG, J. Irvin—Brevet Brigadier General, USV. Commander of the 2nd Brigade of Crook's 2nd Division of cavalry in Meade's Army of the Potomac.

GREGORY, Edgar M.—Brevet Brigadier General, USV. Commander of the 2nd Brigade of Griffin's 1st Division of Warren's 5th Corps in Meade's Army of the Potomac.

GRIERSON, Benjamin H.—Brigadier General, USV. Commander of a division of cavalry in Dana's Department of the Mississippi in

Canby's Military Division of West Mississippi.

GRIFFIN, Charles—Brigadier General, USV (USMA 1847). Commander of the 1st Division of Warren's 5th Corps in Meade's Army of the Potomac. Succeeded to command of the corps.

GRIFFIN, Simon G.—Brigadier General, USV. Commander of the 2nd Brigade of Potter's 2nd Division of Parke's 9th Corps in Meade's Army of the Potomac.

GRIMES, Bryan—Major General, CSA. Commander of a division in Gordon's 2nd Corps of Lee's Army of Northern Virginia.

GROVER, Cuvier—Brigadier General, USV (USMA 1850). Commander of the 2nd Division of the 19th Corps in Sheridan's Army of the Shenandoah (Middle Military Division), which was shipped down the coast to Savannah, where it became Grover's Division of Foster's Department of the South.

GWYN, James—Brevet Brigadier General, USV. Commander of the 3rd Brigade of Ayres' 2nd Division of Warren's (later Griffin's) 5th Corps in Meade's Army of the Potomac.

HALLECK, Henry Wager—Major General, USA (USMA 1839). Grant's predecessor as general-in-chief and former boss in the trans-Allegheny West. Named by Grant as the first chief of staff of the U.S. Army to take care of the paperwork in Washington while he ran the armies from the field.

HAMLIN, Hannibal—Vice President of the United States during Lincoln's first term.

HAMMOND, John H.—Brevet Brigadier General, USV. Commander of the 1st Brigade in Knipe's 7th Division of Wilson's Cavalry Corps of Sherman's Military Division of the Mississippi.

HAMPTON, Wade—Major (later Lieutenant) General, CSA. Commander of the Cavalry Corps of Lee's Army of Northern Virginia. Sent to South Carolina to help raise troops to oppose Sherman's advance and put in command of all the cavalry in the Carolinas.

HANCOCK, Winfield Scott—Major General, USV (USMA 1840). Temporary commander of the Middle Military Division in Sheridan's absence. Former commander of the 2nd Corps in Meade's Army of the Potomac.

HARBIN, Thomas H. (alias Thomas A. Wilson)—agent of the Confederate Secret Service involved in Booth's plot to capture

President Lincoln.

HARDEE, William J.—Lieutenant General, CSA (USMA 1838). Commander of the Department of South Carolina, Georgia and Florida.

HARNDEN, Henry—Lieutenant Colonel, USV. Commander of the 1st Wisconsin Cavalry Regiment in La Grange's 2nd Brigade of McCook's, later Croxton's, 1st Division of Wilson's Cavalry Corps of Sherman's Military Division of the Mississippi. One of two regiments involved in the capture of Jefferson Davis.

HARNEY, Thomas F.—Lieutenant, CSA. Explosives expert sent to blow up the White House.

HARRIMAN, Samuel—Colonel, USV. Commander of the 1st Brigade of Willcox's 1st Division of Parke's 9th Corps in Meade's Army of the Potomac.

HARRIS, Clara—The young lady who was with the Lincolns in the state box at Ford's Theatre when the president was shot. Daughter of Senator Ira Harris of New York.

HARRIS, Nathaniel H. ("Nate")—Brigadier General, CSA. Commander of a brigade in Mahone's Division of Hill's 3rd Corps of Lee's Army of Northern Virginia.

HARRIS, Thomas M.—Brigadier General, USV. Commander of the 3rd Brigade of Turner's Independent Division of Gibbon's 24th Corps in Ord's Army of the James (Department of Virginia). Member of the military commission that tried Booth's conspirators.

HARRISON, Burton—Colonel, CSA. Jefferson Davis's secretary. Escorted Davis's wife and family south from Richmond.

HARRISON, Thomas Jefferson—Colonel, USV. Commander of the 1st Brigade of Johnson's 6th Division of Wilson's Cavalry Corps of Sherman's Military Division of the Mississippi.

HARTRANFT, John F.—Brigadier General, USV. Commander of the 3rd Division of Parke's 9th Corps in Meade's Army of the Potomac. Special provost marshal for the trial of Booth's conspirators.

HATCH, Edward—Brigadier General, USV. Commander of the 5th Division of Wilson's Cavalry Corps in Sherman's Military Division of the Mississippi.

HATCH, John P.—Brigadier General, USV (USMA 1845). Commander of a division in Foster's Department of the South.

HAWKINS, John P.—Brigadier General, USV (USMA 1852).

Commander of the 1st Division of United States Colored Troops in Steele's District of West Florida in Hurlbut's Department of the Gulf in Canby's Military Division of West Mississippi.

HAYS, William—Brigadier General, USV (USMA 1840). Commander of the 2nd Division of Humphreys' 2nd Corps in Meade's Army of the Potomac.

HAZEN, William B.—Brigadier General, USV (USMA 1855). Commander of the 2nd Division of Logan's 15th Corps in Howard's Army of the Tennessee in Sherman's Military Division of the Mississippi. Succeeded to command of the corps when Logan succeeded to command of the army after Howard was assigned to the Freedmen's Bureau.

HENDERSON, Thomas Jefferson—Brigadier General, USV. Commander of the 3rd Brigade of Cox's 3rd Division of the 23rd Corps in Schofield's Army of the Ohio (Department of North Carolina).

HEROLD, David—A member of John Wilkes Booth's group of Confederate sympathizers who planned to capture President Lincoln and later decided to assassinate him instead.

HETH (pronounced heath), Henry—Major General, CSA (USMA 1847). Commander of a division in A.P. Hill's 3rd Corps of Lee's Army of Northern Virginia. Succeeded to the command of the corps after Hill was shot.

HILL, Ambrose Powell—Lieutenant General, CSA (USMA 1847). Commander of the 3rd Corps in Lee's Army of Northern Virginia.

HILL, Daniel Harvey—Major General, CSA (USMA 1842). Commander of a division in Johnston's Army of Tennessee.

HINES, Thomas—Captain, CSA. Confederate secret agent in charge of military operations out of Canada.

HOBART, Harrison—Colonel, USV. Commander of the 1st Brigade of Carlin's 1st Division of Davis's 14th Corps in Slocum's Army of Georgia in Sherman's Military Division of the Mississippi.

HOFFMAN, John S.—Colonel, CSA. Temporary commander of Walker's Brigade in Pegram's (Early's) Division of Gordon's 2nd Corps in Lee's Army of Northern Virginia.

HOKE, Robert F.—Major General, CSA. Commander of a division in Anderson's 4th Corps of Lee's Army of Northern Virginia sent to North Carolina to defend Wilmington and later to oppose Sherman's march.

HOLT, Joseph—Brigadier General, USV. Judge Advocate General of the United States Army.

HOOD, John Bell—General, CSA (USMA 1853). Commander of the Army of Tennessee.

HOWARD, Oliver Otis—Major General, USV (USMA 1854). Commander of the Army of the Tennessee (also known as the Right Wing) in Sherman's Military Division of the Mississippi. Commissioner of the Freedman's Bureau.

HUMPHREYS, Andrew A.—Major General, USV (USMA 1831). Commander of the 2nd Corps in Meade's Army of the Potomac.

HUNT, Henry J.—Brevet Major General, USV (USMA 1839). Chief of Artillery of Meade's Army of the Potomac.

HUNTER, David—Major General, USV (USMA 1822). Senior officer on the miltary commission appointed to try Booth's conspirators. Former commander of the Department and Army of West Virginia.

HUNTER, Robert M.T.—President pro tempore of the Confederate Senate. A former U.S. Senator. One of the three peace commissioners who met with Lincoln near Fortress Monroe.

HUNTON, Eppa—Brigadier General, CSA. Brigade commander in Pickett's Division of Longstreet's 1st Corps of Lee's Army of Northern Virginia.

HYDE, Thomas—Colonel, USV. Commander of the 3rd Brigade of Getty's 2nd Division of Wright's 6th Corps in Meade's Army of the Potomac.

INGALLS, Rufus—Brigadier General, USV (USMA 1843). Chief quartermaster of Grant's Armies Operating Against Richmond.

IZLAR, James F.—Captain, CSA. Senior officer among the reinforcements from Hagood's Brigade of Hoke's Division who reached the land face in time to help defend Fort Fisher.

JACKSON, William H. ("Red")—Brigadier General, CSA (USMA 1856). Commander of a division of Forrest's cavalry corps in Taylor's Department of Alabama, Mississippi and East Louisiana.

JOHNSON, Andrew—Brigadier General, USV. Military governor of Tennessee. Then vice president of the United States. Became the 17th president of the United States when Lincoln was assassinated.

JOHNSON, Bushrod R.—Major General, CSA (USMA 1840).

Commander of a division in Anderson's 4th Corps of Lee's Army of Northern Virginia.

JOHNSTON, Joseph Eggleston—General, CSA (USMA 1829). Hood's predecessor in command of the Department and Army of Tennessee. Appointed by Lee to command all the Confederate troops in North and South Carolina.

KARGÉ, Joseph—Colonel, USV. Commander of the 1st Brigade of Grierson's Cavalry Division of Dana's Department of the Mississippi in Canby's Military Division of West Mississippi.

KAUTZ, August V.—Brigadier General, USV (USMA 1852). Commander of the Cavalry Division of Ord's Army of the James (Department of Virginia). Later Commander of the 1st Division of Weitzel's 25th Corps in Ord's Army of the James. Member of the military commission that tried Booth's conspirators.

KELLEY, Benjamin Franklin—Brigadier General, USV. Commander of forces west of Sleepy Hollow in Crook's Department of West Virginia in Sheridan's Middle Military Division.

KENNEDY, Robert Cobb—Captain, CSA. One of the Confederate officers who tried to burn New York City in November 1864.

KILPATRICK, Hugh Judson—Brigadier General, USV (USMA 1861). Commander of the 3rd Cavalry Division of Wilson's Cavalry Corps of Sherman's Military Division of the Mississippi, the only cavalry taken on the March to the Sea and through the Carolinas.

KIRKLAND, William W.—Brigadier General, CSA. Commander of a brigade in Hoke's Division of Anderson's 4th Corps of Lee's Army of Northern Virginia, sent to help defend Wilmington, North Carolina, and later to oppose Sherman's march through the Carolinas.

La GRANGE, Oscar H.—Colonel, USV. Commander of the 2nd Brigade of McCook's 1st Division of Wilson's Cavalry Corps of Sherman's Military Division of the Mississippi.

LAMB, William—Colonel, CSA. Commander of the 36th North Carolina Artillery Regiment and of Fort Fisher, North Carolina.

LANE, James H.—Brigadier General, CSA. Commander of a brigade in Wilcox's Division of Hill's 3rd Corps of Lee's Army of Northern Virginia.

LEE, Edwin G.—Brigadier General, CSA. In charge of Confederate operations from Canada. Cousin of R.E. Lee.

LEE, Fitzhugh ("Fitz")—Major General, CSA (USMA 1856). Commander of a cavalry division in R.E. Lee's Army of Northern Virginia. Later commanded the Cavalry Corps of Lee's army. Nephew of R.E. Lee.

LEE, George Washington Custis—Major General, CSA (USMA 1854). Commander of a division in Ewell's Department of Richmond. Oldest son of R.E. Lee.

LEE, Robert Edward—General, CSA (USMA 1829). Commander of the Army of Northern Virginia and, for the last few months of the war, general-in-chief of the Confederate army.

LEE, Robert Edward, Jr.—Captain, CSA. Third son of the commander of the Army of Northern Virginia.

LEE, Stephen Dill—Lieutenant General, CSA (USMA 1854). Commander of the 2nd Corps of Hood's (later Johnston's) Army of Tennessee. Only very distantly related to the Virginia Lees.

LEE, William Henry Fitzhugh ("Rooney")—Major General, CSA. Commander of a cavalry division in R.E. Lee's Army of Northern Virginia. Second son of R.E. Lee; brother of G.W.C. Lee; cousin of Fitzhugh Lee.

LIDDELL, St. John R.—Brigadier General, CSA. Commander of Fort Blakely in the defenses of Mobile, Alabama.

LINCOLN, Abraham—Sixteenth president of the United States and the first Republican to ever be elected to that office.

LINCOLN, Mary Todd—Wife of Abraham Lincoln.

LINCOLN, Robert—Captain, USV. Aide on Grant's staff. Oldest son of Abraham Lincoln.

LLOYD, John—Tavernkeeper at Surrattsville, Maryland.

LOGAN, John A.—Major General, USV. Commander of the 15th Corps in Howard's Army of the Tennessee in Sherman's Military Division of the Mississippi. Succeeded to command of that army when Howard became commissioner of the Freedmen's Bureau.

LOMAX, Lunsford L.—Major General, CSA (USMA 1856). Commander of a cavalry division in Early's Army of the Valley.

LONG, Eli—Brigadier General, USV. Commander of the 2nd Division of Wilson's Cavalry Corps of Sherman's Military Division of the Mississippi until wounded during the capture of Selma, Alabama.

LONGSTREET, James—Lieutenant General, CSA (USMA 1842).

Commander of the 1st Corps of Lee's Army of Northern Virginia.

LUCAS, Thomas J.—Brigadier General, USV. Commander of the Separate Cavalry Brigade of Steele's District of West Florida in Hurlbut's Department of the Gulf in Canby's Military Division of West Mississippi.

LYON, Hylan B.—Brigadier General, CSA (USMA 1856). Commander of the Department of Western Kentucky and a division of Kentucky recruits that made a raid into that state during Hood's Nashville campaign.

MACKENZIE, Ranald S.—Brigadier General, USV (USMA 1862). Commander of the Cavalry Division of Ord's Army of the James (Department of Virginia).

MacRAE, William—Brigadier General, CSA. Commander of a brigade in Heth's Division of Hill's 3rd Corps of Lee's Army of Northern Virginia.

MAGRUDER, John B.—Lieutenant General, CSA (USMA 1830). Commander of the District of Texas in Kirby Smith's Trans-Mississippi Department.

MAHONE, William—Major General, CSA. Commander of a division in Hill's 3rd Corps of Lee's Army of Northern Virginia.

MARSHALL, CHARLES—Colonel, CSA. R.E. Lee's military secretary.

MAYO, Robert—Colonel, CSA. Temporary commander of a brigade of Heth's Division of A.P. Hill's 3rd Corps of Lee's Army of Northern Virginia that was moved north of the James River and assigned to the Department of Richmond so that some of its members could be sent home to northern Virginia to provide security for bringing a kidnapped President Lincoln to Richmond.

McALLISTER, Robert—Colonel, USV. Commander of the 3rd Brigade of Mott's 3rd Division of Humphreys' 2nd Corps in Meade's Army of the Potomac.

McCOOK, Edward M.—Brigadier General, USV. Commander of the 1st Division of Wilson's Cavalry Corps of Sherman's Military Division of the Mississippi.

McGOWAN, Samuel—Brigadier General, CSA. Commander of a brigade in Wilcox's Division of Hill's 3rd Corps in Lee's Army of Northern Virginia.

McLAUGHLEN, Napoleon Bonaparte—Colonel, USV. Commander of the 3rd Brigade of Willcox's 1st Division of Parke's 9th Corps in

Meade's Army of the Potomac.

McLAWS, Lafayette—Major General, CSA (USMA 1842). Commander of a division in Hardee's Department of South Carolina, Georgia and Florida, which, at Bentonville, became Hardee's corps of Johnston's army.

McPHERSON, James B.,—Major General, USV (USMA 1853). Howard's predecessor as commander of the Army of the Tennessee in Sherman's Military Division of the Mississippi. Killed during the battle of Atlanta, 22 July 1864.

McQUISTON, John C.—Colonel, USV. Commander of the 2nd Brigade of Ruger's 1st Division of the 23rd Corps in Schofield's Army of the Ohio (Department of North Carolina).

MEADE, George Gordon—Major General, USV (USMA 1835). Commander of the Army of the Potomac.

MEIGS, Montgomery C.—Brevet Major General, USV (USMA 1836). Quartermaster General of the Union army.

MERRITT, Wesley—Brigadier General, USV (USMA 1860). Commander of the Cavalry Corps in Sheridan's Army of the Shenandoah (Middle Military Division).

MILES, David—Colonel, USV. Commander of the 3rd Brigade of Carlin's 1st Division of Davis's 14th Corps in Slocum's Army of Georgia in Sherman's Military Division of the Mississippi.

MILES, Nelson A.—Brevet Major General, USV. Commander of the 1st Division of Humphreys' 2nd Corps in Meade's Army of the Potomac.

MILLER, Abram—Colonel, USV. Commander of the 1st Brigade of Long's (later Minty's) 2nd Division of Wilson Cavalry Corps of Sherman's Military Division of the Mississippi.

MINTY, Robert—Colonel, USV. Commander of the 2nd Brigade of Long's 2nd Division of Wilson's Cavalry Corps of Sherman's Military Division of the Mississippi. Succeeded to command of the division after Long was wounded at Selma.

MOORE, Orlando H.—Colonel, USV. Commander of the 2nd Brigade of Couch's 2nd Division of the 23rd Corps in Schofield's Army of the Ohio (Department of North Carolina).

MORGAN, James D.—Brigadier General, USV. Commander of the 2nd Division of Davis's 14th Corps in Slocum's Army of Georgia in Sherman's Military Division of the Mississippi.

MOSBY, John Singleton—Colonel, CSA. Commander of a battalion of partisan rangers in northern Virginia.

MOTT, Gershom—Brigadier General, USV. Commander of the 3rd Division of Humphreys' 2nd Corps in Meade's Army of the Potomac.

MOWER, Joseph A.—Major General, USV. Commander of the 1st Division of Blair's 17th Corps in Howard's Army of the Tennessee in Sherman's Military Division of the Mississippi. Later commander of the 20th Corps in Slocum's Army of Georgia in Sherman's Military Division of the Mississippi.

MUDD, Dr. Samuel—A pro-Confederate medical doctor who lived on a Maryland farm southeast of Washington, D.C., and became entangled in John Wilkes Booth's plot against President Lincoln.

MUNFORD, Thomas T.—Brigadier General, CSA. Commander of a brigade of Fitzhugh Lee's cavalry division in Lee's Army of Northern Virginia. Took command of the division when Fitz Lee was put in command of all of Lee's cavalry south of the James River.

O'BEIRNE, James—Major, USV. Provost marshal of Washington, D.C.

O'LAUGHLIN, Michael—A member of John Wilkes Booth's conspiracy to capture President Lincoln and take him to Richmond.

ORD, Edward O. C.—Major General, USV (USMA 1839). Commander of the 24th Corps in Butler's Army of the James (Department of Virginia and North Carolina) and Butler's successor in command of that army and department.

OSBORN, Thomas O.—Colonel, USV. Commander of the 1st Brigade of Foster's 1st Division of Gibbon's 24th Corps in Ord's Army of the James (Department of Virginia).

OSTERHAUS, Peter J.—Major General, USV. Chief of staff in Canby's Military Division of West Mississippi.

PALMER, Innis N.—Brigadier General, USV (USMA 1846). Commander of the 1st Division of Cox's District of Beaufort in Schofield's Department of North Carolina.

PALMER, John M.—Major General, USV. Commander of the Department of Kentucky in Sherman's Military Division of the Mississippi.

PALMER, William J.—Colonel (later Brevet Brigadier General), USV. Commander of a small brigade of cavalry that captured Hood's pontoon train and one of his supply trains. Then commander of a brigade of Gillem's cavalry division that raided under Stoneman from east Tennessee into Virginia and North Carolina. Succeeded to command of the division and led it in pursuit of Jefferson Davis.

PARKE, John G.—Major General, USV (USMA 1849). Commander of the 9th Corps in Meade's Army of the Potomac.

PARKER, Ely Samuel—Lieutenant Colonel, USV. One of Grant's military secretaries. A sachem of the Seneca tribe of Iroquois Indians and son of a famous chief.

PARKER, James—Lieutenant Commander, USN. Commander of the second division of Breese's naval brigade in the attack on Fort Fisher. Executive officer of the USS *Minnesota.*

PEARSON, Alfred—Brevet Brigadier General, USV. Colonel of the 155th Pennsylvania in Bartlett's 3rd Brigade of Griffin's 1st Division of Warren's (later Griffin's) 5th Corps in Meade's Army of the Potomac. Put in temporary charge of three regiments of Bartlett's brigade, including his own.

PEGRAM, John—Brigadier General, CSA (USMA 1854). Temporary commander of Early's Division of Gordon's 2nd Corps of Lee's Army of Northern Virginia.

PENDLETON, William Nelson—Brigadier General, CSA (USMA 1830). Chief of artillery of Lee's Army of Northern Virginia.

PENNINGTON, Alexander—Colonel, USV (USMA 1860). Commander of the 1st Brigade of Custer's 3rd Division of Merritt's Cavalry Corps of Sheridan's Army of the Shenandoah.

PENNYPACKER, Galusha—Colonel, USV. Commander of the 2nd Brigade of Ames' 2nd Division of the 24th Corps in Butler's, later Ord's, Army of the James (Department of Virginia). Badly wounded at Fort Fisher.

PICKETT, George E.—Major General, CSA (USMA 1846). Commander of a division in Longstreet's 1st Corps of Lee's Army of Northern Virginia.

PIERCE, Bryon R.—Brigadier General, USV. Commander of the 2nd Brigade of Mott's (later de Trobriand's) 3rd Division of Humphreys' 2nd Corps in Meade's Army of the Potomac.

POPE, John—Major General, USV (USMA 1842). Commander of the Military Division of the Missouri.

PORTER, David Dixon—Rear Admiral, USN. Commander of the North Atlantic Blockading Squadron and the naval forces attacking Fort Fisher.

PORTER, Horace—Lieutenant Colonel, USA (USMA 1860). An aide on Grant's staff. His book *Campaigning with Grant* is frequently quoted in these pages.

POTTER, Robert B.—Brigadier General, USV. Commander of the 2nd Division of Parke's 9th Corps in Meade's Army of the Potomac.

POWELL (alias Paine), Lewis—Private, CSA. Member of Mosby's command sent to Washington to aid in Booth's plot to capture Lincoln.

PRITCHARD, Benjamin—Lieutenant Colonel, USV. Commander of the 4th Michigan Cavalry Regiment in Minty's 2nd Brigade of Long's, later Minty's, 2nd Division of Wilson's Cavalry Corps of Sherman's Military Division of the Mississippi. One of the two regiments involved in the capture of Jefferson Davis.

QUANTRILL, William Clarke—Captain, CSA. Confederate guerilla in Missouri and Kentucky.

RAMSEY, John—Brevet Brigadier General, USV. Commander of the 4th Brigade of Miles' 1st Division of Humphreys' 2nd Corps in Meade's Army of the Potomac.

RATHBONE, Henry R.—Major, USV. The officer who was in the state box with the Lincolns when the president was shot. Stepson of Senator Ira Harris of New York.

RAWLINS, John A.—Brigadier General, USV. Grant's chief of staff.

READ, Theodore—Brevet Brigadier General, USV. Chief of staff of Ord's Army of the James (Department of Virginia).

REAGAN, John—Postmaster General in Jefferson Davis's cabinet.

REILLY, James—Major, CSA. Succeeded Lamb as commander of the Fort Fisher garrison after Lamb was wounded.

REYNOLDS, Joseph J.—Major General, USV (USMA 1843). Commander of the Department of Arkansas (7th Army Corps) in Pope's Military Division of the Missouri.

RHIND, Alexander—Commander, USN. Officer in charge of blowing up the powder boat *Louisiana.*

RHODES, Elisha Hunt—Lieutenant Colonel, USV. Commander of the 2nd Rhode Island Volunteers in Edwards' 3rd Brigade of Wheaton's 1st Division of Wright's 6th Corps in Meade's Army of the Potomac.

RICHARDS, A.C.—Major, USV. Superintendent of police of

Washington, D.C.

RIPLEY, Edward H.—Colonel, USV. Commander of the 1st Brigade of Devens' 3rd Division of Gibbon's 24th Corps in Ord's Army of the James (Department of Virginia).

ROBERTS, Samuel H.—Colonel, USV. Commander of the 3rd Brigade of the 3rd Division of Gibbon's 24th Corps in Ord's Army of the James (Department of Virginia). Led the amphibious raid on Fredericksburg and the Northern Neck.

ROBINSON, James—Brigadier General, USV. Commander of the 3rd Brigade of the 1st Division of Williams' 20th Corps in Slocum's Army of Georgia in Sherman's Military Division of the Mississippi.

RODDEY, Philip D.—Brigadier General, CSA. Commander of a small division of cavalry and the District of Northern Alabama in Taylor's Department of Alabama, Mississippi and East Louisiana in Beauregard's Division of the West. His division was later reorganized as a brigade that was intended to form part of Buford's Division of Forrest's cavalry corps of Taylor's department.

ROSSER, Thomas L.—Major General, CSA (USMA ex-1861). Commander of a division of cavalry in Early's Army of the Valley. Later commander of a somewhat altered cavalry division in Fitzhugh Lee's Cavalry Corps of Lee's Army of Northern Virginia.

RUGER, Thomas H.—Brigadier General, USV (USMA 1854). Commander of the 1st Division of the 23rd Corps in Schofield's Army of the Ohio (Department of North Carolina).

SCHOFIELD, John M.—Major General, USV (USMA 1853). Commander of the Department and Army of the Ohio in Sherman's Military Division of the Mississippi. Later commander of the Department of North Carolina.

SEDDON, James—Secretary of War in Jefferson Davis's cabinet until replaced by Breckinridge.

SELFRIDGE, Thomas O., Jr.—Lieutenant Commander, USN. Commander of the third division of Breese's naval brigade in the attack on Fort Fisher.

SEMMES, Raphael—Rear Admiral, CSN. Commander of the James River squadron.

SEWARD, Frederick—Assistant Secretary of State of the United States. Son of William Henry Seward. Acting Secretary of State after his father was injured in a carriage accident.

SEWARD, William Henry—Secretary of State in Lincoln's cabinet.

SHELBY, Joseph O. ("Jo")—Brigadier General, CSA. Commander of a cavalry division in Kirby Smith's Trans-Mississippi Department.

SHERIDAN, Philip Henry—Major General, USV (USMA 1853). Commander of the Army of the Shenandoah and the Middle Military Division. Later, replaced in the latter capacity by Hancock, he became the unofficial commander of all of the cavalry with Grant's "armies operating against Richmond."

SHERMAN, John. United States Senator from Ohio. Brother of William T. Sherman.

SHERMAN, William Tecumseh—Major General, USA (USMA 1840). Grant's favorite subordinate and his successor in command, first of the Army of the Tennessee, and then of the Military Division of the Mississippi.

SICKEL, Hotatio G.—Colonel and Brevet Brigadier General, USV. Commander of the 198th Pennsylvania Volunteer Infantry Regiment in Chamberlain's 1st Brigade of Griffin's 1st Division of Warren's 5th Corps in Meade's Army of the Potomac.

SIMMS, James P.—Brigadier General, CSA. Commander of a brigade in Kershaw's Division of Longstreet's 1st Corps (part of Ewell's informal corps during the retreat from Richmond) of Lee's Army of Northern Virginia.

SINGLETON, James Washington ("General"). Illinois politician married to a cousin of Lincoln's wife. Tried to make a fortune trading for Confederate cotton.

SLOCUM, Henry W.—Major General, USV (USMA 1852). Commander of the Left Wing, or Army of Georgia, in Sherman's Military Division of the Mississippi.

SMITH, Andrew Jackson—Major General, USV (USMA 1838). Commander of a force known as Detachment Army of the Tennessee as part of Thomas's army that defeated Hood at Nashville and later served in Canby's campaign against Mobile as the 16th Corps.

SMITH, Charles H.—Colonel, USV. Commander of the 2nd Brigade of Crook's 2nd Division of cavalry in Meade's Army of the Potomac.

SMITH, Edmund Kirby—General, CSA (USMA 1838). Commander of the Trans-Mississippi Department.

SMITH, John E.—Brigadier General, USV. Commander of the 3rd Division of Logan's 15th Corps in Howard's Army of the Tennessee in Sherman's Military Division of the Mississippi.

SNIPER, Gustavus—Colonel, USV. Commander of the 185th New York Volunteer Infantry Regiment in Chamberlain's 1st Brigade of Griffin's 1st Division of Warren's 5th Corps in Meade's Army of the Potomac.

SPANGLER, Ned—Stagehand at Ford's Theatre who had worked for John Wilkes Booth's father.

SPRAGUE, John T.—Lieutenant Colonel, USV. Chief of staff of Pope's Military Division of the Missouri.

STAGG, Peter—Colonel, USV. Commander of the 1st (Michigan) Brigade of Devin's 1st Division of Merritt's Cavalry Corps of Sheridan's Army of the Shenandoah.

STANTON, Edwin McMasters—Secretary of War in Lincoln's cabinet.

STEEDMAN, James B.—Major General, USV. Commander of the District of the Etowah in Thomas's Department of the Cumberland in Sherman's Military Division of the Mississippi, and of a corps-sized provisional detachment at the battle of Nashville.

STEELE, Frederick—Major General, USV (USMA 1843). Commander of the District of West Florida in Hurlbut's Department of the Gulf in Canby's Military Division of West Mississippi.

STEPHENS, Alexander Hamilton—Vice President of the Confederate States. One of the three Confederate peace commissioners who met with Lincoln near Fortress Monroe.

STEWART, Alexander P.—Lieutenant General, CSA (USMA 1842). Commander of the Army of Mississippi, or Stewart's Corps, in Hood's (later Johnston's) Army of Tennessee. At Bentonville he commanded all of the troops from the old Army of Tennessee in Johnston's army.

STONEMAN, George—Major General, USV (USMA 1846). Chief of cavalry and second in command of Schofield's Department of the Ohio in Sherman's Military Division of the Mississippi.

SURRATT, John H., Jr.—Courier on the Confederate Secret Service's clandestine line of communication between Washington and Richmond and member of John Wilke's Booth's conspiracy against Lincoln. Son of Mary Surratt.

SURRATT, Mary—Owner of a boardinghouse in Washington, D.C. where Booth's conspirators sometimes met and of a tavern in Surrattsville, Maryland. Mother of John H. Surratt, Jr.

TAYLOR, Richard ("Dick")—Lieutenant General, CSA. Commander of the Department of Alabama, Mississippi and East Louisiana. Son of President Zachary Taylor and brother-in-law to Confederate president Jefferson Davis.

TERRY, Alfred H.—Brevet Major General, USV. Temporary commander of the 24th Corps in Butler's Army of the James (Department of Virginia and North Carolina). Then put in command of the second expedition against Fort Fisher. His expeditionary force was later designated the 10th Corps in Schofield's Army of the Ohio (Department of North Carolina).

THOMAS, Edward L.—Brigadier General, CSA. Commander of a brigade in Wharton's Division of Early's Army of the Valley.

THOMAS, George H.—Major General, USV (USMA 1840). Commander of the Department and Army of the Cumberland in Sherman's Military Division of the Mississippi. Left in charge of most of Sherman's division after the latter marched across Georgia to the east coast.

THOMPSON, Jacob—Confederate commissioner to Canada. Secretary of the Interior in the administration of James Buchanan, Lincoln's predecessor.

THOMPSON, M. Jeff—Colonel, CSA. Commander of a force of cavalry in Kirby Smith's Trans-Mississippi Department.

TORBERT, Alfred T. A.—Brevet Major General, USV (USMA 1855). Commander of the Cavalry Corps in Sheridan's Army of the Shenandoah (Middle Military Division).

TUCKER, G.W.—Sergeant, CSA. Chief courier of A.P. Hill's 3rd Corps in Lee's Army of Northern Virginia. Hill's sole companion at Hill's death. Accompanied Lee and Col. Marshall to McLean's house for the surrender to Grant.

UPTON, Emory—Brigadier General, USV (USMA May 1861). Commander of the 4th Division in Wilson's Cavalry Corps of Sherman's Military Division of the Mississippi.

VAUGHN, John C.—Brigadier General, CSA. Commander of one of the brigades of cavalry that escorted Jefferson Davis through the Carolinas.

VENABLE, Charles—Colonel, CSA. An aide on R.E. Lee's staff.

WALKER, Henry H.—Brigadier General, CSA (USMA 1853). In charge of defending the railroads south of Petersburg.

WALKER, James—Brigadier General, CSA. Commander of a division in Gordon's 2nd Corps of Lee's Army of Northern Virginia.

WALTHALL, Edward C.—Major General, CSA. Commander of a division in Stewart's Corps of Hood's Army of Tennessee in Beauregard's Division of the West and of the ad hoc division of infantry in the rear guard after Hood's defeat at Nashville.

WARNER, James M.—Colonel, USV (USMA 1860). Commander of the 2nd Brigade of Getty's 2nd Division of Wright's 6th Corps in Meade's Army of the Potomac.

WARREN, Gouverneur K.—Major General, USV (USMA 1850). Commander of the 5th Corps in Meade's Army of the Potomac.

WASHBURNE, Elihu B.—Congressman from northwestern Illinois. Grant's political sponsor.

WEBB, Alexander S.—Brevet Major General, USV (USMA, 1855). Chief of staff of Meade's Army of the Potomac.

WEICHMANN, Louis J.—Clerk at the United States War Department, boarder at Mary Surratt's boarding house, and old friend of John H. Surratt, Jr.

WEITZEL, Godfrey—Major General, USV (USMA 1855). Commander of the 25th Corps in Butler's (later Ord's) Army of the James (Dept. of Virginia), and commander, under Butler, of the army's forces in the first expedition against Fort Fisher. Left in charge of the department when Ord moved south of the James with part of his army.

WELLES, Gideon—Secretary of the Navy in Lincoln's cabinet.

WHARTON, Gabriel C.—Brigadier General, CSA. Commander of the only infantry division left in Early's Army of the Valley.

WHEATON, Frank—Brigadier General, USV. Commander of the 1st Division of Wright's 6th Corps in Meade's Army of the Potomac.

WHEELER, Joseph—Major General, CSA (USMA 1859). Commander of the Cavalry Corps of Hood's Army of Tennessee. Left behind to oppose Sherman's march across Georgia when Hood moved northward into Tennessee.

WHITING, William Henry Chase—Major General, CSA (USMA 1845). Commander of the 3rd Military District of Beauregard's Department of Southern Virginia and North Carolina, whose primary responsibility was the defense of Wilmington, N.C.

WILCOX, Cadmus Marcellus—Major General, CSA (USMA 1846). Commander of a division in A.P. Hill's 3rd Corps of Lee's Army of Northern Virginia.

WILLCOX, Orlando B.—Brigadier General, USV (USMA 1847). Commander of the 1st Division of Parke's 9th Corps in Meade's Army of the Potomac.

WILLIAMS, Alpheus S.—Brevet Major General, USA. Commander of the 20th Corps in Slocum's Army of Georgia in Sherman's Military Division of the Mississippi. Later commander of the 1st Division of the same corps.

WILLIAMS, Seth—Brevet Major General, USV (USMA 1842). Inspector general on Grant's staff.

WILSON, James Harrison—Brevet Major General, USV (USMA 1860). Commander of the Cavalry Corps of Sherman's Military Division of the Mississippi.

WINTHROP, Frederick—Brevet Brigadier General, USV. Commander of the 1st Brigade of Ayres' 2nd Division of Warren's 5th Corps in Meade's Army of the Potomac.

WISE, Henry A.—Brigadier General, CSA. Commander of a brigade in Johnson's Division of Anderson's 4th Corps of Lee's Army of Northern Virginia. Former governor of Virginia.

WISE, John—Lieutenant, CSA. Officer sent to find Lee for Jefferson Davis. Son of Henry A. Wise.

WOOD, John Taylor—Colonel, CSA and Captain, CSN (USNA 1853). Aide to President Jefferson Davis. Nephew of Davis's first wife; grandson of President Zachary Taylor.

WOOD, Thomas J.—Brigadier General, USV (USMA 1845). Commander of the 4th Corps in Thomas's Army of the Cumberland in Sherman's Military Division of the Mississippi.

WOODS, Charles R.—Brevet Major General, USV (USMA 1852). Commander of the 1st Division of Logan's 15th Corps in Howard's Army of the Tennessee in Sherman's Military Division of the Mississippi.

WRIGHT, Horatio G.—Major General, USV (USMA 1841). Commander of the 6th Corps in Meade's Army of the Potomac.

APPENDIX B

Military Organizations

(Late December 1864)

UNITED STATES ARMY:
Commander-in-Chief—President Abraham Lincoln
Secretary of War—Edwin McMasters Stanton
General-in-Chief—Lieutenant General Ulysses S. Grant
Chief of Staff—Major General Henry W. Halleck
Quartermaster General—Brevet Major General Montgomery Meigs

DEPARTMENT OF THE EAST:
Commanding General—Major General John Adams Dix
Second in Command—Major General John J. Peck

DEPARTMENT OF THE SOUTH:
Commanding General—Major General John G. Foster
Coast Division: Brigadier General John P. Hatch
1st Separate Brigade: Brig. General Alexander Schimmelfennig
  Morris Island, S.C.: Colonel Edward N. Hallowell
  Folly Island, S.C.: Colonel Eugene A. Kozlay
2nd Separate Brigade: Brigadier General Rufus Saxton
3rd Separate Brigade: Bvt. Brig. Gen. Milton S. Littlefield

4th Separate Brigade: Brigadier General Eliakim P. Scammon

NORTHERN DEPARTMENT:
Commanding General—Major General Joseph Hooker

DEPARTMENT OF THE NORTHWEST:
Commanding General—Major General John Pope
District of Iowa: Brigadier General Alfred Sully
District of Minnesota: Brigadier General Henry H. Sibley
District of Wisconsin: Brigadier General Thomas C. H. Smith

DEPARTMENT OF KANSAS:
Commanding General—Major General Samuel R. Curtis
District of Colorado: Colonel John M. Chivington
District of Nebraska: Brigadier General Robert B. Mitchell
District of North Kansas: Brigadier General Thomas A. Davies
District of South Kansas: Major General James G. Blunt
District of the Upper Arkansas: Colonel James H. Ford

DEPARTMENT OF NEW MEXICO:
Commanding General—Brigadier General James H. Carleton
District of Arizona: Major Joseph Smith

DEPARTMENT OF THE PACIFIC:
Commanding General—Major General Irvin McDowell

Armies Operating Against Richmond:

Commanding General—(Lieutenant General Ulysses S. Grant)
Chief of Staff—Brigadier General John A. Rawlins
Chief Quartermaster—Brigadier General Rufus Ingalls
Chief Engineer—Brigadier General John G. Barnard

ARMY OF THE POTOMAC:
Commanding General—Major General George Gordon Meade
Adjutant General—Major General Seth Williams
Provost Guard: Brigadier General Marsena R. Patrick

Engineer Brigade and Defenses of City Point:

Brigadier General Henry W. Benham
Artillery: Brevet Major General Henry J. Hunt
Artillery Reserve: Captain Ezekiel R. Mayo
Siege Artillery: Colonel Henry L. Abbot
Cavalry: 2nd Division: Brevet Major General David M. Gregg
1st Brigade: Brigadier General Henry Davies, Jr.
2nd Brigade: Brevet Brigadier General J. Irvin Gregg

3rd Brigade: Brevet Brigadier General Charles H. Smith

2nd ARMY CORPS: Major General Andrew A. Humphreys
1st Division: Brigadier General Nelson A. Miles
1st Brigade: Brevet Brigadier General George N. Macy
2nd Brigade: Colonel Robert Nugent
3rd Brigade: Colonel Clinton D. MacDougall
4th Brigade: Lieutenant Colonel William Glenny
2nd Division: Major General John Gibbon
1st Brigade: Colonel James M. Willett
2nd Brigade: Colonel Mathew Murphy
3rd Brigade: Lieutenant Colonel Francis E. Pierce
3rd Division: Brevet Major General Gershom Mott
1st Brigade: Brigadier General P. Regis de Trobriand
2nd Brigade: Brigadier General Bryon R. Pierce
3rd Brigade: Brevet Brigadier General John Ramsey
Artillery Brigade: Brevet Lieutenant Colonel John G. Hazard

5th ARMY CORPS: Major General Gouverneur K. Warren
1st Division: Brigader General Charles Griffin
1st Brigade: Brigadier General Joshua L. Chamberlain
2nd Brigade: Brevet Brigadier General Edgar M. Gregory
3rd Brigade: Brigadier General Joseph J. Bartlett
2nd Division: Brigadier General Romeyn B. Ayres
1st Brigade: Brevet Brigadier General Frederick Winthrop
2nd Brigade: Brevet Brigadier General Andrew W. Denison
3rd Brigade: Brevet Brigadier General James Gwyn
3rd Division: Brevet Major General Samuel W. Crawford
1st Brigade: Brigadier General Edward S. Bragg
2nd Brigade: Brigadier General Henry Baxter
3rd Brigade: Brevet Brigadier General J. William Hofmann
Artillery Brigade: Brevet Brig. General Charles S. Wainwright

6th ARMY CORPS: Major General Horatio G. Wright
1st Division: Brevet Major General Frank Wheaton
1st Brigade: Captain Baldwin Hufty
2nd Brigade: Brigadier General Ranald S. Mackenzie
3rd Brigade: Colonel Thomas S. Allen
2nd Division: Brevet Major General George W. Getty
1st Brigade: Colonel James M. Warner
2nd Brigade: Brigadier General Lewis A. Grant
3rd Brigade: Colonel Thomas W. Hyde
3rd Division: Brigadier General Truman Seymour

1st Brigade: Colonel William S. Truex
2nd Brigade: Colonel Benjamin F. Smith
Artillery Brigade: Colonel Charles H. Tompkins

9th ARMY CORPS: Brevet Major General Orlando B. Willcox
1st Division: Brevet Brigadier General Napoleon B. McLaughlen
1st Brigade: Colonel Samuel Harriman
2nd Brigade: Colonel Bryon M. Cutcheon
3rd Brigade: Brevet Colonel Gilbert P. Robinson
2nd Division: Brevet Major General Robert B. Potter
1st Brigade: Brevet Brigadier General John I. Curtin
2nd Brigade: Brigadier General Simon G. Griffin
3rd Division: Brigadier General John F. Hartranft
1st Brigade: Colonel Charles W. Diven
2nd Brigade: Colonel Joseph A. Mathews
Artillery Brigade: Brevet Brigadier General John C. Tidball

DEPARTMENT OF VIRGINIA AND NORTH CAROLINA:
Commanding General—Major General Benjamin F. Butler
Chief of Staff—Brigadier General John W. Turner

District of Eastern Virginia: Brig. Gen. George F. Shepley
Portsmouth: Brigadier General Israel Vogdes
Norfolk: Major Harvey W. Brown
Newport News: Lieutenant Colonel Loren Burritt
Fort Monroe: Colonel Joseph Roberts
Fort Magruder: Colonel Joseph J. Morrison
Eastern Shore: Lieutenant Colonel Frank J. White
District of North Carolina: Brigadier General Innis N. Palmer
Sub-district of the Albemarle: Colonel Theodore F. Lehmann
Sub-district of Beaufort: Colonel Joseph M. McChesney
Sub-district of New Berne: Brig. Gen. Edward Harland
Plymouth: Colonel Jones Frankle

ARMY OF THE JAMES:
Commanding General—(Major General Benjamin F. Butler)

24th ARMY CORPS: Major General Edward O.C. Ord (on leave), Brigadier General Alfred H. Terry (temporary)
1st Division: Brigadier General Robert S. Foster
1st Brigade: Colonel Thomas O. Osborn
2nd Brigade: Colonel Joseph R. Hawley
3rd Brigade: Colonel Harris M. Plaisted
4th Brigade: Brevet Brigadier General James Jourdan

2nd Division: Brigadier General Adelbert Ames
1st Brigade: Brevet Brigadier General N. Martin Curtis
2nd Brigade: Colonel Galusha Pennypacker
3rd Brigade: Colonel Louis Bell
3rd Division: Brigadier General Charles Devens
1st Brigade: Lieutenant Colonel John B. Raulston
2nd Brigade: Colonel Joseph H. Potter
3rd Brigade: Brevet Brigadier General Guy V. Henry
Independent Division: Brevet Brigadier General Thomas Harris
1st Brigade: Lieutenant Colonel Thomas F. Wildes
2nd Brigade: Colonel William B. Curtis
3rd Brigade: Colonel Lieutenant Colonel Moses S. Hall
Artillery Brigade: Major Charles C. Abell

25th ARMY CORPS: Major General Godfrey Weitzel
1st Division: Brigadier General Charles J. Paine
1st Brigade: Brevet Brigadier General Delevan Bates
2nd Brigade: Colonel John W. Ames
3rd Brigade: Colonel Elias Wright
2nd Division: Brigadier General William Birney
1st Brigade: Brevet Brigadier General Charles S. Russell
2nd Brigade: Colonel Ulysses Doubleday
3rd Brigade: Colonel Henry C. Ward
3rd Division: Brigadier General Edward A. Wild
1st Brigade: Brevet Brigadier General Alonzo G. Draper
2nd Brigade: Colonel Edward Martindale
3rd Brigade: Brigadier General Henry G. Thomas
Artillery Brigade: Lieutenant Colonel Richard H. Jackson

Cavalry Division: Brigadier General August V. Kautz
1st Brigade: Colonel Robert West
2nd Brigade: Colonel Samuel P. Spear
3rd Brigade: Colonel Andrew W. Evans

Defenses of Bermuda Hundred: Bvt. Maj. General Edward Ferrero
1st Brigade: Colonel William Heine
2nd Brigade: Lieutenant Colonel G. De Peyster Arden
Provisional Brigade: Colonel William M. McClure

Separate Brigade: Colonel Wardwell G. Robinson
Fort Pocahontas: Major William H. Tantum
Harrison's Landing: Lieutenant Colonel William P. McKinley

Fort Powhatan: Colonel William J. Sewell

MIDDLE MILITARY DIVISION:

Commanding General—Major General Philip H. Sheridan

DEPARTMENT OF WASHINGTON:

Commanding General—Major General Christopher C. Augur
Light Artillery Camp: Brigadier General Albion P. Howe
Provisional Brigades: Major General Silas Casey
Hardin's Division: Brigadier General Martin D. Hardin
1st Brigade: Colonel Charles H. Long
2nd Brigade: Colonel William S. Abert
3rd Brigade: Lieutenant Colonel John H. Oberteuffer
Fort Foote, Md.: Lieutenant Colonel Thomas Allcock
District of St. Mary's, Md.: Brigadier General James Barnes
Fort Washington, Md.: Colonel Horace Brooks
District of Washington: Colonel Moses N. Wisewell
1st Brigade: Colonel George W. Gile
De Russy's Division: Brigadier General Gustavus A. De Russy
1st Brigade: Colonel Joseph N. G. Whistler
2nd Brigade: Colonel Charles Barnes
3rd Brigade: Colonel William S. King
4th Brigade: Major Charles C. Meservey
District of Alexandria: Brigadier General John P. Slough
Provost Detachments: Lieutenant Colonel Henry H. Wells
Rendezvous of Distribution: Lieutenant Colonel Samuel McKelvy
1st Separate (cavalry) Brigade: Colonel William Gamble
Cavalry Forces Upper Potomac: Major Joseph F. Andrews

MIDDLE DEPARTMENT (8th ARMY CORPS):

Commanding General—Major General Lewis Wallace
1st Seperate Brigade: Brigadier General Erastus B. Tyler
2nd Seperate Brigade: Brigadier General William W. Morris
3rd Seperate Brigade: Brigadier General Henry H. Lockwood
Annapolis, Md.: Colonel Adrian R. Root
Wilmington, Del.: Colonel Samuel M. Bowman
District of the Eastern Shore: Brig. Gen. John R. Kenly

DEPARTMENT OF PENNSYLVANIA:

Commanding General—Major General George Cadwalader

DEPARTMENT OF WEST VIRGINIA:

Commanding General—Brevet Major General George Crook
District of Harper's Ferry: Brigadier General John Stevenson

West of Hancock, Md.: Brevet Major General Benjamin Kelley
2nd Division: Brigadier General Isaac H. Duval
1st Brigade: Colonel Rutherford B. Hayes
2nd Brigade: Colonel Daniel D. Johnson
1st Separate (cavalry) Brigade: Colonel John H. Oley

ARMY OF THE SHENANDOAH:
Commanding General—(Major General Philip H. Sheridan)

CAVALRY CORPS: Brevet Major General Alfred T. A. Torbert
1st Division: Brigadier General Alfred Gibbs
1st Brigade: Colonel Peter Stagg
2nd Brigade: Lieutenant Colonel George S. Nichols
Reserve Brigade: Major Archibald McKendry
2nd Division (W. Va.): Brigadier General William H. Powell
1st Brigade: Brevet Brigadier General William B. Tibbits
2nd Brigade: Colonel Henry Capehart
3rd Division: Brevet Major General George Armstrong Custer
1st Brigade: Colonel Alexander C. M. Pennington, Jr.
2nd Brigade: Brigadier General George H. Chapman
Horse Artillery Brigade: Captain La Rhett L. Livingston

19th ARMY CORPS: Brevet Major General William H. Emory
1st Division: Brigadier General William Dwight
1st Brigade: Brigadier General George L. Beal
2nd Brigade: Brigadier General James W. McMillan
3rd Brigade: Brigadier General James D. Fessenden
2nd Division: Brevet Major General Cuvier Grover
1st Brigade: Brigadier General Henry W. Birge
2nd Brigade: Brevet Brigadier General Edward L. Molineux
3rd Brigade: Lieutenant Colonel James P. Richardson
4th Brigade: Colonel Henry D. Washburn
Artillery Brigade: Major Albert W. Bradbury

MILITARY DIVISION OF THE MISSISSIPPI:

Commanding General—Major General William T. Sherman
Second in Command—Major General George H. Thomas

CAVALRY CORPS: Brevet Major General James H. Wilson
1st Division: Brigadier General Edward M. McCook
1st Brigade: Brigadier General John T. Croxton
2nd Brigade: Colonel Oscar H. La Grange
3rd Brigade: Brevet Brigadier General Louis D. Watkins
2nd Division: Brigadier General Eli Long

1st Brigade: Colonel Abram O. Miller
2nd Brigade: Colonel Robert H. G. Minty
4th Division: Brevet Major General Emory Upton
1st Brigade: Lieutenant Colonel Frederick W. Benteen
2nd Brigade: Colonel Joseph Kargé
5th Division: Brigadier General Edward Hatch
1st Brigade: Colonel Robert R. Stewart
2nd Brigade: Colonel Datus E. Coon
6th Division: Brigadier General Richard W. Johnson
1st Brigade: Colonel Thomas J. Harrison
2nd Brigade: Colonel James Biddle
7th Division: Brigadier General Joseph F. Knipe
1st Brigade: Brevet Brigadier General John H. Hammond
2nd Brigade: Colonel Gilbert M. L. Johnson

DEPARTMENT OF THE CUMBERLAND:
Commanding General—Major General George H. Thomas
Chief of Artillery—Brigadier General John M. Brannan

Reserve Brigade: Colonel Heber Le Favour
Veteran Reserve Corps: Major Audley W. Gazzam
Post of Nashville: Brigadier General John F. Miller
2nd Brig., 4th Div., 20th Corps: Colonel Edwin C. Mason
Garrison Artillery: Major John J. Ely

4th ARMY CORPS: Brigadier General Thomas J. Wood
1st Division: Brigadier General Nathan Kimball
1st Brigade: Colonel Isaac M. Kirby
2nd Brigade: Brigadier General Walter C. Whittaker
3rd Brigade: Brigadier General William Grose
2nd Division: Brigadier General Washington L. Elliott
1st Brigade: Colonel Emerson Opdycke
2nd Brigade: Colonel John Q. Lane
3rd Brigade: Colonel Joseph Conrad
3rd Division: Brigadier General Samuel Beatty
1st Brigade: Colonel Abel D. Streight
2nd Brigade: Lieutenant Colonel Robert L. Kimberly
3rd Brigade: Colonel Frederick Knefler
Artillery Brigade: Major Wilbur F. Goodspeed

DETACHMENT ARMY OF THE TENNESSEE:
Major General A.J. Smith
1st Division: Brigadier General John McArthur

1st Brigade: Colonel William L. McMillen
2nd Brigade: Colonel Lucius F. Hubbard
3rd Brigade: Colonel William R. Marshall
2nd Division: Brigadier General Kenner Garrard
1st Brigade: Colonel David Moore
2nd Brigade: Colonel James I. Gilbert
3rd Brigade: Colonel Edward H. Wolfe
3rd Division: Colonel Jonathan B. Moore
1st Brigade: Colonel Lyman M. Ward
2nd Brigade: Colonel Leander Blanden

23rd ARMY CORPS (ARMY OF THE OHIO):
Commanding General—Major General John M. Schofield
2nd Division: Major General Darius N. Couch
1st Brigade: Brigadier General Joseph A. Cooper
2nd Brigade: Colonel Orlando H. Moore
3rd Brigade: Colonel John Mehringer
3rd Division: Brigadier General Jacob D. Cox
1st Brigade: Colonel Charles C. Doolittle
2nd Brigade: Colonel John S. Casement
3rd Brigade: Colonel Israel N. Stiles

PROVISIONAL DETACHMENT: Major General James B. Steedman
1st Colored Brigade: Colonel Thomas J. Morgan
2nd Colored Brigade: Colonel Charles R. Thompson
Provisional Division: Brigadier General Charles Cruft
1st Brigade: Colonel Benjamin Harrison
2nd Brigade: Colonel John G. Mitchell
3rd Brigade: Lieutenant Colonel Charles H. Grosvenor
2nd Brigade (Army of the Tenn.): Colonel Adam G. Malloy

DISTRICT OF TENNESSEE: Major General Lovell H. Rousseau
1st Brigade, 4th Div., 20th Corps: Colonel William P. Lyon
Nashville & Northwestern RR: Colonel Charles R. Thompson
Nashville & Chattanooga RR: Major General Robert H. Milroy
1st Brigade: Brigadier General Horatio P. Van Cleve
3rd Brigade: Colonel Wladimir Krzyzanowski

DEPARTMENT OF THE OHIO (23rd ARMY CORPS):
Commanding General—(Major General John M. Schofield)
Second in Command—Major General George Stoneman
4th Division (East Tenn.): Brigadier General Jacob Ammen
1st Brigade: Colonel William Y. Dillard
2nd Brigade: Brigadier General Davis Tillson

3rd Brigade: Lieutenant Colonel Michael L. Patterson

DISTRICT OF KENTUCKY: Bvt. Major General Stephen G. Burbridge

1st Division: Brigadier General Nathaniel C. McLean

1st Brigade: Brigadier General Edward H. Hobson
2nd Brigade: Colonel John M. Brown
3rd Brigade: Colonel Charles S. Hanson
4th Brigade: Colonel Robert W. Ratliff
Camp Nelson: Brigadier General Speed S. Fry

2nd Division: Brigadier General Hugh Ewing

1st Brigade: Lieutenant Colonel Thomas B. Fairleigh
2nd Brigade: Colonel Cicero Maxwell

District of Western Kentucky: Brig. Gen. Eleazer A. Paine

Cairo, Ill.: Brigadier General Solomon Meredith
Paducah, Ky.: Colonel Henry W. Barry
Columbus, Ky.: Colonel James N. McArthur
Mayfield, Ky.: Lieutenant Colonel John C. Bigelow

"ARMY OF THE WEST":

Commanding General—(Major General William T. Sherman)
Chief of Artillery—Brigadier General William F. Barry

LEFT WING (ARMY OF GEORGIA):

Commanding General—Major General Henry W. Slocum

14th ARMY CORPS: Brevet Major General Jefferson C. Davis

1st Division: Brigadier General William P. Carlin

1st Brigade: Colonel Harrison C. Hobart
2nd Brigade: Lieutenant Colonel Joseph H. Brigham
3rd Brigade: Lieutenant Colonel David Miles

2nd Division: Brigadier General James D. Morgan

1st Brigade: Colonel Robert F. Smith
2nd Brigade: Lieutenant Colonel John S. Pearce
3rd Brigade: Lieutenant Colonel James W. Langley

3rd Division: Brigadier General Absalom Baird

1st Brigade: Colonel Marton C. Hunter
2nd Brigade: Colonel Newell Gleason
3rd Brigade: Colonel George P. Este

Artillery Brigade: Major Charles Houghtaling

20th ARMY CORPS: Brigadier General Alpheus S. Williams

1st Division: Brigadier General Nathaniel J. Jackson

1st Brigade: Colonel James L. Selfridge

2nd Brigade: Colonel Ezra A. Carman
3rd Brigade: Colonel James S. Robinson
2nd Division: Brigadier General John W. Geary
1st Brigade: Colonel Ario Pardee, Jr.
2nd Brigade: Colonel Patrick H. Jones
3rd Brigade: Colonel Henry A. Barnum
3rd Division: Brigadier General William T. Ward
1st Brigade: Colonel Henry Case
2nd Brigade: Colonel Daniel Dustin
3rd Brigade: Colonel Samuel Ross
Artillery Brigade: Major John A. Reynolds

Cavalry: 3rd Division: Brigadier General Judson Kilpatrick
1st Brigade: Colonel Thomas J. Jordan
2nd Brigade: Colonel Smith D. Atkins

RIGHT WING (ARMY OF THE TENNESSEE):
Commanding General—Major General Oliver O. Howard

15th ARMY CORPS: Major General Peter J. Osterhaus
1st Division: Brigadier General Charles R. Woods
1st Brigade: Colonel Milo Smith
2nd Brigade: Colonel Robert F. Catterson
3rd Brigade: Colonel James A. Williamson
2nd Division: Brigadier General William B. Hazen
1st Brigade: Colonel Theodore Jones
2nd Brigade: Colonel James S. Martin
3rd Brigade: Colonel John M. Oliver
3rd Division: Brigadier General John E. Smith
1st Brigade: Colonel Joseph B. McCown
2nd Brigade: Colonel Green B. Raum
4th Division: Brigadier General John M. Corse
1st Brigade: Brigadier General Elliott W. Rice
2nd Brigade: Colonel Robert N. Adams
3rd Brigade: Lieutenant Colonel Frederick J. Hurlbut
Artillery: Major Charles J. Stolbrand

17th ARMY CORPS: Major General Francis P. Blair, Jr.
1st Division: Major General Joseph A. Mower
1st Brigade: Colonel Charles S. Sheldon
2nd Brigade: Brigadier General John W. Sprague
3rd Brigade: Colonel John Tillson
3rd Division: Brigadier General Mortimer D. Leggett

1st Brigade: Brigadier General Manning F. Force
2nd Brigade: Colonel Greenberry F. Wiles
4th Division: Brigadier General Giles A. Smith
1st Brigade: Colonel Benjamin F. Potts
3rd Brigade: Brigadier General William W. Belknap
Artillery: Major Allen C. Waterhouse

MILITARY DIVISION OF WEST MISSISSIPPI:

Commanding General—Major General E.R.S. Canby

RESERVE CORPS: Major General Joseph J. Reynolds
1st Brigade: Brigadier General Michael K. Lawler
2nd Brigade: Brigadier General Elias S. Dennis
3rd Brigade: Colonel William T. Spicely
4th Brigade: Colonel Charles Black
Forces at Mouth of White River: Brig. Gen. George McGinnis
Cavalry Forces: Colonel Edmund J. Davis
Artillery: Captain Benjamin Nields

DEPARTMENT OF THE GULF:
Commanding General—Major General Stephen A. Hurlbut
Cavalry Division: Brigadier General Joseph Bailey
Morganza, La.: Brigadier General Daniel Ullman
1st Brigade, 1st Div. U.S.C.T.: Colonel William H. Dickey
2nd Brigade, 1st Div. U.S.C.T.: Colonel Alonzo J. Edgerton
Defenses of New Orleans: Brigadier General Thomas W. Sherman
District of Carrollton, La.: Lieutenant Colonel Nelson Viall
District of La Fourche: Brigadier General Robert A. Cameron
District of Bonnet Carré: Colonel Cyrus Hamlin
Forces Lake Ponchartrain: Colonel Robert B. Jones
Forts Jackson and St. Philip: Major Joseph J. Comstock, Jr.
District of Baton Rouge and Port Hudson:
Brigadier General George L. Andrews
District of Baton Rouge: Brigadier General Joseph Bailey
Forces at Port Hudson: Colonel Charles W. Drew
District of West Florida and South Alabama:
Brigadier General George H. Gordon
District of West Florida: Brigadier General Thomas McKean
1st Brigade: Lieutenant Colonel George E. Yarrington
2nd Brigade: Colonel Ephraim W. Woodman
District of South Alabama: Colonel Henry Bertram
District of Key West and Tortugas: Colonel Charles Hamilton
Brazos Santiago, Texas: Brigadier General William A. Pile

DEPARTMENT OF THE MISSOURI:
Commanding General—Major General Grenville M. Dodge
District of St. Louis: Brigadier General Thomas Ewing, Jr.
District of Rolla: Colonel Edwin C. Catherwood
District of Central Missouri: Colonel John F. Philips
District of North Missouri: Brigadier General Clinton B. Fisk
District of Southwest Missouri: Brig. Gen. John B. Sanborn
Alton, Illinois: Brevet Brigadier General Roy Stone

DEPARTMENT OF ARKANSAS (7th ARMY CORPS):
Commanding General—(Major General Joseph J. Reynolds)

DISTRICT OF LITTLE ROCK: Brigadier General Eugene A. Carr
1st Division: Brigadier General Frederick Salomon
1st Brigade: Colonel Cyrus H. Mackey
2nd Brigade: Colonel John A. Garrett
2nd Division: Brigadier General Alexander Shaler
1st Brigade: Colonel Hans Mattson
2nd Brigade: Colonel James M. True
Cavalry Division: Brigadier General Joseph R. West
1st Brigade: Colonel Albert Erskine
2nd Brigade: Brigadier General Cyrus Bussey
3rd Brigade: Colonel Washington F. Geiger
4th Brigade: Colonel John K. Mizner
District of Eastern Arkansas: Brig. Gen. Napoleon B. Buford
District of the Frontier: Brigadier General John M. Thayer
1st Brigade: Colonel Charles W. Adams
2nd Brigade: Colonel James M. Williams
3rd Brigade: Colonel William R. Judson
Indian Brigade: Colonel William A. Phillips

DEPARTMENT OF MISSISSIPPI:
Commanding General—Major General Napoleon J. T. Dana

DISTRICT OF VICKSBURG: Major General Cadwallader C. Washburn
Reserve Artillery: Captain William H. Bolton
Enrolled Militia: Brigadier General George C. McKee
Post and Defenses of Vicksburg: Brig. Gen. Morgan L. Smith
Maltby's Brigade: Brigadier General Jasper A. Maltby
1st Division U.S.C.T.: Brigadier General John P. Hawkins
1st Brigade: Colonel Frederick M. Crandal
2nd Brigade: Colonel Hiram Scofield

Post and Defenses of Natchez: Brigadier General Mason Brayman

DISTRICT OF WEST TENNESSEE: Brig. Gen. James C. Veatch
Post and Defenses of Memphis: (Brig. Gen. James C. Veatch)
1st Brigade: Colonel George B. Hoge
1st Brigade, USCT: Colonel Frank A. Kendrick
Fort Pickering: Colonel Ignatz G. Kappner
Enrolled Militia: Brigadier General Charles W. Dustan
Light Artillery: Major Raphael G. Rombauer
Cavalry Division: Brigadier General Benjamin H. Grierson
1st Brigade: Lieutenant Colonel Samuel O. Shorey
2nd Brigade: Colonel Edward F. Winslow
3rd Brigade: Colonel Embury D. Osband

CONFEDERATE STATES ARMY:

Commander-in-Chief—President Jefferson Davis
Secretary of War—James Alexander Seddon
Commanding General—General Braxton Bragg
Adjutant and Inspector General—General Samuel Cooper

DEPARTMENT AND ARMY OF NORTHERN VIRGINIA:
Commanding General—General Robert Edward Lee
Chief of Artillery—Brigadier General William N. Pendleton

1st ARMY CORPS: Lieutenant General James Longstreet
Pickett's Division: Major General George E. Pickett
Steuart's Brigade: Brigadier General George H. Steuart
Hunton's Brigade: Colonel Henry Gantt
Corse's Brigade: Brigadier General Montgomery D. Corse
Terry's Brigade: Brigadier General William R. Terry
Field's Division: Major General Charles W. Field
Anderson's Brigade: Brigadier General George T. Anderson
Law's Brigade: Colonel William F. Perry
Bratton's Brigade: Brigadier General John Bratton
Benning's Brigade: Brigadier General Henry L. Benning
Texas Brigade: Colonel Frederick S. Bass
Kershaw's Division: Major General Joseph B. Kershaw
Wofford's Brigade: Brigadier General Dudley M. Du Bose
Bryan's Brigade: Colonel James P. Simms
Humphrey's Brigade: Major G. B. Gerald
Conner's Brigade: Colonel John D. Kennedy
Artillery: Brigadier General E. Porter Alexander

2nd ARMY CORPS: Major General John B. Gordon

Rodes' Division: Brigadier General Bryan Grimes

Grimes' Brigade: Colonel David G. Cowand
Battle's Brigade: Colonel Charles Forsyth
Cook's Brigade: Colonel William H. Peebles
Cox's Brigade: Brigadier General William R. Cox

Early's Division: Brigadier General John Pegram

Pegram's Brigade: Colonel John S. Hoffman
Johnston's Brigade: Brigadier General Robert D. Johnston
Lewis's Brigade: Brigadier General William G. Lewis

Gordon's Division: Brigadier General Clement A. Evans

Evans' Brigade: Colonel John H. Baker
Terry's Brigade: Brigadier General William Terry
York's Brigade: Colonel William R. Peck

3rd ARMY CORPS: Lieutenant General A.P. Hill

Mahone's Division: Major General William Mahone

Sander's Brigade: Colonel William H. Forney
Weisiger's Brigade: Brigadier General David A. Weiseger
Harris's Brigade: Brigadier General Nathaniel H. Harris
Sorrel's Brigade: Brigadier General G. Moxley Sorrel
Finegan's Brigade: Brigadier General Joseph Finegan

Wilcox's Division: Major General Cadmus Wilcox

Thomas' Brigade: Brigadier General Edward L. Thomas
McGowan's Brigade: Brigadier General Samuel McGowan
Lane's Brigade: Brigadier General James H. Lane
Scale's Brigade: Brigadier General Alfred M. Scales

Heth's Division: Major General Henry Heth

Davis's Brigade: Brigadier General Joseph R. Davis
MacRae's Brigade: Brigadier General William MacRae
Cooke's Brigade: Brigadier General John R. Cooke
Johnson's Brigade: Colonel John M. Hughs

Artillery: Colonel R. Lindsey Walker

ANDERSON'S CORPS: Lieutenant General Richard H. Anderson

Hoke's Division: Major General Robert F. Hoke

Clingman's Brigade: Colonel Hector M. McKethan
Colquitt's Brigade: Brigadier General Alfred H. Colquitt
Hagood's Brigade: Brigadier General Johnson Hagood
Kirkland's Brigade: Brigadier General William W. Kirkland

Johnson's Division: Major General Bushrod R. Johnson

Wise's Brigade: Colonel John Thomas Goode

Ransom's Brigade: Colonel Henry M. Rutledge
Gracie's Brigade: Colonel Young M. Moody
Elliott's Brigade: Brigadier General William H. Wallace
Artillery: Colonel H. P. Jones
1st Military District: Brigadier General Henry A. Wise
Walker's Brigade: Brigadier General James A. Walker
Garnett's Brigade: Lieutenant Colonel John J. Garnett
Petersburg: Major William H. Ker

CAVALRY CORPS: Major General Wade Hampton
1st Division: Major General M. C. Butler
Butler's Brigade: Colonel B. Huger Rutledge
Young's Brigade: Lieutenant Colonel William W. Rich
Dearing's Brigade: Brigadier General James Dearing
3rd Division: Major General W. H. F. "Rooney"Lee
Barringer's Brigade: Brigadier General Rufus Barringer
Chambliss' Brigade: Colonel Richard L. T. Beale
Horse Artillery: Major R. P. Chew

ARMY OF THE VALLEY DISTRICT: Lieutenant General Jubal Early
Breckinridge's Division: Brigadier General Gabriel Wharton
Wharton's Brigade: Major Peter Otey
Echol's Brigade: Lieutenant Colonel John C. McDonald
Smith's Brigade: Colonel Thomas Smith
Lee's (cavalry) Division: Brigadier General Thomas L. Rosser
Wickham's Brigade: Brigadier General Williams C. Wickham
Payne's Brigade: Colonel William H. Payne
The Laurel Brigade: Colonel Oliver R. Funsten
Lomax's (cavalry) Division: Major General Lunsford L. Lomax
Imboden's Brigade: Brigadier General John Imboden
McCausland's Brigade: Brigadier General John McCausland
Davidson's Brigade: Brigadier General Henry B. Davidson
Artillery: Colonel Thomas H. Carter

DEPARTMENT OF RICHMOND:
Commanding General—Lieutenant General Richard S. Ewell*
Walker's Brigade: Colonel Robert M. Mayo
Barton's Brigade: Colonel Meriwether Lewis Clark
1st Brigade Va. Reserves: Brig. General Patrick T. Moore
Local Defense Forces: Brigadier General G. W. Custis Lee
Gary's Cavalry Brigade: Major Edward M. Boykin
Artillery Defenses: Lieutenant Colonel John C. Pemberton

DEPARTMENT OF SOUTHWESTERN VIRGINIA AND EAST TENNESSEE:

Commanding General—Major General John C. Breckinridge*

Giltner's Brigade: Colonel A. L. Pridemore
Cosby's Brigade: Brigadier General George Cosby
Morgan's Brigade: Colonel Basil Duke
Vaughn's Brigade: Brigadier General John Vaughn

DEPARTMENT OF NORTH CAROLINA:

Commanding General—General Braxton Bragg

2nd Military District: Brigadier General Lawrence S. Baker

1st Sub-District, Goldsborough: Colonel Stephen D. Pool
2nd Sub-District, Kinston: Lt. Colonel Rufus W. Wharton
3rd Sub-District, Fort Branch: Colonel Frank S. Armistead
4th Sub-District, Weldon: Colonel William F. Martin

3rd Military District: Major General William H. C. Whiting

Fort Fisher: Colonel William Lamb
Hedrick's Brigade (Fort Anderson): Colonel John J. Hedrick
Batteries at the Obstructions: Colonel Peter C. Gaillard
Post and Garrison of Wilmington: Colonel George Jackson

DEPARTMENT OF SOUTH CAROLINA, GEORGIA AND FLORIDA:

Commanding General—Lieutenant General William J. Hardee

McLaw's Division: Major General Lafayette McLaws

Ripley's Brigade: Brigadier General Roswell S. Ripley
Trapier's Brigade: Brigadier General James H. Trapier
Robertson's Brigade: Brigadier General Beverly H. Robertson
Taliaferro's Brigade: Brigadier General William B. Taliaferro
Miller's Brigade: Brigadier General William Miller

Post of Florence, S.C.: Colonel George P. Harrison, Jr.

Post of Columbia, S.C.: Lieutenant Colonel Robert S. Means

Cavalry Corps Army of Tennessee: Major General Joseph Wheeler

DIVISION OF THE WEST:

Commanding General—General Pierre G. T. Beauregard

DEPARTMENT OF TENNESSEE AND GEORGIA (ARMY OF TENNESSEE):

Commanding General—General John Bell Hood

Chief Engineer—Major General Martin Luther Smith

Chief of Artillery—Colonel Robert F. Beckham

CHEATHAM'S CORPS: Major General Benjamin Franklin Cheatham

Brown's Division: Brigadier General Mark P. Lowrey

Gist's Brigade: Lieutenant Colonel Zachariah L. Watters
Maney's Brigade: Colonel Hume R. Field
Strahl's Brigade: Colonel Andrew J. Kellar
Vaughn's Brigade: Colonel William M. Watkins

Cleburne's Division: Brigadier General James A. Smith

Lowrey's Brigade: commander unknown
Granbury's Brigade: Captain E. T. Broughton
Govan's Brigade: Brigadier General Daniel C. Govan
Smith's Brigade: Colonel Charles H. Olmstead

Bate's Division: Major General William B. Bate

Tyler's Brigade: commander unknown
Finley's Brigade: Major Jacob A. Lash
Jackson's Brigade: commander unknown

Artillery: Colonel Melancthon Smith

LEE'S CORPS: Lieutenant General Stephen Dill Lee

Stevenson's Division: Major General Carter L. Stevenson

Brown's and Reynold's Brigades: Colonel Joseph B. Palmer
Pettus' Brigade: Brigadier General Edmund W. Pettus
Cumming's Brigade: Colonel Elihu P. Watkins

Johnson's Division: commander unknown

Deas' Brigade: Brigadier General Zachariah C. Deas
Manigault's Brigade: Lieutenant Colonel William L. Butler
Brantly's Brigade: Brigadier General William F. Brantly
Sharp's Brigade: Brigadier General Jacob H. Sharp

Clayton's Division: Major General Henry D. Clayton

Stovall's Brigade: Brigadier General Marcellus A. Stovall
Gibson's Brigade: Brigadier General Randall L. Gibson
Holtzclaw's Brigade: Colonel Bushrod Jones

Artillery: Major John W. Johnston

STEWART'S CORPS: Lieutenant General Alexander P. Stewart

Loring's Division: Major General William W. Loring

Featherston's Brigade: Brig. Gen. Winfield S. Featherston
Adams' Brigade: Colonel Robert Lowry
Scott's Brigade: Colonel John Snodgrass

French's Division: commander unknown

Ector's Brigade: Colonel David Coleman
Cockrell's Brigade: Colonel Peter C. Flournoy
Sears' Brigade: Lieutenant Colonel Rueben H. Shotwell

Walthall's Division: Major General Edward C. Walthall
Quarles' Brigade: Brigadier General George D. Johnson
Cantey's Brigade: Brigadier General Charles M. Shelley
Reynolds' Brigade: Brigadier General Daniel H. Reynolds
Artillery: Lieutenant Colonel Samuel C. Williams

DEPARTMENT OF ALABAMA, MISSISSIPPI, AND EAST LOUISIANA:
Commanding General—Lieutenant General Richard Taylor

CAVALRY CORPS (with Hood): Major General Nathan B. Forrest
Chalmers' Division: Brigadier General James R. Chalmers
Rucker's Brigade: commander unknown
Biffle's Brigade: Colonel Jacob B. Biffle
Buford's Division: Brigadier General Abraham Buford
Crossland's Brigade: Colonel Edward Crossland
Bell's Brigade: Colonel Tyree H. Bell
Jackson's Division: Brigadier General William H. Jackson
Armstrong's Brigade: Brigadier General Frank C. Armstrong
Ross's Brigade: Brigadier General Lawrence S. Ross
Artillery: Captain John Morton

DISTRICT OF THE GULF: Major General Dabney H. Maury
Liddell's Division: Brigadier General St. John R. Liddell
Baker's Brigade: Brigadier General Alpheus Baker
Artillery: Colonel Isaac W. Patton
Cavalry: Colonel Henry Maury
Thomas' Command: Brigadier General Bryan M. Thomas
Fuller's Command: Colonel Charles A. Fuller
Burnet's Command: Colonel William E. Burnet
McCulloch's Cavalry Brigade: Colonel Robert McCulloch
District of North Alabama: Brigadier General Philip D. Roddey
District of Central Alabama: Brigadier General Daniel Adams
Armistead's Cavalry Brigade: Colonel Charles G. Armistead
Clanton's Brigade: Brigadier General James H. Clanton

DISTRICT OF MISSISSIPPI AND EAST LOUSIANA: Major General Franklin Gardner
Northern Sub-District: Brigadier General Wirt Adams
Denis's (cavalry) Brigade: Colonel Jules C. Denis
Mabry's (cavalry) Brigade: Brigadier General Hinchie Mabry
Central Sub-District: Colonel Robert C. Wood, Jr.
District of Southwest Mississippi and East Lousiana: Brigadier General George B. Hodge

TRANS-MISSISSIPPI DEPARTMENT:
Commanding General—General E. Kirby Smith

1st ARMY CORPS: Lieutenant General Simon Bolivar Buckner
1st Texas Infantry Division: Major General John H. Forney
1st Texas Infantry Brigade: Brigadier General Thomas Waul
2nd Texas Infantry Brigade: Brig. Gen. Richard Waterhouse
3rd Texas Infantry Brigade: Brig. Gen. Robert P. Maclay
2nd Infantry Division: Major General Camille J. Polignac
4th Texas Infantry Brigade: Brig. General William H. King
1st Louisiana Infantry Brigade: Brig. General Allen Thomas
2nd Louisiana Infantry Brigade: *commander unknown*
2nd Texas Cavalry Division: Major General Samuel B. Maxey
4th Texas Cavalry Brigade: Brig. General Arthur P. Bagby
5th Texas Cavalry Brigade: Brig. General Richard M. Gano
6th Texas Cavalry Brigade: Brig. General Xavier B. Debray
1st Louisiana Cavalry Brigade: Brig. Gen. Joseph L. Brent
3rd Louisiana Cavalry Brigade: Colonel Isaac F. Harrison

2nd ARMY CORPS: Major General John B. Magruder
1st Arkansas Infantry Division: Major Gen. Thomas Churchill
1st Arkansas Infantry Brigade: Brig. General John S. Roane
2nd Arkansas Infantry Brigade: Brig. Gen. Evander McNair
3rd Arkansas Infantry Brigade: Brig. Gen. James C. Tappan
4th Arkansas Infantry Brigade: Brig. Gen. Alex. Hawthorn
1st Missouri Infantry Division: Major General Mosby Parsons
1st Missouri Infantry Brigade: Colonel Charles S. Mitchell
2nd Missouri Infantry Brigade: Colonel Simon P. Burns
1st Texas Cavalry Division: Major General John A. Wharton
1st Texas Cavalry Brigade: Brig. General William Steele
2nd Texas Cavalry Brigade: Brig. General James P. Major
3rd Texas Cavalry Brigade: Colonel William P. Hardeman

3rd ARMY CORPS: Major General John G. Walker
2nd Texas Division: *commander unknown*
5th Texas Infantry Brigade: Brig. General James M. Hawes
6th Texas Infantry Brigade: Brig. General Paul O. Hebert
3rd Texas Cavalry Division: Brigadier General Thomas Drayton
7th Texas Cavalry Brigade: Brig. General James Slaughter
8th Texas Cavarly Brigade: Brig. General Henry McCulloch

CAVALRY CORPS: Major General Sterling Price
1st Missouri Cavalry Division: Major General John Marmaduke

1st Missouri Cavalry Brigade: Brig. Gen. Joseph O. Shelby
2nd Missouri Cavalry Brigade: Brig. Gen. John B. Clark

1st Arkansas Cavalry Division: Major General James F. Fagan

1st Arkansas Cavalry Brigade: Brig. Gen. William Cabell
2nd Arkansas Cavalry Brigade: Colonel W. F. Slemons

Indian Cavalry Division: Brigadier General Douglas H. Cooper

1st Indian Cavalry Brigade: Brigadier General Stand Watie
2nd Indian Cavalry Brigade: Colonel Tandy Walker

APPENDIX C

Bibliography

BOOKS

Ammen, Daniel. *The Atlantic Coast.* New York, 1883.

Angle, Paul M., editor. *The Lincoln Reader*, New Brunswick, N.J., 1947.

Basler, Roy P., editor. *The Collected Works of Abraham Lincoln.* Eight volumes. New Brunswick, N.J., 1953-1955.

Bearss, Ed and Chris Calkins. *The Battle of Five Forks.* Lynchburg, Va., 1985.

Bergeron, Arthur W., Jr. *Confederate Mobile.* Jackson, Miss., 1991.

Bishop, Jim. *The Day Lincoln Was Shot.* New York, 1955.

Boatner, Mark Mayo III. *The Civil War Dictionary.* New York, 1959.

Boritt, Gabor S. ed. *Why the Confederacy Lost.* New York, 1992.

Brandt, Nat. *The Man Who Tried to Burn New York.* Syracuse, 1986.

Brooks, Noah. *Washington in Lincoln's Time.* New York, 1958.

Catton, Bruce. *A Stillness at Appomattox.* Garden City, N.Y., 1957.

——. *Grant Takes Command.* Boston, 1968, 1969.

——. *Never Call Retreat.* Garden City, N.Y., 1965.

——. *This Hallowed Ground: The Story of the Union Side ofthe Civil War.* New York, 1956.

Chamberlain, Joshua Lawrence. *The Passing of the Armies: An Account of the Final Campaign of the Army of the Potomac, Based Upon Personal Reminiscences of the Fifth Army Corps.* New York, 1915. Bantom Books paperback edition, 1993.

Coggins, Jack. *Arms and Equipment of the Civil War.* Garden City, N.Y., 1962.

Connelly, Thomas L. *Autumn of Glory: The Army of Tennessee,1862-1865.* Baton Rouge, 1971.

——. *The Marble Man: Robert E. Lee and His Image in American Society.* Baton Rouge, 1977.

Cox, Jacob D. *The March to the Sea, Franklin and Nashville.* New York, 1882.

Dana, Charles A. *Recollections of the Civil War.* New York, 1898. Collier Books paperback edition. New York, 1963.

Davis, Burke. *Sherman's March.* New York, 1980.

——. *The Long Surrender.* New York, 1985.

——. *To Appomattox: Nine April Days, 1865.* New York, 1959.

Douglas, Henry Kyd. *I Rode with Stonewall.* Chapel Hill, 1940. Mockingbird Books paperback edition, 1961.

Dowdey, Clifford, and Louis H. Manarin, editors. *The Wartime Papers of R.E. Lee.* New York, 1961.

Dyer, Frederick H. *A Compendium of the War of the Rebellion.* 3 vols. Des Moines, Iowa, 1908.

Easton, Clement. *Jefferson Davis.* New York, 1977.

Faust, Patricia L., Editor. *Historical Times Illustrated Encyclopedia of the Civil War.* New York, 1986.

Foote, Shelby. *The Civil War: A Narrative.* 3 vols. New York, 1958-1974.

Fowler, William M., Jr. *Under Two Flags: The American Navy in the Civil War.* New York, 1990.

Frassanito, William A. *Grant and Lee: The Virginia Campaigns, 1864-1865.* New York, 1983.

Freeman, Douglas Southall. *Lee's Lieutenants: A Study in Command.* 3 vols. New York, 1942-1944.

——. *R.E. Lee: A Biography.* 4 vols. New York, 1934-1935.

Glatthaar, Joseph T. *The March to the Sea and Beyond: Sherman's Troops in the Savannah and Carolinas Campaigns.* New York, 1986.

Gragg, Rod. *Confederate Goliath: The Battle of Fort Fisher.* New York, 1991.

Grant, Julia Dent. *The Personal Memoirs of Julia Dent Grant.* New York, 1975.

Grant, Ulysses S. *Personal Memoirs of U.S. Grant.* 2 vols. New York, 1886.

Hallock, Judith Lee. *Braxton Bragg and Confederate Defeat.* Vol. 2. Tuscaloosa, 1991.

Hanna, A. J. *Flight into Oblivion.* New York, 1938.

Hassler, William Woods. *A.P. Hill: Lee's Forgotten General.* Richmond, 1962.

Henry, Robert Selph. *"First with the Most" Forrest.* New York, 1991.

Hoehling, A.A., and Mary Hoehling. *The Last Days of the Confederacy.* New York, 1981. (Originally published as *The Day Richmond Died.*)

Horan, James D. *Confederate Agent: A Discovery in History.* New York, 1954.

Horn, Stanley F. *The Decisive Battle of Nashville.* Baton Rouge, 1956.

Humphreys, Andrew A. *The Virginia Campaign of '64 and '65.* New York, 1883.
Jones, James Pickett. *Yankee Blitzkrieg: Wilson's Raid Through Alabama and Georgia.* Athens, Ga., 1976.
Jones, John B. *A Rebel War Clerk's Diary.* New York, 1866. Condensed edition, Earl Schenck Miers, editor. New York, 1958.
Jones, Virgil Carrington. *Ranger Mosby.* Chapel Hill, 1944.
Lee, Fitzhugh. *General Lee.* New York, 1894. Fawcett paperback edition, 1961.
Leech, Margaret. *Reveille in Washington, 1860-1865.* New York, 1941.
Long, E. B. with Barbara Long. *The Civil War Day by Day: An Almanac, 1861-1865.* Garden City, New York, 1971.
Longstreet, James. *From Manassas to Appomattox: Memoirs of the Civil War in America.* Philadelphia, 1896.
Marszalek, John F. *Sherman: A Soldier's Passion for Order.* New York, 1993.
McFeely, William S. *Grant: A Biography.* New York, 1981.
McMurry, Richard M. *Two Great Rebel Armies: An Essay in Confederate Military History.* Chapel Hill, 1989.
McPherson, James M. *Abraham Lincoln and the Second American Revolution.* New York, 1990.
——. *Battle Cry of Freedom: The Civil War Era.* New York, 1988.
Miers, Earl Schenk. *The General Who Marched to Hell.* New York, 1951.
Morris, Roy, Jr. *Sheridan: The Life and Wars of General Phil Sheridan.* New York, 1992.
Mosby, John S. *Gray Ghost: The Memoirs of Colonel John S.Mosby.* Boston, 1917. Bantam Eyewitness to the Civil War edition. New York, 1992.
Nevins, Allan. *The War for the Union.* 4 vols. New York, 1959-1971.
Nicolay, John G., and John Hay. *Abraham Lincoln: A History.* 10 vols. New York, 1886-1890.
Nolan, Alan T. *Lee Considered: General Robert E. Lee and Civil War History.* Chapel Hill, 1991.
O'Flaherty, Daniel. *General Jo Shelby: Undefeated Rebel.* Chapel Hill, 1954.
Porter, Horace. *Campaigning with Grant.* New York, 1897.
Pratt, Fletcher. *Ordeal by Fire.* New York, 1935.
Pullen, John J. *The Twentieth Maine: A Volunteer Regiment in the Civil War.* New York, 1957.
Reed, Rowena. *Combined Operations in the Civil War.* Annapolis, 1978.
Rhodes, Robert Hunt, editor. *All For the Union: The Civil War Diary and Letters of Elisha Hunt Rhodes.* New York, 1985.
Rodick, Burleigh Cushing. *Appomattox: The Last Campaign.* New York, 1965.

Roske, Ralph J. and Charles Van Doren. *Lincoln's Commando: The Biography of Commander W. B. Cushing, USN.* New York, 1957.

Ross, Ishbell. *The General's Wife: The Life of Mrs. Ulysses S. Grant.* New York, 1959.

Sandburg, Carl. *Abraham Lincoln: The War Years, 1864-1865.* New York, 1926.

Sheridan, Philip. *Civil War Memoirs.* New York 1991. This is part of the Bantam Domain paperback "Eyewitness to the Civil War" series and contains the complete text of the *Personal Memoirs of P.H. Sheridan* (New York, 1888, 2 vols.) that pertains to the Civil War but omits the chapters concerning events before and after the war.

Sherman, William Tecumseh. *Memoirs of General W. T. Sherman.* New York, 1886. Library of America edition.

Siepel, Kevin H. *Rebel: The Life and Times of John Singleton Mosby.* New York, 1983.

Starr, Stephen Z. *The Union Cavalry in the Civil War.* 3 vols. Baton Rouge, 1979-1985.

Stern, Philip Van Doren. *An End to Valor: The Last Days of the Civil War.* Boston, 1958.

Sword, Wiley. *Embrace an Angry Wind: The Confederacy's Last Hurrah: Spring Hill, Franklin, and Nashville.* New York, 1992.

Taylor, Dudley Cornish. *The Sable Arm: Black Troops in the Union Army, 1861-1865.* Lawrence, Kansas, 1956.

Thomas, Benjamin P., and Harold M. Hyman. *Stanton: The Life and Times of Lincoln's Secretary of War.* New York, 1962.

Tidwell, William A., with James O. Hall and David Winfred Gaddy. *Come Retribution: The Confederate Secret Service and the Assassination of Lincoln.* Jackson, Miss., 1988.

Trotter, William R. *Ironclads and Columbiads: The Civil War in North Carolina: The Coast.* Winston-Salem, 1989.

Trudeau, Noah Andre. *The Last Citadel: Petersburg, Virginia, June 1864-April 1865.* Boston, 1991.

——. *Out of the Storm: The End of the Civil War, April-June 1865.* Boston, 1994.

Turner, Thomas Reed. *Beware the People Weeping: Public Opinion and the Assassination of Abraham Lincoln.* Baton Rouge, 1982.

Urwin, Gregory J. W. *Custer Victorious: The Civil War Battles of General George Armstrong Custer.* East Brunswick, N.J., 1983.

U.S. War Department. *The War of the Rebellion: a Compilation of the Official Records of the Union and Confederate Armies.* Seventy volumes in 128 parts. Washington, 1891-1895. All references in the notes are to Series I unless otherwise indicated.

Waddell, James I. *C.S.S. Shenandoah: The Memoirs of Lieutenant Commanding James I Waddell.* New York, 1960.
Wainwright, Charles S. *A Diary of Battle: The Personal Journals of Colonel Charles S. Wainwright, 1861-1865.* New York, 1962.
Watkins, Sam R. *Co. Aytch: A Side Show of the Big Show.* Nashville, 1882. Collier Books paperback edition, 1962.
Weichmann, Louis J. *A True History of the Assassination of Abraham Lincoln and of the Conspiracy of 1865.* New York, 1975.
Wells, Edward L. *Hampton and His Cavalry in '64.* New York, 1899.
Wheeler, Richard. *Witness to Appomattox.* New York, 1989.
Woodward, W.E. *Meet General Grant.* New York, 1928.
Woodworth, Steven E. *Jefferson Davis and His Generals: The Failure of Command in the West.* Lawrence, 1990.

ARTICLES

Blakeman, Noel. "Noel Blakeman Recalls the Trials of Blockading." In *The Blue and the Gray* edited by Henry Steele Commager. New York, 1950.
Calkins, Chris. "The Battle of Five Forks: Final Push for the South Side." *Blue and Gray Magazine.* April 1992.
Cochran, Darrell. "Confederates' Brilliant Exploit." *America's Civil War.* September 1991.
Duke, Basil W. "Last Days of the Confederacy."In *Battles and Leaders of the Civil War,* edited by Robert Underwood Johnson and Clarence Clough Buel. Volume Four. New York, 1888.
Ewing, Joseph H. "The New Sherman Letters." *American Heritage.* July-August 1987.
Graves, Thomas Thatcher. "The Occupation." In *Battles and Leaders.* Vol. 4. See Duke.
Gray, John Chipman. "He Might Sit for a Portrait of an Ideal Yankee." In *The Blue and the Gray.* See Blakeman.
Hanchett, William. "Lincoln's Murder: The Simple Conspiracy Theory." *Civil War Times Illustrated.* November-December 1991.
Hitchcock, Henry. "The Sort of Power Which a Flash of Lightning Suggests."In *The Blue and the Gray.* See Blakeman.
Jones, Mary Cadwalader. "The Stars and Stripes Are Raised Over Fort Sumter." In *The Blue and the Gray* See Blakeman.
Kilmer, George L. "Gordon's Attack at Fort Stedman." In *Battles and Leaders.* Vol. 4. See Duke.

Lamb, William. "The Defense of Fort Fisher."
In *Battle and Leaders*. Vol. 4. See Duke.
Prescott, R. B. "The Poor Colored People Thanked God That Their Sufferings Were Ended."In *The Blue and the Gray*. See Blakeman.
Selfridge, Thomas O., Jr. "The Navy at Fort Fisher."In *Battles and Leaders*, Vol. 4. See Duke.
Wilkinson, John. "Wilmington Is Turned Topsy-Turvy by the War." In *The Blue and the Gray*. See Blakeman.

Index

HIPPOCRENE'S
MILITARY & HISTORY BOOKS

CONTEMPORARY

TRIAL BY FIRE: The 1972 Easter Offensive, America's Last Vietnam Battle
by Dale Andradé

"A masterful account of the last great engagement of the Vietnam War in which American forces participated." —*Kirkus Reviews*

A MILITARY BOOK CLUB SELECTION

maps, b&w photos, index, 600 pages, 0-7818-0286-5, $24.95 hc (#366)

TWENTIETH-CENTURY AMERICAN WARS
by Wilbur H. Morrison

"This book is as much a survey of 20th century American history as it is a feature book on the U.S. war experience. If you own just one book on the headlines and headliners of 20th century America, this should be it. A superb reference." —*Military Review*

"A worthwhile, readable addition to popular military history." —Booklist

436 pages, 0-7818-0120-6, $29.50 hc (#47)

ELEPHANT AND TIGER:
The Full Story of the War in Vietnam
by Wilbur H. Morrison

"A comprehensive, hard-nosed exploration of the question, how did we win every battle yet lose the war?... Includes a full account of South Vietnamese military operations, an element of the war usually ignored."
—*Publishers Weekly*

MILITARY BOOK CLUB DUAL SELECTION

640 pages, 16 b&w photos, 0-87052-623-5, $24.95 hc (#78)

KOREA: The First War We Lost
(3rd Edition) Revised with Epilogue
by Bevin Alexander

"Well-researched and readable." —*The New York Times*

"This is arguably the most reliable and fully-realized one-volume history of the Korean War since David Rees' *Korea.*" —*Publisher's Weekly*

"Bevin Alexander does a superb job... this respectable and fast-moving study is the first to be written by a professional army historian." —*Library Journal*

13 maps, index, 82 b&w photos, 580 pages, 0-7818-0065-X, $16.95pb (#107)

SECRETS OF THE VIET CONG
by James W. McCoy

"... this book is an eye-opener that belongs on military professionals' bookshelves." *—Military Review*

549 pages, 0-7818-0028-5, $24.95 hc (#532)

WORLD WAR I

VICTORY MUST BE OURS:
Germany in the Great War, 1914-1918
by Laurence V. Moyer, Introduction by John Keegan

"A stark, well-documented study of the hardships suffered by German civilians during WWI and how Germany's defeat influenced much of the world's history over the next three decades." — *Publisher's Weekly*

"... a very good book that will be new to most Western historians of the War." *—The New York Review of Books*

"A specialist in German history, [Moyer] has full command of the facts and relates his account with analytical skill and compassion." *—Booklist*

"Recommended for world war collections."*—Library Journal*

324 pages, illustrated, 0-7818-0370-5, $24.95 hc (#575)

WORLD WAR II

Available in Winter '96....

YOUR LIFE IS WORTH MINE:
The Story—Never-Told Before—of How Polish Nuns in World War II Saved Hundreds of Jewish Lives in German-Occupied Poland, 1939-1945
by Ewa Kurek, Introduction by Jan Karski

The first historical study of the role played by Polish nuns in saving Jewish children from the Nazis in World War II.

272 pages, 0-7818-0409-4, $22.50hc (#240)

POLISH CAMPAIGN OF 1939
by V. Madej and S. Zaloga

"This is the first major work in English to explain the genesis and conduct of the campaign with a Polish view." *—U.S. Army Armor Magazine*

"A valuable and timely book." *—Nowj Dziennik*

0-87052-013-X, $11.95pb (#152)

PATTON'S THIRD ARMY:
A Chronology of the Third Army Advance, August 1944 to May 1945
by Charles M. Province

"This book forms an invaluable work of reference which contains a wealth of facts and figures." —*British Army Review*

336 pages, 0-7818-0239-3, $11.95pb (#205)

OVERLORD COASTLINE: The Major D-Day Locations
by Stephen Chicken

A travel guide and military manual which shows you with 87 photographs, and 37 maps and plans, what was happening where on June 6, 1944.

104 pages, 0-7818-0274-7, $14.95pb (#374)

STALINGRAD
by V.E. Tarrant

"... a solid contribution to the study of a pivotal World War II battle."
—*Academic Library Book Review*

A MILITARY BOOK CLUB SELECTION

272 pages, illustrations, maps, 0-7818-0154-0, $24.95 (#566)

FORGOTTEN FEW:
The Polish Air Force in the Second World War
by Adam Zamoyski

Some 17,000 men and women passed through the ranks of the Polish Air Force while it was stationed on British soil in World War II. This is the story of who they were, where they came from, what they did, and their fate after the war's end.

272 pages, 30 illustrations, 30 maps, 0-7818-0421-3, $24.95hc (#493)

BATAAN: Our Last Ditch
by Lt. Col. John Whitman

"... a masterful job... " —*Ex-POW Bulletin*

"This is a superb tactical study.... Recommended for all World War II collections." —*Library Journal*

700 pages, 16 b&w photos, maps, 0-87052-877-7, $29.95 hc (#334)

DID THE CHILDREN CRY?
Hitler's War Against Jewish and Polish Children
by Richard C. Lukas

"[Lukas] intersperses the endless numbers, dates, locations and losses with personal accounts of tragedy and triumph. ...A well-researched book.... "
—*Catalyst*

263 pages, 15 b&w photos, 0-7818-0242-3, $24.95 hc (#145)

THE FORGOTTEN HOLOCAUST:
The Poles Under German Occupation, 1939-1944
by Richard C. Lukas

"Contains excellent analyses of the relationship of Poland's Jewish and Gentile communities, the development of the resistance, the exile leadership, and the Warsaw uprisings.... A superior work." —*Library Journal*

"An absorbing, meticulously documented study." —*National Review*

300 pages, illustrated, 0-87052-632-4, $9.95pb (#340)

WORLD WAR II COLLECTOR'S GUIDES

A COLLECTOR'S GUIDE TO THE WAFFEN-SS
by Robin Lumsden

160 pages, 180 illustrations, 0-7818-0357-8, $19.95pb (#475)

A COLLECTOR'S GUIDE TO GERMAN WORLD WAR II COMBAT MEDALS AND POLITICAL AWARDS
by Chris Ailsby

160 pages, 150 illustrations, 0- 7818-0225-3, $19.95pb (#265)

A COLLECTOR'S GUIDE TO THE HISTORY AND UNIFORMS OF DAS HEER: THE GERMAN ARMY 1933-1945
by Chris Ellis

160 pages, historical photos & illustrations, 0-7818-0226-1, $19.95pb (#279)

THE BLACK CORPS: A COLLECTOR'S GUIDE TO THE HISTORY AND REGALIA OF THE SS
by Robin Lumsden

235 pages, 150 illustrations, 0-7818-0112-5, $19.95pb (#315)

A COLLECTOR'S GUIDE TO THE THIRD REICH MILITARIA
by Robin Lumsden

176 pages, 150 b&w photos, illustrations, 0-711017-239, $19.95 (#3)

DETECTING THE FAKES: A Collector's Guide to Third Reich Militaria
by Robin Lumsden

144 pages, 150 b&w photos, illustrations, 0-7818-0324-1, $19.95pb (#592)

THE CIVIL WAR

SPIES AND SPYMASTERS OF THE CIVIL WAR
by Donald E. Markle

"The single, most valuable contribution to general Civil War literature so far this year." *—Booklist*

"Provides deep detail for operational topics... quite readable... the most general account in print." *—Library Journal*

A MILITARY BOOK CLUB SELECTION

235 pages, 0-7818-0428-0, $11.95pb (#531)

U.S.A. GUIDE TO CIVIL WAR SITES
by Tom Weil

With over 1,300 listings in both northern and southern states, this is a comprehensive guide to historic sites associated with the Civil War.

map overview, photos, 0-7818-0302-0, $14.95pb (#178)

Previous volumes by Don Lowry....

NO TURNING BACK:
The End of the Civil War, May-June 1864

"Lowry's highly readable command study of Ulysses S. Grant's Wilderness Campaign (March-June 1864) reveals a sure grasp of Civil War history and military strategy." —*Library Journal*

576 pages, index, appendices, 4 maps, 0-87052-010-5, $27.50hc (#271)

FATE OF THE COUNTRY:
The Civil War from June to September 1864

"An excellent account of the period... recommended." —*Booklist*

"Lowry's frame-by-frame chronology succeeds in heightening the natural drama of the events." —*Library Journal*

555 pages, 4 maps, 0-7818-0064-1, $27.50hc (#154)

DARK AND CRUEL WAR:
The Decisive Months of the Civil War, September-December 1864

"The third of four massive volumes constituting a comprehensive history of the Civil War's last year suggests that Lowry will complete the whole project admirably.... This is a superior contribution to the narrative histories of the Civil War." —Booklist

780 pages, 4 maps, 0-7818-0168-0, $29.50hc (#94)

TO ORDER HIPPOCRENE BOOKS, contact your local bookstore or send a check or money order payable to Hippocrene Books, 171 Madison Avenue, New York, NY 10016. Include $5.00 for shipping (UPS) for the first book, 50 cents for each additional book.